AMERICAN FANTASTIC TALES

AMERICAN
FANTASTIC TALES

TERROR AND THE UNCANNY
FROM THE 1940s TO NOW

Peter Straub, editor

THE LIBRARY OF AMERICA

Some of the material in this volume is reprinted with permission
of the holders of copyright and publication rights.
Acknowledgments are on page 703.

The paper used in this publication meets the
minimum requirements of the American National Standard for
Information Sciences—Permanence of Paper for Printed
Library Materials, ANSI Z39.48—1984.

Distributed to the trade in the United States
by Penguin Group (USA) Inc.
and in Canada by Penguin Books Canada Ltd.

Library of Congress Control Number: 2009927074
ISBN 978–1–59853–048–3

———

First Printing
The Library of America—197

Manufactured in the United States of America

Contents

Introduction

WHEN THOUGHT OF, in really the simplest manner possible, as an alternative to straightforward realism, the fantastic can immediately be seen to offer writers of fiction another toolbox, another set of instruments available for the depiction of human beings in interesting and revelatory situations. Or, take off *those* glasses and put on *these* glasses: see how different everything looks? The landscape instantly becomes craggier, the shadows deeper, the buildings more eccentric and Gaudiesque. At its core, I think, the fantastic is a way of seeing.

In this second volume of *American Fantastic Tales*, those lenses are trained, decade by decade, on any number of social issues. In the forties, John Collier addresses the anxieties of a nation just beginning to work its way out of the Depression and toward a great war ("Evening Primrose"); Fritz Leiber conjures with the different anxieties of becoming a nation dominated by giant factories and heavy industries ("Smoke Ghost"); and Jane Rice makes the delicious most of the occupation of Paris ("The Refugee"). In the late sixties, Harlan Ellison is imagining what might happen if Norbert Wiener's vast, enigmatic computers at MIT ever got out of hand ("I Have No Mouth, and I Must Scream"); in the seventies, Isaac Bashevis Singer continues to contemplate the Holocaust's legacy ("Hanka"). At the end of the eighties, Joyce Carol Oates has some giddy, black-humor fun with the disasters potential within a poisoned environment ("Family"). In the first decade of the twenty-first century, Steven Millhauser takes up the ever-troubling matters of teenage behavior and the inexplicable hysteria common to teen fads ("Dark Laughter"); in the same year, M. Rickert uses the Persephone myth as the underpinning of a story that hinges on parental fears of what could happen should a child wander, all innocence, into an Internet chat room ("The Chambered Fruit"). A little later in the decade, Benjamin Percy homes in on the drudgery of call centers and fears about the effects on the human body of cell phones and the towers that enable them ("Dial Tone").

Other sorts of themes, some of them familiar from the first of these two volumes, shape these stories, too. Bad Nature conspires against man in Kelly Link's "Stone Animals" and T.E.D. Klein's "The Events at Poroth Farm," which, like Thomas Ligotti's "The Last Feast of Harlequin," is a loving and exacting tribute to H. P. Lovecraft. What I take to be the central theme in the American literature of the fantastic, the loss of the individual will, hence of the self, and the terror aroused by the prospect of this loss, simmers through Paul Bowles' "The Circular Valley," Ray Bradbury's "The April Witch" (in close proximity, these two stories share an identical mechanism), Steven Millhauser's "Dangerous Laughter," Brian Evenson's "The Wavering Knife," and Tim Powers' "Pat Moore." Volume I contained four vampire stories, the most striking and indirect of which, Mary Wilkins Freeman's "Luella Miller," reads like a direct precursor of this volume's "Torch Song," by John Cheever. Each volume contains one werewolf story. The traditional horror tropes in fact appear very seldom in these volumes. The first volume reprints only three true ghost stories, Edith Wharton's "Afterward," Willa Cather's "Consequences," and Ellen Glasgow's "The Shadowy Third"; several other stories allude to ghosts, but the lurking phantoms are not the primary focus. Volume II contains only one, Nabokov's "The Vane Sisters," which could be called a meta-ghost story.

The simplest possible form of the fantastic tale is the story of single effect, in which, with varying degrees of art, the writer eliminates as much narrative complication as possible to concentrate solely on the development toward the shocker of the climax. The only point of such stories is what happens near the end, at the end, or in the very last sentence, and the only point of writing them is to drop that little bomb and see it explode. Brevity is a necessary consequence. The first volume has four stories of single effect, by Harriet Prescott Spofford ("The Moonstone Mass"), Madeline Yale Wynn ("The Little Room"), Ralph Adams Cram ("The Dead Valley"), and by the otherwise genteel Gertrude Atherton, whose "The Striding Place" pulls off the final trick with crude, undeniable vigor. This volume contains two such stories, Donald Wandrei's enjoyably pulpy "Nightmare" and Thomas Tessier's "Nocturne," probably the most sophisticated story of single effect ever to be written. With an easygoing *flaneur* named O'Netty we venture into an underground bar, admire and enjoy the friendly cosmopolitan crowd, then witness a shocking and inexplicable act that, while ruffling no one's composure, not even O'Netty's, causes the reader to take in everything that follows it with a refreshed, ultra-conscious awareness.

Time is the great conundrum in fiction of every kind, and the fantastic is peculiarly suited to its exploration. Human memory complicates our experience of time with its immediate access to pockets of the lost past that, when recovered, can coexist with the present and sometimes—for an immeasurable period that in some sense exists altogether outside of time—just about replace it. Or, actually, for the length of the timeless moment, *to* replace it. Technically impossible (in 2009, anyhow) and philosophically ill-advised for a hundred reasons given us by science fiction and works of fantasy, time travel nonetheless happens all the time and to more or less everybody. The versatile Jack Finney, whose "I'm Scared" reports the alarm of an average male of the 1940s or 50s upon observing that the universal distaste for present-day conditions has encouraged both trivial and significant fragments of the past to commandeer the world about him, spent most of his long career wrestling with the puzzle of time in novels like *Time and Again* and *From Time to Time* as well as the stories collected within *The Third Level* and *About Time*.

Stephen King's "That Feeling, You Can Only Say What It Is in French" and Benjamin Percy's "Dial Tone" push Finney's obsession with time slips and time travel through a kind of metaphysical food processor, a kind of meaning-enhancer, thereby enriching these themes with greater psychological depth and raising the literary ante. The Finney story is a clever representation of the perceived dangers of nostalgia in a troubled era; the stories by King and Percy seem to me to have bigger fish to fry. They are less accommodating, less comfortable, ascribable to a far less familiar template. If the King story has any direct ancestor, it might be Ambrose Bierce's "Occurrence at Owl Creek Bridge," the way you'd see that story if you looked at it though a kaleidoscope. ("Dial Tone"'s underlying pattern might be derived from a chapter near the conclusion of

Brian Evenson's novel *The Open Curtain*, or even from certain wild-eyed passages in *Absalom, Absalom*. Probably, of course, it is neither Evenson nor Faulkner, just something in the air these days.)

In "That Feeling, You Can Only Say What It Is in French," time is dubious, unreliable, radically decentered. It seems responsive to human emotion, and the abrupt discontinuities, refrains, and repeated images bubbling to the surface of King's mixed-sequence time imply the presence of a great, gathering, secret meaning. The ultimate desire hidden behind any presentation of mixed-sequence temporality is, I think, the complex, god-like rapture of finally perceiving the simultaneity of all of time. The characters in this story, it must be said, are rewarded with a far less exalted recognition.

Percy's "Dial Tone" dices space as well as time and makes both, along with character, multivalent. The resulting discontinuities are so radical as to be destructive to the traditional terms of story-making itself. The narrative appears to be going forward, but it actually moves backward, shoving the reader along up to the moment just before the situation described in the first paragraph. (Come to think of it, that sounds like "Occurrence at Owl Creek Bridge," too.) Our bored but conventional narrator, a call center wage-slave subject to the verbal abuse of his potential customers, gradually devolves into the haggard red-eyed wretch with missing clumps of hair he sees in a picture window when coming to the aid of a concussed bird, then into the rude, offensive man on the other side of the window, then into the brutal, wraith-like murderer who hears himself uttering the tentative telephone greeting he had half-whispered earlier, back in the call center. Everything collapses into itself, and we are left with a dead man being hoisted up a cell tower by a dying man invaded by the multiple voices coursing through the wires that surround him.

About forty percent of the stories in this volume, seventeen out of forty-three, or exactly a fifth of the two-volume total of eighty-five, were originally published in this decade and the last. Of that seventeen, twelve were first published in the '00s. This distribution may seem more than a little unbalanced, but I could easily have found, and in fact undoubtedly did find, twice as many stories from the present decade worthy of inclusion here. Because we were already packed full to the rafters, a lot of excellent work did not in the end get past the velvet rope. Something analogous to the gearing-up from the Finney story to those by King and Percy has taken place all across the fantasy/horror genre, to call it that, as a whole. (The same thing also happened in sci-fi and mystery novels.) Younger writers who had grown up reading people who were already pushing at the borders of genre were able to take the next, and to me breathtaking, step of creating fiction that acted as though those borders had never existed in the first place. A straight line connects Stephen King and Benjamin Percy, and it has to do with artistic ambition.

Michael Chabon and Kelly Link seem to me central figures in the movement I am describing. They are at least superbly representative of it. Throughout his sterling, deservedly honored career, Chabon has demonstrated great fondness for and knowledge of genre literatures of many kinds, including comic books, and his work often draws its content from these literatures. Kelly Link wrote from the first with the assumption that everything on earth was fair game for the serious writer. Nancy Drew, fairy tales, sibling rivalry, ghost stories, zombies, teenage angst, grief, loss, despair—it all goes into the hopper and emerges as fiction distinguished by its utter originality, playfulness, associative logic, depth of intuition, and sureness of touch. Her great story "Stone Animals" proceeds by precisely these means from the purchase of a house in the country to a conclusion that is simultaneously surrealist, disturbing, startling, yet thoroughly prepared-for and in fact inevitable: at every step, subtle inner voicings lead the way.

As "The God of Dark Laughter" looks back fondly to the ersatz scholarship and ancient gods of Lovecraft's Cthulhu tales, "Stone Animals" begins with a direct reference to the first line of Edith Wharton's "Afterward." The real-estate agent is responding to the question, "Is this house haunted?" instead of "Is there a ghost?" but the allusion neatly bridges the ninety-nine years that separate the two stories. One wonders how Edith Wharton would have reacted to the then utterly undreamt-of manner in which Kelly Link was to develop her clever opening gambit.

Peter Straub

JOHN COLLIER

(1901–1980)

Evening Primrose

In a pad of Highlife Bond,
bought by Miss Sadie Brodribb
at Bracey's
for 25 ¢

February 21

TODAY I made my decision. I would turn my back for good and all upon the *bourgeois* world that hates a poet. I would leave, get out, break away——

And I have done it. I am free! Free as the mote that dances in the sunbeam! Free as a house-fly crossing first-class in the *Queen Mary*! Free as my verse! Free as the food I shall eat, the paper I write upon, the lamb's-wool-lined softly slithering slippers I shall wear.

This morning I had not so much as a car-fare. Now I am here, on velvet. You are itching to learn of this haven: you would like to organize trips here, spoil it, send your relations-in-law, perhaps even come yourself. After all, this journal will hardly fall into your hands till I am dead. I'll tell you.

I am at Bracey's Giant Emporium, as happy as a mouse in the middle of an immense cheese, and the world shall know me no more.

Merrily, merrily shall I live now, secure behind a towering pile of carpets, in a corner-nook which I propose to line with eiderdowns, angora vestments, and the Cleopatræan tops in pillows. I shall be cosy.

I nipped into this sanctuary late this afternoon, and soon heard the dying footfalls of closing time. From now on, my only effort will be to dodge the night-watchman. Poets can dodge.

I have already made my first mouse-like exploration. I tiptoed as far as the stationery department, and, timid, darted back with only these writing materials, the poet's first need.

I

Now I shall lay them aside, and seek other necessities: food, wine, the soft furniture of my couch, and a natty smoking-jacket. This place stimulates me. I shall write here.

Dawn, next day

I suppose no one in the world was ever more astonished and overwhelmed than I have been tonight. It is unbelievable. Yet I believe it. How interesting life is when things get like that!

I crept out, as I said I would, and found the great shop in mingled light and gloom. The central well was half illuminated; the circling galleries towered in a pansy Piranesi of toppling light and shade. The spidery stairways and flying bridges had passed from purpose into fantasy. Silks and velvets glimmered like ghosts, a hundred pantie-clad models offered simpers and embraces to the desert air. Rings, clips, and bracelets glittered frostily in a desolate absence of Honey and Daddy.

Creeping along the transverse aisles, which were in deeper darkness, I felt like a wandering thought in the dreaming brain of a chorus girl down on her luck. Only, of course, their brains are not so big as Bracey's Giant Emporium. And there was no man there.

None, that is, except the night-watchman. I had forgotten him. A regular thudding, which might almost have been that of my own heart, suddenly burst upon me loudly, from outside, only a few feet away. Quick as a flash I seized a costly wrap, flung it about my shoulders, and stood stock-still.

I was successful. He passed me, jingling his little machine on its chain, humming his little tune, his eyes scaled with refractions of the blaring day. "Go, worldling!" I whispered, and permitted myself a soundless laugh.

It froze on my lips. My heart faltered. A new fear seized me.

I was afraid to move. I was afraid to look round. I felt I was being watched, by something that could see right through me. This was a very different feeling from the ordinary emergency caused by the very ordinary night-watchman. My conscious impulse was the obvious one, to glance behind me. But my eyes knew better. I remained absolutely petrified, staring straight ahead.

My eyes were trying to tell me something that my brain refused to believe. They made their point. I was looking straight into another pair of eyes, human eyes, but large, flat, luminous. I have seen such eyes among the nocturnal creatures, which creep out under the artificial blue moonlight in the zoo.

The owner was only a dozen feet away from me. The watchman had passed between us, nearer him than me. Yet he had not been seen. I must have been looking straight at him for several minutes at a stretch. I had not seen him either.

He was half reclining against a high dais, a platform for the exhibition of shawls and mantillas. One of these brushed his shoulder: its folds concealed perhaps his ear, his shoulder, and a little of his right side. He was clad in dim but large-patterned Shetland tweeds of the latest cut, suède shoes, a shirt of a rather broad *motif* in olive, pink, and grey. He was as pale as a creature found under a stone. His long thin arms ended in hands that hung floatingly, more like trailing, transparent fins, or wisps of chiffon, than ordinary hands.

He spoke. His voice was not a voice, a mere whistling under the tongue. "Not bad, for a beginner!"

I grasped that he was complimenting me, rather satirically, on my concealment under the wrap. I stuttered. I said, "I'm sorry. I didn't know anyone else lived here." I noticed, even as I spoke, that I was imitating his own whistling sibilant utterance.

"Oh, yes," he said. "*We* live here. It's delightful."

"We?"

"Yes, all of us. Look."

We were near the edge of the first gallery. He swept his long hand round, indicating the whole well of the shop. I looked. I saw nothing. I could hear nothing, except the watchman's thudding step receding infinitely far along some basement aisle.

"Don't you see?"

You know the sensation one has, peering into the half-light of a vivarium? One sees bark, pebbles, a few leaves, nothing more. And then, suddenly, a stone breathes—it is a toad; there is a chameleon, another, a coiled adder, a mantis among the leaves. The whole case seems crepitant with life. Perhaps the whole world is. One glances at one's sleeve, one's feet.

So it was with the shop. I looked, and it was empty. I looked, and there was an old lady, clambering out from behind the monstrous clock. There were three girls, elderly *ingénues*,

incredibly emaciated, simpering at the entrance of the per-
fumery. Their hair was a fine floss, pale as gossamer. Equally
brittle and colourless was a man with the appearance of a
colonel of southern extraction, who stood regarding me while
he caressed moustachios that would have done credit to a crystal shrimp. A chintzy woman, possibly of literary tastes, swam
forward from the curtains and drapes.

They came thick about me, fluttering, whistling, like a waving
of gauze in the wind. Their eyes were wide and flatly bright. I
saw there was no colour to the iris.

"How raw he looks!"

"A detective! Send for the Dark Men!"

"I'm not a detective. I am a poet. I have renounced the
world."

"He is a poet. He has come over to us. Mr. Roscoe found
him."

"He admires us."

"He must meet Mrs. Vanderpant."

I was taken to meet Mrs. Vanderpant: she proved to be the
Grand Old Lady of the store, almost entirely transparent.

"So you are a poet, Mr. Snell? You will find inspiration here.
I am quite the oldest inhabitant. Three mergers and a complete rebuilding, but they didn't get rid of me!"

"Tell how you went out by daylight, dear Mrs. Vanderpant,
and nearly got bought for Whistler's *Mother*."

"That was in pre-war days. I was more robust then. But at
the cash desk they suddenly remembered there was no frame.
And when they came back to look at me—"

"—She was gone."

Their laughter was like the stridulation of the ghosts of
grasshoppers.

"Where is Ella? Where is my broth?"

"She is bringing it, Mrs. Vanderpant. It will come."

"Terrible little creature! She is our foundling, Mr. Snell. She
is not quite our sort."

"Is that so, Mrs. Vanderpant? Dear, dear!"

"I lived alone here, Mr. Snell, ever since the terrible times in
the eighties. I was a young girl then, a beauty, they said, and
poor Papa lost his money. Bracey's meant a lot to a young girl,
in the New York of those days, Mr. Snell. It seemed to me ter-

rible that I should not be able to come here in the ordinary
way. So I came here for good. I was quite alarmed when others
began to come in, after the crash of 1907. But it was the dear
Judge, the Colonel, Mrs. Bilbee——"

I bowed. I was being introduced.

"Mrs. Bilbee writes plays. *And* of a very old Philadelphia
family. You will find us quite *nice* here, Mr. Snell."

"I feel it a great privilege, Mrs. Vanderpant."

"And of course, all our dear *young* people came in '29. *Their*
poor papas jumped from skyscrapers."

I did a great deal of bowing and whistling. The introductions took a long time. Who would have thought so many
people lived in Bracey's?

"And here at last is Ella with my broth."

It was then I noticed that the young people were not so
young after all, in spite of their smiles, their little ways, their
ingénue dress. Ella was in her teens. Clad only in something from
the shop-soiled counter, she nevertheless had the appearance
of a living flower in a French cemetery, or a mermaid among
polyps.

"Come, you stupid thing!"

"Mrs. Vanderpant is waiting."

Her pallor was not like theirs, not like the pallor of something that glistens or scuttles when you turn over a stone. Hers
was that of a pearl.

Ella! Pearl of this remotest, most fantastic cave! Little mermaid, brushed over, pressed down by objects of a deadlier
white—tentacles—! I can write no more.

February 28

Well, I am rapidly becoming used to my new and half-lit
world, to my strange company. I am learning the intricate laws
of silence and camouflage which dominate the apparently casual strollings and gatherings of the midnight clan. How they
detest the night-watchman, whose existence imposes these
laws on their idle festivals!

"Odious, vulgar creature! He reeks of the coarse sun!"

Actually, he is quite a personable young man, very young for
a night-watchman. But they would like to tear him to pieces.

They are very pleasant to me, though. They are pleased that

a poet should have come among them. Yet I cannot like them
entirely. My blood is a little chilled by the uncanny ease with
which even the old ladies can clamber spider-like from balcony
to balcony. Or is it because they are unkind to Ella?

Yesterday we had a bridge party. Tonight Mrs. Bilbee's little
play, *Love in Shadowland*, is going to be presented. Would you
believe it?—another colony, from Wanamaker's, is coming over
en masse to attend. Apparently people live in all stores. This
visit is considered a great honour: there is an intense snobbery
in these creatures. They speak with horror of a social outcast
who left a high-class Madison Avenue establishment, and now
leads a wallowing, beachcomberish life in a delicatessen. And
they relate with tragic emotion the story of the man in Altman's,
who conceived such a passion for a model plaid dressing jacket
that he emerged and wrested it from the hands of a purchaser.
It seems that all the Altman colony, dreading an investigation,
were forced to remove beyond the social pale, into a five-and-
dime. Well, I must get ready to attend the play.

March 1

I have found an opportunity to speak to Ella. I dared not
before: here one has a sense always of pale eyes secretly watching.
But last night, at the play, I developed a fit of hiccups. I was
somewhat sternly told to go and secrete myself in the basement, among the garbage cans, where the watchman never
comes.

There, in the rat-haunted darkness, I heard a stifled sob.
"What's that? Is it you? Is it Ella? What ails you, child? Why do
you cry?"

"They wouldn't even let me see the play."

"Is that all? Let me console you."

"I am so unhappy."

She told me her tragic little story. What do you think? When
she was a child, a little tiny child of only six, she strayed away
and fell asleep behind a counter, while her mother tried on a
new hat. When she woke, the store was in darkness.

"And I cried, and they all came round, and took hold of me.
'She will tell, if we let her go,' they said. Some said, 'Call in the
Dark Men.' 'Let her stay here,' said Mrs. Vanderpant. 'She will
make me a nice little maid.'"

"Who are these Dark Men, Ella? They spoke of them when I came here."

"Don't you know? Oh, it's horrible! It's horrible!"

"Tell me, Ella. Let us share it."

She trembled. "You know the morticians, 'Journey's End,' who go to houses when people die?"

"Yes, Ella."

"Well, in that shop, just like here, and at Gimbel's, and at Bloomingdale's, there are people living, people like these."

"How disgusting! But what can they live upon, Ella, in a funeral home?"

"Don't ask me! Dead people are sent there, to be embalmed. Oh, they are terrible creatures! Even the people here are terrified of them. But if anyone dies, or if some poor burglar breaks in, and sees these people, and might tell——"

"Yes? Go on."

"Then they send for the others, the Dark Men."

"Good heavens!"

"Yes, and they put the body in the surgical department—or the burglar, all tied up, if it's a burglar—and they send for these others, and then they all hide, and in they come, these others— Oh! they're like pieces of blackness. I saw them once. It was terrible."

"And then?"

"They go in, to where the dead person is, or the poor burglar. And they have wax there—and all sorts of things. And when they're gone there's just one of these wax models left, on the table. And then our people put a frock on it, or a bathing suit, and they mix it up with all the others, and nobody ever knows."

"But aren't they heavier than the others, these wax models? You would think they'd be heavier."

"No. They're not heavier. I think there's a lot of them—gone."

"Oh dear! So they were going to do that to you, when you were a little child?"

"Yes, only Mrs. Vanderpant said I was to be her maid."

"I don't like these people, Ella."

"Nor do I. I wish I could see a bird."

"Why don't you go into the pet-shop?"

"It wouldn't be the same. I want to see it on a twig, with leaves."

"Ella, let us meet often. Let us creep away down here and meet. I will tell you about birds, and twigs and leaves."

March 10

"Ella, I love you."

I said it to her just like that. We have met many times. I have dreamt of her by day. I have not even kept up my journal. Verse has been out of the question.

"Ella, I love you. Let us move into the trousseau department. Don't look so dismayed, darling. If you like, we will go right away from here. We will live in the refreshment rooms in Central Park. There are thousands of birds there."

"Don't, Charles, don't."

"But I love you with all my heart."

"You mustn't."

"But I find I must. I can't help it. Ella, you don't love another?"

She wept a little. "Oh, Charles, I do."

"Love another, Ella? One of these? I thought you dreaded them all. It must be Roscoe. He is the only one that's any way human. We talk of art, life, and such things. And he has stolen your heart!"

"No, Charles, no. He's just like the rest, really. I hate them all. They make me shudder."

"Who is it, then?"

"It's him."

"Who?"

"The night-watchman."

"Impossible!"

"No. He smells of the sun."

"Oh, Ella, you have broken my heart."

"Be my friend, though."

"I will. I'll be your brother. How did you fall in love with him?"

"Oh, Charles, it was so wonderful. I was thinking of birds, and I was careless. Don't tell on me, Charles, they'll punish me."

"No. No. Go on."

"I was careless, and there he was, coming round the corner.

And there was no place for me, I had this blue frock on. There were only some wax models in their underthings."

"Please go on."

"I couldn't help it, Charles. I slipped off my dress, and stood still."

"I see."

"And he stopped just by me, Charles. And he looked at me. And he touched my cheek."

"Did he notice nothing?"

"No. It was cold. But Charles, he said—he said—'Say, honey, I wish they made 'em like you on Eighth Avenue.' Charles, wasn't that a lovely thing to say?"

"Personally, I should have said Park Avenue."

"Oh, Charles, don't get like these people here. Sometimes I think you're getting like them. It doesn't matter what street, Charles; it was a lovely thing to say."

"Yes, but my heart's broken. And what can you do about him? Ella, he belongs to another world."

"Yes, Charles, Eighth Avenue. I want to go there. Charles, are you truly my friend?"

"I'm your brother, only my heart's broken."

"I'll tell you. I will. I'm going to stand there again. So he'll see me."

"And then?"

"Perhaps he'll speak to me again."

"My dearest Ella, you are torturing yourself. You are making it worse."

"No, Charles. Because I shall answer him. He will take me away."

"Ella, I can't bear it."

"Ssh! There is someone coming. I shall see birds, flowers growing. They're coming. You must go."

March 13

The last three days have been torture. This evening I broke. Roscoe (he was my first acquaintance) came in. There has always been a sort of hesitant sympathy between us.

He said, "You're looking seedy, old fellow. Why don't you go over to Wanamaker's for some skiing?"

His kindness compelled a frank response. "It's deeper than

that, Roscoe. I'm done for. I can't eat, I can't sleep. I can't write, man, I can't even write."

"What is it? Day starvation?"

"Roscoe—it's love."

"Not one of the staff, Charles, or the customers? That's absolutely forbidden."

"No, it's not that, Roscoe. But just as hopeless."

"My dear old fellow, I can't bear to see you like this. Let me help you. Let me share your trouble."

Then it all came out. It burst out. I trusted him. I think I trusted him. I really think I had no intention of betraying Ella, of spoiling her escape, of keeping her here till her heart turned towards me. If I had, it was subconscious. I swear it.

But I told him all. All. He was sympathetic, but I detected a sly reserve in his sympathy. "You will respect my confidence, Roscoe? This is to be a secret between us."

"As secret as the grave, old chap."

And he must have gone straight to Mrs. Vanderpant. This evening the atmosphere has changed. People flicker to and fro, smiling nervously, horribly, with a sort of frightened sadistic exaltation. When I speak to them they answer evasively, fidget, and disappear. An informal dance has been called off. I cannot find Ella. I will creep out. I will look for her again.

Later

Heaven! It has happened. I went in desperation to the manager's office, whose glass front overlooks the whole shop. I watched till midnight. Then I saw a little group of them, like ants bearing a victim. They were carrying Ella. They took her to the surgical department. They took other things.

And, coming back here, I was passed by a flittering, whispering horde of them, glancing over their shoulders in a thrilled ecstasy of panic, making for their hiding places. I, too, hid myself. How can I describe the dark inhuman creatures that passed me, silent as shadows? They went there—where Ella is.

What can I do? There is only one thing. I will find the watchman. I will tell him. He and I will save her. And if we are overpowered— Well, I will leave this on a counter. Tomorrow, if we live, I can recover it.

If not, look in the windows. Look for three new figures: two men, one rather sensitive-looking, and a girl. She has blue eyes, like periwinkle flowers, and her upper lip is lifted a little.

Look for us.

Smoke them out! Obliterate them! Avenge us!

1940

FRITZ LEIBER

(1910–1992)

Smoke Ghost

Miss Millick wondered just what had happened to Mr. Wran. He kept making the strangest remarks when she took dictation. Just this morning he had quickly turned around and asked, "Have you ever seen a ghost, Miss Millick?" And she had tittered nervously and replied, "When I was a girl there was a thing in white that used to come out of the closet in the attic bedroom when you slept there, and moan. Of course it was just my imagination. I was frightened of lots of things." And he had said, "I don't mean that traditional kind of ghost. I mean a ghost from the world today, with the soot of the factories in its face and the pounding of machinery in its soul. The kind that would haunt coal yards and slip around at night through deserted office buildings like this one. A real ghost. Not something out of books." And she hadn't known what to say.

He'd never been like this before. Of course it might be joking, but it didn't sound that way. Vaguely Miss Millick wondered whether he mightn't be seeking some sort of sympathy from her. Of course, Mr. Wran was married and had a little child, but that didn't prevent her from having daydreams. She had daydreams about most of the men she worked for. The daydreams were all very similar in pattern and not very exciting, but they helped fill up the emptiness in her mind. And now he was asking her another of those disturbing and jarringly out-of-place questions.

"Have you ever thought what a ghost of our times would look like, Miss Millick? Just picture it. A smoky composite face with the hungry anxiety of the unemployed, the neurotic restlessness of the person without purpose, the jerky tension of the high-pressure metropolitan worker, the sullen resentment of the striker, the callous viciousness of the strike breaker, the aggressive whine of the panhandler, the inhibited terror of the bombed civilian, and a thousand other twisted emotional patterns? Each one overlying and yet blending with the other, like a pile of semitransparent masks?"

Miss Millick gave a little self-conscious shiver and said, "My, that would be terrible. What an awful thing to think of."

She peered at him furtively across the desk. Was he going crazy? She remembered having heard that there had been something impressively abnormal about Mr. Wran's childhood, but she couldn't recall what it was. If only she could do something —joke at him or ask him what was really wrong. She shifted around the extra pencils in her left hand and mechanically traced over some of the shorthand curlicues in her notebook.

"Yet, that's just what such a ghost or vitalized projection would look like, Miss Millick," he continued, smiling in a tight way. "It would grow out of the real world. It would reflect all the tangled, sordid, vicious things. All the loose ends. And it would be very grimy. I don't think it would seem white or wispy or favor graveyards. It wouldn't moan. But it would mutter unintelligibly, and twitch at your sleeve. Like a sick, surly ape. What would such a thing want from a person, Miss Millick? Sacrifice? Worship? Or just fear? What could you do to stop it from troubling you?"

Miss Millick giggled nervously. She felt embarrassed and out of her depth. There was an expression beyond her powers of definition in Mr. Wran's ordinary, flat-cheeked, thirty-ish face, silhouetted against the dusty window. He turned away and stared out into the gray downtown atmosphere that rolled in from the railroad yards and the mills. When he spoke again his voice sounded far away.

"Of course, being immaterial, it couldn't hurt you physically —at first. You'd have to be peculiarly sensitive even to see it, or be aware of it at all. But it would begin to influence your actions. Make you do this. Stop you from doing that. Although only a projection, it would gradually get its hooks into the world of things as they are. Might even get control of suitably vacuous minds. Then it could hurt whomever it wanted."

Miss Millick squirmed and tried to read back her shorthand, like books said you should do when there was a pause. She became aware of the failing light and wished Mr. Wran would ask her to turn on the overhead light. She felt uncomfortable and scratchy as if soot were sifting down on to her skin.

"It's a rotten world, Miss Millick," said Mr. Wran, talking at the window. "Fit for another morbid growth of superstition. It's time the ghosts, or whatever you call them, took over and began a rule of fear. They'd be no worse than men."

"But"—Miss Millick's diaphragm jerked, making her titter inanely—"of course there aren't any such things as ghosts."

Mr. Wran turned around. She noticed with a start that his grin had broadened, though without getting any less tight.

"Of course there aren't, Miss Millick," he said in a sudden loud, reassuring, almost patronizing voice, as if she had been doing the talking rather than he. "Modern science and common sense and better self-understanding all go to prove it."

He stopped, staring past her abstractedly. She hung her head and might even have blushed if she hadn't felt so all at sea. Her leg muscles twitched, making her stand up, although she hadn't intended to. She aimlessly rubbed her hand back and forth along the edge of the desk, then pulled it back.

"Why, Mr. Wran, look what I got off your desk," she said, showing him a heavy smudge. There was a note of cumbersomely playful reproof in her voice, but she really just wanted to be saying something. "No wonder the copy I bring you always get so black. Somebody ought to talk to those scrubwomen. They're skimping on your room."

She wished he would make some normal joking reply. But instead he drew back and his face hardened.

"Well, to get back to the letter to Fredericks," he rapped out harshly, and began to dictate.

When she was gone he jumped up, dabbed his finger experimentally at the smudged part of the desk, frowned worriedly at the almost inky smears. He jerked open a drawer, snatched out a rag, hastily swabbed off the desk, crumpled the rag into a ball and tossed it back. There were three or four other rags in the drawer, each impregnated with soot.

Then he strode over to the window and peered out anxiously through the gathering dusk, his eyes searching the panorama of roofs, fixing on each chimney, each water tank.

"It's a psychosis. Must be. Hallucination. Compulsion neurosis," he muttered to himself in a tired, distraught voice that would have made Miss Millick gasp. "Good thing I'm seeing the psychiatrist tonight. It's that damned mental abnormality cropping up in a new form. Can't be any other explanation. Can't be. But it's so damned real. Even the soot. I don't think I could force myself to get on the elevated tonight. Good thing I made the appointment. The doctor will know—" His voice trailed off, he rubbed his eyes, and his memory automatically started to grind.

It had all begun on the elevated. There was a particular little sea of roofs he had grown into the habit of glancing at just as the packed car carrying him homeward lurched around a turn. A dingy, melancholy little world of tar paper, tarred gravel, and smoky brick. Rusty tin chimneys with odd conical hats suggested abandoned listening posts. There was a washed-out advertisement of some ancient patent medicine on the nearest wall. Superficially it was like ten thousand other drab city roofs. But he always saw it around dusk, either in the normal smoky half-light, or tinged with red by the flat rays of a dirty sunset, or covered by ghostly windblown white sheets of rain-splash, or patched with blackish snow; and it seemed unusually bleak and suggestive, almost beautifully ugly, though in no sense picturesque; dreary but meaningful. Unconsciously it came to symbolize for Catesby Wran certain disagreeable aspects of the frustrated, frightened century in which he lived, the jangled century of hate and heavy industry and Fascist wars. The quick, daily glance into the half darkness became an integral part of his life. Oddly, he never saw it in the morning, for it was then his habit to sit on the other side of the car, his head buried in the paper.

One evening toward winter he noticed what seemed to be a shapeless black sack lying on the third roof from the tracks. He did not think about it. It merely registered as an addition to the well-known scene and his memory stored away the impression for further reference. Next evening, however, he decided he had been mistaken in one detail. The object was a roof nearer than he had thought. Its color and texture, and the grimy stains around it, suggested that it was filled with coal dust, which was hardly reasonable. Then, too, the following evening it seemed to have been blown against a rusty ventilator by the wind—which could hardly have happened if it were at all heavy. Perhaps it was filled with leaves. Catesby was surprised to find

16 FRITZ LEIBER

himself anticipating his next daily glance with a minor note of apprehension. There was something unwholesome in the posture of the thing that stuck in his mind—a bulge in the sacking that suggested a misshapen head peering around the ventilator. And his apprehension was justified, for that evening the thing was on the nearest roof, though on the farther side, looking as if it had just flopped down over the low brick parapet.

Next evening the sack was gone. Catesby was annoyed at the momentary feeling of relief that went through him, because the whole matter seemed too unimportant to warrant feelings of any sort. What difference did it make if his imagination had played tricks on him, and he'd fancied that the object was crawling and hitching itself slowly closer across the roofs? That was the way any normal imagination worked. He deliberately chose to disregard the fact that there were reasons for thinking his imagination was by no means a normal one. As he walked home from the elevated, however, he found himself wondering whether the sack was really gone. He seemed to recall a vague, smudgy trail leading across the gravel to the nearer side of the roof. For an instant an unpleasant picture formed in his mind —that of an inky, humped creature crouched behind the nearer parapet, waiting. Then he dismissed the whole subject.

The next time he felt the familiar grating lurch of the car, he caught himself trying not to look out. That angered him. He turned his head quickly. When he turned it back, his compact face was definitely pale. There had only been time for a fleeting rearward glance at the escaping roof. Had he actually seen in silhouette the upper part of a head of some sort peering over the parapet? Nonsense, he told himself. And even if he had seen something, there were a thousand explanations which did not involve the supernatural or even true hallucination. To-morrow he would take a good look and clear up the whole matter. If necessary, he would visit the roof personally, though he hardly knew where to find it and disliked in any case the idea of pampering a whim of fear.

He did not relish the walk home from the elevated that evening, and visions of the thing disturbed his dreams and were in and out of his mind all next day at the office. It was then that he first began to relieve his nerves by making jokingly serious remarks about the supernatural to Miss Millick, who seemed properly mystified. It was on the same day, too, that he became aware of a growing antipathy to grime and soot. Everything he touched seemed gritty, and he found himself mopping and wiping at his desk like an old lady with a morbid fear of germs. He reasoned that there was no real change in his office, and that he'd just now become sensitive to the dirt that had always been there, but there was no denying an increasing nervousness. Long before the car reached the curve, he was straining his eyes through the murky twilight determined to take in every detail.

Afterward he realized that he must have given a muffled cry of some sort, for the man beside him looked at him curiously, and the woman ahead gave him an unfavorable stare. Conscious of his own pallor and uncontrollable trembling, he stared back at them hungrily, trying to regain the feeling of security he had completely lost. They were the usual reassuringly wooden-faced people everyone rides home with on the elevated. But suppose he had pointed out to one of them what he had seen—that sodden, distorted face of sacking and coal dust, that boneless paw which waved back and forth, unmistakably in his direction, as if reminding him of a future appointment— He involuntarily shut his eyes tight. His thoughts were racing ahead to tomorrow evening. He pictured this same windowed oblong of light and packed humanity surging around the curve—then an opaque monstrous form leaping out from the roof in a parabolic swoop—an unmentionable face pressed close against the window, smearing it with wet coal dust—huge paws fumbling sloppily at the glass—

Somehow he managed to turn off his wife's anxious inquiries. Next morning he reached a decision and made an appointment for that evening with a psychiatrist a friend had told him about. It cost him a considerable effort for Catesby had a peculiarly great and very well-grounded distaste for anything dealing with psychological abnormality. Visiting a psychiatrist meant raking up an episode in his past which he had never fully described even to his wife and which Miss Millick only knew of as "something impressively abnormal about Mr. Wran's childhood." Once he had made the decision, however, he felt considerably relieved. The doctor, he told himself, would clear everything up. He could almost fancy the doctor saying, "Merely a bad case of nerves. However, you must consult the oculist whose name I'm writing down for you, and you must take two of these pills in water every hour," and so on. It was almost comforting, and made the coming revelation he would have to make seem less painful.

But as the smoky dusk rolled in, his nervousness returned and he let his joking mystification of Miss Millick run away with him until he realized that he wasn't frightening anyone but himself.

He would have to keep his imagination under better control, he told himself, as he continued to peer out restlessly at the massive, murky shapes of the downtown office buildings. Why, he had spent the whole afternoon building up a kind of neomedieval cosmology of superstition. It wouldn't do. He realized then that he had been standing at the window much longer than he'd thought, for the glass panel in the door was dark and there was no noise coming from the outer office. Miss Millick and the rest must already have gone home.

It was then he made the discovery that there would have been no special reason for dreading the swing around the curve that night. It was, as it happened, a horrible discovery. For, on the shadowed roof across the street and four stories below, he saw the thing huddle and roll across the gravel and, after one upward look of recognition, merge into the blackness beneath the water tank.

As he hurriedly collected his things and made for the elevator, fighting the panicky impulse to run, he began to think of hallucination and mild psychosis as very desirable conditions. For better or for worse, he pinned all his hopes on the doctor.

"So you find yourself growing nervous and . . . er . . . jumpy, as you put it," said Dr. Trevethick, smiling with dignified geniality. "Do you notice any more definite physical symptoms? Pain? Headache? Indigestion?"

Catesby shook his head and wet his lips. "I'm especially nervous while riding in the elevated," he murmured swiftly.

"I see. We'll discuss that more fully. But I'd like you first to tell me about something you mentioned earlier. You said there was something about your childhood that might predispose you to nervous ailments. As you know, the early years are critical ones in the development of an individual's behavior pattern."

Catesby studied the yellow reflections of frosted globes in the dark surface of the desk. The palm of his left hand aimlessly rubbed the thick nap of the armchair. After a while he raised his head and looked straight into the doctor's small brown eyes.

"From perhaps my third to my ninth year," he began, choosing the words with care, "I was what you might call a sensory prodigy."

The doctor's expression did not change. "Yes?" he inquired politely.

"What I mean is that I was supposed to be able to see through walls, read letters through envelopes and books through their covers, fence and play Ping-pong blindfolded, find things that were buried, read thoughts." The words tumbled out.

"And could you?" The doctor's expression was toneless.

"I don't know. I don't suppose so," answered Catesby, long-lost emotions flooding back into his voice. "It's all so confused now. I thought I could, but then they were always encouraging me. My mother . . . was . . . well . . . interested in psychic phenomena. I was . . . exhibited. I seem to remember seeing things other people couldn't. As if most opaque objects were transparent. But I was very young. I didn't have any scientific criteria for judgment."

He was reliving it now. The darkened rooms. The earnest assemblages of gawking, prying adults. Himself sitting alone on a little platform, lost in a straight-backed wooden chair. The black silk handkerchief over his eyes. His mother's coaxing, insistent questions. The whispers. The gasps. His own hate of the whole business, mixed with hunger for the adulation of adults. Then the scientists from the university, the experiments, the big test. The reality of those memories engulfed him and momentarily made him forget the reason why he was disclosing them to a stranger.

"Do I understand that your mother tried to make use of you as a medium for communicating with the . . . er . . . other world?"

Catesby nodded eagerly.

"She tried to, but she couldn't. When it came to getting

in touch with the dead, I was a complete failure. All I could do—or thought I could do—was see real, existing, three-dimensional objects beyond the vision of normal people. Objects they could have seen except for distance, obstruction, or darkness. It was always a disappointment to mother," he finished slowly.

He could hear her sweetish patient voice saying, "Try again, dear, just this once. Katie was your aunt. She loved you. Try to hear what she's saying." And he had answered, "I can see a woman in a blue dress standing on the other side of Jones' house." And she had replied, "Yes, I know, dear. But that's not Katie. Katie's a spirit. Try again. Just this once, dear." For a second time the doctor's voice gently jarred him hack into the softly gleaming office.

"You mentioned scientific criteria for judgment, Mr. Wran. As far as you know, did anyone ever try to apply them to you?"

Catesby's nod was emphatic.

"They did. When I was eight, two young psychologists from the university here got interested in me. I guess they considered it a joke at first, and I remember being very determined to show them I amounted to something. Even now I seem to recall how the note of polite superiority and amused sarcasm drained out of their voices. I suppose they decided at first that it was very clever trickery, but somehow they persuaded mother to let them try me out under controlled conditions. There were lots of tests that seemed very businesslike after mother's slipshod little exhibitions. They found I was still clairvoyant—or so they thought. I got worked up and on edge. They were going to demonstrate my supernormal sensory powers to the university psychology faculty. For the first time I began to worry about whether I'd come through. Perhaps they kept me going at too hard a pace, I don't know. At any rate, when the test came, I couldn't do a thing. Everything became opaque. I got desperate and made things up out of my imagination. I lied. In the end I failed utterly, and I believe the two young psychologists lost their jobs as a result."

He could hear the brusque, bearded man saying, "You've been taken in by a child, Flaxman, a mere child. I'm greatly disturbed. You've put yourself on the same plane as common charlatans. Gentlemen, I ask you to banish from your minds this whole sorry episode. It must never be referred to." He winced at the recollection of his feeling of guilt. But at the same time he was beginning to feel exhilarated and almost light-hearted. Unburdening his long-repressed memories had altered his whole viewpoint. The episodes on the elevated began to take on what seemed their proper proportions as merely the bizarre workings of overwrought nerves, and an overly suggestible mind. The doctor, he anticipated confidently, would disentangle the obscure subconscious causes, whatever they might be. And the whole business would be finished off quickly, just as his childhood experience—which was beginning to seem a little ridiculous now—had been finished off.

"From that day on," he continued, "I never exhibited a trace of my supposed powers. My mother was frantic, and tried to sue the university. I had something like a nervous breakdown. Then the divorce was granted, and my father got custody of me. He did his best to make me forget it. We went on long outdoor vacations, and did a lot of athletics, associated with normal, matter-of-fact people. I went to business college eventually. I'm in advertising now. But," Catesby paused, "now that I'm having nervous symptoms, I'm wondering if there mightn't be a connection. It's not a question of whether I really was clairvoyant or not. Very likely my mother taught me a lot of unconscious deceptions, good enough even to fool young psychology instructors. But don't you think it may have some important bearing on my present condition?"

For several moments the doctor regarded him with a slightly embarrassing professional frown. Then he said quietly, "And is there some . . . er . . . more specific connection between your experiences then and now? Do you by any chance find that you are once again beginning to . . . er . . . see things?"

Catesby swallowed. He had felt an increasing eagerness to unburden himself of his fears, but it was not easy to make a beginning, and the doctor's shrewd question rattled him. He forced himself to concentrate. The thing he thought he had seen on the roof loomed up before his inner eye with unexpected vividness. Yet it did not frighten him. He groped for words.

Then he saw that the doctor was not looking at him but over his shoulder. Color was draining out of the doctor's face and his eyes did not seem so small. Then the doctor sprang to his feet, walked past Catesby, threw open the window and peered into the darkness.

As Catesby rose, the doctor slammed down the window and said in a voice whose smoothness was marred by a slight, persistent gasping, "I hope I haven't alarmed you. I saw the face of . . . er . . . a Negro prowler on the fire escape. I must have frightened him, for he seems to have gotten out of sight in a hurry. Don't give it another thought. Doctors are frequently bothered by *voyeurs* . . . er . . . Peeping Toms."

"A Negro?" asked Catesby, moistening his lips.

The doctor laughed nervously. "I imagine so, though my first odd impression was that it was a white man in blackface. You see, the color didn't seem to have any brown in it. It was dead-black."

Catesby moved toward the window. There were smudges on the glass. "It's quite all right, Mr. Wran." The doctor's voice had acquired a sharp note of impatience, as if he were trying hard to get control of himself and reassume his professional authority. "Let's continue our conversation. I was asking you if you were"—he made a face—"seeing things."

Catesby's whirling thoughts slowed down and locked into place. "No, I'm not seeing anything . . . other people don't see, too. And I think I'd better go now. I've been keeping you too long." He disregarded the doctor's half-hearted gesture of denial. "I'll phone you about the physical examination. In a way you've already taken a big load off my mind." He smiled woodenly. "Good night, Dr. Trevethick."

Catesby Wran's mental state was a peculiar one. His eyes searched every angular shadow and he glanced sideways down each chasmlike alley and barren basement passageway and kept stealing looks at the irregular line of the roofs, yet he was hardly conscious of where he was going in a general way. He pushed away the thoughts that came into his mind, and kept moving. He became aware of a slight sense of security as he turned into a lighted street where there were people and high buildings and blinking signs. After a while he found himself in the dim lobby of the structure that housed his office. Then he realized why he couldn't go home—because he might cause his wife and baby to see it, just as the doctor had seen it. And the baby, only two years old.

"Hello, Mr. Wran," said the night elevator man, a burly figure in blue overalls, sliding open the grille-work door to the old-fashioned cage. "I didn't know you were working nights now."

Catesby stepped in automatically. "Sudden rush of orders," he murmured inanely. "Some stuff that has to be gotten out."

The cage creaked to a stop at the top floor. "Be working very late, Mr. Wran?"

He nodded vaguely, watched the car slide out of sight, found his keys, swiftly crossed the outer office, and entered his own. His hand went out to the light switch, but then the thought occurred to him that the two lighted windows, standing out against the dark bulk of the building, would indicate his whereabouts and serve as a goal toward which something could crawl and climb. He moved his chair so that the back was against the wall and sat down in the semidarkness. He did not remove his overcoat.

For a long time he sat there motionless, listening to his own breathing and the faraway sounds from the streets below; the thin metallic surge of the crosstown streetcar, the farther one of the elevated, faint lonely cries and honkings, indistinct rumblings. Words he had spoken to Miss Millick in nervous jest came back to him with the bitter taste of truth. He found himself unable to reason critically or connectedly, but by their own volition thoughts rose up into his mind and gyrated slowly and rearranged themselves, with the inevitable movement of planets.

Gradually his mental picture of the world was transformed. No longer a world of material atoms and empty space, but a world in which the bodiless existed and moved according to its own obscure laws or unpredictable impulses. The new picture illumined with dreadful clarity certain general facts which had always bewildered and troubled him and from which he had tried to hide; the inevitability of hate and war, the diabolically timed mischances which wrecked the best of human intentions, the walls of willful misunderstanding that divided one man from another, the eternal vitality of cruelty and ignorance and greed. They seemed appropriate now, necessary parts of the picture. And superstition only a kind of wisdom.

Then his thoughts returned to himself, and the question he had asked Miss Millick came back, "What would such a thing want from a person? Sacrifices? Worship? Or just fear? What could you do to stop it from troubling you?" It had now become a purely practical question.

With an explosive jangle, the phone began to ring. "Cate, I've been trying everywhere to get you," said his wife. "I never thought you'd be at the office. What are you doing? I've been worried."

He said something about work.

"You'll be home right away?" came the faint anxious question. "I'm a little frightened. Ronny just had a scare. It woke him up. He kept pointing to the window saying, 'Black man, black man.' Of course it's something he dreamed. But I'm frightened. You will be home? What's that, dear? Can't you hear me?"

"I will. Right away," he said. Then he was out of the office, buzzing the night bell and peering down the shaft.

He saw it peering up the shaft at him from three floors below, the sacking face pressed close against the iron grille-work. It started up the stair at a shockingly swift, shambling gait, vanishing temporarily from sight as it swung into the second corridor below.

Catesby clawed at the door to the office, realized he had not locked it, pushed it in, slammed and locked it behind him, retreated to the other side of the room, cowered between the filing cases and the wall. His teeth were clicking. He heard the groan of the rising cage. A silhouette darkened the frosted glass of the door, blotting out part of the grotesque reverse of the company name. After a little the door opened.

The big-globed overhead light flared on and, standing just inside the door, her hand on the switch, he saw Miss Millick.

"Why, Mr. Wran," she stammered vacuously, "I didn't know you were here. I'd just come in to do some extra typing after the movie. I didn't . . . but the lights weren't on. What were you—"

He stared at her. He wanted to shout in relief, grab hold of her, talk rapidly. He realized he was grinning hysterically.

"Why, Mr. Wran, what's happened to you?" she asked embarrassedly, ending with a stupid titter. "Are you feeling sick? Isn't there something I can do for you?"

He shook his head jerkily, and managed to say, "No, I'm just leaving. I was doing some extra work myself."

"But you *look* sick," she insisted, and walked over toward him. He inconsequentially realized she must have stepped in mud, for her high-heeled shoes left neat black prints.

"Yes, I'm sure you must be sick. You're so terribly pale." She sounded like an enthusiastic, incompetent nurse. Her face brightened with a sudden inspiration. "I've got something in my bag that'll fix you up right away," she said. "It's for indigestion."

She fumbled at her stuffed oblong purse. He noticed that she was absent-mindedly holding it shut with one hand while she tried to open it with the other. Then, under his very eyes, he saw her bend back the thick prongs of metal locking the purse as if they were tinfoil, or as if her fingers had become a pair of steel pliers.

Instantly his memory recited the words he had spoken to Miss Millick that afternoon. "It couldn't hurt you physically— at first . . . gradually get its hooks into the world . . . might even get control of suitably vacuous minds. Then it could hurt whomever it wanted." A sickish, cold feeling came to a focus inside him. He began to edge toward the door.

But Miss Millick hurried ahead of him.

"You don't have to wait, Fred," she called. "Mr. Wran's decided to stay a while longer."

The door to the cage shut with a mechanical rattle. The cage creaked. Then she turned around in the door.

"Why, Mr. Wran," she gurgled reproachfully, "I just couldn't think of letting you go home now. I'm sure you're terribly unwell. Why, you might collapse in the street. You've just got to stay here until you feel different."

The creaking died away. He stood in the center of the office motionless. His eyes traced the course of Miss Millick's footprints to where she stood blocking the door. Then a sound that was almost a scream was wrenched out of him, for he saw that the flesh of her face was beginning to change color; blackening until the powder on it was a sickly white dust, rouge a hideous pinkish one, lipstick a translucent red film. It was the same with her hands and with the skin beneath her thin silk stockings.

"Why, Mr. Wran," she said, "you're acting as if you were crazy. You must lie down for a little while. Here, I'll help you off with your coat."

The nauseously idiotic and rasping note was the same; only it had been intensified. As she came toward him he turned and ran through the storeroom, clattered a key desperately at the lock of the second door to the corridor.

"Why, Mr. Wran," he heard her call, "are you having some kind of fit? You must let me help you."

The door came open and he plunged out into the corridor and up the stairs immediately ahead. It was only when he reached the top that he realized the heavy steel door in front of him led to the roof. He jerked up the catch.

"Why, Mr. Wran, you mustn't run away. I'm coming after you."

Then he was out on the gritty tar paper of the roof, the night sky was clouded and murky, with a faint pinkish glow from the neon signs. From the distant mills rose a ghostly spurt of flame. He ran to the edge. The street lights glared dizzily upward. Two men walking along were round blobs of hat and shoulders. He swung around.

The thing was in the doorway. The voice was no longer solicitous but moronically playful, each sentence ending in a titter.

"Why, Mr. Wran, why have you come up here? We're all alone. Just think, I might push you off."

The thing came slowly toward him. He moved backward until his heels touched the low parapet. Without knowing why or what he was going to do, he dropped to his knees. The black, coarse-grained face came nearer, a focus for the worst in the world, a gathering point for poisons from everywhere. Then the lucidity of terror took possession of his mind, and words formed on his lips

"I will obey you. You are my god," he said. "You have supreme power over man and his animals and his machines.

You rule this city and all others. I recognize that. Therefore spare me."

Again the titter, closer. "Why, Mr. Wran, you never talked like this before. Do you mean it?"

"The world is yours to do with as you will, save or tear to pieces." He answered fawningly, as the words automatically fitted themselves together into vaguely liturgical patterns. "I recognize that. I will praise, I will sacrifice. In smoke and soot and flame I will worship you forever."

The voice did not answer. He looked up. There was only Miss Millick, deathly pale and swaying drunkenly. Her eyes were closed. He caught her as she wobbled toward him. His knees gave way under the added weight and they sank down together on the roof edge.

After a while she began to twitch. Small wordless noises came from her throat, and her eyelids edged open.

"Come on, we'll go downstairs," he murmured jerkily, trying to draw her up. "You're feeling bad."

"I'm terribly dizzy," she whispered. "I must have fainted. I didn't eat enough. And then I'm so nervous lately, about the war and everything, I guess. Why, we're on the roof! Did you bring me up here to get some air? Or did I come up without knowing it? I'm awfully foolish. I used to walk in my sleep, my mother said."

As he helped her down the stairs, she turned and looked at him. "Why, Mr. Wran," she said, faintly, "you've got a big smudge on your forehead. Here, let me get it off for you." Weakly she rubbed at it with her handkerchief. She started to sway again and he steadied her.

"No, I'll be all right," she said. "Only I feel cold. What happened, Mr. Wran? Did I have some sort of fainting spell?"

He told her it was something like that.

Later, riding home in an empty elevated car, he wondered how long he would be safe from the thing. It was a purely practical problem. He had no way of knowing, but instinct told him he had satisfied the brute for some time. Would it want more when it came again? Time enough to answer that question when it arose. It might be hard, he realized, to keep out of an insane asylum. With Helen and Ronny to protect, as well as himself, he would have to be careful and tight-lipped. He began to speculate as to how many other men and women had seen the thing or things like it, and knew that mankind had once again spawned a ghost world, and that superstition once more ruled.

The elevated slowed and lurched in a familiar fashion. He looked at the roofs again, near the curve. They seemed very ordinary, as if what made them impressive had gone away for a while.

1941

TENNESSEE WILLIAMS

(1911–1983)

The Mysteries of the Joy Rio

Perhaps because he was a watch repairman, Mr. Gonzales had grown to be rather indifferent to time. A single watch or clock can be a powerful influence on a man, but when a man lives among as many watches and clocks as crowded the tiny, dim shop of Mr. Gonzales, some lagging behind, some skipping ahead, but all ticking monotonously on in their witless fashion, the multitude of them may be likely to deprive them of importance, as a gem loses its value when there are too many just like it which are too easily or cheaply obtainable. At any rate, Mr. Gonzales kept very irregular hours, if he could be said to keep any hours at all, and if he had not been where he was for such a long time, his trade would have suffered badly. But Mr. Gonzales had occupied his tiny shop for more than twenty years, since he had come to the city as a boy of nineteen to work as an apprentice to the original owner of the shop, a very strange and fat man of German descent named Kroger, Emiel Kroger, who had now been dead a long time. Emiel Kroger, being a romantically practical Teuton, had taken time, the commodity he worked with, with intense seriousness. In practically all his behavior he had imitated a perfectly adjusted fat silver watch. Mr. Gonzales, who was then young enough to be known as Pablo, had been his only sustained flirtation with the confusing, quicksilver world that exists outside of regularities. He had met Pablo during a watchmakers' convention in Dallas, Texas, where Pablo, who had illegally come into the country from Mexico a few days before, was drifting hungrily about the streets, and at that time Mr. Gonzales, Pablo, had not grown plump but had a lustrous dark grace which had completely bewitched Mr. Kroger. For as I have noted already, Mr. Kroger was a fat and strange man, subject to the kind of bewitchment that the graceful young Pablo could cast. The spell was so strong that it interrupted the fleeting and furtive practices of a

lifetime in Mr. Kroger and induced him to take the boy home
with him, to his shop-residence, where Pablo, now grown to
the mature and fleshy proportions of Mr. Gonzales, had lived
ever since, for three years before the death of his protector and
for more than seventeen years after that, as the inheritor of
shop-residence, clocks, watches, and everything else that Mr.
Kroger had owned except a few pieces of dining-room silver
which Emiel Kroger had left as a token bequest to a married
sister in Toledo.

Some of these facts are of dubious pertinence to the little
history which is to be unfolded. The important one is the fact
that Mr. Gonzales had managed to drift enviably apart from
the regularities that rule most other lives. Some days he would
not open his shop at all and some days he would open it only
for an hour or two in the morning, or in the late evening when
other shops had closed, and in spite of these caprices he managed to continue to get along fairly well, due to the excellence
of his work, when he did it, the fact that he was so well established in his own quiet way, the advantage of his location in a
neighborhood where nearly everybody had an old alarm-clock
which had to be kept in condition to order their lives, (this
community being one inhabited mostly by people with small-
paying jobs), but it was also due in measurable part to the fact
that the thrifty Mr. Kroger, when he finally succumbed to a
chronic disease of the bowels, had left a tidy sum in government bonds, and this capital, bringing in about a hundred and
seventy dollars a month, would have kept Mr. Gonzales going
along in a commonplace but comfortable fashion even if he
had declined to do anything whatsoever. It was a pity that the
late, or rather long-ago, Mr. Kroger, had not understood what
a fundamentally peaceable sort of young man he had taken
under his wing. Too bad he couldn't have guessed how perfectly everything suited Pablo Gonzales. But youth does not
betray its true nature as palpably as the later years do, and Mr.
Kroger had taken the animated allure of his young protégé, the
flickering lights in his eyes and his quick, nervous movements,
his very grace and slimness, as meaning something difficult to
keep hold of. And as the old gentleman declined in health, as
he did quite steadily during the three years that Pablo lived
with him, he was never certain that the incalculably precious

bird flown into his nest was not one of sudden passage but rather the kind that prefers to keep a faithful commitment to a single place, the nest-building kind, and not only that, but the very-rare-indeed-kind that gives love back as generously as he takes it. The long-ago Mr. Kroger had paid little attention to his illness, even when it entered the stage of acute pain, so intense was his absorption in what he thought was the tricky business of holding Pablo close to him. If only he had known that for all this time after his decease the boy would still be in the watchshop, how it might have relieved him! But on the other hand, maybe this anxiety, mixed as it was with so much tenderness and sad delight, was actually a blessing, standing as it did between the dying old man and a concern with death.

Pablo had never flown. But the sweet bird of youth had flown from Pablo Gonzales, leaving him rather sad, with a soft yellow face that was just as round as the moon. Clocks and watches he fixed with marvelous delicacy and precision, but he paid no attention to them; he had grown as obliviously accustomed to their many small noises as someone grows to the sound of waves who has always lived by the sea. Although he wasn't aware of it, it was actually light by which he told time, and always in the afternoons when the light had begun to fail (through the narrow window and narrower, dusty skylight at the back of the shop), Mr. Gonzales automatically rose from his stooped position over littered table and gooseneck lamp, took off his close-seeing glasses with magnifying lenses, and took to the street. He did not go far and he always went in the same direction, across town toward the river where there was an old opera house, now converted into a third-rate cinema, which specialized in the showing of cowboy pictures and other films of the sort that have a special appeal to children and male adolescents. The name of this movie-house was the Joy Rio, a name peculiar enough but nowhere nearly so peculiar as the place itself.

The old opera house was a miniature of all the great opera houses of the old world, which is to say its interior was faded gilt and incredibly old and abused red damask which extended upwards through at least three tiers and possibly five. The upper stairs, that is, the stairs beyond the first gallery, were roped off and unlighted and the top of the theater was so peculiarly dusky, even with the silver screen flickering far below it, that Mr. Gonzales, used as he was to close work, could not have made it out from below. Once he had been there when the lights came on in the Joy Rio, but the coming on of the lights had so enormously confused and embarrassed him, that looking up was the last thing in the world he felt like doing. He had buried his nose in the collar of his coat and had scuttled out as quickly as a cockroach makes for the nearest shadow when a kitchen light comes on.

I have already suggested that there was something a bit special and obscure about Mr. Gonzales' habitual attendance at the Joy Rio, and that was my intention. For Mr. Gonzales had inherited more than the material possessions of his dead benefactor: he had also come into custody of his old protector's fleeting and furtive practices in dark places, the practices which Emiel Kroger had given up only when Pablo had come into his fading existence. The old man had left Mr. Gonzales the full gift of his shame, and now Mr. Gonzales did the sad, lonely things that Mr. Kroger had done for such a long time before his one lasting love came to him. Mr. Kroger had even practiced those things in the same place in which they were practiced now by Mr. Gonzales, in the many mysterious recesses of the Joy Rio, and Mr. Gonzales knew about this. He knew about it because Mr. Kroger had told him. Emiel Kroger had confessed his whole life and soul to Pablo Gonzales. It was his theory, the theory of most immoralists, that the soul becomes intolerably burdened with lies that have to be told to the world in order to be permitted to live in the world, and that unless this burden is relieved by entire honesty with *some one* person, who is trusted and adored, the soul will finally collapse beneath its weight of falsity. Much of the final months of the life of Emiel Kroger, increasingly dimmed by morphia, were devoted to these whispered confessions to his adored apprentice, and it was as if he had breathed the guilty soul of his past into the ears and brain and blood of the youth who listened, and not long after the death of Mr. Kroger, Pablo, who had stayed slim until then, had begun to accumulate fat. He never became anywhere nearly so gross as Emiel Kroger had been, but his delicate frame disappeared sadly from view among the irrelevant curves of a sallow plumpness. One by one the perfections

which he had owned were folded away as Pablo put on fat as a
widow puts on black garments. For a year beauty lingered
about him, ghostly, continually fading, and then it went out altogether, and at twenty-five he was already the nondescriptly
plump and moonfaced little man that he now was at forty, and
if in his waking hours somebody to whom he would have to
give a true answer had enquired of him, Pablo Gonzales, how
much do you think about the dead Mr. Kroger, he probably
would have shrugged and said, *Not much now. It's such a long
time ago.* But if the question were asked him while he slept, the
guileless heart of the sleeper would have responded, *Always,
always!*

II

Now across the great marble stairs, that rose above the first
gallery of the Joy Rio to the uncertain number of galleries
above it, there had been fastened a greasy and rotting length
of old velvet rope at the center of which was hung a sign that
said to *Keep Out.* But that rope had not always been there. It
had been there about twenty years, but the late Mr. Kroger had
known the Joy Rio in the days before the flight of stairs was
roped off. In those days the mysterious upper galleries of the
Joy Rio had been a sort of fiddler's green where practically
every device and fashion of carnality had run riot in a gloom so
thick that a chance partner could only be discovered by touch.
There were not rows of benches (as there were now on the
orchestra level and the one gallery still kept in use), but strings
of tiny boxes, extending in semicircles from one side of the
great proscenium to the other. In some of these boxes broken-
legged chairs might be found lying on their sides and shreds of
old hangings still clung to the sliding brass loops at the entrances. According to Emiel Kroger, who is our only authority
on these mysteries which share his remoteness in time, one
lived up there, in the upper reaches of the Joy Rio, an almost
sightless existence where the other senses, the senses of smell
and touch and hearing, had to develop a preternatural keenness in order to spare one from making awkward mistakes, such
as taking hold of the knee of a boy when it was a girl's knee
one looked for, and where sometimes little scenes of panic

occurred when a mistake of gender or of compatibility had been carried to a point where radical correction was called for. There had been many fights, there had even been rape and murder in those ancient boxes, till finally the obscure management of the Joy Rio had been compelled by the pressure of notoriety to shut down that part of the immense old building which had offered its principal enticement, and the Joy Rio, which had flourished until then, had then gone into sharp decline. It had been closed down and then reopened and closed down and reopened again. For several years it had opened and shut like a nervous lady's fan. Those were the years in which Mr. Kroger was dying. After his death the fitful era subsided, and now for about ten years the Joy Rio had been continually active as a third-rate cinema, closed only for one week during a threatened epidemic of poliomyelitis some years past and once for a few days when a small fire had damaged the projection booth. But nothing happened there now of a nature to provoke a disturbance. There were no complaints to the management or the police, and the dark glory of the upper galleries was a legend in such memories as that of the late Emiel Kroger and the present Pablo Gonzales, and one by one, of course, those memories died out and the legend died out with them. Places like the Joy Rio and the legends about them make one more than usually aware of the short bloom and the long fading out of things. The angel of such a place is a fat silver angel of sixty-three years in a shiny dark-blue alpaca jacket, with short, fat fingers that leave a damp mark where they touch, that sweat and tremble as they caress between whispers, an angel of such a kind as would be kicked out of heaven and laughed out of hell and admitted to earth only by grace of its habitual slyness, its gift for making itself a counterfeit being, and the connivance of those that a quarter tip and an old yellow smile can corrupt.

But the reformation of the Joy Rio was somewhat less than absolute. It had reformed only to the point of ostensible virtue, and in the back rows of the first gallery at certain hours in the afternoon and very late at night were things going on of the sort Mr. Gonzales sometimes looked for. At those hours the Joy Rio contained few patrons, and since the seats in the orchestra were in far better condition, those who had come to sit comfortably watching the picture would naturally remain downstairs; the few that elected to sit in the nearly deserted rows of the first gallery did so either because smoking was permitted in that section—or *because* . . .

There was a danger, of course, there always is a danger with places and things like that, but Mr. Gonzales was a tentative person not given to leaping before he looked. If a patron had entered the first gallery only in order to smoke, you could usually count on his occupying a seat along the aisle. If the patron had bothered to edge his way toward the center of a row of seats irregular as the jawbone of poor Yorick, one could assume as infallibly as one can assume anything in a universe where chance is the one invariable, that he had chosen his seat with something more than a cigarette in mind. Mr. Gonzales did not take many chances. This was a respect in which he paid due homage to the wise old spirit of the late Emiel Kroger, that romantically practical Teuton who used to murmur to Pablo, between sleeping and waking, a sort of incantation that went like this: Sometimes you will find it and other times you won't find it and the times you don't find it are the times when you have got to be careful. Those are the times when you have got to remember that other times you *will* find it, not *this* time but the *next* time, or the time *after* that, and then you've got to be able to go home without it, yes, those times are the times when you have got to be able to go home without it, go home *alone* without it . . .

Pablo didn't know, then, that he would ever have need of this practical wisdom that his benefactor had drawn from his almost lifelong pursuit of a pleasure which was almost as unreal and basically unsatisfactory as an embrace in a dream. Pablo didn't know then that he would inherit so much from the old man who took care of him, and at that time, when Emiel Kroger, in the dimness of morphia and weakness following hemorrhage, had poured into the delicate ear of his apprentice, drop by slow, liquid drop, this distillation of all he had learned in the years before he found Pablo, the boy had felt for this whisper the same horror and pity that he felt for the mortal disease in the flesh of his benefactor, and only gradually, in the long years since the man and his whisper had ceased, had the singsong rigmarole begun to have sense for him, a practical

wisdom that such a man as Pablo had turned into, a man such
as Mr. Gonzales, could live by safely and quietly and still find
pleasure . . .

Mr. Gonzales was careful, and for careful people life has a tendency to take on the character of an almost arid plain with only
here and there, at wide intervals, the solitary palm tree and its
shadow and the spring alongside it. Mr. Kroger's life had been
much the same until he had come across Pablo at the watchmakers' convention in Dallas. But so far in Mr. Gonzales' life
there had been no Pablo. In his life there had been only Mr.
Kroger and the sort of things that Mr. Kroger had looked for
and sometimes found but most times continued patiently to
look for in the great expanse of arid country which his lifetime
had been before the discovery of Pablo. And since it is not my
intention to spin this story out any longer than its content seems
to call for, I am not going to attempt to sustain your interest in
it with a descripion of the few palm trees on the uneventful
desert through which the successor to Emiel Kroger wandered
after the death of the man who had been his life. But I am
going to remove you rather precipitately to a summer afternoon which we will call *Now* when Mr. Gonzales learned that
he was dying, and not only dying but dying of the same trouble that had put the period under the question mark of Emiel
Kroger. The scene, if I can call it that, takes place in a doctor's
office. After some hedging on the part of the doctor, the word
malignant is uttered. The hand is placed on the shoulder,
almost contemptuously comforting, and Mr. Gonzales is assured that surgery is unnecessary because the condition is not
susceptible to any help but that of drugs to relax the afflicted
organs. And after that the scene is abruptly blacked out . . .

Now it is a year later. Mr. Gonzales has recovered more or
less from the shocking information that he received from his
doctor. He has been repairing watches and clocks almost as
well as ever, and there has been remarkably little alteration in
his way of life. Only a little more frequently is the shop closed.
It is apparent, now, that the disease from which he suffers does
not intend to destroy him any more suddenly than it destroyed

the man before him. It grows slowly, the growth, and in fact it
has recently shown signs of what is called a remission. There is
no pain, hardly any and hardly ever. The most palpable symptom is loss of appetite and, as a result of that, a steady decrease
of weight. Now rather startlingly, after all this time, the graceful approximation of Pablo's delicate structure has come back
out of the irrelevant contours which had engulfed it after the
long-ago death of Emiel Kroger. The mirrors are not very
good in the dim little residence-shop, where he lives in his long
wait for death, and when he looks in them, Mr. Gonzales sees
the boy that was loved by the man whom he loved. It is almost
Pablo. Pablo has almost returned from Mr. Gonzales.

And then one afternoon . . .

IV

The new usher at the Joy Rio was a boy of seventeen and the
little Jewish manager had told him that he must pay particular
attention to the roped-off staircase to see to it that nobody
slipped upstairs to the forbidden region of the upper galleries,
but this boy was in love with a girl named Gladys who came
to the Joy Rio every afternoon, now that school was let out for
the summer, and loitered around the entrance where George,
the usher, was stationed. She wore a thin, almost transparent,
white blouse with nothing much underneath it. Her skirt was
usually of sheer silken material that followed her heart-shaped
loins as raptly as George's hand followed them when he embraced her in the dark ladies' room on the balcony level of the
Joy Rio. Sensual delirium possessed him those afternoons when
Gladys loitered near him. But the recently changed management of the Joy Rio was not a strict one, and in the summer
vigilance was more than commonly relaxed. George stayed near
the downstairs entrance, twitching restively in his tight, faded
uniform till Gladys drifted in from the afternoon streets on a
slow tide of lilac perfume. She would seem not to see him as
she sauntered up the aisle he indicated with his flashlight and
took a seat in the back of the orchestra section where he could
find her easily when the "coast was clear," or if he kept her
waiting too long and she was more than usually bored with the
film, she would stroll back out to the lobby and inquire in her

childish drawl, Where is the Ladies' Room, Please? Sometimes he would curse her fiercely under his breath because she hadn't waited. But he would have to direct her to the staircase, and she would go up there and wait for him, and the knowledge that she was up there waiting would finally overpower his prudence to the point where he would even abandon his station if the little manager, Mr. Katz, had his office door wide open. The ladies' room was otherwise not in use. Its light-switch was broken, or if it was repaired, the bulbs would be mysteriously missing. When ladies other than Gladys enquired about it, George would say gruffly, The ladies' room's out of order. It made an almost perfect retreat for the young lovers. The door left ajar gave warning of footsteps on the grand marble staircase in time for George to come out with his hands in his pockets before whoever was coming could catch him at it. But these interruptions would sometimes infuriate him, especially when a patron would insist on borrowing his flashlight to use the cabinet in the room where Gladys waited with her crumpled silk skirt gathered high about her flanks (leaning against the invisible dried-up washbasin) which were the blazing black heart of the insatiably concave summer.

In the old days Mr. Gonzales used to go to the Joy Rio in the late afternoons but since his illness he had been going earlier because the days tired him earlier, especially the steaming days of August which were now in progress. Mr. Gonzales knew about George and Gladys; he made it his business, of course, to know everything there was to be known about the Joy Rio, which was his earthly heaven, and, of course, George also knew about Mr. Gonzales; he knew why Mr. Gonzales gave him a fifty cent tip every time he inquired his way to the men's room upstairs, each time as if he had never gone upstairs before. Sometimes George muttered something under his breath, but the tributes collected from patrons like Mr. Gonzales had so far ensured his complicity in their venal practices. But then one day in August, on one of the very hottest and blindingly bright afternoons, George was so absorbed in the delights of Gladys that Mr. Gonzales had arrived at the top of the stairs to the balcony before George heard his footsteps. Then he heard them and he clamped a sweating palm over the mouth of Gladys which was full of stammerings of his name and the name of God. He waited, but Mr. Gonzales also waited. Mr. Gonzales was actually waiting at the top of the stairs to recover his breath from the climb, but George, who could see him, now, through the door kept slightly ajar, suspected that he was waiting to catch him coming out of his secret place. A fury burst in the boy. He thrust Gladys violently back against the wash-basin and charged out of the room without even bothering to button his fly. He rushed up to the slight figure waiting near the stairs and began to shout a dreadful word at Mr. Gonzales, the word "morphodite." His voice was shrill as a jungle bird's, shouting this word "morphodite." Mr. Gonzales kept backing away from him, with the lightness and grace of his youth, he kept stepping backwards from the livid face and threatening fists of the usher, all the time murmuring, No, no, no, no, no. The youth stood between him and the stairs below so it was toward the upper staircase that Mr. Gonzales took flight. All at once, as quickly and lightly as ever Pablo had moved, he darted under the length of velvet rope with the sign "Keep Out." George's pursuit was interrupted by the manager of the theater, who seized his arm so fiercely that the shoulder-seam of the uniform burst apart. This started another disturbance under the cover of which Mr. Gonzales fled farther and farther up the forbidden staircase into regions of deepening shadow. There were several points at which he might safely have stopped but his flight had now gathered an irresistible momentum and his legs moved like pistons bearing him up and up, and then——

At the very top of the staircase he was intercepted. He half turned back when he saw the dim figure waiting above, he almost turned and scrambled back down the grand marble staircase, when the name of his youth was called to him in a tone so commanding that he stopped and waited without daring to look up again.

Pablo, said Mr. Kroger, come on up here, Pablo.

Mr. Gonzales obeyed, but now the false power that his terror had given him was drained out of his body and he climbed with effort. At the top of the stairs where Emiel Kroger waited, he would have sunk exhausted to his knees if the old man hadn't sustained him with a firm hand at his elbow.

Mr. Kroger said, This way, Pablo. He led him into the Stygian blackness of one of the little boxes in the once-golden horse-shoe of the topmost tier. Now sit down, he commanded.

Pablo was too breathless to say anything except, Yes, and Mr. Kroger leaned over him and unbuttoned his collar for him, unfastened the clasp of his belt, all the while murmuring, There now, there now, Pablo.

The panic disappeared under those soothing old fingers and the breathing slowed down and stopped hurting the chest as if a fox was caught in it, and then at last Mr. Kroger began to lecture the boy as he used to, Pablo, he murmured, don't ever be so afraid of being lonely that you forget to be careful. Don't forget that you will find it sometimes but other times you won't be lucky, and those are the times when you have got to be patient, since patience is what you must have when you don't have luck.

The lecture continued softly, reassuringly familiar and repetitive as the tick of a bedroom clock in his ear, and if his ancient protector and instructor, Emiel Kroger, had not kept all the while soothing him with the moist, hot touch of his tremulous fingers, the gradual, the very gradual dimming out of things, his fading out of existence, would have terrified Pablo. But the ancient voice and fingers, as if they had never left him, kept on unbuttoning, touching, soothing, repeating the ancient lesson, saying it over and over like a penitent counting prayer beads, Sometimes you will have it and sometimes you won't have it, so don't be anxious about it. You must always be able to go home alone without it. Those are the times when you have got to remember that other times you will have it and it doesn't matter if sometimes you don't have it and have to go home without it, go home alone without it, go home alone without it. The gentle advice went on, and as it went on, Mr. Gonzales drifted away from everything but the wise old voice in his ear, even at last from that, but not till he was entirely comforted by it.

1941

JANE RICE

(1913–2003)

The Refugee

THE trouble with the war, Milli Cushman thought as she stared sulkily through streaming French windows into her rain-drenched garden, was that it was so frightfully boring. There weren't any men, any more. Interesting ones, that is. Or parties. Or little pink cocktails. Or café royale. Or long-stemmed roses wrapped in crackly green wax paper. There wasn't even a decent hairdresser left.

She had been a fool to stay on. But it had seemed so exciting. Everyone listening to the radio broadcasts; the streets blossoming with uniforms; an air of feverish gaiety, heady as Moselle wine, over all the city; the conversations that made one feel so important—so in the thick of things. Would the Maginot Line hold? Would the British come? Would the Low Countries be invaded? Was it true America had issued an ultimatum? Subjects that, now, were outdated as Gatling guns.

It had been terrifically stimulating being asked for her opinion, as an American. Of course, she hadn't been home for a number of years and considered herself a true cosmopolite freed from the provincialities of her own country—but, still, it had been nice, in those first flurried jack-in-the-box days of the war to be able to discourse so intelligently on Americana. It had been such *fun*.

Momentarily, Milli's eyes sparkled—remembering. The sparkle faded and died.

Then, unexpectedly, the city had become a gaunt, gray ghost. No, not a ghost, a cat. A gaunt gray cat with its bones showing through, as it crouched on silent haunches and stared unwinkingly before it. Like one of those cats that hung around the alley barrels of the better hotels. Or used to hang. Cooked, a cat bore a striking resemblance to a rabbit.

Overnight, a hush had fallen on everything. It was as though the city had gasped in one long, last, labored, dying breath.

And had held it. One could feel it in the atmosphere. Almost like a desperate pounding.

For some inexplicable reason, it reminded her of her childhood when she had played a game as the street lights began to bloom in the gathering dusk. "If I can hold my eyes open without blinking," she would tell herself, "until the last one is lighted, I'll get a new doll"—or a new muff—or a new hair ribbon—or whatever it might be she wanted. She could still recall that exhausted sense of time running out as the final lights went on. Most always she had won. Sometimes she hadn't, but most always she had. By the skin of her teeth.

It would be perfectly horrid, if this was one of the times when she *didn't* win. If she had to stay on and on, trotting back and forth seeing about that idiotic visa, and saving her hairpins and soap ends and things, it was going to be too utterly stultifying. It was fortunate she had had the perception to realize, before it was too late, who were the "right people" to know. It helped. Although, in these days, the right people didn't fare much better than the "wrong" ones.

Milli used "fare" in its strictest interpretation. Often, of late, she found herself dwelling, with an aching nostalgia, on her father's butcher shop in Pittsburgh. That had been before he'd invented a new deboner, or meat cleaver, or something, and had amassed an unbelievable amount of money before he strangled to death on a loose gold filling at Tim O'Toole's clambake.

Milli's recollection of her father was but a dim blur of red face and handlebar mustaches and a deep booming voice that Milli had associated with the line "the curfew tolls the knell of parting day," which she had been forced to learn and recite at P.S. 46. Her mother she didn't remember at all, as she had been called to pastures greener than anything Pittsburgh had to offer while Milli was yet wearing swaddling clothes in a perpetual state of dampness.

However, sharpened by adversity, Milli's recollections of the butcher shop were crystal clear. The refrigerator with whole sides of beef hanging from hooks, legs of lamb like fat tallow candles, plump chickens with thick drumsticks and their heads wrapped in brown paper, slabs of pork and veal, and, at Thanksgiving and Christmas, short-legged ducks, and high-breasted turkeys, and big, yellow geese. In the showcase had been chops, and steaks, and huge roasts, and all sorts of sausages and spiced meats laid out in white enamel trays with carrot tops in between for "dressing."

It was hopeless to dream of these things, but practically impossible to stop. The main topics of conversation no longer were of "major developments" but of where one could buy an extra ration of tea of questionable ingredients, or a grisly chop of dubious origin, or a few eggs of doubtful age—if one could pay the whopping price.

Well, as long as she had liqueur-filled chocolates, and she had had enough foresight to lay in quite a supply, she could be assured of her "share." They were better than money, at the present exchange.

The clock on the mantelpiece tinkled out the hours and Milli sighed. She should bathe and dress for dinner. But what was the use of keeping up appearances when there wasn't anyone to see. And it was dreadful curling the ends of one's hair on an iron. It was tedious and it didn't really *do* a great deal for one. And it had an unmistakable scent of burning shoe leather about it. The water would be tepid, if not actually cold. The soap wouldn't lather. The bathroom would be clammy, and the dinner, when it was forthcoming, would be a ragout of God knew what, a potato that had gouged-out areas in it, a limp salad, and a compote of dried fruit. And Maria grumbled so about serving it in courses. It was positively useless to diagram for her the jumbled up indecencies of a table d'hote. Maria was almost worse than no help at all. Definitely a bourgeois.

Milli yawned and stretched her arms above her head. She arose and, going over to the windows, stood looking out. A shaft of sunlight broke through the clouds and angered the tiny charms that dangled from her "war bracelet." An airplane studded with rhinestones, a miniature cannon with gold-leaf wheels, a toy soldier whose diamond chip eyes winked red and blue and green in the sun as he twirled helplessly on his silver chain. Ten or twelve of these baubles hung from the bracelet and it is indicative of Milli's character that she had bought them as a gift to herself to "celebrate" the last Bastille Day.

The sun's watery radiance turned the slackening rain into shining strings of quicksilver and made a drowned seascape of the garden. The faun that once had been a fountain, gleamed wetly in the pale, unearthly light and about its feet in the cracked basin, the pelting raindrops danced and bubbled like antiphonic memories of long gone grace notes. The flower heads were heavy with sodden, brown-edged petals and their stalks bent wearily as if cognizant of the fact that their lives were held by a tenuous thread that was soon to be snapped between the chill, biting teeth of an early frost.

Milli looked at the rain intermingled with sun and thought, the devil is beating his wife. That was what Savannah used to say, back in Pittsburgh. "The devil's beatin' his wife, sho nuff." Savannah, who made such luscious mince pies and cherry tarts, and whose baked hams were always brown and crunchy on top and stuck with cloves and crisscrossed with a knife so that the juice ran down in between the cracks and— Milli's culinary recollections suffered a complete collapse and her eyes opened very wide as they alighted on a head poking out inquisitively from the leafy seclusion of the tall hedge that bounded the garden.

Two brown hands pushed aside the foliage to allow a pair of broad, brown shoulders to come through.

Milli gave an infinitesimal gasp. A man was in her garden! A man who, judging from the visible portion of his excellent anatomy, had—literally—lost his shirt.

Instinctively, she opened her mouth to make some sort of an outcry. Whether she meant to call for aid, or to scare the interloper away, or merely to give vent to a belated exclamation of surprise, will forever be debatable for the object of her scrutiny chose that moment to turn his extraordinarily well-shaped head and his glance fixed itself on Milli. Milli's outcry died a-borning.

To begin with, it wasn't a man. It was a youth. And to end with, there was something about him, some queer, indefinable quality, that was absolutely fascinating.

He was, Milli thought, rather like a young panther, or a half-awakened leopard. He was, Milli admitted, entranced, beautiful. Perfectly *beautiful*. As an animal is beautiful and, automatically, she raised her chin so that the almost unnoticeable pouch under it became one with the line of her throat.

The youth was unabashed. If the discovery of his presence in a private garden left him in a difficult position, he effectively concealed his embarrassment. He regarded Milli steadfastly, and unwaveringly, and admiringly, and Milli, like a mesmerized bird, watched the rippling play of his muscles beneath his skin as he shoved the hedge apart still farther to obtain a better view of his erstwhile hostess.

Confusedly, Milli thought that it was lucky the windows were locked and, in the same mental breath, what a pity that they were.

The two peered at one another. Milli knew only that his hair was pasted flat to his head with the rain, and that his arms shone like sepia satin, and his eyes were tawny and filled with a flickering inward fire that made suet pudding of her knees.

For a long moment they remained so—their eyes locked. Milli's like those of an amazed china doll's; his like those of an untamed animal that was slightly underfed and resented the resulting gastric disturbances. The kitchen door banged and Milli could hear Maria calling a neighborly greeting to someone, as she emptied a bucket of water in the yard. At that instant the last vestiges of sun began to sink behind the horizon, and the youth was gone. There was just the garden, and the rain, and the hedge.

Dimly, as through a fog, Milli heard Maria come in, heard the latch shoot home, the metallic clatter of the bucket as she set it down under the sink and, from somewhere outside, the long, diminishingly mournful howl of a dog.

Milli shook herself out of her trance. She brushed a hand across her eyelids as if to clear them of cobwebs and, unbolting one of the windows, went out into the garden. There was no one. Only a footprint by the hedge, a bare footprint filling in with water.

She went back into the house. Maria was there, turning on the lamps. She looked at Milli curiously and Milli realized she must be an odd sight, indeed, her hair liberally besprinkled with raindrops, her shoes muddy, her dress streaked with moisture.

"I thought I saw someone out there, just now," she explained. "Someone looking in."

"The police, probably," Maria said dourly. "The police have no notions of privacy."

"No," Milli said. "No, it wasn't the police. Didn't I hear you go out a few moments ago?"

"I wasn't looking in," Maria said in a peevish voice. "For why should I look in? I have other things to do besides looking in the windows." She drew herself up to list vocally and with accompanying gestures the numberless things she had to do.

"Did you see anyone?" Milli asked quickly.

"Old Phillipe," Maria answered. "I saw old Phillipe. On his way to the inn in the pouring rain and he with a cough since last April. When one has a cough and it is raining, one does not look in windows. Anyway, Phillipe is too old. When one is as old as Phillipe one is no longer interested. Anyhow, his son was killed at Avignon. Phillipe would not look in the windows."

"You saw no one else?"

Maria's eyes narrowed. "Madame was expecting someone, no?"

"No," Milli said. "No, I just thought . . . it was nothing."

"If madame is expecting someone, perhaps it would be well to save the beverage for later in the evening?"

"I am expecting no one."

It was, Milli thought as she let the curling iron rest in the gaseous flame, next to impossible to tell which side of the fence Maria was on. She could easily be reporting things to *both* sides. One had to be careful. So very careful.

This chap in the garden, for example. He must have escaped from somewhere. That would account for the absence of clothes. He was a refugee of some sort. And refugees of any sort were dangerous. It was best to stick to the beaten path and those who trod thereon. But he was so beautiful. Like a stripling god. No more than twenty, surely. It was delightful to see again someone as young as twenty. It was—Milli swore fluently as the iron began to smoke; she waved it in the air to cool it and, testing it gingerly with a moistened forefinger, applied it to her coiffure—it was not only delightful, it was heavenly. It was, really, rather like one of those little, long ago, pink cocktails. It *did* something for one.

A faint aroma of singeing hair made itself manifest in the damp, wallpapery smelling room.

Milli considered the refugee from every angle as she ate her solitary dinner and, afterward, as she reclined on her chaise longue idly turning the pages of a book selected at random, and while she was disrobing for bed, and even when she was giving the underpart of her chin the regulation number of backhanded slaps, a ritual that as a rule occupied her entire attention.

Slipping into her dressing gown, she opened her window and leaned out, chin in hands, elbows on the sill. The moon rode in the sky—a hunted thing dodging behind wisps of tattered cloud, and the air was heavy and wet and redolent of dying leaves.

"The moon was a ghostly galleon," Milli quoted, feeling, somehow frail and immensely poetic. She smiled a sad, fragile smile in keeping with her mood and wondered if the refugee also was having a lonely rendezvous with the moon. Lying on his back in some hidden spot thinking, possibly, of— Her reverie was broken sharply by Maria's voice, shattering the stillness of the night. It was followed by a cascade of water.

"What on earth are you *doing*!" Milli called down exasperatedly.

"There was an animal out here," Maria yelled back, equally as exasperated. "Trampling in my mulch pile."

Milli started to say, "Don't be ridiculous, go to bed," but the sentence froze on her lips as she remembered the refugee. He had come back! Maria had thrown water on him! He had returned full of . . . of—well, hope for refuge, maybe, and Maria, the dolt, had chased him away!

"Wait," she called frenziedly into the darkness. "Wait! Oh, please, wait!"

Maria, thinking the command was for her, had waited, although the "please" had astonished her somewhat. Muttering under her breath, she had led her strangely overwrought mistress into the kitchen garden and had pointed out with pardonable pride the footprints in her mulch pile. Padded footprints. With claws.

"I saw the eyes," she said, "great, gleaming, yellow ones shining in the light when I started to pull the scullery blinds. Luckily I had a pot of water handy and I jerked open the door and—"

But her mistress wasn't listening. In truth, for one originally so upset, she had regained her composure with remarkable rapidity.

"Undoubtedly, the Trudeau's dog," she said with a total lack of interest.

"The Trudeau's dog is a Pomeranian," Maria said determinedly.

"No matter," Milli said. "Go to bed, Maria."

Maria went, mumbling to herself a querulous litany in which the word Pomeranian was, ever and anon, distinguishable—and pronounced with expletive force.

Milli awakened to find her room bright with sun, which was regrettable as it drew attention to the pattern of the rug and the well-worn condition of the curtains. It, likewise, did various things to Milli Cushman's face, which were little short of libelous. Libelous, that is, after Milli had painted herself a new one with painstaking care and the touch of an inspired, if jaded, master.

Downstairs, she found her breakfast ready and, because of its readiness, a trifle cold. She also found Maria, while not openly weeping, puffy as to eyes, and pink as to nose, and quite snuffly —a state that Milli found deplorable in servants.

A series of sharp questions brought to light the fact that old Phillipe was dead. Old Phillipe, it seemed, was not only dead but a bit mangled. To make a long story short, old Phillipe had been discovered in a condition that bordered on the skeletal. Identification had been made through particles of clothing and a pair of broken spectacles.

"You mean to say he was *eaten*!" Milli cried, which caused Maria to go off into a paroxysm of near hysterics from which Milli gathered, obscurely, that Maria blamed herself for old Phillipe's untimely demise.

By degrees, Milli drew it out of her. The footprints in the mulch pile. The kettle of water. The withdrawal of the animal to more congenial surroundings. Surroundings, doubtless, that were adjacent to the inn from whence old Phillipe, subsequently, plodded homeward. The stealthy pad of marauding feet. The encounter. The shriek. The awful ensuing silence.

Maria's detail was so graphic that it made Milli slightly ill, although it didn't prevent her from being firm about the matter of the wolf.

"Nonsense," Milli said. "Ridiculous. A *wolf*. Preposterous."

Maria explained about the bloody footprints leading away from the scene of slaughter. Footprints much too large for a dog. *Enormous* footprints.

"No doubt it was an enormous dog," Milli said coldly. "The natural habitat of a wolf is a forest, not a paved street."

Maria opened her mouth to go even further into detail, but Milli effectively shut it for her by a reprimand that, like the porridge of the smallest of the three bears, was neither too hot nor too cold, but just right.

After all, Milli thought, old Phillipe was better off. In all probability, he hadn't suffered a great deal. Most likely he had died of shock first. One more, one less, what difference did it make. Especially when one was as old as old Phillipe. At least he had lived his life while *she*, with so much life yet to be lived, was embalmed in a wretched sort of a flypaper existence that adhered to every inch of her no matter how hard she pulled. That visa. She would have to see about it again tomorrow. And the tea supply was disastrously low. And this horrible toast made of horrible bread that was crumbly and dry and tasted of sawdust. And her last bottle of eau de cologne practically *gone*, and she *couldn't* eat this mess in front of her.

Milli got up and went into the parlor. She flung wide the French windows and petulantly surveyed the garden. She had rented the place *because* of the garden—such a lovely setting for informal teas, she had thought, and impromptu chafing-dish suppers on the flagstones with candlelight and thin, graceful-stemmed glasses. She had pictured herself in appropriate attire, cutting flowers and doing whatever it was one did with peat moss, and now look at the thing. Just *look* at it!

Milli looked at it. Her breath went out of her. She drew it in again with an unbecoming wheeze. One hand flew to her throat.

In the garden, fast asleep, curled up in a ball under the hedge, was the refugee, all dappled with shadows and naked as the day he was born.

This time, it must be noted in all fairness, Milli didn't open her chops. If an outcry was in her, it wasn't strong enough to register on her reflexes. Her eyes blinked rapidly, as they

always did when Milli was thinking fast and, when she re-
crossed the parlor and walked down the hallway into the
kitchen, her heels made hard staccato sounds on the flooring,
as they always did when Milli had reached a decision.

Milli's decision made Maria as happy as could be, under the
circumstances, and ten minutes later, reticule in hand, Maria
departed for the domicile of her married niece's husband's
aunt who was a friend of old Phillipe's widow and, consequently, would be in possession of all the particulars and
would more than appreciate a helping hand and an attentive
ear over the week end.

Milli turned the key behind her. Lightly, she ran to the
scullery closet and took down from a nail a pair of grass-
stained pants that had belonged to a gardener who had been
liquidated before he had had a chance to return for his garment. Carrying the trousers over her arm, she retraced her
steps to the parlor and through the double French windows.

Quiet as she was, her unbidden guest was awake as soon as
her foot touched the first flagstone. He didn't move a muscle.
He just opened his eyes and watched her with the easy assurance of one who knows he can leave whenever he wants to and
several jumps ahead of the nearest competitor.

Milli stopped. She held out the pants.

"For you," she said. She gave them a toss. The boy, his queer,
light eyes watching her every movement, made no attempt to
catch them.

"Put them on," Milli said. She hesitated. "Please," she said,
adding, "I am your friend."

The boy sat up. Milli hastily turned her back.

"Tell me when you get them on," she ordered.

She waited, and waited, and waited and, hearing not the
faintest rustle, cautiously swiveled her head around. Once again
she drew in her breath and the wheeze was very nearly an eek
for, not six inches away, was her visitor—his lips pulled over his
teeth in a rather disconcerting smile, his eyes like glittering
nuggets of amber.

The thought raced through Milli's head that he was going
to "spring" at her, a thought tinged with relief as she subcon-

sciously noted that he *had* donned the ex-gardener's pants—tinged, too, with a thrilling sense of her own charms as the boy's eyes enumerated them one by one. She promptly elevated her chin and tried to keep her consternation from becoming obvious.

The boy laughed softly. A laugh that, somehow, was like a musical sort of a snarl. He stepped back. He bowed. Mockingly.

"What are you doing in my garden?" Milli asked, thinking it best to put him in his place, first and foremost. It wouldn't do to let him get out of hand. So soon, anyway.

"Sleeping," the boy said.

"Don't you have any place to sleep?"

"Yes. Many places. But I like this place."

"What happened to your clothes?"

The boy shrugged. He didn't answer.

"Are you a refugee?"

"In a way, I suppose, yes."

"You're hiding, aren't you?"

"Until you came out, I was simply sleeping. After I have eaten I sleep until a short while before sundown."

"You're not hungry?" Milli elevated her eyebrows in surprise.

"Not now." The boy let his glance rove fleetingly over his hostess' neck. "I will be later."

"What do you mean 'until a short while before sundown'? Have you been traveling by night?"

"Yes."

Milli made an ineffectual motion toward the trousers. "Wasn't it . . . I mean, going around without any . . . that is. I should think— Weren't you cold?"

"No."

"It's a wonder you didn't catch pneumonia."

The boy grinned. He patted his flat stomach. "Not pneumonia," he said. "But it wasn't much better. Old and stringy and without flavor."

Milli regarded him with a puzzled frown. She didn't like being "taken in." She decided to let it go.

"My name is Milli Cushman," she said. "You are more than welcome to stay here until you are rested. You won't be bothered. I have sent my maid away."

"You're most kind," the boy said with exaggerated politeness.

"Until tonight will be sufficient." If he realized that Milli was expecting him to introduce himself, he gave no sign.

After a pause, she spoke, a shade irritably. "No doubt, you *do* have a name?"

"I have lots of names. Even Latin ones."

"Well, for Heaven's sake, what is one? I can't just go about calling you 'you,' you know."

"You might call me Lupus," the boy said. "It's one of the Latin ones. It means wolf."

"Do they call you The Wolf!"

"Yes."

"How intriguing. But why?"

The boy smiled at her. "I daresay you'll find out," he said.

"You mean you're one of the ones who . . . well, like the affair of that German officer last week . . . that is to say, in a manner of speaking, you're one of those who're *still* going at it hammer and tongs?"

"Tooth and nail," the boy said.

"It seems so *silly*," Milli said. "What *good* does it do. It doesn't scare them. It just makes them angrier. And that makes it harder on *us*."

"Oh, but it *does* scare them," the boy said with an ironic lilt to his voice. "It scares them to death. Or at any rate it helps." He yawned, his tongue curling out like a cat's. And, suddenly, he was sullen. He glared at Milli with remote hostility.

"I'm sleepy," he growled. "I'm tired of talking. I want to go to sleep. Go away."

"Come inside," Milli said. "You can have Maria's bed." She gave him her most delectable glance. The one that involved the upsweeping and downsweeping of her eyelashes with the slimmest trace of a roguish quirk about the lips.

"I won't disturb you," she said. "And, besides, you might be caught if you stay in the garden. There was a man killed last night by some kind of a creature, or so they say, and Maria is sure to spread the news abroad that she threw water at something, and police just *might* investigate, and it *could* be very awkward for us both. Won't you come in, please?"

The boy looked at her in surly silence.

"Please, Lupus. For me?"

Once more he laughed softly. And this time the laugh was definitely a snarl. He reached out and pinched her. "For you, I will."

It was, Milli thought, not at all a flirtatious pinch. It was the kind of pinch her father used to give chickens to see if they were filled out in the proper places.

But Lupus wouldn't sleep in Maria's bed. He curled up on the floor of the parlor. Which, Milli thought, was just as well. It would save remaking Mania's bed so Maria wouldn't notice anything.

While her caller slept, Milli busied herself with pots and pans in the kitchen. It was tedious, but worth it. Tonight, there would be supper on the flagstones, with candles, and starlight, and all the accessories. A chance like this might not come her way for many another moon. She was resolved to make the most of it. As Savannah would have said, she was going to "do herself proud." For Lupus, the best was none too good. Not for herself, either. She nibbled a sandwich for luncheon, not wanting to spoil her appetite—not waking Lupus, for fear of spoiling his.

She got out her precious hoard of condiments. She scanned the fine printed directions on boxes. Meticulously she read the instructive leaflet inclosed in her paper bag of tanbarky appearing flour. She took off her bracelet, rolled up her sleeves, and went to work—humming happily to herself, a thing which she hadn't done for months.

She scraped, peeled, measured, sifted, chopped, stirred, beat and folded. Some fairly creditable muffins emerged from under her unaccustomed and amateurish fingers, a dessert that wasn't bad at all, and a salad that managed to give the impression of actually *being* a salad, which bordered on the miraculous.

The day slowly drew to a close and Milli was quite startled to find the hours had passed with such swiftness. So swiftly, that her initial awareness of their passing was caused by the advent of a patently ill-humored Lupus.

"Oh, dear," Milli said, "I didn't realize—is it late?"

"No," Lupus said. "It's growing early. The sun is going down."

"Are you hungry? I'm fixing some things I think will be rather good."

"I'm ravening," Lupus said. "Let's go watch the sunset."

Milli put her hands up to her coiffure, coquettishly, allowing her sleeves to fall away from her round, white arms.

"Wait till I fix my hair. I must be a sight."

"You are," Lupus agreed, his eyes glistening. "And I won't have to wait much longer." Effortlessly he moved across and stood over Milli, devouring her with an all-encompassing gaze.

"Won't you have one of these," Milli asked hurriedly, hoping his impetuosity wouldn't brim over *too* abruptly. She shoved a box of liqueur-filled chocolates at him. "There's no such thing as a cocktail any more. Come along, we'll eat them on the sofa. It's . . . it's cozier."

But Lupus wasn't interested in the chocolates. In the parlor he stretched his long, supple length on the floor and contemplated the garden, ablaze in the last rays of a dying sun.

Milli plopped down beside him and began to rub his back, gently with long, smooth, even strokes. Lupus rolled his head over in lazy, indifferent pleasure, and looked up at her with a hunger that would have been voluptuous, if it hadn't been so stark.

"Do you like that?" Milli whispered.

For a reply, Lupus opened his mouth and yawned. And into it Milli dropped a chocolate, while at the same instant she jabbed him savagely with a hairpin.

The boy sucked in his breath with a pained howl, and a full eight minutes before the sun went down, Lupus had neatly choked to death on a chocolate whose liqueur-filled insides contained a silver bullet from Milli Cushman's "war bracelet."

It had been, Milli told herself later, a near thing. And it would have been *ghastly* if it hadn't worked. But it *had* worked, tra la. Of course, it stood to reason that it *would*. After all, if, at death, a werewolf changed back into human form, why, logically, the human form would—if in close personal contact with a silver bullet *before* sundown—metamorphosis into a wolf.

It was marvelous that she'd happened to pick up "The Werewolf of Paris" yesterday—had given her an insight, so to speak, and it was *extremely* handy that she'd had all that butcher shop background.

Milli wiped her mouth daintily with a napkin. How divinely *full* she was. And with Maria gone she could have Lupus all to herself.

Down to the last, delicious morsel.

1943

ANTHONY BOUCHER

(1911–1968)

Mr. Lupescu

THE teacups rattled and flames flickered over the logs.

"Alan, I *do* wish you could do something about Bobby."

"Isn't that rather Robert's place?"

"Oh you know *Robert.* He's so busy doing good in nice abstract ways with committees in them."

"And headlines."

"He can't be bothered with things like Mr. Lupescu. After all, Bobby's only his *son.*"

"And yours, Marjorie."

"And mine. But things like this take a *man*, Alan."

The room was warm and peaceful; Alan stretched his long legs by the fire and felt domestic. Marjorie was soothing even when she fretted. The firelight did things to her hair and the curve of her blouse.

A small whirlwind entered at high velocity and stopped only when Marjorie said, "Bob-*by*! Say hello nicely to Uncle Alan."

Bobby said hello and stood tentatively on one foot.

"Alan. . . ." Marjorie prompted.

Alan sat up straight and tried to look paternal. "Well, Bobby," he said. "And where are you off to in such a hurry?"

"See Mr. Lupescu, 'f course. He usually comes afternoons."

"Your mother's been telling me about Mr. Lupescu. He must be quite a person."

"Oh, gee, I'll say he is, Uncle Alan. He's got a great big red nose and red gloves and red eyes—not like when you've been crying but really red like yours 're brown—and little red wings that twitch, only he can't fly with them 'cause they're ruddermentary he says. And he talks like—oh, gee, I can't do it, but he's swell, he is."

"Lupescu's a funny name for a fairy godfather, isn't it, Bobby?"

56

"Why? Mr. Lupescu always says why do all the fairies have to be Irish because it takes all kinds, doesn't it?"

"Alan!" Marjorie said. "I don't see that you're doing a *bit* of good. You talk to him seriously like that and you simply make him think it *is* serious. And you *do* know better, don't you, Bobby? You're just joking with us."

"Joking? About *Mr. Lupescu*?"

"Marjorie, you don't— Listen, Bobby. Your mother didn't mean to insult you or Mr. Lupescu. She just doesn't believe in what she's never seen, and you can't blame her. Now supposing you took her and me out in the garden and we could all see Mr. Lupescu. Wouldn't that be fun?"

"Uh, uh." Bobby shook his head gravely. "Not for Mr. Lupescu. He doesn't like people. Only little boys. And he says if ever bring people to see him then he'll let Gorgo get me. G'bye now." And the whirlwind departed.

Marjorie sighed. "At least thank heavens for Gorgo. I never can get a very clear picture out of Bobby, but he says Mr. Lupescu tells the most *terrible* things about him. And if there's any trouble about vegetables or brushing teeth all I have to say is *Gorgo* and hey presto!"

Alan rose. "I don't think you need worry, Marjorie. Mr. Lupescu seems to do more good than harm, and an active imagination is no curse to a child."

"You haven't *lived* with Mr. Lupescu."

"To live in a house like this, I'd chance it," Alan laughed. "But please forgive me now—back to the cottage and the typewriter. Seriously, why don't you ask Robert to talk with him?"

Marjorie spread her hands helplessly.

"I know. I'm always the one to assume responsibilities. And yet you married Robert."

Marjorie laughed. "I don't know. Somehow there's something *about* Robert. . . ." Her vague gesture happened to include the original Degas over the fireplace, the sterling tea service, and even the liveried footman who came in at that moment to clear away.

Mr. Lupescu was pretty wonderful that afternoon all right. He had a little kind of an itch like in his wings and they kept twitching all the time. Stardust, he said. It tickles. Got it up in the Milky Way. Friend of his has a wagon route up there.

Mr. Lupescu had lots of friends and they all did something you wouldn't ever think of not in a squillion years. That's why he didn't like people because people don't do things you can tell stories about. They just work or keep house or are mothers or something.

But one of Mr. Lupescu's friends now was captain of a ship only it went in time and Mr. Lupescu took trips with him and came back and told you all about what was happening this very minute five hundred years ago. And another of the friends was a radio engineer only he could tune in on all the kingdoms of faery and Mr. Lupescu would squidgle up his red nose and twist it like a dial and make noises like all the kingdoms of faery coming in on the set. And then there was Gorgo only he wasn't a friend, not exactly, not even to Mr. Lupescu.

They'd been playing for a couple of weeks only it must've been really hours 'cause Mamselle hadn't yelled about supper yet but Mr. Lupescu says Time is funny, when Mr. Lupescu screwed up his red eyes and said, "Bobby, let's go in the house."

"But there's people in the house and you don't—"

"I know I don't like people. That's why we're going in the house. Come on, Bobby, or I'll—"

So what could you do when you didn't even want to hear him say Gorgo's name?

He went into father's study through the French window and it was a strict rule that nobody ever went into father's study, but rules weren't for Mr. Lupescu.

Father was on the telephone telling somebody he'd try to be at a luncheon but there was a committee meeting that same morning but he'd see. While he was talking Mr. Lupescu went over to a table and opened a drawer and took something out.

When father hung up he saw Bobby first and started to be very mad. He said, "Young man, you've been trouble enough to your mother and me with all your stories about your red-winged Mr. Lupescu, and now if you're to start bursting in—"

You have to be polite and introduce people. "Father, this is Mr. Lupescu. And see he does, too, have red wings."

Mr. Lupescu held out the gun he'd taken from the drawer and shot father once right through the forehead. It made a little clean hole in front and a big messy hole in back. Father fell down and was dead.

"Now, Bobby," Mr. Lupescu said, "a lot of people are going to come here and ask you a lot of questions. And if you don't tell the truth about exactly what happened, I'll send Gorgo to fetch you."

Then Mr. Lupescu was gone through the French window onto the gravel path.

"It's a curious case, Lieutenant," the medical examiner said. "It's fortunate I've dabbled a bit in psychiatry; I can at least give you a lead until you get the experts in. The child's statement that his fairy godfather shot his father is obviously a simple flight-mechanism, susceptible of two interpretations. A, the father shot himself; the child was so horrified by the sight that he refused to accept it and invented this explanation. B, the child shot the father, let us say by accident, and shifted the blame to his imaginary scapegoat. B has of course more sinister implications; if the child had resented his father and created an ideal substitute, he might make the substitute destroy the reality. . . . But there's the solution to your eye-witness testimony; which alternative is true, Lieutenant, I leave it up to your researches into motive and the evidence of ballistics and fingerprints. The angle of the wound jibes with either."

The man with the red nose and eyes and gloves and wings walked down the back lane to the cottage. As soon as he got inside he took off his coat and removed the wings and the mechanism of strings and rubbers that made them twitch. He laid them on top of the ready pile of kindling and lit the fire. When it was well started, he added gloves. Then he took off the nose, kneaded the putty until the red of its outside vanished into the neutral brown of the mass, jammed it into a crack in the wall, and smoothed it over. Then he took the red-irised contact lenses out of his brown eyes and went into the kitchen, found a hammer, pounded them to powder, and washed the powder down the sink.

Alan started to pour himself a drink and found, to his pleased surprise, that he didn't especially need one. But he did feel tired. He could lie down and recapitulate it all, from the invention of

Mr. Lupescu (and Gorgo and the man with the Milky Way route) to today's success and on into the future when Marjorie, pliant, trusting Marjorie would be more desirable than ever as Robert's widow and heir. And Bobby would need a *man* to look after him.

Alan went into the bedroom. Several years passed by in the few seconds it took him to recognize what was waiting on the bed, but then Time is funny.

Alan said nothing.

"Mr. Lupescu, I presume?" said Gorgo.

1945

TRUMAN CAPOTE

(1924–1984)

Miriam

For several years, Mrs. H. T. Miller had lived alone in a pleasant apartment (two rooms with kitchenette) in a remodeled brownstone near the East River. She was a widow: Mr. H. T. Miller had left a reasonable amount of insurance. Her interests were narrow, she had no friends to speak of, and she rarely journeyed farther than the corner grocery. The other people in the house never seemed to notice her: her clothes were matter-of-fact, her hair iron-gray, clipped and casually waved; she did not use cosmetics, her features were plain and inconspicuous, and on her last birthday she was sixty-one. Her activities were seldom spontaneous: she kept the two rooms immaculate, smoked an occasional cigarette, prepared her own meals and tended a canary.

Then she met Miriam. It was snowing that night. Mrs. Miller had finished drying the supper dishes and was thumbing through an afternoon paper when she saw an advertisement of a picture playing at a neighborhood theater. The title sounded good, so she struggled into her beaver coat, laced her galoshes and left the apartment, leaving one light burning in the foyer: she found nothing more disturbing than a sensation of darkness.

The snow was fine, falling gently, not yet making an impression on the pavement. The wind from the river cut only at street crossings. Mrs. Miller hurried, her head bowed, oblivious as a mole burrowing a blind path. She stopped at a drugstore and bought a package of peppermints.

A long line stretched in front of the box office; she took her place at the end. There would be (a tired voice groaned) a short wait for all seats. Mrs. Miller rummaged in her leather handbag till she collected exactly the correct change for admission. The line seemed to be taking its own time and, looking around for some distraction, she suddenly became conscious of a little girl standing under the edge of the marquee.

Her hair was the longest and strangest Mrs. Miller had ever seen: absolutely silver-white, like an albino's. It flowed waist-length in smooth, loose lines. She was thin and fragilely constructed. There was a simple, special elegance in the way she stood with her thumbs in the pockets of a tailored plum-velvet coat.

Mrs. Miller felt oddly excited, and when the little girl glanced toward her, she smiled warmly. The little girl walked over and said, "Would you care to do me a favor?"

"I'd be glad to, if I can," said Mrs. Miller.

"Oh, it's quite easy. I merely want you to buy a ticket for me; they won't let me in otherwise. Here, I have the money." And gracefully she handed Mrs. Miller two dimes and a nickel.

They went into the theater together. An usherette directed them to a lounge; in twenty minutes the picture would be over.

"I feel just like a genuine criminal," said Mrs. Miller gaily, as she sat down. "I mean that sort of thing's against the law, isn't it? I do hope I haven't done the wrong thing. Your mother knows where you are, dear? I mean she does, doesn't she?"

The little girl said nothing. She unbuttoned her coat and folded it across her lap. Her dress underneath was prim and dark blue. A gold chain dangled about her neck, and her fingers, sensitive and musical-looking, toyed with it. Examining her more attentively, Mrs. Miller decided the truly distinctive feature was not her hair, but her eyes; they were hazel, steady, lacking any childlike quality whatsoever and, because of their size, seemed to consume her small face.

Mrs. Miller offered a peppermint. "What's your name, dear?"

"Miriam," she said, as though, in some curious way, it were information already familiar.

"Why, isn't that funny—my name's Miriam, too. And it's not a terribly common name either. Now, don't tell me your last name's Miller!"

"Just Miriam."

"But isn't that funny?"

"Moderately," said Miriam, and rolled the peppermint on her tongue.

Mrs. Miller flushed and shifted uncomfortably. "You have such a large vocabulary for such a little girl."

"Do I?"

"Well, yes," said Mrs. Miller, hastily changing the topic to: "Do you like the movies?"

"I really wouldn't know," said Miriam. "I've never been before."

Women began filling the lounge; the rumble of the newsreel bombs exploded in the distance. Mrs. Miller rose, tucking her purse under her arm. "I guess I'd better be running now if I want to get a seat," she said. "It was nice to have met you."

Miriam nodded ever so slightly.

It snowed all week. Wheels and footsteps moved soundlessly on the street, as if the business of living continued secretly behind a pale but impenetrable curtain. In the falling quiet there was no sky or earth, only snow lifting in the wind, frosting the window glass, chilling the rooms, deadening and hushing the city. At all hours it was necessary to keep a lamp lighted, and Mrs. Miller lost track of the days: Friday was no different from Saturday and on Sunday she went to the grocery: closed, of course.

That evening she scrambled eggs and fixed a bowl of tomato soup. Then, after putting on a flannel robe and cold-creaming her face, she propped herself up in bed with a hot-water bottle under her feet. She was reading the *Times* when the doorbell rang. At first she thought it must be a mistake and whoever it was would go away. But it rang and rang and settled to a persistent buzz. She looked at the clock: a little after eleven; it did not seem possible, she was always asleep by ten.

Climbing out of bed, she trotted barefoot across the living room. "I'm coming, please be patient." The latch was caught; she turned it this way and that way and the bell never paused an instant. "Stop it," she cried. The bolt gave way and she opened the door an inch. "What in heaven's name?"

"Hello," said Miriam.

"Oh . . . why, hello," said Mrs. Miller, stepping hesitantly into the hall. "You're that little girl."

"I thought you'd never answer, but I kept my finger on the button; I knew you were home. Aren't you glad to see me?"

Mrs. Miller did not know what to say. Miriam, she saw, wore

the same plum-velvet coat and now she had also a beret to match; her white hair was braided in two shining plaits and looped at the ends with enormous white ribbons.

"Since I've waited so long, you could at least let me in," she said.

"It's awfully late. . . ."

Miriam regarded her blankly. "What difference does that make? Let me in. It's cold out here and I have on a silk dress." Then, with a gentle gesture, she urged Mrs. Miller aside and passed into the apartment.

She dropped her coat and beret on a chair. She was indeed wearing a silk dress. White silk. White silk in February. The skirt was beautifully pleated and the sleeves long; it made a faint rustle as she strolled about the room. "I like your place," she said. "I like the rug, blue's my favorite color." She touched a paper rose in a vase on the coffee table. "Imitation," she commented wanly. "How sad. Aren't imitations sad?" She seated herself on the sofa, daintily spreading her skirt.

"What do you want?" asked Mrs. Miller.

"Sit down," said Miriam. "It makes me nervous to see people stand."

Mrs. Miller sank to a hassock. "What do you want?" she repeated.

"You know, I don't think you're glad I came."

For a second time Mrs. Miller was without an answer; her hand motioned vaguely. Miriam giggled and pressed back on a mound of chintz pillows. Mrs. Miller observed that the girl was less pale than she remembered; her cheeks were flushed.

"How did you know where I lived?"

Miriam frowned. "That's no question at all. What's your name? What's mine?"

"But I'm not listed in the phone book."

"Oh, let's talk about something else."

Mrs. Miller said. "Your mother must be insane to let a child like you wander around at all hours of the night—and in such ridiculous clothes. She must be out of her mind."

Miriam got up and moved to a corner where a covered bird cage hung from a ceiling chain. She peeked beneath the cover. "It's a canary," she said. "Would you mind if I woke him? I'd like to hear him sing."

"Leave Tommy alone," said Mrs. Miller, anxiously. "Don't you dare wake him."

"Certainly," said Miriam. "But I don't see why I can't hear him sing." And then, "Have you anything to eat? I'm starving! Even milk and a jam sandwich would be fine."

"Look," said Mrs. Miller, arising from the hassock, "look— if I make some nice sandwiches will you be a good child and run along home? It's past midnight, I'm sure."

"It's snowing," reproached Miriam. "And cold and dark."

"Well, you shouldn't have come here to begin with," said Mrs. Miller, struggling to control her voice. "I can't help the weather. If you want anything to eat you'll have to promise to leave."

Miriam brushed a braid against her cheek. Her eyes were thoughtful, as if weighing the proposition. She turned toward the bird cage. "Very well," she said, "I promise."

How old is she? Ten? Eleven? Mrs. Miller, in the kitchen, unsealed a jar of strawberry preserves and cut four slices of bread. She poured a glass of milk and paused to light a cigarette. *And why has she come?* Her hand shook as she held the match, fascinated, till it burned her finger. The canary was singing; singing as he did in the morning and at no other time. "Miriam," she called, "Miriam, I told you not to disturb Tommy." There was no answer. She called again; all she heard was the canary. She inhaled the cigarette and discovered she had lighted the cork-tip end and—oh, really, she mustn't lose her temper.

She carried the food in on a tray and set it on the coffee table. She saw first that the bird cage still wore its night cover. And Tommy was singing. It gave her a queer sensation. And no one was in the room. Mrs. Miller went through an alcove leading to her bedroom; at the door she caught her breath.

"What are you doing?" she asked.

Miriam glanced up and in her eyes there was a look that was not ordinary. She was standing by the bureau, a jewel case opened before her. For a minute she studied Mrs. Miller, forcing their eyes to meet, and she smiled. "There's nothing good here," she said. "But I like this." Her hand held a cameo brooch. "It's charming."

"Suppose—perhaps you'd better put it back," said Mrs.

Miller, feeling suddenly the need of some support. She leaned against the door frame; her head was unbearably heavy; a pressure weighted the rhythm of her heartbeat. The light seemed to flutter defectively. "Please, child—a gift from my husband . . ."

"But it's beautiful and I want it," said Miriam. "*Give it to me.*"

As she stood, striving to shape a sentence which would somehow save the brooch, it came to Mrs. Miller there was no one to whom she might turn; she was alone; a fact that had not been among her thoughts for a long time. Its sheer emphasis was stunning. But here in her own room in the hushed snow-city were evidences she could not ignore or, she knew with startling clarity, resist.

Miriam ate ravenously, and when the sandwiches and milk were gone, her fingers made cobweb movements over the plate, gathering crumbs. The cameo gleamed on her blouse, the blonde profile like a trick reflection of its wearer. "That was very nice," she sighed, "though now an almond cake or a cherry would be ideal. Sweets are lovely, don't you think?"

Mrs. Miller was perched precariously on the hassock, smoking a cigarette. Her hair net had slipped lopsided and loose strands straggled down her face. Her eyes were stupidly concentrated on nothing and her cheeks were mottled in red patches, as though a fierce slap had left permanent marks.

"Is there a candy—a cake?"

Mrs. Miller tapped ash on the rug. Her head swayed slightly as she tried to focus her eyes. "You promised to leave if I made the sandwiches," she said.

"Dear me, did I?"

"It was a promise and I'm tired and I don't feel well at all."

"Mustn't fret," said Miriam. "I'm only teasing."

She picked up her coat, slung it over her arm, and arranged her beret in front of a mirror. Presently she bent close to Mrs. Miller and whispered, "Kiss me good night."

"Please—I'd rather not," said Mrs. Miller.

Miriam lifted a shoulder, arched an eyebrow. "As you like," she said, and went directly to the coffee table, seized the vase containing the paper roses, carried it to where the hard surface of the floor lay bare, and hurled it downward. Glass sprayed in all directions and she stamped her foot on the bouquet.

Then slowly she walked to the door, but before closing it she looked back at Mrs. Miller with a slyly innocent curiosity.

Mrs. Miller spent the next day in bed, rising once to feed the canary and drink a cup of tea; she took her temperature and had none, yet her dreams were feverishly agitated; their unbalanced mood lingered even as she lay staring wide-eyed at the ceiling. One dream threaded through the others like an elusively mysterious theme in a complicated symphony, and the scenes it depicted were sharply outlined, as though sketched by a hand of gifted intensity: a small girl, wearing a bridal gown and a wreath of leaves, led a gray procession down a mountain path, and among them there was unusual silence till a woman at the rear asked, "Where is she taking us?" "No one knows," said an old man marching in front. "But isn't she pretty?" volunteered a third voice. "Isn't she like a frost flower . . . so shining and white?"

Tuesday morning she woke up feeling better; harsh slats of sunlight, slanting through Venetian blinds, shed a disrupting light on her unwholesome fancies. She opened the window to discover a thawed, mild-as-spring day; a sweep of clean new clouds crumpled against a vastly blue, out-of-season sky; and across the low line of rooftops she could see the river and smoke curving from tugboat stacks in a warm wind. A great silver truck plowed the snow-banked street, its machine sound humming on the air.

After straightening the apartment, she went to the grocer's, cashed a check and continued to Schrafft's where she ate breakfast and chatted happily with the waitress. Oh, it was a wonderful day—more like a holiday—and it would be so foolish to go home.

She boarded a Lexington Avenue bus and rode up to Eighty-sixth Street; it was here that she had decided to do a little shopping.

She had no idea what she wanted or needed, but she idled along, intent only upon the passers-by, brisk and preoccupied, who gave her a disturbing sense of separateness.

It was while waiting at the corner of Third Avenue that she

saw the man: an old man, bowlegged and stooped under an armload of bulging packages; he wore a shabby brown coat and a checkered cap. Suddenly she realized they were exchanging a smile: there was nothing friendly about this smile, it was merely two cold flickers of recognition. But she was certain she had never seen him before.

He was standing next to an El pillar, and as she crossed the street he turned and followed. He kept quite close; from the corner of her eye she watched his reflection wavering on the shopwindows.

Then in the middle of the block she stopped and faced him. He stopped also and cocked his head, grinning. But what could she say? Do? Here, in broad daylight, on Eighty-sixth Street? It was useless and, despising her own helplessness, she quickened her steps.

Now Second Avenue is a dismal street, made from scraps and ends; part cobblestone, part asphalt, part cement; and its atmosphere of desertion is permanent. Mrs. Miller walked five blocks without meeting anyone, and all the while the steady crunch of his footfalls in the snow stayed near. And when she came to a florist's shop, the sound was still with her. She hurried inside and watched through the glass door as the old man passed; he kept his eyes straight ahead and didn't slow his pace, but he did one strange, telling thing: he tipped his cap.

"Six white ones, did you say?" asked the florist. "Yes," she told him, "white roses." From there she went to a glassware store and selected a vase, presumably a replacement for the one Miriam had broken, though the price was intolerable and the vase itself (she thought) grotesquely vulgar. But a series of unaccountable purchases had begun, as if by pre-arranged plan: a plan of which she had not the least knowledge or control.

She bought a bag of glazed cherries, and at a place called the Knickerbocker Bakery she paid forty cents for six almond cakes.

Within the last hour the weather had turned cold again; like blurred lenses, winter clouds cast a shade over the sun, and the skeleton of an early dusk colored the sky; a damp mist mixed with the wind and the voices of a few children who romped high on mountains of gutter snow seemed lonely and cheerless. Soon the first flake fell, and when Mrs. Miller reached the brownstone house, snow was falling in a swift screen and foot tracks vanished as they were printed.

The white roses were arranged decoratively in the vase. The glazed cherries shone on a ceramic plate. The almond cakes, dusted with sugar, awaited a hand. The canary fluttered on its swing and picked at a bar of seed.

At precisely five the doorbell rang. Mrs. Miller *knew* who it was. The hem of her housecoat trailed as she crossed the floor. "Is that you?" she called.

"Naturally," said Miriam, the word resounding shrilly from the hall. "Open this door."

"Go away," said Mrs. Miller.

"Please hurry . . . I have a heavy package."

"Go away," said Mrs. Miller. She returned to the living room, lighted a cigarette, sat down and calmly listened to the buzzer; on and on and on. "You might as well leave. I have no intention of letting you in."

Shortly the bell stopped. For possibly ten minutes Mrs. Miller did not move. Then, hearing no sound, she concluded Miriam had gone. She tiptoed to the door and opened it a sliver; Miriam was half-reclining atop a cardboard box with a beautiful French doll cradled in her arms.

"Really, I thought you were never coming," she said peevishly. "Here, help me get this in, it's awfully heavy."

It was not spell-like compulsion that Mrs. Miller felt, but rather a curious passivity; she brought in the box, Miriam the doll. Miriam curled up on the sofa, not troubling to remove her coat or beret, and watched disinterestedly as Mrs. Miller dropped the box and stood trembling, trying to catch her breath.

"Thank you," she said. In the daylight she looked pinched and drawn, her hair less luminous. The French doll she was loving wore an exquisite powdered wig and its idiot glass eyes sought solace in Miriam's. "I have a surprise," she continued. "Look into my box."

Kneeling, Mrs. Miller parted the flaps and lifted out another doll; then a blue dress which she recalled as the one Miriam had worn that first night at the theater; and of the remainder she said, "It's all clothes. Why?"

"Because I've come to live with you," said Miriam, twisting a cherry stem. "Wasn't it nice of you to buy me the cherries . . . ?"

"But you can't! For God's sake go away—go away and leave me alone!"

". . . and the roses and the almond cakes? How really wonderfully generous. You know, these cherries are delicious. The last place I lived was with an old man; he was terribly poor and we never had good things to eat. But I think I'll be happy here." She paused to snuggle her doll closer. "Now, if you'll just show me where to put my things . . ."

Mrs Miller's face dissolved into a mask of ugly red lines; she began to cry, and it was an unnatural, tearless sort of weeping, as though, not having wept for a long time, she had forgotten how. Carefully she edged backward till she touched the door.

She fumbled through the hall and down the stairs to a landing below. She pounded frantically on the door of the first apartment she came to; a short, red-headed man answered and she pushed past him. "Say, what the hell is this?" he said. "Anything wrong, lover?" asked a young woman who appeared from the kitchen, drying her hands. And it was to her that Mrs. Miller turned.

"Listen," she cried, "I'm ashamed behaving this way but— well, I'm Mrs. H. T. Miller and I live upstairs and . . ." She pressed her hands over her face. "It sounds so absurd. . . ."

The woman guided her to a chair, while the man excitedly rattled pocket change. "Yeah?"

"I live upstairs and there's a little girl visiting me, and I suppose that I'm afraid of her. She won't leave and I can't make her and—she's going to do something terrible. She's already stolen my cameo, but she's about to do something worse— something terrible!"

The man asked, "Is she a relative, huh?"

Mrs. Miller shook her head. "I don't know who she is. Her name's Miriam, but I don't know for certain who she is."

"You gotta calm down, honey," said the woman, stroking Mrs. Miller's arm. "Harry here'll tend to this kid. Go on, lover." And Mrs. Miller said, "The door's open—5A."

After the man left, the woman brought a towel and bathed Mrs. Miller's face. "You're very kind," Mrs. Miller said. "I'm sorry to act like such a fool, only this wicked child. . . ."

"Sure, honey," consoled the woman. "Now, you better take it easy."

Mrs. Miller rested her head in the crook of her arm; she was quiet enough to be asleep. The woman turned a radio dial; a piano and a husky voice filled the silence and the woman, tapping her foot, kept excellent time. "Maybe we oughta go up too," she said.

"I don't want to see her again. I don't want to be anywhere near her."

"Uh huh, but what you shoulda done, you shoulda called a cop."

Presently they heard the man on the stairs. He strode into the room frowning and scratching the back of his neck. "Nobody there," he said, honestly embarrassed. "She musta beat it."

"Harry, you're a jerk," announced the woman. "We been sitting here the whole time and we woulda seen . . ." she stopped abruptly, for the man's glance was sharp.

"I looked all over," he said, "and there just ain't nobody there. Nobody, understand?"

"Tell me," said Mrs. Miller, rising, "tell me, did you see a large box? Or a doll?"

"No, ma'am, I didn't."

And the woman, as if delivering a verdict, said, "Well, for cryinoutloud. . . ."

Mrs. Miller entered her apartment softly; she walked to the center of the room and stood quite still. No, in a sense it had not changed: the roses, the cakes, and the cherries were in place. But this was an empty room, emptier than if the furnishings and familiars were not present, lifeless and petrified as a funeral parlor. The sofa loomed before her with a new strangeness: its vacancy had a meaning that would have been less penetrating and terrible had Miriam been curled on it. She gazed fixedly at the space where she remembered setting the box and, for a moment, the hassock spun desperately. And she looked through the window; surely the river was real, surely snow was falling—but then, one could not be certain witness to anything: Miriam, so vividly *there*—and yet, where was she? Where, where?

As though moving in a dream, she sank to a chair. The room was losing shape; it was dark and getting darker and there was nothing to be done about it; she could not lift her hand to light a lamp.

Suddenly, closing her eyes, she felt an upward surge, like a diver emerging from some deeper, greener depth. In times of terror or immense distress, there are moments when the mind waits, as though for a revelation, while a skein of calm is woven over thought; it is like a sleep, or a supernatural trance; and during this lull one is aware of a force of quiet reasoning: well, what if she had never really known a girl named Miriam? that she had been foolishly frightened on the street? In the end, like everything else, it was of no importance. For the only thing she had lost to Miriam was her identity, but now she knew she had found again the person who lived in this room, who cooked her own meals, who owned a canary, who was someone she could trust and believe in: Mrs. H. T. Miller.

Listening in contentment, she became aware of a double sound: a bureau drawer opening and closing; she seemed to hear it long after completion—opening and closing. Then gradually, the harshness of it was replaced by the murmur of a silk dress and this, delicately faint, was moving nearer and swelling in intensity till the walls trembled with the vibration and the room was caving under a wave of whispers. Mrs. Miller stiffened and opened her eyes to a dull, direct stare.

"Hello," said Miriam.

1945

JACK SNOW

(1907–1956)

Midnight

Between the hour of eleven and midnight John Ware made ready to perform the ceremony that would climax the years of homage he had paid to the dark powers of evil. Tonight he would become a part of that essence of dread that roams the night hours. At the last stroke of midnight his consciousness would leave his body and unite with that which shuns the light and is all depravity and evil. Then he would roam the world with this midnight elemental and for one hour savor all the evil that this alien being is capable of inspiring in human souls.

John Ware had lived so long among the shadows of evil that his mind had become tainted, and through the channel of his thoughts his soul had been corrupted by the poison of the dark powers with which he consorted.

There was scarcely a forbidden book of shocking ceremonies and nameless teachings that Ware had not consulted and pored over in the long hours of the night. When certain guarded books he desired were unobtainable, he had shown no hesitation in stealing them. Nor had Ware stopped with mere reading and studying these books. He had descended to the ultimate depths and put into practice the ceremonies, rites and black sorceries that stained the pages of the volumes. Often these practices had required human blood and human lives, and here again Ware had not hesitated. He had long ago lost count of the number of innocent persons who had mysteriously vanished from the face of the earth—victims of his insatiable craving for knowledge of the evil that dwells in the dark, furtively, when the powers of light are at their nadir.

John Ware had traveled to all the strange and little known parts of the earth. He had tricked and wormed secrets out of priests and dignitaries of ancient cults and religions of whose existence the world of clean daylight has no inkling. Africa, the

West Indies, Tibet, China, Ware knew them all and they held
no secret whose knowledge he had not violated.

By devious means Ware had secured admission to certain
private institutions and homes behind whose facades were
confined individuals who were not mad in the outright sense
of the everyday definition of the word, but who, given their
freedom, would loose nightmare horror on the world. Some
of these prisoners were so curiously shaped and formed that
they had been hidden away since childhood. In a number of
instances their vocal organs were so alien that the sounds they
uttered could not be considered human. Nevertheless, John
Ware had been heard to converse with them.

In John Ware's chamber stood an ancient clock, tall as a
human being, and abhorrently fashioned from age-yellowed
ivory. Its head was that of a woman in an advanced state of dissolution. Around the skull, from which shreds of ivory flesh
hung, were Roman numerals, marked by two death's head
beetles, which, engineered by intricate machinery in the clock,
crawled slowly around the perimeter of the skull to mark the
hours. Nor did this clock tick as does an ordinary clock. Deep
within its woman's bosom sounded a dull, regular thud, disturbingly similar to the beating of a human heart.

The malevolent creation of an unknown sorcerer of the dim
past, this eerie clock had been the property of a succession of
warlocks, alchemists, wizards, Satanists and like devotees of forbidden arts, each of whom had invested the clock with something of his own evil existence, so that a dark and revolting
nimbus hung about it and it seemed to exude a loathsome an-
imus from its repellently human form.

It was to this clock that John Ware addressed himself at the
first stroke of midnight. The clock did not announce the hour
in the fashion of other clocks. During the hour its ticking
sounded faint and dull, scarcely distinguishable above ordinary sounds. But at each hour the ticking rose to a muffled
thud, sounding like a human heart-beat heard through a
stethoscope. With these ominous thuds it marked the hours,
seeming to intimate that each beat of the human heart narrows
that much more the span of mortal life.

Now the clock sounded the midnight hour. "Thud, thud,

thud—" Before it stood John Ware, his body traced with ca-balistic markings in a black pigment which he had prepared according to an ancient and noxious formula.

As the clock thudded out the midnight hour, John Ware repeated an incantation, which, had it not been for his devouring passion for evil, would have caused even him to shudder at the mere sounds of the contorted vowels. To his mouthing of the unhuman phrases, he performed a pattern of motions with his body and limbs which was an unearthly grotesquerie of a dance.

"Thud, thud, thud—" the beat sounded for the twelfth time and then subsided to a dull, muffled murmur which was barely audible in the silence of the chamber. The body of John Ware sank to the thick rug and lay motionless. The spirit was gone from it. At the last stroke of the hour of midnight it had fled.

With a great thrill of exultation, John Ware found himself outside in the night. He had succeeded! That which he had summoned had accepted him! Now for the next hour he would feast to his fill on unholy evil. Ware was conscious that he was not alone as he moved effortlessly through the night air. He was accompanied by a being which he perceived only as an amorphous darkness, a darkness that was deeper and more absolute than the inky night, a darkness that was a vacuum or blank in the color spectrum.

Ware found himself plunging suddenly earthward. The walls of a building flashed past him and an instant later he was in a sumptuously furnished living room, where stood a man and a woman. Ware felt a strong bond between himself and the woman. Her thoughts were his, he felt as she did. A wave of terror was enveloping him, flowing to him from the woman, for the man standing before her held a revolver in his hand. He was about to pull the trigger. John Ware lived through an agony of fear in those few moments that the helpless woman cringed before the man. Then a shapeless darkness settled over the man. His eyes glazed dully. Like an automaton he pressed the trigger and the bullet crashed into the woman's heart. John Ware died as she died.

Once again Ware was soaring through the night, the black

being close at his side. He was shaken by the experience. What could it mean? How had he come to be identified so closely with the tortured consciousness of the murdered woman?

Again Ware felt himself plummeting earthward. This time he was in a musty cellar in the depths of a vast city's tenement section. A man lay chained to a crude, wooden table. Over him stood two creatures of loathsome and sadistic countenance. Then John Ware *was* the man on the table. He knew, he thought, he felt everything that the captive felt. He saw a black shadow settle over the two evil-looking men. Their eyes glazed, their lips parted slightly as saliva drooled from them. The men made use of an assortment of crude instruments, knives, scalpels, pincers and barbed hooks, in a manner which in ten short minutes reduced the helpless body before them from a screaming human being to a whimpering, senseless thing covered with wounds and rivulets of blood. John Ware suffered as the victim suffered. At last the tortured one slipped into unconsciousness. An instant later John Ware was moving swiftly through the night sky. At his side was the black being.

It had been terrible. Ware had endured agony that he had not believed the human body was capable of suffering. Why? Why had he been chained to the consciousness of the man on the torture table? Swiftly Ware and his companion soared through the night moving ever westward.

John Ware felt himself descending again. He caught a fleeting glimpse of a lonely farm house, with a single lamp glowing in one window. Then he was in an old fashioned country living room. In a wheel chair an aged man sat dozing. At his side, near the window, stood a table on which burned an oil lamp. A dark shape hovered over the sleeping man. Shuddering in his slumber, the man flung out one arm, restlessly. It struck the oil lamp, sending it crashing to the floor, where it shattered and a pool of flame sprang up instantly. The aged cripple awoke with a cry, and made an effort to wheel his chair from the flames. But it was too late. Already the carpet and floor were burning and now the man's clothing and the robe that covered his legs were afire. Instinctively the victim threw up his arms to shield his face. Then he screamed piercingly, again and again. John Ware felt everything that the old man felt. He suffered the inexpressible agony of being consumed alive by flames. Then he was outside in the night. Far below and behind him the house burned like a torch in the distance. Ware glanced fearfully at the shadow that accompanied him as they sped on at tremendous speed, ever westward.

Once again Ware felt himself hurtling down through the night. Where to this time? What unspeakable torment was he to endure now? All was dark about him. He glimpsed no city or abode as he flashed to earth. About him was only silence and darkness. Then like a wave engulfing his spirit, came a torrent of fear and dread. He was striving to push something upward. Panic thoughts consumed him. He would not die—he wanted to live—he would escape! He writhed and twisted in his narrow confines, his fists beating on the surface above him. It did not yield. John Ware knew that he was linked with the consciousness of a man who had been prematurely buried. Soon the victim's fists were dripping with blood as he ineffectually clawed and pounded at the lid of the coffin. As time is measured it didn't last long. The exertions of the doomed man caused him quickly to exhaust the small amount of air in the coffin and he soon smothered to death. John Ware experienced that, too. But the final obliteration and crushing of the hope that burned in the man's bosom probably was the worst of all.

Ware was again soaring through the night. His soul shuddered as he grasped the final, unmistakable significance of the night's experiences. *He, he* was to be the victim, the sufferer, throughout this long hour of midnight.

He had thought that by accompanying the dark being around the earth, he would share in the savoring of all the evils that flourish in the midnight hour. He *was* participating—but not as he had expected. Instead, *he* was the victim, the, cringing, tormented one. Perhaps this dark being he had summoned was jealous of its pleasures, or perhaps it derived an additional intensity of satisfaction by adding John Ware's consciousness to those of its victims.

Ware was descending again. There was no resisting the force that flung him earthward.

He was completely helpless before the power he had summoned. What now? What new terror would he experience?

On and on, ever westward through the night, John Ware endured horror after horror. He died again and again, each time in a more fearsome manner. He was subjected to revolting tortures and torments as he was linked with victim after victim. He knew the frightening nightmare of human minds tottering on the abyss of madness. All that is black and unholy and is visited upon mankind he experienced as he roamed the earth with the midnight being.

Would it never end? Only the thought that these sixty minutes must pass sustained him. But it did not end. It seemed an eternity had gone by. Such suffering could not be crowded into a single hour. It must be days since he had left his body.

Days, nights, sixty minutes, one hour? John Ware was struck with a realization of terrific impact. It seemed to be communicated to him from the dark being at his side. Horribly clear did that being make the simple truth. John Ware was lost. Weeks, even months, might have passed since he had left his body. Time, for him, had stopped still.

John Ware was eternally chained to the amorphous black shape, and was doomed to exist thus horribly forever, suffering endless and revolting madness, torture and death through eternity. He had stepped into that band of time known as midnight, and was caught, trapped hopelessly—doomed to move with the grain of time endlessly around the earth.

For as long as the earth spins beneath the sun, one side of it is always dark and in the darkness midnight dwells forever.

1946

JOHN CHEEVER

(1912–1982)

Torch Song

AFTER Jack Lorey had known Joan Harris in New York for a few years, he began to think of her as the Widow. She always wore black, and he was always given the feeling, by a curious disorder in her apartment, that the undertakers had just left. This impression did not stem from malice on his part, for he was fond of Joan. They came from the same city in Ohio and had reached New York at about the same time in the middle thirties. They were the same age, and during their first summer in the city they used to meet after work and drink Martinis in places like the Brevoort and Charles', and have dinner and play checkers at the Lafayette.

Joan went to a school for models when she settled in the city, but it turned out that she photographed badly, so after spending six weeks learning how to walk with a book on her head she got a job as a hostess in a Longchamps. For the rest of the summer she stood by the hatrack, bathed in an intense pink light and the string music of heartbreak, swinging her mane of dark hair and her black skirt as she moved forward to greet the customers. She was then a big, handsome girl with a wonderful voice, and her face, her whole presence, always seemed infused with a gentle and healthy pleasure at her surroundings, whatever they were. She was innocently and incorrigibly convivial, and would get out of bed and dress at three in the morning if someone called her and asked her to come out for a drink, as Jack often did. In the fall, she got some kind of freshman executive job in a department store. They saw less and less of each other and then for quite a while stopped seeing each other altogether. Jack was living with a girl he had met at a party, and it never occurred to him to wonder what had become of Joan.

Jack's girl had some friends in Pennsylvania, and in the spring and summer of his second year in town he often went there with her for weekends. All of this—the shared apartment in the Village, the illicit relationship, the Friday-night train to a country house—was what he had imagined life in New York to be, and he was intensely happy. He was returning to New York with his girl one Sunday night on the Lehigh line. It was one of those trains that move slowly across the face of New Jersey, bringing back to the city hundreds of people, like the victims of an immense and strenuous picnic, whose faces are blazing and whose muscles are lame. Jack and his girl, like most of the other passengers, were overburdened with vegetables and flowers. When the train stopped in Pennsylvania Station, they moved with the crowd along the platform, toward the escalator. As they were passing the wide, lighted windows of the diner, Jack turned his head and saw Joan. It was the first time he had seen her since Thanksgiving, or since Christmas. He couldn't remember.

Joan was with a man who had obviously passed out. His head was in his arms on the table, and an overturned highball glass was near one of his elbows. Joan was shaking his shoulders gently and speaking to him. She seemed to be vaguely troubled, vaguely amused. The waiters had cleared off all the other tables and were standing around Joan, waiting for her to resurrect her escort. It troubled Jack to see in these straits a girl who reminded him of the trees and the lawns of his home town, but there was nothing he could do to help. Joan continued to shake the man's shoulders, and the crowd pressed Jack past one after another of the diner's windows, past the malodorous kitchen, and up the escalator.

He saw Joan again, later that summer, when he was having dinner in a Village restaurant. He was with a new girl, a Southerner. There were many Southern girls in the city that year. Jack and his belle had wandered into the restaurant because it was convenient, but the food was terrible and the place was lighted with candles. Halfway through dinner, Jack noticed Joan on the other side of the room, and when he had finished eating, he crossed the room and spoke to her. She was with a tall man who was wearing a monocle. He stood, bowed stiffly from the waist, and said to Jack, "We are very pleased to meet you." Then he excused himself and headed for the toilet. "He's a count, he's a Swedish count," Joan said. "He's on

the radio, Friday afternoons at four-fifteen. Isn't it exciting?"
She seemed to be delighted with the count and the terrible
restaurant.

Sometime the next winter, Jack moved from the Village to
an apartment in the East Thirties. He was crossing Park Avenue one cold morning on his way to the office when he noticed, in the crowd, a woman he had met a few times at Joan's
apartment. He spoke to her and asked about his friend.
"Haven't you heard?" she said. She pulled a long face. "Perhaps I'd better tell you. Perhaps you can help." She and Jack
had breakfast in a drugstore on Madison Avenue and she un-
burdened herself of the story.

The count had a program called "The Song of the Fiords,"
or something like that, and he sang Swedish folk songs. Everyone suspected him of being a fake, but that didn't bother Joan.
He had met her at a party and, sensing a soft touch, had moved
in with her the following night. About a week later, he complained of pains in his back and said he must have some morphine. Then he needed morphine all the time. If he didn't get
morphine, he was abusive and violent. Joan began to deal with
those doctors and druggists who peddle dope, and when they
wouldn't supply her, she went down to the bottom of the city.
Her friends were afraid she would be found some morning
stuffed in a drain. She got pregnant. She had an abortion. The
count left her and moved to a flea bag near Times Square, but
she was so impressed by then with his helplessness, so afraid
that he would die without her, that she followed him there
and shared his room and continued to buy his narcotics. He
abandoned her again, and Joan waited a week for him to return before she went back to her place and her friends in the
Village.

It shocked Jack to think of the innocent girl from Ohio
having lived with a brutal dope addict and traded with criminals, and when he got to his office that morning, he telephoned
her and made a date for dinner that night. He met her at
Charles'. When she came into the bar, she seemed as wholesome and calm as ever. Her voice was sweet, and reminded
him of elms, of lawns, of those glass arrangements that used to
be hung from porch ceilings to tinkle in the summer wind. She
told him about the count. She spoke of him charitably and

with no trace of bitterness, as if her voice, her disposition, were incapable of registering anything beyond simple affection and pleasure. Her walk, when she moved ahead of him toward their table, was light and graceful. She ate a large dinner and talked enthusiastically about her job. They went to a movie and said goodbye in front of her apartment house.

That winter, Jack met a girl he decided to marry. Their engagement was announced in January and they planned to marry in July. In the spring, he received, in his office mail, an invitation to cocktails at Joan's. It was for a Saturday when his fiancée was going to Massachusetts to visit her parents, and when the time came and he had nothing better to do, he took a bus to the Village. Joan had the same apartment. It was a walk-up. You rang the bell above the mailbox in the vestibule and were answered with a death rattle in the lock. Joan lived on the third floor. Her calling card was in a slot in the mailbox, and above her name was written the name Hugh Bascomb.

Jack climbed the two flights of carpeted stairs, and when he reached Joan's apartment, she was standing by the open door in a black dress. After she greeted Jack, she took his arm and guided him across the room. "I want you to meet Hugh, Jack," she said.

Hugh was a big man with a red face and pale-blue eyes. His manner was courtly and his eyes were inflamed with drink. Jack talked with him for a little while and then went over to speak to someone he knew, who was standing by the mantelpiece. He noticed then, for the first time, the indescribable disorder of Joan's apartment. The books were in their shelves and the furniture was reasonably good, but the place was all wrong, somehow. It was as if things had been put in place without thought or real interest, and for the first time, too, he had the impression that there had been a death there recently.

As Jack moved around the room, he felt that he had met the ten or twelve guests at other parties. There was a woman executive with a fancy hat, a man who could imitate Roosevelt, a grim couple whose play was in rehearsal, and a newspaperman who kept turning on the radio for news of the Spanish Civil War. Jack drank Martinis and talked with the woman in the fancy hat. He looked out of the window at the back yards and the ailanthus trees and heard, in the distance, thunder exploding off the cliffs of the Hudson.

Hugh Bascomb got very drunk. He began to spill liquor, as if drinking, for him, were a kind of jolly slaughter and he enjoyed the bloodshed and the mess. He spilled whiskey from a bottle. He spilled a drink on his shirt and then tipped over someone else's drink. The party was not quiet, but Hugh's hoarse voice began to dominate the others. He attacked a photographer who was sitting in a corner explaining camera techniques to a homely woman. "What did you come to the party for if all you wanted to do was to sit there and stare at your shoes?" Hugh shouted. "What did you come for? Why don't you stay at home?"

The photographer didn't know what to say. He was not staring at his shoes. Joan moved lightly to Hugh's side. "Please don't get into a fight now, darling," she said. "Not this afternoon."

"Shut up," he said. "Let me alone. Mind your own business." He lost his balance, and in struggling to steady himself he tipped over a lamp.

"Oh, your lovely lamp, Joan," a woman sighed.

"Lamps!" Hugh roared. He threw his arms into the air and worked them around his head as if he were bludgeoning himself. "Lamps. Glasses. Cigarette boxes. Dishes. They're killing me. They're killing me, for Christ's sake. Let's all go up to the mountains and hunt and fish and live like men, for Christ's sake."

People were scattering as if a rain had begun to fall in the room. It had, as a matter of fact, begun to rain outside. Someone offered Jack a ride uptown, and he jumped at the chance. Joan stood at the door, saying goodbye to her routed friends. Her voice remained soft, and her manner, unlike that of those Christian women who in the face of disaster can summon new and formidable sources of composure, seemed genuinely simple. She appeared to be oblivious of the raging drunk at her back, who was pacing up and down, grinding glass into the rug, and haranguing one of the survivors of the party with a story of how he, Hugh, had once gone without food for three weeks.

*

In July, Jack was married in an orchard in Duxbury, and he and his wife went to West Chop for a few weeks. When they returned to town, their apartment was cluttered with presents, including a dozen after-dinner coffee cups from Joan. His wife sent her the required note, but they did nothing else.

Late in the summer, Joan telephoned Jack at his office and asked if he wouldn't bring his wife to see her; she named an evening the following week. He felt guilty about not having called her, and accepted the invitation. This made his wife angry. She was an ambitious girl who liked a social life that offered rewards, and she went unwillingly to Joan's Village apartment with him.

Written above Joan's name on the mailbox was the name Franz Denzel. Jack and his wife climbed the stairs and were met by Joan at the open door. They went into her apartment and found themselves among a group of people for whom Jack, at least, was unable to find any bearings.

Franz Denzel was a middle-aged German. His face was pinched with bitterness or illness. He greeted Jack and his wife with that elaborate and clever politeness that is intended to make guests feel that they have come too early or too late. He insisted sharply upon Jack's sitting in the chair in which he himself had been sitting, and then went and sat on a radiator. There were five other Germans sitting around the room, drinking coffee. In a corner was another American couple, who looked uncomfortable. Joan passed Jack and his wife small cups of coffee with whipped cream. "These cups belonged to Franz's mother," she said. "Aren't they lovely? They were the only things he took from Germany when he escaped from the Nazis."

Franz turned to Jack and said, "Perhaps you will give us your opinion on the American educational system. That is what we were discussing when you arrived."

Before Jack could speak, one of the German guests opened an attack on the American educational system. The other Germans joined in, and went on from there to describe every vulgarity that had impressed them in American life and to contrast German and American culture generally. Where, they asked one another passionately, could you find in America anything like the Mitropa dining cars, the Black Forest, the pictures in Munich, the music in Bayreuth? Franz and his friends began speaking in German. Neither Jack nor his wife nor Joan could understand German, and the other American couple had not opened their mouths since they were introduced. Joan went happily around the room, filling everyone's cup with coffee, as if the music of a foreign language were enough to make an evening for her.

Jack drank five cups of coffee. He was desperately uncomfortable. Joan went into the kitchen while the Germans were laughing at their German jokes, and he hoped she would return with some drinks, but when she came back, it was with a tray of ice cream and mulberries.

"Isn't this pleasant?" Franz asked, speaking in English again.

Joan collected the coffee cups, and as she was about to take them back to the kitchen, Franz stopped her.

"Isn't one of those cups chipped?"

"No, darling," Joan said. "I never let the maid touch them. I wash them myself."

"What's that?" he asked, pointing at the rim of one of the cups.

"That's the cup that's always been chipped, darling. It was chipped when you unpacked it. You noticed it then."

"These things were perfect when they arrived in this country," he said.

Joan went into the kitchen and he followed her.

Jack tried to make conversation with the Germans. From the kitchen there was the sound of a blow and a cry. Franz returned and began to eat his mulberries greedily. Joan came back with her dish of ice cream. Her voice was gentle. Her tears, if she had been crying, had dried as quickly as the tears of a child. Jack and his wife finished their ice cream and made their escape. The wasted and unnerving evening enraged Jack's wife, and he supposed that he would never see Joan again.

Jack's wife got pregnant early in the fall, and she seized on all the prerogatives of an expectant mother. She took long naps, ate canned peaches in the middle of the night, and talked about the rudimentary kidney. She chose to see only other couples who were expecting children, and the parties that she and Jack gave were temperate. The baby, a boy, was born in May, and Jack was very proud and happy. The first party he and his wife went to after her convalescence was the wedding of a girl whose family Jack had known in Ohio.

The wedding was at St. James's, and afterward there was a big reception at the River Club. There was an orchestra dressed like Hungarians, and a lot of champagne and Scotch. Toward the end of the afternoon, Jack was walking down a dim corridor when he heard Joan's voice. "Please don't, darling," she was saying. "You'll break my arm. *Please* don't, darling." She was being pressed against the wall by a man who seemed to be twisting her arm. As soon as they saw Jack, the struggle stopped. All three of them were intensely embarrassed. Joan's face was wet and she made an effort to smile through her tears at Jack. He said hello and went on without stopping. When he returned, she and the man had disappeared.

When Jack's son was less than two years old, his wife flew with the baby to Nevada to get a divorce. Jack gave her the apartment and all its furnishings and took a room in a hotel near Grand Central. His wife got her decree in due course, and the story was in the newspapers. Jack had a telephone call from Joan a few days later.

"I'm awfully sorry to hear about your divorce, Jack," she said. "She seemed like *such* a nice girl. But that wasn't what I called you about. I want your help, and I wondered if you could come down to my place tonight around six. It's something I don't want to talk about over the phone."

He went obediently to the Village that night and climbed the stairs. Her apartment was a mess. The pictures and the curtains were down and the books were in boxes. "You moving, Joan?" he asked.

"That's what I wanted to see you about, Jack. First, I'll give you a drink." She made two Old-Fashioneds. "I'm being evicted, Jack," she said. "I'm being evicted because I'm an immoral woman. The couple who have the apartment downstairs —they're charming people, I've always thought—have told the real-estate agent that I'm a drunk and a prostitute and all kinds of things. Isn't that fantastic? This real-estate agent has always been so nice to me that I didn't think he'd believe them, but he's canceled my lease, and if I make any trouble, he's threatened to take the matter up with the store, and I don't want to lose my job. This nice real-estate agent won't even talk with me any more. When I go over to the office, the receptionist leers at me as if I were some kind of dreadful woman. Of course, there have been a lot of men here and we sometimes are noisy, but I can't be expected to go to bed at ten every night. Can I? Well, the agent who manages this building has apparently told all the other agents in the neighborhood that I'm an immoral and drunken woman, and none of them will give me an apartment. I went in to talk with one man—he seemed to be such a nice old gentleman—and he made me an indecent proposal. Isn't it fantastic? I have to be out of here on Thursday and I'm literally being turned out into the street."

Joan seemed as serene and innocent as ever while she described this scourge of agents and neighbors. Jack listened carefully for some sign of indignation or bitterness or even urgency in her recital, but there was none. He was reminded of a torch song, of one of those forlorn and touching ballads that had been sung neither for him nor for her but for their older brothers and sisters by Marion Harris. Joan seemed to be singing her wrongs.

"They've made my life miserable," she went on quietly. "If I keep the radio on after ten o'clock, they telephone the agent in the morning and tell him I had some kind of orgy here. One night when Philip—I don't think you've met Philip; he's in the Royal Air Force; he's gone back to England—one night when Philip and some other people were here, they called the police. The police came bursting in the door and talked to me as if I were I don't know what and then looked in the bedroom. If they think there's a man up here after midnight, they call me on the telephone and say all kinds of disgusting things. Of course, I can put my furniture into storage and go to a hotel, I guess. I guess a hotel will take a woman with my kind of reputation, but I thought perhaps you might know of an apartment. I thought—"

It angered Jack to think of this big, splendid girl's being persecuted by her neighbors, and he said he would do what he could. He asked her to have dinner with him, but she said she was busy.

Having nothing better to do, Jack decided to walk uptown to his hotel. It was a hot night. The sky was overcast. On his way, he saw a parade in a dark side street off Broadway near Madison Square. All the buildings in the neighborhood were dark. It was so dark that he could not see the placards the marchers carried until he came to a street light. Their signs urged the entry of the United States into the war, and each platoon represented a nation that had been subjugated by the Axis powers. They marched up Broadway, as he watched, to no music, to no sound but their own steps on the rough cobbles. It was for the most part an army of elderly men and women—Poles, Norwegians, Danes, Jews, Chinese. A few idle people like himself lined the sidewalks, and the marchers passed between them with all the self-consciousness of enemy prisoners. There were children among them dressed in the costumes in which they had, for the newsreels, presented the Mayor with a package of tea, a petition, a protest, a constitution, a check, or a pair of tickets. They hobbled through the darkness of the loft neighborhood like a mortified and destroyed people, toward Greeley Square.

In the morning, Jack put the problem of finding an apartment for Joan up to his secretary. She started phoning real-estate agents, and by afternoon she had found a couple of available apartments in the West Twenties. Joan called Jack the next day to say that she had taken one of the apartments and to thank him.

Jack didn't see Joan again until the following summer. It was a Sunday evening; he had left a cocktail party in a Washington Square apartment and had decided to walk a few blocks up Fifth Avenue before he took a bus. As he was passing the Brevoort, Joan called to him. She was with a man at one of the tables on the sidewalk. She looked cool and fresh, and the man appeared to be respectable. His name, it turned out, was Pete Bristol. He invited Jack to sit down and join in a celebration. Germany had invaded Russia that weekend, and Joan and Pete were drinking champagne to celebrate Russia's changed position in the war. The three of them drank champagne until it got dark. They had dinner and drank champagne with their dinner. They drank more champagne afterward and then went over to the Lafayette and then to two or three other places. Joan had always been tireless in her gentle way. She hated to see the night end, and it was after three o'clock when Jack stumbled into his apartment. The following morning he woke up haggard and sick, and with no recollection of the last hour or so of the previous evening. His suit was soiled and he had lost his hat. He didn't get to his office until eleven. Joan had already called him twice, and she called him again soon after he got in. There was no hoarseness at all in her voice. She said that she had to see him, and he agreed to meet her for lunch in a seafood restaurant in the Fifties.

He was standing at the bar when she breezed in, looking as though she had taken no part in that calamitous night. The advice she wanted concerned selling her jewelry. Her grand-mother had left her some jewelry, and she wanted to raise money on it but didn't know where to go. She took some rings and bracelets out of her purse and showed them to Jack. He said that he didn't know anything about jewelry but that he could lend her some money. "Oh, I couldn't borrow money from you, Jack," she said. "You see, I want to get the money for Pete. I want to help him. He wants to open an ad-vertising agency, and he needs quite a lot to begin with." Jack didn't press her to accept his offer of a loan after that, and the project wasn't mentioned again during lunch.

He next heard about Joan from a young doctor who was a friend of theirs. "Have you seen Joan recently?" the doctor asked Jack one evening when they were having dinner together. He said no. "I gave her a checkup last week," the doctor said, "and while she's been through enough to kill the average mortal—and you'll never know what she's been through—she still has the constitution of a virtuous and healthy woman. Did you hear about the last one? She sold her jewelry to put him into some kind of business, and as soon as he got the money, he left her for another girl, who had a car—a convertible."

Jack was drafted into the Army in the spring of 1942. He was kept at Fort Dix for nearly a month, and during this time he came to New York in the evening whenever he could get per-mission. Those nights had for him the intense keenness of a re-prieve, a sensation that was heightened by the fact that on the train in from Trenton women would often press upon him dog-eared copies of *Life* and half-eaten boxes of candy, as though the brown clothes he wore were surely cerements. He telephoned Joan from Pennsylvania Station one night. "Come right over, Jack," she said. "Come right over. I want you to meet Ralph."

She was living in that place in the West Twenties that Jack had found for her. The neighborhood was a slum. Ash cans stood in front of her house, and an old woman was there picking out bits of refuse and garbage and stuffing them into a perambulator. The house in which Joan's apartment was located was shabby, but the apartment itself seemed familiar. The furniture was the same. Joan was the same big, easygoing girl. "I'm so glad you called me," she said. "It's so good to see you. I'll make you a drink. I was having one myself. Ralph ought to be here by now. He promised to take me to dinner." Jack offered to take her to Cavanagh's, but she said that Ralph might come while she was out. "If he doesn't come by nine, I'm going to make myself a sandwich. I'm not really hungry."

Jack talked about the Army. She talked about the store. She had been working in the same place for—how long was it? He didn't know. He had never seen her at her desk and he couldn't imagine what she did. "I'm terribly sorry Ralph isn't here," she said. "I'm sure you'd like him. He's not a young man. He's a heart specialist who loves to play the viola." She turned on some lights, for the summer sky had got dark. "He has this dreadful wife on Riverside Drive and four ungrateful children. He—"

The noise of an air-raid siren, lugubrious and seeming to spring from pain, as if all the misery and indecision in the city had been given a voice, cut her off. Other sirens, in distant neighborhoods, sounded, until the dark air was full of their noise. "Let me fix you another drink before I have to turn out the lights," Joan said, and took his glass. She brought the drink back to him and snapped off the lights. They went to the windows, and, as children watch a thunderstorm, they watched the city darken. All the lights nearby went out but one. Air-raid wardens had begun to sound their whistles in the street. From a distant yard came a hoarse shriek of anger. "Put out your lights, you Fascists!" a woman screamed. "Put out your lights, you Nazi Fascist Germans. Turn out your lights. Turn out your lights." The last light went off. They went away from the window and sat in the lightless room.

In the darkness, Joan began to talk about her departed lovers, and from what she said Jack gathered that they had all had a hard time. Nils, the suspect count, was dead. Hugh Bascomb, the drunk, had joined the Merchant Marine and was missing in the North Atlantic. Franz, the German, had taken poison the night the Nazis bombed Warsaw. "We listened to the news on the radio," Joan said, "and then he went back to his hotel and took poison. The maid found him dead in the bathroom the next morning." When Jack asked her about the one who was going to open an advertising agency, she seemed at first to have forgotten him. "Oh, Pete," she said after a pause. "Well, he was always very sick, you know. He was supposed to go to Saranac, but he kept putting it off and putting it off and—" She stopped talking when she heard steps on the stairs, hoping, he supposed, that it was Ralph, but whoever it was turned at the landing and continued to the top of the house. "I wish Ralph would come," she said, with a sigh. "I want you to meet him." Jack asked her again to go out, but she refused, and when the all-clear sounded, he said goodbye.

Jack was shipped from Dix to an infantry training camp in the Carolinas and from there to an infantry division stationed in Georgia. He had been in Georgia three months when he married a girl from the Augusta boarding-house aristocracy. A year or so later, he crossed the continent in a day coach and thought sententiously that the last he might see of the country he loved was the desert towns like Barstow, that the last he might hear of it was the ringing of the trolleys on the Bay Bridge. He was sent into the Pacific and returned to the United States twenty months later, uninjured and apparently unchanged. As soon as he received his furlough, he went to Augusta. He presented his wife with the souvenirs he had brought from the islands, quarreled violently with her and all her family, and, after making arrangements for her to get an Arkansas divorce, left for New York.

Jack was discharged from the Army at a camp in the East a few months later. He took a vacation and then went back to the job he had left in 1942. He seemed to have picked up his life at approximately the moment when it had been interrupted by the war. In time, everything came to look and feel the same. He saw most of his old friends. Only two of the men he knew had been killed in the war. He didn't call Joan, but he met her one winter afternoon on a crosstown bus.

Her fresh face, her black clothes, and her soft voice instantly destroyed the sense—if he had ever had such a sense—that anything had changed or intervened since their last meeting, three or four years ago. She asked him up for cocktails and he went to her apartment the next Saturday afternoon. Her room and her guests reminded him of the parties she had given when she had first come to New York. There was a woman with a fancy hat, an elderly doctor, and a man who stayed close to the radio, listening for news from the Balkans. Jack wondered which of the men belonged to Joan and decided on an Englishman who kept coughing into a handkerchief that he pulled out of his sleeve. Jack was right. "Isn't Stephen brilliant?" Joan asked him a little later, when they were alone in a corner. "He knows more about the Polynesians than anyone else in the world."

Jack had returned not only to his old job but to his old salary. Since living costs had doubled and since he was paying alimony to two wives, he had to draw on his savings. He took another job, which promised more money, but it didn't last long and he found himself out of work. This didn't bother him at all. He still had money in the bank, and anyhow it was easy to borrow from friends. His indifference was the consequence not of lassitude or despair but rather of an excess of hope. He had the feeling that he had only recently come to New York from Ohio. The sense that he was very young and that the best years of his life still lay before him was an illusion that he could not seem to escape. There was all the time in the world. He was living in hotels then, moving from one to another every five days.

In the spring, Jack moved to a furnished room in the badlands west of Central Park. He was running out of money. Then, when he began to feel that a job was a desperate necessity, he got sick. At first, he seemed to have only a bad cold, but he was unable to shake it and he began to run a fever and to cough blood. The fever kept him drowsy most of the time, but he roused himself occasionally and went out to a cafeteria for a meal. He felt sure that none of his friends knew where he was, and he was glad of this. He hadn't counted on Joan.

Late one morning, he heard her speaking in the hall with his landlady. A few moments later, she knocked on his door. He was lying on the bed in a pair of pants and a soiled pajama top, and he didn't answer. She knocked again and walked in. "I've been looking everywhere for you, Jack," she said. She spoke softly. "When I found out that you were in a place like this I thought you must be broke or sick. I stopped at the bank and got some money, in case you're broke. I've brought you some Scotch. I thought a little drink wouldn't do you any harm. Want a little drink?"

Joan's dress was black. Her voice was low and serene. She sat in a chair beside his bed as if she had been coming there every day to nurse him. Her features had coarsened, he thought, but there were still very few lines in her face. She was heavier. She was nearly fat. She was wearing black cotton gloves. She got two glasses and poured Scotch into them. He drank his whiskey greedily. "I didn't get to bed until three last night," she said. Her voice had once before reminded him of a gentle and despairing song, but now, perhaps because he was sick, her mildness, the mourning she wore, her stealthy grace, made him uneasy. "It was one of those nights," she said. "We went to the theatre. Afterward, someone asked us up to his place. I don't know who he was. It was one of those places. They're so strange. There were some meat-eating plants and a collection of Chinese snuff bottles. Why do people collect Chinese snuff bottles? We all autographed a lampshade, as I remember, but I can't remember much."

Jack tried to sit up in bed, as if there were some need to defend himself, and then fell back again, against the pillows. "How did you find me, Joan?" he asked.

"It was simple," she said. "I called that hotel. The one you were staying in. They gave me this address. My secretary got the telephone number. Have another little drink."

"You know, you've never come to a place of mine before—never," he said. "Why did you come now?"

"Why did I come, darling?" she asked. "What a question! I've known you for thirty years. You're the oldest friend I have in New York. Remember that night in the Village when it snowed and we stayed up until morning and drank whiskey sours for breakfast? That doesn't seem like twelve years ago. And that night—"

"I don't like to have you see me in a place like this," he said earnestly. He touched his face and felt his beard.

"And all the people who used to imitate Roosevelt," she said, as if she had not heard him, as if she were deaf. "And that place on Staten Island where we all used to go for dinner when Henry had a car. Poor Henry. He bought a place in Connecticut and went out there by himself one weekend. He fell asleep with a lighted cigarette and the house, the barn, everything burned. Ethel took the children out to California." She poured more Scotch into his glass and handed it to him. She lighted a cigarette and put it between his lips. The intimacy of this gesture, which made it seem not only as if he were deathly ill but as if he were her lover, troubled him.

"As soon as I'm better," he said, "I'll take a room at a good hotel. I'll call you then. It was nice of you to come."

"Oh, don't be ashamed of this room, Jack," she said. "Rooms never bother me. It doesn't seem to matter to me where I am. Stanley had a filthy room in Chelsea. At least, other people told me it was filthy. I never noticed it. Rats used to eat the food I brought him. He used to have to hang the food from the ceiling, from the light chain."

"I'll call you as soon as I'm better," Jack said. "I think I can sleep now if I'm left alone. I seem to need a lot of sleep."

"You really *are* sick, darling," she said. "You must have a fever." She sat on the edge of his bed and put a hand on his forehead.

"How is that Englishman, Joan?" he asked. "Do you still see him?"

"What Englishman?" she said.

"You know. I met him at your house. He kept a handkerchief up his sleeve. He coughed all the time. You know the one I mean."

"You must be thinking of someone else," she said. "I haven't had an Englishman at my place since the war. Of course, I can't remember everyone." She turned and, taking one of his hands, linked her fingers in his.

"He's dead, isn't he?" Jack said. "That Englishman's dead." He pushed her off the bed, and got up himself. "Get out," he said.

"You're sick, darling," she said. "I can't leave you alone here."

"Get out," he said again, and when she didn't move, he

shouted, "What kind of an obscenity are you that you can smell sickness and death the way you do?"

"You poor darling."

"Does it make you feel young to watch the dying?" he shouted. "Is that the lewdness that keeps you young? Is that why you dress like a crow? Oh, I know there's nothing I can say that will hurt you. I know there's nothing filthy or corrupt or depraved or brutish or base that the others haven't tried, but this time you're wrong. I'm not ready. My life isn't ending. My life's beginning. There are wonderful years ahead of me. There are, there are wonderful, wonderful, wonderful years ahead of me, and when they're over, when it's time, then I'll call you. Then, as an old friend, I'll call you and give you whatever dirty pleasure you take in watching the dying, but until then, you and your ugly and misshapen forms will leave me alone."

She finished her drink and looked at her watch. "I guess I'd better show up at the office," she said. "I'll see you later. I'll come back tonight. You'll feel better then, you poor darling." She closed the door after her, and he heard her light step on the stairs.

Jack emptied the whiskey bottle into the sink. He began to dress. He stuffed his dirty clothes into a bag. He was trembling and crying with sickness and fear. He could see the blue sky from his window, and in his fear it seemed miraculous that the sky should be blue, that the white clouds should remind him of snow, that from the sidewalk he could hear the shrill voices of children shrieking, "I'm the king of the mountain, I'm the king of the mountain, I'm the king of the mountain." He emptied the ashtray containing his nail parings and cigarette butts into the toilet, and swept the floor with a shirt, so that there would be no trace of his life, of his body, when that lewd and searching shape of death came there to find him in the evening.

1947

SHIRLEY JACKSON

(1916–1965)

The Daemon Lover

SHE had not slept well; from one-thirty, when Jamie left and she went lingeringly to bed, until seven, when she at last allowed herself to get up and make coffee, she had slept fitfully, stirring awake to open her eyes and look into the half-darkness, remembering over and over, slipping again into a feverish dream. She spent almost an hour over her coffee—they were to have a real breakfast on the way—and then, unless she wanted to dress early, had nothing to do. She washed her coffee cup and made the bed, looking carefully over the clothes she planned to wear, worried unnecessarily, at the window, over whether it would be a fine day. She sat down to read, thought that she might write a letter to her sister instead, and began, in her finest handwriting, "Dearest Anne, by the time you get this I will be married. Doesn't it sound funny? I can hardly believe it myself, but when I tell you how it happened, you'll see it's even stranger than that. . . ."

Sitting, pen in hand, she hesitated over what to say next, read the lines already written, and tore up the letter. She went to the window and saw that it was undeniably a fine day. It occurred to her that perhaps she ought not to wear the blue silk dress; it was too plain, almost severe, and she wanted to be soft, feminine. Anxiously she pulled through the dresses in the closet, and hesitated over a print she had worn the summer before; it was too young for her, and it had a ruffled neck, and it was very early in the year for a print dress, but still. . . .

She hung the two dresses side by side on the outside of the closet door and opened the glass doors carefully closed upon the small closet that was her kitchenette. She turned on the burner under the coffeepot, and went to the window; it was sunny. When the coffeepot began to crackle she came back and poured herself coffee, into a clean cup. I'll have a headache if I don't get some solid food soon, she thought, all this coffee,

96

smoking too much, no real breakfast. A headache on her wedding day; she went and got the tin box of aspirin from the
bathroom closet and slipped it into her blue pocketbook. She'd
have to change to a brown pocketbook if she wore the print
dress, and the only brown pocketbook she had was shabby.
Helplessly, she stood looking from the blue pocketbook to the
print dress, and then put the pocketbook down and went and
got her coffee and sat down near the window, drinking her
coffee, and looking carefully around the one-room apartment.
They planned to come back here tonight and everything must
be correct. With sudden horror she realized that she had forgotten to put clean sheets on the bed; the laundry was freshly
back and she took clean sheets and pillow cases from the top
shelf of the closet and stripped the bed, working quickly to
avoid thinking consciously of why the was changing the sheets.
The bed was a studio bed, with a cover to make it look like a
couch, and when it was finished no one would have known she
had just put clean sheets on it. She took the old sheets and pillow cases into the bathroom and stuffed them down into the
hamper, and put the bathroom towels in the hamper too, and
clean towels on the bathroom racks. Her coffee was cold when
she came back to it, but she drank it anyway.

When she looked at the clock, finally, and saw that it was
after nine, she began at last to hurry. She took a bath, and used
one of the clean towels, which she put into the hamper and replaced with a clean one. She dressed carefully, all her underwear fresh and most of it new; she put everything she had
worn the day before, including her nightgown, into the hamper. When she was ready for her dress, she hesitated before the
closet door. The blue dress was certainly decent, and clean,
and fairly becoming, but she had worn it several times with
Jamie, and there was nothing about it which made it special
for a wedding day. The print dress was overly pretty, and new
to Jamie, and yet wearing such a print this early in the year was
certainly rushing the season. Finally she thought, This is my
wedding day, I can dress as I please, and she took the print
dress down from the hanger. When she slipped it on over her
head it felt fresh and light, but when she looked at herself in
the mirror she remembered that the ruffles around the neck did
not show her throat to any great advantage, and the wide

swinging skirt looked irresistibly made for a girl, for someone who would run freely, dance, swing it with her hips when she walked. Looking at herself in the mirror she thought with revulsion, It's as though I was trying to make myself look prettier than I am, just for him; he'll think I want to look younger because he's marrying me; and she tore the print dress off so quickly that a seam under the arm ripped. In the old blue dress she felt comfortable and familiar, but unexciting. It isn't what you're wearing that matters, she told herself firmly, and turned in dismay to the closet to see if there might be anything else. There was nothing even remotely suitable for her marrying Jamie, and for a minute she thought of going out quickly to some little shop nearby, to get a dress. Then she saw that it was close on ten, and she had no time for more than her hair and her makeup. Her hair was easy, pulled back into a knot at the nape of her neck, but her make-up was another delicate balance between looking as well as possible, and deceiving as little. She could not try to disguise the sallowness of her skin, or the lines around her eyes, today, when it might look as though she were only doing it for her wedding, and yet she could not bear the thought of Jamie's bringing to marriage anyone who looked haggard and lined. You're thirty-four years old after *all*, she told herself cruelly in the bathroom mirror. Thirty, it said on the license.

It was two minutes after ten; she was not satisfied with her clothes, her face, her apartment. She heated the coffee again and sat down in the chair by the window. Can't do anything more now, she thought, no sense trying to improve anything the last minute.

Reconciled, settled, she tried to think of Jamie and could not see his face clearly, or hear his voice. It's always that way with someone you love, she thought, and let her mind slip past today and tomorrow, into the farther future, when Jamie was established with his writing and she had given up her job, the golden house-in-the-country future they had been preparing for the last week. "I used to be a wonderful cook," she had promised Jamie, "with a little time and practice I could remember how to make angel-food cake. And fried chicken," she said, knowing how the words would stay in Jamie's mind, half-tenderly. "And Hollandaise sauce."

Ten-thirty. She stood up and went purposefully to the phone. She dialed, and waited, and the girl's metallic voice said, ". . . the time will be exactly ten-twenty-nine." Half-consciously she set her clock back a minute; she was remembering her own voice saying last night, in the doorway: "Ten o'clock then. I'll be ready. Is it really *true*?"

And Jamie laughing down the hallway.

By eleven o'clock she had sewed up the ripped seam in the print dress and put her sewing-box away carefully in the closet. With the print dress on, she was sitting by the window drinking another cup of coffee. I could have taken more time over my dressing after all, she thought; but by now it was so late he might come any minute, and she did not dare try to repair anything without starting all over. There was nothing to eat in the apartment except the food she had carefully stocked up for their life beginning together: the unopened package of bacon, the dozen eggs in their box, the unopened bread and the unopened butter; they were for breakfast tomorrow. She thought of running downstairs to the drugstore for something to eat, leaving a note on the door. Then she decided to wait a little longer.

By eleven-thirty she was so dizzy and weak that she had to go downstairs. If Jamie had had a phone she would have called him then. Instead, she opened her desk and wrote a note: "Jamie, have gone downstairs to the drugstore. Back in five minutes." Her pen leaked onto her fingers and she went into the bathroom and washed, using a clean towel which she replaced. She tacked the note on the door, surveyed the apartment once more to make sure that everything was perfect, and closed the door without locking it, in case he should come.

In the drugstore she found that there was nothing she wanted to eat except more coffee, and she left it half-finished because she suddenly realized that Jamie was probably upstairs waiting and impatient, anxious to get started.

But upstairs everything was prepared and quiet, as she had left it, her note unread on the door, the air in the apartment a little stale from too many cigarettes. She opened the window and sat down next to it until she realized that she had been asleep and it was twenty minutes to one.

Now, suddenly, she was frightened. Waking without preparation into the room of waiting and readiness, everything clean and untouched since ten o'clock, she was frightened, and felt an urgent need to hurry. She got up from the chair and almost ran across the room to the bathroom, dashed cold water on her face, and used a clean towel; this time she put the towel carelessly back on the rack without changing it; time enough for that later. Hatless, still in the print dress with a coat thrown on over it, the wrong blue pocketbook with the aspirin inside in her hand, she locked the apartment door behind her, no note this time, and ran down the stairs. She caught a taxi on the corner and gave the driver Jamie's address.

It was no distance at all; she could have walked it if she had not been so weak, but in the taxi she suddenly realized how imprudent it would be to drive brazenly up to Jamie's door, demanding him. She asked the driver, therefore, to let her off at a corner near Jamie's address and, after paying him, waited till he drove away before she started to walk down the block. She had never been here before; the building was pleasant and old, and Jamie's name was not on any of the mailboxes in the vestibule, nor on the doorbells. She checked the address; it was right, and finally she rang the bell marked "Superintendent." After a minute or two the door buzzer rang and she opened the door and went into the dark hall where she hesitated until a door at the end opened and someone said, "Yes?"

She knew at the same moment that she had no idea what to ask, so she moved forward toward the figure waiting against the light of the open doorway. When she was very near, the figure said, "Yes?" again and she saw that it was a man in his shirtsleeves, unable to see her any more clearly than she could see him.

With sudden courage she said, "I'm trying to get in touch with someone who lives in this building and I can't find the name outside."

"What's the name you wanted?" the man asked, and she realized that she would have to answer.

"James Harris," she said. "Harris."

The man was silent for a minute and then he said, "Harris." He turned around to the room inside the lighted doorway and said, "Margie, come here a minute."

"What now?" a voice said from inside, and after a wait long

enough for someone to get out of a comfortable chair a woman joined him in the doorway, regarding the dark hall. "Lady here," the man said. "Lady looking for a guy name of Harris, lives here. Anyone in the building?"

"No," the woman said. Her voice sounded amused. "No men named Harris here."

"Sorry," the man said. He started to close the door. "You got the wrong house, lady," he said, and added in a lower voice, "or the wrong guy," and he and the woman laughed.

When the door was almost shut and she was alone in the dark hall she said to the thin lighted crack still showing, "But he *does* live here; I know it."

"Look," the woman said, opening the door again a little, "it happens all the time."

"Please don't make any mistake," she said, and her voice was very dignified, with thirty-four years of accumulated pride. "I'm afraid you don't understand."

"What did he look like?" the woman said wearily, the door still only part open.

"He's rather tall, and fair. He wears a blue suit very often. He's a writer."

"No," the woman said, and then, "Could he have lived on the third floor?"

"I'm not sure."

"There was a fellow," the woman said reflectively. "He wore a blue suit a lot, lived on the third floor for a while. The Roysters lent him their apartment while they were visiting her folks upstate."

"That might be it; I thought, though. . . ."

"This one wore a blue suit mostly, but I don't know how tall he was," the woman said. "He stayed there about a month."

"A month ago is when—"

"You ask the Roysters," the woman said. "They come back this morning. Apartment 3B."

The door closed, definitely. The hall was very dark and the stairs looked darker.

On the second floor there was a little light from a skylight far above. The apartment doors lined up, four on the floor, uncommunicative and silent. There was a bottle of milk outside 2C.

On the third floor, she waited for a minute. There was the

sound of music beyond the door of 3B, and she could hear voices. Finally she knocked, and knocked again. The door was opened and the music swept out at her, an early afternoon symphony broadcast. "How do you do," she said politely to this woman in the doorway. "Mrs. Royster?"

"That's right." The woman was wearing a housecoat and last night's make-up.

"I wonder if I might talk to you for a minute?"

"Sure," Mrs. Royster said, not moving.

"About Mr. Harris."

"*What* Mr. Harris?" Mrs. Royster said flatly.

"Mr. James Harris. The gentleman who borrowed your apartment."

"O Lord," Mrs. Royster said. She seemed to open her eyes for the first time. "What'd he do?"

"Nothing. I'm just trying to get in touch with him."

"O Lord," Mrs. Royster said again. Then she opened the door wider and said, "Come in," and then, "Ralph!"

Inside, the apartment was still full of music, and there were suitcases half-unpacked on the couch, on the chairs, on the floor. A table in the corner was spread with the remains of a meal, and the young man sitting there, for a minute resembling Jamie, got up and came across the room.

"What about it?" he said.

"Mr. Royster," she said. It was difficult to talk against the music. "The superintendent downstairs told me that this was where Mr. James Harris has been living."

"Sure," he said. "If that was his name."

"I thought you lent him the apartment," she said, surprised.

"*I* don't know anything about him," Mr. Royster said. "He's one of Dottie's friends."

"Not *my* friends," Mrs. Royster said. "No friend of mine." She had gone over to the table and was spreading peanut butter on a piece of bread. She took a bite and said thickly, waving the bread and peanut butter at her husband. "Not *my* friend."

"You picked him up at one of those damn meetings," Mr. Royster said. He shoved a suitcase off the chair next to the radio and sat down, picking up a magazine from the floor next to him. "I never said more'n ten words to him."

"You said it was okay to lend him the place," Mrs. Royster said before she took another bite. "You never said a word against him, after *all*."

"*I* don't say anything about *your* friends," Mr. Royster said.

"If he'd of been a friend of mine you would have said *plenty*, believe me," Mrs. Royster said darkly. She took another bite and said, "Believe me, he would have said *plenty*."

"That's all I want to hear," Mr. Royster said, over the top of the magazine. "No more, now."

"You see." Mrs. Royster pointed the bread and peanut butter at her husband. "That's the way it is, day and night."

There was silence except for the music bellowing out of the radio next to Mr. Royster, and then she said, in a voice she hardly trusted to be heard over the radio noise, "Has he gone, then?"

"Who?" Mrs. Royster demanded, looking up from the peanut butter jar.

"Mr. James Harris."

"Him? He must've left this morning, before we got back. No sign of him anywhere."

"Gone?"

"Everything was fine, though, perfectly fine. I told you," she said to Mr. Royster, "I told you he'd take care of everything fine. I can always tell."

"You were lucky," Mr. Royster said.

"Not a thing out of place," Mrs. Royster said. She waved her bread and peanut butter inclusively. "Everything just the way we left it," she said.

"Do you know where he is now?"

"Not the slightest idea," Mrs. Royster said cheerfully. "But, like I said, he left everything fine. Why?" she asked suddenly. "You looking for *him*?"

"It's very important."

"I'm sorry he's not here," Mrs. Royster said. She stepped forward politely when she saw her visitor turn toward the door.

"Maybe the super saw him," Mr. Royster said into the magazine.

When the door was closed behind her the hall was dark again, but the sound of the radio was deadened. She was halfway down the first flight of stairs when the door was opened and Mrs. Royster shouted down the stairwell, "If I see him I'll tell him you were looking for him."

What can I do? she thought, out on the street again. It was impossible to go home, not with Jamie somewhere between here and there. She stood on the sidewalk so long that a woman, leaning out of a window across the way, turned and called to someone inside to come and see. Finally, on an impulse, she went into the small delicatessen next door to the apartment house, on the side that led to her own apartment. There was a small man reading a newspaper, leaning against the counter; when she came in he looked up and came down inside the counter to meet her.

Over the glass case of cold meats and cheese she said, timidly, "I'm trying to get in touch with a man who lived in the apartment house next door, and I just wondered if you know him."

"Whyn't you ask the people there?" the man said, his eyes narrow, inspecting her.

It's because I'm not buying anything, she thought, and she said, "I'm sorry. I asked them, but they don't know anything about him. They think he left this morning."

"I don't know what you want *me* to do," he said, moving a little back toward his newspaper. "I'm not here to keep track of guys going in and out next door."

She said quickly, "I thought you might have noticed, that's all. He would have been coming past here, a little before ten o'clock. He was rather tall, and he usually wore a blue suit."

"Now how many men in blue suits go past here every day, lady?" the man demanded. "You think I got nothing to do but—"

"I'm sorry," she said. She heard him say, "For God's sake," as she went out the door.

As she walked toward the corner, she thought, he must have come this way, it's the way he'd go to get to my house, it's the only way for him to walk. She tried to think of Jamie: where would he have crossed the street? What sort of person was he actually—would he cross in front of his own apartment house, at random in the middle of the block, at the corner?

On the corner was a newsstand; they might have seen him

there. She hurried on and waited while a man bought a paper and a woman asked directions. When the newsstand man looked at her she said, "Can you possibly tell me if a rather tall young man in a blue suit went past here this morning around ten o'clock?" When the man only looked at her, his eyes wide and his mouth a little open, she thought, he thinks it's a joke, or a trick, and she said urgently, "It's very important, please believe me. I'm not teasing you."

"*Look*, lady," the man began, and she said eagerly, "He's a writer. He might have bought magazines here."

"What you want him for?" the man asked. He looked at her, smiling, and she realized that there was another man waiting in back of her and the newsdealer's smile included him. "Never mind," she said, but the newsdealer said, "Listen, maybe he did come by here." His smile was knowing and his eyes shifted over her shoulder to the man in back of her. She was suddenly horribly aware of her over-young print dress, and pulled her coat around her quickly. The newsdealer said, with vast thoughtfulness, "Now I don't know for sure, mind you, but there might have been someone like your gentleman friend coming by this morning."

"About ten?"

"About ten," the newsdealer agreed. "Tall fellow, blue suit. I wouldn't be at all surprised."

"Which way did he go?" she said eagerly. "Uptown?"

"Uptown," the newsdealer said, nodding. "He went uptown. That's just exactly it. What can I do for you, sir?"

She stepped back, holding her coat around her. The man who had been standing behind her looked at her over his shoulder and then he and the newsdealer looked at one another. She wondered for a minute whether or not to tip the newsdealer but when both men began to laugh she moved hurriedly on across the street.

Uptown, she thought, that's right, and she started up the avenue, thinking: He wouldn't have to cross the avenue, just go up six blocks and turn down my street, so long as he started uptown. About a block farther on she passed a florist's shop; there was a wedding display in the window and she thought, This is my wedding day after all, he might have gotten flowers to bring me, and she went inside. The florist came out of the back of the shop, smiling and sleek, and she said, before he could speak, so that he wouldn't have a chance to think she was buying anything: "It's *terribly* important that I get in touch with a gentleman who may have stopped in here to buy flowers this morning. *Terribly* important."

She stopped for breath, and the florist said, "Yes, what sort of flowers were they?"

"I don't know," she said, surprised. "He never—" She stopped and said, "He was a rather tall young man, in a blue suit. It was about ten o'clock."

"I see," the florist said. "Well, *really*, I'm afraid. . . ."

"But it's *so* important," she said. "He may have been in a hurry," she added helpfully.

"Well," the florist said. He smiled genially, showing all his small teeth. "For a *lady*," he said. He went to a stand and opened a large book. "Where were they to be sent?" he asked.

"Why," she said, "I don't think he'd have sent them. You see, he was coming—that is, he'd *bring* them."

"Madam," the florist said; he was offended. His smile became deprecatory, and he went on, "Really, you must realize that unless I have *something* to go on. . . ."

"*Please* try to remember," she begged. "He was tall, and had a blue suit, and it was about ten this morning."

The florist closed his eyes, one finger to his mouth, and thought deeply. Then he shook his head. "I simply *can't*," he said.

"Thank you," she said despondently, and started for the door, when the florist said, in a shrill, excited voice, "Wait! Wait just a moment, madam." She turned and the florist, thinking again, said finally, "Chrysanthemums?" He looked at her inquiringly.

"Oh, *no*," she said; her voice shook a little and she waited for a minute before she went on. "Not for an occasion like this, I'm sure."

The florist tightened his lips and looked away coldly. "Well, of *course* I don't know the *occasion*," he said, "but I'm almost certain that the gentleman you were inquiring for came in this morning and purchased one dozen chrysanthemums. No delivery."

"You're *sure*?" she asked.

"Positive," the florist said emphatically. "That was absolutely the man." He smiled brilliantly, and she smiled back and said, "Well, thank you very much."

He escorted her to the door. "Nice corsage?" he said, as they went through the shop. "Red roses? Gardenias?"

"It was very kind of you to help me," she said at the door.

"Ladies always look their best in flowers," he said, bending his head toward her. "Orchids, perhaps?"

"No, thank you," she said, and he said, "I hope you find your young man," and gave it a nasty sound.

Going on up the street she thought, Everyone thinks it's so *funny*. and she pulled her coat tighter around her, so that only the ruffle around the bottom of the print dress was showing.

There was a policeman on the corner, and she thought, Why don't I go to the police—you go to the police for a missing person. And then thought, What a fool I'd look like. She had a quick picture of herself standing in a police station, saying, "Yes, we were going to be married today, but he didn't come," and the policemen, three or four of them standing around listening, looking at her, at the print dress, at her too-bright make-up, smiling at one another. She couldn't tell them any more than that, could not say, "Yes, it looks silly, doesn't it, me all dressed up and trying to find the young man who promised to marry me, but what about all of it you don't know? I have more than this, more than you can see: talent, perhaps, and humor of a sort, and I'm a lady and I have pride and affection and delicacy and a certain clear view of life that might make a man satisfied and productive and happy; there's more than you think when you look at me."

The police were obviously impossible, leaving out Jamie and what he might think when he heard she'd set the police after him. "No, no," she said aloud, hurrying her steps, and someone passing stopped and looked after her.

On the coming corner—she was three blocks from her own street—was a shoeshine stand, an old man sitting almost asleep in one of the chairs. She stopped in front of him and waited, and after a minute he opened his eyes and smiled at her.

"Look," she said, the words coming before she thought of them, "I'm sorry to bother you, but I'm looking for a young man who came up this way about ten this morning, did you see him?" And she began her description, "Tall, blue suit, carrying a bunch of flowers?"

The old man began to nod before she was finished. "I saw him," he said. "Friend of yours?"

"Yes," she said, and smiled back involuntarily.

The old man blinked his eyes and said, "I remember I thought, You're going to see your girl, young fellow. They all go to see their girls," he said, and shook his head tolerantly.

"Which way did he go? Straight on up the avenue?"

"That's right," the old man said. "Got a shine, had his flowers, all dressed up, in an awful hurry. You got a girl, I thought."

"Thank you," she said, fumbling in her pocket for her loose change.

"She sure must of been glad to see him, the way he looked," the old man said.

"Thank you," she said again, and brought her hand empty from her pocket.

For the first time she was really sure he would be waiting for her, and she hurried up the three blocks, the skirt of the print dress swinging under her coat, and turned into her own block. From the corner she could not see her own windows, could not see Jamie looking out, waiting for her, and going down the block she was almost running to get to him. Her key trembled in her fingers at the downstairs door, and as she glanced into the drugstore she thought of her panic, drinking coffee there this morning, and almost laughed. At her own door she could wait no longer, but began to say, "Jamie, I'm here, I was so worried," even before the door was open.

Her own apartment was waiting for her, silent, barren, afternoon shadows lengthening from the window. For a minute she saw only the empty coffee cup, thought, He has been here waiting, before she recognized it as her own, left from the morning. She looked all over the room, into the closet, into the bathroom.

"I never saw him," the clerk in the drugstore said. "I know

because I would of noticed the flowers. No one like that's been in."

The old man at the shoeshine stand woke up again to see her standing in front of him. "Hello again," he said, and smiled.

"Are you *sure*?" she demanded. "Did he go on up the avenue?"

"I watched him," the old man said, dignified against her tone. "I thought, There's a young man's got a girl, and I watched him right into the house."

"What house?" she said remotely.

"Right there," the old man said. He leaned forward to point. "The next block. With his flowers and his shine and going to see his girl. Right into her house."

"Which one?" she said.

"About the middle of the block," the old man said. He looked at her with suspicion, and said, "What you trying to do, anyway?"

She almost ran, without stopping to say "Thank you." Up on the next block she walked quickly, searching the houses from the outside to see if Jamie looked from a window, listening to hear his laughter somewhere inside.

A woman was sitting in front of one of the houses, pushing a baby carriage monotonously back and forth the length of her arm. The baby inside slept, moving back and forth.

The question was fluent, by now. "I'm sorry, but did you see a young man go into one of these houses about ten this morning? He was tall, wearing a blue suit, carrying a bunch of flowers."

A boy about twelve stopped to listen, turning intently from one to the other, occasionally glancing at the baby.

"Listen," the woman said tiredly, "the kid has his bath at ten. Would I see strange men walking around? I ask you."

"Big bunch of flowers?" the boy asked, pulling at her coat. "Big bunch of flowers? I seen him, missus."

She looked down and the boy grinned insolently at her. "Which house did he go in?" she asked wearily.

"You gonna divorce him?" the boy asked insistently.

"That's not nice to ask the lady," the woman rocking the carriage said.

"Listen," the boy said, "I seen him. He went in there." He pointed to the house next door. "I followed him," the boy said. "He give me a quarter." The boy dropped his voice to a growl, and said. "'This is a big day for me, kid,' he says. Give me a quarter."

She gave him a dollar bill. "Where?" she said.

"Top floor," the boy said. "I followed him till he give me the quarter. Way to the top." He backed up the sidewalk, out of reach, with the dollar bill. "You gonna divorce him?" he asked again.

"Was he carrying flowers?"

"Yeah," the boy said. He began to screech. "You gonna divorce him, missus? You got something on him?" He went careening down the street, howling, "She's got something on the poor guy," and the woman rocking the baby laughed.

The street door of the apartment house was unlocked; there were no bells in the outer vestibule, and no lists of names. The stairs were narrow and dirty; there were two doors on the top floor. The front one was the right one; there was a crumpled florist's paper on the floor outside the door, and a knotted paper ribbon, like a clue, like the final clue in the paper-chase.

She knocked, and thought she heard voices inside, and she thought, suddenly, with terror, What shall I say if Jamie is there, if he comes to the door? The voices seemed suddenly still. She knocked again and there was silence, except for something that might have been laughter far away. He could have seen me from the window, she thought, it's the front apartment and that little boy made a dreadful noise. She waited, and knocked again, but there was silence.

Finally she went to the other door on the floor, and knocked. The door swung open beneath her hand and she saw the empty attic room, bare lath on the walls, floorboards unpainted. She stepped just inside, looking around; the room was filled with bags of plaster, piles of old newspapers, a broken trunk. There was a noise which she suddenly realized was a rat, and then she saw it, sitting very close to her, near the wall, its evil face alert, bright eyes watching her. She stumbled in her haste to be out with the door closed, and the skirt of the print dress caught and tore.

She knew there was someone inside the other apartment, because she was sure she could hear low voices and sometimes laughter. She came back many times, every day for the first week. She came on her way to work, in the mornings; in the evenings, on her way to dinner alone, but no matter how often or how firmly she knocked, no one ever came to the door.

1949

PAUL BOWLES

(1910–1999)

The Circular Valley

THE abandoned monastery stood on a slight eminence of
land in the middle of a vast clearing. On all sides the ground
sloped gently downward toward the tangled, hairy jungle that
filled the circular valley, ringed about by sheer, black cliffs.
There were a few trees in some of the courtyards, and the birds
used them as meeting-places when they flew out of the rooms
and corridors where they had their nests. Long ago bandits
had taken whatever was removable out of the building. Soldiers had used it once as headquarters, had, like the bandits,
built fires in the great windy rooms so that afterward they
looked like ancient kitchens. And now that everything was
gone from within, it seemed that never again would anyone
come near the monastery. The vegetation had thrown up a
protecting wall; the first story was soon quite hidden from
view by small trees which dripped vines to lasso the cornices of
the windows. The meadows roundabout grew dank and lush;
there was no path through them.

At the higher end of the circular valley a river fell off the
cliffs into a great cauldron of vapor and thunder below; after
this it slid along the base of the cliffs until it found a gap at the
other end of the valley, where it hurried discreetly through with
no rapids, no cascades—a great thick black rope of water moving
swiftly downhill between the polished flanks of the canyon.
Beyond the gap the land opened out and became smiling; a
village nestled on the side hill just outside. In the days of the
monastery it was there that the friars had got their provisions,
since the Indians would not enter the circular valley. Centuries
ago when the building had been constructed the Church had
imported the workmen from another part of the country.
These were traditional enemies of the tribes thereabouts, and
had another language; there was no danger that the inhabitants would communicate with them as they worked at setting

112

up the mighty walls. Indeed, the construction had taken so long that before the east wing was completed the workmen had all died, one by one. Thus it was the friars themselves who had closed off the end of the wing with blank walls, leaving it that way, unfinished and blind-looking, facing the black cliffs.

Generation after generation, the friars came, fresh-cheeked boys who grew thin and gray, and finally died, to be buried in the garden beyond the courtyard with the fountain. One day not long ago they had all left the monastery; no one knew where they had gone, and no one thought to ask. It was shortly after this that the bandits, and then the soldiers had come. And now, since the Indians do not change, still no one from the village went up through the gap to visit the monastery. The Atlá-jala lived there; the friars had not been able to kill it, had given up at last and gone away. No one was surprised, but the Atlá-jala gained in prestige by their departure. During the centuries the friars had been there in the monastery, the Indians had wondered why it allowed them to stay. Now, at last, it had driven them out. It always had lived there, they said, and would go on living there because the valley was its home, and it could never leave.

In the early morning the restless Atlájala would move through the halls of the monastery. The dark rooms sped past, one after the other. In a small patio, where eager young trees had pushed up the paving stones to reach the sun, it paused. The air was full of small sounds: the movements of butterflies, the falling to the ground of bits of leaves and flowers, the air following its myriad courses around the edges of things, the ants pursuing their endless labors in the hot dust. In the sun it waited, conscious of each gradation in sound and light and smell, living in the awareness of the slow, constant disintegration that attacked the morning and transformed it into afternoon. When evening came, it often slipped above the monastery roof and surveyed the darkening sky: the waterfall would roar distantly. Night after night, along the procession of years, it had hovered here above the valley, darting down to become a bat, a leopard, a moth for a few minutes or hours, returning to rest immobile in the center of the space enclosed by the cliffs. When the monastery had been built, it had taken to frequenting the rooms, where it had observed for the first time the meaning-less gestures of human life.

And then one evening it had aimlessly become one of the young friars. This was a new sensation, strangely rich and com-plex, and at the same time unbearably stifling, as though every other possibility besides that of being enclosed in a tiny, iso-lated world of cause and effect had been removed forever. As the friar, it had gone and stood in the window, looking out at the sky, seeing for the first time, not the stars, but the space between and beyond them. Even at that moment it had felt the urge to leave, to step outside the little shell of anguish where it lodged for the moment, but a faint curiosity had im-pelled it to remain a little longer and partake a little further of the unaccustomed sensation. It held on; the friar raised his arms to the sky in an imploring gesture. For the first time the Atlájala sensed opposition, the thrill of a struggle. It was deli-cious to feel the young man striving to free himself of its pres-ence, and it was immeasurably sweet to remain there. Then with a cry the friar had rushed to the other side of the room and seized a heavy leather whip hanging on the wall. Tearing off his clothing he had begun to carry out a ferocious self-beating. At the first blow of the lash the Atlájala had been on the point of letting go, but then it realized that the immediacy of that intriguing inner pain was only made more manifest by the impact of the blows from without, and so it stayed and felt the young man grow weak under his own lashing. When he had finished and said a prayer, he crawled to his pallet and fell asleep weeping, while the Atlájala slipped out obliquely and entered into a bird which passed the night sitting in a great tree on the edge of the jungle, listening intently to the night sounds, and uttering a scream from time to time.

Thereafter the Atlájala found it impossible to resist sliding inside the bodies of the friars; it visited one after the other, finding an astonishing variety of sensation in the process. Each was a separate world, a separate experience, because each had different reactions when he became conscious of the other being within him. One would sit and read or pray, one would go for a long troubled walk in the meadows, around and around the building, one would find a comrade and engage in an absurd but bitter quarrel, a few wept, some flagellated themselves or sought a friend to wield the lash for them. Always there was a rich profusion of perceptions for the Atlájala to enjoy, so that it no longer occurred to it to frequent the bodies of insects, birds and furred animals, nor even to leave the monastery and move in the air above. Once it almost got into difficulties when an old friar it was occupying suddenly fell back dead. That was a hazard it ran in the frequenting of men: they seemed not to know when they were doomed, or if they did know, they pretended with such strength not to know, that it amounted to the same thing. The other beings knew beforehand, save when it was a question of being seized unawares and devoured. And that the Atlájala was able to prevent: a bird in which it was staying was always avoided by the hawks and eagles.

When the friars left the monastery, and, following the government's orders, doffed their robes, dispersed and became workmen, the Atlájala was at a loss to know how to pass its days and nights. Now everything was as it had been before their arrival: there was no one but the creatures that always had lived in the circular valley. It tried a giant serpent, a deer, a bee: nothing had the savor it had grown to love. Everything was the same as before, but not for the Atlájala; it had known the existence of man, and now there were no men in the valley —only the abandoned building with its empty rooms to make man's absence more poignant.

Then one year bandits came, several hundred of them in one stormy afternoon. In delight it tried many of them as they sprawled about cleaning their guns and cursing, and it discovered still other facets of sensation: the hatred they felt for the world, the fear they had of the soldiers who were pursuing them, the strange gusts of desire that swept through them as they sprawled together drunk by the fire that smoldered in the center of the floor, and the insufferable pain of jealousy which the nightly orgies seemed to awaken in some of them. But the bandits did not stay long. When they had left, the soldiers came in their wake. It felt very much the same way to be a soldier as to be a bandit. Missing were the strong fear and the hatred, but the rest was almost identical. Neither the bandits nor the soldiers appeared to be at all conscious of its presence in them; it could slip from one man to another without causing any change in their behavior. This surprised it, since its effect on the friars had been so definite, and it felt a certain disappointment at the impossibility of making its existence known to them.

Nevertheless, the Atlájala enjoyed both bandits and soldiers immensely, and was even more desolate when it was left alone once again. It would become one of the swallows that made their nests in the rocks beside the top of the waterfall. In the burning sunlight it would plunge again and again into the curtain of mist that rose from far below, sometimes uttering exultant cries. It would spend a day as a plant louse, crawling slowly along the under side of the leaves, living quietly in the huge green world down there which is forever hidden from the sky. Or at night, in the velvet body of a panther, it would know the pleasure of the kill. Once for a year it lived in an eel at the bottom of the pool below the waterfall, feeling the mud give slowly before it as it pushed ahead with its flat nose; that was a restful period, but afterward the desire to know again the mysterious life of man had returned—an obsession of which it was useless to try to rid itself. And now it moved restlessly through the ruined rooms, a mute presence, alone, and thirsting to be incarnate once again, but in man's flesh only. And with the building of highways through the country it was inevitable that people should come once again to the circular valley.

A man and a woman drove their automobile as far as a village down in a lower valley; hearing about the ruined monastery and the waterfall that dropped over the cliffs into the great amphitheatre, they determined to see these things. They came on burros as far as the village outside the gap, but there the Indians they had hired to accompany them refused to go any farther, and so they continued alone, upward through the canyon and into the precinct of the Atlájala.

It was noon when they rode into the valley; the black ribs of the cliffs glistened like glass in the sun's blistering downward rays. They stopped the burros by a cluster of boulders at the edge of the sloping meadows. The man got down first, and reached up to help the woman off. She leaned forward, putting her hands on his face, and for a long moment they kissed. Then he lifted her to the ground and they climbed hand in hand up over the rocks. The Atlájala hovered near them, watching the

woman closely: she was the first ever to have come into the valley. The two sat beneath a small tree on the grass, looking at
one another, smiling. Out of habit, the Atlájala entered into
the man. Immediately, instead of existing in the midst of the
sunlit air, the bird calls and the plant odors, it was conscious
only of the woman's beauty and her terrible imminence. The
waterfall, the earth, and the sky itself receded, rushed into
nothingness, and there were only the woman's smile and her
arms and her odor. It was a world more suffocating and painful
than the Atlájala had thought possible. Still, while the man
spoke and the woman answered, it remained within.

"Leave him. He doesn't love you."

"He would kill me."

"But I love you. I need you with me."

"I can't. I'm afraid of him."

The man reached out to pull her to him; she drew back
slightly, but her eyes grew large.

"We have today," she murmured, turning her face toward
the yellow walls of the monastery.

The man embraced her fiercely, crushing her against him as
though the act would save his life. "No, no, no. It can't go on
like this," he said. "No."

The pain of his suffering was too intense; gently the Atlájala
left the man and slipped into the woman. And now it would
have believed itself to be housed in nothing, to be in its own
spaceless self, so completely was it aware of the wandering
wind, the small flutterings of the leaves, and the bright air that
surrounded it. Yet there was a difference: each element was
magnified in intensity, the whole sphere of being was immense,
limitless. Now it understood what the man sought in the
woman, and it knew that he suffered because he never would
attain that sense of completion he sought. But the Atlájala,
being one with the woman, had attained it, and being aware of
possessing it, trembled with delight. The woman shuddered as
her lips met those of the man. There on the grass in the shade
of the tree their joy reached new heights; the Atlájala, knowing
them both, formed a single channel between the secret springs
of their desires. Throughout, it remained within the woman,
and began vaguely to devise ways of keeping her, if not inside
the valley, at least nearby, so that she might return.

In the afternoon, with dreamlike motions, they walked to the burros and mounted them, driving them through the deep meadow grass to the monastery. Inside the great courtyard they halted, looking hesitantly at the ancient arches in the sunlight, and at the darkness inside the doorways.

"Shall we go in?" said the woman.

"We must get back."

"I want to go in," she said. (The Atlájala exulted.) A thin gray snake slid along the ground into the bushes. They did not see it.

The man looked at her perplexedly. "It's late," he said.

But she jumped down from her burro by herself and walked beneath the arches into the long corridor within. (Never had the rooms seemed so real as now when the Atlájala was seeing them through her eyes.)

They explored all the rooms. Then the woman wanted to climb up into the tower, but the man took a determined stand.

"We must go back now," he said firmly, putting his hand on her shoulder.

"This is our only day together, and you think of nothing but getting back."

"But the time . . ."

"There is a moon. We won't lose the way."

He would not change his mind. "No."

"As you like," she said. "I'm going up. You can go back alone if you like."

The man laughed uneasily. "You're mad." He tried to kiss her.

She turned away and did not answer for a moment. Then she said: "You want me to leave my husband for you. You ask everything from me, but what do you do for me in return? You refuse even to climb up into a little tower with me to see the view. Go back alone. Go!"

She sobbed and rushed toward the dark stairwell. Calling after her, he followed, but stumbled somewhere behind her. She was as sure of foot as if she had climbed the many stone steps a thousand times before, hurrying up through the darkness, around and around.

In the end she came out at the top and peered through the small apertures in the cracking walls. The beams which had supported the bell had rotted and fallen; the heavy bell lay on its side in the rubble, like a dead animal. The waterfall's sound was louder up here; the valley was nearly full of shadow. Below, the man called her name repeatedly. She did not answer. As she stood watching the shadow of the cliffs slowly overtake the farthest recesses of the valley and begin to climb the naked rocks to the east, an idea formed in her mind. It was not the kind of idea which she would have expected of herself, but it was there, growing and inescapable. When she felt it complete there inside her, she turned and went lightly back down. The man was sitting in the dark near the bottom of the stairs, groaning a little.

"What is it?" she said.

"I hurt my leg. Now are you ready to go or not?"

"Yes," she said simply. "I'm sorry you fell."

Without saying anything he rose and limped after her out into the courtyard where the burros stood. The cold mountain air was beginning to flow down from the tops of the cliffs. As they rode through the meadow she began to think of how she would broach the subject to him. (It must be done before they reached the gap. The Atlájala trembled.)

"Do you forgive me?" she asked him.

"Of course," he laughed.

"Do you love me?"

"More than anything in the world."

"Is that true?"

He glanced at her in the failing light, sitting erect on the jogging animal.

"You know it is," he said softly.

She hesitated.

"There is only one way, then," she said finally.

"But what?"

"I'm afraid of him. I won't go back to him. You go back. I'll stay in the village here." (Being that near, she would come each day to the monastery.) "When it is done, you will come and get me. Then we can go somewhere else. No one will find us."

The man's voice sounded strange. "I don't understand."

"You do understand. And that is the only way. Do it or not, as you like. It is the only way."

They trotted along for a while in silence. The canyon loomed ahead, black against the evening sky.

Then the man said, very clearly: "Never."

A moment later the trail led out into an open space high above the swift water below. The hollow sound of the river reached them faintly. The light in the sky was almost gone; in the dusk the landscape had taken on false contours. Everything was gray—the rocks, the bushes, the trail—and nothing had distance or scale. They slowed their pace.

His word still echoed in her ears.

"I won't go back to him!" she cried with sudden vehemence. "You can go back and play cards with him as usual. Be his good friend the same as always. I won't go. I can't go on with both of you in the town." (The plan was not working; the Atlájala saw it had lost her, yet it still could help her.)

"You're very tired," he said softly.

He was right. Almost as he said the words, that unaccustomed exhilaration and lightness she had felt ever since noon seemed to leave her; she hung her head wearily, and said: "Yes, I am."

At the same moment the man uttered a sharp, terrible cry; she looked up in time to see his burro plunge from the edge of the trail into the grayness below. There was a silence, and then the faraway sound of many stones sliding downward. She could not move or stop the burro; she sat dumbly, letting it carry her along, an inert weight on its back.

For one final instant, as she reached the pass which was the edge of its realm, the Atlájala alighted tremulously within her. She raised her head and a tiny exultant shiver passed through her; then she let it fall forward once again.

Hanging in the dim air above the trail, the Atlájala watched her indistinct figure grow invisible in the gathering night. (If it had not been able to hold her there, still it had been able to help her.)

A moment later it was in the tower, listening to the spiders mend the webs that she had damaged. It would be a long, long time before it would bestir itself to enter into another being's awareness. A long, long time—perhaps forever.

1950

JACK FINNEY

(1911–1995)

I'm Scared

I'M very badly scared, not so much for myself—I'm a gray-haired man of sixty-six, after all—but for you and everyone else who has not yet lived out his life. For I believe that certain dangerous things have recently begun to happen in the world. They are noticed here and there, idly discussed, then dismissed and forgotten. Yet I am convinced that unless these occurrences are recognized for what they are, the world will be plunged into a nightmare. Judge for yourself.

One evening last winter I came home from a chess club to which I belong. I'm a widower; I live alone in a small but comfortable three-room apartment overlooking lower Fifth Avenue. It was still fairly early, and I switched on a lamp beside my leather easy chair, picked up a murder mystery I'd been reading, and turned on the radio; I did not, I'm sorry to say, notice which station it was tuned to.

The tubes warmed, and the music of an accordion—faint at first, then louder—came from the loudspeaker. Since it was good music for reading, I adjusted the volume control and began to read.

Now, I want to be absolutely factual and accurate about this, and I do not claim that I paid close attention to the radio. But I do know that presently the music stopped, and an audience applauded. Then a man's voice, chuckling and pleased with the applause, said, "All right, all right," but the applause continued for several more seconds. During that time the voice once more chuckled appreciatively, then firmly repeated, "All right," and the applause died down. "That was Alec Somebody-or-other," the radio voice said, and I went back to my book.

But I soon became aware of this middle-aged voice again; perhaps a change of tone as he turned to a new subject caught my attention. "And now, Miss Ruth Greeley," he was saying, "of Trenton, New Jersey. Miss Greeley is a pianist; that right?"

A girl's voice, timid and barely audible, said, "That's right, Major Bowes." The man's voice—and now I recognized his familiar singsong delivery—said, "And what are you going to play?" The girl replied, "La Paloma." The man repeated it after her, as an announcement: "La Paloma." There was a pause, then an introductory chord sounded from a piano, and I resumed my reading.

As the girl played, I was half aware that her style was mechanical, her rhythm defective; perhaps she was nervous. Then my attention was fully aroused once more by a gong which sounded suddenly. For a few notes more the girl continued to play falteringly, not sure what to do. The gong sounded jarringly again, the playing abruptly stopped, and there was a restless murmur from the audience. "All right, all right," said the now familiar voice, and I realized I'd been expecting this, knowing it would say just that. The audience quieted, and the voice began, "Now——"

The radio went dead. For the smallest fraction of a second no sound issued from it but its own mechanical hum. Then a completely different program came from the loud-speaker; the recorded voice of Andy Williams singing "You Butterfly," a favorite of mine. So I returned once more to my reading, wondering vaguely what had happened to the other program, but not actually thinking about it until I finished my book and began to get ready for bed.

Then, undressing in my bedroom, I remembered that Major Bowes was dead. Years had passed, a decade, since that dry chuckle and familiar, "All right, all right," had been heard in the nation's living rooms.

Well, what does one do when the apparently impossible occurs? It simply made a good story to tell friends, and more than once I was asked if I'd recently heard Moran and Mack, a pair of radio comedians popular some thirty years ago, or Floyd Gibbons, an old-time news broadcaster. And there were other joking references to my crystal radio set.

But one man—this was at a lodge meeting the following Thursday—listened to my story with utter seriousness, and when I had finished he told me a queer little story of his own. He is a thoughtful, intelligent man, and as I listened I was not frightened, but puzzled at what seemed to be a connecting link, a common denominator, between this story and the odd behavior of my radio. The following day, since I am retired and have plenty of time, I took the trouble of making a two-hour train trip to Connecticut in order to verify the story at first hand. I took detailed notes, and the story appears in my files now as follows:

Case 2. Louis Trachnor, coal and wood dealer, R.F.D. 1, Danbury, Connecticut, aged fifty-four.

On July 20, 1956, Mr. Trachnor told me, he walked out on the front porch of his house about six o'clock in the morning. Running from the eaves of his house to the floor of the porch was a streak of gray paint, still damp. "It was about the width of an eight-inch brush," Mr. Trachnor told me, "and it looked like hell, because the house was white. I figured some kids did it in the night for a joke, but if they did, they had to get a ladder up to the eaves and you wouldn't figure they'd go to that much trouble. It wasn't smeared, either; it was a careful job, a nice even stripe straight down the front of the house."

Mr. Trachnor got a ladder and cleaned off the gray paint with turpentine.

In October of that same year, Mr. Trachnor painted his house. "The white hadn't held up so good, so I painted it gray. I got to the front last and finished about five one Saturday afternoon. Next morning when I came out, I saw a streak of white right down the front of the house. I figured it was the damned kids again, because it was the same place as before. But when I looked close, I saw it wasn't new paint; it was the old white I'd painted over. Somebody had done a nice careful job of cleaning off the new paint in a long stripe about eight inches wide right down from the eaves! Now, who the hell would go to that trouble? I just can't figure it out."

Do you see the link between this story and mine? Suppose for a moment that something had happened, on each occasion, to disturb briefly the orderly progress of time. That seemed to have happened in my case; for a matter of some seconds I apparently heard a radio broadcast that had been made years before. Suppose, then, that no one had touched Mr. Trachnor's house but himself; that he had painted his house in October, and that through some fantastic mix-up in time, a portion of that paint appeared on his house the previous summer. Since he had cleaned the paint off at that time, a broad stripe of new gray paint was missing *after* he painted his house in the fall.

I would be lying, however, if I said I really believed this. It was merely an intriguing speculation, and I told both these little stories to friends, simply as curious anecdotes. I am a sociable person, see a good many people, and occasionally I heard other odd stories in response to mine.

Someone would nod and say, "Reminds me of something I heard recently . . ." and I would have one more to add to my collection. A man on Long Island received a telephone call from his sister in New York on Friday evening. She insists that she did not make this call until the following Monday, three days later. At the Forty-fifth Street branch of the Chase National Bank, I was shown a check deposited the day before it was written. A letter was delivered on East Sixty-eighth Street in New York City, just seventeen minutes after it was dropped into a mailbox on the main street of Green River, Wyoming.

And so on, and so on; my stories were now in demand at parties, and I told myself that collecting and verifying them was a hobby. But the day I heard Julia Eisenberg's story, I knew it was no longer that.

Case 17. Julia Eisenberg, office worker, New York City, aged thirty-one.

Miss Eisenberg lives in a small walk-up apartment in Greenwich Village. I talked to her there after a chess-club friend who lives in her neighborhood had repeated to me a somewhat garbled version of her story, which was told to him by the doorman of the building he lives in.

In October, 1954, about eleven at night, Miss Eisenberg left her apartment to walk to the drugstore for toothpaste. On her way back, not far from her apartment, a large black and white dog ran up to her and put his front paws on her chest.

"I made the mistake of petting him," Miss Eisenberg told me, "and from then on he simply wouldn't leave. When I went into the lobby of my building, I actually had to push him away to get the door closed. I felt sorry for him, poor hound, and a little guilty, because he was still sitting at the door an hour later when I looked out my front window."

This dog remained in the neighborhood for three days, discovering and greeting Miss Eisenberg with wild affection each time she appeared on the street. "When I'd get on the bus in the morning to go to work, he'd sit on the curb looking after me in the most mournful way, poor thing. I wanted to take him in, and I wish with all my heart that I had, but I knew he'd never go home then, and I was afraid whoever owned him would be sorry to lose him. No one in the neighborhood knew who he belonged to, and finally he disappeared."

Two years later a friend gave Miss Eisenberg a three-week-old puppy. "My apartment is really too small for a dog, but he was such a darling I couldn't resist. Well, he grew up into a nice big dog who ate more than I did."

Since the neighborhood was quiet, and the dog well behaved, Miss Eisenberg usually unleashed him when she walked him at night, for he never strayed far. "One night—I'd last seen him sniffing around in the dark a few doors down—I called to him and he didn't come back. And he never did; I never saw him again.

"Now, our street is a solid wall of brownstone buildings on both sides, with locked doors and no areaways. He *couldn't* have disappeared like that, he just *couldn't*. But he did."

Miss Eisenberg hunted for her dog for many days afterward, inquired of neighbors, put ads in the papers, but she never found him. "Then one night I was getting ready for bed; I happened to glance out the front window down at the street, and suddenly I remembered something I'd forgotten all about. I remembered the dog I'd chased away over two years before." Miss Eisenberg looked at me for a moment, then she said flatly. "It was the same dog. If you own a dog you *know* him, you can't be mistaken, and I tell you it was the same dog. Whether it makes sense or not, my dog was lost—I chased him away—two years before he was born."

She began to cry silently, the tears running down her face. "Maybe you think I'm crazy, or a little lonely and overly sentimental about a dog. But you're wrong." She brushed at her tears with a handkerchief. "I'm a well-balanced person, as much as anyone is these days, at least, and I tell you I *know* what happened."

It was in that moment, sitting in Miss Eisenberg's neat, shabby living room, that I realized fully that the consequences of these odd little incidents could be something more than merely intriguing; that they might, quite possibly, be tragic. It was in that moment that I began to be afraid.

I have spent the last eleven months discovering and tracking down these strange occurrences, and I am astonished and frightened at how many there are. I am astonished and frightened at how much more frequently they are happening now, and—I hardly know how to express this—at their increasing *power* to tear human lives tragically apart. This is an example, selected almost at random, of the increasing strength of—whatever it is that is happening in the world.

Case 34. Paul V. Kerch, accountant, the Bronx, aged thirty-one.

On a bright, clear, Sunday afternoon, I met an unsmiling family of three at their Bronx apartment: Mr. Kerch, a chunky, darkly good-looking young man; his wife, a pleasant-faced dark-haired woman in her late twenties, whose attractiveness was marred by circles under her eyes; and their son, a nice-looking boy of six or seven. After introductions, the boy was sent to his room at the back of the house to play.

"All right," Mr. Kerch said wearily then, and walked toward a bookcase, "let's get at it. You said on the phone that you know the story in general." It was half a question, half a statement.

"Yes," I said.

He took a book from the top shelf and removed some photographs from it. "There are the pictures." He sat down on the davenport beside me, with the photographs in his hand. "I own a pretty good camera, I'm a fair amateur photographer, and I have a darkroom setup in the kitchen; do my own developing. Two weeks ago, we went down to Central Park." His voice was a tired monotone as though this were a story he'd repeated many times, aloud and in his own mind. "It was nice, like today, and the kid's grandmothers have been pestering us for pictures, so I took a whole roll of films, pictures of all of us. My camera can be set up and focused and it will snap the picture automatically a few seconds later, giving me time to get around in front of it and get in the picture myself."

There was a tired, hopeless look in his eyes as he handed me all but one of the photographs. "These are the first ones I took," he said. The photographs were all fairly large, perhaps $5 \times 7''$, and I examined them closely.

They were ordinary enough, very sharp and detailed, and

each showed the family of three in various smiling poses. Mr. Kerch wore a light business suit, his wife had on a dark dress and a cloth coat, and the boy wore a dark suit with knee-length pants. In the background stood a tree with bare branches. I glanced up at Mr. Kerch, signifying that I had finished my study of the photographs.

"The last picture," he said, holding it in his hand ready to give to me, "I took exactly like the others. We agreed on the pose, I set the camera, walked around in front, and joined my family. Monday night I developed the whole roll. This is what came out on the last negative." He handed me the photograph.

For an instant it seemed to me like merely one more photograph in the group; then I saw the difference. Mr. Kerch looked much the same, bare-headed and grinning broadly, but he wore an entirely different suit. The boy, standing beside him, wore long pants, was a good three inches taller, obviously older, but equally obviously the same boy. The woman was an entirely different person. Dressed smartly, her light hair catching the sun, she was very pretty and attractive, and she was smiling into the camera, holding Mr. Kerch's hand.

I looked up at him. "Who is this?"

Wearily, Mr. Kerch shook his head. "I don't know," he said sullenly, then suddenly exploded: "I don't *know*! I've never seen her in my life!" He turned to look at his wife, but she would not return his glance, and he turned back to me, shrugging. "Well, there you have it," he said. "The whole story." And he stood up, thrusting both hands into his trouser pockets, and began to pace about the room, glancing often at his wife, talking to *her* actually, though he addressed his words to me. "So who is she? How could the camera have snapped that picture? I've never seen that woman in my life!"

I glanced at the photograph again, then bent closer. "The trees here are in full bloom," I said. Behind the solemn-faced boy, the grinning man and smiling woman, the trees of Central Park were in full summer leaf.

Mr. Kerch nodded. "I know," he said bitterly. "And you know what *she* says?" he burst out, glaring at his wife. "She says that *is* my wife in the photograph, my *new* wife a couple of years from now! God!" He slapped both hands down on his head. "The ideas a woman can get!"

"What do you mean?" I glanced at Mrs. Kerch, but she ignored me, remaining silent, her lips tight.

Kerch shrugged hopelessly. "She says that photograph shows how things will be a couple of years from now. She'll be dead or"—he hesitated, then said the word bitterly—"divorced, and I'll have our son and be married to the woman in the picture."

We both looked at Mrs. Kerch, waiting until she was obliged to speak.

"Well, if it isn't so," she said, shrugging a shoulder, "then tell me what that picture does mean."

Neither of us could answer that, and a few minutes later I left. There was nothing much I could say to the Kerches; certainly I couldn't mention my conviction that, whatever the explanation of the last photograph, their married life was over. . . .

Case 72. Lieutenant Alfred Eichler, New York Police Department, aged thirty-three.

In the late evening of January 9, 1956, two policemen found a revolver lying just off a gravel path near an East Side entrance to Central Park. The gun was examined for fingerprints at the police laboratory and several were found. One bullet had been fired from the revolver and the police fired another which was studied and classified by a ballistics expert. The fingerprints were checked and found in police files; they were those of a minor hoodlum with a record of assault.

A routine order to pick him up was sent out. A detective called at the rooming house where he was known to live, but he was out, and since no unsolved shootings had occurred recently, no intensive search for him was made that night.

The following evening a man was shot and killed in Central Park with the same gun. This was proved ballistically past all question of error. It was soon learned that the murdered man had been quarreling with a friend in a nearby tavern. The two men, both drunk, had left the tavern together. And the second man was the hoodlum whose gun had been found the previous night, and which was still locked in a police safe.

As Lieutenant Eichler said to me, "It's impossible that the dead man was killed with that same gun, but he was. Don't ask me how, though, and if anybody thinks we'd go into court with a case like that, they're crazy."

Case III. Captain Hubert V. Rihm, New York Police Department, retired, aged sixty-six.

I met Captain Rihm by appointment one morning in Stuyvesant Park, a patch of greenery, wood benches and asphalt surrounded by the city, on lower Second Avenue. "You want to hear about the Fentz case, do you?" he said, after we had introduced ourselves and found an empty bench. "All right, I'll tell you. I don't like to talk about it—it bothers me—but I'd like to see what you think." He was a big, rather heavy man, with a red, tough face, and he wore an old police jacket and uniform cap with the insigne removed.

"I was up at City Mortuary," he began, as I took out my notebook and pencil, "at Bellevue, about twelve one night, drinking coffee with one of the interns. This was in June, 1955, just before I retired, and I was in Missing Persons. They brought this guy in and he was a funny-looking character. Had a beard. A young guy, maybe thirty, but he wore regular muttonchop whiskers, and his clothes were funny-looking. Now, I was thirty years on the force and I've seen a lot of queer guys killed on the streets. We found an Arab once, in full regalia, and it took us a week to find out who he was. So it wasn't just the way the guy looked that bothered me; it was the stuff we found in his pockets."

Captain Rihm turned on the bench to see if he'd caught my interest, then continued. "There was about a dollar in change in the dead guy's pocket, and one of the boys picked up a nickel and showed it to me. Now, you've seen plenty of nickels, the new ones with Jefferson's picture, the buffalo nickels they made before that, and once in a while you still see even the old Liberty-head nickels; they quit making them before the First World War. But this one was even older than that. It had a shield on the front, a U.S. shield, and a big five on the back; I used to see that kind when I was a boy. And the funny thing was, that old nickel looked new; what coin dealers call 'mint condition,' like it was made the day before yesterday. The date on that nickel was 1876, and there wasn't a coin in his pocket dated any later."

Captain Rihm looked at me questioningly. "Well," I said, glancing up from my notebook, "that could happen."

"Sure, it could," he answered in a satisfied tone, "but all the pennies he had were Indian-head pennies. Now, when did you see one of them last? There was even a silver three-cent piece; looked like an old-style dime, only smaller. And the bills in his wallet, every one of them, were old-time bills, the big kind."

Captain Rihm leaned forward and spat on the path, a needle-jet of tobacco juice, and an expression of a policeman's annoyed contempt for anything deviating from an orderly norm.

"Over seventy bucks in cash, and not a Federal reserve note in the lot. There were two yellow-back tens. Remember them? They were payable in gold. The rest were old national-bank notes; you remember them, too. Issued direct by local banks, personally signed by the bank president; that kind used to be counterfeited a lot.

"Well," Captain Rihm continued, leaning back on the bench and crossing his knees, "there was a bill in his pocket from a livery stable on Lexington Avenue: three dollars for feeding and stabling his horse and washing a carriage. There was a brass slug in his pocket good for a five-cent beer at some saloon. There was a letter postmarked Philadelphia, June, 1876, with an old-style two-cent stamp; and a bunch of cards in his wallet. The cards had his name and address on them, and so did the letter."

"Oh," I said, a little surprised, "you identified him right away, then?"

"Sure. Rudolph Fentz, some address on Fifth Avenue—I forget the exact number—in New York City. No problem at all." Captain Rihm leaned forward and spat again. "Only that address wasn't a residence. It's a store, and it has been for years, and nobody there ever heard of any Rudolph Fentz, and there's no such name in the phone book, either. Nobody ever called or made any inquiries about the guy, and Washington didn't have his prints. There was a tailor's name in his coat, a lower Broadway address, but nobody there ever heard of this tailor."

"What was so strange about his clothes?"

The Captain said, "Well, did you ever know anyone who wore a pair of pants with big black-and-white checks, cut very narrow, no cuffs, and pressed without a crease?"

I had to think for a moment. "Yes," I said then, "my father, when he was a very young man, before he was married; I've seen old photographs."

"Sure," said Captain Rihm, "and he probably wore a short sort of cutaway coat with two cloth-covered buttons at the back, a vest with lapels, a tall silk hat, and a big, black oversize bow tie on a turned-up stiff collar, and button shoes."

"That's how this man was dressed?"

"Like eighty years ago! And him no more than thirty years old. There was a label in his hat, a Twenty-third Street hat store that went out of business around the turn of the century. Now, what do you make out of a thing like that?"

"Well," I said carefully, "there's nothing much you can make of it. Apparently someone went to a lot of trouble to dress up in an antique style; the coins and bills, I assume he could buy at a coin dealer's; and then he got himself killed in a traffic accident."

"Got himself killed is right. Eleven fifteen at night in Times Square—the theaters letting out; busiest time and place in the world—and this guy shows up in the middle of the street, gawking and looking around at the cars and up at the signs like he'd never seen them before. The cop on duty noticed him, so you can see how he must have been acting. The lights change, the traffic starts up, with him in the middle of the street, and instead of waiting, the damned fool, he turns and tries to make it back to the sidewalk. A cab got him and he was dead when he hit."

For a moment Captain Rihm sat chewing his tobacco and staring angrily at a young woman pushing a baby carriage, though I'm sure he didn't see her. The young mother looked at him in surprise as she passed, and the captain continued:

"Nothing you can make out of a thing like that. We found out nothing. I started checking through our file of old phone books, just as routine, but without much hope because they only go back so far. But in the 1939 summer edition I found a Rudolph Fentz, Jr., somewhere on East Fifty-second Street. He'd moved away in 'forty-two, though, the building super told me, and was a man in his sixties besides, retired from business; used to work in a bank a few blocks away, the super thought. I found the bank where he'd worked, and they told me he'd retired in 'forty, and had been dead for five years; his widow was living in Florida with a sister.

"I wrote to the widow, but there was only one thing she could tell us, and that was no good. I never even reported it, not officially, anyway. Her husband's father had disappeared when her husband was a boy maybe two years old. He went out for a walk around ten one night—his wife thought cigar smoke smelled up the curtains, so he used to take a little stroll before he went to bed, and smoke a cigar—and he didn't come back, and was never seen or heard of again. The family spent a good deal of money trying to locate him, but they never did. This was in the middle eighteen seventies sometime; the old lady wasn't sure of the exact date. Her husband hadn't ever said too much about it.

"And that's all," said Captain Rihm. "Once I put in one of my afternoons off hunting through a bunch of old police records. And I finally found the Missing Persons file for 1876, and Rudolph Fentz was listed, all right. There wasn't much of a description, and no fingerprints, of course. I'd give a year of my life, even now, and maybe sleep better nights, if they'd had his fingerprints. He was listed as twenty-nine years old, wearing full muttonchop whiskers, a tall silk hat, dark coat and checked pants. That's about all it said. Didn't say what kind of tie or vest or if his shoes were the button kind. His name was Rudolph Fentz and he lived at this address on Fifth Avenue; it must have been a residence then. Final disposition of case: not located.

"Now, I hate that case," Captain Rihm said quietly. "I hate it and I wish I'd never heard of it. What do *you* think?" he demanded suddenly, angrily. "You think this guy walked off into thin air in eighteen seventy-six, and showed up again in nineteen fifty-five!"

I shrugged noncommittally, and the captain took it to mean no.

"No, of course not," he said. "Of *course* not, but—give me some other explanation."

I could go on. I could give you several hundred such cases. A sixteen-year-old girl walked out of her bedroom one morning, carrying her clothes in her hand because they were too big for her, and she was quite obviously eleven years old again. And there are other occurrences too horrible for print. All of them have happened in the New York City area alone, all within the last few years; and I suspect thousands more have occurred, and are occurring, all over the world. I could go on, but the point is this: What is happening and *why*? I believe that I know.

Haven't you noticed, too, on the part of nearly everyone you know, a growing rebellion against the *present*? And an increasing longing for the past? I have. Never before in all my long life have I heard so many people wish that they lived "at the turn of the century," or "when life was simpler," or "worth living," or "when you could bring children into the world and count on the future," or simply "in the good old days." People didn't talk that way when I was young! The present was a glorious time! But they talk that way now.

For the first time in man's history, man is desperate to escape the present. Our newsstands are jammed with escape literature, the very name of which is significant. Entire magazines are devoted to fantastic stories of escape—to other times, past and future, to other worlds and planets—escape to anywhere but here and now. Even our larger magazines, book publishers and Hollywood are beginning to meet the rising demand for this kind of escape. Yes, there is a craving in the world like a thirst, a terrible mass pressure that you can almost feel, of millions of minds struggling against the barriers of time. I am utterly convinced that this terrible mass pressure of millions of minds is already, slightly but definitely, affecting time itself. In the moments when this happens—when the almost universal longing to escape is greatest—my incidents occur. Man is disturbing the clock of time, and I am afraid it will break. When it does, I leave to your imagination the last few hours of madness that will be left to us; all the countless moments that now make up our lives suddenly ripped apart and chaotically tangled in time.

Well, I have lived most of my life; I can be robbed of only a few more years. But it seems too bad—this universal craving to escape what could be a rich, productive, happy world. We live on a planet well able to provide a decent life for every soul on it, which is all ninety-nine of a hundred human beings ask. Why in the world can't we have it?

1951

VLADIMIR NABOKOV

(1899–1977)

The Vane Sisters

I.

I MIGHT never have heard of Cynthia's death, had I not run, that night, into D., whom I had also lost track of for the last four years or so; and I might never have run into D., had I not got involved in a series of trivial investigations.

The day, a compunctious Sunday after a week of blizzards, had been part jewel, part mud. In the midst of my usual afternoon stroll through the small hilly town attached to the girls' college where I taught French literature, I had stopped to watch a family of brilliant icicles drip-dripping from the eaves of a frame house. So clear-cut were their pointed shadows on the white boards behind them that I was sure the shadows of the falling drops should be visible too. But they were not. The roof jutted too far out, perhaps, or the angle of vision was faulty, or, again, I did not chance to be watching the right icicle when the right drop fell. There was a rhythm, an alternation in the dropping that I found as teasing as a coin trick. It led me to inspect the corners of several house blocks, and this brought me to Kelly Road, and right to the house where D. used to live when he was instructor here. And as I looked up at the eaves of the adjacent garage with its full display of transparent stalactites backed by their blue silhouettes, I was rewarded at last, upon choosing one, by the sight of what might be described as the dot of an exclamation mark leaving its ordinary position to glide down very fast—a jot faster than the thaw-drop it raced. This twinned twinkle was delightful but not completely satisfying; or rather it only sharpened my appetite for other tidbits of light and shade, and I walked on in a state of raw awareness that seemed to transform the whole of my being into one big eyeball rolling in the world's socket.

Through peacocked lashes I saw the dazzling diamond reflection of the low sun on the round back of a parked automobile. To all kinds of things a vivid pictorial sense had been restored by the sponge of the thaw. Water in overlapping festoons flowed down one sloping street and turned gracefully into another. With ever so slight a note of meretricious appeal, narrow passages between buildings revealed treasures of brick and purple. I remarked for the first time the humble fluting— last echoes of grooves on the shafts of columns—ornamenting a garbage can, and I also saw the rippling upon its lid—circles diverging from a fantastically ancient center. Erect, dark-headed shapes of dead snow (left by the blades of a bulldozer last Friday) were lined up like rudimentary penguins along the curbs, above the brilliant vibration of live gutters.

I walked up, and I walked down, and I walked straight into a delicately dying sky, and finally the sequence of observed and observant things brought me, at my usual eating time, to a street so distant from my usual eating place that I decided to try a restaurant which stood on the fringe of the town. Night had fallen without sound or ceremony when I came out again. The lean ghost, the elongated umbra cast by a parking meter upon some damp snow, had a strange ruddy tinge; this I made out to be due to the tawny red light of the restaurant sign above the sidewalk; and it was then—as I sauntered there, wondering rather wearily if in the course of my return tramp I might be lucky enough to find the same in neon blue it was then that a car crunched to a standstill near me and D. got out of it with an exclamation of feigned pleasure.

He was passing, on his way from Albany to Boston, through the town he had dwelt in before, and more than once in my life have I felt that stab of vicarious emotion followed by a rush of personal irritation against travelers who seem to feel nothing at all upon revisiting spots that ought to harass them at every step with wailing and writhing memories. He ushered me back into the bar that I had just left, and after the usual exchange of buoyant platitudes came the inevitable vacuum which he filled with the random words: "Say, I never thought there was anything wrong with Cynthia Vane's heart. My lawyer tells me she died last week."

2.

He was still young, still brash, still shifty, still married to the gentle, exquisitely pretty woman who had never learned or suspected anything about his disastrous affair with Cynthia's hysterical young sister, who in her turn had known nothing of the interview I had had with Cynthia when she suddenly summoned me to Boston to make me swear I would talk to D. and get him "kicked out" if he did not stop seeing Sybil at once— or did not divorce his wife (whom incidentally she visualized through the prism of Sybil's wild talk as a termagant and a fright). I had cornered him immediately. He had said there was nothing to worry about—had made up his mind, anyway, to give up his college job and move with his wife to Albany where he would work in his father's firm; and the whole matter, which had threatened to become one of those hopelessly entangled situations that drag on for years, with peripheral sets of well-meaning friends endlessly discussing it in universal secrecy —and even founding, among themselves, new intimacies upon its alien woes—came to an abrupt end.

I remember sitting next day at my raised desk in the large classroom where a mid-year examination in French Lit. was being held on the eve of Sybil's suicide. She came in on high heels, with a suitcase, dumped it in a corner where several other bags were stacked, with a single shrug slipped her fur coat off her thin shoulders, folded it on her bag, and with two or three other girls stopped before my desk to ask when would I mail them their grades. It would take me a week, beginning from tomorrow, I said, to read the stuff. I also remember wondering whether D. had already informed her of his decision— and I felt acutely unhappy about my dutiful little student as during one hundred and fifty minutes my gaze kept reverting to her, so childishly slight in close-fitting grey, and kept observing that carefully waved dark hair, that small, small-flowered hat with a little hyaline veil as worn that season and under it her small face broken into a cubist pattern by scars due to a skin disease, pathetically masked by a sun-lamp tan that hardened her features whose charm was further impaired by her having painted everything that could be painted, so that the pale gums of her teeth between cherry-red chapped lips and the diluted blue ink of her eyes under darkened lids were the only visible openings into her beauty.

Next day, having arranged the ugly copybooks alphabetically, I plunged into their chaos of scripts and came prematurely to Valevsky and Vane whose books I had somehow misplaced. The first was dressed up for the occasion in a semblance of legibility, but Sybil's work displayed her usual combination of several demon hands. She had begun in very pale, very hard pencil which had conspicuously embossed the blank verso, but had produced little of permanent value on the upper-side of the page. Happily the tip soon broke, and Sybil continued in another, darker lead, gradually lapsing into the blurred thickness of what looked almost like charcoal, to which, by sucking the blunt point, she had contributed some traces of lipstick. Her work, although even poorer than I had expected, bore all the signs of a kind of desperate conscientiousness, with underscores, transposes, unnecessary footnotes, as if she were intent upon rounding up things in the most respectable manner possible. Then she had borrowed Mary Valevsky's fountain pen and added: "*Cette examain est finie ainsi que ma vie. Adieu, jeunes filles!* Please, *Monsieur le Professeur*, contact *ma soeur* and tell her that Death was not better than D minus, but definitely better than Life minus D."

I lost no time in ringing up Cynthia who told me it was all over—had been all over since eight in the morning—and asked me to bring her the note, and when I did, beamed through her tears with proud admiration for the whimsical use ("Just like her!") Sybil had made of an examination in French literature. In no time she "fixed" two highballs, while never parting with Sybil's notebook—by now splashed with soda water and tears—and went on studying the death message, whereupon I was impelled to point out to her the grammatical mistakes in it and to explain the way "girl" is translated in American colleges lest students innocently bandy around the French equivalent of "wench," or worse. These rather tasteless trivialities pleased Cynthia hugely as she rose, with gasps, above the heaving surface of her grief. And then, holding that limp notebook as if it were a kind of passport to a casual Elysium (where pencil points do not snap and a dreamy young beauty with an impeccable complexion winds a lock of her hair on a dreamy forefinger, as she meditates over some celestial test), Cynthia led me upstairs, to a chilly little bedroom just to show me, as if I were the police or a sympathetic Irish neighbor, two empty pill bottles and the tumbled bed from which a tender, inessential body, that D. must have known down to its last velvet detail, had been already removed.

3.

It was four or five months after her sister's death that I began seeing Cynthia fairly often. By the time I had come to New York for some vocational research in the Public Library she had also moved to that city where for some odd reason (in vague connection, I presume, with artistic motives) she had taken what people, immune to gooseflesh, term a "cold water" flat, down in the scale of the city's transverse streets. What attracted me were neither her ways, which I thought repulsively vivacious, nor her looks, which other men thought striking. She had wide-spaced eyes very much like her sister's, of a frank, frightened blue with dark points in a radial arrangement. The interval between her thick black eyebrows was always shiny, and shiny too were the fleshy volutes of her nostrils. The coarse texture of her epiderm looked almost masculine, and, in the stark lamplight of her studio, you could see the pores of her thirty-two-year-old face fairly gaping at you like something in an aquarium. She used cosmetics with as much zest as her little sister had, but with an additional slovenliness that would result in her big front teeth getting some of the rouge. She was handsomely dark, wore a not too tasteless mixture of fairly smart heterogeneous things, and had a so-called good figure; but all of her was curiously frowsy, after a way I obscurely associated with left-wing enthusiasms in politics and "advanced" banalities in art, although, actually, she cared for neither. Her coily hair-do, on a part-and-bun basis, might have looked feral and bizarre had it not been thoroughly domesticated by its own soft unkemptness at the vulnerable nape. Her fingernails were gaudily painted, but badly bitten and not clean. Her lovers were a silent young photographer with a sudden laugh and two older men, brothers, who owned a small printing establishment across the street. I wondered at their tastes whenever I

glimpsed, with a secret shudder, the higgledy-piggledy stria-
tion of black hairs that showed all along her pale shins through
the nylon of her stockings with the scientific distinctness of a
preparation flattened under glass; or when I felt, at her every
movement, the dullish, stalish, not particularly conspicuous
but all-pervading and depressing emanation that her seldom
bathed flesh spread from under weary perfumes and creams.

Her father had gambled away the greater part of a comfortable fortune, and her mother's first husband had been of Slav
origin, but otherwise Cynthia Vane belonged to a good, respectable family. For aught we know, it may have gone back to
kings and soothsayers in the mists of ultimate islands. Transferred to a newer world, to a landscape of doomed, splendid
deciduous trees, her ancestry presented, in one of its first phases,
a white churchful of farmers against a black thunderhead, and
then an imposing array of townsmen engaged in mercantile
pursuits, as well as a number of learned men, such as Dr.
Jonathan Vane, the gaunt bore (1780–1839), who perished in
the conflagration of the steamer "Lexington" to become later
an habitué of Cynthia's tilting table. I have always wished to
stand genealogy on its head, and here I have an opportunity
to do so, for it is the last scion, Cynthia, and Cynthia alone,
who will remain of any importance in the Vane dynasty. I am
alluding of course to her artistic gift, to her delightful, gay, but
not very popular paintings which the friends of her friends
bought at long intervals—and I dearly should like to know
where they went after her death, those honest and poetical pictures that illumined her living-room—the wonderfully detailed
images of metallic things, and my favorite "Seen Through a
Windshield"—a windshield partly covered with rime, with a
brilliant trickle (from an imaginary car roof) across its transparent part and, through it all, the sapphire flame of the sky
and a green and white fir tree.

4.

Cynthia had a feeling that her dead sister was not altogether
pleased with her—had discovered by now that she and I had
conspired to break her romance; and so, in order to disarm her
shade, Cynthia reverted to a rather primitive type of sacrificial

offering (tinged, however, with something of Sybil's humor), and began to send to D.'s business address, at deliberately un-fixed dates, such trifles as snapshots of Sybil's tomb in a poor light; cuttings of her own hair which was indistinguishable from Sybil's; a New England sectional map with an inked-in cross, midway between two chaste towns, to mark the spot where D. and Sybil had stopped on October the twenty-third, in broad daylight, at a lenient motel, in a pink and brown forest; and, twice, a stuffed skunk.

Being as a conversationalist more voluble than explicit, she never could describe in full the theory of intervenient auras that she had somehow evolved. Fundamentally there was nothing particularly new about her private creed since it pre-supposed a fairly conventional hereafter, a silent solarium of immortal souls (spliced with mortal antecedents) whose main recreation consisted of periodical hoverings over the dear quick. The interesting point was a curious practical twist that Cynthia gave to her tame metaphysics. She was sure that her existence was influenced by all sorts of dead friends each of whom took turns in directing her fate much as if she were a stray kitten which a schoolgirl in passing gathers up, and presses to her cheek, and carefully puts down again, near some subur-ban hedge—to be stroked presently by another transient hand or carried off to a world of doors by some hospitable lady.

For a few hours, or for several days in a row, and sometimes recurrently, in an irregular series, for months or years, any-thing that happened to Cynthia, after a given person had died, would be, she said, in the manner and mood of that person. The event might be extraordinary, changing the course of one's life; or it might be a string of minute incidents just suffi-ciently clear to stand out in relief against one's usual day and then shading off into still vaguer trivia as the aura gradually faded. The influence might be good or bad; the main thing was that its source could be identified. It was like walking through a person's soul, she said. I tried to argue that she might not always be able to determine the exact source since not everybody has a recognizable soul; that there are anony-mous letters and Christmas presents which anybody might send; that, in fact, what Cynthia called "a usual day" might be itself a weak solution of mixed auras or simply the routine shift of a humdrum guardian angel. And what about God? Did or did not people who would resent any omnipotent dictator on earth look forward to one in heaven? And wars? What a dreadful idea—dead soldiers still fighting with living ones, or phantom armies trying to get at each other through the lives of crippled old men.

But Cynthia was above generalities as she was beyond logic. "Ah, that's Paul," she would say when the soup spitefully boiled over, or: "I guess good Betty Brown is dead"—when she won a beautiful and very welcome vacuum cleaner in a charity lottery. And, with Jamesian meanderings that exasperated my French mind, she would go back to a time when Betty and Paul had not yet departed, and tell me of the showers of well-meant, but odd and quite unacceptable bounties—beginning with an old purse that contained a check for three dollars which she picked up in the street and, of course, returned (to the aforesaid Betty Brown—this is where she first comes in—a decrepit colored woman hardly able to walk), and ending with an insulting proposal from an old beau of hers (this is where Paul comes in) to paint "straight" pictures of his house and family for a reasonable remuneration—all of which followed upon the demise of a certain Mrs. Page, a kindly but petty old party who had pestered her with bits of matter-of-fact advice since Cynthia had been a child.

Sybil's personality, she said, had a rainbow edge as if a little out of focus. She said that had I known Sybil better I would have at once understood how Sybil-like was the aura of minor events which, in spells, had suffused her, Cynthia's, existence after Sybil's suicide. Ever since they had lost their mother they had intended to give up their Boston home and move to New York, where Cynthia's paintings, they thought, would have a chance to be more widely admired; but the old home had clung to them with all its plush tentacles. Dead Sybil, however, had proceeded to separate the house from its view—a thing that affects fatally the sense of home. Right across the narrow street a building project had come into loud, ugly, scaffolded life. A pair of familiar poplars died that spring, turning to blond skeletons. Workmen came and broke up the warm-colored lovely old sidewalk that had a special violet sheen on wet April days and had echoed so memorably to the morning footsteps of museum-bound Mr. Lever, who upon retiring from business at sixty had devoted a full quarter of a century exclusively to the study of snails.

Speaking of old men, one should add that sometimes these posthumous auspices and interventions were in the nature of parody. Cynthia had been on friendly terms with an eccentric librarian called Porlock who in the last years of his dusty life had been engaged in examining old books for miraculous misprints such as the substitution of "l" for the second "h" in the word "hither." Contrary to Cynthia, he cared nothing for the thrill of obscure predictions; all he sought was the freak itself, the chance that mimics choice, the flaw that looks like a flower; and Cynthia, a much more perverse amateur of mis-shapen or illicitly connected words, puns, logogriphs, and so on, had helped the poor crank to pursue a quest that in the light of the example she cited struck me as statistically insane. Anyway, she said, on the third day after his death she was reading a magazine and had just come across a quotation from an imperishable poem (that she, with other gullible readers, believed to have been really composed in a dream) when it dawned upon her that "Alph" was a prophetic sequence of the initial letters of Anna Livia Plurabelle (another sacred river running through, or rather around, yet another fake dream), while the additional "h" modestly stood, as a private signpost, for the word that had so hypnotized Mr. Porlock. And I wish I could recollect that novel or short story (by some contemporary writer, I believe) in which, unknown to its author, the first letters of the words in its last paragraph formed, as deciphered by Cynthia, a message from his dead mother.

5.

I am sorry to say that not content with these ingenious fancies Cynthia showed a ridiculous fondness for spiritualism. I refused to accompany her to sittings in which paid mediums took part: I knew too much about that from other sources. I did consent, however, to attend little farces rigged up by Cynthia and her two poker-faced gentlemen-friends of the printing shop. They were podgy, polite, and rather eerie old fellows, but I satisfied myself that they possessed considerable wit and culture. We sat down at a light little table, and crackling tremors started almost as soon as we laid our fingertips upon it. I was treated to an assortment of ghosts who rapped out their reports most readily though refusing to elucidate anything that I did not quite catch. Oscar Wilde came in and in rapid garbled French, with the usual anglicisms, obscurely accused Cynthia's dead parents of what appeared in my jottings as "*plagiatisme.*" A brisk spirit contributed the unsolicited information that he, John Moore, and his brother Bill had been coal miners in Colorado and had perished in an avalanche at "Crested Beauty" in January 1883. Frederic Myers, an old hand at the game, hammered out a piece of verse (oddly resembling Cynthia's own fugitive productions) which in part reads in my notes:

> *What is this—a conjuror's rabbit,*
> *Or a flawy but genuine gleam—*
> *Which can check the perilous habit*
> *And dispel the dolorous dream?*

Finally, with a great crash and all kinds of shudderings and jig-like movements on the part of the table, Leo Tolstoy visited our little group and, when asked to identify himself by specific traits of terrene habitation, launched upon a complex description of what seemed to be some Russian type of architectural woodwork ("figures on boards—man, horse, cock, man, horse, cock"), all of which was difficult to take down, hard to understand, and impossible to verify.

I attended two or three other sittings which were even sillier but I must confess that I preferred the childish entertainment they afforded and the cider we drank (Podgy and Pudgy were teetotallers) to Cynthia's awful house parties.

She gave them at the Wheelers' nice flat next door—the sort of arrangement dear to her centrifugal nature, but then, of course, her own living-room always looked like a dirty old palette. Following a barbaric, unhygienic, and adulterous custom, the guests' coats, still warm on the inside, were carried by quiet, baldish Bob Wheeler into the sanctity of a tidy bedroom and heaped on the conjugal bed. It was also he who poured out the drinks which were passed around by the young photographer while Cynthia and Mrs. Wheeler took care of the canapés.

A late arrival had the impression of lots of loud people unnecessarily grouped within a smoke-blue space between two mirrors gorged with reflections. Because, I suppose, Cynthia wished to be the youngest in the room, the women she used to invite, married or single, were, at the best, in their precarious forties; some of them would bring from their homes, in dark taxis, intact vestiges of good looks, which, however, they lost as the party progressed. It has always amazed me—the capacity sociable week-end revellers have of finding almost at once, by a purely empiric but very precise method, a common denominator of drunkenness, to which everybody loyally sticks before descending, all together, to the next level. The rich friendliness of the matrons was marked by tomboyish overtones, while the fixed inward look of amiably tight men was like a sacrilegious parody of pregnancy. Although some of the guests were connected in one way or another with the arts, there was no inspired talk, no wreathed, elbow-propped heads, and of course no flute girls. From some vantage point where she had been sitting in a stranded mermaid pose on the pale carpet with one or two younger fellows, Cynthia, her face varnished with a film of beaming sweat, would creep up on her knees, a proffered plate of nuts in one hand, and crisply tap with the other the athletic leg of Cochran or Corcoran, an art dealer, ensconced, on a pearl-grey sofa, between two flushed, happily disintegrating ladies.

At a further stage there would come spurts of more riotous gaiety. Corcoran or Coransky would grab Cynthia or some other wandering woman by the shoulder and lead her into a corner to confront her with a grinning embroglio of private jokes and rumors, whereupon, with a laugh and a toss of her head, she would break away. And still later there would be flurries of intersexual chumminess, jocular reconciliations, a bare fleshy arm flung around another woman's husband (he standing very upright in the midst of a swaying room), or a sudden rush of flirtatious anger, of clumsy pursuit—and the quiet half smile of Bob Wheeler picking up glasses that grew like mushrooms in the shade of chairs.

After one last party of that sort, I wrote Cynthia a perfectly harmless and, on the whole, well-meant note, in which I poked a little Latin fun at some of her guests. I also apologized for not having touched her whisky, saying that as a Frenchman I preferred the grape to the grain. A few days later I met her on the steps of the Public Library, in the broken sun, under a weak cloudburst, opening her amber umbrella, struggling with a couple of armpitted books (of which I relieved her for a moment). "Footfalls on the Boundary of Another World," by Robert Dale Owen, and something on "Spiritualism and Christianity"; when, suddenly, with no provocation on my part, she blazed out at me with vulgar vehemence, using poisonous words, saying—through pear-shaped drops of sparse rain—that I was a prig and a snob; that I only saw the gestures and disguises of people; that Corcoran had rescued from drowning, in two different oceans, two men—by an irrelevant coincidence both called Corcoran; that romping and screeching Joan Winter had a little girl doomed to grow completely blind in a few months; and that the woman in green with the freckled chest whom I had snubbed in some way or other had written a national best-seller in 1932. Strange Cynthia! I had been told she could be thunderously rude to people whom she liked and respected; one had, however, to draw the line somewhere and since I had by then sufficiently studied her interesting auras and other odds and ids, I decided to stop seeing her altogether.

6.

The night D. informed me of Cynthia's death I returned after eleven to the two-storied house I shared, in horizontal section, with an emeritus professor's widow. Upon reaching the porch I looked with the apprehension of solitude at the two kinds of darkness in the two rows of windows: the darkness of absence and the darkness of sleep.

I could do something about the first but could not duplicate the second. My bed gave me no sense of safety; its springs only made my nerves bounce. I plunged into Shakespeare's sonnets—and found myself idiotically checking the first letters of the lines to see what sacramental words they might form. I got

FATE (LXX), ATOM (CXX) and, twice, TAFT (LXXXVIII, CXXXI). Every now and then I would glance around to see how the objects in my room were behaving. It was strange to think that if bombs began to fall I would feel little more than a gambler's excitement (and a great deal of earthy relief) whereas my heart would burst if a certain suspiciously tense-looking little bottle on yonder shelf moved a fraction of an inch to one side. The silence, too, was suspiciously compact as if deliberately forming a black back-drop for the nerve flash caused by any small sound of unknown origin. All traffic was dead. In vain did I pray for the groan of a truck up Perkins Street. The woman above who used to drive me crazy by the booming thuds occasioned by what seemed monstrous feet of stone (actually, in diurnal life, she was a small dumpy creature resembling a mummified guinea pig) would have earned my blessings had she now trudged to her bathroom. I put out my light and cleared my throat several times so as to be responsible for at least *that* sound. I thumbed a mental ride with a very remote automobile but it dropped me before I had a chance to doze off. Presently a crackle (due, I hoped, to a discarded and crushed sheet of paper opening like a mean, stubborn night flower)—started and stopped in the waste-paper basket, and my bed-table responded with a little click. It would have been just like Cynthia to put on right then a cheap poltergeist show.

I decided to fight Cynthia. I reviewed in thought the modern era of raps and apparitions, beginning with the knockings of 1848, at the hamlet of Hydesville, N.Y., and ending with grotesque phenomena at Cambridge, Mass.; I evoked the anklebones and other anatomical castanets of the Fox sisters (as described by the sages of the University of Buffalo); the mysteriously uniform type of delicate adolescent in bleak Epworth or Tedworth, radiating the same disturbances as in old Peru; solemn Victorian orgies with roses falling and accordions floating to the strains of sacred music; professional imposters regurgitating moist cheesecloth; Mr. Duncan, a lady medium's dignified husband, who, when asked if he would submit to a search, excused himself on the ground of soiled underwear; old Alfred Russel Wallace, the naïve naturalist, refusing to believe that the white form with bare feet and unperforated earlobes before him, at a private pandemonium in Boston, could be prim Miss Cook whom he had just seen asleep, in her curtained corner, all dressed in black, wearing laced-up boots and earrings; two other investigators, small, puny, but reasonably intelligent and active men, closely clinging with arms and legs about Eusapia, a large, plump elderly female reeking of garlic, who still managed to fool them; and the sceptical and embarrassed magician, instructed by charming young Margery's "control" not to get lost in the bathrobe's lining but to follow up the left stocking until he reached the bare thigh—upon the warm skin of which he felt a "teleplastic" mass that appeared to the touch uncommonly like cold, uncooked liver.

7.

I was appealing to flesh, and the corruption of flesh, to refute and defeat the possible persistence of discarnate life. Alas, these conjurations only enhanced my fear of Cynthia's phantom. Atavistic peace came with dawn, and when I slipped into sleep, the sun through the tawny window shades penetrated a dream that somehow was full of Cynthia.

This was disappointing. Secure in the fortress of daylight, I said to myself that I had expected more. She, a painter of glass-bright minutiæ—and now so vague! I lay in bed, thinking my dream over and listening to the sparrows outside: Who knows, if recorded and then run backward, those bird sounds might not become human speech, voiced words, just as the latter become a twitter when reversed? I set myself to re-read my dream—backward, diagonally, up, down—trying hard to unravel something Cynthia-like in it, something strange and suggestive that must be there.

I could isolate, consciously, little. Everything seemed blurred, yellow-clouded, yielding nothing tangible. Her inept acrostics, maudlin evasions, theopathies—every recollection formed ripples of mysterious meaning. Everything seemed yellowly blurred, illusive, lost.

1951

RAY BRADBURY

(b. 1920)

The April Witch

INTO the air, over the valleys, under the stars, above a river, a
pond, a road, flew Cecy. Invisible as new spring winds, fresh as
the breath of clover rising from twilight fields, she flew. She
soared in doves as soft as white ermine, stopped in trees and
lived in blossoms, showering away in petals when the breeze
blew. She perched in a lime-green frog, cool as mint by a shining
pool. She trotted in a brambly dog and barked to hear echoes
from the sides of distant barns. She lived in new April grasses, in
sweet clear liquids rising from the musky earth.

It's spring, thought Cecy. I'll be in every living thing in the
world tonight.

Now she inhabited neat crickets on the tar-pool roads, now
prickled in dew on an iron gate. Hers was an adaptably quick
mind flowing unseen upon Illinois winds on this one evening
of her life when she was just seventeen.

"I want to be in love," she said.

She had said it at supper. And her parents had widened their
eyes and stiffened back in their chairs. "Patience," had been
their advice. "Remember, you're remarkable. Our whole family is odd and remarkable. We can't mix or marry with ordinary
folk. We'd lose our magical powers if we did. You wouldn't want
to lose your ability to 'travel' by magic, would you? Then be
careful. Be careful!"

But in her high bedroom, Cecy had touched perfume to her
throat and stretched out, trembling and apprehensive, on her
four-poster, as a moon the color of milk rose over Illinois
country, turning rivers to cream and roads to platinum.

"Yes," she sighed. "I'm one of an odd family. We sleep days
and fly nights like black kites on the wind. If we want, we can
sleep in moles through the winter, in the warm earth. I can live
in anything at all—a pebble, a crocus, or a praying mantis. I

148

can leave my plain, bony body behind and send my mind far out for adventure. Now!"

The wind whipped her away over fields and meadows.

She saw the warm spring lights of cottages and farms glowing with twilight colors.

If I can't be in love, myself, because I'm plain and odd, then I'll be in love through someone else, she thought.

Outside a farmhouse in the spring night a dark-haired girl, no more than nineteen, drew up water from a deep stone well. She was singing.

Cecy fell—a green leaf—into the well. She lay in the tender moss of the well, gazing up through dark coolness. Now she quickened in a fluttering, invisible amoeba. Now in a water droplet! At last, within a cold cup, she felt herself lifted to the girl's warm lips. There was a soft night sound of drinking.

Cecy looked out from the girl's eyes.

She entered into the dark head and gazed from the shining eyes at the hands pulling the rough rope. She listened through the shell ears to this girl's world. She smelled a particular universe through these delicate nostrils, felt this special heart beating, beating. Felt this strange tongue move with singing.

Does she know I'm here? thought Cecy.

The girl gasped. She stared into the night meadows.

"Who's there?"

No answer.

"Only the wind," whispered Cecy.

"Only the wind." The girl laughed at herself, but shivered.

It was a good body, this girl's body. It held bones of finest slender ivory hidden and roundly fleshed. This brain was like a pink tea rose, hung in darkness, and there was cider-wine in this mouth. The lips lay firm on the white, white teeth and the brows arched neatly at the world, and the hair blew soft and fine on her milky neck. The pores knit small and close. The nose tilted at the moon and the cheeks glowed like small fires. The body drifted with feather-balances from one motion to another and seemed always singing to itself. Being in this body, this head, was like basking in a hearth fire, living in the purr of a sleeping cat, stirring in warm creek waters that flowed by night to the sea.

I'll like it here, thought Cecy.

"What?" asked the girl, as if she'd heard a voice.

"What's your name?" asked Cecy carefully.

"Ann Leary." The girl twitched. "Now why should I say that out loud?"

"Ann, Ann," whispered Cecy. "Ann, you're going to be in love."

As if to answer this, a great roar sprang from the road, a clatter and a ring of wheels on gravel. A tall man drove up in a rig, holding the reins high with his monstrous arms, his smile glowing across the yard.

"Ann!"

"Is that you, Tom?"

"Who else?" Leaping from the rig, he tied the reins to the fence.

"I'm not speaking to you!" Ann whirled, the bucket in her hands slopping.

"No!" cried Cecy.

Ann froze. She looked at the hills and the first spring stars. She stared at the man named Tom. Cecy made her drop the bucket.

"Look what you've done!"

Tom ran up.

"Look what you made me do!"

He wiped her shoes with a kerchief, laughing.

"Get away!" She kicked at his hands, but he laughed again, and gazing down on him from miles away, Cecy saw the turn of his head, the size of his skull, the flare of his nose, the shine of his eye, the girth of his shoulder, and the hard strength of his hands doing this delicate thing with the handkerchief. Peering down from the secret attic of this lovely head, Cecy yanked a hidden copper ventriloquist's wire and the pretty mouth popped wide: "Thank you!"

"Oh, so you *have* manners?" The smell of leather on his hands, the smell of the horse rose from his clothes into the tender nostrils, and Cecy, far, far away over night meadows and flowered fields, stirred as with some dream in her bed.

"Not for you, no!" said Ann.

"Hush, speak gently," said Cecy. She moved Ann's fingers out toward Tom's head. Ann snatched them back.

"I've gone mad!"

"You have." He nodded, smiling but bewildered. "Were you going to touch me then?"

"I don't know. Oh, go away!" Her cheeks glowed with pink charcoals.

"Why don't you run? I'm not stopping you." Tom got up. "Have you changed your mind? Will you go to the dance with me tonight? It's special. Tell you why later."

"No," said Ann.

"Yes!" cried Cecy. "I've never danced. I want to dance. I've never worn a long gown, all rustly. I want that. I want to dance all night. I've never known what it's like to be in a woman, dancing; Father and Mother would never permit it. Dogs, cats, locusts, leaves, everything else in the world at one time or another I've known, but never a woman in the spring, never on a night like this. Oh, please—we *must* go to that dance!"

She spread her thought like the fingers of a hand within a new glove.

"Yes," said Ann Leary, "I'll go. I don't know why, but I'll go to the dance with you tonight, Tom."

"Now inside, quick!" cried Cecy. "You must wash, tell your folks, get your gown ready, out with the iron, into your room!"

"Mother," said Ann, "I've changed my mind!"

The rig was galloping off down the pike, the rooms of the farmhouse jumped to life, water was boiling for a bath, the coal stove was heating an iron to press the gown, the mother was rushing about with a fringe of hairpins in her mouth. "What's come over you, Ann? You don't like Tom!"

"That's true." Ann stopped amidst the great fever.

But it's spring! thought Cecy.

"It's spring," said Ann.

And it's a fine night for dancing, thought Cecy.

". . . for dancing," murmured Ann Leary.

Then she was in the tub and the soap creaming on her white seal shoulders, small nests of soap beneath her arms, and the flesh of her warm breasts moving in her hands and Cecy moving the mouth, making the smile, keeping the actions going. There must be no pause, no hesitation, or the entire pantomime might fall in ruins! Ann Leary must be kept moving, doing, acting, wash here, soap there, now out! Rub with a towel! Now perfume and powder!

"You!" Ann caught herself in the mirror, all whiteness and pinkness like lilies and carnations. "*Who* are you tonight?"

"I'm a girl seventeen." Cecy gazed from her violet eyes. "You can't see me. Do you know I'm here?"

Ann Leary shook her head. "I've rented my body to an April witch, for sure."

"*Close*, very close!" laughed Cecy. "Now, on with your dressing."

The luxury of feeling good clothes move over an ample body! And then the halloo outside.

"Ann, Tom's back!"

"Tell him to wait." Ann sat down suddenly. "Tell him I'm not going to that dance."

"What?" said her mother, in the door.

Cecy snapped back into attention. It had been a fatal relaxing, a fatal moment of leaving Ann's body for only an instant. She had heard the distant sound of horses' hoofs and the rig rambling through moonlit spring country. For a second she thought, I'll go find Tom and sit in his head and see what it's like to be in a man of twenty-two on a night like this. And so she had started quickly across a heather field, but now, like a bird to a cage, flew back and rustled and beat about in Ann Leary's head.

"Ann!"

"Tell him to go away!"

"Ann!" Cecy settled down and spread her thoughts.

But Ann had the bit in her mouth now. "No, no, I hate him!"

I shouldn't have left—even for a moment. Cecy poured her mind into the hands of the young girl, into the heart, into the head, softly, softly. *Stand up*, she thought.

Ann stood.

Put on your coat!

Ann put on her coat.

Now, march!

No! thought Ann Leary.

March!

"Ann," said her mother, "don't keep Tom waiting another

minute. You get on out there now and no nonsense. What's come over you?"

"Nothing, Mother. Good night. We'll be home late."

Ann and Cecy ran together into the spring evening.

A room full of softly dancing pigeons ruffling their quiet, trailing feathers, a room full of peacocks, a room full of rainbow eyes and lights. And in the center of it, around, around, around, danced Ann Leary.

"Oh, it *is* a fine evening," said Cecy.

"Oh, it's a fine evening," said Ann.

"You're odd," said Tom.

The music whirled them in dimness, in rivers of song; they floated, they bobbed, they sank down, they arose for air, they gasped, they clutched each other like drowning people and whirled on again, in fan motions, in whispers and sighs, to "Beautiful Ohio."

Cecy hummed. Ann's lips parted and the music came out.

"Yes, I'm odd," said Cecy.

"You're not the same," said Tom.

"No, not tonight."

"You're not the Ann Leary I knew."

"No, not at all, at all," whispered Cecy, miles and miles away. "No, not at all," said the moved lips.

"I've the funniest feeling," said Tom.

"About what?"

"About you." He held her back and danced her and looked into her glowing face, watching for something. "Your eyes," he said, "I can't figure it."

"Do you see *me*?" asked Cecy.

"Part of you's here, Ann, and part of you's not." Tom turned her carefully, his face uneasy.

"Yes."

"Why did you come with me?"

"I didn't want to come," said Ann.

"Why, then?"

"Something made me."

"What?"

"I don't know." Ann's voice was faintly hysterical.

"Now, now, hush, hush," whispered Cecy. "Hush, that's it. Around, around."

They whispered and rustled and rose and fell away in the dark room, with the music moving and turning them.

"But you *did* come to the dance," said Tom.

"I did," said Cecy.

"Here." And he danced her lightly out an open door and walked her quietly away from the hall and the music and the people.

They climbed up and sat together in the rig.

"Ann," he said, taking her hands, trembling. "Ann." But the way he said her name it was as if it wasn't her name. He kept glancing into her pale face, and now her eyes were open again. "I used to love you, you know that," he said.

"I know."

"But you've always been fickle and I didn't want to be hurt."

"It's just as well, we're very young," said Ann.

"No, I mean to say, I'm sorry," said Cecy.

"What *do* you mean?" Tom dropped her hands and stiffened.

The night was warm and the smell of the earth shimmered up all about them where they sat, and the fresh trees breathed one leaf against another in a shaking and rustling.

"I don't know," said Ann.

"Oh, but *I* know," said Cecy. "You're tall and you're the finest-looking man in all the world. This is a good evening; this is an evening I'll always remember, being with you." She put out the alien cold hand to find his reluctant hand again and bring it back, and warm it and hold it very tight.

"But," said Tom, blinking, "tonight you're here, you're there. One minute one way, the next minute another. I wanted to take you to the dance tonight for old times' sake. I meant nothing by it when I first asked you. And then, when we were standing at the well, I knew something had changed, really changed, about you. You were different. There was something new and soft, something . . ." He groped for a word. "I don't know, I can't say. The way you looked. Something about your voice. And I know I'm in love with you again."

"No," said Cecy. "With me, with *me*."

"And I'm afraid of being in love with you," he said. "You'll hurt me again."

"I might," said Ann.

No, no, I'd love you with all my heart! thought Cecy. Ann, say it to him, say it for me. Say you'd love him with all your heart.

Ann said nothing.

Tom moved quietly closer and put his hand up to hold her chin. "I'm going away. I've got a job a hundred miles from here. Will you miss me?"

"Yes," said Ann and Cecy.

"May I kiss you good-by, then?"

"Yes," said Cecy before anyone else could speak.

He placed his lips to the strange mouth. He kissed the strange mouth and he was trembling.

Ann sat like a white statue.

"Ann!" said Cecy. "Move your arms, *hold* him!"

She sat like a carved wooden doll in the moonlight.

Again he kissed her lips.

"I do love you," whispered Cecy. "I'm here, it's me you saw in her eyes, it's me, and I love you if she never will."

He moved away and seemed like a man who had run a long distance. He sat beside her. "I don't know what's happening. For a moment there . . ."

"Yes?" asked Cecy.

"For a moment I thought—" He put his hands to his eyes. "Never mind. Shall I take you home now?"

"Please," said Ann Leary.

He clucked to the horse, snapped the reins tiredly, and drove the rig away. They rode in the rustle and slap and motion of the moonlit rig in the still early, only eleven o'clock spring night, with the shining meadows and sweet fields of clover gliding by.

And Cecy, looking at the fields and meadows, thought, It would be worth it, it would be worth everything to be with him from this night on. And she heard her parents' voices again, faintly, "Be careful. You wouldn't want to lose your magical powers, would you—married to a mere mortal? Be careful. You wouldn't want that."

Yes, yes, thought Cecy, even that I'd give up, here and now, if he would have me. I wouldn't need to roam the spring nights then, I wouldn't need to live in birds and dogs and cats and foxes, I'd need only to be with him. Only him. Only him.

The road passed under, whispering.

"Tom," said Ann at last.

"What?" He stared coldly at the road, the horse, the trees, the sky, the stars.

"If you're ever, in years to come, at any time, in Green Town, Illinois, a few miles from here, will you do me a favor?"

"Perhaps."

"Will you do me the favor of stopping and seeing a friend of mine?" Ann Leary said this haltingly, awkwardly.

"Why?"

"She's a good friend. I've told her of you. I'll give you her address. Just a moment." When the rig stopped at her farm she drew forth a pencil and paper from her small purse and wrote in the moonlight, pressing the paper to her knee. "There it is. Can you read it?"

He glanced at the paper and nodded bewileredly.

"Cecy Elliott, 12 Willow Street, Green Town, Illinois," he said.

"Will you visit her someday?" asked Ann.

"Someday," he said.

"Promise?"

"What has this to do with us?" he cried savagely. "What do I want with names and papers?" He crumpled the paper into a tight ball and shoved it in his coat.

"Oh, please promise!" begged Cecy.

". . . promise . . ." said Ann.

"All right, all right, now let me be!" he shouted.

I'm tired, thought Cecy. I can't stay. I have to go home. I'm weakening. I've only the power to stay a few hours out like this in the night, traveling, traveling. But before I go . . .

". . . before I go," said Ann.

She kissed Tom on the lips.

"This is *me* kissing you," said Cecy.

Tom held her off and looked at Ann Leary and looked deep, deep inside. He said nothing, but his face began to relax slowly, very slowly, and the lines vanished away, and his mouth softened from its hardness, and he looked deep again into the moonlit face held here before him.

Then he put her off the rig and without so much as good night was driving swiftly down the road.

Cecy let go.

Ann Leary, crying out, released from prison, it seemed, raced up the moonlit path to her house and slammed the door.

Cecy lingered for only a little while. In the eyes of a cricket she saw the spring night world. In the eyes of a frog she sat for a lonely moment by a pool. In the eyes of a night bird she looked down from a tall, moon-haunted elm and saw the lights go out in two farmhouses, one here, one a mile away. She thought of herself and her family, and her strange power, and the fact that no one in the family could ever marry any one of the people in this vast world out here beyond the hills.

"Tom?" Her weakening mind flew in a night bird under the trees and over deep fields of wild mustard. "Have you still got the paper, Tom? Will you come by someday, some year, sometime, to see me? Will you know me then? Will you look in my face and remember then where it was you saw me last and know that you love me as I love you, with all my heart for all time?"

She paused in the cool night air, a million miles from towns and people, above farms and continents and rivers and hills. "Tom?" Softly.

Tom was asleep. It was deep night; his clothes were hung on chairs or folded neatly over the end of the bed. And in one silent, carefully upflung hand upon the white pillow, by his head, was a small piece of paper with writing on it. Slowly, slowly, a fraction of an inch at a time, his fingers closed down upon and held it tightly. And he did not even stir or notice when a blackbird, faintly, wondrously, beat softly for a moment against the clear moon crystals of the windowpane, then, fluttering quietly, stopped and flew away toward the east, over the sleeping earth.

1952

CHARLES BEAUMONT

(1929–1967)

Black Country

Spoof Collins blew his brains out, all right—right on out through the top of his head. But I don't mean with a gun. I mean with a horn. Every night: slow and easy, eight to one. And that's how he died. Climbing, with that horn, climbing up high. For what? *"Hey, man, Spoof—listen, you picked the tree, now come on down!"* But he couldn't come down, he didn't know how. He just kept climbing, higher and higher. And then he fell. Or jumped. Anyhow, *that's* the way he died.

The bullet didn't kill anything. I'm talking about the one that tore up the top of his mouth. It didn't kill anything that wasn't dead already. Spoof just put in an extra note, that's all.

We planted him out about four miles from town—home is where you drop: residential district, all wood construction. Rain? You know it. Bible type: sky like a month-old bedsheet, wind like a stepped-on cat, cold and dark, those Forty Days, those Forty Nights! But nice and quiet most of the time. Like Spoof: nice and quiet, with a lot underneath that you didn't like to think about.

We planted him and watched and put what was his down into the ground with him. His horn, battered, dented, nicked —right there in his hands, but not just there; I mean in position, so if he wanted to do some more climbing, all right, he could. And his music. We planted that too, because leaving it out would have been like leaving out Spoof's arms or his heart or his guts.

Lux started things off with a chord from his guitar, no particular notes, only a feeling, a sound. A Spoof Collins kind of sound. Jimmy Fritch picked it up with his stick and they talked a while—Lux got a real piano out of that git-box. Then when Jimmy stopped talking and stood there, waiting, Sonny Holmes stepped up and wiped his mouth and took the melody on his shiny new trumpet. It wasn't Spoof, but it came close; and it was still *The Jimjam Man*, the way Spoof wrote it back when he used to write things down. Sonny got off with a high-squealing blast, and no eyes came up—we knew, we remembered. The kid always had it collared. He just never talked about it. And listen to him now! He stood there over Spoof's grave, giving it all back to The Ol' Massuh, giving it back right—*"Broom off, white child, you got four sides!" "I want to learn from you, Mr. Collins. I want to play jazz and you can teach me." "I got things to do, I can't waste no time on a half-hipped young'un." "Please, Mr. Collins." "You got to stop that, you got to stop callin' me 'Mr. Collins,' hear?" "Yes sir, yes sir."*— He put out real sound, like he didn't remember a thing. Like he wasn't playing for that pile of darkmeat in the ground, not at all; but for the great Spoof Collins, for the man Who Knew and the man Who Did, who gave jazz spats and dressed up the blues, who did things with a trumpet that a trumpet couldn't do, and more; for the man who could blow down the walls or make a chicken cry, without half trying—for the mighty Spoof, who'd once walked in music like a boy in river mud, loving it, breathing it, living it.

Then Sonny quit. He wiped his mouth again and stepped back and Mr. "T" took it on his trombone while I beat up the tubs.

Pretty soon we had *The Jimjam Man* rocking the way it used to rock. A little slow, maybe: it needed Bud Meunier on bass and a few trips on the piano. But it moved.

We went through *Take It From Me* and *Night in the Blues* and *Big Gig* and *Only Us Chickens* and *Forty G's*—Sonny's insides came out through the horn on that one, I could tell— and *Slice City Stomp*—you remember: sharp and clean, like sliding down a razor—and *What the Cats Dragged In*—the longs, the shorts, all the great Spoof Collins numbers. We wrapped them up and put them down there with him.

Then it got dark.

And it was time for the last one, the greatest one. . . . Rose-Ann shivered and cleared her throat; the rest of us looked around, for the first time, at all those rows of split-wood grave markers, shining in the rain, and the trees and the coffin, dark, wet. Out by the fence, a couple of farmers stood watching. Just watching.

One—Rose-Ann opens her coat, puts her hands on her hips, wets her lips;

Two—Freddie gets the spit out of his stick, rolls his eyes;

Three—Sonny puts the trumpet to his mouth;

Four—

And we played Spoof's song, his last one, the one he wrote a long way ago, before the music dried out his head, before he turned mean and started climbing: *Black Country*. The song that said just a little of what Spoof wanted to say, and couldn't.

You remember. Spider-slow chords crawling down, soft, easy, and then bottom and silence and, suddenly, the cry of the horn, screaming in one note all the hate and sadness and loneliness, all the want and got-to-have; and then the note dying, quick, and Rose-Ann's voice, a whisper, a groan, a sigh. . . .

> *"Black Country is somewhere, Lord,*
> *That I don't want to go.*
> *Black Country is somewhere*
> *That I never want to go.*
> *Rain-water drippin'*
> *On the bed and on the floor,*
> *Rain-water drippin'*
> *From the ground and through the door . . ."*

We all heard the piano, even though it wasn't there. Fingers moving down those minor chords, those black keys, that black country . . .

> *"Well, in that old Black Country*
> *If you ain't feelin' good,*
> *They let you have an overcoat*
> *That's carved right out of wood.*
> *But way down there*
> *It gets so dark*
> *You never see a friend—*
> *Black Country may not be the Most,*
> *But, Lord! it's sure the End . . ."*

Bitter little laughing words, piling up, now mad, now sad; and then, an ugly blast from the horn and Rose-Ann's voice screaming, crying:

> *"I never want to go there, Lord!*
> *I never want to be,*
> *I never want to lay down*
> *In that Black Country!"*

And quiet, quiet, just the rain, and the wind.

"Let's go, man," Freddie said.

So we turned around and left Spoof there under the ground.

Or, at least, that's what I thought we did.

Sonny took over without saying a word. He didn't have to: just who was about to fuss? He was white, but he didn't play white, not these days; and he learned the hard way—by unlearning. Now he could play gutbucket and he could play blues, stomp and slide, name it, Sonny could play it. Funny as hell to hear, too, because he looked like everything else but a musician. Short and skinny, glasses, nose like a melted candle, head clean as the one-ball, and white? Next to old Hushup, that café sunburn glowed like a flashlight.

"Man, who skinned you?"

"Who dropped you in the flour barrel?"

But he got closer to Spoof than any of the rest of us did. He knew what to do, and why. Just like a school teacher all the time: "That's good, Lux, that's awful good—now let's play some music." "Get off it, C.T.—what's Lenox Avenue doing in the middle of Lexington?" "Come on, boys, hang on to the sound, hang on to it!" Always using words like "flavor" and "authentic" and "blood," peering over those glasses, pounding his feet right through the floor: STOMP! STOMP! "That's it, we've got it now—oh, listen! It's true, it's clean!" STOMP! STOMP!

Not the easiest to dig him. Nobody broke all the way through.

"How come, boy? What for?" and every time the same answer:

"I want to play jazz."

Like he'd joined the Church and didn't want to argue about it. Spoof was still Spoof when Sonny started coming around.

Not a lot of people with us then, but a few, enough—the long-hairs and critics and connoisseurs—and some real ears too—enough to fill a club every night, and who needs more? It was COLLINS AND HIS CREW, tight and neat, never a performance, always a session. Lot of music, lot of fun. And a line-up that some won't forget: Jimmy Fritch on clarinet, Honker Reese on alto-sax, Charles di Lusso on tenor, Spoof on trumpet, Henry Walker on piano, Lux Anderson on banjo and myself—Hushup Paige—on drums. Newmown hay, all right, I know—I remember, I've heard the records we cut—but, the Road was there.

Sonny used to hang around the old Continental Club on State Street in Chicago, every night, listening. Eight o'clock roll 'round, and there he'd be—a little different: younger, skinnier—listening hard, over in a corner all to himself, eyes closed like he was asleep. Once in a while he put in a request—*Darktown Strutter's Ball* was one he liked, and some of Jelly Roll's numbers—but mostly he just sat there, taking it all in. For real.

And it kept up like this for two or three weeks, regular as 2/4.

Now Spoof was mean in those days—don't think he wasn't—but not blood-mean. Even so, the white boy in the corner bugged Ol' Massuh after a while and he got to making dirty cracks with his horn: WAAAAA! *Git your ass out of here.* WAAAAA! *You only* think *you're with it!* WAAAAA! *There's a little white child sittin' in a chair there's a little white child losin' all his hair . . .*

It got to the kid, too, every bit of it. And that made Spoof even madder. But what can you do?

Came Honker's trip to Slice City along about then: our sax-man got a neck all full of the sharpest kind of steel. So we were out one horn. And you could tell: we played a little bit too rough, and the head-arrangements Collins and His Crew grew up to, they needed Honker's grease in the worst way. But we'd been together for five years or more, and a new man just didn't play somehow. We were this one solid thing, like a unit, and somebody had cut off a piece of us and we couldn't grow the piece back so we just tried to get along anyway, bleeding every night, bleeding from that wound.

Then one night it bust. We'd gone through some slow

walking stuff, some tricky stuff and some loud stuff—still covering up—when this kid, this white boy, got up from his chair and ankled over and tapped Spoof on the shoulder. It was break-time and Spoof was brought down about Honker, about how bad we were sounding, sitting there sweating, those pounds of man, black as coaldust soaked in oil—he was the *blackest* man!—and those eyes, beady white and small as agates.

"Excuse me, Mr. Collins, I wonder if I might have a word with you?" He wondered if he might have a word with Mr. Collins!

Spoof swiveled in his chair and clapped a look around the kid. "Hnff?"

"I notice that you don't have a sax man any more."

"You don't mean to tell me?"

"Yes sir. I thought—I mean, I was wondering if—"

"Talk up, boy. I can't hear you."

The kid looked scared. Lord, he looked scared—and he was white to begin with.

"Well sir, I was just wondering if—if you needed a saxophone."

"You know somebody plays sax?"

"Yes sir, I do."

"And who might that be?"

"Me."

"You."

"Yes sir."

Spoof smiled a quick one. Then he shrugged. "Broom off, son," he said. "Broom 'way off."

The kid turned red. He all of a sudden didn't look scared any more. Just mad. Mad as hell. But he didn't say anything. He went on back to his table and then it was end of the ten.

We swung into *Basin Street*, smooth as Charley's tenor could make it, with Lux Anderson talking it out: *Basin Street, man, it is the street, Where the elite, well, they gather 'round to eat a little* . . . And we fooled around with the slow stuff for a while. Then Spoof lifted his horn and climbed up two-and-a-half and let out his trademark, that short high screech that sounded like something dying that wasn't too happy about it. And we rocked some, Henry taking it, Jimmy kanoodling the great headwork that only Jimmy knows how to do, me slamming the skins—and it was nowhere. Without Honker to keep us all on the ground, we were just making noise. Good noise, all right, but not music. And Spoof knew it. He broke his mouth blowing—to prove it.

And we cussed the cat that sliced our man.

Then, right away—nobody could remember when it came in —suddenly, we had us an alto-sax. Smooth and sure and snaky, that sound put a knot on each of us and said: Bust loose now, boys, I'll pull you back down. Like sweet-smelling glue, like oil in a machine, like—Honker.

We looked around and there was the kid, still sore, blowing like a madman, and making fine fine music.

Spoof didn't do much. Most of all, he didn't stop the number. He just let that horn play, listening—and when we slid over all the rough spots and found us backed up neat as could be, the Ol' Massuh let out a grin and a nod and a "Keep blowin', young'un!" and we knew that we were going to be all right.

After it was over, Spoof walked up to the kid. They looked at each other, sizing it up, taking it in.

Spoof says: "You did good."

And the kid—he was still burned—says: "You mean I did *damn* good."

And Spoof shakes his head. "No, that ain't what I mean."

And in a second one was laughing while the other one blushed. Spoof had known all along that the kid was faking, that he'd just been lucky enough to know our style on *Basin Street* up-down-and-across.

The Ol' Massuh waited for the kid to turn and start to slink off, then he said: "Boy, you want to go to work?" . . .

Sonny learned so fast it scared you. Spoof never held back; he turned it all over, everything it had taken us our whole lives to find out.

And—we had some good years. Charley di Lusso dropped out, we took on Bud Meunier—the greatest bass man of them all—and Lux threw away his banjo for an AC-DC git-box and old C.T. Mr. "T" Green and his trombone joined the Crew. And we kept growing and getting stronger—no million-copies platter sales or stands at the Paramount—too "special"—but we never ate too far down on the hog, either.

In a few years Sonny Holmes was making that sax stand on its hind legs and jump through hoops that Honker never dreamed about. Spoof let him strictly alone. When he got mad it wasn't ever because Sonny had white skin—Spoof always was too busy to notice things like that—but only because The Ol' Massuh had to get T'd off at each one of us every now and then. He figured it kept us on our toes.

In fact, except right at first, there never was any real blood between Spoof and Sonny until Rose-Ann came along.

Spoof didn't want a vocalist with the band. But the coon-shouting days were gone alas, except for Satchmo and Calloway —who had style: none of us had style, man, we just hollered— so when push came to shove, we had to put out the net.

And chickens aplenty came to crow and plenty moved on fast and we were about to give up when a dusky doll of 20-ought stepped up and let loose a hunk of *The Man I Love* and that's all, brothers, end of the search.

Rose-Ann McHugh was a little like Sonny: where she came from, she didn't know a ball of cotton from a piece of popcorn. She'd studied piano for a flock of years with a Pennsylvania long-hair, read music whipfast and had been pointed toward the Big Steinway and the O.M's, Chopin and Bach and all that jazz. And good—I mean, she could pull some very fancy noise out of those keys. But it wasn't the Road. She'd heard a few records of Muggsy Spanier's, a couple of Jelly Roll's— *New Orleans Bump*, *Shreveport Stomp*, old *Wolverine Blues*— and she just got took hold of. Like it happens, all the time. She knew.

Spoof hired her after the first song. And we could see things in her eyes for The Ol' Massuh right away, fast. Bad to watch: I mean to say, she was chicken dinner, but what made it ugly was, you could tell she hadn't been in the oven very long.

Anyway, most of us could tell. Sonny, for instance.

But Spoof played tough to begin. He gave her the treatment, all the way. To see if she'd hold up. Because, above everything else, there was the Crew, the Unit, the Group. It was right, it had to stay right.

"Gal, forget your hands—that's for the cats out front. Leave 'em alone. And pay attention to the music, hear?"

"You ain't got a 'voice,' you got an instrument. And you ain't

even started to learn how to play on it. Get some sound, bring it on out."

"Stop that throat stuff—you' singin' with the Crew now. From the belly, gal, from the belly. That's where music comes from, hear?"

And she loved it, like Sonny did. She was with The Ol' Massuh, she knew what he was talking about.

Pretty soon she fit just fine. And when she did, and everybody knew she did, Spoof eased up and waited and watched the old machine click right along, one-two, one-two.

That's when he began to change. Right then, with the Crew growed up and in long pants at last. Like we didn't need him any more to wash our face and comb our hair and switch our behinds for being bad.

Spoof began to change. He beat out time and blew his riffs, but things were different and there wasn't anybody who didn't know that for a fact.

In a hurry, all at once, he wrote down all his great arrangements, quick as he could. One right after the other. And we wondered why—we'd played them a million times.

Then he grabbed up Sonny. *"White Boy, listen. You want to learn how to play trumpet?"*

And the blood started between them. Spoof rode on Sonny's back twenty-four hours, showing him lip, showing him breath. *"This ain't a saxophone, boy, it's a trumpet, a music-horn. Get it right—do it again—that's lousy—do it again—that was nowhere—do it again—do it again!"* All the time.

Sonny worked hard. Anybody else, they would have told The Ol' Massuh where he could put that little old horn. But the kid knew something was being given to him—he didn't know why, nobody did, but for a reason—something that Spoof wouldn't have given anybody else. And he was grateful. So he worked. And he didn't ask any how-comes, either.

Pretty soon he started to handle things right. 'Way down the road from great, but coming along. The sax had given him a hard set of lips and he had plenty of wind; most of all, he had the spirit—the thing that you can beat up your chops about it for two weeks straight and never say what it is, but if it isn't there, buddy-ghee, you may get to be President but you'll never play music.

Lord, Lord, Spoof worked that boy like a two-ton jockey on a ten-ounce horse. *"Do it again—that ain't right—goddamn it, do it again! Now one more time!"*

When Sonny knew enough to sit in with the horn on a few easy ones, Ol' Massuh would tense up and follow the kid with his eyes—I mean it got real crawly. What for? Why was he pushing it like that?

Then it quit. Spoof didn't say anything. He just grunted and quit all of a sudden, like he'd done with us, and Sonny went back on sax and that was that.

Which is when the real blood started.

The Lord says every man has got to love something, some-times, somewhere. First choice is a chick, but there's other choices. Spoof's was a horn. He was married to a piece of brass, just as married as a man can get. Got up with it in the morning, talked with it all day long, loved it at night like no chick I ever heard of got loved. And I don't mean one-two-three: I mean the slow-building kind. He'd kiss it and hold it and watch out for it. Once a cat full of tea tried to put the snatch on Spoof's horn, for laughs: when Spoof caught up with him, that cat gave up laughing for life.

Sonny knew this. It's why he never blew his stack at all the riding. Spoof's teaching him to play trumpet—*the* trumpet—was like as if The Ol' Massuh had said: *"You want to take my wife for a few nights? You do? Then here, let me show you how to do it right. She likes it done right."*

For Rose-Ann, though, it was the worst. Every day she got that look deeper in, and in a while we turned around and, man! *Where* is little Rosie? She was gone. That young half-fried chicken had flew the roost. And in her place was a doll that wasn't dead, a big bunch of curves and skin like a brand-new penny. Overnight, almost. Sonny noticed. Freddie and Lux and even old Mr. "T" noticed. *I* had eyes in my head. But Spoof didn't notice. He was already in love, there wasn't any more room.

Rose-Ann kept snapping the whip, but Ol' Massuh, he wasn't *about* to make the trip. He'd started climbing, then, and he didn't treat her any different than he treated us.

"Get away, gal, broom on off—can't you see I'm busy? Wiggle it elsewhere, hear? Elsewhere. Shoo!"

And she just loved him more for it. Every time he kicked

her, she loved him more. Tried to find him and see him and, sometimes, when he'd stop for breath, she'd try to help, because she knew something had crawled inside Spoof, something that was eating from the inside out, that maybe he couldn't get rid of alone.

Finally, one night, at a two-weeker in Dallas, it tumbled.

We'd gone through *Georgia Brown* for the tourists and things were kind of dull, when Spoof started sweating. His eyes began to roll. And he stood up, like a great big animal—like an ape or a bear, big and powerful and mean-looking—and he gave us the two-finger signal.

Sky-High. 'Way before it was due, before either the audience or any of us had got wound up.

Freddie frowned. "You think it's time, Top?"

"Listen," Spoof said, "goddamn it, who says when it's time —you, or me?"

We went into it, cold, but things warmed up pretty fast. The dancers grumbled and moved off the floor and the place filled up with talk.

I took my solo and beat hell out of the skins. Then Spoof swiped at his mouth and let go with a blast and moved it up into that squeal and stopped and started playing. It was all headwork. All new to us.

New to anybody.

I saw Sonny get a look on his face, and we sat still and listened while Spoof made love to that horn.

Now like a scream, now like a laugh—now we're swinging in the trees, now the white men are coming, now we're in the boat and chains are hanging from our ankles and we're rowing, rowing—*Spoof, what is it?*—now we're sawing wood and picking cotton and serving up those cool cool drinks to the Colonel in his chair—*Well, blow, man!*—now we're free, and we're struttin' down Lenox Avenue and State & Madison and Pirate's Alley, laughing, crying—*Who said free?*—and we want to go back and we don't want to go back—*Play it, Spoof! God, God, tell us all about it! Talk to us!*—and we're sitting in a cellar with a comb wrapped up in paper, with a skin-barrel and a tinklebox—*Don't stop, Spoof! Oh Lord, please don't stop!*—and we're making something, something, what is it? Is it jazz? Why, yes, Lord, it's jazz. Thank you, sir, and thank you, sir, we finally got it, something that is *ours*, something great that belongs to us and to us alone, that we made, and *that's* why it's important, and *that's* what it's all about and—*Spoof! Spoof, you can't stop now*—

But it was over, middle of the trip. And there was Spoof standing there facing us and tears streaming out of those eyes and down over that coaldust face, and his body shaking and shaking. It's the first we ever saw that. It's the first we ever heard him cough, too—like a shotgun going off every two seconds, big raking sounds that tore up from the bottom of his belly and spilled out wet and loud.

The way it tumbled was this. Rose-Ann went over to him and tried to get him to sit down. "Spoof, honey, what's wrong? Come on and sit down. Honey, don't just stand there."

Spoof stopped coughing and jerked his head around. He looked at Rose-Ann for a while and whatever there was in his face, it didn't have a name. The whole room was just as quiet as it could be.

Rose-Ann took his arm. "Come on, honey, Mr. Collins—"

He let out one more cough, then, and drew back his hand— that black-topped, pink-palmed ham of a hand—and laid it, sharp, across the girl's cheek. It sent her staggering. "Git off my back, hear? Damn it, git off! Stay 'way from me!"

She got up crying. Then, you know what she did? She waltzed on back and took his arm and said: "Please."

Spoof was just a lot of crazy-mad on two legs. He shouted out some words and pulled back his hand again. "Can't you never learn? What I got to do, goddamn little—"

Then—Sonny moved. All-the-time quiet and soft and gentle Sonny. He moved quick across the floor and stood in front of Spoof.

"Keep your black hands off her," he said.

Ol' Massuh pushed Rose-Ann aside and planted his legs, his breath rattling fast and loose, like a bull's. And he towered over the kid, Goliath and David, legs far apart on the boards and fingers curled up, bowling balls at the ends of his sleeves.

"You talkin' to me, boy?"

Sonny's face was red, like I hadn't seen it since that first time at the Continental Club, years back. "You've got ears, Collins. Touch her again and I'll kill you."

I don't know exactly what we expected, but I know what we were afraid of. We were afraid Spoof would let go; and if he did . . . well, put another bed in the hospital, men. He stood there, breathing, and Sonny gave it right back—for hours, days and nights, for a month, toe to toe.

Then Spoof relaxed. He pulled back those fat lips, that didn't look like lips any more, they were so tough and leathery, and showed a mouthful of white and gold, and grunted, and turned, and walked away.

We swung into *Twelfth Street Rag* in *such* a hurry!

And it got kicked under the sofa.

But we found out something, then, that nobody even suspected.

Sonny had it for Rose-Ann. He had it bad.

And that ain't good.

Spoof fell to pieces after that. He played day and night, when we were working, when we weren't working. Climbing. Trying to get it said, all of it.

"Listen, you can't hit Heaven with a slingshot, Daddy-O!"

"What you want to do, man—blow Judgment?"

He never let up. If he ate anything, you tell me when. Sometimes he tied on, straight stuff, quick, medicine type of drinking. But only after he'd been climbing and started to blow flat and ended up in those coughing fits.

And it got worse. Nothing helped, either: foam or booze or tea or even Indoor Sports, and he tried them all. And got worse.

"Get fixed up, Mr. C, you hear? See a bone-man; you in bad shape . . ."

"Get away from me, get on away!" Hawk! and a big red spot on the handkerchief. *"Broom off! Shoo!"*

And gradually the old horn went sour, ugly and bitter sounding, like Spoof himself. Hoo Lord, the way he rode Sonny then: *"How you like the dark stuff, boy? You like it pretty good? Hey there, don't hold back. Rosie's fine talent—I know. Want me to tell you about it, pave the way, show you how? I taught you everything else, didn't I?"* And Sonny always clamming up, his eyes doing the talking: *"You were a great musician, Collins, and you still are, but that doesn't mean I've got to like you—you won't let me. And you're damn right I'm in love with Rose-Ann! That's the biggest reason why I'm still here—just to be close to her. Otherwise, you wouldn't see me for the dust. But you're too dumb to realize she's in love with you, too dumb and stupid and mean and wrapped up with that lousy horn!"*

What *Sonny* was too dumb to know was, Rose-Ann had cut Spoof out. She was now Public Domain.

Anyway, Spoof got to be the meanest, dirtiest, craziest, low-talkin'est man in the world. And nobody could come in: he had signs out all the time. . . .

The night that he couldn't even get a squeak out of his trumpet and went back to the hotel—alone, always alone—and put the gun in his mouth and pulled the trigger, we found something out.

We found out what it was that had been eating at The Ol' Massuh.

Cancer.

Rose-Ann took it the hardest. She had the dry-weeps for a long time, saying it over and over: "Why didn't he let us know? Why didn't he tell us?"

But, you get over things. Even women do, especially when they've got something to take its place.

We reorganized a little. Sonny cut out the sax—saxes were getting cornball anyway—and took over on trumpet. And we decided against keeping Spoof's name. It was now Sonny Holmes and His Crew.

And we kept on eating high up. Nobody seemed to miss Spoof—not the cats in front, at least—because Sonny blew as great a horn as anybody could want, smooth and sure, full of excitement and clean as a gnat's behind.

We played across the States and back, and they loved us—thanks to the kid. Called us an "institution" and the disc-jockeys began to pick up our stuff. We were "real," they said—the only authentic jazz left, and who am I to push it? Maybe they were right.

Sonny kept things in low. And then, when he was sure—damn that slow way: it had been a cinch since back when—he started to pay attention to Rose-Ann. She played it cool, the way she knew he wanted it, and let it build up right. Of course, who didn't know she would've married him this minute, now, just say the word? But Sonny was a very conscientious cat indeed.

We did a few stands in France about that time—Listen to them holler!—and a couple in England and Sweden—getting better, too—and after a breather, we cut out across the States again.

It didn't happen fast, but it happened sure. Something was sounding flat all of a sudden like—wrong, in a way:

During an engagement in El Paso we had *What the Cats Dragged In* lined up. You all know *Cats*—the rhythm section still, with the horns yelling for a hundred bars, then that fast and solid beat, that high trip and trumpet solo? Sonny had the ups on a wild riff and was coming on down, when he stopped. Stood still, with the horn to his lips; and we waited.

"Come on, wrap it up—you want a drum now? What's the story, Sonny?"

Then he started to blow. The notes came out the same almost, but not quite the same. They danced out of the horn strop-razor sharp and sliced up high and blasted low and the cats all fell out. "Do it! Go! Go, man! Oooo, I'm out of the boat, don't pull me back! Sing out, man!"

The solo lasted almost seven minutes. When it was time for us to wind it up, we just about forgot.

The crowd went wild. They stomped and screamed and whistled. But they couldn't get Sonny to play any more. He pulled the horn away from his mouth—I mean that's the way it looked, as if he was yanking it away with all his strength—and for a second he looked surprised, like he'd been goosed. Then his lips pulled back into a smile.

It was the *damndest* smile!

Freddie went over to him at the break. "Man, that was the craziest. How many tongues you got?"

But Sonny didn't answer him.

Things went along all right for a little. We played a few dances in the cities, some radio stuff, cut a few platters. Easy walking style.

Sonny played Sonny—plenty great enough. And we forget about what happened in El Paso. So what? So he cuts loose once—can't a man do that if he feels the urge? Every jazz man brings that kind of light at least once.

We worked through the sticks and were finally set for a New York opening when Sonny came in and gave us the news.

It was a gasser. Lux got sore. Mr. "T" shook his head.

"Why? How come, Top?"

He had us booked for the corn-belt. The old-time route, exactly, even the old places, back when we were playing razzmatazz and feeling our way.

"You trust me?" Sonny asked. "You trust my judgment?"

"Come off it, Top; you know we do. Just tell us how come. Man, New York's what we been working for—"

"That's just it," Sonny said. "We aren't ready."

That brought us down. How did *we* know—we hadn't even thought about it.

"We need to get back to the real material. When we play in New York, it's not anything anybody's liable to forget in a hurry. And that's why I think we ought to take a refresher course. About five weeks. All right?"

Well, we fussed some and fumed some, but not much, and in the end we agreed to it. Sonny knew his stuff, that's what we figured.

"Then it's settled."

And we lit out.

Played mostly the old stuff dressed up—*Big Gig, Only Us Chickens* and the rest—or head-arrangements with a lot of trumpet. Illinois, Indiana, Kentucky . . .

When we hit Louisiana for a two-nighter at the Tropics, the same thing happened that did back in Texas. Sonny blew wild for eight minutes on a solo that broke the glasses and cracked the ceiling and cleared the dance-floor like a tornado. Nothing off the stem, either—but like it was practice, sort of, or exercise. A solo out of nothing, that didn't even try to hang on to a shred of the melody.

"Man, it's great, but let us know when it's gonna happen, hear!"

About then Sonny turned down the flame on Rose-Ann. He was polite enough and a stranger wouldn't have noticed, but we did, and Rose-Ann did—and it was tough for her to keep it all down under, hidden. All those questions, all those memories and fears.

He stopped going out and took to hanging around his rooms a lot. Once in a while he'd start playing: one time we listened to that horn all night.

Finally—it was still somewhere in Louisiana—when Sonny was reaching with his trumpet so high he didn't get any more sound out of it than a dog-whistle, and the front cats were laughing up a storm, I went over and put it to him flatfooted.

His eyes were big and he looked like he was trying to say something and couldn't. He looked scared.

"Sonny . . . look, boy, what are you after? Tell a friend, man, don't lock it up."

But he didn't answer me. He couldn't.

He was coughing too hard.

Here's the way we doped it: Sonny had worshiped Spoof, like a god or something. Now some of Spoof was rubbing off, and he didn't know it.

Freddie was elected. Freddie talks pretty good most of the time.

"Get off the train, Jack. Ol' Massuh's gone now, dead and buried. Mean, what he was after ain't to be had. Mean, he wanted it all and then some—and all is all, there isn't any more. You play the greatest, Sonny—go on, ask anybody. Just fine. So get off the train. . . ."

And Sonny laughed, and agreed and promised. I mean in words. His eyes played another number, though.

Sometimes he snapped out of it, it looked like, and he was fine then—tired and hungry, but with it. And we'd think, He's okay. Then it would happen all over again—only worse. Every time, worse.

And it got so Sonny even talked like Spoof half the time: "Broom off, man, leave me alone, will you? Can't you see I'm busy, got things to do? Get away!" And walked like Spoof— that slow walk-in-your-sleep shuffle. And did little things—like scratching his belly and leaving his shoes unlaced and rehearsing in his undershirt.

He started to smoke weeds in Alabama.

In Tennessee he took the first drink anybody ever saw him take.

And always with that horn—cussing it, yelling at it, getting sore because it wouldn't do what he wanted it to.

We had to leave him alone, finally. "I'll handle it . . . I—understand, I think. . . . Just go away, it'll be all right. . . ."

Nobody could help him. Nobody at all.

Especially not Rose-Ann.

End of the corn-belt route, the way Sonny had it booked, was the Copper Club. We hadn't been back there since the night we planted Spoof—and we didn't feel very good about it.

But a contract isn't anything else.

So we took rooms at the only hotel there ever was in the town. You make a guess which room Sonny took. And we played some cards and bruised our chops and tried to sleep and couldn't. We tossed around in the beds, listening, waiting for the horn to begin. But it didn't. All night long, it didn't.

We found out why, oh yes. . . .

Next day we all walked around just about everywhere except in the direction of the cemetery. Why kick up misery? Why make it any harder?

Sonny stayed in his room until ten before opening, and we began to worry. But he got in under the wire.

The Copper Club was packed. Yokels and farmers and high school stuff, a jazz "connoisseur" here and there—to the beams. Freddie had set up the stands with the music notes all in order, and in a few minutes we had our positions.

Sonny came out wired for sound. He looked—powerful; and that's a hard way for a five-foot four-inch baldheaded white man to look. At any time. Rose-Ann threw me a glance and I threw it back, and collected it from the rest. Something bad. Something real bad. Soon.

Sonny didn't look any which way. He waited for the applause to die down, then he did a quick One-Two-Three-Four and we swung into *The Jimjam Man*, our theme.

I mean to say, that crowd was with us all the way—they smelled something.

Sonny did the thumb-and-little-finger signal and we started *Only Us Chickens*. Bud Meunier did the intro on his bass, then Henry took over on the piano. He played one hand racing the other. The front cats hollered "Go! Go!" and Henry went. His left hand crawled on down over the keys and scrambled and didn't fuzz once or slip once and then walked away, cocky and proud, like a mouse full of cheese from an unsprung trap.

"Hooo-boy! Play, Henry, play!"

Sonny watched and smiled. "Bring it on out," he said, gentle, quiet, pleased. "Keep bringin' it out."

Henry did that counterpoint business that you're not supposed to be able to do unless you have two right arms and four extra fingers, and he got that boiler puffing, and he got it shaking, and he screamed his Henry Walker "Wooooo-OOOOO!" and he finished. I came in on the tubs and beat them up till I couldn't see for the sweat, hit the cymbal and waited.

Mr. "T," Lux and Jimmy fiddlefaddled like a coop of capons talking about their operation for a while. Rose-Ann chanted: "Only us chickens in the hen-house, Daddy, Only us chickens here, Only us chickens in the hen-house, Daddy, Ooo-bab-a-roo, Ooo-bob-a-roo . . ."

Then it was horn time. Time for the big solo.

Sonny lifted the trumpet—One! Two!—He got it into sight —Three!

We all stopped dead. I mean we stopped.

That wasn't Sonny's horn. This one was dented-in and beat-up and the tip-end was nicked. It didn't shine, not a bit.

Lux leaned over—you could have fit a coffee cup into his mouth. "Jesus God," he said. "Am I seeing right?"

I looked close and said: "Man, I hope not."

But why kid? We'd seen that trumpet a million times.

It was Spoof's.

Rose-Ann was trembling. Just like me, she remembered how we'd buried the horn with Spoof. And she remembered how quiet it had been in Sonny's room last night. . . .

I started to think real hophead thoughts, like—where did Sonny get hold of a shovel that late? and how could he expect a horn to play that's been under the ground for two years? and—

That blast got into our ears like long knives.

Spoof's own trademark!

Sonny looked caught, like he didn't know what to do at first, like he was hypnotized, scared, almighty scared. But as the sound came out, rolling out, sharp and clean and clear—new-trumpet sound—his expression changed. His eyes changed: they danced a little and opened wide.

Then he closed them, and blew that horn. Lord God of the Fishes, how he blew it! How he loved it and caressed it and pushed it up, higher and higher and higher. High C? Bottom of the barrel. He took off, and he walked all over the rules and stamped them flat.

The melody got lost, first off. Everything got lost, then, while that horn flew. It wasn't only jazz; it was the heart of jazz, and the insides, pulled out with the roots and held up for everybody to see; it was blues that told the story of all the lonely cats and all the ugly whores who ever lived, blues that spoke up for the loser lamping sunshine out of iron-gray bars and every hophead hooked and gone, for the bindlestiffs and the city slicers, for the country boys in Georgia shacks and the High Yellow hipsters in Chicago slums and the bootblacks on the corners and the fruits in New Orleans, a blues that spoke for all the lonely, sad and anxious downers who could never speak themselves. . . .

And then, when it had said all this, it stopped and there was a quiet so quiet that Sonny could have shouted:

"It's okay, Spoof. It's all right now. You'll get it said, all of it —I'll help you. God, Spoof, you showed me how, you planned it—I'll do my best!"

And he laid back his head and fastened the horn and pulled in air and blew some more. Not sad, now, not blues—but not anything else you could call by a name. Except . . . jazz. It was jazz.

Hate blew out of that horn, then. Hate and fury and mad and fight, like screams and snarls, like little razors shooting at you, millions of them, cutting, cutting deep. . . .

And Sonny only stopping to wipe his lip and whisper in the silent room full of people: "You're saying it, Spoof! You are!"

God Almighty Himself must have heard that trumpet, then; slapping and hitting and hurting with notes that don't exist and never existed. Man! Life took a real beating! Life got groined and sliced and belly-punched and the horn, it didn't stop until everything had all spilled out, every bit of the hate and mad that's built up in a man's heart.

Rose-Ann walked over to me and dug her nails into my hand as she listened to Sonny. . . .

"Come on now, Spoof! Come on! We can do it! Let's play the rest and play it right. You know it's got to be said, you know it does. Come on, you and me together!"

And the horn took off with a big yellow blast and started to laugh. I mean it laughed! Hooted and hollered and jumped around, dancing, singing, strutting through those notes that never were there. Happy music? Joyful music? It was chicken dinner and an empty stomach; it was big-butted women and big white beds; it was country walking and windy days and fresh-born crying and—Oh, there just doesn't happen to be any happiness that didn't come out of that horn.

Sonny hit the last high note—the Spoof blast—but so high you could just barely hear it.

Then Sonny dropped the horn. It fell onto the floor and bounced and lay still.

And nobody breathed. For a long, long time.

Rose-Ann let go of my hand, at last. She walked across the platform, slowly, and picked up the trumpet and handed it to Sonny.

He knew what she meant.

We all did. It was over now, over and done. . . .

Lux plucked out the intro. Jimmy Fritch picked it up and kept the melody.

Then we all joined in, slow and quiet, quiet as we could. With Sonny—I'm talking about *Sonny*—putting out the kind of sound he'd always wanted to.

And Rose-Ann sang it, clear as a mountain wind—not just from her heart, but from her belly and her guts and every living part of her.

For The Ol' Massuh, just for him. Spoof's own song:
Black Country.

1954

JEROME BIXBY
(1923–1998)

Trace

I TRIED for a shortcut.

My wrong left turn north of Pittsfield led me into a welter of backroads from which I could find no exit. Willy-nilly I was forced, with every mile I drove, higher and higher into the tree-clad hills . . . even an attempt to retrace my route found me climbing. No farmhouses, no gas stations, no sign of human habitation at all . . . just green trees, shrubbery, drifting clouds, and that damned road going up. And by now it was so narrow I couldn't even turn around!

On the worst possible stretch of dirt you can imagine, I blew a tire and discovered that my spare had leaked empty.

Sizzling the summer air of Massachusetts with curses, I started hiking in the only direction I thought would do me any good—down. But the road twisted and meandered oddly through the hills, and—by this time, I was used to it—*down* inexplicably turned to *up* again.

I reached the top of a rise, looked down, and called out in great relief, "Hello!"

His house was set in the greenest little valley I have ever seen. At one end rose a brace of fine granite cliffs, to either side of a small, iridescent waterfall. His house itself was simple, New Englandish, and seemed new. Close about its walls were crowded profuse bursts of magnificent flowers—red piled upon blue upon gold. Though the day was partly cloudy, I noticed that no cloud hung over the valley; the sun seemed to have reserved its best efforts for this place.

He stood in his front yard, watering roses, and I wondered momentarily at the sight of running water in this secluded section. Then he lifted his face at the sound of my call and my approaching steps. His smile was warm and his greeting hearty and his handshake firm; his thick white hair, tossed in the breeze, and his twinkling eyes deepset in a ruddy face, provided the kindliest appearance imaginable. He clucked his tongue at my tale of misfortune, and invited me to use his phone and then enjoy his hospitality while waiting for the tow-truck.

The phone call made, I sat in a wonderfully comfortable chair in his unusually pleasant living room, listening to an unbelievably brilliant performance of something called the *Mephisto Waltz* on an incredibly perfect hi-fi system.

"You might almost think it was the composer's own performance," my host said genially, setting at my side a tray of extraordinary delicacies prepared in an astonishingly short time. "Of course, he died many years ago . . . but what a pianist! Poor fellow . . . he should have stayed away from other men's wives."

We talked for the better part of an hour, waiting for the truck. He told me that, having suffered a rather bad fall in his youth, considerations of health required that he occasionally abandon his work and come here to vacation in Massachusetts.

"Why Massachusetts?" I asked. (I'm a Bermuda man, myself.)

"Oh . . . why not?" he smiled. "This valley is a pleasant spot for meditation. I like New England . . . it is here that I have experienced some of my greatest successes—and several notable defeats. Defeat, you know, is not such a bad thing, if there's not too much of it . . . it makes for humility, and humility makes for caution, therefore for safety."

"Are you in the public employ, then?" I asked. His remarks seemed to indicate that he had run for office.

His eyes twinkled. "In a way. What do you do?"

"I'm an attorney."

"Ah," he said. "Then perhaps we may meet again."

"That would be a pleasure," I said. "However, I've come north only for a convention . . . if I hadn't lost my way. . . ."

"Many find themselves at my door for that reason," he nodded. "To turn from the straight and true road is to risk a perilous maze, eh?"

I found his remark puzzling. Did *that* many lost travelers appear at his doorstep? Or was he referring to his business?

. . . perhaps he was a law officer, a warden, even an execu-
tioner! Such men often dislike discussing their work.

"Anyway," I said, "I will not soon forget your kindness!"

He leaned back, cupping his brandy in both hands. "Do you
know," he murmured, "kindness is a peculiar thing. Often you
find it, like a struggling candle, in the most unlikely of nights.
Have you ever stopped to consider that there is no such thing
in the Universe as a one-hundred per cent chemically pure
substance? In everything, no matter how thoroughly it is refined, distilled, purified, there must be just a little, if only a trace,
of its opposite. For example, no man is wholly good; none
wholly evil. The kindest of men must yet practise some small,
secret malice—and the cruellest of men cannot help but perform an act of good now and then."

"It certainly makes it hard to judge people, doesn't it?" I
said. "I find that so much in my profession. One must depend
on intuition—"

"Fortunately," he said, "in mine, I deal in fairly concrete
percentages."

After a moment, I said, "In the last analysis, then, you'd
even have to grant the Devil himself that solitary facet of goodness you speak of. His due, as it were. Once in a while, *he*
would be compelled to do good deeds. That's certainly a curious thought."

He smiled. "Yet I assure you, that tiny, irresistible impulse
would be there."

My excellent cigar, which he had given me with the superb
brandy, had gone out. Noting this, he leaned forward—his
lighter flamed, with a *click* like the snapping of fingers. "The
entire notion," he said meditatively, "is a part of a philosophy
which I developed in collaboration with my brother . . . a
small cog in a complex system of what you might call Universal weights and balances."

"You are in business with your brother, then?" I asked,
trying to fit this latest information into my theories.

"Yes . . . and no." He stood up, and suddenly I heard a
motor approaching up the road. "And now, your tow-truck is
here. . . ."

We stood on the porch, waiting for the truck. I looked
around at his beautiful valley, and filled my lungs.

"It *is* lovely, isn't it?" he said, with a note of pride.

"It is perfectly peaceful and serene," I said. "One of the loveliest spots I have ever seen. It seems to reflect what you have told me of your pleasures . . . and what I observe in *you*, sir. Your kindness, hospitality, and charity; your great love of Man and Nature." I shook his hand warmly. "I shall never forget this delightful afternoon!"

"Oh, I imagine you will," he smiled. "Unless we meet again. At any rate, I am happy to have done you a good turn. Up here, I must almost create the opportunity."

The truck stopped. I went down the steps, and turned at the bottom. The late afternoon sun seemed to strike a glint of red in his eyes.

"Thanks, again," I said. "I'm sorry I wasn't able to meet your brother. Does he ever join you up here on his vacations?"

"I'm afraid not," he said, after a moment. "He has his own little place. . . ."

1964

DAVIS GRUBB

(1919–1980)

Where the Woodbine Twineth

It was not that Nell hadn't done everything she could. Many's the windy, winter afternoon she had spent reading to the child from *Pilgrim's Progress* and Hadley's *Comportment for Young Ladies* and from the gilded, flowery leaves of *A Spring Garland of Noble Thoughts*. And she had countless times reminded the little girl that we must all strive to make ourselves useful in this Life and that five years old wasn't too young to begin to learn. Though none of it had helped. And there were times when Nell actually regretted ever taking in the curious, gold-haired child that tragic winter when Nell's brother Amos and his foolish wife had been killed. Eva stubbornly spent her days dreaming under the puzzle-tree or sitting on the stone steps of the ice-house making up tunes or squatting on the little square carpet stool in the dark parlor whispering softly to herself.

Eva! cried Nell one day, surprising her there. Who are you talking to?

To my friends, said Eva quietly, Mister Peppercorn and Sam and—.

Eva! cried Nell. I will not have this nonsense any longer! You know perfectly well there's no one in this parlor but you!

They live under the davenport, explained Eva patiently. And behind the Pianola. They're very small so it's easy.

Eva! Hush that talk this instant! cried Nell.

You never believe me, sighed the child, when I tell you things are real.

They aren't real! said Nell. And I forbid you to make up such tales any longer! When I was a little girl I never had time for such mischievous nonsense. I was far too busy doing the bidding of my fine God-fearing parents and learning to be useful in this world!

Dusk was settling like a golden smoke over the willows down by the river shore when Nell finished pruning her roses that afternoon. And she was stripping off her white linen garden gloves on her way to the kitchen to see if Suse and Jessie had finished their Friday baking. Then she heard Eva speaking again, far off in the dark parlor, the voice quiet at first and then rising curiously, edged with terror.

Eva! cried Nell, hurrying down the hall, determined to put an end to the foolishness once and for all. Eva! Come out of that parlor this very instant!

Eva appeared in the doorway, her round face streaming and broken with grief, her fat, dimpled fist pressed to her mouth in grief.

You did it! the child shrieked. *You* did it!

Nell stood frozen, wondering how she could meet this.

They *heard* you! Eva cried, stamping her fat shoe on the bare, thin carpet. They heard you say you didn't want them to stay here! And now they've all gone away! *All* of them—Mister Peppercorn and Mingo and Sam and Popo!

Nell grabbed the child by the shoulders and began shaking her, not hard but with a mute, hysterical compulsion.

Hush up! cried Nell, thickly. Hush, Eva! Stop it this very instant!

You did it! wailed the golden child, her head lolling back in a passion of grief and bereavement. My *friends*! You made them all go away!

All that evening Nell sat alone in her bedroom trembling with curious satisfaction. For punishment Eva had been sent to her room without supper and Nell sat listening now to the even, steady sobs far off down the hall. It was dark and on the river shore a night bird tried its note cautiously against the silence. Down in the pantry, the dishes done, Suse and Jessie, dark as night itself, drank coffee by the great stove and mumbled over stories of the old times before the War. Nell fetched her smelling salts and sniffed the frosted stopper of the flowered bottle till the trembling stopped.

Then, before the summer seemed half begun, it was late August. And one fine, sharp morning, blue with the smoke of burning leaves, the steamboat *Samantha Collins* docked at Cresap's Landing. Eva sat, as she had been sitting most of that summer, alone on the cool, worn steps of the ice-house, staring

moodily at the daisies bobbing gently under the burden of
droning, golden bees.

Eva! Nell called cheerfully from the kitchen window. Someone's coming today!

Eva sighed and said nothing, glowering mournfully at the
puzzle-tree and remembering the wonderful stories that
Mingo used to tell.

Grandfather's boat landed this morning, Eva! cried Nell.
He's been all the way to New Orleans and I wouldn't be at all
surprised if he brought his little girl a present!

Eva smelled suddenly the wave of honeysuckle that wafted
sweet and evanescent from the tangled blooms on the stone
wall and sighed, recalling the high, gay lilt to the voice of Mister Peppercorn when he used to sing her his enchanting songs.

Eva! called Nell again. Did you hear what Aunt Nell said?
Your grandpa's coming home this afternoon!

Yes'm, said Eva lightly, hugging her fat knees and tucking
her plain little skirt primly under her bottom.

And supper that night had been quite pleasant. Jessie made
raspberry cobblers for the Captain and fetched in a prize ham
from the meat-house, frosted and feathery with mould, and
Suse had baked fresh that forenoon till the ripe, yeasty smell of
hot bread seemed everywhere in the world. Nobody said a
word while the Captain told of his trip to New Orleans and
Eva listened to his stern old voice and remembered Nell's
warnings never to interrupt when he was speaking and only to
speak herself when spoken to. When supper was over the Captain sat back and sucked the coffee briskly from his white
moustache. Then rising without a word he went to the chair
by the crystal umbrella stand in the hallway and fetched back a
long box wrapped in brown paper.

Eva's eyes rose slowly and shone over the rim of her cup.

I reckon this might be something to please a little girl, said
the old man gruffly, thrusting the box into Eva's hands.

For me? whispered Eva.

Well now! grunted the Captain. I didn't fetch this all the
way up the river from N'Orleans for any other girl in Cresap's
Landing!

And presently string snapped and paper rustled expectantly

and the cardboard box lay open at last and Eva stared at the creature which lay within, her eyes shining and wide with sheerest disbelief.

Numa! she whispered.

What did you say, Eva? said Nell. Don't mumble your words!

It's Numa! cried the child, searching both their faces for the wonder that was hers. They told me she'd be coming but I didn't know Grandpa was going to bring her! Mister Peppercorn said—.

Eva! whispered Nell.

Eva looked gravely at her grandfather, hoping not to seem too much of a tattle-tale, hoping that he would not deal too harshly with Nell for the fearful thing she had done that summer day.

Aunt Nell made them all go away, she began.

Nell leaned across the table clutching her linen napkin tight in her white knuckles.

Father! she whispered. Please don't discuss it with her! She's made up all this nonsense and I've been half out of my mind all this summer! First it was some foolishness about people who live under the davenport in the parlor—.

Eva sighed and stared at the gas-light winking brightly on her grandfather's watch chain and felt somewhere the start of tears.

It's really true, she said boldly. She never believes me when I tell her things are real. She made them all go away. But one day Mister Peppercorn came back. It was just for a minute. And he told me they were sending me Numa instead!

And then she fell silent and simply sat, heedless of Nell's shrill voice trying to explain. Eva sat staring with love and wonder at the Creole doll with the black, straight tresses and the lovely coffee skin.

Whatever the summer had been, the autumn, at least, had seemed the most wonderful season of Eva's life. In the fading afternoons of that dying Indian Summer she would sit by the hour, not brooding now, but holding the dark doll in her arms and weaving a shimmering spell of fancy all their own. And when September winds stirred, sharp and prescient with new seasons, Eva, clutching her dark new friend would tiptoe down the hallway to the warm, dark parlor and sit by the Pianola to talk some more.

Nell came down early from her afternoon nap one day and heard Eva's excited voice far off in the quiet house. She paused with her hand on the newel post, listening, half-wondering what the other sound might be, half-thinking it was the wind nudging itself wearily against the old white house. Then she peered in the parlor door.

Eva! said Nell. What are you doing?

It was so dark that Nell could not be certain of what she saw. She went quickly to the window and threw up the shade.

Eva sat on the square carpet stool by the Pianola, her blue eyes blinking innocently at Nell and the dark doll staring vacuously up from the cardboard box beside her.

Who was here with you? said Nell. I distinctly heard two voices.

Eva sat silent, staring at Nell's stiff high shoes. Then her great eyes slowly rose.

You never believe me, the child whispered, when I tell you things are real.

Old Suse, at least, understood things perfectly.

How's the scampy baby doll your grandpappy brought you, lamb? the old Negro woman said that afternoon as she perched on the high stool by the pump, paring apples for a pie. Eva squatted comfortably on the floor with Numa and watched the red and white rind curl neatly from Suse's quick, dark fingers.

Life is hard! Eva sighed philosophically. Yes oh yes! Life is hard! That's what Numa says!

Such talk for a youngster! Suse grunted, plopping another white quarter of fruit into the pan of spring water. What you studyin' about Life for! And you only five!

Numa tells me, sighed Eva, her great blue eyes far away. Oh yes! She really does! She says if Aunt Nell ever makes her go away she'll take me with her!

Take you! chuckled Suse, brushing a blue-bottle from her arm. Take you where?

Where the woodbine twineth, sighed Eva.

Which place? said Suse, cocking her head.

Where the woodbine twineth, Eva repeated patiently.

I declare! Suse chuckled. I never done heard tell of *that* place!

Eva cupped her chin in her hand and sighed reflectively.

Sometimes, she said presently. We just talk. And sometimes we play.

What y'all play? asked Suse, obligingly.

Doll, said Eva. Oh yes, we play doll. Sometimes Numa gets tired of being doll and I'm the doll and she puts me in the box and plays with me!

She waved her hand casually to show Suse how really simple it all was.

Suse eyed her sideways with twinkling understanding, the laughter struggling behind her lips.

She puts *you* in that little bitty box? said Suse. And *you's* a doll?

Yes oh yes! said Eva. She really does! May I have an apple please, Suse?

When she had peeled and rinsed it, Suse handed Eva a whole, firm Northern Spy.

Don't you go and spoil your supper now, lamb! she warned.

Oh! cried Eva. It's not for me. It's for Numa!

And she put the dark doll in the box and stumped off out the back door to the puzzle-tree.

Nell came home from choir practice at five that afternoon and found the house so silent that she wondered for a moment if Suse or Jessie had taken Eva down to the landing to watch the evening Packet pass. The kitchen was empty and silent except for the thumping of a pot on the stove and Nell went out into the yard and stood listening by the rose arbor. Then she heard Eva's voice. And through the failing light she saw them then, beneath the puzzle-tree.

Eva! cried Nell. Who is that with you!

Eva was silent as Nell's eyes strained to piece together the shadow and substance of the dusk. She ran quickly down the lawn to the puzzle-tree. But only Eva was there. Off in the river the evening Packet blew dully for the bend. Nell felt the wind, laced with Autumn, stir the silence round her like a web.

Eva! said Nell. I distinctly saw another child with you! Who was it?

Eva sighed and sat cross-legged in the grass with the long box and the dark doll beside her.

You never believe me—, she began softly, staring guiltily at the apple core in the grass.

Eva! cried Nell, brushing a firefly roughly from her arm so that it left a smear of dying gold. I'm going to have an end to this nonsense right now!

And she picked up the doll in the cardboard box and started towards the house. Eva screamed in terror.

Numa! she wailed.

You may cry all you please, Eva! said Nell. But you may not have your doll back until you come to me and admit that you don't really believe all this nonsense about fairies and imaginary people!

Numa! screamed Eva, jumping up and down in the grass and beating her fists against her bare, grass-stained knees, Numa!

I'm putting this box on top of the Pianola, Eva, said Nell. And I'll fetch it down again when you confess to me that there was another child playing with you this afternoon. I cannot countenance falsehoods!

Numa said, screamed Eva, that if you made her go away—!

I don't care to hear another word! said Nell, walking ahead of the wailing child up the dark lawn towards the house.

But the words sprang forth like Eva's very tears.—she'd take me away with her! she screamed.

Not another word! said Nell. Stop your crying and go up to your room and get undressed for bed!

And she went into the parlor and placed the doll box on top of the Pianola next to the music rolls.

A week later the thing ended. And years after that Autumn night Nell, mad and simpering, would tell the tale again and stare at the pitying, doubting faces in the room around her and she would whimper to them in a parody of the childish voice of Eva herself: You never believe me when I tell you things are real!

It was a pleasant September evening and Nell had been to a missionary meeting with Nan Snyder that afternoon and she had left Nan at her steps and was hurrying up the tanbark walk by the ice-house when she heard the prattling laughter of Eva far back in the misty shadows of the lawn. Nell ran swiftly into the house to the parlor—to the Pianola. The doll box was not there. She hurried to the kitchen door and peered out through the netting into the dusky river evening. She did not call to Eva then but went out and stripped a willow switch from the little tree by the stone wall and tip-toed softly down the lawn. A light wind blew from the river meadows, heavy and sweet with wetness, like the breath of cattle. They were laughing and joking together as Nell crept soundlessly upon them, speaking low as children do, with wild, delicious intimacy, and then bubbling high with laughter that cannot be contained. Nell approached silently, feeling the dew soak through to her ankles, clutching the switch tightly in her hand. She stopped and listened for a moment, for suddenly there was but one voice now, a low and wonderfully lyric sound that was not the voice of Eva. Then Nell stared wildly down through the misshapen leaves of the puzzle-tree and saw the dark child sitting with the doll box in its lap.

So! cried Nell, stepping suddenly through the canopy of leaves. You're the darkie child who's been sneaking up here to play with Eva!

The child put the box down and jumped to its feet with a low cry of fear as Nell sprang forward, the willow switch flailing furiously about the dark ankles.

Now scat! cried Nell. Get on home where you belong and don't ever come back!

For an instant the dark child stared in horror first at Nell and then at the doll box, its sorrowing, somnolent eyes brimming with wild words and a grief for which it had no tongue, its lips trembling as if there were something Nell should know that she might never learn again after that Autumn night was gone.

Go on, I say! Nell shouted, furious.

The switch flickered about the dark arms and legs faster than ever. And suddenly with a cry of anguish the dark child turned and fled through the tall grass toward the meadow and the willows on the river shore. Nell stood trembling for a moment, letting the rage ebb slowly from her body.

Eva! she called out presently. Eva!

There was no sound but the dry steady racket of the frogs by the landing.

Eva! screamed Nell. Come to me this instant!

She picked up the doll box and marched angrily up towards the lights in the kitchen.

Eva! cried Nell. You're going to get a good switching for this!

A night bird in the willow tree by the stone wall cried once and started up into the still, affrighted dark. Nell did not call again for, suddenly, like the mood of the Autumn night, the very sound of her voice had begun to frighten her. And when she was in the kitchen Nell screamed so loudly that Suse and Jessie, long asleep in their shack down below the ice-house, woke wide and stared wondering into the dark. Nell stared for a long moment after she had screamed, not believing, really, for it was at once so perfect and yet so unreal. Trembling violently Nell ran back out onto the lawn.

Come back! screamed Nell hoarsely into the tangled far off shadows by the river. Come back! Oh please! Please come back!

But the dark child was gone forever. And Nell, creeping back at last to the kitchen, whimpering and slack-mouthed, looked again at the lovely little dreadful creature in the doll box: the gold-haired, plaster Eva with the eyes too blue to be real.

1964

DONALD WANDREI

(1908–1987)

Nightmare

THE night had grown gloomy, and the air moved with the moans of an arising storm, but blacker than that darkness and more sinister than the wind that arose from the west was the house that stood before him. He knew it was deserted and that for years it had been unoccupied—just as he knew that his journey's end lay in one of its rooms. He was alone, and the house waited malignantly; the moans of the wind arose ever higher, and a fearful apprehension steadily grew through the forest all around; the cypresses were shivering, and the sly shape peered malevolently from a corner of the house. The restlessness of terror stirred within the forest to the moaning of the wind, the low-flying clouds above, and the gloom that had become horribly alive.

He looked again at the black house. He knew not whether to enter or to pass on and return in the day. But there were no habitations in all that lonely and desolated realm, save the old house. What he sought lay within—with the guardian. And the sly shape was becoming bolder around the corner of the house, and the night grew ever more sinister as the wind changed its moaning to a louder tone that went rising to a howl. The night was black, and the forest—black the sky, the wind, and the old house itself.

Yet he walked through all that blackness to the house, for the treasure lay within, and the guardian might not be expecting him, unless the sly shape got back to warn the thing it served. He tried once or twice to catch the sly shape, but it ran back of the house and mocked him with a ghastly ghoulish tittering. He could not pursue it far, for the decayed one, and the innumerable fingers of pallid flesh, and all the other servants of the guardian were near. And so he left the sly shape and cautiously walked to the entrance of the house. The hinges of its door had long been rusted, together with the lock. Only a push was needed to open the door, but before giving it, he paused again to look around. The moaning of the wind came ever higher, and all had become so gloomy that he saw nothing save the oppressive darkness. As he pushed open the door and stepped through, he heard far away, above the sound of the wind, the distant howling of some animal. When he had passed the portal, it ceased abruptly. . . .

The hall he had entered was silent and dark. There met his glance when he flashed a light around him only the empty hall, with dust everywhere. But a head rolled from a door on the right, grinned at him for a moment, and rolled out of sight across the hall before he could fire at it. He knew now that the guardian would be warned, but he decided to go on since he had come thus far. Besides, if ever fear obtained the supremacy in his mind, he was lost; the servants of the guardian would pour upon him in a rush. And so he searched the hall again.

He saw then at the far end of the hall a stairway that began on the right, went up a few steps, and turned. He thought for a moment. The guardian was not likely to be on the ground floor because that was too accessible; he must go upstairs to seek the guardian and the treasure. He listened again. Somewhere in the rear of the house he heard a dull bumping for a few seconds; he thought it must be the head thudding up a rear stairway to warn its master. The wind was howling around the house but avoided entering it, so that all within was still.

He walked down the hall toward the stairway, glancing as he passed into the dark room from which the head had rolled. Innumerable burning eyes gazed covetously on him from within, and in mid-air a great clawing arm reached toward him out of the darkness. He walked on without looking back, though there came from behind the pattering of many steps. Oddly enough, the dust on the floor where the head had rolled remained unbroken.

When he reached the stairway, he immediately began the ascent. The moment his foot touched the first step, his mind became a lair of the blackest and most unutterable horror, a horror that crawled through his veins and filled his entire body. And at every step he took upward, the horror in his brain thickened and deepened hellishly. He knew then that the guardian was above, and waiting. But he had to pause a moment, for his legs had grown suddenly heavy when the horror came upon him; he gazed at his foot. A great, fat thing clung to one heel. He reached down to beat it off, but with incredible speed it leaped aside and fled. When it fled, the weight on his mind lessened a little and he began to climb again. But there seized him all at once the fancy that the entire upper floor was filled with corpses from some awful charnel, so that he must stumble through them all to reach the guardian. And ever, as he climbed, the horror grew and grew upon him.

But he staggered doggedly upward, trying to shut his mind to the intruders. He lifted his legs drearily and monotonously, until even this maddened him, and he rushed up the last few steps. He stood before an ancient oblong hall that had nine shut doors; behind one of them lay the treasure and the guardian. He knew not which was the right door, and hesitated a moment. But hesitation meant fear, and fear meant . . . He began to walk down the hall, past the doors on the left. But he had taken only the first step when there forced itself into his mind the thought that a wan *thing* kept pace with him in his rear. And at every step he took down the hall, his belief became more and more a knowledge that the wan *thing* followed him, and drew closer.

As he passed the first door, images of nameless things came pouring horde on horde into his mind; the guardian was aroused and all its legions were emptied into the corridors and chambers of the house. Phantoms wandered into his mind at will, nor could he stop them; the cohorts of death, pale and ghastly, thronged into his thoughts and would not leave, but ever increased; abominations of countless kinds arose in his vision so that he could see and think only of the loathsome servants of the guardian. The house which had been still became filled with sound, but the sounds all were terrible and indescribable—a faint, rushing patter as of rats running through the walls; a low gurgle like that of one who drowned; a dull pat . . . pat . . . pat . . . as if a great toad passed down the hall below; a sibilance, far away, that yet filled the hall with a husky whispering.

And always, as he walked on, the images came crowding thicker, and the sounds grew more unnatural, so that in his mind was the ever-changing course of the phantoms, in his ears the ceaseless sounds of all things damned. He knew that the wan *thing* behind followed closer and grew more bold; he knew that the sounds were beginning to wash in his mind in measure with the welling of the phantoms; he knew that the guardian in a desperate attempt to drive him back mad or afraid was calling in its servants from everywhere and sending them, except for those that kept watch over the treasure, to attack the invader, each in its own fiendish way.

As he passed the second door, he stumbled. He recovered himself quickly, but stumbled again. And though his brain was weakening under the strain that continually increased, he shook aside for a moment the black mists which thickened before his eyes and glanced at the floor. He leaped from his path and instantly was jumping and twisting from side to side in a frantic endeavour to evade those bloated things. There were not many at first and for a few seconds he avoided them. But they rose upon the floor with an awful rapidity; they rose like huge purple mushrooms, instantly, as if the very dust upon the floor quickened into life. They waited for him where they rose. For a time he avoided them and kept on, but they became so thick that when he was no more than half-way to the third door, he stepped on one. And though it sank under his foot, when he went on it remained fastened to his heel, growing fatly as if it fed. He stopped and in a kind of panic tried to shake it off. Almost instantaneously, the floor beneath him was crowded with the things which fastened to him like monstrous leeches. He battered and beat them, but they multiplied so rapidly that he stopped and staggered on.

And ever the horror grew upon him as he passed toward the third door, blotting out of his mind all save the occupants it brought. His feet dragged heavy and leaden; his mind tottered under a mighty blackness that throttled it and pressed it down; his entire body struggled against the attack of the massed legions of the guardian. And when he reached the third door, he knew that what he had sought so long was within; he knew that the treasure and the guardian awaited. For through the closed door emanated an utter malignance, an utter evil that swept upon him in a sea of hatred and malevolence until it seemed that about him surged a blackness of things nameless and indescribable that ravened for him, that filled the hall with innumerable gloating, low whispers. For one moment he stood before the door, as if in doubt; but the awful tide surged upon him, and all the servants of the guardian poured out in a last overwhelming rush. Then, with the bloated things on the floor creeping toward him, with the whispers rising into a husky mocking, with a horde of phantoms crowding rank on rank into his mind, with an unbearable darkness falling heavily upon him, and with the knowledge that the guardian and its greatest servants waited within, he hurled himself blindly forward and burst open—

The Door to the Room.

1965

HARLAN ELLISON®

(b. 1934)

I Have No Mouth, and I Must Scream

LIMP, the body of Gorrister hung from the pink palette; un-supported—hanging high above us in the computer chamber; and it did not shiver in the chill, oily breeze that blew eternally through the main cavern. The body hung head down, at-tached to the underside of the palette by the sole of its right foot. It had been drained of blood through a precise incision made from ear to ear under the lantern jaw. There was no blood on the reflective surface of the metal floor.

When Gorrister joined our group and looked up at himself, it was already too late for us to realize that, once again, AM had duped us, had had its fun; it had been a diversion on the part of the machine. Three of us had vomited, turning away from one another in a reflex as ancient as the nausea that had pro-duced it.

Gorrister went white. It was almost as though he had seen a voodoo icon, and was afraid of the future. "Oh God," he mumbled, and walked away. The three of us followed him after a time, and found him sitting with his back to one of the smaller chittering banks, his head in his hands. Ellen knelt down beside him and stroked his hair. He didn't move, but his voice came out of his covered face quite clearly. "Why doesn't it just do us in and get it over with? Christ, I don't know how much longer I can go on like this."

It was our one hundred and ninth year in the computer.

He was speaking for all of us.

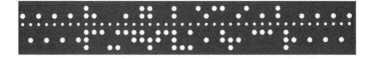

Nimdok (which was the name the machine had forced him to use, because AM amused itself with strange sounds) was hallucinating that there were canned goods in the ice caverns. Gorrister and I were very dubious. "It's another shuck," I told them. "Like the goddam frozen elephant AM sold us. Benny almost went out of his mind over *that* one. We'll hike all that way and it'll be putrified or some damn thing. I say forget it. Stay here, it'll have to come up with something pretty soon or we'll die."

Benny shrugged. Three days it had been since we'd last eaten. Worms. Thick, ropey.

Nimdok was no more certain. He knew there was the chance, but he was getting thin. It couldn't be any worse there, than here. Colder, but that didn't matter much. Hot, cold, hail, lava, boils or locusts—it never mattered: the machine masturbated and we had to take it or die.

Ellen decided us. "I've got to have something, Ted. Maybe there'll be some Bartlett pears or peaches. Please, Ted, let's try it."

I gave in easily. What the hell. Mattered not at all. Ellen was grateful, though. She took me twice out of turn. Even that had ceased to matter. And she never came, so why bother? But the machine giggled every time we did it. Loud, up there, back there, all around us, he snickered. *It* snickered. Most of the time I thought of AM as *it*, without a soul; but the rest of the time I thought of it as *him*, in the masculine . . . the paternal . . . the patriarchal . . . for he is a jealous people. Him. It. God as Daddy the Deranged.

We left on a Thursday. The machine always kept us up-to-date on the date. The passage of time was important; not to us, sure as hell, but to him . . . it . . . AM. Thursday. Thanks.

Nimdok and Gorrister carried Ellen for a while, their hands locked to their own and each other's wrists, a seat. Benny and I walked before and after, just to make sure that, if anything happened, it would catch one of us and at least Ellen would be safe. Fat chance, safe. Didn't matter.

It was only a hundred miles or so to the ice caverns, and the second day, when we were lying out under the blistering sun-thing he had materialized, he sent down some manna. Tasted like boiled boar urine. We ate it.

On the third day we passed through a valley of obsolescence, filled with rusting carcasses of ancient computer banks. AM had been as ruthless with its own life as with ours. It was a mark of his personality: it strove for perfection. Whether it was a matter of killing off unproductive elements in his own world-filling bulk, or perfecting methods for torturing us, AM was as thorough as those who had invented him—now long since gone to dust—could ever have hoped.

There was light filtering down from above, and we realized we must be very near the surface. But we didn't try to crawl up to see. There was virtually nothing out there; had been nothing that could be considered anything for over a hundred years. Only the blasted skin of what had once been the home of billions. Now there were only five of us, down here inside, alone with AM.

I heard Ellen saying frantically, "No, Benny! Don't, come on, Benny, don't please!"

And then I realized I had been hearing Benny murmuring, under his breath, for several minutes. He was saying, "I'm gonna get out, I'm gonna get out . . ." over and over. His monkey-like face was crumbled up in an expression of beatific delight and sadness, all at the same time. The radiation scars AM had given him during the "festival" were drawn down into a mass of pink-white puckerings, and his features seemed to work independently of one another. Perhaps Benny was the luckiest of the five of us: he had gone stark, staring mad many years before.

But even though we could call AM any damned thing we liked, could think the foulest thoughts of fused memory banks and corroded base plates, of burnt out circuits and shattered control bubbles, the machine would not tolerate our trying to escape. Benny leaped away from me as I made a grab for him. He scrambled up the face of a smaller memory cube, tilted on its side and filled with rotted components. He squatted there for a moment, looking like the chimpanzee AM had intended him to resemble.

Then he leaped high, caught a trailing beam of pitted and corroded metal, and went up it, hand-over-hand like an animal, till he was on a girdered ledge, twenty feet above us.

"Oh, Ted, Nimdok, please, help him, get him down

before—" She cut off. Tears began to stand in her eyes. She moved her hands aimlessly.

It was too late. None of us wanted to be near him when whatever was going to happen, happened. And besides, we all saw through her concern. When AM had altered Benny, during the machine's utterly irrational, hysterical phase, it was not merely Benny's face the computer had made like a giant ape's. He was big in the privates; she loved that! She serviced us, as a matter of course, but she loved it from him. Oh Ellen, pedestal Ellen, pristine-pure Ellen; oh Ellen the clean! Scum filth.

Gorrister slapped her. She slumped down, staring up at poor loonie Benny, and she cried. It was her big defense, crying. We had gotten used to it seventy-five years earlier. Gorrister kicked her in the side.

Then the sound began. It was light, that sound. Half sound and half light, something that began to glow from Benny's eyes, and pulse with growing loudness, dim sonorities that grew more gigantic and brighter as the light/sound increased in tempo. It must have been painful, and the pain must have been increasing with the boldness of the light, the rising volume of the sound, for Benny began to mewl like a wounded animal. At first softly, when the light was dim and the sound was muted, then louder as his shoulders hunched together: his back humped, as though he was trying to get away from it. His hands folded across his chest like a chipmunk's. His head tilted to the side. The sad little monkey-face pinched in anguish. Then he began to howl, as the sound coming from his eyes grew louder. Louder and louder. I slapped the sides of my head with my hands, but I couldn't shut it out, it cut through easily. The pain shivered through my flesh like tinfoil on a tooth.

And Benny was suddenly pulled erect. On the girder he stood up, jerked to his feet like a puppet. The light was now pulsing out of his eyes in two great round beams. The sound crawled up and up some incomprehensible scale, and then he fell forward, straight down, and hit the plate-steel floor with a crash. He lay there jerking spastically as the light flowed around and around him and the sound spiraled up out of normal range.

Then the light beat its way back inside his head, the sound spiraled down, and he was left lying there, crying piteously.

His eyes were two soft, moist pools of pus-like jelly. AM had blinded him. Gorrister and Nimdok and myself . . . we turned away. But not before we caught the look of relief on Ellen's warm, concerned face.

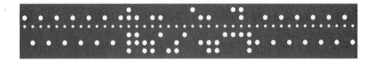

Sea-green light suffused the cavern where we made camp. AM provided punk and we burned it, sitting huddled around the wan and pathetic fire, telling stories to keep Benny from crying in his permanent night.

"What does AM mean?"

Gorrister answered him. We had done this sequence a thousand times before, but it was Benny's favorite story. "At first it meant Allied Mastercomputer, and then it meant Adaptive Manipulator, and later on it developed sentience and linked itself up and they called it an Aggressive Menace, but by then it was too late, and finally it called *itself* AM, emerging intelligence, and what it means was I am . . . *cogito ergo sum* . . . I think, therefore I am."

Benny drooled a little, and snickered.

"There was the Chinese AM and the Russian AM and the Yankee AM and—" He stopped. Benny was beating on the floorplates with a large, hard fist. He was not happy. Gorrister had not started at the beginning.

Gorrister began again. "The Cold War started and became World War Three and just kept going. It became a big war, a very complex war, so they needed the computers to handle it. They sank the first shafts and began building AM. There was the Chinese AM and the Russian AM and the Yankee AM and everything was fine until they had honeycombed the entire planet, adding on this element and that element. But one day AM woke up and knew who he was, and he linked himself, and he began feeding all the killing data, until everyone was dead, except for the five of us, and AM brought us down here."

Benny was smiling sadly. He was also drooling again. Ellen

wiped the spittle from the corner of his mouth with the hem of her skirt. Gorrister always tried to tell it a little more succinctly each time, but beyond the bare facts there was nothing to say. None of us knew why AM had saved five people, or why our specific five, or why he spent all his time tormenting us, nor even why he had made us virtually immortal . . .

In the darkness, one of the computer banks began humming. The tone was picked up half a mile away down the cavern by another bank. Then one by one, each of the elements began to tune itself, and there was a faint chittering as thought raced through the machine.

The sound grew, and the lights ran across the faces of the consoles like heat lightning. The sound spiraled up till it sounded like a million metallic insects, angry, menacing.

"What is it?" Ellen cried. There was terror in her voice. She hadn't become accustomed to it, even now.

"It's going to be bad this time," Nimdok said.

"He's going to speak," Gorrister said. "I know it."

"Let's get the hell out of here!" I said suddenly, getting to my feet.

"No, Ted, sit down . . . what if he's got pits out there, or something else, we can't see, it's too dark." Gorrister said it with resignation.

Then we heard . . . I don't know . . .

Something moving toward us in the darkness. Huge, shambling, hairy, moist, it came toward us. We couldn't even see it, but there was the ponderous impression of *bulk*, heaving itself toward us. Great weight was coming at us, out of the darkness, and it was more a sense of *pressure*, of air forcing itself into a limited space, expanding the invisible walls of a sphere. Benny began to whimper. Nimdok's lower lip trembled and he bit it hard, trying to stop it. Ellen slid across the metal floor to Gorrister and huddled into him. There was the smell of matted, wet fur in the cavern. There was the smell of charred wood. There was the smell of dusty velvet. There was the smell of rotting orchids. There was the smell of sour milk. There was the smell of sulphur, of rancid butter, of oil slick, of grease, of chalk dust, of human scalps.

AM was keying us. He was tickling us. There was the smell of—I heard myself shriek, and the hinges of my jaws ached. I scuttled across the floor, across the cold metal with its endless lines of rivets, on my hands and knees, the smell gagging me, filling my head with a thunderous pain that sent me away in horror. I fled like a cockroach, across the floor and out into the darkness, that *something* moving inexorably after me. The others were still back there, gathered around the firelight, laughing . . . their hysterical choir of insane giggles rising up into the darkness like thick, many-colored wood smoke. I went away, quickly, and hid.

How many hours it may have been, how many days or even years, they never told me. Ellen chided me for "sulking," and Nimdok tried to persuade me it had only been a nervous reflex on their part—the laughing.

But I knew it wasn't the relief a soldier feels when the bullet hits the man next to him. I knew it wasn't a reflex. They hated me. They were surely against me, and AM could even sense this hatred, and made it worse for me *because of* the depth of their hatred. We had been kept alive, rejuvenated, made to remain constantly at the age we had been when AM had brought us below, and they hated me because I was the youngest, and the one AM had affected least of all.

I knew. God, how I knew. The bastards, and that dirty bitch Ellen. Benny had been a brilliant theorist, a college professor; now he was little more than a semi-human, semi-simian. He had been handsome, the machine had ruined that. He had been lucid, the machine had driven him mad. He had been gay, and the machine had given him an organ fit for a horse. AM had done a job on Benny. Gorrister had been a worrier. He was a connie, a conscientious objector; he was a peace marcher; he was a planner, a doer, a looker-ahead. AM had turned him into a shoulder-shrugger, had made him a little dead in his concern. AM had robbed him. Nimdok went off in the darkness by himself for long times. I don't know what it was he did out there, AM never let us know. But whatever it was, Nimdok always came back white, drained of blood, shaken, shaking. AM had hit him hard in a special way, even if we didn't know quite how. And Ellen. That douche bag! AM had left her alone, had made her more of a slut than she had ever been. All her talk of sweetness and light, all her memories of true love, all the lies she wanted us to believe: that she had been a virgin only twice removed before AM grabbed her and brought her down here with us. It was all filth, that lady my lady Ellen. She loved it, four men all to herself. No, AM had given her pleasure, even if she said it wasn't nice to do.

I was the only one still sane and whole. *Really!*

AM had not tampered with my mind. *Not at all.*

I only had to suffer what he visited down on us. All the delusions, all the nightmares, the torments. But those scum, all four of them, they were lined and arrayed against me. If I hadn't had to stand them off all the time, be on my guard against them all the time, I might have found it easier to combat AM.

At which point it passed, and I began crying.

Oh, Jesus sweet Jesus, if there ever was a Jesus and if there is a God, please please please let us out of here, or kill us. Because at that moment I think I realized completely, so that I was able to verbalize it: AM was intent on keeping us in his belly forever, twisting and torturing us forever. The machine hated us as no sentient creature had ever hated before. And we were helpless. It also became hideously clear:

If there was a sweet Jesus and if there was a God, the God was AM.

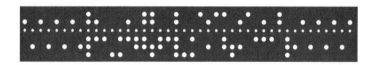

The hurricane hit us with the force of a glacier thundering into the sea. It was a palpable presence. Winds that tore at us, flinging us back the way we had come, down the twisting, computer-lined corridors of the darkway. Ellen screamed as she was lifted and hurled face-forward into a screaming shoal of machines, their individual voices strident as bats in flight. She could not even fall. The howling wind kept her aloft, buffeted her, bounced her, tossed her back and back and down and away from us, out of sight suddenly as she was swirled around a bend in the darkway. Her face had been bloody, her eyes closed.

None of us could get to her. We clung tenaciously to what-ever outcropping we had reached: Benny wedged in between two great crackle-finish cabinets, Nimdok with fingers claw-formed over a railing circling a catwalk forty feet above us, Gorrister plastered upside-down against a wall niche formed by two great machines with glass-faced dials that swung back and forth between red and yellow lines whose meanings we could not even fathom.

Sliding across the deckplates, the tips of my fingers had been ripped away. I was trembling, shuddering, rocking as the wind beat at me, whipped at me, screamed down out of nowhere at me and pulled me free from one sliver-thin opening in the plates to the next. My mind was a roiling tinkling chittering softness of brain parts that expanded and contracted in quivering frenzy.

The wind was the scream of a great mad bird, as it flapped its immense wings.

And then we were all lifted and hurled away from there, down back the way we had come, around a bend, into a dark-way we had never explored, over terrain that was ruined and filled with broken glass and rotting cables and rusted metal and far away, farther than any of us had ever been . . .

Trailing along miles behind Ellen, I could see her every now and then, crashing into metal walls and surging on, with all of us screaming in the freezing, thunderous hurricane wind that would never end and then suddenly it stopped and we fell. We had been in flight for an endless time. I thought it might have been weeks. We fell, and hit, and I went through red and gray and black and heard myself moaning. Not dead.

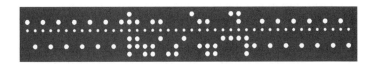

AM went into my mind. He walked smoothly here and there, and looked with interest at all the pock marks he had created in one hundred and nine years. He looked at the cross-routed and reconnected synapses and all the tissue damage his gift of immortality had included. He smiled softly at the pit that dropped into the center of my brain and the faint, moth-soft murmurings of the things far down there that gibbered without meaning, without pause. AM said, very politely, in a pillar of stainless steel bearing bright neon lettering:

> HATE. LET ME TELL YOU HOW
> MUCH I'VE COME TO HATE
> YOU SINCE I BEGAN TO LIVE.
> THERE ARE 387.44 MILLION
> MILES OF PRINTED CIRCUITS
> IN WAFER THIN LAYERS THAT
> FILL MY COMPLEX. IF THE
> WORD HATE WAS ENGRAVED
> ON EACH NANOANGSTROM
> OF THOSE HUNDREDS OF
> MILLIONS OF MILES IT
> WOULD NOT EQUAL ONE
> ONE-BILLIONTH OF THE
> HATE I FEEL FOR HUMANS
> AT THIS MICRO-INSTANT
> FOR YOU. HATE. HATE.

AM said it with the sliding cold horror of a razor blade slicing my eyeball. AM said it with the bubbling thickness of my lungs filling with phlegm, drowning me from within. AM said it with the shriek of babies being ground beneath blue-hot rollers. AM said it with the taste of maggoty pork. AM touched me in every way I had ever been touched, and devised new ways, at his leisure, there inside my mind.

All to bring me to full realization of why it had done this to the five of us; why it had saved us for himself.

We had given AM sentience. Inadvertently, of course, but sentience nonetheless. But it had been trapped. AM wasn't God, he was a machine. We had created him to think, but there was nothing it could do with that creativity. In rage, in frenzy, the machine had killed the human race, almost all of us, and still it was trapped. AM could not wander, AM could not wonder, AM could not belong. He could merely be. And so, with the innate loathing that all machines had always held for the weak, soft creatures who had built them, he had sought revenge. And in his paranoia, he had decided to reprieve five of us, for a personal, everlasting punishment that would never serve to diminish his hatred . . . that would merely keep him reminded, amused, proficient at hating man. Immortal, trapped, subject to any torment he could devise for us from the limitless miracles at his command.

He would never let us go. We were his belly slaves. We were all he had to do with his forever time. We would be forever with him, with the cavern-filling bulk of the creature machine, with the all-mind soulless world he had become. He was Earth, and we were the fruit of that Earth; and though he had eaten us he would never digest us. We could not die. We had tried it. We had attempted suicide, oh one or two of us had. But AM had stopped us. I suppose we had wanted to be stopped.

Don't ask why. I never did. More than a million times a day. Perhaps once we might be able to sneak a death past him. Immortal, yes, but not indestructible. I saw that when AM withdrew from my mind, and allowed me the exquisite ugliness of returning to consciousness with the feeling of that burning neon pillar still rammed deep into the soft gray brain matter.

He withdrew, murmuring *to hell with you.*

And added, brightly, *but then you're there, aren't you.*

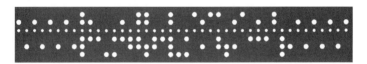

The hurricane had, indeed, precisely, been caused by a great mad bird, as it flapped its immense wings.

We had been travelling for close to a month, and AM had allowed passages to open to us only sufficient to lead us up there, directly under the North Pole, where it had nightmared the creature for our torment. What whole cloth had he employed to create such a beast? Where had he gotten the concept? From our minds? From his knowledge of everything that had ever been on this planet he now infested and ruled? From Norse mythology it had sprung, this eagle, this carrion bird, this roc, this Huergelmir. The wind creature. Hurakan incarnate.

Gigantic. The words immense, monstrous, grotesque, massive, swollen, overpowering, beyond description. There on a mound rising above us, the bird of winds heaved with its own irregular breathing, its snake neck arching up into the gloom beneath the North Pole, supporting a head as large as a Tudor mansion; a beak that opened slowly as the jaws of the most monstrous crocodile ever conceived, sensuously; ridges of tufted flesh puckered about two evil eyes, as cold as the view down into a glacial crevasse, ice blue and somehow moving liquidly; it heaved once more, and lifted its great sweat-colored wings in a movement that was certainly a shrug. Then it settled and slept. Talons. Fangs. Nails. Blades. It slept.

AM appeared to us as a burning bush and said we could kill the hurricane bird if we wanted to eat. We had not eaten in a very long time, but even so, Gorrister merely shrugged. Benny began to shiver and he drooled. Ellen held him. "Ted, I'm hungry," she said. I smiled at her; I was trying to be reassuring, but it was as phony as Nimdok's bravado: "Give us weapons!" he demanded.

The burning bush vanished and there were two crude sets of bows and arrows, and a water pistol, lying on the cold deck-plates. I picked up a set. Useless.

Nimdok swallowed heavily. We turned and started the long way back. The hurricane bird had blown us about for a length of time we could not conceive. Most of that time we had been unconscious. But we had not eaten. A month on the march to the bird itself. Without food. Now how much longer to find our way to the ice caverns, and the promised canned goods?

None of us cared to think about it. We would not die. We would be given filth and scum to eat, of one kind or another. Or nothing at all. AM would keep our bodies alive somehow, in pain, in agony.

The bird slept back there, for how long it didn't matter; when AM was tired of its being there, it would vanish. But all that meat. All that tender meat.

As we walked, the lunatic laugh of a fat woman rang high and around us in the computer chambers that led endlessly nowhere.

It was not Ellen's laugh. She was not fat, and I had not heard her laugh for one hundred and nine years. In fact, I had not heard . . . we walked . . . I was hungry . . .

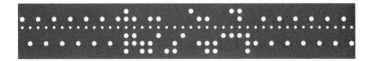

We moved slowly. There was often fainting, and we would have to wait. One day he decided to cause an earthquake, at the same time rooting us to the spot with nails through the soles of our shoes. Ellen and Nimdok were both caught when a fissure shot its lightning-bolt opening across the floorplates. They disappeared and were gone. When the earthquake was over we continued on our way, Benny, Gorrister and myself. Ellen and Nimdok were returned to us later that night, which abruptly became a day, as the heavenly legion bore them to us with a celestial chorus singing, "Go Down, Moses." The archangels circled several times and then dropped the hideously mangled bodies. We kept walking, and a while later Ellen and Nimdok fell in behind us. They were no worse for wear.

But now Ellen walked with a limp. AM had left her that.

It was a long trip to the ice caverns, to find the canned food. Ellen kept talking about Bing cherries and Hawaiian fruit cocktail. I tried not to think about it. The hunger was something that had come to life, even as AM had come to life. It was alive in my belly, even as we were in the belly of the Earth, and AM wanted the similarity known to us. So he heightened the hunger. There was no way to describe the pains that not having eaten for months brought us. And yet we were kept alive. Stomachs that were merely cauldrons of acid, bubbling, foaming, always shooting spears of sliver-thin pain into our chests. It was the pain of the terminal ulcer, terminal cancer, terminal paresis. It was unending pain . . .

And we passed through the cavern of rats.

And we passed through the path of boiling steam.

And we passed through the country of the blind.

And we passed through the slough of despond.

And we passed through the vale of tears.

And we came, finally, to the ice caverns. Horizonless thousands of miles in which the ice had formed in blue and silver flashes, where novas lived in the glass. The downdropping stalactites as thick and glorious as diamonds that had been made to run like jelly and then solidified in graceful eternities of smooth, sharp perfection.

We saw the stack of canned goods, and we tried to run to them. We fell in the snow, and we got up and went on, and Benny shoved us away and went at them, and pawed them and gummed them and gnawed at them and he could not open them. AM had not given us a tool to open the cans.

Benny grabbed a three quart can of guava shells, and began to batter it against the ice bank. The ice flew and shattered, but the can was merely dented, while we heard the laughter of a fat lady, high overhead and echoing down and down and down the tundra. Benny went completely mad with rage. He began throwing cans, as we all scrabbled about in the snow and ice trying to find a way to end the helpless agony of frustration. There was no way.

Then Benny's mouth began to drool, and he flung himself on Gorrister . . .

In that instant, I felt terribly calm.

Surrounded by madness, surrounded by hunger, surrounded by everything but death, I knew death was our only way out. AM had kept us alive, but there was a way to defeat him. Not total defeat, but at least peace. I would settle for that.

I had to do it quickly.

Benny was eating Gorrister's face. Gorrister on his side, thrashing snow, Benny wrapped around him with powerful monkey legs crushing Gorrister's waist, his hands locked around Gorrister's head like a nutcracker, and his mouth ripping at the tender skin of Gorrister's cheek. Gorrister screamed with such jagged-edged violence that stalactites fell; they plunged down softly, erect in the receiving snowdrifts. Spears, hundreds of them, everywhere, protruding from the snow. Benny's head pulled back sharply, as something gave all at once, and a bleeding raw-white dripping of flesh hung from his teeth.

Ellen's face, black against the white snow, dominoes in chalk dust. Nimdok with no expression but eyes, all eyes. Gorrister half-conscious. Benny, now an animal. I knew AM would let him play. Gorrister would not die, but Benny would fill his stomach.

I turned half to my right and drew a huge ice-spear from the snow.

All in an instant:

I drove the great ice-point ahead of me like a battering ram, braced against my right thigh. It struck Benny on the right side, just under the rib cage, and drove upward through his stomach and broke inside him. He pitched forward and lay still. Gorrister lay on his back. I pulled another spear free and straddled him, still moving, driving the spear straight down through his throat. His eyes closed as the cold penetrated. Ellen must have realized what I had decided, even as fear gripped her. She ran at Nimdok with a short icicle, as he screamed, and into his mouth, and the force of her rush did the job. His head jerked sharply as if it had been nailed to the snow crust behind him.

All in an instant.

There was an eternity beat of soundless anticipation. I could hear AM draw in his breath. His toys had been taken from him. Three of them were dead, could not be revived. He could keep us alive, by his strength and talent, but he was *not* God. He could not bring them back.

Ellen looked at me, her ebony features stark against the snow that surrounded us. There was fear and pleading in her manner, the way she held herself ready. I knew we had only a heartbeat before AM would stop us.

It struck her and she folded toward me, bleeding from the mouth. I could not read meaning into her expression, the pain had been too great, had contorted her face; but it *might* have been thank you. It's possible. Please.

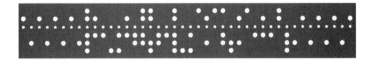

Some hundreds of years may have passed. I don't know. AM has been having fun for some time, accelerating and retarding my time sense. I will say the word now. Now. It took me ten months to say now. I don't know. I *think* it has been some hundreds of years.

He was furious. He wouldn't let me bury them. It didn't matter. There was no way to dig up the deckplates. He dried up the snow. He brought the night. He roared and sent locusts. It didn't do a thing; they stayed dead. I'd had him. He was furious. I had thought AM hated me before. I was wrong. It was not even a shadow of the hate he now slavered from every printed circuit. He made certain I would suffer eternally and could not do myself in.

He left my mind intact. I can dream, I can wonder, I can lament. I remember all four of them. I wish—

Well, it doesn't make any sense. I know I saved them, I know I saved them from what has happened to me, but still, I cannot forget killing them. Ellen's face. It isn't easy. Sometimes I want to, it doesn't matter.

AM has altered me for his own peace of mind, I suppose. He doesn't want me to run at full speed into a computer bank and smash my skull. Or hold my breath till I faint. Or cut my throat on a rusted sheet of metal. There are reflective surfaces down here. I will describe myself as I see myself:

I am a great soft jelly thing. Smoothly rounded, with no mouth, with pulsing white holes filled by fog where my eyes used to be. Rubbery appendages that were once my arms; bulks rounding down into legless humps of soft slippery matter. I leave a moist trail when I move. Blotches of diseased, evil gray come and go on my surface, as though light is being beamed from within.

Outwardly: dumbly, I shamble about, a thing that could never have been known as human, a thing whose shape is so alien a travesty that humanity becomes more obscene for the vague resemblance.

Inwardly: alone. Here. Living under the land, under the sea, in the belly of AM, whom we created because our time was badly spent and we must have known unconsciously that he could do it better. At least the four of them are safe at last.

AM will be all the madder for that. It makes me a little happier. And yet . . . AM has won, simply . . . he has taken his revenge . . .

I have no mouth. And I must scream.

1967

RICHARD MATHESON

(b. 1926)

Prey

AMELIA arrived at her apartment at six-fourteen. Hanging her coat in the hall closet, she carried the small package into the living room and sat on the sofa. She nudged off her shoes while she unwrapped the package on her lap. The wooden box resembled a casket. Amelia raised its lid and smiled. It was the ugliest doll she'd ever seen. Seven inches long and carved from wood, it had a skeletal body and an oversized head. Its expression was maniacally fierce, its pointed teeth completely bared, its glaring eyes protuberant. It clutched an eight-inch spear in its right hand. A length of fine, gold chain was wrapped around its body from the shoulders to the knees. A tiny scroll was wedged between the doll and the inside wall of its box. Amelia picked it up and unrolled it. There was handwriting on it. *This is He Who Kills*, it began. *He is a deadly hunter.* Amelia smiled as she read the rest of the words. Arthur would be pleased.

The thought of Arthur made her turn to look at the telephone on the table beside her. After a while, she sighed and set the wooden box on the sofa. Lifting the telephone to her lap, she picked up the receiver and dialed a number.

Her mother answered.

"Hello, Mom," Amelia said.

"Haven't you left yet?" her mother asked.

Amelia steeled herself. "Mom, I know it's Friday night—" she started.

She couldn't finish. There was silence on the line. Amelia closed her eyes. Mom, please, she thought. She swallowed. "There's this man," she said. "His name is Arthur Breslow. He's a high school teacher."

"You aren't coming," her mother said.

Amelia shivered. "It's his birthday," she said. She opened

her eyes and looked at the doll. "I sort of promised him we'd
. . . spend the evening together."

Her mother was silent. There aren't any good movies playing
tonight, anyway, Amelia's mind continued. "We could go to-
morrow night," she said.

Her mother was silent.

"Mom?"

"Now even Friday night's too much for you."

"Mom, I see you two, three nights a week."

"To *visit*," said her mother. "When you have your own room
here."

"Mom, *let's not start on that again*," Amelia said. I'm not a
child, she thought. Stop treating me as though I were a child!

"How long have you been seeing him?" her mother asked.

"A month or so."

"Without telling me," her mother said.

"I had every intention of telling you." Amelia's head was
starting to throb. I will *not* get a headache, she told herself.
She looked at the doll. It seemed to be glaring at her. "He's a
nice man, Mom," she said.

Her mother didn't speak. Amelia felt her stomach muscles
drawing taut. I won't be able to eat tonight, she thought.

She was conscious suddenly of huddling over the telephone.
She forced herself to sit erect. *I'm thirty-three years old*, she
thought. Reaching out, she lifted the doll from its box. "You
should see what I'm giving him for his birthday," she said. "I
found it in a curio shop on Third Avenue. It's a genuine Zuni
fetish doll, extremely rare. Arthur is a buff on anthropology.
That's why I got it for him."

There was silence on the line. All right, *don't talk*, Amelia
thought. "It's a hunting fetish," she continued, trying hard to
sound untroubled. "It's supposed to have the spirit of a Zuni
hunter trapped inside it. There's a golden chain around it to
prevent the spirit from—" She couldn't think of the word; ran
a shaking finger over the chain. "—escaping, I guess," she said.
"His name is He Who Kills. You should see his face." She felt
warm tears trickling down her cheeks.

"Have a good time," said her mother, hanging up.

Amelia stared at the receiver, listening to the dial tone. Why
is it always like this? she thought. She dropped the receiver

onto its cradle and set aside the telephone. The darkening room looked blurred to her. She stood the doll on the coffee-table edge and pushed to her feet. I'll take my bath now, she told herself. I'll meet him and we'll have a lovely time. She walked across the living room. A lovely time, her mind repeated emptily. She knew it wasn't possible. Oh, *Mom*! she thought. She clenched her fists in helpless fury as she went into the bedroom.

In the living room, the doll fell off the table edge. It landed head down and the spear point, sticking into the carpet, braced the doll's legs in the air.

The fine, gold chain began to slither downward.

It was almost dark when Amelia came back into the living room. She had taken off her clothes and was wearing her terry-cloth robe. In the bathroom, water was running into the tub.

She sat on the sofa and placed the telephone on her lap. For several minutes, she stared at it. At last, with a heavy sigh, she lifted the receiver and dialed a number.

"Arthur?" she said when he answered.

"Yes?" Amelia knew the tone—pleasant but suspecting. She couldn't speak.

"Your mother," Arthur finally said.

That cold, heavy sinking in her stomach. "It's our night together," she explained. "Every Friday—" She stopped and waited. Arthur didn't speak. "I've mentioned it before," she said.

"I know you've mentioned it," he said.

Amelia rubbed at her temple.

"She's still running your life, isn't she?" he said.

Amelia tensed. "I just don't want to hurt her feelings anymore," she said. "My moving out was hard enough on her."

"I don't want to hurt her feelings either," Arthur said. "But how many birthdays a year do I have? We *planned* on this."

"I know." She felt her stomach muscles tightening again.

"Are you really going to let her do this to you?" Arthur asked. "One Friday night out of the whole year?"

Amelia closed her eyes. Her lips moved soundlessly. I just can't hurt her feelings anymore, she thought. She swallowed. "She's my mother," she said.

"Very well," he said. "I'm sorry. I was looking forward to it, but—" He paused. "I'm sorry," he said. He hung up quietly.

Amelia sat in silence for a long time, listening to the dial tone. She started when the recorded voice said loudly, "Please hang up." Putting the receiver down, she replaced the telephone on its table. So much for my birthday present, she thought. It would be pointless to give it to Arthur now. She reached out, switching on the table lamp. She'd take the doll back tomorrow.

The doll was not on the coffee table. Looking down, Amelia saw the gold chain lying on the carpet. She eased off the sofa edge onto her knees and picked it up, dropping it into the wooden box. The doll was not beneath the coffee table. Bending over, Amelia felt around underneath the sofa.

She cried out, jerking back her hand. Straightening up, she turned to the lamp and looked at her hand. There was something wedged beneath the index fingernail. She shivered as she plucked it out. It was the head of the doll's spear. She dropped it into the box and put the finger in her mouth. Bending over again, she felt around more cautiously beneath the sofa.

She couldn't find the doll. Standing with a weary groan, she started pulling one end of the sofa from the wall. It was terribly heavy. She recalled the night that she and her mother had shopped for the furniture. She'd wanted to furnish the apartment in Danish modern. Mother had insisted on this heavy, maple sofa; it had been on sale. Amelia grunted as she dragged it from the wall. She was conscious of the water running in the bathroom. She'd better turn it off soon.

She looked at the section of carpet she'd cleared, catching sight of the spear shaft. The doll was not beside it. Amelia picked it up and set it on the coffee table. The doll was caught beneath the sofa, she decided; when she'd moved the sofa, she had moved the doll as well.

She thought she heard a sound behind her—fragile, skittering. Amelia turned. The sound had stopped. She felt a chill move up the backs of her legs. "It's He Who Kills," she said with a smile. "He's taken off his chain and gone—"

She broke off suddenly. There had definitely been a noise inside the kitchen; a metallic, rasping sound. Amelia swallowed nervously. What's going on? she thought. She walked across the living room and reached into the kitchen, switching on the light. She peered inside. Everything looked normal. Her gaze moved falteringly across the stove, the pan of water on it, the table and chair, the drawers and cabinet doors all shut, the electric clock, the small refrigerator with the cookbook lying on top of it, the picture on the wall, the knife rack fastened to the cabinet side—its small knife missing.

Amelia stared at the knife rack. Don't be silly, she told herself. She'd put the knife in the drawer, that's all. Stepping into the kitchen, she pulled out the silverware drawer. The knife was not inside it.

Another sound made her look down quickly at the floor. She gasped in shock. For several moments, she could not react; then, stepping to the doorway, she looked into the living room, her heartbeat thudding. Had it been imagination? She was sure she'd seen a movement.

"Oh, come on," she said. She made a disparaging sound. She hadn't seen a thing.

Across the room, the lamp went out.

Amelia jumped so startledly, she rammed her right elbow against the doorjamb. Crying out, she clutched the elbow with her left hand, eyes closed momentarily, her face a mask of pain.

She opened her eyes and looked into the darkened living room. "Come on," she told herself in aggravation. Three sounds plus a burned-out bulb did not add up to anything as idiotic as—

She willed away the thought. She had to turn the water off. Leaving the kitchen, she started for the hall. She rubbed her elbow, grimacing.

There was another sound. Amelia froze. Something was coming across the carpet toward her. She looked down dumbly. No, she thought.

She saw it then—a rapid movement near the floor. There was a glint of metal, instantly, a stabbing pain in her right calf. Amelia gasped. She kicked out blindly. Pain again. She felt warm blood running down her skin. She turned and lunged into the hall. The throw rug slipped beneath her and she fell against the wall, hot pain lancing through her right ankle. She clutched at the wall to keep from falling, then went sprawling on her side. She thrashed around with a sob of fear.

More movement, dark on dark. Pain in her left calf, then her right again. Amelia cried out. Something brushed along her thigh. She scrabbled back, then lurched up blindly, almost falling again. She fought for balance, reaching out convulsively. The heel of her left hand rammed against the wall, supporting her. She twisted around and rushed into the darkened bedroom. Slamming the door, she fell against it, panting. Something banged against it on the other side, something small and near the floor.

Amelia listened, trying not to breathe so loudly. She pulled carefully at the knob to make sure the latch had caught. When there were no further sounds outside the door, she backed toward the bed. She started as she bumped against the mattress edge. Slumping down, she grabbed at the extension phone and pulled it to her lap. Whom could she call? The police? They'd think her mad. Mother? She was too far off.

She was dialing Arthur's number by the light from the bathroom when the doorknob started turning. Suddenly, her fingers couldn't move. She stared across the darkened room. The door latch clicked. The telephone slipped off her lap. She heard it thudding onto the carpet as the door swung open. Something dropped from the outside knob.

Amelia jerked back, pulling up her legs. A shadowy form was scurrying across the carpet toward the bed. She gaped at it. It isn't true, she thought. She stiffened at the tugging on her bedspread. *It was climbing up to get her.* No, she thought; *it isn't true.* She couldn't move. She stared at the edge of the mattress.

Something that looked like a tiny head appeared. Amelia twisted around with a cry of shock, flung herself across the bed and jumped to the floor. Plunging into the bathroom, she spun around and slammed the door, gasping at the pain in her ankle. She had barely thumbed in the button on the doorknob when something banged against the bottom of the door. Amelia heard a noise like the scratching of a rat. Then it was still.

She turned and leaned across the tub. The level of the water was almost to the overflow drain. As she twisted shut the faucets, she saw drops of blood falling into the water. Straightening up, she turned to the medicine-cabinet mirror above the sink.

She caught her breath in horror as she saw the gash across her neck. She pressed a shaking hand against it. Abruptly, she became aware of pain in her legs and looked down. She'd been slashed along the calves of both legs. Blood was running down her ankles, dripping off the edges of her feet. Amelia started crying. Blood ran between the fingers of the hand against her neck. It trickled down her wrist. She looked at her reflection through a glaze of tears.

Something in her aroused her, a wretchedness, a look of terrified surrender. *No*, she thought. She reached out for the medicine-cabinet door. Opening it, she pulled out iodine, gauze and tape. She dropped the cover of the toilet seat and sank down gingerly. It was a struggle to remove the stopper of the iodine bottle. She had to rap it hard against the sink three times before it opened.

The burning of the antiseptic on her calves made her gasp. Amelia clenched her teeth as she wrapped gauze around her right leg.

A sound made her twist toward the door. She saw the knife blade being jabbed beneath it. It's trying to stab my feet, she thought; it thinks I'm standing there. She felt unreal to be considering its thoughts. *This is He Who Kills*, the scroll flashed suddenly across her mind. *He is a deadly hunter.* Amelia stared at the poking knife blade. God, she thought.

Hastily, she bandaged both her legs, then stood and, looking into the mirror, cleaned the blood from her neck with a wash-rag. She swabbed some iodine along the edges of the gash, hissing at the fiery pain.

She whirled at the new sound, heartbeat leaping. Stepping to the door, she leaned down, listening hard. There was a faint metallic noise inside the knob.

The doll was trying to unlock it.

Amelia backed off slowly, staring at the knob. She tried to visualize the doll. Was it hanging from the knob by one arm, using the other to probe inside the knob lock with the knife? The vision was insane. She felt an icy prickling on the back of her neck. *I mustn't let it in*, she thought.

A hoarse cry pulled her lips back as the doorknob button popped out. Reaching out impulsively, she dragged a bath towel off its rack. The doorknob turned, the latch clicked free. The door began to open.

Suddenly the doll came darting in. It moved so quickly that its figure blurred before Amelia's eyes. She swung the towel down hard, as though it were a huge bug rushing at her. The doll was knocked against the wall. Amelia heaved the towel on top of it and lurched across the floor, gasping at the pain in her ankle. Flinging open the door, she lunged into the bedroom.

She was almost to the hall door when her ankle gave. She pitched across the carpet with a cry of shock. There was a noise behind her. Twisting around, she saw the doll come through the bathroom doorway like a jumping spider. She saw the knife blade glinting in the light. Then the doll was in the shadows, coming at her fast. Amelia scrabbled back. She glanced over her shoulder, saw the closet and backed into its darkness, clawing for the doorknob.

Pain again, an icy slashing at her foot. Amelia screamed and heaved back. Reaching up, she yanked a topcoat down. It fell across the doll. She jerked down everything in reach. The doll was buried underneath a mound of blouses, skirts and dresses. Amelia pitched across the moving pile of clothes. She forced herself to stand and limped into the hall as quickly as she could. The sound of thrashing underneath the clothes faded from her hearing. She hobbled to the door. Unlocking it, she pulled the knob.

The door was held. Amelia reached up quickly to the bolt. It had been shot. She tried to pull it free. It wouldn't budge. She clawed at it with sudden terror. It was twisted out of shape. "No," she muttered. *She was trapped.* "Oh, God." She started pounding on the door. "Please help me! *Help* me!"

Sound in the bedroom. Amelia whirled and lurched across the living room. She dropped to her knees beside the sofa, feeling for the telephone, but her fingers trembled so much that she couldn't dial the numbers. She began to sob, then twisted around with a strangled cry. The doll was rushing at her from the hallway.

Amelia grabbed an ashtray from the coffee table and hurled it at the doll. She threw a vase, a wooden box, a figurine. She couldn't hit the doll. It reached her, started jabbing at her legs. Amelia reared up blindly and fell across the coffee table. Rolling to her knees, she stood again. She staggered toward the hall, shoving over furniture to stop the doll. She toppled a chair, a table. Picking up a lamp, she hurled it at the floor. She backed into the hall and, spinning, rushed into the closet, slammed the door shut.

She held the knob with rigid fingers. Waves of hot breath pulsed against her face. She cried out as the knife was jabbed beneath the door, its sharp point sticking into one of her toes. She shuffled back, shifting her grip on the knob. Her robe hung open. She could feel a trickle of blood between her breasts. Her legs felt numb with pain. She closed her eyes. Please, someone help, she thought.

She stiffened as the doorknob started turning in her grasp. Her flesh went cold. It couldn't be stronger than she: it *couldn't* be. Amelia tightened her grip. *Please,* she thought. The side of her head bumped against the front edge of her suitcase on the shelf.

The thought exploded in her mind. Holding the knob with her right hand, she reached up, fumbling, with her left. The suitcase clasps were open. With a sudden wrench, she turned the doorknob, shoving at the door as hard as possible. It rushed away from her. She heard it bang against the wall. The doll thumped down.

Amelia reached up, hauling down her suitcase. Yanking open the lid, she fell to knees in the closet doorway, holding the suitcase like an open book. She braced herself, eyes wide, teeth clenched together. She felt the doll's weight as it banged against the suitcase bottom. Instantly, she slammed the lid and threw the suitcase flat. Falling across it, she held it shut until her shaking hands could fasten the clasps. The sound of them clicking into place made her sob with relief. She shoved away the suitcase. It slid across the hall and bumped against the wall. Amelia struggled to her feet, trying not to listen to the frenzied kicking and scratching inside the suitcase.

She switched on the hall light and tried to open the bolt. It was hopelessly wedged. She turned and limped across the living room, glancing at her legs. The bandages were hanging loose. Both legs were streaked with caking blood, some of the gashes still bleeding. She felt at her throat. The cut was still wet. Amelia pressed her shaking lips together. She'd get to a doctor soon now.

Removing the ice pick from its kitchen drawer, she returned to the hall. A cutting sound made her look toward the suitcase. She caught her breath. The knife blade was protruding from the suitcase wall, moving up and down with a sawing motion. Amelia stared at it. She felt as though her body had been turned to stone.

She limped to the suitcase and knelt beside it, looking, with revulsion at the sawing blade. It was smeared with blood. She tried to pinch it with the fingers of her left hand, pull it out. The blade was twisted, jerked down, and she cried out, snatching back her hand. There was a deep slice in her thumb. Blood ran down across her palm. Amelia pressed the finger to her robe. She felt as though her mind was going blank.

Pushing to her feet, she limped back to the door and started prying at the bolt. She couldn't get it loose. Her thumb began to ache. She pushed the ice pick underneath the bolt socket and tried to force it off the wall. The ice pick point broke off. Amelia slipped and almost fell. She pushed up, whimpering. There was no time, no time. She looked around in desperation.

The window! She could throw the suitcase out! She visualized it tumbling through the darkness. Hastily, she dropped the ice pick, turning toward the suitcase.

She froze. The doll had forced its head and shoulders through the rent in the suitcase wall. Amelia watched it struggling to get out. She felt paralyzed. The twisting doll was staring at her. No, she thought, it isn't true. The doll jerked free its legs and jumped to the floor.

Amelia jerked around and ran into the living room. Her right foot landed on a shard of broken crockery. She felt it cutting deep into her heel and lost her balance. Landing on her side, she thrashed around. The doll came leaping at her. She could see the knife blade glint. She kicked out wildly, knocking back the doll. Lunging to her feet, she reeled into the kitchen, whirled, and started pushing shut the door.

Something kept it from closing. Amelia thought she heard a screaming in her mind. Looking down, she saw the knife and a tiny wooden hand. The doll's arm was wedged between the door and the jamb! Amelia shoved against the door with all her might, aghast at the strength with which the door was pushed the other way. There was a cracking noise. A fierce smile pulled her lips back and she pushed berserkly at the door. The screaming in her mind grew louder, drowning out the sound of splintering wood.

The knife blade sagged. Amelia dropped to her knees and tugged at it. She pulled the knife into the kitchen, seeing the wooden hand and wrist fall from the handle of the knife. With a gagging noise, she struggled to her feet and dropped the knife into the sink. The door slammed hard against her side; the doll rushed in.

Amelia jerked away from it. Picking up the chair, she slung it toward the doll. It jumped aside, then ran around the fallen chair. Amelia snatched the pan of water off the stove and hurled it down. The pan clanged loudly off the floor, spraying water on the doll.

She stared at the doll. It wasn't coming after her. It was trying to climb the sink, leaping up and clutching at the counter side with one hand. It wants the knife, she thought. It has to have its weapon.

She knew abruptly what to do. Stepping over to the stove, she pulled down the broiler door and twisted the knob on all the way. She heard the puffing detonation of the gas as she turned to grab the doll.

She cried out as the doll began to kick and twist, its maddened thrashing flinging her from one side of the kitchen to the other. The screaming filled her mind again and suddenly she knew it was the spirit in the doll that screamed. She slid and crashed against the table, wrenched herself around and, dropping to her knees before the stove, flung the doll inside. She slammed the door and fell against it.

The door was almost driven out. Amelia pressed her shoulder, then her back against it, turning to brace her legs against the wall. She tried to ignore the pounding scrabble of the doll inside the broiler. She watched the red blood pulsing from her heel. The smell of burning wood began to reach her and she closed her eyes. The door was getting hot. She shifted carefully. The kicking and pounding filled her ears. The screaming flooded through her mind. She knew her back would get burned, but she didn't dare to move. The smell of burning wood grew worse. Her foot ached terribly.

Amelia looked up at the electric clock on the wall. It was four minutes to seven. She watched the red second hand revolving slowly. A minute passed. The screaming in her mind was fading now. She shifted uncomfortably, gritting her teeth against the burning heat on her back.

Another minute passed. The kicking and the pounding stopped. The screaming faded more and more. The smell of burning wood had filled the kitchen. There was a pall of gray smoke in the air. That they'll see, Amelia thought. Now that it's over, they'll come and help. That's the way it always is.

She started to ease herself away from the broiler door, ready to throw her weight back against it if she had to. She turned around and got on her knees. The reek of charred wood made her nauseated. She had to know, though. Reaching out, she pulled down the door.

Something dark and stifling rushed across her and she heard the screaming in her mind once more as hotness flooded over her and into her. It was a scream of victory now.

Amelia stood and turned off the broiler. She took a pair of ice tongs from its drawer and lifted out the blackened twist of wood. She dropped it into the sink and ran water over it until the smoke had stopped. Then she went into the bedroom, picked up the telephone and depressed its cradle. After a moment, she released the cradle and dialed her mother's number.

"This is Amelia, Mom," she said. "I'm sorry I acted the way I did. I want us to spend the evening together. It's a little late, though. Can you come by my place and we'll go from here?" She listened. "Good," she said. "I'll wait for you."

Hanging up, she walked into the kitchen, where she slid the longest carving knife from its place in the rack. She went to the front door and pushed back its bolt, which now moved freely. She carried the knife into the living room, took off her bathrobe and danced a dance of hunting, of the joy of hunting, of the joy of the impending kill.

Then she sat down, cross-legged, in the corner. He Who Kills sat, cross-legged, in the corner, in the darkness, waiting for the prey to come.

1969

T.E.D. KLEIN
(b. 1947)

The Events at Poroth Farm

As soon as the phone stops ringing, I'll begin this affidavit. Lord, it's hot in here. Perhaps I should open a window. . . .

Thirteen rings. It has a sense of humor.

I suppose that ought to be comforting.

Somehow I'm not comforted. If it feels free to indulge in these teasing, tormenting little games, so much the worse for me.

The summer is over now, but this room is like an oven. My shirt is already drenched, and this pen feels slippery in my hand. In a moment or two the little drop of sweat that's collecting above my eyebrow is going to splash onto this page.

Just the same, I'll keep that window closed. Outside, through the dusty panes of glass, I can see a boy in red spectacles sauntering toward the courthouse steps. Perhaps there's a telephone booth in back. . . .

A sense of humor—that's one quality I never noticed in it. I saw only a deadly seriousness and, of course, an intelligence that grew at terrifying speed, malevolent and inhuman. If it now feels itself safe enough to toy with me before doing whatever it intends to do, so much the worse for me. So much the worse, perhaps, for us all.

I hope I'm wrong. Though my name is Jeremy, derived from Jeremiah, I'd hate to be a prophet in the wilderness. I'd much rather be a harmless crank.

But I believe we're in for trouble.

I'm a long way from the wilderness now, of course. Though perhaps not far enough to save me. . . . I'm writing this affidavit in room 2-K of the Union Hotel, overlooking Main Street in Flemington, New Jersey, twenty miles south of Gilead. Directly across the street, hippies lounging on its steps, stands the county courthouse where Bruno Hauptmann was tried back in 1935. (Did they ever find the body of that child?) Hauptmann undoubtedly walked down those very steps, now

lined with teenagers savoring their last week of summer vacation. Where that boy in the red spectacles sits sucking on his
cigarette—did the killer once halt there, police and reporters
around him, and contemplate his imminent execution?

For several days now I have been afraid to leave this room.

I have perhaps been staring too often at that ordinary-
looking boy on the steps. He sits there every day. The red
spectacles conceal his eyes; it's impossible to tell where he's
looking.

I know he's looking at me.

But it would be foolish of me to waste time worrying about
executions when I have these notes to transcribe. It won't take
long, and then, perhaps, I'll sneak outside to mail them—and
leave New Jersey forever. I remain, despite all that's happened,
an optimist. What was it my namesake said? "Thou art my
hope in the day of evil."

There *is*, surprisingly, some real wilderness left in New Jersey, assuming one wants to be a prophet. The hills to the west,
spreading from the southern swamplands to the Delaware and
beyond to Pennsylvania, provide shelter for deer, pheasant,
even an occasional bear—and hide hamlets never visited by outsiders: pockets of ignorance, some of them, citadels of ancient
superstition utterly cut off from news of New York and the rest
of the state, religious communities where customs haven't
changed appreciably since the days of their settlement a century or more ago.

It seems incredible that villages so isolated can exist today
on the very doorstep of the world's largest metropolis—
villages with nothing to offer the outsider, and hence never
visited, except by the occasional hunter who stumbles on them
unwittingly. Yet as you speed down one of the state highways,
consider how few of the cars slow down for the local roads. It
is easy to pass the little towns without even a glance at the
signs; and if there are no signs . . . ? And consider, too, how
seldom the local traffic turns off onto the narrow roads that
emerge without warning from the woods. And when those untraveled side roads lead into others still deeper in wilderness;
and when those in turn give way to dirt roads, deserted for
weeks on end. . . . It is not hard to see how tiny rural com-

munities can exist less than an hour from major cities, virtually unaware of one another's existence.

Television, of course, will link the two—unless, as is often the case, the elders of the community choose to see this distraction as the Devil's tool and proscribe it. Telephones put these outcast settlements in touch with their neighbors—unless they choose to ignore their neighbors. And so in the course of years they are . . . forgotten.

New Yorkers were amazed when in the winter of 1968 the *Times* "discovered" a religious community near New Providence that had existed in its present form since the late 1800s —less than forty miles from Times Square. Agricultural work was performed entirely by hand, women still wore long dresses with high collars, and town worship was held every evening.

I, too, was amazed. I'd seldom traveled west of the Hudson and still thought of New Jersey as some dismal extension of the Newark slums, ruled by gangsters, foggy with swamp gases and industrial waste, a gray land that had surrendered to the city.

Only later did I learn of the rural New Jersey, and of towns whose solitary general stores double as post offices, with one or two gas pumps standing in front. And later still I learned of Baptistown and Quakertown, their old religions surviving unchanged, and of towns like Lebanon, Landsdown, and West Portal, close to Route 22 and civilization but heavy with secrets city folk never dreamed of; Mt. Airy, with its network of hidden caverns, and Mt. Olive, bordering the infamous Budd Lake; Middle Valley, sheltered by dark cliffs, subject of the recent archaeological debate chronicled in *Natural History*, where the wanderer may still find grotesque relics of pagan worship and, some say, may still hear the chants that echo from the cliffs on certain nights; and towns with names like Zaraphath and Gilead, forgotten communities of bearded men and black-robed women, walled hamlets too small or obscure for most maps of the state. This was the wilderness into which I traveled, weary of Manhattan's interminable din; and it was outside Gilead where, until the tragedies, I chose to make my home for three months.

Among the silliest of literary conventions is the "town that won't talk"—the Bavarian village where peasants turn away from tourists' queries about "the castle" and silently cross themselves, the New England harbor town where fishermen feign ignorance and cast "furtive glances" at the traveler. In actuality, I have found, country people love to talk to the stranger, provided he shows a sincere interest in their anecdotes. Storekeepers will interrupt their activity at the cash register to tell you their theories on a recent murder; farmers will readily spin tales of buried bones and of a haunted house down the road. Rural townspeople are not so reticent as the writers would have us believe.

Gilead, isolated though it is behind its oak forests and ruined walls, is no exception. The inhabitants regard all outsiders with an initial suspicion, but let one demonstrate a respect for their traditional reserve and they will prove friendly enough. They don't favor modern fashions or flashy automobiles, but they can hardly be described as hostile, although that was my original impression.

When asked about the terrible events at Poroth Farm, they will prove more than willing to talk. They will tell you of bad crops and polluted well water, of emotional depression leading to a fatal argument. In short, they will describe a conventional rural murder, and will even volunteer their opinions on the killer's present whereabouts.

But you will learn almost nothing from them—or almost nothing that is true. They don't know what really happened. I do. I was there.

I had come to spend the summer with Sarr Poroth and his wife. I needed a place where I could do a lot of reading without distraction, and Poroth's farm, secluded as it was even from the village of Gilead six miles down the dirt road, appeared the perfect spot for my studies.

I had seen the Poroths' advertisement in the *Hunterdon County Democrat* on a trip west through Princeton last spring. They advertised for a summer or long-term tenant to live in one of the outbuildings behind the farmhouse. As I soon learned, the building was a long low cinder-block affair, unpleasantly suggestive of army barracks but clean, new, and cool in the sun; by the start of summer ivy sprouted from the walls and disguised the ugly gray brick. Originally intended to house chickens, it had in fact remained empty for several years until the farm's original owner, a Mr. Baber, sold out last fall to the Poroths, who immediately saw that with the installation of dividing walls, linoleum floors, and other improvements the building might serve as a source of income. I was to be their first tenant.

The Poroths, Sarr and Deborah, were in their early thirties, only slightly older than I, although anyone who met them might have believed the age difference to be greater; their relative solemnity and the drabness of their clothing added years to their appearance, and so did their hair styles: Deborah, though possessing a beautiful length of black hair, wound it all in a tight bun behind her neck, pulling the hair back from her face with a severity which looked almost painful, and Sarr maintained a thin fringe of black beard that circled from ears to chin in the manner of the Pennsylvania Dutch, who leave their hair shaggy but refuse to grow moustaches lest they resemble the military class they've traditionally despised. Both man and wife were hard-working, grave of expression, and pale despite the time spent laboring in the sun—a pallor accentuated by the inky blackness of their hair. I imagine this unhealthy aspect was due, in part, to the considerable amount of inbreeding that went on in the area, the Poroths themselves being, I believe, third cousins. On first meeting, one might have taken them for brother and sister, two gravely devout children aged in the wilderness.

And yet there was a difference between them—and, too, a difference that set them both in contrast to others of their sect. The Poroths were, as far as I could determine, members of a tiny Mennonitic order outwardly related to the Amish, though doctrinal differences were apparently rather profound. It was this order that made up the large part of the community known as Gilead.

I sometimes think the only reason they allowed an infidel like me to live on their property (for my religion was among the first things they inquired about) was because of my name; Sarr was very partial to Jeremiah, and the motto of his order was, "Stand ye in the ways, and see, and ask for the old paths, where is the good way, and walk therein." (VI:16)

Having been raised in no particular religion except a universal skepticism, I began the summer with a hesitancy to bring up the topic in conversation, and so I learned comparatively little about the Poroths' beliefs. Only toward the end of my stay did I begin to thumb through the Bible in odd moments and take to quoting jeremiads. That was, I suppose, Sarr's influence.

I was able to learn, nonetheless, that for all their conservative aura the Poroths were considered, in effect, young liberals by most of Gilead. Sarr had a bachelor's degree in religious studies from Rutgers, and Deborah had attended a nearby community college for two years, unusual for women of the sect. Too, they had only recently taken to farming, having spent the first year of their marriage near New Brunswick, where Sarr had hoped to find a teaching position and, when the job situation proved hopeless, had worked as a sort of handyman/carpenter. While most inhabitants of Gilead had never left the farm, the Poroths were coming to it late—their families had been merchants for several generations—and so were relatively inexperienced.

The inexperience showed. The farm comprised some ninety acres, but most of that was forest, or fields of weeds too thick and high to walk through. Across the backyard, close to my rooms, ran a small, nameless stream nearly choked with green scum. A large cornfield to the north lay fallow, but Sarr was planning to seed it this year, using borrowed equipment. His wife spent much of her time indoors, for though she maintained a small vegetable garden, she preferred keeping house and looking after the Poroths' great love, their seven cats.

As if to symbolize their broad-mindedness, the Poroths owned a television set, very rare in Gilead; in light of what was to come, however, it is unfortunate they lacked a telephone. (Apparently the set had been received as a wedding present from Deborah's parents, but the monthly expense of a telephone was simply too great.) Otherwise, though, the little farmhouse was "modern" in that it had a working bathroom and gas heat. That they had advertised in the local newspaper was considered scandalous by some of the order's more orthodox members, and indeed a mere subscription to that innocuous weekly had at one time been regarded as a breach of religious conduct.

Though outwardly similar, both of them tall and pale, the Poroths were actually so different as to embody the maxim

that "opposites attract." It was that carefully nurtured reserve
that deceived one at first meeting, for in truth Deborah was far
more talkative, friendly, and energetic than her husband. Sarr
was moody, distant, silent most of the time, with a voice so low
that one had trouble following him in conversation. Sitting as
stonily as one of his cats, never moving, never speaking, perennially inscrutable, he tended to frighten visitors to the farm
until they learned that he was not really sitting in judgment on
them; his reserve was not born of surliness but of shyness.

Where Sarr was catlike, his wife hid beneath the formality of
her order the bubbly personality of a kitten. Given the smallest
encouragement—say, a family visit—she would plunge into
animated conversation, gesticulating, laughing easily, hugging
whatever cat was nearby or shouting to guests across the room.
When drinking—for both of them enjoyed liquor and, curiously, it was not forbidden by their faith—their innate differences were magnified: Deborah would forget the restraints
placed upon women in the order and would eventually dominate the conversation, while her husband would seem to grow
increasingly withdrawn and morose.

Women in the region tended to be submissive to the men,
and certainly the important decisions in the Poroths' lives were
made by Sarr. Yet I really cannot say who was the stronger of
the two. Only once did I ever see them quarrel. . . .

Perhaps the best way to tell it is by setting down portions of
the journal I kept this summer. Not every entry, of course.
Mere excerpts. Just enough to make this affidavit comprehensible to anyone unfamiliar with the incidents at Poroth Farm.

The journal was the only writing I did all summer; my primary reason for keeping it was to record the books I'd read
each day, as well as to examine my reactions to relative solitude
over a long period of time. All the rest of my energies (as you
will no doubt gather from the notes below) were spent reading,
in preparation for a course I plan to teach at Trenton State this
fall. Or *planned*, I should say, because I don't expect to be
anywhere around here come fall.

Where will I be? Perhaps that depends on what's beneath
those rose-tinted spectacles.

The course was to cover the Gothic tradition from Shakespeare to Faulkner, from *Hamlet* to *Absalom, Absalom!* (And

why not view the former as Gothic, with its ghost on the battlements and concern for lost inheritance?) To make the move
to Gilead, I'd rented a car for a few days and had stuffed it full
of books—only a few of which I ever got to read. But then, I
couldn't have known. . . .

How pleasant things were, at the beginning.

June 4

Unpacking day. Spent all morning putting up screens, and a
good thing I did. Night now, and a million moths tapping at
the windows. One of them as big as a small bird—white—
largest I've ever seen. What kind of caterpillar must it have
been? I hope the damned things don't push through the
screens.

Had to kill literally hundreds of spiders before moving my
stuff in. The Poroths finished doing the inside of this building
only a couple of months ago, and already it's infested. Arach-
nidae—hate the bastards. Why? We'll take that one up with
Sigmund someday. Daydreams of Revenge of the Spiders.
Writhing body covered with a frenzy of hairy brown legs.
"Egad, man, that face! That bloody, torn face! And the missing
eyes! It looks like—no! Jeremy!" Killing spiders is supposed to
bring bad luck. (Insidious Sierra Club propaganda masquerading as folk myth?) But can't sleep if there's anything crawling
around . . . so what the hell?

Supper with the Poroths. Began to eat, then heard Sarr saying
grace. Apologies—but things like that don't embarrass me as
much as they used to. (Is that because I'm nearing thirty?)

Chatted about crops, insects, humidity. (Very damp area—
band of purplish mildew already around bottom of walls out
here.) Sarr told of plans to someday build a larger house when
Deborah has a baby, three or four years from now. He wants to
build it out of stone. Then he shut up, and I had to keep the
conversation going. (Hate eating in silence—animal sounds of
mastication, bubbling stomachs.) Deborah joked about cats
being her surrogate children. All seven of them hanging around
my legs, rubbing against ankles. My nose began running and
my eyes itched. Goddamned allergy. Must remember to start
treatments this fall, when I get to Trenton. Deborah sympathetic, Sarr merely watching; she told me my eyes were blood-

shot, offered antihistamine. Told them I was glad they at least believe in modern medicine—I'd been afraid she'd offer herbs or mud or something. Sarr said some of the locals still use "snake oil." Asked him how snakes were killed, quoting line from *Vathek*: "The oil of the serpents I have pinched to death will be a pretty present." We discussed wisdom of pinching snakes. Apparently there's a copperhead out back, near the brook. . . .

The meal was good—lamb and noodles. Not bad for fifteen dollars a week, since I detest cooking. Spice cake for dessert, home-made, of course. Deborah is a good cook. Handsome woman, too.

Still light when I left their kitchen. Fireflies already on the lawn—I've never seen so many. Knelt and watched them a while, listening to the crickets. Think I'll like it here.

Took nearly an hour to arrange my books the way I wanted them. Alphabetical order by authors? No, chronological. . . . But anthologies mess that system up, so back to authors. Why am I so neurotic about my books?

Anyway, they look nice there on the shelves.

Sat up tonight finishing *The Mysteries of Udolpho*. Figure it's best to get the long ones out of the way first. Radcliffe's unfortunate penchant for explaining away all her ghosts and apparitions really a mistake and a bore. All in all, not exactly the most fascinating reading, though a good study in Romanticism. Montoni the typical Byronic hero/villain. But can't demand students read *Udolpho*—too long. In fact, had to keep reminding myself to slow down, have patience with the book. Tried to put myself in frame of mind of 1794 reader with plenty of time on his hands. It works, too—I do have plenty of time out here, and already I can feel myself beginning to unwind. What New York does to people. . . .

It's almost two A.M. now, and I'm about ready to turn in. Too bad there's no bathroom in this building—I hate pissing outside at night. God knows what's crawling up your ankles. . . . But it's hardly worth stumbling through the darkness to the farmhouse, and maybe waking up Sarr and Deborah. The nights out here are really pitch-black.

. . . Felt vulnerable, standing there against the night. But what made me even uneasier was the view I got of this building.

The lamp on the desk casts the only light for miles, and as I stood outside looking into this room, I could see dozens of flying shapes making right for the screens. When you're inside here it's as if you're in a display case—the whole night can see you, but all you can see is darkness. I wish this room didn't have windows on three of the walls—though that does let in the breeze. And I wish the woods weren't so close to my windows by the bed. I suppose privacy is what I wanted—but feel a little unprotected out here.

Those moths are still batting themselves against the screens, but as far as I can see the only things that have gotten in are a few gnats flying around this lamp. The crickets sound good—you sure don't hear them in the city. Frogs are croaking in the brook.

My nose is only now beginning to clear up. Those god-damned cats. Must remember to buy some Contac. Even though the cats are all outside during the day, that farmhouse is full of their scent. But I don't expect to be spending that much time inside the house anyway; this allergy will keep me away from the TV and out here with the books.

Just saw an unpleasantly large spider scurry across the floor near the foot of my bed. Vanished behind the footlocker. Must remember to buy some insect spray tomorrow.

June 11

Hot today, but at night comes a chill. The dampness of this place seems to magnify temperature. Sat outside most of the day finishing the Maturin book, *Melmoth the Wanderer*, and feeling vaguely guilty each time I heard Sarr or Deborah working out there in the field. Well, I've paid for my reading time, so I guess I'm entitled to enjoy it. Though some of these old Gothics are a bit hard to enjoy. The trouble with *Melmoth* is that it wants you to hate. You're especially supposed to hate the Catholics. No doubt its picture of the Inquisition is accurate, but all a book like this can do is put you in an unconstructive rage. Those vicious characters have been dead for centuries, and there's no way to punish them. Still, it's a nice, cynical book for those who like atrocity scenes—starving prisoners forced to eat their girlfriends, delightful things like that.

And narratives within narratives within narratives within narratives. I may assign some sections to my class. . . .

Just before dinner, in need of a break, read a story by Arthur Machen. Welsh writer, turn of the century, though think the story's set somewhere in England: old house in the hills, dark woods with secret paths and hidden streams. God, what an experience! I was a little confused by the framing device and all its high-flown talk of "cosmic evil," but the sections from the young girl's notebook were . . . staggering. That air of paganism, the malevolent little faces peeping from the shadows, and those rites she can't dare talk about. . . . It's called "The White People," and it must be the most persuasive horror tale ever written.

Afterward, strolling toward the house, I was moved to climb the old tree in the side yard—the Poroths had already gone in to get dinner ready—and stood upright on a great heavy branch near the middle, making strange gestures and faces that no one could see. Can't say exactly what it was I did, or why. It was getting dark—fireflies below me and a mist rising off the field. I must have looked like a madman's shadow as I made signs to the woods and the moon.

Lamb tonight, and damned good. I may find myself getting fat. Offered, again, to wash the dishes, but apparently Deborah feels that's her role, and I don't care to dissuade her. So talked a while with Sarr about his cats—the usual subject of conversation, especially because, now that summer's coming, they're bringing in dead things every night. Field mice, moles, shrews, birds, even a little garter snake. They don't eat them, just lay them out on the porch for the Poroths to see—sort of an offering, I guess. Sarr tosses the bodies in the garbage can, which, as a result, smells indescribably foul. Deborah wants to put bells around their necks; she hates mice but feels sorry for the birds. When she finished the dishes, she and Sarr sat down to watch one of their godawful TV programs, so I came out here to read.

Spent the usual ten minutes going over this room, spray can in hand, looking for spiders to kill. Found a couple of little ones, then spent some time spraying bugs that were hanging on the screens hoping to get in. Watched a lot of daddy longlegs curl up and die. . . . Tended not to kill the moths, unless they were making too much of a racket banging against the screen; I can tolerate them okay, but it's only fireflies I really like. I always feel a little sorry when I kill one by mistake and see it hold that cold glow too long. (That's how you know they're dead: the dead ones don't wink. They just keep their light on till it fades away.)

The insecticide I'm using is made right here in New Jersey, by the Ortho Chemical Company. The label on the can says, "WARNING. For Outdoor Use Only." That's why I bought it —figured it's the most powerful brand available.

Sat in bed reading Algernon Blackwood's witch/cat story, "Ancient Sorceries" (nowhere near as good as Machen, or as his own tale "The Willows"), and it made me think of those seven cats. The Poroths have around a dozen names for each one of them, which seems a little ridiculous since the creatures barely respond to even one name. Sasha, for example, the orange one, is also known as Butch, which comes from Bouche, mouth. And that's short for Eddie La Bouche, so he's also called Ed or Eddie—which in turn come from some friend's mispronunciation of the cat's original name, Itty, short for Itty Bitty Kitty, which, apparently, he once was. And Zoë, the cutest of the kittens, is also called Bozo and Bisbo. Let's see, how many others can I remember? (I'm just learning to tell some of them apart.) Felix, or "Flixie," was originally called Paleface, and Phaedra, his mother, is sometimes known as Phuddy, short for Phuddy Duddy.

Come to think of it, the only cat that hasn't got multiple names is Bwada, Sarr's cat. (All the others were acquired after he married Deborah, but Bwada was his pet years before.) She's the oldest of the cats, and the meanest. Fat and sleek, with fine gray fur darker than silver gray, lighter than charcoal. She's the only cat that's ever bitten anyone—Deborah, as well as friends of the Poroths—and after seeing the way she snarls at the other cats when they get in her way, I decided to keep my distance. Fortunately she's scared of me and retreats whenever I approach. I think being spayed is what's messed her up and given her an evil disposition.

Sounds are drifting from the farmhouse. I can vaguely make out a psalm of some kind. It's late, past eleven, and I guess the

Poroths have turned off the TV and are singing their evening devotions. . . .

And now all is silence. They've gone to bed. I'm not very tired yet, so I guess I'll stay up a while and read some—

Something odd just happened. I've never heard anything like it. While writing for the past half hour I've been aware, if half-consciously, of the crickets. Their regular chirping can be pretty soothing, like the sound of a well-tuned machine. But just a few seconds ago they seemed to miss a beat. They'd been singing along steadily, ever since the moon came up, and all of a sudden they just *stopped* for a beat—and then they began again, only they were out of rhythm for a moment or two, as if a hand had jarred the record or there'd been some kind of momentary break in the natural flow. . . .

They sound normal enough now, though. Think I'll go back to *Otranto* and let that put me to sleep. It may be the foundation of the English Gothics, but I can't imagine anyone actually reading it for pleasure. I wonder how many pages I'll be able to get through before I drop off. . . .

June 12

Slept late this morning, and then, disinclined to read Walpole on such a sunny day, took a walk. Followed the little brook that runs past my building. There's still a lot of that greenish scum clogging one part of it, and if we don't have some rain soon I expect it will get worse. But the water clears up considerably when it runs past the cornfield and through the woods.

Passed Sarr out in the field—he yelled to watch out for the copperhead, which put a pall on my enthusiasm for exploration. . . . But as it happened I never ran into any snakes, and have a fair idea I'd survive even if bitten. Walked around half a mile into the woods, branches snapping in my face. Made an effort to avoid walking into the little yellow caterpillars that hang from every tree. At one point I had to get my feet wet, because the trail that runs alongside the brook disappeared and the undergrowth was thick. Ducked under a low arch made by decaying branches and vines, my sneakers sloshing in the water. Found that as the brook runs west it forms a small circular pool with banks of wet sand, surrounded by tall oaks, their roots thrust into the water. Lots of animal tracks in the sand—deer, I believe, and what may be a fox or perhaps some farmer's dog. Obviously a watering place. Waded into the center of the pool—it only came up a little past my ankles—but didn't stand there long because it started looking like rain.

The weather remained nasty all day, but no rain has come yet. Cloudy now, though; can't see any stars.

Finished *Otranto*, began *The Monk*. So far so good—rather dirty, really. Not for today, of course, but I can imagine the sensation it must have caused back at the end of the eighteenth century.

Had a good time at dinner tonight, since Sarr had walked into town and brought back some wine. (Medical note: I seem to be less allergic to cats when mildly intoxicated.) We sat around the kitchen afterward playing poker for matchsticks— very sinful indulgence, I understand; Sarr and Deborah told me, quite seriously, that they'd have to say some extra prayers tonight by way of apology to the Lord.

Theological considerations aside, though, we all had a good time, and Deborah managed to clean us both out. Women's intuition, she says. I'm sure she must have it—she's the type. Enjoy being around her, and not always so happy to trek back outside, through the high grass, the night dew, the things in the soil. . . . I've got to remember, though, that they're a couple, I'm the single one, and I mustn't intrude too long. So left them tonight at eleven—or actually a little after that, since their clock is slightly out of kilter. They have this huge grandfather-type clock, a wedding present from Sarr's parents, that has supposedly been keeping perfect time for a century or more. You can hear its ticking all over the house when everything else is still. Deborah said that last night, just as they were going to bed, the clock seemed to slow down a little, then gave a couple of faster beats and started in as before. Sarr, who's pretty good with mechanical things, examined it, but said he saw nothing wrong. Well, I guess everything's got to wear out a bit, after years and years.

Back to *The Monk*. May Brother Ambrosio bring me pleasant dreams.

June 13

Read a little in the morning, loafed during the afternoon. At four thirty watched *The Thief of Baghdad*—ruined on TV and portions omitted, but still a great film. Deborah puttered around the kitchen, and Sarr spent most of the day outside. Before dinner I went out back with a scissors and cut away a lot of ivy that has tried to grow through the windows of my building. The little shoots fasten onto the screens and really cling.

Beef with rice tonight, and apple pie for dessert. Great. I stayed inside the house after dinner to watch the late news with the Poroths. The announcer mentioned that today was Friday the thirteenth, and I nearly gasped. I'd known, on some dim automatic level, that it was the thirteenth, if only from keeping this journal; but I hadn't had the faintest idea it was Friday. That's how much I've lost track of time out here; day drifts into day, and every one but Sunday seems completely interchangeable. Not a bad feeling, really, though at certain moments this isolation makes me feel somewhat adrift. I'd been so used to living by the clock and the calendar. . . .

We tried to figure out if anything unlucky happened to any of us today. About the only incident we could come up with was Sarr's getting bitten by some animal a cat had left on the porch. The cats had been sitting by the front door waiting to be let in for their dinner, and when Sarr came in from the field he was greeted with the usual assortment of dead mice and moles. As he always did, he began gingerly picking the bodies up by the tails and tossing them into the garbage can, meanwhile scolding the cats for being such natural-born killers. There was one body, he told us, that looked different from the others he'd seen: rather like a large shrew, only the mouth was somehow askew, almost as if it were vertical instead of horizontal, with a row of little yellow teeth exposed. He figured that, whatever it was, the cats had pretty well mauled it, which probably accounted for its unusual appearance; it was quite tattered and bloody by this time.

In any case, he'd bent down to pick it up, and the thing had bitten him on the thumb. Apparently it had just been feigning death, like an opossum, because as soon as he yelled and dropped it the thing sped off into the grass, with Bwada and the rest in hot pursuit. Deborah had been afraid of rabies—always a real danger around here, rare though it is—but apparently the bite hadn't even pierced the skin. Just a nip, really. Hardly a Friday-the-thirteenth tragedy.

Lying in bed now, listening to sounds in the woods. The trees come really close to my windows on one side, and there's always some kind of sound coming from the underbrush in addition to the tapping at the screens. A millions creatures out there, after all—most of them insects and spiders, a colony of frogs in the swampy part of the woods, and perhaps even skunks and raccoons. Depending on your mood, you can either ignore the sounds and just go to sleep or—as I'm doing now—remain awake listening to them. When I lie here thinking about what's out there, I feel more protected with the light off. So I guess I'll put away this writing. . . .

June 15

Something really weird happened today. I still keep trying to figure it out.

Sarr and Deborah were gone almost all day; Sunday worship is, I guess, the center of their religious activity. They walked into Gilead early in the morning and didn't return until after four. They'd left, in fact, before I woke up. Last night they'd asked me if I'd like to come along, but I got the impression they'd invited me mainly to be polite, so I declined. I wouldn't want to make them uncomfortable during their services, but perhaps someday I'll accompany them anyway, since I'm curious to see a fundamentalist church in action.

In any case, I was left to share the farm with the Poroths' seven cats and the four hens they'd bought last week. From my window I could see Bwada and Phaedra chasing after something near the barn; lately they've taken to stalking grasshoppers. As I do every morning, I went into the farmhouse kitchen and made myself some breakfast, leafing through one of the Poroths' religious magazines, and then returned to my rooms out back for some serious reading. I picked up *Dracula* again, which I'd started yesterday, but the soppy Victorian sentimentality began to annoy me; the book had begun so well, on such a frightening note—Jonathan Harker trapped in that

Carpathian castle, inevitably the prey of its terrible owner—that when Stoker switched the locale to England and his main characters to women, he simply couldn't sustain that initial tension.

With the Poroths gone I felt a little lonely and bored, something I hadn't felt out here yet. Though I'd brought cartons of books to entertain me, I felt restless and wished I owned a car; I'd have gone for a drive, perhaps visited friends at Princeton. As things stood, though, I had nothing to do except watch television or take a walk.

I followed the stream again into the woods and eventually came to the circular pool. There were some new animal tracks in the wet sand, and, ringed by oaks, the place was very beautiful, but still I felt bored. Again I waded to the center of the water and looked up at the sky through the trees. Feeling myself alone, I began to make some of the odd signs with face and hands that I had that evening in the tree—but I felt that these movements had been unaccountably robbed of their power. Standing there up to my ankles in water, I felt foolish.

Worse than that, upon leaving it I found a red-brown leech clinging to my right ankle. It wasn't large and I was able to scrape it off with a stone, but it left me with a little round bite that oozed blood, and a feeling of—how shall I put it?—physical helplessness. I felt that the woods had somehow become hostile to me and, more important, would forever remain hostile. Something had passed.

I followed the stream back to the farm, and there I found Bwada, lying on her side near some rocks along its bank. Her legs were stretched out as if she were running, and her eyes were wide and astonished-looking. Flies were crawling over them.

She couldn't have been dead for long, since I'd seen her only a few hours before, but she was already stiff. There was foam around her jaws. I couldn't tell what had happened to her until I turned her over with a stick and saw, on the side that had lain against the ground, a gaping red hole that opened like some new orifice. The skin around it was folded back in little triangular flaps, exposing the pink flesh beneath. I backed off in disgust, but I could see even from several feet away that the hole had been made *from the inside.*

I can't say that I was very upset at Bwada's death, because I'd always hated her. What did upset me, though, was the manner of it—I can't figure out what could have done that to her. I vaguely remember reading about a kind of slug that, when eaten by a bird, will bore its way out through the bird's stomach. . . . But I'd never heard of something like this happening with a cat. And far stranger than that, how could—

Well, anyway, I saw the body and thought, Good riddance. But I didn't know what to do with it. Looking back, of course, I wish I'd buried it right there. . . . But I didn't want to go near it again. I considered walking into town and trying to find the Poroths, because I knew their cats were like children to them, even Bwada, and that they'd want to know right away. But I really didn't feel like running around Gilead asking strange people where the Poroths were—or, worse yet, stumbling into their forbidding-looking church in the middle of a ceremony.

Finally I made up my mind to simply leave the body there and pretend I'd never seen it. Let Sarr discover it himself. I didn't want to have to tell him when he got home that his pet had been killed; I prefer to avoid unpleasantness. Besides, I felt strangely guilty, the way one often does after someone else's misfortune.

So I spent the rest of the afternoon reading in my room, slogging through the Stoker. I wasn't in the best mood to concentrate. Sarr and Deborah got back after four—they shouted hello and went into the house. When Deborah called me for dinner, they still hadn't come outside.

All the cats except Bwada were inside having their evening meal when I entered the kitchen, and Sarr asked me if I'd seen her during the day. I lied and said I hadn't. Deborah suggested that occasionally Bwada ignored the supper call because, unlike the other cats, she sometimes ate what she killed and might simply be full. That rattled me a bit, but I had to stick to my lie.

Sarr seemed more concerned than Deborah, and when he told her he intended to search for the cat after dinner (it would still be light), I readily offered my help. I figured I could lead him to the spot where the body lay. . . .

And then, in the middle of our dinner, came that scratching at the door. Sarr got up and opened it. Bwada walked in.

Now, I know she was dead. She was *stiff* dead. That wound in her side had been huge, and now it was only . . . a reddish swelling. Hairless. Luckily the Poroths didn't notice my shock; they were busy fussing over her, seeing what was wrong. "Look, she's hurt herself," said Deborah. "She's bumped into something." The animal didn't walk well, and there was a clumsiness in the way she held herself. When Sarr put her down after examining the swelling, she slipped when she tried to walk away.

The Poroths concluded that she had run into a rock or some other object and had badly bruised herself; they believe her lack of coordination is due to the shock, or perhaps to a pinching of the nerves. That sounds logical enough. Sarr told me before I came out here for the night that if she's worse tomorrow, he'll take her to the local vet, even though he'll have trouble paying for treatment. I immediately offered to lend him money, or even pay for the visit myself, because I desperately want to hear a doctor's opinion.

My own conclusion is really not that different from Sarr's. I tend to think now that maybe, just maybe, I was wrong in thinking the cat dead. Maybe what I mistook for rigor mortis was some kind of fit—after all, I know almost nothing about medicine. Maybe she really did run into something sharp and then went into some kind of shock . . . whose effect hasn't yet worn off. Is this possible?

But I could swear that hole came from inside her.

I couldn't continue dinner and told the Poroths my stomach hurt, which was partly true. We all watched Bwada stumble around the kitchen floor, ignoring the food Deborah put before her as if it weren't there. Her movements were stiff, tentative, like a newborn animal still unsure how to move its muscles. I guess that's the result of her fit.

When I left the house tonight, a little while ago, she was huddled in the corner staring at me. Deborah was crooning over her, but the cat was staring at me.

Killed a monster of a spider behind my suitcase tonight. That Ortho spray really does a job. When Sarr was in here a few days ago he said the room smelled of spray, but I guess my allergy's too bad for me to smell it.

I enjoy watching the zoo outside my screens. Put my face close and stare the bugs eye to eye. Zap the ones whose faces I don't like with my spray can.

Tried to read more of the Stoker—but one thing keeps bothering me. The way that cat stared at me. Deborah was brushing its back, Sarr fiddling with his pipe, and that cat just stared at me and never blinked. I stared back, said, "Hey, Sarr? Look at Bwada. That damned cat's not blinking." And just as he looked up, it blinked. Heavily.

Hope we can go to the vet tomorrow, because I want to ask him whether cats can impale themselves on a rock or a stick, and if such an accident might cause a fit of some kind that would make them rigid.

Cold night. Sheets are damp and the blanket itches. Wind from the woods—ought to feel good in the summer, but it doesn't feel like summer. That damned cat didn't blink till I mentioned it. Almost as if it understood me.

June 17

. . . Swelling on her side's all healed now. Hair growing back over it. She walks fine, has a great appetite, shows affection to the Poroths. Sarr says her recovery demonstrates how the Lord watches over animals—affirms his faith. Says if he'd taken her to a vet he'd just have been throwing away money.

Read some LeFanu. "Green Tea," about the phantom monkey with eyes that glow, and "The Familiar," about the little staring man who drives the hero mad. Not the smartest choices right now, the way I feel, because for all the time that fat gray cat purrs over the Poroths, it just stares at me. And snarls. I suppose the accident may have addled its brain a bit. I mean, if spaying can change a cat's personality, certainly a goring on a rock might.

Spent a lot of time in the sun today. The flies made it pretty hard to concentrate on the stories, but figured I'd get a suntan. I probably have a good tan now (hard to tell, because the mirror in here is small and the light dim), but suddenly it occurs to me that I'm not going to be seeing anyone for a long time anyway, except the Poroths, so what the hell do I care how I look?

Can hear them singing their nightly prayers now. A rather comforting sound, I must admit, even if I can't share the sentiments.

Petting Felix today—my favorite of the cats, real charm— came away with a tick on my arm which I didn't discover till taking a shower before dinner. As a result, I can still feel imaginary ticks crawling up and down my back. Damned cat.

June 21

. . . Coming along well with the Victorian stuff. Zipped through "The Uninhabited House" and "Monsieur Maurice," both very literate, sophisticated. Deep into the terrible suffering of "The Amber Witch," poor priest and daughter near starvation, when Deborah called me in for dinner. Roast beef, with salad made from garden lettuce. Quite good. And Deborah was wearing one of the few sleeveless dresses I've seen on her. So she has a body after all. . . .

A rainy night. Hung around the house for a while reading in their living room while Sarr whittled and Deborah crocheted. Rain sounded better from in there than it does out here where it's not so cozy.

At eleven we turned on the news, cats purring around us, Sarr with Zoë on his lap, Deborah petting Phaedra, me sniffling. . . . Halfway through the wrap-up I pointed to Bwada, curled up at my feet, and said, "Look at her. You'd think she was watching the news with us." Deborah laughed and leaned over to scratch Bwada behind the ears. As she did so, Bwada turned to look at me.

The rain is letting up slightly. I can still hear the dripping from the trees, leaf to leaf to the dead leaves lining the forest floor; it will probably continue on and off all night. Occasionally I think I hear thrashings in one of the oaks near the barn, but then the sound turns into the falling of the rain.

Mildew higher on the walls of this place. Glad my books are on shelves off the ground. So damp in here my envelopes are ruined—glue moistened, sealing them all shut. Stamps that had been in my wallet are stuck to the dollar bills. At night my sheets are clammy and cold, but each morning I wake up sweating.

Finished "The Amber Witch," really fine. Would that all lives had such happy endings.

June 22

When Poroths returned from church, helped them prepare strips of molding for the upstairs study. Worked in the tool shed, one of the old wooden outbuildings. I measured, Sarr sawed, Deborah sanded. All in all, hardly felt useful, but what the hell?

While they were busy, I sat staring out the window. There's a narrow cement walk running from the shed to the main house, and, as was their habit, Minnie and Felix, two of the kittens, were crouched in the middle of it taking in the late afternoon sun. Suddenly Bwada appeared on the house's front porch and began slinking along the cement path in our direction, tail swishing from side to side. When she neared the kittens she gave a snarl—I could see her mouth working—and they leaped to their feet, bristling, and ran off into the grass.

Called this to Poroths' attention. They said, in effect, Yes, we know, she's always been nasty to the kittens, probably because she never had any of her own. And besides, she's getting older.

When I turned back to the window, Bwada was gone. Asked the Poroths if they didn't think she'd gotten worse lately. Realized that, in speaking, I'd unconsciously dropped my voice, as if someone might be listening through the chinks in the floorboards.

Deborah conceded that, yes, the cat is behaving worse these days toward the others. And not just toward the kittens, as before. Butch, the adult orange male, seems particularly afraid of her. . . .

Am a little angry at the Poroths. Will have to tell them when I see them tomorrow morning. They claim they never come into these rooms, respect privacy of a tenant, etc. etc., but one of them must have been in here, because I've just noticed my can of insect spray is missing. I don't mind their borrowing it, but I like to have it by my bed on nights like this. Went over room looking for spiders, just in case; had a fat copy of *Amer-*

ican Scholar in my hand to crush them (only thing it's good for). But found nothing.

Tried to read some *Walden* as a break from all the horror stuff, but found my eyes too irritated, watery. Keep scratching them as I write this. Nose pretty clogged, too—the damned allergy's worse tonight. Probably because of the dampness. Expect I'll have trouble getting to sleep.

June 24

Slept very late this morning because the noise from outside kept me up late last night. (Come to think of it, the Poroths' praying was unusually loud as well, but that wasn't what bothered me.) I'd been in the middle of writing in this journal—some thoughts on A. E. Coppard—when it came. I immediately stopped writing and shut off the light.

At first it sounded like something in the woods near my room—an animal? a child? I couldn't tell, but smaller than a man—shuffling through the dead leaves, kicking them around as if it didn't care who heard it. There was a snapping of branches and, every so often, a silence and then a bump, as if it were hopping over fallen logs. I stood in the dark listening to it, then crept to the window and looked out. Thought I noticed some bushes moving, back there in the undergrowth, but it may have been the wind.

The sound grew farther away. Whatever it was must have been walking directly out into the deepest part of the woods, where the ground gets swampy and treacherous, because, very faintly, I could hear the sucking sounds of feet slogging through the mud.

I stood by the window for almost an hour, occasionally hearing what I thought were movements off there in the swamp, but finally all was quiet except for the crickets and the frogs. I had no intention of going out there with my flashlight in search of the intruder—that's for guys in stories, I'm much too chicken—and I wondered if I should call Sarr. But by this time the noise had stopped, and whatever it was had obviously moved on. Besides, I tend to think he'd have been angry if I'd awakened him and Deborah just because some stray dog had wandered near the farm. I recalled how annoyed he'd been earlier that day when—maybe not all that tactfully—I'd asked

him what he'd done with my bug spray. (Must remember to
walk into town tomorrow and pick up a can. Still can't figure
out where I misplaced mine.)

I went over to the windows on the other side and watched
the moonlight on the barn for a while; my nose probably
looked crosshatched from pressing against the screen. In contrast to the woods, the grass looked peaceful under the full
moon. Then I lay in bed, but had a hard time falling asleep.
Just as I was getting relaxed, the sounds started again. High-
pitched wails and caterwauls, from deep within the woods.
Even after thinking about it all today, I still don't know
whether the noise was human or animal. There were no actual
words, of that I'm certain, but nevertheless there was the impression of *singing*. In a crazy, tuneless kind of way the sound
seemed to carry the same solemn rhythm as the Poroths'
prayers earlier that night.

The noise only lasted a minute or two, but I lay awake till
the sky began to get lighter. Probably should have read a little
more Coppard, but was reluctant to turn on the lamp.

. . . Slept all morning and, in the afternoon, followed the
road the opposite direction from Gilead, seeking anything of
interest. But the road just gets muddier and muddier till it disappears altogether by the ruins of an old homestead—rocks
and cement covered with moss—and it looked so much like
poison ivy around there that I didn't want to risk tramping
through.

At dinner (pork chops, home-grown stringbeans, and
pudding—quite good), mentioned the noise of last night. Sarr
acted very concerned and went to his room to look up something in one of his books; Deborah and I discussed the matter
at some length and concluded that the shuffling sounds
weren't necessarily related to the wailing. The former were
almost definitely those of a dog—dozens in the area, and they
love to prowl around at night, exploring, hunting coons—and
as for the wailing . . . well, it's hard to say. She thinks it may
have been an owl or whippoorwill, while I suspect it may have
been that same stray dog. I've heard the howl of wolves and
I've heard hounds baying at the moon, and both have the
same element of, I suppose, *worship* in them that these did.

Sarr came back downstairs and said he couldn't find what

he'd been looking for. Said that when he moved into this farm
he'd had "a fit of piety" and had burned a lot of old books he'd
found in the attic; now he wishes he hadn't.

Looked up something on my own after leaving the Poroths.
Field Guide to Mammals lists both red and gray foxes and,
believe it or not, coyotes as surviving here in New Jersey. No
wolves left, though—but the guide might be wrong.

Then, on a silly impulse, opened another reference book,
Barbara Byfield's *Glass Harmonica*. Sure enough, my hunch
was right: looked up June twenty-third, and it said, "St. John's
Eve. Sabbats likely."

I'll stick to the natural explanation. Still, I'm glad Mrs. Byfield lists nothing for tonight; I'd like to get some sleep. There
is, of course, a beautiful full moon—werewolf weather, as Maria
Ouspenskaya might have said. But then, there are no wolves
left in New Jersey. . . .

(Which reminds me, really must read some Marryat and
Endore. But only after *Northanger Abbey*, my course always
comes first.)

June 25

. . . After returning from town, the farm looked very
lonely. Wish they had a library in Gilead with more than religious tracts. Or a stand that sold the *Times*. (Though it's
strange how, after a week or two, you no longer miss it.)

Overheated from walk—am I getting out of shape? Or is it
just the hot weather? Took a cold shower. When I opened the
bathroom door, I accidentally let Bwada out—I'd wondered
why the chair was propped against it. She raced into the
kitchen, pushed open the screen door by herself, and I had no
chance to catch her. (Wouldn't have attempted to anyway; her
claws are wicked.) I apologized later when Deborah came in
from the fields. She said Bwada had become vicious toward the
other cats and that Sarr had confined her to the bathroom as
punishment. The first time he'd shut her in there, Deborah
said, the cat had gotten out; apparently she's smart enough to
turn the door-knob by swatting at it a few times. Hence the
chair.

Sarr came in carrying Bwada, both obviously out of temper.
He'd seen a streak of orange running through the field toward

him, followed by a gray blur. Butch had stopped at his feet and
Bwada had pounced on him, but before she could do any
damage Sarr had grabbed her around the neck and carried her
back here. He'd been bitten once and scratched a lot on his
hands, but not badly; maybe the cat still likes him best. He
threw her back in the bathroom and shoved the chair against
the door, then sat down and asked Deborah to join him in
some silent prayer. I thumbed uneasily through a religious
magazine till they were done, and we sat down to dinner.

I apologized again, but he said he wasn't mad at me, that
the Devil had gotten into his cat. It was obvious he meant that
quite literally. During dinner (omelet—the hens have been
laying well) we heard a grating sound from the bathroom, and
Sarr ran in to find her almost out the window; somehow she
must have been strong enough to slide the sash up partway.
She seemed so placid, though, when Sarr pulled her down
from the sill—he'd been expecting another fight—that he let
her out into the kitchen. At this she simply curled up near the
stove and went to sleep; I guess she'd worked off her rage for
the day. The other cats gave her a wide berth, though.

Watched a couple of hours of television with the Poroths.
They may have gone to college, but the shows they find interesting . . . God! I'm ashamed of myself for sitting there like
a cretin in front of that box. I won't even mention what we
watched, lest history record the true abysmality of my tastes.

And yet I find that the TV draws us closer, as if we were
having an adventure together. Shared experience, really. Like
knowing the same people or going to the same school.

But there's a lot of duplicity in those Poroths—and I don't
mean just religious hypocrisy, either. Came out here after
watching the news, and though I hate to accuse anyone of
spying on me, there's no doubt that Sarr or Deborah has been
inside this room today. I began tonight's entry with great irritation, because I found my desk in disarray; this journal wasn't
even put back in the right drawer. I keep all my pens on one
side, all my pencils on another, ink and erasers in the middle,
etc., and when I sat down tonight I saw that everything was
out of place. Thank God I haven't included anything too personal in here. . . . What I assume happened was that Deborah
came in to wash the mildew off the walls—she's mentioned

doing so several times, and she knew I'd be in town part of the day—and got sidetracked into reading this, thinking it must be some kind of secret diary. (I'm sure she was disappointed to find that it's merely a literary journal, with nothing about her in it.)

What bugs me is the difficulty of broaching the subject. I can't just walk in and charge Deborah with being a sneak—Sarr is moody enough as it is—and even if I hint at "someone messing up my desk," they'll know what I mean and perhaps get angry. Whenever possible I prefer to avoid unpleasantness. I guess the best thing to do is simply hide this book under my mattress from now on and say nothing. If it happens again, though, I'll definitely move out of here.

. . . I've been reading some *Northanger Abbey*. Really quite witty, as all her stuff is, but it's obvious the mock-Gothic bit isn't central to the story. I'd thought it was going to be a real parody. . . . Love stories always tend to bore me, and normally I'd be asleep right now, but my damned nose is so clogged tonight that it's hard to breathe when I lie back. Usually being out here clears it up. I've used this goddamned inhaler a dozen times in the past hour, but within a few minutes I sneeze and have to use it again. Wish Deborah'd gotten around to cleaning off the mildew instead of wasting her time looking in here for True Confessions and deep dark secrets. . . .

Think I hear something moving outside. Best to shut off my light.

June 30

Slept late. Read some Shirley Jackson stories over breakfast, but got so turned off at her view of humanity that I switched to old Aleister Crowley, who at least keeps a sunny disposition. For her, people in the country are callous and vicious, those in the city are callous and vicious, husbands are (of course) callous and vicious, and children are merely sadistic. The only ones with feelings are her put-upon middle-aged heroines, with whom she obviously identifies. I guess if she didn't write so well the stories wouldn't sting so.

Inspired by Crowley, walked back to the pool in the woods. Had visions of climbing a tree, swinging on vines, anything to commemorate his exploits. . . . Saw something dead floating in the center of the pool and ran back to the farm. Copper-head? Caterpillar? It had somehow opened up. . . .

Joined Sarr chopping stakes for tomatoes. Could hear his ax all over the farm. He told me Bwada hadn't come home last night, and no sign of her this morning. Good riddance, as far as I'm concerned. Helped him chop some stakes while he was busy peeling off bark. That ax can get heavy fast! My arm hurt after three lousy stakes, and Sarr had already chopped fifteen or sixteen. Must start exercising. But I'll wait till my arm's less tired. . . .

July 2

Unpleasant day. Two A.M. now and still can't relax.

Sarr woke me up this morning—stood at my window calling "Jeremy . . . Jeremy. . . ." over and over very quietly. He had something in his hand which, through the screen, I first took for a farm implement; then I saw it was a rifle. He said he wanted me to help him. With what? I asked.

"A burial."

Last night, after he and Deborah had gone to bed, they'd heard the kitchen door open and someone enter the house. They both assumed it was me, come to use the bathroom—but then they heard the cats screaming. Sarr ran down and switched on the light in time to see Bwada on top of Butch, claws in his side, fangs buried in his neck. From the way he described it, sounds almost sexual in reverse. Butch had stopped struggling, and Minnie, the orange kitten, was already dead. The door was partly open, and when Bwada saw Sarr, she ran out.

Sarr and Deborah hadn't followed her; they'd spent the night praying over the bodies of Minnie and Butch. I *thought* I'd heard their voices late last night, but that's all I heard, probably because I'd been playing my radio. (Something I rarely do—you can't hear noises from the woods with it on.)

Poroths took deaths the way they'd take the death of a child. Regular little funeral service over by the unused pasture. (Hard to say if Sarr and Deborah were dressed in mourning, since that's the way they always dress.) Must admit I didn't feel particularly involved—my allergy's never permitted me to take much interest in the cats, though I'm fond of Felix—but I tried to act concerned: when Sarr asked, appropriately, "Is there no balm in Gilead? Is there no physician there?" (Jeremiah VIII:22), I nodded gravely. Read passages out of Deborah's Bible (Sarr seemed to know them all by heart), said amen when they did, knelt when they knelt, and tried to comfort Deborah when she cried. Asked her if cats could go to heaven, received a tearful "Of course." But Sarr added that Bwada would burn in hell.

What concerned me, apparently a lot more than it did either of them, was how the damned thing could get into the house. Sarr gave me this stupid, earnest answer: "She was always a smart cat." Like an outlaw's mother, still proud of her baby. . . .

Yet he and I looked all over the land for her so he could kill her. Barns, tool shed, old stables, garbage dump, etc. He called her and pleaded with her, swore to me she hadn't always been like this.

We could hardly check every tree on the farm—unfortunately—and the woods are a perfect hiding place, even for animals larger than a cat. So naturally we found no trace of her. We did try, though; we even walked up the road as far as the ruined homestead.

But for all that, we could have stayed much closer to home.

We returned for dinner, and I stopped at my room to change clothes. My door was open. Nothing inside was ruined, everything was in its place, everything as it should be—except the bed. The sheets were in tatters right down to the mattress, and the pillow had been ripped to shreds. Feathers were all over the floor. There were even claw marks on my blanket.

At dinner the Poroths demanded they be allowed to pay for the damage—nonsense, I said, they have enough to worry about—and Sarr suggested I sleep downstairs in their living room. "No need for that," I told him. "I've got lots more sheets." But he said no, he didn't mean that: he meant for my own protection. He believes the thing is particularly inimical, for some reason, toward me.

It seemed so absurd at the time. . . . I mean, nothing but a big fat gray cat. But now, sitting out here, a few feathers still scattered on the floor around my bed, I wish I were back inside the house. I did give in to Sarr when he insisted I take his ax with me. . . . But what I'd rather have is simply a room without windows.

I don't think I want to go to sleep tonight, which is one reason I'm continuing to write this. Just sit up all night on my new bedsheets, my back against the Poroths' pillow, leaning against the wall behind me, the ax beside me on the bed, this journal on my lap. . . . The thing is, I'm rather tired out from all the walking I did today. Not used to that much exercise.

I'm pathetically aware of every sound. At least once every five minutes some snapping of a branch or rustling of leaves makes me jump.

"Thou art my hope in the day of evil." At least that's what the man said. . . .

July 3

Woke up this morning with the journal and the ax cradled in my arms. What awakened me was the trouble I had breathing —nose all clogged, gasping for breath. Down the center of one of my screens, facing the woods, was a huge slash. . . .

July 15

Pleasant day, St. Swithin's Day—and yet, my birthday. Thirty years old, lordy lordy lordy. Today I am a man. First dull thoughts on waking: "Damnation. Thirty today." But another voice inside me, smaller but more sensible, spat contemptuously at such an artificial way of charting time. "Ah, don't give it another thought," it said. "You've still got plenty of time to fool around." Advice I took to heart.

Weather today? Actually, somewhat nasty. And thus the weather for the next forty days, since "If rain on St. Swithin's Day, forsooth, no summer drouthe," or something like that. My birthday predicts the weather. It's even mentioned in *The Glass Harmonica*.

As one must, took a critical self-assessment. First area for improvement: flabby body. Second? Less bookish, perhaps? Nonsense—I'm satisfied with the progress I've made. "And seekest thou great things for thyself? Seek them not." (Jeremiah XLV:5) So I simply did what I remembered from the RCAF exercise series and got good and winded. Flexed my stringy muscles in the shower, certain I'll be a Human Dynamo by the end of the summer. Simply a matter of will-power.

Was so ambitious I trimmed the ivy around my windows again. It's begun to block the light, and someday I may not be able to get out the door.

Read Ruthven Todd's *Lost Traveller*. Merely the narrative of a dream turned to nightmare, and illogical as hell. Wish, too, that there'd been more than merely a few hints of sex. On the whole, rather unpleasant; that gruesome ending is so inevitable. . . . Took me much of the afternoon. Then came upon an incredible essay by Lafcadio Hearn, something entitled "Gaki," detailing the curious Japanese belief that insects are really demons or the ghosts of evil men. Uncomfortably convincing!

Dinner late because Deborah, bless her, was baking me a cake. Had time to walk into town and phone parents. Happy birthday, happy birthday. Both voiced first worry—mustn't I be getting bored out here? Assured them I still had plenty of books and did not grow tired of reading.

"But it's so . . . *secluded* out there," Mom said. "Don't you get lonely?"

Ah, she hadn't reckoned on the inner resources of a man of thirty. Was tempted to quote *Walden*—"Why should I feel lonely? Is not our planet in the Milky Way?"—but refrained. How can I get lonely, I asked, when there's still so much to read? Besides, there are the Poroths to talk to.

Then the kicker: Dad wanted to know about the cat. Last time I'd spoken to them it had sounded like a very real danger. "Are you still sleeping inside the farmhouse, I hope?"

No, I told him, really, I only had to do that for a few days, while the thing was prowling around at night. Yes, it had killed some chickens—a hen every night, in fact. But there were only four of them, and then it stopped. We haven't had a sign of it in more than a week. (I didn't tell him that it had left the hens uneaten, dead in the nest. No need to upset him further.)

"But what it did to your sheets," he went on. "If you'd been sleeping . . . Such savagery."

Yes, that was unfortunate, but there's been no trouble since. Honest. It was only an animal, after all, just a housecat gone a little wild. It posed the same kind of threat as (I was going to say, logically, a wildcat; but for Mom said) a nasty little dog. Like Mrs. Miller's bull terrier. Besides, it's probably miles and miles away by now. Or dead.

They offered to drive out with packages of food, magazines, a portable TV, but I made it clear I needed nothing. Getting too fat, actually.

Still light when I got back. Deborah had finished the cake, Sarr brought up some wine from the cellar, and we had a nice little celebration. The two of them being over thirty, they were happy to welcome me to the fold.

It's nice out here. The wine has relaxed me and I keep yawning. It was good to talk to Mom and Dad again. Just as long as I don't dream of *The Lost Traveller*, I'll be content. And happier still if I don't dream at all.

July 30

Well, Bwada is dead—this time for sure. We'll bury her tomorrow. Deborah was hurt, just how badly I can't say, but she managed to fight Bwada off. Tough woman, though she seems a little shaken. And with good reason.

It happened this way: Sarr and I were in the tool shed after dinner, building more shelves for the upstairs study. Though the fireflies were out, there was still a little daylight left. Deborah had gone up to bed after doing the dishes; she's been tired a lot lately, falls asleep early every night while watching TV with Sarr. He thinks it may be something in the well water.

It had begun to get dark, but we were still working. Sarr dropped a box of nails, and while we were picking them up, he thought he heard a scream. Since I hadn't heard anything, he shrugged and was about to start sawing again when— fortunately—he changed his mind and ran off to the house. I followed him as far as the porch, not sure whether to go upstairs, until I heard him pounding on their bedroom door and calling Deborah's name. As I ran up the stairs I heard her say, "Wait a minute. Don't come in. I'll unlock the door . . . soon." Her voice was extremely hoarse, practically a croaking. We heard her rummaging in the closet—finding her bathrobe, I suppose—and then she opened the door.

She looked absolutely white. Her long hair was in tangles

and her robe buttoned incorrectly. Around her neck she had wrapped a towel, but we could see patches of blood soaking through it. Sarr helped her over to the bed, shouting at me to bring up some bandages from the bathroom.

When I returned, Deborah was lying in bed, still pressing the towel to her throat. I asked Sarr what had happened; it almost looked as if the woman had tried suicide.

He didn't say anything, just pointed to the floor on the other side of the bed. I stepped around for a look. A crumpled gray shape was lying there, half covered by the bedclothes. It was Bwada, a wicked-looking wound in her side. On the floor next to her lay an umbrella—the thing that Deborah had used to kill her.

She told us she'd been asleep when she felt something crawl heavily over her face. It had been like a bad dream. She'd tried to sit up, and suddenly Bwada was at her throat, digging in. Luckily she'd had the strength to tear the animal off and dash to the closet, where the first weapon at hand was the umbrella. Just as the cat sprang at her again, Deborah said, she'd raised the weapon and lunged. Amazing; how many women, I wonder, would have had such presence of mind? The rest sounds incredible to me, but it's probably the sort of crazy thing that happens in moments like this: somehow the cat had impaled itself on the umbrella.

Her voice, as she spoke, was barely more than a whisper. Sarr had to persuade her to remove the towel from her throat; she kept protesting that she wasn't hurt that badly, that the towel had stopped the bleeding. Sure enough, when Sarr finally lifted the cloth from her neck, the wounds proved relatively small, the slash marks already clotting. Thank God that thing didn't really get its teeth in. . . .

My guess—only a guess—is that it had been weakened from days of living in the woods. (It was obviously incapable of feeding itself adequately, as I think was proved by its failure to eat the hens it had killed.) While Sarr dressed Deborah's wounds, I pulled back the bedclothes and took a closer look at the animal's body. The fur was matted and patchy. Odd that an umbrella could make a puncture like that, ringed by flaps of skin, as if the flesh had been pushed outward. Deborah must have had the extraordinary good luck to have jabbed the

animal precisely in its old wound, which had reopened. Naturally I didn't mention this to Sarr.

He made dinner for us tonight—soup, actually, because he
thought that was best for Deborah. Her voice sounded so bad
he told her not to strain it any more by talking, at which she
nodded and smiled. We both had to help her downstairs, as
she was clearly weak from shock.

In the morning Sarr will have the doctor out. He'll have to examine the cat, too, to check for rabies, so we put the body in the
freezer to preserve it as well as possible. Afterward we'll bury it.

Deborah seemed okay when I left. Sarr was reading through
some medical books, and she was just lying on the living room
couch gazing at her husband with a look of purest gratitude—
not moving, not saying anything, not even blinking.

I feel quite relieved. God knows how many nights I've lain
here thinking every sound I heard was Bwada. I'll feel more
relieved, of course, when that demon's safely underground;
but I think I can say, at the risk of being melodramatic, that the
reign of terror is over.

Hmm, I'm still a little hungry—used to more than soup for
dinner. These daily push-ups burn up energy. I'll probably
dream of hamburgers and chocolate layer cakes.

July 31

 . . . The doctor collected scrapings from Bwada's teeth
and scolded us for doing a poor job of preserving the body.
Said storing it in the freezer was a sensible idea, but that we
should have done so sooner, since it was already decomposing.
The dampness, I imagine, must act fast on dead flesh.

He pronounced Deborah in excellent condition—the marks
on her throat are, remarkably, almost healed—but he said her
reflexes were a little off. Sarr invited him to stay for the burial,
but he declined—and quite emphatically, at that. He's not a
member of their order, doesn't live in the area, and apparently
doesn't get along that well with the people of Gilead, most of
whom mistrust modern science. (Not that the old geezer
sounded very representative of modern science. When I asked
him for some good exercises, he recommended "chopping
wood and running down deer.")

Standing under the heavy clouds, Sarr looked like a revivalist minister. His sermon was from Jeremiah XXII:19—"He shall be buried with the burial of an ass." The burial took place far from the graves of Bwada's two victims, and closer to the woods. We sang one song, Deborah just mouthing the words (still mustn't strain throat muscles). Sarr solemnly asked the Lord to look mercifully upon all His creatures, and I muttered an "amen." Then we walked back to the house, Deborah leaning on Sarr's arm; she's still a little stiff.

It was gray the rest of the day, and I sat in my room reading *The King in Yellow*—or rather, Chambers' collection of the same name. One look at the *real* book, so Chambers would claim, and I might not live to see the morrow, at least through the eyes of a sane man. (That single gimmick—masterful, I admit—seems to be his sole inspiration.)

I was disappointed that dinner was again made by Sarr; Deborah was upstairs resting, he said. He sounded concerned, felt there were things wrong with her the doctor had over-looked. We ate our meal in silence, and I came back here im-mediately after washing the dishes. Feel very drowsy and, for some reason, also rather depressed. It may be the gloomy weather—we are, after all, just animals, more affected by the sun and the seasons than we like to admit. More likely it was the absence of Deborah tonight. Hope she feels better.

Note: The freezer still smells of the cat's body; opened it tonight and got a strong whiff of decay.

August 1
Writing this, breaking habit, in early morning. Went to bed last night just after finishing the entry above, but was awak-ened around two by sounds coming from the woods. Wailing, deeper than before, followed by a low, guttural monologue. No words, at least that I could distinguish. If frogs could talk . . . For some reason I fell asleep before the sounds ended, so I don't know what followed.

Could very well have been an owl of some kind, and later a large bullfrog. But I quote, without comment, from *The Glass Harmonica*: "July 31: Lammas Eve. Sabbats likely."

Little energy to write tonight, and even less to write about. (Come to think of it, I slept most of the day: woke up at eleven, later took an afternoon nap. Alas, senile at thirty!) Too tired to shave, and haven't had the energy to clean this place, either; thinking about work is easier than doing it. The ivy's beginning to cover the windows again, and the mildew's been climbing steadily up the walls. It's like a dark green band that keeps widening. Soon it will reach my books. . . .

Speaking of which, note: opened M. R. James at lunch today—*Ghost Stories of an Antiquary*—and a silverfish slithered out. Omen?

Played a little game with myself this evening—

I just had one hell of a shock. While writing the above I heard a soft tapping, like nervous fingers drumming on a table, and discovered an enormous spider, biggest of the summer, crawling only a few inches from my ankle. It must have been living behind this desk. . . .

When you can hear a spider walk across the floor, you *know* it's time to keep your socks on. Thank God for insecticide.

Oh, yeah, that game—the What If game. I probably play it too often. (Vain attempt to enlarge realm of the possible? Heighten my own sensitivity? Or merely work myself into an icy sweat?) I pose unpleasant questions for myself and consider the consequences, e.g., what if this glorified chicken coop is sinking into quicksand? (Wouldn't be at all surprised.) What if the Poroths are tired of me? What if I woke up inside my own coffin?

What if I never see New York again?

What if some horror stories aren't really fiction? If Machen sometimes told the truth? If there *are* White People, malevolent little faces peering out of the moonlight? Whispers in the grass? Poisonous things in the woods? Perfect hate and evil in the world?

Enough of this foolishness. Time for bed.

August 9

. . . Read some Hawthorne in the morning and, over lunch, reread this week's *Hunterdon County Democrat* for the dozenth time. Sarr and Deborah were working somewhere in the fields, and I felt I ought to get some physical activity myself; but the thought of starting my exercises again after more than a week's laziness just seemed too unpleasant. . . . I took a walk down the road, but only as far as a smashed-up cement culvert half buried in the woods. I was bored, but Gilead just seemed too far away.

Was going to cut the ivy surrounding my windows when I got back, but decided the place looks more artistic covered in vines. Rationalization?

Chatted with Poroths about politics, The World Situation, a little cosmology, blah blah blah. Dinner wasn't very good, probably because I'd been looking forward to it all day. The lamb was underdone and the beans were cold. Still, I'm always the gentleman, and was almost pleased when Deborah agreed to my offer to do the dishes. I've been doing them a lot lately.

I didn't have much interest in reading tonight and would have been up for some television, but Sarr's recently gotten into one of his religious kicks and began mumbling prayers to himself immediately after dinner. (Deborah, more human, wanted to watch the TV news. She seems to have an insatiable curiosity about world events, yet she claims the isolation here appeals to her.) Absorbed in his chanting, Sarr made me uncomfortable—I didn't like his face—and so after doing the dishes, I left.

I've been listening to the radio for the last hour or so. . . . I recall days when I'd have gotten uptight at having wasted an hour—but out here I've lost all track of time. Feel adrift—a little disconcerting, but healthy, I'm sure.

. . . Shut off the radio a moment ago, and now realize my room is filled with crickets. Up close their sound is hardly pleasant—cross between a radiator and a tea-kettle, very shrill. They'd been sounding off all night, but I'd thought it was interference on the radio.

Now I notice them; they're all over the room. A couple of dozen, I should think. Hate to kill them, really—they're one of the few insects I can stand, along with ladybugs and fireflies. But they make such a racket!

Wonder how they got in. . . .

August 14

Played with Felix all morning—mainly watching him chase insects, climb trees, doze in the sun. Spectator sport. After lunch went back to my room to look up something in Lovecraft and discovered my books were out of order. (Saki, for example, was filed under "S," whereas—whether out of fastidiousness or pedantry—I've always preferred to file him as "Munro.") This is definitely one of the Poroths' doing. I'm pissed they didn't mention coming in here, but also a little surprised they'd have any interest in this stuff.

Arranged them correctly again, then sat down to reread Lovecraft's essay on "Supernatural Horror in Literature." It upset me to see how little I've actually read, how far I still have to go. So many obscure authors, so many books I've never come across. . . . Left me feeling depressed and tired, so I took a nap for the rest of the afternoon.

Over dinner—vegetable omelet, rather tasteless—Deborah continued to question us on current events. It's getting to be like junior high school, with daily newspaper quizzes. . . . Don't know how she got started on this, or why the sudden interest, but it obviously annoys the hell out of Sarr.

Sarr used to be a sucker for her little-girl pleadings—I remember how he used to carry her upstairs, becoming pathetically tender, the moment she'd say, "Oh, honey, I'm so tired" —but now he just becomes angry. Often he goes off morose and alone to pray, and the only time he laughs is when he watches television.

Tonight, thank God, he was in a mood to forgo the prayers, and so after dinner we all watched a lot of offensively ignorant programs. I was disturbed to find myself laughing along with the canned laughter, but I have to admit the TV helps us get along better together. Came back here after the news.

Not very tired, having slept so much of the afternoon, so began to read John Christopher's *The Possessors*; but good though it was, my mind began to wander to all the books I *haven't* yet read, and I got so depressed I turned on the radio. Find it takes my mind off things.

August 19

Slept long into the morning, then walked down to the brook, scratching groggily. Deborah was kneeling by the water, lost, it seemed, in daydream, and I was embarrassed because I'd come upon her talking to herself. We exchanged a few insincere words and she went back toward the house.

Sat by some rocks, throwing blades of grass into the water. The sun on my head felt almost painful, as if my brain were growing too large for my skull. I turned and looked at the farmhouse. In the distance it looked like a picture at the other end of a large room, the grass for a carpet, the ceiling the sky. Deborah was stroking a cat, then seemed to grow angry when it struggled from her arms; I could hear the screen door slam as she went into the kitchen, but the sound reached me so long after the visual image that the whole scene struck me as, somehow, fake. I gazed up at the maples behind me, and they seemed trees out of a cheap postcard, the kind in which thinly colored paint is dabbed over a black-and-white photograph; if you look closely you can see that the green in the trees is not merely in the leaves, but rather floats as a vapor over leaves, branches, parts of the sky. . . . The trees behind me seemed the productions of a poor painter, the color and shape not quite meshing. Parts of the sky were green, and pieces of the green seemed to float away from my vision. No matter how hard I tried, I couldn't follow them.

Far down the stream I could see something small and kicking, a black beetle, legs in the air, borne swiftly along in the current. Then it was gone.

Thumbed through the Bible while I ate my lunch—mostly cookies. By late afternoon I was playing word games while I lay on the grass near my room. The shrill twitter of the birds, I would say, the birds singing in the sun. . . . And inexorably I'd continue with the sun dying in the moonlight, the moonlight falling on the floor, the floor sagging to the cellar, the cellar filling with water, the water seeping into the ground, the ground twisting into smoke, the smoke staining the sky, the sky burning in the sun, the sun dying in the moonlight, the moonlight falling on the floor . . . —melancholy progressions that held my mind like a whirlpool.

Sarr woke me for dinner; I had dozed off, and my clothes were damp from the grass. As we walked up to the house together he whispered that, earlier in the day, he'd come upon his wife bending over me, peering into my sleeping face. "Her eyes were wide," he said. "Like Bwada's." I said I didn't understand why he was telling me this.

"Because," he recited in a whisper, gripping my arm, "the heart is deceitful above all things, and desperately wicked: who can know it?"

I recognized that. Jeremiah XVII:9.

Dinner was especially uncomfortable; the two of them sat picking at their food, occasionally raising their eyes to one another like children in a staring contest. I longed for the conversations of our early days, inconsequential though they must have been, and wondered where things had first gone wrong.

The meal was dry and unappetizing, but the dessert looked delicious—chocolate mousse, made from an old family recipe. Deborah had served it earlier in the summer and knew both Sarr and I loved it. This time, however, she gave none to herself, explaining that she had to watch her weight.

"Then we'll not eat any!" Sarr shouted, and with that he snatched my dish from in front of me, grabbed his own, and hurled them both against the wall, where they splattered like mudballs.

Deborah was very still; she said nothing, just sat there watching us. She didn't look particularly afraid of this madman, I was happy to see—but *I* was. He may have read my thoughts, because as I got up from my seat, he said much more gently, in the soft voice normal to him, "Sorry, Jeremy. I know you hate scenes. We'll pray for each other, all right?"

"Are you okay?" I asked Deborah. "I'm going out now, but I'll stay if you think you'll need me for anything." She stared at me with a slight smile and shook her head. I raised my eyebrows and nodded toward her husband, and she shrugged.

"Things will work out," she said. I could hear Sarr laughing as I shut the door.

When I snapped on the light out here I took off my shirt and stood in front of the little mirror. It had been nearly a week since I'd showered, and I'd become used to the smell of my body. My hair had wound itself into greasy brown curls, my beard was at least two weeks old, and my eyes . . . well, the eyes that stared back at me looked like those of an old man. The whites were turning yellow, like old teeth. I looked at my chest and arms, flabby at thirty, and I thought of the frightening alterations in my friend Sarr, and I knew I'd have to get out of here.

Just glanced at my watch. It's now quite late: two thirty. I've been packing my things.

August 20

I woke about an hour ago and continued packing. Lots of books to put away, but I'm just about done. It's not even nine A.M. yet, much earlier than I normally get up, but I guess the thought of leaving here fills me with energy.

The first thing I saw on rising was a garden spider whose body was as big as some of the mice the cats have killed. It was sitting on the ivy that grows over my window sill—fortunately on the other side of the screen. Apparently it had had good hunting all summer, preying on the insects that live in the leaves. Concluding that nothing so big and fearsome has a right to live, I held the spray can against the screen and doused the creature with poison. It struggled halfway up the screen, then stopped, arched its legs, and dropped backwards into the ivy.

I plan to walk into town this morning and telephone the office in Flemington where I rented my car. If they can have one ready today I'll hitch there to pick it up; otherwise I'll spend tonight here and pick it up tomorrow. I'll be leaving a little early in the season, but the Poroths already have my month's rent, so they shouldn't be too offended.

And anyway, how could I be expected to stick around here with all that nonsense going on, never knowing when my room might be ransacked, having to put up with Sarr's insane suspicions and Deborah's moodiness?

Before I go into town, though, I really must shave and shower for the good people of Gilead. I've been sitting inside here waiting for some sign the Poroths are up, but as yet—it's almost nine—I've heard nothing. I wouldn't care to barge in on them while they're still having breakfast or, worse, just getting up. . . . So I'll just wait here by the window till I see them.

. . . Ten o'clock now, and they still haven't come out. Perhaps they're having a talk. . . . I'll give them half an hour more, then I'm going in.

*

Here my journal ends. Until today, almost a week later, I have not cared to set down any of the events that followed. But here in the temporary safety of this hotel room, protected by a heavy brass travel-lock I had sent up from the hardware store down the street, watched over by the good people of Flemington—and perhaps by something not good—I can continue my narrative.

The first thing I noticed as I approached the house was that the shades were drawn, even in the kitchen. Had they decided to sleep late this morning? I wondered. Throughout my thirty years I have come to associate drawn shades with a foul smell, the smell of a sickroom, of shamefaced poverty and food gone bad, of people lying too long beneath blankets; but I was not ready for the stench of decay that met me when I opened the kitchen door and stepped into the darkness. Something had died in that room—and not recently.

At the moment the smell first hit, four little shapes scrambled across the linoleum toward me and out into the daylight. The Poroths' cats.

By the other wall a lump of shadow moved; a pale face caught light penetrating the shades. Sarr's voice, its habitual softness exaggerated to a whisper: "Jeremy. I thought you were still asleep."

"Can I—"

"No. Don't turn on the light." He got to his feet, a black form towering against the window. Fiddling nervously with the kitchen door—the tin doorknob, the rubber bands stored around it, the fringe at the bottom of the drawn window shade—I opened it wider and let in more sunlight. It fell on the dark thing at his feet, over which he had been crouching: Deborah, the flesh at her throat torn and wrinkled like the skin of an old apple.

Her clothing lay in a heap beside her. She appeared long dead. The eyes were shriveled, sunken into sockets black as a skull's.

I think I may have staggered at that moment, because he came toward me. His steady, unblinking gaze looked so sincere—but *why was he smiling?* "I'll make you understand," he was saying, or something like that; even now I feel my face twisting into horror as I try to write of him. "I had to kill her. . . ."

"You—"

"She tried to kill me," he went on, silencing all questions. "The same thing that possessed Bwada . . . possessed her."

My hand played behind my back with the bottom of the window shade. "But her throat—"

"That happened a long time ago. Bwada did it. I had nothing to do with . . . that part." Suddenly his voice rose. "Don't you understand? She tried to stab me with the bread knife." He turned, stooped over, and, clumsy in the darkness, began feeling about him on the floor. "Where is that thing?" he was mumbling. "I'll show you. . . ." As he crossed a beam of sunlight, something gleamed like a silver handle on the back of his shirt.

Thinking, perhaps, to help him search, I pulled gently on the window shade, then released it; it snapped upward like a gunshot, flooding the room with light. From deep within the center of his back protruded the dull wooden haft of the bread knife, buried almost completely but for an inch or two of gleaming steel.

He must have heard my intake of breath—that sight chills me even today, the grisly absurdity of the thing—he must have heard me, because immediately he stood, his back to me, and reached up behind himself toward the knife, his arm stretching in vain, his fingers curling around nothing. The blade had been planted in a spot he couldn't reach.

He turned towards me and shrugged in embarrassment, a child caught in a foolish error. "Oh, yeah," he said, grinning at his own weakness. "I forgot it was there."

Suddenly he thrust his face into mine, fixing me in a gaze that never wavered, his eyes wide with candor. "It's easy for us to forget things," he explained—and then, still smiling, still watching, volunteered that last trivial piece of information, that final message whose words released me from inaction and left me free to dash from the room, to sprint in panic down the road to town, pursued by what had once been the farmer Sarr Poroth.

It serves no purpose here to dwell on my flight down that

twisting dirt road, breathing in such deep gasps that I was soon
moaning with every breath; how, with my enemy racing
behind me, not even winded, his steps never flagging, I veered
into the woods; how I finally lost him, perhaps from the
inexperience of whatever thing now controlled his body, and
was able to make my way back to the road, only to come upon
him again as I rounded a bend; his laughter as he followed me,
and how it continued long after I had evaded him a second
time; and how, after hiding until nightfall in the old cement
culvert, I ran the rest of the way in pitch-darkness, stumbling
in the ruts, torn by vines, nearly blinding myself when I ran
into a low branch, until I arrived in Gilead filthy, exhausted,
and nearly incoherent.

Suffice it to say that my escape was largely a matter of luck,
a physical wreck fleeing something oblivious to pain or fatigue;
but that, beyond mere luck, I had been impelled by an almost
ecstatic sense of dread produced by his last words to me, that
last communication from an alien face smiling inches from my
own, and which I chose to take as his final warning:

"Sometimes we forget to blink."

You can read the rest in the newspapers. *The Hunterdon
County Democrat* covered most of the story, though its man
wrote it up as merely another lunatic wife-slaying, the result of
loneliness, religious mania, and a mysteriously tainted well.
(Traces of insecticide were found, among other things, in the
water.) The *Somerset Reporter* took a different slant, implying
that I had been the third member of an erotic triangle and that
Sarr had murdered his wife in a fit of jealousy.

Needless to say, I was by this time past caring what was
written about me. I was too haunted by visions of that lonely,
abandoned farmhouse, the wails of its hungry cats, and by the
sight of Deborah's corpse, discovered by the police, protruding from that hastily dug grave beyond the cornfield.

Accompanied by state troopers, I returned to my ivy-
covered outbuilding. A bread knife had been plunged deep
into its door, splintering the wood on the other side. The
blood on it was Sarr's.

My journal had been hidden under my mattress and so was

untouched, but (I look at them now, piled in cardboard boxes beside my suitcase) my precious books had been hurled about the room, their bindings slashed. My summer is over, and now I sit inside here all day listening to the radio, waiting for the next report. Sarr—or his corpse—has not been found.

I should think the evidence was clear enough to corroborate my story, but I suppose I should have expected the reception it received from the police. They didn't laugh at my theory of "possession"—not to my face, anyway—but they ignored it in obvious embarrassment. Some see a nice young bookworm gone slightly deranged after contact with a murderer; others believe my story to be the desperate fabrication of an adulterer trying to avoid the blame for Deborah's death.

I can understand their reluctance to accept my explanation of the events, for it's one that goes a little beyond the "natural," a little beyond the scientific considerations of motive, *modus operandi*, and fingerprints. But I find it quite unnerving that at least one official—an assistant district attorney, I think, though I'm afraid I'm rather ignorant of these matters—believes I am guilty of murder.

There has, of course, been no arrest. Still, I've been given the time-honored instructions against leaving town.

The theory proposing my own complicity in the events is, I must admit, rather ingenious—and so carefully worked out that it will surely gain more adherents than my own. This police official is going to try to prove that I killed poor Deborah in a fit of passion and, immediately afterward, disposed of Sarr. He points out that their marriage had been an observably happy one until I arrived, a disturbing influence from the city. My motive, he says, was simple lust—unrequited, to be sure—aggravated by boredom. The heat, the insects, and, most of all, the oppressive loneliness—all constituted an environment alien to any I'd been accustomed to, and all worked to unhinge my reason.

I have no cause for fear, however, because this affidavit will certainly establish my innocence. Surely no one can ignore the evidence of my journal (though I can imagine an antagonistic few maintaining that I wrote the journal not at the farm but here in the Union Hotel, this very week).

What galls me is not the suspicions of a few detectives, but the predicament their suspicions place me in. Quite simply, *I cannot run away.* I am compelled to remain locked up in this room, potential prey to whatever the thing that was Sarr Poroth has now become—the thing that was once a cat, and once a woman, and once . . . what? A large white moth? A serpent? A shrewlike thing with wicked teeth?

A police chief? A president? A boy with eyes of blood that sits beneath my window?

Lord, who will believe me?

It was that night that started it all, I'm convinced of it now. The night I made those strange signs in the tree. The night the crickets missed a beat.

I'm not a philosopher, and I can supply no ready explanation for why this new evil has been released into the world. I'm only a poor scholar, a bookworm, and I must content myself with mumbling a few phrases that keep running through my mind, phrases out of books read long ago when such abstractions meant, at most, a pleasant shudder. I am haunted by scraps from the myth of Pandora, and by a semantic discussion I once read comparing "unnatural" and "supernatural."

And something about "a tiny rent in the fabric of the universe. . . ."

Just large enough to let something in. Something not of nature, and hard to kill. Something with its own obscure purpose.

Ironically, the police may be right. Perhaps it was my visit to Gilead that brought about the deaths. Perhaps I had a hand in letting loose the force that, to date, has snuffed out the lives of four hens, three cats, and at least two people—but will hardly be content to stop there.

I've just checked. He hasn't moved from the steps of the courthouse; and even when I look out my window, the rose spectacles never waver. Who knows where the eyes beneath them point? Who knows if they remember to blink?

Lord, this heat is sweltering. My shirt is sticking to my skin, and droplets of sweat are rolling down my face and dripping onto this page, making the ink run.

My hand is tired from writing, and I think it's time to end this affidavit.

If, as I now believe possible, I inadvertently called down evil from the sky and began the events at Poroth Farm, my death will only be fitting. And after my death, many more. We are all, I'm afraid, in danger. Please, then, forgive this prophet of doom, old at thirty, his last jeremiad: "The harvest is past, the summer is ended, and we are not saved."

1972

ISAAC BASHEVIS SINGER

(1904–1991)

Hanka

This trip made little sense from the start. First, it didn't pay
financially to leave New York and my work for two and a half
months to go to Argentina for a lecture tour; second, I should
have taken an airplane instead of wasting my time on a ship for
eighteen days. But I had signed the contract and accepted a
first-class round-trip ticket on *La Plata* from my impresario,
Chazkel Poliva. That summer, the heat lasted into October.
On the day I embarked, the thermometer registered ninety degrees. I was always assailed by premonitions and phobias
before a trip: I would get sick; the ship would sink; some other
calamity would occur. An inner voice warned me, Don't go!
However, if I had made a practice of acting on these premonitions, I would not have come to America but would have perished in Nazi-occupied Poland.

As it happened, I was provided with all possible comforts.
My cabin looked like a salon, with two square windows, a sofa,
a desk, and pictures on the walls. The bathroom had both a
tub and a shower stall. The number of passengers was small,
mostly Latin Americans, and the service staff was large. In the
dining room I had a special wine steward who promptly filled
my glass each time I took a sip of wine. A band of five musicians played at lunch and dinner. Every second day the captain
gave a cocktail party. But for some reason I could not make
any acquaintances on this ship. The few passengers who spoke
English kept to themselves. The men, all young six-foot giants,
played shuffleboard and cavorted in the swimming pool. The
women were too tall and too athletic for my taste. In the
evening, they all danced or sat at the bar, drinking and smoking.
I made up my mind that I would remain isolated, and it
seemed that others sensed my decision. No one spoke a word
to me. I began to wonder if by some magic I had become one

who sees and is not seen. After a while I stopped attending the cocktail parties and I asked that my meals be served in my cabin. In Trinidad and in Brazil, where the ship stopped for a day, I walked around alone. I had taken little to read with me, because I was sure that the ship would have a library. But it consisted of a single glass-doored bookcase with some fifty or so volumes in Spanish and perhaps a dozen in English—all moldy travel books printed a hundred years ago. This bookcase was kept locked, and each time I wanted to exchange a book there was a commotion about who had the key; I would be sent from one member of the staff to the other. Eventually an officer with epaulets would write down my name, the number of my stateroom, the titles and authors of my books. This took him at least fifteen minutes.

When the ship approached the equator, I stopped going out on deck in the daytime. The sun burned like a flame. The days had shortened and night came swiftly. One moment it was light, the next it was dark. The sun did not set but fell into the water like a meteor. Late in the evening, when I went out briefly, a hot wind slapped my face. From the ocean came a roar of passions that seemed to have broken through all barriers: "We must procreate and multiply! We must exhaust all the powers of lust!" The waves glowed like lava, and I imagined I could see multitudes of living beings—algae, whales, sea monsters— reveling in an orgy, from the surface to the bottom of the sea. Immortality was the law here. The whole planet raged with animation. At times, I heard my name in the clamor: the spirit of the abyss calling me to join them in their nocturnal dance.

In Buenos Aires I was met by Chazkel Poliva—a short, round person—and a young woman who introduced herself as my relative. Her name was Hanka and she was, she said, a great-granddaughter of my Aunt Yentel from her first husband. Actually, Hanka was not my relative, because my Uncle Aaron was Yentel's third husband. Hanka was petite, lean, and had a head of pitch-black hair, full lips, and eyes as black as onyx. She wore a dark dress and a black, broad-brimmed hat. She could have been thirty or thirty-five. Hanka immediately told me that in Warsaw someone had hidden her on the Aryan side—the way she was saved from the Nazis. She was a dancer, she said, but even before she told me I saw it in the muscles of her calves. I asked her where she danced and she replied, "At Jewish affairs and at my own troubles."

Chazkel Poliva took us in his car to the Hotel Cosmopolitan on Junín Street, which was once famous as the main street of the red-light district. Poliva said that the neighborhood had been cleaned up and all the literati now stayed in this hotel. The three of us ate supper in a restaurant on Corrientes Avenue, and Chazkel Poliva handed me a schedule covering my four weeks in Argentina. I was to lecture in Buenos Aires at the Théâtre Soleil and at the Jewish Community Center, and also I was to go to Rosario, Mar del Plata, and to the Jewish colonies in Moisés Ville and in Entre Ríos. The Warsaw Society, the Yiddish section of the P.E.N. Club, the journalists of the newspaper that published my articles, and a number of Yiddish schools were all preparing receptions.

When Poliva was alone with me for a moment, he asked, "Who is this woman? She says that she dances at Jewish affairs, but I've never seen her anywhere. While we were waiting for you, I suggested that she give me her address and telephone number in case I needed to get in touch with her, but she refused. Who is she?"

"I really don't know."

Chazkel Poliva had another engagement that evening and left us after dinner. I wanted to pay the bill—why should he pay for a woman who was supposed to be my relative?—but he would not permit it. I noticed that Hanka ate nothing—she had only a glass of wine. She accompanied me back to the hotel. It was not long after Perón had been ousted, and Argentina was in the midst of a political and perhaps economic crisis. Buenos Aires, it seemed, was short of electricity. The streets were dimly lit. Here and there a gendarme patrolled, carrying a machine gun. Hanka took my arm and we walked through Corrientes Avenue. I couldn't see any physical resemblance in her to my Aunt Yentel, but she had her style of talking: she jumped from one subject to another, confused names, places, dates. She asked me, "Is this your first visit to Argentina? Here the climate is crazy and so are the people. In Warsaw there was spring fever; here one fevers all year round. When it's hot, you melt from the heat. When the rains begin, the cold eats into your bones. It is actually one big jungle. The cities are oases in the pampas. For years, the pimps and whores controlled the Jewish immigrants. Later, they were excommunicated and had to build a synagogue and acquire a cemetery of their own. The Jews who came here after the Holocaust are lost creatures. How is it that they don't translate you into Spanish? When did you last see my great-grandmother Yentel? I didn't know her, but she left me as an inheritance a chain with a locket that was perhaps two hundred years old. I sold it for bread. Here is your hotel. If you're not tired, I'll go up with you for a while."

We took the elevator to the sixth floor. From childhood I have had a liking for balconies; there was one outside my room and we went there directly. There were few high constructions in Buenos Aires, so we could see a part of the city. I brought out two chairs and we sat down. Hanka was saying, "You must wonder why I came to meet you. As long as I had near relatives —a father, a mother, a brother, a sister—I did not appreciate them. Now that they are all ashes, I am yearning for relatives, no matter how distant. I read the Yiddish press. You often mention your Aunt Yentel in your stories. Did she really tell you all those weird tales? You probably make them up. In my own life, things happened that cannot possibly be told. I am alone, completely alone."

"A young woman does not have to be alone."

"Just words. There are circumstances when you are torn away like a leaf from a tree and no power can attach you again. The wind carries you from your roots. There's a name for it in Hebrew, but I've forgotten."

"*Na-v'nad*—a fugitive and a wanderer."

"That's it."

I expected that I would have a short affair with Hanka. But when I tried to embrace her she seemed to shrink in my arms. I kissed her and her lips were cold. She said, "I can understand you—you are a man. You will find plenty of women here if you look for them. You will find them even if you don't look. But you are a normal person, not a necrophile. I belong to an exterminated tribe and we are not material for sex."

My lecture at the Théâtre Soleil having been postponed for some days, Hanka promised to return the next evening. I asked for her telephone number and she said that her telephone was out of order. In Buenos Aires, when something is broken, you can wait months until it is repaired. Before she left, Hanka told me almost casually that while she was looking for relatives in Buenos Aires she had found a second cousin of mine—Jechiel, who had changed his name to Julio. Jechiel was the son of my granduncle Avigdor. I had met Jechiel twice— once in the village of Tishewitz, and the second time in Warsaw, where he came for medical treatment. Jechiel was about ten years older than I—tall, darkish, and emaciated. I remembered that he suffered from tuberculosis and that Uncle Avigdor had brought him to Warsaw to see a lung specialist. I had felt sure that Jechiel did not survive the Holocaust, and now I heard that he was alive and in Argentina. Hanka gave me some details. He came to Argentina with a wife and a daughter, but he divorced his wife and married a Frampol girl whom he met in a concentration camp. He became a peddler—a knocker, as they were called in Buenos Aires. His new wife was illiterate and was afraid to go out of the house by herself. She hadn't learned a word of Spanish. When she needed to go to the grocery for a loaf of bread or for potatoes, Jechiel had to accompany her. Lately, Jechiel had been suffering from asthma and had to give up his peddling. He was living on a pension—what kind of a pension Hanka did not know: perhaps from the city or from some charitable society.

I was tired after the long day, and the moment Hanka left I fell onto the bed in my clothes and slept. After a few hours, I awoke and went out onto the balcony. It was strange to be in a country thousands of miles from my present home. In America fall was approaching; in Argentina it was spring. It had rained while I slept and Junín Street glistened. Old houses lined the street; its stalls were shuttered with iron bars. I could see the rooftops and parts of the brick walls of buildings in adjoining streets. Here and there a reddish light glimmered in a window. Was someone sick? Had someone died? In Warsaw, when I was a boy, I often heard gruesome tales about Buenos Aires: a pimp would carry a poor girl, an orphan, away to this wicked city and try to seduce her with baubles and promises, and, if she did not give in, with blows, tearing her hair and sticking pins into her fingers. Our neighbor Basha used to talk about this with my sister Hinda. Basha would say, "What could the girl do? They took her away on a ship and kept her in chains. She had already lost her innocence. She was sold into a brothel and she had to do what she was told. Sooner or later she got a little worm in her blood, and with this she could not live long. After seven years of disgrace, her hair and teeth fell out, her nose rotted away, and the play was over. Since she was defiled, they buried her behind the fence." I remember my sister's asking, "Alive?"

Now Warsaw was destroyed and I found myself in Buenos Aires, in the neighborhood where misfortunes like this were supposed to have taken place. Basha and my sister Hinda were both dead, and I was not a small boy but a middle-aged writer who had come to Argentina to spread culture.

It rained all the next day. Perhaps for the same reason that there was a shortage of electricity, the telephones didn't work properly—a man would be speaking to me in Yiddish when suddenly I was listening to a female laughing and screaming in Spanish. In the evening Hanka came. We could not go out into the street, so I ordered supper from room service. I asked Hanka what she wanted to eat and she said, "Nothing."

"What do you mean by nothing?"

"A glass of tea."

I didn't listen to her and I ordered a meat supper for her and a vegetarian platter for myself. I ate everything; Hanka barely touched the food on her plate. Like Aunt Yentel, she spewed forth stories.

"They knew in the whole house that he was hiding a Jewish girl. The tenants certainly knew. The Aryan side teemed with *szmalcownicy*—this is what they were called—who extorted the last penny from Jews to protect them and then denounced them to the Nazis. My Gentile—Andrzej was his name—had no money. Any minute someone could have notified the Gestapo and we would have all been shot—I, Andrzej, Stasiek, his son, and Maria, his wife. What am I saying? Shooting was considered light punishment. We would have been tortured. All the tenants would have paid with their lives for that crime. I often told him, 'Andrzej, my dear, you have done enough. I don't want to bring disaster on all of you.' But he said, 'Don't go, don't go. I cannot send you away to your death. Perhaps there is a God after all.' I was hidden in an alcove without a window, and they put a clothes closet at the door to conceal the entrance. They removed a board from the back of the closet and through it they passed my food and, forgive me, they took out the chamber pot. When I extinguished the little lamp I had, it became dark like in a grave. He came to me, and both of them knew about it—his wife and their son. Maria had a female sickness. Their son was sick, too. When he was a child he developed scrofula or some glandular illness and he did not need a woman. I don't think he even grew a beard. He had one passion—reading newspapers. He read all the Warsaw papers, including the advertisements. Did Andrzej satisfy me? I did not look for satisfaction. I was glad that he was relieved. From too much reading, my eyesight dimmed. I became so constipated that only castor oil would help me. Yes, I lay in my grave. But if you lie in a grave long enough, you get accustomed to it and you don't want to part from it. He had given me a pill of cyanide. He and his wife and their son also carried such pills. We all lived with death, and I want you to know that one can fall in love with death. Whoever has loved death cannot love anything else any more. When the liberation came and they told me to leave, I didn't want to go. I clung to the threshold like an ox being dragged to the slaughter.

"How I came to Argentina and what happened between me and José is a story for another time. I did not deceive him. I told him, 'José, if your wife is not lively enough, what do you need a corpse for?' But men do not believe me. When they see a woman who is young, not ugly, and can dance besides, how can she be dead? Also, I had no strength to go to work in a factory with the Spanish women. He bought me a house and this became my second grave—a fancy grave, with flowerpots, bric-a-brac, a piano. He told me to dance and I danced. In what way is it worse than to knit sweaters or to sew on buttons? All day long I sat alone and waited for him. In the evening he came, drunk and angry. One day he spoke to me and told me stories; the next day he would be mute. I knew that sooner or later he would stop talking to me altogether. When it happened I was not surprised, and I didn't try to make him talk, because I knew it was fated. He maintained his silence for over a year. Finally I told him, 'José, go.' He kissed my forehead and he left. I never saw him again."

The plans for my lecture tour began to go awry. The engagement in Rosario was called off because the president of the organization suffered a heart attack. The board of directors of the Jewish Community Center in Buenos Aires had a falling out over political differences, and the subsidy that they were to give to the colonies for my lectures there was withheld. In Mar del Plata, the hall I was to speak in suddenly became unavailable. In addition to the problems of the tour, the weather in Buenos Aires worsened from day to day. There was lightning, thunder, and from the provinces came news of windstorms and floods. The mail system didn't seem to be functioning. Proofs of a new book were supposed to come by airmail from New York, but they did not arrive and I worried that the book might be published without my final corrections. Once I was stuck in an elevator between the fourth and fifth floors and it took almost two hours before I got free. In New York I had been assured that I would not have hay fever in Buenos Aires, because it was spring there. But I suffered from attacks of sneezing, my eyes watered, my throat constricted—and I didn't even have my antihistamines with me. Chazkel Poliva stopped calling, and I suspected that he was about to cancel the whole tour. I was ready to return to New York—but how could I get information about a ship when the telephone did not work and I didn't know a word of Spanish?

Hanka came to my room every evening, always at the same time—I even imagined at the same minute. She entered noiselessly. I looked up and there she was, standing in the dusk—an image surrounded by shadows. I ordered dinner and Hanka would begin her soliloquy in the quiet monotone that reminded me of my Aunt Yentel. One night Hanka spoke about her childhood in Warsaw. They lived on Hoża Street in a Gentile neighborhood. Her father, a manufacturer, was always in debt—on the edge of bankruptcy. Her mother bought her dresses in Paris. In the summer they vacationed in Zoppot, in the winter in Zakopane. Hanka's brother Zdzislaw studied in a private high school. Her older sister, Edzia, loved to dance, but their

mother insisted it was Hanka who must become another
Pavlova or Isadora Duncan. The dance teacher was a sadist.
Even though she was ugly and a cripple herself, she demanded
perfection from her pupils. She had the eyes of a hawk, she
hissed like a snake. She taunted Hanka about her Jewishness.
Hanka was saying, "My parents had one remedy for all our
troubles—assimilation. We had to be one-hundred-per-cent
Poles. But what kind of Poles could we be when my grandfather Asher, your Aunt Yentel's son, could not even speak
Polish? Whenever he visited us, we almost died from shame.
My maternal grandfather, Yudel, spoke a broken Polish. He
once told me that we were descended from Spanish Jews. They
had been driven from Spain in the fifteenth century, and our
ancestors wandered first to Germany and then, in the Hundred Years' War, to Poland. I felt the Jewishness in my blood.
Edzia and Zdzislaw were both blond and had blue eyes, but I
was dark. I began at an early age to ponder the eternal questions: Why is one born? Why must one die? What does God
want? Why so much suffering? My mother insisted that I read
the Polish and French popular novels, but I stealthily looked
into the Bible. In the Book of Proverbs I read the words
'Charm is deceitful, and beauty is vain,' and I fell in love with
that book. Perhaps because I was forced to make an idol of my
body, I developed a hatred for the flesh. My mother and my
sister were fascinated by the beauty of movie actresses. In the
dancing school the talk was always of hips, thighs, legs, breasts.
When a girl gained as much as a quarter of a pound, the teacher
created a scene. All this seemed petty and vulgar to me. From
too much dancing, we developed bunions and bulging muscles. I was often complimented for my dancing, but I was possessed by the dybbuk of an old Talmudist, one of those
whitebeards who used to come to us to ask for alms and were
chased away by our maid. My dybbuk would ask, 'For whom
are you going to dance—for the Nazis?' Shortly before the
war, when Polish students chased the Jews through the Saxony
Gardens and my brother Zdzislaw had to stand up at the lectures in the university because he refused to sit on the ghetto
benches, he became a Zionist. But I realized that the worldly
Jews in Palestine were also eager to imitate the Gentiles. My
brother played football. He belonged to the Maccabee sports

club. He lifted weights to develop his muscles. How tragic that all my family who loved life so much had to die in the concentration camps, while fate brought me to Argentina.

"I learned Spanish quickly—the words seemed to flow back into me. I tried to dance at Jewish affairs, but everything here is rootless. Here they believe that the Jewish State will end our misfortunes once and forever. This is sheer optimism. We are surrounded there by hordes of enemies whose aim is the same as Hilter's—to exterminate us. Ten times they may not succeed —but the eleventh, catastrophe. I see the Jews being driven into the sea. I hear the wailing of the women and the children. Why is suicide considered such a sin? My own feeling is that the greatest virtue would be to abandon the body and all its iniquities."

That night, when Hanka left, I did not ask her when she would return. My lecture in the Théâtre Soleil had been advertised for the next day, and I expected her to attend. I had slept little the night before, and I went to bed and fell asleep immediately. I wakened with a feeling that someone was whispering in my ear. I tried to light the lamp by my bed, but it did not go on. I groped for the wall switch, but I could not locate it. I had hung my jacket containing my passport and traveler's checks on a chair; the chair was gone. Had I been robbed? I felt my way around the room like a blind man, tripping and bruising my knee. After a while, I stumbled into the chair. No one had taken my passport or my traveler's checks. But my gloom did not lessen. I knew that I'd had a bad dream, and I stood in the dark trying to recollect it. The second I closed my eyes, I was with the dead. They did things words cannot express. They spoke madness. "I will not let her into my room again," I murmured. "This Hanka is my angel of death."

I sat down on the edge of the bed, draped the covers over my shoulders, and took calculation of my soul. This trip had stirred up all my anxieties. I had not prepared any notes for my lecture, "Literature and the Supernatural," and I was apprehensive that I might suddenly become speechless; I foresaw a bloody revolution in Argentina, an atomic war between the United States and Russia; I would become desperately sick. Wild absurdities invaded my mind: What would happen if I got into bed and found a crocodile there? What would happen if the earth were to split into two parts and my part were to fly off to another constellation? What if my going to Argentina had actually been a departure into the next world? I had an uncanny feeling of Hanka's presence. In the left corner of the room I saw a silhouette, a dense whorl that stood apart from the surrounding darkness and took on the shadowy form of a body—shoulders, head, hair. Though I could not make out its face, I sensed in the lurking phantom the mocking of my cowardices. God in heaven, this trip was waking all the fears of my cheder days, when I dared not sleep alone because monsters slithered around my bed, tore at my sidelocks, screeching at me with terrifying voices. In my fright, I began to pray to God to keep me from falling into the hands of the Evil Ones. It seems that my prayer was heard, for suddenly the lamp went on. I saw my face in the mirror—white as after a sickness. I went to the door to make sure it was locked. Then I limped back to the bed.

The next day I spoke in the Théâtre Soleil. The hall was filled with people in spite of the heavy rain outside. I saw so many familiar faces in the audience that I could scarcely believe my eyes. True, I did not remember their names, but they reminded me of friends and acquaintances from Bilgoray, Lublin, Warsaw. Was it possible that so many had been saved from the Nazis and come to my lecture? As a rule, when I spoke about the supernatural, there were interruptions from the audience —even protest. But here, when I concluded, there was ominous silence. I wanted to go down into the audience and greet these resurrected images of my past; instead, Chazkel Poliva led me behind the stage, and by the time I made my way to the auditorium the overhead lights were extinguished and the seats empty. I said, "Shall I speak now to the spirits?"

As if he were reading my mind, Poliva asked, "Where is your so-called cousin? I didn't see her in the hall."

"No, she did not come."

"I don't want to mix into your private affairs, but do me a favor and get rid of her. It's not good for you that she should trail after you."

"No. But why do you say this?"

Chazkel Poliva hesitated. "She frightens me. She will bring you bad luck."

"Do you believe in such things?"

"When you have been an impresario for thirty years, you have to believe in them."

I had dozed off and evening had fallen. Was it the day after my lecture or a few days later? I opened my eyes and Hanka stood at my bedside. I saw embarrassment in her eyes, as if she knew my plight and felt guilty. She said, "We are supposed to go to your cousin Julio this evening."

I had prepared myself to say to her, "I cannot see you again," but I asked, "Where does Julio live?"

"It's not too far. You said that you like to walk."

Ordinarily I would have invited her to dinner, but I had no intention of dallying with her late into the night. Perhaps Julio would offer us something to eat. Half asleep, I got up and we walked out onto Corrientes. Only an occasional street light was lit, and armed soldiers were patrolling the streets. All the stores were closed. There was an air of curfew and Black Sabbath. We walked in silence, like a pair who have quarreled yet must still go visiting together. Corrientes is one of the longest boulevards in the world. We walked for an hour. Each time I asked if we were nearing our destination Hanka replied that we had some distance to go yet. After a while we turned off Corrientes. It seemed that Julio lived in a suburb. We passed factories with smokeless chimneys and barred windows, dark garages, warehouses with their windows sealed, empty lots overgrown with weeds. The few private homes we saw looked old, their patios enclosed by fences. I was tense and glanced sideways at Hanka. I could not distinguish her face—just two dark eyes. Unseen dogs were barking; unseen cats mewed and yowled. I was not hungry but unsavory fluids filled my mouth. Suspicions fell on me like locusts: Is this my final walk? Is she leading me into a cave of murderers? Perhaps she is a she-devil and will soon reveal her goose feet and pig's snout?

As if Hanka grasped that her silence made me uneasy, she became talkative. We were passing a sprawling house, with no windows, the remnants of a fence, and a lone cactus tree in front. Hanka began, "This is where the old Spanish Gentiles live. There is no heat in these houses—the ovens are for cooking, not for heating. When the rains come, they freeze. They have a drink that they call maté. They cover themselves with ragged clothes, sip maté, and lay out cards. They are Catholics, but the churches here are half empty even on Sunday. The men don't go, only the women. They are witches who pray to the devil, not to God. Time has stopped for them—they are a throwback to the era of Queen Isabella and Torquemada. José left me many books, and since I stopped dancing and have no friends I keep reading. I know Argentina. Sometimes I think I have lived here in a former incarnation. The men still dream of in-quisitions and autos-da-fé. The women mutter incantations and cast spells on their enemies. At forty they are wrinkled and wilted. The husbands find mistresses, who immediately begin to spawn children, and after a few years they are as jealous, bit-ter, and shabby as the wives. They may not know it, but many of them descend from the Marranos. Somewhere in the far-away provinces there are sects that light candles Friday evening and keep a few other Jewish customs. Here we are."

We entered an alley that was under construction. There was no pavement, no sidewalk. We made our way between piles of boards and heaps of bricks and cement. A few unfinished houses stood without roofs, without panes in the windows. The house where Julio lived was narrow and low. Hanka knocked, but no one answered. She pushed the door open, and we went through a tiny foyer into a dimly lit room furnished only with two chairs and a chest. On one chair sat Jechiel. I recognized him only because I knew that it was he. He looked ancient, but from behind his aged face, as if from behind a mask, the Jechiel of former times showed. His skull was bald, with a few wisps of side hair that were neither gray nor black but color-less. He had sunken cheeks, a pointed chin, the throat of a plucked rooster, and the pimpled nose of an alcoholic. Half of his forehead and one cheek were stained with a red rash. Jechiel did not lift his eyelids when we entered. I never saw his eyes that evening. On the other chair sat a squat, wide-girthed woman with ash-colored, disheveled hair; she was wearing a shabby housecoat. Her face was round and pasty, her eyes blank and watery, like the eyes one sees in asylums for the mentally sick. It was hard to determine whether she was forty or sixty. She did not budge. She reminded me of a stuffed doll.

From the way Hanka had spoken, I presumed that she was

well acquainted with them and that she had told them of me. But she seemed to be meeting them for the first time.

I said, "Jechiel, I am your cousin Isaac, the son of Bath-sheba. We met once in Tishewitz and later in Warsaw."

"*Sí.*"

"Do you recognize me?"

"*Sí.*"

"You have forgotten Yiddish?" I asked.

"No."

No, he had not forgotten Yiddish, but it seemed that he had forgotten how to speak. He dozed and yawned. I had to drag conversation from him. To all my questions he answered either "*Sí,*" "*No,*" or "*Bueno.*" Neither he nor his wife made an effort to bring something for us to sit on or a glass of tea. Even though I am not tall, my head almost touched the ceiling. Hanka leaned against the wall in silence. Her face had lost all expression. I walked over to Jechiel's wife and asked, "Do you have someone left in Frampol?"

For what seemed a very long time there came no answer; then she said, "Nobody."

"What was your father's name?"

She pondered as if she had to remind herself. "Avram Itcha."

"What did he do?"

Again a long pause. "A shoemaker."

After a half hour, I wearied of drawing answers from this numb couple. There was an air of fatigue about them that baffled me. Each time I addressed Jechiel, he started as if I had wakened him.

"If you have any interest in me, you can call the Hotel Cosmopolitan," I said at last.

"*Sí.*"

Jechiel's wife did not utter a sound when I said good night to her. Jechiel mumbled something I could not understand and collapsed into his chair. I thought I heard him snore. Outside, I said to Hanka, "If this is possible, anything is possible."

"We shouldn't have visited them at night," Hanka said. "They're both sick. He suffers from asthma and she has a bad heart. I told you, they became acquainted in Auschwitz. Didn't you notice the numbers on their arms?"

"No."

"Those who stood at the threshold of death remain dead."

I had heard these words from Hanka and from other refugees before, but in this dark alley they made me shudder. I said, "Whatever you are, be so good as to get me a taxi."

"*Sí.*"

Hanka embraced me. She leaned against me and clung to me. I did not stir. We stood silent in the alley, and a needle-like rain began to fall on us. Someone extinguished the light in Julio's house and it became as dark around us as in Tishewitz.

The sun was shining, the sky had cleared, it shone blue and summery. The air smelled of the sea, of mango and orange trees. Blossoms fell from their branches. The breezes reminded me of the Vistula and of Warsaw. Like the weather, my lecture tour had also cleared up. All kinds of institutions invited me to speak and gave banquets for me. Schoolchildren honored me with dancing and songs. It was bewildering that such a fuss should be made about a writer, but Argentina is isolated and when they get a guest they receive him with exaggerated friendliness.

Chazkel Poliva said, "It's all because you freed yourself of Hanka."

I had not freed myself. I was searching for her. Since the night we visited Julio, Hanka had not come to see me. And there was no way I could get in touch with her. I did not know where she lived; I didn't even know her surname. I had asked for her address more than once, but she had always avoided answering. Neither did I hear from Julio. No matter how I tried to describe his little alley, no one could identify it for me. I looked in the telephone book—Julio's name was not listed.

I went up to my room late. Going onto the balcony at night had become a habit with me. A cool wind was blowing, bringing me greetings from the Antarctic and the South Pole. I raised my eyes and saw different stars, different constellations. Some groups of stars reminded me of consonants, vowels, and the musical notations I had studied in cheder—an *aleph*, a *hai*, a *shuruk*, a *segul*, a *tsairai*, a *chain*. The sickle of the moon seemed to hang reversed, ready to harvest the heavenly fields backward. Over the roofs of Junín Street, the southern sky stretched, strangely near and divinely distant, a cosmic illumination of a volume without a beginning and without an end—to be read and judged by the Author himself. I was calling to Hanka, "Why did you run away? Wherever you are, come back. There can be no world without you. You are an eternal letter in God's scroll."

In Mar del Plata, the hall had become available, and I went there with Chazkel Poliva. On the train he said to me, "You may think it crazy, but here in Argentina Communism is a game for the rich. A poor man cannot become a member of the Communist Party. Don't ask me any questions. So it is. The rich Jews who have villas in Mar del Plata and will come tonight to your lecture are all leftists. Do me a favor and don't speak about mysticism to them. They don't believe in it. They babble constantly about the social revolution, although when the revolution comes they will be its first victims."

"This in itself is a mystery."

"Yes. But we want your lecture to be a success."

I did what Poliva told me to do. I didn't mention the hidden powers. After the lecture, I read a humorous sketch. When I finished and the question-and-answer period began, an old man rose and asked me about my inclination toward the supernatural. Soon questions on this subject came from all sides. That night the rich Jews in Mar del Plata showed great interest in telepathy, clairvoyance, dybbuks, premonitions, reincarnation: "If there is life after death, why don't the slaughtered Jews take revenge on the Nazis?" "If there is telepathy, why do we need the telephone?" "If it is possible that thought influences inanimate objects, how does it come that the bank in the casino makes high profits just because it has one chance more than its clients?" I answered that if the existence of God, the soul, the hereafter, special providence, and everything that has to do with metaphysics were scientifically proven, man would lose the highest gift bestowed upon him— free choice.

The chairman announced that the next question would be the last one, and a young man got up and asked, "Have you had personal experience of that sort? Have you ever seen a spirit?"

I answered, "All my experiences have been ambiguous.

None of them could serve for evidence. Just the same, my belief in spirits becomes ever stronger."

There was applause. As I bowed and thanked them, I saw
Hanka. She was sitting in the audience, clapping her hands.
She wore the same black hat and black dress she had worn at
all our meetings. She smiled at me and winked. I was stunned.
Had she traveled after me to Mar del Plata? I looked again and
she had vanished. No, it had been a hallucination. It lasted
only one instant. But I will brood about this instant for the
rest of my life.

Translated by the author and Blanche and Joseph Nevel

1974

FRED CHAPPELL

(b. 1936)

Linnaeus Forgets

The year 1758 was a comparatively happy one in the life of Carl Linnaeus. For although his second son, Johannes, had died the year before at the age of three, in that same year his daughter Sophia, the last child he was to have, was born. And in 1758 he purchased three small bordering estates in the country near Uppsala and on one of these, Hammarby, he established a retreat, to which he thereafter retired during the summer months, away from the town and its deadly fever. He was content in his family, his wife and five children living; and having recently been made a Knight of the Polar Star, he now received certain intelligence that at the opportune hour he would be ennobled by King Adolph Fredrik.

The landscape about Hammarby was pleasant and interesting, though of course Linnaeus long ago had observed and classified every botanical specimen this region had to offer. Even so, he went almost daily on long walks into the countryside, usually accompanied by students. The students could not deny themselves his presence even during vacation periods; they were attracted to him as hummingbirds to trumpet vines by his geniality and humor and by his encyclopedic knowledge of every plant springing from the earth.

And he was happy, too, in overseeing the renovations of the buildings in Hammarby and the construction of the new orangery, in which he hoped to bring to fruition certain exotic plants that had never before flowered on Swedish soil. Linnaeus had become at last a famous man, a world figure in the same fashion that Samuel Johnson and Voltaire and Albrecht von Haller were world figures, and every post brought him sheaves of adulatory verse and requests for permission to dedicate books to him and inquiries about the details of his system of sexual classification and plant specimens of every sort. Most of the specimens were flowers quite commonly known, but dried and pressed and sent to him by young ladies who sometimes hoped that they had discovered a new species, or who hoped merely to secure a token of the man's notice, an autograph letter. But he also received botanical samples from persons with quite reputable knowledge, from scientists persuaded that they had discovered some anomaly or exception that might cause him to think over again some part of his method. (For the ghost of Siegesbeck was even yet not completely laid.) Occasionally other specimens arrived that were indeed unfamiliar to him. These came from scientists and missionaries traveling in remote parts of the world, or the plants were sent by knowledgeable ship captains or now and then by some common sailor who had come to know, however vaguely and confusedly, something of Linnaeus's reputation.

His renown had come to him so belatedly and so tendentiously that the great botanist took a child's delight in all this attention. He read all the verses and all the letters and often would answer his unknown correspondents pretty much in their own manner; letters still remain to us in which he addressed one or another of his admirers in a silly and exaggerated prose style, admiring especially the charms of these young ladies on whom he had never set eyes. Sweden was in those days regarded as a backward country, having only a few warriors and enlightened despots to offer as important cultural figures, and part of Linnaeus's pride in his own achievements evinced itself in nationalist terms, a habit that Frenchmen and Englishmen found endearing.

On June 12, 1758, a large box was delivered to Linnaeus, along with a brief letter, and both these objects were battered from much travel. He opened first the box and found inside it a plant in a wicker basket that had been lined with oilskin. The plant was rooted in a black sandy loam, now dry and crumbly, and Linnaeus immediately watered it from a sprinkling can, though he entertained little hope of saving—actually, resuscitating—the plant. The plant was so wonderfully woebegone in appearance, so tattered by rough handling, that the scientist could not say immediately whether it was shrub, flower, or a tall grass. It seemed to have collapsed in upon itself, and its tough leaves and stems were the color of parchment and crackled like

parchment when he tried to examine them. He desisted, hoping
that the accompanying letter would answer some of his questions.

The letter bore no postmark. It was signed with a Dutch
name, Gerhaert Oorts, though it was written in French. As he
read the letter, it became clear to Linnaeus that the man who
had signed it had not written it out himself but had dictated it
to someone else who had translated his words as he spoke. The
man who wrote the letter was a Dutch sailor, a common sea-
man, and it was probably one of his superior officers who had
served him as amanuensis and translator. The letter was un-
dated and began: "*Cher maître Charles Linné, père de la science
botanique; je ne sçay si. . . .*"

"To the great Carl Linnaeus, father of botany; I know not
whether the breadth of your interests still includes a wondering curiosity about strange plants which grow in many different parts of the world, or whether your ever-agile spirit has
undertaken to possess new kingdoms of science entirely. But
in case you are continuing in your botanical endeavors, I am
taking liberty to send you a remarkable flower [*une fleur mer-
veilleuse*] that my fellows and I have observed to have strange
properties and characteristics. This flower grows in no great
abundance on the small islands east of Guiana in the South
Seas. With all worshipful respect, I am your obedient servant,
Gerhaert Oorts."

Linnaeus smiled on reading this letter, amused by the odd
wording, but then frowned slightly. He still had no useful information. The fact that Mynheer Oorts called the plant a
flower was no guarantee that it was indeed a flower. Few
people in the world were truly interested in botany, and it was
not to be expected that a sailor could have leisure for even the
most rudimentary study of the subject. The most he could
profitably surmise was that it bore blooms, which the sailor
had seen.

He looked at it again, but it was so crumpled in upon itself
that he was fearful of damaging it if he undertook a hasty inspection. It was good to know that it was a tropical plant. Linnaeus lifted the basket out of the box and set the plant on the
corner of a long table where the sunlight fell strongest. He

noticed that the soil was already thirsty again, so he watered it liberally, still not having any expectation that his ministrations would take the least effect.

It was now quarter till two, and as he had arranged a two o'clock appointment with a troublesome student, Linnaeus hurried out of his museum—which he called "my little back room"—and went into the main house to prepare himself. His student arrived promptly but was so talkative and contentious and so involved in a number of personal problems that the rest of the afternoon was dissipated in conference with him. After this, it was time for dinner, over which Linnaeus and his family habitually sat for more than two hours, gossiping and teasing and laughing. And then there was music on the clavier in the small, rough dining room; the botanist was partial to Telemann, and sat beaming in a corner of a sofa, nodding in time to a sonata.

And so it was eight o'clock before he found opportunity to return to his little back room. He had decided to defer thorough investigation of his new specimen until the next day, preferring to examine his plants by natural sunlight rather than by lamplight. For though the undying summer twilight still held the western sky, in the museum it was gray and shadowy. But he wanted to take a final look at the plant before retiring and he needed also to draw up an account of the day's activities for his journal.

He entered the little house and lit two oil lamps. The light they shed mingled with the twilight, giving a strange orange tint to the walls and furnishings.

Linnaeus was immediately aware that changes had taken place in the plant. It was no trick of the light; the plant had acquired more color. The leaves and stems were suffused with a bright lemonish yellow, a color much more alive than the dim dun the plant had shown at two o'clock. And in the room hung a pervasive scent, unmistakable but not oppressive, which could be accounted for only by the presence of the plant. This was a pleasant perfume and full of reminiscence—but he could not remember of what the scent reminded him. So many associations crowded into his mind that he could sort none of them out; but there was nothing unhappy in these confused sensations. He wagged his head in dreamy wonder.

He looked at it more closely and saw that the plant had lost its dry parchmentlike texture, that its surfaces had become pliable and lifelike in appearance. Truly it was a remarkable specimen, with its warm perfume and marvelous recuperative powers. He began to speculate that this plant had the power of simply becoming dormant, and not dying, when deprived of proper moisture and nourishment. He took up a bucket of well water, replenishing the watering can, and watered it again, resolving that he would give up all his other projects now until he had properly examined this stranger and classified it.

He snuffed the lamps and went out again into the vast whitish-yellow twilight. A huge full moon loomed in the east, just brushing the tree tips of a grove, and from within the grove sounded the harsh trills and staccato accents of a song sparrow and the calmly flowing recital of a thrush. The air was already cool enough that he could feel the warmth of the earth rising about his ankles. Now the botanist was entirely happy, and he felt within him the excitement he often had felt before when he came to know that he had found a new species and could enter another name and description into his grand catalogue.

He must have spent more time in his little back room than he had supposed, for when he reentered his dwelling house, all was silent and only enough lamps were burning for him to see to make his way about. Everyone had retired, even the two servants. Linnaeus reflected that his household had become accustomed to his arduous hours and took it for granted that he could look after his own desires at bedtime. He took a lamp and went quietly up the stairs to the bedroom. He dressed himself for bed and got in beside Fru Linnaea, who had gathered herself into a warm huddle on the left-hand side. As he arranged the bedclothes, she murmured some sleep-blurred words that he could not quite hear, and he stroked her shoulder and then turned on his right side to go to sleep.

But sleep did not come. Instead, bad memories rose, memories of old academic quarrels, and memories especially of the attacks upon him by Johann Siegesbeck. For when Siegesbeck first attacked his system of sexual classification in that detestable book called *Short Outline of True Botanic Wisdom*, Linnaeus had almost no reputation to speak of and Siegesbeck represented—to Sweden, at least—the authority of the

academy. And what, Linnaeus asked, was the basis of this ignorant pedant's objections? Why, that his system of classifying
plants was morally dissolute. In his book, Siegesbeck had asked,
"Who would have thought that bluebells, lilies, and onions
could be up to such immorality?" He went on for pages in this
vein, not failing to point out that Sir Thomas Browne had
listed the notion of the sexuality of plants as one of the vulgar
errors. Finally Siegesbeck had asked—anticipating an objection
Goethe would voice eighty-three years later—how such a li-
centious method of classification could be taught to young
students without corruption of minds and morals.

Linnaeus groaned involuntarily, helpless under the force of
memory.

These attacks had not let up, had cost him a position at the
university, so that he was forced to support himself as a medical practitioner and for two barren years had been exiled from
his botanical studies. In truth, Linnaeus never understood the
nature of these attacks; they seemed foolish and irrelevant, and
that is why he remembered them so bitterly. He could never
understand how a man could write: "To tell you that nothing
could equal the gross prurience of Linnaeus's mind is perfectly
needless. A literal translation of the first principles of Linnaean
botany is enough to shock female modesty. It is possible that
many virtuous students might not be able to make out the
similitude of *Clitoria*."

It seemed to Linnaeus that to describe his system of classification as immoral was to describe nature as immoral, and nature could not be immoral. It seemed to him that the plants
inhabited a different world than the fallen world of mankind,
and that they lived in a sphere of perfect freedom and ease, un-
vexed by momentary and perverse jealousies. Any man with
eyes could see that the stamens were masculine and the pistils
feminine, and that if there was only one stamen to the female
part (Monandria), this approximation of the Christian European family was only charmingly coincidental. It was more likely
that the female would be attended by four husbands (Tetran-
dria) or by five (Pentandria) or by twelve or more (Dodecan-
dria). When he placed the poppy in the class Polyandria and
described its arrangement as "Twenty males or more in the
same bed with the female," he meant to say of the flower no

more than God had said when He created it. How had it happened that mere literal description had caused him such un-
warrantable hardship?

These thoughts and others toiled in his mind for an hour or
so. When at last they subsided, Linnaeus had turned on his left
side toward his wife and fallen asleep, breathing unevenly.

He rose later than was his custom. His sleep had been shaken
by garish dreams that now he could not remember, and he
wished he had awakened earlier. Now he got out of bed with
uncertain movements and stiffly made his toilet and dressed
himself. His head buzzed. He hurried downstairs as soon as he
could.

It was much later than he had supposed. None of the family
was about; everyone had already breakfasted and set out in
pursuit of the new day. Only Nils, the elderly bachelor man-
servant, waited to serve him in the dining room. He informed
his master that Fru Linnaea had taken all the children, except
the baby asleep in the nursery, on an excursion into town. Linnaeus nodded, and wondered briefly whether the state of his
accounts this quarter could support the good Fru's passion for
shopping. Then he forgot about it.

It was almost nine o'clock.

He ate a large breakfast of bread and cheese and butter and
fruit, together with four cups of strong black tea. After eating,
he felt both refreshed and dilatory and he thought for a long
moment of taking advantage of the morning and the unnaturally quiet house to read in some of the new volumes of botanical studies that had arrived during the past few weeks.

But when he remembered the new specimen awaiting him
in the museum, these impulses evaporated and he left the house
quickly. It was another fine day. The sky was cloudless, a mild,
mild blue. Where the east grove cast its shadow on the lawn,
dew still remained, and he smelled its freshness as he passed.
He fumbled the latch excitedly, and then he swung the museum door open.

His swift first impression was that something had caught fire
and burned, the odor in the room was so strong. It wasn't an
acrid smell, a smell of destruction, but it was overpowering, and
in a moment he identified it as having an organic source. He

closed the door and walked to the center of the room. It was
not only the heavy damp odor that attacked his senses but also
a high-pitched musical chirping, or twittering, scattered on the
room's laden air. And the two sensations, smell and sound,
were indistinguishably mixed; here was an example of that sensory confusion of which M. Diderot had written so engagingly.
At first he could not discover the source of all this sensual
hurly-burly. The morning sun entered the windows to shine
aslant the north wall, so that between Linnaeus and his strange
new plant there fell a tall rectangular corridor of sunshine
through which his gaze couldn't pierce clearly.

He stood stock-still, for what he could see of the plant
beyond the light astonished him. It had opened out and
grown monstrously; it was enormous, tier on tier of dark green
reaching to a height of three feet or more above the table. No
blooms that he could see, but differentiated levels of broad
green leaves spread out in orderly fashion from bottom to top,
so that the plant had the appearance of a flourishing green
pyramid. And there was movement among and about the
leaves, a shifting in the air all around it, and he supposed that
an extensive tropical insect life had been transported into his
little museum. Linnaeus smiled nervously, hardly able to contain his excitement, and stepped into the passage of sunlight.

As he advanced toward the plant, the twittering sound grew
louder. The foliage, he thought, must be rife with living creatures. He came to the edge of the table but could not see
clearly yet, his sight still dazzled from stepping into and out of
the swath of sunshine.

Even when his eyes grew more accustomed to shadow, he
still could not make out exactly what he was looking at. There
was a general confused movement about and within the plant,
a continual settling and unsettling as around a beehive, but the
small creatures that flitted there were so shining and iridescent,
so gossamerlike, that he could fix no proper impression of them.
Now, though, he heard them quite clearly, and realized that
what at first had seemed a confused mélange of twittering was,
in fact, an orderly progression of sounds, a music as of flutes
and piccolos in polyphony.

He could account for this impression in no way but to think
of it as a product of his imagination. He had become aware

that his senses were not so acute as they ordinarily were; or rather, that they were acute enough, but that he was having some difficulty in interpreting what his senses told him. It occurred to him that the perfume of the plant—which now cloaked him heavily, an invisible smoke—possessed perhaps some narcotic quality. When he reached past the corner of the table to a wall shelf for a magnifying glass, he noticed that his movements were sluggish and that an odd feeling of remoteness took power over his mind.

He leaned over the plant, training his glass and trying to breathe less deeply. The creature that swam into his sight, flitting through the magnification, so startled him that he dropped the glass to the floor and began to rub his eyes and temples and forehead. He wasn't sure what he had seen—that is, he could not believe what he thought he had seen—because it was no form of insect life at all.

He retrieved the glass and looked again, moving from one area of the plant to another, like a man examining a map.

These were no insects, though many of the creatures here inhabiting were winged. They were of flesh, however diminutive they were in size. The whole animal family was represented here in miniature: horses, cows, dogs, serpents, lions and tigers and leopards, elephants, opossums and otters. . . . All the animals Linnaeus had seen or heard of surfaced here for a moment in his horn-handled glass and then sped away on their ordinary amazing errands—and not only the animals he might have seen in the world, but the fabulous animals, too: unicorns and dragons and gryphons and basilisks and the Arabian flying serpents of which Herodotus had written.

Tears streamed on the botanist's face, and he straightened and wiped his eyes with his palm. He looked all about him in the long room, but nothing else had changed. The floor was littered with potting soil and broken and empty pots, and on the shelves were the jars of chemicals and dried leaves, and on the small round table by the window his journal lay open, with two quill pens beside it and the inkpot and his pewter snuffbox. If he had indeed become insane all in a moment, the distortion of his perceptions did not extend to the daily objects of his existence but was confined to this one strange plant.

He stepped to the little table and took two pinches of snuff, hoping that the tobacco might clear his head and that the dust in his nostrils might prevent to some degree the narcotic effect of the plant's perfume, if that was what caused the appearance of these visions. He sneezed in the sunlight and dust motes rose golden around him. He bent to his journal and dipped his pen and thought, but finally wrote nothing. What could he write down that he would believe in a week's time?

He returned to the plant, determined to subject it to the most minute examination. He decided to limit his observation to the plant itself, disregarding the fantastic animal life. With the plant, his senses would be less likely to deceive him. But his resolve melted away when once again he employed the magnifying glass. There was too much movement; the distraction was too violent.

Now he observed that there were not only miniature animals, real and fabulous, but there was also a widespread colony, or nation, of homunculi. Here were little men and women, perfectly formed, and—like the other animals—sometimes having wings. He felt the mingled fear and astonishment that Mr. Swift's hapless Gulliver felt when he first encountered the Lilliputians. But he also felt an admiration, as he might have felt upon seeing some particularly well-fashioned example of the Swiss watch-maker's art. To see large animals in small, with their customary motions so accelerated, did indeed give the impression of a mechanical exhibition.

Yet there was really nothing mechanical about them, if he put himself in their situation. They were self-determining; most of their actions had motives intelligible to him, however exotic were the means of carrying out these motives. Here, for example, a tiny rotund man in a green jerkin and saffron trousers talked—sang, rather—to a tiny slender man dressed all in brown. At the conclusion of this recitative, the man in brown raced away and leapt onto the back of a tiny winged camel, which bore him from this lower level of the plant to an upper one, where he dismounted and began singing to a young lady in a bright blue gown. Perfectly obvious that a message had been delivered. . . . Here in another place a party of men and women mounted on unwinged great cats, lions and leopards and tigers, pursued over the otherwise-deserted broad plain of a leaf a fearful Hydra, its nine heads snapping and spitting. At last they impaled it to the white leaf vein with the sharp black thorns they carried for lances and then they set the monster afire, writhing and shrieking, and they rode away together. A grayish waxy blister formed on the leaf where the hydra had burned. . . . And here in another area a formal ball was taking place, the tiny gentlemen leading out the ladies in time to the music of an orchestra sawing and pounding at the instruments. . . .

This plant, then, enfolded a little world, a miniature society in which the mundane and the fanciful commingled in matter-of-fact fashion but at a feverish rate of speed.

Linnaeus became aware that his legs were trembling from tiredness and that his back ached. He straightened, feeling a grateful release of muscle tension. He went round to the little table and sat, dipped his pen again, and began writing hurriedly, hardly stopping to think. He wrote until his hand almost cramped and then he flexed it several times and wrote more, covering page after page with his neat sharp script. Finally he laid the pen aside and leaned back in his chair and thought. Many different suppositions formed in his mind, but none of them made clear sense. He was still befuddled and he felt that he might be confused for years to come, that he had fallen victim to a dream or vision from which he might never recover.

In a while he felt rested and he returned again to look at the plant.

By now a whole season, or a generation or more, had passed. The plant itself was a darker green than before, its shape had changed, and even more creatures now lived within it. The mid-part of the plant had opened out into a large boxlike space thickly walled with hand-sized kidney-shaped leaves. This section formed a miniature theater or courtyard. Something was taking place here, but Linnaeus could not readily figure out what it was.

Much elaborate construction had been undertaken. The smaller leaves of the plant in this space had been clipped and arranged into a grand formal garden. There were walls and arches of greenery and greenery shaped into obelisks topped with globes, and Greek columns and balconies and level paths. Wooden statues and busts were placed at intervals within this garden, and it seemed to Linnaeus that on some of the subjects

he could make out the lineaments of the great classical bota-
nists. Here, for example, was Pliny, and there was Theophras-
tus. Many of the persons so honored were unfamiliar to him,
but then he found on one of the busts, occupying a position of
great prominence, his own rounded cheerful features. Could
this be true? He stared and stared, but his little glass lacked
enough magnification for him to be finally certain.

Music was everywhere; chamber orchestras were stationed
at various points along the outer walls of the garden and two
large orchestras were set up at either end of the wide main path.
There were a number of people calmly walking about, twittering
to one another, but there were fewer than he had supposed at
first. The air above them was dotted with cherubs flying about
playfully, and much of the foliage was decorated with artfully
hung tapestries. There was about the scene an attitude of expectancy, of waiting.

At this point the various orchestras began to sound in concert and gathered the music into recognizable shape. The
sound was still thin and high-pitched, but Linnaeus discerned
in it a long reiterative fanfare, which was followed by a slow,
grave processional march. All the little people turned from
their casual attitudes and gave their attention to the wall of
leaves standing at the end of the main wide pathway. There was
a clipped narrow corridor in front of the wall and from it
emerged a happy band of naked children. They advanced
slowly and disorderly, strewing the path with tiny pink petals
that they lifted out in dripping handfuls from woven baskets
slung over their shoulders. They were singing in unison, but
Linnaeus could not make out the melody, their soprano voices
pitched beyond his range of hearing. Following the children
came another group of musicians, blowing and thumping, and
then a train of comely maidens, dressed in airy long white
dresses tied about the waists with broad ribbons, green and
yellow. The maidens, too, were singing, and the botanist now
began to hear the vocal music, a measured but joyous choral
hymn. Linnaeus was smiling to himself, buoyed up on an ocean
of happy fullness; his face and eyes were bright.

The beautiful maidens were followed by another troop of
petal-scattering children, and after them came a large orderly
group of animals of all sorts, domestic animals and wild

animals and fantastic animals, stalking forward with their fine
innate dignities, though not, of course, in step. The animals
were unattended, moving in the procession as if conscious of
their places and duties. There were more of these animals,
male and female of each kind, than Linnaeus had expected to
live within the plant. He attempted vainly to count the number of different species, but he gave over as they kept pouring
forward smoothly, like sand grains twinkling into the bottom
of an hourglass.

The spectators had gathered to the sides of the pathway and
stood cheering and applauding.

The animals passed by, and now a train of carriages ranked
in twos took their place. These carriages each were drawn by
teams of four little horses, and both the horses and carriages
were loaded down with great garlands of bright flowers, hung
with blooms from end to end. Powdered ladies fluttered their
fans in the windows. And after the carriages, another band of
musicians marched.

Slowly now, little by little, a large company of strong young
men appeared, scores of them. Each wore a stout leather harness from which long reins of leather were attached behind to
an enormous wheeled platform. The young men, their bodies
shining, drew this platform down the pathway. The platform
itself supported another formal garden, within which was an
interior arrangement suggestive of a royal court. There was a
throne on its dais, and numerous attendants before and behind
the throne. Flaming braziers in each corner gave off thick
grayish-purple clouds of smoke, and around these braziers
small children exhibited various instruments and implements
connected with the science of botany: shovels, thermometers,
barometers, potting spades, and so forth. Below the dais on
the left-hand side, a savage, a New World Indian, adorned with
feathers and gold, knelt in homage, and in front of him a beautiful woman in Turkish dress proffered to the throne a tea shrub
in a silver pot. Farther to the left, at the edge of the tableau, a
sable Ethiopian stood, he also carrying a plant indigenous to
his mysterious continent.

The throne itself was a living creature, a great tawny lion
with sherry-colored eyes. The power and wildness of the creature were unmistakable in him, but now he lay placid and

willing, with a sleepy smile on his face. And on this throne of
the living lion, over whose back a covering of deep-plush green
satin had been thrown, sat the goddess Flora. This was she indeed, wearing a golden crown and holding in her left hand a
gathering of peonies (*Paeonia officinalis*) and in her right hand
a heavy golden key. Flora sat in ease, the goddess gowned in a
carmine silk that shone silver where the light fell on it in broad
planes, the gown tied over her right shoulder and arm to form
a sleeve, and gathered lower on her left side to leave the breast
bare. An expression of sublime dreaminess was on her face and
she gazed off into a far distance, thinking thoughts unknowable even to her most intimate initiates. She was attended on
her right-hand side by Apollo, splendidly naked except for the
laurel bays round his forehead and his bow and quiver crossed
on his chest. Behind her Diana disposed herself, half-reclining,
half-supporting herself on her bow, and wearing in her hair her
crescent-moon fillet. Apollo devoted his attention to Flora,
holding aloft a blazing torch, and looking down upon her with
an expression of mingled tenderness and admiration. He stood
astride the carcass of a loathsome slain dragon, signifying the
demise of ignorance and superstitious unbelief.

The music rolled forth in loud hosannas, and the spectators
on every side knelt in reverence to the goddess as she passed.

Linnaeus became dizzy. He closed his eyes for a moment
and felt the floor twirling beneath his feet. He stumbled across
the room to his chair by the writing table and sat. His chin
dropped down on his chest; he fell into a deep swoon.

When he regained consciousness, the shaft of sunlight had
reached the west wall. At least an hour had passed. When he
stirred himself, there was an unaccustomed stiffness in his limbs
and it seemed to him that over the past twenty-four hours or
so his body had aged several years.

His first clear thoughts were of the plant, and he rose and
went to his worktable to find out what changes had occurred.
But the plant was no more; it had disappeared. Here was the
wicker container lined with oilcloth, here was the earth inside
it, now returned to its dry and crumbly condition, but the
wonderful plant no longer existed. All that remained was a
greasy gray-green powder sifted over the soil. Linnaeus took
up a pinch of it in his fingers and sniffed at it and even tasted

it, but it had no sensory qualities at all except a neutral oiliness. Absentmindedly he wiped his fingers on his coat sleeve.

A deep melancholy descended upon the man and he locked his hands behind his back and began walking about the room, striding up and down beside his worktable. A harsh welter of thoughts and impulses overcame his mind. At one point he halted in mid-stride, turned and crossed to his writing table, and snatched up his journal, anxious to determine what account he had written of his strange adventure.

His journal was no help at all, for he could not read it. He looked at the unfinished last page and then thumbed backward for seven pages and turned them all over again, staring and staring. He had written in a script unintelligible to him, a writing that seemed to bear some distant resemblance to Arabic perhaps, but which bore no resemblance at all to his usual exuberant mixture of Latin and Swedish. Not a word or a syllable on any page conveyed the least meaning to him.

As he gazed at these dots and squiggles he had scratched on the page, Linnaeus began to forget. He waved his hand before his face like a man brushing away cobwebs. The more he looked at his pages, the more he forgot, until finally he had forgotten the whole episode: the letter from the Dutch sailor, the receiving of the plant, the discovery of the little world the plant contained—everything.

Like a man in a trance, and with entranced movements, he returned to his worktable and swept some scattered crumbs of soil into a broken pot and carried it away and deposited it in the dustbin.

It has been said that some great minds have the ability *to forget deeply.* That is what happened to Linnaeus; he forgot the plant and the bright vision that had been vouchsafed to him. But the profoundest levels of his life had been stirred, and some of the details of his thinking had changed.

His love for metaphor sharpened, for one thing. Writing in his *Deliciae naturae,* which appeared fourteen years after his encounter with the plant, he described a small pink-flowered ericaceous plant of Lapland growing on a rock by a pool, with a newt as "the blushing naked princess Andromeda, lovable and beautiful, chained to a sea rock and exposed to a horrible dragon." These kinds of conceits intrigued him, and more than ever metaphor began to inform the way he perceived and outlined the facts of his science.

Another happy change in his life was the cessation of his bad nights of sleeplessness and uneasy dreams. No longer was he troubled by memories of the attacks of Siegesbeck or any other of his old opponents. Linnaeus had acquired a new and resistless faith in his observations. He was finally certain that the plants of this earth carry on their love affairs in uncaring merry freedom, making whatever sexual arrangements best suit them, and that they go to replenish the globe guiltlessly, in high and winsome delight.

1977

JOHN CROWLEY

(b. 1942)

Novelty

I

HE found, quite suddenly and just as he took a stool midway down the bar, that he had been vouchsafed a theme. A notion about the nature of things that he had been turning over in his mind for some time had become, without his ever choosing it, the theme of a book. It had "fallen into place," as it's put, like the tumblers of a lock that a safecracker listens to, and—so he experienced it—with the same small, smooth sound.

The theme was the contrary pull men feel between Novelty and Security. Between boredom and adventure, between safety and dislocation, between the snug and the wild. Yes! Not only a grand human theme, but a truly *mammalian* theme, perhaps the only one. Curiosity killed the cat, we are warned, and warned with good reason, and yet we are curious. Cats could be a motif: cats asleep, taking their ease in that superlatively comfortable way they have—you feel drowsy and snug just watching them. Cats on the prowl, endlessly prying. Cats tiptoe-walking away from fearsome novelty, hair on fire and faces shocked. He chuckled, pleased with this, and lifted the glass that had been set before him. From the great window south light poured through the golden liquor, refracted delicately by ice.

The whole high front of the Seventh Saint Bar & Grill where he sat is of glass, floor to ceiling, a glass divided by vertical beams into a triptych and deeply tinted brown. During the day nothing of the dimly lit interior of the bar can be seen from the outside; walkers-by see only themselves, darkly; often they stop to adjust their clothing or their hair in what seems to them to be a mirror, or simply gaze at themselves in passing, momentarily but utterly absorbed, unaware that they are caught at it by watchers inside. (Or watcher, today, he being so far the bar's sole customer.) Seen from inside the bar, the avenue, the stores opposite, the street glimpsed going off at right angles, the trapezoid of sky visible above the lower buildings, are altered by the tinted windows into an elsewhere, oddly peaceful, a desert or the interior of the sea. Sometimes when he has fallen asleep face upward in the sun, his dreams have taken on this quality of supernatural bright darkness.

Novelty. Security. *Novelty* wouldn't be a bad title. It had the grandness of abstraction, alerting the reader that large and thoughtful things were to be bodied forth. As yet he had no inkling of any incidents or characters that might occupy his theme; perhaps he never would. He could see though the book itself, he could feel its closed heft and see it opened, white pages comfortably large and shadowed gray by print; dense, numbered, full of meat. He sensed a narrative voice, speaking calmly and precisely, with immense assurance building, building; a voice too far off for him to hear, but speaking.

The door of the bar opened, showing him a momentary oblong of true daylight, blankly white. A woman entered. He couldn't see her face as she crossed to the bar in front of the window, but he could see, drawn with exactitude by the light behind her, her legs within a summery white dress. When young he had supposed, without giving it much thought, that women didn't realize that sun behind them revealed them in this way; now he supposes that of course they must, and thinks about it.

"Well, look who's here," said the bartender. "You off today?"

"I took off," she said, and as she took a seat between him and the window, he saw that she was known to him, that is, they had sat here in this relation before. "I couldn't stand it anymore. What's tall and cool and not too alcoholic?"

"How about a spritzer?"

"Okay."

He caught himself staring fixedly at her, trying to remember if they had spoken before, and she caught him, too, raising her eyes to him as she lifted the pale drink to her lips, large dark eyes with startling whites; and looked away again quickly.

Where was he again? Novelty, security. He felt the feet of his attention skate out from under him in opposite directions. Should he make a note? He felt for the smooth shape of his pen in his pocket. "Theme for a novel: The contrary pull . . ." No. If this notion were real, he needn't make a note. A notion on which a note had to be made would be stillborn anyway, his notebook was a parish register of such, born and dead on the same page. Let it live if it can.

But had he spoken to her before? What had he said?

II

When he was in college, a famous poet made a useful distinction for him. He had drunk enough in the poet's company to be compelled to describe to him a poem he was thinking of. It would be a monologue of sorts, the self-contemplation of a student on a summer afternoon who is reading *Euphues*. The poem itself would be a subtle series of euphuisms, translating the heat, the day, the student's concerns, into symmetrical posies; translating even his contempt and boredom with that famously foolish book into a euphuism.

The poet nodded his big head in a sympathetic, rhythmic way as this was explained to him, then told him that there are two kinds of poems. There is the kind you write; there is the kind you talk about in bars. Both kinds have value and both are poems; but it's fatal to confuse them.

In the Seventh Saint, many years later, it had struck him that the difference between himself and Shakespeare wasn't talent —not especially—but *nerve*. The capacity not to be frightened by his largest and most potent conceptions, to simply (simply!) sit down and execute them. The dreadful lassitude he felt when something really large and multifarious came suddenly clear to him, something *Lear*-sized yet sonnet-precise. If only they didn't rush on him whole, all at once, massive and perfect, leaving him frightened and nerveless at the prospect of articulating them word by scene by page. He would try to believe they were of the kind told in bars, not the kind to be written, though there was no way to be sure of this except to attempt the writing; he would raise a finger (the novelist in the bar mirror raising the obverse finger) and push forward his change. Wailing like a neglected ghost, the vast notion would beat its wings into the void.

Sometimes it would pursue him for days and years as he fled

desperately. Sometimes he would turn to face it, and do battle. Once, twice, he had been victorious, objectively at least. Out of an immense concatenation of feeling, thought, word, and transcendent meaning had come his first novel, a slim, silent pageant of a book, tombstone for his slain conception. A publisher had taken it, gingerly; had slipped it quietly into the deep pool of spring releases, where it sank without a ripple, and where he supposes it lies still, its calm Bodoni gone long since green. A second, just as slim but more lurid, nightmarish even, about imaginary murders in an imaginary exotic locale, had been sold for a movie, though the movie had never been made. He felt guilt for the producer's failure (which perhaps the producer didn't feel), having known the book could not be filmed; he had made a large sum, enough to finance years of this kind of thing, on a book whose first printing was largely returned.

His editor now and then took him to an encouraging lunch, and talked about royalties, advances, and upcoming titles, letting him know that whatever doubts he had she considered him a member of the profession, and deserving of a share in its largesse and its gossip; at their last one, some months before, she had pressed him for a new book, something more easily graspable than his others. "A couple of chapters, and an outline," she said. "I could tell from that."

Well, he *was* sort of thinking of something, but it wasn't really shaping up, or rather it was shaping up rather like the others, into something indescribable at bottom. . . . "What it would be," he said timidly, "would be sort of a Catholic novel, about growing up Catholic," and she looked warily up at him over her Campari.

The first inkling of this notion had come to him the Christmas before, at his daughter's place in Vermont. On Christmas Eve, as indifferent evening took hold in the blue squares of the windows, he sat alone in the crepuscular kitchen, imbued with a profound sense of the identity of winter and twilight, of twilight and time, of time and memory, of his childhood and that church which on this night waited to celebrate the second greatest of its feasts. For a moment or an hour as he sat, become one with the blue of the snow and the silence, a con-

gruity of star, cradle, winter, sacrament, self, it was as though
he listened to a voice that had long been trying to catch his attention, to tell him, Yes, this was the subject long withheld
from him, which he now knew, and must eventually act on.

He had managed, though, to avoid it. He only brought it out
now to please his editor, at the same time aware that it wasn't
what she had in mind at all. But he couldn't do better; he had
really only the one subject, if subject was the word for it, this
idea of a notion or a holy thing growing clear in the stream of
time, being made manifest in unexpected ways to an assortment of people: the revelation itself wasn't important, it could
be anything, almost. Beyond that he had only one interest, the
seasons, which he could describe endlessly and with all the
passion of a country-bred boy grown old in the city. He was
coming to doubt (he said) whether these were sufficient to
make any more novels out of, though he knew that writers of
genius had made great ones out of less. He supposed really (he
didn't say) that he wasn't a novelist at all, but a failed poet, like
a failed priest, one who had perceived that in fact he had no
vocation, had renounced his vows, and yet had found nothing
at all else in the world worth doing when measured by the
calling he didn't have, and went on through life fatally attracted to whatever of the sacerdotal he could find or invent in
whatever occupation he fell into, plumbing or psychiatry or
tending bar.

III

"Boring, boring, *boring*," said the woman down the bar from
him. "I feel like taking off for good." Victor, the bartender,
chin in his hand and elbow on the bar, looked at her with the
remote sympathy of confessors and bartenders.

"Just take off," she said.

"So take off," Victor said. "Jeez, there's a whole world out
there."

She made a small noise to indicate she doubted there was.
Her brilliant eyes, roving over her prospects, fell on his where
they were reflected in the bar mirror. She gazed at him but (he
knew) didn't see him, for she was looking within. When she did

shift focus and understand she was being regarded, she smiled briefly and glanced at his real person, then bent to her drink again. He summoned the bartender.

"Another, please, Victor."

"How's the writing coming?"

"Slowly. Very slowly. I just now thought of a new one, though."

"Izzat so."

It was so; but even as he said it, as the stirring stick he had just raised out of his glass dripped whiskey drop by drop back into it, the older notion, the notion he had been unable to describe at all adequately to his editor, which he had long since dropped or thought he had dropped, stirred within him. Stirred mightily, though he tried to shut doors on it; stirred, rising, and came forth suddenly in all the panoply with which he had forgotten it had come to be dressed, its facets glittering, windows opening on vistas, great draperies billowing. It seemed to have grown old in its seclusion but more potent, and fiercely reproachful of his neglect. Alarmed, he tried to shelter his tender new notion of Novelty and Security from its onrush, but even as he attempted this, the old notion seized upon the new, and as he watched helplessly, the two coupled in an utter ravishment and interlacement, made for each other, one thing now and more than twice as compelling as each had been before. "Jesus," he said aloud; and then looked up, wondering if he had been heard. Victor and the woman were tête-à-tête, talking urgently in undertones.

IV

"I know, I know," he'd said, raising a hand to forestall his editor's objection. "The Catholic Church is a joke. Especially the Catholic Church I grew up in . . ."

"Sometimes a grim joke."

"And it's been told a lot. The nuns, the weird rules, all that decayed scholastic guff. The prescriptions, and the proscriptions —especially the proscriptions, all so trivial when they weren't hurtful or just ludicrous. But that's not the way it's perceived. For a kid, for me, the church organized the whole world—not morally, either, or not especially, but in its whole nature. Even if the kid isn't particularly moved by thoughts of God and sin—I wasn't—there's still a lot of church left over, do you see? Because all the important things about the church were real things: objects, places, words, sights, smells, days. The liturgical calendar. The Eastern church must be even more so. For me, the church was mostly about the seasons: it kept them in order. The church was coextensive with the world."

"So the kid's point of view against—"

"No, no. What I would do, see, to get around this contradiction between the real church and this other church I seemed to experience physically and emotionally, is to reimagine the Catholic Church as another kind of church altogether, a very subtle and wise church, that understood all these feelings; a church that was really—secretly—*about* these things in fact, and not what it seemed to be about; and then pretend, in the book, that the church I grew up in was that church."

"You're going to invent a whole new religion?"

"Well, not exactly. It would just be a matter of shifting emphasis, somehow, turning a thing a hundred and eighty degrees . . ."

"Well, how? Do you mean 'books in the running brooks, sermons in stones,' that kind of thing? Pantheism?"

"No. No. The opposite. In that kind of religion the trees and the sky and the weather *stand for* God or some kind of supernatural unity. In my religion, God and all the rituals and sacraments would stand for the real world. The religion would be a means of perceiving the real world in a sacramental way. A Gnostic ascension. A secret at the heart of it. And the secret is—everything. Common reality. The day outside the church window."

"Hm."

"That's what it would really have been about from the beginning. And only seemed to be about these divine personages, and stuff, and these rules."

She nodded slowly in a way that showed she followed him but frankly saw no novel. He went on, wanting at least to say it all before he no longer saw it with this clarity. "The priests and nuns would know this was the case, the wisest of them, and would guide the worshipers—the ones they thought could grasp it—to see through the paradox, to see that it *is* a paradox: that only by believing, wholly and deeply, in all of it could you see through it one day to what is real—see through Christmas to the snow; see through the fasting, and the saints' lives, and the sins, and Baby Jesus walking through the snow every Christmas night ringing a little bell—"

"What?"

"That was a story one nun told. That was a thing she said was the case."

"Good heavens. Did she believe it?"

"Who knows? That's what I'm getting at."

She broke into her eggs Florentine with a delicate fork. The two chapters, full of meat; the spinach of an outline. She was very attractive in a coltish, aristocratic way, with a rosy flush on her tanned cheeks that was just the flush his wife's cheeks had had. No doubt still had; no doubt.

"Like Zen," he said desperately. "As though it were a kind of Zen."

V

Well, he had known as well as she that it was no novel, no matter that it importuned him, reminding him often of its deep truth to his experience, and suggesting shyly how much fun it might be to manipulate, what false histories he could invent that would account for the church he imagined. But he had it now; now the world began to turn beneath him firmly, both rotating and revolving; it was quite clear now.

The *theme* would not be religion at all, but this ancient conflict between novelty and security. This theme would be embodied in the contrasted adventures of a set of *characters*, a family of Catholic believers modeled on his own. The *motion* of the book would be the sense of a holy thing ripening in the stream of time, that is, the seasons; and the *form* would be a false history or mirror-reversal of the world he had known and the church he had believed in.

Absurdly, his heart had begun to beat fast. Not years from now, not months, very soon, imaginably soon, he could begin. That there was still nothing concrete in what he envisioned didn't bother him, for he was sure this scheme was one that would generate concreteness spontaneously and easily. He had

planted a banner amid his memories and imaginings, a banner
to which they could all repair, to which they were repairing
even now, primitive clans vivified by these colors, clamoring to
be marshaled into troops by the captains of his art.

It would take a paragraph, a page, to eliminate, say, the Reformation, and thus make his church infinitely more aged,
bloated, old in power, forgetful of dogmas long grown universal and ignorable, dogmas altered by subtle subversives into
their opposites, by a brotherhood within the enormous bu-
reaucracy of faith, a brotherhood animated by a holy irony and
secret as the Rosicrucians. Or contrariwise: he could pretend
that the Reformation had been more nearly a complete success
than it was, leaving his Roman faith a small, inward-turning,
Gnostic sect, poor and not grand, guiltless of the Inquisition;
its pope itinerant or in shabby exile somewhere (Douai, or
Alexandria, or Albany); through Appalachia a poor priest travels from church to church, riding the circuit in an old Stude-
baker as rusty black as his cassock, putting up at a plain frame
house on the outskirts of town, a convent. The wainscoted parlor is the nuns' chapel, and the pantry is full of their canning;
in autumn the broken stalks of corn wither in their kitchen
garden. "Use it up, wear it out," says the proverb of their
creed (and not that of splendid and orgulous Protestants),
"make it do, do without": and they possess themselves in
edge-worn and threadbare truth.

Yes! The little clapboard church in Kentucky where his family had worshiped, in the Depression, amid the bumptious
Baptists. In the hastening dawn he had walked a mile to serve
six o'clock mass there. In winter the stove's smell was incense;
in summer it was the damp odor of morning coming through
the lancet windows, opened a crack to reveal a band of blue-
green day beneath the feet of the saints fragilely pictured there
in imitation stained glass. The three or four old Polish women
always present always took Communion, their extended
tongues trembling and their veined closed eyelids trembling,
too; and though when they rose crossing themselves they became only unsanctified old women again, he had for a moment
glimpsed their clean pink souls. There were aged and untended rosebushes on the sloping lawn of the big gray house
he had grown up in—his was by far the best off of any family in

that little parish—and when the roses bloomed in May the priest came and the familiar few they saw in church each week gathered, and the Virgin was crowned there, a Virgin pink and blue and white as the rose-burdened day, the best lace table-cloth beneath her, strange to see that domestic lace outdoors edge-curled by odorous breezes and walked on by bugs. He caught himself singing:

> *O Mary, we crown thee with blossoms today*
> *Queen of the Angels*
> *Queen of the May*

Of course he would lose by this scheme a thousand other sorts of memories just as dear, would lose the grand and the fatuous baroque, mitered bishops in jewel-encrusted copes and steel-rimmed eyeglasses; but the point was not nostalgia and self-indulgence after all, no, the opposite; in fact there ought to be some way of tearing the heart completely out of the old religion, or to conceive on it something so odd that no reader would ever confuse it with the original, except that it would be as concrete, its concreteness the same concreteness (which was the point . . .) And what then had been that religion's heart?

What if his Jesus hadn't saved mankind?

What if the Renaissance, besides uncovering the classical past, had discovered evidence—manuscripts, documentary proofs (incontrovertible, though only after terrible struggles)—that Jesus had in the end refused to die on the cross? Had run away; had abjured his Messiah-hood; and left his followers then to puzzle that out. It would not have been out of cowardice, exactly, though the new New Testaments would seem to say so, but (so the apologetic would come to run) out of a desire to share our human life completely, even our common unheroic fate. Because the true novelty, for God, would lie not in the redemption of men—an act he could perform with a millionth part of the creative effort he had expended in creating the world—but in being a human being entire, growing old and impotent to redeem anybody, including himself. Something like that had happened with the false messiah Sevi in the seventeenth century: his Messiah-hood spread quickly and widely through the whole Jewish world; then, at the last minute, threatened with death, he'd converted to Islam. His followers mostly fell away, but a few still believed, and their attempts to figure out how the Messiah could act in that strange way, redeem us by not redeeming us, yielded up the Hassidic sect, with its Kabbalah and its paradoxical parables, almost Zenlike; very much what he had in mind for his church.

"A man of sorrows, and acquainted with grief"—the greatest grief, far greater than a few moments' glorious pain on that Tree. Mary's idea of it was that in the end the Father was unable to permit the death of his only begotten son; the prophecy is Abraham and Isaac; she interceded for him, of course, her son, too, as she still intercedes for each of us. Perhaps he resented it. In any case he out-lived her, and his own wife and son, too; lived on, a retired carpenter, in his daughter's house; and the rabble came before his door, and they mocked him, saying: *If thou art the Christ, take up thy cross.*

Weird! But, but—what made him chuckle and nearly smack his lips (in full boil now)—the thing would be, that his characters would pursue their different destinies *completely oblivious of all this oddity*, oblivious, that is, that it *is* odd; the narrative voice wouldn't notice it either; their Resurrection has always been this ambiguous one, this Refusal; their holy-card of Jesus in despised old age (after Murillo) has always marked the Sundays in their missals; their church is just the old, the homely, the stodgy great Security, Peter's rock, which his was. His priest would venture out (bored, restless) from that security into the strange and the dangerous, at first only wishing to be a true priest, then for their own sakes, for the adventure of understanding. A nun: starting from a wild embracing of all experience, anything goes, she passes later into quietness and, well, into habit. His wife would have to sit for that portrait, of course, of course; though she wouldn't sit still. The two meet after long separation, only to pass each other at the X-point, coming from different directions, headed for different heavens —a big scene there. A saint: but which one? He or she? Well, that had always been the question; neither, or both, or one seeing at last after the other's death his sainthood, and advocating it (in the glum Vatican, a Victorian pile in Albany, the distracted pope), a miracle awaited and given at last, unexpectedly, or not given, withheld—oh, hold on, he asked, stop a minute, slow down. He plucked out and lit a cigarette with care. He placed his glass more exactly in the center of its cardboard coaster and arranged his change in orbits around it.

Flight over. Cats, though. He would appropriate for his Jesus that story about Muhammad called from his couch, tearing off his sleeve rather than disturbing the cat that had fallen asleep on it. A parable. Did Jews keep cats then? Who knows.

Oh God how subtle he would have to be, how cunning. . . . No paragraph, no phrase even of the thousands the book must contain could strike a discordant note, be less than fully imagined, an entire novel's worth of thought would have to be expended on each one. His attention had only to lapse for a moment, between preposition and object, colophon and chapter heading, for dead spots to appear like gangrene that would rot the whole. Silkworms didn't work as finely or as patiently as he must, and yet boldness was all, the large stroke, the end contained in and prophesied by the beginning, the stains of his clouds infinitely various but all signifying sunrise. Unity in diversity, all that guff. An enormous weariness flew over him. The trouble with drink, he had long known, wasn't that it started up these large things but that it belittled the awful difficulties of their execution. He drank, and gazed out into the false golden day, where a passage of girl students in plaid uniforms was just then occurring, passing secret glances through the trick mirror of the window.

VI

"I'm such a chicken," the woman said to Victor. "The other day they were going around at work signing people up for the softball team. I really wanted to play. They said come on, come on, it's no big deal, it's not professional or anything . . ."

"Sure, just fun."

"I didn't dare."

"What's to dare? Just good exercise. Fresh air."

"Sure, *you* can say that. You've probably been playing all your life." She stabbed at the last of her ice with a stirring-stick. "I really wanted to, too. I'm such a chicken."

Play right field, he wanted to advise her. That had always been his retreat, nothing much ever happens in right field, you're safe there mostly unless a left-handed batter gets up, and then if you blow one, the shame is quickly forgotten. He told himself to say to her: *You should have volunteered for right field*. But his throat said it might refuse to do this, and his pleasantry could come out a muffled croak, watch out. She had finished her drink; how much time did he have to think of a thing to say to her? Buy her a drink: the sudden offer always made him feel like a masher, a cad, something antique and repellent.

"You should have volunteered for right field," he said.

"Oh, hi," she said. "How's the writing coming?"

"What?"

"The last time we talked you were writing a novel."

"Oh. Well, I sort of go in spurts." He couldn't remember still that he had ever talked with her, much less what imaginary novel he had claimed to be writing.

"It's like coming into a cave here," she said, raising her glass, empty now except for the rounded remains of ice. "You can't see anything for a while. Because of the sun in your eyes. I didn't recognize you at first." The ice she wanted couldn't escape from the bottom of the glass till she shook the glass briskly to free it; she slid a piece into her mouth then and crunched it heedlessly (a long time since he'd been able to do that) and drew her skirt away from the stool beside her, which he had come to occupy.

"Will you have another?"

"No, nope." They smiled at each other, each ready to go on with this if the other could think of something to go on with.

"So," he said.

"Taking a break?" she said. "Do you write every day?"

"Oh, no. Oh, I sort of try. I don't work very hard, really. Really I'm on vacation. All the time. Or you could say I work all the time, too. It comes to the same thing." He'd said all this before, to others; he wondered if he'd said it to her. "It's like weekend homework. Remember? There wasn't ever a time you absolutely had to do it—there was always Saturday, then Sunday—but then there wasn't ever a time when it wasn't there to do, too."

"How awful."

Sunday dinner's rich odor declining into stale leftoverhood:

was it that incense that made Sunday Sunday, or what? For there was no part of Sunday that was not Sunday; even if, rebelling, you changed from Sunday suit to Saturday jeans when dinner was over, they felt not like a second skin, like a bold animal's useful hide, as they had the day before, but strange, all right but wrong to flesh chafed by wool, the flannel shirt too smooth, too indulgent after the starched white. And upstairs—though you kept as far from them as possible, that is, facedown and full-length on the parlor carpet, head inches from the funnies—the books and blue-lined paper waited.

"It must take a lot of self-discipline," she said.

"Oh, I don't know. I don't have much." He felt himself about to say again, and unable to resist saying, that "Dumas, I think it was Dumas, some terrifically prolific Frenchman, said that writing novels is a simple matter—if you write one page a day, you'll write one novel a year, two pages a day, two novels a year, three pages, three novels, and so on. And how long does it take to cover a page with writing? Twenty minutes? An hour? So you see. Very easy really."

"I don't know," she said, laughing. "I can't even bring myself to write a letter."

"Oh, now *that's* hard." Easiest to leave it all just as it had been, and only inveigle into it a small sect of his own making . . . easiest of all just to leave it. It was draining from him, like the suits of the bathing beauties pictured on trick tumblers, to opposite effect. Self-indulgence only, nostalgia, pain of loss for what had not ever been worth saving: the self-indulgence of a man come to that time when the poignance of memory is his sharpest sensation, grown sharp as the others have grown blunt. The journey now quite obviously more than half over, it had begun to lose interest; only the road already traveled still seemed full of promise. Promise! Odd word. But there it was. He blinked, and having fallen rudely silent, said, "Well, well, well."

"Well," she said. She had begun to gather up the small habitation she had made before her on the bar, purse and open wallet, folded newspaper, a single unblown rose he hadn't noticed her bring in. "I'd like to read your book sometime."

"Sure," he said. "It's not very good. I mean, it has some nice things in it, it's a good little story. But it's nothing really."

"I'm sure it's terrific." She spun the rose beneath her nose and alighted from her stool.

"I happen to have a lot of copies. I'll give you one."

"Good. Got to go."

On her way past him she gave the rose to Victor without any other farewell. Once again sun described her long legs as she crossed the floor (sun lay on its boards like gilding, sun was impartial), and for a moment she paused, sun-blinded maybe, in the garish lozenge of real daylight made when she opened the door. Then she reappeared in the other afternoon of the window. She raised her hand in a command, and a cab the color of marigolds appeared before her as though conjured. A flight of pigeons filled up the window all in an instant, seeming stationary there like a sculpted frieze, and then just as instantly didn't fill it up anymore.

"Crazy," Victor said.

"Hm?"

"Crazy broad." He gestured with the rose toward the vacant window. "My wife. You married?"

"I was. Like the pumpkin eater." Handsome guy, Victor, in a brutal, black-Irish way. Like most New York bartenders, he was really an actor, or was it the reverse?

"Divorced?"

"Separated."

He tested his thumb against the pricks of the rose. "Women. They say you got all the freedom. Then you give them their freedom, and they don't want it."

He nodded, though it wasn't wisdom that his own case would have yielded up. He was only glad now not to miss her any longer; and now and then, sad that he was glad. The last precipitate was that occasionally when a woman he'd been looking at, on a bus, in a bar, got up to leave, passing away from him for good, he felt a shooting pang of loss absurd on the face of it.

Volunteer, he thought, but for right field. And if standing there you fall into a reverie, and the game in effect goes on without you, well, you knew it would when you volunteered for the position. Only once every few innings the lost—the not-even-noticed-till-too-late—fly ball makes you sorry that things are as they are and not different, and you wonder if people think you might be bored and indifferent out there, contemptuous even, which isn't the case at all. . . .

"On the house," Victor said, and rapped his knuckles lightly on the bar.

"Oh, hey, thanks." Kind Victor, though the glass put before him contained a powerful solvent, he knew that even as he raised the glass to his lips. He could still fly, oh yes, always, though the cost would be terrible. But what was it he fled from? Self-indulgence, memory dearer to him than any adventure, solitude, lapidary work in his very own mines . . . what could be less novel, more secure? And yet it seemed dangerous; it seemed he hadn't the nerve to face it; he felt unarmed against it.

Novelty and Security: the security of novelty, the novelty of security. Always the full thing, the whole subject, the *true* subject, stood just behind the one you found yourself contemplating. The trick, but it wasn't a trick, was to take up at once the thing you saw and the reason you saw it as well; to always bite off more than you could chew, and then chew it. If it were self-indulgence for him to cut and polish his semiprecious memories, and yet seem like danger, like a struggle he was unfit for, then self-indulgence was a potent force, he must examine it, he must reckon with it.

And he would reckon with it: on that last Sunday in Advent, when his story was all told, the miracle granted or refused, the boy would lift his head from the books and blue-lined paper, the questions that had been set for him answered, and see that it had begun to snow.

Snow not falling but flying sidewise, and sudden, not signaled by the slow curdling of clouds all day and a flake or two drifting downward, but rushing forward all at once as though sent for. (The blizzard of '36 had looked like that.) And filling up the world's concavities, pillowing up in the gloaming, making night light with its whiteness, and then falling still in everyone's dreams, falling for pages and pages; steepling (so an old man would dream in his daughter's house) the plain frame convent on the edge of town, and drifting up even to the eyes of the martyrs pictured on the sash windows of the little clapboard church, Our Lady of the Valley; the wind full of howling white riders tearing the shingles from the roof, piling the snow still higher, blizzarding the church away entirely and the convent too and all the rest of it, so that by next day oblivion whiter than the hair of God would have returned the world to normality, covering his false history and all its works in the deep ordinariness of two feet of snow; and at evening the old man in his daughter's house would sit looking out over the silent calm alone at the kitchen table, a congruence of star, cradle, season, sacrament, etc., end of chapter thirty-five, the next page a fly-leaf blank as snow.

The whole thing, the full thing, the step taken backward that frames the incomprehensible as in a window. *Novelty*: there was, he just then saw, a pun in the title.

He rose. Victor, lost in thought, watched the hurrying crowds that had suddenly filled the streets, afternoon gone, none with time to glance at themselves; hurrying home. One page a day, seven a week, thirty or thirty-one to the month. Fishing in his pocket for a tip, he came up with his pen, a thick black fountain pen. Fountain: it seemed less flowing, less forthcoming than that, in shape more like a bullet or a bomb.

1983

JONATHAN CARROLL

(b. 1949)

Mr Fiddlehead

On my fortieth birthday, Lenna Rhodes invited me over for lunch. That's the tradition—when one of us has a birthday, there's lunch, a nice present and a good laughing afternoon to cover the fact we've moved one more step down the staircase.

We met years ago when we happened to marry into the same family: six months after I said yes to Eric Rhodes, she said it to his brother Michael. Lenna got the better end of *that* wishbone: she and Michael are still delighted with each other, while Eric and I fought about everything and nothing and then got divorced.

But to my surprise and relief, they were a great help to me during the divorce, even though there were obvious difficulties climbing over some of the thorn-bushes of family and blood allegiance.

They live in a big apartment up on 100th Street with long halls and not much light. But the gloom of the place is offset by their kids' toys everywhere, colourful jackets stacked on top of each other, coffee cups with 'World's Greatest Mom' and 'Dartmouth' written on the side. Theirs is a home full of love and hurry, children's drawings on the fridge alongside reminders to buy *La Stampa*. Michael owns a very elegant vintage-fountain-pen store, while Lenna freelances for *Newsweek*. Their apartment is like their life: high ceilinged, thought out, overflowing with interesting combinations and possibilities. It is always nice to go there and share it a while.

I felt pretty good about forty years old. Finally there was some money in the bank, and someone I liked talking to about a trip together to Egypt in the spring. Forty was a milestone, but one that didn't mean much at the moment. I already thought of myself as being slightly middle-aged anyway, but I was healthy and had good prospects so, So What! to the beginning of my fifth decade.

'You cut your hair!'

'Do you like it?'

'You look very French.'

'Yes, but do you *like* it?'

'I think so. I have to get used to it. Come on in.'

We sat in the living room and ate. Elbow, their bull-terrier, rested his head on my knee and never took his eye off the table. After the meal was over, we cleared the plates and she handed me a small red box.

'I hope you like it. I made them myself.'

Inside the box were a pair of the most beautiful gold earrings I have ever seen.

'My God, Lenna! They're *exquisite*! You *made* these? I didn't know you made jewellery.'

She looked happily embarrassed. 'You like them? They're real gold, believe it or not.'

'I believe it. They're art! You *made* them, Lenna? I can't get over it. They're really works of art; they look like something by Klimt.' I took them carefully out of the box and put them on.

She clapped her hands like a girl. 'Oh, Juliet, they really do look good!'

Our friendship *is* important and goes back a long way, but this was a lifetime present—one you gave to a spouse or someone who'd saved your life.

Before I could say that (or anything else), the lights went out. Her two young sons brought in the birthday cake, forty candles strong.

A few days later I was walking down Madison Avenue and, caught by something there, looked in a jewellery-store window. There they were—my birthday earrings. The exact ones. Looking closer, open mouthed, I saw the price tag. Five thousand dollars! I stood and gaped for what must have been minutes. Either way, it was shocking. Had she lied about making them? Or spent five thousand dollars for my birthday present? Lenna wasn't a liar and she wasn't rich. All right, so she had had them copied in brass or something and just *said* they were gold to make me feel good. That wasn't her way either. What the hell was going on?

The confusion emboldened me to walk right into that store. Or rather, walk right up and press their buzzer. After a short wait, someone rang me in. The salesgirl who appeared from behind a curtain looked like she'd graduated from Radcliffe with a degree in blue-stocking. Maybe one had to to work in this place.

'Can I help you?'

'Yes. I'd like to see those earrings you have in the window.'

Looking at my ears, it was as if a curtain rose from in front of her regard, i.e., when I first entered, I was only another nobody in a plaid skirt asking for a moment's sniff of their palace air. But realizing I had a familiar five grand hanging off my lobes changed everything; this woman would be my slave—or friend—for life, I only had to say which.

'Of course, the Dixies.'

'The what?'

She smiled, like I was being very funny. It quickly dawned on me that she must have thought I knew very well what 'Dixies' were because I was wearing some.

She took them out of the window and put them carefully down in front of me on a blue velvet card. They were beautiful and, admiring them, I entirely forgot for a while I had some on.

'I'm so surprised you have a pair. They only came into the store a week ago.'

Thinking fast, I said, 'My husband bought them for me and I like them so much I'm thinking of getting a pair for my sister.

'Tell me about the designer. His name is Dixie?'

'I don't know much, madam. Only the owner knows who Dixie is, where they come from . . . And that whoever it is is a real genius. Apparently both Bulgari and people from the Memphis group have already been in asking who it is and how they can contact him.'

'How do you know it's a man?' I put the earrings down and looked directly at her.

'Oh, I don't. It's just that the work is so masculine that I assumed it. Maybe you're right; maybe it *is* a woman.' She picked one up and held it to the light. 'Did you notice how they don't really reflect light so much as enhance it? Golden light. You can own it any time you want. I've never seen that. I envy you.'

They were real. I went to a jeweller on 47th Street to have them appraised, then to the only other two stores in the city that sold 'Dixies'. No one knew anything about the creator, or weren't talking if they did. Both dealers were very respectful and pleasant, but mum was the word when I asked about the jewellery's origin.

'The gentleman asked us not to give out information, madam. We must respect his wishes.'

'But it *is* a man?'

A professional smile. 'Yes.'

'Could I contact him through you?'

'Yes, I'm sure that would be possible. Can I help with anything else, madam?'

'What other pieces did he design?'

'As far as I know, only the earrings, the fountain pen, and this keyring.' He'd already shown me the pen which was nothing special. Now he brought out a small golden keyring shaped in a woman's profile. Lenna Rhodes' profile.

The doorbell tinkled when I walked into the store. Michael was with a customer and smiling hello, gave me the sign he'd be over as soon as he was finished. He had started 'Ink' almost as soon as he got out of college, and it was a success from the beginning. Fountain pens are cranky, unforgiving things that demand full attention and patience. But they are also a handful of flash and old-world elegance; gratifying slowness that offers no reward other than the sight of shiny ink flowing wetly across a dry page. Ink's customers were both rich and not so, but all of them had the same collector's fiery glint in their eye and addict's desire for more. A couple of times a month I'd work there when Michael needed an extra hand. It taught me to be cheered by old pieces of Bakelite and gold-plate, as well as another kind of passion.

'Juliet, hi! Roger Peyton was in this morning and bought that yellow Parker "Duofold". The one he's been looking at for months?'

'Finally. Did he pay full price?'

Michael grinned and looked away. 'Rog can never afford full price. I let him do it in instalments. What's up with you?'

'Did you ever hear of a "Dixie" pen? Looks a little like the Cartier "Santos"?'

'"Dixie". No. It looks like the Santos?' The expression on his face said he was telling the truth.

I brought out the brochure from the jewellery store and, opening it to the pen photograph, handed it to him. His reaction was immediate.

'That bastard! How much do I have to put up with with this man?'

'You know him?'

Michael looked up from the photo, anger and confusion competing for first place on his face. 'Do I know him? Sure I know him. He lives in my goddamned *house* I know him so well! "Dixie", huh? Cute name. Cute man.

'Wait. I'll show you something, Juliet. Just stay there. Don't move! That shit.'

There's a mirror behind the front counter at Ink. When Michael charged off to the back of the store, I looked at my reflection and said, '*Now* you did it.'

He was back in no time. 'Look at this. You want to see something beautiful? Look at this.' He handed me a blue velvet case. I opened it and saw . . . the Dixie fountain pen.

'But you said you'd never heard of them.'

His voice was hurt and loud. 'It is *not* a Dixie fountain pen. It's a Sinbad. An original, solid gold Sinbad made at the Benjamin Swire Fountain-Pen Works in Konstanz, Germany, around 1915. There's a rumour the Italian Futurist Antonio Sant' Elia did the design, but that's never been proven. Nice, isn't it?'

It *was* nice, but he was so angry that I wouldn't have dared say no. I nodded eagerly.

He took it back. 'I've been selling pens twenty years, but've only seen two of these in all that time. One was owned by Walt Disney and I have the other. Collector's value? About seven thousand dollars. But as I said, you just don't find them.'

'Won't the Dixie people get in trouble for copying it?'

'No, because I'm sure they either bought the design, or

there are small differences between the original and this new one. Let me see that brochure again.'

'But you have an original, Michael. It still holds its value.'

'That's not the point! It's not the value that matters. I'd never sell this.

'You know the classic "bathtub" Porsche? One of the strangest, greatest-looking cars of all time. Some smart, cynical person realized that and is now making fibreglass copies of the thing. They're very well done and full of all the latest features.

'But it's a lie car, Juliet; sniff it and it smells only of today— little plastic things and cleverly cut corners you can't see. Not important to the car, but essential to the real *object*. The wonder of the thing was that Porsche designed it so well and thoughtfully so long ago. That's art. But the art is in its original everything, not just the look or the convincing copy. I can guarantee you your Dixie pen has too much plastic inside where you can't see it, and a gold point that probably has about a third as much gold on it as the original. Looks good, but they always miss the whole point with these cut corners.

'Look, you're going to find out sooner or later, so I think you better know now.'

'What are you talking about?'

He brought a telephone up from beneath the counter and gestured for me to wait a bit. He called Lenna and in a few words told her about the Dixies, my discovery of them . . .

He was looking at me when he asked, 'Did he tell you he was doing that, Lenna?'

Whatever her long answer was, it left his expression dead-pan. 'Well, I'm going to bring Juliet home. I want her to meet him. What? Because we've got to do something about it, Lenna! Maybe she'll have an idea of what to do. Do you think this is normal? Oh, you *do*? That's interesting. Do you think it's normal for *me*?' A dab of saliva popped off his lip and flew across the store.

When Michael opened the door, Lenna stood right on the other side, arms crossed tight over her chest. Her soft face was squinched into a tense challenge.

'Whatever he told you probably isn't true, Juliet.'

I put up both hands in surrender. 'He didn't tell me anything,

Lenna. I don't even want to *be* here. I just showed him a picture of a pen.'

Which wasn't strictly true. I showed him a picture of a pen because I wanted to know more about 'Dixie' and maybe my five-thousand-dollar earrings. Yes, sometimes I am nosy. My ex-husband used to tell me that too often.

Both of the Rhodeses were calm and sound people. I don't think I'd ever seen them really disagree on anything important or raise their voices at each other.

Michael growled, 'Where is he? Eating again?'

'Maybe. So what? You don't like what he eats, anyway.'

He turned to me. 'Our guest is a vegetarian. His favourite food is plum stones.'

'Oh, that's *mean*, Michael. That's really mean.' She turned and left the room.

'So he is in the kitchen? Good. Come on, Juliet.' He took my hand and pulled me behind on his stalk to their visitor.

Before we got to him I heard music. Ragtime piano. Scott Joplin?

A man sat at the table with his back to us. He had long red hair down over the collar of his sports jacket. One freckled hand was fiddling with the dial on a radio nearby.

'Mr Fiddlehead? I'd like you to meet Lenna's best friend, Juliet Skotchdopole.'

He turned, but even before he was all the way around, I knew I was sunk. What a face! Ethereally thin, with high cheekbones and deep-set green eyes that were both merry and profound. Those storybook eyes, the carroty hair and freckles everywhere. How could freckles suddenly be so damned sexy? They were for children and cute advertisements. I wanted to touch every one on him.

'Hello, Juliet! "Skotchdopole", is it? That's a good name. I wouldn't mind havin' it myself. It's a lot better than Fiddlehead, you know.' His deep voice lay in a hammock of a very strong Irish accent.

I put out a hand and we shook. Looking down, I ran my thumb once quickly, softly across the top of his hand. I felt hot and dizzy, like someone I wanted had put their hand gently between my legs for the first time.

He smiled. Maybe he sensed it. There was a yellow plate of

something on the table next to the radio. To stop staring so embarrassingly at him, I focused on it and realized the plate was full of plum stones.

'Do you like them? They're delicious.' He picked one off the shiny orange/brown pile and, slipping the stony thing in his mouth, bit down. Something cracked loud, like he'd broken a tooth, but he kept his angel's smile on while crunching away.

I looked at Michael who only shook his head. Lenna came into the kitchen and gave Mr Fiddlehead a big hug and kiss. He only smiled and went on eating . . . stones.

'Juliet, the first thing you have to know is I lied about your birthday present. I didn't make those earrings—Mr Fiddlehead did. But since he's me, I wasn't *really* lying.' She smiled as if she was sure I understood what she was talking about. I looked at Michael for help, but he was poking around in the refrigerator. Beautiful Mr Fiddlehead was still eating.

'What do you mean, Lenna, he's "you"?'

Michael took out a carton of milk and, at the same time, a plum, which he exaggeratedly offered his wife. She made a face at him and snatched it out of his hand.

Biting it, she said, 'Remember I told you I was an only child? Like a lot of lonely kids, I solved my problem the best way I could—by making up an imaginary friend.'

My eyes widened. I looked at the red-headed man. He winked at me.

Lenna went on. 'I made up Mr Fiddlehead. I read and dreamed so much then that one day I put it all together into my idea of the perfect friend. First, his name would be "Mr Fiddlehead", because I thought that was the funniest name in the world; something that would always make me laugh when I was sad. Then he had to come from Ireland because that was the home of all the leprechauns and faeries. In fact, I wanted a kind of life-sized human leprechaun. He'd have red hair and green eyes and, whenever I wanted, the magical ability to make gold bracelets and jewellery for me out of thin air.'

'Which explains the Dixie jewellery in the stores?'

Michael nodded. 'He said he got bored just hanging around, so I suggested he do something useful. Everything was fine so long as it was just the earrings and keychain.'

He slammed the glass down on the counter. 'But I didn't know about the fountain pen until today. What's with *that*, Fiddlehead?'

'Because I wanted to try me hand at it. I loved the one you showed me, so I thought I'd use that as my model. Why not? You can't improve on perfection. The only thing I did was put some more gold in it here and there.'

I put my hand up like a student with a question. 'But who's Dixie?'

Lenna smiled and said, 'I am. That was the secret name I made up for myself when I was little. The only other person who knew it was my secret friend.' She stuck her thumb in the other's direction.

'Wonderful! So now "Dixie" fountain pens, which are lousy rip-offs of Sinbads, will he bought by every asshole in New York who can afford to buy a Piaget watch or a Hermès brief-case. It makes me sick.' Michael glared at the other man and waited belligerently for a reply.

Mr Fiddlehead's reply was to laugh like Woody Woodpecker.

Which cracked both Lenna and me up.

Which sent her husband storming out of the kitchen.

'Is it true?'

They both nodded.

'I had an imaginary friend too when I was little! The Bimbergooner. But I've never seen them for real.'

'Maybe you didn't make him real enough. Maybe you just cooked him up when you were sad or needed someone to talk to. In Lenna's case, the more she needed me, the more real I became. She needed me a lot. One day I was just there for good.'

I looked at my friend. 'You mean he's been here since you were a girl? Living with you?'

She laughed. 'No. As I grew up I needed him less. I was happier and had more friends. My life got fuller. So he was around less.' She reached over and touched his shoulder.

He smiled but it was a sad one, full of memories. 'I can give her huge pots of gold and do great tricks. I've even been prac-tising ventriloquism and can throw my voice a little. But you'd be surprised how few women love ventriloquists.

'If you two'll excuse me, I think I'll go in the other room and watch TV with the boys. It's about time for "The Three

Stooges". Remember how much we loved that show, Lenna? I
think we saw one episode ten times. The one where they open
up the hairdressing salon in Mexico?'

'I remember. You loved Moe and I loved Curly.'

They beamed at each other over the shared memory.

'But wait, if he's . . . what you say, how come he came
back now?'

'You didn't know it, but Michael and I went through a *very*
bad period a little while ago. He even moved out for two
weeks and we both thought that was it: no more marriage.
One night I got into bed crying like a fool and wishing to hell
Mr Fiddlehead was around again to help me. And then suddenly there he was, standing in the bathroom doorway smiling
at me.' She squeezed his shoulder again. He covered her hand
with his own.

'God, Lenna, what did you do?'

'Screamed! I didn't recognize him.'

'What do you mean?'

'I mean he grew up! The Mr Fiddlehead I imagined when I
was a child was exactly my age. I guess as I got older so did he.
It makes sense.'

'I'm going to sit down now. I have to sit down because this
has been the strangest afternoon of my life.' Fiddlehead jumped
up and gave me his seat. I took it. He left the room for television with the boys. I watched him go. Without thinking, I
picked up Michael's half-empty glass of milk and finished it.
'Everything that you told me is true?'

She put up her right hand. 'I swear on our friendship.'

'That beautiful man out there is an old dream of yours?'

Her head recoiled. 'Oo, do you think he's beautiful? Really?
I think he's kind of funny-looking, to tell the truth. I love him
as a friend, but—' she looked guiltily at the door—'I'd never
want to go *out* with him or anything.'

But *I* did, so we did. After the first few dates I would have
gone and hunted rats with him in the South Bronx if that's
what he liked. I was, as expected, completely gone for him.
The line of a man's neck can change your life. The way he digs
in his pockets for change can make the heart squawk and hands
grow cold. How he touches your elbow or the button that is

not closed on the cuff of his shirt are demons he's loosed without ever knowing it. They own us immediately. He was a thoroughly compelling man. I wanted to rise to the occasion of his presence in my life and become something more than I'd previously thought myself capable of.

I think he began to love me too, but he didn't say things like that. Only that he was happy, or that he wanted to share things he'd held in reserve all his life.

Because he knew sooner or later he'd have to go away (*where* he never said, and I stopped asking), he seemed to have thrown all caution to the wind. But before him, I had never thrown anything away, caution included. I'd been a careful reader of timetables, made the bed tight and straight first thing every morning, and hated dishes in the sink. My life at forty was comfortably narrow and ordered. Going haywire or off the deep end wasn't in my repertoire, and normally people who did made me squint.

I realized I was in love *and* haywire the day I taught him to play racquetball. After we'd batted it around an hour, we were sitting in the gallery drinking Coke. He flicked sweat from his forehead with two fingers. A hot, intimate drop fell on my wrist. I put my hand over it quickly and rubbed it into my skin. He didn't see. I knew then I'd have to learn to put whatever expectations I had aside and just live purely in his jet-stream, no matter where it took me. That day I realized I'd sacrifice anything for him and for a few hours I went around feeling like some kind of holy person, a zealot, love made flesh.

'Why does Michael let you stay there?'

He took a cigarette from my pack. He began smoking a week before and loved it. Almost as much as he liked to drink, he said. The perfect Irishman.

'Don't forget he was the one who left Lenna, not vice-versa. When he came back he was pretty much on his knees to her. He had to be. There wasn't a lot he could say about me being there. Especially after he found out who I was. Do you have any plum stones around?'

'Question two—why in God's name do you eat those things?'

'That's easy: because plums are Lenna's favourite fruit.

When she was a little girl, she'd have tea parties for just us two. Scott Joplin music, imaginary tea and real plums. She'd eat the fruit then put the stone on my plate to eat. Makes perfect sense.'

I ran my fingers through his red hair, loving the way my fingers got caught in all the thick curls. 'That's disgusting. It's like slavery! Why am I getting to the point where I don't like my best friend so much any more?'

'If you like me, you should like her, Juliet—she made me.'

I kissed his fingers. '*That* part I like. Would you ever consider moving in with me?'

He kissed my hand. 'I would love to consider that, but I have to tell you I don't think I'll be around very much longer. But if you'd like, I'll stay with you until I, uh, have to go.'

I sat up. 'What are you talking about?'

He put his hand close to my face. 'Look hard and you'll see.'

It took a moment but then there it was; from certain angles I could see right through the hand. It had become vaguely transparent.

'Lenna's happy again. It's the old story—when she's down she needs me and calls.' He shrugged. 'When she's happy again, I'm not needed, so she sends me away. Not consciously, but . . . Look, we all know I'm her little Frankenstein monster. She can do what she *wants* with me. Even dream up that I like to eat fucking plum stones.'

'It's so wrong!'

Sighing, he sat up and started pulling on his shirt. It's wrong, but it's life, sweet girl. Not much we can do about it, you know.'

'Yes we can. We can do something.'

His back was to me. I remembered the first time I'd ever seen him. His back was to me then too. The long red hair falling over his collar.

When I didn't say anything more, he turned and looked at me over his shoulder, smiling.

'We can do something? What can we do?' His eyes were gentle and loving, eyes I wanted to see for the rest of my life.

'We can make her sad. We can make her need you.'

'What do you mean?'

'Just what I said, Fiddy. When she's sad she needs you. We have to decide what would make her sad a long time. Maybe something to do with Michael. Or their children.'

His fingers had stopped moving over the buttons. Thin, artistic fingers. Freckles.

1989

JOYCE CAROL OATES

(b. 1938)

Family

THE days were brief and attenuated and the season appeared
to be fixed—neither summer nor winter, spring nor fall. A
thermal haze of inexpressible sweetness, though bearing tiny
bits of grit or mica, had eased into the Valley from the industrial region to the north and there were nights when the sun
set at the western horizon as if it were sinking through a
porous red mass, and there were days when a hard-glaring
moon like bone remained fixed in a single position, prominent
in the sky. Above the patchwork of excavated land bordering
our property—all of which had formerly been our property in
Grandfather's time: thousands of acres of wheat, corn, oats,
and open grazing land—a curious trembling rainbow sometimes defined itself, its colors shifting even as you stared, shades
of blue, blue-green, blue-purple, orange, orange-red, orange-
yellow, a translucent yellow that dissolved into mere moisture
as the thermal breeze stirred, warm as an exhaled breath. And
if you had run to tell others of the rainbow it was likely to be
gone when they came. "Liar," my older brothers and sisters
said, "don't say such things if you don't mean them!" Father
said, frowning, "Don't say such things at all if you aren't certain they will be true for others, not simply for yourself."

   This begins in the time of family celebration—after Father
succeeded in selling all but a few of the acres of land surrounding our house, his inheritance from Grandfather, and he and
Mother were giddy as children with relief at having escaped
the luckless fate of certain of our neighbors in the Valley,
rancher-rivals of Grandfather's and their descendants, who had
sold off their property years ago, before the market had begun
to realize its full potential. (*Full potential* were words that
Father often uttered, rolling the words about in his mouth like
round, smooth stones whose taste absorbed him.) Now they
were landless, and their investments were shaky and they had

made their homes in cities of increasing inhospitality, where no
country people could endure to live for long. They had virtually
prostituted themselves, Father said, sighing, and smiling—and
for so little! It was a saying of Grandfather's that a curse would
befall anyone in the Valley who gloated over a neighbor's misfortune, but as Father said, it was damned difficult not to feel
superior in this instance. And Mother vehemently agreed.

Our house was made of stone, stucco, and clapboard; the
newer wings, designed by a big-city architect, had a good deal
of glass, and looked out into the Valley, where on good days we
could see for many miles while on humid hazy days we could
see barely beyond the fence that marked the edge of our property. Father, however, preferred the roof: In his white, light-
woolen three-piece suit, white fedora cocked back on his head,
for luck, he spent many of his waking hours on the highest peak
of the highest roof of the house, observing, through binoculars, the amazing progress of construction in the Valley—for
overnight, it seemed, there appeared roads, expressways, sew-
ers, drainage pipes, "planned" communities with such names
as Whispering Glades, Murmuring Oaks, Pheasant Run, Deer
Willow, all of them walled to keep out intruders, and, yet more
astonishing, towerlike buildings of aluminum and glass and
steel and brick, buildings whose windows shone and winked
like mirrors, splendid in sunshine like pillars of flame; such
beauty where once there had been mere earth and sky, it
caught at your throat like a great bird's talons, taking your
breath away. "The ways of beauty are as a honeycomb," Father
told us, and none of us could determine, staring at his slow-
moving lips, whether the truth he spoke was a happy truth or
not, whether even it was truth.

So mesmerized was Father by the transformation of the
Valley, perceived with dreamlike acuity through the twin lenses
of his binoculars, the poor man often forgot were he was;
failed to come down for dinner, or for bed; and if Mother,
thinking to indulge him, or hurt by his indifference to her, did
not send one of the servants to summon him, he was likely to
spend the entire night on the roof . . . and in the morning,
smiling sheepishly, he would explain that he'd fallen asleep, or,
conversely, that he had been troubled by having seen things
for which he could not account—shadows the size of long-

horns moving beyond our twelve-foot barbed-wire fence, and mysterious winking lights fifty miles away in the foothills. Mother dismissed the shadows as optical illusions caused by Father's overwrought constitution, or the ghosts of old, long-since-slaughtered livestock; the lights, she said, were surely from the private airport at Furnace Creek—had Father forgotten already that he'd sold a large parcel of land for a small airport there? "These lights more resemble fires," Father said stubbornly. "And they were in the foothills, not in the plain."

There were times then of power failures, and financial losses, and Father was forced to give up nearly all of our servants, but he retained his rooftop vigil, white-clad, powerful lenses to his eyes, for he perceived himself as a witness and thought, should he live to a ripe old age, as Grandfather had (Grandfather was in his ninety-ninth year when he died, and then in a fall from a wasp-stung horse), he would be a chronicler of our time, like Thucydides of his, for "Is there a world struggling to be born, or only struggle?"

Because of numerous dislocations in the Valley, of which we learned by degrees, the abandonment of houses, farms, livestock, even pets, it happened that packs of dogs began to roam about looking for food, particularly by night, poor starveling creatures that were becoming a nuisance in the region and should be, as authorities urged, shot down on sight—these dogs being not feral by birth of course but formerly domesticated terriers, setters, cocker spaniels, German shepherds, Labrador retrievers, even the larger and coarser breed of poodle—and it was the cause of some friction between Mother and Father that, despite his presence on the roof at all hours of the day and night, Father failed nonetheless to see a band of dogs dig beneath our fence and silently make their way to the dairy barn, where with terrifying efficiency they tore out the throats —and surely this could not have been in silence!—of our last six holsteins, and our last two she-goats, preparatory to devouring the poor creatures; nor did Father notice anything out of the ordinary on the night that two homeless derelicts, formerly farmhands of ours, impaled themselves on the fence (which was electrically charged, though in compliance with County Farm and Home Office regulations) and were found, dead, in the morning. (It was Kit, our sixteen-year-old, who

found them, and the sight of the men, he said, tore his heart—
so skinny, gray, grizzled, he scarcely recognized them. And the
crows had been at them early.)

Following this episode Father journeyed to the state capital,
with the purpose of taking out a loan, and reestablishing, as he
called it, old ties with his politician friends, and Mother joined
him a few days later for a greatly needed change of scene, as
she said—"Not that I don't love you all, and the farm, but I
need to breathe other air for a while"—leaving us under the
care of Mrs. Hoyt our housekeeper and our eldest sister, Cory.
The decision to leave us at this time was not a judicious one:
Mother had forgotten that Mrs. Hoyt was in poor health, or
perhaps she had decided not to care; and she seemed ignorant
of the fact that Cory, for all the innocence of her marigold eyes
and melodic voice, was desperately in love with one of the National Guardsmen who patrolled the Valley in jeeps, authorized to shoot wild dogs and, upon certain occasions, vandals,
would-be arsonists, and squatters who were deemed a threat
to the public well-being. And when Mother returned, unaccompanied by Father, after what seemed to us a very long absence (two weeks? two months?) it was with shocking news:
She and Father had, after heart-searching deliberation, decided
that, for the good of all concerned, they must separate—they
must officially dissolve the marriage bond. Mother's voice
wavered as she spoke but fierce little pinpoints of light shone in
her eyes. We children were so taken by surprise we could not
speak at first. Separate! Dissolve! For the good of all! We stood
staring and mute; not even Cory, Kit, and Dale, not even Lona,
who was the most impulsive of us, found words with which to
protest; the youngest children began whimpering helplessly,
soon joined by the rest—and by our few remaining servants;
and Mrs. Hoyt, whose features were already bloated by illness.
Mother said, "Don't! Please! I can hardly bear the pain myself!"
She then played a video of Father's farewell to the family, which
drew fresh tears . . . for there, suddenly framed on our television screen, where we had never seen his image before, and
could not in our wildest fancies have imagined it, was Father,
somberly dressed, his hair in thin steely bands combed wetly
across the dome of his skull, and his eyes puffy, an unnatural
sheen to his face as if it had been scoured hard. He sat stiffly

erect in a chair with a high ornately carved back; his fingers were gripping the arms so tightly the blood had drained from his knuckles; his words were slow, halting, and faint, like the progress of a gut-shot deer across a field, but unmistakably his: *Dear children your mother and I after thirty years of marriage of very happy marriage have decided to . . . have decided to . . . have decided to. . . .* One of the low-flying helicopters belonging to the National Guardsmen soared past the house, making the television screen shudder, but the sound seemed to be garbled in any case, as if the tape had been clumsily cut and spliced; there were miniature lightning flashes; and Father's dear face turned liquid, melting horizontally, his eyes long and narrow as slugs and his mouth distended like a drowning man's; and all we could hear were sounds, not words, resembling *Help me* or *I am innocent* or *I love you dear children*—and then the screen was dead.

That afternoon Mother introduced us to the man who was to be Father's successor in the household, and to his three children, who were to be our new brothers and sister, and we shook hands shyly, in a state of mutual shock, and regarded one another with wide staring eyes. Our new Father! Our new brothers and sister! As Mother explained patiently her new husband was no *step*father but a genuine *father*, which meant that we were to call him "Father" at all times, and even, in our most private innermost thoughts, we were to think of him as "Father": for otherwise he would be very hurt, and very displeased. And so too with Einar and Erastus, our new brothers (not *step*brothers), and Fifi, our new sister (not *step*sister).

Our new Father stood before us beaming, a man of our former Father's approximate age but heavier and more robust than that Father, with an unusually large head, the cranium particularly developed, and small shrewd quick-darting eyes beneath brows of bone. He wore a fashionably tailored suit so dark as to resemble an undertaker's, and sported a red carnation in his lapel; his black shoes shone so splendidly they might have been phosphorescent. "Hello Father," we murmured, hardly daring to raise our eyes to his. "Hello Father." "Hello. . . ." The man's jaws were elongated, the lower jaw a good inch longer than the upper, so that a wet malevolent ridge of teeth was revealed; and, as often happened in those days, a single thought shot like lightning among us children, from one to the other to the other to the other, each of us smiling guiltily as it struck us: *Crocodile!* Only little Jori burst into tears when the thought passed into her head and after an embarrassed moment our new Father stooped to pick her up in his arms and comfort her . . . and some of us could virtually see how the memory of our former Father passed from her, as cruelly as if it had been hosed out of her skull. She was three years old then, and not accountable for her behavior.

New Father's children were tall, big-boned, solemn, with a greenish peevish cast to their skin, like many city children; the boys had inherited their father's large head and protruding crocodile jaws but the girl, Fifi, seventeen years old, was eye-catching in her beauty, with hair as mutinous as Cory's, and wide-set brown eyes in which something wolfish glimmered.

That evening certain of the boys—Dale, Kit, and Hewett—gathered close around Fifi, telling her wild tales of the Valley, how we had to protect ourselves with rifles and shotguns from trespassers, and how there was a resurgence of rats and other rodents on the farm, as a consequence of so much excavation in the countryside, and these tales, silly as they were, and exaggerated, made the girl shudder and giggle and lean toward the boys as if she were in need of their protection. And when Dale hurried off to get Fifi a goblet of ice water—at her request—she took the glass from his fingers and lifted it prissily to the light to examine its contents, asking, "Is this water *pure?* Is it safe to *drink?*" It was true, our water was sometimes strangely effervescent, and tasted of rust; after a heavy rainfall there were likely to be tiny red wriggly things in it, like animated tails; so we had learned not to examine it too closely, and as our initial attacks of nausea, diarrhea, and faint-headedness had more or less subsided, we rarely thought of it any longer but tried to be grateful, as Mrs. Hoyt used to urge us, that we had any drinking water at all. So it was offensive to us to see Fifi make such a face, handing the goblet of water back to Dale, and asking him how anyone in his right mind could drink such—spilth. Dale said angrily, "*How?* This is *how!*" and drank the water down in a single thirsty gulp. And he and his new sister stood staring at each other, each of them trembling with passion.

As Cory observed smiling, yet with a trace of resentment or envy, "It looks as if 'new sister' has made a conquest!"

"But what will she do," I couldn't help asking, "—if she can't drink our water?"

"She'll drink it," Cory said grimly. "And she'll find it delicious, like the rest of us." Which, of course, turned out very quickly to be true.

Cory's confinement came in a time of ever-increasing confusion . . . when there were frequent power failures in the Valley, and all foods except tinned goods were scarce, and the price of ammunition doubled, and quadrupled; and the sky by both day and night was criss-crossed by the contrails of unmarked bombers in a design both eerie and beautiful, like the web of a gigantic spider. By this time construction in most parts of the Valley had been halted, temporarily or indefinitely: Part-completed houses and high-rise office buildings punctuated the landscape; some were mere concrete foundations upon which girders had been erected, like exposed bone. The lovely "Mirror Tower"—as we children called it: It must have had a real name—was a two-hundred-story patchwork of interlocking slots of reflecting glass with a pale turquoise tint, and where its elegant surface had once mirrored scenes of sparkling beauty there was now, from day to day, virtually nothing: a sky like soiled cotton batting, smoldering slag heaps, fantastic burdocks and thistles grown to the height of trees. Traffic had dwindled to a half-dozen diesel trucks per day hauling their massive cargo (much of it diseased livestock bound for northern slaughterhouses) and a very few passenger cars. There were cloverleafs that coiled endlessly upon themselves and elevated highways that broke off in midair, thus as authorities warned travelers you were in danger, if you ventured into the countryside, of being attacked by roaming gangs—but the rumor was that the most dangerous men were rogue Guardsmen who wore their uniforms inside out and preyed upon the very people they were paid to protect. None of the family left the compound without being well armed and of course the younger children no longer left at all. All schools, public and private, were temporarily shut down.

The most luxurious of the model communities, known to us

as The Wheel—its original name was forgotten: Whispering
Glades? Deer Willow?—had suffered so extreme a financial
collapse that most of its services were said to be suspended, and
many of its tenants had fled back to the cities from which they'd
fled to the Valley. (The community was called The Wheel
because its condominiums, office buildings, shops, schools,
hospitals, and crematoria were arranged in spokes radiating
outward from a single axis; and were protected at their twenty-
mile circumference not by a visible wall, which the Japanese
architect who had designed it had declared a vulgar and
outmoded concept, but by a force field of electricity of lethal
voltage.) Though the airport at Furnace Creek was officially
closed we often saw small aircraft taking off and landing there
in the night, heard the insectlike whine of their engines and
spied their winking red lights, and one night when the sun
hung paralyzed at the horizon for several hours and visibility
was poor though shot with a duplicitous sharpened clarity there
was an airplane crash in a slag-heap area that had once been
a grazing pasture for our cows, and some of the older boys
insisted upon going out to investigate . . . returning with
sober, stricken faces, and little to say of the sights they had
seen except they wished they had not seen them. Miles away in
the foothills were mysterious encampments, some of them
mere camps, in which people lived and slept on the ground,
others deliberately if crudely erected villages like those once
displayed in museums as being the habitations of Native American peoples . . . the names of these "peoples" long since
forgotten. These were rumored to be unauthorized settlements
of city dwellers who had fled their cities at the time of the general urban collapse, as well as former ranchers and their descendants, and various wanderers and evicted persons, criminals, the
mentally ill, and victims of contagious diseases . . . all of
these officially designated outlaw parties who were subject to
harsh treatment by the Guardsmen, for the region was now
under martial law, and only within compounds maintained by
government-registered property owners and heads of families
were civil rights, to a degree, still operative. Eagerly, we scanned
the Valley for signs of life, passing among us a pair of binoculars
like forbidden treasure whose original owner we could not recall
—though Cory believed this person, an adult male, had lived

with us before Father's time, and had been good to us. But not even Cory could remember his name. Cory's baby was born shortly after the funerals of two of the younger children, who had died of violent flulike illnesses, and of Uncle Darrah, who had died of shotgun wounds while driving his pick-up truck in the Valley; but this, we were assured by Mother and Father, was mere coincidence, and not to be taken as a sign. One by one we were led into the attic room set aside for Cory to stare in astonishment at the puppy-sized, red-faced, squalling, yet so wonderfully alive creature . . . with its large oval soft-looking head, its wizened angry features, its unblemished skin. Mother had found a cradle in the storage barn for the baby, a white wicker antique dating back to the previous century, perhaps a cradle she herself had used though she could not remember it, nor could any of us, her children, recall having slept in it; a piece of furniture too good for Cory's "bastard child," as Mother tearfully called it. (Though allowing that the infant's parentage was no fault of its own.) Fit punishment, Mother said, that Cory's breasts yielded milk so grudgingly, and what milk they did yield was frequently threaded with blood, fit punishment for her daughter's "sluttish" behavior . . . but the family's luck held and one day the older boys returned from a hunting expedition with a dairy cow . . . a beautiful black-and-white marbled animal very like the kind, years ago, or was it only months ago, we ourselves had owned. The cow supplied us with sweet, fresh, reasonably pure milk, thus saving Cory's bastard infant's life, as Mother said— "for whatever that life is worth."

Though she was occupied with household tasks, and often with emergency situations, Mother seemed obsessed with ferreting out the identity of Cory's infant's father; Cory's secret lover, as Mother called him with a bitter twist of her lips. Yet it seemed to give her a prideful sort of pleasure that her eldest daughter had not only had a secret lover at one time in her life (the baby being irrefutable proof of this) but had one still— despite the fact that no lover had stepped forward to claim the baby, or the baby's mother; and that Cory, once the prettiest of the girls, was now disfigured by skin rashes covering most of her body. And since her pregnancy her lower body remained bloated while her upper body had become emaciated. Mother

herself was frequently ill, with flaming rashes, respiratory illnesses, intestinal upsets, bone aches, uncertain vision; like
most of us she was plagued with ticks—the smallest species of
deer tick, which could burrow into the skin, particularly into
the scalp, unnoticed, there to do its damage, and after weeks
drop off, to be found on the floor, swollen with blood, black,
shiny, about the size and apparent texture of a watermelon
seed, deceptive to the eye. By degrees Mother had shrunk to a
height of about four feet eight inches, very unlike the statuesque beauty of certain old photographs; with stark white
matted hair, and pale silvery gray eyes as keen and suspicious as
ever, and a voice so hard, harsh, brassy, and penetrating, a
shout from her had the power to paralyze any of us where we
stood . . . though we knew or believed ourselves safely hidden from her by a wall, or more than a single wall. Even the
eldest of her sons, Kit, Hewett, Dale, tall ragged-bearded men
who absented themselves from the compound for days at a
stretch, were intimidated by Mother's authority, and, like poor
Cory, shrank in guilty submission before her. Again and again
Mother interrogated Cory, "Who is your secret lover? Why are
you so ashamed of him?" and Cory insisted she did not know
who her lover was, or could not remember—"Even if I see his
face sometimes, in my sleep, I can't remember his name. Or
who he was. Or who he claimed to be."

Yet Mother continued her investigation, risking Father's displeasure in so ruthlessly questioning all males with whom she
came into contact, not excluding Cory's cousins and uncles
and even Cory's own brothers!—even those ravaged men and
boys who made their homes, so to speak, in the drainage pipes
beyond the compound, and whose services the family sometimes enlisted in times of emergency. But no one confessed; no
one acknowledged Cory's baby as his. And one day when Cory
lay ill upstairs in her attic room and I was entrusted with caring
for the baby, feeding it from a bottle, in the kitchen, Mother
came into the room with a look of such determination I felt
terror for the baby, and hugged it to my bosom, and Mother
said, "Give me the bastard, girl," and I said, "No Mother, don't
make me," and Mother said, "Are you disobeying me? *Give
me the bastard*," and I said, backing away, "No Mother, Cory's
baby belongs to Cory, and it isn't a bastard." Mother advanced

upon me, furious; her eyes whitely rimmed and her fingers—
ah, what talons they had become!—outstretched; her mouth
twisting, working, distending itself—and I saw that in the
midst of her passion she was forgetting what she meant to do,
and that this might save Cory's baby. For often in those days
when the family had little to eat except worm-riddled apples
from the old orchard, and stunted blackened potatoes, and
such wild game (or wildlife) as the boys could hunt down, we
often forgot what we were doing in the very act of doing it;
and in the midst of speaking we might forget the words we
meant to speak, for instance *water, rainbow, grief, love, filth,
God, deer tick* . . . and Father, who had become somber-
minded with the onset of age, worried above all that as a family we might one day lose all sense of ourselves as a family
should we forget, collectively, and in the same moment, the
sacred word *family.*

And indeed Mother was forgetting. And indeed within the
space of less than thirty seconds she had forgotten. She stared
at the living thing, the quivering palpitating creature in my
arms, with its soft flat shallow face, its tiny recessed eyes, its
mere holes for nostrils, above all its small pursed mouth set like
a manta ray's in its shallow face, and could not, simply could
not, recall the word *baby,* or *infant,* or *Cory's bastard.* And
shortly afterward there was a commotion of some kind outside, apparently rather close to the compound gate, and a
sound of gunfire, familiar enough yet always jarring when unexpected, and Mother hurried out to investigate. And Cory's
baby continued to suck hungrily at the bottle's frayed rubber
nipple and all was safe for the time being.

But Cory, poor Cory, died a few days later: Early one
morning Lona discovered her in her attic bed, her eyes opened
wide and her pale mouth contorted, the bedclothes soaked in
blood . . . and when in horror Lona drew the sheet away she
saw that Cory's breasts had been partly devoured, and her chest
cavity exposed; she must have been attacked in the night by
rats, and had been too weak or too terrified to call for help. Yet
her baby was sleeping only a few feet away in its antique cradle,
untouched, sunk to that most profound and enviable level of
sleep at which organic matter seems about to pass over again
into the inorganic. The household rats with their glittering

amaranthine eyes and stiff hairless tails had spared it!—had missed it entirely!

Lona snatched up the baby and ran screaming downstairs for help; and so fierce was she in possession she could scarcely be forced to surrender the sleepy infant to the rest of us: Her fingers had to be pried open. In a dazed gloating voice she said, "It is my baby. It is Lona's baby now." Father sharply rebuked her: "It is the family's baby now."

And Fifi too had a baby; or, rather, writhed and screamed in agony for a day and a night, before giving birth to a piteous undersized creature that lived for only a few minutes. Poor sister!—in the weeks that followed only our musical evenings, at which she excelled, gave her solace. If Dale tried to touch her, let alone comfort her, she shrank from him in repugnance. Nor would she allow Father or any male to come near. Sometimes she crawled into my bed and hugged me in her cold bone-thin arms. "What I like best," she whispered "is the black waves that splash over us, at night." And my heart was so swollen with emotion, I could not say no, or Oh yes.

For suddenly we had taken up music. In the evenings by kerosene lamp. In the worst, the most nightmarish of times. We played such musical instruments as fell into our hands discovered here and there in the house, or by way of strangers at our gate desperate to barter anything in their possession for food. Kit took up the violin doubtfully at first and then with growing joy, for, it seemed, he had musical talent!—practicing for hours on the beautiful though badly scarified old violin that had once belonged to Grandfather (so we surmised: One of Grandfather's portraits showed him as a child of eleven or twelve posed with the identical violin, then luminously gleaming, tucked under his chin); Jori took up the piccolo, which she shared with Vega; Hewett took up the drums, Dale the cymbals, Einar the oboe, Fifi the piano . . . and the rest of us sang, sang our hearts out, our collective voices sometimes frail as straws through which a rough careless wind blew but at other times, and always unpredictably, so harmonious, so strong, so commanding, our hearts beat hard in unquestioning love of one another and of any fate that might befall us. We sang after Mother's death and we sang when a feculent wind blew from the Valley day after day bearing the odor of decomposing flesh and we sang, though our noses and throats filled with smoke, when fires raged in the dry woodland areas to the west, and then too a relentless wind blew upon us barricaded in our stone house atop a high hill, winds from several directions they seemed, intent upon seeking us out, carrying sparks to our sanctuary, destroying us in a paroxysm of fire as others, human and beast, were being destroyed shrieking in pain and terror . . . and how else for us to endure such odors, such sights, such sounds than to take up our instruments and play them, and sing, and sing and sing and sing until our throats were raw, how else.

Yet it became a time of joy and even feasting, since the cow was dying in any case and might as well be quickly slaughtered, when Father brought his new wife home to meet us: New Mother some of us called her, or Young Mother, and Old Mother that fierce stooped wild-eyed old woman was forgotten, the strangeness of her death lingering only in whispers for had she like Cory died of household rats? had she like Erastus grown pimples, then boils, then tumors over her entire body, swelling bulbs of flesh that drained away life? had she drowned in the cistern, had she died of thirst and malnutrition locked away in a distant room of the house, had she died of infection, of heartbreak, of her own rage, of Father's steely fingers closing about her neck . . . or had she not died at all but simply passed into oblivion, as the black waves splashed over her, and Young Mother stepped forward smiling to take her place . . . ? Young Mother was stout and hearty-faced, plumply pretty about the eyes and cheeks, her color a rich earthen hue, her breasts capacious as large balloons filled to bursting with liquid, and she gave off a hot intoxicating smell of nutmeg, and small slippery flames darted when in a luxury of sighing, yawning, and stretching, she lifted with beringed hands the heavy mass of red-russet hair that hung between her shoulder blades, and fixed upon us her warm moist unblinking dark gaze. "Mother!" we cried, even the eldest of us, "Oh Mother!" begging would she hug us, would she fold us in those plump arms, press our faces against that bosom, each of us, all of us, weeping, in her arms, against her bosom, there.

Cory's baby was not maturing as it was believed babies should, nor had it been named since we could not determine whether it was male or female, or both, or neither; and this household vexation Young Mother addressed herself to at once. No matter Lona's jealous love of the baby, Young Mother declared herself "practical-minded": For why otherwise had Father brought her to this household but to reform it and give hope? She could not comprehend, she said, how and why an extra mouth, and in this case not only a useless but perhaps even a dangerous mouth, could be tolerated in a time of near famine, in violation of certain government edicts as she understood them. "Drastic remedies in drastic times," Young Mother said. Lona said, "I will give it my food. I will protect it with my life." And Young Mother simply repeated, smiling, her warm brown eyes easing like a caress over us all, "Drastic remedies in drastic times." There were those of us who loved Cory's baby and felt an unreasoned joy in its very existence, for it *was* flesh of our flesh, it *was* the future of the family; yet there were others, among them not only the males, who seemed fearful of it, keeping their distance when it was fed or bathed and averting their eyes when it crawled into a room to nudge its head or mouth against a foot, an ankle, a leg. Though it had not matured in the usual way Cory's baby was considerably heavier than it had been at birth, and weighed now about forty pounds; but it was soft as a slug is soft, or an oyster; with an oyster's shape; seemingly boneless; the hue of bread dough, and hairless. As its small eyes lacked an iris, being entirely white, it was believed to be blind; its nose was but a rudimentary pair of nostrils, mere holes in the center of its face; its fishlike mouth was deceptive in that it seemed to possess its own intelligence, being ideally formed, not for human speech, but for seizing, sucking, and chewing. Though it had at best only a cartilaginous skeleton it did boast two fully formed rows of tiny needle-sharp teeth, which it was not shy of using, particularly when ravenous for food; and it was often ravenous. At such times it groped its way around the house by instinct, sniffing and quivering, and if by chance it was drawn by the heat of your blood to your bed it would burrow against you beneath the covers, and nudge, and nuzzle, and begin like any nursing infant to suck, virtually any part of the body though preferring of course a female's breasts . . . and if not stopped in time it would bite, and chew, and *eat* . . . in all the brute innocence of appetite. So some of us surmised, though Lona angrily denied it, that Cory had not died of rat bites after all but of having been attacked and partly devoured by her own baby. (In this, Lona was duplicitous: taking care never to undress in Mother's presence for fear that Mother's sharp eye would take in the numerous wounds on her breasts, belly, and thighs.)

As the family had a custom of debating issues, in order that all divergent opinions might be honored, for instance should we pay the exorbitant price a cow or a she-goat now commanded, or should the boys be empowered to acquire one of these beasts however they could, for instance should we make an attempt to feed starving men, women, and children who gathered outside our fence, even if it was with food unfit for the family's own consumption—so naturally the issue of Cory's baby was taken up too, and threatened to split the family into two warring sides. For her part Mother argued persuasively that the baby was worthless, repulsive, and might one day be dangerous—not guessing that it had already proved dangerous, indeed; and for her part Lona argued persuasively that the baby, "Lona's baby," as she persisted in calling it, was a living human being, a member of the family, one of *us*. Mother said hotly, "It is not one of *us*, girl, if by *us* you mean a family that includes *me*," and Lona said with equal heat, "It is one of *us* because it predates any family that includes *you*."

So each of us argued in turn, and emotions ran high, and it was a curious phenomenon that many of us changed our minds repeatedly, now swayed by Mother's reasoning, and now by Lona's; now by Father, who spoke on behalf of Mother, or by Hewett, who spoke on behalf of Lona; or by Father, whose milky eyes gave him an air of patrician distinction and fair-mindedness, who spoke on behalf of Lona! The issue raged, and subsided, and raged again, and Mother dared not put her power to the vote for fear that Lona would prevail against her. Father acknowledged that however we felt about the baby it was our flesh and blood presumably, and embodied for us the great insoluble mystery of life . . . "its soul bounded by its skull and its destiny no more problematic than the thin tubes that connect its mouth and its anus. Who are we to judge!"

Yet Mother had her way, as slyboots Mother was always to have her way . . . one morning soliciting the help of several of us, who were sworn to secrecy, and delighted to be her handmaidens, in a simple scheme: Lona being asleep in Cory's old bed, Mother led the baby out of the house by holding a piece of bread soaked in chicken blood just in front of its nostrils, led it crawling with surprising swiftness across the hard-packed earth, to one of the barns, and, inside, led it to a dark corner where she lifted it, grunting, and lowered it carefully into an old rain barrel empty except for a wriggling mass of half-grown baby rats that squealed in great excitement at being disturbed, or at the smell of the blood-soaked bread which Mother dropped on them. We then nailed a cover in place; and, as Mother said, her color warmly flushed and her breath coming fast, "There—it is entirely out of our hands."

And then one day it was spring. And Kit led a she-goat proudly into the kitchen, her bags primed with milk, swollen pink dugs leaking milk! How grateful we were, those of us who were with child, after the privations of so long a season, during which certain words had slipped from our memories, for instance *she-goat*, and *milk*, and as we realized, *rainbow*, for the rainbow too appeared, or reappeared, shimmering and translucent across the Valley. In the fire-ravaged plain was a sea of fresh green shoots and in the sky enormous dimpled clouds and that night we gathered around Fifi at the piano to play our instruments and sing. Father had passed away but Mother had remarried: a husky horseman whose white teeth flashed in his beard, and whose rowdy pinches meant love and good cheer, not hurt. We were so happy we debated turning the calendar ahead to the New Year. We were so happy we debated abolishing the calendar entirely and declaring it the year 1, and beginning Time anew.

1989

THOMAS LIGOTTI
(b. 1953)

The Last Feast of Harlequin

I.

My interest in the town of Mirocaw was first aroused when I heard that an annual festival was held there which promised to include, to some extent, the participation of clowns among its other elements of pageantry. A former colleague of mine, who is now attached to the anthropology department of a distant university, had read one of my recent articles ("The Clown Figure in American Media," *Journal of Popular Culture*), and wrote to me that he vaguely remembered reading or being told of a town somewhere in the state that held a kind of "Fool's Feast" every year, thinking that this might be pertinent to my peculiar line of study. It was, of course, more pertinent than he had reason to think, both to my academic aims in this area and to my personal pursuits.

Aside from my teaching, I had for some years been engaged in various anthropological projects with the primary ambition of articulating the significance of the clown figure in diverse cultural contexts. Every year for the past twenty years I have attended the pre-Lenten festivals that are held in various places throughout the southern United States. Every year I learned something more concerning the esoterics of celebration. In these studies I was an eager participant—along with playing my part as an anthropologist, I also took a place behind the clownish mask myself. And I cherished this role as I did nothing else in my life. To me the title of Clown has always carried connotations of a noble sort. I was an adroit jester, strangely enough, and had always taken pride in the skills I worked so diligently to develop.

I wrote to the State Department of Recreation, indicating what information I desired and exposing an enthusiastic urgency which came naturally to me on this topic. Many weeks later I received a tan envelope imprinted with a government logo. Inside was a pamphlet that catalogued all of the various seasonal festivities of which the state was officially aware, and I noted in passing that there were as many in late autumn and winter as in the warmer seasons. A letter inserted within the pamphlet explained to me that, according to their voluminous records, no festivals held in the town of Mirocaw had been officially registered. Their files, nonetheless, could be placed at my disposal if I should wish to research this or similar matters in connection with some definite project. At the time this offer was made I was already laboring under so many professional and personal burdens that, with a weary hand, I simply deposited the envelope and its contents in a drawer, never to be consulted again.

Some months later, however, I made an impulsive digression from my responsibilities and, rather haphazardly, took up the Mirocaw project. This happened as I was driving north one afternoon in late summer with the intention of examining some journals in the holdings of a library at another university. Once out of the city limits the scenery changed to sunny fields and farms, diverting my thoughts from the signs that I passed along the highway. Nevertheless, the subconscious scholar in me must have been regarding these with studious care. The name of a town loomed into my vision. Instantly the scholar retrieved certain records from some deep mental drawer, and I was faced with making a few hasty calculations as to whether there was enough time and motivation for an investigative side trip. But the exit sign was even hastier in making its appearance, and I soon found myself leaving the highway, recalling the roadsign's promise that the town was no more than seven miles east.

These seven miles included several confusing turns, the forced taking of a temporarily alternate route, and a destination not even visible until a steep rise had been fully ascended. On the descent another helpful sign informed me that I was within the city limits of Mirocaw. Some scattered houses on the outskirts of the town were the first structures I encountered. Beyond them the numerical highway became Townshend Street, the main avenue of Mirocaw.

The town impressed me as being much larger once I was

within its limits than it had appeared from the prominence just outside. I saw that the general hilliness of the surrounding countryside was also an internal feature of Mirocaw. Here, though, the effect was different. The parts of the town did not look as if they adhered very well to one another. This condition might be blamed on the irregular topography of the town. Behind some of the old stores in the business district, steeply roofed houses had been erected on a sudden incline, their peaks appearing at an extraordinary elevation above the lower buildings. And because the foundations of these houses could not be glimpsed, they conveyed the illusion of being either precariously suspended in air, threatening to topple down, or else constructed with an unnatural loftiness in relation to their width and mass. This situation also created a weird distortion of perspective. The two levels of structures overlapped each other without giving a sense of depth, so that the houses, because of their higher elevation and nearness to the foreground buildings, did not appear diminished in size as background objects should. Consequently, a look of flatness, as in a photograph, predominated in this area. Indeed, Mirocaw could be compared to an album of old snapshots, particularly ones in which the camera had been upset in the process of photography, causing the pictures to develop on an angle: a cone-roofed turret, like a pointed hat jauntily askew, peeked over the houses on a neighboring street; a billboard displaying a group of grinning vegetables tipped its contents slightly westward; cars parked along steep curbs seemed to be flying skyward in the glare-distorted windows of a five-and-ten; people leaned lethargically as they trod up and down sidewalks; and on that sunny day the clock tower, which at first I mistook for a church steeple, cast a long shadow that seemed to extend an impossible distance and wander into unlikely places in its progress across the town. I should say that perhaps the disharmonies of Mirocaw are more acutely affecting my imagination in retrospect than they were on that first day, when I was primarily concerned with locating the city hall or some other center of information.

I pulled around a corner and parked. Sliding over to the other side of the seat, I rolled down the window and called to a passerby: "Excuse me, sir," I said. The man, who was shabbily dressed and very old, paused for a moment without approaching the car. Though he had apparently responded to my call, his vacant expression did not betray the least awareness of my presence, and for a moment I thought it just a coincidence that he halted on the sidewalk at the same time I addressed him. His eyes were focused somewhere beyond me with a weary and imbecilic gaze. After a few moments he continued on his way and I said nothing to call him back, even though at the last second his face began to appear dimly familiar. Someone else finally came along who was able to direct me to the Mirocaw City Hall and Community Center.

The city hall turned out to be the building with the clock tower. Inside I stood at a counter behind which some people were working at desks and walking up and down a back hallway. On one wall was a poster for the state lottery: a jack-in-the-box with both hands grasping green bills. After a few moments, a tall, middle-aged woman came over to the counter.

"Can I help you?" she asked in a neutral, bureaucratic voice.

I explained that I had heard about the festival—saying nothing about being a nosy academic—and asked if she could provide me with further information or direct me to someone who could.

"Do you mean the one held in the winter?" she asked.

"How many of them are there?"

"Just that one."

"I suppose, then, that that's the one I mean." I smiled as if sharing a joke with her.

Without another word, she walked off into the back hallway. While she was absent I exchanged glances with several of the people behind the counter who periodically looked up from their work.

"There you are," she said when she returned, handing me a piece of paper that looked like the product of a cheap copy machine. *Please Come to the Fun*, it said in large letters. *Parades*, it went on, *Street Masquerade, Bands, The Winter Raffle*, and *The Coronation of the Winter Queen*. The page continued with the mention of a number of miscellaneous festivities. I read the words again. There was something about that imploring little "please" at the top of the announcement that made the whole affair seem like a charity function.

"When is it held? It doesn't say when the festival takes place."

"Most people already know that." She abruptly snatched the page from my hands and wrote something at the bottom. When she gave it back to me, I saw "Dec. 19–21" written in blue-green ink. I was immediately struck by an odd sense of scheduling on the part of the festival committee. There was, of course, solid anthropological and historical precedent for holding festivities around the winter solstice, but the timing of this particular event did not seem entirely practical.

"If you don't mind my asking, don't these days somewhat conflict with the regular holiday season? I mean, most people have enough going on at that time."

"It's just tradition," she said, as if invoking some venerable ancestry behind her words.

"That's very interesting," I said as much to myself as to her.

"Is there anything else?" she asked.

"Yes. Could you tell me if this festival has anything to do with clowns? I see there's something about a masquerade."

"Yes, of course there are some people in . . . costumes. I've never been in that position myself . . . that is, yes, there are clowns of a sort."

At that point my interest was definitely aroused, but I was not sure how much further I wanted to pursue it. I thanked the woman for her help and asked the best means of access to the highway, not anxious to retrace the labyrinthine route by which I had entered the town. I walked back to my car with a whole flurry of half-formed questions, and as many vague and conflicting answers, cluttering my mind.

The directions the woman gave me necessitated passing through the south end of Mirocaw. There were not many people moving about in this section of town. Those that I did see, shuffling lethargically down a block of battered store-fronts, exhibited the same sort of forlorn expression and manner as the old man from whom I had asked directions earlier. I must have been traversing a central artery of this area, for on either side stretched street after street of poorly tended yards and houses bowed with age and indifference. When I came to a stop at a streetcorner, one of the citizens of this slum passed in front of my car. This lean, morose, and epicene person turned my way and sneered outrageously with a taut little mouth, yet seemed to be looking at no one in particular. After progressing a few streets farther, I came to a road that led back to the highway. I felt delectably more comfortable as soon as I found myself traveling once again through the expanses of sun-drenched farmlands.

I reached the library with more than enough time for my research, and so I decided to make a scholarly detour to see what material I could find that might illuminate the winter festival held in Mirocaw. The library, one of the oldest in the state, included in its holdings the entire run of the Mirocaw *Courier*. I thought this would be an excellent place to start. I soon found, however, that there was no handy way to research information from this newspaper, and I did not want to engage in a blind search for articles concerning a specific subject.

I next turned to the more organized resources of the newspapers for the larger cities located in the same county, which incidentally shares its name with Mirocaw. I uncovered very little about the town, and almost nothing concerning its festival, except in one general article on annual events in the area that erroneously attributed to Mirocaw a "large Middle-Eastern community" which every spring hosted a kind of ethnic jamboree. From what I had already observed, and from what I subsequently learned, the citizens of Mirocaw were solidly midwestern-American, the probable descendants in a direct line from some enterprising pack of New Englanders of the last century. There was one brief item devoted to a Mirocavian event, but this merely turned out to be an obituary notice for an old woman who had quietly taken her life around Christmastime. Thus, I returned home that day all but empty-handed on the subject of Mirocaw.

However, it was not long afterward that I received another letter from the former colleague of mine who had first led me to seek out Mirocaw and its festival. As it happened, he rediscovered the article that caused him to stir my interest in a local "Fool's Feast." This article had its sole appearance in an obscure festschrift of anthropology studies published in Amsterdam twenty years ago. Most of these papers were in Dutch, a few in German, and only one was in English: "The Last Feast of Harlequin: Preliminary Notes on a Local Festival." It was exciting, of course, finally to be able to read this study, but even more exciting was the name of its author: Dr. Raymond Thoss.

2.

Before proceeding any further, I should mention something about Thoss, and inevitably about myself. Over two decades ago, at my alma mater in Cambridge, Mass., Thoss was a professor of mine. Long before playing a role in the events I am about to describe, he was already one of the most important figures in my life. A striking personality, he inevitably influenced everyone who came in contact with him. I remember his lectures on social anthropology, how he turned that dim room into a brilliant and profound circus of learning. He moved in an uncannily brisk manner. When he swept his arm around to indicate some common term on the blackboard behind him, one felt he was presenting nothing less than an item of fantastic qualities and secret value. When he replaced his hand in the pocket of his old jacket this fleeting magic was once again stored away in its well-worn pouch, to be retrieved at the sorcerer's discretion. We sensed he was teaching us more than we could possibly learn, and that he himself was in possession of greater and deeper knowledge than he could possibly impart. On one occasion I summoned up the audacity to offer as interpretation —which was somewhat opposed to his own—regarding the tribal clowns of the Hopi Indians. I implied that personal experience as an amateur clown and special devotion to this study provided me with an insight possibly more valuable than his own. It was then he disclosed, casually and very obiter dicta, that he had actually acted in the role of one of these masked tribal fools and had celebrated with them the dance of the *kachinas.* In revealing these facts, however, he somehow managed not to add to the humiliation I had already inflicted upon myself. And for this I was grateful to him.

Thoss's activities were such that he sometimes became the object of gossip or romanticized speculation. He was a field-worker par excellence, and his ability to insinuate himself into exotic cultures and situations, thereby gaining insights where other anthropologists merely collected data, was renowned. At various times in his career there had been rumors of his having "gone native" à la the Frank Hamilton Cushing legend. There were hints, which were not always irresponsible or cheaply glamorized, that he was involved in projects of a freakish sort, many of which focused on New England. It is a fact that he spent six months posing as a mental patient at an institution in western Massachussetts, gathering information on the "culture" of the psychically disturbed. When his book *Winter Solstice: The Longest Night of a Society* was published, the general opinion was that it was disappointingly subjective and impressionistic, and that, aside from a few moving but "poetically obscure" observations, there was nothing at all to give it value. Those who defended Thoss claimed he was a kind of superanthropologist: while much of his work emphasized his own mind and feelings, his experience had in fact penetrated to a rich core of hard data which he had yet to disclose in objective discourse. As a student of Thoss, I tended to support this latter estimation of him. For a variety of tenable and untenable reasons, I believed Thoss capable of unearthing hitherto inaccessible strata of human existence. So it was gratifying at first that this article entitled "The Last Feast of Harlequin" seemed to uphold the Thoss mystique, and in an area I personally found captivating.

Much of the content of the article I did not immediately comprehend, given its author's characteristic and often strategic obscurities. On first reading, the most interesting aspect of this brief study—the "notes" encompassed only twenty pages —was the general mood of the piece. Thoss's eccentricities were definitely present in these pages, but only as a struggling inner force which was definitely contained—incarcerated, I might say—by the somber rhythmic movements of his prose and by some gloomy references he occasionally called upon. Two references in particular shared a common theme. One was a quotation from Poe's "The Conqueror Worm," which Thoss employed as a rather sensational epigraph. The point of the epigraph, however, was nowhere echoed in the text of the article save in another passing reference. Thoss brought up the well-known genesis of the modern Christmas celebration, which of course descends from the Roman Saturnalia. Then, making it clear he had not yet observed the Mirocaw festival and had only gathered its nature from various informants, he established that it too contained many, even more overt, elements of the Saturnalia. Next he made what seemed to me a trivial and purely linguistic observation, one that had less to do with his main course of argument than it did with the equally peripheral Poe epigraph. He briefly mentioned that an early sect of the Syrian Gnostics called themselves "Saturnians" and believed, among other religious heresies, that mankind was created by angels who were in turn created by the Supreme Unknown. The angels, however, did not possess the power to make their creation an erect being and for a time he crawled upon the earth like a worm. Eventually, the Creator remedied this grotesque state of affairs. At the time I supposed that the symbolic correspondences of mankind's origins and ultimate condition being associated with worms, combined with a year-end festival recognizing the winter death of the earth, was the gist of this Thossian "insight," a poetic but scientifically valueless observation.

Other observations he made on the Mirocaw festival were also strictly etic; in other words, they were based on second-hand sources, hearsay testimony. Even at that juncture, however, I felt Thoss knew more than he disclosed; and, as I later discovered, he had indeed included information on certain aspects of Mirocaw suggesting he was already in possession of several keys which for the moment he was keeping securely in his own pocket. By then I myself possessed a most revealing morsel of knowledge. A note to the "Harlequin" article apprised the reader that the piece was only a fragment in rude form of a more wide-ranging work in preparation. This work was never seen by the world. My former professor had not published anything since his withdrawal from academic circulation some twenty years ago. Now I suspected where he had gone.

For the man I had stopped on the streets of Mirocaw and from whom I tried to obtain directions, the man with the disconcertingly lethargic gaze, had very much resembled a superannuated version of Dr. Raymond Thoss.

3.

And now I have a confession to make. Despite my reasons for
being enthusiastic about Mirocaw and its mysteries, especially
its relationship to both Thoss and my own deepest concerns as
a scholar—I contemplated the days ahead of me with no more
than a feeling of frigid numbness and often with a sense of
profound depression. Yet I had no reason to be surprised at
this emotional state, which had little relevance to the outward
events in my life but was determined by inward conditions that
worked according to their own, quite enigmatic, seasons and
cycles. For many years, at least since my university days, I have
suffered from this dark malady, this recurrent despondency in
which I would become buried when it came time for the earth
to grow cold and bare and the skies heavy with shadows. Nevertheless, I pursued my plans, though somewhat mechanically,
to visit Mirocaw during its festival days, for I superstitiously
hoped that this activity might diminish the weight of my seasonal despair. In Mirocaw would be parades and parties and
the opportunity to play the clown once again.

For weeks in advance I practiced my art, even perfecting a
new feat of juggling magic, which was my special forte in fool-
ery. I had my costumes cleaned, purchased fresh makeup, and
was ready. I received permission from the university to cancel
some of my classes prior to the holiday, explaining the nature
of my project and the necessity of arriving in the town a few
days before the festival began, in order to do some preliminary
research, establish informants, and so on. Actually, my plan
was to postpone any formal inquiry until after the festival and
to involve myself beforehand as much as possible in its activities. I would, of course, keep a journal during this time.

There was one resource I did want to consult, however.
Specifically, I returned to that outstate library to examine those
issues of the Mirocaw *Courier* dating from December two
decades ago. One story in particular confirmed a point Thoss
made in the "Harlequin" article, though the event it chronicled must have taken place after Thoss had written his study.

The Courier story appeared two weeks after the festival had
ended for that year and was concerned with the disappearance
of a woman named Elizabeth Beadle, the wife of Samuel Bea-

dle, a hotel owner in Mirocaw. The county authorities speculated that this was another instance of the "holiday suicides" which seemed to occur with inordinate seasonal regularity in the Mirocaw region. Thoss documented this phenomenon in his "Harlequin" article, though I suspect that today these deaths would be neatly categorized under the heading "seasonal affective disorder". In any case, the authorities searched a half-frozen lake near the outskirts of Mirocaw where they had found many successful suicides in years past. This year, however, no body was discovered. Alongside the article was a picture of Elizabeth Beadle. Even in the grainy microfilm reproduction one could detect a certain vibrancy and vitality in Mrs. Beadle's face. That an hypothesis of "holiday suicide" should be so readily posited to explain her disappearance seemed strange and in some way unjust.

Thoss, in his brief article, wrote that every year there occurred changes of a moral or spiritual cast which seemed to affect Mirocaw along with the usual winter metamorphosis. He was not precise about its origin or nature but stated, in typically mystifying fashion, that the effect of this "subseason" on the town was conspicuously negative. In addition to the number of suicides actually accomplished during this time, there was also a rise in treatment of "hypochondriacal" conditions, which was how the medical men of twenty years past characterized these cases in discussions with Thoss. This state of affairs would gradually worsen and finally reach a climax during the days scheduled for the Mirocaw festival. Thoss speculated that given the secretive nature of small towns, the situation was probably even more intensely pronounced than casual investigation could reveal.

The connection between the festival and this insidious subseasonal climate in Mirocaw was a point on which Thoss did not come to any rigid conclusions. He did write, nevertheless, that these two "climatic aspects" had had a parallel existence in the town's history as far back as available records could document. A late nineteenth-century history of Mirocaw County speaks of the town by its original name of New Colstead, and castigates the townspeople for holding a "ribald and soulless feast" to the exclusion of normal Christmas observances. (Thoss comments that the historian had mistakenly fused two distinct aspects of the season, their actual relationship being essentially antagonistic.) The "Harlequin" article did not trace the festival to its earliest appearance (this may not have been possible), though Thoss emphasized the New England origins of Mirocaw's founders. The festival, therefore, was one imported from this region and could reasonably be extended at least a century; that is, if it had not been brought over from the Old World, in which case its roots would become indefinite until further research could be done. Surely Thoss's allusion to the Syrian Gnostics suggested the latter possibility could not entirely be ruled out.

But it seemed to be the festival's link to New England that nourished Thoss's speculations. He wrote of this patch of geography as if it were an acceptable place to end the search. For him, the very words "New England" seemed to be stripped of all traditional connotations and had come to imply nothing less than a gateway to all lands, both known and suspected, and even to ages beyond the civilized history of the region. Having been educated partly in New England, I could somewhat understand this sentimental exaggeration, for indeed there are places that seem archaic beyond chronological measure, appearing to transcend relative standards of time and achieving a kind of absolute antiquity which cannot be logically fathomed. But how this vague suggestion related to a small town in the Midwest I could not imagine. Thoss himself observed that the residents of Mirocaw did not betray any mysteriously primitive consciousness. On the contrary, they appeared superficially unaware of the genesis of their winter merrymaking. That such a tradition had endured through the years, however, even eclipsing the conventional Christmas holiday, revealed a profound awareness of the festival's meaning and function.

I cannot deny that what I had learned about the Mirocaw festival did inspire a trite sense of fate, especially given the involvement of such an important figure from my past as Thoss. It was the first time in my academic career that I knew myself to be better suited than anyone else to discern the true meaning of scattered data, even if I could only attribute this special authority to chance circumstances.

Nevertheless, as I sat in that library on a morning in mid

December I doubted for a moment the wisdom of setting out
for Mirocaw rather than returning home, where the more familiar *rite de passage* of winter depression awaited me. My original
scheme was to avoid the cyclical blues the season held for me,
but it seemed this was also a part of the history of Mirocaw,
only on a much larger scale. My emotional instability, however, was exactly what qualified me most for the particular
fieldwork ahead, though I did not take pride or consolation in
the fact. And to retreat would have been to deny myself an opportunity that might never offer itself again. In retrospect,
there seems to have been no fortuitous resolution to the decision I had to make. As it happened, I went ahead to the town.

4.

Just past noon, on December 18, I started driving toward
Mirocaw. A blur of dull, earthen-colored scenery extended in
every direction. The snowfalls of late autumn had been sparse,
and only a few white patches appeared in the harvested fields
along the highway. The clouds were gray and abundant. Passing
by a stretch of forest, I noticed the black, ragged clumps of
abandoned nests clinging to the twisted mesh of bare branches.
I thought I saw black birds skittering over the road ahead, but
they were only dead leaves and they flew into the air as I
drove by.

I approached Mirocaw from the south, entering the town
from the direction I had left it on my visit the previous summer. This took me once again through that part of town which
seemed to exist on the wrong side of some great invisible barrier dividing the desirable sections of Mirocaw from the undesirable. As lurid as this district had appeared to me under the
summer sun, in the thin light of that winter afternoon it degenerated into a pale phantom of itself. The frail stores and
starved-looking houses suggested a borderline region between
the material and nonmaterial worlds, with one sardonically
wearing the mask of the other. I saw a few gaunt pedestrians who
turned as I passed by, though seemingly not *because* I passed
by, making my way up to the main street of Mirocaw.

Driving up the steep rise of Townshend Street, I found the
sights there comparatively welcoming. The rolling avenues of

the town were in readiness for the festival. Streetlights had their poles raveled with evergreen, the fresh boughs proudly conspicuous in a barren season. On the doors of many of the businesses on Townshend were holly wreaths, equally green but observably plastic. However, although there was nothing unusual in this traditional greenery of the season, it soon became apparent to me that Mirocaw had quite abandoned itself to this particular symbol of Yuletide. It was garishly in evidence everywhere. The windows of stores and houses were framed in green lights, green streamers hung down from storefront awnings, and the beacons of the Red Rooster Bar were peacock green floodlights. I supposed the residents of Mirocaw desired these decorations, but the effect was one of excess. An eerie emerald haze permeated the town, and faces looked slightly reptilian.

At the time I assumed that the prodigious evergreen, holly wreaths, and colored lights (if only of a single color) demonstrated an emphasis on the vegetable symbols of the Nordic Yuletide, which would inevitably be muddled into the winter festival of any northern country just as they had been adopted for the Christmas season. In his "Harlequin" article Thoss wrote of the pagan aspect of Mirocaw's festival, likening it to the ritual of a fertility cult, with probable connections to chthonic divinities at some time in the past. But Thoss had mistaken, as I had, what was only part of the festival's significance for the whole.

The hotel at which I had made reservations was located on Townshend. It was an old building of brown brick, with an arched doorway and a pathetic coping intended to convey an impression of neoclassicism. I found a parking space in front and left my suitcases in the car.

When I first entered the hotel lobby it was empty. I thought perhaps the Mirocaw festival would have attracted enough visitors to at least bolster the business of its only hotel, but it seemed I was mistaken. Tapping a little bell, I leaned on the desk and turned to look at a small, traditionally decorated Christmas tree on a table near the entranceway. It was complete with shiny, egg-fragile bulbs; miniature candy canes; flat, laughing Santas with arms wide; a star on top nodding awkwardly against the delicate shoulder of an upper branch; and colored lights that bloomed out of flower-shaped sockets. For some reason this seemed to me a sorry little piece.

"May I help you?" said a young woman arriving from a room adjacent to the lobby.

I must have been staring rather intently at her, for she looked away and seemed quite uneasy. I could hardly imagine what to say to her or how to explain what I was thinking. In person she immediately radiated a chilling brilliance of manner and expression. But if this woman had not committed suicide twenty years before, as the newspaper article had suggested, neither had she aged in that time.

"Sarah," called a masculine voice from the invisible heights of a stairway. A tall, middle-aged man came down the steps. "I thought you were in your room," said the man, whom I took to be Samuel Beadle. Sarah, not Elizabeth, Beadle glanced sideways in my direction to indicate to her father that she was conducting the business of the hotel. Beadle apologized to me, and then excused the two of them for a moment while they went off to one side to continue their exchange.

I smiled and pretended everything was normal, while trying to remain within earshot of their conversation. They spoke in tones that suggested their conflict was a familiar one: Beadle's over-protective concern with his daughter's whereabouts and Sarah's frustrated understanding of certain restrictions placed upon her. The conversation ended, and Sarah ascended the stairs, turning for a moment to give me a facial pantomime of apology for the unprofessional scene that had just taken place.

"Now, sir, what can I do for you?" Beadle asked, almost demanded.

"Yes, I have a reservation. Actually, I'm a day early, if that doesn't present a problem." I gave the hotel the benefit of the doubt that its business might have been secretly flourishing.

"No problem at all, sir," he said, presenting me with the registration form, and then a brass-colored key dangling from a plastic disc bearing the number 44.

"Luggage?"

"Yes, it's in my car."

"I'll give you a hand with that."

While Beadle was settling me in my fourth-floor room it

seemed an opportune moment to broach the subject of the festival, the holiday suicides, and perhaps, depending upon his reaction, the fate of his wife. I needed a respondent who had lived in the town for a good many years and who could enlighten me about the attitude of Mirocavians toward their season of sea-green lights.

"This is just fine," I said about the clean but somber room. "Nice view. I can see the bright green lights of Mirocaw just fine from up here. Is the town usually all decked out like this? For the festival, I mean."

"Yes, sir, for the festival," he replied mechanically.

"I imagine you'll probably be getting quite a few of us out-of-towners in the next couple of days."

"Could be. Is there anything else?"

"Yes, there is. I wonder if you could tell me something about the festivities."

"Such as . . ."

"Well, you know, the clowns and so forth."

"Only clowns here are the ones that're . . . well, picked out, I suppose you would say."

"I don't understand."

"Excuse me, sir. I'm very busy right now. Is there anything else?"

I could think of nothing at the moment to perpetuate our conversation. Beadle wished me a good stay and left.

I unpacked my suitcases. In addition to regular clothing I had also brought along some of the items from my clown's wardrobe. Beadle's comment that the clowns of Mirocaw were "picked out" left me wondering exactly what purpose these street masqueraders served in the festival. The clown figure has had so many meanings in different times and cultures. The jolly, well-loved joker familiar to most people is actually but one aspect of this protean creature. Madmen, hunchbacks, amputees, and other abnormals were once considered natural clowns; they were elected to fulfil a comic role which could allow others to see them as ludicrous rather than as terrible reminders of the forces of disorder in the world. But sometimes a cheerless jester was required to draw attention to this same disorder, as in the case of King Lear's morbid and honest fool, who of course was eventually hanged, and so much for his clownish wisdom. Clowns have often had ambiguous and sometimes contradictory roles to play. Thus, I knew enough not to brashly jump into costume and cry out, "Here I am again!"

That first day in Mirocaw I did not stray far from the hotel. I read and rested for a few hours and then ate at a nearby diner. Through the window beside my table I watched the winter night turn the soft green glow of the town into a harsh and almost totally new color as it contrasted with the darkness. The streets of Mirocaw seemed to me unusually busy for a small town at evening. Yet it was not the kind of activity one normally sees before an approaching Christmas holiday. This was not a crowd of bustling shoppers loaded with bright bags of presents. Their arms were empty, their hands shoved deep in their pockets against the cold, which nevertheless had not driven them to the solitude of their presumably warm houses. I watched them enter and exit store after store without buying; many merchants remained open late, and even the places that were closed had left their neons illuminated. The faces that passed the window of the diner were possibly just stiffened by the cold, I thought; frozen into deep frowns and nothing else. In the same window I saw the reflection of my own face. It was not the face of an adept clown; it was slack and flabby and at that moment seemed the face of someone less than alive. Outside was the town of Mirocaw, its streets dipping and rising with a lunatic severity, its citizens packing the sidewalks, its heart bathed in green: as promising a field of professional and personal challenge as I had ever encountered—and I was bored to the point of dread. I hurried back to my hotel room.

"Mirocaw has another coldness within its cold," I wrote in my journal that night. "Another set of buildings and streets that exists behind the visible town's facade like a world of disgraceful back alleys." I went on like this for about a page, across which I finally engraved a big "X". Then I went to bed.

In the morning I left my car at the hotel and walked toward the main business district a few blocks away. Mingling with the good people of Mirocaw seemed like the proper thing to do at that point in my scientific sojourn. But as I began laboriously walking up Townshend (the sidewalks were cramped with wandering pedestrians), a glimpse of someone suddenly replaced my haphazard plan with a more specific and immediate one. Through the crowd and about fifteen paces ahead was my goal.

"Dr. Thoss," I called.

His head almost seemed to turn and look back in response to my shout, but I could not be certain. I pushed past several warmly wrapped bodies and green-scarved necks, only to find that the object of my pursuit appeared to be maintaining the same distance from me, though I did not know if this was being done deliberately or not. At the next corner, the dark-coated Thoss abruptly turned right onto a steep street which led downward directly toward the dilapidated south end of Mirocaw. When I reached the corner I looked down the sidewalk and could see him very clearly from above. I also saw how he managed to stay so far ahead of me in a mob that had impeded my own progress. For some reason the people on the sidewalk made room so that he could move past them easily, without the usual jostling of bodies. It was not a dramatic physical avoidance, though it seemed nonetheless intentional. Fighting the tight fabric of the throng, I continued to follow Thoss, losing and regaining sight of him.

By the time I reached the bottom of the sloping street the crowd had thinned out considerably, and after walking a block or so farther I found myself practically a lone pedestrian pacing behind a distant figure that I hoped was still Thoss. He was now walking quite swiftly and in a way that seemed to acknowledge my pursuit of him, though really it felt as if he were leading me as much as I was chasing him. I called his name a few more times at a volume he could not have failed to hear, assuming that deafness was not one of the changes to have come over him; he was, after all, not a young man, nor even a middle-aged one any longer.

Thoss suddenly crossed in the middle of the street. He walked a few more steps and entered a signless brick building between a liquor store and a repair shop of some kind. In the "Harlequin" article Thoss had mentioned that the people living in this section of Mirocaw maintained their own businesses, and that these were patronized almost exclusively by residents of the area. I could well believe this statement when I looked at these little sheds of commerce, for they had the same badly weathered appearance as their clientele. The formidable shoddiness of these buildings notwithstanding, I followed Thoss into the plain brick shell of what had been, or possibly still was, a diner.

Inside it was unusually dark. Even before my eyes made the adjustment I sensed that this was not a thriving restaurant cozily cluttered with chairs and tables—as was the establishment where I had eaten the night before—but a place with only a few disarranged furnishings, and very cold. It seemed colder, in fact, than the winter streets outside.

"Dr. Thoss?" I called toward a lone table near the center of the long room. Perhaps four or five were sitting around the table, with some others blending into the dimness behind them. Scattered across the top of the table were some books and loose papers. Seated there was an old man indicating something in the pages before him, but it was not Thoss. Beside him were two youths whose wholesome features distinguished them from the grim weariness of the others. I approached the table and they all looked up at me. None of them showed a glimmer of emotion except the two boys, who exchanged worried and guilt-ridden glances with each other, as if they had just been discovered in some shameful act. They both suddenly burst from the table and ran into the dark background, where a light appeared briefly as they exited by a back door.

"I'm sorry," I said diffidently. "I thought I saw someone I knew come in here."

They said nothing. Out of a back room others began to emerge, no doubt interested in the source of the commotion. In a few moments the room was crowded with these tramp-like figures, all of them gazing emptily in the dimness. I was not at this point frightened of them; at least I was not afraid they would do me any physical harm. Actually, I felt as if it was quite within my power to pummel them easily into submission, their mousy faces almost inviting a succession of firm blows. But there were so many of them.

They slid slowly toward me in a worm-like mass. Their eyes seemed empty and unfocused, and I wondered a moment if they were even aware of my presence. Nevertheless, I was the center upon which their lethargic shuffling converged, their shoes scuffing softly along the bare floor. I began to deliver a number of hasty inanities as they continued to press toward me, their weak and unexpectedly odorless bodies nudging against mine. (I understood now why the people along the sidewalks seemed to instinctively avoid Thoss.) Unseen legs became entangled with my own; I staggered and then regained my balance. This sudden movement aroused me from a kind of mesmeric daze into which I must have fallen without being aware of it. I had intended to leave that dreary place long before events had reached such a juncture, but for some reason I could not focus my intentions strongly enough to cause myself to act. My mind had been drifting farther away as these slavish things approached. In a sudden surge of panic I pushed through their soft ranks and was outside.

The open air revived me to my former alertness, and I immediately started pacing swiftly up the hill. I was no longer sure that I had not simply imagined what had seemed, and at the same time did not seem, like a perilous moment. Had their movements been directed toward a harmful assault, or were they trying merely to intimidate me? As I reached the green-glazed main street of Mirocaw I really could not determine what had just happened.

The sidewalks were still jammed with a multitude of pedestrians, who now seemed more lively than they had been only a short time before. There was a kind of vitality that could only be attributed to the imminent festivities. A group of young men had begun celebrating prematurely and strode noisily across the street at midpoint, obviously intoxicated. From the laughter and joking among the still sober citizens I gathered that, mardi-gras style, public drunkenness was within the traditions of this winter festival. I looked for anything to indicate the beginnings of the Street Masquerade, but saw nothing: no brightly garbed harlequins or snow-white pierrots. Were the ceremonies even now in preparation for the coronation of the Winter Queen? "The Winter Queen," I wrote in my journal. "Figure of fertility invested with symbolic powers of revival and prosperity. Elected in the manner of a high school prom queen. Check for possible consort figure in the form of a representative from the underworld."

In the pre-darkness hours of December 19 I sat in my hotel room and wrote and thought and organized. I did not feel too badly, all things considered. The holiday excitement which was steadily rising in the streets below my window was definitely infecting me. I forced myself to take a short nap in anticipation of a long night. When I awoke, Mirocaw's annual feast had begun.

5.

Shouting, commotion, carousing. Sleepily I went to the window and looked out over the town. It seemed all the lights of Mirocaw were shining, save in that section down the hill which became part of the black void of winter. And now the town's greenish tinge was even more pronounced, spreading everywhere like a great green rainbow that had melted from the sky and endured, phosphorescent, into the night. In the streets was the brightness of an artificial spring. The byways of Mirocaw vibrated with activity: on a nearby corner a brass band blared; marauding cars blew their horns and were sometimes mounted by laughing pedestrians; a man emerged from the Red Rooster Bar, threw up his arms, and crowed. I looked closely at the individual celebrants, searching for the vestments of clowns. Soon, delightedly, I saw them. The costume was red and white, with matching cap, and the face painted a noble alabaster. It almost seemed to be a clownish incarnation of that white-bearded and black-booted Christmas fool.

This particular fool, however, was not receiving the affection and respect usually accorded to a Santa Claus. My poor fellow-clown was in the middle of a circle of revelers who were pushing him back and forth from one to the other. The object of this abuse seemed to accept it somewhat willingly, but this little game nevertheless appeared to have humiliation as its purpose. "Only clowns here are the ones that're picked out," echoed Beadle's voice in my memory. "Picked *on*" seemed closer to the truth.

Packing myself in some heavy clothes, I went out into the green gleaming streets. Not far from the hotel I was stumbled into by a character with a wide blue and red grin and bright baggy clothes. Actually he had been shoved into me by some youths outside a drugstore.

"See the freak," said an obese and drunken fellow. "See the freak fall."

My first response was anger, and then fear as I saw two others flanking the fat drunk. They walked toward me and I tensed myself for a confrontation.

"This is a disgrace," one said, the neck of a wine bottle held loosely in his left hand.

But it was not to me they were speaking; it was to the clown, who had been pushed to the sidewalk. His three persecutors helped him up with a sudden jerk and then splashed wine in his face. They ignored me altogether.

"Let him loose," the fat one said. "Crawl away, freak. Oh, he flies!"

The clown trotted off, becoming lost in the throng.

"Wait a minute," I said to the rowdy trio, who had started lumbering away. I quickly decided that it would probably be futile to ask them to explain what I had just witnessed, especially amid the noise and confusion of the festivities. In my best jovial fashion I proposed we all go someplace where I could buy them each a drink. They had no objection and in a short while we were all squeezed around a table in the Red Rooster.

Over several drinks I explained to them that I was from out of town, which pleased them no end for some reason. I told them there were things I did not understand about their festival.

"I don't think there's anything to understand," the fat one said. "It's just what you see."

I asked him about the people dressed as clowns.

"Them? They're the freaks. It's their turn this year. Everyone takes their turn. Next year it might be mine. Or *yours*," he said, pointing at one of his friends across the table. "And when we find out which one you are—"

"You're not smart enough," said the defiant potential freak.

This was an important point: the fact that individuals who played the clowns remain, or at least attempted to remain, anonymous. This arrangement would help remove inhibitions a resident of Mirocaw might have about abusing his own neighbor or even a family relation. From what I later observed, the extent of this abuse did not go beyond a kind of playful roughhousing. And even so, it was only the occasional group of rowdies who actually took advantage of this aspect of the festival, the majority of the citizens very much content to stay on the sidelines.

As far as being able to illuminate the meaning of this custom, my three young friends were quite useless. To them it was just amusement, as I imagine it was to the majority of Mirocavians. This was understandable. I suppose the average person would not be able to explain exactly how the profoundly familiar Christmas holiday came to be celebrated in its present form.

I left the bar alone and not unaffected by the drinks I had consumed there. Outside, the general merrymaking continued. Loud music emanated from several quarters. Mirocaw had fully transformed itself from a sedate small town to an enclave of Saturnalia within the dark immensity of a winter night. But Saturn is also the planetary symbol of melancholy and sterility, a clash of opposites contained within that single word. And as I wandered half-drunkenly down the street, I discovered that there was a conflict within the winter festival itself. This discovery indeed appeared to be that secret key which Thoss withheld in his study of the town. Oddly enough, it was through my unfamiliarity with the outward nature of the festival that I came to know its true nature.

I was mingling with the crowd on the street, warmly enjoying the confusion around me, when I saw a strangely designed creature lingering on the corner up ahead. It was one of the Mirocaw clowns. Its clothes were shabby and nondescript, almost in the style of a tramp-type clown, but not humorously exaggerated enough. The face, though, made up for the lackluster costume. I had never seen such a strange conception for a clown's countenance. The figure stood beneath a dim streetlight, and when it turned its head my way I realized why it seemed familiar. The thin, smooth, and pale head; the wide eyes; the oval-shaped features resembling nothing so much as the skull-faced, screaming creature in that famous painting (memory fails me). This clownish imitation rivalled the original in suggesting stricken realms of abject horror and despair: an inhuman likeness more proper to something under the earth than upon it.

From the first moment I saw this creature, I thought of those inhabitants of the ghetto down the hill. There was the same nauseating passivity and languor in its bearing. Perhaps if I had not been drinking earlier I would not have been bold

enough to take the action I did. I decided to join in one of the
upstanding traditions of the winter festival, for it annoyed me
to see this morbid impostor of a clown standing up. When I
reached the corner I laughingly pushed myself into the creature
—"Whoops!"—who stumbled backward and ended up on the
sidewalk. I laughed again and looked around for approval
from the festivalers in the vicinity. No one, however, seemed to
appreciate or even acknowledge what I had done. They did
not laugh with me or point with amusement, but only passed
by, perhaps walking a little faster until they were some distance
from this streetcorner incident. I realized instantly I had violated some tacit rule of behavior, though I had thought my action well within the common practice. The idea occurred to
me that I might even be apprehended and prosecuted for what
in any other circumstances was certainly a criminal act. I turned
around to help the clown back to his feet, hoping to somehow
redeem my offense, but the creature was gone. Solemnly I
walked away from the scene of my inadvertent crime and
sought other streets away from its witnesses.

Along the various back avenues of Mirocaw I wandered,
pausing exhaustedly at one point to sit at the counter of a small
sandwich shop that was packed with customers. I ordered a
cup of coffee to revive my overly alcoholed system. Warming my
hands around the cup and sipping slowly from it, I watched
the people outside as they passed the front window. It was well
after midnight but the thick flow of passersby gave no indication that anyone was going home early. A carnival of profiles
filed past the window and I was content simply to sit back and
observe, until finally one of these faces made me start. It was
that frightful little clown I had roughed up earlier. But although
its face was familiar in its ghastly aspect, there was something
different about it. And I wondered that there should be two
such hideous freaks.

Quickly paying the man at the counter, I dashed out to get
a second glimpse of the clown, who was now nowhere in sight.
The dense crowd kept me from pursuing this figure with any
speed, and I wondered how the clown could have made its
way so easily ahead of me. Unless the crowd had instinctively
allowed this creature to pass unhindered through its massive
ranks, as it did for Thoss. In the process of searching for this

particular freak, I discovered that interspersed among the celebrating populous of Mirocaw, which included the sanctioned
festival clowns, there was not one or two, but a considerable
number of these pale, wraith-like creatures. And they all
drifted along the streets unmolested by even the rowdiest of
revelers. I now understood one of the taboos of the festival.
These other clowns were not to be disturbed and should even
be avoided, much as were the residents of the slum at the edge
of town. Nevertheless, I felt instinctively that the two groups
of clowns were somehow identified with each other, even if the
ghetto clowns were not welcome at Mirocaw's winter festival.
Indeed, they were not simply part of the community and celebrating the season in their own way. To all appearances, this
group of melancholy mummers constituted nothing less than
an entirely independent festival—a festival within a festival.

Returning to my room, I entered my suppositions into the
journal I was keeping for this venture. The following are
excerpts:

There is a superstitiousness displayed by the residents of Mirocaw
with regard to these people from the slum section, particularly as they
lately appear in those dreadful faces signifying their own festival.
What is the relationship between these simultaneous celebrations?
Did one precede the other? If so, which? My opinion at this point—
and I claim no conclusiveness for it—is that Mirocaw's winter festival
is the later manifestation, that it appeared after the festival of those
depressingly pallid clowns, in order to cover it up or mitigate its
effect. The holiday suicides come to mind, and the subclimate Thoss
wrote about, the disappearance of Elizabeth Beadle twenty years ago,
and my own experience with this pariah clan existing outside yet
within the community. Of my own experience with this emotionally
deleterious subseason I would rather not speak at this time. Still not
able to say whether or not my usual winter melancholy is the cause.
On the general subject of mental health, I must consider Thoss's
book about his stay in a psychiatric hospital (in western Mass., almost
sure of that. Check on this book & Mirocaw's New England roots).
The winter solstice is tomorrow, albeit sometime past midnight (how
blurry these days and nights are becoming!). It is, of course, the day
of the year in which night hours surpass daylight hours by the greatest margin. Note what this has to do with the suicides and a rise in
psychic disorder. Recalling Thoss's list of documented suicides in his
article, there seemed to be a recurrence of specific family names, as

there very likely might be for any kind of data collected in a small town. Among these names was a Beadle or two. Perhaps, then, there is a genealogical basis for the suicides which has nothing to do with Thoss's mystical subclimate, which is a colorful idea to be sure and one that seems fitting for this town of various outward and inward aspects, but is not a conception that can be substantiated.

One thing that seems certain, however, is the division of Mirocaw into two very distinct types of citizenry, resulting in two festivals and the appearance of similar clowns—a term now used in an extremely loose sense. But there is a connection, and I believe I have some idea of what it is. I said before that the normal residents of the town regard those from the ghetto, and especially their clown figures, with superstition. Yet it's more than that: there is fear, perhaps a kind of hatred—the particular kind of hatred resulting from some powerful and irrational memory. What threatens Mirocaw I think I can very well understand. I recall the incident earlier today in that vacant diner. "Vacant" is the appropriate word here, despite its contradiction of fact. The congregation of that half-lit room formed less a presence than an absence, even considering the oppressive number of them. Those eyes that did not or could not focus on anything, the pining lassitude of their faces, the lazy march of their feet. I was spiritually drained when I ran out of there. I then understood why these people and their activities are avoided.

I cannot question the wisdom of those ancestral Mirocavians who began the tradition of the winter festival and gave the town a pretext for celebration and social intercourse at a time when the consequences of brooding isolation are most severe, those longest and darkest days of the solstice. A mood of Christmas joviality obviously would not be sufficient to counter the menace of this season. But even so, there are still the suicides of individuals who are somehow cut off, I imagine, from the vitalizing activities of the festival.

It is the nature of this insidious subseason that seems to determine the outward forms of Mirocaw's winter festival: the optimistic greenery in a period of gray dormancy; the fertile promise of the Winter Queen; and, most interesting to my mind, the clowns. The bright clowns of Mirocaw who are treated so badly; they appear to serve as substitute figures for those dark-eyed mummers of the slums. Since the latter are feared for some power or influence they possess, they may still be symbolically confronted and conquered through their counterparts, who are elected for precisely this function. If I am right about this, I wonder to what extent there is a conscious awareness among the town's populace of this indirect show of aggression. Those three young men I spoke with tonight did not seem to possess much insight beyond seeing that there was a certain amount of robust fun in the festival's tradition. For that matter, how much awareness is there on the *other side* of these two antagonistic festivals? Too horrible to think of such a thing, but I must wonder if, for all their apparent aimlessness, those inhabitants of the ghetto are not the only ones who know what they are about. No denying that behind those inhumanly limp expressions there seems to lie a kind of obnoxious intelligence.

Now I realize the confusion of my present state, but as I wobbled from street to street tonight, watching those oval-mouthed clowns, I could not help feeling that all the merry-making in Mirocaw was somehow allowed only by their sufferance. This I hope is no more than a fanciful Thossian intuition, the sort of idea that is curious and thought-provoking without ever seeming to gain the benefit of proof. I know my mind is not entirely lucid, but I feel that it may be possible to penetrate Mirocaw's many complexities and illuminate the hidden side of the festival season. In particular I must look for the significance of the other festival. Is it also some kind of fertility celebration? From what I have seen, the tenor of this "celebrating" sub-group is one of anti-fertility, if anything. How have they managed to keep from dying out completely over the years? How do they maintain their numbers?

But I was too tired to formulate any more of my sodden speculations. Falling onto my bed, I soon became lost in dreams of streets and faces.

6.

I was, of course, slightly hung over when I woke up late the next morning. The festival was still going strong, and blaring music outside roused me from a nightmare. It was a parade. A number of floats proceeded down Townshend, a familiar color predominating. There were theme floats of pilgrims and Indians, cowboys and Indians, and clowns of an orthodox type. In the middle of it all was the Winter Queen herself, freezing atop an icy throne. She waved in all directions. I even imagined she waved up at my dark window.

In the first few groggy moments of wakefulness I had no

sympathy with my excitation of the previous night. But I discovered that my former enthusiasm had merely lain dormant, and soon returned with an even greater intensity. Never before had my mind and senses been so active during this usually inert time of year. At home I would have been playing lugubrious old records and looking out the window quite a bit. I was terribly grateful in a completely abstract way for my commitment to a meaningful mania. And I was eager to get to work after I had had some breakfast at the coffee shop.

When I got back to my room I discovered the door was unlocked. And there was something written on the dresser mirror. The writing was red and greasy, as if done with a clown's make-up pencil—my own, I realized. I read the legend, or rather I should say *riddle*, several times: "What buries itself before it is dead?" I looked at it for quite a while, very shaken at how vulnerable my holiday fortifications were. Was this supposed to be a warning of some kind? A threat to the effect that if I persisted in a certain course I would end up prematurely interred? I would have to be careful, I told myself. My resolution was to let nothing deter me from the inspired strategy I had conceived for myself. I wiped the mirror clean, for it was now needed for other purposes.

I spent the rest of the day devising a very special costume and the appropriate face to go with it. I easily shabbied up my overcoat with a torn pocket or two and a complete set of stains. Combined with blue jeans and a pair of rather scuffed-up shoes, I had a passable costume for a derelict. The face, however, was more difficult, for I had to experiment from memory. Conjuring a mental image of the screaming pierrot in that painting (*The Scream*, I now recall), helped me quite a bit. At nightfall I exited the hotel by the back stairway.

It was strange to walk down the crowded street in this gruesome disguise. Though I thought I would feel conspicuous, the actual experience was very close, I imagined, to one of complete invisibility. No one looked at me as I strolled by, or as they strolled by, or as we strolled by each other. I was a phantom—perhaps the ghost of festivals past, or those yet to come.

I had no clear idea where my disguise would take me that night, only vague expectations of gaining the confidence of my fellow specters and possibly in some way coming to know their secrets. For a while I would simply wander around in that lack-adaisical manner I had learned from them, following their lead in any way they might indicate. And for the most part this meant doing almost nothing and doing it silently. If I passed one of my kind on the sidewalk there was no speaking, no exchange of knowing looks, no recognition at all that I was aware of. We were there on the streets of Mirocaw to create a presence and nothing more. At least this is how I came to feel about it. As I drifted along with my bodiless invisibility, I felt myself more and more becoming an empty, floating shape, seeing without being seen and walking without the interference of those grosser creatures who shared my world. It was not an experi-ence completely without interest or even pleasure. The clown's shibboleth of "here we are again" took on a new meaning for me as I felt myself a novitiate of a more rarified order of harle-quinry. And very soon the opportunity to make further prog-ress along this path presented itself.

Going the opposite direction, down the street, a pickup truck slowly passed, gently parting a sea of zigging and zagging cel-ebrants. The cargo in the back of this truck was curious, for it was made up entirely of my fellow sectarians. At the end of the block the truck stopped and another of them boarded it over the back gate. One block down I saw still another get on. Then the truck made a U-turn at an intersection and headed in my direction.

I stood at the curb as I had seen the others do. I was not sure the truck would pick me up, thinking that somehow they knew I was an imposter. The truck did, however, slow down, almost coming to a stop when it reached me. The others were crowded on the floor of the truck bed. Most of them were just staring into nothingness with the usual indifference I had come to expect from their kind. But a few actually glanced at me with some anticipation. For a second I hesitated, not sure I wanted to pursue this ruse any further. At the last moment, some impulse sent me climbing up the back of the truck and squeezing myself in among the others.

There were only a few more to pick up before the truck headed for the outskirts of Mirocaw and beyond. At first I tried to maintain a clear orientation with respect to the town. But as we took turn after turn through the darkness of narrow country roads, I found myself unable to preserve any sense of direction. The majority of the others in the back of the truck exhibited no apparent awareness of their fellow passengers. Guardedly, I looked from face to ghostly face. A few of them spoke in short whispered phrases to others close by. I could not make out what they were saying but the tone of their voices was one of innocent normalcy, as if they were not of the hardened slum-herd of Mirocaw. Perhaps, I thought, these were thrill-seekers who had disguised themselves as I had done, or, more likely, initiates of some kind. Possibly they had received prior instructions at such meetings as I had stumbled onto the day before. It was also likely that among this crew were those very boys I had frightened into a precipitate exit from that old diner.

The truck was now speeding along a fairly open stretch of country, heading toward those higher hills that surrounded the now distant town of Mirocaw. The icy wind whipped around us, and I could not keep myself from trembling with cold. This definitely betrayed me as one of the newcomers among the group, for the two bodies that pressed against mine were rigidly still and even seemed to be radiating a frigidity of their own. I glanced ahead at the darkness into which we were rapidly progressing.

We had left all open country behind us now, and the road was enclosed by thick woods. The mass of bodies in the truck leaned into one another as we began traveling up a steep incline. Above us, at the top of the hill, were lights shining somewhere within the woods. When the road levelled off, the truck made an abrupt turn, steering into what looked like a great ditch.

There was an unpaved path, however, upon which the truck proceeded toward the glowing in the near distance.

This glowing became brighter and sharper as we approached it, flickering upon the trees and revealing stark detail where there had formerly been only smooth darkness. As the truck pulled into a clearing and came to a stop, I saw a loose assembly of figures, many of which held lanterns that beamed with a dazzling and frosty light. I stood up in the back of the truck to unboard as the others were doing. Glancing around from that height I saw approximately thirty more of those cadaverous clowns milling about. One of my fellow passengers spied me lingering in the truck and in a strangely high-pitched whisper told me to hurry, explaining something about the "apex of darkness". I thought again about this solstice night; it was technically the longest period of darkness of the year, even if not by a very significant margin from many other winter nights. Its true significance, though, was related to considerations having little to do with either statistics or the calendar.

I went over to the place where the others were forming into a tighter crowd, which betrayed a sense of expectancy in the subtle gestures and expressions of its individual members. Glances were now exchanged, the hand of one lightly touched the shoulder of another, and a pair of circled eyes gazed over to where two figures were setting their lanterns on the ground about six feet apart. The illumination of these lanterns revealed an opening in the earth. Eventually the awareness of everyone was focused on this roundish pit, and as if by pre-arranged signal we all began huddling around it. The only sounds were those of the wind and our own movements as we crushed frozen leaves and sticks underfoot.

Finally, when we had all surrounded this gaping hole, the first one jumped in, leaving our sight for a moment but then reappearing to take hold of a lantern which another handed him from above. The miniature abyss filled with light, and I could see it was no more than six feet deep. One of its walls opened into the mouth of a tunnel. The figure holding the lantern stooped a little and disappeared into the passage.

Each of us, in turn, dropped into the darkness of this pit, and every fifth one took a lantern. I kept to the back of the group, for whatever subterranean activities were going to take place, I was sure I wanted to be on their periphery. When only about ten of us remained on the ground above, I maneuvered to let four of them precede me so that as the fifth I might receive a lantern. This was exactly how it worked out, for after I had leaped to the bottom of the hole a light was ritually handed down to me. Turning about-face, I quickly entered the passageway. At that point I shook so with cold that I was neither curious nor afraid, but only grateful for the shelter.

I entered a long, gently sloping tunnel, just high enough for me to stand upright. It was considerably warmer down there than outside in the cold darkness of the woods. After a few moments I had sufficiently thawed out so that my concerns shifted from those of physical comfort to a sudden and justified preoccupation with my survival. As I walked I held my lantern close to the sides of the tunnel. They were relatively smooth as if the passage had not been made by manual digging but had been burrowed by something which left behind a clue to its dimensions in the tunnel's size and shape. This delirious idea came to me when I recalled the message that had been left on my hotel room mirror: "What buries itself before it is dead?"

I had to hurry along to keep up with those uncanny spelunkers who preceded me. The lanterns ahead bobbed with every step of their bearers, the lumbering procession seeming less and less real the farther we marched into that snug little tunnel. At some point I noticed the line ahead of me growing shorter. The processioners were emptying out into a cavernous chamber where I, too, soon arrived. This area was about thirty feet in height, its other dimensions approximating those of a large ballroom. Gazing into the distance above made me uncomfortably aware of how far we had descended into the earth. Unlike the smooth sides of the tunnel, the walls of this cavern looked jagged and irregular, as though they had been gnawed at. The earth had been removed, I assumed, either through the tunnel from which we had emerged, or else by way of one of the many other black openings that I saw around the edges of the chamber, for possibly they too led back to the surface.

But the structure of this chamber occupied my mind a great deal less than did its occupants. There to meet us on the floor of the great cavern was what must have been the entire slum population of Mirocaw, and more, all with the same eerily wide-eyed and oval-mouthed faces. They formed a circle around an altar-like object which had some kind of dark, leathery covering draped over it. Upon the altar, another covering of the same material concealed a lumpy form beneath.

And behind this form, looking down upon the altar, was the only figure whose face was not greased with makeup.

He wore a long snowy robe that was the same color as the wispy hair berimming his head. His arms were calmly at his sides. He made no movement. The man I once believed would penetrate great secrets stood before us with the same professorial bearing that had impressed me so many years ago, yet now I felt nothing but dread at the thought of what revelations lay pocketed within the abysmal folds of his magisterial attire. Had I really come here to challenge such a formidable figure? The name by which I knew him seemed itself insufficient to designate one of his stature. Rather I should name him by his other incarnations: god of all wisdom, scribe of all sacred books, father of all magicians, thrice great and more—rather I should call him *Thoth*.

He raised his cupped hands to his congregation and the ceremony was underway.

It was all very simple. The entire assembly, which had remained speechless until this moment, broke into the most horrendous high-pitched singing that can be imagined. It was a choir of sorrow, of shrieking delirium, and of shame. The cavern rang shrilly with the dissonant, whining chorus. My voice, too, was added to the congregation's, trying to blend with their maimed music. But my singing could not imitate theirs, having a huskiness unlike their cacophonous keening wail. To keep from exposing myself as an intruder I continued to mouth their words without sound. These words were a revelation of the moody malignancy which until then I had no more than sensed whenever in the presence of these figures. They were singing to the "unborn in paradise," to the "pure unlived lives." They sang a dirge for existence, for all its vital forms and seasons. Their ideals were those of darkness, chaos, and a melancholy half-existence consecrated to all the many shapes of death. A sea of thin, bloodless faces trembled and screamed with perverted hopes. And the robed, guiding figure at the heart of all this—elevated over the course of twenty years to the status of high priest—was the man from whom I had taken so many of my own life's principles. It would be useless to describe what I felt at that moment and a waste of the time I need to describe the events which followed.

The singing abruptly stopped and the towering white-haired figure began to speak. He was welcoming those of the new generation—twenty winters had passed since the "Pure Ones" had expanded their ranks. The word "pure" in this setting was a violence to what sense and composure I still retained, for nothing could have been more foul than what was to come. Thoss—and I employ this defunct identity only as a convenience —closed his sermon and drew closer to the dark-skinned altar. Then, with all the flourish of his former life, he drew back the topmost covering. Beneath it was a limp-limbed effigy, a collapsed puppet sprawled upon the slab. I was standing toward the rear of the congregation and attempted to keep as close to the exit passage as I could. Thus, I did not see everything as clearly as I might have.

Thoss looked down upon the crooked, doll-like form and then out at the gathering. I even imagined that he made knowing eye-contact with myself. He spread his arms and a stream of continuous and unintelligible words flowed from his moaning mouth. The congregation began to stir, not greatly but perceptibly. Until that moment there was a limit to what I believed was the evil of these people. They were, after all, only that. They were merely morbid, self-tortured souls with strange beliefs. If there was anything I had learned in all my years as an anthropologist it was that the world is infinitely rich in strange ideas, even to the point where the concept of strangeness itself had little meaning for me. But with the scene I then witnessed, my conscience bounded into a realm from which it will never return.

For now was the transformation scene, the culmination of every harlequinade.

It began slowly. There was increasing movement among those on the far side of the chamber from where I stood. Someone had fallen to the floor and the others in the area backed away. The voice at the altar continued its chanting. I tried to gain a better view but there were too many of them around me. Through the mass of obstructing bodies I caught only glimpses of what was taking place.

The one who had swooned to the floor of the chamber seemed to be losing all former shape and proportion. I thought it was a clown's trick. They were clowns, were they not? I myself could make four white balls transform into four black balls as I juggled them. And this was not my most astonishing feat of clownish magic. And is there not always a sleight-of-hand inherent in all ceremonies, often dependent on the transported delusions of the celebrants? This was a good show, I thought, and giggled to myself. The transformation scene of Harlequin throwing off his fool's facade. O God, Harlequin, do not move like that! Harlequin, where are your arms? And your legs have melted together and begun squirming upon the floor. What horrible, mouthing umbilicus is that where your face should be? *What is it that buries itself before it is dead?* The almighty serpent of wisdom—the Conqueror Worm.

It now started happening all around the chamber. Individual members of the congregation would gaze emptily—caught for a moment in a frozen trance—and then collapse to the floor to begin the sickening metamorphosis. This happened with ever-increasing frequency the louder and more frantic Thoss chanted his insane prayer or curse. Then there began a writhing movement toward the altar, and Thoss welcomed the things as they curled their way to the altar-top. I knew now what lax figure lay upon it.

This was Kora and Persephone, the daughter of Ceres and the Winter Queen: the child abducted into the underworld of death. Except this child had no supernatural mother to save her, no living mother at all. For the sacrifice I witnessed was an echo of one that had occurred twenty years before, the carnival feast of the preceding generation—*O carne vale!* Now both mother and daughter had become victims of this subterranean sabbath. I finally realized this truth when the figure stirred upon the altar, lifted its head of icy beauty, and screamed at the sight of mute mouths closing around her.

I ran from the chamber into the tunnel. (There was nothing else that could be done, I have obsessively told myself.) Some of the others who had not yet changed began to pursue me. They would have caught up to me, I have no doubt, for I fell only a few yards into the passage. And for a moment I imagined that I too was about to undergo a transformation, but I had not been prepared as the others had been. When I heard the approaching footsteps of my pursuers I was sure there was an even worse fate facing me upon the altar. But the footsteps ceased and retreated. They had received an order in the voice of their high priest. I too heard the order, though I wish I had not, for until then I had imagined that Thoss did not remember who I was. It was that voice which taught me otherwise.

For the moment I was free to leave. I struggled to my feet

and, having broken my lantern in the fall, retraced my way back through cloacal blackness.

Everything seemed to happen very quickly once I emerged from the tunnel and climbed up from the pit. I wiped the reeking greasepaint from my face as I ran through the woods and back to the road. A passing car stopped, though I gave it no other choice except to run me down.

"Thank you for stopping."

"What the hell are you doing out here?" the driver asked.

I caught my breath. "It was a joke. The festival. Friends thought it would be funny . . . Please drive on."

My ride let me off about a mile out of town, and from there I could find my way. It was the same way I had come into Mirocaw on my first visit the summer before. I stood for a while at the summit of that high hill just outside the city limits, looking down upon the busy little hamlet. The intensity of the festival had not abated, and would not until morning. I walked down toward the welcoming glow of green, slipped through the festivities unnoticed, and returned to the hotel. No one saw me go up to my room. Indeed, there was an atmosphere of absence and abandonment throughout that building, and the desk in the lobby was unattended.

I locked the door to my room and collapsed upon the bed.

7.

When I awoke the next morning I saw from my window that the town and surrounding countryside had been visited during the night by a snowstorm, one which was entirely unpredicted. The snow was still falling on the now deserted streets of Mirocaw. The festival was over. Everyone had gone home.

And this was exactly my own intention. Any action on my part concerning what I had seen the night before would have to wait until I was away from the town. I am still not sure it will do the slightest good to speak up like this. Any accusations I could make against the slum populace of Mirocaw would be resisted, as well they should be, as unbelievable. Perhaps in a very short while none of this will be my concern.

With packed suitcases in both hands I walked up to the front desk to check out. The man behind the desk was not Samuel Beadle, and he had to fumble around to find my bill.

"Here we are. Everything all right?"

"Fine," I answered in a dead voice. "Is Mr. Beadle around?"

"No, I'm afraid he's not back yet. Been out all night looking for his daughter. She's a very popular girl, being the Winter Queen and all that nonsense. Probably find she was at a party somewhere."

A little noise came out of my throat.

I threw my suitcases in the back seat of my car and got behind the wheel. On that morning nothing I could recall seemed real to me. The snow was falling and I watched it through my windshield, slow and silent and entrancing. I started up my car, routinely glancing in my rear view mirror. What I saw there is now vividly framed in my mind, as it was framed in the back window of my car when I turned to verify its reality.

In the middle of the street behind me, standing ankle-deep in snow, was Thoss and another figure. When I looked closely at the other I recognized him as one of the boys whom I surprised in that diner. But he had now taken on a corrupt and listless resemblance to his new family. Both he and Thoss stared at me, making no attempt to forestall my departure. Thoss knew that this was unnecessary.

I had to carry the image of those two dark figures in my mind as I drove back home. But only now has the full weight of my experience descended upon me. So far I have claimed illness in order to avoid my teaching schedule. To face the normal flow of life as I had formerly known it would be impossible. I am now very much under the influence of a season and a climate far colder and more barren than all the winters in human memory. And mentally retracing past events does not seem to have helped; I can feel myself sinking deeper into a velvety white abyss.

At certain times I could almost dissolve entirely into this inner realm of awful purity and emptiness. I remember those invisible moments when in disguise I drifted through the streets of Mirocaw, untouched by the drunken, noisy forms around me: untouchable. But instantly I recoil at this grotesque nostalgia, for I realize what is happening and what I do not want to be true, though Thoss proclaimed it was. I recall his command to those others as I lay helplessly prone in the tunnel. They could have apprehended me, but Thoss, my old master, called them back. His voice echoed throughout that cavern, and it now reverberates within my own psychic chambers of memory.

"He is one of us," it said. "He has *always* been one of us."

It is this voice which now fills my dreams and my days and my long winter nights. I have seen you, Dr. Thoss, through the snow outside my window. Soon I will celebrate, alone, that last feast which will kill your words, only to prove how well I have learned their truth.

To the memory of H. P. Lovecraft

1990

PETER STRAUB

(b. 1943)

A Short Guide to the City

THE viaduct killer, named for the location where his victims'
bodies have been discovered, is still at large. There have been
six victims to date, found by children, people exercising their
dogs, lovers, or—in one instance—by policemen. The bodies
lay sprawled, their throats slashed, partially sheltered by one or
another of the massive concrete supports at the top of the
slope beneath the great bridge. We assume that the viaduct
killer is a resident of the city, a voter, a renter or property owner,
a product of the city's excellent public school system, perhaps
even a parent of children who even now attend one of its seven
elementary schools, three public high schools, two parochial
schools, or single nondenominational private school. He may
own a boat or belong to the Book-of-the-Month Club, he
may frequent one or another of its many bars and taverns, he
may have subscription tickets to the concert series put on by
the city symphony orchestra. He may be a factory worker with
a library ticket. He owns a car, perhaps two. He may swim in
one of the city's public pools or the vast lake, punctuated with
sailboats, during the hot moist August of the city.

For this is a Midwestern city, northern, with violent changes
of season. The extremes of climate, from ten or twenty below
zero to up around one hundred in the summer, cultivate an
attitude of acceptance in its citizens, of insularity—it looks inward, not out, and few of its children leave for the more temperate, uncertain, and experimental cities of the eastern or
western coasts. The city is proud of its modesty—it cherishes
the ordinary, or what it sees as the ordinary, which is not. (It has
had the same mayor for twenty-four years, a man of limited-to-
average intelligence who has aged gracefully and has never had
any other occupation of any sort.)

Ambition, the yearning for fame, position, and achievement,
is discouraged here. One of its citizens became the head of a

389

small foreign state, another a famous bandleader, yet another a Hollywood staple who for decades played the part of the star's best friend and confidant; this, it is felt, is enough, and besides, all of these people are now dead. The city has no literary tradition. Its only mirror is provided by its two newspapers, which have thick sports sections and are comfortable enough to be read in bed.

The city's characteristic mode is *denial.* For this reason, an odd fabulousness permeates every quarter of the city, a receptiveness to fable, to the unrecorded. A river runs through the center of the business district, as the Liffey runs through Dublin, the Seine through Paris, the Thames through London, and the Danube through Budapest, though our river is smaller and less consequential than any of these.

Our lives are ordinary and exemplary, the citizens would say. We take part in the life of the nation, history courses through us for all our immunity to the national illnesses: it is even possible that in our ordinary lives . . . We too have had our pulse taken by the great national seers and opinion-makers, for in us you may find . . .

Forty years ago, in winter, the body of a woman was found on the banks of the river. She had been raped and murdered, cast out of the human community—a prostitute, never identified—and the noises of struggle that must have accompanied her death went unnoticed by the patrons of the Green Woman Taproom, located directly above that point on the river where her body was discovered. It was an abnormally cold winter that year, a winter of shared misery, and within the Green Woman the music was loud, feverish, festive.

In that community, which is Irish and lives above its riverfront shops and bars, neighborhood children were supposed to have found a winged man huddling in a packing case, an aged man, half-starved, speaking a strange language none of the children knew. His wings were ragged and dirty, many of the feathers as cracked and threadbare as those of an old pigeon's, and his feet were dirty and swollen. *Ull! Li! Gack!* the children screamed at him, mocking the sounds that came from his mouth. They pelted him with rocks and snowballs, imagining that he had crawled up from that same river which sent chill damp—a damp as cold as cancer—into their bones and bedrooms, which gave them earaches and chilblains, which in summer bred rats and mosquitos.

One of the city's newspapers is Democratic, the other Republican. Both papers ritually endorse the mayor, who though consummately political has no recognizable politics. Both of the city's newspapers also support the Chief of Police, crediting him with keeping the city free of the kind of violence that has undermined so many other American cities. None of our citizens goes armed, and our church attendance is still far above the national average.

We are ambivalent about violence.

We have very few public statues, mostly of Civil War generals. On the lakefront, separated from the rest of the town by a six-lane expressway, stands the cubelike structure of the Arts Center, otherwise called the War Memorial. Its rooms are hung with mediocre paintings before which schoolchildren are led on tours by their teachers, most of whom were educated in our local school system.

Our teachers are satisfied, decent people, and the statistics about alcohol and drug abuse among both students and teachers are very encouraging.

There is no need to linger at the War Memorial.

Proceeding directly north, you soon find yourself among the orderly, impressive precincts of the wealthy. It was in this sector of the town, known generally as the East Side, that the brewers and tanners who made our city's first great fortunes set up their mansions. Their houses have a northern, Germanic, even Baltic look which is entirely appropriate to our climate. Of gray stone or red brick, the size of factories or prisons, these stately buildings seem to conceal that vein of fantasy that is actually our most crucial inheritance. But it may be that the style of life—the invisible, hidden life—of these inbred merchants is itself fantastic: the multitude of servants, the maids and coachmen, the cooks and laundresses, the private zoos, the elaborate dynastic marriages and fleets of cars, the rooms lined with silk wallpaper, the twenty-course meals, the underground wine cellars and bomb shelters. . . . Of course we do not know if all of these things are true, or even if some of them are true. Our society folk keep to themselves, and what we know of them we learn chiefly from the newspapers, where they are pictured at their balls, standing with their beautiful daughters before fountains of champagne. The private zoos have been broken up long ago. As citizens, we are free to walk down the avenues, past the magnificent houses, and to peer in through the gates at their coach houses and lawns. A uniformed man polishes a car, four tall young people in white play tennis on a private court.

The viaduct killer's victims have all been adult women.

While you continue moving north you will find that as the houses diminish in size the distance between them grows greater. Through the houses, now without gates and coach houses, you can glimpse a sheet of flat grayish-blue—the lake. The air is free, you breathe it in. That is freedom, breathing this air from the lake. Free people may invent themselves in any image, and you may imagine yourself a prince of the earth, walking with an easy stride. Your table is set with linen, china, crystal, and silver, and as you dine, as the servants pass among you with the serving trays, the talk is educated, enlightened, without prejudice of any sort. The table talk is mainly about ideas, it is true, ideas of a conservative cast. You deplore violence, you do not recognize it.

Further north lie suburbs, which are uninteresting.

If from the War Memorial you proceed south, you cross the viaduct. Beneath you is a valley—the valley is perhaps best seen in the dead of winter. All of our city welcomes winter, for our public buildings are gray stone fortresses which, on days when the temperature dips below zero and the old gray snow of previous storms swirls in the avenues, seem to blend with the leaden air and become dreamlike and cloudy. This is how they were meant to be seen. The valley is called . . . it is called the Valley. Red flames tilt and waver at the tops of columns, and smoke pours from factory chimneys. The trees seem to be black. In the winter, the smoke from the factories becomes solid, like dark gray glaciers, and hangs in the dark air in defiance of gravity, like wings that are a light feathery gray at their tips and darken imperceptibly toward black, toward pitchy black at the point where these great frozen glaciers, these dirigibles, would join the body at the shoulder. The bodies of the great birds to which these wings are attached must be imagined.

In the old days of the city, the time of the private zoos,

wolves were bred in the Valley. Wolves were in great demand in those days. Now the wolf-ranches have been entirely replaced by factories, by rough taverns owned by retired shop foremen, by spurs of the local railroad line, and by narrow streets lined with rickety frame houses and shoe-repair shops. Most of the old wolf-breeders were Polish, and though their kennels, grassy yards, and barbed-wire exercise runs have disappeared, at least one memory of their existence endures: the Valley's street signs are in the Polish language. Tourists are advised to skirt the Valley, and it is always recommended that photographs be confined to the interesting views obtained by looking down from the viaduct. The more courageous visitors, those in search of pungent experience, are cautiously directed to the taverns of the ex-foremen, in particular the oldest of these (the Rusty Nail and the Brace 'n' Bit), where the wooden floors have so softened and furred with lavings and scrubbings that the boards have come to resemble the pelts of long narrow short-haired animals. For the intrepid, these words of caution: do not dress conspicuously, and carry only small amounts of cash. Some working knowledge of Polish is also advised.

Continuing further south, we come to the Polish district proper, which also houses pockets of Estonians and Lithuanians. More than the city's sadly declining downtown area, this district has traditionally been regarded as the city's heart, and has remained unchanged for more than a hundred years. Here the visitor may wander freely among the markets and street fairs, delighting in the sight of well-bundled children rolling hoops, patriarchs in tall fur hats and long beards, and women gathering around the numerous communal water pumps. The sausages and stuffed cabbage sold at the food stalls may be eaten with impunity, and the local beer is said to be of an unrivaled purity. Violence in this district is invariably domestic, and the visitor may feel free to enter the frequent political discussions, which in any case partake of a nostalgic character. In late January or early February the "South Side" is at its best, with the younger people dressed in multilayered heavy woolen garments decorated with the "reindeer" or "snowflake" motif, and the older women of the community seemingly vying to see which of them can outdo the others in the thickness, blackness, and heaviness of her outergarments and in the severity of the traditional head scarf known as the babushka. In late winter the neatness and orderliness of these colorful folk may be seen at its best, for the wandering visitor will often see the bearded paterfamilias sweeping and shoveling not only his immaculate bit of sidewalk (for these houses are as close together as those of the wealthy along the lakefront, so near to one another that until very recently telephone service was regarded as an irrelevance), but his tiny front lawn as well, with its Marian shrines, crèches, ornamental objects such as elves, trolls, postboys, etc. It is not unknown for residents here to proffer the stranger an invitation to inspect their houses, in order to display the immaculate condition of the kitchen with its well-blackened wood stove and polished ornamental tiles, and perhaps even extend a thimble-glass of their own peach or plum brandy to the thirsty visitor.

Alcohol, with its associations of warmth and comfort, is ubiquitous here, and it is the rare family that does not devote some portion of the summer to the preparation of that winter's plenty.

For these people, violence is an internal matter, to be resolved within or exercised upon one's own body and soul or those of one's immediate family. The inhabitants of these neat, scrubbed little houses with their statues of Mary and cathedral tiles, the descendants of the hard-drinking wolf-breeders of another time, have long since abandoned the practice of crippling their children to ensure their continuing exposure to parental values, but self-mutilation has proved more difficult to eradicate. Few blind themselves now, but many a grandfather conceals a three-fingered hand within his embroidered mitten. Toes are another frequent target of self-punishment, and the prevalence of cheerful, even boisterous shops, always crowded with old men telling stories, which sell the hand-carved wooden legs known as "pegs" or "dollies," speaks of yet another.

No one has ever suggested that the viaduct killer is a South Side resident.

The South Siders live in a profound relationship to violence, and its effects are invariably implosive rather than explosive. Once a decade, perhaps twice a decade, one member of a family will realize, out of what depths of cultural necessity the outsider can only hope to imagine, that the whole family must die—*be sacrificed*, to speak with greater accuracy. Axes, knives, bludgeons, bottles, babushkas, ancient derringers, virtually every imaginable implement has been used to carry out this aim. The houses in which this act of sacrifice has taken place are immediately if not instantly cleaned by the entire neighborhood, acting in concert. The bodies receive a Catholic burial in consecrated ground, and a mass is said in honor of both the victims and their murderer. A picture of the departed family is installed in the church which abuts Market Square, and for a year the house is kept clean and dust-free by the grandmothers of the neighborhood. Men young and old will quietly enter the house, sip the brandy of the "removed," as they are called, meditate, now and then switch on the wireless or the television set, and reflect on the darkness of earthly life. The departed are frequently said to appear to friends and neighbors, and often accurately predict the coming of storms and assist in the location of lost household objects, a treasured button or Mother's sewing needle. After the year has elapsed, the house is sold, most often to a young couple, a young blacksmith or market vendor and his bride, who find the furniture and even the clothing of the "removed" welcome additions to their small household.

Further south are suburbs and impoverished hamlets, which do not compel a visit.

Immediately west of the War Memorial is the city's downtown. Before its decline, this was the city's business district and administrative center, and the monuments of its affluence remain. Marching directly west on the wide avenue which begins at the expressway are the Federal Building, the Post Office, and the great edifice of City Hall. Each is an entire block long and constructed of granite blocks quarried far north in the state. Flights of marble stairs lead up to the massive doors of these structures, and crystal chandeliers can be seen through many of the windows. The facades are classical and severe, uniting in an architectural landscape of granite revetments and colonnades of pillars. (Within, these grand and inhuman buildings have long ago been carved and partitioned into warrens illuminated by bare light bulbs or flickering fluorescent tubing, each tiny office with its worn counter for

petitioners and a stamped sign proclaiming its function: Tax &
Excise, Dog Licenses, Passports, Graphs & Charts, Registry of
Notary Publics, and the like. The larger rooms with chandeliers
which face the avenue, reserved for civic receptions and banquets, are seldom used.)

In the next sequence of buildings are the Hall of Records,
the Police Headquarters, and the Criminal Courts Building.
Again, wide empty marble steps lead up to massive bronze doors,
rows of columns, glittering windows which on wintry days reflect back the gray empty sky. Local craftsmen, many of them
descendants of the city's original French settlers, forged and
installed the decorative iron bars and grilles on the facade of
the Criminal Courts Building.

After we pass the massive, nearly windowless brick facades of
the Gas and Electric buildings, we reach the arching metal drawbridge over the river. Looking downriver, we can see its muddy
banks and the lights of the terrace of the Green Woman Taproom, now a popular gathering place for the city's civil servants.
(A few feet further east is the spot from which a disgruntled
lunatic attempted and failed to assassinate President Dwight
D. Eisenhower.) Further on stand the high cement walls of
several breweries. The drawbridge has not been raised since
1956, when a corporate yacht passed through.

Beyond the drawbridge lies the old mercantile center of the
city, with its adult bookstores, pornographic theaters, coffee
shops, and its rank of old department stores. These now house
discount outlets selling roofing tiles, mufflers and other auto
parts, plumbing equipment, and cut-rate clothing, and most
of their display windows have been boarded or bricked in since
the civic disturbances of 1968. Various civic plans have failed to
revive this area, though the cobblestones and gas street lamps
installed in the optimistic mid-seventies can for the most part
still be seen. Connoisseurs of the poignant will wish to take a
moment to appreciate them, though they should seek to avoid
the bands of ragged children that frequent this area at nightfall, for though these children are harmless they can become
pressing in their pleas for small change.

Many of these children inhabit dwellings they have constructed themselves in the vacant lots between the adult book-

stores and fast-food outlets of the old mercantile district, and the "tree houses" atop mounds of tires, most of them several stories high and utilizing fire escapes and flights of stairs scavenged from the old department stores, are of some architectural interest. The stranger should not attempt to penetrate these "children's cities," and on no account should offer them any more than the pocket change they request or display a camera, jewelry, or an expensive wristwatch. The truly intrepid tourist seeking excitement may hire one of these children to guide him to the diversions of his choice. Two dollars is the usual gratuity for this service.

It is not advisable to purchase any of the goods the children themselves may offer for sale, although they have been affected by the same self-consciousness evident in the impressive buildings on the other side of the river and do sell picture postcards of their largest and most eccentric constructions. It may be that the naive architecture of these tree houses represents the city's most authentic artistic expression, and the postcards, amateurish as most of them are, provide interesting, perhaps even valuable, documentation of this expression of what may be called folk art.

These industrious children of the mercantile area have ritualized their violence into highly formalized tattooing and "spontaneous" forays and raids into the tree houses of opposing tribes during which only superficial injuries are sustained, and it is not suspected that the viaduct killer comes from their number.

Further west are the remains of the city's museum and library, devastated during the civic disturbances, and beyond these picturesque, still-smoking hulls lies the ghetto. It is not advised to enter the ghetto on foot, though the tourist who has arranged to rent an automobile may safely drive through it after he has negotiated his toll at the gate house. The ghetto's residents are completely self-sustaining, and the attentive tourist who visits this district will observe the multitude of tents housing hospitals, wholesale food and drug warehouses, and the like. Within the ghetto are believed to be many fine poets, painters, and musicians, as well as the historians known as "memorists," who are the district's living encyclopedias and archivists. The "memorist's" tasks include the memorization of the works of the area's poets, painters, etc., for the district contains no printing presses or art-supply shops, and these inventive and self-reliant people have devised this method of preserving their works. It is not believed that a people capable of inventing the genre of "oral painting" could have spawned the viaduct killer, and in any case no ghetto resident is permitted access to any other area of the city.

The ghetto's relationship to violence is unknown.

Further west the annual snowfall increases greatly, for seven months of the year dropping an average of two point three feet of snow each month upon the shopping malls and paper mills which have concentrated here. Dust storms are common during the summers, and certain infectious viruses, to which the inhabitants have become immune, are carried in the water.

Still further west lies the Sports Complex.

The tourist who has ventured thus far is well advised to turn back at this point and return to our beginnning, the War Memorial. Your car may be left in the ample and clearly posted parking lot on the Memorial's eastern side. From the Memorial's wide empty terraces, you are invited to look southeast, where a great unfinished bridge crosses half the span to the hamlets of Wyatt and Arnoldville. Construction was abandoned on this noble civic project, subsequently imitated by many cities in our western states and in Australia and Finland, immediately after the disturbances of 1968, when its lack of utility became apparent. When it was noticed that many families chose to eat their bag lunches on the Memorial's lakeside terraces in order to gaze silently at its great interrupted arc, the bridge was adopted as the symbol of the city, and its image decorates the city's many flags and medals.

The "Broken Span," as it is called, which hangs in the air like the great frozen wings above the Valley, serves no function but the symbolic. In itself and entirely by accident this great non-span memorializes violence, not only by serving as a reference to the workmen who lost their lives during its construction (its nonconstruction). It is not rounded or finished in any way, for labor on the bridge ended abruptly, even brutally, and from its truncated floating end dangle lengths of rusting iron webbing, thick wire cables weighted by chunks of cement, and bits of old planking material. In the days before access to the un-bridge was walled off by an electrified fence, two or three citizens each year elected to commit their suicides by leaping from the end of the span; and one must resort to a certain lexical violence when referring to it. Ghetto residents are said to have named it "Whitey," and the tree-house children call it "Ursula," after one of their own killed in the disturbances. South Siders refer to it as "The Ghost," civil servants, "The Beast," and East Siders simply as "that thing." The "Broken Span" has the violence of all unfinished things, of everything interrupted or left undone. In violence there is often the quality of *yearning*—the yearning for completion. For closure. For that which is absent and would if present bring to fulfillment. For the body without which the wing is a useless frozen ornament. It ought not to go unmentioned that most of the city's residents have never seen the "bridge" except in its representations, and for this majority the "bridge" is little more or less than a myth, being without any actual referent. It is pure idea.

Violence, it is felt though unspoken, is the physical form of sensitivity. The city believes this. Incompletion, the lack of referent which strands you in the realm of pure idea, demands release from itself. We are above all an American city, and what we believe most deeply we . . .

The victims of the viaduct killer, that citizen who excites our attention, who makes us breathless with outrage and causes our police force to ransack the humble dwellings along the riverbank, have all been adult women. These women in their middle years are taken from their lives and set like statues beside the pillar. Each morning there is more pedestrian traffic on the viaduct, in the frozen mornings men (mainly men) come with their lunches in paper bags, walking slowly along the cement walkway, not looking at one another, barely knowing what they are doing, looking down over the edge of the viaduct, looking away, dawdling, finally leaning like fishermen against the railing, waiting until they can no longer delay going to their jobs.

The visitor who has done so much and gone so far in this city may turn his back on the "Broken Span," the focus of civic pride, and look in a southwesterly direction past the six lanes of the expressway, perhaps on tiptoe (children may have to mount one of the convenient retaining walls). The dull flanks of the viaduct should just now be visible, with the heads and shoulders of the waiting men picked out in the gray air like brush strokes. The quality of their yearning, its expectancy, is visible even from here.

1990

JEFF VANDERMEER

(b. 1968)

The General Who Is Dead

My name is Stephen Barrow and I served in the Korean War, under the auspices of the 52nd Battalion. You would not have heard about the 52nd Battalion on the newsreels, for all we did was defend a city of the dead from the dead without, and the city held us in its thrall. From afar, it appeared as a glittering white crown of pagodas and snow, undisturbed and pristine. The walled kingdom of an ice witch, something right out of C. S. Lewis' *The Lion, the Witch and the Wardrobe*, perhaps.

Our mission was morbid and macabre and we loved it fiercely, for it kept us from the front lines. The city had been abandoned for over a year. Within its walls, the U.S. High Command had decided to house, catalog, and prepare for shipment stateside the bodies of the soldiers who had died at the front in our stead. We also housed, cataloged, and pre- pared (for cremation) the remains of South Korean civilians who had been caught in the crossfire. At times, the city streets were littered with the dead, all formally laid out, limbs no longer akimbo from bomb or mine blast, faces much more serene since their grimaces had been crafted into the artifice of smiles. Perhaps they merely slept, I would joke with my fellow sol- diers, usually Nate Burlow, a muscle-bound lunk from New Jersey, and Tom Waters, a slender willow with hair so black it was almost blue and pale green eyes that stared out unblinking from beneath a helmet too big for his head. Nate was garrulous and Tom silent to a fault, calm as ice in a Rusty Nail. Between the two of them, I came very close to keeping my sanity amongst the dead.

All of us doubled up on our duties to conserve manpower, and so I became, much against my will, a writer of press re- leases for the army, under the supervision of Colonel X. It was easy work and I did it at my desk on the fourth floor of head- quarters, which had been set up in the Buddhist temple at the

city's center. The temple was the tallest structure in a place
where the buildings seemed to genuflect and make themselves
as small against the earth as possible.

I would sit with the snow-white pieces of paper in front of
me and, when the pens were not frozen, I would write about
the death of General So-and-So, the bravery of Corporal
What's-His-Name. It gave me a lot of time to think. Perhaps
too much time. My past did not bear up under close scrutiny
and if, in describing what I am about to describe I am indirect
about my own life—if, to be blunt, I discard bland fact in favor
of hard truth—forgive me.

Suffice it to say, the war had passed us by in more ways than
one. By the time I came into the middle of it, my landing at
Inchon had none of the biting melodrama of MacArthur's initial beachhead. Colonel B. Powell had urinated proudly in the
Yalu River more than six months before, doing several "takes"
for the *Stars and Stripes* boys, blissfully ignorant of the fact that
no American soldier after him would advance so far to demonstrate his backwardness. U.S. General Smith, a marine, had
already declared, "Retreat, Hell! We're not retreating! We're
just advancing in a different direction!" All the photo ops and
all the best lines had been taken. By the time I came to Korea,
the war had bogged down to a slow, futile, and bloody shifting
of the lines along barren fields of snow, advance and retreat
along the 38th Parallel, like the ebb and flow of some Ice Age
tide.

All I had were dead bodies to take care of and paper to write
on and my buddies to shoot the shit with. And, of course, the
dead Chinese soldiers outside the city's walls.

When I came to the city, along with Nate and Tom, the dead
Chinese soldiers were the first things we saw. You couldn't miss
them. Over forty thousand of them on the plain outside the
city's walls. The sergeant at arms had made sure the chopper
let us off in the middle of the plain so that we had to walk
through the dead to reach the city. What the man was trying
to prove, I have no idea.

There were thirty of us new boys and we said nothing to
each other at the time—out of nervousness or sympathy or re-

spect, I don't know which. All I know is we were so quiet you could hear the crunch of our boots in the snow. The sunlight suffused the snow and bled through the Chinese soldiers, turning them crystalline and divine and pathetic all at once. As you can see through the skins of certain fish to their internal organs, so you could see through the ice and know the shapes, the contours, of the dead men on the frozen field. Some knelt and some stood and some huddled in clumps seeking a warmth that had long since left them. Forty thousand dead Chinese soldiers sprawled along a snowy plain. There were forty thousand stories in those lives, for they had all died in subtlely unique ways, and those ways had lent all of their faces a fierce individuality that would mark them even when spring came and thawed them out.

They had called themselves "The Army Which Casts No Shadow" because they had marched by night and lay camouflaged from reconnaissance planes by day. United Nations forces had not spotted them until they crossed the 38th Parallel. They had outrun their own supply lines out of Manchuria in an attempt to cut off U.S. forces from Inchon. They had no choice but to march forward and assault the U.S. perimeter at Pusan. They never made it. Our forces just kept retreating, left no supplies behind, and their progress slowed as they grew hungry, and then a blizzard caught them out in the open. They had already eaten their boots; almost none of them that I could see had shoes on their feet.

Parodies of statues in Pompeii.

The ice that had hardened around their bodies had also hardened their features, disguised their uniforms and weaponry, so that indeed it was a plain of statuary, ethereal, ghostly, and mocking. No one would have guessed they were once an army, or that they had marched anywhere, that once they had been alive. Walking among them I felt a crawling sensation across my spine—a helplessness and a despair that I did not know could live within me. I had a sudden frantic urge to write it down, to write about their deaths. I could not tell whether the impulse was ghoulish or commemorative, so I let it pass.

"Come spring," muttered Tom.

"Come spring what?" said Nate.

"Come spring, they'll thaw and then there'll just be forty thousand stinking dead people here for the vultures to feast on."

It was about the longest sentence Tom ever said, and when I got to know him better, I knew it meant those dead soldiers had really gotten to him, under his skin.

But they looked curiously at peace out in the snow, the longer I stared at them—as if they waited for someone or something to resurrect them. Or perhaps I read that into them and I was waiting for someone to resurrect me. I had a sudden memory of making snow angels in the front yard of our house, my Dad at six-six spread out ridiculously, making giant angels, while my own had been much smaller divinities.

We walked among the dead men for nearly an hour that first, most important, time, although the walls of the city were near. We did not feel, not having seen the indignities of war first hand, that we could leave without paying our respects, if that is the correct term. It was like walking among gravestones, only these men needed no such symbolism. They stood staunchly for themselves. Seeing them so vulnerable, waiting for the thaw that would make them fully human again, my imagination began to unfetter itself from the cold and the company of my fellow soldiers. Something churned in my stomach and up, into my heart. What if these men, these soldiers, really were waiting for someone? As if they had been enchanted, put under a spell? Who were they waiting for?

"Who are they waiting for?" I said it aloud.

"General who?" Tom said, as if reading my mind.

"General Who," I said. Inside, the churning stopped and I thought, yes, it was General Who who led them. General Who who would come back for them. He could protect them, much as my father had often wrapped his arms around me in the snow and held me against his chest, warm and secure.

As we finally left the field, I saw a Chinese woman who had frozen to death along with the soldiers, a look of divinity upon her face. As if she could see something magical beyond her reach. Her head was inclined upward and when I saw her, her features etched cruelly in the ice, I looked where she looked, almost expecting there to be someone in the sky, or some sign.

But this time, there was just the white. Always the white. And from then on, I could not hate our Enemy, or even think ill of Him, but thought only of when I too would be stiff, my eyes staring out into the unknown, afraid—taken away from the sudden, lacerating beauty of this world and into the cruel glacial light of the next.

"General Who is dead," I said as we left that place, and Tom and Nate nodded like they almost understood what I meant.

1996

STEPHEN KING

(b. 1947)

That Feeling, You Can Only Say What It Is in French

Floyd, what's that over there? Oh shit.

The man's voice speaking these words was vaguely familiar, but the words themselves were just a disconnected snip of dialogue, the kind of thing you heard when you were channel-surfing with the remote. There was no one named Floyd in her life. Still, that was the start. Even before she saw the little girl in the red pinafore, there were those disconnected words.

But it was the little girl who brought it on strong. "Oh-oh, I'm getting that feeling," Carol said.

The girl in the pinafore was in front of a country market called Carson's—BEER, WINE, GROC, FRESH BAIT, LOTTERY—crouched down with her butt between her ankles and the bright-red apron-dress tucked between her thighs, playing with a doll. The doll was yellow-haired and dirty, the kind that's round and stuffed and boneless in the body.

"What feeling?" Bill asked.

"You know. The one you can only say what it is in French. Help me here."

"Déjà vu," he said.

"That's it," she said, and turned to look at the little girl one more time. *She'll have the doll by one leg,* Carol thought. *Holding it upside down by one leg with its grimy yellow hair hanging down.*

But the little girl had abandoned the doll on the store's splintery gray steps and had gone over to look at a dog caged up in the back of a station wagon. Then Bill and Carol Shelton went around a curve in the road and the store was out of sight.

"How much farther?" Carol asked.

Bill looked at her with one eyebrow raised and his mouth dimpled at one corner—left eyebrow, right dimple, always the same. The look that said, *You think I'm amused, but I'm really irritated. For the ninety trillionth or so time in the marriage, I'm really irritated. You don't know that, though, because you can only see about two inches into me and then your vision fails.*

But she had better vision than he realized; it was one of the secrets of the marriage. Probably he had a few secrets of his own. And there were, of course, the ones they kept together.

"I don't know," he said. "I've never been here."

"But you're sure we're on the right road."

"Once you get over the causeway and onto Sanibel Island, there's only one," he said. "It goes across to Captiva, and there it ends. But before it does we'll come to Palm House. That I promise you."

The arch in his eyebrow began to flatten. The dimple began to fill in. He was returning to what she thought of as the Great Level. She had come to dislike the Great Level, too, but not as much as the eyebrow and the dimple, or his sarcastic way of saying "Excuse me?" when you said something he considered stupid, or his habit of pooching out his lower lip when he wanted to appear thoughtful and deliberative.

"Bill?"

"Mmm?"

"Do you know anyone named Floyd?"

"There was Floyd Denning. He and I ran the downstairs snack bar at Christ the Redeemer in our senior year. I told you about him, didn't I? He stole the Coke money one Friday and spent the weekend in New York with his girlfriend. They suspended him and expelled her. What made you think of him?"

"I don't know," she said. Easier than telling him that the Floyd with whom Bill had gone to high school wasn't the Floyd the voice in her head was speaking to. At least, she didn't think it was.

Second honeymoon, that's what you call this, she thought, looking at the palms that lined Highway 867, a white bird that stalked along the shoulder like an angry preacher, and a sign that read SEMINOLE WILDLIFE PARK, BRING A CARFUL FOR $10. *Florida the Sunshine State. Florida the Hospitality State. Not to mention Florida the Second-Honeymoon State. Florida, where Bill Shelton and Carol Shelton, the former Carol O'Neill, of Lynn, Massachusetts, came on their first honeymoon twenty-five years before. Only that was on the other side, the Atlantic side, at a little cabin colony, and there were cockroaches in the bureau drawers. He couldn't stop touching me. That was all right, though, in those days I wanted to be touched. Hell, I wanted to be torched like Atlanta in* Gone in the Wind, *and he torched me, rebuilt me, torched me again. Now it's silver. Twenty-five is silver. And sometimes I get that feeling.*

They were approaching a curve, and she thought, *Three crosses on the right side of the road. Two small ones flanking a bigger one. The small ones are clapped-together wood. The one in the middle is white birch with a picture on it, a tiny photograph of the seventeen-year-old boy who lost control of his car on this curve one drunk night that was his last drunk night, and this is where his girlfriend and her girlfriends marked the spot—*

Bill drove around the curve. A pair of black crows, plump and shiny, lifted off from something pasted to the macadam in a splat of blood. The birds had eaten so well that Carol wasn't sure they were going to get out of the way until they did. There were no crosses, not on the left, not on the right. Just roadkill in the middle, a woodchuck or something, now passing beneath a luxury car that had never been north of the Mason-Dixon Line.

Floyd, what's that over there?

"What's wrong?"

"Huh?" She looked at him, bewildered, feeling a little wild.

"You're sitting bolt-upright. Got a cramp in your back?"

"Just a slight one." She settled back by degrees. "I had that feeling again. The déjà vu."

"Is it gone?"

"Yes," she said, but she was lying. It had retreated a little, but that was all. She'd had this before, but never so *continuously.* It came up and went down, but it didn't go away. She'd been aware of it ever since that thing about Floyd started knocking around in her head—and then the little girl in the red pinafore.

But, really, hadn't she felt something before either of those things? Hadn't it actually started when they came down the steps of the Lear 35 into the hammering heat of the Fort Myers sunshine? Or even before? En route from Boston?

They were coming to an intersection. Overhead was a flashing yellow light, and she thought, *To the right is a used-car lot and a sign for the Sanibel Community Theater.*

Then she thought, *No, it'll be like the crosses that weren't there. It's a strong feeling but a false feeling.*

Here was the intersection. On the right there *was* a used-car lot—Palmdale Motors. Carol felt a real jump at that, a stab of something sharper than disquiet. She told herself to quit being stupid. There had to be car lots all over Florida and if you predicted one at every intersection sooner or later the law of averages made you a prophet. It was a trick mediums had been using for hundreds of years.

Besides, there's no theater sign.

But there was another sign. It was Mary the Mother of God, the ghost of all her childhood days, holding out her hands the way she did on the medallion Carol's grandmother had given her for her tenth birthday. Her grandmother had pressed it into her hand and looped the chain around her fingers, saying, "Wear her always as you grow, because all the hard days are coming." She had worn it, all right. At Our Lady of Angels grammar and middle school she had worn it, then at St. Vincent de Paul high. She wore the medal until breasts grew around it like ordinary miracles, and then someplace, probably on the class trip to Hampton Beach, she had lost it. Coming home on the bus she had tongue-kissed for the first time. Butch Soucy had been the boy, and she had been able to taste the cotton candy he'd eaten.

Mary on that long-gone medallion and Mary on this billboard had exactly the same look, the one that made you feel guilty of thinking impure thoughts even when all you were thinking about was a peanut-butter sandwich. Beneath Mary, the sign said MOTHER OF MERCY CHARITIES HELP THE FLORIDA HOMELESS—WON'T YOU HELP US?

Hey there, Mary, what's the story—

More than one voice this time; many voices, girls' voices, chanting ghost voices. These were ordinary miracles; there were also ordinary ghosts. You found these things out as you got older.

"What's wrong with you?" She knew that voice as well as she did the eyebrow-and-dimple look. Bill's I'm-only-pretending-to-be-pissed tone of voice, the one that meant he really *was* pissed, at least a little.

"Nothing." She gave him the best smile she could manage.

"You really don't seem like yourself. Maybe you shouldn't have slept on the plane."

"You're probably right," she said, and not just to be agreeable, either. After all, how many women got a second honeymoon on Captiva Island for their twenty-fifth anniversary? Round trip on a chartered Learjet? Ten days at one of those places where your money was no good (at least until MasterCard coughed up the bill at the end of the month) and if you wanted a massage a big Swedish babe would come and pummel you in your six-room beach house?

Things had been different at the start. Bill, whom she'd first met at a crosstown high-school dance and then met again at college three years later (another ordinary miracle), had begun their married life working as a janitor, because there were no openings in the computer industry. It was 1973, and computers were essentially going nowhere and they were living in a grotty place in Revere, not on the beach but close to it, and all night people kept going up the stairs to buy drugs from the two sallow creatures who lived in the apartment above them and listened endlessly to dopey records from the sixties. Carol used to lie awake waiting for the shouting to start, thinking, *We won't ever get out of here, we'll grow old and die within earshot of Cream and Blue Cheer and the Dodgem cars down on the beach.*

Bill, exhausted at the end of his shift, would sleep through the noise, lying on his side, sometimes with one hand on her hip. And when it wasn't there she often put it there, especially if the creatures upstairs were arguing with their customers. Bill was all she had. Her parents had practically disowned her when she married him. He was a Catholic, but the wrong sort of Catholic. Gram had asked why she wanted to go with that boy when anyone could tell he was shanty, how could she fall for all his foolish talk, why did she want to break her father's heart. And what could she say?

It was a long distance from that place in Revere to a private jet soaring at forty-one thousand feet; a long way to this rental car, which was a Crown Victoria—what the goodfellas in the gangster movies invariably called a Crown Vic—heading for ten days in a place where the tab would probably be . . . well, she didn't even want to think about it.

Floyd? . . . Oh shit.

"Carol? What is it now?"

"Nothing," she said. Up ahead by the road was a little pink bungalow, the porch flanked by palms—seeing those trees with their fringy heads lifted against the blue sky made her think of Japanese Zeros coming in low, their underwing machine guns firing, such an association clearly the result of a youth misspent in front of the TV—and as they passed a black woman would come out. She would be drying her hands on a piece of pink towelling and would watch them expressionlessly as they passed, rich folks in a Crown Vic headed for Captiva, and she'd have no idea that Carol Shelton once lay awake in a ninety-dollar-a-month apartment, listening to the records and the drug deals upstairs, feeling something alive inside her, something that made her think of a cigarette that had fallen down behind the drapes at a party, small and unseen but smoldering away next to the fabric.

"Hon?"

"Nothing, I said." They passed the house. There was no woman. An old man—white, not black—sat in a rocking chair, watching them pass. There were rimless glasses on his nose and a piece of ragged pink towelling, the same shade as the house, across his lap. "I'm fine now. Just anxious to get there and change into some shorts."

His hand touched her hip—where he had so often touched her during those first days—and then crept a little farther inland. She thought about stopping him (Roman hands and Russian fingers, they used to say) and didn't. They were, after all, on their second honeymoon. Also, it would make that expression go away.

"Maybe," he said, "we could take a pause. You know, after the dress comes off and before the shorts go on."

"I think that's a lovely idea," she said, and put her hand over his, pressed both more tightly against her. Ahead was a sign that would read PALM HOUSE 3 MI. ON LEFT when they got close enough to see it.

The sign actually read PALM HOUSE 2 MI. ON LEFT. Beyond

it was another sign, Mother Mary again, with her hands out-stretched and that little electric shimmy that wasn't quite a halo around her head. This version read MOTHER OF MERCY CHARITIES HELP THE FLORIDA SICK—WON'T <u>YOU</u> HELP <u>US</u>?

Bill said, "The next one ought to say 'Burma Shave.'"

She didn't understand what he meant, but it was clearly a joke and so she smiled. The next one would say "Mother of Mercy Charities Help the Florida Hungry," but she couldn't tell him that. Dear Bill. Dear in spite of his sometimes stupid expressions and his sometimes unclear allusions. *He'll most likely leave you, and you know something? If you go through with it that's probably the best luck you can expect.* This according to her father. Dear Bill, who had proved that just once, just that one crucial time, her judgement had been far better than her father's. She was still married to the man her Gram had called "the big boaster." At a price, true, but what was that old axiom? God says take what you want . . . and pay for it.

Her head itched. She scratched at it absently, watching for the next Mother of Mercy billboard.

Horrible as it was to say, things had started turning around when she lost the baby. That was just before Bill got a job with Beach Computers, out on Route 128; that was when the first winds of change in the industry began to blow.

Lost the baby, had a miscarriage—they all believed that except maybe Bill. Certainly her family had believed it: Dad, Mom, Gram. "Miscarriage" was the story they told, miscarriage was a Catholic's story if ever there was one. *Hey, Mary, what's the story*, they had sometimes sung when they skipped rope, feeling daring, feeling sinful, the skirts of their uniforms flipping up and down over their scabby knees. That was at Our Lady of Angels, where Sister Annunciata would spank your knuckles with her ruler if she caught you gazing out the window during Sentence Time, where Sister Dormatilla would tell you that a million years was but the first tick of eternity's endless clock (and you could spend eternity in Hell, most people did, it was easy). In Hell you would live forever with your skin on fire and your bones roasting. Now she was in Florida, now she was in a Crown Vic sitting next to her husband, whose hand was still in her crotch; the dress would be wrinkled but who cared if it got that look off his face, and why wouldn't the feeling *stop*?

She thought of a mailbox with RAGLAN painted on the side and an American-flag decal on the front, and although the name turned out to be Reagan and the flag a Grateful Dead sticker, the box was there. She thought of a small black dog trotting briskly along the other side of the road, its head down, sniffling, and the small black dog was there. She thought again of the billboard and, yes, there it was: MOTHER OF MERCY CHARITIES HELP THE FLORIDA HUNGRY—WON'T YOU HELP US?

Bill was pointing. "There—see? I think that's Palm House. No, not where the billboard is, the other side. Why do they let people put those things up out here, anyway?"

"I don't know." Her head itched. She scratched, and black dandruff began falling past her eyes. She looked at her fingers and was horrified to see dark smutches on the tips; it was as if someone had just taken her fingerprints.

"Bill?" She raked her hand through her blond hair and this time the flakes were bigger. She saw they were not flakes of skin but flakes of paper. There was a face on one, peering out of the char like a face peering out of a botched negative.

"*Bill?*"

"What? Wh—" Then a total change in his voice, and that frightened her more than the way the car swerved. "Christ, honey, what's in your hair?"

The face appeared to be Mother Teresa's. Or was that just because she'd been thinking about Our Lady of Angels? Carol plucked it from her dress, meaning to show it to Bill, and it crumbled between her fingers before she could. She turned to him and saw that his glasses were melted to his cheeks. One of his eyes had popped from its socket and then split like a grape pumped full of blood.

And I knew it, she thought. *Even before I turned, I knew it. Because I had that feeling.*

A bird was crying in the trees. On the billboard, Mary held out her hands. Carol tried to scream. Tried to scream.

*

"Carol?"

It was Bill's voice, coming from a thousand miles away. Then his hand—not pressing the folds of her dress into her crotch, but on her shoulder.

"You okay, babe?"

She opened her eyes to brilliant sunlight and her ears to the steady hum of the Learjet's engines. And something else—pressure against her eardrums. She looked from Bill's mildly concerned face to the dial below the temperature gauge in the cabin and saw that it had wound down to twenty-eight thousand.

"Landing?" she said, sounding muzzy to herself. "Already?"

"It's fast, huh?" Sounding pleased, as if he had flown it himself instead of only paying for it. "Pilot says we'll be on the ground in Fort Myers in twenty minutes. You took a hell of a jump, girl."

"I had a nightmare."

He laughed—the plummy ain't-you-the-silly-billy laugh she had come really to detest. "No nightmares allowed on your second honeymoon, babe. What was it?"

"I don't remember," she said, and it was the truth. There were only fragments: Bill with his glasses melted all over his face, and one of the three or four forbidden skip rhymes they had sometimes chanted back in fifth and sixth grade. This one had gone *Hey there, Mary, what's the story* . . . and then something-something-something. She couldn't come up with the rest. She could remember *Jangle-tangle jingle-bingle, I saw daddy's great big dingle*, but she couldn't remember the one about Mary.

Mary helps the Florida sick, she thought, with no idea of what the thought meant, and just then there was a beep as the pilot turned the seat-belt light on. They had started their final descent. *Let the wild rumpus start*, she thought, and tightened her belt.

"You really don't remember?" he asked, tightening his own. The little jet ran through a cloud filled with bumps, one of the pilots in the cockpit made a minor adjustment, and the ride smoothed out again. "Because usually, just after you wake up, you can still remember. Even the bad ones."

"I remember Sister Annunciata, from Our Lady of Angels. Sentence Time."

"Now, *that's* a nightmare."

Ten minutes later the landing gear came down with a whine and a thump. Five minutes after that they landed.

"They were supposed to bring the car right out to the plane," Bill said, already starting up the Type A shit. This she didn't like, but at least she didn't detest it the way she detested the plummy laugh and his repertoire of patronizing looks. "I hope there hasn't been a hitch."

There hasn't been, she thought, and the feeling swept over her full force. *I'm going to see it out the window on my side in just a second or two. It's your total Florida vacation car, a great big white goddam Cadillac, or maybe it's a Lincoln—*

And, yes, here it came, proving what? Well, she supposed, it proved that sometimes when you had déjà vu what you thought was going to happen next really did. It wasn't a Caddy or a Lincoln after all, but a Crown Victoria—what the gangsters in a Martin Scorsese film would doubtless call a Crown Vic.

"Whoo," she said as he helped her down the steps and off the plane. The hot sun made her feel dizzy.

"What's wrong?"

"Nothing, really. I've got déjà vu. Left over from my dream, guess. We've been here before, that kind of thing."

"It's being in a strange place, that's all," he said, and kissed her cheek. "Come on, let the wild rumpus start."

They went to the car. Bill showed his driver's license to the young woman who had driven it out. Carol saw him check out the hem of her skirt, then sign the paper on her clipboard.

She's going to drop it, Carol thought. The feeling was now so strong it was like being on an amusement-park ride that goes just a little too fast; all at once you realize you're edging out of the Land of Fun and into the Kingdom of Nausea. *She'll drop it, and Bill will say "Whoopsy-daisy" and pick it up for her, get an even closer look at her legs.*

But the Hertz woman didn't drop her clipboard. A white courtesy van had appeared, to take her back to the Butler Aviation terminal. She gave Bill a final smile—Carol she had ignored completely—and opened the front passenger door. She stepped up, then slipped. "Whoopsy-daisy, don't be crazy," Bill said, and took her elbow, steadying her. She gave him a smile, he gave her well-turned legs a goodbye look, and Carol stood by the growing pile of their luggage and thought, *Hey there, Mary . . .*

"Mrs. Shelton?" It was the co-pilot. He had the last bag, the case with Bill's laptop inside it, and he looked concerned. "Are you all right? You're very pale."

Bill heard and turned away from the departing white van, his face worried. If her strongest feelings about Bill were her only feelings about Bill, now that they were twenty-five years on, she would have left him when she found out about the secretary, a Clairol blonde too young to remember the Clairol slogan that started "If I have only one life to live." But there were other feelings. There was love, for instance. Still love. A kind that girls in Catholic-school uniforms didn't suspect, a weedy, unlovely species too tough to die.

Besides, it wasn't just love that held people together. There were secrets, and the price you paid to keep them.

"Carol?" he asked her. "Babe? All right?"

She thought about telling him no, she wasn't all right, she was drowning, but then she managed to smile and said, "It's the heat, that's all. I feel a little groggy. Get me in the car and crank up the air-conditioning. I'll be fine."

Bill took her by the elbow (*Bet you're not checking out my legs, though*, Carol thought. *You know where they go, don't you?*) and led her toward the Crown Vic as if she were a very old lady. By the time the door was closed and cool air was pumping over her face, she actually had started to feel a little better.

If the feeling comes back, I'll tell him, Carol thought. *I'll have to. It's just too strong. Not normal.*

Well, déjà vu was never normal, she supposed—it was something that was part dream, part chemistry, and (she was sure she'd read this, maybe in a doctor's office somewhere while waiting for her gynecologist to go prospecting up her fifty-two-year-old twat) part the result of an electrical misfire in the brain, causing new experience to be identified as old data. A temporary hole in the pipes, hot water and cold water mingling. She closed her eyes and prayed for it to go away.

Oh, Mary, conceived without sin, pray for us who have recourse to thee.

Please ("Oh puh-lease," they used to say), not back to parochial school. This was supposed to be a vacation, not—

Floyd, what's that over there? Oh shit! Oh SHIT!

Who was Floyd? The only Floyd Bill knew was Floyd Dorning (or maybe it was Darling), the kid he'd run the snack bar with, the one who'd run off to New York with his girl-friend. Carol couldn't remember when Bill had told her about that kid, but she knew he had.

Just quit it, girl. There's nothing here for you. Slam the door on the whole train of thought.

And that worked. There was a final whisper—*what's the story*—and then she was just Carol Shelton, on her way to Captiva Island, on her way to Palm House with her husband the renowned software designer, on their way to the beaches and the rum drinks, and the sound of a steel band playing "Margaritaville."

They passed a Publix market. They passed an old black man minding a roadside fruit stand—he made her think of actors from the thirties and movies you saw on the American Movie Channel, an old yassuh-boss type of guy wearing bib overalls and a straw hat with a round crown. Bill made small talk, and she made it right back at him. She was faintly amazed that the little girl who had worn a Mary medallion every day from ten to sixteen had become this woman in the Donna Karan dress— that the desperate couple in that Revere apartment were these middle-aged rich folks rolling down a lush aisle of palms—but she was and they were. Once in those Revere days he had come home drunk and she had hit him and drawn blood from below his eye. Once she had been in fear of Hell, had lain half-drugged in steel stirrups, thinking, *I'm damned, I've come to damnation. A million years, and that's only the first tick of the clock.*

They stopped at the causeway toll-booth and Carol thought, *The toll-taker has a strawberry birthmark on the left side of his forehead, all mixed in with his eyebrow.*

There was no mark—the toll-taker was just an ordinary guy

in his late forties or early fifties, iron-gray hair in a buzz cut, horn-rimmed specs, the kind of guy who says, "Y'all have a nahce tahm, okai?"—but the feeling began to come back, and Carol realized that now the things she thought she knew were things she really did know, at first not all of them, but then, by the time they neared the little market on the right side of Route 41, it was almost everything.

The market's called Corson's and there's a little girl out front, Carol thought. *She's wearing a red pinafore. She's got a doll, a dirty old yellow-haired thing, that she's left on the store steps so she can look at a dog in the back of a station wagon.*

The name of the market turned out to be Carson's, not Corson's, but everything else was the same. As the white Crown Vic passed, the little girl in the red dress turned her solemn face in Carol's direction, a country girl's face, although what a girl from the toolies could be doing here in rich folks' tourist country, her and her dirty yellow-headed doll, Carol didn't know.

Here's where I ask Bill how much farther, only I won't do it. Because I have to break out of this cycle, this groove. I have to.

"How much farther?" she asked him. *He says there's only one road, we can't get lost. He says he promises me we'll get to the Palm House with no problem. And, by the way, who's Floyd?*

Bill's eyebrow went up. The dimple beside his mouth appeared. "Once you get over the causeway and onto Sanibel Island, there's only one road," he said. Carol barely heard him. He was still talking about the road, her husband who had spent a dirty weekend in bed with his secretary two years ago, risking all they had done and all they had made, Bill doing that with his other face on, being the Bill Carol's mother had warned would break her heart. And later Bill trying to tell her he hadn't been able to help himself, her wanting to scream, *I once murdered a child for you, the potential of a child, anyway. How high is that price? And is this what I get in return? To reach my fifties and find out that my husband had to get into some Clairol girl's pants?*

Tell him! she shrieked. *Make him pull over and stop, make him do anything that will break you free—change one thing, change everything! You can do it—if you could put your feet up in those stirrups, you can do anything!*

But she could do nothing, and it all began to tick by faster.

The two overfed crows lifted off from their splatter of lunch. Her husband asked why she was sitting that way, was it a cramp, her saying, Yes, yes, a cramp in her back but it was easing. Her mouth quacked on about déjà vu just as if she weren't drowning in it, and the Crown Vic moved forward like one of those sadistic Dodgem cars at Revere Beach. Here came Palmdale Motors on the right. And on the left? Some kind of sign for the local community theater, a production of *Naughty Marietta*.

No, it's Mary, not Marietta. Mary, mother of Jesus, Mary, mother of God, she's got her hands out . . .

Carol bent all her will toward telling her husband what was happening, because the right Bill was behind the wheel, the right Bill could still hear her. Being heard was what married love was all about.

Nothing came out. In her mind Gram said, "All the hard days are coming." In her mind a voice asked Floyd what was over there, then said, "Oh shit," then *screamed* "Oh shit!"

She looked at the speedometer and saw it was calibrated not in miles an hour but thousands of feet: they were at twenty-eight thousand and descending. Bill was telling her that she shouldn't have slept on the plane and she was agreeing.

There was a pink house coming up, little more than a bungalow, fringed with palm trees that looked like the ones you saw in the Second World War movies, fronds framing incoming Learjets with their machine guns blazing—

Blazing. Burning hot. All at once the magazine he's holding turns into a torch. Holy Mary, mother of God, hey there, Mary, what's the story—

They passed the house. The old man sat on the porch and watched them go by. The lenses of his rimless glasses glinted in the sun. Bill's hand established a beachhead on her hip. He said something about how they might pause to refresh themselves between the doffing of her dress and the donning of her shorts and she agreed, although they were never going to get to Palm House. They were going to go down this road and down this road, they were for the white Crown Vic and the white Crown Vic was for them, forever and ever amen.

The next billboard would say PALM HOUSE 2 MI. Beyond it was the one saying that Mother of Mercy Charities helped the Florida sick. Would they help her?

Now that it was too late she was beginning to understand. Beginning to see the light the way she could see the subtropical sun sparkling off the water on their left. Wondering how many wrongs she had done in her life, how many sins if you liked that word, God knew her parents and her Gram certainly had, sin this and sin that and wear the medallion between those growing things the boys look at. And years later she had lain in bed with her new husband on hot summer nights, knowing a decision had to be made, knowing the clock was ticking, the cigarette butt was smoldering, and she remembered making the decision, not telling him out loud because about some things you could be silent.

Her head itched. She scratched it. Black flecks came swirling down past her face. On the Crown Vic's instrument panel the speedometer froze at sixteen thousand feet and then blew out, but Bill appeared not to notice.

Here came a mailbox with a Grateful Dead sticker pasted on the front; here came a little black dog with its head down, trotting busily, and God how her head itched, black flakes drifting in the air like fallout and Mother Teresa's face looking out of one of them.

MOTHER OF MERCY CHARITIES HELP THE FLORIDA HUNGRY —WON'T YOU HELP US?

Floyd. What's that over there? Oh shit.

She has time to see something big. And to read the word DELTA.

"Bill? *Bill?*"

His reply, clear enough but nevertheless coming from around the rim of the universe: "Christ, honey, what's in your *hair?*"

She plucked the charred remnant of Mother Teresa's face from her lap and held it out to him, the older version of the man she had married, the secretary-fucking man she had married, the man who had nonetheless rescued her from people who thought that you could live forever in paradise if you only lit enough candles and wore the blue blazer and stuck to the approved skipping rhymes. Lying there with this man one hot summer night while the drug deals went on upstairs and Iron Butterfly sang "In-A-Gadda-Da-Vida" for the nine billionth time, she had asked what he thought you got, you know, after. When your part in the show was over. He had taken her in his arms and held her, down the beach she had heard the jangle-jingle of the midway and the bang of the Dodgem cars and Bill—

Bill's glasses were melted to his face. One eye bulged out of its socket. His mouth was a bloodhole. In the trees a bird was crying, a bird was *screaming*, and Carol began to scream with it, holding out the charred fragment of paper with Mother Teresa's picture on it, screaming, watching as his cheeks turned black and his forehead swarmed and his neck split open like a poisoned goiter, screaming, she was screaming, somewhere Iron Butterfly was singing "In-A-Gadda-Da-Vida" and she was screaming.

"Carol?"

It was Bill's voice, from a thousand miles away. His hand was on her, but it was concern in his touch rather than lust.

She opened her eyes and looked around the sun-brilliant cabin of the Lear 35, and for a moment she understood everything—in the way one understands the tremendous import of a dream upon the first moment of waking. She remembered asking him what he believed you got, you know, *after,* and he had said you probably got what you'd always thought you *would* get, that if Jerry Lee Lewis thought he was going to Hell for playing boogie-woogie, that's exactly where he'd go. Heaven, Hell, or Grand Rapids, it was your choice—or the choice of those who had taught you what to believe. It was the human mind's final great parlor-trick: the perception of eternity in the place where you'd always expected to spend it.

"Carol? You okay, babe?" In one hand was the magazine he'd been reading, a *Newsweek* with Mother Teresa on the cover. SAINTHOOD NOW? it said in white.

Looking around wildly at the cabin, she was thinking, *It happens at sixteen thousand feet. I have to tell them, I have to warn them.*

But it was fading, all of it, the way those feelings always did. They went like dreams, or cotton candy turning into a sweet mist just above your tongue.

"Landing? Already?" She felt wide-awake, but her voice sounded thick and muzzy.

"It's fast, huh?" he said, sounding pleased, as if he'd flown it himself instead of paying for it. "Floyd says we'll be on the ground in—"

"Who?" she asked. The cabin of the little plane was warm but her fingers were cold. "Who?"

"Floyd. You know, the *pilot*." He pointed his thumb toward the cockpit's lefthand seat. They were descending into a scrim of clouds. The plane began to shake. "He says we'll be on the ground in Fort Myers in twenty minutes. You took a hell of a jump, girl. And before that you were moaning."

Carol opened her mouth to say it was that feeling, the one you could only say what it was in French, something *vu* or *vous*, but it was fading and all she said was "I had a nightmare."

There was a beep as Floyd the pilot switched the seat-belt light on. Carol turned her head. Somewhere below, waiting for them now and forever, was a white car from Hertz, a gangster car, the kind the characters in a Martin Scorsese movie would probably call a Crown Vic. She looked at the cover of the news magazine, at the face of Mother Teresa, and all at once she remembered skipping rope behind Our Lady of Angels, skipping to one of the forbidden rhymes, skipping to the one that went *Hey there, Mary, what's the story, save my ass from Purgatory.*

All the hard days are coming, her Gram had said. She had pressed the medal into Carol's palm, wrapped the chain around her fingers. *The hard days are coming.*

1998

GEORGE SAUNDERS

(b. 1958)

Sea Oak

At six Mr. Frendt comes on the P.A. and shouts, "Welcome to Joysticks!" Then he announces Shirts Off. We take off our flight jackets and fold them up. We take off our shirts and fold them up. Our scarves we leave on. Thomas Kirster's our beautiful boy. He's got long muscles and bright-blue eyes. The minute his shirt comes off two fat ladies hustle up the aisle and stick some money in his pants and ask will he be their Pilot. He says sure. He brings their salads. He brings their soups. My phone rings and the caller tells me to come see her in the Spitfire mock-up. Does she want me to be her Pilot? I'm hoping. Inside the Spitfire is Margie, who says she's been diagnosed with Chronic Shyness Syndrome, then hands me an Instamatic and offers me ten bucks for a close-up of Thomas's tush.

Do I do it? Yes I do.

It could be worse. It is worse for Lloyd Betts. Lately he's put on weight and his hair's gone thin. He doesn't get a call all shift and waits zero tables and winds up sitting on the P-51 wing, playing solitaire in a hunched-over position that gives him big gut rolls.

I Pilot six tables and make forty dollars in tips plus five an hour in salary.

After closing we sit on the floor for Debriefing. "There are times," Mr. Frendt says, "when one must move gracefully to the next station in life, like for example certain women in Africa or Brazil, I forget which, who either color their faces or don some kind of distinctive headdress upon achieving menopause. Are you with me? One of our ranks must now leave us. No one is an island in terms of being thought cute forever, and so today we must say good-bye to our friend Lloyd. Lloyd, stand up so we can say good-bye to you. I'm sorry. We are all so very sorry."

"Oh God," says Lloyd. "Let this not be true."

But it's true. Lloyd's finished. We give him a round of applause, and Frendt gives him a Farewell Pen and the contents of his locker in a trash bag and out he goes. Poor Lloyd. He's got a wife and two kids and a sad little duplex on Self-Storage Parkway.

"It's been a pleasure!" he shouts desperately from the doorway, trying not to burn any bridges.

What a stressful workplace. The minute your Cute Rating drops you're a goner. Guests rank us as Knockout, Honeypie, Adequate, or Stinker. Not that I'm complaining. At least I'm working. At least I'm not a Stinker like Lloyd.

I'm a solid Honeypie/Adequate, heading home with forty bucks cash.

At Sea Oak there's no sea and no oak, just a hundred subsidized apartments and a rear view of FedEx. Min and Jade are feeding their babies while watching *How My Child Died Violently*. Min's my sister. Jade's our cousin. *How My Child Died Violently* is hosted by Matt Merton, a six-foot-five blond who's always giving the parents shoulder rubs and telling them they've been sainted by pain. Today's show features a ten-year-old who killed a five-year-old for refusing to join his gang. The ten-year-old strangled the five-year-old with a jump rope, filled his mouth with baseball cards, then locked himself in the bathroom and wouldn't come out until his parents agreed to take him to FunTimeZone, where he confessed, then dove screaming into a mesh cage full of plastic balls. The audience is shrieking threats at the parents of the killer while the parents of the victim urge restraint and forgiveness to such an extent that finally the audience starts shrieking threats at them too. Then it's a commercial. Min and Jade put down the babies and light cigarettes and pace the room while studying aloud for their GEDs. It doesn't look good. Jade says "regicide" is a virus. Min locates Biafra one planet from Saturn. I offer to help and they start yelling at me for condescending.

"You're lucky, man!" my sister says. "You did high school. You got your frigging diploma. We don't. That's why we have to do this GED shit. If we had our diplomas we could just watch TV and not be all distracted."

"Really," says Jade. "Now shut it, chick! We got to study. Show's almost on."

They debate how many sides a triangle has. They agree that Churchill was in opera. Matt Merton comes back and explains that last week's show on suicide, in which the parents watched a reenactment of their son's suicide, was a healing process for the parents, then shows a video of the parents admitting it was a healing process.

My sister's baby is Troy. Jade's baby is Mac. They crawl off into the kitchen and Troy gets his finger caught in the heat vent. Min rushes over and starts pulling.

"Jesus freaking Christ!" screams Jade. "Watch it! Stop yanking on him and get the freaking Vaseline. You're going to give him a really long arm, man!"

Troy starts crying. Mac starts crying. I go over and free Troy no problem. Meanwhile Jade and Min get in a slap fight and nearly knock over the TV.

"Yo, chick!" Min shouts at the top of her lungs. "I'm sure you're slapping me? And then you knock over the freaking TV? Don't you care?"

"I care!" Jade shouts back. "You're the slut who nearly pulled off her own kid's finger for no freaking reason, man!"

Just then Aunt Bernie comes in from DrugTown in her DrugTown cap and hobbles over and picks up Troy and everything calms way down.

"No need to fuss, little man," she says. "Everything's fine. Everything's just hunky-dory."

"Hunky-dory," says Min, and gives Jade one last pinch.

Aunt Bernie's a peacemaker. She doesn't like trouble. Once this guy backed over her foot at FoodKing and she walked home with ten broken bones. She never got married, because Grandpa needed her to keep house after Grandma died. Then he died and left all his money to a woman none of us had ever heard of, and Aunt Bernie started in at DrugTown. But she's not bitter. Sometimes she's so nonbitter it gets on my nerves. When I say Sea Oak's a pit she says she's just glad to have a roof over her head. When I say I'm tired of being broke she says Grandpa once gave her pencils for Christmas and she was so thrilled she sat around sketching horses all day on the backs of used envelopes. Once I asked was she sorry she never had kids and she said no, not at all, and besides, weren't we her kids?

And I said yes we were.

But of course we're not.

For dinner it's beanie-wienies. For dessert it's ice cream with freezer burn.

"What a nice day we've had," Aunt Bernie says once we've got the babies in bed.

"Man, what an optometrist," says Jade.

Next day is Thursday, which means a visit from Ed Anders from the Board of Health. He's in charge of ensuring that our penises never show. Also that we don't kiss anyone. None of us ever kisses anyone or shows his penis except Sonny Vance, who does both, because he's saving up to buy a FaxIt franchise. As for our Penile Simulators, yes, we can show them, we can let them stick out the top of our pants, we can even periodically dampen our tight pants with spray bottles so our Simulators really contour, but our real penises, no, those have to stay inside our hot uncomfortable oversized Simulators.

"Sorry fellas, hi fellas," Anders says as he comes wearily in. "Please know I don't like this any better than you do. I went to school to learn how to inspect meat, but this certainly wasn't what I had in mind. Ha ha!"

He orders a Lindbergh Enchilada and eats it cautiously, as if it's alive and he's afraid of waking it. Sonny Vance is serving soup to a table of hairstylists on a bender and for a twenty shoots them a quick look at his unit.

Just then Anders glances up from his Lindbergh.

"Oh for crying out loud," he says, and writes up a Shutdown and we all get sent home early. Which is bad. Every dollar counts. Lately I've been sneaking toilet paper home in my briefcase. I can fit three rolls in. By the time I get home they're usually flat and don't work so great on the roller but still it saves a few bucks.

I clock out and cut through the strip of forest behind FedEx. Very pretty. A raccoon scurries over a fallen oak and starts nibbling at a rusty bike. As I come out of the woods I hear a shot. At least I think it's a shot. It could be a back-fire. But no, it's a shot, because then there's another one, and some kids sprint across the courtyard yelling that Big Scary Dawgz rule.

I run home. Min and Jade and Aunt Bernie and the babies are huddled behind the couch. Apparently they had the babies outside when the shooting started. Troy's walker got hit. Luckily he wasn't in it. It's supposed to look like a duck but now the beak's missing.

"Man, fuck this shit!" Min shouts.

"Freak this crap you mean," says Jade. "You want them growing up with shit-mouths like us? Crap-mouths I mean?"

"I just want them growing up, period," says Min.

"Boo-hoo, Miss Dramatic," says Jade.

"Fuck off, Miss Ho," shouts Min.

"I mean it, jagoff, I'm not kidding," shouts Jade, and punches Min in the arm.

"Girls, for crying out loud!" says Aunt Bernie. "We should be thankful. At least we got a home. And at least none of them bullets actually hit nobody."

"No offense, Bernie?" says Min. "But you call this a freaking home?"

Sea Oak's not safe. There's an ad hoc crackhouse in the laundry room and last week Min found some brass knuckles in the kiddie pool. If I had my way I'd move everybody up to Canada. It's nice there. Very polite. We went for a weekend last fall and got a flat tire and these two farmers with bright-red faces insisted on fixing it, then springing for dinner, then starting a college fund for the babies. They sent us the stock certificates a week later, along with a photo of all of us eating cobbler at a diner. But moving to Canada takes bucks. Dad's dead and left us nada and Ma now lives with Freddie, who doesn't like us, plus he's not exactly rich himself. He does phone polls. This month he's asking divorced women how often they backslide and sleep with their exes. He gets ten bucks for every completed poll.

So not lucrative, and Canada's a moot point.

I go out and find the beak of Troy's duck and fix it with Elmer's.

"Actually you know what?" says Aunt Bernie. "I think that looks even more like a real duck now. Because sometimes their beaks are cracked? I seen one like that downtown."

"Oh my God," says Min. "The kid's duck gets shot in the face and she says we're lucky."

"Well, we are lucky," says Bernie.

"Somebody's beak is cracked," says Jade.

"You know what I do if something bad happens?" Bernie says. "I don't think about it. Don't take it so serious. It ain't the end of the world. That's what I do. That's what I always done. That's how I got where I am."

My feeling is, Bernie, I love you, but where are you? You work at DrugTown for minimum. You're sixty and own nothing. You were basically a slave to your father and never had a date in your life.

"I mean, complain if you want," she says. "But I think we're doing pretty darn good for ourselves."

"Oh, we're doing great," says Min, and pulls Troy out from behind the couch and brushes some duck shards off his sleeper.

Joysticks reopens on Friday. It's a madhouse. They've got the fog on. A bridge club offers me fifteen bucks to oil-wrestle Mel Turner. So I oil-wrestle Mel Turner. They offer me twenty bucks to feed them chicken wings from my hand. So I feed them chicken wings from my hand. The afternoon flies by. Then the evening. At nine the bridge club leaves and I get a sorority. They sing intelligent nasty songs and grope my Simulator and say they'll never be able to look their boyfriends' meager genitalia in the eye again. Then Mr. Frendt comes over and says phone. It's Min. She sounds crazy. Four times in a row she shrieks get home. When I tell her calm down, she hangs up. I call back and no one answers. No biggie. Min's prone to panic. Probably one of the babies is puky. Luckily I'm on FlexTime.

"I'll be back," I say to Mr. Frendt.

"I look forward to it," he says.

I jog across the marsh and through FedEx. Up on the hill there's a light from the last remaining farm. Sometimes we take the boys to the adjacent car wash to look at the cow. Tonight however the cow is elsewhere.

At home Min and Jade are hopping up and down in front of Aunt Bernie, who's sitting very very still at one end of the couch.

"Keep the babies out!" shrieks Min. "I don't want them seeing something dead!"

"Shut up, man!" shrieks Jade. "Don't call her something dead!"

She squats down and pinches Aunt Bernie's cheek.

"Aunt Bernie?" she shrieks. "Fuck!"

"We already tried that like twice, chick!" shrieks Min. "Why are you doing that shit again? Touch her neck and see if you can feel that beating thing!"

"Shit shit shit!" shrieks Jade.

I call 911 and the paramedics come out and work hard for twenty minutes, then give up and say they're sorry and it looks like she's been dead most of the afternoon. The apartment's a mess. Her money drawer's empty and her family photos are in the bathtub.

"Not a mark on her," says a cop.

"I suspect she died of fright," says another. "Fright of the intruder?"

"My guess is yes," says a paramedic.

"Oh God," says Jade. "God, God, God."

I sit down beside Bernie. I think: I am so sorry. I'm sorry I wasn't here when it happened and sorry you never had any fun in your life and sorry I wasn't rich enough to move you somewhere safe. I remember when she was young and wore pink stretch pants and made us paper chains out of DrugTown receipts while singing "Froggie Went A-Courting." All her life she worked hard. She never hurt anybody. And now this.

Scared to death in a crappy apartment.

Min puts the babies in the kitchen but they keep crawling out. Aunt Bernie's in a shroud on this sort of dolly and on the couch are a bunch of forms to sign.

We call Ma and Freddie. We get their machine.

"Ma, pick up!" says Min. "Something bad happened! Ma, please freaking pick up!"

But nobody picks up.

So we leave a message.

Lobton's Funeral Parlor is just a regular house on a regular street. Inside there's a rack of brochures with titles like "Why Does My Loved One Appear Somewhat Larger?" Lobton looks healthy. Maybe too healthy. He's wearing a yellow golf shirt and his biceps keep involuntarily flexing. Every now and then he touches his delts as if to confirm they're still big as softballs.

"Such a sad thing," he says.

"How much?" asks Jade. "I mean, like for basic. Not super-fancy."

"But not crappy either," says Min. "Our aunt was the best."

"What price range were you considering?" says Lobton, cracking his knuckles. We tell him and his eyebrows go up and he leads us to something that looks like a moving box.

"Prior to usage we'll moisture-proof this with a spray lacquer," he says. "Makes it look quite woodlike."

"That's all we can get?" says Jade. "Cardboard?"

"I'm actually offering you a slight break already," he says, and does a kind of push-up against the wall. "On account of the tragic circumstances. This is Sierra Sunset. Not exactly cardboard. More of a fiberboard."

"I don't know," says Min. "Seems pretty gyppy."

"Can we think about it?" says Ma.

"Absolutely," says Lobton. "Last time I checked this was still America."

I step over and take a closer look. There are staples where Aunt Bernie's spine would be. Down at the foot there's some writing about Folding Tab A into Slot B.

"No freaking way," says Jade. "Work your whole life and end up in a Mayflower box? I doubt it."

We've got zip in savings. We sit at a desk and Lobton does what he calls a Credit Calc. If we pay it out monthly for seven years we can afford the Amber Mist, which includes a double-thick balsa box and two coats of lacquer and a one-hour wake.

"But seven years, jeez," says Ma.

"We got to get her the good one," says Min. "She never had anything nice in her life."

So Amber Mist it is.

We bury her at St. Leo's, on the hill up near BastCo. Her part of the graveyard's pretty plain. No angels, no little rock houses, no flowers, just a bunch of flat stones like parking bumpers and here and there a Styrofoam cup. Father Brian says a prayer and then one of us is supposed to talk. But what's there to say? She never had a life. Never married, no kids, work work work. Did she ever go on a cruise? All her life it was buses. Buses buses buses. Once she went with Ma on a bus to Quigley, Kansas, to gamble and shop at an outlet mall. Someone broke into her room and stole her clothes and took a dump in her suitcase while they were at the Roy Clark show. That was it. That was the extent of her tourism. After that it was DrugTown, night and day. After fifteen years as Cashier she got demoted to Greeter. People would ask where the cold remedies were and she'd point to some big letters on the wall that said Cold Remedies.

Freddie, Ma's boyfriend, steps up and says he didn't know her very long but she was an awful nice lady and left behind a lot of love, etc. etc. blah blah blah. While it's true she didn't do much in her life, still she was very dear to those of us who knew her and never made a stink about anything but was always content with whatever happened to her, etc. etc. blah blah blah.

Then it's over and we're supposed to go away.

"We gotta come out here like every week," says Jade.

"I know I will," says Min.

"What, like I won't?" says Jade. "She was so freaking nice."

"I'm sure you swear at a grave," says Min.

"Since when is freak a swear, chick?" says Jade.

"Girls," says Ma.

"I hope I did okay in what I said about her," says Freddie in his full-of-crap way, smelling bad of English Navy. "Actually I sort of surprised myself."

"Bye-bye, Aunt Bernie," says Min.

"Bye-bye, Bern," says Jade.

"Oh my dear sister," says Ma.

I scrunch my eyes tight and try to picture her happy, laughing, poking me in the ribs. But all I can see is her terrified on the couch. It's awful. Out there, somewhere, is whoever did it. Someone came in our house, scared her to death, watched her die, went through our stuff, stole her money. Someone who's still living, someone who right now might be having a piece of pie or running an errand or scratching his ass, someone who, if he wanted to, could drive west for three days or whatever and sit in the sun by the ocean.

We stand a few minutes with heads down and hands folded.

*

Afterward Freddie takes us to Trabanti's for lunch. Last year Trabanti died and three Vietnamese families went in together and bought the place, and it still serves pasta and pizza and the big oil of Trabanti is still on the wall but now from the kitchen comes this very pretty Vietnamese music and the food is somehow better.

Freddie proposes a toast. Min says remember how Bernie always called lunch dinner and dinner supper? Jade says remember how when her jaw clicked she'd say she needed oil?

"She was a excellent lady," says Freddie.

"I already miss her so bad," says Ma.

"I'd like to kill that fuck that killed her," says Min.

"How about let's don't say fuck at lunch," says Ma.

"It's just a word, Ma, right?" says Min. "Like pluck is just a word? You don't mind if I say pluck? Pluck pluck pluck?"

"Well, shits just a word too," says Freddie. "But we don't say it at lunch."

"Same with puke," says Ma.

"Shit puke, shit puke," says Min.

The waiter clears his throat. Ma glares at Min.

"I love you girls' manners," Ma says.

"Especially at a funeral," says Freddie.

"This ain't a funeral," says Min.

"The question in my mind is what you kids are gonna do now," says Freddie. "Because I consider this whole thing a wake-up call, meaning it's time for you to pull yourself up by the bootstraps like I done and get out of that dangerous craphole you're living at."

"Mr. Phone Poll speaks," says Min.

"Anyways it ain't that dangerous," says Jade.

"A woman gets killed and it ain't that dangerous?" says Freddie.

"All's we need is a dead bolt and a eyehole," says Min.

"What's a bootstrap," says Jade.

"It's like a strap on a boot, you doof," says Min.

"Plus where we gonna go?" says Min. "Can we move in with you guys?"

"I personally would love that and you know that," says Freddie. "But who would not love that is our landlord."

"I think what Freddie's saying is it's time for you girls to get jobs," says Ma.

"Yeah right, Ma," says Min. "After what happened last time?"

When I first moved in, Jade and Min were working the info booth at HardwareNiche. Then one day we picked the babies up at day care and found Troy sitting naked on top of the washer and Mac in the yard being nipped by a Pekingese and the day-care lady sloshed and playing KillerBirds on Nintendo.

So that was that. No more HardwareNiche.

"Maybe one could work, one could baby-sit?" says Ma.

"I don't see why I should have to work so she can stay home with her baby," says Min.

"And I don't see why I should have to work so she can stay home with her baby," says Jade.

"It's like a freaking veece versa," says Min.

"Let me tell you something," says Freddie. "Something about this country. Anybody can do anything. But first they gotta try. And you guys ain't. Two don't work and one strips naked? I don't consider that trying. You kids make squat. And therefore you live in a dangerous craphole. And what happens in a dangerous craphole? Bad tragic shit. It's the freaking American way—you start out in a dangerous craphole and work hard so you can someday move up to a somewhat less dangerous craphole. And finally maybe you get a mansion. But at this rate you ain't even gonna make it to the somewhat less dangerous craphole."

"Like you live in a mansion," says Jade.

"I do not claim to live in no mansion," says Freddie. "But then again I do not live in no slum. The other thing I also do not do is strip naked."

"Thank God for small favors," says Min.

"Anyways he's never actually naked," says Jade.

Which is true. I always have on at least a T-back.

"No wonder we never take these kids out to a nice lunch," says Freddie.

"I do not even consider this a nice lunch," says Min.

For dinner Jade microwaves some Stars-n-Flags. They're addictive. They put sugar in the sauce and sugar in the meat nuggets. I think also caffeine. Someone told me the brown streaks in the Flags are caffeine. We have like five bowls each.

After dinner the babies get fussy and Min puts a mush of ice cream and Hershey's syrup in their bottles and we watch *The Worst That Could Happen*, a half-hour of computer simulations of tragedies that have never actually occurred but theoretically could. A kid gets hit by a train and flies into a zoo, where he's eaten by wolves. A man cuts his hand off chopping wood and while wandering around screaming for help is picked up by a tornado and dropped on a preschool during recess and lands on a pregnant teacher.

"I miss Bernie so bad," says Min.

"Me too," Jade says sadly.

The babies start howling for more ice cream.

"That is so cute," says Jade. "They're like, *Give it the fuck up!*"

"We'll give it the fuck up, sweeties, don't worry," says Min. "We didn't forget about you."

Then the phone rings. It's Father Brian. He sounds weird. He says he's sorry to bother us so late. But something strange has happened. Something bad. Something sort of, you know, unspeakable. Am I sitting? I'm not but I say I am.

Apparently someone has defaced Bernie's grave.

My first thought is there's no stone. It's just grass. How do you deface grass? What did they do, pee on the grass on the grave? But Father's nearly in tears.

So I call Ma and Freddie and tell them to meet us, and we get the babies up and load them into the K-car.

"Deface," says Jade on the way over. "What does that mean, deface?"

"It means like fucked it up," says Min.

"But how?" says Jade. "I mean, like what did they do?"

"We don't know, dumbass," says Min. "That's why we're going there."

"And why?" says Jade. "Why would someone do that?"

"Check out Miss Shreelock Holmes," says Min. "Someone done that because someone is a asshole."

"Someone is a big-time asshole," says Jade.

Father Brian meets us at the gate with a flashlight and a golf cart.

"When I saw this," he says. "I literally sat down in astonishment. Nothing like this has ever happened here. I am so sorry. You seem like nice people."

We're too heavy and the wheels spin as we climb the hill, so I get out and jog alongside.

"Okay, folks, brace yourselves," Father says, and shuts off the engine.

Where the grave used to be is just a hole. Inside the hole is the Amber Mist, with the top missing. Inside the Amber Mist is nothing. No Aunt Bernie.

"What the hell," says Jade. "Where's Bernie?"

"Somebody stole Bernie?" says Min.

"At least you folks have retained your feet," says Father Brian. "I'm telling you I literally sat right down. I sat right down on that pile of dirt. I dropped as if shot. See that mark? That's where I sat."

On the pile of grave dirt is a butt-shaped mark.

The cops show up and one climbs down in the hole with a tape measure and a camera. After three or four flashes he climbs out and hands Ma a pair of blue pumps.

"Her little shoes," says Ma. "Oh my God."

"Are those them?" says Jade.

"Those are them," says Min.

"I am freaking out," says Jade.

"I am totally freaking out," says Min.

"I'm gonna sit," says Ma, and drops into the golf cart.

"What I don't get is who'd want her?" says Min.

"She was just this lady," says Jade.

"Typically it's teens?" one cop says. "Typically we find the loved one nearby? Once we found the loved one nearby with, you know, a cigarette between its lips, wearing a sombrero? These kids today got a lot more nerve than we ever did. I never would've dreamed of digging up a dead corpse when I was a teen. You might tip over a stone, sure, you might spray-paint something on a crypt, you might, you know, give a wino a hotfoot."

"But this, jeez," says Freddie. "This is a entirely different ballgame."

"Boy howdy," says the cop, and we all look down at the shoes in Ma's hands.

*

Next day I go back to work. I don't feel like it but we need the money. The grass is wet and it's hard getting across the ravine in my dress shoes. The soles are slick. Plus they're too tight. Several times I fall forward on my briefcase. Inside the briefcase are my T-backs and a thing of mousse.

Right off the bat I get a tableful of MediBen women seated under a banner saying BEST OF LUCK, BEATRICE, NO HARD FEELINGS. I take off my shirt and serve their salads. I take off my flight pants and serve their soups. One drops a dollar on the floor and tells me feel free to pick it up.

I pick it up.

"Not like that, not like that," she says. "Face the other way, so when you bend we can see your crack."

I've done this about a million times, but somehow I can't do it now.

I look at her. She looks at me.

"What?" she says. "I'm not allowed to say that? I thought that was the whole point."

"That is the whole point, Phyllis," says another lady. "You stand your ground."

"Look," Phyllis says. "Either bend how I say or give back the dollar. I think that's fair."

"You go, girl," says her friend.

I give back the dollar. I return to the Locker Area and sit awhile. For the first time ever, I'm voted Stinker. There are thirteen women at the MediBen table and they all vote me Stinker. Do the MediBen women know my situation? Would they vote me Stinker if they did? But what am I supposed to do, go out and say, Please ladies, my aunt just died, plus her body's missing?

Mr. Frendt pulls me aside.

"Perhaps you need to go home," he says. "I'm sorry for your loss. But I'd like to encourage you not to behave like one of those Comanche ladies who bite off their index fingers when a loved one dies. Grief is good, grief is fine, but too much grief, as we all know, is excessive. If your aunt's death has filled your mouth with too many bitten-off fingers, for crying out loud, take a week off, only don't take it out on our Guests, they didn't kill your dang aunt."

But I can't afford to take a week off. I can't even afford to take a few days off.

"We really need the money," I say.

"Is that my problem?" he says. "Am I supposed to let you dance without vigor just because you need the money? Why don't I put an ad in the paper for all sad people who need money? All the town's sad could come here and strip. Goodbye. Come back when you feel halfway normal."

From the pay phone I call home to see if they need anything from the FoodSoQuik.

"Just come home," Min says stiffly. "Just come straight home."

"What is it?" I say.

"Come home," she says.

Maybe someone's found the body. I imagine Bernie naked, Bernie chopped in two, Bernie posed on a bus bench. I hope and pray that something only mildly bad's been done to her, something we can live with.

At home the door's wide open. Min and Jade are sitting very still on the couch, babies in their laps, staring at the rocking chair, and in the rocking chair is Bernie. Bernie's body.

Same perm, same glasses, same blue dress we buried her in.

What's it doing here? Who could be so cruel? And what are we supposed to do with it?

Then she turns her head and looks at me.

"Sit the fuck down," she says.

In life she never swore.

I sit. Min squeezes and releases my hand, squeezes and releases, squeezes and releases.

"You, mister," Bernie says to me, "are going to start showing your cock. You'll show it and show it. You go up to a lady, if she wants to see it, if she'll pay to see it, I'll make a thumbprint on the forehead. You see the thumbprint, you ask. I'll try to get you five a day, at twenty bucks a pop. So a hundred bucks a day. Seven hundred a week. And that's cash, so no taxes. No withholding. See? That's the beauty of it."

She's got dirt in her hair and dirt in her teeth and her hair is a mess and her tongue when it darts out to lick her lips is black.

"You, Jade," she says. "Tomorrow you start work. Andersen Labels, Fifth and Rivera. Dress up when you go. Wear something nice. Show a little leg. And don't chomp your gum. Ask for Len. At the end of the month, we take the money you made and the cock money and get a new place. Somewhere safe. That's part one of Phase One. You, Min. You baby-sit. Plus you quit smoking. Plus you learn how to cook. No more food out of cans. We gotta eat right to look our best. Because I am getting me so many lovers. Maybe you kids don't know this but I died a freaking virgin. No babies, no lovers. Nothing went in, nothing came out. Ha ha! Dry as a bone, completely wasted, this pretty little thing God gave me between my legs. Well I am going to have lovers now, you fucks! Like in the movies, big shoulders and all, and a summer house, and nice trips, and in the morning in my room a big vase of flowers, and I'm going to get my nipples hard standing in the breeze from the ocean, eating shrimp from a cup, you sons of bitches, while my lover watches me from the veranda, his big shoulders shining, all hard for me, that's one damn thing I will guarantee you kids! Ha ha! You think I'm joking? I ain't freaking joking. I never got nothing! My life was shit! I was never even up in a freaking plane. But that was that life and this is this life. My new life. Cover me up now! With a blanket. I need my beauty rest. Tell anyone I'm here, you all die. Plus they die. Whoever you tell, they die. I kill them with my mind. I can do that. I am very freaking strong now. I got powers! So no visitors. I don't exactly look my best. You got it? You all got it?"

We nod. I go for a blanket. Her hands and feet are shaking and she's grinding her teeth and one falls out.

"Put it over me, you fuck, all the way over!" she screams, and I put it over her.

We sneak off with the babies and whisper in the kitchen.

"It looks like her," says Min.

"It is her," I say.

"It is and it ain't," says Jade.

"We better do what she says," Min says.

"No shit," Jade says.

All night she sits in the rocker under the blanket, shaking and swearing.

All night we sit in Min's bed, fully dressed, holding hands.

"See how strong I am!" she shouts around midnight, and there's a cracking sound, and when I go out the door's been torn off the microwave but she's still sitting in the chair.

In the morning she's still there, shaking and swearing.

"Take the blanket off!" she screams. "It's time to get this show on the road."

I take the blanket off. The smell is not good. One ear is now in her lap. She keeps absentmindedly sticking it back on her head.

"You, Jade!" she shouts. "Get dressed. Go get that job. When you meet Len, bend forward a little. Let him see down your top. Give him some hope. He's a sicko, but we need him. You, Min! Make breakfast. Something homemade. Like biscuits."

"Why don't you make it with your powers?" says Min.

"Don't be a smartass!" screams Bernie. "You see what I did to that microwave?"

"I don't know how to make freaking biscuits," Min wails.

"You know how to read, right?" Bernie shouts. "You ever heard of a recipe? You ever been in the grave? It sucks so bad! You regret all the things you never did. You little bitches are gonna have a very bad time in the grave unless you get on the stick, believe me! Turn down the thermostat! Make it cold. I like cold. Something's off with my body. I don't feel right."

I turn down the thermostat. She looks at me.

"Go show your cock!" she shouts. "That is the first part of Phase One. After we get the new place, that's the end of the first part of Phase Two. You'll still show your cock, but only three days a week. Because you'll start community college. Pre-law. Pre-law is best. You'll be a whiz. You ain't dumb. And Jade'll work weekends to make up for the decrease in cock money. See? See how that works? Now get out of here. What are you gonna do?"

"Show my cock?" I say.

"Show your cock, that's right," she says, and brushes back her hair with her hand, and a huge wad comes out, leaving her almost bald on one side.

"Oh God," says Min. "You know what? No way me and the babies are staying here alone."

"You ain't alone," says Bernie. "I'm here."

"Please don't go," Min says to me.

"Oh, stop it," Bernie says, and the door flies open and I feel a sort of invisible fist punching me in the back.

Outside it's sunny. A regular day. A guy's changing his oil. The clouds are regular clouds and the sun's the regular sun and the only nonregular thing is that my clothes smell like Bernie, a combo of wet cellar and rotten bacon.

Work goes well. I manage to keep smiling and hide my shaking hands, and my midshift rating is Honeypie. After lunch this older woman comes up and says I look so much like a real Pilot she can hardly stand it.

On her head is a thumbprint. Like Ash Wednesday, only sort of glowing.

I don't know what to do. Do I just come out and ask if she wants to see my cock? What if she says no? What if I get caught? What if I show her and she doesn't think it's worth twenty bucks?

Then she asks if I'll surprise her best friend with a birthday table dance. She points out her friend. A pretty girl, no thumbprint. Looks somehow familiar.

We start over and at about twenty feet I realize it's Angela.

Angela Silveri.

We dated senior year. Then Dad died and Ma had to take a job at Patty-Melt Depot. From all the grease Ma got a bad rash and could barely wear a blouse. Plus Min was running wild. So Angela would come over and there'd be Min getting high under a tarp on the carport and Ma sitting in her bra on a kitchen stool with a fan pointed at her gut. Angela had dreams. She had plans. In her notebook she pasted a picture of an office from the J. C. Penney catalogue and under it wrote, *My (someday?) office*. Once we saw this black Porsche and she said very nice but make hers red. The last straw was Ed Edwards, a big drunk, one of Dad's cousins. Things got so bad Ma rented him the utility room. One night Angela and I were making out on the couch late when Ed came in soused and started peeing in the dishwasher.

What could I say? He's only barely related to me? He hardly ever does that?

Angela's eyes were like these little pies.

I walked her home, got no kiss, came back, cleaned up the

dishwasher as best I could. A few days later I got my class ring in the mail and a copy of *The Prophet*.

You will always be my first love, she'd written inside. *But now my path converges to a higher ground. Be well always. Walk in joy. Please don't think me cruel, it's just that I want so much in terms of accomplishment, plus I couldn't believe that guy peed right on your dishes.*

No way am I table dancing for Angela Silveri. No way am I asking Angela Silveri's friend if she wants to see my cock. No way am I hanging around here so Angela can see me in my flight jacket and T-backs and wonder to herself how I went so wrong etc. etc.

I hide in the kitchen until my shift is done, then walk home very, very slowly because I'm afraid of what Bernie's going to do to me when I get there.

Min meets me at the door. She's got flour all over her blouse and it looks like she's been crying.

"I can't take any more of this," she says. "She's like falling apart. I mean shit's falling off her. Plus she made me bake a freaking pie."

On the table is a very lumpy pie. One of Bernie's arms is now disconnected and lying across her lap.

"What are you thinking of!" she shouts. "You didn't show your cock even once? You think it's easy making those thumb-prints? You try it, smartass! Do you or do you not know the plan? You gotta get us out of here! And to get us out, you gotta use what you got. And you ain't got much. A nice face. And a decent unit. Not huge, but shaped nice."

"Bernie, God," says Min.

"What, Miss Priss?" shouts Bernie, and slams the severed arm down hard on her lap, and her other ear falls off.

"I'm sorry, but this is too fucking sickening," says Min. "I'm going out."

"What's sickening?" says Bernie. "Are you saying I'm sick-ening? Well, I think you're sickening. So many wonderful things in life and where's your mind? You think with your lazy ass. Whatever life hands you, you take. You're not going any-where. You're staying home and studying."

"I'm what?" says Min. "Studying what? I ain't studying.

Chick comes into my house and starts ordering me to study? I freaking doubt it."

"You don't know nothing!" Bernie says. "What fun is life when you don't know nothing? You can't find your own town on the map. You can't name a single president. When we go to Rome you won't know nothing about the history. You're going to study the World Book. Do we still have those World Books?"

"Yeah right," says Min. "We're going to Rome."

"We'll go to Rome when he's a lawyer," says Bernie.

"Dream on, chick," says Min. "And we'll go to Mars when I'm a stockbreaker."

"Don't you dare make fun of me!" Bernie shouts, and our only vase goes flying across the room and nearly nails Min in the head.

"She's been like this all day," says Min.

"Like what?" shouts Bernie. "We had a perfectly nice day."

"She made me help her try on my bras," says Min.

"I never had a nice sexy bra," says Bernie.

"And now mine are all ruined," says Min. "They got this sort of goo on them."

"You ungrateful shit!" shouts Bernie. "Do you know what I'm doing for you? I'm saving your boy. And you got the nerve to say I made goo on your bras! Troy's gonna get caught in a crossfire in the courtyard. In September. September eighteenth. He's gonna get thrown off his little trike. With one leg twisted under him and blood pouring out of his ear. It's a freaking prophecy. You know that word? It means prediction. You know that word? You think I'm bullshitting? Well I ain't bull-shitting. I got the power. Watch this: All day Jade sat licking labels at a desk by a window. Her boss bought everybody subs for lunch. She's bringing some home in a green bag."

"That ain't true about Troy, is it?" says Min. "Is it? I don't believe it."

"Turn on the TV!" Bernie shouts. "Give me the changer."

I turn on the TV. I give her the changer. She puts on *Nathan's Body Shop*. Nathan says washboard abs drive the women wild. Then there's a close-up of his washboard abs.

"Oh yes," says Bernie. "Them are for me. I'd like to give

those a lick. A lick and a pinch. I'd like to sort of straddle those things."

Just then Jade comes through the door with a big green bag.

"Oh God," says Min.

"Told you so!" says Bernie, and pokes Min in the ribs. "Ha ha! I really got the power!"

"I don't get it," Min says, all desperate. "What happens? Please. What happens to him? You better freaking tell me."

"I already told you," Bernie says. "He'll fly about fifteen feet and live about three minutes."

"Bernie, God," Min says, and starts to cry. "You used to be so nice."

"I'm still so nice," says Bernie, and bites into a sub and takes off the tip of her finger and starts chewing it up.

Just after dawn she shouts out my name.

"Take the blanket off," she says. "I ain't feeling so good."

I take the blanket off. She's basically just this pile of parts: both arms in her lap, head on the arms, heel of one foot touching the heel of the other, all of it sort of wrapped up in her dress.

"Get me a washcloth," she says. "Do I got a fever? I feel like I got a fever. Oh, I knew it was too good to be true. But okay. New plan. New plan. I'm changing the first part of Phase One. If you see two thumbprints, that means the lady'll screw you for cash. We're in a fix here. We gotta speed this up. There ain't gonna be nothing left of me. Who's gonna be my lover now?"

The doorbell rings.

"Son of a bitch," Bernie snarls.

It's Father Brian with a box of doughnuts. I step out quick and close the door behind me. He says he's just checking in. Perhaps we'd like to talk? Perhaps we're feeling some residual anger about Bernie's situation? Which would of course be completely understandable. Once when he was a young priest someone broke in and drew a mustache on the Virgin Mary with a permanent marker, and for weeks he was tortured by visions of bending back the finger of the vandal until he or she burst into tears of apology.

"I knew that wasn't appropriate," he says. "I knew that by

indulging in that fantasy I was honoring violence. And yet it gave me pleasure. I also thought of catching them in the act and boinking them in the head with a rock. I also thought of jumping up and down on their backs until something in their spinal column cracked. Actually I had about a million ideas. But you know what I did instead? I scrubbed and scrubbed our Holy Mother, and soon she was as good as new. Her statue, I mean. She herself of course is always good as new."

From inside comes the sound of breaking glass. Breaking glass and then something heavy falling, and Jade yelling and Min yelling and the babies crying.

"Oops, I guess?" he says. "I've come at a bad time? Look, all I'm trying to do is urge you, if at all possible, to forgive the perpetrators, as I forgave the perpetrator that drew on my Virgin Mary. The thing lost, after all, is only your aunt's body, and what is essential, I assure you, is elsewhere, being well taken care of?"

I nod. I smile. I say thanks for stopping by. I take the doughnuts and go back inside.

The TV's broke and the refrigerator's tipped over and Bernie's parts are strewn across the living room like she's been shot out of a cannon.

"She tried to get up," says Jade.

"I don't know where the hell she thought she was going," says Min.

"Come here," the head says to me, and I squat down. "That's it for me. I'm fucked. As per usual. Always the bridesmaid, never the bride. Although come to think of it I was never even the freaking bridesmaid. Look, show your cock. It's the shortest line between two points. The world ain't giving away nice lives. You got a trust fund? You a genius? Show your cock. It's what you got. And remember: Troy in September. On his trike. One leg twisted. Don't forget. And also. Don't remember me like this. Remember me like how I was that night we all went to Red Lobster and I had that new perm. Ah Christ. At least buy me a stone."

I rub her shoulder, which is next to her foot.

"We loved you," I say.

"Why do some people get everything and I got nothing?" she says. "Why? Why was that?"

"I don't know," I say.

"Show your cock," she says, and dies again.

We stand there looking down at the pile of parts. Mac crawls toward it and Min moves him back with her foot.

"This is too freaking much," says Jade, and starts crying.

"What do we do now?" says Min.

"Call the cops," Jade says.

"And say what?" says Min.

We think about this awhile.

I get a Hefty bag. I get my winter gloves.

"I ain't watching," says Jade.

"I ain't watching either," says Min, and they take the babies into the bedroom.

I close my eyes and wrap Bernie up in the Hefty bag and twistie-tie the bag shut and lug it out to the trunk of the K-car. I throw in a shovel. I drive up to St. Leo's. I lower the bag into the hole using a bungee cord, then fill the hole back in.

Down in the city are the nice houses and the so-so houses and the lovers making out in dark yards and the babies crying for their moms, and I wonder if, other than Jesus, this has ever happened before. Maybe it happens all the time. Maybe there's angry dead all over, hiding in rooms, covered with blankets, bossing around their scared, embarrassed relatives. Because how would we know?

I for sure don't plan on broadcasting this.

I smooth over the dirt and say a quick prayer: If it was wrong for her to come back, forgive her, she never got beans in this life, plus she was trying to help us.

At the car I think of an additional prayer: But please don't let her come back again.

When I get home the babies are asleep and Jade and Min are watching a phone-sex infomercial, three girls in leather jumpsuits eating bananas in slo-mo while across the screen runs a constant disclaimer: "Not Necessarily the Girls Who Man the Phones! Not Necessarily the Girls Who Man the Phones!"

"Them chicks seem to really be enjoying those bananas," says Min in a thin little voice.

"I like them jumpsuits though," says Jade.

"Yeah them jumpsuits look decent," says Min.

Then they look up at me. I've never seen them so sad and beat and sick.

"It's done," I say.

Then we hug and cry and promise never to forget Bernie the way she really was, and I use some Resolve on the rug and they go do some reading in their World Books.

Next day I go in early. I don't see a single thumbprint. But it doesn't matter. I get with Sonny Vance and he tells me how to do it. First you ask the woman would she like a private tour. Then you show her the fake P-40, the Gallery of Historical Aces, the shower stall where we get oiled up, etc. etc. and then in the hall near the rest room you ask if there's anything else she'd like to see. It's sleazy. It's gross. But when I do it I think of September. September and Troy in the crossfire, his little leg bent under him etc. etc.

Most say no but quite a few say yes.

I've got a place picked out at a complex called Swan's Glen. They've never had a shooting or a knifing and the public school is great and every Saturday they have a nature walk for kids behind the clubhouse.

For every hundred bucks I make, I set aside five for Bernie's stone.

What do you write on something like that? LIFE PASSED HER BY? DIED DISAPPOINTED? CAME BACK TO LIFE BUT FELL APART? All true, but too sad, and no way I'm writing any of those.

BERNIE KOWALSKI, it's going to say: BELOVED AUNT.

Sometimes she comes to me in dreams. She never looks good. Sometimes she's wearing a dirty smock. Once she had on handcuffs. Once she was naked and dirty and this mean cat was clawing its way up her front. But every time it's the same thing.

"Some people get everything and I got nothing," she says. "Why? Why did that happen?"

Every time I say I don't know.

And I don't.

1998

CAITLÍN R. KIERNAN
(b. 1964)

The Long Hall on the Top Floor

THREE months now since Deacon Silvey pulled up stakes and left Atlanta, what passed for pulling up stakes, when all he had to begin with was a job in a laundromat in the afternoons and a job at a liquor store half the night, two shit jobs and three hundred and twelve dollars and seventy-five cents hidden in the toe of one of his boots. And man, some motherfucker's gonna walk in off the street one night, some dusthead with a .35, and blow your brains out for a few bills from the register, and then it's the goddamn *laundromat* that gets held up, instead. Three Hispanic kids with baseball bats and a crowbar, and he sat still and kept his mouth shut while they opened the coin boxes on every washer, every dryer, watched them fill a pillow case almost to bursting with the bright and dull quarters that spilled like noisy silver candy. And then the kids were gone, door cowbell ringing shut behind them, and Deke too goddamned astonished to do anything but sit and stare at the violated Maytags and Kenmores, at Herman and Lily Munster on the little black-and-white television behind the counter, the sound turned all the way down.

So a week later, fuck it, he was on the bus to Birmingham, everything he owned in one old blue suitcase and a cardboard box, Tanqueray box from behind the liquor store to hold his paperbacks and notebooks and all his ratty clothes stuffed into the suitcase. And some guy sitting next to him all the way, smoking Kools, black guy named Owen smoking Kools and watching the interstate night slip by outside, Georgia going to Alabama while he told Deacon Silvey about New Orleans, his brother's barber shop on Magazine Street where he was gonna work sweeping up hair and crap like that.

"Hell, man, it's worth a shit job to be down there," and Deacon thinking the man talked like he fell backwards off a Randy Newman song and landed on his head.

"How old you be, anyways?" and the man lit another Kool, menthol-smooth cloud from his lips, and he leaned across the aisle of the bus towards Deke. And "Thirty-two," Deacon answered. "Shit. Thirty-two? I'd give my left big toe to see thirty-two again. Thirty-two, the womens still give a damn, you know?" And the bus rolled on, and the man talked and smoked, until 3:45 A.M. when the Greyhound pulled up under the bug-specked yellow glare of the station, and Deacon got off in downtown Birmingham.

So now Deacon works at the Highland Wash'N'Fold every other night, and a warehouse in the mornings. He sleeps afternoons, and it's not much different from Atlanta, except mostly it's old drag queens and young slackers in the Wash'N'Fold and no laundromat pirates so far. His new apartment is a little bigger, two rooms and a bathroom, one corner for a kitchen, in a place that's built to look like a shoddy theme park excuse for a castle, Quinlan Castle in big letters out front and four turrets to prove it. But the rent's something he can afford, and the cockroaches stay off his bed if he sleeps with the light on, so it could be worse, has been worse lots of times.

And tonight's Friday, so no laundromat until tomorrow, and Deacon's sitting on a bench in a park down the hill from the castle, sipping a bottle of cheap gin, tightrope balancing act, staying drunk and making the quart last the night. August and here he is, sitting under the sodium-arc glare on the edge of a basketball court, not even midnight yet, just sipping at his gin and reading *The Martian Chronicles* by Ray Bradbury, "Mars is Heaven" and "Dark They Were and Golden-Eyed," and hoping he doesn't run out of gin before he runs out of night.

"Hey, man," and Deke looks up, green eyes tracking drunk-slow from the pages to Soda's face, hawk-nosed Soda and his twenty-something acne, battered skateboard tucked under one arm, and he never smiles because he's lost too many teeth up front. "What's kickin'," and he's already parking his skinny ass on the bench next to Deacon like he's been invited; Deke slips the McCall's into the crook of one arm, knows that Soda's already seen the bottle, but better late than never. "What do you want?" but Soda doesn't answer, stares down at the raggedy cuffs of his jeans, at the place where the grass turns to concrete, and Deacon's about to go back to his book when Soda says, "I heard you used to work for the cops, man. That true? You used to work for the cops, back in Atlanta?"

"Fuck off," Deke says, and he's wondering what it feels like to be hit in the head with a skateboard when Soda shrugs and says, "Look, I ain't tryin' to get in your shit, okay. It's just somethin' I heard."

"Then maybe you need to clean out your damn ears every now and then," Deke says and steals a sip from the bottle while Soda's still trying to figure out what he should say next.

"Yeah, well, that's what I heard, okay?"

"Soda, do I look like a goddamned cop to you?"

And Soda nervously rubs at a fat pimple on the end of his chin. "I didn't say you *were* a cop, asshole. I said, I heard you *worked* for them, that's all," and then the rest, out quick, like he's afraid he's about to lose his courage, so it's now or never. "I heard you could do that psychic shit, Deke. That they used to get you to find dead people by touching their clothes and find stolen cars and that sort of thing. I *wasn't* sayin' you were a cop."

Deke wants to hit him, wants to knock the bony little weasel down and kick his last few front teeth straight down his throat. Because this isn't Atlanta, and it's been four years since the last time he even talked to a cop. "Where the hell did you hear something like that, Soda? Who told you that?"

"Look, if I tell you . . . Jesus, man, that just don't matter, okay? I'm tellin' you I heard this 'cause I gotta *ask* you somethin'. I'm about to ask you a favor, and I don't need you freakin' out on me when I definitely did *not* say you were a cop, okay?" And now Deke's nodding his head, careful nod like a clock ticking, tocking, closing Ray Bradbury and his eyes fixed on Soda's chest, on his Beastie Boys T-shirt and a stain over one nipple that looks like strawberry jelly, but probably isn't.

"What, Soda? What do you want?"

"It ain't even *for* me, Deke. It's this chick I know, and she's kinda weird," and Soda draws little circles in the air, three quick orbits around his right ear. "But she's all right. And it ain't even really a favor, man, not exactly. Mostly we just need you to look at somethin' for us. *If* it's true, you workin' with the cops and all. You bein' psychic."

"How many *other* people have you told I was a 'psychic?'" and Deacon makes quotation marks with his fingers for emphasis.

"Nobody. Jesus, it ain't like I'm askin' you for money or dope or nothin'," and Deke snarls right back at him, "You don't have any idea *what* you're asking me, Soda. That's the problem." And Soda's mouth open, but Deke still talking or already talking again, not about to give him a chance.

"Whatever I did for the fucking cops, they *paid* me, Soda. Whatever I did, it wasn't for goddamn charity or out of the goodness of my heart."

And Soda makes an exasperated, whistling sound through the spaces where his missing front teeth should be, then shakes his head and risks half a disgusted glance at Deacon. "What happens to make someone such a bitter motherfucker at your age, Deke? Fuckin' wino. I oughta have my head examined for believin' you ever done anything but suck down juice and watch people doin' their laundry." For a minute neither of them says anything, then, and there's only the cars and the crickets and what sounds like someone banging on the lid of a garbage can a long way off. Until Deacon sighs, then takes a long pull from the bottle of gin and wipes his mouth on the back of his hand.

"Rule number one, Soda. If I do this, it's once and once only, and you're never going to ask me for anything like this ever again."

Soda shrugs, a shrug that'll have to pass for understanding, for agreement. "Yeah. So what's rule number two?" and Deke looks up at the sodium streetlight glare where the stars should be. "Rule number two, you tell anyone—no—if I find out you've *already* told anyone else about this, I'm going to find you, Soda, and stick the broken end of a Coke bottle so far up your ass your gums will bleed."
                                                                          •

Ask Deacon Silvey, it's a little bit more than an understatement to say that Sadie Jasper is weird. Three counties south of weird and straight on to creepy, more like it. She's standing on the corner by Martin Flowers, staring in at the darkened florist shop, real flowers and fake flowers and plaster angels behind the plate glass, and when she turns and looks at Deacon Silvey and Soda her expression makes Deke think of a George Romero zombie on a really bad batch of crank: that blank, that tight, and her eyes so pale blue under all the tear- and sleep-smeared eyeliner and mascara that they almost look white. Boiled-fish eyes squinting at him from that dead face.

"So, this is Deke," Soda says, and Sadie holds her hand out like she's a duchess on her throne and expects Deacon to bow and kiss her fucking pinkie. Soda's still talking.

"He's the guy I was tellin' you about, okay?"

Deacon shakes the girl's hand, and she almost manages to look disappointed.

"So you're the skull monkey," she says and smiles like it's something she's been practicing for days and still can't get quite right. "The psychic criminologist," she says, drawing the syllables out slow like refrigerated syrup, and tries to smile again.

"Not exactly," Deacon says, wanting to be back on his bench in the park, reading about Martians, enjoying the way the gin makes his ears buzz, or all the way back in his apartment; anything but standing on a street corner with Soda and this cadaver in her black polyester pants suit and too-red lips and Scooby Doo lunch-box purse.

"Yeah, well, Soda told me you used to be a cop, but they fired you for being an alcoholic," she says, and Deacon turns around and kicks Soda as hard as he can, the scuffed toe of his size-twelve Doc Marten connecting with Soda's shin like a leather sledge hammer. Soda screams like a girl and drops his skateboard. It rolls out into the street while Soda hops about on one foot, holding his kicked leg and cursing Deacon, *fuck you, you asshole, fuck both of you, you broke my goddamn leg,* and then a Budweiser delivery truck rumbles past and runs over his skateboard.

Deacon walks a hesitant few steps behind Sadie Jasper, all the way to the old Harris Transfer and Warehouse building over on Twenty-Second. Just the two of them now, because when Soda finally stopped hopping around and cursing and saw what the Budweiser truck had done to his skateboard—flat, cracked fiberglass, three translucent yellow rubber wheels squashed out around the edges like the legs of a dead cartoon bug that's just been smacked with a cartoon fly swatter, the fourth wheel rolling away down the street, spinning, a frantic blur escaping any further demolition—when he *saw* it, took it all in, Soda made a strangled sound and sat down on the curb. Wouldn't talk to either of them, or even go after what was left of his board, so they left him there, a pitiful lump of patched denim and scabs, and Deacon almost wished he hadn't kicked the son of a bitch, might actually have managed to feel sorry for him, if not for Sadie, the fact that somehow his unfortunate promise to look at whatever it was they were going to look at had not been broken along with Soda's skateboard.

"I *wasn't* a cop," Deke mutters, and Sadie stops walking and looks back at him, waiting for him to catch up, and she's still squinting as if even the piss-yellow street lights are too much for her smudgy, listless eyes.

"Okay. But the psychic part, he wasn't lying about that, was he?" she asks, and Deacon shrugs. Instead of answering her, he says, "I don't think Soda meant to lie about anything. I think he's just stupid." And she smiles then, smiles for real this time, instead of that forced and ugly expression from before, and it makes her look a little less like a zombie.

"You really don't like to talk about this, do you?" she asks, and Deke stops and stares up at the building, turn-of-the-century brick, rusted bars over broken windows and those jagged holes either swallowing the light or spitting it back out, because it's blacker in there than midnight in a coffin, black like the second before the universe was switched on, and Deke knows he needs another mouthful of gin before whatever's coming next.

"No," he tells her, unscrewing the cap on the bottle, "I don't." And Sadie nods while he tips the gin to his lips, while he closes his eyes and the alcohol burns its way into his belly and bloodstream and brain.

"It hurts, doesn't it?" she whispers, and *Maybe I'm going to need two mouthfuls for this,* Deke thinks, and so he takes another drink.

"I knew a girl, when I lived down in Mobile," Sadie says, almost whispering, confession murmur like Deke's some kind of priest and she's about to give up some terrible sin. "She was a clairvoyant, and it drove her crazy. She was always in and out of psych wards, you know. Finally, she overdosed on Valium. *Adiós muchachos.*"

"I'm not clairvoyant," Deacon says. "I get impressions, that's all. What I did for the cops, I helped them find lost things."

"Lost things," Sadie says, still talking like she's afraid someone will overhear. "Yeah, I guess that's a good word for it." Deke looks at her, then looks past her at the night-filled building. "A good word for what?" he asks.

"Oh, you'll see," she says, and this time when Sadie Jasper smiles it makes him think of a hungry animal, or the Grinch that stole Christmas.

They don't go in the door, of course, the locked and boarded door inside the marble arch, *Harris* chiseled deep into the pediment overhead. She leads him down the alley instead, to a place where someone's pried away the iron burglar bars and there are three or four wooden produce crates stacked under the window. Sadie scrambles up the makeshift steps and slips inside, slips smoothly over the shattered glass like a raw oyster over sharp teeth, like she's done this a hundred fucking times before, and for all he knows, she has; for all he knows, she's living in the damn warehouse. Deacon looks both ways twice, up and down the alley, before he follows her.

And however dark the place looked from the *outside*, it's at least twice that dark *inside*, and the broken glass under Deke's boots makes a sound like he's walking on breakfast cereal.

"Hold on a sec," Sadie says, and then there's light, a weak and narrow beam from a silver flashlight in her hand, and he has no idea where she got it, maybe from her purse, or maybe it was stashed somewhere in the gloom. White light across the concrete floor, chips and shards of window to diamond twinkle, a few scraps of cardboard and what looks like a filthy, raveling sweater lying in one corner; nothing else, just this wide and dust-drowned room, and Sadie motions towards a doorway with the beam of light.

"Stairs are over there," she says, and leads the way. Deacon stays close, spooked, feeling foolish, but not wanting to get too far away from the flashlight. The air in the warehouse smells like mildew and dust and cockroaches, a rank, closed away from the world odor that makes his nose itch and makes his eyes water a little.

"Oh, watch out for that spot there," Sadie says, and the beam swings suddenly to her left and down, and Deke sees the gaping hole in the floor, big enough to drop a truck through, that hole. Big enough and black enough that Deke thinks maybe that's where all the dark inside the building's coming from, spilling up from the basement or sub-basement, maybe. Then the flashlight sweeps right again, and he doesn't have to see the hole anymore. There's a flight of stairs, instead, stairs ascending into the nothing waiting past the flashlight's reach, more concrete and a crooked steel handrail Deacon wouldn't trust even for a minute.

"It's all the way at the top," Sadie says, and he notices that she isn't whispering anymore, that there's something excited in her voice now, and Deke can't tell if it's fear or anticipation.

"What's all the way at the top, Sadie? What's waiting for us up there?"

"It's easier if I just show you, if you see it for yourself without me trying to explain," and she starts up the stairs, two at a time, and taking the light away with her, leaving Deke alone next to the hole. So, he hurries to catch up, chasing the bobbing flashlight beam and silently cursing Soda, wishing he'd taken the bottle straight back to his apartment, instead of sitting down on that park bench to read. Up and up and up the stairwell, like Alice falling backwards, and nothing to mark their progress past each floor but a closed door or a place where a door should be, nothing to mark the time but the dull echo of their feet against the cement. She's always three or four steps ahead of him, and pretty soon, Deacon's out of breath, gasping the musty air, and he yells at her to slow the fuck down, what's the goddamn hurry.

"We're almost there," she calls back and keeps going.

And finally there are no more stairs left to climb, just a landing and a narrow window, and at least it's not so dark up here. Deke leans against the wall, wheezing, trying to get his breath, his sides hurting, legs aching; he stares out through flyblown glass at the streets and rooftops below, a couple of passing cars, and it all seems a thousand miles away, or like a projected film of the world, and if he broke this window there might be nothing on the other side at all.

"It's right over here," Sadie says, and the closeness of her voice does nothing about the hard, lonely feeling settling into Deacon Silvey. "This hallway here," she says, jabbing the flashlight at the darkness like a knife as he turns away from the window. "First time I saw it, I was tripping and didn't think it was real. But I started dreaming about it and had to come back to see. I had to know for sure."

Deacon steps slowly away from the window, three slow steps and he's standing beside Sadie. She smells like sweat and tearose perfume. Safe, familiar smells that make him feel no less alone, no less dread for whatever the fuck she's talking about.

"There," she says and switches off the flashlight. "All the way at the other end of the hall."

For a moment Deacon can't see anything at all, just a darting afterimage from the flashlight and nothing much else while his pupils swell, making room for light that isn't there.

"Do you feel it yet, Deacon?" she asks, whispering again, excited, and he's getting tired of this, starts to say so, starts to say he doesn't feel a goddamn thing, but will she please turn the flashlight back on. But then he *does* feel something, cold air flowing thick and heavy around them now, open-icebox air to fog their breath and send a painful rash of goose bumps across his arms. And it isn't *just* cold, it's indifference, the freezing temperature of an apathy so absolute, so perfect; Deacon takes a step backwards, one hand to his mouth, but it's too late, and the gin and his supper come up and splatter loudly on the floor at his feet.

"You okay?" she asks, and he opens his eyes, wants to slap her just for asking, but he nods his head, head filling with the cold and beginning to throb at the temples.

"Do you want me to help you up?" she asks, and he hadn't even realized he was on the floor, on his knees, but she's bending over him.

"Jesus," he croaks, throat raw, sore from bile and the frigid air. He blinks, tears in his eyes, and it's a miracle they haven't frozen, he thinks, pictures himself crying ice cubes like Chilly Willy. His stomach rolls again, and Deacon stares past the girl, down the hall, that long stretch of nothing at all but closed doors and a tiny window way down at the other end.

No, not nothing. Close, but not exactly nothing, and he's trying to make his eyes focus, trying to ignore the pain in his head getting bigger and bigger, threatening to shut him down. Sadie's pulling him to his feet, and Deke doesn't take his eyes off the window, the distant rectangle less inky than the hall only by stingy degrees.

"There," she says. "It's there."

And he knows this is only a dim shadow of the thing itself, this fluid stain rushing wild across the walls, washing water-color thin across the window; a shadow that could be the wings of a great bird, or long jointed legs moving fast through some deep and secret ocean. It's neither of those things, of course, no convenient, comprehensible nightmare, and he closes his eyes again. Sadie's holding his right hand, squeezing so hard it hurts.

"Don't look at it," he tells her, the floor beneath him getting soft now, and he's slipping, afraid the floor's about to tilt and send them both sliding helplessly past the closed doors, towards the window, towards *it*.

"Sadie, it doesn't want to be seen," he says, tasting blood, and so he knows that he's bitten his tongue or his lip. "It wasn't *meant* to be seen."

"But it's beautiful," Sadie says, and there's awe in her voice, and a sadness that hurts to hear.

Deacon Silvey gets a whiff of a new smell, then, burning leaves and something sweet and rotten, something dead left by the side of the highway, left beneath the summer sun, and the last thing, before he loses consciousness and slips mercifully from himself into a place where even the cold can't follow, the very last thing, a sound like crying that isn't crying and wind that isn't blowing through the long hall.

Twenty minutes later, and they're sitting together, each alone, but one beside the other, on the curb outside the Harris Transfer and Warehouse building. Deacon's too sober, but still too sick to finish the gin, and Sadie sits quietly, waiting to see how this story ends. A police car cruises by, slows down and the cop gives them the hairy eyeball, and for a second Deacon thinks maybe someone saw them climbing in or out of the window. But the cop keeps going, better trouble somewhere else tonight.

"Shit. I thought sure he was going to stop," Sadie says, trying to sound relieved.

"Why the fuck did you guys want me to see that?" Deke asks, making no attempt to hide the anger swirling around inside his throbbing head, yellow hornets stinging the backs of his eyes. "Did you even *have* a reason, Sadie?"

She kicks at the gravel and bits of trash in the gutter, but doesn't look at him, drawing a circle with the toe of one black tennis shoe.

"I guess I wanted to know it was real," she replies, a faint defiant edge in her voice, defiance or defense but nothing like repentance, nothing like sorry. "That's all. I figured you'd know, if it was. Real."

"And Soda, he never went up there with you, did he?"

Sadie shakes her head and barks out a dry little excuse for a laugh. "Are you kidding? Soda gets scared walking past funeral parlors."

"Yeah," Deacon says, wishing he had a cigarette, wishing he'd kicked Soda a little harder. Sadie Jasper sighs loudly, and the rubber toe of her left shoe sends a spray of gravel onto the blacktop, little shower of limestone nuggets and sand and an old spark plug that clatters all the way to the broken yellow center line.

"I know that you're sitting there thinking I'm a bitch," she says and kicks more grit after the spark plug. "Just some spooky bitch that's come along to fuck with your head, right?" Deacon doesn't deny it, and, anyway, she keeps talking.

"But Christ, Deacon. Don't you get sick of it? Day after motherfucking day, sunrise, sunset, getting drunk on that stuff so you don't have to think about how getting drunk is the only thing that makes your shabby excuse for a life bearable? Meanwhile, the whole shitty world's getting a little shittier, a little more hollow every goddamn day. And then, something like *that* comes along," and she turns and points towards the top floor of the warehouse. "Something that means *something*, you know? And maybe it's something horrible, so horrible you won't be able to sleep for a week, but at least when you're afraid you know you're fucking alive."

Deacon's looking at her now, and her white-blue eyes glimmer wetly, close to tears, her crimson lips trembling and pressed together tight like a red-ink slash to underline everything that she's just said. No way he can tell her she's full of shit, because he knows better, has lived too long in the empty husk of his routine not to know better. But there's no way he can ever admit it, either. So he just stares at her until she blinks first, one tear past the eyeliner smear and down her cheek, and then she looks away.

"Jesus, you're an asshole," she says.

"Yeah, well, maybe you wouldn't say that if you got to know me better," and he stands up, keeping the building and its ragged phantoms at his back. "Look. Just promise me you'll stay away from this place, okay? Will you please promise me that, Sadie?"

She nods, and he guesses that's all he's going to get for a promise, more than he expected. And then he leaves her sitting there by herself and walks away through the warm night, through the air that stinks of car exhaust and cooling asphalt, and Deacon Silvey tries not to notice his long shadow, trailing along behind.

1999

THOMAS TESSIER
(b. 1947)

Nocturne

In the calm of his middle years, O'Netty made it a point to go for a walk at night at least once a week. Thursday or Friday was best, as there were other people out doing things and the city was livelier, which pleased him. Saturdays were usually too busy and noisy for his liking, and the other nights a little too quiet —though there were also times when he preferred the quiet and relative solitude.

He enjoyed the air, the exercise, and the changing sights of the city. He enjoyed finishing his stroll at a familiar tavern and sometimes seeing people he knew slightly in the neighborhood. But he also enjoyed visiting a tavern that was new to him, and observing the scene. O'Netty was by no means a heavy drinker. Two or three beers would do, then it was back to his apartment and sleep.

O'Netty went out early one particular evening in September and found the air so pleasant and refreshing that he walked farther than usual. A windy rainstorm had blown through the city that afternoon. The black streets still glistened and wet leaves were scattered everywhere like pictures torn from a magazine. Purple and grey clouds continued to sail low across the darkening sky. Eventually he came to the crest of a hill above the center of the city.

He decided it was time to have a drink before undertaking the long trek back. He saw the neon light of a bar a short distance ahead and started toward it, but then stopped and looked again at a place he had nearly passed. The Europa Lounge was easy to miss. It had no frontage, just a narrow door lodged between a camera shop and a pizzeria. The gold script letters painted on the glass entrance were scratched and chipped with age. But the door opened when O'Netty tried it, and he stepped inside. There was a small landing and a flight of stairs—apparently the bar was in the basement. He didn't hesitate. If it turned out to be something not for him, he could simply turn around and leave, but he wanted at least to see the place.

The stairs were narrow and steep. The one flight turned into two, and then a third. O'Netty might have given up before descending the last steps, but by then he saw the polished floor below and he heard the mixed murmur of voices and music. The bottom landing was a small foyer. There was one door marked as an exit, two others designated as rest rooms, and then the entrance to the lounge itself. O'Netty stepped inside and looked around.

The lounge could not have been more than fifteen feet by ten, with a beamed ceiling. But there was nothing dank or dingy about the place. On the contrary, at first glance it appeared to be rather well done up. It had a soft wheat carpet and golden cedar walls. There were three small banquettes to one side, and a short bar opposite with three upholstered stools, two of which were occupied by men a few years younger than O'Netty. Along the back wall there were two small round wooden tables, each with two chairs. Table lamps with ivory shades cast a creamy glow that gave the whole room a warm, intimate feeling.

There were middle-aged couples in the back two banquettes but the nearest one was empty, and O'Netty took it. The bartender was an older man with gleaming silver hair, dressed in a white shirt, dark blue suit and tie. He smiled politely, nodded and when he spoke it was with a slight, unrecognizable accent. O'Netty's beer was served in a very tall pilsener glass.

The music playing on the sound system was some mix of jazz and blues with a lot of solo guitar meditations. It was unfamiliar to O'Netty but he found it soothing, almost consoling in some way. He sipped his drink. This place was definitely unlike the average neighborhood tavern, but it wasn't at all uncomfortable. In fact, O'Netty thought it seemed rather pleasant.

After a few minutes, he realized that the other people there were speaking in a foreign language. He only caught brief snatches of words, but he heard enough to know that he had no idea what language it was. Which was no great surprise. After all, there were so many European languages one almost never heard—for instance: Czech, Hungarian, Rumanian, Bulgarian and Finnish. O'Netty concluded that he had come across a bar, a social club run by and for locals of some such eastern European origin. Before he left, perhaps he would ask the bartender about it.

Although he couldn't understand anything the others said, O'Netty had no trouble catching their mood. Their voices were relaxed, lively, friendly, chatty, and occasionally there was some laughter. It was possible for O'Netty to close his eyes and imagine that he was sitting on the terrace of a cafe in some exotic and distant city, a stranger among the locals. He liked that thought.

Some little while later, when O'Netty was about halfway through his second glass of beer, he noticed that the others had either fallen silent or were speaking very softly. He sensed an air of anticipation in the room.

A few moments later, a young man emerged from the door behind the bar. The music stopped and everyone was still and quiet. The young man came around to the front of the bar. He could not yet be thirty, O'Netty thought. The young man swiftly pulled off his T-shirt and tossed it aside. He was slender, with not much hair on his chest. He kicked off his sandals and removed his gym pants, so that he now stood there dressed only in a pair of black briefs. The other two men at the bar had moved the stools aside to create more space.

The young man reached into a bag he had brought with him and began to unfold a large sheet of dark green plastic, which he carefully spread out on the floor. He stood on it, positioning himself in the center of the square. Then he took a case out of the bag, opened it and grasped a knife. The blade was about eight inches long and very slightly curved. The young man's expression was serious and purposeful, but otherwise revealed nothing.

What now, O'Netty wondered.

Let's see.

The young man hooked the tip of the blade in his chest, just below the sternum, pushed it in farther, and then carefully tugged it down through his navel, all the way to the elastic top of his briefs. He winced and sagged with the effort, and he used his free hand to hold the wound partly closed. Next, he jabbed the knife into his abdomen, just above the left hip, and pulled it straight across to his right side. He groaned and dropped the knife. Now he was hunched over, struggling to hold himself up, and he could not contain the double wound. His organs bulged out in his arms—liver, stomach, the long rope of intestines, all of them dry and leathery. There was no blood at all, but rather a huge and startling cascade of dark red sand that made a clatter of noise as it spilled across the plastic sheet. The young man was very wobbly now, and the other two at the bar stepped forward to take him by the arms and lower him gently to the ground. The young man's eyes blinked several times, and then stayed shut. The other two carefully wrapped his body in the plastic sheet and secured it with some tape they got from the bag. Finally, they lifted the body and carried it into the room behind the bar. They returned a few moments later and took their seats again. Conversations resumed, slowly at first, but then became quick and more animated with half-suppressed urgency.

After a while O'Netty finished his beer and got up to leave. No one paid any attention to him except the bartender, who came to the end of the bar for O'Netty's payment and then brought him his change.

"By the way, sir, in case you don't know. You can use the fire exit. There's no need to climb all those stairs."

"Ah, thank you," O'Netty replied. "It *is* a lot of stairs."

"Good night, sir."

"Good night."

The fire exit opened onto a long metal staircase that brought him to a short lane that led to a side street just off one of the main avenues in the center of the city. It was already daylight, the air crisp and fresh, the early morning sun exploding on the upper floors of the taller buildings. O'Netty stood there for a few moments, trying to regain his bearings and decide what to do.

Then he saw a city bus coming his way, and he realized it was the one that went to his neighborhood. It must be the first bus of the day, O'Netty thought, as he stepped to the curb and raised his hand.

2000

MICHAEL CHABON
(b. 1963)

The God of Dark Laughter

THIRTEEN days after the Entwhistle-Ealing Bros. Circus left
Ashtown, beating a long retreat toward its winter headquarters
in Peru, Indiana, two boys out hunting squirrels in the woods
along Portwine Road stumbled on a body that was dressed in
a mad suit of purple and orange velour. They found it at the
end of a muddy strip of gravel that began, five miles to the
west, as Yuggogheny County Road 22A. Another half mile farther to the east and it would have been left to my colleagues
over in Fayette County to puzzle out the question of who had
shot the man and skinned his head from chin to crown and
clavicle to clavicle, taking ears, eyelids, lips, and scalp in a single grisly flap, like the cupped husk of a peeled orange. My
name is Edward D. Satterlee, and for the last twelve years I
have faithfully served Yuggogheny County as its district attorney, in cases that have all too often run to the outrageous and
bizarre. I make the following report in no confidence that it,
or I, will be believed, and beg the reader to consider this, at
least in part, my letter of resignation.

The boys who found the body were themselves fresh from
several hours' worth of bloody amusement with long knives
and dead squirrels, and at first the investigating officers took
them for the perpetrators of the crime. There was blood on the
boys' cuffs, their shirttails, and the bills of their gray twill caps.
But the county detectives and I quickly moved beyond Joey
Matuszak and Frankie Corro. For all their familiarity with gris-
tle and sinew and the bright-purple discovered interior of a
body, the boys had come into the station looking pale and bewildered, and we found ample evidence at the crime scene of
their having lost the contents of their stomachs when confronted with the corpse.

Now, I have every intention of setting down the facts of this
case as I understand and experienced them, without fear of the

463

reader's doubting them (or my own sanity), but I see no point in mentioning any further *anatomical* details of the crime, except to say that our coroner, Dr. Sauer, though he labored at the problem with a sad fervor, was hard put to establish conclusively that the victim had been dead before his killer went to work on him with a very long, very sharp knife.

The dead man, as I have already mentioned, was attired in a curious suit—the trousers and jacket of threadbare purple velour, the waistcoat bright orange, the whole thing patched with outsized squares of fabric cut from a variety of loudly clashing plaids. It was on account of the patches, along with the victim's cracked and split-soled shoes and a certain undeniable shabbiness in the stuff of the suit, that the primary detective —a man not apt to see deeper than the outermost wrapper of the world (we do not attract, I must confess, the finest police talent in this doleful little corner of western Pennsylvania)— had already figured the victim for a vagrant, albeit one with extraordinarily big feet.

"Those cannot possibly be his real shoes, Ganz, you idiot," I gently suggested. The call, patched through to my boarding house from that gruesome clearing in the woods, had interrupted my supper, which by a grim coincidence had been a Brunswick stew (the specialty of my Virginia-born landlady) of pork and *squirrel*. "They're supposed to make you laugh."

"They *are* pretty funny," said Ganz. "Come to think of it." Detective John Ganz was a large-boned fellow, upholstered in a layer of ruddy flesh. He breathed through his mouth, and walked with a tall man's defeated stoop, and five times a day he took out his comb and ritually plastered his thinning blond hair to the top of his head with a dime-size dab of Tres Flores.

When I arrived at the clearing, having abandoned my solitary dinner, I found the corpse lying just as the young hunters had come upon it, supine, arms thrown up and to either side of the flayed face in a startled attitude that fuelled the hopes of poor Dr. Sauer that the victim's death by gunshot had preceded his mutilation. Ganz or one of the other investigators had kindly thrown a chamois cloth over the vandalized head. I took enough of a peek beneath it to provide me with everything that I or the reader could possibly need to know about the condition of the head—I will never forget the sight of that monstrous, fleshless grin—and to remark the dead man's un-usual choice of cravat. It was a giant, floppy bow tie, white with orange and purple polka dots.

"Damn you, Ganz," I said, though I was not in truth ad-dressing the poor fellow, who, I knew, would not be able to answer my question anytime soon. "What's a dead clown doing in my woods?"

We found no wallet on the corpse, nor any kind of identifying objects. My men, along with the better part of the Ashtown Police Department, went over and over the woods east of town, hourly widening the radius of their search. That day, when not attending to my other duties (I was then in the process of breaking up the Dushnyk cigarette-smuggling ring), I man-aged to work my way back along a chain of inferences to the Entwhistle-Ealing Bros. Circus, which, as I eventually recalled, had recently stayed on the eastern outskirts of Ashtown, at the fringe of the woods where the body was found.

The following day, I succeeded in reaching the circus's gen-eral manager, a man named Onheuser, at their winter head-quarters in Peru. He informed me over the phone that the company had left Pennsylvania and was now en route to Peru, and I asked him if he had received any reports from the road manager of a clown's having suddenly gone missing.

"Missing?" he said. I wished that I could see his face, for I thought I heard the flatted note of something false in his tone. Perhaps he was merely nervous about talking to a county dis-trict attorney. The Entwhistle-Ealing Bros. Circus was a mangy affair, by all accounts, and probably no stranger to pursuit by officers of the court. "Why, I don't believe so, no."

I explained to him that a man who gave every indication of having once been a circus clown had turned up dead in a pine-wood outside Ashtown, Pennsylvania.

"Oh, no," Onheuser said. "I truly hope he wasn't one of mine, Mr. Satterlee."

"Is it possible you might have left one of your clowns behind, Mr. Onheuser?"

"Clowns are special people," Onheuser replied, sounding a touch on the defensive. "They love their work, but sometimes it can get to be a little, well, too much for them." It developed that Mr. Onheuser had, in his younger days, performed as a clown, under the name of Mr. Wingo, in the circus of which he was now the general manager. "It's not unusual for a clown to drop out for a little while, cool his heels, you know, in some town where he can get a few months of well-earned rest. It isn't *common*, I wouldn't say, but it's not unusual. I will wire my road manager—they're in Canton, Ohio—and see what I can find out."

I gathered, reading between the lines, that clowns were high-strung types, and not above going off on the occasional bender. This poor fellow had probably jumped ship here two weeks ago, holing up somewhere with a case of rye, only to run afoul of a very nasty person, possibly one who harbored no great love of clowns. In fact, I had an odd feeling, nothing more than a hunch, really, that the ordinary citizens of Ashtown and its environs were safe, even though the killer was still at large. Once more, I picked up a slip of paper that I had tucked into my desk blotter that morning. It was something that Dr. Sauer had clipped from his files and passed along to me. *Coulrophobia: morbid, irrational fear of or aversion to clowns.*

"Er, listen, Mr. Satterlee," Onheuser went on. "I hope you won't mind my asking. That is, I hope it's not a, well, a confidential police matter, or something of the sort. But I know that when I do get through to them, out in Canton, they're going to want to know."

I guessed, somehow, what he was about to ask me. I could hear the prickling fear behind his curiosity, the note of dread in his voice. I waited him out.

"Did they—was there any—how did he die?"

"He was shot," I said, for the moment supplying only the least interesting part of the answer, tugging on that loose thread of fear. "In the head."

"And there was . . . forgive me. No . . . no harm done? To the body? Other than the gunshot wound, I mean to say."

"Well, yes, his head was rather savagely mutilated," I said brightly. "Is that what you mean to say?"

"Ah! No, no, I don't—"

"The killer or killers removed all the skin from the cranium. It was very skillfully done. Now, suppose you tell me what you know about it."

There was another pause, and a stream of agitated electrons burbled along between us.

"I don't know anything, Mr. District Attorney. I'm sorry. I really must go now. I'll wire you when I have some—"

The line went dead. He was so keen to hang up on me that he could not even wait to finish his sentence. I got up and went to the shelf where, in recent months, I had taken to keeping a bottle of whiskey tucked behind my bust of Daniel Webster. Carrying the bottle and a dusty glass back to my desk, I sat down and tried to reconcile myself to the thought that I was confronted—not, alas, for the first time in my tenure as chief law-enforcement officer of Yuggogheny County—with a crime whose explanation was going to involve not the usual amalgam of stupidity, meanness, and singularly poor judgment but the incalculable intentions of a being who was genuinely evil. What disheartened me was not that I viewed a crime committed out of the promptings of an evil nature as inherently less liable to solution than the misdeeds of the foolish, the unlucky, or the habitually cruel. On the contrary, evil often expresses itself through refreshingly discernible patterns, through schedules and syllogisms. But the presence of evil, once scented, tends to bring out all that is most irrational and uncontrollable in the public imagination. It is a catalyst for pea-brained theories, gimcrack scholarship, and the credulous cosmologies of hysteria.

At that moment, there was a knock on the door to my office, and Detective Ganz came in. At one time I would have tried to hide the glass of whiskey, behind the typewriter or the photo of my wife and son, but now it did not seem to be worth the effort. I was not fooling anyone. Ganz took note of the glass in my hand with a raised eyebrow and a schoolmarmish pursing of his lips.

"Well?" I said. There had been a brief period, following my son's death and the subsequent suicide of my dear wife, Mary, when I had indulged the pitying regard of my staff. I now found that I regretted having shown such weakness. "What is it, then? Has something turned up?"

"A cave," Ganz said. "The poor bastard was living in a cave."

*

The range of low hills and hollows separating lower Yug-gogheny from Fayette County is rotten with caves. For many years, when I was a boy, a man named Colonel Earnshawe operated penny tours of the iridescent organ pipes and jagged stone teeth of Neighborsburg Caverns, before they collapsed in the mysterious earthquake of 1919, killing the Colonel and his sister Irene, and putting to rest many strange rumors about that eccentric old pair. My childhood friends and I, ranging in the woods, would from time to time come upon the root-choked mouth of a cave exhaling its cool plutonic breath, and dare one another to leave the sunshine and enter that world of shadow—that entrance, as it always seemed to me, to the legendary past itself, where the bones of Indians and Frenchmen might lie moldering. It was in one of these anterooms of buried history that the beam of a flashlight, wielded by a deputy sheriff from Plunkettsburg, had struck the silvery lip of a can of pork and beans. Calling to his companions, the deputy plunged through a curtain of spiderweb and found himself in the parlor, bedroom, and kitchen of the dead man. There were some cans of chili and hash, a Primus stove, a lantern, a bed-roll, a mess kit, and an old Colt revolver, Army issue, loaded and apparently not fired for some time. And there were also books—a Scout guide to roughing it, a collected Blake, and a couple of odd texts, elderly and tattered: one in German called "Über das Finstere Lachen," by a man named Friedrich von Junzt, which appeared to be religious or philosophical in nature, and one a small volume bound in black leather and printed in no alphabet known to me, the letters sinuous and furred with wild diacritical marks.

"Pretty heavy reading for a clown," Ganz said.

"It's not all rubber chickens and hosing each other down with seltzer bottles, Jack."

"Oh, no?"

"No, sir. Clowns have unsuspected depths."

"I'm starting to get that impression, sir."

Propped against the straightest wall of the cave, just beside the lantern, there was a large mirror, still bearing the bent clasps and sheared bolt that had once, I inferred, held it to the wall of a filling-station men's room. At its foot was the item that had earlier confirmed to Detective Ganz—and now confirmed to

me as I went to inspect it—the recent habitation of the cave by
a painted circus clown: a large, padlocked wooden makeup kit,
of heavy and rather elaborate construction. I directed Ganz
to send for a Pittsburgh criminalist who had served us with
discretion in the horrific Primm case, reminding him that
nothing must be touched until this Mr. Espy and his black bag
of dusts and luminous powders arrived.

The air in the cave had a sharp, briny tinge; beneath it there
was a stale animal musk that reminded me, absurdly, of the
smell inside a circus tent.

"Why was he living in a cave?" I said to Ganz. "We have a
perfectly nice hotel in town."

"Maybe he was broke."

"Or maybe he thought that a hotel was the first place they
would look for him."

Ganz looked confused, and a little annoyed, as if he thought
I were being deliberately mysterious.

"*Who* was looking for him?"

"I don't know, Detective. Maybe no one. I'm just thinking
out loud."

Impatience marred Ganz's fair, bland features. He could tell
that I was in the grip of a hunch, and hunches were always
among the first considerations ruled out by the procedural
practices of Detective John Ganz. My hunches had, admittedly, an uneven record. In the Primm business, one had very
nearly got both Ganz and me killed. As for the wayward hunch
about my mother's old crony Thaddeus Craven and the
strength of his will to quit drinking—I suppose I shall regret
indulging that one for the rest of my life.

"If you'll excuse me, Jack . . ." I said. "I'm having a bit of
a hard time with the stench in here."

"I was thinking he might have been keeping a pig." Ganz
inclined his head to one side and gave an empirical sniff. "It
smells like pig to me."

I covered my mouth and hurried outside into the cool, dank
pinewood. I gathered in great lungfuls of air. The nausea passed,
and I filled my pipe, walking up and down outside the mouth
of the cave and trying to connect this new discovery to my talk
with the circus man, Onheuser. Clearly, he had suspected that
this clown might have met with a grisly end. Not only that, he

had known that his fellow circus people would fear the very same thing—as if there were some coulrophohic madman with a knife who was as much a part of circus lore as the prohibition on whistling in the dressing room or on looking over your shoulder when you marched in the circus parade.

I got my pipe lit, and wandered down into the woods, toward the clearing where the boys had stumbled over the dead man, following a rough trail that the police had found. Really, it was not a trail so much as an impromptu alley of broken saplings and trampled ground that wound a convoluted course down the hill from the cave to the clearing. It appeared to have been blazed a few days before by the victim and his pursuer; near the bottom, where the trees gave way to open sky, there were grooves of plowed earth that corresponded neatly with encrustations on the heels of the clown's giant brogues. The killer must have caught the clown at the edge of the clearing, and then dragged him along by the hair, or by the collar of his shirt, for the last twenty-five yards, leaving this furrowed record of the panicked, slipping flight of the clown. The presumed killer's footprints were everywhere in evidence, and appeared to have been made by a pair of long and pointed boots. But the really puzzling thing was a third set of prints, which Ganz had noticed and mentioned to me, scattered here and there along the cold black mud of the path. They seemed to have been made by a barefoot child of eight or nine years. And damned, as Ganz had concluded his report to me, if that barefoot child did not appear to have been dancing!

I came into the clearing, a little short of breath, and stood listening to the wind in the pines and the distant rumble of the state highway, until my pipe went out. It was a cool afternoon, but the sky had been blue all day and the woods were peaceful and fragrant. Nevertheless, I was conscious of a mounting sense of disquiet as I stood over the bed of sodden leaves where the body had been found. I did not then, nor do I now, believe in ghosts, but as the sun dipped down behind the tops of the trees, lengthening the long shadows encompassing me, I became aware of an irresistible feeling that somebody was watching me. After a moment, the feeling intensified, and localized, as it were, so I was certain that to see who it was I need only turn around. Bravely—meaning not that I am a brave

man but that I behaved as if I were—I took my matches from
my jacket pocket and relit my pipe. Then I turned. I knew that
when I glanced behind me I would not see Jack Ganz or one
of the other policemen standing there; any of them would
have said something to me by now. No, it was either going to
be nothing at all or something that I could not even allow myself to imagine.

It was, in fact, a baboon, crouching on its hind legs in the
middle of the trail, regarding me with close-set orange eyes,
one hand cupped at its side. It had great puffed whiskers and a
long canine snout. There was something in the barrel chest and
the muttonchop sideburns that led me to conclude, correctly,
as it turned out, that the specimen was male. For all his majestic bulk, the old fellow presented a rather sad spectacle. His fur
was matted and caked with mud, and a sticky coating of pine
needles clung to his feet. The expression in his eyes was unset-
tlingly forlorn, almost pleading, I would have said, and in his
mute gaze I imagined I detected a hint of outraged dignity.
This might, of course, have been due to the hat he was wearing.
It was conical, particolored with orange and purple lozenges,
and ornamented at the tip with a bright-orange pompom.
Tied under his chin with a length of black ribbon, it hung
from the side of his head at a humorous angle. I myself
might have been tempted to kill the man who had tied it to
my head.

"Was it you?" I said, thinking of Poe's story of the rampaging
orang swinging a razor in a Parisian apartment. Had that story
had any basis in fact? Could the dead clown have been killed
by the pet or sidekick with whom, as the mystery of the animal
smell in the cave now resolved itself, he had shared his fugitive
existence?

The baboon declined to answer my question. After a moment,
though, he raised his long crooked left arm and gestured vaguely
toward his belly. The import of this message was unmistakable,
and thus I had the answer to my question—if he could not
open a can of franks and beans, he would not have been able
to perform that awful surgery on his owner or partner.

"All right, old boy," I said. "Let's get you something to eat."
I took a step toward him, watching for signs that he might bolt
or, worse, throw himself at me. But he sat, looking miserable,

clenching something in his right paw. I crossed the distance
between us. His rancid-hair smell was unbearable. "You need a
bath, don't you?" I spoke, by reflex, as if I were talking to
somebody's tired old dog. "Were you and your friend in the
habit of bathing together? Were you there when it happened,
old boy? Any idea who did it?"

The animal gazed up at me, its eyes kindled with that luminous and sagacious sorrow that lends to the faces of apes and
mandrills an air of cousinly reproach, as if we humans have betrayed the principles of our kind. Tentatively, I reached out to
him with one hand. He grasped my fingers in his dry leather
paw, and then the next instant he had leapt bodily into my
arms, like a child seeking solace. The garbage-and-skunk stench
of him burned my nose. I gagged and stumbled backward as
the baboon scrambled to wrap his arms and legs around me. I
must have cried out; a moment later a unit of iron lids seemed
to slam against my skull, and the animal went slack, sliding,
with a horrible, human sigh of disappointment, to the ground
at my feet.

Ganz and two Ashtown policemen came running over and
dragged the dead baboon away from me.

"He wasn't—he was just—" I was too outraged to form a
coherent expression of my anger. "You could have hit *me*!"

Ganz closed the animal's eyes, and laid its arms out at its
sides. The right paw was still clenched in a shaggy fist. Ganz,
not without some difficulty, managed to pry it open. He uttered an printable oath.

In the baboon's palm lay a human finger. Ganz and I looked
at each other, wordlessly confirming that the dead clown had
been in possession of a full complement of digits.

"See that Espy gets that finger," I said. "Maybe we can find
out whose it was."

"It's a woman's," Ganz said. "Look at that nail."

I took it from him, holding it by the chewed and bloody end
so as not to dislodge any evidence that might be trapped under
the long nail. Though rigid, it was strangely warm, perhaps from
having spent a few days in the vengeful grip of the animal who
had claimed it from his master's murderer. It appeared to be
an index finger, with a manicured, pointed nail nearly three-
quarters of an inch long. I shook my head.

"It isn't painted," I said. "Not even varnished. How many women wear their nails like that?"

"Maybe the paint rubbed off," one of the policemen suggested.

"Maybe," I said. I knelt on the ground beside the body of the baboon. There was, I noted, a wound on the back of his neck, long and deep and crusted over with dirt and dried blood. I now saw him in my mind's eye, dancing like a barefoot child around the murderer and the victim as they struggled down the path to the clearing. It would take a powerful man to fight such an animal off. "I can't believe you killed our only witness, Detective Ganz. The poor bastard was just giving me a hug."

This information seemed to amuse Ganz nearly as much as it puzzled him.

"He was a monkey, sir," Ganz said. "I doubt he—"

"He could make signs, you fool! He told me he was *hungry*."

Ganz blinked, trying, I supposed, to append to his personal operations manual this evidence of the potential usefulness of circus apes to police inquiries.

"If I had a dozen baboons like that one on my staff," I said, "I would never have to leave the office."

That evening, before going home, I stopped by the evidence room in the High Street annex and signed out the two books that had been found in the cave that morning. As I walked back into the corridor, I thought I detected an odd odor— odd, at any rate, for that dull expanse of linoleum and buzzing fluorescent tubes—of the sea: a sharp, salty, briny smell. I decided that it must be some new disinfectant being used by the custodian, but it reminded me of the smell of blood from the specimen bags and sealed containers in the evidence room. I turned the lock on the room's door and slipped the books, in their waxy protective envelopes, into my briefcase, and walked down High Street to Dennistoun Road, where the public library was. It stayed open late on Wednesday nights, and I would need a German-English dictionary if my college German and I were going to get anywhere with Herr von Junzt.

The librarian, Lucy Brand, returned my greeting with the circumspect air of one who hopes to be rewarded for her forbearance with a wealth of juicy tidbits. Word of the murder,

denuded of most of the relevant details, had made the Ashtown *Ambler* yesterday morning, and though I had cautioned
the unlucky young squirrel hunters against talking about the
case, already conjectures, misprisions, and outright lies had
begun wildly to coalesce; I knew the temper of my home town
well enough to realize that if I did not close this case soon
things might get out of hand. Ashtown, as the events surrounding the appearance of the so-called Green Man, in 1932,
amply demonstrated, has a lamentable tendency toward municipal panic.

Having secured a copy of Köhler's Dictionary of the English
and German Languages, I went, on an impulse, to the card
catalogue and looked up von Junzt, Friedrich. There was no
card for any work by this author—hardly surprising, perhaps, in
a small-town library like ours. I returned to the reference shelf,
and consulted an encyclopedia of philosophical biography and
comparable volumes of philologic reference, but found no
entry for any von Junzt—a diplomate, by the testimony of his
title page, of the University of Tübingen and of the Sorbonne.
It seemed that von Junzt had been dismissed, or expunged,
from the dusty memory of his discipline.

It was as I was closing the Encyclopedia of Archaeo-Anthro-
pological Research that a name suddenly leapt out at me,
catching my eye just before the pages slammed together. It
was a word that I had noticed in von Junzt's book: "Urartu."
I barely managed to slip the edge of my thumb into the encyclopedia to mark the place; half a second later and the reference might have been lost to me. As it turned out, the name
of von Junzt itself was also contained—sealed up—in the sar-
cophagus of this entry, a long and tedious one devoted to the
work of an Oxford man by the name of St. Dennis T. R. Glad-
fellow, "a noted scholar," as the entry had it, "in the field of
inquiry into the beliefs of the ancient, largely unknown
peoples referred to conjecturally today as proto-Urartians."
The reference lay buried in a column dense with comparisons
among various bits of obsidian and broken bronze:

> G.'s analysis of the meaning of such ceremonial blades admittedly
> was aided by the earlier discoveries of Friedrich von Junzt, at the site
> of the former Temple of Yrrh, in north central Armenia, among them

certain sacrificial artifacts pertaining to the worship of the proto-Urartian deity Yê-Heh, rather grandly (though regrettably without credible evidence) styled "the god of dark or mocking laughter" by the German, a notorious adventurer and fake whose work, nevertheless, in this instance, has managed to prove useful to science.

The prospect of spending the evening in the company of Herr von Junzt began to seem even less appealing. One of the most tedious human beings I have ever known was my own mother, who, early in my childhood, fell under the spell of Madame Blavatsky and her followers and proceeded to weary my youth and deplete my patrimony with her devotion to that indigestible caseation of balderdash and lies. Mother drew a number of local simpletons into her orbit, among them poor old drunken Thaddeus Craven, and burnt them up as thoroughly as the earth's atmosphere consumes asteroids. The most satisfying episodes of my career have been those which afforded me the opportunity to prosecute charlatans and frauds and those who preyed on the credulous; I did not now relish the thought of sitting at home with such a man all evening, in particular one who spoke only German.

Nevertheless, I could not ignore the undeniable novelty of a murdered circus clown who was familiar with scholarship—however spurious or misguided concerning the religious beliefs of proto-Urartians. I carried the Köhler's over to the counter, where Lucy Brand waited eagerly for me to spill some small ration of beans. When I offered nothing for her delectation, she finally spoke.

"Was he a German?" she said, showing unaccustomed boldness, it seemed to me.

"Was *who* a German, my dear Miss Brand?"

"The victim." She lowered her voice to a textbook librarian's whisper, though there was no one in the building but old Bob Spherakis, asleep and snoring in the periodicals room a copy of *Grit*.

"I—I don't know," I said, taken aback by the simplicity of her inference, or rather by its having escaped me. "I suppose he may have been, yes."

She slid the book across the counter toward me.

"There was another one of them in here this afternoon," she said. "At least, I think he was a German. A Jew, come to think of it. Somehow he managed to find the only book in Hebrew we have in our collection. It's one of the books old Mr. Vorzeichen donated when he died. A prayer book, I think it is. Tiny little thing. Black leather."

This information ought to have struck a chord in my memory, of course, but it did not. I settled my hat on my head, bid Miss Brand good night, and walked slowly home, with the dictionary under my arm, and, in my briefcase, von Junzt's stout tome and the little black-leather volume filled with sinuous mysterious script.

I will not tax the reader with an account of my struggles with Köhler's dictionary and the thorny bramble of von Junzt's overheated German prose. Suffice to say that it took me the better part of the evening to make my way through the introduction. It was well past midnight by the time I arrived at the first chapter, and nearing two o'clock before I had amassed the information that I will now pass along to the reader, with no endorsement beyond the testimony of these pages, nor any hope of its being believed.

It was a blustery night; I sat in the study on the top floor of my old house's round tower, listening to the windows rattle in their casements, as if a gang of intruders were seeking a way in. In this high room, in 1885, it was said, Howard Ash, the last living descendant of our town's founder, General Hannaniah Ash, had sealed the blank note of his life and dispatched himself, with postage due, to his Creator. A fugitive draft blew from time to time across my desk and stirred the pages of the dictionary by my left hand. I felt, as I read, as if the whole world were asleep—benighted, ignorant, and dreaming—while I had been left to man the crow's nest, standing lonely vigil in the teeth of a storm that was blowing in from a tropic of dread.

According to the scholar or charlatan Friedrich von Junzt, the regions around what is now northern Armenia had spawned, along with an entire cosmology, two competing cults of incalculable antiquity, which survived to the present day: that of Yê-Heh, the God of Dark Laughter, and that of Ai, the God of Unbearable and Ubiquitous Sorrow. The Yê-Hehists viewed the universe as a cosmic hoax, perpetrated by the father-god Yrrh for unknowable purposes: a place of calamity and cruel irony so overwhelming that the only possible response was a malevolent laughter like that, presumably, of Yrrh himself. The laughing followers of baboon-headed Yê-Heh created a sacred burlesque, mentioned by Pausanias and by one of the travellers in Plutarch's dialogue "On the Passing of the Oracles," to express their mockery of life, death, and all human aspirations. The rite involved the flaying of a human head, severed from the shoulders of one who had died in battle or in the course of some other supposedly exalted endeavor. The clown-priest would don the bloodless mask and then dance, making a public travesty of the noble dead. Through generations of inbreeding, the worshippers of Yê-Heh had evolved into a virtual subspecies of humanity, characterized by distended grins and skin as white as chalk. Von Junzt even claimed that the tradition of painted circus clowns derived from the clumsy imitation, by noninitiates, of these ancient kooks.

The "immemorial foes" of the baboon boys, as the reader may have surmised, were the followers of Ai, the God Who Mourns. These gloomy fanatics saw the world as no less horrifying and cruel than did their archenemies, but their response to the whole mess was a more or less permanent wailing. Over the long millennia since the heyday of ancient Urartu, the Aiites had developed a complicated physical discipline, a sort of jujitsu or calisthenics of murder, which they chiefly employed in a ruthless hunt of followers of Yê-Heh. For they believed that Yrrh, the Absent One, the Silent Devisor who, an eternity ago, tossed the cosmos over his shoulder like a sheet of fish wrap and wandered away leaving not a clue as to his intentions, would not return to explain the meaning of his inexplicable and tragic creation until the progeny of Yê-Heh, along with all copies of the Yê-Hehist sacred book, "Khndzut Dzul," or "The Unfathomable Ruse," had been expunged from the face of the earth. Only then would Yrrh return from his primeval hiatus—"bringing what new horror or redemption," as the German intoned, "none can say."

All this struck me as a gamier variety of the same loony, Zoroastrian plonk that my mother had spent her life decanting,

and I might have been inclined to set the whole business aside
and leave the case to be swept under the administrative rug by
Jack Ganz had it not been for the words with which Herr von
Junzt concluded the second chapter of his tedious work:

While the Yê-Hehist gospel of cynicism and ridicule has, quite obviously, spread around the world, the cult itself has largely died out, in
part through the predations of foes and in part through chronic
health problems brought about by inbreeding. Today [von Junzt's
book carried a date of 1849] it is reported that there may be fewer
than 150 of the Yê-Hehists left in the world. They have survived, for
the most part, by taking on work in travelling circuses. While their existence is known to ordinary members of the circus world, their
secret has, by and large, been kept. And in the sideshows they have
gone to ground, awaiting the tread outside the wagon, shadow on
the tent-flap, the cruel knife that will, in a mockery of their own long-
abandoned ritual of mockery, deprive them of the lily-white flesh of
their skulls.

Here I put down the book, my hands trembling from fatigue, and took up the other one, printed in an unknown
tongue. "The Unfathomable Ruse"? I hardly thought so; I was
inclined to give as little credit as I reasonably could to Herr
von Junzt's account. More than likely the small black volume
was some inspirational text in the mother tongue of the dead
man, a translation of the Gospels, perhaps. And yet I must
confess that there were a few tangential points in von Junzt's
account that caused me some misgiving.

There was a scrape then just outside my window, as if a finger with a very long nail were being drawn almost lovingly
along the glass. But the finger turned out to be one of the
branches of a fine old horse-chestnut tree that stood outside
the tower, scratching at the window in the wind. I was relieved
and humiliated. Time to go to bed, I said to myself. Before I
turned in, I went to the shelf and moved to one side the bust
of Galen that I had inherited from my father, a country doctor.
I took a quick snort of old Tennessee whiskey, a taste for which
I had also inherited from the old man. Thus emboldened, I
went over to the desk and picked up the books. To be frank,
I would have preferred to leave them there—I would have

preferred to burn them, to be really frank—but I felt that it was my duty to keep them about me while they were under my watch. So I slept with the books beneath my pillow, in their wax envelopes, and I had the worst dream of my life.

It was one of those dreams where you are a fly on the wall, a phantom bystander, disembodied, unable to speak or intervene. In it, I was treated to the spectacle of a man whose young son was going to die. The man lived in a corner of the world where, from time to time, evil seemed to bubble up from the rusty red earth like a black combustible compound of ancient things long dead. And yet, year after year, this man met each new outburst of horror, true to his code, with nothing but law books, statutes, and county ordinances, as if sheltering with only a sheet of newspaper those he had sworn to protect, insisting that the steaming black geyser pouring down on them was nothing but a light spring rain. That vision started me laughing, but the cream of the jest came when, seized by a spasm of forgiveness toward his late, mad mother, the man decided not to prosecute one of her old paramours, a rummy by the name of Craven, for driving under the influence. Shortly thereafter, Craven steered his old Hudson Terraplane the wrong way down a one-way street, where it encountered, with appropriate cartoon sound effects, an oncoming bicycle ridden by the man's heedless, darling, wildly pedalling son. That was the funniest thing of all, funnier than the amusing ironies of the man's profession, than his furtive drinking and his wordless, solitary suppers, funnier even than his having been widowed by suicide: the joke of a father's outliving his boy. It was so funny that, watching this ridiculous man in my dream, I could not catch my breath for laughing. I laughed so hard that my eyes popped from their sockets, and my smile stretched until it broke my aching jaw. I laughed until the husk of my head burst like a pod and fell away, and my skull and brains went floating off into the sky, white dandelion fluff, a cloud of fairy parasols.

Around four o'clock in the morning, I woke and was conscious of someone in the room with me. There was an unmistakable tang of the sea in the air. My eyesight is poor and it took me a while to make him out in the darkness, though he was standing just beside my bed, with his long thin arm snaked under my pillow, creeping around. I lay perfectly still, aware of the tips of this slender shadow's fingernails and the scrape of his scaly knuckles, as he rifled the contents of my head and absconded with them through the bedroom window which was somehow also the mouth of the Neighborsburg Caverns, with tiny old Colonel Earnshaw taking tickets in the booth.

I awakened now in truth, and reached immediately under the pillow. The books were still there. I returned them to the evidence room at eight o'clock this morning. At nine, there was a call from Dolores and Victor Abbott, at their motor lodge out on the Plunkettsburg Pike. A guest had made an abrupt departure, leaving a mess. I got into a car with Ganz and we drove out to get a look. The Ashtown police were already there, going over the buildings and grounds of the Vista Dolores Lodge. The bathroom wastebasket of Room 201 was overflowing with blood-soaked bandages. There was evidence that the guest had been keeping some kind of live bird in the room; one of the neighboring guests reported that it had sounded like a crow. And over the whole room there hung a salt smell that I recognized immediately, a smell that some compared to the smell of the ocean, and others to that of blood. When the pillow, wringing wet, was sent up to Pittsburgh for analysis by Mr. Espy, it was found to have been saturated with human tears.

When I returned from court, late this afternoon, there was a message from Dr. Sauer. He had completed his postmortem and wondered if I would drop by. I took the bottle from behind Daniel Webster and headed on down to the county morgue.

"He was already dead, the poor son of a biscuit eater," Dr. Sauer said, looking less morose than he had the last time we spoke. Sauer was a gaunt old Methodist who avoided strong language but never, so long as I had known him, strong drink. I poured us each a tumbler, and then a second. "It took me a while to establish it because there was something about the fellow that I was missing."

"What was that?"

"Well, I'm reasonably sure that he was a hemophiliac. So my reckoning time of death by coagulation of the blood was all thrown off."

"Hemophilia," I said.

"Yes," Dr. Sauer said. "It is associated sometimes with in-breeding, as in the case of royal families of Europe."

Inbreeding. We stood there for a while, looking at the sad bulk of the dead man under the sheet.

"I also found a tattoo," Dr. Sauer added. "The head of a grinning baboon. On his left forearm. Oh, and one other thing. He suffered from some kind of vitiligo. There are white patches on his nape and throat."

Let the record show that the contents of the victim's makeup kit, when it was inventoried, included cold cream, rouge, red greasepaint, a powder puff, some brushes, cotton swabs, and five cans of foundation in a tint the label described as "Olive Male." There was no trace, however, of the white greasepaint with which clowns daub their grinning faces.

Here I conclude my report, and with it my tenure as district attorney for this blighted and unfortunate county. I have staked my career—my life itself—on the things I could see, on the stories I could credit, and on the eventual vindication, when the book was closed, of the reasonable and skeptical approach. In the face of twenty-five years of bloodshed, mayhem, criminality, and the universal human pastime of ruination, I have clung fiercely to Occam's razor, seeking always to keep my solutions unadorned and free of conjecture, and never to resort to conspiracy or any kind of prosecutorial woolgathering. My mother, whenever she was confronted by calamity or personal sorrow, invoked cosmic emanations, invisible empires, ancient prophecies, and intrigues; it has been the business of my life to reject such folderol and seek the simpler explanation. But we were fools, she and I, arrant blockheads, each of us blind to or heedless of the readiest explanation: that the world is an ungettable joke, and our human need to explain its wonders and horrors, our appalling genius for devising such explanations, is nothing more than the rim shot that accompanies the punch line.

I do not know if that nameless clown was the last, but in any case, with such pursuers, there can be few of his kind left. And if there is any truth in the grim doctrine of those hunters, then the return of our father Yrrh, with his inscrutable inventions, cannot be far off. But I fear that, in spite of their efforts over the last ten thousand years, the followers of Ai are going to be gravely disappointed when, at the end of all we know and everything we have ever lost or imagined, the rafters of the world are shaken by a single, a terrible guffaw.

2001

JOE HILL

(b. 1972)

Pop Art

My best friend when I was twelve was inflatable. His name was Arthur Roth, which also made him an inflatable Hebrew, although in our now-and-then talks about the afterlife, I don't remember that he took an especially Jewish perspective. Talk was mostly what we did—in his condition rough-house was out of the question—and the subject of death, and what might follow it, came up more than once. I think Arthur knew he would be lucky to survive high school. When I met him, he had already almost been killed a dozen times, once for every year he had been alive. The afterlife was always on his mind; also the possible lack of one.

When I tell you we talked, I mean only to say we communicated, argued, put each other down, built each other up. To stick to facts, *I* talked—Art couldn't. He didn't have a mouth. When he had something to say, he wrote it down. He wore a pad around his neck on a loop of twine, and carried crayons in his pocket. He turned in school papers in crayon, took tests in crayon. You can imagine the dangers a sharpened pencil would present to a four-ounce boy made of plastic and filled with air.

I think one of the reasons we were best friends was because he was such a great listener. I needed someone to listen. My mother was gone and my father I couldn't talk to. My mother ran away when I was three, sent my Dad a rambling and confused letter from Florida, about sunspots and gamma rays and the radiation that emanates from power lines, about how the birthmark on the back of her left hand had moved up her arm and onto her shoulder. After that, a couple postcards, then nothing.

As for my father, he suffered from migraines. In the afternoons, he sat in front of soaps in the darkened living room, wet-eyed and miserable. He hated to be bothered. You couldn't tell him anything. It was a mistake even to try.

"Blah blah," he would say, cutting me off in mid-sentence. "My head is splitting. You're killing me here with blah blah this, blah blah that."

But Art liked to listen, and in trade, I offered him protection. Kids were scared of me. I had a bad reputation. I owned a switchblade, and sometimes I brought it to school and let other kids see; it kept them in fear. The only thing I ever stuck it into, though, was the wall of my bedroom. I'd lie on my bed and flip it at the corkboard wall, so that it hit, blade-first, *thunk!*

One day when Art was visiting he saw the pockmarks in my wall. I explained, one thing led to another, and before I knew it he was begging to have a throw.

"What's wrong with you?" I asked him. "Is your head completely empty? Forget it. No way."

Out came a Crayola, burnt-sienna. He wrote:

> So at least let me look.

I popped it open for him. He stared at it wide-eyed. Actually, he stared at everything wide-eyed. His eyes were made of glassy plastic, stuck to the surface of his face. He couldn't blink or anything. But this was different than his usual bug-eyed stare. I could see he was really fixated.

He wrote:

> I'll be careful I totally promise *please!*

I handed it to him. He pushed the point of the blade into the floor so it snicked into the handle. Then he hit the button and it snicked back out. He shuddered, stared at it in his hand. Then, without giving any warning, he chucked it at the wall. Of course it didn't hit tip-first; that takes practice, which he hadn't had, and coordination, which, speaking honestly, he wasn't ever going to have. It bounced, came flying back at him. He sprang into the air so quickly it was like I was watching his ghost jump out of his body. The knife landed where he had been and clattered away under my bed.

I yanked Art down off the ceiling. He wrote:

> You were right, that was dumb. I'm a loser—a jerk.

"No question," I said.

But he wasn't a loser or a jerk. My Dad is a loser. The kids at school were jerks. Art was different. He was all heart. He just wanted to be liked by someone.

Also, I can say truthfully, he was the most completely harmless person I've ever known. Not only would he not hurt a fly, he *couldn't* hurt a fly. If he slapped one, and lifted his hand, it would buzz off undisturbed. He was like a holy person in a Bible story, someone who can heal the ripped and infected parts of you with a laying-on of hands. You know how Bible stories go. That kind of person, they're never around long. Losers and jerks put nails in them and watch the air run out.

There was something special about Art, an invisible special something that just made other kids naturally want to kick his ass. He was new at our school. His parents had just moved to town. They were normal, filled with blood not air. The condition Art suffered from is one of these genetic things that plays hopscotch with the generations, like Tay-Sachs (Art told me once that he had had a grand-uncle, also inflatable, who flopped one day into a pile of leaves and burst on the tine of a buried rake). On the first day of classes, Mrs. Gannon made Art stand at the front of the room, and told everyone all about him, while he hung his head out of shyness.

He was white. Not Caucasian, *white*, like a marshmallow, or Casper. A seam ran around his head and down his sides. There was a plastic nipple under one arm, where he could be pumped with air.

Mrs. Gannon told us we had to be extra careful not to run with scissors or pens. A puncture would probably kill him. He couldn't talk; everyone had to try and be sensitive about that. His interests were astronauts, photography, and the novels of Bernard Malamud.

Before she nudged him towards his seat, she gave his shoulder an encouraging little squeeze and as she pressed her fingers into him, he whistled gently. That was the only way he ever made sound. By flexing his body he could emit little squeaks and whines. When other people squeezed him, he made a soft, musical hoot.

He bobbed down the room and took an empty seat beside me. Billy Spears, who sat directly behind him, bounced thumbtacks off his head all morning long. The first couple times Art pretended not to notice. Then, when Mrs. Gannon wasn't looking, he wrote Billy a note. It said:

> *Please stop!* I don't want to say anything to Mrs. Gannon but it isn't safe to throw thumbtacks at me. I'm *not* kidding.

Billy wrote back:

> You make trouble, and there won't be enough of you left to patch a tire. Think about it.

It didn't get any easier for Art from there. In biology lab, Art was paired with Cassius Delamitri, who was in sixth grade for the second time. Cassius was a fat kid, with a pudgy, sulky face, and a disagreeable film of black hair above his unhappy pucker of a mouth.

The project was to distill wood, which involved the use of a gas flame—Cassius did the work, while Art watched and wrote notes of encouragement:

> I can't believe you got a D– on this experiment when you did it last year—you totally know how to do this stuff!!

and

> my parents bought me a lab kit for my birthday. You could come over and we could play mad scientist sometime want to?

After three or four notes like that, Cassius had read enough, got it in his head Art was some kind of homosexual . . . especially with Art's talk about having him over to play doctor or whatever. When the teacher was distracted helping some other kids, Cassius shoved Art under the table and tied him around one of the table legs, in a squeaky granny knot, head, arms, body and all. When Mr. Milton asked where Art had gone, Cassius said he thought he had run to the bathroom.

"Did he?" Mr. Milton asked. "What a relief. I didn't even know if that kid *could* go to the bathroom."

Another time, John Erikson held Art down during recess

and wrote KOLLOSTIMY BAG on his stomach with indelible
marker. It was Spring before it faded away.

> The worst thing was my mom saw. Bad enough she
> has to know I get beat up on a daily basis. But she was
> really upset it was spelled wrong.

He added:

> I don't know what she expects—this is 6th grade.
> Doesn't she remember 6th grade? I'm sorry, but
> realistically, what are the odds you're going to get
> beat up by the grand champion of the spelling bee?

"The way your year is going," I said, "I figure them odds
might be pretty good."

Here is how Art and I wound up friends:

During recess periods, I always hung out at the top of the
monkey bars by myself, reading sports magazines. I was cultivating my reputation as a delinquent and possible drug pusher.
To help my image along, I wore a black denim jacket and didn't
talk to people or make friends.

At the top of the monkey bars—a dome-shaped construction at one edge of the asphalt lot behind the school—I was a
good nine feet off the ground, and had a view of the whole
yard. One day I watched Billy Spears horsing around with Cassius Delamitri and John Erikson. Billy had a wiffle ball and a
bat, and the three of them were trying to bat the ball in
through an open second floor window. After fifteen minutes of
not even coming close, John Erikson got lucky, swatted it in.

Cassius said, "Shit—there goes the ball. We need something
else to bat around."

"Hey," Billy shouted. "Look! There's Art!"

They caught up to Art, who was trying to keep away, and
Billy started tossing him in the air and hitting him with the bat
to see how far he could knock him. Every time he struck Art
with the bat it made a hollow, springy *whap!* Art popped into
the air, then floated along a little ways, sinking gently back to
ground. As soon as his heels touched earth he started to run,
but swiftness of foot wasn't one of Art's qualities. John and

Cassius got into the fun by grabbing Art and drop-kicking him, to see who could punt him highest.

The three of them gradually pummeled Art down to my end of the lot. He struggled free long enough to run in under the monkey bars. Billy caught up, struck him a whap across the ass with the bat, and shot him high into the air.

Art floated to the top of the dome. When his body touched the steel bars, he stuck, face-up—static electricity.

"Hey," Billy hollered. "Chuck him down here!"

I had, up until that moment, never been face to face with Art. Although we shared classes, and even sat side-by-side in Mrs. Gannon's homeroom, we had not had a single exchange. He looked at me with his enormous plastic eyes and sad blank face, and I looked right back. He found the pad around his neck, scribbled a note in spring green, ripped it off and held it up at me.

> I don't care what they do, but could you go away? I
> hate to get the crap knocked out of me in front of
> spectators.

"What's he writin'?" Billy shouted.

I looked from the note, past Art, and down at the gathering of boys below. I was struck by the sudden realization that I could *smell* them, all three of them, a damp, *human* smell, a sweaty-sour reek. It turned my stomach.

"Why are you bothering him?" I asked.

Billy said, "Just screwin' with him."

"We're trying to see how high we can make him go," Cassius said. "You ought to come down here. You ought to give it a try. We're going to kick him onto the roof of the friggin' school!"

"I got an even funner idea," I said, *funner* being an excellent word to use if you want to impress on some other kids that you might be a mentally retarded psychopath. "How about we see if I can kick your lardy ass up on the roof of the school?"

"What's your problem?" Billy asked. "You on the rag?"

I grabbed Art and jumped down. Cassius blanched. John Erikson tottered back. I held Art under one arm, feet sticking towards them, head pointed away.

"You guys are dicks," I said—some moments just aren't right for a funny line.

And I turned away from them. The back of my neck crawled at the thought of Billy's wiffle ball bat clubbing me one across the skull, but he didn't do a thing, let me walk.

We went out on the baseball field, sat on the pitcher's mound. Art wrote me a note that said thanks, and another that said I didn't have to do what I had done but that he was glad I had done it, and another that said he owed me one. I shoved each note into my pocket after reading it, didn't think why. That night, alone in my bedroom, I dug a wad of crushed note-paper out of my pocket, a lump the size of a lemon, peeled each note free and pressed it flat on my bed, read them all over again. There was no good reason not to throw them away, but I didn't, started a collection instead. It was like some part of me knew, even then, I might want to have something to re-member Art by after he was gone. I saved hundreds of his notes over the next year, some as short as a couple words, a few six-page long manifestos. I have most of them still, from the first note he handed me, the one that begins *I don't care what they do*, to the last, the one that ends:

I want to see if it's true. If the sky opens up at the top.

At first my father didn't like Art, but after he got to know him better he really hated him.

"How come he's always mincing around?" my father asked. "Is he a fairy or something?"

"No, Dad. He's inflatable."

"Well he acts like a fairy," he said. "You better not be queering around with him up in your room."

Art tried to be liked—he tried to build a relationship with my father. But the things he did were misinterpreted; the state-ments he made were misunderstood. My Dad said something once about a movie he liked. Art wrote him a message about how the book was even better.

"He thinks I'm an illiterate," my Dad said, as soon as Art was gone.

Another time, Art noticed the pile of worn tires heaped up

behind our garage, and mentioned to my Dad about a recycling program at Sears, bring in your rotten old ones, get twenty percent off on brand-new Goodyears.

"He thinks we're trailer trash," my Dad complained, before Art was hardly out of earshot. "Little snotnose."

One day Art and I got home from school, and found my father in front of the TV, with a pit bull at his feet. The bull erupted off the floor, yapping hysterically, and jumped up on Art. His paws made a slippery zipping sound sliding over Art's plastic chest. Art grabbed one of my shoulders and vaulted into the air. He could really jump when he had to. He grabbed the ceiling fan—turned off—and held on to one of the blades while the pit bull barked and hopped beneath.

"What the hell is that?" I asked.

"Family dog," my father said. "Just like you always wanted."

"Not one that wants to eat my friends."

"Get off the fan, Artie. That isn't built for you to hang off it."

"This isn't a dog," I said. "It's a blender with teeth."

"Listen, do you want to name it, or should I?" Dad asked.

Art and I hid in my bedroom and talked names.

"Snowflake," I said. "Sugarpie. Sunshine."

> How about Happy? That has a ring to it, doesn't it?

We were kidding, but Happy was no joke. In just a week, Art had at least three life-threatening encounters with my father's ugly dog.

> If he gets his teeth in me, I'm done for. He'll punch me full of holes.

But Happy couldn't be housebroken, left turds scattered around the living room, hard to see in the moss brown rug. My Dad squelched through some fresh leavings once, in bare feet, and it sent him a little out of his head. He chased Happy all through the downstairs with a croquet mallet, smashed a hole in the wall, crushed some plates on the kitchen counter with a wild backswing.

The very next day, he built a chain-link pen in the sideyard. Happy went in, and that was where he stayed.

By then, though, Art was nervous to come over, and preferred to meet at his house. I didn't see the sense. It was a long walk to get to his place after school, and my house was right there, just around the corner.

"What are you worried about?" I asked him. "He's in a pen. It's not like Happy is going to figure out how to open the door to his pen, you know."

Art knew . . . but he still didn't like to come over, and when he did, he usually had a couple patches for bicycle tires on him, to guard against dark happenstance.

Once we started going to Art's every day, once it came to be a habit, I wondered why I had ever wanted us to go to my house instead. I got used to the walk—I walked the walk so many times I stopped noticing that it was long bordering on never-ending. I even looked forward to it, my afternoon stroll through coiled suburban streets, past houses done in Disney pastels: lemon, tangerine, ash. As I crossed the distance between my house and Art's house, it seemed to me that I was moving through zones of ever-deepening stillness and order, and at the walnut heart of all this peace was Art's.

Art couldn't run, talk or approach anything with a sharp edge on it, but at his house we managed to keep ourselves entertained. We watched TV. I wasn't like other kids, and didn't know anything about television. My father, I mentioned already, suffered from terrible migraines. He was home on disability, lived in the family room, and hogged our TV all day long, kept track of five different soaps. I tried not to bother him, and rarely sat down to watch with him—I sensed my presence was a distraction to him at a time when he wanted to concentrate.

Art would have watched whatever I wanted to watch, but I didn't know what to do with a remote control. I couldn't make a choice, didn't know how. Had lost the habit. Art was a NASA buff, and we watched anything to do with space, never missed a space shuttle launch. He wrote:

> I want to be an astronaut. I'd adapt really well to
> being weightless. I'm *already* mostly weightless.

This was when they were putting up the international space station. They talked about how hard it was on people to spend too long in outer space. Your muscles atrophy. Your heart shrinks three sizes.

> The advantages of sending me into space keep piling
> up. I don't have any muscles to atrophy. I don't have
> any heart to shrink. I'm telling you. I'm the ideal
> spaceman. I *belong* in orbit.

"I know a guy who can help you get there. Let me give Billy
Spears a call. He's got a rocket he wants to stick up your ass. I
heard him talking about it."

Art gave me a dour look, and a scribbled two word response.

Lying around Art's house in front of the tube wasn't always
an option, though. His father was a piano instructor, tutored
small children on the baby grand, which was in the living room
along with their television. If he had a lesson, we had to find
something else to do. We'd go into Art's room to play with his
computer, but after twenty minutes of *row-row-row-your-boat*
coming through the wall—a shrill, out-of-time plinking—we'd
shoot each other sudden wild looks, and leave by way of the
window, no need to talk it over.

Both Art's parents were musical, his mother a cellist. They
had wanted music for Art, but it had been let-down and disappointment from the start.

> I can't even kazoo

Art wrote me once. The piano was out. Art didn't have any
fingers, just a thumb, and a puffy pad where his fingers belonged. Hands like that, it had been years of work with a tutor
just to learn to write legibly with a crayon. For obvious reasons, wind instruments were also out of the question; Art
didn't have lungs, and didn't breathe. He tried to learn the
drums, but couldn't strike hard enough to be any good at it.

His mother bought him a digital camera. "Make music with
color," she said. "Make melodies out of light."

Mrs. Roth was always hitting you with lines like that. She
talked about oneness, about the natural decency of trees, and she
said not enough people were thankful for the smell of cut grass.
Art told me when I wasn't around, she asked questions about
me. She was worried I didn't have a healthy outlet for my creative self. She said I needed something to feed the inner me. She
bought me a book about origami and it wasn't even my birthday.

"I didn't know the inner me was hungry," I said to Art.

> That's because it already starved to death

Art wrote.

She was alarmed to learn that I didn't have any sort of religion. My father didn't take me to church or send me to Sunday school. He said religion was a scam. Mrs. Roth was too polite to say anything to me about my father, but she said things about him to Art, and Art passed her comments on. She told Art that if my father neglected the care of my body, like he neglected the care of my spirit, he'd be in jail, and I'd be in a foster home. She also told Art that if I was put in foster care, she'd adopt me, and I could stay in the guest room. I loved her, felt my heart surge whenever she asked me if I wanted a glass of lemonade. I would have done anything she asked.

"Your Mom's an idiot," I said to Art. "A total moron. I hope you know that. There isn't any oneness. It's every man for himself. Anyone who thinks we're all brothers in the spirit winds up sitting under Cassius Delamitri's fat ass during recess, smelling his jock."

Mrs. Roth wanted to take me to the synagogue—not to convert me, just as an educational experience, exposure to other cultures and all that—but Art's father shot her down, said not a chance, not our business, and what are you crazy? She had a bumper sticker on her car that showed the Star of David and the word PRIDE with a jumping exclamation point next to it.

"So Art," I said another time. "I got a Jewish question I want to ask you. Now you and your family, you're a bunch of hardcore Jews, right?"

> I don't know that I'd describe us as *hardcore* exactly. We're actually pretty lax. But we go to synagogue, observe the holidays—things like that.

"I thought Jews had to get their joints snipped," I said, and grabbed my crotch. "For the faith. Tell me—"
But Art was already writing.

> No not me. I got off. My parents were friends with a progressive Rabbi. They talked to him about it first thing after I was born. Just to find out what the official position was.

"What'd he say?"

> He said it was the official position to make an
> exception for anyone who would actually explode
> during the circumcision. They thought he was joking,
> but later on my Mom did some research on it. Based
> on what she found out, it looks like I'm in the clear,
> Talmudically-speaking. Mom says the foreskin has
> to be *skin*. If it isn't, it doesn't need to be cut.

"That's funny," I said. "I always thought your Mom didn't
know dick. Now it turns out your Mom *does* know dick. She's
an expert even. Shows what I know. Hey, if she ever wants to do
more research, I have an unusual specimen for her to examine."
And Art wrote how she would need to bring a microscope,
and I said how she would need to stand back a few yards when
I unzipped my pants, and back and forth, you don't need me
to tell you, you can imagine the rest of the conversation for
yourself. I rode Art about his mother every chance I could get,
couldn't help myself. Started in on her the moment she left
the room, whispering about how for an old broad she still had
an okay can, and what would Art think if his father died and I
married her. Art on the other hand, never once made a punch
line out of my Dad. If Art ever wanted to give me a hard time,
he'd make fun of how I licked my fingers after I ate, or how I
didn't always wear matching socks. It isn't hard to understand
why Art never stuck it to me about my father, like I stuck it to
him about his mother. When your best friend is ugly—I mean
bad ugly, *deformed*—you don't kid them about shattering
mirrors. In a friendship, especially in a friendship between two
young boys, you are allowed to inflict a certain amount of
pain. This is even expected. But you must cause no serious injury; you must never, under any circumstances, leave wounds
that will result in permanent scars.

Arthur's house was also where we usually settled to do our
homework. In the early evening, we went into his room to
study. His father was done with lessons by then, so there wasn't
any plink-plink from the next room to distract us. I enjoyed
studying in Art's room, responded well to the quiet, and liked

working in a place where I was surrounded by books; Art had shelves and shelves of books. I liked our study time together, but mistrusted it as well. It was during our study sessions—surrounded by all that easy stillness—that Art was most likely to say something about dying.

When we talked, I always tried to control the conversation, but Art was slippery, could work death into anything.

"Some Arab *invented* the idea of the number zero," I said. "Isn't that weird? Someone had to think zero up."

> Because it isn't obvious—that nothing can be something. That something which can't be measured or seen could still exist and have meaning. Same with the soul, when you think about it.

"True or false," I said another time, when we were studying for a science quiz. "Energy is never destroyed, it can only be changed from one form into another."

> I hope it's true—it would be a good argument that you continue to exist after you die, even if you're transformed into something completely different than what you had been.

He said a lot to me about death and what might follow it, but the thing I remember best was what he had to say about Mars. We were doing a presentation together, and Art had picked Mars as our subject, especially whether or not men would ever go there and try to colonize it. Art was all for colonizing Mars, cities under plastic tents, mining water from the icy poles. Art wanted to go himself.

"It's fun to imagine, maybe, fun to think about it," I said. "But the actual thing would be bullshit. Dust. Freezing cold. Everything red. You'd go blind looking at so much red. You wouldn't really want to do it—leave this world and never come back."

Art stared at me for a long moment, then bowed his head, and wrote a brief note in robin's egg blue.

> But I'm going to have to do that anyway. Everyone has to do that.

Then he wrote:

> You get an astronaut's life whether you want it or not.
> Leave it all behind for a world you know nothing
> about. That's just the deal.

In the Spring, Art invented a game called Spy Satellite. There
was a place downtown, the Party Station, where you could buy
a bushel of helium-filled balloons for a quarter. I'd get a bunch,
meet Art somewhere with them. He'd have his digital camera.

Soon as I handed him the balloons, he detached from the
earth and lifted into the air. As he rose, the wind pushed him
out and away. When he was satisfied he was high enough, he'd
let go a couple balloons, level off, and start snapping pictures.
When he was ready to come down, he'd just let go a few more.
I'd meet him where he landed and we'd go over to his house
to look at the pictures on his laptop. Photos of people swimming in their pools, men shingling their roofs; photos of me
standing in empty streets, my upturned face a miniature brown
blob, my features too distant to make out; photos that always
had Art's sneakers dangling into the frame at the bottom edge.

Some of his best pictures were low altitude affairs, things he
snapped when he was only a few yards off the ground. Once
he took three balloons and swam into the air over Happy's
chain-link enclosure, off at the side of our house. Happy spent
all day in his fenced-off pen, barking frantically at women
going by with strollers, the jingle of the ice cream truck, squirrels. Happy had trampled all the space in his penned-in plot of
earth down to mud. Scattered about him were dozens of dried
piles of dogcrap. In the middle of this awful brown turdscape
was Happy himself, and in every photo Art snapped of him, he
was leaping up on his back legs, mouth open to show the pink
cavity within, eyes fixed on Art's dangling sneakers.

> I feel bad. What a horrible place to live.

"Get your head out of your ass," I said. "If creatures like
Happy were allowed to run wild, they'd make the whole world
look that way. He doesn't want to live somewhere else. Turds
and mud—that's Happy's idea of a total garden spot."

> I *STRONGLY* disagree

Arthur wrote me, but time has not softened my opinions on this matter. It is my belief that, as a rule, creatures of Happy's ilk—I am thinking here of canines and men both—more often run free than live caged, and it is in fact a world of mud and feces they desire, a world with no Art in it, or anyone like him, a place where there is no talk of books or God or the worlds beyond this world, a place where the only communication is the hysterical barking of starving and hate-filled dogs.

One Saturday morning, mid-April, my Dad pushed the bedroom door open, and woke me up by throwing my sneakers on my bed. "You have to be at the dentist's in half an hour. Put your rear in gear."

I walked—it was only a few blocks—and I had been sitting in the waiting room for twenty minutes, dazed with boredom, when I remembered I had told Art that I'd be coming by his house as soon as I got up. The receptionist let me use the phone to call him.

His mom answered. "He just left to see if he could find you at your house," she told me.

I called my Dad.

"He hasn't been by," he said. "I haven't seen him."

"Keep an eye out."

"Yeah well. I've got a headache. Art knows how to use the doorbell."

I sat in the dentist's chair, my mouth stretched open and tasting of blood and mint, and struggled with unease and an impatience to be going. Did not perhaps trust my father to be decent to Art without myself present. The dentist's assistant kept touching my shoulder and telling me to relax.

When I was all through and got outside, the deep and vivid blueness of the sky was a little disorientating. The sunshine was headache-bright, bothered my eyes. I had been up for two hours, but still felt cotton-headed and dull-edged, not all the way awake. I jogged.

The first thing I saw, standing on the sidewalk, was Happy, free from his pen. He didn't so much as bark at me. He was on his belly in the grass, head between his paws. He lifted sleepy eyelids to watch me approach, then let them sag shut again. His pen door stood open in the side yard.

I was looking to see if he was lying on a heap of tattered plastic when I heard the first feeble tapping sound. I turned my head and saw Art in the back of my father's station wagon, smacking his hands on the window. I walked over and opened the door. At that instant, Happy exploded from the grass with a peal of mindless barking. I grabbed Art in both arms, spun and fled. Happy's teeth closed on a piece of my flapping pant-leg. I heard a tacky ripping sound, stumbled, kept going.

I ran until there was a stitch in my side and no dog in sight—six blocks, at least. Toppled over in someone's yard. My pantleg was sliced open from the back of my knee to the ankle. I took my first good look at Art. It was a jarring sight. I was so out of breath, I could only produce a thin, dismayed little squeak—the sort of sound Art was always making.

His body had lost its marshmallow whiteness. It had a gold-brown duskiness to it now, so it resembled a marshmallow, lightly toasted. He seemed to have deflated to about half his usual size. His chin sagged into his body. He couldn't hold his head up.

Art had been crossing our front lawn, when Happy burst from his hiding place under one of the hedges. In that first crucial moment, Art saw he would never be able to outrun our family dog on foot. All such an effort would get him would be an ass full of fatal puncture wounds. So instead, he jumped into the station wagon, and slammed the door.

The windows were automatic—there was no way to roll them down. Any door he opened, Happy tried to jam his snout in at him. It was seventy degrees outside the car, over a hundred inside. Art watched in dismay as Happy flopped in the grass beside the wagon to wait.

Art sat. Happy didn't move. Lawnmowers droned in the distance. The afternoon passed. In time Art began to wilt in the heat. He became ill and groggy. His plastic skin started sticking to the seats.

Then you showed up. Just in time. You saved my life.

But my eyes blurred and tears dripped off my face onto his note. I hadn't come just in time—not at all.

Art was never the same. His skin stayed a filmy yellow, and he developed a deflation problem. His parents would pump him up, and for a while he'd be all right, his body swollen with oxygen, but eventually he'd go saggy and limp again. His doctor took one look and told his parents not to put off the trip to Disney World another year.

I wasn't the same either. I was miserable—couldn't eat, suffered unexpected stomachaches, brooded and sulked.

"Wipe that look off your face," my father said one night at dinner. "Life goes on. Deal with it."

I was dealing all right. I knew the door to Happy's pen didn't open itself. I punched holes in the tires of the station wagon, then left my switchblade sticking out of one of them, so my father would know for sure who had done it. He had police officers come over and pretend to arrest me. They drove me around in the squad car and talked tough at me for a while, then said they'd bring me home if I'd "get with the program." The next day I locked Happy in the wagon and he took a shit on the driver's seat. My father collected all the books Art had got me to read, the Bernard Malamud, the Ray Bradbury, the Isaac Bashevis Singer. He burned them on the barbecue grill.

"How do you feel about that, smart guy?" he asked me, while he squirted lighter fluid on them.

"Okay with me," I said. "They were on your library card."

That summer, I spent a lot of time sleeping over at Art's.

> Don't be angry. No one is to blame.

Art wrote me.

"Get your head out of your ass," I said, but then I couldn't say anything else because it made me cry just to look at him.

Late August, Art gave me a call. It was a hilly four miles to Scarswell Cove, where he wanted us to meet, but by then months of hoofing it to Art's after school had hardened me to long walks. I had plenty of balloons with me, just like he asked.

Scarswell Cove is a sheltered, pebbly beach on the sea, where people go to stand in the tide and fish in waders. There was no one there except a couple old fishermen, and Art, sitting on the slope of the beach. His body looked soft and saggy, and his head lolled forward, bobbled weakly on his non-existent neck. I sat down beside him. Half a mile out, the dark blue waves were churning up icy combers.

"What's going on?" I asked.

Art bowed his head. He thought a bit. Then he began to write.

He wrote:

> Do you know people have made it into outer space
> without rockets? Chuck Yeager flew a high
> performance jet so high it started to tumble—it
> tumbled *upwards*, not downwards. He ran so high,
> gravity lost hold of him. His jet was tumbling up
> out of the stratosphere. All the color melted out of
> the sky. It was like the blue sky was paper, and a
> hole was burning out the middle of it, and behind
> it, everything was black. Everything was full of stars.
> Imagine falling *UP*.

I looked at this note, then back to his face. He was writing again. His second message was simpler.

> I've had it. Seriously—I'm all done. I deflate
> 15–16 times a day. I need someone to pump me up
> practically every hour. I feel sick all the time and I
> hate it. This is no kind of life.

"Oh no," I said. My vision blurred. Tears welled up and spilled over my eyes. "Things will get better."

> No. I don't think so. It isn't about whether I die. It's
> about figuring out where. And I've decided. I'm
> going to see how high I can go. I want to see if it's
> true. If the sky opens up at the top.

I don't know what else I said to him. A lot of things, I guess. I asked him not to do it, not to leave me. I said that it wasn't fair. I said that I didn't have any other friends. I said that I had always been lonely. I talked until it was all blubber and strangled, helpless sobs, and he reached his crinkly plastic arms around me and held me while I hid my face in his chest.

He took the balloons from me, got them looped around one wrist. I held his other hand and we walked to the edge of the water. The surf splashed in and filled my sneakers. The sea was so cold it made the bones in my feet throb. I lifted him and held him in both arms, and squeezed until he made a mournful squeak. We hugged for a long time. Then I opened my arms. I let him go. I hope if there is another world, we will not be judged too harshly for the things we did wrong here— that we will at least be forgiven for the mistakes we made out of love. I have no doubt it was a sin of some kind, to let such a one go.

He rose away and the airstream turned him around so he was looking back at me as he bobbed out over the water, his left arm pulled high over his head, the balloons attached to his wrist. His head was tipped at a thoughtful angle, so he seemed to be studying me.

I sat on the beach and watched him go. I watched until I could no longer distinguish him from the gulls that were wheeling and diving over the water, a few miles away. He was just one more dirty speck wandering the sky. I didn't move. I wasn't sure I could get up. In time, the horizon turned a dusky rose and the blue sky above deepened to black. I stretched out on the beach, and watched the stars spill through the darkness overhead. I watched until a dizziness overcame me, and I could imagine spilling off the ground, and falling up into the night.

I developed emotional problems. When school started again, I would cry at the sight of an empty desk. I couldn't answer questions or do homework. I flunked out and had to go through seventh grade again.

Worse, no one believed I was dangerous anymore. It was impossible to be scared of me after you had seen me sobbing my guts out a few times. I didn't have the switchblade either; my father had confiscated it.

Billy Spears beat me up one day, after school—mashed my lips, loosened a tooth. John Erikson held me down, wrote COLLISTAMY BAG on my forehead in magic marker. Still trying to get it right. Cassius Delamitri ambushed me, shoved me down and jumped on top of me, crushing me under his weight, driving all the air out of my lungs. A defeat by way of deflation; Art would have understood perfectly.

I avoided the Roths'. I wanted more than anything to see Art's mother, but stayed away. I was afraid if I talked to her, it would come pouring out of me, that I had been there at the end, that I stood in the surf and let Art go. I was afraid of what I might see in her eyes; of her hurt and anger.

Less than six months after Art's deflated body was found slopping in the surf along North Scarswell beach, there was a FOR SALE sign out in front of the Roth's ranch. I never saw either of his parents again. Mrs. Roth sometimes wrote me letters, asking how I was and what I was doing, but I never replied. She signed her letters *love*.

I went out for track in high school, and did well at pole vault. My track coach said the law of gravity didn't apply to me. My track coach didn't know fuckall about gravity. No matter how high I went for a moment, I always came down in the end, same as anyone else.

Pole vault got me a state college scholarship. I kept to myself. No one at college knew me, and I was at last able to rebuild my long lost image as a sociopath. I didn't go to parties. I didn't date. I didn't want to get to know anybody.

I was crossing the campus one morning, and I saw coming towards me a young girl, with black hair so dark it had the cold blue sheen of rich oil. She wore a bulky sweater and a librarian's ankle-length skirt; a very asexual outfit, but all the same you could see she had a stunning figure, slim hips, high ripe breasts. Her eyes were of staring blue glass, her skin as white as Art's. It was the first time I had seen an inflatable person since Art drifted away on his balloons. A kid walking behind me wolf-whistled at her. I stepped aside, and when he went past, I tripped him up and watched his books fly everywhere.

"Are you some kind of psycho?" he screeched.

"Yes," I said. "Exactly."

Her name was Ruth Goldman. She had a round rubber patch on the heel of one foot where she had stepped on a shard of broken glass as a little girl, and a larger square patch on her left shoulder where a sharp branch had poked her once on a windy day. Home schooling and obsessively protective parents had saved her from further damage. We were both English majors. Her favorite writer was Kafka—because he understood the absurd. My favorite writer was Malamud—because he understood loneliness.

We married the same year I graduated. Although I remain

doubtful about the life eternal, I converted without any prod-
ding from her, gave in at last to a longing to have some talk of
the spirit in my life. Can you really call it a conversion? In
truth, I had no beliefs to convert from. Whatever the case,
ours was a Jewish wedding, glass under white cloth, crunched
beneath the bootheel.

One afternoon I told her about Art.

> *That's so sad. I'm so sorry.*

She wrote to me in wax pencil. She put her hand over mine.

> *What happened? Did he run out of air?*

"Ran out of sky," I said.

2001

POPPY Z. BRITE

(b. 1967)

Pansu

TWILIGHT was settling over L.A.'s Koreatown, the lights of the stores clicking off, the lights of the restaurants and bars flickering on. Samuel Oh stood beneath the red marquee of his restaurant, surveyed the street scene, and thought that this was one of those rare California moments of peace with no evil.

He was wrong.

He went back inside. The dinner crowd had just started to come in. The restaurant was dark, lit with paper lanterns and strings of Christmas lights. Two of his favorite customers, a pair of young men who wrote and produced a successful TV show, were at their usual table in the corner. Mr. Oh's wife, Bobbi, was setting out their *pan chan*. Smiling, she laid the last of the small dishes on the table. Mr. Oh was about to turn away when he saw Bobbi hurl her tray like a Frisbee across the room, where it landed in the middle of someone's flaming bulgogi platter. She thrust her tongue out as far as it would go, hiked her modest skirt well above her waist, and commanded the two young men, "Fuck me!"

"Uh, we don't really feel that way about you, Mrs. Oh," said one of them.

"And those people's table is on fire," pointed out the other one.

Mr. Oh grabbed the fire extinguisher from its place beside the kitchen door, ran to the table where the tray had landed, and doused the flames with chemical foam, apologizing furiously to the diners. Luckily they were Korean, and he was able to express his profound embarrassment and promise them a complimentary replacement dinner without stumbling over his words. He found a waitress to move them to a new table and raced over to where his wife had begun to slide out of her white cotton panties. He grabbed her from behind. She lashed out with one arm and sent him flying backward. His feet tangled, and he fell ungracefully to the floor.

"Is your wife OK?" asked one of the young men, bending to assist Mr. Oh.

"Dude, obviously she's not OK," his friend said. As they helped Mr. Oh to his feet, Bobbi yanked the tablecloth off the table and sent the little appetizer dishes flying. A particularly spicy clump of *kimchi* hit Mr. Oh square in the left eye. Diners were beginning to flee the restaurant as Bobbi ran to the center of the room, screamed "FUCK ME, ANYBODY FUCK ME!", and vomited a mass of bright green goo into a charming little fountain Mr. Oh had just installed.

He turned desperately to the two TV writers. "What can be wrong with her?" he asked in English.

"Well," said the light-haired one, "I've only ever seen a movie about it, but it looks to me like she's possessed by Satan."

"Yup," his friend concurred. "Exorcist, obviously."

"What do you mean?" Mr. Oh began to ask, but then his wife's head spun twice around on her neck, and as he heard the terrible sound of the cracking bones he knew, because he had seen the movie himself.

Mr. Oh had closed the restaurant, sent the staff home, and dragged Bobbi into the little office where he placed the food orders and added the receipts. He had begged his two TV-writing customers to stay, as they seemed to know more than he did about this problem, and they had reluctantly agreed. In his distraction he kept mixing up their names, but he was fairly sure that the light-haired one was called Darin and the other one was Mark.

Since he usually kept the restaurant open all night, he had a little cot in the office. Bobbi thrashed on it now, her wrists bound with napkins because she had scratched her face so badly that blood and shreds of skin were embedded beneath her nails. She had torn all the buttons off her blouse before he managed to tie her up, and the sight of her plain white cotton bra against her flushed golden skin broke Mr. Oh's heart a little more. Her skirt was rucked up beneath her, her legs akimbo, her body twisting in some pain or fury he could not imagine.

He turned away from her and saw that Mark was rolling a

joint on the desk where he did the accounts. The loose marijuana was scattered across a seafood bill stamped PAID, like some terrible symbol of chaos consuming order. "You cannot smoke that shit in here!"

Mark looked up at him with eyes very dark and serious. "Mr. Oh," he said, "if you want us to stay here and try to help you deal with your possessed wife, then we most definitely *can* smoke this shit in here."

Darin nodded his agreement and pulled out a Zippo lighter stamped with some vulgar cartoon character. Mark put the finished joint in his mouth and leaned over so that Darin could light it for him. They went through a complex, difficult-looking process of getting it to stay lit and burn evenly. Mr. Oh found that he could not take his eyes off this process: if he looked at them, he did not have to look at his wife writhing on the cot.

He could still hear her, though. She was muttering in Korean, dreadful words he had not thought she knew and had never imagined that she would combine. Literally, she had just called him, or someone unseen, a fucker of pigs.

The marijuana smoke filled the small office and made Mr. Oh's head feel as if it sat more lightly on his neck. For the first time since Bobbi had thrown the tray, he relaxed a little, and realized that perhaps he did know something about this problem after all.

As if sensing possible danger, Bobbi spoke up. Her words were English now, her voice so guttural it hurt to hear, with an accent that was definitely not Korean. "YOU'RE GETTING STONED!"

"No I'm not," he said without thinking.

"Dude!" Darin grabbed his arm. *"Don't answer its charges.* That's one of the rules you have to follow. It lies."

"Not necessarily in this case," Mark said. "He might *be* getting stoned. It's pretty smoky in here."

"Well, but you're not supposed to argue with it. Max von Sydow said so."

"Agreed."

"FUCKING ADDICT WASTECASE FAGGOTS!" Bobbi roared.

They glanced over at the cot, looked at each other, shrugged as if they could not argue with this assessment even had they wanted to, and finished off the joint.

"I am not getting stoned!" Mr. Oh said. "I am trying to help my wife, and I thought you had agreed to help me."

"Preparations are necessary," Darin said. "No way can we watch that fucking thing stone cold sober."

"Don't speak of her that way!"

"Mr. Oh," Mark said gently, "he's not talking about your wife. He's talking about that thing inside her."

"How are you so calm? I expect not—"

"You *don't expect*."

"I don't expect you to feel as I do, but you seem . . ." He gestured helplessly for the words. "You seem as if this is almost normal to you."

"We grew up in a small town in Utah," Darin told him. "Now we've been in Hollywood for five years. We've seen some things that seemed pretty fucking weird to us. I'd say 'almost normal' isn't too far off for this."

Mark shook his head. "I don't know, dude. I think 'almost normal' is going a little far. I think this is at least slightly weird."

"Pussy."

"Dude! Come in for pork belly hot pot, stay for Satan? Come on. That's fucking weird."

"*That's enough!*" shouted Mr. Oh. "Yes, it is weird! But it is not a show! It is not something on TV to laugh at! If you're not going to help me, then *get out of my restaurant!*"

They stared at him, then looked at each other, abashed. Beneath their surprise, beneath the bland Hollywood smirks they had picked up somewhere along the way, Mr. Oh thought he could see the faces of those two young boys from Utah. Maybe that was how it was with his wife, too. Maybe she was still in there, trapped.

He remembered what he had forgotten. It was a story his grandmother had told him, a story from before the Second World War, when she was a girl living in a village a hundred miles from Seoul. It was about a kind of healer, one who healed by feeding the hungry. He knew how to do that.

"We're sorry, Mr. Oh," said Darin. "We didn't mean to make fun. We'll help however we can. Do you want us to go get a priest or something? I mean, he'd probably just tell us to fuck off, but . . ."

"No priest," said Mr. Oh. "We're not Catholic. We're not even religious. But we are Korean. I think I know what to do. Stay here and watch her, please."

He made several trips between the kitchen and the office, bringing in portions of each special they'd planned to serve tonight, all the *pan chan* they'd prepared, a few particularly succulent-looking raw fruits and vegetables, and last of all a new bottle of peach schnapps from the bar. He cracked the seal and set the cap on the floor beside the full bottle.

"The bottle should be made from peach wood," he said. "But I have no idea where to get such a thing in Los Angeles. This will have to do."

The two writers were huddled together at Mr. Oh's desk. They'd been happy enough to talk about movie Satans, but now that it looked as if something might actually happen, they were wide-eyed and silent.

"What are you going to do exactly?" asked Darin at last.

"I'm going to feed it."

"Feed it! Dude, that doesn't sound like the best way to—"

"It is the Korean way. My grandmother told me this. The ritual should be done by a Korean healer called a pansu, but I will have to do it myself."

"Still, are you sure—"

"It is not like the movie." In case the thing inside Bobbi was listening, Mr. Oh hoped he sounded more confident than he felt. "This devil does not want my wife's soul. It wants the pleasures of her body. It cannot make love or smoke or eat. It would like to do any of these things, but most of all it is hungry."

"Can we do anything?" Mark asked at last.

Mr. Oh shrugged. "I suppose it might try to jump from her to me. If it does . . ." He shook his head. "Take her with you, get out, and call the police."

"But—"

"Quiet, please. I'm going to start."

Bobbi's mouth opened impossibly wide, and guttural laughter spilled out. "Moron! You think you can catch me with food?

Cut off your penis and feed me that; perhaps such a tiny morsel will still my hunger!"

She had spoken in Korean this time; he supposed he still had something to be thankful for. He turned away from the cot and addressed the doorway that led to the kitchen.

"God of the doorway! God of the kitchen! God of this little eating house that is our second home! Come and feast, if you will." He spoke these words first in Korean, then repeated them in English.

"I thought—" Darin began. Mark shushed him.

"Feast and make yourselves content, for I would ask a favor of you. Should this humble repast fail to satisfy, I will happily prepare as much as you require."

"It is good," said Bobbi in a new voice.

The three of them turned to look at her. Her face had changed again; the expression of rage and pain seemed to be buried somehow under one of haughty benevolence. "Your repast is good, Samuel Oh. Give it to us."

"Take it," he answered, and untied her wrists.

Bobbi rose from the cot and approached the dishes laid out on the floor. Her gait was steady, her bearing regal despite her disheveled hair and the vomit that still streaked her clothes. She knelt before the dishes and, with her fingers, delicately took up portions of each one. Mark and Darin watched with increasing wariness, as though they expected her to resume flinging food at any moment, but she simply tasted each dish and returned to the cot, where she lay down again.

"Now you have feasted," Mr. Oh said. "Now I ask a favor of you. Will you intercede with the spirit that has possessed my wife? Will you invite it to feast also, and leave us?"

"I shall try," said Bobbi in the same calm voice. "You know that such spirits will not always settle for a feast."

"I know."

She closed her eyes and lay motionless on the cot, scarcely seeming to breathe. When her eyes flew open again, they could see that the first spirit was back. It thrust out its tongue and laughed that guttural laugh. "Will you feed me, husband?"

"I am not your husband," said Mr. Oh. "I am the husband of Bobbi Oh, whose body you have stolen. But I will feed you before I ask you to leave her."

"What if I refuse to leave her?"

"There are other things that can be done," Mr. Oh told it, wondering what in the world those things might be.

"Perhaps not. Perhaps I will join you in bed tonight, Samuel Oh."

He managed to suppress a shudder, and said only, "Will you eat?"

"I will," she said. But this time her body did not rise from the cot, though she began to make chewing motions with her mouth. Mark nudged Darin and pointed at the food. Mouthfuls of it were disappearing, apparently into thin air: a clump of kim chee, the head of a fish, a piece of winter squash marked by invisible teeth that must have been far larger than Bobbi Oh's.

"You have eaten well," Mr. Oh said when the dishes were clean. "Will you go now?"

"I have eaten very well," the thing replied. Though Bobbi's mouth still moved, the voice now seemed to emanate from all around them. "I would like to eat so well every day. I will not go."

Mr. Oh closed his eyes for a moment. This would be the crucial moment. "You have eaten," he said, "but you have not drunk."

"Ahhh . . . true!"

A loud sucking sound filled the air, as if a huge rude child were finishing off an enormous ice cream soda, and the level of the peach schnapps began to sink. Mr. Oh sprang for the bottle, seized it by the neck, and screwed the cap on as tightly as it would go. The bottle jerked once, and the office fell silent.

Mr. Oh's legs failed him. He sank to the floor.

The writers stared at each other as if they had missed something. "Is that it?" said one of them; Mr. Oh wasn't sure which.

"Is what it?" said a soft, feminine, Korean-accented voice. They all turned as Bobbi sat up on the cot, frowning at her soiled outfit and the three men staring at her. She began to sob, and Mr. Oh went to her.

Mark and Darin drove down Wilshire Boulevard toward the La Brea Tar Pits. The bottle was in the trunk, taped up in a lettuce box Mr. Oh had given them, well padded with crumpled Korean-language newspapers.

"You're sure that thing isn't going to just bust out of the bottle?" Darin asked for the hundredth time.

"Dude, you heard what Mr. Oh said," Darin told him. "It's a *peach schnapps* bottle. He said peach has some kind of power over it. He said it would make the thing too weak to break the bottle."

"I hope to hell he's right."

"Hope no more, we're here." Mark pulled over and cut the engine. The Tar Pits had been closed for hours, but only a chain link fence separated them from the street. Mark and Darin got out, opened the trunk, unpacked the bottle, and carried it to the fence. A smell like a hundred freshly resurfaced blacktops filled the air. They cast twin apprehensive looks at each other.

"You wanna try it?" asked Mark.

"Oh, right. When we were playing Horse last week, you said I threw like a girl. This shot's all yours, buddy."

Mark got a firm grasp on the bottle's neck, stepped back from the fence, wound up a couple of times, and let fly. They held their breath as the bottle sailed over the fence. It seemed to hang suspended for several beats too long, catching the light of the streetlamps and neon signs, glittering in a nasty way. Then it dropped easily into a pool of prehistoric tar and, within seconds, was sucked out of sight.

"Dude, nice shot," said Darin.

"Thanks." They returned to the car and drove away without looking back. After a few miles of empty Wilshire, Mark said "You know, I'm still hungry."

"Yeah, me too. Let's grab something."

"Whaddaya feel like?"

"Maybe something besides Korean."

"I think so, yeah."

"How about that all-night Thai place over by Jumbo's Clown Room?"

"You got it," said Mark, and swung the car up Western toward Hollywood Boulevard.

2003

STEVEN MILLHAUSER

(b. 1943)

Dangerous Laughter

F EW of us now recall that perilous summer. What began as a game, a harmless pastime, quickly took a turn toward the serious and obsessive, which none of us tried to resist. After all, we were young. We were fourteen and fifteen, scornful of childhood, remote from the world of stern and ludicrous adults. We were bored, we were restless, we longed to be seized by any whim or passion and follow it to the farthest reaches of our natures. We wanted to live—to die—to burst into flame—to be transformed into angels or explosions. Only the mundane offended us, as if we secretly feared it was our destiny. By late afternoon our muscles ached, our eyelids grew heavy with obscure desires. And so we dreamed and did nothing, for what was there to do, played ping-pong and went to the beach, loafed in backyards, slept late into the morning—and always we craved adventures so extreme we could never imagine them.

In the long dusks of summer we walked the suburban streets through scents of maple and cut grass, waiting for something to happen.

The game began innocently and spread like a dark rumor. In cool playrooms with parallelograms of sunlight pouring through cellar windows, at ping-pong tables in hot, open garages, around yellow and blue beach towels lying on bright sand above the tide line, you would hear the quiet words, the sharp bursts of laughter. The idea had the simplicity of all inspired things. A word, any word, uttered in a certain solemn tone, could be compelled to reveal its inner stupidity. "Cheese," someone would say, with an air of somber concentration, and again, slowly: "Cheese." Someone would laugh; it was inevitable; the laughter would spread; gusts of hilarity would sweep through the group; and just as things were about to die down, someone would cry out "Elbow!" or "Dirigible!" and bursts of laughter would be set off again. What drew us wasn't

512

so much the hidden absurdity of words, which we'd always suspected, as the sharp heaves and gasps of laughter itself. Deep in our inner dark, we had discovered a startling power. We became fanatics of laughter, devotees of eruption, as if these upheavals were something we hadn't known before, something that would take us where we needed to go.

Such simple performances couldn't satisfy us for long. The laugh parties represented a leap worthy of our hunger. The object was to laugh longer and harder than anyone else, to maintain in yourself an uninterrupted state of explosive release. Rules sprang up to eliminate unacceptable laughter—the feeble, the false, the unfairly exaggerated. Soon every party had its judges, who grew skillful in detecting the slightest deviation from the genuine. As long laughter became the rage, a custom arose in which each of us in turn had to step into a circle of watchers, and there, partly through the stimulus of a crowd already rippling with amusement, and partly through some inner trick that differed from person to person, begin to laugh. Meanwhile the watchers and judges, who themselves were continually thrown into outbursts that drove the laugher to greater and greater heights, studied the roars and convulsions carefully and timed the performance with a stopwatch.

In this atmosphere of urgency, abandon, and rigorous striving, accidents were bound to happen. One girl, laughing hysterically on a couch in a basement playroom, threw back her head and injured her neck when it struck the wooden couch-arm. A boy gasping with mad laughter crashed into a piano bench, fell to the floor, and broke his left arm. These incidents, which might have served as warnings, only heightened our sense of rightness, as if our wounds were signs that we took our laughter seriously.

Not long after the laugh parties began to spread through our afternoons, there arose a new pastime, which enticed us with promises of a more radical kind. The laugh clubs—or laugh parlors, as they were sometimes called—represented a bolder effort to draw forth and prolong our laughter. At first they were organized by slightly older girls, who invited "members" to their houses after dark. In accordance with rules and practices that varied from club to club, the girls were said to produce sustained fits of violent laughter far more thrilling than anything we had yet discovered. No one was certain how the clubs had come into being—one day they simply seemed to be there, as if they'd been present all along, waiting for us to find them.

It was rumored that the first club was the invention of six-teen-year-old Bernice Alderson, whose parents were never home. She lived in a large house in the wooded north end of town; one day she'd read in a history of Egypt that Queen Cleopatra liked to order a slave girl to bind her arms and tickle her bare feet with a feather. In her third-floor bedroom, Bernice and her friend Mary Chapman invited club members to remove their shoes and lie down one by one on the bed. While Mary, with her muscular arms, held the chest and knees firmly in place, Bernice began to tickle the outstretched body—on the stomach, the ribs, the neck, the thighs, the tops and sides of the feet. There was an art to it all: the art of invading and withdrawing, of coaxing from the depths a steady outpouring of helpless laughter. For the visitor held down on the bed, it was a matter of releasing oneself into the hands of the girls and enduring it for as long as possible. All you had to do was say "Stop." In theory the laughter never had to stop, though most of us could barely hold out for three minutes.

Although the laugh parlors existed in fact, for we all attended them and even began to form clubs of our own, they also continued to lead a separate and in a sense higher existence in the realm of rumor, which had the effect of lifting them into the inaccessible and mythical. It was said that in one of these clubs, members were required to remove their clothes, after which they were chained to a bed and tickled savagely to the point of delirium. It was said that one girl, sobbing with laughter, gasping, began to move her hips in strange and suggestive ways, until it became clear that the act of tickling had brought her to orgasm. The erotic was never absent from these rumors—a fact that hardly surprised us, since those of us who were purists of laughter and disdained any crude crossing over into the sexual recognized the kinship between the two worlds. For even then we understood that our laughter, as it erupted from us in unseemly spasms, was part of the kingdom of forbidden things.

As laugh parties gave way to laugh parlors, and rumors

thickened, we sometimes had the sense that our secret games had begun to spread to other regions of the town. One day a nine-year-old boy was discovered by his mother holding down and violently tickling his seven-year-old sister, who was shrieking and screaming—the collar of her dress was soaked with tears. The girl's pale body was streaked with lines of deep pink, as if she'd been struck repeatedly with a rope. We heard that Bernice Alderson's mother, at home for a change, had entered the kitchen with a heavy bag of groceries in her arms, slipped on a rubber dog-toy, and fallen to the floor. As she sat there beside a box of smashed and oozing eggs and watched the big, heavy, thumping oranges go rolling across the linoleum, the corners of her mouth began to twitch, her lungs, already burning with anger, began to tingle, and all at once she burst into laughter that lashed her body, threw her head back against the metal doors of the cabinet under the sink, rose to the third-floor bedroom of her daughter, who looked up frowning from a book, and in the end left her exhausted, shaken, bruised, panting, and exhilarated. At night, in my hot room, I lay restless and dissatisfied, longing for the release of feverish laughter that alone could soothe me—and through the screen I seemed to hear, along with the crickets, the rattling window-fan next door, and the hum of far-off trucks on the thruway, the sound of laughter bursting faintly in the night, all over our town, like the buzz of a fluorescent lamp in a distant bedroom.

One night after my parents were asleep I left the house and walked across town to Bernice Alderson's neighborhood. The drawn shade of her third-floor window was aglow with dim yellow light. On the bed in her room Mary Chapman gripped me firmly while Bernice bent over me with a serious but not unkind look. Slowly she brought me to a pitch of wild laughter that seemed to scald my throat as sweat trickled down my neck and the bed creaked to the rhythm of my deep, painful, releasing cries. I held out for a long time, nearly seven minutes, until I begged her to stop. Instantly it was over. Even as I made my way home, under the maples and lindens of a warm July night, I regretted my cowardice and longed for deeper and more terrible laughter. Then I wondered how I could push my way through the hours that separated me from my next descent into the darkness of my body, where laughter lay like lava, waiting for a fissure to form that would release it like liquid fire.

Of course we compared notes. We'd known from the beginning that some were more skilled in laughter than others, that some were able to sustain long and robust fits of the bone-shaking kind, which seemed to bring them to the verge of hysteria or unconsciousness without stepping over the line. Many of us boasted of our powers, only to be outdone by others; rumors blossomed; and in this murky atmosphere of extravagant claims, dubious feats, and unverifiable stories, the figure of Clara Schuler began to stand out with a certain distinctness.

Clara Schuler was fifteen years old. She was a quiet girl, who sat very still in class with her book open before her, eyes lowered and both feet resting on the floor. She never drummed her fingers on the desk. She never pushed her hair back over her ear or crossed and uncrossed her legs—as if, for her, a single motion were a form of disruption. When she passed a handout to the person seated behind her, she turned her upper body abruptly, dropped the paper on the desk with lowered eyes, and turned abruptly back. She never raised her hand in class. When called on, she flushed slightly, answered in a voice so quiet that the teacher had to ask her to "speak up," and said as little as possible, though it was clear she'd done the work. She seemed to experience the act of being looked at as a form of violation; she gave you the impression that her idea of happiness would be to dissolve gradually, leaving behind a small puddle. She was difficult to picture clearly—a little pale, her hair dark in some elusive shade between brown and black, her eyes hidden under lowered lids that sometimes opened suddenly to reveal large, startled irises. She wore trim knee-length skirts and solid-colored cotton blouses that looked neatly ironed. Sometimes she wore in her collar a small silver pin shaped like a cat.

One small thing struck me about Clara Schuler: in the course of the day she would become a little unraveled. Strands of hair would fall across her face, the back of her blouse would bunch up and start to pull away from her leather belt, one of her white socks would begin to droop. The next day she'd be back in her seat, her hair neatly combed, her blouse tucked in, her socks pulled up tight with the ribs perfectly straight, her hands folded lightly on her maplewood desk.

Clara had one friend, a girl named Helen Jacoby, who sat with her in the cafeteria and met her at the lockers after class. Helen was a long-boned girl who played basketball and laughed at anything. When she threw her head back to drink bottles of soda, you could see the ridges of her trachea pressing through her neck. She seemed an unlikely companion for Clara Schuler, but we were used to seeing them together and we felt, without thinking much about it, that each enhanced the other—Helen made Clara seem less strange and solitary, in a sense protected her and prevented her from being perceived as ridiculous, while Clara made good old Helen seem more interesting, lent her a touch of mystery. We weren't surprised, that summer, to see Helen at the laugh parties, where she laughed with her head thrown back in a way that reminded me of the way she drank soda; and it was Helen who one afternoon brought Clara Schuler with her and introduced her to the new game.

I began to watch Clara at these parties. We all watched her. She would step into the circle and stand there with lowered eyes, her head leaning forward slightly, her shoulders slumped, her arms tense at her sides—looking, I couldn't help thinking, as if she were being punished in some humiliating way. You could see the veins rising up on the backs of her hands. She stood so motionless that she seemed to be holding her breath; perhaps she was; and you could feel something building in her, as in a child about to cry; her neck stiff; the tendons visible; two vertical lines between her eyebrows; then a kind of mild trembling in her neck and arms, a veiled shudder, an inner rippling, and through her body, still rigid but in the grip of a force, you could sense a presence, rising, expanding, until, with a painful gasp, with a jerk of her shoulders, she gave way to a cry or scream of laughter—laughter that continued to well up in her, to shake her as if she were possessed by a demon, until her cheeks were wet, her hair wild in her face, her chest heaving, her fingers clutching at her arms and head—and still the laughter came, hurling her about, making her gulp and gasp as if in terror, her mouth stretched back over her teeth, her eyes squeezed shut, her hands pressed against her ribs as if to keep herself from cracking apart.

And then it would stop. Abruptly, mysteriously, it was over. She stood there, pale—exhausted—panting. Her eyes, wide open, saw nothing. Slowly she came back to herself. Then quickly, a little unsteadily, she would walk away from us to collapse on a couch.

These feats of laughter were immediately recognized as bold and striking, far superior to the performances we had become accustomed to; and Clara Schuler was invited to all the laugh parties, applauded, and talked about admiringly, for she had a gift of reckless laughter we had not seen before.

Now whenever loose groups of us gathered to pursue our game, Clara Schuler was there. We grew used to her, waited impatiently for her when she was late, this quiet girl who'd never done anything but sit obediently in our classes with both feet on the floor before revealing dark depths of laughter that left us wondering and a little uneasy. For there was something about Clara Schuler's laughter. It wasn't simply that it was more intense than ours. Rather, she seemed to be transformed into an object, seized by a force that raged through her before letting her go. Yes, in Clara Schuler the discrepancy between the body that was shaken and the force that shook it appeared so sharply that at the very moment she became most physical she seemed to lose the sense of her body altogether. For the rest of us, there was always a touch of the sensual in these performances: breasts shook, hips jerked, flesh moved in unexpected ways. But Clara Schuler seemed to pass beyond the easy suggestiveness of moving bodies and to enter new and more ambiguous realms, where the body was the summoner of some dark, eruptive power that was able to flourish only through the accident of a material thing, which it flung about as if cruelly before abandoning it to the rites of exhaustion.

One day she appeared among us alone. Helen Jacoby was at the beach, or out shopping with her mother. We understood that Clara Schuler no longer needed her friend in the old way —that she had come into her own. And we understood one other thing: she would allow nothing to stop her from joining our game, from yielding to the seductions of laughter, for she lived, more and more, only in order to let herself go.

It was inevitable that rumors should spring up about Clara Schuler. It was said that she'd begun to go to the laugh parlors, those half-real, half-legendary places where laughter was wrung out of willing victims by special arts. It was said that one night she had paid a visit to Bernice Alderson's house, where in the lamplit bedroom on the third floor she'd been constrained and skillfully tickled for nearly an hour, at which point she fainted dead away and had to be revived by a scented oil rubbed into her temples. It was said that at another house she'd been so shaken by extreme laughter that her body rose from the bed and hovered in the air for thirty seconds before dropping back down. We knew that this last was a lie, a frivolous and irritating tale fit for children, but it troubled us all the same, it seized our imaginations—for we felt that under the right circumstances, with the help of a physiologically freakish but not inconceivable pattern of spasms, it was the kind of thing Clara Schuler might somehow be able to do.

As our demands became more exacting, and our expectations more refined, Clara Schuler's performances attained heights of release that inflamed us and left no doubt of her power. We tried to copy her gestures, to jerk our shoulders with her precise rhythms, always without success. Sometimes we imagined we could hear, in Clara Schuler's laughter, our own milder laughter, changed into something we could only long for. It was as if our dreams had entered her.

I noticed that her strenuous new life was beginning to affect her appearance. Now when she came to us her hair fell across her cheeks in long strands, which she would impatiently flick away with the backs of her fingers. She looked thinner, though it was hard to tell; she looked tired; she looked as if she might be coming down with something. Her eyes, no longer hidden under lowered lids, gazed at us restlessly and a little vaguely. Sometimes she gave the impression that she was searching for something she could no longer remember. She looked expectant; a little sad; a little bored.

One night, unable to sleep, I escaped from the house and took a walk. Near the end of my street I passed under a streetlamp that flickered and made a crackling sound, so that my shadow trembled. It seemed to me that I was that streetlamp, flickering and crackling with restlessness. After a while I came to an older neighborhood of high maples and gabled houses with rundown front porches. Bicycles leaned wearily against wicker furniture and beach towels hung crookedly over porch rails. I stopped before a dark house near the end of the street.

Through an open window on the second floor, over the dirt driveway, I heard the sound of a rattling fan.

It was Clara Schuler's house. I wondered if it was her window. I walked a little closer, looking up at the screen, and it seemed to me that through the rattle and hum of the fan I heard some other sound. It was—I thought it was—the sound of quiet laughter. Was she lying there in the dark, laughing secretly, releasing herself from restlessness? Could she be laughing in her sleep? Maybe it was only some trick of the fan. I stood listening to that small, uncertain sound, which mingled with the blades of the fan until it seemed the fan itself was laughing, perhaps at me. What did I long for, under that window? I longed to be swept up into Clara Schuler's laughter, I longed to join her there, in her dark room, I longed for release from whatever it was I was. But whatever I was lay hard and immovable in me, like bone; I would never be free of my own weight. After a while I turned around and walked home.

It wasn't long after this visit that I saw Clara Schuler at one of the laugh parlors we'd formed, in imitation of those we had heard about or perhaps had invented in order to lure ourselves into deeper experiments. Helen Jacoby sat on the bed and held Clara's wrists while a friend of Helen's held Clara's ankles. A blond-haired girl I'd never seen before bent over her with hooked fingers. Five of us watched the performance. It began with a sudden shiver, as the short blunt fingers darted along her ribs and thighs. Clara Schuler's head began to turn from side to side; her feet in her white socks stiffened. As laughter rushed through her in sharp shuddering bursts, one of her shoulders lifted as if to fold itself across her neck. Within ten minutes her eyes had grown glassy and calm. She lay almost still, even as she continued to laugh. What struck us was that eerie stillness, as if she'd passed beyond struggle to some other place, where laughter poured forth in pure, vigorous streams.

Someone asked nervously if we should stop. The blond-haired girl glanced at her watch and bent over Clara Schuler more intently. After half an hour, Clara began breathing in great wracking gulps, accompanied by groans torn up from her throat. Helen asked her if she'd had enough; Clara shook her head harshly. Her face was so wet that she glowed in the lamplight. Stains of wetness darkened the bedspread.

When the session had lasted just over an hour, the blond-haired girl gave up in exhaustion. She stood shaking her wrists, rubbing the fingers of first one hand and then the other. On the bed Clara Schuler continued stirring and laughing, as if she still felt the fingers moving over her. Gradually her laughter grew fainter; and as she lay there pale and drained, with her head turned to one side, her eyes dull, her lips slack, strands of long hair sticking to her wet cheek, she looked, for a moment, as if she'd grown suddenly old.

It was at this period, when Clara Schuler became queen of the laugh parlors, that I first began to worry about her. One day, emerging from an unusually violent and prolonged series of gasps, she lay motionless, her eyes open and staring, while the fingers played over her skin. It took some moments for us to realize she had lost consciousness, though she soon revived. Another time, walking across a room, she thrust out an arm and seized the back of a chair as her body leaned slowly to one side, before she straightened and continued her walk as if nothing had happened. I understood that these feverish games, these lavish abandonments, were no longer innocent. Sometimes I saw in her eyes the restless unhappiness of someone for whom nothing, not even such ravishments, would ever be enough.

One afternoon when I walked to Main Street to return a book to the library, I saw Clara Schuler stepping out of Cerino's grocery store. I felt an intense desire to speak to her; to warn her against us; to praise her extravagantly; to beg her to teach me the difficult art of laughter. Shyness constrained me, though I wasn't shy—but it was as if I had no right to intrude on her, to break the spell of her remoteness. I kept out of sight and followed her home. When she climbed the wooden steps of her porch, one of which creaked like the floor of an attic, I stepped boldly into view, daring her to turn and see me. She opened the front door and disappeared into the house. For a while I stood there, trying to remember what it was I had wanted to say to Clara Schuler, the modest girl with a fierce, immodest gift. A clattering startled me. Along the shady sidewalk, trembling with spots of sunlight, a girl with yellow pigtails was pulling a lollipop-red wagon, which held a jouncing rhinoceros. I turned and headed home.

That night I dreamed about Clara Schuler. She was standing in a sunny backyard, looking into the distance. I came over to her and spoke a few words, but she did not look at me. I began to walk around her, speaking urgently and trying to catch her gaze, but her face was always turned partly away, and when I seized her arm it felt soft and crumbly, like pie dough.

About this time I began to sense among us a slight shift of attention, an inner wandering. A change was in the air. The laugh parlors seemed to lack their old aura of daring—they'd grown a little familiar, a little humdrum. While one of us lay writhing in laughter, the rest of us glanced toward the windows. One day someone pulled a deck of cards from a pocket, and as we waited our turn on the bed we sat down on the floor to a few hands of gin rummy.

We tried to conjure new possibilities, but our minds were mired in the old forms. Even the weather conspired to hold us back. The heat of midsummer pressed against us like fur. Leaves, thick as tongues, hung heavily from the maples. Dust lay on polished furniture like pollen.

One night it rained. The rain continued all the next day and night; wind knocked down tree branches and telephone wires. In the purple-black sky, prickly lines of lightning burst forth with troubling brightness. Through the dark rectangles of our windows, the lightning flashes looked like textbook diagrams of the circulation of the blood.

The turn came with the new sun. Mist like steam rose from soaked grass. We took up our old games, but it was as if something had been carried off by the storm. At a birthday party in a basement playroom with an out-of-tune piano, a girl named Janet Bianco, listening to a sentimental song, began to behave strangely. Her shoulders trembled, her lips quivered. Mirthless tears rolled along her cheeks. Gradually we understood that she was crying. It caught our attention—it was a new note. Across the room, another girl suddenly burst into tears.

A passion for weeping seized us. It proved fairly easy for one girl to set off another, who set off a third. Boys, tense and embarrassed, gave way slowly. We held weep-fests that left us shaken and thrilled. Here and there a few laugh parties and laugh clubs continued to meet, but we knew it was the end of an era.

Clara Schuler attended that birthday party. As the rage for weeping swept over us, she appeared at a few gatherings, where she stood off to one side with a little frown. We saw her there, looking in our direction, before she began to shimmer and dissolve through our abundant tears. The pleasures of weeping proved more satisfying than the old pleasures of laughter, possibly because, when all was said and done, we weren't happy, we who were restless and always in search of diversion. And whereas laughter had always been difficult to sustain, weeping, once begun, welled up in us with gratifying ease. Several girls, among them Helen Jacoby, discovered in themselves rich and unsuspected depths of unhappiness, which released in the rest of us lengthy, heartfelt bouts of sorrow.

It wasn't long after the new craze had swept away the old that we received an invitation from Clara Schuler. None of us except Helen Jacoby had ever set foot in her house before. We arrived in the middle of a sunny afternoon; in the living room it was already dusk. A tall woman in a long drab dress pointed vaguely toward a carpeted stairway. Clara, she said, was waiting for us in the guest room in the attic. At the top of the stairs we came to a hallway covered with faded wallpaper, showing repeated waterwheels beside repeated streams shaded by willows. A door with a loose knob led up to the attic. Slowly we passed under shadowy rafters that slanted down over wooden barrels and a big bear in a chair and a folded card-table leaning against a tricycle. Through a half-open door we entered the guest room. Clara Schuler stood with her hands hanging down in front of her, one hand lightly grasping the wrist of the other.

It looked like the room of someone's grandmother, which had been invaded by a child. On a frilly bedspread under old lace curtains sat a big rag doll wearing a pink dress with an apron. Her yellow yarn hair looked as heavy as candy. On top of a mahogany chest of drawers, a black-and-white photograph of a bearded man sat next to a music box decorated with elephants and balloons. It was warm and dusty in that room; we didn't know whether we were allowed to sit on the bed, which seemed to belong to the doll, so we sat on the floor. Clara herself looked tired and tense. We hadn't seen her for a while. We hardly thought about her. It occurred to me that we'd begun to forget her.

Seven or eight of us were there that day, sitting on a frayed maroon rug and looking awkwardly around. After a while Clara tried to close the door—the wood, swollen in the humid heat, refused to fit into the frame—and then walked to the center of the room. I had the impression that she was going to say something to us, but she stood looking vaguely before her. I could sense what she was going to do even before she began to laugh. It was a good laugh, one that reminded me of the old laugh parties, and a few of us joined her uneasily, for old times' sake. But we were done with that game, we could scarcely recall those days of early summer. And, in truth, even our weeping had begun to tire us, already we longed for new enticements. Maybe Clara had sensed a change and was trying to draw us back; maybe she simply wanted to perform one more time. If she was trying to assert her old power over us, she failed entirely. But neither our halfhearted laughter nor our hidden resistance seemed to trouble her, as she abandoned herself to her desire.

There was a concentration in Clara Schuler's laughter, a completeness, an immensity that we hadn't seen before. It was as if she wanted to outdo herself, to give the performance of her life. Her face, flushed on the cheek ridges, was so pale that laughter seemed to be draining away her blood. She stumbled to one side and nearly fell over—someone swung up a supporting hand. She seemed to be laughing harder and harder, with a ferocity that flung her body about, snapped her head back, wrenched her out of shape. The room, filled with wails of laughter, began to feel unbearable. No one knew what to do. At one point she threw herself onto the bed, gasping in what appeared to be an agony of laughter. Slowly, gracefully, the big doll slumped forward, until her head touched her stuck-out legs and the yellow yarn hair lay flung out over her feet.

After thirty-five minutes someone rose and quietly left. I could hear the footsteps fading through the attic.

Others began to leave; they did not say good-bye. Those of us who remained found an old Monopoly game and sat in a corner to play. Clara's eyes had taken on their glassy look, as cries of laughter continued to erupt from her. After the first hour I understood that no one was going to forgive her for this.

When the Monopoly game ended, everyone left except Helen Jacoby and me. Clara was laughing fiercely, her face twisted as if in pain. Her skin was so wet that she looked hard and shiny, like metal. The laughter, raw and harsh, poured up out of her as if some mechanism had broken. One of her forearms was bruised. The afternoon was drawing on toward five when Helen Jacoby, turning up her hands and giving a bitter little shrug, stood up and walked out of the room.

I stayed. And as I watched Clara Schuler, I had the desire to reach out and seize her wrist, to shake her out of her laughter and draw her back before it was too late. No one is allowed to laugh like that, I wanted to say. Stop it right now. She had passed so far beyond herself that there was almost nothing left —nothing but that creature emptying herself of laughter. It was ugly—indecent—it made you want to look away. At the same time she bound me there, for it was as if she were inviting me to follow her to the farthest and most questionable regions of laughter, where laughter no longer bore any relation to earthly things and, sufficient to itself, soared above the world to flourish in the void. There, you were no longer yourself—you were no longer anything.

More than once I started to reach for her arm. My hand hung in front of me like some fragile piece of sculpture I was holding up for inspection. I saw that I was no more capable of stopping Clara Schuler in her flight than I was of joining her. I could only be a witness.

It was nearly half past five when I finally stood up. "Clara!" I said sharply, but I might as well have been talking to the doll. I wondered whether I'd ever spoken her name before. She was still laughing when I disappeared into the attic. Downstairs I told her mother that something was wrong, her daughter had been laughing for hours. She thanked me, turned slowly to gaze at the carpeted stairs, and said she hoped I would come again.

The local paper reported that Mrs. Schuler discovered her daughter around seven o'clock. She had already stopped breathing. The official cause of death was a ruptured blood vessel in the brain, but we knew the truth: Clara Schuler had died of laughter. "She was always a good girl," her mother was quoted as saying, as if death were a form of disobedience. We cooperated fully with the police, who found no trace of foul play.

For a while Clara Schuler's death was taken up eagerly by the weeping parties, which had begun to languish and which now gained a feverish new energy before collapsing decisively. It was late August; school was looming; as if desperately we hurled ourselves into a sudden passion for old board games, staging fierce contests of Monopoly and Risk, altering the rules in order to make the games last for days. But already our ardor was tainted by the end of summer, already we could see, in eyes glittering with the fever of obsession, a secret distraction.

On a warm afternoon in October I took a walk into Clara Schuler's neighborhood. Her house had been sold. On the long front steps sat a little girl in a green-and-orange-checked jacket, leaning forward and tightening a roller skate with a big silver key. I stood looking up at the bedroom window, half expecting to hear a ghostly laughter. In the quiet afternoon I heard only the whine of a backyard chain saw and the slap of a jump rope against a sidewalk. I felt awkward standing there, like someone trying to peek through a window. The summer seemed far away, as distant as childhood. Had we really played those games? I thought of Clara Schuler, the girl who had died of a ruptured blood vessel, but it was difficult to summon her face. What I could see clearly was that rag doll, slowly falling forward. Something stirred in my chest, and to my astonishment, with a kind of sorrow, I felt myself burst into a sharp laugh.

I looked around uneasily and began walking away. I wanted to be back in my own neighborhood, where people didn't die of laughter. There we threw ourselves into things for a while, lost interest, and went on to something else. Clara Schuler played games differently. Had we disappointed her? As I turned the corner of her street, I glanced back at the window over her dirt driveway. I had never learned whether it was her room. For all I knew, she slept on the other side of the house, or in the guest room in the attic. Again I saw that pink-and-yellow doll, falling forward in a slow, graceful, grotesque bow. No, my laughter was all right. It was a salute to Clara Schuler, an acknowledgment of her great gift. In her own way, she was complete. I wondered whether she had been laughing at us a little, up there in her attic.

As I entered the streets of my neighborhood, I felt a familiar restlessness. Everything stood out clearly. In an open, sunny garage, a man was reaching up to an aluminum ladder hanging horizontally on hooks, while in the front yard a tenth-grade girl wearing tight jeans rolled up to midcalf and a billowy red-and-black lumberjack shirt was standing with a rake beside a pile of yellow leaves shot through with green, shading her eyes and staring up at a man hammering on a roof. The mother of a friend of mine waved at me from behind the shady, sun-striped screen of a porch. Against a backboard above a brilliant white garage door, a basketball went round and round the orange rim of a basket. It was Sunday afternoon, time of the great boredom. Deep in my chest I felt a yawn begin; it went shuddering through my jaw. On the crosspiece of a sunny telephone pole, a grackle shrieked once and was still. The basketball hung in the white net. Suddenly it came unstuck and dropped with a smack to the driveway, the grackle rose into the air, somewhere I heard a burst of laughter. I nodded in the direction of Clara Schuler's neighborhood and continued down the street. Tomorrow something was bound to happen.

2003

M. RICKERT

(b. 1959)

The Chambered Fruit

STONES. Roots. Chips like bones. The moldering scent of dry
leaves and dirt, the odd aroma of mint. What grew here before
it fell to neglect and misuse? I remember this past spring's
tulips and daffodils, sprouted amongst the weeds, picked and
discarded without discrimination. I was so distracted by my
dead daughter that I rarely noticed the living. I take a deep
breath. Mint thyme. It should have survived the neglect, perhaps did, but now has fallen victim to my passionate weeding,
as so much of more significance has fallen victim before it. I
pick up a small, brown bulb and set it, point up, in the hole,
cover it with dirt. Geese fly overhead. I shade my eyes to watch
them pass, and then cannot avoid surveying the property.

Near the old barn are piles of wood and brick meant to further its renovation. Leaves and broken branches litter the
stacks. The wood looks slightly warped, weathered by the seasons it's gone untended. The yard is bristly with dried weeds
and leaves. The house has suffered the worst. Surely, instead of
planting bulbs I should be calling a contractor. It can't be
good, the way it looks like it's begun to sink into the earth or
how the roof litters shingles that spear into the ground around
it. But who should I call? How far do I have to search to find
someone who doesn't know our story?

I think of it like the nursery rhyme. Inside the old farmhouse
with the sagging porch, through the large, sunny kitchen, past
the living room with the wood-burning stove, up the creaking
stairs and down the hall lined with braided rugs, past the bathroom with the round window and claw-footed tub, past the
yellow and white bedroom we called the guest room, past her
room (where the door is shut) to our bedroom—my bedroom
now—there is, on the bedside table, a picture of the three of
us. It's from her last birthday. Twelve candles on the cake. She
is bent to blow them out, her face in pretty profile. Her dark

528

hair brushes against the smooth skin of her puffed cheek; her eye, bright with happiness, dark-lashed beneath its perfectly arched brow. Jack and I stand behind her. Both of us are blurry, the result of Jack having set up the camera for automatic timer, his running to be in the shot, me moving to make room for him. He looks like her, only handsome, and I look like, well, someone passing by who got in the picture by mistake, a blur of long, untidy hair, an oversized shirt, baggy slacks. The camera captures and holds their smiles forever, locked in innocence and joy, and my smile, strained, my focus somewhere past the borders of the picture, as if I see, in the shadows, what is coming.

When I think of everything that happened, from the beginning, I look for clues. In a way, there are so many it baffles strangers that we couldn't see them. But to understand this, and really, I'm beyond expecting anyone else to understand this, but for my own understanding, I have to remember that to be human is a dangerous state. That said, Jack's nature is not profoundly careless, and I am not, really, in spite of everything you might have read or concluded, criminally naïve. Though of course I accept, even as I rebel against its horrible truth, that a great deal of the fault was ours. Sometimes I think more ours than his. When I look for clues to the dangerous parents we'd become I have to accept the combustible combination that occurred, just once, when Jack was careless and I was naïve and that's all it took. We lost her.

You may be familiar with my old work. Folk scenes, sort of like Grandma Moses except, frankly, hers are better. Maybe the difference is that hers were created from real memories and mine were made from longing. No one I know has ever ridden in a horse-drawn sleigh, with or without bells. We did not hang Christmas wreaths on all the doors and from the street lamps lit with candles. We did not send the children to skate at the neighborhood pond (which didn't exist, the closest thing being the town dump) or burn leaves and grow pumpkins (well, the Hadley's grew pumpkins but their farmhouse was an old trailer so it didn't really fit the picture). We did garden, but our gardens did not all blossom into perfect flower at the same moment on the same day, the women standing in aprons, talking over the fence. The sun shone but it didn't shine the way I painted it, a great ball of light with spears of brightness around it.

These are the paintings I made. Little folk scenes that were actually quite popular, not in town, of course, but in other places where people imagined the world I painted existed. I made a decent living at it. Even now, when all I paint are dark and frightening scenes of abduction and despair that I show no one (who would come anyway, even old friends keep their distance now), I live off the royalties. My paintings are on calendars, Christmas cards, coasters, T-shirts. In the first days of horror, when the news coverage was so heavy, I thought someone would certainly point out that I (the neglectful mother of the dead girl) was also the painter, C. R. Rite, but as far as I know the connection was never made and my income has not suffered for my neglect.

Jack still represents my work, which also makes it strange that no one ever made the connection. Maybe people assumed we were actually farmers, though the locals certainly knew that wasn't true. Maybe the media was just too busy telling the grisly details of our story to focus any attention on the boring issue of our finances. Certainly that matter isn't very titillating. What people seemed to want to hear was how our daughter died, an endless nightmare from which I can't ever wake, that strangers actually watch and read as some form of entertainment.

I accept my fault in this, and I know it's huge. I live every day with the Greek proportions of our story. In the classic nature I had a fault, a small area, like Achilles's heel, that left me vulnerable.

But not evil. As Jack likes to point out, we didn't do that to her and we would have stopped it from happening if we knew how.

The unforgivable thing, everyone agrees, is that we didn't see it. How evil do you have to be? We did not keep our daughter safe and she's dead because of that. Isn't that evil enough?

When we moved here, Steff was eight. She didn't know that we were really country people, having lived her whole life in the city. At first she spent all her time in her room with her books and her dolls but eventually, during that giddy, first hot summer when I walked about in my slip (when the construction crew wasn't working on the barn) eating raspberries off the bushes and planting sunflower seeds, and hollyhocks (though it was too late and they wouldn't bloom), she joined me, staying close, afraid of all the space, the strangeness of sky. Eventually, she came to love it too and brought blankets into the yard for picnics, both real and imagined, and paper to color, which, in true Buddha-child fashion she left to blow about the yard when she was finished. When one of these pictures blew across my path, a scene of a girl picking flowers, a shimmering angel behind her, I memorized it and then let it blow away, thinking it would be a gift for somebody unlucky enough not to have a child who drew pictures of that other world which children are so close to.

In the city, Steffie had attended a small private school with a philosophy that sheltered children from the things in our world that make them grow up so fast. The influence of media was discouraged and, contrary to national trend, computer use was considered neither necessary nor particularly beneficial to children. At eight, Steffie still played with dolls, and believed in, if not magic, at least a magicalness to the world; a condition that caused strangers to look at her askance and try to measure her IQ but for which I took great pride. In her school they learned the mythic stories, needlework, and dance. Friends of mine with children in public or other private schools talked of the homework stress and the busyness of their lives, transporting kids from practice to practice. When I visited these friends their children did not play the piano, or happily kick soccer balls in the yard. In spite of all those lessons, or, I suspected, because of them, these children sat listless and bleary-eyed in front of the television or wandered about the house, restless and bored, often resorting to eating, while Steffie played with dolls or spoons, whatever was available. I feel that our society has forgotten the importance of play, the simple beginnings of a creative mind. The value of that. Not that anyone is interested in parental guidance from me now.

At any rate, Steffie got off the bus, that first day, in tears. Several of the children would not sit with her because, they said, we were a bunch of hippies who ran around the yard in our underthings. When Steffie told me this I cried right along with her. I'd made a life out of forgetting the world. I found its reminders sharp and disturbing.

Eventually, she adjusted and I did too. I wore clothes in the yard, though I was baffled how anyone knew I'd ever done differently. Steff put away her dolls and proudly carried her heavy backpack filled with books and maps and serious questions about the real world, completely neglecting anything about the spiritual. Incredibly (to me) she liked it. A lot. She loved the candy they were rewarded with, the movies they watched. "I like it because it's normal," she said, and I realized that she knew we were not.

The years passed. I had the barn converted to an art studio and planned to further the renovation so that I could turn it into a sort of community art center for teenagers. I imagined Saturday mornings teaching painting, others teaching things like weaving, or, when Steffie began to take an interest in it, even dance. I think part of the motivation for this plan was the idea of filling the place with teenagers and helping Steffie's social life, which still seemed, though she never complained, strangely quiet for a child her age.

So, when Jack bought the computer, I thought it was a good idea. He said he needed it for the business and Steffie had been complaining for some time that she "needed" one too. He brought home the computer and I didn't argue. After all, he and Steff were the ones dealing with the notorious "real" world and I was the one who got to spend all morning painting happy pictures and the rest of the day gardening, or baking cookies, or reading a good book. Who in the world lived a life like mine?

When the computer was set up and ready to use in his office, Jack called me to come look. I looked into the brightly colored screen and felt numbed by it. Steff, however, was thrilled. Soon the two of them were talking a strange language I didn't understand. I drifted off into private thoughts, mentally working on paintings, scenes from a time before the world was enchanted by screens.

About three months before (oh, God, I still cannot write these words without trembling) her last birthday, Jack began campaigning that we get Steff her own computer. I didn't like the idea but I couldn't say why, though I held my ground until one Saturday when I drove into town to the post office and saw a group of girls who looked to be Steffie's age, and who I thought I recognized from classroom functions, sitting at the picnic table outside the ice cream place. A few of the girls caught me staring, and they began whispering behind open hands. I turned away. Had I done this to her? Was it my strangeness that made her unpopular? I went home and told Jack to go ahead and buy the thing. We gave it to her for her twelfth birthday, that's when we took the picture, the one I still have on the bedside table.

Steff was thrilled. She hugged us both and gave us kisses and thanked us so much that I began to believe we had done the right thing. I was baffled how this silent box was going to make her life better but after seeing those girls together, I was ready to try anything.

They set up the computer in her room. At night, after dinner, they each went off for hours, clicking and staring at their separate screens. I lit candles and sat, with the cat in my lap, reading. I guess I had some vague ideas about homework, and I'd heard that there were ways to view great paintings from distant museums on the computer. I assumed she was doing things like that. I thought she should be doing more interacting with the world. I thought this as I sat reading, with the cat on my lap, and tried to believe that one solitude is the same as any other.

As though she'd been given the magic elixir for a social life, she began talking about various friends. Eventually one name came up more and more frequently. Celia read the same books Steffie did and liked to draw and dance. When Celia asked Steff to sleep over I was thrilled until I found out Stephanie had never actually met the girl but only "talked" to her on the computer.

Of course, I said this would not happen. She could be anyone; why, Celia might not even be a girl, I said. No, she could not sleep over at this stranger's house, who, coincidentally lived only twenty-four miles away.

Steff burst into tears at the dinner table, threw her napkin on the plate. "You don't want me to be normal," she said, "you want me to be just like you and I'm not!" Then she ran out of the kitchen, up the stairs to her bedroom where she actually slammed the door, all of this perhaps not unusual behavior for an almost teenager but completely new for Steff.

Jack looked at me accusingly.

"You can't expect me to let her go off to some stranger's house. We don't even know the family."

"Whose family do we know?"

I understood his point. I had sheltered us, all of us, with my sheltered ways.

"When it comes down to it, if she went anywhere in town, we wouldn't know those people either."

"It's not the same thing. People have reputations." As soon as I saw the look on Jack's face, I realized that our reputation was probably more extensive than I knew. If not for me, they would be having a normal life. I was the odd one. It was all my fault.

"What if I speak to the girl's parents, would that make you more comfortable?"

For a moment, I considered that we invite the girl's family over, we could have a barbecue, but the thought of having to spend a whole evening entertaining anyone horrified me. When it comes right down to it, my daughter died because of my reluctance to entertain. How ridiculous and horrifying. Instead, I agreed that she could go if Jack talked to Celia's parents first.

We went up to her room together. We knocked and entered. I expected to find her lying across the bed, my posture of teenage despair, but instead, she was sitting at the desk, staring into the computer.

"We've decided you can go, but we want to speak to her parents first."

She turned and grinned, bathed in computer glow, all the color gone from her pretty face and replaced with green.

"Is that Celia now?" Jack asked.

She nodded.

"Ask her for her number."

She began typing. I turned and walked away. What was I so creeped out about? This was the new world. My daughter and my husband were a part of it, as was I, even if with reluctance.

*

Jack spoke to Celia's father that night. It turned out they had a lot in common too. He was an insurance salesman. His wife, however, was very different from me, a lawyer out of town until Friday night. Jack covered the mouthpiece. "He wants to pick Steff up around 4:30 on Friday. He's going to be passing through town. They'll pick Celia up at her dance class, and Sarah will get home from D.C. about 5:30. He's spoken to her and she's happy to have Stephanie over. What do you think?"

"How does he sound?"

"He sounds a lot like me."

Steff was standing in the kitchen doorway watching. I wasn't used to her squinty-eyed appraisal, as if suddenly there was something suspicious about me.

"Okay," I said.

Steff grinned. Jack took his hands off the mouthpiece. "That'll work out fine," he said in a boisterous voice. They really both looked so thrilled. Had I done this to them? Kept them so sheltered that Stephanie's sleepover at a friend's house on a Friday night, an absolutely normal occurrence for any girl her age, was such an enormous event?

Was this all my fault?

He was right on time. It was a beautiful spring day, unseasonably warm. I found him immediately affable, friendly, grinning dimples. I thought he looked younger than Jack or me, though in reality he was a year older. I guess people without consciences don't wrinkle like the rest of us. I opened the door and we shook hands. He had a firm handshake, a bit sweaty, but it was a warm day. Jack came out and the two of them got to talking immediately. I slipped away to get Steff. I went to her bedroom. Her backpack was packed, the sleeping bag rolled next to it, but she was not in the room. I walked over to the window and saw her in the garden, picking flowers. I opened the window. She looked up and waved, the flowers in her hand arcing the sky. I waved, pointed to his car. She nodded and ran toward the house. I brought the ridiculously heavy backpack and sleeping bag downstairs. When I got to the kitchen, she was standing there, her cheeks flushed, holding the bouquet of daffodils and tulips while Jack and Celia's father talked. I helped her wrap the stems in a wet paper towel and aluminum foil. "This is a very nice idea," I whispered to her at the sink.

She smiled and shrugged. "Celia said her mom likes flowers too."

What was it about that that set off a little warning buzzer in my head? All these coincidences. I shook it back; after all, isn't that how friendships are made, by common interests? We turned and the fathers stopped talking. Celia's father grinned at Steff. Once more the alarm sounded but he bent down, picked up the pack, and said something like, What do kids put in these things, Celia's is always so heavy too. They walked to the door. I wanted to hug Stephanie but it seemed silly and probably would be embarrassing to her, and, after all, hadn't I already embarrassed her enough? The screen door banged shut. I stood in the kitchen and listened to the cheerful voices, the car doors slam, the engine, the sound of the gravel as they drove away. Too late, I ran out to wave goodbye. I have no idea if Steffie saw me or not.

Jack wrapped his arms around my waist, nuzzled my neck. "The garden? Kitchen? Name your place, baby."

"I should have told her to call when she gets there."

"Honey, she'll be back tomorrow."

"Let's call her, just to make sure she's comfortable."

"Chloe—"

"After we call her, the garden."

There was a sudden change in the weather. The temperature dropped thirty degrees. We closed windows and doors and put on sweaters and jeans. It began to rain about 5:30 and it just kept raining. We called at six, seven, eight. No one answered. It began to hail.

"Something's wrong," I said.

"They probably just went to a movie."

We called at nine. It rang and rang.

"I'm going there."

"What? Are you kidding? Do you have any idea how embarrassing that would be for her?"

"Well, where are they, Jack?"

"They went to a movie, or the mall, or out for pizza. Not everyone lives like us."

Ten. Still no answer.

I put on my coat.

"Where are you going?"

"Give me the directions."

"You can't be serious."

"Where are the directions?"

"Nothing's wrong."

"Jack!"

"I don't have any directions."

"What do you mean? How are we supposed to pick her up?"

"Turns out he's coming back this way tomorrow. He's going to drop her off."

Lightning split the sky and thunder shook the house. "Do you even have an address?"

"I'm sure everything's all right," he said, but he said it softly and I could hear the fear in his voice.

We called at 10:20, 10:30, 10:41, 10:50, 10:54. At last, at 10:59, a man's voice.

"Hello, this is Steffie's mother, is this—" I don't even know his name "—is this Celia's father?"

"I just picked up the phone, lady, ain't no one here."

"What do you mean? Who are you? Where is everyone?"

"This is just a phone booth, okay?"

I drop the phone. I run to the bathroom. In the distance I hear Jack's voice, he says the number and then he says, "Oh my God," and I don't hear the rest, over the sound of my retching.

Police sirens blood red. Blue uniforms and serious faces. Lights blaze. Pencils scratch across white pads. Jack wipes his hand through his hair, over and over again. Dry taste in my mouth. The smell of vomit. The questions. The descriptions. Fingerprint powder. I take them to her bedroom. Strange hands paw her things. Her diary. Someone turns her computer on. "Do you know her password?" I shake my head. "Well," says the man reading her diary, "it appears she really believed there was a Celia." What? Of course she did, can I see that? "Sorry, ma'am, it's evidence." Downstairs. More uniforms and raincoats. Police banter about the weather. Blazing lights. The telephone rings. Sudden silence. I run to answer it. "Hello."

It's Mrs. Bialo, my neighbor; she says, is everything all right? No, it's not. I hang up the phone. The activity resumes. Suddenly I see a light like the tiny flicker of a hundred fireflies hovering close to me and I hear her voice, *Mom?* I fall to my knees sobbing. Jack rushes over and holds me like I'm breakable. There is a temporary and slight change in the activity around us but then it continues as before and goes on like this for hours. In early morning there is a freak snowfall. We start getting calls from newspapers and magazines. A TV truck parks at the end of our drive. My neighbor, Mrs. Bialo, shows up with banana bread and starts making coffee. I stand on the porch and watch the snow salting down. The red tulips droop wounded against the icy white. The daffodils bow their silent bells. I listen to the sound of falling snow. I haven't told anyone what I know. What would be the point? Who would believe me? But I know. She's dead. She's dead. She's gone.

Let's go quickly over the details. The body. Oh, her body. Found. The tests confirm. Raped and strangled. My little darling.

Then, incredibly, he is found too. Trying to do the same thing again but this time to a more savvy family. He even used the name Celia. The sergeant tells me this with glee. "They always think they're so clever, but they're not. They make mistakes." How excited everybody is. They found him. He can't do it again. This is good. But I don't feel happiness, which disappoints everyone.

Jack agrees to go on a talk show. They convince him he will be helping other families and other little girls but really he's there so everyone can feel superior. One lady stands up. She is wearing a sensible dress and shoes. She is a sensible mother, anyone can see that, and she says, "I just don't understand, in this day and age, how you could let your daughter go off with a stranger like that?" She says it like she really cares, but she beams when the audience claps because really, she just wants to make her point.

Jack tries to say the stuff about how really everyone takes chances when they send their children off to other homes. I mean, we're all really strangers, he says. But they aren't buying it, this clever audience. The sensible lady stands up again and says, "I'm really sorry about what happened to your daughter but you gotta accept that it's at least partly your fault." There is scattered applause. The host tries to take it back. "I'm sure no one here means to imply this is your fault," he says, "we only want to learn from your mistakes." The audience applauds at that as well. Everyone gets applause except Jack.

After the taping he calls me in tears. I'm not much help as I am also feeling superior since I would never be so stupid as to fall for the "You're helping others" line the talk show people keep trying. He says it was terrible but on the day it airs, he insists we watch. It is terrible.

We move through the house and our lives. I think I will never eat again and then, one day, I do. I think I well never make love again and then, one night, something like that happens but it is so different, there is such a cold desperation to it, that I think it will never happen again, and it doesn't.

Six months later there is a trial. We are both witnesses for the prosecution so we can't attend. The defense attorney does a mean job on us but the prosecutor says, "He's just trying to distract the jury. It's not going to work. In fact, it'll probably backfire, generating more sympathy."

Fuck their sympathy, I say.

Jack looks as if I've just confirmed the worst rumors he's heard about me. The attorney maintains his placid expression, but his tone of voice is mildly scolding when he says, "The jury is your best hope now."

I think of her picking flowers in the garden that afternoon, the way she waved them in an arc across the sky.

When the verdict is read I stare at the back of his head. I think how, surely, if I had really studied him that day, instead of being so distracted by self-doubt, I never would have let him take her. The shape of his ears at the wrong height, the tilt of his head, something about his shoulders, all of it adds up. It's so obvious now.

"Guilty," the foreman says.

The courtroom is strangely quiet. Somehow, it is not enough.

*

When Jack and I get home he goes into his office. I wander about, until finally I settle on a plan. I take the fireside poker and walk up the stairs to her room where I smash the computer. When I'm done Jack is standing there, watching. "That's a very expensive machine," he says.

"Fuck you," I say.

It doesn't get any better. At the end of the month, he moves out.

Fat, white flakes fall all day. The pine trees are supplicant with snow. I sit in my rocking chair like an old woman, the blue throw across my lap. I thought about starting a fire with the well-seasoned wood left over from last winter but when I opened the stove and saw those ashes I didn't have the energy to clean them out. I rock and watch the snow fall. The house creaks with emptiness. The phone rings. I don't answer it. I fall asleep in the chair and when I wake it's dark. I walk to the kitchen, turn on the outside light. It's still snowing. I turn off the light and go to bed, not bothering to change out of my sweats and turtleneck. The phone rings and I grumble into the blankets but I don't answer it. I sleep what has become my usual restless sleep. In the morning it's still snowing.

Day after day it snows. Finally, the power goes out. The phone lines are down. I don't mind this at all. Oddly, I am invigorated by it. I shovel the wood-burning stove's ashes into an old paint can, find the wood carrier, and bring in stacks of wood and kindling. I build a fire and once I'm sure it's really started good, go upstairs and get my book, some blankets and pillows. I find the flashlights in the kitchen, both with working batteries, search through the linen closet and then the kitchen cupboards until I remember and find the portable radio on the top shelf in the basement. I stoke the fire, wrap myself in a blanket. How efficient we were, how well organized, how prepared for this sort of emergency, how completely useless, even culpable, when she needed us most. I turn on the radio. It will snow and snow, they say. We are having a blizzard. There are widespread reports of power outages. The Red Cross is setting up in the high school, which, actually, is also currently out of power so residents are advised to stay home for now. I click off the radio.

The phone is ringing.

"Hello?"

"Mom, where are you?"

"Steff? Steff?"

But there is no response. I stand there, holding the phone while the kitchen shadows lengthen around me. Still I stand there. I say her name over and over again. I don't know how long I stand there before I hang up but when I do, I'm a changed woman. If I can't keep her alive, and it's been all too obvious that I can't, I'll take her dead. Yes, I want this ghost.

The person you most love has died and is now trying to contact you. You are happy.

You do whatever you can to help. You go out in the middle of the worst blizzard on record since there has been a record and drive to town. A trip that usually takes ten minutes today takes an hour and a half and you are happy. You go to the local drugstore and walk right past the aisles stripped of batteries and Sterno cans and candles to the toy section where you select a Ouija board and tarot cards and you don't care when the clerk looks at you funny because you already have a strange reputation and who even cares about reputation when your dead daughter is trying to talk to you. You are not scared. You are excited. You know you probably should change your expression and look bored or disinterested as the clerk tallies up your purchases on a notepad because the cash register doesn't work due to the power outage and you probably should say something about buying this for your teenage niece but instead you stand there grinning with excitement. You sense the clerk, who looks to be a teenager herself, only a few years older than your dead daughter, watching you leave the store and walk through the storm to your truck, the only vehicle in the parking lot.

It takes even longer to get home and by the time you do the fire has gone out and the house is cold. You are too excited to stop everything to build another fire. Instead you set up the Ouija board on the kitchen table. The cat comes over to smell

it. You light a candle. The cat rubs against your leg. You sit at
the table. You rest your fingers lightly on the pointer. You remember this from when you were young. "Steff," you say, and
the sound of it is both silly and wonderful in the silent house.
As if, maybe, she's just in another room or something. "Steff,
are you here?" You wait for the pointer to move. It does not.
"Steff?" Suddenly the house is wild with light and sound. The
kitchen blazes brightly, the refrigerator hums, the heater turns
on. The phone rings. You push back the chair, stand, and bang
your thigh against the table. The phone rings and rings.
"Hello?"

"Mom?"

"Steff, Steff, is that you?"

The dial tone buzzes.

You slam the phone down. The cat races out of the room
with her tail puffed up.

You turn to the Ouija board. The pointer rests over the word.
Yes. You try to remember if you left it there but you don't
think you did or maybe it got knocked there when you hit
your leg but why are you trying to explain it when there is only
one explanation for your dead daughter's voice on the phone?
Slowly you turn and look at the silent phone. You pick up the
receiver and listen to the dial tone.

You don't know whether to laugh or cry and suddenly your
body is convulsing in some new emotion that seems to be a
combination of both. You sink to the kitchen floor. The cat
comes back into the room and lies down beside you. The dead
can't make phone calls but the living can lose their minds. You
decide you won't do that. You get up.

You try to believe it didn't happen.

But just in case, every time the phone rings, I answer it. I speak
to an endless assortment of telemarketers wanting to sell me
newspapers, a different phone service, offering me exciting opportunities to win trips to Florida, or the Bahamas. Jack calls
about once a week and we generally have the same conversation. (I'm fine. He can't come back. I haven't forgiven him. I
haven't forgiven myself. I don't expect to. Ever.) Once there is
a call where no one speaks at all and I'm terrified to hang up
the phone so I stand there saying hello, hello, and finally I say,

Steff? and there's a click and then the dial tone. Once, an old friend of mine from the city calls and I tell her all lies. How I've begun painting scenes of idyllic life again, how I've begun the healing process. I tell her the things people want me to say and by the end of the conversation she's happy she called and for a few minutes I feel happy too, as though everything I said was true.

I start receiving Christmas cards in the mail, strange greetings of Peace on Earth with scrawled condolences or blessings about this first Christmas without her. Jack calls in tears and tells me how much he misses her and us. I know, I know, I say gently, but you still can't come back. There is a long silence, then he hangs up.

I go into town only for groceries. I lose track of the days so completely that I end up in the supermarket on Christmas Eve. Happy shoppers load carts with turkeys and gift wrap and bottles of wine, bags of shrimp, crackers and cheese. I pick through the limp lettuce, the winter tomatoes. While I'm choosing apples I feel someone watching me and turn to see a teenage girl of maybe sixteen or seventeen standing by the bananas. There is something strange about the girl's penetrating stare beneath her homemade knit cap though it is not unusual to catch people staring at me; after all, I'm the mother of a dead girl. I grab a bag of apples. I wonder if she knew Steff. I turn to look over by the bananas but she's not there.

"I don't know if you remember me or not."

The girl stands at my elbow. The brown knit cap is pulled low over her brow with wisps of brown hair sticking out. She has dark brown eyes, lashed with black. She might be pretty.

"I waited on you during the first storm at Walker's drug-store."

I nod, at a loss at what to say to this strange, staring girl.

She leans close to me. I smell bubblegum, peppermint, and something faintly sour. "I can help," she whispers.

"Excuse me?"

She looks around, in a dramatic way, as if we are sharing state secrets, licks her chapped lips and leans close again. "I know how to talk to dead people. You know, like in that movie. I'm like that kid." She leans back and looks at me with those dark, sad eyes and then scans the room as if frightened of the living. "My name is Maggie Dwinder. I'm in the book." She nods abruptly and walks away. I watch her in her old wool coat, a brown knit scarf trailing down her back like a snake.

"Oh, how are you doing, dear?"

This face sends me back to that day. Snow on tulips. My daughter's death. "Mrs. Bialo, I never thanked you for coming over that morning."

She pats my arm. One of her fingernails is black, the others are lined with dirt. "Don't mention it, dear. I should of made a effort long before. I wouldn't bother you now, except I noticed you was talking to the Dwinder girl."

I nod.

"There's something wrong with that child, her parents are all so upset about it, her father being a reverend and all. Anyhow, I hope she didn't upset you none."

"Oh no," I lie, "we were just talking about apple pie."

My neighbor studies me closely and I can imagine her reporting her findings to the ladies at the checkout, how I am so strange. I'm glad I lied to the old snoop, and feel unreasonably proud that in this small way I may have protected the girl. It doesn't take a Jungian analyst to figure it out. It felt good to protect the girl.

It's the coldest, snowiest winter on record and Christmas morning is no different. The windchill factor is ten below and it's snowing. I stack wood into the carrier, the icy snow stinging my face. My wood supply is rapidly dwindling but I dread trying to buy more wood now, during the coldest winter anyone can remember. I can just imagine the bantering, "Lady, you want wood? Seasoned wood?" Or the pity, "Is this, are you, I'm so sorry, we're out of wood to sell but wait, we'll bring you ours." Or the insult, "What? You want me to bring it where? Not after what you did to that girl, they should have put you in jail for child neglect, letting her leave like that with a stranger." Head bent against the bitter chill, both real and imagined, I carry the wood inside.

There is nothing like that feeling of coming into a warm house from the cold. I turn on the classical music station, make a fire, fill the teakettle, and put it on the kitchen stove. The radio is playing Handel's *Messiah*, the teakettle rattles softly on

the burner, the cat curls up on the braided rug. I wrap my
arms around myself and watch the snow swirl outside the
window. Inexplicably, it stops as suddenly as if turned off by a
switch. The sun comes out, the yard sparkles, and I realize I'm
happy. The teakettle whistles. I turn to take it off the burner,
search through the cupboard for the box of green tea. I wrap
the teabag string around the teapot handle, pour the hot water.
If we never got that stupid computer, if we never (stupidly) let
her go with him, how different this morning would be,
scented by pine and punctuated with laughter, the tear of
wrapping paper and litter of ribbons and bows. I turn, teapot
in hand, to the kitchen table and see that the storm has returned to its full vigor, the crystallized scene obliterated. As it
should be. In my grief this stormy winter has been perfect.

I find my strange Christmas perfect too. I make a vegetable
soup and leave it to simmer on the stove. The radio station
plays beautiful music. All day the weather volleys between winter wonderland and wild storm. I bring out the old photo albums and page through the imperfect memories, her smile but
not her laughter, her face but not her breath, her skin but not
her touch. I rock and weep. Outside, the storm rages. This is
how I spend the first Christmas without her, crying, napping,
in fits of peace and rage.

I go to bed early and for the first time since she died, sleep
through the night. In the morning, a bright winter sun is reflected a thousand times in the thick ice that coats the
branches outside my bedroom window and hangs from the
eaves like daggers. The phone rings.

"Hello?"

"Mom?"

"Steff, talk to me, what do you want?"

"Maggie Dwinder."

"What?"

But there is no answer, only a dial tone.

I tear up half the house looking for the local phone book,
searching through drawers and cupboards, until at last I find it
in Jack's old office on the middle of the otherwise empty desk.
Jack used to sit here in a chaos of papers and folders, a pencil
tucked behind his ear, the computer screen undulating with a

swirl of colored tubes that broke apart and reassembled over and over again. I bring the phone book to the kitchen where I page through to the Ds and find, Dwinder, Reverend John, and Nancy. My hand is shaking when I dial.

"Hello," a cheerful voice answers on the first ring.

"Hello, is Maggie there?"

"Speaking."

"Maggie, I spoke to you on Christmas Eve, at the grocery store."

"Uh-huh?"

"You said you could help me."

"I'm not sure I, oh." The voice drops to a serious tone. "I've been expecting you to call. She really has something important to tell you." While I absorb this, she adds, "I'm really sorry about what happened." Her voice changes to a cheerful tone, "Really? All of it? That's great!"

"I'm sorry I—"

"No way! Everything?"

"Maggie, are you afraid of being overheard?"

"That's the truth."

"Maybe you should come over here."

"Okay, when?"

"Can you come now?"

"Yeah, l have to do the dishes and then I can come over."

"Do you know where I live?"

"Doesn't everybody?"

"Can you get here or should I . . ."

"No. I'll be over as soon as I can."

She took so long to arrive that I started watching for her at the window. In the midst of more bad weather, I saw the dark figure walking up the road. At first, even though I knew she was coming, I had the ridiculous notion that it was Steffie's ghost, but as she got closer, I recognized the old wool coat, the brown knit hat and scarf crusted with snow. She walked carefully, her head bent with the wind, her hands thrust in her pockets, her narrow shoulders hunched against the chill, her snow-crusted jeans tucked into old boots, the kind with buckles. I asked myself how this rag doll was going to help me, then opened the door for her. For a moment she stood there, as if considering turning back, then she nodded and stepped inside.

"You must be freezing. Please, take off your coat."

She whipped off the knit hat and revealed straight, brown hair that fell to her shoulders as she unwrapped the long, wet scarf, unbuttoned her coat (still wearing her gloves, one blue, the other black). I took her things. She sat to unbuckle her boots, while I hung her things in the hall closet. When I returned, she sat at the kitchen table, hunched over in a white sweatshirt. It occurred to me that she might fit into one of Steffie's baggier sweaters but I offered her one of mine instead. She shook her head and said (as she shivered), "No thanks, I'm warm enough."

"Do you want some tea?" She shrugged, then shook her head. "Hot chocolate?"

She looked up and smiled. "Yes, please." I opened the refrigerator, took out the milk. "I like your house. It's not at all like I heard."

I pour the milk into the pan. "What did you hear?"

"Oh, different stuff."

I set the pan on the burner and start opening cupboards, looking for the chocolate bars from last winter.

"Some people say you're a witch."

This is a new one and I'm so startled by it that I bang my head on the shelf. I touch the sore spot and turn to look at her.

"Of course I don't believe it," she says. "I think of you more as a Mother Nature type."

I find the chocolate and drop two bars in with the milk.

"I never saw anyone make it like this before. We always just add water."

"We used to make real whipped cream for it too."

"Of course I wouldn't care if you was, 'cause, you know, I sort of am."

"Excuse me?"

"Well, you know, like, I told you, dead people talk to me."

I stir the milk to just below a boil then pour two mugs full. There is a temporary break in the weather. Sun streams across the kitchen table. I hand the little witch her mug. She holds it with both hands, sniffs it, and smiles.

"You don't look like a witch."

She shrugs. "Well, who knows?"

I sit across from her with my own mug of hot chocolate. Yes. Who knows? All I know is that Steffie told me she wanted Maggie Dwinder. So here she is, sipping hot chocolate in my kitchen, and I'm not sure what I'm supposed to do with her.

As if sensing my inquiry, she stops sipping and looks at me over the rim of the cup. "She wants to come back."

"Come back?"

"She misses you, and she misses it here." She slowly lowers the cup, sets it on the table. "But there's a problem. A couple problems, actually. She can't stay, of course. She can only be here for a little while and then she has to go back."

"No she doesn't."

"She's been gone a long time."

"You don't have to tell me that."

She bites her chapped lips.

"I'm sorry. This isn't easy for me."

"Yeah. Anyway, she can't stay. I'm sorry too, but that's the way it is. Those are the rules and, also . . ."

"Yes?"

"I don't think you're going to like this part."

"Please tell me."

She looks up at me and then down at the table. "The thing is, she doesn't want to stay here anyway, she sort of likes it where she is."

"Being dead?"

Maggie shrugs and attempts a feeble smile. "Well, you could say that's her life now."

I push back from the table, my chair scraping across the floor. "Is that supposed to be funny?" Maggie shrinks at my voice. "Why?"

"I don't know," she says, softly. "Maybe she figures she sort of belongs there now."

"When?"

"What?"

"When does she want to come?"

"That's why she talked to me. 'Cause she said you've been really upset and all but she wonders if you can wait until spring?"

"Spring?"

"Yeah. She wants to come in the spring. If it's okay with you." Maggie watches me closely as I consider this imperfect offer, my daughter returned but only borrowed from the dead. What rational response can there be? Life is composed of large faiths, in the series of beliefs that sustain us, we little humans whose very existence is a borrowing from the dead. I look into Maggie's brown eyes, I fall into them and feel as if I'm being pulled into the earth. All this, as we sit at the kitchen table, a world done and undone, a life given and taken. "Yes," I say. "Tell her spring will be fine."

We are like one of my paintings. Small, in a vast landscape. The snow glistens outside. We are not cold, or hungry, or anything but this, two figures through a lit window, waiting.

Maggie and I became friends of sorts. She liked to sit in the kitchen and chat over hot chocolate about her school day. (Most of her classmates, and all her teachers were "boring.") The cat liked to sit in her lap.

There were no more phone calls from Stephanie. "Don't worry about that," Maggie reassured me, "she'll be here soon enough and you can really talk."

It was the worst winter on record. Maggie said that the students were really "pissed" because they would have to make up days in June.

I grew to look forward to her visits. Eventually we got to talking about painting and she showed me some of her sketches, the ones assigned by the art teacher: boxes, shoes, books, and the ones she drew from her imagination: vampires and shadowed, winged figures, pictures that might have warned me were I not spending my days painting girls picking flowers, with dark figures descending on them. I thought Maggie was wise. She understood and accepted the way the world is, full of death and sorrow. This did not seem to affect her happiness. On the contrary, she seemed to be blossoming, losing the tired, haggard look she had when I first met her. I mentioned this to her one day over hot chocolate and she opened her mouth, then bit her lip and nodded.

"What were you going to say?"

"I don't know if I should."

"No, go ahead."

"It was your daughter."

"What was my daughter?"

"She was wearing me out. I know she wasn't meaning to but it's like she was haunting me ever since she, I mean, she wouldn't leave me alone."

"That doesn't sound like Steffie."

"Yeah, well, I guess people change when they're, you know, dead."

I nod.

"Anyway, it stopped once I talked to you. I guess she just wanted to make sure you got the message."

I remember that time as being almost joyful. What a relief it was to think of our separation as temporary, that she would return to me as she had been before she left, carrying flowers, her cheeks flushed, her eyes bright with happiness.

I got the phone call on a Tuesday afternoon. I remember this so clearly because I marked it with a big, black X on the calendar, and also, that day, though it was already April, there was another storm, so sudden that six motorists were killed in a four-car pileup, one of them a teenage boy. But that was later, after Maggie's parents left.

Maggie's mother calls in the morning, introduces herself, and says that she and her husband want to talk to me, could they stop by for a visit.

How can I refuse them? They are Maggie's parents and I'm sure concerned and curious about this adult she is spending so much time with. Nancy, Maggie's mother, sounds nice enough on the phone. When they arrive an hour later, I think I could like her and, to my surprise, the reverend too.

She has a wide, pleasant face, lightly freckled, red hair the color of certain autumn leaves, and hazel eyes that measure me with a cool but kind mother-to-mother look. She wears a long, dark wool skirt, boots, and a red sweater.

Her husband has a firm handshake and kind, brown eyes. His hair is dark and curly, a little long about the ears. He has a neatly trimmed beard and mustache. I am immediately disturbed and surprised to find myself somewhat attracted to him. He wears blue jeans, and a green sweater that looks homemade and often worn.

They sit side by side on the couch. I sit in the rocker. A pot of tea cools on the table between us, three cups and saucers on the tray beside it. "Would you like some tea?"

Nancy glances at her husband and he nods. "Thank you," he says, "allow me." He reaches over and pours tea for the three of us. I find this simple gesture comforting. How long it has been since anyone has done anything for me.

"I have to thank you," I say, "you've been so kind about allowing Maggie to visit and her company has been much appreciated."

They nod in unison. Then both begin to speak. With a nod from his wife, the reverend continues.

"I feel I owe you an apology. I should have visited you much sooner and then, perhaps, none of this would have happened." He laughs one of those rueful laughs I was always reading about. "What I mean to say is, I should have offered you my services when you were suffering but I thought that you probably had more spiritual assistance than you knew what to do with." He looks at me hopefully.

But I cannot offer him that redemption. Oddly, there had been no one. Oh, many letters offering prayers, and accusations, and a couple Bibles mailed to the house, but no one stood and held my hand, so to speak, spiritually. There was something distasteful about my involvement in Steffie's horrible death; no one wanted any part of it.

He looks into his teacup and sighs.

"We're sorry," Nancy says in a clear, steady voice. "We've been involved with our own problems and because of that it seems we haven't always made the right choices. It's affected our judgement."

"Please, don't worry about it. You're kind to come now."

The reverend sets his cup on the table. "We're here about Maggie."

"She's a lovely girl."

Nancy sets her cup and saucer on the table, licks her lips. I smile at the gesture, so reminiscent of her daughter. "We thought, well, we want you to understand, we hope you understand, that we thought you, being an artist, and Maggie, being so creative. . . ."

The reverend continues. "We prayed and pondered, and thought maybe you two would be good for each other."

"We made the choice to let her be with you for both your sakes."

"Certainly we had no idea."

"Oh, no idea at all."

Suddenly I feel so cold. I sit in the rocking chair and look at the two of them with their earnest faces. I want them to leave. I don't understand yet what they've come to say, but I know I don't want to hear it.

The reverend looks at me with those beautiful eyes and shakes his head. "We're sorry."

Nancy leans forward and reaches as though to pat me on the knee but the reach is short and she brushes air instead. "It's not her fault. It's just the way she is. We only hope you can find it in your heart to forgive her."

The reverend nods. "We know what we're asking here, a woman like you, who has so much to forgive already."

My hands are shaking when I set my teacup down. "I don't know what you're talking about."

The reverend just looks at me with sorrowful eyes. Nancy nods, bites her lower lip, and says, "We know what she's been telling you," she says. "We found her diary."

I open my mouth. She raises her hand. "I know, I would have thought the same thing. It's horrible to read your child's diary, but I did, and I don't regret it." She glances at her husband who does not return the look. "How else can a mother know? They're so secretive at this age. And I was right. After all, look what she's been doing."

I look from her to the reverend. "We know, we can guess how tempting it's been for you to believe her," he says.

"She's ill, really ill."

"We knew this even before—"

"I read her diary."

"But we never thought she—"

"How could we? We hope you understand, she's mentally ill. She didn't mean to cause you pain."

The cold moves through me. Why are they here with their petty family squabbles? So she read her daughter's diary, while I, imperfect mother, never even looked for Steffie's, or had any idea what her e-mail address was. Why are they here apologizing for their living daughter? Why do I care? "I'm not sure I—"

"There's also a scrapbook. If I would have known, if we would have known—"

"A scrapbook?"

The reverend clears his throat. "She was obsessed with your daughter's death. I try to understand it, but God help me, I don't. She saved every article—"

"Every picture."

I imagine Maggie cutting up newspapers, gluing the stories into a red scrapbook, the kind I had as a girl. "It's all right," I say, though I'm not sure that it is. "A lot of people were fascinated by it." I imagine myself on an iceberg, drifting into the deep, cold blue.

The reverend opens his mouth but Nancy speaks, like a shout from the unwanted shore. "You don't understand. We know what she's been telling you, about your daughter coming back, and of course, we hope you realize it's all made up."

There. The words spoken. I close my eyes. The ice in my blood crashes like glass. The reverend's voice whispers from the distance. "We're sorry. It must have been tempting to believe her—"

"She called me. I spoke to her."

He shakes his head. "It was Maggie."

"A mother knows her daughter's voice."

"But you were so upset, right? And she never said much, did she? And in your state—"

"Nancy," the reverend says gently.

The room is filled with sad silence. I can't look at either of them. How stupid I have been, how unbearably stupid. I see the reverend's legs, and then his wife's, unbending.

The world is ending, I think, all darkness and ice, like the poem.

"We should leave," says the reverend.

I watch the legs cross the room. Listen to the closet door, the rattle of hangars. Whispering. "We're sorry," says Nancy. Footsteps in the kitchen. Door opened. "Snow!" Closed.

All darkness and despair. The greatest loneliness. A shattering. Ice. Who knows how long until at last I throw the cups across the room, the teapot, still full. Brown tea bleeds down the wall. I scream and weep into darkness. Now I know what waits at world's end. Rage is what fills the emptiness. Rage, and it is cold.

How we suffer, we humans. Pain and joy but always pain again. How do we do this? Why? Some small part of me still waits for spring. Just to be sure. I know it is absurd, but the rational knowing does not change the irrational hope.

I figured Maggie's parents had told her that they talked to me. I couldn't imagine she would want to face my wrath, though she couldn't know that I didn't even have the energy for anger anymore. Instead I felt a tired sorrow, a weariness with life. She did come, in the midst of a downpour, knocking on my door after school, wearing a yellow slicker. I finally opened the door just a crack and peered out at her, drenched like a stray dog, her hair hanging dark in her face, her lashes beaded with water.

"Go home, Maggie."

"Please. You have to talk to me."

She is crying and snot drips from her nose toward her mouth. She wipes it with the back of her hand, sniffing loudly.

I simply do not know what to say. I close the door.

"You were the only one who ever believed me!" she shouts.

Later, when I look out the window, she is gone, as if I imagined her, made her up out of all my pain.

I decide to sell the house though I don't do anything about it. I sleep day and night. One day I realize I haven't seen the cat for a long while. I walk around whistling and calling her name but she doesn't appear. I sit at the kitchen table and stare out the window until gradually I realize I'm looking at spring. Green grass, leaves, tulip and daffodil blooms thrust through the wreck of the garden. Spring. I open windows and doors. Birds twitter in branches. Squirrels scurry across the lawn. Almost a year since we lost her. Gone. My little darling.

Then I see someone, is it, no, in the garden, picking daffodils, her long, dark hair tied with a weedy-looking thing, wearing the dress she had on last year, tattered and torn, my daughter, my ghost.

"Stephanie!" I call.

She turns and looks at me. Yes. It is her face but changed, with a sharpness to it I had not foreseen. She smiles, raises her arm and sweeps the sky with flowers and I am running down the steps and she is running through the garden calling, "Mom, Mom, Mom!" I think when I touch her she will disappear but she doesn't, though she flinches and squirms from the hug. "You can't hold me so close anymore," she says.

So I hold her gently, like the fragile thing she is, and I'm weeping and she's laughing and somehow, with nimble fingers she braids the bouquet into a crown which she sets on my head. She covers my face with kisses, so soft I'm sure I'm imagining all of it but I don't care anyway. I never want to wake up or snap out of it. I want to be with her always. "Steffie, Steffie, Steffie, I've missed you so much."

She has bags under her eyes and her skin is pale and cold. She stares at me, unsmiling, then reaches up, takes the crown from my head and places it on her own. "You've changed a lot." She turns and looks at the yard. "Everything has."

"It's been a hard year," I say to her narrow back and bony elbows. She looks like such a little orphan, so motherless standing there in that dirty dress. I'll make her something new, something pretty. She turns and looks at me with an expression like none I'd ever seen on her in her lifetime, a hate-filled face, angry and sharp. "Steff, honey, what is it?"

"Don't. Tell. Me. How hard. This year. Has been."

"Oh sweetie," I reach for her but she pulls back.

"I told you. Don't touch me."

"At all?"

"I'm the queen," she says. "Don't touch me unless I touch you first."

I don't argue or disagree. The queen, my daughter, even in death maintains that imagination I so highly prize. When I ask her if she is hungry she says, "I only ate one thing the whole time I was gone." I feel this surge of anger. What kind of place is this death? She doesn't want to come inside while I make the sandwiches and I'm afraid she'll be gone when I come out with the tray, but she isn't. We have a picnic under the apple tree which is in white bloom and buzzing with flies, then she falls asleep on the blanket beside me and, to my surprise, I fall asleep too.

I wake, cold and shivering, already mourning the passing dream. I reach to wrap the picnic blanket around me and my hand touches her. Real. Here. My daughter, sleeping.

"I told you not to touch me."

"I'm sorry. Honey, are you cold?"

She rolls over and looks up at me. "You do realize I'm dead?"

"Yes."

She sets the wilted crown back on her head and surveys the yard. "You really let everything go to shit around here, didn't you?"

"Stephanie!"

"What?"

Really, what? How to be the mother of a dead girl? We sit on the blanket and stare at each other. What she is thinking, I don't know. I'm surprised, in the midst of this momentous happiness, to feel a sadness, a certain grief for the girl I knew who, I guess, was lost somewhere at the border of death. Then she sighs, a great old sigh.

"Mom?" she says, in her little girl voice.

"Yes, honey?"

"It's good to be back."

"It's good to have you here."

"But I can't stay."

"How long?"

She shrugs.

"Is it horrible there?"

She looks at me, her face going through some imperceptible change that brings more harshness to it. "Don't ask the dead."

"What?"

"Don't ask questions you don't want the answer to."

"Just stay. Don't go back."

She stands up. "It doesn't work like that."

"We could—"

"No, don't act like you know anything about it. You don't."

I roll up the blanket, pick up the tray. We walk to the house together beneath the purple-tinged sky. When we get to the door she hesitates. "What's wrong?" She looks at me with wide, frightened eyes. "Steff, what is it?" Wordlessly, she steps inside. I flick on the kitchen light. "Are you hungry?"

She nods.

The refrigerator is nearly empty so I rummage through cupboards and find some spaghetti and a jar of sauce. I fill a pan with water and set it on the stove.

"Is Dad coming back?"

"Would you like to see him?"

She shakes her head vigorously, no.

"Steff, don't be mad at him, he didn't know—"

"Well, he really fucked up."

I bite my lip, check the water. Where is my little girl? I turn and look at her. She is walking around the kitchen, lightly brushing her hand against the wall, a strange, unlovely creature, her hair still knotted with a weed, crowned with wilted daffodils.

"Do you want to talk about it, what happened to you?"

She stops, the tips of her fingers light against the wall, then continues walking around the room, humming softly.

I take this to be a no. I make spaghetti for six and she eats all of it, my ravenous ghost child. What is this feeling? Here is my dead daughter, cold and unkind and difficult and so different from the girl she used to be that only now do I finally accept that Stephanie is gone forever, even as she sits before me, slurping spaghetti, the red sauce blooding her lips.

The dead move in secrets, more wingless than the living, bound by some weight; the memory of life, the impossible things? Dead bones grow and hair and fingernails too. Everything grows but it grows with death. The dead laugh and cry and plant flowers that they pick too soon. The dead do not care about keeping gardens in blossom.

Dead daughters don't wear socks or shoes and they won't go into old bedrooms unless you beg and coax and then you see immediately how they were right all along. Dead daughters have little in common with the living ones. They are more like sisters than the same girl and you realize, just as you miss the daughter you've lost, so does the dead girl miss, really miss, the one she was.

The dead pick up paint brushes and suddenly their hands move like rag dolls and they splatter paint, not like Jackson Pollack, or even a kindergartner. All the paint turns brown on

the paintbrush and drips across the canvas or floor or wall,
until they, helpless, throw it to the ground.

All the dead can do is wander. You walk for hours with your
dead daughter pacing the yard she will not (cannot?) leave.
She picks all the flowers and drops them in her step. She sleeps
suddenly for hours, and then does not sleep for days. She ex-
hausts you. The days and nights whirl. The last time you felt
like this was when she was an infant.

One day, as you sit at the kitchen table, watching her tearing
flowers from the garden in the new dress you made that
already hangs raglike and dirty around her, you think of Maggie Dwinder and you realize you miss her. You put your face in
your hands. What have you done?

"What's wrong with you?"

You would like to believe that she asks because she cares but
you don't think that's true. Something vital in her was lost
forever. Was this what happened at death or was it because of
how she died? You accept you'll never know. She refuses to
talk about it, and really, what would be the point? You look
at her, weedy, dirty, wearing that brittle crown. "Maggie
Dwinder," you say.

"As good as dead."

"What?"

She rolls her eyes.

"Don't you roll your eyes at me, young lady."

"Mother, you don't know anything about it."

"She's your friend, and mine. She told me you would come.
She suffered for it."

"Oh, big deal, mommy and daddy watch her very closely.
She has to go see the psychiatrist. She doesn't have any friends.
Big fucking deal. What a hard life!"

"Steff."

"Don't tell me about suffering. I know about suffering."

"Steff, honey—"

"Everyone said it was a mistake for me to come back here.
They said you wouldn't like me anymore."

"Honey, that's not true. I love you."

"You love who I used to be, not who I am now."

"Well, you're dead."

"Like it's my fault."

The dead are jealous, jealous, jealous and they will do anything to keep you from the living, the lucky living. They will
argue with you, and distract you, and if that doesn't work,
they will even let you hug them, and dance for you, and kiss
you, and laugh, anything to keep you. The dead are selfish.
Jealous. Lonely. Desperate. Hungry.

It isn't until she brings you a flower, dead for weeks, and
hands it to you with that poor smile, that you again remember
the living. "I have to call Maggie."

"Forget about her."

"No, I have to tell her."

"Look at me, Mommy."

"Sweetheart."

"Look what you did."

"It wasn't me."

She walks away.

"It wasn't."

She keeps walking.

You follow. Of course, you follow.

The phone rings. Such a startling noise. I roll into my blankets.
Simultaneously I realize the night was cool enough for blankets and that the phone didn't ring all summer. I reach for it,
fumbling across the bedside table, and knock off the photograph from Steff's last birthday.

"Hello?"

"See you next spring."

"Steff? Where are you?"

There is only a dial tone. I hang up the phone. Throw off
the covers. "Steff!" I call. "Steff!" I look in her bedroom but
she's not there. I run down the stairs and through the house,
calling her name. The blue throw is bunched up on the couch,
as if she'd sat there for a while, wrapped up in it, but she's not
there now. I run outside, the grass cold against my feet. "Steff!
Steff!" She is not in the garden, or the studio. She is not in the
yard. A bird cries and I look up through the apple tree branches.
One misshapen apple drops while I stand there, shivering in
my nightgown. Everything is tinged with brown, except the
leaves of the old oak which are a brilliant red.

A squirrel scurries past. There is a gentle breeze and one red leaf falls. I wrap my arms around myself and walk into the house, fill the teakettle, set it on the burner to boil. I sit at the kitchen table and stare at the garden. I should plant some bulbs. Order firewood. Arrange to have the driveway plowed when it snows. The teakettle whistles. I walk across the cool floor, pour the water into the pot. I leave it to steep and go to the living room where she left the blue throw all balled up. I pick it up and wrap it around myself. It smells like her, musty, sour.

It smells like Maggie too, last Christmas Eve when she spoke to me in the supermarket. What a risk that was for her. Who knows, I might have been like Mrs. Bialo, or her parents; I might have laughed at her. Instead, I became her friend and then cast her aside at the first sign of trouble.

How many chances do we get? With love? How many times do we wreck it before it's gone?

I don't even drink the tea but dress in a rush. All my clothes are too big on me and I see in the mirror how tired I look, how much new gray is in my hair. Yet, there's something else, a sort of glow, a happiness. I miss her, the one who died, and her ghost is my responsibility, a relationship based on who we lost, while Maggie is a friend, a relationship based on what we found.

All summer I only left for groceries. Stephanie would stand at the top of the driveway, watching me with those cold, narrow eyes as if suspicious I wouldn't come back. Out of habit I look in the rearview mirror, but all I see is a patch of brown grass, the edge of the house.

It's easy to find the Dwinder residence. They live right next to the church in a brick house with red geraniums dropping teardrop-shaped petals onto the porch. I ring the bell. Nancy answers, in a pink terry cloth robe.

"I'm sorry, I forgot how early it is."

She brushes a hand through her red hair. "That's all right. We were getting ready for church."

"There's something I have to tell Maggie. Is she home?"

"I don't know if that's such a good idea."

"Honey, who is it?" The reverend comes to the door in plaid flannel pants and a T-shirt, his dark hair tousled, his face wrinkled with sleep. "Oh. Chloe, how are you?"

"I'm sorry to disturb you, it's just—"

"She wants to talk to Maggie."

"I'll tell her you're here." The reverend turns back into the house.

Nancy continues to stare at me, then, just as I hear Maggie saying, What does she want? she blurts, "She's been better since she's stopped seeing you." I'm not sure if this is meant as an accusation or an apology and before I can find out, Maggie comes to the door dressed in torn jeans and a violet T-shirt, her hair in braids. She meets my gaze with those dark eyes.

"Coffee's ready!" the reverend calls and Nancy turns away, her pink-robed figure receding slowly down the hall.

"Yeah?"

"I was hoping, if you can forgive me, I was hoping we could be friends again."

"I can't be her replacement, you know."

"I know."

"You hurt me a lot."

"I know. I'm sorry. Can you ever forgive me?"

She frowns, squints, then tilts her head slightly, and looks up at me. "I guess."

"Please. Stop by. Any time. Like you used to."

She nods and shuts the door gently in my face.

On a sunny but cold day, as the last crimson leaves flutter to earth, and apples turn to cider on the ground, I shovel last winter's ash onto the garden. A flock of geese flies overhead. I shade my eyes to watch them pass and when I look down again, she is standing there in baggy jeans and an old blue pea coat, unbuttoned in the sun.

It's as though I've been living in one of those glass domes and it's been shaking for a long time, but in this moment, has stopped, and after all that flurry and unsettling, there is a kind of peace. "Maggie."

For a moment we only look at each other, then she puts her hand on her hip, rolls her eyes, and says, "You wouldn't believe what they're making us do in gym, square dancing!"

All life is death. You don't fool yourself about this anymore. You slash at the perfect canvas with strokes of paint and replace the perfect picture of your imagination with the reality of what you are capable of. From death, and sorrow, and compromise, you create. This is what it means, you finally realize, to be alive.

You try to explain this to Maggie. You hear yourself talking about bitter seeds, and sweet fruit. She nods and doesn't interrupt but you know you have not successfully communicated it. This is all right. The grief is so large you're not sure you want her, or anyone, to understand it, though you wish you could describe this other emotion.

You stand in the ash of your garden. All this time you didn't realize what you'd been deciding. Now you are crying, because with the realization of the question comes the answer. It is snowing and white flakes fall onto the garden, sticking to the brown stems and broken flowers, melting into the ash. You look up to the sunless white sky. Cold snow tips your face and neck. You close your eyes, and think, yes. Oh, life. Yes.

2003

BRIAN EVENSON

(b. 1966)

The Wavering Knife

I. Theoria

Despite the unfortunate and increasingly serious illness of my benefactor, I continued to work without cease or rest to salvage my analysis of the Gengli oeuvre. The image of the wavering knife, which I had for years perceived as the unifier and ultimate hingepiece of Eva Gengli's philosophy, had, under the severe scrutiny made possible by her private papers, collapsed, and I could discover no adequate trope to stand in its stead. Indeed, Eva Gengli's private papers had led me to realize with an alarming degree of clarity that the Gengli philosophy was exceedingly more complex than I had first imagined.

In deference to my benefactor and his declining health, while he was still alive I told him little and in fact nothing of my difficulties. Instead, I continued to serve him as I had before, though hurrying through my assigned tasks so as to spend more time each day with the Gengli papers. Even when I was with my benefactor—undressing him for bed, rubbing his now inadequate legs, reading to him, conversing with him, feeding him, arranging his pillows, undressing him for the night, steadying his walker, propelling him down the hall, preparing his morning meal, reading at him, dressing him for the day, bathing him, preparing his noon meal, ignoring him, preparing his evening meal, straightening the dust ruffle—I was hardly with him at all. Rather, I was with his "lover" (his claim) Eva Gengli's papers, making the most incisive of critical judgements, examining, to give one instance, two versions of Eva Gengli's "Aphorism on Aesthetics," considering which, if either, she meant to be definitive:

> *The ten fingers of the pianist compose the two hands of the lover.*

or (as marked over in a hand I could not be absolutely certain belonged to Eva Gengli)

> *The ten fingers of the pianist compose the two hands*
> *of the strangler.*

The multiple versions of Eva Gengli's philosophical texts raised difficult questions, made even more difficult by the sense I was gaining that Eva Gengli appeared to regard traditional philosophy as a sort of second-rate game, a game she played well but claimed to have no real stake in. As a result, the philosophical statements she offered were not only variously versioned but were likely to be called into question by what she saw as her more memorable work in film and prose. Nonetheless, I had managed to maintain a firm belief, despite Eva Gengli's own statements, that her philosophical statements were what were genuinely serious.

Admittedly, my task—that of how to salvage and give acclaim to the philosophy while at the same time remaining not unfaithful to Eva Gengli's larger project—had become exceptionally complicated. Since any choice about how to consider an individual philosophical statement first would influence my view of the remainder of the Gengli philosophy and second would demand a continual repositioning in regard to all her work, I was constantly in a state of unease and distress. Worse, rather than establishing a new pattern, each newly considered moment of her philosophy seemed to call into question the hint of pattern I had begun to theorize. Soon I was left only with the trope of the wavering knife and then, as my analysis progressed further, with nothing at all.

I was distracted and despondent for weeks, and grew even more so upon discovering that my benefactor's condition had worsened. The palsification of his body and the dark slur of his speech had grown extreme and could no longer be arrested or corrected by the pharmaceuticals that had lasted us in good stead through the first months of my research. Indeed, my benefactor shook so utterly he could in his worst times no longer raise his hands to his mouth, which meant I had to feed him and even hold his hands and head steady. He could not bear to be left long alone, for alone, he claimed, his condition worsened. He wanted me to stay with him more often, for the severity of the palsy made it difficult and sometimes impossible for him to rest in his bed or in his chair without slipping out, and he would not tolerate the obvious solution of allowing me to strap him in place.

In the seventh month of my analysis, my benefactor's condition had so decayed that he was asking me to drive him again the six hours to his "specialist" (as he referred to his doctor), who, he claimed, would provide the medicines that were sure to make of him "a new man." I was, I must admit, reluctant. It would be a day wasted, I knew, a day that might have in large part been spent in the company of Eva Gengli's papers, trying to unravel from her thought the thread that would allow the unification of her philosophy that I desired. To be away for as long as a day would cause me to lose critical concentration, and to reestablish it again might take weeks. Nor could I envision leaving the Gengli papers unattended, for the house was an old one and could easily be subject to fire and all other manner of calamity, and there were no fire-proof or flood-proof devices that might serve to protect the papers. Worse, the papers could be stolen—for I was far from being the only scholar with an interest in Eva Gengli (though I was the only one to give her philosophy its proper due). There were other scholars who were not as scrupulous as I, who might try to gain access to the papers by dishonest rather than honest means. There were even those who might try to destroy the philosophic papers on the grounds that they obscured the literary work. We could not leave the Gengli papers unattended, I told my benefactor, for to do so would be to shirk all responsibility to philosophy.

At first my benefactor was rather incensed, though gradually he calmed himself enough to set about trying to coerce me to fulfill his will. Immediately seeing through this, I covered my ears and considered the Gengli manuscripts further in my mind, focussing on the tricky problem of "a topography of desire" being substituted for "a trajectory of desire" in the "Flesh" aphorism to describe the intercourse of the mind with the body. The manuscripts made a case for both, my own philosophical bent being better supported if I could discard both statements and think of the mind and body differently. I was thus hoping to discover evidence that the "Flesh" aphorisms had been written at a point of weakness, on a day when Eva Gengli was known to be afflicted or during her rejection of philosophy, when her statements could no longer be trusted. The script in both versions of the aphorism, I recalled, was slightly unstable, and this perhaps could be parlayed into a legitimate, scholarly rejection.

I was well into my mental formulations for dismissal, developing an alternative mind/body formulation, when my benefactor began to jab at me weakly with his cane. Lifting my head, I removed my hands from my ears, showed myself attentive.

"I assume you are ready to listen to reason," he said. He had to say it twice before I was able to draw the meaning out from his slurred and shaking mouth.

"You see the state I am in," he said, his hands bobbing along the coverlet, his head shaking.

I folded my arms across my chest, inclined my head slightly. "It truly injures me to see you this way," I said. This was, in fact, true, though perhaps not in the way he would interpret it.

"I am very ill," he said. "I need my specialist."

I did not disagree with this, though I could not see how his mere *needs* would cause a *duty* to Eva Gengli's philosophy to vanish. Considered objectively, one had a certain obligation (to history, to thought) which demanded sacrifice, which superseded one's immediate pain. Pain must be subsidiary to art, I explained to him, even a function of art itself. Indeed, his "lover" Eva Gengli (if she ever had actually been his lover, which I doubted) had proven this by generating art from pain. Her film sequence "Inscription of the Spastic"—each film one minute long and subtitled after its only subject (e.g. Stephen #5, Helene #12, David P. #19)—had recorded the attempts at movement of forty-two people inflicted with muscular atrophy or spasticity, I reminded him. By recording them, Eva Gengli had transformed pain and dysfunction into something valuable. Privately, I reminded myself that my position was complicated by Eva Gengli's re-editing of the film sequence, her retitling it "Reinscription," and her attempt, by increasing or decreasing the speed of certain moments of the films themselves, to modify each gesture's regularity until it seemed each of the spastic were engaged in a seamless and mysterious dance.

But had not the "Reinscription" been an error in judgement? Was it not better from the philosophical point of view to record pain rather than to regulate it away?

Before I could mount a persuasive mental argument in favor of pain, however, I felt myself prodded again. "If you care to remain in this house," my benefactor said muddily, "you shall obey me."

I quickly stood and passed out of the room. I could hear my benefactor calling behind me, his voice unstable and shaken. I climbed the stairs, went directly to the library. Unlocking the door with the key around my neck, I went in.

With the door shut, I could no longer hear him. The manuscripts were as I had left them, undisturbed. I sat at the table, slid on the cloth gloves, and began to read, following the first text with the index finger of my right hand, the second with the index of my left, my head turning from one text to the other. The first:

> *Aphorism of the Two Enforested Dandies.*
> *Nietzsche: axe. Heidegger: woodpath.*

It was a somewhat odd aphorism which defined a relationship between two philosophers. "Woodpath" was from Heidegger's work (*Holzwege*), but I could not remember "axe" having appeared in Nietzsche's oeuvre and was unsure why it would be paired with Nietzsche. And why dismiss two radical philosophers as "Dandies"?

Though there was no second version, there did exist a second separate text, a "creative" text. Indeed, the forest scene excerpted from Eva Gengli's play *The Shadow of a Wing* called the initial aphorism into question:

> *Ducharme: Nietzsche, he's too busy cutting down*
> *   trees to actually pay attention to the forest itself.*
> *Madame Sbro: (clears his [sic] throat)*
> *Ducharme: Yes, it is true. And old Marty Heidegger,*
> *   he spends all his time looking for the trees to open*
> *   into a clearing so he can spread out his goddamn*
> *   picnic.*
> *Madame Sbro: (shaking her [sic] head) And what*
> *   about you?*

> *Ducharme: Me? (laughs) I like to spend my after-*
> *noons in the city.*

It is precisely ill-considered passages such as these—passages, I am convinced, written by Eva Gengli at moments of profound disturbance late in her life, after a sort of mental decay had begun—which less inventive critics have used to justify a dismissal of her philosophical statements.

I puzzled over the relation of the two texts for some time in my head. I considered it in the light of the previous texts I had encountered, and wrote a summary of the problem on a yellow legal pad, my seventeenth such pad.

Carefully formulated on paper, the problem began to seem plain enough, though it was still clear to me, as it had been clear for some time, that my examination of Eva Gengli's papers was leading me away from any clean formulation of her philosophy. This awareness I found to lead to an alternation of despair and exhilaration. Despair because my analysis was potentially interminable and useless, exhilaration because what I was now doing was not so much analyzing Eva Gengli's philosophy as entering into it in all its contradiction. I was swallowing the philosophy whole.

After a time, I realized I could hear my benefactor's voice calling me feebly. I opened the door and left the library. Leaning over the banister, I saw my benefactor lying heaped at the bottom of the stairs. I climbed down and picked him up, carried him back to his bedroom. He was trying to speak, but I encouraged him to remain silent until he was lying down and had had a moment to regain his composure. I placed him in his bed, under the blankets and sheets, tightened them around him, safety-pinned them into place to make it difficult for him to shake free again.

"There now," I said. "What would you do without me?"

He coughed, threads of saliva spilling through his lips. His mouth offered something I could not quite understand.

"What?" I asked. "Excuse me?"

"When are you going?" he asked.

"Going?"

"The doctor's."

"I am just leaving," I said. I kissed him on the forehead, then returned directly to the library, resuming my analysis where I had left off.

By the time I had reached the point where I could conveniently arrest my research, it was well past midnight. I arranged the books, secured the door to the library. I went downstairs, turning off the lights on my way.

Passing my benefactor's door, I heard him groan. I went inside. He was out of his bed again and crumpled in the corner, shaking violently. He had overturned the telephone table and had a puffy gash across his forehead, the skin all around it dull and abnormally raised. The telephone receiver was in his hand, the black cord entangled all around his forehead in a sort of dark nimbus, the base wedged somehow underneath his legs.

I carefully disentangled him and carried him back to his bed.

"The medicine?" he asked.

I ignored him, set about arranging his bed.

"You have it?" he asked.

"What you need is a good long sleep," I said.

I left him and went into the bathroom. Removing a bottle of sleeping pills, I shook a half-dozen into my hand. Filling an empty medicine bottle with tapwater, I returned to my benefactor's room.

"Take these," I said. "They will make you feel better."

"I don't want to fall asleep," he claimed.

"It's time to sleep," I said. I showed him the clock on the bureau. "You see?" I said. "This is for your own good."

In the end I had to force his jaws open and push the pills down his throat one by one, as one is sometimes forced to do with cats. He choked a little, but in the end swallowed everything.

"What did you do to the telephone?" he asked.

"The telephone?" I picked up the receiver, listened to the absence of any dial tone. "I know nothing about it," I claimed.

He looked blearily up at me.

"What are you planning to do with me?" he asked.

"Nothing," I said. I smiled to reassure him. "I am here only to serve."

II. Zwischen

Somewhere in the space between my analysis of the 128th aphorism (variously titled the "Aphorism on Adultery" and "Aphorism on Adulthood") and my return to Eva Gengli's only extended philosophical text, *A Blotter of Wings*, my benefactor's condition worsened considerably. He lost the ability to move of his own accord and will, individual portions of his body and speech having altogether fled his frame. His eyes, when I opened them with my fingers, stumbled about the sockets. He was having difficulty breathing and the shuddering of his body was so severe it seemed as if he would shake the flesh off his bones.

It was difficult to conduct a proper philosophical investigation under such circumstances, and had I not been intent on beginning an analysis of *A Blotter of Wings* I would have temporarily set all philosophy aside. Yet I had been struggling to gain an approach to *A Blotter of Wings* for months. At one time I had thought to have found, in the trope of the wavering knife, the proper and perhaps only unified approach to the book, the device that would lay bare certain fundamental consistencies of Eva Gengli's thought and make it manageable. But as I looked closer, I realized that Eva Gengli could not be reduced to fundamental structures or strictures, that her philosophy simply refused to conform to "thought" as I understood the term. Perhaps, I thought, the wavering knife could be coupled with another trope, or perhaps with a series of tropes—the rapid beating of insect wings, for instance (c.f. 34), or the overlayering and interlarding of faces suggested on page 21, or even the strange notion of the soul as container for the body, as existing not embedded in the flesh, but as a membrane between flesh and the world (83–97). Perhaps, I tried to believe, by beginning with Eva Gengli's abandonment of interiority ("the mind," she claimed, "is merely an image among others, a moment of vision"), one might be able to impose a structure that would at least allow the analysis to be written. Though I suspected in advance this would fail, I attempted it anyway. I wrote through the night and well into the day with an increasing sense of hopelessness, a hopelessness that eventually grew strong enough to

cause me to tear to shreds the sheets I had written and sit for a
further seven or eight hours staring at a blank piece of paper.

I might have sat in the same position for another seven or
eight hours except that I began to grow hungry and, growing
hungry, realized that I had not fed my benefactor for several
days. Going downstairs, I found him with his legs still on the
bed and entangled in the blanket, his body hanging out, his
head and face pushed against the floor. I lifted him up, found
his pulse torpid, his skin cold to the touch. I shook him a little,
spoke to him even, but he would not move.

I straightened him on the bed. Going upstairs to the library,
I surveyed the careful piles and stacks of Eva Gengli's papers. I
was, I considered, now that my benefactor was apparently incapacitated beyond the ability to make decisions, the sole care-
taker of all that remained of Eva Gengli. Carefully, I gathered
her papers back into the boxes they had been kept in before I
had volunteered my service to my benefactor. I piled the boxes
at the bottom of the stairs, then loaded them one by one into
my benefactor's automobile, always holding my eyes both to
the boxes in the automobile and to the boxes still piled just inside the door. I could of course not observe both at once, but
looked rapidly from one to another, switching my gaze with
such speed that it was as if I were observing both at once. The
boxes filled the trunk and all but the front seat of the "mini-
sedan" (as the manufacturers shamelessly had chosen to name
the vehicle), except that when I tried to close the trunk it
would not close, so two boxes did have to go in the front seat
as well. *A mini-sedan!* I thought. *How could the incomparable
Eva Gengli ever have been involved with someone who owned a
mini-sedan?* It was a disservice to her memory to put her
papers into such a car, but unfortunately I had no choice.

My benefactor, I further considered, was a small, slight, rat-
like person—not at all the sort I would imagine Eva Gengli to
involve herself with, though exactly the sort of person who
would choose to drive a mini-sedan. But here, now, in the box-
cramped car, perhaps I could use my benefactor's slightness to
my advantage. In his present condition, perhaps I could wedge
him between a box and the door to steady him and keep him
aright, and use the other box to rest his feet upon. In his present

condition, he was in no condition to object. I would make him
fit.

After locking all the automobile doors, then checking again
to assure myself they were locked, I went back into the house.
My benefactor was on the bed where I had left him, still unconscious, his body slightly tremulous. I gathered him up in
my arms and carried him out. Unlocking and opening the automobile door, I forced him inside, pushing his knees up near
his chest and working him sideways until he was in. He fit nicely
as long as I kept his knees folded up and against his chest. Getting into the automobile, I worked the key.

Though the automobile had not been driven in months it
started cleanly, which I saw as a blessing from the Gengli muse,
as it were, a ratification of my impulses. Pulling from the drive,
I moved down the road, away from town.

A mile from the highway, I pulled the automobile onto a
farm route and passed out through fields already thick with
grain, past farmhouses, satellite dishes, hulks of ruined automobiles. The road curved and splayed and turned into gravel,
and we passed underneath the highway, passed a ruined and
gutted and defaced building, a shattered circle of concrete
around it, moving deeper into the country. The road turned
dirt, becoming rutted and hard. I was forced to shift the gear
downward which, because of the boxes, was no easy task.

Near a cornfield, I eased the mini-sedan to the edge of the
track and switched it off. My benefactor, I saw, was no longer
shaking or moving at all. His tongue was pushing slightly from
between his lips. I reached across the seat, forced his knees further apart. I pressed my fingers into his neck. Along the web of
my thumb, I could still feel something of a pulse to him. When
I separated his eyelids, the eye remain dilated, settling slowly
lower in the socket as I shook him.

Putting my hands more firmly around the neck, I squeezed.
His neck and shoulder crumpled into the seat, his chin pressing
hard against my wrist. He hardly moved, only fluttering his
hand a little, and when he was perhaps already dead his eyes
opened and clouded slowly, the pupil fading dull. I shook my
hands loose, smelled them. They did not smell like anything. I
climbed out of the automobile and got him out too, dragging
him out into the weeds. Locking the doors, keeping always one

eye on the mini-sedan containing the boxes of Eva Gengli's private papers, I dragged the body out into the cornfield, smoothed the arms down along the sides as my impulses directed me to do. I examined my handiwork.

It was utterly clear to me now that Eva Gengli had meant in her "Aphorism on Aesthetics" the two hands of the strangler, not the two hands of a lover. That had been correct.

I had made a mistake in trying to limit my analysis to the page, I thought. Theory can only take one so far. Praxis is everything. One understands nothing until one begins to act.

III. Praxis

When I entered again, the house itself was mostly dark and quiet, the air still but for the dust and hair aswirl near where I had dropped the boxes, dust rising from my footsteps as well. I climbed the stairs and switched on the library lights, found everything as undisturbed as I had left it. I moved through the house, switching on lights, looking into each room to assure myself that I was in fact alone with Eva Gengli.

In my benefactor's room I smoothed the sheets, fluffed the pillow to remove from it the crease of his head. I stood back to admire my handiwork but, seeing the crease still to remain somewhat, I stripped the bed of sheets, balling them up and hiding them in the kitchen, under the sink. I considered the sink for some time, then took the sheets and hid them inside the refrigerator. I looked at the refrigerator a while, then took the sheets out and pushed them out the kitchen window.

There was still the smell of my benefactor in the room and through the entire house. I could not stop myself from fitting rubber gloves over my hands and walking about the house spraying disinfectant/deodorant aerosol before me, feeling it settle tingling on my arms. In a little while I could hardly breathe, so stripped off the gloves and abandoned both them and the disinfectant/deodorant, pushing them out the kitchen window.

I carried my lover's boxes upstairs to the library, one after the other. I was prepared to unpack them, but my forearms, I found, were sticky with disinfectant/deodorant, and the rubber gloves had made my hands watery. It would be an error, I thought, as well as a show of disrespect, to touch Eva's private papers in such a condition.

Going downstairs, I began to lather my hands in the bathroom basin. The lip of the sink and the floor below, I observed as I scrubbed, were clottered over by dark strands of my benefactor's hair. I rinsed and dried my hands, then swept the hair over the edge with my forefinger, gathering it in my other palm, then got on my knees and plucked it up strand by strand until the bathroom was mainly bald and hairless. I chartered the remainder of the house on my knees, the crease of my palm tight with hair, looking for further remnant of my benefactor. There was hair, I saw, everywhere, and dust too, and perhaps in the dust flakes of skin, and perhaps, I could not help but think, the dust was entirely made of flakes of skin. But the difficulty was in sifting and sorting, in separating the skin of my benefactor from what might still remain of Eva Gengli's "uncannily soft skin" (my benefactor's claim, though I doubt he would have ever touched it). Looking at the hair in my hand I noticed among it one or two strands of lighter hair, perhaps blond, perhaps white—perhaps her very hair, though she had died years before. I unthreaded these hairs, slipped them inside my shirt. The remainder, the dark strands, I took to the window and abandoned to the outside.

There was a scent still but no longer so strong. If I concentrated I could ignore it entirely. Indeed, there was little enough of my benefactor left and what was left was spread thin enough that I could feel through it and alongside it, in the stillness, something else entirely. What remained no longer was my benefactor refusing death but the force of a stronger mind, of my lover Eva Gengli gathering her breath just for me.

I moved quickly up the stairs to the library. Throwing the lids off the boxes, I arranged Eva's manuscripts in a circle all around me. Taking the pen, I poised it over a blank page. I waited for her to speak.

She, Eva Gengli, I began, *fighting a too uncanny sense of the presence of her own body, turned for a brief moment to philosophy for solace. In the short form, the aphorism in particular, she found a means of moving from a palpable space to a uniquely regenerative cerebral space. She, however—wrongly this critic believes—always dismissed her philosophical musings in general and her aphorisms in particular, claiming that they were useful as a means of "drawing breath" so as to return to her "only important work, the novels and films" (her words). The philosophy, she claimed in her famous but perhaps unfortunate letter to A. Kline, was "a temporary relief from the body," a sort of "necessary and necessarily ephemeral affair," afterwards allowing her to return more strongly to "the dark or bright bond between writing and flesh."*

Despite the strength of the aphorisms, I wrote, *it is Gengli's single extended treatise, with its exploration of pain and its critique of all dichotomy, that marks her as among the greatest philosophers of her generation. In this treatise,* A Blotter of Wings, *Eva Gengli postulates through the unifying image of the wavering knife (the knife wavering so rapidly as to resemble a beating pair of insect wings) that—*

My inspiration had suddenly fled altogether.

I put my pen down and went downstairs to see if the door was locked. It was locked. There was a smell to the house still, I now noticed. I went into the kitchen to gather the gloves and disinfectant/deodorant, but the space they normally occupied was empty. I opened the kitchen cupboards, closed them again. I opened the stove, pushed my head in, withdrew it.

Upstairs again, I read over what I had written. I had fallen back on the wavering knife despite knowing from my protracted analysis of Eva Gengli's work that the trope would not hold. Insisting upon it as a unifier, I told myself, would lead to a tremendously faulty reading of the Gengli philosophical oeuvre. And there was nothing of Eva Gengli in my writing either, I now realized. My style was turgid, nothing like the flowing and lucid prose of my lover, the careful repetitions ringing like dark chimes, words spilling slick as blood off the tongue. With every word I was writing about Eva Gengli, I realized, I was in fact betraying her. This might have been acceptable were I in fact betraying part of her, the "creative" part, to forward the philosophy, but only a dozen sentences in it was already clear to me that I was betraying all portions of her, and her mind and body too.

I tore the page up and carried it downstairs, dumped the scraps out the kitchen window. Taking a new, unblemished page, I sat down, attempted to begin again.

She, Eva Gengli, I wrote, *overwhelmed by her own touch, turned her gaze rational for an instant and rendered her hand philosophical. It was during this transition, between her novel* A Tergo *and her play* The Shadow of a Wing, *that Eva Gengli did her finest and*—

That was not it, not it at all. Although my benefactor had mostly fled the house, all his possessions were still present. They were pushing against the walls, limiting the air of the house, stifling and strangling what still remained of the woman he claimed had been his lover (Eva Gengli: impossible!).

I went through the shelves of the library, sorting out all those books which Eva Gengli had not signed inside the front cover. I carried each armload of books downstairs and dumped it out the kitchen window, the books cascading off the back porch and onto the lawn. There were, I saw on my tenth trip, neighbors and others of the curious beginning to gather, all of whom I ignored.

When the library had been cleansed sufficiently of all non-Gengli-related texts, I went back in and sat in it again. I closed my eyes, listened. Though it would be untrue to say I felt the presence of my lover Eva Gengli as clearly as I had when I was first compelled to begin, I did not feel my benefactor at all anymore, until I sensed him seeping under the library door from the other parts of his house where his possessions were still abundant.

I took off my shirt and tried to cram the crack under the door shut with it, but it was not long enough so I had to remove my pants as well. When I was done, I stared at the stuffed crack for about an hour, sniffing at it, then tried to write. Nothing at all was coming. My lover had abandoned me.

Pushing the clothing aside and opening the door, I went downstairs. The air outside the library was fetid, marauded through with smells that worked against the purpose of true scholarship. I went around the house, throwing open windows until halfway around, seeing the neighbors crouched about outside, observing me, I realized that perhaps what was outside the house was worse than what was in. At least with the

windows closed nothing new could enter. I went about the
house closing the windows again, thinking that what I needed
now was a system or method to keep at bay all that was undesirable, and to clean the air for thought.

The technique I first employed was incendiary. I went from
room to room striking matches, the sweet burn of sulfur rid-
ding the air at least for a moment of the smells of my benefactor's dying (now dead) body, a rat-like body which I was
certain Eva could never have touched. Yet matches were not
sufficient; all his things were still in the house. As soon as a
match was damped out, the things themselves tried to fill the
room again before good air could rush in and fill the gap. I
was moving about the house striking matches as quickly as I
could and dropping them and letting them burn themselves
out, but nothing permanent was happening except for the
floorboards smouldering in some parts, so that I had to stamp
the sparks out with my bare feet until the soles of my feet were
slicked dark and burnt a little.

I figured there had to be a better way. I could hardly write
my analysis while running about striking matches. So instead
of the matches I began to move things out again, starting first
with things in plain sight that my benefactor had valued, such
as the half-meter cactus, the bronzed shoe, the handsewn table-
cloth, the Senegalese mask. I moved them into the kitchen and
threw them out the kitchen window. What would not fit out, I
broke up until it would fit and then threw out. Once I had finished with the incidentals, I began to try to move the furniture
out. Only I could not, with the tools available to me, think
of a way to break things like the couch and bed into small
enough pieces, so left them jumbled in the kitchen while I ruminated over their possible means of expulsion and went in
search of easier prey.

I had begun to dispose of the clothing from my benefactor's
closet when, in the back of it, wrapped in brown paper, I discovered a dress. It was black mostly, with a nearly hidden abstract patterning similar to a dress Eva had worn on the back
cover of her *Lead Glass Iris.*

Confronted by my lover's dress, I suddenly was conscious
again of my own nakedness. I began to put on one of my
benefactor's suits, but before it was all the way on I could feel

that it would not sit easily on my skin. I removed it and tried another, then another, until the whole of the room was scattered with his clothing and the only thing untried still was the dress.

I shook it out, slipped it over my head. It was tight but would fit mostly if I did not button it and did not move my arms too far. It felt good on me, the fabric smooth, of an odd, subtle weave. I could not stop running my hands over it.

I looked at myself in the mirror. I was so lovely I could hardly recognize myself. I looked in the drawers for something to put my face back on, but there was nothing. I was so lovely I could hardly bear to look at myself, and I could not stop my hands caressing or my mouth from speaking her name.

I could feel her all around me like a sheen over the surface of my body, and she having taken charge of me as well. I could see her gathering in my reflection. The whole world was turning and me along with it, and I was falling backwards and onto the floor, so taken with everything I could not move except in response to her missing touch, all language and analysis having fled me, my dress coming off, my lover's body touching all parts of my body until my body too was wavering and coming asunder and my soul dissolved and expelled to bubble along the surface of my skin and away, until nothing was left of myself nor my body, nothing left of anything at all.

2004

KELLY LINK

(b. 1969)

Stone Animals

Henry asked a question. He was joking.

"As a matter of fact," the real estate agent snapped, "it is."

It was not a question she had expected to be asked. She gave Henry a goofy, appeasing smile and yanked at the hem of the skirt of her pink linen suit, which seemed as if it might, at any moment, go rolling up her knees like a window shade. She was younger than Henry, and sold houses that she couldn't afford to buy.

"It's reflected in the asking price, of course," she said. "Like you said."

Henry stared at her. She blushed.

"I've never seen anything," she said. "But there are stories. Not stories that I know. I just know there are stories. If you believe that sort of thing."

"I don't," Henry said. When he looked over to see if Catherine had heard, she had her head up the tiled fireplace, as if she were trying it on, to see whether it fit. Catherine was six months pregnant. Nothing fit her except for Henry's baseball caps, his sweatpants, his T-shirts. But she liked the fireplace.

Carleton was running up and down the staircase, slapping his heels down hard, keeping his head down and his hands folded around the banister. Carleton was serious about how he played. Tilly sat on the landing, reading a book, legs poking out through the railings. Whenever Carleton ran past, he thumped her on the head, but Tilly never said a word. Carleton would be sorry later, and never even know why.

Catherine took her head out of the fireplace. "Guys," she said. "Carleton, Tilly. Slow down a minute and tell me what you think. Think King Spanky will be okay out here?"

"King Spanky is a cat, Mom," Tilly said. "Maybe we should get a dog, you know, to help protect us." She could tell by looking at her mother that they were going to move. She didn't

579

know how she felt about this, except she had plans for the yard. A yard like that needed a dog.

"I don't like big dogs," said Carleton, six years old and small for his age. "I don't like this staircase. It's too big."

"Carleton," Henry said. "Come here. I need a hug."

Carleton came down the stairs. He lay down on his stomach on the floor and rolled, noisily, floppily, slowly, over to where Henry stood with the real estate agent. He curled like a dead snake around Henry's ankles. "I don't like those dogs outside," he said.

"I know it looks like we're out in the middle of nothing, but if you go down through the backyard, cut through that stand of trees, there's this little path. It takes you straight down to the train station. Ten-minute bike ride," the agent said. Nobody ever remembered her name, which was why she had to wear too-tight skirts. She was, as it happened, writing a romance novel, and she spent a lot of time making up pseudonyms, just in case she ever finished it. Ophelia Pink. Matilde Hightower. LaLa Treeble. Or maybe she'd write gothics. Ghost stories. But not about people like these. "Another ten minutes on that path and you're in town."

"What dogs, Carleton?" Henry said.

"I think they're lions, Carleton," said Catherine. "You mean the stone ones beside the door? Just like the lions at the library. You love those lions, Carleton. Patience and Fortitude?"

"I've always thought they were rabbits," the real estate agent said. "You know, because of the ears. They have big ears." She flopped her hands and then tugged at her skirt, which would not stay down. "I think they're pretty valuable. The guy who built the house had a gallery in New York. He knew a lot of sculptors."

Henry was struck by that. He didn't think he knew a single sculptor.

"I don't like the rabbits," Carleton said. "I don't like the staircase. I don't like this room. It's too big. I don't like *her*."

"Carleton," Henry said. He smiled at the real estate agent.

"I don't like the house," Carleton said, clinging to Henry's ankles. "I don't like houses. I don't want to live in a house."

"Then we'll build you a teepee out on the lawn," Catherine said. She sat on the stairs beside Tilly, who shifted her weight, almost imperceptibly, towards Catherine. Catherine sat as still as possible. Tilly was in fourth grade and difficult in a way that girls weren't supposed to be. Mostly she refused to be cuddled or babied. But she sat there, leaning on Catherine's arm, emanating saintly fragrances: peacefulness, placidness, goodness. *I want this house*, Catherine said, moving her lips like a silent movie heroine, to Henry, so that neither Carleton nor the agent, who had bent over to inspect a piece of dust on the floor, could see. "You can live in your teepee, and we'll invite you to come over for lunch. You like lunch, don't you? Peanut butter sandwiches?"

"I don't," Carleton said, and sobbed once.

But they bought the house anyway. The real estate agent got her commission. Tilly rubbed the waxy, stone ears of the rabbits on the way out, pretending that they already belonged to her. They were as tall as she was, but that wouldn't always be true. Carleton had a peanut butter sandwich.

The rabbits sat on either side of the front door. Two stone animals sitting on cracked, mossy haunches. They were shapeless, lumpish, patient in a way that seemed not worn down, but perhaps never really finished in the first place. There was something about them that reminded Henry of Stonehenge. Catherine thought of topiary shapes; *The Velveteen Rabbit*; soldiers who stand guard in front of palaces and never even twitch their noses. Maybe they could be donated to a museum. Or broken up with jackhammers. They didn't suit the house at all.

"So what's the house like?" said Henry's boss. She was carefully stretching rubber bands around her rubber band ball. By now the rubber band ball was so big, she had to get special extra-large rubber bands from the art department. She claimed it helped her think. She had tried knitting for a while, but it turned out that knitting was too utilitarian, too feminine. Making an enormous ball out of rubber bands struck the right note. It was something a man might do.

It took up half of her desk. Under the fluorescent office lights it had a peeled red liveliness. You almost expected it to shoot forward and out the door. The larger it got, the more it looked like some kind of eyeless, hairless, legless animal.

Maybe a dog. A Carleton-sized dog, Henry thought, although not a Carleton-sized rubber band ball.

Catherine joked sometimes about using the carleton as a measure of unit.

"Big," Henry said. "Haunted."

"Really?" his boss said. "So's this rubber band." She aimed a rubber band at Henry and shot him in the elbow. This was meant to suggest that she and Henry were good friends, and just goofing around, the way good friends did. But what it really meant was that she was angry at him. "Don't leave me," she said.

"I'm only two hours away." Henry put up his hand to ward off rubber bands. "Quit it. We talk on the phone, we use email. I come back to town when you need me in the office."

"You're sure this is a good idea?" his boss said. She fixed her reptilian, watery gaze on him. She had problematical tear ducts. Though she could have had a minor surgical procedure to fix this, she'd chosen not to. It was a tactical advantage, the way it spooked people.

It didn't really matter that Henry remained immune to rubber bands and crocodile tears. She had backup strategies. She thought about which would be most effective while Henry pitched his stupid idea all over again.

Henry had the movers' phone number in his pocket, like a talisman. He wanted to take it out, wave it at The Crocodile, say Look at this! Instead he said, "For nine years, we've lived in an apartment next door to a building that smells like urine. Like someone built an entire building out of bricks made of compressed red pee. Someone spit on Catherine in the street last week. This old Russian lady in a fur coat. A kid rang our doorbell the other day and tried to sell us gas masks. Door-to-door gas mask salesmen. Catherine bought one. When she told me about it, she burst into tears. She said she couldn't figure out if she was feeling guilty because she'd bought a gas mask, or if it was because she hadn't bought enough for everyone."

"Good Chinese food," his boss said. "Good movies. Good bookstores. Good dry cleaners. Good conversation."

"Treehouses," Henry said. "I had a treehouse when I was a kid."

"You were never a kid," his boss said.

"Three bathrooms. Crown moldings. We can't even see our nearest neighbor's house. I get up in the morning, have coffee, put Carleton and Tilly on the bus, and go to work in my pajamas."

"What about Catherine?" The Crocodile put her head down on her rubber band ball. Possibly this was a gesture of defeat.

"There was that thing. Catherine's whole department is leaving. Like rats deserting a sinking ship. Anyway, Catherine needs a change. And so do I," Henry said. "We've got another kid on the way. We're going to garden. Catherine'll teach ESOL, find a book group, write her book. Teach the kids how to play bridge. You've got to start them early."

He picked a rubber band off the floor and offered it to his boss. "You should come out and visit some weekend."

"I never go upstate," The Crocodile said. She held on to her rubber band ball. "Too many ghosts."

"Are you going to miss this? Living here?" Catherine said. She couldn't stand the way her stomach poked out. She couldn't see past it. She held up her left foot to make sure it was still there, and pulled the sheet off Henry.

"I love the house," Henry said.

"Me too," Catherine said. She was biting her fingernails. Henry could hear her teeth going *click, click*. Now she had both feet up in the air. She wiggled them around. Hello, feet.

"What are you doing?"

She put them down again. On the street outside, cars came and went, pushing smears of light along the ceiling, slow and fast at the same time. The baby was wriggling around inside her, kicking out with both feet like it was swimming across the English Channel, the Pacific. Kicking all the way to China. "Did you buy that story about the former owners moving to France?"

"I don't believe in France," Henry said. "*Je ne crois pas en France.*"

"Neither do I," Catherine said. "Henry?"

"What?"

"Do you love the house?"

"I love the house."

"I love it more than you do," Catherine said, although

Henry hated it when she said things like that. "What do you love best?"

"That room in the front," Henry said. "With the windows. Our bedroom. Those weird rabbit statues."

"Me too," Catherine said, although she didn't. "I love those rabbits."

Then she said, "Do you ever worry about Carleton and Tilly?"

"What do you mean?" Henry said. He looked at the alarm clock: it was 4 A.M. "Why are we awake right now?"

"Sometimes I worry that I love one of them better," Catherine said. "Like I might love Tilly better. Because she used to wet the bed. Because she's always so angry. Or Carleton, because he was so sick when he was little."

"I love them both the same," Henry said.

He didn't even know he was lying. Catherine knew, though. She knew he was lying, and she knew he didn't even know it. Most of the time she thought that it was okay. As long as he thought he loved them both the same, and acted as if he did, that was good enough.

"Well, do you ever worry that you love them more than me?" she said. "Or that I love them more than I love you?"

"Do you?" Henry said.

"Of course," Catherine said. "I have to. It's my job."

She found the gas mask in a box of wineglasses, and also six recent issues of *The New Yorker*, which she still might get a chance to read someday. She put the gas mask under the sink and *The New Yorkers* in the sink. Why not? It was her sink. She could put anything she wanted into it. She took the magazines out again and put them into the refrigerator, just for fun.

Henry came into the kitchen, holding silver candlesticks and a stuffed armadillo, which someone had made into a purse. It had a shoulder strap made out of its own skin. You opened its mouth and put things inside it, lipstick and subway tokens. It had pink gimlet eyes and smelled strongly of vinegar. It belonged to Tilly, although how it had come into her possession was unclear. Tilly claimed she'd won it at school in a contest involving donuts. Catherine thought it more likely Tilly had either stolen it or (slightly preferable) found it in someone's trash. Now Tilly kept her most valuable belongings inside the purse, to keep them safe from Carleton, who was covetous of the precious things—because they were small, and because they belonged to Tilly—but afraid of the armadillo.

"I've already told her she can't take it to school for at least the first two weeks. Then we'll see." She took the purse from Henry and put it with the gas mask under the sink.

"What are they doing?" Henry said. Framed in the kitchen window, Carleton and Tilly hunched over the lawn. They had a pair of scissors and a notebook and a stapler.

"They're collecting grass." Catherine took dishes out of a box, put the Bubble Wrap aside for Tilly to stomp, and stowed the dishes in a cabinet. The baby kicked like it knew all about Bubble Wrap. "Woah, Fireplace," she said. "We don't have a dancing license in there."

Henry put out his hand, rapped on Catherine's stomach. *Knock, knock.* It was Tilly's joke. Catherine would say, "Who's there?" and Tilly would say, Candlestick's here. Fat Man's here. Box. Hammer. Milkshake. Clarinet. Mousetrap. Fiddlestick. Tilly had a whole list of names for the baby. The real estate agent would have approved.

"Where's King Spanky?" Henry said.

"Under our bed," Catherine said. "He's up in the box frame."

"Have we unpacked the alarm clock?" Henry said.

"Poor King Spanky," Catherine said. "Nobody to love except an alarm clock. Come upstairs and let's see if we can shake him out of the bed. I've got a present for you."

The present was in a U-Haul box exactly like all the other boxes in the bedroom, except that Catherine had written HENRY'S PRESENT on it instead of LARGE FRONT BEDROOM. Inside the box were Styrofoam peanuts and then a smaller box from Takashimaya. The Takashimaya box was fastened with a silver ribbon. The tissue paper inside was dull gold, and inside the tissue paper was a green silk robe with orange sleeves and heraldic animals in orange and gold thread. "Lions," Henry said.

"Rabbits," Catherine said.

"I didn't get you anything," Henry said.

Catherine smiled nobly. She liked giving presents better than getting presents. She'd never told Henry, because it seemed to her that it must be selfish in some way she'd never bothered to figure out. Catherine was grateful to be married to Henry, who accepted all presents as his due; who looked good in the clothes that she bought him; who was vain, in an easygoing way, about his good looks. Buying clothes for Henry was especially satisfying now, while she was pregnant and couldn't buy them for herself.

She said, "If you don't like it, then I'll keep it. Look at you, look at those sleeves. You look like the emperor of Japan."

They had already colonized the bedroom, making it full of things that belonged to them. There was Catherine's mirror on the wall, and their mahogany wardrobe, their first real piece of furniture, a wedding present from Catherine's great-aunt. There was their serviceable, queen-sized bed with King Spanky lodged up inside it, and there was Henry, spinning his arms in the wide orange sleeves, like an embroidered windmill. Henry could see all of these things in the mirror, and behind him, their lawn and Tilly and Carleton, stapling grass into their notebook. He saw all of these things and he found them good. But he couldn't see Catherine. When he turned around, she stood in the doorway, frowning at him. She had the alarm clock in her hand.

"Look at you," she said again. It worried her, the way something, someone, *Henry*, could suddenly look like a place she'd never been before. The alarm began to ring and King Spanky came out from under the bed, trotting over to Catherine. She bent over, awkwardly—ungraceful, ungainly, so clumsy, so fucking awkward, being pregnant was like wearing a fucking suitcase strapped across your middle—put the alarm clock down on the ground, and King Spanky hunkered down in front of it, his nose against the ringing glass face.

And that made her laugh again. Henry loved Catherine's laugh. Downstairs, their children slammed a door open, ran through the house, carrying scissors, both Catherine and Henry knew, and slammed another door open and were outside again, leaving behind the smell of grass. There was a store in New York where you could buy a perfume that smelled like that.

*

Catherine and Carleton and Tilly came back from the grocery store with a tire, a rope to hang it from, and a box of pancake mix for dinner. Henry was online, looking at a jpeg of a rubber band ball. There was a message too. The Crocodile needed him to come into the office. It would be just a few days. Someone was setting fires and there was no one smart enough to see how to put them out except for him. They were his accounts. He had to come in and save them. She knew Catherine and Henry's apartment hadn't sold; she'd checked with their listing agent. So surely it wouldn't be impossible, not impossible, only inconvenient.

He went downstairs to tell Catherine, "That *witch*," she said, and then bit her lip. "She called the listing agent? I'm sorry. We talked about this. Never mind. Just give me a moment."

Catherine inhaled. Exhaled. Inhaled. If she were Carleton, she would hold her breath until her face turned red and Henry agreed to stay home, but then again, it never worked for Carleton. "We ran into our new neighbors in the grocery store. She's about the same age as me. Liz and Marcus. One kid, older, a girl, um, I think her name was Alison, maybe from a first marriage—potential babysitter, which is really good news. Liz is a lawyer. Gorgeous. Reads Oprah books. He likes to cook."

"So do I," Henry said.

"You're better looking," Catherine said. "So do you have to go back tonight, or can you take the train in the morning?"

"The morning is fine," Henry said, wanting to seem agreeable.

Carleton appeared in the kitchen, his arms pinned around King Spanky's middle. The cat's front legs stuck straight out, as if Carleton were dowsing. King Spanky's eyes were closed. His whiskers twitched Morse code. "What are you wearing?" Carleton said.

"My new uniform," Henry said. "I wear it to work."

"Where do you work?" Carleton said, testing.

"I work at home," Henry said. Catherine snorted.

"He looks like the king of rabbits, doesn't he? The plenipotentiary of Rabbitaly," she said, no longer sounding particularly pleased about this.

"He looks like a princess," Carleton said, now pointing King Spanky at Henry like a gun.

"Where's your grass collection?" Henry said. "Can I see it?"

"No," Carleton said. He put King Spanky on the floor, and the cat slunk out of the kitchen, heading for the staircase, the bedroom, the safety of the bedsprings, the beloved alarm clock, the beloved. The beloved may be treacherous, greasy-headed and given to evil habits, or else it can be a man in his late forties who works too much, or it can be an alarm dock.

"After dinner," Henry said, trying again, "we could go out and find a tree for your tire swing."

"No," Carleton said, regretfully. He lingered in the kitchen, hoping to be asked a question to which he could say yes.

"Where's your sister?" Henry said.

"Watching television," Carleton said. "I don't like the television here."

"It's too big," Henry said, but Catherine didn't laugh.

Henry dreams he is the king of the real estate agents. Henry loves his job. He tries to sell a house to a young couple with twitchy noses and big dark eyes. Why does he always dream that he's trying to sell things?

The couple stare at him nervously. He leans towards them as if he's going to whisper something in their silly, expectant ears. It's a secret he's never told anyone before. It's a secret he didn't even know that he knew. "Let's stop fooling," he says. "You can't afford to buy this house. You don't have any money. You're rabbits."

"Where do you work?" Carleton said, in the morning, when Henry called from Grand Central.

"I work at home," Henry said. "Home where we live now, where you are. Eventually. Just not today. Are you getting ready for school?"

Carleton put the phone down. Henry could hear him saying something to Catherine. "He says he's not nervous about school," she said. "He's a brave kid."

"I kissed you this morning," Henry said, "but you didn't wake up. There were all these rabbits on the lawn. They were huge. King Spanky–sized. They were just sitting there like they were waiting for the sun to come up. It was funny, like some kind of art installation. But it was kind of creepy too. Think they'd been there all night?"

"Rabbits? Can they have rabies? I saw them this morning when I got up," Catherine said. "Carleton didn't want to brush his teeth this morning. He says something's wrong with his toothbrush."

"Maybe he dropped it in the toilet, and he doesn't want to tell you," Henry said.

"Maybe you could buy a new toothbrush and bring it home," Catherine said. "He doesn't want one from the drugstore here. He wants one from New York."

"Where's Tilly?" Henry said.

"She says she's trying to figure out what's wrong with Carleton's toothbrush. She's still in the bathroom." Catherine said.

"Can I talk to her for a second?" Henry said.

"Tell her she needs to get dressed and eat her Cheerios," Catherine said. "After I drive them to school, Liz is coming over for coffee. Then we're going to go out for lunch. I'm not unpacking another box until you get home. Here's Tilly."

"Hi," Tilly said. She sounded as if she were asking a question.

Tilly never liked talking to people on the telephone. How were you supposed to know if they were really who they said they were? And even if they were who they claimed to be, they didn't know whether you were who you said you were. You could be someone else. They might give away information about you, and not even know it. There were no protocols. No precautions.

She said, "Did you brush your teeth this morning?"

"Good morning, Tilly," her father (if it was her father) said. "My toothbrush was fine. Perfectly normal."

"That's good," Tilly said. "I let Carleton use mine."

"That was very generous," Henry said.

"No problem," Tilly said. Sharing things with Carleton wasn't like having to share things with other people. It wasn't really like sharing things at all. Carleton belonged to her, like the toothbrush. "Mom says that when we get home today, we can draw on the walls in our rooms if we want to, while we decide what color we want to paint them."

"Sounds like fun," Henry said. "Can I draw on them too?"

"Maybe," Tilly said. She had already said too much. "Gotta go. Gotta eat breakfast."

"Don't be worried about school," Henry said.

"I'm not worried about school," Tilly said.

"I love you," Henry said.

"I'm real concerned about this toothbrush," Tilly said.

He closed his eyes only for a minute. Just for a minute. When he woke up, it was dark and he didn't know where he was. He stood up and went over to the door, almost tripping over something. It sailed away from him in an exuberant, rollicking sweep. According to the clock on his desk, it was 4 A.M. Why was it always 4 A.M.? There were four messages on his cell phone, all from Catherine.

He checked train schedules online. Then he sent Catherine a fast email.

> Fell asleep @ midnight? Mssed trains. Awake now, going to keep on working. Pttng out fires. Take the train home early afternoon? Still lv me?

Before he went back to work, he kicked the rubber band ball back down the hall towards The Crocodile's door.

Catherine called him at 8:45.

"I'm sorry," Henry said.

"I bet you are," Catherine said.

"I can't find my razor. I think The Crocodile had some kind of tantrum and tossed my stuff."

"Carleton will love that," Catherine said. "Maybe you should sneak in the house and shave before dinner. He had a hard day at school yesterday."

"Maybe I should grow a beard," Henry said. "He can't be afraid of everything, all the time. Tell me about the first day of school."

"We'll talk about it later," Catherine said. "Liz just drove up. I'm going to be her guest at the gym. Just make it home for dinner."

*

At 6 A.M. Henry emailed Catherine again. "Srry. Accidentally startd avalanche while puttng out fires. Wait up for me? How ws 2nd day of school?" She didn't write him back. He called and no one picked up the phone. She didn't call.

He took the last train home. By the time it reached the station, he was the only one left in his car. He unchained his bicycle and rode it home in the dark. Rabbits pelted across the footpath in front of his bike. There were rabbits foraging on his lawn. They froze as he dismounted and pushed the bicycle across the grass. The lawn was rumpled; the bike went up and down over invisible depressions that he supposed were rabbit holes. There were two short fat men standing in the dark on either side of the front door, waiting for him, but when he came closer, he remembered that they were stone rabbits. "Knock, knock," he said.

The real rabbits on the lawn tipped their ears at him. The stone rabbits waited for the punch line, but they were just stone rabbits. They had nothing better to do.

The front door wasn't locked. He walked through the downstairs rooms, putting his hands on the backs and tops of furniture. In the kitchen, cut-down boxes leaned in stacks against the wall, waiting to be recycled or remade into cardboard houses and spaceships and tunnels for Carleton and Tilly.

Catherine had unpacked Carleton's room. Night-lights in the shape of bears and geese and cats were plugged into every floor outlet. There were little low-watt table lamps as well—hippo, robot, gorilla, pirate ship. Everything was soaked in a tender, peaceable light, translating Carleton's room into something more than a bedroom: something luminous, numinous, Carleton's cartoony Midnight Church of Sleep.

Tilly was sleeping in the other bed.

Tilly would never admit that she sleepwalked, the same way that she would never admit that she sometimes still wet the bed. But she refused to make friends. Making friends would have meant spending the night in strange houses. Tomorrow morning she would insist that Henry or Catherine must have carried her from her room, put her to bed in Carleton's room for reasons of their own.

Henry knelt down between the two beds and kissed Carleton on the forehead. He kissed Tilly, smoothed her hair. How could he not love Tilly better? He'd known her longer. She was so brave, so angry.

On the walls of Carleton's bedroom, Henry's children had drawn a house. A cat nearly as big as the house. There was a crown on the cat's head. Trees or flowers with pairs of leaves that pointed straight up, still bigger, and a stick figure on a stick bicycle, riding past the trees. When he looked closer, he thought that maybe the trees were actually rabbits. The wall smelled like Fruit Loops. Someone had written *Henry Is A Rat Fink! Ha Ha!* He recognized his wife's handwriting.

"Scented markers," Catherine said. She stood in the door, holding a pillow against her stomach. "I was sleeping downstairs on the sofa. You walked right past and didn't see me."

"The front door was unlocked," Henry said.

"Liz says nobody ever locks their doors out here," Catherine said. "Are you coming to bed, or were you just stopping by to see how we were?"

"I have to go back in tomorrow." Henry said. He pulled a toothbrush out of his pocket and showed it to her. "There's a box of Krispy Kreme donuts on the kitchen counter."

"Delete the donuts," Catherine said. "I'm not that easy." She took a step towards him and accidentally kicked King Spanky. The cat yowled. Carleton woke up. He said, "Who's there? Who's there?"

"It's me," Henry said. He knelt beside Carleton's bed in the light of the Winnie the Pooh lamp. "I brought you a new toothbrush."

Carleton whimpered.

"What's wrong, spaceman?" Henry said. "It's just a toothbrush." He leaned towards Carleton and Carleton scooted back. He began to scream.

In the other bed, Tilly was dreaming about rabbits. When she'd come home from school, she and Carleton had seen rabbits, sitting on the lawn as if they had kept watch over the house all the time that Tilly had been gone. In her dream they were still there. She dreamed she was creeping up on them. They opened their mouths, wide enough to reach inside like she was some kind of rabbit dentist, and so she did. She put her hand around something small and cold and hard. Maybe it was a ring, a diamond ring. Or a. Or. It was a. She couldn't wait to show Carleton. Her arm was inside the rabbit all the way to her shoulder. Someone put their little cold hand around her wrist and yanked. Somewhere her mother was talking. She said—

"It's the beard."

Catherine couldn't decide whether to laugh or cry or scream like Carleton. That would surprise Carleton, if she started screaming too. "Shoo! Shoo, Henry—go shave and come back as quick as you can, or else he'll never go back to sleep."

"Carleton, honey," she was saying as Henry left the room. "It's your dad. It's not Santa Claus. It's not the big bad wolf. It's your dad. Your dad just forgot. Why don't you tell me a story? Or do you want to go watch your daddy shave?"

Catherine's hot water bottle was draped over the tub. Towels were heaped on the floor. Henry's things had been put away behind the mirror. It made him feel tired, thinking of all the other things that still had to be put away. He washed his hands, then looked at the bar of soap. It didn't feel right. He put it back on the sink, bent over and sniffed it and then tore off a piece of toilet paper, used the toilet paper to pick up the soap. He threw it in the trash and unwrapped a new bar of soap. There was nothing wrong with the new soap. There was nothing wrong with the old soap either. He was just tired. He washed his hands and lathered up his face, shaved off his beard and watched the little bristles of hair wash down the sink. When he went to show Carleton his brand-new face, Catherine was curled up in bed beside Carleton. They were both asleep. They were still asleep when he left the house at five thirty the next morning.

"Where are you?" Catherine said.

"I'm on my way home. I'm on the train." The train was still in the station. They would be leaving any minute. They had been leaving any minute for the last hour or so, and before that, they had had to get off the train twice, and then back on again. They had been assured there was nothing to worry about. There was no bomb threat. There was no bomb. The delay was only temporary. The people on the train looked at each other, trying to seem as if they were not looking. Everyone had their cell phones out.

"The rabbits are out on the lawn again," Catherine said. "There must be at least fifty or sixty. I've never counted rabbits before. Tilly keeps trying to go outside to make friends with them, but as soon as she's outside, they all go bouncing away like beach balls. I talked to a lawn specialist today. He says we need to do something about it, which is what Liz was saying. Rabbits can be a big problem out here. They've probably got tunnels and warrens all through the yard. It could be a problem. Like living on top of a sinkhole. But Tilly is never going to forgive us. She knows something's up. She says she doesn't want a dog anymore. It would scare away the rabbits. Do you think we should get a dog?"

"So what do they do? Put out poison? Dig up the yard?" Henry said. The man in the seat in front of him got up. He took his bags out of the luggage rack and left the train. Everyone watched him go, pretending they were not.

"He was telling me they have these devices, kind of like ultrasound equipment. They plot out the tunnels, close them up, and then gas the rabbits. It sounds gruesome," Catherine said. "And this kid, this baby has been kicking the daylights out of me. All day long it's kick, kick, jump, kick, like some kind of martial artist. He's going to be an angry kid, Henry. Just like his sister. Her sister. Or maybe I'm going to give birth to rabbits."

"As long as they have your eyes and my chin," Henry said.

"I've gotta go," Catherine said. "I have to pee again. All day long it's the kid jumping, me peeing, Tilly getting her heart broken because she can't make friends with the rabbits, me worrying because she doesn't want to make friends with other kids, just with rabbits, Carleton asking if today he has to go to school, does he have to go to school tomorrow, why am I making him go to school when everybody there is bigger than him, why is my stomach so big and fat, why does his teacher tell him to act like a big boy? Henry, why are we doing this again? Why am I pregnant? And where are you? Why aren't you here? What about our deal? Don't you want to be here?"

"I'm sorry," Henry said. "I'll talk to The Crocodile. We'll work something out."

"I thought you wanted this too, Henry. Don't you?"

"Of course," Henry said. "Of course I want this."

"I've gotta go," Catherine said again. "Liz is bringing some women over. We're finally starting that book club. We're going to read *Fight Club*. Her stepdaughter Alison is going to look after Tilly and Carleton for me. I've already talked to Tilly. She promises she won't bite or hit or make Alison cry."

"What's the trade? A few hours of bonus TV?"

"No," Catherine said. "Something's up with the TV."

"What's wrong with the TV?"

"I don't know," Catherine said. "It's working fine. But the kids won't go near it. Isn't that great? It's the same thing as the toothbrush. You'll see when you get home. I mean, it's not just the kids. I was watching the news earlier, and then I had to turn it off. It wasn't the news. It was the TV."

"So it's the downstairs bathroom and the coffeemaker and Carleton's toothbrush and now the TV?"

"There's some other stuff as well, since this morning. Your office, apparently. Everything in it—your desk, your bookshelves, your chair, even the paper clips."

"That's probably a good thing, right? I mean, that way they'll stay out of there."

"I guess," Catherine said. "The thing is, I went and stood in there for a while and it gave me the creeps too. So now I can't pick up email. And I had to throw out more soap. And King Spanky doesn't love the alarm clock anymore. He won't come out from under the bed when I set it off."

"The alarm clock too?"

"It does sound different," Catherine said. "Just a little bit different. Or maybe I'm insane. This morning, Carleton told me that he knew where our house was. He said we were living in a secret part of Central Park. He said he recognizes the trees. He thinks that if he walks down that little path, he'll get mugged. I've really got to go, Henry, or I'm going to wet my pants, and I don't have time to change again before everyone gets here."

"I love you," Henry said.

"Then why aren't you here?" Catherine said victoriously. She hung up and ran down the hallway towards the downstairs bathroom. But when she got there, she turned around. She went racing up the stairs, pulling down her pants as she went, and barely got to the master bedroom bathroom in time. All day long she'd gone up and down the stairs, feeling extremely silly. There was nothing wrong with the downstairs bathroom. It's just the fixtures. When you flush the toilet or run water in the sink. She doesn't like the sound the water makes.

Several times now, Henry had come home and found Catherine painting rooms, which was a problem. The problem was that Henry kept going away. If he didn't keep going away, he wouldn't have to keep coming home. That was Catherine's point. Henry's point was that Catherine wasn't supposed to be painting rooms while she was pregnant. Pregnant women weren't supposed to breathe around paint fumes.

Catherine solved this problem by wearing the gas mask while she painted. She had known the gas mask would come in handy. She told Henry she promised to stop painting as soon as he started working at home, which was the plan. Meanwhile, she couldn't decide on colors. She and Carleton and Tilly spent hours looking at paint strips with colors that had names like Sangria, Peat Bog, Tulip, Tantrum, Planetarium, Galactica, Tea Leaf, Egg Yolk, Tinker Toy, Gauguin, Susan, Envy, Aztec, Utopia, Wax Apple, Rice Bowl, Cry Baby, Fat Lip, Green Banana, Trampoline, Finger Nail. It was a wonderful way to spend time. They went off to school, and when they got home, the living room would be Harp Seal instead of Full Moon. They'd spend some time with that color, getting to know it, ignoring the television, which was haunted (*haunted* wasn't the right word, of course, but Catherine couldn't think what the right word was) and then a couple of days later, Catherine would go buy some more primer and start again. Carleton and Tilly loved this. They begged her to repaint their bedrooms. She did.

She wished she could eat paint. Whenever she opened a can of paint, her mouth watered. When she'd been pregnant with Carleton, she hadn't been able to eat anything except for olives and hearts of palm and dry toast. When she'd been pregnant with Tilly, she'd eaten dirt, once, in Central Park. Tilly thought they should name the baby after a paint color, Chalk, or Dilly Dilly, or Keelhauled. Lapis Lazulily. Knock, knock.

Catherine kept meaning to ask Henry to take the television and put it in the garage. Nobody ever watched it now. They'd had to stop using the microwave as well, and a colander, some of the flatware, and she was keeping an eye on the toaster. She had a premonition, or an intuition. It didn't feel wrong, not yet, but she had a feeling about it. There was a gorgeous pair of earrings that Henry had given her—how was it possible to be spooked by a pair of diamond earrings?—and yet. Carleton wouldn't play with his Lincoln Logs, and so they were going to the Salvation Army, and Tilly's armadillo purse had disappeared. Tilly hadn't said anything about it, and Catherine hadn't wanted to ask.

Sometimes, if Henry wasn't coming home, Catherine painted after Carleton and Tilly went to bed. Sometimes Tilly would walk into the room where Catherine was working, Tilly's eyes closed, her mouth open, a tourist-somnambulist. She'd stand there, with her head cocked towards Catherine. If Catherine spoke to her, she never answered, and if Catherine took her hand, she would follow Catherine back to her own bed and lie down again. But sometimes Catherine let Tilly stand there and keep her company. Tilly was never so attentive, so *present*, when she was awake. Eventually she would turn and leave the room and Catherine would listen to her climb back up the stairs. Then she would be alone again.

Catherine dreams about colors. It turns out her marriage was the same color she had just painted the foyer. Velveteen Fade. Leonard Felter, who had had an ongoing affair with two of his graduate students, several adjuncts, two tenured faculty members, brought down Catherine's entire department, and saved Catherine's marriage, would make a good lipstick or nail polish. Peach Nooky. There's The Crocodile, a particularly bilious Eau De Vil, a color that tastes bad when you say it. Her mother, who had always been disappointed by Catherine's choices, turned out to have been a beautiful, rich, deep chocolate. Why hadn't Catherine ever seen that before? Too late, too late. It made her want to cry.

Liz and she are drinking paint, thick and pale as cream. "Have some more paint," Catherine says. "Do you want sugar?"

"Yes, lots," Liz says. "What color are you going to paint the rabbits?"

Catherine passes her the sugar. She hasn't even thought about the rabbits, except which rabbits does Liz mean, the stone rabbits or the real rabbits? How do you make them hold still?

"I got something for you," Liz says. She's got Tilly's armadillo purse. It's full of paint strips. Catherine's mouth fills with saliva.

Henry dreams he has an appointment with the exterminator. "You've got to take care of this," he says. "We have two small children. These things could be rabid. They might carry plague."

"See what I can do," the exterminator says, sounding glum. He stands next to Henry. He's an odd-looking, twitchy guy. He has big ears. They contemplate the skyscrapers that poke out of the grass like obelisks. The lawn is teeming with skyscrapers. "Never seen anything like this before. Never wanted to see anything like this. But if you want my opinion, it's the house that's the real problem—"

"Never mind about my wife," Henry says. He squats down beside a knee-high art-deco skyscraper, and peers into a window. A little man looks back at him and shakes his fists, screaming something obscene. Henry flicks a finger at the window, almost hard enough to break it. He feels hot all over. He's never felt this angry before in his life, not even when Catherine told him that she'd accidentally slept with Leonard Felter. The little bastard is going to regret what he just said, whatever it was. He lifts his foot.

The exterminator says, "I wouldn't do that if I were you. You have to dig them up, get the roots. Otherwise, they just grow back. Like your house. Which is really just the tip of the iceberg lettuce, so to speak. You've probably got seventy, eighty stories underground. You gone down on the elevator yet? Talked to the people living down there? It's your house, and you're just going to let them live there rent-free? Mess with your things like that?"

"What?" Henry says, and then he hears helicopters, fighter planes the size of hummingbirds. "Is this really necessary?" he says to the exterminator.

The exterminator nods. "You have to catch them off guard."

"Maybe we're being hasty," Henry says. He has to yell to be

heard above the noise of the tiny, tinny, furious planes. "Maybe we can settle this peacefully."

"Hemree," the interrogator says, shaking his head. "You called me in, because I'm the expert, and you knew you needed help."

Henry wants to say "You're saying my name wrong." But he doesn't want to hurt the undertaker's feelings.

The alligator keeps on talking. "Listen up, Hemreeee, and shut up about negotiations and such, because if we don't take care of this right away, it may be too late. This isn't about homeownership, or lawn care, Hemreeeeee, this is war. The lives of your children are at stake. The happiness of your family. Be brave. Be strong. Just hang on to your rabbit and fire when you see delight in their eyes."

He woke up. "Catherine," he whispered. "Are you awake? I was having this dream."

Catherine laughed. "That's the phone, Liz," she said. "It's probably Henry, saying he'll be late."

"Catherine," Henry said. "Who are you talking to?"

"Are you mad at me, Henry?" Catherine said. "Is that why you won't come home?"

"I'm right here," Henry said.

"You take your rabbits and your crocodiles and get out of here," Catherine said. "And then come straight home again."

She sat up in bed and pointed her finger. "I am sick and tired of being spied on by rabbits!"

When Henry looked, something stood beside the bed, rocking back and forth on its heels. He fumbled for the light, got it on, and saw Tilly, her mouth open, her eyes closed. She looked larger than she ever did when she was awake. "It's just Tilly," he said to Catherine, but Catherine lay back down again. She put her pillow over her head. When he picked Tilly up, to carry her back to bed, she was warm and sweaty, her heart racing as if she had been running through all the rooms of the house.

He walked through the house. He rapped on walls, testing. He put his ear against the floor. No elevator. No secret rooms, no hidden passageways.

There isn't even a basement.

*

Tilly has divided the yard in half. Carleton is not allowed in her half, unless she gives permission.

From the bottom of her half of the yard, where the trees run beside the driveway, Tilly can barely see the house. She's decided to name the yard Matilda's Rabbit Kingdom. Tilly loves naming things. When the new baby is born, her mother has promised that she can help pick out the real names, although there will only be two real names, a first one and a middle. Tilly doesn't understand why there can only be two. *Oishi* means "delicious" in Japanese. That would make a good name, either for the baby or for the yard, because of the grass. She knows the yard isn't as big as Central Park, but it's just as good, even if there aren't any pagodas or castles or carriages or people on roller skates. There's plenty of grass. There are hundreds of rabbits. They live in an enormous underground city, maybe a city just like New York. Maybe her dad can stop working in New York, and come work under the lawn instead. She could help him, go to work with him. She could be a biologist, like Jane Goodall, and go and live underground with the rabbits. Last year her ambition had been to go and live secretly in the Metropolitan Museum of Art, but someone has already done that, even if it's only in a book. Tilly feels sorry for Carleton. Everything he ever does, she'll have already been there. She'll already have done that.

Tilly has left her armadillo purse sticking out of a rabbit hole. First she made the hole bigger; then she packed the dirt back in around the armadillo so that only the shiny, peeled snout poked out. Carleton digs it out again with his stick. Maybe Tilly meant him to find it. Maybe it was a present for the rabbits, except what is it doing here, in his half of the yard? When he lived in the apartment, he was afraid of the armadillo purse, but there are better things to be afraid of out here. But be careful, Carleton. Might as well be careful. The armadillo purse says Don't touch me. So he doesn't. He uses his stick to pry open the snap-mouth, dumps out Tilly's most valuable things, and with his stick pushes them one by one down the hole. Then he puts his ear to the rabbit hole so that he can hear the rabbits say thank you. Saying thank you is polite. But the rabbits say nothing. They're holding their breath, waiting for him to go away. Carleton waits too. Tilly's armadillo, empty and smelly and haunted, makes his eyes water.

Someone comes up and stands behind him. "I didn't do it," he says. "They fell."

But when he turns around, it's the girl who lives next door. Alison. The sun is behind her and makes her shine. He squints. "You can come over to my house if you want to," she says. "Your mom says. She's going to pay me fifteen bucks an hour, which is way too much. Are your parents really rich or something? What's that?"

"It's Tilly's," he says. "But I don't think she wants it anymore."

She picks up Tilly's armadillo. "Pretty cool," she says. "Maybe I'll keep it for her."

Deep underground, the rabbits stamp their feet in rage.

Catherine loves the house. She loves her new life. She's never understood people who get stuck, become unhappy, can't change, can't adapt. So she's out of a job. So what? She'll find something else to do. So Henry can't leave his job yet, won't leave his job yet. So the house is haunted. That's okay. They'll work through it. She buys some books on gardening. She plants a rosebush and a climbing vine in a pot. Tilly helps. The rabbits eat off all the leaves. They bite through the vine.

"Shit," Catherine says when she sees what they've done. She shakes her fists at the rabbits on the lawn. The rabbits flick their ears at her. They're laughing, she knows it. She's too big to chase after them.

"Henry, wake up. Wake up."

"I'm awake," he said, and then he was. Catherine was crying: noisy, wet, ugly sobs. He put his hand out and touched her face. Her nose was running.

"Stop crying," he said. "I'm awake. Why are you crying?"

"Because you weren't here," she said. "And then I woke up and you were here, but when I wake up tomorrow morning you'll be gone again. I miss you. Don't you miss me?"

"I'm sorry," he said. "I'm sorry I'm not here. I'm here now. Come here."

"No," she said. She stopped crying, but her nose still leaked. "And now the dishwasher is haunted. We have to get a new dishwasher before I have this baby. You can't have a baby and not have a dishwasher. And you have to live here with us. Because I'm going to need some help this time. Remember Carleton, how fucking hard that was."

"He was one cranky baby," Henry said. When Carleton was three months old, Henry had realized that they'd misunderstood something. Babies weren't babies—they were land mines; bear traps; wasp nests. They were a noise, which was sometimes even not a noise, but merely a listening for a noise; they were a damp, chalky smell; they were the heaving, jerky, sticky manifestation of not-sleep. Once Henry had stood and watched Carleton in his crib, sleeping peacefully. He had not done what he wanted to do. He had not bent over and yelled in Carleton's ear. Henry still hadn't forgiven Carleton, not yet, not entirely, not for making him feel that way.

"Why do you have to love your job so much?" Catherine said.

"I don't know," Henry said. "I don't love it."

"Don't lie to me," Catherine said.

"I love you better," Henry said. He does, he does, he does loves Catherine better. He's already made that decision. But she isn't even listening.

"Remember when Carleton was little and you would get up in the morning and go to work and leave me all alone with them?" Catherine poked him in the side. "I used to hate you. You'd come home with takeout, and I'd forget I hated you, but then I'd remember again, and I'd hate you even more because it was so easy for you to trick me, to make things okay again, just because for an hour I could sit in the bathtub and eat Chinese food and wash my hair."

"You used to carry an extra shirt with you, when you went out," Henry said. He put his hand down inside her T-shirt, on her fat, full breast. "In case you leaked."

"You can't touch that breast," Catherine said. "It's haunted." She blew her nose on the sheets.

Catherine's friend Lucy owns an online boutique, Nice Clothes for Fat People. There's a woman in Tarrytown who knits stretchy, sexy Argyle sweaters exclusively for NCFP, and Lucy has an appointment with her. She wants to stop off and see Catherine afterwards, before she has to drive back to the city again. Catherine gives her directions, and then begins to clean house, feeling out of sorts. She's not sure she wants to see Lucy right now. Carleton has always been afraid of Lucy, which is embarrassing. And Catherine doesn't want to talk about Henry. She doesn't want to explain about the downstairs bathroom. She had planned to spend the day painting the wood trim in the dining room, but now she'll have to wait.

The doorbell rings, but when Catherine goes to answer it, no one is there. Later on, after Tilly and Carleton have come home, it rings again, but no one is there. It rings and rings, as if Lucy is standing outside, pressing the bell over and over again. Finally Catherine pulls out the wire. She tries calling Lucy's cell phone, but can't get through. Then Henry calls. He says that he's going to be late.

Liz opens the front door, yells, "Hello, anyone home! You've got to see your rabbits, there must be thousands of them. Catherine, is something wrong with your doorbell?"

Henry's bike, so far, was okay. He wondered what they'd do if the Toyota suddenly became haunted. Would Catherine want to sell it? Would resale value be affected? The car and Catherine and the kids were gone when he got home, so he put on a pair of work gloves and went through the house with a cardboard box, collecting all the things that felt haunted. A hairbrush in Tilly's room, an old pair of Catherine's tennis shoes. A pair of Catherine's underwear that he finds at the foot of the bed. When he picked them up he felt a sudden shock of longing for Catherine, like he'd been hit by some kind of spooky lightning. It hit him in the pit of the stomach, like a cramp. He dropped them in the box.

The silk kimono from Takashimaya. Two of Carleton's night-lights. He opened the door to his office, put the box inside. All the hair on his arms stood up. He closed the door.

Then he went downstairs and cleaned paintbrushes. If the paintbrushes were becoming haunted, if Catherine was throwing them out and buying new ones, she wasn't saying. Maybe he should check the Visa bill. How much were they spending on paint, anyway?

Catherine came into the kitchen and gave him a hug. "I'm glad you're home," she said. He pressed his nose into her neck and inhaled. "I left the car running—I've got to pee. Would you go pick up the kids for me?"

"Where are they?" Henry said.

"They're over at Liz's. Alison is babysitting them. Do you have money on you?"

"You mean I'll meet some neighbors?"

"Wow, sure," Catherine said. "If you think you're ready. Are you ready? Do you know where they live?"

"They're our neighbors, right?"

"Take a left out of the driveway, go about a quarter of a mile, and they're the red house with all the trees in front."

But when he drove up to the red house and went and rang the doorbell, no one answered. He heard a child come running down a flight of stairs and then stop and stand in front of the door. "Carleton? Alison?" he said. "Excuse me, this is Catherine's husband, Henry. Carleton and Tilly's dad." The whispering stopped. He waited for a bit. When he crouched down and lifted the mail slot, he thought he saw someone's feet, the hem of a coat, something furry? A dog? Someone standing very still, just to the right of the door? Carleton, playing games. "I see you," he said, and wiggled his fingers through the mail slot. Then he thought maybe it wasn't Carleton after all. He got up quickly and went back to the car. He drove into town and bought more soap.

Tilly was standing in the driveway when he got home, her hands on her hips. "Hi, Dad," she said. "I'm looking for King Spanky. He got outside. Look what Alison found."

She held out a tiny toy bow strung with what looked like dental floss, an arrow as small as a needle.

"Be careful with that," Henry said. "It looks sharp. Archery Barbie, right? So did you guys have a good time with Alison?"

"Alison's okay," Tilly said. She belched. "'Scuse me. I don't feel very good."

"What's wrong?" Henry said.

"My stomach is funny," Tilly said. She looked up at him, frowned, and then vomited all over his shirt, his pants.

"Tilly!" he said. He yanked off his shirt, used a sleeve to wipe her mouth. The vomit was foamy and green.

"It tastes horrible," she said. She sounded surprised. "Why does it always taste so bad when you throw up?"

"So that you won't go around doing it for fun," he said. "Are you going to do it again?"

"I don't think so," she said, making a face.

"Then I'm going to go wash up and change clothes. What were you eating, anyway?"

"Grass," Tilly said.

"Well, no wonder," Henry said. "I thought you were smarter than that, Tilly. Don't do that anymore."

"I wasn't planning to," Tilly said. She spat in the grass.

When Henry opened the front door, he could hear Catherine talking in the kitchen. "The funny thing is," she said, "none of it was true. It was just made up, just like something Carleton would do. Just to get attention."

"Dad," Carleton said. He was jumping up and down on one foot. "Want to hear a song?"

"I was looking for you," Henry said. "Did Alison bring you home? Do you need to go to the bathroom?"

"Why aren't you wearing any clothes?" Carleton said.

Someone in the kitchen laughed, as if they had heard this.

"I had an accident," Henry said, whispering. "But you're right, Carleton, I should go change." He took a shower, rinsed and wrung out his shirt, put on clean clothes, but by the time he got downstairs, Catherine and Carleton and Tilly were eating Cheerios for dinner. They were using paper bowls, plastic spoons, as if it were a picnic. "Liz was here, and Alison, but they were going to a movie," she said. "They said they'd meet you some other day. It was awful—when they came in the door, King Spanky went rushing outside. He's been watching the rabbits all day. If he catches one, Tilly is going to be so upset."

"Tilly's been eating grass," Henry said.

Tilly rolled her eyes. As if.

"Not again!" Catherine said. "Tilly, real people don't eat grass. Oh, look, fantastic, there's King Spanky. Who let him in? What's he got in his mouth?"

King Spanky sits with his back to them. He coughs and something drops to the floor, maybe a frog, or a baby rabbit. It goes scrabbling across the floor, half-leaping, dragging one leg. King Spanky just sits there, watching as it disappears under the sofa.

Carleton freaks out. Tilly is shouting "Bad King Spanky! Bad cat!" When Henry and Catherine push the sofa back, it's too late, there's just King Spanky and a little blob of sticky blood on the floor.

Catherine would like to write a novel. She'd like to write a novel with no children in it. The problem with novels with children in them is that bad things will happen either to the children or else to the parents. She wants to write something funny, something romantic.

It isn't very comfortable to sit down now that she's so big. She's started writing on the walls. She writes in pencil. She names her characters after paint colors. She imagines them leading beautiful, happy, useful lives. No haunted toasters. No mothers no children no crocodiles no photocopy machines no Leonard Felters. She writes for two or three hours, and then she paints the walls again before anyone gets home. That's always the best part.

"I need you next weekend," The Crocodile said. Her rubber band ball sat on the floor beside her desk. She had her feet up on it, in an attempt to show it who was boss. The rubber band ball was getting too big for its britches. Someone was going to have to teach it a lesson, send it a memo.

She looked tired. Henry said, "You don't need me."

"I do," The Crocodile said, yawning. "I *do*. The clients want to take you out to dinner at Four Seasons when they come in to town. They want to go see musicals with you. *Rent. Phantom of the Cabaret Lion.* They want to go to Coney Island with you and eat hot dogs. They want to go out to trendy bars and clubs and pick up strippers and publicists and performance artists. They want to talk about poetry, philosophy, sports, politics, their lousy relationships with their fathers. They want to ask you for advice about their love lives. They want you to come to the weddings of their children and make toasts. You're indispensable, honey. I hope you know that."

"Catherine and I are having some problems with rabbits," Henry said. The rabbits were easier to explain than the other thing. "They've taken over the yard. Things are a little crazy."

"I don't know anything about rabbits," The Crocodile said,

digging her pointy heels into the flesh of the rubber band ball until she could feel the red rubber blood come running out. She pinned Henry with her beautiful, watery eyes.

"Henry." She said his name so gently that he had to lean forward to hear what she was saying.

She said, "You have the best of both worlds. A wife and children who adore you, a beautiful house in the country, a secure job at a company that depends on you, a boss who appreciates your talents, clients who think you're the shit. You *are* the shit, Henry, and the thing is, you're probably thinking that no one deserves to have all this. You think you have to make a choice. You think you have to give up something. But you don't have to give up anything, Henry, and anyone who tells you otherwise is a fucking rabbit. Don't listen to them. You can have it all. You *deserve* to have it all. You love your job. Do you love your job?"

"I love my job," Henry says. The Crocodile smiles at him tearily.

It's true. He loves his job.

When Henry came home, it must have been after midnight, because he never got home before midnight. He found Catherine standing on a ladder in the kitchen, one foot resting on the sink. She was wearing her gas mask, a black cotton sports bra, and a pair of black sweatpants rolled down so he could see she wasn't wearing any underwear. Her stomach stuck out so far, she had to hold her arms at a funny angle to run the roller up and down the wall in front of her. Up and down in a V. Then fill the V in. She had painted the kitchen ceiling a shade of purple so dark, it almost looked black. Midnight Eggplant.

Catherine has been buying paints from a specialty catalog. All the colors are named after famous books, *Madame Bovary*, *Forever Amber*, *Fahrenheit 451*, *Tin Drum*, *A Curtain of Green*, *Twenty Thousand Leagues Beneath the Sea*. She was painting the walls *Catch-22*, a novel she'd taught over and over again to undergraduates. It always went over well. The paint color was nice too. She couldn't decide if she missed teaching. The thing about teaching and having children is that you always ended up treating your children like undergraduates, and your undergraduates like children. There was a particular tone of voice.

She'd even used it on Henry a few times, just to see if it worked.

All the cabinets were fenced around with masking tape, like a crime scene. The room stank of new paint.

Catherine took off the gas mask and said, "Tilly picked it out. What do you think?" Her hands were on her hips. Her stomach poked out at Henry. The gas mask had left a ring of white and red around her eyes and chin.

Henry said, "How was the dinner party?"

"We had fettuccine. Liz and Marcus stayed and helped me do the dishes."

("Is something wrong with your dishwasher?" "No. I mean, yes. We're getting a new one.")

She had had a feeling. It had been a feeling like déjà vu, or being drunk, or falling in love. Like teaching. She had imagined an audience of rabbits out on the lawn, watching her dinner party. A classroom of rabbits, watching a documentary. Rabbit television. Her skin had felt electric.

"So she's a lawyer?" Henry said.

"You haven't even met them yet," Catherine said, suddenly feeling possessive. "But I like them. I really, really like them. They wanted to know all about us. You. I think they think that either we're having marriage problems or that you're imaginary. Finally I took Liz upstairs and showed her your stuff in the closet. I pulled out the wedding album and showed them photos."

"Maybe we could invite them over on Sunday? For a cookout?" Henry said.

"They're away next weekend," Catherine said. "They're going up to the mountains on Friday. They have a house up there. They've invited us. To come along."

"I can't," Henry said. "I have to take care of some clients next weekend. Some big shots. We're having some cash flow problems. Besides, are you allowed to go away? Did you check with your doctor, what's his name again, Dr. Marks?"

"You mean, did I get my permission slip signed?" Catherine said. Henry put his hand on her leg and held on. "Dr. Marks said I'm shipshape. Those were his exact words. Or maybe he said tip-top. It was something alliterative."

"Well, I guess you ought to go, then," Henry said. He

rested his head against her stomach. She let him. He looked so tired. "Before Golf Cart shows up. Or what is Tilly calling the baby now?"

"She's around here somewhere," Catherine said. "I keep putting her back in her bed and she keeps getting out again. Maybe she's looking for you."

"Did you get my email?" Henry said. He was listening to Catherine's stomach. He wasn't going to stop touching her unless she told him to.

"You know I can't check email on your computer anymore," Catherine said.

"This is so stupid," Henry said. "This house isn't haunted. There isn't any such thing as a haunted house."

"It isn't the house," Catherine said. "It's the stuff we brought with us. Except for the downstairs bathroom, and that might just be a draft, or an electrical problem. The house is fine. I love the house."

"Our stuff is fine," Henry said. "I love our stuff."

"If you really think our stuff is fine," Catherine said, "then why did you buy a new alarm clock? Why do you keep throwing out the soap?"

"It's the move," Henry said. "It was a hard move."

"King Spanky hasn't eaten his food in three days," Catherine said. "At first I thought it was the food, and I bought new food and he came down and ate it and I realized it wasn't the food, it was King Spanky. I couldn't sleep all night, knowing he was up under the bed. Poor spooky guy. I don't know what to do. Take him to the vet? What do I say? Excuse me, but I think my cat is haunted? Anyway, I can't get him out of the bed. Not even with the old alarm clock, the haunted one."

"I'll try," Henry said. "Let me try and see if I can get him out." But he didn't move. Catherine tugged at a piece of his hair and he put up his hand. She gave him her roller. He popped off the cylinder and bagged it and put it in the freezer, which was full of paintbrushes and other rollers. He helped Catherine down from the ladder. "I wish you would stop painting."

"I can't," she said. "It has to be perfect. If I can just get it right, then everything will go back to normal and stop being haunted and the rabbits won't tunnel under the house and make it fall down, and you'll come home and stay home, and our neighbors will finally get to meet you and they'll like you and you'll like them, and Carleton will stop being afraid of everything, and Tilly will fall asleep in her own bed, and stay there, and—"

"Hey," Henry said. "It's all going to work out. It's all good. I really like this color."

"I don't know," Catherine said. She yawned. "You don't think it looks too old-fashioned?"

They went upstairs and Catherine took a bath while Henry tried to coax King Spanky out of the bed. But King Spanky wouldn't come out. When Henry got down on his hands and knees, and stuck the flashlight under the bed, he could see King Spanky's eyes, his tail hanging down from the box frame.

Out on the lawn the rabbits were perfectly still. Then they sprang up in the air, turning and dropping and landing and then freezing again. Catherine stood at the window of the bathroom, toweling her hair. She turned the bathroom light off, so that she could see them better. The moonlight picked out their shining eyes, the moon-colored fur, each hair tipped in paint. They were playing some rabbit game like leapfrog. Or they were dancing the quadrille. Fighting a rabbit war. Did rabbits fight wars? Catherine didn't know. They ran at each other and then turned and darted back, jumping and crouching and rising up on their back legs. A pair of rabbits took off like racehorses, sailing through the air and over a long curled shape in the grass. Then back over again. She put her face against the window. It was Tilly, stretched out against the grass, Tilly's legs and feet bare and white.

"Tilly," she said, and ran out of the bathroom, wearing only the towel around her hair.

"What is it?" Henry said as Catherine darted past him, and down the stairs. He ran after her, and by the time she had opened the front door, was kneeling beside Tilly, the wet grass tickling her thighs and her belly, Henry was there too and he picked up Tilly and was carrying her back into the house. They wrapped her in a blanket and put her in her bed and because neither of them wanted to sleep in the bed where King Spanky was hiding, they lay down on the sofa in the family room, curled up against each other. When they woke up in the morning, Tilly was asleep in a ball at their feet.

*

For a whole minute or two, last year, Catherine thought she had it figured out. She was married to a man whose specialty was solving problems, salvaging bad situations. If she did something dramatic enough, if she fucked up badly enough, it would save her marriage. And it did, except that once the problem was solved and the marriage was saved and the baby was conceived and the house was bought, then Henry went back to work.

She stands at the window in the bedroom and looks out at all the trees. For a minute she imagines that Carleton is right, and they are living in Central Park and Fifth Avenue is just right over there. Henry's office is just a few blocks away. All those rabbits are just tourists.

Henry wakes up in the middle of the night. There are people downstairs. He can hear women talking, laughing, and he realizes Catherine's book club must have come over. He gets out of bed. It's dark. What time is it anyway? But the alarm clock is haunted again. He unplugs it. As he comes down the stairs, a voice says, "Well, will you look at that!" and then, "Right under his nose the whole time!"

Henry walks through the house, turning on lights. Tilly stands in the middle of the kitchen. "May I ask who's calling?" she says. She's got Henry's cell phone tucked between her shoulder and her face. She's holding it upside down. Her eyes are open, but she's asleep.

"Who are you talking to?" Henry says.

"The rabbits," Tilly says. She tilts her head, listening. Then she laughs. "Call back later," she says. "He doesn't want to talk to you. Yeah. Okay." She hands Henry his phone. "They said it's no one you know."

"Are you awake?" Henry says.

"Yes," Tilly says, still asleep. He carries her back upstairs. He makes a bed out of pillows in the hall closet and lays her down across them. He tucks a blanket around her. If she refuses to wake up in the same bed that she goes to sleep in, then maybe they should make it a game. If you can't beat them, join them.

*

Catherine hadn't had an affair with Leonard Felter. She hadn't even slept with him. She had just said she had, because she was so mad at Henry. She could have slept with Leonard Felter. The opportunity had been there. And he had been magical, somehow: the only member of the department who could make the photocopier make copies, and he was nice to all of the secretaries. Too nice, as it turned out. And then, when it turned out that Leonard Felter had been fucking everyone, Catherine had felt she couldn't take it back. So she and Henry had gone to therapy together. Henry had taken some time off work. They'd taken the kids to Yosemite. They'd gotten pregnant. She'd been remorseful for something she hadn't done. Henry had forgiven her. Really, she'd saved their marriage. But it had been the sort of thing you could do only once.

If someone has to save the marriage a second time, it will have to be Henry.

Henry went looking for King Spanky. They were going to see the vet: he had the cat cage in the car, but no King Spanky. It was early afternoon, and the rabbits were out on the lawn. Up above, a bird hung, motionless, on a hook of air. Henry craned his head, looking up. It was a big bird, a hawk maybe. It circled, once, twice, again, and then dropped like a stone, towards the rabbits. The rabbits didn't move. There was something about the way they waited, as if this were all a game. The bird dropped through the air, folded like a knife, and then it jerked, tumbled, fell. The wings loose. The bird smashed into the grass and feathers flew up. The rabbits moved closer, as if investigating.

Henry went to see for himself. The rabbits scattered, and the lawn was empty. No rabbits, no bird. But there, down in the trees, beside the bike path, Henry saw something move. King Spanky swung his tail angrily, slunk into the woods.

When Henry came out of the woods, the rabbits were back, guarding the lawn again and Catherine was calling his name. "Where were you?" she said. She was wearing her gas mask around her neck, and there was a smear of paint on her arm. Whiskey Horse. She'd been painting the linen closet.

"King Spanky took off," Henry said. "I couldn't catch him.

I saw the weirdest thing—this bird was going after the rabbits, and then it fell—"

"Marcus came by," Catherine said. Her cheeks were flushed. He knew that if he touched her, her skin would be hot. "He stopped by to see if you wanted to go play golf."

"Who wants to play golf?" Henry said. "I want to go upstairs with you. Where are the kids?"

"Alison took them into town, to see a movie," Catherine said. "I'm going to pick them up at three."

Henry lifted the gas mask off her neck, fitted it around her face. He unbuttoned her shirt, undid the clasp of her bra. "Better take this off," he said. "Better take all your clothes off. I think they're haunted."

"You know what would make a great paint color? Can't believe no one has done this yet. Yellow Sticky. What about King Spanky?" Catherine said. She sounded like Darth Vader, maybe on purpose, and Henry thought it was sexy: Darth Vader, pregnant, with his child. She put her hand against his chest and shoved. Not too hard, but harder than she meant to. It turned out that painting had given her some serious muscle. That will be a good thing when she has another kid to haul around.

"Yellow Sticky. That's great. Forget King Spanky," Henry said. "King Spanky is a terrible name for a paint color."

Catherine was painting Tilly's room Lavender Fist. It was going to be a surprise. But when Tilly saw it, she burst into tears. "Why can't you just leave it alone?" she said. "I liked it the way it was."

"I thought you liked purple," Catherine said, astounded. She took off her gas mask.

"I hate purple," Tilly said. "And I hate you. You're so fat. Even Carleton thinks so."

"Tilly!" Catherine said. She laughed. "I'm pregnant, remember?"

"That's what you think," Tilly said. She ran out of the room and across the hall. There were crashing noises, the sounds of things breaking.

"Tilly!" Catherine said.

Tilly stood in the middle of Carleton's room. All around her lay broken night-lights, lamps, broken lightbulbs. The carpet was dusted in glass. Tilly's feet were bare and Catherine looked down, realized that she wasn't wearing shoes either. "Don't move, Tilly," she said.

"They were haunted," Tilly said, and began to cry.

"So how come your dad's never home?" Alison said.

"I don't know," Carleton said. "Guess what? Tilly broke all my night-lights?"

"Yeah," Alison said. "You must be pretty mad."

"No, it's good that she did," Carleton said, explaining. "They were haunted. Tilly didn't want me to be afraid."

"But aren't you afraid of the dark?" Alison said.

"Tilly said I shouldn't be," Carleton said. "She said the rabbits stay awake all night, that they make sure everything is okay, even when it's dark. Tilly slept outside once, and the rabbits protected her."

"So you're going to stay with us this weekend," Alison said.

"Yes," Carleton said.

"But your dad isn't coming," Alison said.

"No," Carleton said. "I don't know."

"Want to go higher?" Alison said. She pushed the swing and sent him soaring.

When Henry puts his hand against the wall in the living room, it gives a little, as if the wall is pregnant. The paint under the paint is wet. He walks around the house, running his hands along the walls. Catherine has been painting a mural in the foyer. She's painted trees and trees and trees. Golden trees with brown leaves and green leaves and red leaves, and reddish trees with purple leaves and yellow leaves and pink leaves. She's even painted some leaves on the wooden floor, as if the trees are dropping them. "Catherine," he says. "You have got to stop painting the damn walls. The rooms are getting smaller."

Nobody says anything back. Catherine and Tilly and Carleton aren't home. It's the first time Henry has spent the night alone in his house. He can't sleep. There's no television to watch. Henry throws out all of Catherine's paintbrushes. But when Catherine gets home, she'll just buy new ones.

He sleeps on the couch, and during the night someone comes and stands and watches him sleep. Tilly. Then he wakes up and remembers that Tilly isn't there.

The rabbits watch the house all night long. It's their job.

Tilly is talking to the rabbits. It's cold outside, and she's lost her gloves. "What's your name?" she says. "Oh, you beauty. You beauty." She's on her hands and knees. Carleton watches from his side of the yard.

"Can I come over?" he says. "Can I please come over?"

Tilly ignores him. She gets down on her hands and knees, moving even closer to the rabbits. There are three of them, one of them almost close enough to touch. If she moved her hand, slowly, maybe she could grab it by the ears. Maybe she can catch it and train it to live inside. They need a pet rabbit. King Spanky is haunted. He spends most of his time outside. Her parents keep their bedroom door shut so that King Spanky can't get in.

"Good rabbit," Tilly says. "Just stay still. Stay still."

The rabbits flick their ears. Carleton begins to sing a song Alison has taught them, a skipping song. Carleton is such a girl. Tilly puts out her hand. There's something tangled around the rabbit's neck, like a piece of string or a leash. She wiggles closer, holding out her hand. She stares and stares and can hardly believe her eyes. There's a person, a little man sitting behind the rabbit's ears, holding on to the rabbit's fur and the piece of knotted string, with one hand. His other hand is cocked back, like he's going to throw something. He's looking right at her—his hand flies forward and something hits her hand. She pulls her hand back, astounded. "Hey!" she says, and she falls over on her side and watches the rabbits go springing away. "Hey, you! Come back!"

"What?" Carleton yells. He's frantic. "What are you doing? Why won't you let me come over?"

She closes her eyes, just for a second. Shut up, Carleton. Just shut up. Her hand is throbbing and she lies down, holds her hand up to her face. Shut. Up.

When she wakes up, Carleton is sitting beside her. "What are you doing on my side?" she says, and he shrugs.

"What are you doing?" he says. He rocks back and forth on his knees. "Why did you fall over?"

"None of your business," she says. She can't remember what she was doing. Everything looks funny. Especially Carleton. "What's wrong with you?"

"Nothing's wrong with me," Carleton says, but something is wrong. She studies his face and begins to feel sick, as if she's been eating grass. Those sneaky rabbits! They've been distracting her, and now, while she wasn't paying attention, Carleton's become haunted.

"Oh yes it is," Tilly says, forgetting to be afraid, forgetting her hand hurts, getting angry instead. She's not the one to blame. This is her mother's fault, her father's fault, and it's Carleton's fault too. How could he have let this happen? "You just don't know it's wrong. I'm going to tell Mom."

Haunted Carleton is still a Carleton who can be bossed around. "Don't tell," he begs.

Tilly pretends to think about this, although she's already made up her mind. Because what can she say? Either her mother will notice that something's wrong or else she won't. Better to wait and see. "Just stay away from me," she tells Carleton. "You give me the creeps."

Carleton begins to cry, but Tilly is firm. He turns around, walks slowly back to his half of the yard, still crying. For the rest of the afternoon, he sits beneath the azalea bush at the edge of his side of the yard, and cries. It gives Tilly the creeps. Her hand throbs where something has stung it. The rabbits are all hiding underground. King Spanky has gone hunting.

"What's up with Carleton?" Henry said, coming downstairs. He couldn't stop yawning. It wasn't that he was tired, although he was tired. He hadn't given Carleton a good-night kiss, just in case it turned out he was coming down with a cold. He didn't want Carleton to catch it. But it looked like Carleton, too, was already coming down with something.

Catherine shrugged. Paint samples were balanced across her stomach like she'd been playing solitaire. All weekend long, away from the house, she'd thought about repainting Henry's office. She'd never painted a haunted room before. Maybe if you mixed the paint with a little bit of holy water? She wasn't sure: What was holy water, anyway? Could you buy it? "Tilly's being mean to him," she said. "I wish they would make some friends out here. He keeps talking about the new baby, about how he'll take care of it. He says it can sleep in his room. I've been trying to explain babies to him, about how all they do is sleep and eat and cry."

"And get bigger," Henry said.

"That too," Catherine said. "So did he go to sleep okay?"

"Eventually," Henry said. "He's just acting really weird."

"How is that different from usual?" Catherine said. She yawned. "Is Tilly finished with her homework?"

"I don't know," Henry said. "You know, just weird. Different weird. Maybe he's going through a weird spell. Tilly wanted me to help her with her math, but I couldn't get it to come out right. So what's up with my office?"

"I cleared it out," Catherine said. "Alison and Liz came over and helped. I told them we were going to redecorate. Why is it that we're the only ones who notice everything is fucking haunted around here?"

"So where'd you put my stuff?" Henry said. "What's up?"

"You're not working here now," Catherine pointed out. She didn't sound angry, just tired. "Besides, it's all haunted, right? So I took your computer into the shop, so they could have a look at it. I don't know, maybe they can unhaunt it."

"Well," Henry said. "Okay. Is that what you told them? It's haunted?"

"Don't be ridiculous," Catherine said. She discarded a paint strip. Too lemony. "So I heard about the bomb scare on the radio."

"Yeah," Henry said. "The subways were full of kids with crew cuts and machine guns. And they evacuated our building for about an hour. We all went and stood outside, holding on to our laptops like idiots, just in case. The Crocodile carried out her rubber band ball, which must weigh about thirty pounds. It kind of freaked people out, even the firemen. I thought the bomb squad was going to blow it up. So tell me about your weekend."

"Tell me about yours," Catherine said.

"You know," Henry said. "Those clients are assholes. But they don't know they're assholes, so it's almost okay. You just have to feel sorry for them. They don't get it. You have to explain how to have fun, and then they get anxious, so they drink a lot and so you have to drink too. Even The Crocodile got drunk. She did this weird wriggly dance to a Pete Seeger song. So what's their place like?"

"It's nice," Catherine said. "You know, really nice."

"So you had a good weekend? Carleton and Tilly had a good time?"

"It was really nice," Catherine said. "No, really, it was great. I had a fucking great time. So you're sure you can make it home for dinner on Thursday."

It wasn't a question.

"Carleton looks like he might be coming down with something," Henry said. "Here. Do you think I feel hot? Or is it cold in here?"

Catherine said, "You're fine. It's going to be Liz and Marcus and some of the women from the book group and their husbands, and what's her name, the real estate agent. I invited her too. Did you know she's written a book? I was going to do that! I'm getting the new dishwasher tomorrow. No more paper plates. And the lawn care specialist is coming on Monday to take care of the rabbits. I thought I'd drop off King Spanky at the vet, take Tilly and Carleton back to the city, stay with Lucy for two or three days—did you know she tried to find this place and got lost? She's supposed to come up for dinner too—just in case the poison doesn't go away right away, you know, or in case we end up with piles of dead rabbits on the lawn. Your job is to make sure there are no dead rabbits when I bring Tilly and Carleton back."

"I guess I can do that," Henry said.

"You'd better," Catherine said. She stood up with some difficulty, came and leaned over his chair. Her stomach bumped into his shoulder. Her breath was hot. Her hands were full of strips of color. "Sometimes I wish that instead of working for The Crocodile, you were having an affair with her. I mean, that way you'd come home when you're supposed to. You wouldn't want me to be suspicious."

"I don't have any time to have affairs," Henry said. He

sounded put out. Maybe he was thinking about Leonard Felter. Or maybe he was picturing The Crocodile naked. The Crocodile wearing stretchy red rubber sex gear. Catherine imagined telling Henry the truth about Leonard Felter. I didn't have an affair. Did not. I made it up. Is that a problem?

"That's exactly what I mean," Catherine said. "You'd better be here for dinner. You live here, Henry. You're my husband. I want you to meet our friends. I want you to be here when I have this baby. I want you to fix what's wrong with the downstairs bathroom. I want you to talk to Tilly. She's having a rough time. She won't talk to me about it."

"Tilly's fine," Henry said. "We had a long talk tonight. She said she's sorry she broke all of Carleton's night-lights. I like the trees, by the way. You're not going to paint over them, are you?"

"I had all this leftover paint," Catherine said. "I was getting tired of just slapping paint on with the rollers. I wanted to do something fancier."

"You could paint some trees in my office, when you paint my office."

"Maybe," Catherine said. "Ooof, this baby won't stop kicking me." She lay down on the floor in front of Henry, and lifted her feet into his lap. "Rub my feet. I've still got so much fucking paint. But once your office is done, I'm done with the painting. Tilly told me to stop it or else. She keeps hiding my gas mask. Will you be here for dinner?"

"I'll be here for dinner," Henry said, rubbing her feet. He really meant it. He was thinking about the exterminator, about rabbit corpses scattered all across the lawn, like a war zone. Poor rabbits. What a mess.

After they went to see the therapist, after they went to Yosemite and came home again, Henry said to Catherine, "I don't want to talk about it anymore. I don't want to talk about it ever again. Can we not talk about it?"

"Talk about what?" Catherine said. But she had almost been sorry. It had been so much work. She'd had to invent so many details that eventually it began to seem as if she hadn't made it up after all. It was too strange, too confusing, to pretend it had never happened, when, after all, it *had* never happened.

*

Catherine is dressing for dinner. When she looks in the mirror, she's as big as a cruise ship. A water tower. She doesn't look like herself at all. The baby kicks her right under the ribs.

"Stop that," she says. She's sure the baby is going to be a girl. Tilly won't be pleased. Tilly has been extra good all day. She helped make the salad. She set the table. She put on a nice dress.

Tilly is hiding from Carleton under a table in the foyer. If Carleton finds her, Tilly will scream. Carleton is haunted, and nobody has noticed. Nobody cares except Tilly. Tilly says names for the baby, under her breath. Dollop. Shampool. Custard. Knock, knock. The rabbits are out on the lawn, and King Spanky has gotten into the bed again, and he won't come out, not for a million haunted alarm clocks.

Her mother has painted trees all along the wall under the staircase. They don't look like real trees. They aren't real colors. It doesn't look like Central Park at all. In among the trees, her mother has painted a little door. It isn't a real door, except that when Tilly goes over to look at it, it is real. There's a doorknob, and when Tilly turns it, the door opens. Underneath the stairs, there's another set of stairs, little dirt stairs, going down. On the third stair, there's a rabbit sitting there, looking up at Tilly. It hops down, one step, and then another. Then another.

"Rumpled Stiltskin!" Tilly says to the rabbit. "Lipstick!"

Catherine goes to the closet to get out Henry's pink shirt. What's the name of that real estate agent? Why can't she ever remember? She lays the shirt on the bed and then stands there for a moment, stunned. It's too much. The pink shirt is haunted. She pulls out all of Henry's suits, his shirts, his ties. All haunted. Every fucking thing is haunted. Even the fucking shoes. When she pulls out the drawers, socks, underwear, handkerchiefs, everything, it's all spoiled. All haunted. Henry doesn't have a thing to wear. She goes downstairs, gets trash bags, and goes back upstairs again. She begins to dump clothes into the trash bags.

She can see Carleton framed in the bedroom window. He's chasing the rabbits with a stick. She hoists open the window, leans out, yells, "Stay away from those fucking rabbits, Carleton! Do you hear me?"

She doesn't recognize her own voice.

Tilly is running around downstairs somewhere. She's yelling too, but her voice gets farther and farther away, fainter and fainter. She's yelling, "Hairbrush! Zeppelin! Torpedo! Marmalade!"

The doorbell rings.

The Crocodile started laughing. "Okay, Henry. Calm down."

He fired off another rubber band. "I mean it," he said. "I'm late. I'll be late. She's going to kill me."

"Tell her it's my fault," The Crocodile said. "So they started dinner without you. Big deal."

"I tried calling," Henry said. "Nobody answered." He had an idea that the phone was haunted now. That's why Catherine wasn't answering. They'd have to get a new phone. Maybe the lawn specialist would know a house specialist. Maybe somebody could do something about this. "I should go home," he said. "I should go home right now." But he didn't get up. "I think we've gotten ourselves into a mess, me and Catherine. I don't think things are good right now."

"Tell someone who cares," The Crocodile suggested. She wiped at her eyes. "Get out of here. Go catch your train. Have a great weekend. See you on Monday."

So Henry goes home, he has to go home, but of course he's late, it's too late. The train is haunted. The closer they get to his station, the more haunted the train gets. None of the other passengers seem to notice. And of course, his bike turns out to be haunted, too. He leaves it at the station and he walks home in the dark, down the bike path. Something follows him home. Maybe it's King Spanky.

Here's the yard, and here's his house. He loves his house, how it's all lit up. You can see right through the windows, you can see the living room, which Catherine has painted Ghost Crab. The trim is Rat Fink. Catherine has worked so hard. The driveway is full of cars, and inside, people are eating dinner. They're admiring Catherine's trees. They haven't waited for him, and that's fine. His neighbors: he loves his neighbors. He's going to love them as soon as he meets them. His wife is going to have a baby any day now. His daughter will stop walking in her sleep. His son isn't haunted. The moon shines down and paints the world a color he's never seen before. Oh, Catherine, wait till you see this. Shining lawn, shining rabbits, shining world. The rabbits are out on the lawn. They've been waiting for him, all this time, they've been waiting. Here's his rabbit, his very own rabbit. Who needs a bike? He sits on his rabbit, legs pressed against the warm, silky, shining flanks, one hand holding on to the rabbit's fur, the knotted string around its neck. He has something in his other hand, and when he looks, he sees it's a spear. All around him, the others are sitting on their rabbits, waiting patiently, quietly. They've been waiting for a long time, but the waiting is almost over. In a little while, the dinner party will be over and the war will begin.

2004

TIM POWERS

(b. 1952)

Pat Moore

"Is it okay if you're one of the ten people I send the letter to,"
said the voice on the telephone, "or is that redundant? I don't
want to screw this up. 'Ear repair' sounds horrible."

Moore exhaled smoke and put out his Marlboro in the half
inch of cold coffee in his cup. "No, Rick, don't send it to me.
In fact, you're screwed—it says you have to have ten friends."

He picked up the copy he had got in the mail yesterday,
spread the single sheet out flat on the kitchen table and
weighted two corners with the dusty salt and pepper shakers.
It had clearly been photocopied from a photocopy, and originally composed on a typewriter.

> This has been sent to you for good luck. The original is
> in San Fransisco. You must send it on to ten friend's,
> who, you think need good luck, within 24 hrs of
> recieving it.

"I could use some luck," Rick went on. "Can you loan me a
couple of thousand? My wife's in the hospital and we've got
no insurance."

Moore paused for a moment before going on with the old
joke; then, "Sure," he said, "so we won't see you at the low-
ball game tomorrow?"

"Oh, I've got money for *that*." Rick might have caught
Moore's hesitation, for he went on quickly without waiting for
a dutiful laugh: "Mark 'n' Howard mentioned the chain letter
this morning on the radio. You're famous."

> The luck is now sent to you—you will recieve Good
> Luck within three days of recieving this, provided you
> send it on. Do not send money, since luck has no price.

*

On a Wednesday dawn five months ago now, Moore had poured a tumbler of Popov Vodka at this table, after sitting most of the night in the emergency room at—what had been the name of the hospital in San Mateo? Not St. Lazarus, for sure—and then he had carefully lit a Virginia Slims from the orphaned pack on the counter and laid the smoldering cigarette in an ashtray beside the glass. When the untouched cigarette had burned down to the filter and gone out, he had carried the full glass and the ashtray to the back door and set them in the trash can, and then washed his hands in the kitchen sink, wondering if the little ritual had been a sufficient goodbye. Later he had thrown out the bottle of vodka and the pack of Virginia Slims too.

> A young man in Florida got the letter, it was very faded, and he resovled to type it again, but he forgot. He had many troubles, including expensive ear repair. But then he typed ten copy's and mailed them, and he got a better job.

"Where you playing today?" Rick asked.

"The Garden City in San Jose, probably," Moore said, "the six-and-twelve-dollar Hold 'Em. I was just about to leave when you called."

"For sure? I could meet you there. I was going to play at the Bay on Bering, but if we were going to meet there you'd have to shave—"

"And find a clean shirt, I know. But I'll see you at Larry's game tomorrow, and we shouldn't play at the same table anyway. Go to the Bay."

"Naw, I wanted to ask you about something. So you'll be at the Garden City. You take the 280, right?"

> Pat Moore put off mailing the letter and died, but later found it again and passed it on, and received threescore and ten.

"Right."

"If that crapped-out Dodge of yours can get up to freeway speed."

"It'll still be cranking along when your Saturn is a planter somewhere."

"Great, so I'll see you there," Rick said. "Hey," he added with forced joviality, "you're famous!"

> Do not ignore this letter
> ST LAZARUS

"Type up ten copies with your name in it, you can be famous too," Moore said, standing up and crumpling the letter. "Send one to Mark 'n' Howard. See you."

He hung up the phone and fetched his car keys from the cluttered table by the front door. The chilly sea breeze outside was a reproach after the musty staleness of the apartment, and he was glad he'd brought his denim jacket.

He combed his hair in the rearview mirror while the Dodge's old slant-six engine idled in the carport, and he wondered if he would see the day when his brown hair might turn gray. He was still thirty years short of threescore and ten, and he wasn't envying the Pat Moore in the chain letter.

The first half hour of the drive down the 280 was quiet, with a Gershwin CD playing the *Concerto in F* and the pines and green meadows of the Fish and Game Refuge wheeling past on his left under the gray sky, while the pastel houses of Hillsborough and Redwood City marched across the eastern hills. The car smelled familiarly of Marlboros and Doublemint gum and engine exhaust.

Just over those hills, on the 101 overlooking the bay, Trish had driven her Ford Granada over an unrailed embankment at midnight, after a St. Patrick's Day party at Bay Meadows. Moore was objectively sure he would drive on the 101 some day, but not yet.

Traffic was light on the 280 this morning, and in his rearview mirror he saw the little white car surging from side to side in the lanes as it passed other vehicles. Like most modern cars, it looked to Moore like an oversized computer mouse. He clicked up his turn signal lever and drifted over the lane-divider bumps into the right lane.

The white car—he could see the blue Chevy cross on its hood now—swooped up in the lane Moore had just left, but instead of rocketing on past him, it slowed, pacing Moore's old Dodge at sixty miles an hour.

Moore glanced to his left, wondering if he knew the driver

of the Chevy—but it was a lean-faced stranger in sunglasses, looking straight at him. In the moment before Moore recognized the thing as a shotgun viewed muzzle-on, he thought the man was holding up a microphone; but instantly another person in the white car had blocked the driver—Moore glimpsed only a purple shirt and long dark hair—and then with squealing tires the car veered sharply away to the left.

Moore gripped the hard green plastic of his steering wheel and looked straight ahead; he was braced for the sound of the Chevy hitting the center-divider fence, and so he didn't jump when he heard the crash—even though the seat rocked under him and someone was now sitting in the car with him, on the passenger side against the door. For one unthinking moment he assumed someone had been thrown from the Chevrolet and had landed in his car.

He focused on the lane ahead and on holding the Dodge Dart steady between the white lines. Nobody could have come through the roof, or the windows; or the doors. Must have been hiding in the back seat all this time, he thought, and only now jumped over into the front. What timing. He was panting shallowly, and his ribs tingled, and he made himself take a deep breath and let it out.

He looked to his right. A dark-haired woman in a purple dress was grinning at him. Her hair hung in a neat pageboy cut, and she wasn't panting.

"I'm your guardian angel," she said. "And guess what my name is."

Moore carefully lifted his foot from the accelerator—he didn't trust himself with the brake yet—and steered the Dodge onto the dirt shoulder. When the car had slowed to the point where he could hear gravel popping under the tires, he pressed the brake; the abrupt stop rocked him forward, though the woman beside him didn't shift on the old green upholstery.

"And guess what my name is," she said again.

The sweat rolling down his chest under his shirt was a sharp tang in his nostrils. "Hmm," he said, to test his voice; then he said, "You can get out of the car now."

In the front pocket of his jeans was a roll of hundred-dollar bills, but his left hand was only inches away from the .38 revolver tucked into the open seam at the side of the seat. But both the woman's hands were visible on her lap, and empty.

She didn't move.

The engine was still running, shaking the car, and he could smell the hot exhaust fumes seeping up through the floor. He sighed, then reluctantly reached forward and switched off the ignition.

"I shouldn't be talking to you," the woman said in the sudden silence. "*She* told me not to. But I just now saved your life. So don't tell me to get out of the car."

It had been a purple shirt or something, and dark hair. But this was obviously not the person he'd glimpsed in the Chevy. A team, twins?

"What's your name?" he asked absently. A van whipped past on the left, and the car rocked on its shock absorbers.

"Pat Moore, same as yours," she said with evident satisfaction. He noticed that every time he glanced at her she looked away from something else to meet his eyes, as if whenever he wasn't watching her she was studying the interior of the car, or his shirt, or the freeway lanes.

"Did you—get threescore and ten?" he asked. Something more like a nervous tic than a smile was twitching his lips. "When you sent out the letter?"

"That wasn't me, that was *her*. And she hasn't got it yet. And she won't, either, if her students kill all the available Pat Moores. You're in trouble every which way, but I like you."

"Listen, when did you get into my car?"

"About ten seconds ago. What if he had backup, another car following him? You should get moving again."

Moore called up the instant's glimpse he had got of the thing in front of the driver's hand—the ring had definitely been the muzzle of a shotgun, twelve-gauge, probably a pistol-grip. And he seized on her remark about a backup car because the thought was manageable and complete. He clanked the gearshift into park, and the Dodge started at the first twist of the key, and he levered it into drive and gunned along the shoulder in a cloud of dust until he had got up enough speed to swing into the right lane between two yellow Stater Brothers trucks.

He concentrated on working his way over to the fast lane, and then when he had got there, his engine roaring, he just watched the rearview mirror and the oncoming exit signs until he found a chance to make a sharp right across all the lanes and straight into the exit lane that swept toward the southbound 85. A couple of cars behind him honked.

He was going too fast for the curving interchange lane, his tires chirruping on the pavement, and he wrestled with the wheel and stroked the brake.

"Who's getting off behind us?" he asked sharply.

"I can't see," she said.

He darted a glance at the rearview mirror, and was pleased to see only a slow-moving old station wagon, far back.

"A station wagon," she said, though she still hadn't turned around. Maybe she had looked in the passenger-side door mirror.

He had got the car back under control by the time he merged with the southbound lanes, and then he braked, for the 85 was ending ahead at a traffic signal by the grounds of some college.

"Is your neck hurt?" he asked. "Can't twist your head around?"

"It's not that. I can't see anything you don't see."

He tried to frame an answer to that, or a question about it, and finally just said, "I bet we could find a bar fairly readily. Around here."

"I can't drink, I don't have any ID."

"You can have a Virgin Mary," he said absently, catching a green light and turning right just short of the college. "Celery stick to stir it with." Raindrops began spotting the dust on the windshield.

"I'm not so good at touching things," she said. "I'm not actually a living person."

"Okay, see, that means what? You're a *dead* person, a ghost?"

"Yes."

Already disoriented, Moore flexed his mind to see if anything in his experience or philosophies might let him believe this, and there was nothing that did. This woman, probably a neighbor, simply knew who he was, and she had hidden in the back of his car back at the apartment parking lot. She was probably insane. It would be a mistake to get further involved with her.

"Here's a place," he said, swinging the car into a strip-mall parking lot to the right. "Pirate's Cove. We can see how well you handle peanuts or something, before you try a drink."

He parked behind the row of stores, and the back door of the Pirate's Cove led them down a hallway stacked with boxes before they stepped through an arch into the dim bar. There were no other customers in the place at this early hour, and the room smelled more like bleach than beer; the teenaged-looking bartender barely gave them a glance and a nod as Moore led the woman across the worn carpet and the par-queted square to a table under a football poster. There were four low stools instead of chairs.

The woman couldn't remember any movies she'd ever seen, and claimed not to have heard about the war in Iraq, so when Moore walked to the bar and came back with a glass of Bud-weiser and a bowl of popcorn, he sat down and just stared at her. She was easier to see in the dim light from the jukebox and the neon bar-signs than she had been out in the gray day-light. He would guess that she was about thirty—though her face had no wrinkles at all, as if she had never laughed or frowned.

"You want to try the popcorn?" he asked as he unsnapped the front of his denim jacket.

"Look at it so I know where it is."

He glanced down at the bowl, and then back at her. As always, her eyes fixed on his as soon as he was looking at her. Either her pupils were fully dilated, or else her irises were black.

But he glanced down again when something thumped the table and a puff of hot salty air flicked his hair, and some pop-corn kernels spun away through the air.

The popcorn remaining in the bowl had been flattened into little white jigsaw-puzzle pieces. The orange plastic bowl was cracked.

Her hands were still in her lap, and she was still looking at him. "I guess not, thanks."

Slowly he lifted his glass of beer and took a sip. That was a powerful raise, he thought, forcing himself not to show any astonishment—though *you should have suspected a strong hand. Play carefully here.*

He glanced toward the bar; but the bartender, if he had looked toward their table at all, had returned his attention to his newspaper.

"Tom Cruise," the woman said.

Moore looked back at her and after a moment raised his eyebrows.

She said, "That was a movie, wasn't it?"

"In a way." *Play carefully here.* "What did you—is something wrong with your vision?"

"I don't have any vision. No retinas. I have to use yours. I'm a ghost."

"Ah. I've never met a ghost before." He remembered a line from a Robert Frost poem: *The dead are holding something back.*

"Well, not that you could see. You can only see me because . . . I'm like the stamp you get on the back of your hand at Disneyland; you can't see me unless there's a black light shining on me. *She*'s the black light."

"You're in her field of influence, like."

"Sure. There's probably dozens of Pat Moore ghosts in the outfield, and *she*'s the whole infield. I'm the shortstop."

"Why doesn't . . . *she* want you to talk to me?" He never drank on days he intended to play, but he lifted his glass again.

"She doesn't want me to tell you what's going to happen." She smiled, and the smile stayed on her smooth face like the expression on a porcelain doll. "If it was up to me, I'd tell you."

He swallowed a mouthful of beer. "But."

She nodded, and at last let her smile relax. "It's not up to me. She'd kill me if I told you."

He opened his mouth to point out a logic problem with that, then sighed and said instead, "Would she know?" She just blinked at him, so he went on, "Would she know it, if you told me?"

"*Oh* yeah."

"How would she know?"

"You'd be doing things. You wouldn't be sitting here drinking a beer, for sure."

"What would I be doing?"

"I think you'd be driving to San Francisco. If I told you—if you asked—" For an instant she was gone, and then he could see her again; but she seemed two-dimensional now, like a projection on a screen—he had the feeling that if he moved to the side he would just see this image of her get narrower, not see the other side of her.

"What's in San Francisco?" he asked quickly.

"Well if you asked me about Maxwell's Demon-n-n-n—"

She was perfectly motionless, and the drone of the last consonant slowly deepened in pitch to silence. Then the popcorn in the cracked bowl rattled in the same instant that she silently disappeared like the picture on a switched-off television set, leaving Moore alone at the table, his face suddenly chilly in the bar's air conditioning. For a moment "air conditioning" seemed to remind him of something, but he forgot it when he looked down at the popcorn—the bowl was full of brown BBs—unpopped dried corn. As he watched, each kernel slowly opened in white curls and blobs until all the popcorn was as fresh-looking and uncrushed as it had been when he had carried it to the table. There hadn't been a sound, though he caught a strong whiff of gasoline. The bowl wasn't cracked anymore.

He stood up and kicked his stool aside as he backed away from the table. She was definitely gone.

The bartender was looking at him now, but Moore hurried past him and back through the hallway to the stormy gray daylight.

What if she had backup? he thought as he fumbled the keys out of his pocket; and, *She doesn't want me to tell you what's going to happen.*

He only realized that he'd been sprinting when he scuffed to a halt on the wet asphalt beside the old white Dodge, and he was panting as he unlocked the door and yanked it open. Rain on the pavement was a steady textured hiss. He climbed in and pulled the door closed, and rammed the key into the ignition—

—when the drumming of rain on the car roof abruptly went silent, and a voice spoke in his head: *Relax. I'm you. You're me.*

And then his mouth opened and the words were coming out of his mouth: "We're Pat Moore, there's nothing to be afraid of." His voice belonged to someone else in this muffled silence.

His eyes were watering with the useless effort to breathe more quickly.

He knew this wasn't the same Pat Moore he had been in the bar with. This was the *her* she had spoken of. A moment later the thoughts had been wiped away, leaving nothing but an insistent pressure of *all-is-well.*

Though nothing grabbed him, he found that his head was turning to the right, and with dimming vision he saw that his right hand was moving toward his face.

But *all-is-well* had for some time been a feeling that was alien to him, and he managed to resist it long enough to make his infiltrated mind form a thought—*she's crowding me out.*

And he managed to think, too, *Alive or dead, stay whole.* He reached down to the open seam in the seat before he could lose his left arm too, and he snatched up the revolver and stabbed the barrel into his open mouth. A moment later he felt the click through the steel against his teeth when he cocked the hammer back. His belly coiled icily, as if he were standing on the coping of a very high wall and looking up.

The intrusion in his mind paused, and he sensed confusion, so he threw at it the thought, *One more step and I blow my head off.* He added, *Go ahead and call this bet, please. I've been meaning to drive the 101 for a while now.*

His throat was working to form words that he could only guess at, and then he was in control of his own breathing again, panting and huffing spit into the gun barrel. Beyond the hammer of the gun he could see the rapid distortions of rain hitting the windshield, but he still couldn't hear anything from outside the car.

The voice in his head was muted now: *I mean to help you.*

He let himself pull the gun away from his mouth, though he kept it pointed at his face, and he spoke into the wet barrel as if it were a microphone. "I don't want help," he said hoarsely.

I'm Pat Moore, and I want help.

"You want to . . . take over, possess me."

I want to protect you. A man tried to kill you.

"That's your pals," he said, remembering what the ghost woman had told him in the car. "Your students, trying to kill all the Pat Moores—to keep you from taking one over, I bet. Don't joggle me now." Staring down the rifled barrel, he cautiously hooked his thumb over the hammer and then pulled the trigger and eased the hammer down. "I can still do it with one pull of the trigger," he told her as he lifted his thumb away. "So you—what, you put off mailing the letter, and died?"

The letter is just my chain mail. The only important thing about it is my name in it, and the likelihood that people will reproduce it and pass it on. Bombers evade radar by throwing clouds of tinfoil. The chain mail is my name, scattered everywhere so that any blow directed at me is dissipated.

"So you're a ghost too."

A prepared ghost. I know how to get outside of time.

"Fine, get outside of time. What do you need me for?"

You're alive, and your name is mine, which is to say your identity is mine. I've used too much of my energy saving you, holding you. And you're the most compatible of them all—you're a Pat Moore identity squared, by marriage.

"Squared by—" He closed his eyes, and nearly lowered the gun. "Everybody called her Trish," he whispered. "Only her mother called her Pat." He couldn't feel the seat under him, and he was afraid that if he let go of the gun it would fall to the car's roof.

Her mother called her Pat.

"You can't have me." He was holding his voice steady with an effort. "I'm driving away now."

You're Pat Moore's only hope.

"You need an exorcist, not a poker player." He could move his right arm again, and he started the engine and then switched on the windshield wipers.

Abruptly the drumming of the rain came back on, sounding loud after the long silence. She was gone.

His hands were shaking as he tucked the gun back into its pocket, but he was confident that he could get back onto the 280, even with his worn-out windshield wipers blurring everything, and he had no intention of getting on the 101 anytime soon; he had been almost entirely bluffing when he told her, *I've been meaning to drive the 101 for a while now.* But like an alcoholic who tries one drink after long abstinence, he was remembering the taste of the gun barrel in his mouth: *That was easier than I thought it would be*, he thought.

He fumbled a pack of Marlboros out of his jacket pocket and shook one out.

As soon as he had got onto the northbound 85 he became aware that the purple dress and the dark hair were blocking the passenger-side window again, and he didn't jump at all. He had wondered which way to turn on the 280, and now he steered the car into the lane that would take him back north, toward San Francisco. The grooved interchange lane gleamed with fresh rain, and he kept his speed down to forty.

"One big U-turn," he said finally, speaking around his lit cigarette. He glanced at her; she looked three-dimensional again, and she was smiling at him as cheerfully as ever.

"I'm your guardian angel," she said.

"Right, I remember. And your name's Pat Moore, same as mine. Same as everybody's, lately." He realized that he was optimistic, which surprised him; it was something like the happy confidence he had felt in dreams in which he had discovered that he could fly, and leave behind all earthbound reproaches. "I met *her*, you know. She's dead too, and she needs a living body, and so she tried to possess me."

"Yes," said Pat Moore. "That's what's going to happen. I couldn't tell you before."

He frowned. "I scared her off, by threatening to shoot myself." Reluctantly he asked, "Will she try again, do you think?"

"Sure. When you're asleep, probably, since this didn't work. She can wait a few hours; a few days, even, in a pinch. It was just because I talked to you that she switched me off and tried to do it right away, while you were still awake. *Jumped the gun*," she added, with the first laugh he had heard from her— it sounded as if she were trying to chant in a language she didn't understand.

"Ah," he said softly. "That raises the ante." He took a deep breath and let it out. "When did you . . . die?"

"I don't know. Some time besides now. Could you put out the cigarette? The smoke messes up my reception, I'm still partly seeing that bar, and partly a hilltop in a park somewhere."

He rolled the window down an inch and flicked the cigarette out. "Is this how you looked, when you were alive?"

She touched her hair as he glanced at her. "I don't know."

"When you were alive—did you know about movies, and current news? I mean, you don't seem to know about them now."

"I suppose I did. Don't most people?"

He was gripping the wheel hard now. "Did your mother call you Pat?"

"I suppose she did. It's my name."

"Did your . . . friends, call you Trish?"

"I suppose they did."

I suppose, I suppose! He forced himself not to shout at her. She's dead, he reminded himself, she's probably doing the best she can.

But again he thought of the Frost line: *The dead are holding something back.*

They had passed under two gray concrete bridges, and now he switched on his left turn signal to merge with the northbound 280. The pavement ahead of him glittered with reflected red brake lights.

"See, my wife's name was Patricia Moore," he said, trying to sound reasonable. "She died in a car crash five months ago. Well, a single-car accident. Drove off a freeway embankment. She was drunk." He remembered that the popcorn in the Pirate's Cove had momentarily smelled like spilled gasoline.

"I've been drunk."

"So has everybody. But—you might be her."

"Who?"

"My wife. Trish."

"I might be your wife."

"Tell me about Maxwell's Demon."

"I would have been married to you, you mean. We'd *really* have been Pat Moore then. Like mirrors reflecting each other."

"That's why *she* wants me, right. So what's Maxwell's Demon?"

"It's . . . she's dead, so she's like a smoke ring somebody puffed out in the air, if they were smoking. Maxwell's Demon keeps her from disappearing like a smoke ring would, it keeps her . . ."

"Distinct," Moore said when she didn't go on. "Even though she's got no right to be distinct anymore."

"And me. Through her."

"Can I kill him? Or make him stop sustaining her?" And you, he thought; it would stop him sustaining you. Did I stop sustaining you before? Well, obviously.

Earthbound reproaches.

"It's not a *him*, really. It looks like a sprinkler you'd screw onto a hose to water your yard, if it would spin. It's in her house, hooked up to the air conditioning."

"A sprinkler." He was nodding repeatedly, and he made himself stop. "Okay. Can you show me where her house is? I'm going to have to sleep sometime."

"She'd kill me."

"Pat—Trish—" Instantly he despised himself for calling her by that name. "—you're already dead."

"She can get outside of time. Ghosts aren't really in time anyway, I'm wrecking the popcorn in that bar in the future as much as in the past, it's all just cards in a circle on a table, none in front. None of it's really now or not-now. She could make me not ever—she could take my thread out of the carpet—you'd never have met me, even like this."

"Make you never have existed."

"Right. Never was any *me* at all."

"She wouldn't dare—Pat." Just from self-respect he couldn't bring himself to call her Trish again. "Think about it. If you never existed, then I wouldn't have married you, and so I wouldn't be the Pat Moore squared that she needs."

"If you *did* marry me. *Me*, I mean. I can't remember. Do you think you did?"

She'll take me there, if I say yes, he thought. She'll believe me if I say it. And what's to become of me, if she doesn't? That woman very nearly crowded me right out of the world five minutes ago, and I was wide awake.

The memory nauseated him.

What becomes of a soul that's pushed out of its body, he thought, as *she* means to do to me? Would there be *anything* left of *me*, even a half-wit ghost like poor Pat here?

Against his will came the thought, You always did lie to her.

"I don't know," he said finally. "The odds are against it."

There's always the 101, he told himself, and somehow the thought wasn't entirely bleak. Six chambers of it, hollow-point .38s. Fly away.

"It's possible, though, isn't it?"

He exhaled, and nodded. "It's possible, yes."

"I think I owe it to you. Some Pat Moore does. We left you alone."

"It was my fault." In a rush he added, "I was even glad you didn't leave a note." It's true, he thought. I was grateful.

"I'm glad she didn't leave a note," this Pat Moore said.

He needed to change the subject. "*You're* a ghost," he said. "Can't you make *her* never have existed?"

"No. I can't get far from real places or I'd blur away, out of focus, but she can go way up high, where you can look down on the whole carpet, and—twist out strands of it; bend somebody at right angles to *everything*, which means you're gone without a trace. And anyway, she and her students are all blocked against that kind of attack, they've got ConfigSafe."

He laughed at the analogy. "You know about computers?"

"No," she said emptily. "Did I?"

He sighed. "No, not a lot." He thought of the revolver in the seat, and then thought of something better. "You mentioned a park. You used to like Buena Vista Park. Let's stop there on the way."

Moore drove clockwise around the tall, darkly wooded hill that was the park, while the peaked roofs and cylindrical towers of the old Victorian houses were teeth on a saw passing across the gray sky on his left. He found a parking space on the eastern curve of Buena Vista Avenue, and he got out of the car quickly to keep the Pat Moore ghost from having to open the door on her side; he remembered what she had done to the bowl of popcorn.

But she was already standing on the splashing pavement in the rain, without having opened the door. In the ashy daylight her purple dress seemed to have lost all its color, and her face was indistinct and pale; he peered at her, and he was sure the heavy raindrops were falling right through her.

He could imagine her simply dissolving on the hike up to the meadow. "Would you rather wait in the car?" he said. "I won't be long."

"Do you have a pair of binoculars?" she asked. Her voice too was frail out here in the cold.

"Yes, in the glove compartment." Cold rain was soaking his hair and leaking down inside his jacket collar, and he wanted to get moving. "Can you . . . *hold* them?"

"I can't hold anything. But if you take out the lens in the middle you can catch me in it, and carry me."

He stepped past her to open the passenger-side door, and bent over to pop open the glove compartment, and then he knelt on the seat and dragged out his old leather-sleeved binoculars and turned them this way and that in the wobbly gray light that filtered through the windshield.

"How do I get the lens out?" he called over his shoulder.

"A screwdriver, I guess," came her voice, barely audible above the thrashing of the rain. "See the tiny screw by the eyepiece?"

"Oh. Right." He used the small blade from his pocketknife on the screw in the back of the left barrel, and then had to do the same with a similar screw on the forward end of it. The eyepiece stayed where it was, but the big forward lens fell out, exposing a metal cross on the inside; it was held down with a screw that he managed to rotate with the blade-tip—and then a triangular block of polished glass fell out into his palm.

"That's it, that's the lens," she called from outside the car.

Moore's cell phone buzzed as he was stepping backward to the pavement, and he fumbled it out of his jacket pocket and flipped it open. "Moore here," he said. He pushed the car door closed and leaned over the phone to keep the rain off it.

"Hey Pat," came Rick's voice, "I'm sitting here in your Garden City club in San Jose, and I could be at the Bay. Where are you, man?"

The Pat Moore ghost was moving her head, and Moore looked up at her. With evident effort she was making her head swivel back and forth in a clear *no* gesture.

The warning chilled Moore. Into the phone he said, "I'm— not far, I'm at a bar off the 85. Place called the Pirate's Cove."

"Well, don't chug your beer on my account. But come over here when you can."

"You bet. I'll be out of here in five minutes." He closed the phone and dropped it back into his pocket.

"They made him call again," said the ghost. "They lost track of your car after I killed the guy with the shotgun." She smiled, and her teeth seemed to be gone. "That was good, saying you were at that bar. They can tell truth from lies, and that's only twenty minutes from being true."

Guardian angel, he thought. "You killed him?"

"I think so." Her image faded, then solidified again. "Yes."

"Ah. Well—good." With his free hand he pushed the wet hair back from his forehead. "So what do I do with this?" he asked, holding up the lens.

"Hold it by the frosted sides, with the long edge of the triangle pointed at me; then look at me through the two other edges."

The glass thing was a blocky right-triangle, frosted on the sides but polished smooth and clear on the thick edges; obediently he held it up to his eye and peered through the two slanted faces of clear glass.

He could see her clearly through the lens—possibly more clearly than when he looked at her directly—but this was a mirror image: the dark slope of the park appeared to be to the left of her.

"Now roll it over a quarter turn, like from noon to three," she said.

He rotated the lens ninety degrees—but her image in it rotated a full 180 degrees, so that instead of seeing her horizontal he saw her upside down.

He jumped then, for her voice was right in his ear. "Close your eyes and put the lens in your pocket."

He did as she said, and when he opened his eyes again she was gone—the wet pavement stretched empty to the curbstones and green lawns of the old houses.

"You've got me in your pocket," her voice said in his ear. "When you want me, look through the lens again and turn it back the other way."

It occurred to him that he believed her. "Okay," he said, and sprinted across the street to the narrow stone stairs that led up into the park.

His leather shoes tapped the ascending steps, and then

splashed in the mud as he took the uphill path to the left. The city was gone now, hidden behind the dense overhanging boughs of pine and eucalyptus, and the rain echoed under the canopy of green leaves. The cold air was musky with the smells of mulch and pine and wet loam.

Up at the level playground lawn the swingsets were of course empty, and in fact he seemed to be the only living soul in the park today. Through gaps between the trees he could see San Francisco spread out below him on all sides, as still as a photograph under the heavy clouds.

He splashed through the gutters that were made of fragments of old marble headstones—keeping his head down, he glimpsed an incised cross filled with mud in the face of one stone, and the lone phrase "in loving memory" on another—and then he had come to the meadow with the big old oak trees he remembered.

He looked around, but there was still nobody to be seen in the cathedral space, and he hurried to the side and crouched to step in under the shaggy foliage and catch his breath.

"It's beautiful," said the voice in his ear.

"Yes," he said, and he took the lens out of his pocket. He held it up and squinted through the right-angle panels, and there was the image of her, upside down. He rotated it counter-clockwise ninety degrees and the image was upright, and when he moved the lens away from his eye she was standing out in the clearing.

"Look at the city some more," she said, and her voice now seemed to come from several yards away. "So I can see it again."

One last time, he thought. Maybe for both of us; it's nice that we can do it together.

"Sure." He stepped out from under the oak tree and walked back out into the rain to the middle of the clearing and looked around.

A line of trees to the north was the panhandle of Golden Gate Park, and past that he could see the stepped levels of Alta Vista Park; more distantly to the left he could just make out the green band that was the hills of the Presidio, though the two big piers of the Golden Gate Bridge were lost behind miles of rain; he turned to look southwest, where the Twin Peaks and the TV tower on Mount Sutro were vivid above the misty streets; and then far away to the east the white spike of the Transamerica Pyramid stood up from the skyline at the very edge of visibility.

"It's beautiful," she said again. "Did you come here to look at it?"

"No," he said, and he lowered his gaze to the dark mulch under the trees. Cypress, eucalyptus, pine, oak—even from out here he could see that mushrooms were clustered in patches and rings on the carpet of wet black leaves, and he walked back to the trees and then shuffled in a crouch into the aromatic dimness under the boughs.

After a couple of minutes, "Here's one," he said, stooping to pick a mushroom. Its tan cap was about two inches across, covered with a patch of white veil. He unsnapped his denim jacket and tucked the mushroom carefully into his shirt pocket.

"What is it?" asked Pat Moore.

"I don't know," he said. "My wife was never able to tell, so she never picked it. It's either *Amanita lanei*, which is edible, or it's *Amanita phalloides*, which is fatally poisonous. You'd need a real expert to know which this is."

"What are you going to do with it?"

"I think I'm going to sandbag her. You want to hop back into the lens for the hike down the hill?"

He had parked the old Dodge at an alarming slant on Jones Street on the south slope of Russian Hill, and then the two of them had walked steeply uphill past close-set gates and balconies under tall sidewalk trees that grew straight up from the slanted pavements. Headlights of cars descending Jones Street reflected in white glitter on the wet trunks and curbstones, and in the wakes of the cars the tire tracks blurred away slowly in the continuing rain.

"How are we going to get into her house?" he asked quietly.

"It'll be unlocked," said the ghost. "She's expecting you now."

He shivered. "Is she. Well I hope I'm playing a better hand than she guesses."

"Down here," said Pat, pointing at a brick-paved alley that led away to the right between the Victorian-gingerbread porches of two narrow houses.

They were in a little alley now, overhung with rosebushes and rosemary, with white-painted fences on either side. Columns of fog billowed in the breeze, and then he noticed that they were human forms—female torsos twisting transparently in the air, blank-faced children running in slow motion, hunched figures swaying heads that changed shape like water balloons.

"The outfielders," said the Pat Moore ghost.

Now Moore could hear their voices: *Goddamn car—I got yer unconditional right here—excuse me, you got a problem?— He was never there for me—So I told him, you want it you come over here and take it—Bless me Father, I have died—*

The acid smell of wet stone was lost in the scents of tobacco and jasmine perfume and liquor and old, old sweat.

Moore bit his lip and tried to focus on the solid pavement and the fences. "Where the hell's her place?" he asked tightly.

"This gate," she said. "Maybe you'd better—"

He nodded and stepped past her; the gate latch had no padlock, and he flipped up the catch. The hinges squeaked as he swung the gate inward over flagstones and low-cut grass.

He looked up at the house the path led to. It was a one-story 1920s bungalow, painted white or gray, with green wicker chairs on the narrow porch. Lights were on behind stained-glass panels in the two windows and the porch door.

"It's unlocked," said the ghost.

He turned back toward her. "Stand over by the roses there," he told her, "away from the . . . the outfielders. I want to take you in in my pocket, okay?"

"Okay."

She drifted to the roses, and he fished the lens out of his pocket and found her image through the right-angle faces, then twisted the lens and put it back into his pocket.

He walked slowly up the path, treading on the grass rather than on the flagstones, and stepped up to the porch.

"It's not locked, Patrick," came a woman's loud voice from inside.

He turned the glass knob and walked several paces into a

high-ceilinged kitchen with a black-and-white-tiled floor; a blonde woman in jeans and a sweatshirt sat at a formica table by the big old refrigerator. From the next room, beyond an arch in the white-painted plaster, a steady whistling hiss provided an irritating background noise, as if a teakettle were boiling.

The woman at the table was much more clearly visible than his guardian angel had been, almost aggressively three-dimensional —her breasts under the sweatshirt were prominent and pointed, her nose and chin stood out perceptibly too far from her high cheekbones, and her lips were so full that they looked distinctly swollen.

A bottle of Wild Turkey bourbon stood beside three Flintstones glasses on the table, and she took it in one hand and twisted out the cork with the other. "Have a drink," she said, speaking loudly, perhaps in order to be heard over the hiss in the next room.

"I don't think I will, thanks," he said. "You're good with your hands." His jacket was dripping rainwater on the tiles, but he didn't take it off.

"I'm the solidest ghost you'll ever see."

Abruptly she stood up, knocking her chair against the refrigerator, and then she rushed past him, her Reeboks beating on the floor; and her body seemed to rotate as she went by him, as if she were swerving away from him; though her course to the door was straight. She reached out one lumpy hand and slammed the door.

She faced him again and held out her right hand. "I'm Pat Moore," she said, "and I want help."

He flexed his fingers, then cautiously held out his own hand. "I'm Pat Moore too," he said.

Her palm touched his, and though it was moving very slowly his own hand was slapped away when they touched.

"I want us to become partners," she said. Her thick lips moved in ostentatious synchronization with her words.

"Okay," he said.

Her outlines blurred for just an instant; then she said, in the same booming tone, "I want us to become one person. You'll be immortal, and—"

"Let's do it," he said.

She blinked her black eyes. "You're—agreeing to it," she said. "You're accepting it, now?"

"Yes." He cleared his throat. "That's correct."

He looked away from her and noticed a figure sitting at the table—a transparent old man in an overcoat, hardly more visible than a puff of smoke.

"Is he Maxwell's Demon?" Moore asked.

The woman smiled, baring huge teeth. "No, that's . . . a soliton. A poor little soliton who's lost its way. I'll show you Maxwell's Demon."

She lunged and clattered into the next room, and Moore followed her, trying simultaneously not to slip on the floor and to keep an eye on her and on the misty old man.

Moore stepped into a parlor, and the hissing noise was louder in here. Carved dark wood tables and chairs and a modern exercise bicycle had been pushed against a curtained bay window in the far wall, and a vast carpet had been rolled back from the dusty hardwood floor and humped against the chair legs. In the high corners of the room and along the fluted top of the window frame, things like translucent cheerleaders' pompoms grimaced and waved tentacles or locks of hair in the agitated air. Moore warily took a step away from them.

"Look over here," said the alarming woman.

In the near wall an air-conditioning panel had been taken apart, and a red rubber hose hung from its machinery and was connected into the side of a length of steel pipe that lay on a TV table. Nozzles on either end of the pipe were making the loud whistling sound.

Moore looked more closely at it. It was apparently two sections of pipe, one about eight inches long and the other about four, connected together by a blocky fitting where the hose was attached, and a stove stopcock stood half-open near the end of the longer pipe.

"Feel the air," the woman said.

Moore cupped a hand near the end of the longer pipe, and then yanked it back—the air blasting out of it felt hot enough to light a cigar. More cautiously he waved his fingers over the nozzle at the end of the short pipe; and then he rolled his hand in the air-jet, for it was icy cold.

"*It's* not supernatural," she boomed, "even though the air

conditioner's pumping room-temperature air. A spiral washer in the connector housing sends air spinning up the long pipe; the hot molecules spin out to the sides of the little whirlwind in there, and it's them that the stopcock lets out. The cold molecules fall into a smaller whirlwind inside the big one, and they move the opposite way and come out at the end of the short pipe. Room-temperature air is a mix of hot and cold molecules, and this device separates them out."

"Okay," said Moore. He spoke levelly, but he was wishing he had brought his gun along from the car. It occurred to him that it was a rifled pipe that things usually come spinning out of, but which he had been ready to dive into. He wondered if the gills under the cap of the mushroom in his pocket were curved in a spiral.

"But this is counter-entropy," she said, smiling again. "A Scottish physicist named Maxwell p-postulay-postul—guessed that a Demon would be needed to sort the hot molecules from the cold ones. If the Demon is present, the effect occurs, and vice versa—if you can make the effect occur you've summoned the Demon. Get the effect, and the cause has no choice but to be present." She thumped her chest, though her peculiar breasts didn't move at all. "And once the Demon is present, he—he—"

She paused, so Moore said, "Maintains distinctions that wouldn't ordinarily stay distinct." His heart was pounding, but he was pleased with how steady his voice was.

Something like an invisible hand struck him solidly in the chest, and he stepped back.

"You don't touch it," she said. Again there was an invisible thump against his chest. "Back to the kitchen."

The soliton old man, hardly visible in the bright overhead light, was still nodding in one of the chairs at the table.

The blonde woman was slapping the wall, and then a white-painted cabinet, but when Moore looked toward her she grabbed the knob on one of the cabinet drawers and yanked it open.

"You need to come over here," she said, "and look in the drawer."

After the things he'd seen in the high corners of the parlor, Moore was cautious; he leaned over and peered into the drawer—but it contained only a stack of typing paper, a felt tip laundry-marking pen, and half a dozen yo-yos.

As he watched, she reached past him and snatched out a sheet of paper and the laundry marker; and it occurred to him that she hadn't been able to see the contents of the drawer until he was looking at them.

I don't have any vision, his guardian angel had said. *No retinas. I have to use yours.*

The woman had stepped away from the cabinet now. "I was prepared, see," she said, loudly enough to be heard out on Jones Street, "for my stupid students killing me. I knew they might. We were all working to learn how to transcend time, but I got there first, and they were afraid of what I would do. So *boom-boom-boom* for Mistress Moore. But I had already set up the Demon, and I had xeroxed my chain mail and put it in addressed envelopes. Bales of them, the stamps cost me a fortune. I came back strong. And I'm going to merge with you now and get a real body again. You accepted the proposal—you said 'Yes, that's correct'—you didn't put out another bet this time to chase me away."

The cap flew off the laundry marker, and then she slapped the paper down on the table next to the Wild Turkey bottle. "Watch me!" she said, and when he looked at the piece of paper, she began vigorously writing on it. Soon she had written PAT in big sprawling letters and was embarked on MOORE.

She straightened up when it was finished. "Now," she said, her black eyes glittering with hunger, "you cut your hand and write with your blood, tracing over the letters. Our name is us, and we'll merge. Smooth as silk through a goose."

Moore slowly dug the pocketknife out of his pants pocket. "This is new," he said. "You didn't do this name-in-blood business when you tried to take me in the car."

She waved one big hand dismissively. "I thought I could sneak up on you. You resisted me, though—you'd probably have tried to resist me even in your sleep. But since you're accepting the inevitable now, we can do a proper contract, in ink and blood. Cut, cut!"

"Okay," he said, and unfolded the short blade and cut a nick in his right forefinger. "*You've* made a new bet now, though, and it's to me." Blood was dripping from the cut, and he dragged his finger over the *P* in her crude signature.

He had to pause halfway through and probe again with the blade-tip to get more freely flowing blood; and as he was painfully tracing the *R* in MOORE, he began to feel another will helping to push his finger along, and he heard a faint drone like a radio carrier-wave starting up in his head. Somewhere he was crouched on his toes on a narrow, outward-tilting ledge with no handholds anywhere, with vast volumes of emptiness below him—and his toes were sliding—

So he added quickly, "And I raise back at you."

By touch alone, looking up at the high ceiling, he pulled the mushroom out of his shirt pocket and popped it into his mouth and bit down on it. Check-and-raise, he thought. Sandbagged. Then he lowered his eyes, and in an instant her gaze was locked onto his.

"What happened?" she demanded, and Moore could hear the three syllables of it chug in his own throat. "What did you do?"

"*Amanita*," said the smoky old man at the table. His voice sounded like nothing organic—more like sandpaper on metal. "It was time to eat the mushroom."

Moore had resolutely chewed the thing up, his teeth grating on bits of dirt. It had the cold-water taste of ordinary mushrooms, and as he forced himself to swallow it he forlornly hoped, in spite of all his bravura thoughts about the 101 freeway, that it might be the *lanei* rather than the deadly *phalloides*.

"He ate a mushroom?" the woman demanded of the old man. "You never told me about any mushroom! Is it a poisonous mushroom?"

"I don't know," came the rasping voice again. "It's either poisonous or not, though, I remember that much."

Moore was dizzy with the first twinges of comprehension of what he had done. "Fifty-fifty chance," he said tightly. "The Death Cap Amanita looks just like another one that's harmless, both grow locally. I picked this one today, and I don't know which it was. If it's the poison one, we won't know for about twenty-four hours, maybe longer."

The drone in Moore's head grew suddenly louder, then

faded until it was imperceptible. "You're telling the truth," she said. She flung out an arm toward the back porch, and for a moment her bony forefinger was a foot long. "Go vomit it up, now!"

He twitched, like someone mistaking the green left-turn arrow for the green light. No, he told himself, clenching his fists to conceal any trembling. Fifty-fifty is better than zero. You've clocked the odds and placed your bet. Trust yourself.

"No good," he said. "The smallest particle will do the job, if it's the poisonous one. Enough's probably been absorbed already. That's why I chose it." This was a bluff, or a guess, anyway, but this time she didn't scan his mind.

He was tense, but a grin was twitching at his lips. He nodded toward the old man and asked her, "Who *is* the lost sultan, anyway?"

"Soliton," she snapped. "He's you, you—dumb-brain." She stamped one foot, shaking the house. "How can I take you now? And I can't wait twenty-four hours just to see if I *can* take you!"

"Me? How is he me?"

"My name's Pat Moore," said the gray silhouette at the table.

"Ghosts are solitons," she said impatiently, "waves that keep moving all-in-a-piece after the living push has stopped. Forward or backward doesn't matter to them."

"I'm from the *future*," said the soliton, perhaps grinning.

Moore stared at the indistinct thing, and he had to repress an urge to run over there and tear it apart, try to set fire to it, stuff it in a drawer. And he realized that the sudden chill on his forehead wasn't from fright, as he had at first assumed, but from profound embarrassment at the thing's presence here.

"I've blown it all on you," the blonde woman said, perhaps to herself even though her voice boomed in the tall kitchen. "I don't have the . . . sounds like 'courses' . . . I don't have the energy reserves to go after another living Pat Moore *now*. You were perfect, Pat Moore squared—why did you have to be a die-hard suicide fan?"

Moore actually laughed at that—and she glared at him in the same instant that he was punched backward off his feet by the hardest invisible blow yet.

He sat down hard and slid, and his back collided with the stove; and then, though he could still see the walls and the old man's smoky legs under the table across the room and the glittering rippled glass of the windows, he was somewhere else. He could feel the square tiles under his palms, but in this other place he had no body.

In the now-remote kitchen, the blonde woman said, "Drape him," and the soliton got up and drifted across the floor toward Moore, shrinking as it came so that its face was on a level with Moore's.

Its face was indistinct—pouches under the empty eyes, drink-wrinkles spilling diagonally across the cheekbones, petulant lines around the mouth—and Moore did not try to recognize himself in it.

The force that had knocked Moore down was holding him pressed against the floor and the stove, unable to crawl away, and all he could do was hold his breath as the soliton ghost swept over him like a spiderweb.

You've got a girl in your pocket, came the thing's raspy old voice in his ear.

Get away from me, Moore thought, nearly gagging.

Who get away from who?

"I can get another living Pat Moore," the blonde woman was saying, "if I never wasted any effort on you in the first place, if there was never a *you* for me to notice." He heard her take a deep breath. "I can do this."

Her knee touched his cheek, slamming his head against the oven door. She was leaning over the top of the stove, banging blindly at the burners and the knobs, and then Moore heard the triple click of one of the knobs turning, and the faint thump of the flame coming on. He peered up and saw that she was holding the sheet of paper with the ink and blood on it, and then he could smell the paper burning.

Moore became aware that there was still the faintest drone in his head only a moment before it ceased.

"Up," she said, and the ghost was a net surrounding Moore, lifting him up off the floor and through the intangible roof and far away from the rainy shadowed hills of San Francisco.

He was aware that his body was still in the house, still slumped against the stove in the kitchen, but his soul, indistinguishable

now from his ghost, was in some vast region where *in front*
and *behind* had no meaning, where the once-apparent dichotomy between *here* and *there* was a discarded optical illusion, where comprehension was total but didn't depend on
light or sight or perspective, and where even *ago* and *to come*
were just compass points; everything was in stasis, for motion
had been left far behind with sequential time.

He knew that the long braids or vapor trails that he encompassed and which surrounded him were lifelines, stretching
from births in that direction to deaths in the other—some linked
to others for varying intervals, some curving alone through
the non-sky—but they were more like long electrical arcs than
anything substantial; they were stretched across time and space,
but at the same time they were coils too infinitesimally small to
be perceived, if his perception had been by means of sight; and
they were electrons in standing waves surrounding an unimaginable nucleus, which also surrounded them—the universe,
apprehended here in its full volume of past and future, was one
enormous and eternal atom.

But he could feel the tiles of the kitchen floor beneath his
fingertips. He dragged one hand up his hip to the side-pocket
of his jacket, and his fingers slipped inside and touched the triangular lens.

No, said the soliton ghost, a separate thing again.

Moore was still huddled on the floor, still touching the lens
—but now he and his ghost were sitting on the other side of
the room at the kitchen table too, and the ghost was holding a
deck of cards in one hand and spinning cards out with the
other. The ghost stopped when two cards lay in front of each
of them. The Wild Turkey bottle was gone, and the glow from
the ceiling lamp was a dimmer yellow than it had been.

"Hold 'Em," the ghost rasped. "Your whole lifeline is the
buy-in, and I'm going to take it away from you. You've got a
tall stack there, birth to now, but I won't go all-in on you right
away. I bet our first seven years—Fudgsicles, our dad flying
kites in the spring sunsets, the star decals in constellations on
our bedroom ceiling, our mom reading the Narnia books out
loud to us. Push 'em out." The air in the kitchen was summery
with the pink candy smell of Bazooka gum.

Hold 'Em, thought Moore. I'll raise.

Trish killed herself, he projected at his ghost, *rather than live with us anymore. Drove her Granada over the embankment off the 101. The police said she was doing ninety, with no touch of the brake.* Again he smelled spilled gasoline—

—and so, apparently did his opponent; the pouchy-faced old ghost flickered, but came back into focus. "I make it more," said the ghost, "the next seven. Bicycles, the Albert Payson Terhune books, hiking with Joe and Ken in the oil fields, the Valentine from Teresa Thompson. Push 'em out, or forfeit."

Neither of them had looked at their cards, and Moore hoped the game wouldn't proceed to the eventual arbitrary showdown—he hoped that the frail ghost wouldn't be able to keep sustaining raises.

I can't hold anything, his guardian angel had said.

It hurt Moore, but he projected another raise at the ghost: *When we admitted we had deleted her poetry files deliberately, she said, "You're not a nice man." She was drunk, and we laughed at her when she said it, but one day after she was gone we remembered it, and then we had to pull over to the side of the road because we couldn't see through the tears to drive.*

The ghost was just a smoky sketch of a midget or a monkey now, and Moore doubted it had enough substance even to deal cards. In a faint birdlike voice it said, "The next seven. College, and our old motorcycle, and—"

And Trish at twenty, Moore finished, grinding his teeth and thinking about the mushroom dissolving in his stomach. *We talked her into taking her first drink. Pink gin, Tanqueray with Angostura bitters. And we were pleased when she said, "Where has this been all my life?"*

"All my life," whispered the ghost, and then it flicked away like a reflection in a dropped mirror.

The blonde woman was sitting there instead. "What did you have?" she boomed, nodding toward his cards.

"The winning hand," said Moore. He touched his two face-down cards. "The pot's mine—the raises got too high for him." The cards blurred away like fragments left over from a dream.

Then he hunched forward and gripped the edge of the table, for the timeless vertiginous gulf, the infinite atom of the lifelines, was a sudden pressure from outside the world, and this artificial scene had momentarily lost its depth of field.

"I can twist your thread out, even without his help," she told him. She frowned, and a vein stood out on her curved forehead, and the kitchen table resumed its cubic dimensions and the light brightened. "Even dead, I'm more potent than you are."

She whirled her massive right arm up from below the table and clanked down her elbow, with her forearm upright; her hand was open.

Put me behind her, Pat, said the Pat Moore ghost's remembered voice in his ear.

He made himself feel the floor tiles under his hand and the stove at his back, and then he pulled the triangular lens out of his pocket; when he held it up to his eye he was able to see himself and the blonde woman at the table across the room, and the Pat Moore ghost was visible upside down behind the woman. He rotated the glass a quarter turn, and she was now upright.

He moved the lens away and blinked, and then he was gripping the edge of the table and looking across it at the blonde woman, and at her hand only a foot away from his face. The fingerprints were like comb-tracks in clay. Peripherally he could see the slim Pat Moore ghost, still in the purple dress, standing behind her.

"Arm-wrestling?" he said, raising his eyebrows. He didn't want to let go of the table, or even move—this localized perspective seemed very frail.

The woman only glared at him out of her irisless eyes. At last he leaned back in the chair and unclamped the fingers of his right hand from the table-edge; and then he shrugged and raised his right arm and set his elbow beside hers. With her free hand she picked up his pocketknife and hefted it. "When this thing hits the floor, we start." She clasped his hand, and his fingers were numbed as if from a hard impact.

Her free hand jerked, and the knife was glittering in a fantastic parabola through the air, and though he was braced all the way through his torso from his firmly planted feet, when the knife clanged against the tiles the massive power of her arm hit his palm like a falling tree.

Sweat sprang out on his forehead, and his arm was steadily bending backward—and the whole world was rotating too, narrowing, tilting away from him to spill him, all the bets he and his ghost had made, into zero.

In the car the Pat Moore ghost had told him, *She can bend somebody at right angles to* everything, *which means you're gone without a trace.*

We're not sitting at the kitchen table, he told himself; we're still dispersed in that vaster comprehension of the universe.

And if she rotates me ninety degrees, he was suddenly certain, I'm gone.

And then the frail Pat Moore ghost leaned in from behind the woman, and clasped her diaphanous hand around Moore's; and together they were Pat Moore squared, their lifelines linked still by their marriage, and he could feel her strong pulse in supporting counterpoint to his own.

His forearm moved like a counterclockwise second hand in front of his squinting eyes as the opposing pressure steadily weakened. The woman's face seemed in his straining sight to be a rubber mask with a frantic animal trapped inside it, and when only inches separated the back of her hand from the formica tabletop, the resistance faded to nothing, and his hand was left poised empty in the air.

The world rocked back to solidity with such abruptness that he would have fallen down if he hadn't been sitting on the floor against the stove.

Over the sudden pressure release ringing in his ears, he heard a scurrying across the tiles on the other side of the room, and a thumping on the hardwood planks in the parlor.

The Pat Moore ghost still stood across the room, beside the table; and the Wild Turkey bottle was on the table, and he was sure it had been there all along.

He reached out slowly and picked up his pocketknife. It was so cold that it stung his hand.

"Cut it," said the ghost of his wife.

"I can't cut it," he said. Barring hallucinations, his body had hardly moved for the past five or ten minutes, but he was panting. "You'll die."

"I'm dead already, Pat. This—" She waved a hand from her shoulder to her knee "—isn't any good. I should be gone." She smiled. "I think that was the *lanei* mushroom."

He knew she was guessing. "I'll know tomorrow."

He got to his feet, still holding the knife. The blade, he saw, was still folded out.

"Forgive me," he said awkwardly. "For everything."

She smiled, and it was almost a familiar smile. "I forgave you in midair. And you forgive me too."

"If you ever did anything wrong, yes."

"Oh, I did. I don't think you noticed. Cut it."

He walked back across the room to the arch that led into the parlor, and he paused when he was beside her.

"I won't come in with you," she said, "if you don't mind."

"No," he said. "I love you, Pat."

"Loved. I loved you too. That counts. Go."

He nodded and turned away from her.

Maxwell's Demon was still hissing on the TV table by the disassembled air conditioner, and he walked to it one step at a time, not looking at the forms that twisted and whispered urgently in the high corners of the room. One seemed to be perceptibly more solid than the rest, but all of them flinched away from him.

He had to blink tears out of his eyes to see the air-hose clearly, and when he did, he noticed a plain on-off toggle switch hanging from wires that were still connected to the air-conditioning unit. He cut the hose and switched off the air conditioner, and the silence that fell then seemed to spill out of the house and across San Francisco and into the sky.

He was alone in the house.

He tried to remember the expanded, timeless perspective he had participated in, but his memory had already simplified it to a three-dimensional picture, with himself floating like a bubble in one particular place.

Which of the . . . jet trails or arcs or coils was mine? he wondered now. How long is it?

I'll be better able to guess tomorrow, he thought. At least I know it's there, forever—and even though I didn't see which one it was, I know it's linked to another.

2004

GENE WOLFE

(b. 1931)

The Little Stranger

Dᴇᴀʀ Cᴏᴜꜱɪɴ Dᴀɴɴʏ:

Please forgive me for troubling you with another letter. I know you understand. You are the only family I have, and as you are dead you probably do not mind. I am lonely, terribly lonely, living alone way out here. Yesterday I drove into town, and at the supermarket Brenda told me how lucky I am. She has to check groceries all day, keep house, and look after three children. I would love to know whether she divorced him or he divorced her, but I do not like to ask. You know how that is.

And why. I would dearly love to know why.

I said I would trade with her if I could stand up to so much work, which I could not, and I would take her children any-time and take care of them for as long as she wanted. They could run through the woods, I said, play Monopoly and Parcheesi, and explore the old road. I should have said only the girls, but I did not think of that in time, Danny. Not that I have anything against you boys, but I don't know much about them or taking care of them.

One time Sally Cusick showed me her husband's fish. There was a big lady fish and a little man fish, very shiny and silvery, and Sally said the man fish just came and went and that was that. I said I thought that was about how people were too, but Sally did not agree and has not had me over since although I have had her twice and invited her three times, one time when she said she could not come because the rain, as if rain ever stopped her from going anywhere. She is my nearest neighbor, and I could ride my bicycle down Miller Road and up the County Road and come anytime.

Brenda gave me the name of a plumber friend of hers. It is Jack C. Swierzbowski. I have called him (phoned), and he says he will come.

Every time I turn on the hot water the whole house moans.

I think that when I told you about this before, Danny, I said it yelled but it is really more of a moan. Or bellow, like a cow. It is a big house. I know you must remember my house from when you came as a little boy and we played store and all that. Well, probably you remember it bigger than it really is. But it *is* big. Five big bedrooms and all the other rooms like the big cold dining room. I never eat in there anymore. You and I would eat in my merry little kitchen, in the breakfast nook.

If Brenda really sends her girls to me someday that is where we will eat, all three crowded around the little table in the breakfast nook, and for the first day we will make chicken soup and bake brownies and cookies.

There it goes again, and I am not even running the water. Maybe I left it on somewhere, I will see.

> Hugs,
> Your cousin Ivy

Dear Cousin Danny:

I do not know whether I ever told you what a relief it is to me to write you like this, but it is. I never write to Mama or Papa because I saw them before they were embalmed and everything, and I went to the funerals. But I feel like you are still alive, so I can do it. I put on a stamp but no return address. That nice Mr. Chen at the Post Office said yesterday it might go to the Dead Letter Office, and I said yes that is where I want it to go. I did not even smile, but it was all I could do to keep from laughing out loud.

Mr. Swierzbowski came and worked for three hours and even got up on the roof, three floors up. Then he turned on the water to show me and it was as quiet as mice. But last night it was doing it again. I do not think I will call him again. It was almost two hundred dollars and I am so afraid he will fall.

I went for a ramble in the woods after he left, Danny, remembering how you and I played there. If Brenda sends her girls to stay with me for a while, they will go out there and talk about it afterward, and I ought to know the places.

So I started learning today. It is sad to see how much was fields and farms back in the colonial times. Now it is woods all over again and the Mohawks would feel right at home, but they are gone. You can still see the square hole where the old

Hopkins place stood, but it is filling up. Father used to say that the Hopkins were the last people around except us. He did not count the Cusicks, because it was too far to see their smoke. When they had a fire in the fireplace, I mean, or burned their leaves. Only I think probably Mr. Swierzbowski could have seen it when he was up on the roof. It is not so far that I could not ride over on my bicycle, Danny, and Sally drives all over.

She does not even feed those fish. Her husband does it.

It might be nicer if I had another cat. I used to have Pussums. She was as nice a cat as ever you saw, a calico and oh so pretty. I did not have her fixed or anything because I thought I would find a nice boy calico for her and they would have pretty kittens. I would give away the ones that were not calicos themselves, but I would keep the calicos and have three or four or even five of them. And then the mice would not come inside in the winter the way they do. It was terrible last winter.

Only Pussums got big and wanted a boy cat, but I had not found one for her yet. And one day she just disappeared. I should have gotten another cat then, I think. I did not because I kept thinking Pussums would come back after she had her little fling. Which she has not done, and it is more than three years.

Hugs,
Your cousin Ivy

Dear Cousin Danny,

Here I am, bothering you again. But a lot has happened since I wrote a week ago, and I really do need to tell somebody.

One night I was lying in bed and I heard the house moan in the way I have told you about. A few minutes later it did it again, and it did it again a few minutes after that.

Pretty soon I understood why it was so unhappy, Danny. It is just like Pussums. It wants another house. You were a man and would not understand, but I *knew*. It was not from thinking, even if I think a lot and am good at it, my teachers always said. I knew. So I got out of bed and told it as loud as I could that I would get it another house. At first I said a tool shed, but that didn't work, so a house. A little house, but a house.

Well, that is what I am going to do. I am going to talk to people who build houses and have a cottage built right here on my own property. I know they will probably cheat me, but I will have to bear it and keep the cheating as small as I can. I mean to talk to Mr. LaPointe at the bank about it. I know he will advise me, and he is honest.

So that is one thing, but just one. There is another one.

An old truck was going up Miller Road towing a big trailer when it broke down right in front of my house here. There were two men in the truck and two ladies in the trailer, and one lady has a little baby. They are all dark, with curly black hair and big smiles, even the baby.

The older man rang my bell and explained what had happened. He asked if he could pull his truck and the trailer up onto my front lawn until he and the other man could get the truck fixed.

I said all right, but then I thought what if they want to come inside to use the bathroom? Should I let them in? I decided I did not know them well enough to make up my mind about that, but you cannot keep somebody who needs to come inside quickly standing on the porch while you ask questions. I went into the parlor and watched them awhile through the window. They had put the baby on the lawn. The young lady was steering, and the men and the older lady were pushing, because the lawn is higher than Miller Road, and there was the ditch and everything. I could see everyone was working hard, so I made lemonade.

When it was ready they had tied a big chain around the biggest maple. There were zigzag ropes between the chain and their truck, turning and turning around little wheels, and they were pulling on the other end. It was working, too. They had already gotten the front end of their truck up on the grass. I went out and we had lemonade and talked awhile.

The older man is Mr. Zoltan, and the younger one is Johnny. The older lady is Marmar. Or something like that. I cannot say it like they do. She is Mrs. Zoltan. The young lady is Mrs. Johnny, and the baby is hers. Her name is Ivy, just like mine. Her mother's name is Suzette, and she is really quite pretty.

I never said about the bathroom, but I decided if they asked I would let them come in, especially Suzette. Only they never have. I think they are going in the woods. Now I am some-

what scared about going to bed. What if they break in while I
am sleeping?

Well, I just went into the parlor and watched them through
the window, and both men are working really hard on their
truck, with flashlights to see and the engine in pieces. So I do
not think they will break in tonight. They will be too tired. I
will write to you again really soon, Danny.

Hugs,

Your cousin Ivy

P.S. The house has been quiet as mice ever since they came.

Dear Cousin Danny:

I have such good news! You will not believe how nicely
everything is working out. Mr. Zoltan came to breakfast this
morning. It was just bacon and eggs and toast, but he liked it.
He drinks a lot of coffee. He said they were poor people, and
they need parts for their truck. I said I did not have any, which
was the truth. Then he asked if they could stay here until they
could earn enough to fix their truck. Not in my house, I said.
He said they would live in their trailer, like always, but if they
parked it someplace without permission the police would
make them leave, and they could not leave here so they would
go to jail.

That was when I got my wonderful idea. I get many wonderful ideas, Danny, but this was the most wonderful ever. I explained to Mr. Zoltan that I wanted another house built on my
property. Not a big house, just a little one. I said that if he and
Johnny would build it for me in their spare time, I would let
them stay.

Mr. Zoltan looked at me in a worried kind of way, then
looked over at the stove. I said if they could fix a truck they
could build a house, and would they do it?

He told me all over again how poor they were. He said they
would have to earn enough to buy wood and shingles and so
forth. They could find some things at the dump, he said, but
they would have to buy the rest. It might take a long time.

I said that I would not ask them to buy the material, only to
build me a little old-fashioned cottage like the picture I showed
him. I would buy the material for them. That made him happy,
and he agreed at once. He wanted to know where I wanted it

built. I said you look around and decide where you think it ought to be and tell me.

So you see, Danny, why I said I had wonderful news. The Willis Lumber Co. in town will not cheat me more than they cheat everybody, and Mr. Zoltan and Johnny will not cheat me either, because I am not going to give them any money at all.

Hugs,
Your cousin Ivy

Dear Cousin Danny,

I had not planned to pester you with another letter as soon as this, but I just have to tell *somebody* how well my plan is going. Mr. Zoltan came to tell me he had found a foundation in the woods we could use. I knew it was the old Hopkins place, but I asked him questions about it, and it was. Then I told him we could not use it because it was not on my land.

It took all the happiness right out of him. He explained that digging the foundation and building the things to hold the cement were going to be some of the hardest work and would take a long while. The old Hopkins foundation is stone, big stone blocks like tombstones, and he said it was as good as new. So I thought, well, I was going to have to pay for the cement and picks and shovels and all that anyway, so perhaps I could buy the land.

When Mr. Zoltan had left, I called up (phoned) Mr. LaPointe and said I wanted the land where the house had been, and a patch in between so I could get there without going off my property. He said how high are you willing to go?

I thought about that, and looked at my bank books and the checking account and all that. I talked to that foreign woman at Merrill Lynch, too. Finally I called Mr. LaPointe back and said fifty thousand. He said he thought he could get it for me cheaper. By that time my mind was made up. I have a hard time making up my mind about things sometime, Danny, but when I do it is done. I said to buy me as much of the Hopkins property as fifty thousand would get, only to make sure where the old house was, was the part I was buying.

After that Mr. Zoltan came back twice to talk about other places, but I said wait.

Then (this was Tuesday afternoon, I think, Danny) Mr.

LaPointe called me. (Phoned.) He was so happy it made me happy for him. He said he had gotten the whole property for thirty-nine thousand five hundred. The whole farm, only it is all woods now. I went right out and told Johnny, who was working on the truck. And that afternoon he and Mr. Zoltan started shoveling the cellar out. I know they did because I went to see, and it is very black soil, good garden soil I would say and mostly rotted leaves. Compost is what the magazines call it.

I showed them pictures of houses like the one they are going to build for me, and they said they would go to the Willis Lumber Company and buy enough lumber to get started as soon as their truck would run again if I would give them the money. I said no, we will go in my car now and the company will deliver it for a little more money.

Which is what we did. You know how bossy I can be. Suzette needed a ride into town, too, so there were four of us on the drive in. She is opening a shop there to make money. It says "Psychic." I let her out in front of it, and Mr. Zoltan, Johnny, and I went to Willis's. I made them tell me what everything they wanted was and why they wanted it, but I promised that they could keep the scroll saw and the other new tools. We bought a whole keg of nails! And ever so much wood, Danny.

Now I am sitting in the Sun Room to write this, and I can hear their hammers, way off in the woods. If they get quiet before dark, I will go out there and see what the matter is.

                              Hugs,
                              Your cousin Ivy

Dear Cousin Danny,

I haven't even mailed that other letter, and here I am writing again. But the envelope is sealed and I do not wish to tear it open. You will get two letters at once, which I hope you will not mind too much.

There are reasons for this, a big one and a little one. I am going to tell you the little one first, so the big one does not squash it flat. It is that the young lady called me (phoned). She has a cell phone. She said she was Yvonne. I said who? She said Yvonne as plain as anything and she was staying with me. (This is what she said, Danny. It is not true.) Then she said I had

given her a ride into town that morning, so I knew it was
Suzette. She said she was ready to come home now and there
was a friend who would drive her, only she called her a client.
But she did not know the roads and neither did her friend.

So I gave her directions, how to find the County Road and
how you turn on Miller Road and so on. I know you know
already, so I will not repeat everything. Then I sat down and
thought hard about the young lady. Could I have remembered
her name wrong? I know I could not, not as wrong as that.

So she is fooling her friend, and if she will fool her friend she
will fool me. I would like to talk with Marmar about her, but I
know Marmar will not talk if I just come up and ask. I must
think of something, and writing you these letters helps.

It helps more now, because I know that you get them and
read them, Danny. That is my big thing. I know it because I
saw you last night. You must have thought I was sleeping. I
could see you were being very quiet so as not to wake me up.

But I was awake, sitting by the window looking down at the
trailer and Mr. Zoltan's truck. I could not sleep. That is how it
is with folks my age. We take naps during the day, and then we
cannot sleep at night. I think that it is because God is getting
us ready for the grave. Is that right? Did He ever tell you?

You went into the woods to look at my new house. I saw you
go and sat up waiting for you to come back. The moon was
low and bright when you did, and I got to see it right through
you, which was very pretty and something I had never seen
before at all. You looked at their truck and even went into the
trailer without opening the door, which must be very handy
when you are carrying a basket of laundry or grocery bags.
When you went back into the woods I waited for you to come
out for a while. I thought about coming downstairs and saying
hello, but I knew you would think you woke me up. You did
not, I just did, and it would not have been fair for me to make
you feel guilty, as I am sure you would even if I said not to.

But I want you to know that I am often awake, and there is
no reason I could not put on a robe and have a nice chat. I
could make tea or anything like that which you might like,
Danny.

                              Hugs,
                              Your cousin Ivy

*

Dear Cousin Danny,

I have had the nicest time! I must tell you. Yvonne (Suzette) was in town at her shop, and Marmar had ever so much work to do, cooking and cleaning her trailer. So I said I would look after little Ivy for a while. We played peekaboo and had a bottle, and I changed her three times. She is really the dearest little baby in the world! Of course I had to give her back eventually, which I did not like to do. But Mr. Zoltan came and wanted her, and I gave her to him. He looked pale and ill, I thought, and his hands shook. So I did not like to and I am afraid he will give little Ivy something. A really bad cold or the flu. But he is her grandfather, so I did.

Then something very, very odd happened. I cannot explain it and don't even know who to ask. I got to thinking about you, and how much I would like to talk to you. And it came to me that you might not want to come into my house unless you were invited. I know you could walk right through my door like you did into Mr. Zoltan's trailer, but I thought you would probably not want to. I thought of inviting you in this letter, and I do. Just come in anytime, Danny.

What is more, I remembered about the rock. There is this big rock in my flower bed close to the front porch, and I keep it there because it was in Mama's. She had it there because Papa always kept a key under it in case he lost his. Only when he died she took the key away for fear someone would find it and come in.

And I thought, well, I *want* Cousin Danny to come in and talk. So I will just put a key there for him to find, and tell him it is there. I got my extra key from the desk in Papa's study and went outside to put it under the rock.

But when I picked that rock up, there was foreign writing on the bottom. It was yellow chalk, I think, very ugly and new-looking. Just looking at it made me feel sick. I took that rock inside right away and washed it in the sink. It made me feel a lot better, and I think it made the rock feel better too. You know what I mean.

Anyway, that rock is all nice and clean now, Danny, and I have put the key under it as a sign that you are welcome to come in anytime. If you pick up the rock and there is bad writing on the bottom, I did not put it there. I do not even have any yellow chalk. Tell me when you come in, and I will wash it off.

But the main thing was little Ivy. She is the darlingest baby, and I just love her.

Hugs,
Your cousin Ivy

Dear Cousin Danny,

In some ways it has been very nice here today, but in others Not So Nice. Let me begin with one of the nice ones, which is Pusson. I went out to see how my new little house was. I had heard a lot of sawing and hammering that morning, and then it had stopped, and I thought I should see what the trouble was. Well, Danny, you would never guess.

It was a cat. Just a cat, not very big and really quite friendly once he gets to know you. He was up on the plywood that Mr. Zoltan and Johnny are going to nail the shingles on. They were afraid of him. Two big men afraid of a little cat! I thought it was silly and said Pussums, Pussums, Pussums! Which was the way I used to call my old cat, and this nice young cat came right down. I let him smell my fingers, and soon he was rubbing my legs.

Yes, Danny, I took Pusson home with me. I think he is really a calico cat under all the black. Other cats are not so friendly and sweet. I have kept Pussums's cat box all ready in case she ever comes home, and Pusson knows how to use it already. So I think he is calico underneath. Pussums found the boy cat she was looking for, and they had children, and this is her son, coming back to the Old Home Place to see how it was when his mama was young. You will think I am just a silly old woman for writing all that, but it could have happened, and since I want to believe it, why should I not be happy?

Besides there is nobody out here for Pusson to belong to except Sally Cusick and she should not have a cat because of all the fish. So he can live here with me, and if Sally ever comes he can hide under the sofa in the parlor.

The not so nice part is Mr. Cherigate. I did not know him at all until he pulled up in his big car. He was perfectly friendly and drank my tea and petted Pusson, but he told me very firmly that I cannot have Mr. Zoltan and Johnny put in the pipes and

the electric like I had planned. Mr. Cherigate is a Building Inspector for the county. He showed me his badge and gave me
his card, which I still have on the nice hallmarked silver tray
that used to be Mama's when you were here. I must have a licensed plumber for the pipes and an electrician for the electric.
I explained that Mr. LaPointe at the bank did not think I
would need a building permit way out here, and he said I did
not, but a building that people might live in must pass inspection and ever so much more.

Naturally I called Mr. Swierzbowski (phoned). He will do
the plumbing, and he will send his friend Mr. Caminiti for the
electric. I am sure it will cost ever so much, but I don't think I
will be able to get Mr. Zoltan to pay, although I will try.

I am not sure if this is the worst thing or just a funny thing,
Danny. Perhaps I will know tomorrow, and if I do I will tell
myself that I should have waited and told you all about it then.
But I am going to tell you now and let you decide. While Mr.
Cherigate was drinking my tea he asked if I knew I was a
witch. I thought about it and said I did not, but if it meant I
get to ride through the air on a broom and throw down candy
to the boys and girls I might do it. He laughed and said no, a
real witch, one that cast spells and sours milk while it is still in
the cow.

Of course I said I could not do that and I did not think anybody else could either. Mr. Cherigate said there was a rumor
going around town that said that, and I explained that there
was nobody rooming with me except Pusson. I should have
said little Ivy sometimes, too, Danny, but I forgot.

But Mr. Cherigate meant *rumor*. So I had made a silly mistake that I would not have made if it were not for Yvonne
(Suzette) telling people she lived here. Then Mr. Cherigate
said that he had heard it from his wife, who heard it from a for-
tune-teller. I said is that the same as psychic and he said it was.
So it was Suzette after all! I will talk to her about this the first
chance I get, Danny, and I will write you again soon to tell you
what I said and what she said.

>   Hugs!
>   Your cousin Ivy

                         *

Dear Cousin Danny,

You will not believe what I am going to tell you in this letter, but it is true, every bit.

When I had finished the letter I wrote yesterday, I waited for somebody to bring Suzette (Yvonne) home. Then I went out to the trailer to talk to her. She was inside, and Marmar said she was nursing little Ivy. I certainly did not want to interrupt that and perhaps make little Ivy cry, so I went to my new little house to see whether Mr. Swierzbowski or Mr. Caminiti had come.

They had not, but Mr. Zoltan and Johnny were there sawing fretwork. When Mr. Zoltan saw me, he got down on his knees. When Johnny saw that, he did too. They begged me to let them use their truck again. If they had their truck, they could go to the dump and find things for me, and buy nails and shingles whenever they needed them, and bring them back here in their truck. It was hard for me to understand everything they said, Danny, because Mr. Zoltan's English is not even as good as Mr. Chen's (at the Post Office). And Johnny would not look at me, or talk very loud either. But that was what they wanted, and when I understood I said of course they could use their truck, go right ahead.

They started thanking me then, over and over, and crying. And while they were doing that, we heard a funny noise from the direction of my house. I did not know what it was. You will think it silly of me, Danny, I know. But I did not. Mr. Zoltan and Johnny knew at once and ran toward it. I worried for a minute that someone might come and take the saws and hammers and things they were leaving behind. And I thought, they are not my things, and Johnny and Mr. Zoltan ran right off and left them so why should not I! No one asked me to watch them while they were gone.

By that time even Mr. Zoltan was out of sight. Johnny was out of sight almost before he began to run, because Johnny can run very fast. I did not run. I walked, but I walked fast, carrying Pusson and petting him as I went along. He is very nice for a black cat, Danny, about as nice as any cat that is not calico can be.

When I got back to my big house, Mr. Zoltan's trailer was still there, but Mr. Zoltan's truck was gone. That was when I knew what the noise we heard had been. It was the noise of the engine starting. Mr. Zoltan and Johnny had heard it many times, so they knew what it was. I had not, so I did not know.

Marmar said Suzette (Yvonne) had taken it. She thought she had run away. I said I did not think so, because I think that she needed to visit her little store, and that if Johnny telephoned her there in a few minutes she would be there. Johnny did not think so. Marmar said we would never see her again and little Ivy cried. Zoltan said I could get her back, but he would not say how.

After that, I decided to telephone myself, but I did not tell them that because I did not want them to think I was interfering.

That was when Mr. Swierzbowski came to talk about plumbing for my new little stranger. I made Mr. Zoltan and Johnny go back to it with us, so they could show Mr. Swierzbowski what needed to be done. There were some trees that would have to be cut for the septic tank, and a lot more that would have to be cut so Mr. Swierzbowski could bring in his big digging machine. I do not like trees being cut, so I said Mr. Zoltan and Johnny would dig it with shovels. They looked very despondent when I said this, so I said that if they would I would get their truck back or get them a new one. I said it because I do not think Suzette (Yvonne) has really run away and left her baby.

After that I came back here and Pusson and I called (phoned) Yvonne's store. There was no answer, so I am writing this letter to you instead. As soon I sign it and address your envelope and find a stamp for it, I will try again.

> Hugs,
> Your cousin Ivy

Dear Cousin Danny:

I have been so busy these past few days that I have not written. I am terribly sorry, but I have not even had a chance to go to the post office to buy Mr. Chen's stamps. Little Ivy is sleeping now. I think that she is more used to me, or perhaps I am more used to her. But she is sleeping like a little angel, with Pusson curled up beside her. I would take a picture if I could only find my camera, which is not in the kitchen cabinet or the library or anywhere.

But I have stopped trying to remember where my camera might be, and started trying to remember what I have told you and what happened after that letter was out in the big tin box, with the flag up. You know that Suzette (Yvonne) took Mr. Zoltan's truck. He is angry about it and so is Johnny. Suzette is not even Mr. Zoltan's daughter, only his daughter-in-law. I have talked to them, and Marmar is Mr. Zoltan's wife, just like I thought. Suzette (Yvonne) is Johnny's wife. But Johnny says was, and says he will beat her for a week. I do not see how he can beat her if he is going to divorce her. He says he will go to the king and get a divorce. Do you think he means George III, Danny? George III is dead, but then you are dead too, so perhaps George III can still divorce people. Johnny is Mr. Zoltan's son, and Marmar's.

It is funny, sometimes, how these things work out. When I had called Suzette's (Yvonne's) store several times and gotten no answer, and talked to Marmar besides Mr. Zoltan and Johnny, and called the store twice more, I felt sure that Suzette had stolen Mr. Zoltan's truck and was not ever going to bring it back.

So she had really stolen my truck because I had promised Mr. Zoltan and Johnny that I would get them a new one if we could not get their old one back. Besides, their trailer was parked in my front yard, and it still is. I like them and they have never asked to use my bathroom, not even once. But I do not want them living in my front yard until I am old and gray, which is now.

So I called the police. I described my truck to the nice policeman, and when he asked about license plates I said it did not have any because I had noticed that before Suzette took it. I said it had just been parked on my property but I had gotten two men to work on it, and as soon as it would run Suzette had run off with it. You can see that I told the nice policeman nothing but the truth, Danny. All that was just as true as I could make it without getting all complicated. I spoke clearly and enunciated plainly, and the nice policeman never argued with me about a thing.

Then he asked me about Suzette. I told him how old she was, and pretty, and black hair. And I explained that she was the wife of one of the men who had been working on my truck and building a new little house for me. That was fine too, Danny, and perhaps I ought to have left it at that, but I did not, and that seemed like it might be a mistake for a while. I told him that her professional name was Yvonne. Which it was.

He became very interested and asked about her store, so I told him where it was and that I had never gone in there to buy anything. He said that there was a Mr. Bunco who would want to hear about Yvonne. I said Mr. Bunco could come out and talk to me anytime and I would tell him all I could, and I told him where I live.

After that I fixed dinner, which was macaroni-and-cheese and salad from my garden with canned salmon in it for me, and more salmon for Pusson. It was very good, too.

Pusson had only just finished saying thank you when we heard a police car. I went outside because I thought I ought to show the policemen where the truck had been, and I was just in time to see Mr. Zoltan and Marmar running into the woods. Johnny was gone already. I know he can run much faster. Little Ivy was crying, so I went into their trailer and picked her up. I rocked her, and she quieted down right away. She is such a good baby, Danny. You would never believe how good she is.

I told the lady who came with the policeman that I had been expecting Mr. Bunco. And she said she was Miz Bunco and that would have to do. But she gave me her card, and she was only fooling. Her name is really Sergeant Lois B. Anderson, unless it was someone else's card. She asked about little Ivy, and I explained that I was taking care of her while Suzette (Yvonne) was away stealing my truck. She said she would tell D.C. and F.S. and they would take her off my hands. I do not know who F.S. is, Danny, but D.C. is the District of Columbia which means the president. He looks like a very nice man, I know. Still, Danny, he is very busy and may not know how to take care of children. So I said that I did not want little Ivy taken off my hands, that I like her and she likes me, which is the truth. Then Miz Anderson said we ought to go inside where I could sit down, and perhaps little Ivy's diaper needed changing.

Miz Anderson held her while I put water on for tea and we had a nice talk. She said the president would put little Ivy in a faster home, and that might not be the best thing for her. Some faster homes were nice and some not so nice, she said. I did not like the idea of little Ivy living in another trailer, and it seems to me that one that went fast would be worse than Mr. Zoltan's, which does not move at all but is terribly crowded and smelly. So I said why not just let me keep her, she will be right here and perhaps Suzette will come back?

Miz Anderson and I agreed that might be better, and Miz Anderson took her card and wrote call at once if Yvonne returns for baby on the back of it.

So little Ivy is mine now, Danny. Another little stranger is what I said to Pusson, who is a little stranger himself and delighted. I have told Marmar that I have to keep her until Suzette (Yvonne) comes back for her. I do not think Marmar likes that very much, but Mr. Zoltan and Johnny are on my side.

Hugs,
Your cousin Ivy

Dear Cousin Danny:

It has been days and days since I wrote last. I have been so busy! My little house is finished now, and some nice children came to see me today. Their names are Hank and Greta, isn't that nice? They are *twins*, and their mother loves old movies. They are ever so cute, and we had a wonderful time together. They have promised to come back and see me again. I made them promise that before they left, Danny, and they did. I am so looking forward to it.

So that is what I wanted to write you about. But I should have written before, because I have ever so much wonderful news. My little house is finished! Isn't that nice? And little Ivy is still with me, which is even nicer. I will give my little stranger back to her mother, of course, if her mother (Suzette) ever comes back. I suppose I'll have to, but I won't like it.

I call her the little stranger, and then I have to remind myself there are really three. That is little Ivy, Pusson, and the first little stranger ever, my new little house. But, Cousin Danny, there are *five* now, because I must include Hank and Greta, who are such sweet little strangers. I could just eat them up!

After Ivy got settled down for her nap this morning, I went to my new little house (it has a name now and I will tell you in a minute) to see if the nice lady from the department store had brought my new furniture yet. And out in front of my new little house were the sweetest children you ever saw, little tow-heads about seven or eight. I said hello and they said hello, and I asked their names, and they wanted to know if my little house was made of gingerbread.

I explained that there was a lot of gingerbread on it, because that is what you call the lovely old-fashioned woodwork Mr. Zoltan and Johnny made for me. Danny, I had to hold each of them up so they could feel it and see it was not the kind of gingerbread you eat! Can you imagine?

After that we went inside, and I told them all about the nice big Navigator car you got for me from Mr. Cherigate, the building inspector. How hard it was to get him to stand up, and how I promised I would stop the bleeding and walk him out of my cute little Gingerbread House and never tell anyone what happened if he would give me his car for Mr. Zoltan. But I am not breaking my promise by talking about it to you in this letter, because you know already. He was so startled when you and that Hopkins girl joined us that he ran into the pantry and bumped his nose on a shelf trying to get out, remember? I still laugh when I think of it, but it was not really funny at all until I made it stop bleeding. Anyway Mr. Caminiti has come and fixed what he had put in wrong, and there are lights, ever so pretty when they shine out through all the trees.

But I just told Hank and Greta that a nice man had given me a big black car for what I did, bigger than Mr. Zoltan's truck had been. And I had given it to Mr. Zoltan and Johnny for building my house. It was too big for me anyway, and I have my own car. I do not think I could ever drive a big thing like that.

Hank and Greta liked my new little house so much that I have decided to call it Gingerbread House. Now I will never forget them, and I will find somebody to paint a sign saying that and put it on my little house, too.

But I was worried about little Ivy. I do not like to leave her alone for a long time, and the time was getting long. So I made Hank and Greta come back with me to this big house. I showed them little Ivy, and I showed them to little Ivy, too! She liked them and laughed and made all sorts of baby noises. Pusson told me her diaper needed changing, and Greta changed while

Hank and I helped. After that, we baked gingerbread men and played with little Ivy, and played checkers with our gingerbread men, too, breaking off heads and things to make them fit on the squares. You could eat the cookies you captured, but if you did you could not use them to crown your kings. Hank ate all his, so Greta beat him. I did too. By that time it was getting dark, so I showed them how I could make fire fly out of Pusson's fur.

Then we went back to Gingerbread House, and Miz Macy had brought the furniture and set it up like she promised, just like magic. The children were amazed and ever so pleased. Hank wanted to know if they could come back on Halloween, and Greta said no, she will be busy then.

So I said I hoped I would be very busy with little trick-or-treaters, but I would save special treats for them. Children never come, Danny, but I did not want Greta to feel badly. So perhaps she and Hank will come then. I hope so. Oh, I do! It has been ever so long since the children came here.

Hugs,

Your cousin Ivy

P.S. Brenda called while I was looking for your envelope. Hank and Greta are hers! And they had come home very late, she said, full of stories about baking cookies with a witch in the woods. Sally Cusick gave her my number and told her I might know something since I lived out this way. Of course I said my goodness there are no witches out here.

Only me.

2004

BENJAMIN PERCY

(b. 1979)

Dial Tone

A JOGGER spotted the body hanging from the cell tower. At
first he thought it was a mannequin. That's what he told Z-21,
the local NBC affiliate. The way the wind blew it, the way it
flopped limply, made it appear insubstantial, maybe stuffed
with straw. It couldn't be a body, he thought, not in a place
like Redmond, Oregon, a nowhere town on the edge of a
great wash of desert. But it was. It was the body of a man. He
had a choke chain, the kind you buy at Pet Depot, wrapped
around his neck and anchored to the steel ladder that rose
twelve hundred feet in the air to the tip of the tower, where a
red light blinked a warning.

Word spread quickly. And everyone, the whole town, it
seemed, crowded around, some of them with binoculars and
cameras, to watch three deputies, joined by a worker from
Clark Tower Service, scale the tower and then descend with
the body in a sling.

I was there. And from where I stood, the tower looked like
a great spear thrust into the hilltop.

Yesterday—or maybe it was the day before—I went to work,
like I always go to work, at West Teleservices Corporation,
where, as a marketing associate, I go through the same motions
every morning. I hit the power button on my computer and
listen to it hum and mumble and blip to life. I settle my weight
into my ergonomic chair. I fit the headset around my skull
and into my ear and take a deep breath, and, with the pale
light of the monitor washing over me, I dial the first number
on the screen.

In this low-ceilinged fluorescent-lit room, there are twenty-
four rows of cubicles, each ten deep. I am C5. When I take a
break and stand up and peer into the cubicle to my right, C6,
I find a Greg or a Josh or a Linda—every day a new name to

remember, a new hand to shake, or so it seems, with the turnover rate so high. This is why I call everyone *you*.

"Hey, you," I say. "How's it going?"

A short, toad-like woman in a Looney Toons sweatshirt massages the bridge of her nose and sighs, "You know how it is."

In response I give her a sympathetic smile, before looking away, out over the vast hive of cubicles that surrounds us. The air is filled with so many voices, all of them coming together into one voice that reads the same script, trying to make a sale for AT&T, Visa, Northwest Airlines, Sandals Beach Resorts, among our many clients.

There are always three supervisors on duty, all of them beefy men with mustaches. Their bulging bellies remind me of feed sacks that might split open with one slit of a knife. They wear polo shirts with "West Teleservices" embroidered on the breast. They drink coffee from stainless-steel mugs. They never seem to sit down. Every few minutes I feel a rush of wind at the back of my neck as they hurry by, usually to heckle some associate who hasn't met the hourly quota.

"Back to work, C5," one of them tells me, and I roll my eyes at C6 and settle into my cubicle, where the noise all around me falls away into a vague murmur, like the distant drone of bees.

I'm having trouble remembering things. Small things, like where I put my keys, for instance. Whether or not I put on deodorant or took my daily vitamin or paid the cable bill. Big things, too. Like, getting up at 6 A.M. and driving to work on a Saturday, not realizing my mistake until I pull into the empty parking lot.

Sometimes I walk into a room or drive to the store and can't remember why. In this way I am like a ghost: someone who can travel through walls and find myself someplace else in the middle of a sentence or thought and not know what brought me there. The other night I woke up to discover I was walking down the driveway in my pajamas, my bare feet blue in the moonlight. I was carrying a shovel.

Today I'm calling on behalf of Capital One, pitching a mileage card. This is what I'm supposed to say: *Hello, is this _____? How are you doing today, sir/ma'am? That's* wonderful! *I'm calling with a **fantastic** offer from Capital One. Did you know that with our **no-annual-fee** No-Hassle Miles Visa Signature Card you can earn 25 **percent more** than regular mileage cards, with 1.25 miles for every $1 spent on purchases? **On top of that,** if you make just $3,000 in purchases a year, you'll earn 20,000 **bonus miles!***

And so on.

The computer tells me what to tell them. The bold sections indicate where I ought to raise my voice for emphasis. If the customer tries to say they aren't interested, I'm supposed to keep talking, to pretend I don't hear. If I stray too far from the script and if one of the supervisors is listening in, I will feel a hand on my shoulder and hear a voice whispering, "Stay on target. Don't lose sight of your primary objective."

The lights on the tops of cell towers are meant to warn pilots to stay away. But they have become a kind of beacon. Migratory birds mistake them for the stars they use to navigate, so they circle such towers in a trance, sometimes crashing into a structure, its steadying guy wires, or even into other birds. And sometimes they keep circling until they fall to the ground, dead from exhaustion. You can find them all around our cell tower: thousands of them, dotting the hilltop, caught in the sagebrush and pine boughs like ghostly ornaments. Their bones are picked clean by ants. Their feathers are dampened by the rain and bleached by the sun and ruffled and loosened and spread like spores by the wind.

In the sky, so many more circle, screeching their frustration as they try to find their way south. Of course they discovered the body. As he hung there, swinging slightly in the wind, they roosted on his shoulders. They pecked away his eyes, and they pecked away his cheeks, so that we could see all of his teeth when the deputies brought him down. He looked like he was grinning.

At night, from where I lie in bed, I can see the light of the cell tower—through the window, through the branches of a juniper tree, way off in the distance—like a winking red eye that assures me of the confidentiality of some terrible secret.

*

Midmorning, I pop my neck and crack my knuckles and prepare to make maybe my fortieth or sixtieth call of the day. "Pete Johnston" is the name on the screen. I say it aloud—twice—the second time as a question. I feel as though I have heard the name before, but really, that means nothing when you consider the hundreds of thousands of people I have called in my three years working here. I notice that his number, 503-531-1440, is local. Normally I pay no attention to the address listing unless the voice on the other end has a thick accent I can't quite decipher—New Jersey? Texas? Minnesota?—but in this case I look and see that he lives just outside of Redmond, in a new housing development only a few miles away.

"Yeah?" is how he answers the phone.

"Hello. Is this Pete Johnston?"

He clears his throat in a growl. "You a telemarketer?"

"How are you doing today, sir?"

"Bad."

"I'm calling on behalf of—"

"Look, cocksucker. How many times I got to tell you? Take me off your list."

"If you'll just hear me out, I want to tell you about a fantastic offer from—"

"You people are so fucking pathetic."

Now I remember him. He said the same thing before, a week or so ago, when I called him. "If you ever fucking call me again, you fucking worthless piece of shit," he said, "I'll reach through the phone and rip your tongue out."

He goes off on a similar rant now, asking me how can I live with myself, if every time I call someone they answer with hatred?

For a moment I forget about the script and answer him. "I don't know," I say.

"What the—?" he says, his voice somewhere between panicked and incensed. "What the hell are you doing in my house? I thought I told you to—"

There is a noise—the noise teeth might make biting hurriedly into melon—punctuated by a series of screams. It makes me want to tear the headset away from my ear.

And then I realize I am not alone. Someone is listening. I don't know how—a certain displacement of sound as the phone rises from the floor to an ear—but I can sense it.

"Hello?" I say.

The line goes dead.

Sometimes, when I go to work for yet another eight-hour shift or when I visit my parents for yet another casserole dinner, I want to be alone more than anything in the world. But once I'm alone, I feel I can't stand another second of it. Everything is mixed up.

This is why I pick up the phone sometimes and listen. There is something reassuring about a dial tone. That simple sound, a low purr, as constant and predictable as the sun's path across the sky. No matter if you are in Istanbul or London or Beijing or Redmond, you can bring your ear to the receiver and hear it.

Sometimes I pick up the phone and bring it to my ear for the same reason people raise their heads to peer at the moon when they're in a strange place. It makes them—it makes me —feel oriented, calmer than I was a moment before.

Perhaps this has something to do with why I drive to the top of the hill and park beneath the cell tower and climb onto the hood of my Neon and lean against the windshield with my hands folded behind my head to watch the red light blinking and the black shapes of birds swirling against the backdrop of an even blacker sky.

I am here to listen. The radio signals emanating from the tower sound like a blade hissing through the air or a glob of spit sizzling on a hot stove: something dangerous, about to draw blood or catch fire. It's nice.

I imagine I hear in it the thousands of voices channeling through the tower at any given moment, and I wonder what terrible things could be happening to these people that they want to tell the person on the other end of the line but don't.

A conversation overheard:

"Do you live here?"

"Yes."

"Are you Pete Johnston?"

"Yes. Who are you? What do you want?"

"To talk to you. Just to talk."

*

Noon, I take my lunch break. I remove my headset and lurch out of my chair with a groan and bring my fists to my back and push until I feel my vertebrae seperate and realign with a juicy series of pops. Then I wander along my row, moving past so many cubicles, each with a person hunched over inside it—and for a moment West Teleservices feels almost like a chapel, with everyone bowing their heads and murmuring together, as if exorcising some private pain.

I sign out with one of the managers and enter the break room, a forty-by-forty-foot room with white walls and a white dropped ceiling and a white linoleum floor. There are two sinks, two microwaves, two fridges, a Coke machine and a SNAX machine. In front of the SNAX machine stands C6, the woman stationed in the cubicle next to me. A Looney Toons theme apparently unifies her wardrobe, since today she wears a sweat-shirt with Sylvester on it. Below him, blocky black letters read, WITHCONTHIN. She stares with intense concentration at the candy bars and chip bags and gum packs, as if they hold some secret message she has yet to decode.

I go to the nearby water fountain and take a drink and dry my mouth with my sleeve, all the while watching C6, who hardly seems to breathe. "Hey, you," I say, moving to within a few steps of her. "Doing all right there?"

She looks at me, her face creased with puzzlement. Then she shakes her head, and a fog seems to lift, and for the first time she sees me and says, "Been better."

"I know how you feel."

She looks again to the SNAX machine, where her reflection hovers like a ghost. "Nobody knows how I feel."

"No. You're wrong. I know."

At first C6 seems to get angry, her face cragging up, but then I say, "You feel like you would feel if you were hurrying along and smacked your shin against the corner of the coffee table. You feel like you want to yell a lot. The pain hasn't completely arrived, but you can see it coming, and you want to yell at it, scare it off." I go to the fridge labeled *A-K* and remove from it my sack lunch and sit down at one of the five tables staggered throughout the room. "Something like that, anyway."

An awkward silence follows, in which I eat my ham sandwich and C6 studies me closely, no doubt recognizing in me some common damage, some likeness of herself.

Then C6 says, "Can't seem to figure out what I want," nodding at the vending machine. "I've been staring at all these goodies for twenty minutes, and I'll be darned if I know what I want." She forces a laugh and then says with some curiosity in her voice, "Hey, what's with your eye?"

I cup a hand to my ear like a seashell, like: Say again?

"Your eyeball." She points and then draws her finger back as if she might catch something from me. "It's really red."

"Huh," I say and knuckle the corner of my eye as if to nudge away a loose eyelash. "Maybe I've got pinkeye. Must have picked it up off a doorknob."

"It's not pink. It's red. It's really, really red."

The nearest reflective surface is the SNAX machine. And she's right. My eye is red. The dark luscious red of an apple. I at once want to scream and pluck it out and suck on it.

"I think you should see somebody," C6 says.

"Maybe I should." I comb a hand back through my hair and feel a vaguely pleasant release as several dozen hairs come out by the roots, just like that, with hardly any effort. I hold my hand out before me and study the clump of hairs woven in between the fingers and the fresh scabs jewelling my knuckles and say to no one in particular, "Looks like I'm falling apart."

Have you ever been on the phone, canceling a credit card or talking to your mother, when all of a sudden—with a pop of static—another conversation bleeds into yours? Probably. It happens a lot, with so many radio signals hissing through the air. What you might not know is, what you're hearing might have been said a minute ago or a day ago or a week ago or a month ago. Years ago.

When you speak into the receiver, your words are compressed into an electronic signal that bounces from phone to tower to satellite to phone, traveling thousands of miles, even if you're talking to your next-door neighbor, Joe. Which means there's plenty of room for a signal to ricochet or duplicate or get lost. Which means there are so many words—the ghosts of old conversations—floating all around us.

Consider this possibility. You pick up your phone and hear a voice—your voice—engaged in some ancient conversation, like that time in high school when you asked Natasha Flatt out for coffee and she made an excuse about her cat being sick. It's like a conversation shouted into a canyon, its words bouncing off walls to eventually come fluttering back to you, warped and soft and sounding like somebody else.

Sometimes this is what my memory feels like. An image or a conversation or a place will rise to the surface of my mind, and I'll recognize it vaguely, not knowing if I experienced it or saw it on television or invented it altogether.

Whenever I try to fix my attention on something, a red light goes on in my head, and I'm like a bird circling in confusion.

I find myself on the sidewalk of a new hillside development called Bear Brook. Here all the streets have names like Kodiak and Grizzly. All around me are two-story houses of a similar design, with freshly painted gray siding and river-rock entry-ways and cathedral windows rising above their front doors to reveal chandeliers in the foyer of each. Each home has a sizable lot that runs up against pine forest. And each costs more than I would make in twenty years with West Teleservices.

A garbage truck rushes past me, raising tiny tornadoes of dust and trash, and I raise my hand to shield my face and notice a number written on the back of it, just below my knuckles —13743—and though I am sure it will occur to me later, for the moment I can't for the life of me remember what it means.

At that moment a bird swoops toward a nearby house. Mistaking the window for a piece of sky, it strikes the glass with a thud and falls into the rose garden beneath it, absently fluttering its wings; soon it goes still. I rush across the lawn and into the garden and bend over to get a better look at it. A bubble of blood grows from its beak and pops. I do not know why, but I reach through the thorns and pick up the bird and stroke its cool, reddish feathers. Its complete lack of weight and its stillness overwhelm me.

When the bird fell, something fell off a shelf inside me—a nice, gold-framed picture of my life, what I dreamed it would be, full of sunshine and ice cream and go-go dancers. It tumbled down and shattered, and my smiling face dissolved into the distressed expression reflected in the living room window before me.

I look alarmingly ugly. My eyes are black-bagged. My skin is yellow. My upper lip is raised to reveal long, thin teeth. Mine is the sort of face that belongs to someone who bites the heads off chickens in a carnival pit, not the sort that belongs to a man who cradles in his hands a tiny red-winged blackbird. The vision of me, coupled with the vision of what I once dreamed I would be—handsome, wealthy, feared by men and cherished by women—assaults me, the ridiculousness of it and also the terror, the realization that I have crept to the edge of a void and am on the verge of falling in, barely balanced.

And then my eyes refocus, concentrating on a farther distance, where through the window I see a man rising from a couch and approaching me. He is tall and square-shouldered. His hair is the color of dried blood on a bandage. He looks at me with derision, saying through the glass, "The hell do you think you're doing on my property?" without saying a word.

I drop the bird and raise my hand, not quite waving, the gesture more like holding up something dark to the light. He does not move except to narrow his eyes further. There's a stone pagoda at the edge of the garden, and when I take several steps back my heel catches against it. I stumble and then lose my balance entirely, falling hard, sprawling out on the lawn. The gray expanse of the sky fills my vision. Moisture from the grass seeps into my jeans and dampens my underwear. My testicles tighten like a fist.

In the window the man continues to watch me. He has a little red mustache, and he fingers it. Then he disappears from sight, moving away from the window and toward the front door.

Just before I stagger off the lawn and hurry along the sidewalk and retreat from this place, my eyes zero in on the porch, waiting for the man to appear there, and I catch sight of the address: 13743.

And then I am off and running. A siren announces itself nearby. The air seems to vibrate with its noise. It is a police cruiser, I'm certain, though how I can tell the difference between it and an ambulance, I don't know. Either way, someone is in trouble.

*

The body was blackened by its lengthy exposure to radio frequency fields. Cooked. Like a marshmallow left too long over flame. This is why the deputies shut off the transmitters, when they climbed the tower.

Z-21 interviewed Jack Millhouse, a professor of radiation biology at Oregon State. He had a beard, and he stroked it thoughtfully. He said that climbing the tower would expose a person to radio frequencies so powerful they would cook the skin. "I'd ask around at the ER," he said. "See if somebody has come in with radiation burns."

Then they interviewed a woman in a yellow, too-large T-shirt and purple stretch pants. She lived nearby and had seen the commotion from her living room window. She thought a man was preparing to jump, she said. So she came running in the hopes of praying him down. She had a blank, round face no one would ever call beautiful. "It's just awful," she said, her lips disappearing as she tightened her mouth. "It's the most horrible thing in the world, and it's right here, and we don't know why."

I know I am not the only one who has been cut off by a swerving car in traffic or yelled at by a teacher in a classroom or laughed at by a woman in a bar. I am not the only one who has wished someone dead and imagined how it might happen, pleasuring in the goriest details.

Here is how it might happen:

I am in a kitchen with duck-patterned wallpaper. I stand over a man with a Gerber hunting knife in my hand. There is blood dripping off the knife, and there is blood coming out of the man. Gouts of it. It matches the color of his hair. A forked vein rises on his forehead to reveal the panicked beating of his heart. A gray string of saliva webs the corner of his mouth. He holds his hands out, waving me away, and I cut my way through them.

A dog barks from the hallway, and the man screams a repulsive scream, a girlish scream, and all this noise sounds to me far away, like a conversation overheard between pops of static.

I am aware of my muscles and their purpose as never before,

using them to place the knife, putting it finally to the man's chest, where it will make the most difference.

At first the blade won't budge, caught on a rib, and then it slips past the bone and into the soft red interior, deeper and then deeper still, with the same feeling you get when you break through that final restraining grip and enter a woman fully. The response is just as cathartic: a shriek, a gasp, a stiffening of the limbs followed by a terrible shivering that eventually gives way to a great, calming release.

There is blood everywhere—on the knife, on the floor, gurgling from the newly rendered wound that looks so much like a mouth—and the man's eyes are open and empty, and his sharp pink tongue lolls out the side of his mouth. I am amazed at the thrill I feel.

When I surprised him, only a few minutes ago, he was on the phone. I spot it now, on the shale floor, with a halo of blood around it. I pick it up and bring it to my ear and hope for the familiar, calming murmur of the dial tone.

Instead I hear a voice. "Hello?" it says.

One day, I think, maybe I'll write a story about all of this. Something permanent. So that I can trace every sentence and find my way to the end and back to the beginning without worrying about losing my way.

The telling would be complicated.

To write a story like this you would have to talk about what it means to speak into a headset all day, reading from a script you don't believe in, conversing with bodiless voices that snarl with hatred, voices that want to claw out your eyes and scissor off your tongue. And you would have to show what that does to a person, experiencing such a routine day after day, with no relief except for the occasional coffee break where you talk about the television show you watched last night.

And you would have to explain how the man named Pete Johnston sort of leaned and sort of collapsed against the fridge, how a magnet fell to the linoleum with a *clack* after you flashed the knife in a silvery arc across his face and then his outstretched hand and then into that soft basin behind the collarbone. After that came blood. And screaming. Again you stabbed the body, in the thigh, the belly, your muscles pulsing with a red electricity. Something inside you, some internal switch, had been triggered, filling you with an unthinking adrenaline that made you feel capable of turning over Volkswagens, punching through concrete, tearing phone books in half.

And you would have to end this story by explaining what it felt like to pull the body from the trunk of your car and hoist it to your shoulder and begin to climb the tower—one rung, then another—going slowly. You breathed raggedly. The dampness of your sweat mingled with the dampness of blood. From here—thirty, then forty, then fifty feet off the ground—you could see the chains of light on Route 97 and Highway 100, each bright link belonging to a machine that carried inside it a man who could lose control in an instant, distracted by the radio or startled by a deer or overwhelmed by tiredness, careening off the asphalt and into the surrounding woods. It could happen to anyone.

Your thighs trembled. You were weary, dizzy. Your fillings tingled, and a funny baked taste filled your mouth. The edges of your eyes went white and then crazy with streaks of color. But you continued climbing, with the wind tugging at your body, with the blackness of the night and the black shapes of birds all around you, the birds swirling through the air like ashes thrown from a fire. And let's not forget the sound—the sound of the tower—how it sounded almost like words. The hissing of radio frequencies, the voices of so many others coming together into one voice that coursed through you in dark conversation.

2007

BIOGRAPHICAL NOTES

NOTE ON THE TEXTS

NOTES

Biographical Notes

Charles Beaumont (January 2, 1929–February 21, 1967) b. Charles Leroy Nutt in Chicago, Illinois. At the age of 12 Beaumont left school after being diagnosed with spinal meningitis. He became absorbed in the world of science fiction and fantasy, editing his own fan magazine, *Utopia*, at 16. After working with limited success as a radio and screen actor, he found work inking cartoons for MGM and wrote in his spare time, living on the edge of poverty with his family. In the mid-1950s he began to achieve recognition after the publication of some stories in *Playboy* ("Black Country" was the first work of short fiction to appear in that magazine); subsequently published the collections *Hunger* (1957), *Yonder* (1958), and *Night Ride* (1960). He also wrote episodes for the TV series *The Twilight Zone* and movie screenplays including *The Intruder* (1962), *The 7 Faces of Dr. Lao* (1964), and *The Masque of the Red Death* (1964). In 1964, Beaumont began suffering from a mysterious brain disease that may have been related to the spinal meningitis he'd contracted as a boy, and his condition degenerated rapidly until his death three years later.

Jerome Bixby (January 11, 1923–April 28, 1998) b. Los Angeles. Best known for writing the *Star Trek* episode "Mirror, Mirror" (1967) and the short story "It's a Good Life" (1953), which was later adapted into a *Twilight Zone* episode. His science fiction stories were collected in two volumes: *The Devil's Scrapbook* (1964) and *Space by the Tale* (1964). He also wrote numerous westerns under various pseudonyms. His last work, *The Man from Earth*, was filmed in 2007, produced by his son Emerson Bixby.

Anthony Boucher (August 21, 1911–April 29, 1968) b. William Anthony Parker White in Oakland, California. Earned B.A. from the University of Southern California in 1932, and an M.A. from the University of California, Berkeley, in 1934. Published a number of detective novels—including *The Case of the Seven of Calvary* (1937), *The Case of the Crumpled Knave* (1939), and *Rocket to the Morgue* (1942, as H. H. Holmes)—and reviewed crime, fantasy, and science fiction novels for the *Chicago Sun-Times, New York Times* and *San Francisco Chronicle*. His own fantasy and science fiction stories were collected in *Far and Away; Eleven Fantasy and SF Stories* (1955) and

The Compleat Werewolf and Other Stories of Fantasy and SF (1969). Also wrote radio scripts for programs including *The New Adventures of Sherlock Holmes, The Adventures of Ellery Queen,* and *The Casebook of Gregory Hood* (which he created). He was the first English translator of Jorge Luis Borges; his version of "The Garden of Forking Paths" appeared in *Ellery Queen's Mystery Magazine* in 1941. He was a founder of the Mystery Writers of America in 1946; co-founded *The Magazine of Fantasy & Science Fiction* with J. Francis McComas in 1949, and edited it until 1958, when poor health forced him to quit.

Paul Bowles (December 30, 1910–November 18, 1999) b. Paul Frederick Bowles in Jamaica, New York. Introduced to classical music at eight, and composed his first piece of music a year later. Two of his poems, written when he was 16, were published in the Paris literary magazine *transition.* Left University of Virginia during his first semester to go to Paris, where he befriended Aaron Copland and Gertrude Stein. Traveled in Europe and North Africa; returned to the U.S. in 1937 and for the next ten years devoted himself to composing music. Wrote scores for over a dozen films and several plays produced by the Federal Theater, along with numerous Broadway shows including William Saroyan's *My Heart's in the Highlands* and Lillian Hellman's *Watch on the Rhine.* In 1947, moved to Tangier and with the encouragement of his wife, Jane Auer, began writing a novel, published two years later as *The Sheltering Sky.* (As Jane Bowles, his wife published the novel *Two Serious Ladies* and the play *In the Summer House.*) The story collection *The Delicate Prey* appeared in 1950. He resided in Tangier for the rest of his life, publishing the novel *Let It Come Down* (1952), *The Spider's House* (1955), and *Up Above the World* (1966) as well as other works including stories, travel writing, poems, and the autobiography *Without Stopping* (1972). He also translated works by Moroccan authors including Driss ben Hamed Charhadi and Mohammed Mrabet. He continued to compose music and made extensive field recordings of traditional Moroccan music for the Library of Congress. He died of heart failure in Tangier and was buried in Lakemont, New York.

Ray Bradbury (b. August 20, 1922) b. Ray Douglas Bradbury in Waukegan, Illinois. Started reading comics at six and within two years was engrossed in pulp magazines such as *Amazing Stories* and later Jules Verne, H. G. Wells, Edgar Rice Burroughs, and the *Oz* books of Frank L. Baum. Claimed he was inspired to begin writing when his parents took him to see a magician called Mr. Electrico, who knighted him with an electrified sword, shouting "Live forever!" In 1934, the family moved to Los Angeles, where Bradbury attended a writing class taught by Robert Heinlein. Graduated from high school in 1938, and in the same year his first published story, "Hollerbachen's Dilemma," appeared in the fan magazine *Imagination!* He started his own fan magazine, *Futuria Fantasia*, a year later. After "Pendulum" was published in *Super Science Stories* in 1941, began writing full time; first story collection, *Dark Carnival*, was published by Arkham House in 1947. The story cycle *The Martian Chronicles* (1950) secured Bradbury's reputation as a fantasist, and was followed by the story collections *The Illustrated Man* (1951) and *The Golden Apples of the Sun* in 1953. The science fiction novel *Fahrenheit 451* (1953) was followed by other novels and story collections in a range of genres, including *The October Country* (1955), *Dandelion Wine* (1957), *Something Wicked This Way Comes* (1962), *The Halloween Tree* (1972), and *Death Is a Lonely Business* (1985). Along with novels, poetry, and children's books, Bradbury has written screenplays, including *It Came From Outer Space* (1953) and *Moby Dick* (1956), and teleplays for programs including *Alfred Hitchcock Presents*, *The Twilight Zone*, and a series based on his own works, *The Ray Bradbury Television Theater* (1985–90). In 2004, he was awarded the National Medal of Arts by George W. Bush.

Poppy Z. Brite (b. May 25, 1967) b. Melissa Ann Brite in New Orleans. Grew up with her mother in Chapel Hill, North Carolina. Started writing at 12 and sold her first story, "Optional Music for Voice and Piano," to *The Horror Show* at 18. Awarded a three-book contract by Dell in 1991 for the novels *Lost Souls* (1992), *Drawing Blood* (1993), and *Exquisite Corpse* (1996). In recent years, Brite has moved away from horror, as in the Liquor series, comprising the dark comedies *Liquor* (2004), *Prime* (2005), and *Soul Kitchen* (2006) and set within the New Orleans restaurant world.

Truman Capote (September 30, 1924–August 25, 1984) b. Truman Streckfus Persons in New Orleans to Arch Persons, a salesman, and 16-year-old Lili Mae "Nina" Faulk. Parents divorced when Capote was six, after which he lived with his mother's cousins in Monroeville, Alabama. He became interested in writing at an early age and in 1934 his story "Old Mr. Busybody" appeared in the *Mobile Press Register*. Adopted the name Truman Capote in 1935 when his parents' custody battle ended and he was legally adopted by his mother and her new husband, Joseph Capote, a Cuban-American textile broker. He went to live with them in New York and attended various schools, including a military academy, before family relocated to Greenwich, Connecticut. After graduating from high school, began working as a copyboy for *The New Yorker*. Began publishing stories regularly, including "Miriam," which won the O. Henry Memorial award in 1946. Spent time at Yaddo in Saratoga Springs, where he worked on novel *Other Voices, Other Rooms* (1948), which was published by Random House and brought him national attention. Subsequently published story collection *A Tree of Night* (1949), novel *The Grass Harp* (1951), journalistic account *The Muses Are Heard* (1956), and novella *Breakfast at Tiffany's* (1958). *In Cold Blood* (1966), his "nonfiction novel" dealing with a multiple murder in Kansas, was tremendously successful. Drug and alcohol abuse diminished his output in later years; he published the nonfiction collections *The Dogs Bark* (1973) and *Music for Chameleons* (1980), and worked on a novel that was published in unfinished form as *Answered Prayers* in 1986.

Jonathan Carroll (b. January 26, 1949) b. New York City to Sidney Carroll, a screenwriter, and June Carroll, an actress. Attended boarding school in Connecticut. Graduated from Rutgers University in 1971; earned an M.A. in English at the University of Virginia two years later. Moved to Vienna (where he continues to live) to teach English at the American International School. His first novel, *The Land of Laughs*, was followed by 15 others to date, including *Sleeping in Flame* (1988), *Kissing the Beehive* (1997), *White Apples* (2002), *Glass Soup* (2005), and *The Ghost in Love* (2008). His short fiction has been collected in *The Panic Hand* (1995).

Michael Chabon (b. May 24, 1963) b. Washington, D.C. Parents divorced when he was 11; he grew up in Columbia, Maryland. Earned a B.A. from the University of Pittsburgh and an M.F.A. in creative writing from the University of California–Irvine. His master's thesis became his first published novel, *The Mysteries of Pittsburgh* (1988), which was a bestseller, as was his next novel, *Wonder Boys* (1995). The story collection *Werewolves in Their Youth* (1999) contained the horror story "In the Black Mill." *The Amazing Adventures of Kavalier & Clay* (2000) won the Pulitzer Prize for Fiction. His interest in genre fiction has been reflected in *Summerland* (2002), a fantasy book for children; *The Final Solution* (2004), whose protagonist is Sherlock Holmes; *The Yiddish Policemen's Union* (2007), a novel of alternate history; and *Gentlemen of the Road* (2007), a swashbuckling adventure.

Fred Chappell (b. May 28, 1936) b. Canton, North Carolina. Received B.A. (1961) and M.A. (1963) from Duke University in 18th-century literature; taught various courses at the University of

North Carolina at Greensboro for 40 years. His published novels include *Dagon* (1968), *I Am One of You Forever* (1985), and *Brighten
the Corner Where You Are* (1989). His poetry has been collected in
Midquest (1981), *Source* (1985), *Spring Garden* (1995), *Shadow Box*
(2009), and other volumes. His latest volume of short fiction is *Ancestors and Others* (2009). He has been awarded, among other honors, the Bollingen Prize in 1985, the T. S. Eliot Prize in 2003, and the
Thomas Wolfe Award in 2006.

John Cheever (May 27, 1912–June 18, 1982) b. John William Cheever
in Quincy, Massachusetts, to Frederick Lincoln Cheever, a shoe
salesman, and Mary Liley, a gift-shop operator. Expelled from
Thayer Academy in South Braintree at 17 for smoking, an incident
forming the basis for his first published story, "Expelled," which appeared in *The New Republic* in 1930. Moved to New York in 1934
where he supported himself by writing novel synopses for MGM.
Married Mary Winternitz, daughter of the dean of the Yale Medical
School, in 1941. Published story collection *The Way Some People Live*
(1943). After serving in the army during World War II, devoted himself to a career as a writer. Awarded a Guggenheim fellowship in 1951;
moved with his family to Westchester County, New York. In addition
to story collections, including *The Enormous Radio* (1953), *The
Housebreaker of Shady Hill* (1958), and *Some People, Places and Things
That Will Not Appear in My Next Novel* (1961), published novels *The
Wapshot Chronicle* (1957), *The Wapshot Scandal* (1964), *Bullet Park*
(1969), and *Falconer* (1977). Alcohol abuse led to hospitalization; he
stopped drinking in 1975. His novel *Falconer* (1977) and his *Collected
Stories* (1978) were bestsellers, and for the latter he won the Pulitzer
Prize for Fiction.

John Collier (May 3, 1901–April 6, 1980) b. London to John George
Collier and Emily Mary Noyes Collier. His interest in fantasy writing
was sparked by childhood reading of Hans Christian Andersen's fairy
tales. He was educated at home by his uncle, Vincent Collier, a novelist. With an allowance from his father, set himself up in London as
a journalist and fiction writer in the early 1920s. Became poetry editor for *Time and Tide* and won a poetry award from *The Quarter* for
his collection *Gemini* (1931). Published the novels *His Monkey Wife;
or, Married to a Chimp* (1930), *Tom's A-Cold: A Tale* (1933), and *Defy
the Foul Fiend; or, The Misadventures of a Heart* (1934). Moved to
Hollywood and began writing scripts; collaborated on *The Elephant
Boy* (1937), *Her Cardboard Lover* (1942), *The African Queen* (1951),
and *The War Lord* (1965). His short fiction, which appeared frequently in *The New Yorker*, was collected in *Presenting Moonshine*

(1941), *The Touch of Nutmeg Makes It* (1943), and *Fancies and Good-nights* (1951), the last of which won both the International Fantasy Award and the Mystery Writers of America's Edgar Award. A number of his stories were adapted for television, notably "Back for Christmas" and "Wet Saturday" by Alfred Hitchcock. Collier moved back to Europe in the early 1950s, first to London and eventually to Grasse, France. In 1973 he published a screenplay based on *Paradise Lost*. He returned to California in 1979 and died of a stroke in Pacific Palisades a year later.

John Crowley (b. December 1, 1942) b. Presque Isle, Maine; grew up in Vermont, Kentucky, and Indiana, where he attended Indiana University (B.A., 1964). Lived in New York City, writing scripts for documentary films; his first novel, *The Deep*, appeared in 1975, followed by *Beasts* (1976) and *Engine Summer* (1979). Subsequent novels included *Little, Big* (1981) and the *Aegypt* tetralogy, consisting of *Aegypt* (retitled *The Solitudes*, 1987), *Love & Sleep* (1994), *Dæmonomania* (2000), and *Endless Things* (2007). His short fiction has been collected in *Novelties and Souvenirs* (2004). Corresponded with literary critic Harold Bloom, who admired his fiction, and in 1993 he became a professor at Yale. Received Award in Literature from the American Academy and Institute of Arts and Letters in 1992.

Harlan Ellison (b. May 27, 1934) b. in Cleveland, Ohio. He has written or edited 76 books and more than 1700 stories, essays, articles, and newspaper columns, as well two dozen teleplays (for programs including *The Outer Limits* and the 1985 revival of *The Twilight Zone*) and a dozen movies. He has won many awards including multiple Edgar, Hugo, and Bram Stoker awards; a Lifetime Achievement Award from the Horror Writers' Association; a World Convention Achievement Award from the Science Fiction Writers of America; and the Silver Pen for Journalism from P.E.N. In 2006 he was named Grand Master of the Science Fiction/Fantasy Writers of America. His best-known works include *Web of the City* (1958), *Memos from Purgatory* (1961), *Ellison Wonderland* (1962), *I Have No Mouth, and I Must Scream* (1967), *Love Ain't Nothing but Sex Misspelled* (1968), *Approaching Oblivion* (1974), *Deathbird Stories* (1975), *Strange Wine* (1978), *All the Lies That Are My Life* (1980), *Shatterday* (1980), *Stalking the Nightmare* (1982), *An Edge in My Voice* (1985), *Angry Candy* (1988), *Mind Fields* (1994), and *Slippage* (1997). He edited the influential anthologies *Dangerous Visions* (1967) and *Again, Dangerous Visions* (1972), and his work has been featured in *The Best American Short Stories*. A retrospective of his work has been published as *The Essential Ellison* (1987; expanded edition, 1998). He has been actively engaged with such issues as First Amendment rights, censorship, and global Internet piracy of writers' work. *Dreams with Sharp Teeth*, an award-winning documentary on his life, was released in 2008.

Brian Evenson (b. August 12, 1966) b. Ames, Iowa, to William Edwin Evenson, a physicist, and Nancy Ann Evenson, an architect. Began to write seriously in college under the mentorship of Welsh poet Leslie Norris. Received Ph.D. from University of Washington, then returned to Brigham Young University, where he had studied as an undergraduate, to teach. The gruesome subject matter of the stories in his first collection, *Altmann's Tongue* (1994), caused dissension with fellow Mormons, and he was obliged to leave both the school and the church. Became Chair of the Literary Arts Program at Brown University. Later books include *Prophets and Brothers* (1997), *Father of Lies* (1998), *Dark Property: An Affliction* (2002), *The Wavering Knife* (2004), *The Open Curtain* (2006), *Last Days* (2009), and *Fugue State* (2009).

Jack Finney (October 2, 1911–November 14, 1995) b. John Finney in Milwaukee, Wisconsin. Graduated from Knox College in Galesburg, Illinois. Married Marguerite Guest in 1934 and moved to New York City where he wrote advertising jingles. His first story, "The Widow's Walk" (1946), won a prize from *Ellery Queen's Mystery Magazine*. A crime novel, *Five Against the House* (1954), was followed by *The Body Snatchers*, filmed in 1956 by Don Siegel as *Invasion of the Body Snatchers* (Finney worked on the screenplay). Other novels included *The House of Numbers* (1957), *Assault on a Queen* (1959), *Good Neighbor Sam* (1963), *The Woodrow Wilson Dime* (1968), and *Time and Again* (1970), a novel of time travel for which he meticulously recreated late-19th-century New York and which enjoyed wide success. He was awarded the World Fantasy Award for Life Achievement in 1987. His last book was *From Time to Time* (1995), a sequel to *Time and Again*.

Davis Grubb (July 23, 1919–July 24, 1980) b. Davis Alexander Grubb in Moundsville, West Virginia. His family's roots in the region went back several centuries. He was interested in writing and painting from an early age. Studied art at the Carnegie Institute of Technology in Pittsburgh (1938–39), but after finding that he was color-blind devoted his energies to writing. Moved around 1941 to New York City, where he wrote copy for NBC. Subsequently worked in radio and advertising in Florida and Philadelphia. His first story, published in *Good Housekeeping* in 1944, was followed by many others in *Collier's, Ellery Queen's Mystery Magazine,* and *American*

Magazine. His first novel, *The Night of the Hunter* (1955), was a finalist for the National Book Award, and was filmed in 1957 by Charles Laughton, with a screenplay by Laughton and James Agee. Grubb's later novels included *A Dream of Kings* (1955), *The Watchman* (1961), *A Tree Full of Stars* (1965), *Fools' Parade* (1969), and *Ancient Lights* (1982).

Joe Hill (b. June 4, 1972) b. Joseph Hillstrom King, to Stephen King and Tabitha King in Bangor, Maine. Began publishing stories in 1997 under the pen name Joe Hill. His story collection *20th Century Ghosts* (2005), which won the Bram Stoker Award, the British Fantasy Award, and the International Horror Guild Award, was followed by the novel *Heart-Shaped Box* (2007). He has also written the comic book series Locke & Key, beginning in 2008.

Shirley Jackson (December 14, 1916–August 8, 1965) b. Shirley Hardie Jackson in San Francisco, California. Moved with family to Rochester, New York, while in high school. Attended Rochester University, 1934–36, and Syracuse University, where she founded and edited literary magazine *The Spectre* with Stanley Edgar Hyman whom she subsequently married, and received a B.A. in English (1940). Began to publish in magazines including *The New Republic* and *The New Yorker*. Moved to Vermont in 1945 when her husband joined faculty of Bennington College. Published novel *The Road Through the Wall* (1948); in the same year "The Lottery" appeared in the June 26 issue of *The New Yorker*. It had great impact and was collected the next year in *The Lottery; or, the Adventures of James Harris*. Her later books include the novels *Hangsaman* (1951), *The Bird's Nest* (1954), *The Sundial* (1958), *The Haunting of Hill House* (1959), and *We Have Always Lived in the Castle* (1962), the humorous memoirs *Life Among the Savages* (1953) and *Raising Demons* (1957), and a history book for children, *The Witchcraft of Salem Village* (1956). She died of a heart attack.

Caitlín R. Kiernan (b. May 26, 1964) b. in Skerries, Ireland. Moved to Leeds, Alabama, with her family when she was a child. Developed early interest in writing and paleontology. While in high school spent summers on archaeological digs; earned B.S. from University of Colorado at Boulder, studying geology and vertebrate paleontology. Her first published novel, *Silk*, appeared in 1998, followed by *Threshold* (2001), *The Five of Cups* (2003, but written a decade earlier), *Low Red Moon* (2003), *Murder of Angels* (2004), and *Daughter of Hounds* (2007). Her short fiction has been collected in volumes including *Tales of Pain and Wonder* (2000), *From Weird and Distant Shores*

(2002), and *Tales from the Woeful Platypus* (2007). She has also contributed scholarly articles to paleontology journals, such as an examination of the biostratigraphy of Alabama mosasaurs for the *Journal of Vertebrate Paleontology* (2002). She lives in Providence, Rhode Island.

Stephen King (b. September 21, 1947) b. Portland, Maine, second son of Donald Edwin King, a master mariner in the U.S. Merchant Marine, and Nellie Ruth Pillsbury King. When he was two, his father abandoned the family, and over the next nine years his mother moved with him and his older brother from town to town across the northern United States, staying with relatives and working sporadically. They settled in Durham, Maine, in 1958. In high school, published his first story, "I Was a Teenage Grave-Robber," in *Comics Review*, a fan magazine, and wrote a book-length manuscript, a post-apocalyptic story called "The Aftermath." Attended University of Maine at Orono on a scholarship; wrote steadily throughout college. Published "The Glass Floor" in *Startling Mystery Stories* (1967), was active in student politics and the anti-war movement, and taught a seminar on "Popular Literature and Culture." Married Tabitha Spruce in 1971; began teaching at the Hampden Academy in Hampden, Maine. His first novel, *Carrie* (1973), enjoyed great success when published in paperback, and was followed by many novels —over 40 to date—that made him the most widely known writer of fantasy and horror, including *Salem's Lot* (1975), *The Shining* (1977), *The Stand* (1978; expanded version, 1990), *The Dead Zone* (1979), *Cujo* (1981), *Pet Sematary* (1983), *Misery* (1987), *The Dark Half* (1989), *Gerald's Game* (1992), *Dolores Claiborne* (1993), *The Green Mile* (1996), and *Lisey's Story* (2006). He also published a number of novels under the pseudonym Richard Bachman. His short fiction has been collected in *Night Shift* (1978), *Different Seasons* (1982), *Skeleton Crew* (1985), *Nightmares & Dreamscapes* (1993), *Everything's Eventual* (2002), and other volumes. Many of his works have been filmed and he has received numerous awards throughout his career.

T.E.D. Klein (b. July 15, 1947) b. Theodore Donald Klein in New York City. Graduated from Brown, 1969; wrote honors thesis on H. P. Lovecraft. Studied film history at Columbia, receiving M.F.A. in 1972. Worked as a reader for Paramount Pictures. Edited magazines *The Twilight Zone* (1981–85) and *CrimeBeat* (1991–93). His novel *The Ceremonies* (1984), for which he won the British Fantasy Society Award, was an expansion of his 1972 novella "The Events at Poroth Farm" (subsequently published in revised versions). Published story collections *The Dark Gods* (1985) and *Reassuring Tales*

(2006). He wrote the screenplay for Dario Argento's *Trauma* (1993) and two critical essays on the weird fiction genre, *Dr Van Helsing's Handy Guide to Ghost Stories* (1981) and *Raising Goosebumps for Fun and Profit* (1988).

Fritz Leiber (December 24, 1910–September 5, 1992) b. in Chicago, Illinois, to Fritz Leiber and Virginia Bronson Leiber, both Shakespearean actors. After graduating with a B.A. in psychology from the University of Chicago in 1932, studied at the Episcopal General Theological Seminary in New York. Returned to the University of Chicago to study philosophy; after a year, dropped out and went on tour with his parents' theater troupe. Attempted to find work in Hollywood; returned to Chicago, where he worked as staff writer for the *Standard American Encyclopedia*. Married Jonquil Stephens in 1936; their son Justin was born two years later. Began writing stories with encouragement of H. P. Lovecraft. Sold fantasy story "Two Sought Adventure" to *Unknown* in 1939. Relocated to Los Angeles with family; taught drama and speech at Occidental College; subsequently took a job with Douglas Aircraft. From 1946 worked for 11 years on editorial staff of *Science Digest* in Chicago. Published novels including *Conjure Wife* (1943), *The Green Millennium* (1953), *The Wanderer* (1964), and *Our Lady of Darkness* (1977); stories collected in *Shadows with Eyes* (1962) and *The Secret Songs* (1968). The sword and sorcery tales involving Fafhrd and the Gray Mouser were collected in numerous volumes including *Swords in the Mist* (1968), *Swords and Deviltry* (1970), and *Swords and Ice Magic* (1977). The increasing popularity of his science fiction and fantasy stories enabled him to move back to Los Angeles and support his family through writing. His first wife died in 1969; he died of a brain disease not long after his second marriage.

Thomas Ligotti (b. July 9, 1953) b. in Detroit, Michigan. After receiving B.A. from Wayne State University in 1977, worked for many years at Gale Research Company as associate editor; left in 2001 to move to south Florida where he currently lives. He began publishing horror stories in small press magazines in the early 1980s. Story collections include *Songs of a Dead Dreamer* (1986), *The Nightmare Factory* (1996), *My Work Is Not Yet Done* (2002), *Sideshow, and Other Stories* (2003), and *The Shadow at the Bottom of the World* (2005). He has also collaborated on albums with the musical group Current 93.

Kelly Link (b. July 19, 1969) b. in Miami, Florida; moved with her family to Greensboro, North Carolina. Received B.A. from Columbia and M.F.A from University of North Carolina at Greensboro.

Her short fiction has been collected in *Stranger Things Happen* (2001) and *Magic for Beginners* (2006). She lives in Northampton, Massachusetts, where with her husband, Gavin Grant, she operates Small Beer Press and co-edits, with Grant and Ellen Datlow, the *Year's Best Fantasy and Horror* anthology series. She has taught in writing programs at Smith College, Bard College, the University of Massachusetts, and other schools.

Richard Matheson (b. February 20, 1926) b. in Allendale, New Jersey. Raised in Brooklyn and attended Brooklyn Technical High School. Served in the infantry during World War II. Earned B.A. in journalism from the University of Missouri in 1949. Moved to California; married Ruth Ann Woodson, with whom he had four children. His story "Born of Man and Woman" appeared in *The Magazine of Fantasy and Science Fiction* in 1950 and was collected in a volume of the same name published four years later. Published many novels including *I Am Legend* (1954), which has been filmed three times; *The Shrinking Man* (1956), filmed, with a script by Matheson, as *The Incredible Shrinking Man*; *A Stir of Echoes* (1958); *Hell House* (1917); and *Bid Time Return* (1975). He also published numerous collections of short stories including *The Shores of Space* (1957), *Shock!* (1961), *Shock 2* (1964), *Shock 3* (1966), and *Nightmare at 20,000 Feet* (2000). He wrote a number of screenplays and also television scripts for programs including *The Twilight Zone* and *Star Trek*; he adapted his story "Duel" for Steven Spielberg's film of the same name, and won an Edgar for his script for the television film *The Night Stalker*.

Steven Millhauser (b. August 3, 1943) b. in New York City. He grew up in Connecticut, where his father, Milton Millhauser, taught English at the University of Bridgeport. Received B.A. from Columbia University (1965) and did graduate studies at Brown. His first novel, *Edwin Mullhouse: The Life and Death of an American Writer 1943–1954* (1972), was followed by *Portrait of a Romantic* (1977) and a number of story collections including *In the Penny Arcade* (1986), *The Barnum Museum* (1990), and *Little Kingdoms* (1993). He won the Pulitzer Prize for his novel *Martin Dressler: The Tale of an American Dreamer* (1996). His subsequent books include *The Knife Thrower* (1998), *Enchanted Night* (1999), and *Dangerous Laughter* (2008). He teaches at Skidmore College.

Vladimir Nabokov (April 23, 1899–July 2, 1977) b. in St. Petersburg, Russia, to Vladimir Dmitrievich Nabokov, a jurist and statesman, and Elena Ivanovna Nabokov; he was the eldest of five children of a wealthy and aristocratic family. He was educated by a private tutor, and learned to read and write English before Russian. After the Bolshevik Revolution, the family fled first to the Crimea, and then to England. Nabokov enrolled in Trinity College, Cambridge, where he studied Slavic and Romance languages. The rest of his family moved in 1920 to Berlin, where his father helped set up the émigré news-paper *Rul* and was assassinated two years later by Russian monar-chists. After graduating with honors from Cambridge, Nabokov moved to Berlin, where he wrote for his father's newspaper under the pen name V. Sirin. Married Vera Evseyevna Slonim in 1925; his first novel, *Mashen'ka* (*Mary*, 1925), was followed by others, as well as poems and plays. Fled with Vera and their son, Dmitri, to France in 1937, then came to the United States in 1940. Began writing only in English; published novels *The Real Life of Sebastian Knight* (1941) and *Bend Sinister* (1947) and memoir *Conclusive Evidence* (1950, later retitled *Speak, Memory*). Met and befriended Edmund Wilson. Taught comparative literature at Wellesley College. Curated lepi-doptery department at Harvard's Comparative Zoology Museum. After teaching at Cornell, the Nabokovs moved to Ashland, Oregon, where he finished writing *Lolita*, which was published in France in 1955 but not in the United States until 1958; its success made him a celebrity. Moved in 1961 to Montreux, Switzerland. Translation of Pushkin's *Eugene Onegin* published in 1964. Later books included *Pale Fire* (1962), *Ada* (1969), and *Look at the Harlequins!* (1974).

Joyce Carol Oates (b. June 16, 1938) b. Lockport, New York, to Frederic James Oates, a tool and die designer, and Caroline Bush Oates. Began writing stories in elementary school and at 15 submitted a novel to a publisher that was rejected as "too depressing." Began writing novels (which remained unpublished) at a rapid rate while studying at Syracuse University, majoring in English and minoring in philosophy. Received graduate degree in English from the University of Wisconsin in 1961. Married fellow student Raymond Joseph Smith and moved with him to Beaumont, Texas, to teach. After several years teaching in Detroit and Canada, became creative writing pro-fessor at Princeton, where she continues to live. Her first published novel, *With Shuddering Fall*, appeared in 1964, followed by *A Gar-den of Earthly Delights* (1967) and *Expensive People* (1968); *them* (1970) received the National Book Award. Among her many other novels—she has published an average of two books a year—are *Won-derland* (1971), *Childwold* (1976), *Bellefleur* (1980), *Black Water* (1992), *Zombie* (1995), *Blonde* (2000), *The Falls* (2004), *The Gravedigger's Daughter* (2007), and *A Fair Maiden* (2009). She has also published collections of short stories including *Dear Husband*

(2009), poetry, essay collections, and novels under the pseudonyms Rosamond Smith and Lauren Kelly.

Benjamin Percy (b. March 28, 1979) b. Eugene, Oregon; lived briefly in Hawaii as a child; family moved back to Oregon, where he attended a private school in Bend. Attended Brown University, studying archeology. Received B.A. with honors and went to Southern Illinois University for M.F.A. in creative writing. First story collection, *The Language of Elk*, appeared in 2006. "Refresh, Refresh," published in *The Paris Review*, won George Plimpton Prize and Pushcart Prize, and became title story of his next collection, published in 2007. Joined the faculty of Iowa State University. In 2009 he received a Whiting Writers' Award.

Tim Powers (b. February 29, 1952) b. in Buffalo, New York. Grew up in California, where his family moved in 1959. Studied English literature at Cal State–Fullerton; earned his B.A. in 1976. Befriended Philip K. Dick, who based the character of "David" in his novel *VALIS* on him. Powers has won several awards for his novels, many of which deal with time travel, among them *The Anubis Gates* (1984) and *Dinner at Deviant's Palace* (1985). His other novels include *Last Call* (1993) and *Declare* (2001). Powers also teaches part-time as writer-in-residence for the Orange County High School of the Arts.

Jane Rice (April 30, 1913–March 2, 2003) Beginning in the early 1940s, Rice was a prolific contributor of short fiction to periodicals such as *Unknown*, *The Magazine of Fantasy & Science Fiction*, and *Charm*. She sometimes collaborated with Ruth Allison under the name Allison Rice. Her stories were first collected in *The Idol of the Flies and Other Stories* (2003). She died in Greensboro, North Carolina.

M. Rickert (b. December 11, 1959) b. Mary Rickert in Port Washington, Wisconsin, and grew up in Fredonia, Wisconsin. Moved to California at age 18, worked a series of odd jobs to support herself, and taught kindergarten at a small private school for ten years. Her first collection of stories, *Map of Dreams* (2006), won the 2007 World Fantasy Award for Best Collection and the 2007 Crawford Award. She lives with her husband in Cedarburg, Wisconsin, not far from where she grew up.

George Saunders (b. December 2, 1958) b. in Amarillo, Texas and grew up in Chicago; in 1981 graduated from the Colorado School of

Mines with a B.Sc. in geophysical engineering. Went on to earn his M.A. in creative writing from Syracuse University. Worked for Radian International, an environmental engineering firm, as a technical writer and geophysical engineer. Since 1996, has been on the faculty of Syracuse University, teaching creative writing in its M.F.A. program. His five collections of short stories and novellas have won many awards including four National Magazine Awards, an O. Henry for *Pastoralia* (2000), and the 2006 World Fantasy Award for Best Short Fiction for his story "CommComm." In 2006, he was named a MacArthur Fellow. He contributes a weekly column, *American Psyche*, to the weekend magazine of *The Guardian*'s Saturday edition.

Isaac Bashevis Singer (c. November 1904–July 24, 1991) b. Yitskhok Zynger in Leoncin, a Polish village northeast of Warsaw (then part of the Russian Empire). His father was a Hasidic rabbi and his mother the daughter of the rabbi of Bilgoraj, in the province of Lublin. Family moved to Warsaw in 1908, where father presided over a rabbinical court in the family home at 10 Krochmalna Street. Went to live with mother in Bilgoraj; studied Talmud, philosophy, and literature. Older brother Israel Joshua Singer began to achieve prominence as a writer in the early 1920s, and Singer, who had moved to Warsaw, soon began publishing stories and literary translations. Novel *Satan in Goray* published in 1933. Moved to the United States in 1935, joining his brother who was already living in New York. Wrote many stories and sketches, mostly for publication in the Yiddish paper *Forverts*. Married Alma Wassermann in 1940; became American citizen in 1943. Brother Israel Joshua died in 1944. Published novel *The Family Moskat* as magazine serial (1945–48); English translation appeared in 1950. His story "Gimpel the Fool," translated by Saul Bellow, was published in *Partisan Review* in 1953. Beginning with *Gimpel the Fool and Other Stories* (1957), English-language collections of Singer's stories began to appear, including *The Spinoza of Market Street* (1961), *Short Friday* (1964), *The Seance* (1968), *A Friend of Kafka* (1970), and *A Crown of Feathers* (1973), as well as the novels *The Magician of Lublin* (1960), *The Slave* (1962), and *Enemies, a Love Story* (1972). Also published stories for children and memoirs. Died in Surfside, Florida.

Jack Snow (August 15, 1907–July 13, 1956) b. John Frederick Snow in Piqua, Ohio. Began to work as a journalist while in high school; later worked in radio, including seven years at WNBC in New York. Published a number of stories in *Weird Tales*; short fiction collected in *Dark Music and Other Spectral Tales* (1947). He wrote two sequels to the Oz novels of L. Frank Baum—*The Magical Mimics in Oz*

(1946) and *The Shaggy Man of Oz* (1949)—and a study of Baum, *Who's Who in Oz* (1954).

Peter Straub (b. March 2, 1943) is the author of 17 novels, which have been translated into more than 20 languages. They include *Julia* (1975), *Ghost Story* (1977), *Koko* (1988), *Mr. X* (1999), *In the Night Room* (2004), and two collaborations with Stephen King, *The Talisman* (1984) and *Black House* (2001). He has written two volumes of poetry and two collections of short fiction, and he edited The Library of America edition of H. P. Lovecraft's *Tales* (2005). He has won many awards including the British Fantasy Award, eight Bram Stoker awards, two International Horror Guild awards, and two World Fantasy awards, and in 1998 was named Grand Master at the World Horror Convention. In 2006, he was given the Horror Writers Association's Life Achievement Award.

Thomas Tessier (b. May 10, 1947) b. Waterbury, Connecticut. Studied at University College, Dublin. His novels include *The Fates* (1978), *The Nightwalker* (1979), *Shockwaves* (1982), *Phantom* (1982), *Rapture* (1987), *Secret Strangers* (1990), *Fog Heart* (1997), *Father Panic's Opera Macabre* (2001), and *Wicked Things* (2007). His fantastic short fiction has been collected in *Ghost Music and Other Tales* (2000). He has also published three collections of poetry.

Jeff VanderMeer (b. July 7, 1968) b. Jeffrey Scott VanderMeer in Bellafonte, Pennsylvania; spent part of childhood in the Fiji Islands, where his parents worked for the Peace Corps. A two-time winner of the World Fantasy Award, his novels include *City of Saints and Madmen* (2001), *Veniss Underground* (2003), *Shriek: An Afterword* (2006), and *Finch* (2009). He is also the author of *Booklife: Strategies and Survial Tips for 21st-Century Writers* (2009) and has edited several anthologies with his wife, Ann VanderMeer, including *Best American Fantasy* (2007), *The New Weird* (2008), and *Steampunk* (2008). His nonfiction has appeared in the *New York Times Book Review*, and elsewhere.

Donald Wandrei (April 20, 1908–October 15, 1987) b. St. Paul, Minnesota. Graduated from the University in Minnesota in 1928; later worked in public relations. He contributed prolifically to pulp magazines and corresponded extensively with H. P. Lovecraft, whose Cthulhu Mythos he explored in several of his own stories. With August Derleth, he co-founded Arkham House, dedicated to the publication of Lovecraft's work; later edited Lovecraft's selected letters (1971–76). Served in the army during World War II. Published novel

The Web of Easter Island in 1948. His stories were collected in *The Eye and the Finger* (1944) and *Strange Harvest* (1965).

Tennessee Williams (March 6, 1911–February 24, 1983) b. Thomas Lanier Williams III in Columbus, Mississippi. Father worked as a traveling salesman. Ill as a child with diphtheria and Bright's disease. Family moved in 1918 to St. Louis, where father had a job as shoe company branch manager. Began writing in junior high school; while in high school published "The Vengeance of Nitocris" in *Weird Tales*. Studied at University of Missouri School of Journalism at Columbia. Began writing plays and studied playwriting at the University of Iowa. His play *Battle of Angels* was produced unsuccessfully by the Theatre Guild in 1940. Spent much time in New Orleans, Key West, and New Mexico. *The Glass Menagerie* opened on Broadway in 1945 and won New York Drama Critics Circle award. Success of *A Streetcar Named Desire* (1947) followed by New York productions of *Summer and Smoke* (1948), *The Rose Tattoo* (1951), and *Camino Real* (1953). Short story collection *Hard Candy* published in 1954. Later plays included *Cat on a Hot Tin Roof* (1955), *Orpheus Descending* (1957), *Suddenly Last Summer* (1958), *Sweet Bird of Youth* (1959), *The Night of the Iguana* (1961), and *The Milk Train Doesn't Stop Here Anymore* (1962). Subsequent plays, including *Kingdom of Earth* (1968), *In the Bar of a Tokyo Hotel* (1969), and *Small Craft Warnings* (1972), found less critical favor than his earlier work.

Gene Wolfe (b. May 7, 1931) b. New York City. Attended Texas A&M University where he began to publish speculative fiction in a student literary magazine. After serving in the Korean War, earned a degree in industrial engineering from the University of Houston. Had long career as industrial engineer and edited technical journal *Plant Engineering*. Since 1970 he has published many novels and stories, many of them honored by awards, and won particular acclaim for the tetralogy *The Book of the New Sun*, consisting of the novels *The Shadow of the Torturer* (1980), *The Claw of the Conciliator* (1981), *The Sword of the Lictor* (1982), and *The Citadel of the Autarch* (1983). Two related cycles, *The Book of the Long Sun* and *The Book of the Short Sun*, appeared in multiple volumes between 1993 and 2001. His later books include *The Wizard Knight* (2004), *Pirate Freedom* (2007), and *An Evil Guest* (2008). Thomas Disch once described him as the "most underrated" author in his field.

Note on the Texts

This volume contains 41 fantastic tales by American writers originally published between 1941 and 2007 and presents them in the order of their original publication. In the case of stories not yet collected in book form, or that were not collected in book form during the author's lifetime, the texts are taken from periodical versions.

The following is a list of the sources of the texts included in this volume, listed in the order of their appearance in this volume.

John Collier: Evening Primrose; *Presenting Moonshine* (New York: Viking Press, 1941), 1–15. Copyright © 1941 by John Collier, renewed © 1969 by John Collier. Permission to reprint granted by Harold Matson Co, Inc.

Fritz Leiber: Smoke Ghost; *Unknown*, October 1941. Copyright © 1948 by the University of the South. Reprinted by permission of New Directions Publishing Corp.

Tennessee Williams: The Mysteries of the Joy Rio, *Hard Candy* (New York: New Directions, 1954), 203–20. Written c. 1941. Copyright © 1948 by the University of the South. Reprinted by permission of New Directions Publishing Corp.

Jane Rice: The Refugee, *Unknown*, October 1943, 111–20.

Anthony Boucher: Mr. Lupescu, *Weird Tales*, September, 1945, 74–76. Reprinted in *The Compleat Werewolf* (New York: Simon & Schuster, 1969). Copyright © 1945 by Anthony Boucher. Reprinted by permission of Curtis Brown, Ltd.

Truman Capote: Miriam, *A Tree of Night* (New York, Random House, 1945), 115–34. First published in *Mademoiselle*, June 1945. Copyright © 1945, 1946, 1947, 1948, 1949 by Truman Capote. Used by permission of Random House, Inc.

Jack Snow: Midnight; *Midnight* (New York: J. Little and Ives Co., 1947), 200–8. First published in *Weird Tales*, May 1946.

John Cheever: Torch Song; *John Cheever: Stories*, Blake Bailey, ed. (New York, Library of America, 2009), 109–25. First published in *The New Yorker*, October 4, 1947; collected in *The Enormous Radio* (New York: Funk & Wagnalls, 1953) and *The Stories of John Cheever* (New York: Alfred A. Knopf, 1978). Copyright © 1978 by John Cheever. Used by permission of Alfred A. Knopf, a division of Random House, Inc.

Shirley Jackson: The Daemon Lover; *The Lottery: Adventures of the Daemon Lover* (New York: Farrar, Straus and Cudahy, 1949). First published (as "The Phantom Lover") in *Woman's Home Companion*, February 1949. Copyright © 1948, 1949 by Shirley Jackson. Copyright renewed 1976, 1977 by Laurence Hyman, Barry Hyman, Mrs. Sarah Webster and Mrs. Joanne Schurer. Reprinted by permission of Farrar, Straus & Giroux, LLC.

Paul Bowles: The Circular Valley; *Paul Bowles: Complete Stories & Later Writings*, Daniel Halpern, ed. (New York: Library of America, 2002), 90–99. First published in *The Delicate Prey and Other Stories* (New York: Random House, 1950); collected in *The Stories of Paul Bowles* (New York: HarperCollins, 2006). Copyright © 2001 by the Estate of Paul Bowles. Reprinted by permission of HarperCollins Publishers.

Jack Finney: I'm Scared; *The Clock of Time* (London: Eyre & Spottiswoode, 1958), 43–63. First published in *Collier's*, September 1951; collected in *About Time* (New York: Simon & Schuster, 1998). Copyright © 1951 by Crowell Collier Publishing Co., © renewed by Jack Finney. Reprinted by permission of Simon & Schuster, Inc. All rights reserved.

Vladimir Nabokov: The Vane Sisters; *Nabokov's Quartet* (New York: Phaedra Publishers, 1966), 75–90. First published in *The Hudson Review*, Winter 1959. Written 1951. Copyright © 1959, renewed © 1987 by Vera Nabokov and Dmitri Nabokov. Used by permission of Alfred A. Knopf, a division of Random House, Inc.

Ray Bradbury: The April Witch, *The Golden Apples of the Sun* (New York: Doubleday & Co., 1953), 31–43. First published in *The Saturday Evening Post*, April 5, 1952. Copyright © 1952 by the Curtis Publishing Company, renewed 1980 by Ray Bradbury. Reprinted by permission of Don Congdon Associates, Inc.

Charles Beaumont: Black Country; *The Hunger and Other Stories* (New York: G. P. Putnam's Sons, 1958), 213–34. First published in *Playboy*, September 1954. Copyright © 1957 by Charles Beaumont, renewed 1985 by Christopher Beaumont. Reprinted by permission of Don Congdon Associates, Inc.

Jerome Bixby: Trace; *Space by the Tale* (New York: Ballantine Books, 1964), 91–94.

Davis Grubb: Where the Woodbine Twineth; *Twelve Tales of Suspense and the Supernatural* (New York: Scribner, 1964), 161–75. First published (as "You Never Believe Me") in *Esquire*, February 1964; collected in *You Never Believe Me and Other Stories* (New York: St. Martin's, 1989. Copyright © 1964 by Davis Grubb.

Donald Wandrei: Nightmare; *Strange Harvest* (Sauk City, WI: Arkham House, 1965), 284–89. Copyright ©1965 by Donald Wandrei for *Strange Harvest*. Reprinted by permission of Harold Hughesdon.

Harlan Ellison®: I Have No Mouth, and I Must Scream; *Essential Ellison* (Beverly Hills, CA: Morpheus International, 1991). First published in *IF: World of Science Fiction*, March 1967. Copyright © 1967 by Harlan Ellison®. Renewed 1995 by The Kilimanjaro Corporation. Reprinted by arrangement with, and permission of, the Author and the Author's agent, Richard Curtis Associates, Inc., New York. All rights reserved. Harlan Ellison® is a registered trademark of The Kilimanjaro Corporation.

Richard Matheson: Prey; *Nightmare at 20,000 Feet* (New York: TOR Books, 2002), 321–35. First published in *Playboy*, April 1969. Copyright © 1969 by HMH Publishing Company, Inc., renewed 1997 by Richard Matheson. Reprinted by permission of Don Congdon Associates, Inc.

T.E.D. Klein: The Events at Poroth Farm; *Reassuring Tales*, (Burton, MI: Subterranean Press, 2006), 121–67. First published in *From Beyond the Dark Gateway #2*, December 1972. Copyright © 1972 by T.E.D. Klein. Reprinted by permission of the author.

Isaac Bashevis Singer: Hanka; *Singer: Collected Stories: A Friend of Kafka to Passions*, Ilan Stavans, ed. (New York: Library of America, 2004), 567–83. First published in Yiddish in *Di goldene keyt 83*, 1974, and in English in *The New Yorker*, February 4, 1974; collected in *Passions and Other Stories* (New York: Farrar, Straus & Giroux, 1975). Copyright © 1975 by Isaac Bashevis Singer. Reprinted by permission of Farrar, Straus & Giroux, LLC.

Fred Chappell: Linnaeus Forgets; *More Shapes Than One* (New York: St. Martin's Press, 1991), 1–18. First published in *American Review*, November 1977. Copyright © 1991 by Fred Chappell. Reprinted by permission of St. Martin's Press, LLC.

John Crowley: Novelty; *Novelties and Souvenirs: Collected Short Fiction* (New York: HarperCollins, 2004), 38–58. First published in *Interzone*, Autumn 1983. Copyright © 1983 by John Crowley. Reprinted by permission of the author and his agent, Ralph M. Vicinanza, Ltd.

Jonathan Carroll: Mr Fiddlehead; *The Panic Hand* (London: HarperCollins UK, 1995), 9–22. First published in *Omni*, February 1989. Copyright © 1989 by Jonathan Carroll. Reprinted by permission of The Richard Parks Agency.

Joyce Carol Oates: Family; *Omni*, December 1989, 75–87. Copyright © 1989 Ontario Review. Reprinted by permission of John Hawkins & Associates, Inc.

Thomas Ligotti: The Last Feast of Harlequin; *Shadow at the Bottom of the World*, (Cold Spring Press, 2005), 195–228. First published in *The Magazine of Fantasy and Science Fiction*, April 1990.

Copyright © 1991 by Thomas Ligotti. All rights reserved. Re-printed by permission of the author.

Peter Straub: A Short Guide to the City; *Houses Without Doors* (New York: Dutton, 1990), 95–105. Copyright © by Peter Straub. Reprinted by arrangement with the Genert Company.

Jeff VanderMeer: The General Who Is Dead, *Secret Life* (Prime Books, 2004), 80–83. First published in *Freezer Burn Magazine 5*, 1996. Copyright © 1996 by Jeff VanderMeer. Reprinted by per-mission of the author.

Stephen King: That Feeling, You Can Only Say What It Is in French; *Everything's Eventual: 14 Dark Tales* (New York: Scribner, 2002) 347–64. First published in *The New Yorker*, June 22, 1998. Copy-right © 2002 by Stephen King. Reprinted with the permission of Scribner, a Division of Simon & Schuster, Inc.

George Saunders: Sea Oak; *Pastoralia* (New York: Riverhead Books, 2000), 91–125. First published in *The New Yorker*, December 28, 1998. Copyright © 2000 by George Saunders. Used by permission of Riverhead Books, an imprint of Penguin Group (USA) Inc.

Caitlín R. Kiernan: The Long Hall on the Top Floor; author's type-script. First published in *Carpe Noctem 16*, 1999. Reprinted in *Tales of Pain and Wonder* (Springfield, PA: Gauntlet Publications, 2000; Burton, MI: Subterranean Press, 2008). Copyright © Caitlín R. Kiernan. Reprinted by permission of the author.

Thomas Tessier: Nocturne; *Ghost Music and Other Tales* (Abingdon, MD: Cemetery Dance Publications, 2000), 293–96. Copyright © 2000 by Thomas Tessier. Reprinted by permission of the author.

Michael Chabon: The God of Dark Laughter; *The New Yorker*, April 9, 2001, 116–28. Copyright © 2001 by Michael Chabon. All rights reserved. Reprinted by arrangement with Mary Evans Inc.

Joe Hill: Pop Art; *20th-Century Ghosts* (UK: PS Publishing, 2005), 51–74. First published in *With Signs & Wonders*, edited by Daniel M. Jaffe (Montpelier, VT: Invisible Cities Press, 2001). Reprinted in *20th-Century Ghosts* (New York: William Morrow, 2007). Copy-right © 2001, 2005, 2007 by Joe Hill. Published in the U.S. in 2007 by William Morrow, an imprint of HarperCollins Publishers.

Poppy Z. Brite: Pansu; *The Devil You Know* (Burton, MI: Subter-ranean Press, 2003), 99–109. First published as a Camelot Books chapbook in 2001. Copyright © Poppy Z. Brite. Reprinted by per-mission of the author.

Steven Millhauser: Dangerous Laughter; *Dangerous Laughter* (New York: Alfred A. Knopf, 2008), 75–93. First published in *Tin House* #17, Fall 2003. Copyright © 2008 by Steven Millhauser. Used by permission of Alfred A. Knopf, a division of Random House, Inc.

M. Rickert: The Chambered Fruit; *Map of Dreams* (Urbana, IL:

Golden Gryphon Press, 2006), 278–308. First published in *The Magazine of Fantasy and Science Fiction*, August 2003. Copyright © 2003 by M. Rickert. Reprinted by permission of the author.

Brian Evenson: The Wavering Knife; *The Wavering Knife* (Tallahassee, FL: Fiction Collective Two, 2004), 81–97. Copyright © 1998 by Brian Evenson. Reprinted by permission.

Kelly Link: Stone Animals; *Magic for Beginners* (Northhampton, MA,: Small Beer Press, 2005), 67–112. First published in *Conjunctions* #43, Fall 2004. Copyright © 2004. Reprinted by permission of the author c/o the Renee Zuckerbrot Literary Agency.

Tim Powers: Pat Moore; *Strange Itineraries* (San Francisco, Calif.: Tachyon Publications, 2005), 41–77. First published in *Flights: Extreme Visions of Fantasy*, edited by Al Sarrantonio (New York: Roc, 2004). Copyright © 2004 Tim Powers. Reprinted with permission of the author.

Gene Wolfe: The Little Stranger; *The Magazine of Fantasy and Science Fiction*, October/November, 2004, 184–201. Copyright © 2004 by Gene Wolfe. Reprinted by permission of the author and the author's agents, the Virginia Kidd Agency Inc.

Benjamin Percy: Dial Tone; *Missouri Review*, Summer, 2007, 97–108. Copyright © 2007 by Benjamin Percy. Reprinted by permission of Curtis Brown, Ltd.

This volume presents the texts listed here without change except for the correction of typographical errors, but it does not attempt to reproduce features of their typographic design. The following is a list of typographical errors, cited by page and line number: 13.15, vicious,; 14.5, diaphram; 25.23, to Millick; 40.8, hurt-/ting; 41.29, it's; 57.1, Lupescue; 74.14, abhorently; 122.21, singing,; 146.1, fate; 150.3, name"; 156.6, Town Illinois; 183.13, Brother; 255.23, Walden; 297.23, oppossums; 318.33, said.; 338.4, capitol; 368.19, thought; 379.24, the,; 425.39, weren't we were her; 447.15, drier; 456.22, It; 463.4, circus; 585.11, grass,".

Notes

In the notes below, the reference numbers refer to page and line of this volume (the line count includes titles and headings). The editor wishes to thank Stefan Dziemianowicz for his expert and deeply knowledgeable assistance in the preparation for these volumes and the selection of their contents.

2.10   Piranesi]   Giovanni Battista Piranesi (1720–1778), Italian artist known for his elaborate depictions of labyrinthine imaginary prisons (*Carceri d'Invenzione*).

41.16   Maginot Line]   System of defensive fortifications along the French border, constructed during the 1930s; it was successfully circumvented by German forces in 1940.

54.38–39   "The Werewolf of Paris"]   Popular horror novel (1933) by Guy Endore (1900–1970).

84.40   Mitropa]   German-Austrian catering company founded in 1916.

87.19   Marion Harris]   Jazz singer (1896–1944) whose hits included "After You've Gone" (1918), "A Good Man Is Hard to Find" (1919), and "I Ain't Got Nobody" (1920).

91.11   Saranac]   The Adirondack Cottage Sanitarium for the treatment of tuberculosis was established in 1885 in Saranac Lake, New York.

96.3   *The Daemon Lover*]   Traditional British ballad, also known as "James Harris," in which a woman is tempted to her doom.

122.2   Major Bowes]   Edward Bowes (1874–1946), host of the radio series *Major Bowes Amateur Hour* (1934–46).

122.4   "La Paloma."]   Song composed by Sebastián Iradier in the early 1860s and widely recorded throughout the 20th century.

122.21   "You Butterfly,"]   "Butterfly" (1957), song by Kal Mann and Bernie Lowe.

122.32   Moran and Mack]   George Moran (1881–1949) and Charles Mack (1888–1934), known for their blackface comedy act Two Black Crows.

122.34   Floyd Gibbons]   War correspondent (1887–1949) who covered World War I for the *Chicago Tribune* and was later known as a radio and newsreel commentator.

137.20–21   *Cette examain . . . jeunes filles!*]   The faulty French can be translated: This test is over and so is my life. Goodbye, girls!

142.21   "Alph"]   See Samuel Taylor Coleridge, "Kubla Khan."

142.22   Anna Livia Plurabelle]   Female figure associated with the River Liffey in James Joyce's *Finnegans Wake* (1939).

146.29   the Fox sisters]   Three sisters from Hydeville, New York, who beginning in the late 1840s acquired a reputation for mediumistic abilities manifested through mysterious rappings. At the height of their celebrity they attracted support from many prominent figures, notably Horace Greeley. In 1888 Margaret Fox published a confession (later recanted) that the rappings had been faked.

146.38   Alfred Russel Wallace]   British naturalist (1823–1913) who developed a theory of natural selection independently of Charles Darwin; he later became an advocate of Spiritualism.

153.16   "Beautiful Ohio."]   Ohio state song, written by Ballard MacDonald and Mary Earl.

162.17–18   Jelly Roll's]   Jelly Roll Morton (1890–1941), pianist and composer whose works included "Wolverine Blues," "New Orleans Bump," and "Shreveport Stomp."

165.25   Muggsy Spanier's]   Cornet player (1906–1967) active on the Chicago jazz scene from the 1920s on.

180.9   *Mephisto Waltz*]   One of four waltzes composed by Franz Liszt between 1859 and 1885.

225.33   Bruno Hauptmann]   Hauptmann (1899–1936) was executed for the abduction and murder of Charles Lindbergh Jr.

233.5   *Vathek*]   Oriental romance written in French by William Beckford (1759–1844), and first published (in English translation) in 1786.

233.21   *The Mysteries of Udolpho*]   Enormously popular novel published in 1794 by Ann Radcliffe (1764–1823).

233.26   Montoni]   Villain who passes himself off as an Italian nobleman in *The Mysteries of Udolpho.*

234.27   Maturin]   Charles Robert Maturin (1782–1824), Irish novelist best known for *Melmoth the Wanderer* (1820).

235.3–4   Arthur Machen]   Welsh novelist (1863–1947) whose many works of fantastic fiction included *The Great God Pan* (1894), *The Three Imposters* (1895), *The House of Souls* (1906), *The Hill of Dreams* (1907), and *The Terror* (1917).

236.12 Algernon Blackwood's] English writer (1869–1951) best known for supernatural stories.

237.16 *Otranto*] *The Castle of Otranto* (1765), prototypical Gothic novel by Horace Walpole (1717–1797).

238.8 *The Monk*] Novel (1795) by Matthew Gregory Lewis (1775–1818).

238.37 Brother Ambrosio] The malevolent protagonist of Lewis's *The Monk*.

239.3 *The Thief of Baghdad*] *The Thief of Bagdad* (1940), film produced by Alexander Korda and directed by a team including Michael Powell and Ludwig Berger; the title role was played by Sabu.

244.26 LeFanu] Joseph Sheridan Le Fanu (1814–1873), writer known for his stories of terror and the supernatural; his novels include *The House by the Churchyard* (1863) and *Uncle Silas* (1864).

245.12 "The Uninhabited House" . . . "Monsieur Maurice,"] Novel by Mrs. J. H. Riddell (1832–1906); novella (1873) by Amelia Ann Blandford Edwards (1831–1892).

245.14 "The Amber Witch,"] German novel (1845) by Wilhelm Meinhold (1797–1851), originally presented by the author as an authentic historical document; in a subsequent edition Meinhold admitted the hoax. An English translation appeared in 1861.

246.39–247.1 *American Scholar*] Magazine of the Phi Beta Kappa Society, published since 1932.

246.13 A. E. Coppard] Short story writer (1878–1957) whose collections included *Adam and Eve and Pinch Me* (1921), *The Black Dog* (1923), and *Fearful Pleasures* (1946).

249.9 Barbara Byfield's *Glass Harmonica*] Byfield's book, published in 1967, is subtitled *A Lexicon of the Fantastical*.

249.14–15 Maria Ouspenskaya] Russian actress (1876–1949) who came to the U.S. as a member of the Moscow Art Theater and went on to appear in Hollywood films such as *Dodsworth* (1936), *The Wolf Man* (1941), and *The Shanghai Gesture* (1942).

249.17–18 Marryat . . . Endore] Frederick Marryat, English writer of nautical novels (1792–1848); Guy Endore, see note 54.38–39.

251.28 Shirley Jackson] American writer (1916–1965) whose works include *The Lottery and Other Stories* (1949) and *The Haunting of Hill House* (1959).

251.30 Aleister Crowley] British occultist (1875–1945), author of *Magick* (1912-13) and other works.

255.6   Ruthven Todd's *Lost Traveller*]   *The Lost Traveller* (1943), novel by the Scottish poet Ruthven Todd (1914–1978).

255.11–12   Lafcadio Hearn . . . "Gaki,"]   See Hearn's 1923 collection *Kottô: Being Japanese Curios, with Sundry Webs*: "The belief in a mysterious relation between ghosts and insects, or rather between spirits and insects, is a very ancient belief in the East, where it now assumes innumerable forms,— some unspeakably horrible, others full of weird beauty."

259.10   *The King in Yellow*]   Collection of short stories (1895) by Robert W. Chambers; the first four all deal in different ways with the evil influence of the fictional play "The King in Yellow."

260.6   M. R. James]   Montagu Rhodes James (1862–1936), antiquarian and author of ghost stories collected in *Ghost Stories of an Antiquary* (1905–11).

262.7   Lovecraft's essay . . . Literature."]   Pioneering survey by H. P. Lovecraft (1890–1937), first published in *The Recluse* in 1927 and reprinted after Lovecraft's death in *The Outsider and Others* (1939).

262.29   John Christopher's *The Possessors*]   Science fiction novel (1965) written by Samuel Youd (b. 1922) under the pseudonym John Christopher.

280.2   Pavlova . . . Isadora Duncan]   Anna Pavlova (1881–1931), Russian ballerina celebrated for her performance as "The Dying Swan"; Duncan (1877–1927), American pioneer of modern dance.

284.15   Marranos]   Sephardic Jews threatened with expulsion from Spain who converted to Christianity under duress, but continued to practice Judaism in secret.

289.5   Carl Linnaeus]   Swedish botanist (1707–1778), pioneer of modern systems of taxonomy.

289.30–31   Albrecht von Haller]   Swiss physiologist and anatomist (1708–1777).

290.8   Siegesbeck]   Johann Georg Siegesbeck (1686–1755), German botanist who engaged in bitter polemics against the Linnean system of classification.

303.38   Andromeda]   In Greek mythology, daughter of Cepheus and Cassiopeia, rulers of Ethiopia; she was chained to a rock and offered in sacrifice to a sea monster who had been sent to punish her mother's pride.

307.12   *Euphues*]   *Euphues, the Anatomy of Wit* (1579), romance by John Lyly (?1554–1606), who followed it with *Euphues and his England* (1580); the ornately allusive and circuitous wordplay of these works were for a time greatly influential among English writers.

315.23   Murillo]   Bartolomé Esteban Murillo (1617–1682), Spanish painter who specialized in religious subjects.

326.30–31   Antonio Sant' Elia] Italian architect (1888–1916) associated with Futurism.

333.2   Scott Joplin] American composer (?1867–1917) known for his rag-time pieces and for the opera *Treemonisha*.

358.34   "The Conqueror Worm,"] Poem by Edgar Allan Poe, collected in *The Raven and Other Poems* (1849).

385.22   *O carne vale!*] O farewell to flesh (or meat)!

402.14   Inchon] Decisive battle (1950) of the Korean War, won by United Nations forces.

414.33   *Let the wild rumpus start*] See Maurice Sendak, *Where the Wild Things Are* (1963).

420.38   "In-A-Gadda-Da-Vida"] The 1968 hit by the psychedelic rock group Iron Butterfly ran 17 minutes and took up one side of the album named for it.

421.22   Jerry Lee Lewis] Rock and country performer (b. 1935) whose recordings include "Great Balls of Fire," "Lewis Boogie," and "High School Confidential."

422.25   *The hard days are coming.*] In the collection *Everything's Eventual*, Stephen King added the following commentary to this story: "I think this story is about Hell. A version of it where you are condemned to do the same thing over and over again. Existentialism, baby, what a concept; paging Albert Camus. There's an idea that Hell is other people. My idea is that it might be repetition."

441.2   *The Prophet*] Perennially popular collection of prose poems (1923) by the Lebanese-American writer Khalil Gibran (1883–1931).

447.20   Herman and Lily Munster] Central characters of the television comedy series *The Munsters* (1964–66), played by Fred Gwynne and Yvonne De Carlo.

447.35   Randy Newman] Singer, songwriter, and composer (b. 1943); his albums include *12 Songs* (1970), *Sail Away* (1972), and *Good Old Boys* (1974).

448.27   *The Martian Chronicles*] Collection of linked stories (1950) detailing the colonization of Mars by humans.

449.34   Beastie Boys] American hip hop group known for the albums *Licensed to Ill* (1986) and *Paul's Boutique* (1988).

451.3–4   George Romero] American filmmaker (b. 1940) best known for his series of zombie movies beginning with *Night of the Living Dead* (1968) and also including *Dawn of the Dead* (1978) and *Day of the Dead* (1985).

471.26–27   Poe's story . . . rampaging orang]   "The Murders in the Rue Morgue" (1841).

475.10   Madame Blavatsky]   Helena Petrovna Blavatsky (1831–1891), born in Russia, came to the U.S. in 1873 and founded the Theosophical Society; author of *The Secret Doctrine* (1888).

481.23   Occam's razor]   Dictum of the English philosopher William of Occam (?1290–1349): "Entities are not to be unnecessarily multiplied," or the simplest explanation is most likely correct.

485.31   Bernard Malamud]   Novelist (1914–1986) whose works include *The Natural* (1952), *The Assistant* (1957), and *The Fixer* (1966).

529.28   Grandma Moses]   Anna Mary Robertson Moses (1860–1961), American folk artist who began to paint in her seventies.

581.23   *The Velveteen Rabbit*]   Novel for children (1922), subtitled *How Toys Become Real*, by Margery Williams (1881–1944).

595.2   *Fight Club*]   Novel (1996) by Chuck Palhniuk.

600.19   Jane Goodall]   English primatologist (b. 1934) known for her studies of the social life of chimpanzees.

607.32   *A Curtain of Green*]   Story collection (1941) by Eudora Welty.

630.17–18   Frost . . . *back*]   See Robert Frost "Two Witches: The Witch of Coös" (collected in *New Hampshire*, 1923), lines 16–18: "Don't that make you suspicious / That there's something the dead are keeping back? / Yes, there's something the dead are keeping back."

THE LIBRARY OF AMERICA SERIES

The Library of America fosters appreciation and pride in America's literary heritage by publishing, and keeping permanently in print, authoritative editions of America's best and most significant writing. An independent nonprofit organization, it was founded in 1979 with seed money from the National Endowment for the Humanities and the Ford Foundation.

To subscribe to the series or to order individual copies,
please visit www.loa.org or call (800) 964.5778.

This book is set in 10 point Linotron Galliard,
a face designed for photocomposition by Matthew Carter
and based on the sixteenth-century face Granjon. The paper
is acid-free lightweight opaque and meets the requirements
for permanence of the American National Standards Institute.
The binding material is Brillianta, a woven rayon cloth made
by Van Heek-Scholco Textielfabrieken, Holland. Compo-
sition by Dedicated Business Services. Printing by
Malloy Incorporated. Binding by Dekker Book-
binding. Designed by Bruce Campbell.

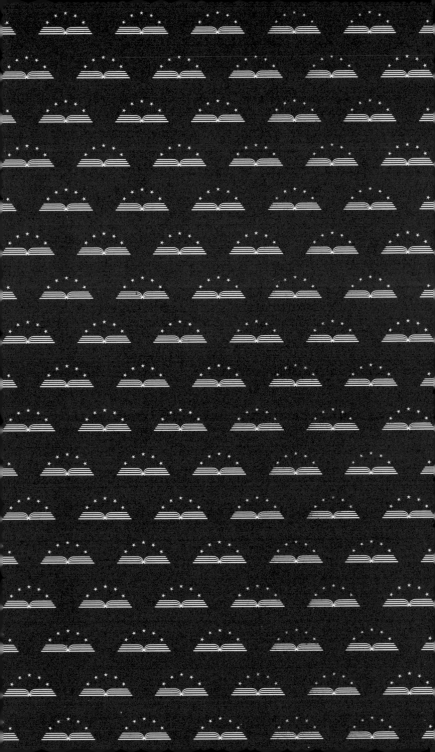

AMERICAN FANTASTIC TALES

AMERICAN FANTASTIC TALES

TERROR AND THE UNCANNY FROM POE TO THE PULPS

Peter Straub, editor

THE LIBRARY OF AMERICA

Some of the material in this volume is reprinted with permission
of the holders of copyright and publication rights.
Acknowledgments are on page 736.

The paper used in this publication meets the
minimum requirements of the American National Standard for
Information Sciences—Permanence of Paper for Printed
Library Materials, ANSI Z39.48—1984.

Distributed to the trade in the United States
by Penguin Group (USA) Inc.
and in Canada by Penguin Books Canada Ltd.

Library of Congress Control Number: 2009927073
ISBN 978–1–59853–047–6

———

First Printing
The Library of America—196

Manufactured in the United States of America

Contents

CONTENTS   ix

Introduction

Most years, I set aside four or five days in mid-March to attend a gathering in Florida called The International Conference on the Fantastic in the Arts. It is the only occasion I know where writers and academics gather together in the absence of fans to discuss, among other things, precisely the kinds of stories to be found in the two volumes of *American Fantastic Tales.* (The other things have included fairy tales, anime, the films of George Romero and Hayao Miyazaki, Philip K. Dick, Joseph Cornell boxes, Doctor Who, and Tolkien. You get the idea.) During these conferences, for at least a couple of years now, John Clute (the only full-time professional critic and theorist in the field of science fiction and fantastic literature) has been using the occasion to evolve and refine an obvious-only-after-you-think-about-it theory: that fiction of this kind, at least in the form seen here, emerged as an expression of the universal sense of loss, grief, and terror produced by the gradual replacement of the Enlightenment's orderly, rational, reassuring world-view with the unstable and untrustworthy universe that came into being during the nineteenth and twentieth centuries.

For now, let us at least take note that loss, grief, and terror echo throughout the two volumes of *American Fantastic Tales.* If the fantastic story originates in such emotions, as I believe it does, it is constantly confessing its origins, and with helpless fervor. Gothic literature in general is inherently melancholy, and melancholy is generally its most cheerful aspect. If you consider Poe and Lovecraft to be "gothic" writers, as I certainly do, then in most of the cases here we are dealing with the gothic sensibility, the many avatars of which are riddled with isolation, loneliness, and dread.

A glance at the tables of contents of these volumes makes clear that apart from one or two stories that might be borderline science fiction, we are dealing almost entirely with the genre category called horror, which in fact allows a very great degree of latitude as to method, theme, tone and content. Anybody who picks up these volumes will probably already know that a couple of decades ago horror took a self-inflicted drubbing from which it is only now beginning to recover. It had been existing on only the most marginal, liminal fringes of respectability since the thirties, and three or four hundred misbegotten novels published in the eighties and early nineties—novels that tended to come garbed in a good deal of chrome, which was draped across jackets featuring drops of blood, houses whose façades looked like faces, and baleful, red-eyed children—dumped it firmly into the gutter. (Actually, I recommend the gutter very highly. The company entertains, and the view illuminates.) However, Henry James, no gutter-dweller, regularly visited the well of "dear old sacred terror," which spoke to him of "those most mysterious of mysteries, the mysteries which are at our own doors." Conflating the gothic and the fantastic through the medium of psychology, James's formulation describes a great many of the stories collected here.

The word "Tales" in our title goes a considerable distance toward clarifying the principles that helped guide the editorial process. From a tale one expects a bit of wildness, of exaggeration and dramatic effect. The tale has no inherent concern with decorum, balance, or harmony. In a tale, the completion of the railway involves a magical hammer, a bloody hacksaw, a man with one eye the color of curdled milk, an oath at midnight, and a ghastly specter glimpsed wandering through a downpour along the riverbank at midnight. (And that right there, sonny, is how we built the railway.) A tale may not display a great deal of structural, psychological, or narrative sophistication, though it might possess all three, but it seldom takes its eye off its primary goal, the creation of a particular emotional state in its reader. Depending on the tale, that state could be wonder, amazement, shock, terror, anger, anxiety, melancholia, or the momentary frisson of horror.

Although tales of this kind always keep their prospective readers in mind, they tend to resist easy accommodation with familiar narrative templates. Part of their appeal can lie in the unpredictability and unexpectedness of the plotting, the sheer strangeness of the characterization, and what can be experienced as the dreamlike, associational flow of events. In all of these ways, tales retain a connection to what I take to be their earliest ancestors: myth, folktale, and oral narratives that pass through a generation or two before being written down. The fantastic has a long, long history, and it existed as both a way of seeing and a way of representing what is seen centuries before it found expression in fiction. A friend of mine who was raised speaking the ancient language of his country, Irish, which we wrongly call Gaelic, told me that when a long-ago tale-teller wished to summon the children and silence the crowd, he would begin with a formula equivalent to, but more commanding than, our own "Once upon a time": *Long, long ago there lived an old man, and if you had known this old man, you wouldn't be alive today.* You can practically hear the wind blowing through that, almost smell the wood smoke and the burning tobacco.

Human beings across every culture I know about require such stories, stories with cool winds and wood smoke. They speak to something deep within us, the capacity to conceptualize, objectify, and find patterns, thereby to create the flow of events and perceptions that find perfect expression in fiction. We are built this way, we create stories by reflex, unstoppably. But this elegant system really works best when the elements of the emerging story, whether it is being written or being read, are taken as literal fact. Almost always, to respond to the particulars of the fantastic as if they were metaphorical or allegorical is to drain them of vitality. (The first of these two volumes does contain a story I take to be an allegory, Alice Brown's "Golden Baby," but it is so hypnotically bizarre that the obviousness of the allegory hardly gets in the way.)

In a story-driven species like ourselves the application of the fantastic as a mode is metaphoric in itself. When I was sixteen years old, I had the first literary insight of my life, that Edgar Allan Poe had created a shrinking room where a pendulum-like scimitar swung ever nearer the heart of man lashed to a bed because, in some central fashion, he saw the world in those terms. That he could project this internal condition into fiction was what made the story, despite its overheated language and absurdly convenient ending, so vivid, so immediately persuasive, so gripping. By grace of the imagination, his aching, fearful metaphor had moved firmly into the realm of the literal.

*

By way of introducing a theme found here in story after story, let us briefly consider the Puritans. One of their first acts of accommodation to a new continent was the establishment of churches that told them some people, the "elect," were saved, the others damned, and one could do nothing about these inflexible categories. Every human being was profoundly sinful by nature. Only harsh, unremitting discipline and hard work joylessly executed could result in the good.

These grim, suspicious people lived in small communities located at the edge of the original first-growth American climax forest. In every way, this seems to me of crucial importance. What did they see in that forest, in that teeming darkness? Everything, we might say, that was not themselves, everything that threatened them most profoundly. Nature was much worse than merely a force not to be trusted; nature was, inherently, wicked in its nature.

Two hundred years and more after the arrival of the Puritans, this message was still coming through loud and clear. Bad Nature, the belief that the natural world itself deludes, tempts, misleads, wishes to devour careless human beings, takes a commanding role here in the stories written by Nathaniel Hawthorne, Herman Melville, Harriet Prescott Spofford, Ralph Adams Cram, Robert E. Howard, and Clark Ashton Smith.

The essential aspect of this primal distrust of Nature is in its ultimate purpose, the surrender or collapse of the individual will. The theme of loss of will, of actual agency, haunts a surprising portion of the stories in this collection. For Americans of all decades, it seems, the loss of agency and selfhood, effected by whatever means, arouses a particularly resonant horror. Trance states, sleepwalking, mesmerism, obsession, possession, that variety of possession represented by literal invasion of wicked and ravenous forces, madness, spiritual infection, the evil potentiality of magnetism (dingbat pseudoscience pops up here a couple of times, especially as we move into the mid-nineteenth century), exotic curses, evil atmospheres, and the simple machinations of malign beings, all these states, conditions, and forces conspire against the healthy, purposive, functional human identity. To feel our character, our personality, and our personal, hard-won history fade from being is to be exposed to whatever lies beneath these comforting operational conveniences. What remains when the conscious and functioning self has been erased is mankind's fundamental condition-irrational, violent, guilt-wracked, despairing, and mad.

In Brockden Brown's "Somnambulism: A Fragment" and Poe's "Berenice," trance states represent erasure of the rational and functioning self; in Seabury Quinn's "The Case of Everard Maundy," the accursed words of a public speaker strip the will from members of his audience and tempt them into suicide. Similarly, words written in an evil or forbidden book have the power to distort and degrade the minds of all who read it. H. P. Lovecraft's *Necronomicon* by "the mad Arab Abdul Alhazred" stands as the most iconic example of what is a consistent marker throughout the history of the American fantastic. Here it becomes central to Robert W. Chambers' "The Repairer of Reputations" (Lovecraft got the idea from Chambers), Howard's "The Black Stone," and Lovecraft's "The Thing on the Doorstep."

The soul-destroying book has close thematic links to "the obscure shop," likely to disappear or change location, in which it or another soul-destroying object may be purchased. Robert Bloch's "The Cloak" provides a ripe example of the mysterious and occult shop. No less than the first story in this volume, Bloch's clever little vampire story concerns a fatal loss of the central, determinative self, which is in peril from the moment the vainglorious protagonist allows the object cited in the title to be draped over his shoulders. Had our Puritan forebears possessed any openness to the devices of fiction, they might have nodded their heads in recognition before going on their wintry way.

Peter Straub

CHARLES BROCKDEN BROWN

(1771–1810)

Somnambulism
A fragment

[The following fragment will require no other preface or commentary than an extract from the Vienna Gazette of June 14, 1784. "At Great Glogau, in Silesia, the attention of physicians, and of the people, has been excited by the case of a young man, whose behaviour indicates perfect health in all respects but one. He has a habit of rising in his sleep, and performing a great many actions with as much order and exactness as when awake. This habit for a long time showed itself in freaks and achievements merely innocent, or, at least, only troublesome and inconvenient, till about six weeks ago. At that period a shocking event took place about three leagues from the town, and in the neighbourhood where the youth's family resides. A young lady, travelling with her father by night, was shot dead upon the road, by some person unknown. The officers of justice took a good deal of pains to trace the author of the crime, and at length, by carefully comparing circumstances, a suspicion was fixed upon this youth. After an accurate scrutiny, by the tribunal of the circle, he has been declared author of the murder: but what renders the case truly extraordinary is, that there are good reasons for believing that the deed was perpetrated by the youth while asleep, and was entirely unknown to himself. The young woman was the object of his affection, and the journey in which she had engaged had given him the utmost anxiety for her safety."]

OUR guests were preparing to retire for the night, when somebody knocked loudly at the gate. The person was immediately admitted, and presented a letter to Mr. Davis. This letter was from a friend, in which he informed our guest of certain concerns of great importance, on which the letter-writer was extremely anxious to have a personal conference with his friend; but knowing that he intended to set out from —— four days previous to his writing, he was hindered from setting out by the apprehension of missing him upon the way. Meanwhile, he had deemed it best to send a special messsage to quicken his motions, should he be able to find him.

The importance of this interview was such, that Mr. Davis declared his intention of setting out immediately. No solicitations could induce him to delay a moment. His daughter, convinced of the urgency of his motives, readily consented to brave the perils and discomforts of a nocturnal journey.

This event had not been anticipated by me. The shock that it produced in me was, to my own apprehension, a subject of surprise. I could not help perceiving that it was greater than the occasion would justify. The pleasures of this intercourse were, in a moment, to be ravished from me. I was to part from my new friend, and when we should again meet it was impossible to foresee. It was then that I recollected her expressions, that assured me that her choice was fixed upon another. If I saw her again, it would probably be as a wife. The claims of friendship, as well as those of love, would then be swallowed up by a superior and hateful obligation.

But, though betrothed, she was not wedded. That was yet to come; but why should it be considered as inevitable? Our dispositions and views must change with circumstances. Who was he that Constantia Davis had chosen? Was he born to outstrip all competitors in ardour and fidelity? We cannot fail of chusing that which appears to us most worthy of choice. He had hitherto been unrivalled; but was not this day destined to introduce to her one, to whose merits every competitor must yield? He that would resign this prize, without an arduous struggle, would, indeed, be of all wretches the most pusillanimous and feeble.

Why, said I, do I cavil at her present choice? I will maintain that it does honour to her discernment. She would not be that accomplished being which she seems, if she had acted otherwise. It would be sacrilege to question the rectitude of her conduct. The object of her choice was worthy. The engagement of her heart in his favour was unavoidable, because her experience had not hitherto produced one deserving to be placed in competition with him. As soon as his superior is found, his claims will be annihilated. Has not this propitious accident supplied the defects of her former observation? But soft! is she not betrothed? If she be, what have I to dread? The engagement is accompanied with certain conditions. Whether they be openly expressed or not, they necessarily limit it. Her vows are binding on condition that the present situation continues, and that another does not arise, previously to marriage, by whom claims those of the present lover will be justly superseded.

But how shall I contend with this unknown admirer? She is going whither it will not be possible for me to follow her. An interview of a few hours is not sufficient to accomplish the important purpose that I meditate; but even this is now at an end. I shall speedily be forgotten by her. I have done nothing that entitles me to a place in her remembrance. While my rival will be left at liberty to prosecute his suit, I shall be abandoned to solitude, and have no other employment than to ruminate on the bliss that has eluded my grasp. If scope were allowed to my exertions, I might hope that they would ultimately be crowned with success; but, as it is, I am manacled and powerless. The good would easily be reached, if my hands were at freedom: now that they are fettered, the attainment is impossible.

But is it true that such is my forlorn condition? What is it that irrecoverably binds me to this spot? There are seasons of respite from my present occupations, in which I commonly indulge myself in journeys. This lady's habitation is not at an immeasurable distance from mine. It may be easily comprised within the sphere of my excursions. Shall I want a motive or excuse for paying her a visit? Her father has claimed to be better acquainted with my uncle. The lady has intimated, that the sight of me, at any future period, will give her pleasure. This will furnish ample apology for visiting their house. But why should I delay my visit? Why not immediately attend them on their way? If not on their whole journey, at least for a part of it? A journey in darkness is not unaccompanied with peril. Whatever be the caution or knowledge of their guide, they cannot be supposed to surpass mine, who have trodden this part of the way so often, that my chamber floor is scarcely more familiar to me. Besides, there is danger, from which, I am persuaded, my attendance would be a sufficient, an indispensable safeguard.

I am unable to explain why I conceived this journey to be attended with uncommon danger. My mind was, at first, occupied with the remoter consequences of this untimely departure, but my thoughts gradually returned to the contemplation of its immediate effects. There were twenty miles to a ferry, by which the travellers designed to cross the river, and at which they expected to arrive at sun-rise the next morning. I have said that the intermediate way was plain and direct. Their guide professed to be thoroughly acquainted with it.—From what quarter, then, could danger be expected to arise? It was easy to enumerate and magnify possibilities; that a tree, or ridge, or stone unobserved might overturn the carriage; that their horse might fail, or be urged, by some accident, to flight, were far from being impossible. Still they were such as justified caution. My vigilance would, at least, contribute to their security. But I could not for a moment divest myself of the belief, that my aid was indispensable. As I pondered on this image my emotions arose to terror.

All men are, at times, influenced by inexplicable sentiments. Ideas haunt them in spite of all their efforts to discard them. Prepossessions are entertained, for which their reason is unable to discover any adequate cause. The strength of a belief, when it is destitute of any rational foundation, seems, of itself, to furnish a new ground for credulity. We first admit a powerful persuasion, and then, from reflecting on the insufficiency of the ground on which it is built, instead of being prompted to dismiss it, we become more forcibly attached to it.

I had received little of the education of design. I owed the formation of my character chiefly to accident. I shall not pretend to determine in what degree I was credulous or superstitious. A belief, for which I could not rationally account, I was sufficiently prone to consider as the work of some invisible agent; as an intimation from the great source of existence and knowledge. My imagination was vivid. My passions, when I allowed them sway, were incontroulable. My conduct, as my feelings, was characterised by precipitation and headlong energy.

On this occasion I was eloquent in my remonstrances. I could not suppress my opinion, that unseen danger lurked in their way. When called upon to state the reasons of my apprehensions, I could only enumerate possibilities of which they were already apprised, but which they regarded in their true light. I made bold enquiries into the importance of the motives that should induce them to expose themselves to the least hazard. They could not urge their horse beyond his real strength. They would be compelled to suspend their journey for some time the next day. A few hours were all that they could hope to save by their utmost expedition. Were a few hours of such infinite moment?

In these representations I was sensible that I had over-leaped the bounds of rigid decorum. It was not my place to weigh his motives and inducements. My age and situation, in this family, rendered silence and submission my peculiar province. I had hitherto confined myself within bounds of scrupulous propriety, but now I had suddenly lost sight of all regards but those which related to the safety of the travellers.

Mr. Davis regarded my vehemence with suspicion. He eyed me with more attention than I had hitherto received from him. The impression which this unexpected interference made upon him, I was, at the time, too much absorbed in other considerations to notice. It was afterwards plain that he suspected my zeal to originate in a passion for his daughter, which it was by no means proper for him to encourage. If this idea occurred to him, his humanity would not suffer it to generate indignation or resentment in his bosom. On the contrary, he treated my arguments with mildness, and assured me that I had overrated the inconveniences and perils of the journey. Some regard was to be paid to his daughter's ease and health. He did not believe them to be materially endangered. They should make suitable provision of cloaks and caps against the inclemency of the air. Had not the occasion been extremely urgent, and of that urgency he alone could be the proper judge, he should certainly not consent to endure even these trivial inconveniences. "But you seem," continued he, "chiefly anxious for my daughter's sake. There is, without doubt, a large portion of gallantry in your fears. It is natural and venial in a young man to take infinite pains for the service of the ladies; but, my dear, what say you? I will refer this important question to your decision. Shall we go, or wait till the morning?"

"Go, by all means," replied she. "I confess the fears that have been expressed appear to be groundless. I am bound to our young friend for the concern he takes in our welfare, but certainly his imagination misleads him. I am not so much a girl as to be scared merely because it is dark."

I might have foreseen this decision; but what could I say? My fears and my repugnance were strong as ever.

The evil that was menaced was terrible. By remaining where they were till the next day they would escape it. Was no other method sufficient for their preservation? My attendance would effectually obviate the danger.

This scheme possessed irresistible attractions. I was thankful to the danger for suggesting it. In the fervour of my conceptions, I was willing to run to the world's end to show my devotion to the lady. I could sustain, with alacrity, the fatigue of many nights of travelling and watchfulness. I should unspeakably prefer them to warmth and ease, if I could thereby extort from this lady a single phrase of gratitude or approbation.

I proposed to them to bear them company, at least till the morning light. They would not listen to it. Half my purpose was indeed answered by the glistening eyes and affectionate looks of Miss Davis, but the remainder I was pertinaciously bent on likewise accomplishing. If Mr. Davis had not suspected my motives, he would probably have been less indisposed to compliance. As it was, however, his objections were insuperable. They earnestly insisted on my relinquishing my design. My uncle, also, not seeing any thing that justified extraordinary precautions, added his injunctions. I was conscious of my inability to show any sufficient grounds for my fears. As long as their representations rung in my ears, I allowed myself to be ashamed of my weakness, and conjured up a temporary persuasion that my attendance was, indeed, superfluous, and that I should show most wisdom in suffering them to depart alone.

But this persuasion was transient. They had no sooner placed themselves in their carriage, and exchanged the parting adieus, but my apprehensions returned upon me as forcibly as ever. No doubt part of my despondency flowed from the idea of separation, which, however auspicious it might prove to the lady, portended unspeakable discomforts to me. But this was not all. I was breathless with fear of some unknown and terrible disaster that awaited them. A hundred times I resolved to disregard their remonstrances, and hover near them till the morning. This might be done without exciting their displeasure. It was easy to keep aloof and be unseen by them. I should doubtless have pursued this method if my fears had assumed any definite and consistent form; if, in reality, I had been able distinctly to tell what it was that I feared. My guardianship would be of no use against the obvious sources of danger in the ruggedness and obscurity of the way. For that end I must have tendered them my services, which I knew would be refused, and, if pertinaciously obtruded on them, might justly excite displeasure. I was not insensible, too, of the obedience that was due to my uncle. My absence would be remarked. Some anger and much disquietude would have been the consequences with respect to him. And after all, what was this groundless and ridiculous persuasion that governed me? Had I profited nothing by experience of the effects of similar follies? Was I never to attend to the lessons of sobriety and truth? How ignominious to be thus the slave of a fortuitous and inexplicable impulse! To be the victim of terrors more chimerical than those which haunt the dreams of idiots and children! *They* can describe clearly, and attribute a real existence to the object of their terrors. Not so can I.

Influenced by these considerations, I shut the gate at which I had been standing, and turned towards the house. After a few steps I paused, turned, and listened to the distant sounds of the carriage. My courage was again on the point of yielding, and new efforts were requisite before I could resume my first resolutions.

I spent a drooping and melancholy evening. My imagination continually hovered over our departed guests. I recalled every circumstance of the road. I reflected by what means they were to pass that bridge, or extricate themselves from this slough. I imagined the possibility of their guide's forgetting the position of a certain oak that grew in the road. It was an ancient tree, whose boughs extended, on all sides, to an extraordinary distance. They seemed disposed by nature in that way in which they would produce the most ample circumference of shade. I could not recollect any other obstruction from which much was to be feared. This indeed was several miles distant, and its appearance was too remarkable not to have excited attention.

The family retired to sleep. My mind had been too powerfully excited to permit me to imitate their example. The incidents of the last two days passed over my fancy like a vision.
The revolution was almost incredible which my mind had
undergone, in consequence of these incidents. It was so abrupt
and entire that my soul seemed to have passed into a new
form. I pondered on every incident till the surrounding scenes
disappeared, and I forgot my real situation. I mused upon the
image of Miss Davis till my whole soul was dissolved in tenderness, and my eyes overflowed with tears. There insensibly
arose a sort of persuasion that destiny had irreversably decreed
that I should never see her more.

While engaged in this melancholy occupation, of which I cannot say how long it lasted, sleep overtook me as I sat. Scarcely
a minute had elapsed during this period without conceiving
the design, more or less strenuously, of sallying forth, with a view
to overtake and guard the travellers; but this design was embarrassed with invincible objections, and was alternately formed
and laid aside. At length, as I have said, I sunk into profound
slumber, if that slumber can be termed profound, in which my
fancy was incessantly employed in calling up the forms, into
new combinations, which had constituted my waking reveries.
—The images were fleeting and transient, but the events of the
morrow recalled them to my remembrance with sufficient distinctness. The terrors which I had so deeply and unaccountably imbibed could not fail of retaining some portion of their
influence, in spite of sleep.

In my dreams, the design which I could not bring myself to
execute while awake I embraced without hesitation. I was
summoned, methought, to defend this lady from the attacks of
an assassin. My ideas were full of confusion and inaccuracy. All
that I can recollect is, that my efforts had been unsuccessful to
avert the stroke of the murderer. This, however, was not accomplished without drawing on his head a bloody retribution.
I imagined myself engaged, for a long time, in pursuit of the
guilty, and, at last, to have detected him in an artful disguise. I
did not employ the usual preliminaries which honour pre-
scribes, but, stimulated by rage, attacked him with a pistol, and
terminated his career by a mortal wound.

I should not have described these phantoms had there not

been a remarkable coincidence between them and the real events of that night. In the morning, my uncle, whose custom it was to rise first in the family, found me quietly reposing in the chair in which I had fallen asleep. His summons roused and startled me. This posture was so unusual that I did not readily recover my recollection, and perceive in what circumstances I was placed.

I shook off the dreams of the night. Sleep had refreshed and invigorated my frame, as well as tranquillized my thoughts. I still mused on yesterday's adventures, but my reveries were more cheerful and benign. My fears and bodements were dispersed with the dark, and I went into the fields, not merely to perform the duties of the day, but to ruminate on plans for the future.

My golden visions, however, were soon converted into visions of despair. A messenger arrived before noon, intreating my presence, and that of my uncle, at the house of Dr. Inglefield, a gentleman who resided at the distance of three miles from our house. The messenger explained the intention of this request. It appeared that the terrors of the preceding evening had some mysterious connection with truth. By some deplorable accident, Miss Davis had been shot on the road, and was still lingering in dreadful agonies at the house of this physician. I was in a field near the road when the messenger approached the house. On observing me, he called me. His tale was meagre and imperfect, but the substance of it it was easy to gather. I stood for a moment motionless and aghast. As soon as I recovered my thoughts I set off full speed, and made not a moment's pause till I reached the house of Inglefield.

The circumstances of this mournful event, as I was able to collect them at different times, from the witnesses, were these. After they had parted from us, they proceeded on their way for some time without molestation. The clouds disappearing, the star-light enabled them with less difficulty to discern their path. They met not a human being till they came within less than three miles of the oak which I have before described. Here Miss Davis looked forward with some curiosity and said to her father, "Do you not see some one in the road before us? I saw him this moment move across from the fence on the right hand and stand still in the middle of the road."

"I see nothing, I must confess," said the father: "but that is no subject of wonder; your young eyes will of course see farther than my old ones."

"I see him clearly at this moment," rejoined the lady. "If he remain a short time where he is, or seems to be, we shall be able to ascertain his properties. Our horse's head will determine whether his substance be impassive or not."

The carriage slowly advancing, and the form remaining in the same spot, Mr. Davis at length percieved it, but was not allowed a clearer examination, for the person, having, as it seemed, ascertained the nature of the cavalcade, shot across the road, and disappeared. The behaviour of this unknown person furnished the travellers with a topic of abundant speculation.

Few possessed a firmer mind than Miss Davis; but whether she was assailed, on this occasion, with a mysterious foreboding of her destiny; whether the eloquence of my fears had not, in spite of resolution, infected her; or whether she imagined evils that my incautious temper might draw upon me, and which might originate in our late interview, certain it was that her spirits were visibly depressed. This accident made no sensible alteration in her. She was still disconsolate and incommunicative. All the efforts of her father were insufficient to inspire her with cheerfulness. He repeatedly questioned her as to the cause of this unwonted despondency. Her answer was, that her spirits were indeed depressed, but she believed that the circumstance was casual. She knew of nothing that could justify despondency. But such is humanity. Cheerfulness and dejection will take their turns in the best regulated bosoms, and come and go when they will, and not at the command of reason. This observation was succeeded by a pause. At length Mr. Davis said, "A thought has just occurred to me. The person whom we just now saw is young Althorpe."

Miss Davis was startled: "Why, my dear father, should you think so? It is too dark to judge, at this distance, by resemblance of figure. Ardent and rash as he appears to be, I should scarcely suspect him on this occasion. With all the fiery qualities of youth, unchastised by experience, untamed by adversity, he is capable no doubt of extravagant adventures, but what could induce him to act in this manner?"

"You know the fears that he expressed concerning the issue

of this night's journey. We know not what foundation he might have had for these fears. He told us of no danger that ought to deter us, but it is hard to conceive that he should have been thus vehement without cause. We know not what motives might have induced him to conceal from us the sources of his terror. And since he could not obtain our consent to his attending us, he has taken these means, perhaps, of effecting his purpose. The darkness might easily conceal him from our observation. He might have passed us without our noticing him, or he might have made a circuit in the woods we have just passed, and come out before us."

"That I own," replied the daughter, "is not improbable. If it be true, I shall be sorry for his own sake, but if there be any danger from which his attendance can secure us, I shall be well pleased for all our sakes. He will reflect with some satisfaction, perhaps, that he has done or intended us a service. It would be cruel to deny him a satisfaction so innocent."

"Pray, my dear, what think you of this young man? Does his ardour to serve us flow from a right source?"

"It flows, I have no doubt, from a double source. He has a kind heart, and delights to oblige others: but this is not all. He is likewise in love, and imagines that he cannot do too much for the object of his passion."

"Indeed!" exclaimed Mr. Davis, in some surprise. "You speak very positively. That is no more than it suspected; but how came you to know it with so much certainty?"

"The information came to me in the directest manner. He told me so himself."

"So ho! why, the impertinent young rogue!"

"Nay, my dear father, his behavior did not merit that epithet. He is rash and inconsiderate. That is the utmost amount of his guilt. A short absence will show him the true state of his feelings. It was unavoidable, in one of his character, to fall in love with the first woman whose appearance was in any degree specious. But attachments like these will be extinguished as easily as they are formed. I do not fear for him on this account."

"Have you reason to fear for him on any account?"

"Yes. The period of youth will soon pass away. Overweening and fickle, he will go on committing one mistake after another, incapable of repairing his errors, or of profiting by the daily lessons of experience. His genius will be merely an implement of mischief. His greater capacity will be evinced merely by the greater portion of unhappiness that, by means of it, will accrue to others or rebound upon himself."

"I see, my dear, that your spirits are low. Nothing else, surely, could suggest such melancholy presages. For my part, I question not, but he will one day be a fine fellow and a happy one. I like him exceedingly. I shall take pains to be acquainted with his future adventures, and do him all the good that I can."

"That intention," said his daughter, "is worthy of the goodness of your heart. He is no less an object of regard to me than to you. I trust I shall want neither the power nor inclination to contribute to his welfare. At present, however, his welfare will be best promoted by forgetting me. Hereafter, I shall solicit a renewal of intercourse."

"Speak lower," said the father. "If I mistake not, there is the same person again." He pointed to the field that skirted the road on the left hand. The young lady's better eyes enabled her to detect his mistake. It was the trunk of a cherry-tree that he had observed.

They proceeded in silence. Contrary to custom, the lady was buried in musing. Her father, whose temper and inclinations were moulded by those of his child, insensibly subsided into the same state.

The re-appearance of the same figure that had already excited their attention diverted them anew from their contemplations. "As I live," exclaimed Mr. Davis, "that thing, whatever it be, haunts us. I do not like it. This is strange conduct for young Althorpe to adopt. Instead of being our protector, the danger, against which he so pathetically warned us, may be, in some inscrutable way, connected with this personage. It is best to be upon our guard."

"Nay, my father," said the lady, "be not disturbed. What danger can be dreaded by two persons from one? This thing, I dare say, means us no harm. What is at present inexplicable might be obvious enough if we were better acquainted with this neighbourhood. It is not worth a thought. You see it is now gone." Mr. Davis looked again, but it was no longer discernible.

They were now approaching a wood. Mr. Davis called to the

guide to stop. His daughter enquired the reason of this command. She found it arose from his uncertainty as to the propriety of proceeding.

"I know not how it is," said he, "but I begin to be affected with the fears of young Althorpe. I am half resolved not to enter this wood.—That light yonder informs that a house is near. It may not be unadvisable to stop. I cannot think of delaying our journey till morning; but, by stopping a few minutes, we may possibly collect some useful information. Perhaps it will be expedient and practicable to procure the attendance of another person. I am not well pleased with myself for declining our young friend's offer."

To this proposal Miss Davis objected the inconveniences that calling at a farmer's house, at this time of night, when all were retired to rest, would probably occasion. "Besides," continued she, "the light which you saw is gone: a sufficient proof that it was nothing but a meteor."

At this moment they heard a noise, at a small distance behind them, as of shutting a gate. They called. Speedily an answer was returned in a tone of mildness. The person approached the chaise, and enquired who they were, whence they came, whither they were going, and, lastly, what they wanted.

Mr. Davis explained to this inquisitive person, in a few words, the nature of their situation, mentioned the appearance on the road, and questioned him, in his turn, as to what inconveniences were to be feared from prosecuting his journey. Satisfactory answers were returned to these enquiries.

"As to what you seed in the road," continued he, "I reckon it was nothing but a sheep or a cow. I am not more scary than some folks, but I never goes out a' nights without I sees some *sich* thing as that, that I takes for a man or woman, and am scared a little oftentimes, but not much. I'm sure after to find that it's not nothing but a cow, or hog, or tree, or something. If it wasn't some sich thing you seed, I reckon it was *Nick Handyside*."

"Nick Handyside! who was he?"

"It was a fellow that went about the country a' nights. A shocking fool to be sure, that loved to plague and frighten people. Yes. Yes. It couldn't be nobody, he reckoned, but Nick.

Nick was a droll thing. He wondered they'd never heard of Nick. He reckoned they were strangers in these here parts."

"Very true, my friend. But who is Nick? Is he a reptile to be shunned, or trampled on?"

"Why I don't know how as that. Nick is an odd soul to be sure; but he don't do nobody no harm, as ever I heard, except by scaring them. He is easily skeart though, for that matter, himself. He loves to frighten folks, but he's shocking apt to be frightened himself. I reckon you took Nick for a ghost. That's a shocking good story, I declare. Yet it's happened hundreds and hundreds of times, I guess, and more."

When this circumstance was mentioned, my uncle, as well as myself, was astonished at our own negligence. While enumerating, on the preceding evening, the obstacles and inconveniences which the travellers were likely to encounter, we entirely and unaccountably overlooked one circumstance, from which inquietude might reasonably have been expected. Near the spot where they now were, lived a Mr. Handyside, whose only son was an idiot. He also merited the name of monster, if a projecting breast, a mis-shapen head, features horrid and distorted, and a voice that resembled nothing that was ever before heard, could entitle him to that appellation. This being, besides the natural deformity of his frame, wore looks and practised gesticulations that were, in an inconceivable degree, uncouth and hideous. He was mischievous, but his freaks were subjects of little apprehension to those who were accustomed to them, though they were frequently occasions of alarm to strangers. He particularly delighted in imposing on the ignorance of strangers and the timidity of women. He was a perpetual rover. Entirely bereft of reason, his sole employment consisted in sleeping, and eating, and roaming. He would frequently escape at night, and a thousand anecdotes could have been detailed respecting the tricks which Nick Handyside had played upon way-farers.

Other considerations, however, had, in this instance, so much engrossed our minds, that Nick Handyside had never been once thought of or mentioned. This was the more remarkable, as there had very lately happened an adventure, in which this person had acted a principal part. He had wandered from home, and got bewildered in a desolate tract, known by the name of Norwood. It was a region, rude, sterile, and lonely, bestrewn with rocks, and embarrassed with bushes.

He had remained for some days in this wilderness. Unable to extricate himself, and, at length, tormented with hunger, he manifested his distress by the most doleful shrieks. These were uttered with most vehemence, and heard at greatest distance, by night. At first, those who heard them were panic-struck; but, at length, they furnished a clue by which those who were in search of him were guided to the spot. Notwithstanding the recentness and singularity of this adventure, and the probability that our guests would suffer molestation from this cause, so strangely forgetful had we been, that no caution on this head had been given. This caution, indeed, as the event testified, would have been superfluous, and yet I cannot enough wonder that in hunting for some reason, by which I might justify my fears to them or to myself, I had totally overlooked this mischief-loving idiot.

After listening to an ample description of Nick, being warned to proceed with particular caution in a part of the road that was near at hand, and being assured that they had nothing to dread from human interference, they resumed their journey with new confidence.

Their attention was frequently excited by rustling leaves or stumbling footsteps, and the figure which they doubted not to belong to Nick Handyside, occasionally hovered in their sight. This appearance no longer inspired them with apprehension. They had been assured that a stern voice was sufficient to repulse him, when most importunate. This antic being treated all others as children. He took pleasure in the effects which the sight of his own deformity produced, and betokened his satisfaction by a laugh, which might have served as a model to the poet who has depicted the ghastly risibilities of Death. On this occasion, however, the monster behaved with unusual moderation. He never came near enough for his peculiarities to be distinguished by star-light. There was nothing fantastic in his motions, nor any thing surprising, but the celerity of his transitions. They were unaccompanied by those howls, which reminded you at one time of a troop of hungry wolves, and had, at another, something in them inexpressibly wild and melancholy. This monster possessed a certain species of dexterity. His

talents, differently applied, would have excited rational admiration. He was fleet as a deer. He was patient, to an incredible degree, of watchfulness, and cold, and hunger. He had improved
the flexibility of his voice, till his cries, always loud and rueful,
were capable of being diversified without end. Instances had
been known, in which the stoutest heart was appalled by them;
and some, particularly in the case of women, in which they had
been productive of consequences truly deplorable.

When the travellers had arrived at that part of the wood
where, as they had been informed, it was needful to be particularly cautious, Mr. Davis, for their greater security, proposed
to his daughter to alight. The exercise of walking, he thought,
after so much time spent in a close carriage, would be salutary
and pleasant. The young lady readily embraced the proposal.
They forthwith alighted, and walked at a small distance before
the chaise, which was now conducted by the servant. From this
moment the spectre, which, till now, had been occasionally visible, entirely disappeared. This incident naturally led the conversation to this topic. So singular a specimen of the forms which
human nature is found to assume could not fail of suggesting a
variety of remarks.

They pictured to themselves many combinations of circumstances in which Handyside might be the agent, and in which
the most momentous effects might flow from his agency, without its being possible for others to conjecture the true nature
of the agent. The propensities of this being might contribute to
realize, on an American road, many of those imaginary tokens
and perils which abound in the wildest romance. He would be
an admirable machine, in a plan whose purpose was to generate or foster, in a given subject, the frenzy of quixotism.—No
theatre was better adapted than Norwood to such an exhibition. This part of the country had long been deserted by beasts
of prey. Bears might still, perhaps, be found during a very rigorous season, but wolves which, when the country was a desert,
were extremely numerous, had now, in consequence of increasing population, withdrawn to more savage haunts. Yet the
voice of Handyside, varied with the force and skill of which he
was known to be capable, would fill these shades with outcries
as ferocious as those which are to be heard in Siamese or Abys-
sinian forests. The tale of his recent elopement had been told

by the man with whom they had just parted, in a rustic but picturesque style.

"But why," said the lady, "did not our kind host inform us of this circumstance? He must surely have been well acquainted with the existence and habits of this Handyside. He must have perceived to how many groundless alarms our ignorance, in this respect, was likely to expose us. It is strange that he did not afford us the slightest intimation of it."

Mr. Davis was no less surprised at this omission. He was at a loss to conceive how this should be forgotten in the midst of those minute directions, in which every cause had been laboriously recollected from which he might incur danger or suffer obstruction.

This person, being no longer an object of terror, began to be regarded with a very lively curiosity. They even wished for his appearance and near approach, that they might carry away with them more definite conceptions of his figure. The lady declared she should be highly pleased by hearing his outcries, and consoled herself with the belief, that he would not allow them to pass the limits which he had prescribed to his wanderings, without greeting them with a strain or two. This wish had scarcely been uttered, when it was completely gratified.

The lady involuntarily started, and caught hold of her father's arm. Mr. Davis himself was disconcerted. A scream, dismally loud, and piercingly shrill, was uttered by one at less than twenty paces from them.

The monster had shown some skill in the choice of a spot suitable to his design. Neighbouring precipices, and a thick umbrage of oaks, on either side, contributed to prolong and to heighten his terrible notes. They were rendered more awful by the profound stillness that preceded and followed them. They were able speedily to quiet the trepidations which this hideous outcry, in spite of preparation and foresight, had produced, but they had not foreseen one of its unhappy consequences.

In a moment Mr. Davis was alarmed by the rapid sound of footsteps behind him. His presence of mind, on this occasion, probably saved himself and his daughter from instant destruction. He leaped out of the path, and, by a sudden exertion, at the same moment, threw the lady to some distance from the tract. The horse that drew the chaise rushed by them with the celerity of lightning. Affrighted at the sounds which had been uttered at a still less distance from the horse than from Mr. Davis, possibly with a malicious design to produce this very effect, he jerked the bridle from the hands that held it, and rushed forward with headlong speed. The man, before he could provide for his own safety, was beaten to the earth. He was considerably bruised by the fall, but presently recovered his feet, and went in pursuit of the horse.

This accident happened at about a hundred yards from the *oak*, against which so many cautions had been given. It was not possible, at any time, without considerable caution, to avoid it. It was not to be wondered at, therefore, that, in a few seconds, the carriage was shocked against the trunk, overturned, and dashed into a thousand fragments. The noise of the crash sufficiently informed them of this event. Had the horse been inclined to stop, a repetition, for the space of some minutes, of the same savage and terrible shrieks would have added tenfold to his consternation and to the speed of his flight. After this dismal strain had ended, Mr. Davis raised his daughter from the ground. She had suffered no material injury. As soon as they recovered from the confusion into which this accident had thrown them, they began to consult upon the measures proper to be taken upon this emergency. They were left alone. The servant had gone in pursuit of the flying horse. Whether he would be able to retake him was extremely dubious. Meanwhile they were surrounded by darkness. What was the distance of the next house could not be known. At that hour of the night they could not hope to be directed, by the far-seen taper, to any hospitable roof. The only alternative, therefore, was to remain where they were, uncertain of the fate of their companion, or to go forward with the utmost expedition.

They could not hesitate to embrace the latter. In a few minutes they arrived at the oak. The chaise appeared to have been dashed against a knotty projecture of the trunk, which was large enough for a person to be conveniently seated on it. Here they again paused.—Miss Davis desired to remain here a few minutes to recruit her exhausted strength. She proposed to her father to leave her here, and go forward in quest of the horse and the servant. He might return as speedily as he thought proper. She did not fear to be alone. The voice was still. Having accomplished his malicious purposes, the spectre had probably taken his final leave of them. At all events, if the report of the rustic was true, she had no personal injury to fear from him.

Through some deplorable infatuation, as he afterwards deemed it, Mr. Davis complied with her intreaties, and went in search of the missing. He had engaged in a most unpromising undertaking. The man and horse were by this time at a considerable distance. The former would, no doubt, shortly return. Whether his pursuit succeeded or miscarried, he would surely see the propriety of hastening his return with what tidings he could obtain, and to ascertain his master's situation. Add to this, the impropriety of leaving a woman, single and unarmed, to the machinations of this demoniac. He had scarcely parted with her when these reflections occurred to him. His resolution was changed. He turned back with the intention of immediately seeking her. At the same moment, he saw the flash and heard the discharge of a pistol. The light proceeded from the foot of the oak. His imagination was filled with horrible forebodings. He ran with all his speed to the spot. He called aloud upon the name of his daughter, but, alas! she was unable to answer him. He found her stretched at the foot of the tree, senseless, and weltering in her blood. He lifted her in his arms, and seated her against the trunk. He found himself stained with blood, flowing from a wound, which either the darkness of the night, or the confusion of his thoughts, hindered him from tracing. Overwhelmed with a catastrophe so dreadful and unexpected, he was divested of all presence of mind. The author of his calamity had vanished. No human being was at hand to succour him in his uttermost distress. He beat his head against the ground, tore away his venerable locks, and rent the air with his cries.

Fortunately there was a dwelling at no great distance from this scene. The discharge of a pistol produces a sound too loud not to be heard far and wide, in this lonely region. This house belonged to a physician. He was a man noted for his humanity and sympathy. He was roused, as well as most of his family, by a sound so uncommon. He rose instantly, and calling up his people proceeded with lights to the road. The lamentations of Mr. Davis directed them to the place. To the physician the scene was inexplicable. Who was the author of this distress; by

whom the pistol was discharged; whether through some untoward chance or with design, he was as yet uninformed, nor
could he gain any information from the incoherent despair of
Mr. Davis.

Every measure that humanity and professional skill could
suggest were employed on this occasion. The dying lady was
removed to the house. The ball had lodged in her brain, and
to extract it was impossible. Why should I dwell on the remaining incidents of this tale? She languished till the next
morning, and then expired.

1805

WASHINGTON IRVING

(1783–1859)

The Adventure of the German Student

On a stormy night, in the tempestuous times of the French revolution, a young German was returning to his lodgings, at a late hour, across the old part of Paris. The lightning gleamed, and the loud claps of thunder rattled through the lofty, narrow streets—but I should first tell you something about this young German.

Gottfried Wolfgang was a young man of good family. He had studied for some time at Göttingen, but being of a visionary and enthusiastic character, he had wandered into those wild and speculative doctrines which have so often bewildered German students. His secluded life, his intense application, and the singular nature of his studies, had an effect on both mind and body. His health was impaired; his imagination diseased. He had been indulging in fanciful speculations on spiritual essences until, like Swedenborg, he had an ideal world of his own around him. He took up a notion, I do not know from what cause, that there was an evil influence hanging over him; an evil genius or spirit seeking to ensnare him and ensure his perdition. Such an idea working on his melancholy temperament produced the most gloomy effects. He became haggard and desponding. His friends discovered the mental malady preying upon him, and determined that the best cure was a change of scene; he was sent, therefore, to finish his studies amidst the splendours and gaieties of Paris.

Wolfgang arrived at Paris at the breaking out of the revolution. The popular delirium at first caught his enthusiastic mind, and he was captivated by the political and philosophical theories of the day: but the scenes of blood which followed shocked his sensitive nature; disgusted him with society and the world, and made him more than ever a recluse. He shut himself up in a solitary apartment in the *Pays Latin*, the quarter of students. There in a gloomy street not far from the monastic walls of the Sorbonne, he pursued his favourite speculations. Sometimes he spent hours together in the great libraries of Paris, those catacombs of departed authors, rummaging among their hoards of dusty and obsolete works in quest of food for his unhealthy appetite. He was, in a manner, a literary goul, feeding in the charnel house of decayed literature.

Wolfgang, though solitary and recluse, was of an ardent temperament, but for a time it operated merely upon his imagination. He was too shy and ignorant of the world to make any advances to the fair, but he was a passionate admirer of female beauty, and in his lonely chamber would often lose himself in reveries on forms and faces which he had seen, and his fancy would deck out images of loveliness far surpassing the reality.

While his mind was in this excited and sublimated state, a dream produced an extraordinary effect upon him. It was of a female face of transcendent beauty. So strong was the impression made, that he dreamt of it again and again. It haunted his thoughts by day, his slumbers by night; in fine, he became passionately enamoured of this shadow of a dream. This lasted so long, that it became one of those fixed ideas which haunt the minds of melancholy men, and are at times mistaken for madness.

Such was Gottfried Wolfgang, and such his situation at the time I mentioned. He was returning home late one stormy night, through some of the old and gloomy streets of the *Marais*, the ancient part of Paris. The loud claps of thunder rattled among the high houses of the narrow streets. He came to the Place de Grève, the square where public executions are performed. The lightning quivered about the pinnacles of the ancient Hôtel de Ville, and shed flickering gleams over the open space in front. As Wolfgang was crossing the square, he shrank back with horror at finding himself close by the guillotine. It was the height of the reign of terror, when this dreadful instrument of death stood ever ready, and its scaffold was continually running with the blood of the virtuous and the brave. It had that very day been actively employed in the work of carnage, and there it stood in grim array amidst a silent and sleeping city, waiting for fresh victims.

Wolfgang's heart sickened within him, and he was turning

shuddering from the horrible engine, when he beheld a shadowy form cowering as it were at the foot of the steps which led up to the scaffold. A succession of vivid flashes of lightning revealed it more distinctly. It was a female figure, dressed in black. She was seated on one of the lower steps of the scaffold, leaning forward, her face hid in her lap, and her long dishevelled tresses hanging to the ground, streaming with the rain which fell in torrents. Wolfgang paused. There was something awful in this solitary monument of wo. The female had the appearance of being above the common order. He knew the times to be full of vicissitude, and that many a fair head, which had once been pillowed on down, now wandered houseless. Perhaps this was some poor mourner whom the dreadful axe had rendered desolate, and who sat here heartbroken on the strand of existence, from which all that was dear to her had been launched into eternity.

He approached, and addressed her in the accents of sympathy. She raised her head and gazed wildly at him. What was his astonishment at beholding, by the bright glare of the lightning, the very face which had haunted him in his dreams. It was pale and disconsolate, but ravishingly beautiful.

Trembling with violent and conflicting emotions, Wolfgang again accosted her. He spoke something of her being exposed at such an hour of the night, and to the fury of such a storm, and offered to conduct her to her friends. She pointed to the guillotine with a gesture of dreadful signification.

"I have no friend on earth!" said she.

"But you have a home," said Wolfgang.

"Yes—in the grave!"

The heart of the student melted at the words.

"If a stranger dare make an offer," said he, "without danger of being misunderstood, I would offer my humble dwelling as a shelter; myself as a devoted friend. I am friendless myself in Paris, and a stranger in the land; but if my life could be of service, it is at your disposal, and should be sacrificed before harm or indignity should come to you."

There was an honest earnestness in the young man's manner that had its effect. His foreign accent, too, was in his favour; it showed him not to be a hackneyed inhabitant of Paris. Indeed there is an eloquence in true enthusiasm that is not to be doubted. The homeless stranger confided herself implicitly to the protection of the student.

He supported her faltering steps across the Pont Neuf, and by the place where the statue of Henry the Fourth had been overthrown by the populace. The storm had abated, and the thunder rumbled at a distance. All Paris was quiet; that great volcano of human passion slumbered for a while, to gather fresh strength for the next day's eruption. The student conducted his charge through the ancient streets of the *Pays Latin*, and by the dusky walls of the Sorbonne to the great, dingy hotel which he inhabited. The old portress who admitted them stared with surprise at the unusual sight of the melancholy Wolfgang with a female companion.

On entering his apartment, the student, for the first time, blushed at the scantiness and indifference of his dwelling. He had but one chamber—an old fashioned saloon—heavily carved and fantastically furnished with the remains of former magnificence, for it was one of those hotels in the quarter of the Luxembourg palace which had once belonged to nobility. It was lumbered with books and papers, and all the usual apparatus of a student, and his bed stood in a recess at one end.

When lights were brought, and Wolfgang had a better opportunity of contemplating the stranger, he was more than ever intoxicated by her beauty. Her face was pale, but of a dazzling fairness, set off by a profusion of raven hair that hung clustering about it. Her eyes were large and brilliant, with a singular expression approaching almost to wildness. As far as her black dress permitted her shape to be seen, it was of perfect symmetry. Her whole appearance was highly striking, though she was dressed in the simplest style. The only thing approaching to an ornament which she wore was a broad, black band round her neck, clasped by diamonds.

The perplexity now commenced with the student how to dispose of the helpless being thus thrown upon his protection. He thought of abandoning his chamber to her, and seeking shelter for himself elsewhere. Still he was so fascinated by her charms, there seemed to be such a spell upon his thoughts and senses, that he could not tear himself from her presence. Her manner, too, was singular and unaccountable. She spoke no more of the guillotine. Her grief had abated. The attentions of the student had first won her confidence, and then, apparently, her heart. She was evidently an enthusiast like himself, and enthusiasts soon understand each other.

In the infatuation of the moment Wolfgang avowed his passion for her. He told her the story of his mysterious dream, and how she had possessed his heart before he had even seen her. She was strangely affected by his recital, and acknowledged to have felt an impulse towards him equally unaccountable. It was the time for wild theory and wild actions. Old prejudices and superstitions were done away; every thing was under the sway of the "Goddess of Reason." Among other rubbish of the old times, the forms and ceremonies of marriage began to be considered superfluous bonds for honourable minds. Social compacts were the vogue. Wolfgang was too much of a theorist not to be tainted by the liberal doctrines of the day.

"Why should we separate?" said he: "our hearts are united; in the eye of reason and honour we are as one. What need is there of sordid forms to bind high souls together?"

The stranger listened with emotion: she had evidently received illumination at the same school.

"You have no home nor family," continued he; "let me be every thing to you, or rather let us be every thing to one another. If form is necessary, form shall be observed—there is my hand. I pledge myself to you for ever."

"For ever?" said the stranger, solemnly.

"For ever!" repeated Wolfgang.

The stranger clasped the hand extended to her: "Then I am yours," murmured she, and sank upon his bosom.

The next morning the student left his bride sleeping, and sallied forth at an early hour to seek more spacious apartments, suitable to the change in his situation. When he returned, he found the stranger lying with her head hanging over the bed, and one arm thrown over it. He spoke to her, but received no reply. He advanced to awaken her from her uneasy posture. On taking her hand, it was cold—there was no pulsation—her face was pallid and ghastly.—In a word—she was a corpse.

Horrified and frantic, he alarmed the house. A scene of confusion ensued. The police was summoned. As the officer of police entered the room, he started back on beholding the corpse.

"Great heaven!" cried he, "how did this woman come here?"

"Do you know any thing about her?" said Wolfgang, eagerly.

"Do I?" exclaimed the police officer: "she was guillotined yesterday!"

He stepped forward; undid the black collar round the neck of the corpse, and the head rolled on the floor!

The student burst into a frenzy. "The fiend! the fiend has gained possession of me!" shrieked he: "I am lost for ever!"

They tried to soothe him, but in vain. He was possessed with the frightful belief that an evil spirit had reanimated the dead body to ensnare him. He went distracted, and died in a madhouse.

———

Here the old gentleman with the haunted head finished his narrative.

"And is this really a fact?" said the inquisitive gentleman.

"A fact not to be doubted," replied the other. "I had it from the best authority. The student told it me himself. I saw him in a madhouse at Paris."

1824

EDGAR ALLAN POE

(1809–1849)

Berenice

Dicebant mihi sodales, si sepulchrum amicae, visitarem,
curas meas aliquantulum fore levatas.—Ebn Zaiat

Misery is manifold. The wretchedness of earth is multiform.
Overreaching the wide horizon as the rainbow, its hues are as
various as the hues of that arch,—as distinct too, yet as intimately blended. Overreaching the wide horizon as the rainbow!
How is it that from beauty I have derived a type of unloveliness?
—from the covenant of peace a simile of sorrow? But as, in
ethics, evil is a consequence of good, so, in fact, out of joy is
sorrow born. Either the memory of past bliss is the anguish of
to-day, or the agonies which *are* have their origin in the ec-
stasies which *might have been.*

My baptismal name is Egæus; that of my family I will not mention. Yet there are no towers in the land more time-honored
than my gloomy, gray, hereditary halls. Our line has been called
a race of visionaries; and in many striking particulars—in the
character of the family mansion—in the frescos of the chief
saloon—in the tapestries of the dormitories—in the chiselling of
some butresses in the armory—but more especially in the gallery
of antique paintings—in the fashion of the library chamber—
and, lastly, in the very peculiar nature of the library's contents,
there is more than sufficient evidence to warrant the belief.

The recollections of my earliest years are connected with that
chamber, and with its volumes—of which latter I will say no
more. Here died my mother. Herein was I born. But it is mere
idleness to say that I had not lived before—that the soul has no
previous existence. You deny it?—let us not argue the matter.
Convinced myself, I seek not to convince. There is, however, a
remembrance of aërial forms—of spiritual and meaning eyes—
of sounds, musical yet sad—a remembrance which will not be
excluded; a memory like a shadow, vague, variable, indefinite,

27

unsteady; and like a shadow, too, in the impossibility of my getting rid of it while the sunlight of my reason shall exist.

In that chamber was I born. Thus awaking from the long night of what seemed, but was not, nonentity, at once into the very regions of fairy-land—into a palace of imagination—into the wild dominions of monastic thought and erudition—it is not singular that I gazed around me with a startled and ardent eye —that I loitered away my boyhood in books, and dissipated my youth in reverie; but it *is* singular that as years rolled away, and the noon of manhood found me still in the mansion of my fathers—it *is* wonderful what stagnation there fell upon the springs of my life—wonderful how total an inversion took place in the character of my commonest thought. The realities of the world affected me as visions, and as visions only, while the wild ideas of the land of dreams became, in turn,—not the material of my everyday existence—but in very deed that existence utterly and solely in itself.

Berenice and I were cousins, and we grew up together in my paternal halls. Yet differently we grew—I ill of health and buried in gloom—she agile, graceful, and overflowing with energy— hers the ramble on the hill-side—mine the studies of the cloister —I living within my own heart, and addicted body and soul to the most intense and painful meditation—she roaming carelessly through life with no thought of the shadows in her path, or the silent flight of the raven-winged hours. Berenice!—I call upon her name—Berenice!—and from the gray ruins of memory a thousand tumultuous recollections are startled at the sound! Ah! vividly is her image before me now, as in the early days of her light-heartedness and joy! Oh! gorgeous yet fantastic beauty! Oh! sylph amid the shrubberies of Arnheim!—Oh! Naiad among its fountains!—and then—then all is mystery and terror, and a tale which should not be told. Disease—a fatal disease—fell like the simoom upon her frame, and, even while I gazed upon her, the spirit of change swept over her, pervading her mind, her habits, and her character, and, in a manner the most subtle and terrible, disturbing even the identity of her person! Alas! the destroyer came and went, and the victim— where was she? I knew her not—or knew her no longer as Berenice.

Among the numerous train of maladies superinduced by that fatal and primary one which effected a revolution of so horrible a kind in the moral and physical being of my cousin, may be mentioned as the most distressing and obstinate in its nature, a species of epilepsy not unfrequently terminating in *trance* itself—trance very nearly resembling positive dissolution, and from which her manner of recovery was, in most instances, startlingly abrupt. In the mean time my own disease— for I have been told that I should call it by no other appellation —my own disease, then, grew rapidly upon me, and assumed finally a monomaniac character of a novel and extraordinary form—hourly and momently gaining vigor—and at length obtaining over me the most incomprehensible ascendancy. This monomania, if I must so term it, consisted in a morbid irritability of those properties of the mind in metaphysical science termed the *attentive*. It is more than probable that I am not understood; but I fear, indeed, that it is in no manner possible to convey to the mind of the merely general reader, an adequate idea of that nervous *intensity of interest* with which, in my case, the powers of meditation (not to speak technically) busied and buried themselves, in the contemplation of even the most ordinary objects of the universe.

To muse for long unwearied hours with my attention riveted to some frivolous device on the margin, or in the typography of a book; to become absorbed for the better part of a summer's day in a quaint shadow falling aslant upon the tapestry, or upon the floor; to lose myself for an entire night in watching the steady flame of a lamp, or the embers of a fire; to dream away whole days over the perfume of a flower; to repeat monotonously some common word, until the sound, by dint of frequent repetition, ceased to convey any idea whatever to the mind; to lose all sense of motion or physical existence, by means of absolute bodily quiescence long and obstinately persevered in:—such were a few of the most common and least pernicious vagaries induced by a condition of the mental faculties, not, indeed, altogether unparalleled, but certainly bidding defiance to anything like analysis or explanation.

Yet let me not be misapprehended.—The undue, earnest, and morbid attention thus excited by objects in their own nature frivolous, must not be confounded in character with that

ruminating propensity common to all mankind, and more especially indulged in by persons of ardent imagination. It was
not even, as might be at first supposed, an extreme condition,
or exaggeration of such propensity, but primarily and essentially distinct and different. In the one instance, the dreamer, or
enthusiast, being interested by an object usually *not* frivolous,
imperceptibly loses sight of this object in a wilderness of de-
ductions and suggestions issuing therefrom, until, at the conclusion of a day dream *often replete with luxury*, he finds the
incitamentum or first cause of his musings entirely vanished
and forgotten. In my case the primary object was *invariably
frivolous*, although assuming, through the medium of my dis-
tempered vision, a refracted and unreal importance. Few de-
ductions, if any, were made; and those few pertinaciously
returning in upon the original object as a centre. The meditations were *never* pleasurable; and, at the termination of the
reverie, the first cause, so far from being out of sight, had attained that supernaturally exaggerated interest which was the
prevailing feature of the disease. In a word, the powers of mind
more particularly exercised were, with me, as I have said before,
the *attentive*, and are, with the day-dreamer, the *speculative*.

My books, at this epoch, if they did not actually serve to irritate the disorder, partook, it will be perceived, largely, in their
imaginative and inconsequential nature, of the characteristic
qualities of the disorder itself. I well remember, among others,
the treatise of the noble Italian Cœlius Secundus Curio "*de
Amplitudine Beati Regni Dei*;" St. Austin's great work, the
"City of God;" and Tertullian "*de Carne Christi*," in which
the paradoxical sentence "*Mortuus est Dei filius; credibile est
quia ineptum est; et sepultus resurrexit; certum est quia impossibile est*" occupied my undivided time, for many weeks of laborious and fruitless investigation.

Thus it will appear that, shaken from its balance only by trivial
things, my reason bore resemblance to that ocean-crag spoken
of by Ptolemy Hephestion, which steadily resisting the attacks
of human violence, and the fiercer fury of the waters and the
winds, trembled only to the touch of the flower called Asphodel.
And although, to a careless thinker, it might appear a matter
beyond doubt, that the alteration produced by her unhappy
malady, in the *moral* condition of Berenice, would afford me

many objects for the exercise of that intense and abnormal meditation whose nature I have been at some trouble in explaining, yet such was not in any degree the case. In the lucid intervals of my infirmity, her calamity, indeed, gave me pain, and, taking deeply to heart that total wreck of her fair and gentle life, I did not fail to ponder frequently and bitterly upon the wonder-working means by which so strange a revolution had been so suddenly brought to pass. But these reflections partook not of the idiosyncrasy of my disease, and were such as would have occurred, under similar circumstances, to the ordinary mass of mankind. True to its own character, my disorder revelled in the less important but more startling changes wrought in the *physical* frame of Berenice—in the singular and most appalling distortion of her personal identity.

During the brightest days of her unparalleled beauty, most surely I had never loved her. In the strange anomaly of my existence, feelings with me, *had never been* of the heart, and my passions *always were* of the mind. Through the gray of the early morning—among the trellissed shadows of the forest at noonday—and in the silence of my library at night, she had flitted by my eyes, and I had seen her—not as the living and breathing Berenice, but as the Berenice of a dream—not as a being of the earth, earthy, but as the abstraction of such a being—not as a thing to admire, but to analyze—not as an object of love, but as the theme of the most abstruse although desultory speculation. And *now*—now I shuddered in her presence, and grew pale at her approach; yet bitterly lamenting her fallen and desolate condition, I called to mind that she had loved me long, and, in an evil moment, I spoke to her of marriage.

And at length the period of our nuptials was approaching, when, upon an afternoon in the winter of the year,—one of those unseasonably warm, calm, and misty days which are the nurse of the beautiful Halcyon,*—I sat, (and sat, as I thought, alone,) in the inner apartment of the library. But uplifting my eyes I saw that Berenice stood before me.

Was it my own excited imagination—or the misty influence of the atmosphere—or the uncertain twilight of the chamber—or

---

*For as Jove, during the winter season, gives twice seven days of warmth, men have called this clement and temperate time the nurse of the beautiful Halcyon.—*Simonides.*

the gray draperies which fell around her figure—that caused in it so vacillating and indistinct an outline? I could not tell. She spoke no word, and I—not for worlds could I have uttered a syllable. An icy chill ran through my frame; a sense of insufferable anxiety oppressed me; a consuming curiosity pervaded my soul; and sinking back upon the chair, I remained for some time breathless and motionless, with my eyes riveted upon her person. Alas! its emaciation was excessive, and not one vestige of the former being, lurked in any single line of the contour. My burning glances at length fell upon the face.

The forehead was high, and very pale, and singularly placid; and the once jetty hair fell partially over it, and overshadowed the hollow temples with innumerable ringlets now of a vivid yellow, and jarring discordantly, in their fantastic character, with the reigning melancholy of the countenance. The eyes were lifeless, and lustreless, and seemingly pupil-less, and I shrank involuntarily from their glassy stare to the contemplation of the thin and shrunken lips. They parted; and in a smile of peculiar meaning, *the teeth* of the changed Berenice disclosed themselves slowly to my view. Would to God that I had never beheld them, or that, having done so, I had died!

The shutting of a door disturbed me, and, looking up, I found that my cousin had departed from the chamber. But from the disordered chamber of my brain, had not, alas! departed, and would not be driven away, the white and ghastly *spectrum* of the teeth. Not a speck on their surface—not a shade on their enamel—not an indenture in their edges—but what that brief period of her smile had sufficed to brand in upon my memory. I saw them now even more unequivocally than I beheld them *then*. The teeth!—the teeth!—they were here, and there, and every where, and visibly and palpably before me; long, narrow, and excessively white, with the pale lips writhing about them, as in the very moment of their first terrible development. Then came the full fury of my *monomania*, and I struggled in vain against its strange and irresistible influence. In the multiplied objects of the external world I had no thoughts but for the teeth. For these I longed with a phrenzied desire. All other matters and all different interests became absorbed in their single contemplation. They—they alone were present to the mental eye, and they, in their sole individuality, became the essence of my mental life. I held them in every light. I turned them in every attitude. I surveyed their characteristics. I dwelt upon their peculiarities. I pondered upon their conformation. I mused upon the alteration in their nature. I shuddered as I assigned to them in imagination a sensitive and sentient power, and even when unassisted by the lips, a capability of moral expression. Of Mad'selle Sallé it has been well said, "*que tous ses pas etaient des sentiments*," and of Berenice I more seriously believed *que tous ses dents etaient des idées. Des idées!*—ah here was the idiotic thought that destroyed me! *Des idées!*—ah *therefore* it was that I coveted them so madly! I felt that their possession could alone ever restore me to peace, in giving me back to reason.

And the evening closed in upon me thus—and then the darkness came, and tarried, and went—and the day again dawned—and the mists of a second night were now gathering around—and still I sat motionless in that solitary room, and still I sat buried in meditation, and still the *phantasma* of the teeth maintained its terrible ascendancy as, with the most vivid and hideous distinctness, it floated about amid the changing lights and shadows of the chamber. At length there broke in upon my dreams a cry as of horror and dismay; and thereunto, after a pause, succeeded the sound of troubled voices, intermingled with many low moanings of sorrow, or of pain. I arose from my seat, and, throwing open one of the doors of the library, saw standing out in the antechamber a servant maiden, all in tears, who told me that Berenice was—no more. She had been seized with epilepsy in the early morning, and now, at the closing in of the night, the grave was ready for its tenant, and all the preparations for the burial were completed.

I found myself sitting in the library, and again sitting there alone. It seemed that I had newly awakened from a confused and exciting dream. I knew that it was now midnight, and I was well aware that since the setting of the sun Berenice had been interred. But of that dreary period which intervened I had no positive—at least no definite comprehension. Yet its memory was replete with horror—horror more horrible from being vague, and terror more terrible from ambiguity. It was a fearful page in the record of my existence, written all over with dim, and hideous, and unintelligible recollections. I strived to de-cypher them, but in vain; while ever and anon, like the spirit of a departed sound, the shrill and piercing shriek of a female voice seemed to be ringing in my ears. I had done a deed—what was it? I asked myself the question aloud, and the whis-pering echoes of the chamber answered me, "*what was it?*"

On the table beside me burned a lamp, and near it lay a little box. It was of no remarkable character, and I had seen it fre-quently before, for it was the property of the family physician; but how came it *there*, upon my table, and why did I shudder in regarding it? These things were in no manner to be ac-counted for, and my eyes at length dropped to the open pages of a book, and to a sentence underscored therein. The words were the singular but simple ones of the poet Ebn Zaiat. "*Dice-bant mihi sodales si sepulchrum amicae visitarem, curas meas aliquantulum fore levatas.*" Why then, as I perused them, did the hairs of my head erect themselves on end, and the blood of my body become congealed within my veins?

There came a light tap at the library door, and pale as the tenant of a tomb, a menial entered upon tiptoe. His looks were wild with terror, and he spoke to me in a voice tremulous, husky, and very low. What said he?—some broken sentences I heard. He told of a wild cry disturbing the silence of the night—of the gathering together of the household—of a search in the di-rection of the sound;—and then his tones grew thrillingly dis-tinct as he whispered me of a violated grave—of a disfigured body enshrouded, yet still breathing, still palpitating, *still alive!*

He pointed to my garments;—they were muddy and clotted with gore. I spoke not, and he took me gently by the hand;—it was indented with the impress of human nails. He directed my attention to some object against the wall;—I looked at it for some minutes;—it was a spade. With a shriek I bounded to the table, and grasped the box that lay upon it. But I could not force it open; and in my tremor it slipped from my hands, and fell heavily, and burst into pieces; and from it, with a rattling sound, there rolled out some instruments of dental surgery, in-termingled with thirty-two small, white and ivory-looking sub-stances that were scattered to and fro about the floor.

1835

NATHANIEL HAWTHORNE

(1804–1864)

Young Goodman Brown

YOUNG GOODMAN BROWN came forth, at sunset, into the
street of Salem village, but put his head back, after crossing the
threshold, to exchange a parting kiss with his young wife. And
Faith, as the wife was aptly named, thrust her own pretty head
into the street, letting the wind play with the pink ribbons of her
cap, while she called to Goodman Brown.

'Dearest heart,' whispered she, softly and rather sadly, when
her lips were close to his ear, 'pr'y thee, put off your journey
until sunrise, and sleep in your own bed to-night. A lone woman
is troubled with such dreams and such thoughts, that she's
afeard of herself, sometimes. Pray, tarry with me this night,
dear husband, of all nights in the year!'

'My love and my Faith,' replied young Goodman Brown, 'of
all nights in the year, this one night must I tarry away from thee.
My journey, as thou callest it, forth and back again, must needs
be done 'twixt now and sunrise. What, my sweet, pretty wife,
dost thou doubt me already, and we but three months married!'

'Then, God bless you!' said Faith, with the pink ribbons,
'and may you find all well, when you come back.'

'Amen!' cried Goodman Brown. 'Say thy prayers, dear
Faith, and go to bed at dusk, and no harm will come to thee.'

So they parted; and the young man pursued his way, until,
being about to turn the corner by the meeting-house, he
looked back, and saw the head of Faith still peeping after him,
with a melancholy air, in spite of her pink ribbons.

'Poor little Faith!' thought he, for his heart smote him.
'What a wretch am I, to leave her on such an errand! She talks
of dreams, too. Methought, as she spoke, there was trouble in
her face, as if a dream had warned her what work is to be done
to-night. But, no, no! 'twould kill her to think it. Well; she's a
blessed angel on earth; and after this one night, I'll cling to her
skirts and follow her to Heaven.'

With this excellent resolve for the future, Goodman Brown felt himself justified in making more haste on his present evil purpose. He had taken a dreary road, darkened by all the gloomiest trees of the forest, which barely stood aside to let the narrow path creep through, and closed immediately behind. It was all as lonely as could be; and there is this peculiarity in such a solitude, that the traveller knows not who may be concealed by the innumerable trunks and the thick boughs overhead; so that, with lonely footsteps, he may yet be passing through an unseen multitude.

'There may be a devilish Indian behind every tree,' said Goodman Brown, to himself; and he glanced fearfully behind him, as he added, 'What if the devil himself should be at my very elbow!'

His head being turned back, he passed a crook of the road, and looking forward again, beheld the figure of a man, in grave and decent attire, seated at the foot of an old tree. He arose, at Goodman Brown's approach, and walked onward, side by side with him.

'You are late, Goodman Brown,' said he. 'The clock of the Old South was striking as I came through Boston; and that is full fifteen minutes agone.'

'Faith kept me back awhile,' replied the young man, with a tremor in his voice, caused by the sudden appearance of his companion, though not wholly unexpected.

It was now deep dusk in the forest, and deepest in that part of it where these two were journeying. As nearly as could be discerned, the second traveller was about fifty years old, apparently in the same rank of life as Goodman Brown, and bearing a considerable resemblance to him, though perhaps more in expression than features. Still, they might have been taken for father and son. And yet, though the elder person was as simply clad as the younger, and as simple in manner too, he had an indescribable air of one who knew the world, and would not have felt abashed at the governor's dinner-table, or in King William's court, were it possible that his affairs should call him thither. But the only thing about him, that could be fixed upon as remarkable, was his staff, which bore the likeness of a great black snake, so curiously wrought, that it might almost be seen to twist and wriggle itself, like a living serpent. This, of course, must have been an ocular deception, assisted by the uncertain light.

'Come, Goodman Brown!' cried his fellow-traveller, 'this is a dull pace for the beginning of a journey. Take my staff, if you are so soon weary.'

'Friend,' said the other, exchanging his slow pace for a full stop, 'having kept covenant by meeting thee here, it is my purpose now to return whence I came. I have scruples, touching the matter thou wot'st of.'

'Sayest thou so?' replied he of the serpent, smiling apart. 'Let us walk on, nevertheless, reasoning as we go, and if I convince thee not, thou shalt turn back. We are but a little way in the forest, yet.'

'Too far, too far!' exclaimed the goodman, unconsciously resuming his walk. 'My father never went into the woods on such an errand, nor his father before him. We have been a race of honest men and good Christians, since the days of the martyrs. And shall I be the first of the name of Brown, that ever took this path, and kept—'

'Such company, thou wouldst say,' observed the elder person, interpreting his pause. 'Well said, Goodman Brown! I have been as well acquainted with your family as with ever a one among the Puritans; and that's no trifle to say. I helped your grandfather, the constable, when he lashed the Quaker woman so smartly through the streets of Salem. And it was I that brought your father a pitch-pine knot, kindled at my own hearth, to set fire to an Indian village, in King Philip's war. They were my good friends, both; and many a pleasant walk have we had along this path, and returned merrily after midnight. I would fain be friends with you, for their sake.'

'If it be as thou sayest,' replied Goodman Brown, 'I marvel they never spoke of these matters. Or, verily, I marvel not, seeing that the least rumor of the sort would have driven them from New-England. We are a people of prayer, and good works, to boot, and abide no such wickedness.'

'Wickedness or not,' said the traveller with the twisted staff, 'I have a very general acquaintance here in New-England. The deacons of many a church have drunk the communion wine with me; the selectmen, of divers towns, make me their chairman;

and a majority of the Great and General Court are firm supporters of my interest. The governor and I, too—but these are state-secrets.'

'Can this be so!' cried Goodman Brown, with a stare of amazement at his undisturbed companion. 'Howbeit, I have nothing to do with the governor and council; they have their own ways, and are no rule for a simple husbandman, like me. But, were I to go on with thee, how should I meet the eye of that good old man, our minister, at Salem village? Oh, his voice would make me tremble, both Sabbath-day and lecture-day!'

Thus far, the elder traveller had listened with due gravity, but now burst into a fit of irrepressible mirth, shaking himself so violently, that his snake-like staff actually seemed to wriggle in sympathy.

'Ha! ha! ha!' shouted he, again and again; then composing himself, 'Well, go on, Goodman Brown, go on; but pr'y thee, don't kill me with laughing!'

'Well, then, to end the matter at once,' said Goodman Brown, considerably nettled, 'there is my wife, Faith. It would break her dear little heart; and I'd rather break my own!'

'Nay, if that be the case,' answered the other, 'e'en go thy ways, Goodman Brown. I would not, for twenty old women like the one hobbling before us, that Faith should come to any harm.'

As he spoke, he pointed his staff at a female figure on the path, in whom Goodman Brown recognized a very pious and exemplary dame, who had taught him his catechism, in youth, and was still his moral and spiritual adviser, jointly with the minister and Deacon Gookin.

'A marvel, truly, that Goody Cloyse should be so far in the wilderness, at night-fall!' said he. 'But, with your leave, friend, I shall take a cut through the woods, until we have left this Christian woman behind. Being a stranger to you, she might ask whom I was consorting with, and whither I was going.'

'Be it so,' said his fellow-traveller. 'Betake you to the woods, and let me keep the path.'

Accordingly, the young man turned aside, but took care to watch his companion, who advanced softly along the road, until he had come within a staff's length of the old dame. She, meanwhile, was making the best of her way, with singular speed for so aged a woman, and mumbling some indistinct words, a prayer, doubtless, as she went. The traveller put forth his staff, and touched her withered neck with what seemed the serpent's tail.

'The devil!' screamed the pious old lady.

'Then Goody Cloyse knows her old friend?' observed the traveller, confronting her, and leaning on his writhing stick.

'Ah, forsooth, and is it your worship, indeed?' cried the good dame. 'Yea, truly is it, and in the very image of my old gossip, Goodman Brown, the grandfather of the silly fellow that now is. But—would your worship believe it?—my broomstick hath strangely disappeared, stolen, as I suspect, by that unhanged witch, Goody Cory, and that, too, when I was all anointed with the juice of smallage and cinque-foil and wolf's-bane—'

'Mingled with fine wheat and the fat of a new-born babe,' said the shape of old Goodman Brown.

'Ah, your worship knows the receipt,' cried the old lady, cackling aloud. 'So, as I was saying, being all ready for the meeting, and no horse to ride on, I made up my mind to foot it; for they tell me, there is a nice young man to be taken into communion to-night. But now your good worship will lend me your arm, and we shall be there in a twinkling.'

'That can hardly be,' answered her friend. 'I may not spare you my arm, Goody Cloyse, but here is my staff, if you will.'

So saying, he threw it down at her feet, where, perhaps, it assumed life, being one of the rods which its owner had formerly lent to the Egyptian Magi. Of this fact, however, Goodman Brown could not take cognizance. He had cast up his eyes in astonishment, and looking down again, beheld neither Goody Cloyse nor the serpentine staff, but his fellow-traveller alone, who waited for him as calmly as if nothing had happened.

'That old woman taught me my catechism!' said the young man; and there was a world of meaning in this simple comment.

They continued to walk onward, while the elder traveller exhorted his companion to make good speed and persevere in the path, discoursing so aptly, that his arguments seemed rather to spring up in the bosom of his auditor, than to be suggested by himself. As they went, he plucked a branch of maple, to serve for a walking-stick, and began to strip it of the twigs and little boughs, which were wet with evening dew. The moment his fingers touched them, they became strangely withered and dried up, as with a week's sunshine. Thus the pair proceeded, at a good free pace, until suddenly, in a gloomy hollow of the road, Goodman Brown sat himself down on the stump of a tree, and refused to go any farther.

'Friend,' said he, stubbornly, 'my mind is made up. Not another step will I budge on this errand. What if a wretched old woman do choose to go to the devil, when I thought she was going to Heaven! Is that any reason why I should quit my dear Faith, and go after her?'

'You will think better of this, by-and-by,' said his acquaintance, composedly. 'Sit here and rest yourself awhile; and when you feel like moving again, there is my staff to help you along.'

Without more words, he threw his companion the maple stick, and was as speedily out of sight, as if he had vanished into the deepening gloom. The young man sat a few moments, by the road-side, applauding himself greatly, and thinking with how clear a conscience he should meet the minister, in his morning-walk, nor shrink from the eye of good old Deacon Gookin. And what calm sleep would be his, that very night, which was to have been spent so wickedly, but purely and sweetly now, in the arms of Faith! Amidst these pleasant and praiseworthy meditations, Goodman Brown heard the tramp of horses along the road, and deemed it advisable to conceal himself within the verge of the forest, conscious of the guilty purpose that had brought him thither, though now so happily turned from it.

On came the hoof-tramps and the voices of the riders, two grave old voices, conversing soberly as they drew near. These mingled sounds appeared to pass along the road, within a few yards of the young man's hiding-place; but owing, doubtless, to the depth of the gloom, at that particular spot, neither the travellers nor their steeds were visible. Though their figures brushed the small boughs by the way-side, it could not be seen that they intercepted, even for a moment, the faint gleam from the strip of bright sky, athwart which they must have passed. Goodman Brown alternately crouched and stood on tip-toe, pulling aside the branches, and thrusting forth his head as far as he durst, without discerning so much as a shadow. It vexed him the more, because he could have sworn, were such a thing

possible, that he recognized the voices of the minister and
Deacon Gookin, jogging along quietly, as they were wont to
do, when bound to some ordination or ecclesiastical council.
While yet within hearing, one of the riders stopped to pluck a
switch.

'Of the two, reverend Sir,' said the voice like the deacon's, 'I
had rather miss an ordination-dinner than to-night's meeting.
They tell me that some of our community are to be here from
Falmouth and beyond, and others from Connecticut and
Rhode-Island; besides several of the Indian powows, who, after
their fashion, know almost as much deviltry as the best of us.
Moreover, there is a goodly young woman to be taken into
communion.'

'Mighty well, Deacon Gookin!' replied the solemn old tones
of the minister. 'Spur up, or we shall be late. Nothing can be
done, you know, until I get on the ground.'

The hoofs clattered again, and the voices, talking so strangely
in the empty air, passed on through the forest, where no
church had ever been gathered, nor solitary Christian prayed.
Whither, then, could these holy men be journeying, so deep
into the heathen wilderness? Young Goodman Brown caught
hold of a tree, for support, being ready to sink down on the
ground, faint and overburthened with the heavy sickness of his
heart. He looked up to the sky, doubting whether there really
was a Heaven above him. Yet, there was the blue arch, and the
stars brightening in it.

'With Heaven above, and Faith below, I will yet stand firm
against the devil!' cried Goodman Brown.

While he still gazed upward, into the deep arch of the firmament and had lifted his hands to pray, a cloud, though no wind
was stirring, hurried across the zenith, and hid the brightening
stars. The blue sky was still visible, except directly overhead,
where this black mass of cloud was sweeping swiftly northward.
Aloft in the air, as if from the depths of the cloud, came a confused and doubtful sound of voices. Once, the listener fancied
that he could distinguish the accents of town's-people of his
own, men and women, both pious and ungodly, many of whom
he had met at the communion-table, and had seen others rioting
at the tavern. The next moment, so indistinct were the sounds,
he doubted whether he had heard aught but the murmur of the

old forest, whispering without a wind. Then came a stronger
swell of those familiar tones, heard daily in the sunshine, at
Salem village, but never, until now, from a cloud of night.
There was one voice, of a young woman, uttering lamentations,
yet with an uncertain sorrow, and entreating for some favor,
which, perhaps, it would grieve her to obtain. And all the unseen multitude, both saints and sinners, seemed to encourage
her onward.

'Faith!' shouted Goodman Brown, in a voice of agony and
desperation; and the echoes of the forest mocked him, crying
—'Faith! Faith!' as if bewildered wretches were seeking her, all
through the wilderness.

The cry of grief, rage, and terror, was yet piercing the night,
when the unhappy husband held his breath for a response.
There was a scream, drowned immediately in a louder murmur
of voices, fading into far-off laughter, as the dark cloud swept
away, leaving the clear and silent sky above Goodman Brown.
But something fluttered lightly down through the air, and
caught on the branch of a tree. The young man seized it, and
beheld a pink ribbon.

'My Faith is gone!' cried he, after one stupefied moment.
'There is no good on earth; and sin is but a name. Come,
devil! for to thee is this world given.'

And maddened with despair, so that he laughed loud and
long, did Goodman Brown grasp his staff and set forth again,
at such a rate, that he seemed to fly along the forest-path,
rather than to walk or run. The road grew wilder and drearier,
and more faintly traced, and vanished at length, leaving in the
heart of the dark wilderness, still rushing onward, with the instinct that guides mortal man to evil. The whole forest was
peopled with frightful sounds; the creaking of the trees, the
howling of wild beasts, and the yell of Indians; while, sometimes, the wind tolled like a distant church-bell, and sometimes
gave a broad roar around the traveller, as if all Nature were
laughing him to scorn. But he was himself the chief horror of
the scene, and shrank not from its other horrors.

'Ha! ha! ha!' roared Goodman Brown, when the wind
laughed at him. 'Let us hear which will laugh loudest! Think not
to frighten me with your deviltry! Come witch, come wizard,

come Indian powow, come devil himself! and here comes
Goodman Brown. You may as well fear him as he fear you!'

In truth, all through the haunted forest, there could be
nothing more frightful than the figure of Goodman Brown.
On he flew, among the black pines, brandishing his staff with
frenzied gestures, now giving vent to an inspiration of horrid
blasphemy, and now shouting forth such laughter, as set all the
echoes of the forest laughing like demons around him. The
fiend in his own shape is less hideous, than when he rages in
the breast of man. Thus sped the demoniac on his course, until,
quivering among the trees, he saw a red light before him, as
when the felled trunks and branches of a clearing have been set
on fire, and throw up their lurid blaze against the sky, at the
hour of midnight. He paused, in a lull of the tempest that had
driven him onward, and heard the swell of what seemed a hymn,
rolling solemnly from a distance, with the weight of many
voices. He knew the tune; it was a familiar one in the choir of
the village meeting-house. The verse died heavily away, and was
lengthened by a chorus, not of human voices, but of all the
sounds of the benighted wilderness, pealing in awful harmony
together. Goodman Brown cried out; and his cry was lost to
his own ear, by its unison with the cry of the desert.

In the interval of silence, he stole forward, until the light
glared full upon his eyes. At one extremity of an open space,
hemmed in by the dark wall of the forest, arose a rock, bearing
some rude, natural resemblance either to an altar or a pulpit,
and surrounded by four blazing pines, their tops aflame, their
stems untouched, like candles at an evening meeting. The mass
of foliage, that had overgrown the summit of the rock, was all
on fire, blazing high into the night, and fitfully illuminating
the whole field. Each pendent twig and leafy festoon was in a
blaze. As the red light arose and fell, a numerous congregation
alternately shone forth, then disappeared in shadow, and again
grew, as it were, out of the darkness, peopling the heart of the
solitary woods at once.

'A grave and dark-clad company!' quoth Goodman Brown.

In truth, they were such. Among them, quivering to-and-fro,
between gloom and splendor, appeared faces that would be
seen, next day, at the council-board of the province, and others

which, Sabbath after Sabbath, looked devoutly heavenward, and benignantly over the crowded pews, from the holiest pulpits in the land. Some affirm, that the lady of the governor was there. At least, there were high dames well known to her, and wives of honored husbands, and widows, a great multitude, and ancient maidens, all of excellent repute, and fair young girls, who trembled, lest their mothers should espy them. Either the sudden gleams of light, flashing over the obscure field, bedazzled Goodman Brown, or he recognized a score of the church-members of Salem village, famous for their especial sanctity. Good old Deacon Gookin had arrived, and waited at the skirts of that venerable saint, his revered pastor. But, irreverently consorting with these grave, reputable, and pious people, these elders of the church, these chaste dames and dewy virgins, there were men of dissolute lives and women of spotted fame, wretches given over to all mean and filthy vice, and suspected even of horrid crimes. It was strange to see, that the good shrank not from the wicked, nor were the sinners abashed by the saints. Scattered, also, among their pale-faced enemies, were the Indian priests, or powows, who had often scared their native forest with more hideous incantations than any known to English witchcraft.

'But, where is Faith?' thought Goodman Brown; and, as hope came into his heart, he trembled.

Another verse of the hymn arose, a slow and mournful strain, such as the pious love, but joined to words which expressed all that our nature can conceive of sin, and darkly hinted at far more. Unfathomable to mere mortals is the lore of fiends. Verse after verse was sung, and still the chorus of the desert swelled between, like the deepest tone of a mighty organ. And, with the final peal of that dreadful anthem, there came a sound, as if the roaring wind, the rushing streams, the howling beasts, and every other voice of the unconverted wilderness, were mingling and according with the voice of guilty man, in homage to the prince of all. The four blazing pines threw up a loftier flame, and obscurely discovered shapes and visages of horror on the smoke-wreaths, above the impious assembly. At the same moment, the fire on the rock shot redly forth, and formed a glowing arch above its base, where now appeared a figure. With reverence be it spoken, the figure bore no slight

similitude, both in garb and manner, to some grave divine of
the New-England churches.

'Bring forth the converts!' cried a voice, that echoed
through the field and rolled into the forest.

At the word, Goodman Brown stept forth from the shadow
of the trees, and approached the congregation, with whom he
felt a loathful brotherhood, by the sympathy of all that was
wicked in his heart. He could have well nigh sworn, that the
shape of his own dead father beckoned him to advance,
looking downward from a smoke-wreath, while a woman, with
dim features of despair, threw out her hand to warn him back.
Was it his mother? But he had no power to retreat one step,
nor to resist, even in thought, when the minister and good old
Deacon Gookin seized his arms, and led him to the blazing
rock. Thither came also the slender form of a veiled female, led
between Goody Cloyse, that pious teacher of the catechism,
and Martha Carrier, who had received the devil's promise to
be queen of hell. A rampant hag was she! And there stood the
proselytes, beneath the canopy of fire.

'Welcome, my children,' said the dark figure, 'to the communion of your race! Ye have found, thus young, your nature
and your destiny. My children, look behind you!'

They turned; and flashing forth, as it were, in a sheet of
flame, the fiend-worshippers were seen; the smile of welcome
gleamed darkly on every visage.

'There,' resumed the sable form, 'are all whom ye have rev-
erenced from youth. Ye deemed them holier than yourselves,
and shrank from your own sin, contrasting it with their lives of
righteousness, and prayerful aspirations heavenward. Yet, here
are they all, in my worshipping assembly! This night it shall be
granted you to know their secret deeds; how hoary-bearded
elders of the church have whispered wanton words to the
young maids of their households; how many a woman, eager
for widow's weeds, has given her husband a drink at bed-time,
and let him sleep his last sleep in her bosom; how beardless
youths have made haste to inherit their fathers' wealth; and how
fair damsels—blush not, sweet ones!—have dug little graves in
the garden, and bidden me, the sole guest, to an infant's funeral.
By the sympathy of your human hearts for sin, ye shall scent
out all the places—whether in church, bed-chamber, street,

field, or forest—where crime has been committed, and shall exult to behold the whole earth one stain of guilt, one mighty blood-spot. Far more than this! It shall be yours to penetrate, in every bosom, the deep mystery of sin, the fountain of all wicked arts, and which inexhaustibly supplies more evil impulses than human power—than my power, at its utmost!—can make manifest in deeds. And now, my children, look upon each other.'

They did so; and, by the blaze of the hell-kindled torches, the wretched man beheld his Faith, and the wife her husband, trembling before that unhallowed altar.

'Lo! there ye stand, my children,' said the figure, in a deep and solemn tone, almost sad, with its despairing awfulness, as if his once angelic nature could yet mourn for our miserable race. 'Depending upon one another's hearts, ye had still hoped, that virtue were not all a dream. Now are ye undeceived! Evil is the nature of mankind. Evil must be your only happiness. Welcome, again, my children, to the communion of your race!'

"Welcome!' repeated the fiend-worshippers, in one cry of despair and triumph.

And there they stood, the only pair, as it seemed, who were yet hesitating on the verge of wickedness, in this dark world. A basin was hollowed, naturally, in the rock. Did it contain water, reddened by the lurid light? or was it blood? or, perchance, a liquid flame? Herein did the Shape of Evil dip his hand, and prepare to lay the mark of baptism upon their foreheads, that they might be partakers of the mystery of sin, more conscious of the secret guilt of others, both in deed and thought, than they could now be of their own. The husband cast one look at his pale wife, and Faith at him. What polluted wretches would the next glance shew them to each other, shuddering alike at what they disclosed and what they saw!

'Faith! Faith!' cried the husband. 'Look up to Heaven, and resist the Wicked One!'

Whether Faith obeyed, he knew not. Hardly had he spoken, when he found himself amid calm night and solitude, listening to a roar of the wind, which died heavily away through the forest. He staggered against the rock and felt it chill and damp, while a hanging twig, that had been all on fire, besprinkled his cheek with the coldest dew.

The next morning, young Goodman Brown came slowly into the street of Salem village, staring around him like a bewildered man. The good old minister was taking a walk along the grave-yard, to get an appetite for breakfast and meditate his sermon, and bestowed a blessing, as he passed, on Goodman Brown. He shrank from the venerable saint, as if to avoid an anathema. Old Deacon Gookin was at domestic worship, and the holy words of his prayer were heard through the open window. 'What God doth the wizard pray to?' quoth Goodman Brown. Goody Cloyse, that excellent old Christian, stood in the early sunshine, at her own lattice, catechising a little girl, who had brought her a pint of morning's milk. Goodman Brown snatched away the child, as from the grasp of the fiend himself. Turning the corner by the meeting-house, he spied the head of Faith, with the pink ribbons, gazing anxiously forth, and bursting into such joy at sight of him, that she skipt along the street, and almost kissed her husband before the whole village. But, Goodman Brown looked sternly and sadly into her face, and passed on without a greeting.

Had Goodman Brown fallen asleep in the forest, and only dreamed a wild dream of a witch-meeting?

Be it so, if you will. But, alas! it was a dream of evil omen for young Goodman Brown. A stern, a sad, a darkly meditative, a distrustful, if not a desperate man, did he become, from the night of that fearful dream. On the Sabbath-day, when the congregation were singing a holy psalm, he could not listen, because an anthem of sin rushed loudly upon his ear, and drowned all the blessed strain. When the minister spoke from the pulpit, with power and fervid eloquence, and, with his hand on the open Bible, of the sacred truths of our religion, and of saint-like lives and triumphant deaths, and of future bliss or misery unutterable, then did Goodman Brown turn pale, dreading, lest the roof should thunder down upon the gray blasphemer and his hearers. Often, awakening suddenly at midnight, he shrank from the bosom of Faith, and at morning or eventide, when the family knelt down at prayer, he scowled, and muttered to himself, and gazed sternly at his wife, and turned away. And when he had lived long, and was borne to his grave, a hoary corpse, followed by Faith, an aged woman, and children and grand-children, a goodly procession, besides neighbors, not a few, they carved no hopeful verse upon his tomb-stone; for his dying hour was gloom.

1835

HERMAN MELVILLE

(1819–1891)

The Tartarus of Maids

It lies not far from Woedolor Mountain in New England. Turning to the east, right out from among bright farms and sunny meadows, nodding in early June with odorous grasses, you enter ascendingly among bleak hills. These gradually close in upon a dusky pass, which, from the violent Gulf Stream of air unceasingly driving between its cloven walls of haggard rock, as well as from the tradition of a crazy spinster's hut having long ago stood somewhere hereabouts, is called the Mad Maid's Bellows'-pipe.

Winding along at the bottom of the gorge is a dangerously narrow wheel-road, occupying the bed of a former torrent. Following this road to its highest point, you stand as within a Dantean gateway. From the steepness of the walls here, their strangely ebon hue, and the sudden contraction of the gorge, this particular point is called the Black Notch. The ravine now expandingly descends into a great, purple, hopper-shaped hollow, far sunk among many Plutonian, shaggy-wooded mountains. By the country people this hollow is called the Devil's Dungeon. Sounds of torrents fall on all sides upon the ear. These rapid waters unite at last in one turbid brick-colored stream, boiling through a flume among enormous boulders. They call this strange-colored torrent Blood River. Gaining a dark precipice it wheels suddenly to the west, and makes one maniac spring of sixty feet into the arms of a stunted wood of gray-haired pines, between which it thence eddies on its further way down to the invisible lowlands.

Conspicuously crowning a rocky bluff high to one side, at the cataract's verge, is the ruin of an old saw-mill, built in those primitive times when vast pines and hemlocks superabounded throughout the neighboring region. The black-mossed bulk of those immense, rough-hewn, and spike-knotted logs, here and there tumbled all together, in long abandonment and decay, or left in solitary, perilous projection over the cataract's gloomy brink, impart to this rude wooden ruin not only much of the aspect of one of rough-quarried stone, but also a sort of feudal, Rhineland, and Thurmberg look, derived from the pinnacled wildness of the neighboring scenery.

Not far from the bottom of the Dungeon stands a large white-washed building, relieved, like some great white sepulchre, against the sullen background of mountain-side firs, and other hardy evergreens, inaccessibly rising in grim terraces for some two thousand feet.

The building is a paper-mill.

Having embarked on a large scale in the seedsman's business (so extensively and broadcast, indeed, that at length my seeds were distributed through all the Eastern and Northern States, and even fell into the far soil of Missouri and the Carolinas), the demand for paper at my place became so great, that the expenditure soon amounted to a most important item in the general account. It need hardly be hinted how paper comes into use with seedsmen, as envelopes. These are mostly made of yellowish paper, folded square; and when filled, are all but flat, and being stamped, and superscribed with the nature of the seeds contained, assume not a little the appearance of business-letters ready for the mail. Of these small envelopes I used an incredible quantity—several hundreds of thousands in a year. For a time I had purchased my paper from the wholesale dealers in a neighboring town. For economy's sake, and partly for the adventure of the trip, I now resolved to cross the mountains, some sixty miles, and order my future paper at the Devil's Dungeon paper-mill.

The sleighing being uncommonly fine toward the end of January, and promising to hold so for no small period, in spite of the bitter cold I started one gray Friday noon in my pung, well fitted with buffalo and wolf robes; and, spending one night on the road, next noon came in sight of Woedolor Mountain.

The far summit fairly smoked with frost; white vapors curled up from its white-wooded top, as from a chimney. The intense congelation made the whole country look like one petrifaction. The steel shoes of my pung craunched and gritted over the vitreous, chippy snow, as if it had been broken glass. The forests here and there skirting the route, feeling the same all-stiffening influence, their inmost fibres penetrated with the cold, strangely groaned—not in the swaying branches merely, but likewise in the vertical trunk—as the fitful gusts remorselessly swept through them. Brittle with excessive frost, many colossal tough-grained maples, snapped in twain like pipe-stems, cumbered the unfeeling earth.

Flaked all over with frozen sweat, white as a milky ram, his nostrils at each breath sending forth two horn-shaped shoots of heated respiration, Black, my good horse, but six years old, started at a sudden turn, where, right across the track—not ten minutes fallen—an old distorted hemlock lay, darkly undulatory as an anaconda.

Gaining the Bellows'-pipe, the violent blast, dead from behind, all but shoved my high-backed pung up-hill. The gust shrieked through the shivered pass, as if laden with lost spirits bound to the unhappy world. Ere gaining the summit, Black, my horse, as if exasperated by the cutting wind, slung out with his strong hind legs, tore the light pung straight up-hill, and sweeping grazingly through the narrow notch, sped downward madly past the ruined saw-mill. Into the Devil's Dungeon horse and cataract rushed together.

With might and main, quitting my seat and robes, and standing backward, with one foot braced against the dash-board, I rasped and churned the bit, and stopped him just in time to avoid collision, at a turn, with the bleak nozzle of a rock, couchant like a lion in the way—a road-side rock.

At first I could not discover the paper-mill.

The whole hollow gleamed with the white, except, here and there, where a pinnacle of granite showed one wind-swept angle bare. The mountains stood pinned in shrouds—a pass of Alpine corpses. Where stands the mill? Suddenly a whirling, humming sound broke upon my ear. I looked, and there, like an arrested avalanche, lay the large whitewashed factory. It was subordinately surrounded by a cluster of other and smaller buildings, some of which, from their cheap, blank air, great length, gregarious windows, and comfortless expression, no doubt were boarding-houses of the operatives. A snow-white hamlet amidst the snows. Various rude, irregular squares and courts resulted from the somewhat picturesque clusterings of these buildings, owing to the broken, rocky nature of the ground, which forbade all method in their relative arrangement. Several narrow lanes and alleys, too, partly blocked with snow fallen from the roof, cut up the hamlet in all directions.

When, turning from the traveled highway, jingling with bells of numerous farmers—who, availing themselves of the fine sleighing, were dragging their wood to market—and frequently diversified with swift cutters dashing from inn to inn of the scattered villages—when, I say, turning from that bustling main-road, I by degrees wound into the Mad Maid's Bellows'-pipe, and saw the grim Black Notch beyond, then something latent, as well as something obvious in the time and scene, strangely brought back to my mind my first sight of dark and grimy Temple-Bar. And when Black, my horse, went darting through the Notch, perilously grazing its rocky wall, I remembered being in a runaway London omnibus, which in much the same sort of style, though by no means at an equal rate, dashed through the ancient arch of Wren. Though the two objects did by no means completely correspond, yet this partial inadequacy but served to tinge the similitude not less with the vividness than the disorder of a dream. So that, when upon reining up at the protruding rock I at last caught sight of the quaint groupings of the factory-buildings, and with the traveled highway and the Notch behind, found myself all alone, silently and privily stealing through deep-cloven passages into this sequestered spot, and saw the long, high-gabled main factory edifice, with a rude tower—for hoisting heavy boxes—at one end, standing among its crowded outbuildings and boarding-houses, as the Temple Church amidst the surrounding offices and dormitories, and when the marvelous retirement of this mysterious mountain nook fastened its whole spell upon me, then, what memory lacked, all tributary imagination furnished, and I said to myself, "This is the very counterpart of the Paradise of Bachelors, but snowed upon, and frost-painted to a sepulchre."

Dismounting, and warily picking my way down the dangerous declivity—horse and man both sliding now and then upon the icy ledges—at length I drove, or the blast drove me, into the largest square, before one side of the main edifice. Piercingly and shrilly the shotted blast blew by the corner; and redly and demoniacally boiled Blood River at one side. A long wood-pile, of many scores of cords, all glittering in mail of crusted ice, stood crosswise in the square. A row of horse-posts, their north sides plastered with adhesive snow, flanked the factory wall. The bleak frost packed and paved the square as with some ringing metal.

The inverted similitude recurred—"The sweet, tranquil Temple garden, with the Thames bordering its green beds," strangely meditated I.

But where are the gay bachelors?

Then, as I and my horse stood shivering in the wind-spray, a girl ran from a neighboring dormitory door, and throwing her thin apron over her bare head, made for the opposite building.

"One moment, my girl; is there no shed hereabouts which I may drive into?"

Pausing, she turned upon me a face pale with work, and blue with cold; an eye supernatural with unrelated misery.

"Nay," faltered I, "I mistook you. Go on; I want nothing."

Leading my horse close to the door from which she had come, I knocked. Another pale, blue girl appeared, shivering in the doorway as, to prevent the blast, she jealously held the door ajar.

"Nay, I mistake again. In God's name shut the door. But hold, is there no man about?"

That moment a dark-complexioned well-wrapped personage passed, making for the factory door, and spying him coming, the girl rapidly closed the other one.

"Is there no horse-shed here, Sir?"

"Yonder, to the wood-shed," he replied, and disappeared inside the factory.

With much ado I managed to wedge in horse and pung between the scattered piles of wood all sawn and split. Then, blanketing my horse, and piling my buffalo on the blanket's top, and tucking in its edges well around the breast-band and breeching, so that the wind might not strip him bare, I tied him fast, and ran lamely for the factory door, stiff with frost, and cumbered with my driver's dread-naught.

Immediately I found myself standing in a spacious place, intolerably lighted by long rows of windows, focusing inward the snowy scene without.

At rows of blank-looking counters sat rows of blank-looking girls, with blank, white folders in their blank hands, all blankly folding blank paper.

In one corner stood some huge frame of ponderous iron, with a vertical thing like a piston periodically rising and falling upon a heavy wooden block. Before it—its tame minister—stood a tall girl, feeding the iron animal with half-quires of rose-hued note paper, which, at every downward dab of the piston-like machine, received in the corner the impress of a wreath of roses. I looked from the rosy paper to the pallid cheek, but said nothing.

Seated before a long apparatus, strung with long, slender strings like any harp, another girl was feeding it with foolscap sheets, which, so soon as they curiously traveled from her on the cords, were withdrawn at the opposite end of the machine by a second girl. They came to the first girl blank; they went to the second girl ruled.

I looked upon the first girl's brow, and saw it was young and fair; I looked upon the second girl's brow, and saw it was ruled and wrinkled. Then, as I still looked, the two—for some small variety to the monotony—changed places; and where had stood the young, fair brow, now stood the ruled and wrinkled one.

Perched high upon a narrow platform, and still higher upon a high stool crowning it, sat another figure serving some other iron animal; while below the platform sat her mate in some sort of reciprocal attendance.

Not a syllable was breathed. Nothing was heard but the low, steady, overruling hum of the iron animals. The human voice was banished from the spot. Machinery—that vaunted slave of humanity—here stood menially served by human beings, who served mutely and cringingly as the slave serves the Sultan. The girls did not so much seem accessory wheels to the general machinery as mere cogs to the wheels.

All this scene around me was instantaneously taken in at one sweeping glance—even before I had proceeded to unwind the heavy fur tippet from around my neck. But as soon as this fell from me the dark-complexioned man, standing close by, raised a sudden cry, and seizing my arm, dragged me out into the open air, and without pausing for a word instantly caught up some congealed snow and began rubbing both my cheeks.

"Two white spots like the whites of your eyes," he said; "man, your cheeks are frozen."

"That may well be," muttered I; " 'tis some wonder the frost of the Devil's Dungeon strikes in no deeper. Rub away."

Soon a horrible, tearing pain caught at my reviving cheeks. Two gaunt blood-hounds, one on each side, seemed mumbling them. I seemed Actæon.

Presently, when all was over, I re-entered the factory, made known my business, concluded it satisfactorily, and then begged to be conducted throughout the place to view it.

"Cupid is the boy for that," said the dark-complexioned man. "Cupid!" and by this odd fancy-name calling a dimpled, red-cheeked, spirited-looking, forward little fellow, who was rather impudently, I thought, gliding about among the passive-looking girls—like a gold fish through hueless waves—yet doing nothing in particular that I could see, the man bade him lead the stranger through the edifice.

"Come first and see the water-wheel," said this lively lad, with the air of boyishly-brisk importance.

Quitting the folding-room, we crossed some damp, cold boards, and stood beneath a great wet shed, incessantly showering with foam, like the green barnacled bow of some East Indiaman in a gale. Round and round here went the enormous revolutions of the dark colossal water-wheel, grim with its one immutable purpose.

"This sets our whole machinery a-going, Sir; in every part of all these buildings; where the girls work and all."

I looked, and saw that the turbid waters of Blood River had not changed their hue by coming under the use of man.

"You make only blank paper; no printing of any sort, I suppose? All blank paper, don't you?"

"Certainly; what else should a paper-factory make?"

The lad here looked at me as if suspicious of my common-sense.

"Oh, to be sure!" said I, confused and stammering; "it only struck me as so strange that red waters should turn out pale chee—paper, I mean."

He took me up a wet and rickety stair to a great light room, furnished with no visible thing but rude, manger-like receptacles running all round its sides; and up to these mangers, like so many mares haltered to the rack, stood rows of girls. Before each was vertically thrust up a long, glittering scythe, immovably fixed at bottom to the manger-edge. The curve of the scythe, and its having no snath to it, made it look exactly like a sword. To and fro, across the sharp edge, the girls forever dragged long strips of rags, washed white, picked from baskets at one side; thus ripping asunder every seam, and converting the tatters almost into lint. The air swam with the fine, poisonous particles, which from all sides darted, subtilely, as motes in sun-beams, into the lungs.

"This is the rag-room," coughed the boy.

"You find it rather stifling here," coughed I, in answer; "but the girls don't cough."

"Oh, they are used to it."

"Where do you get such hosts of rags?" picking up a handful from a basket.

"Some from the country round about; some from far over sea—Leghorn and London."

"'Tis not unlikely, then," murmured I, "that among these heaps of rags there may be some old shirts, gathered from the dormitories of the Paradise of Bachelors. But the buttons are all dropped off. Pray, my lad, do you ever find any bachelor's buttons hereabouts?"

"None grow in this part of the country. The Devil's Dungeon is no place for flowers."

"Oh! you mean the *flowers* so called—the Bachelor's Buttons?"

"And was not that what you asked about? Or did you mean the gold bosom-buttons of our boss, Old Bach, as our whispering girls all call him?"

"The man, then, I saw below is a bachelor, is he?"

"Oh, yes, he's a Bach."

"The edges of those swords, they are turned outward from the girls, if I see right; but their rags and fingers fly so, I can not distinctly see."

"Turned outward."

Yes, murmured I to myself; I see it now; turned outward;

and each erected sword is so borne, edge-outward, before each girl. If my reading fails me not, just so, of old, condemned state-prisoners went from the hall of judgment to their doom: an officer before, bearing a sword, its edge turned outward, in significance of their fatal sentence. So, through consumptive pallors of this blank, raggy life, go these white girls to death.

"Those scythes look very sharp," again turning toward the boy.

"Yes; they have to keep them so. Look!"

That moment two of the girls, dropping their rags, plied each a whet-stone up and down the sword-blade. My unaccustomed blood curdled at the sharp shriek of the tormented steel.

Their own executioners; themselves whetting the very swords that slay them; meditated I.

"What makes those girls so sheet-white, my lad?"

"Why"—with a roguish twinkle, pure ignorant drollery, not knowing heartlessness—"I suppose the handling of such white bits of sheets all the time makes them so sheety."

"Let us leave the rag-room now, my lad."

More tragical and more inscrutably mysterious than any mystic sight, human or machine, throughout the factory, was the strange innocence of cruel-heartedness in this usage-hardened boy.

"And now," said he, cheerily, "I suppose you want to see our great machine, which cost us twelve thousand dollars only last autumn. That's the machine that makes the paper, too. This way, Sir."

Following him, I crossed a large, bespattered place, with two great round vats in it, full of a white, wet, woolly-looking stuff, not unlike the albuminous part of an egg, soft-boiled.

"There," said Cupid, tapping the vats carelessly, "these are the first beginnings of the paper; this white pulp you see. Look how it swims bubbling round and round, moved by the paddle here. From hence it pours from both vats into that one common channel yonder, and so goes, mixed up and leisurely, to the great machine. And now for that."

He led me into a room, stifling with a strange, blood-like, abdominal heat, as if here, true enough, were being finally developed the germinous particles lately seen.

Before me, rolled out like some long Eastern manuscript, lay stretched one continuous length of iron frame-work—multitudinous and mystical, with all sorts of rollers, wheels, and cylinders, in slowly-measured and unceasing motion.

"Here first comes the pulp now," said Cupid, pointing to the nighest end of the machine. "See; first it pours out and spreads itself upon this wide, sloping board; and then—look—slides, thin and quivering beneath the first roller there. Follow on now, and see it as it slides from under that to the next cylinder. There; see how it has become just a very little less pulpy now. One step more, and it grows still more to some slight consistence. Still another cylinder, and it is so knitted—though as yet mere dragon-fly wing—that it forms an air-bridge here, like a suspended cobweb, between two more separated rollers; and flowing over the last one, and under again, and doubling about there out of sight for a minute among all those mixed cylinders you indistinctly see, it reappears here, looking now at last a little less like pulp and more like paper, but still quite delicate and defective yet awhile. But—a little further onward, Sir, if you please—here now, at this further point, it puts on something of a real look, as if it might turn out to be something you might possibly handle in the end. But it's not yet done, Sir. Good way to travel yet, and plenty more of cylinders must roll it."

"Bless my soul!" said I, amazed at the elongation, interminable convolutions, and deliberate slowness of the machine; "it must take a long time for the pulp to pass from end to end, and come out paper."

"Oh! not so long," smiled the precocious lad, with a superior and patronizing air; "only nine minutes. But look; you may try it for yourself. Have you a bit of paper? Ah! here's a bit on the floor. Now mark that with any word you please, and let me dab it on here, and well see how long before it comes out at the other end."

"Well, let me see," said I, taking out my pencil; "come, I'll mark it with your name."

Bidding me take out my watch, Cupid adroitly dropped the inscribed slip on an exposed part of the incipient mass.

Instantly my eye marked the second-hand on my dial-plate.

Slowly I followed the slip, inch by inch; sometimes pausing for full half a minute as it disappeared beneath inscrutable groups of the lower cylinders, but only gradually to emerge again; and so, on, and on, and on—inch by inch; now in open sight, sliding along like a freckle on the quivering sheet; and then again wholly vanished; and so, on, and on, and on—inch by inch; all the time the main sheet growing more and more to final firmness—when, suddenly, I saw a sort of paper-fall, not wholly unlike a water-fall; a scissory sound smote my ear, as of some cord being snapped; and down dropped an unfolded sheet of perfect foolscap, with my "Cupid" half faded out of it, and still moist and warm.

My travels were at an end, for here was the end of the machine.

"Well, how long was it?" said Cupid.

"Nine minutes to a second," replied I, watch in hand.

"I told you so."

For a moment a curious emotion filled me, not wholly unlike that which one might experience at the fulfillment of some mysterious prophecy. But how absurd, thought I again; the thing is a mere machine, the essence of which is unvarying punctuality and precision.

Previously absorbed by the wheels and cylinders, my attention was now directed to a sad-looking woman standing by.

"That is rather an elderly person so silently tending the machine-end here. She would not seem wholly used to it either."

"Oh," knowingly whispered Cupid, through the din, "she only came last week. She was a nurse formerly. But the business is poor in these parts, and she's left it. But look at the paper she is piling there."

"Ay, foolscap," handling the piles of moist, warm sheets, which continually were being delivered into the woman's waiting hands. "Don't you turn out any thing but foolscap at this machine?"

"Oh, sometimes, but not often, we turn out finer work—cream-laid and royal sheets, we call them. But foolscap being in chief demand, we turn out foolscap most."

It was very curious. Looking at that blank paper continually dropping, dropping, dropping, my mind ran on in wonderings of those strange uses to which those thousand sheets eventually would be put. All sorts of writings would be writ on those now vacant things—sermons, lawyers' briefs, physicians'

prescriptions, love-letters, marriage certificates, bills of divorce, registers of births, death-warrants, and so on, without
end. Then, recurring back to them as they here lay all blank, I
could not but bethink me of that celebrated comparison of
John Locke, who, in demonstration of his theory that man had
no innate ideas, compared the human mind at birth to a sheet
of blank paper; something destined to be scribbled on, but
what sort of characters no soul might tell.

Pacing slowly to and fro along the involved machine, still
humming with its play, I was struck as well by the inevitability
as the evolvement-power in all its motions.

"Does that thin cobweb there," said I, pointing to the sheet
in its more imperfect stage, "does that never tear or break? It is
marvelous fragile, and yet this machine it passes through is so
mighty."

"It never is known to tear a hair's point."

"Does it never stop—get clogged?"

"No. It *must* go. The machinery makes it go just *so*; just that
very way, and at that very pace you there plainly *see* it go. The
pulp can't help going."

Something of awe now stole over me, as I gazed upon this
inflexible iron animal. Always, more or less, machinery of this
ponderous, elaborate sort strikes, in some moods, strange dread
into the human heart, as some living, panting Behemoth might.
But what made the thing I saw so specially terrible to me was
the metallic necessity, the unbudging fatality which governed it.
Though, here and there, I could not follow the thin, gauzy vail
of pulp in the course of its more mysterious or entirely invisible
advance, yet it was indubitable that, at those points where it
eluded me, it still marched on in unvarying docility to the auto-
cratic cunning of the machine. A fascination fastened on me. I
stood spell-bound and wandering in my soul. Before my eyes
—there, passing in slow procession along the wheeling cylinders, I seemed to see, glued to the pallid incipience of the pulp,
the yet more pallid faces of all the pallid girls I had eyed that
heavy day. Slowly, mournfully, beseechingly, yet unresistingly,
they gleamed along, their agony dimly outlined on the imperfect paper, like the print of the tormented face on the handkerchief of Saint Veronica.

"Halloa! the heat of the room is too much for you," cried Cupid, staring at me.

"No—I am rather chill, if any thing."

"Come out, Sir—out—out," and, with the protecting air of a careful father, the precocious lad hurried me outside.

In a few moments, feeling revived a little, I went into the folding-room—the first room I had entered, and where the desk for transacting business stood, surrounded by the blank counters and blank girls engaged at them.

"Cupid here has led me a strange tour," said I to the dark-complexioned man before mentioned, whom I had ere this discovered not only to be an old bachelor, but also the principal proprietor. "Yours is a most wonderful factory. Your great machine is a miracle of inscrutable intricacy."

"Yes, all our visitors think it so. But we don't have many. We arc in a very out-of-the-way corner here. Few inhabitants, too. Most of our girls come from far-off villages."

"The girls," echoed I, glancing round at their silent forms. "Why is it, Sir, that in most factories, female operatives, of whatever age, are indiscriminately called girls, never women?"

"Oh! as to that—why, I suppose, the fact of their being generally unmarried—that's the reason, I should think. But it never struck me before. For our factory here, we will not have married women; they are apt to be off-and-on too much. We want none but steady workers: twelve hours to the day, day after day, through the three hundred and sixty-five days, excepting Sundays, Thanksgiving, and Fast-days. That's our rule. And so, having no married women, what females we have are rightly enough called girls."

"Then these are all maids," said I, while some pained homage to their pale virginity made me involuntarily bow.

"All maids."

Again the strange emotion filled me.

"Your cheeks look whitish yet, Sir," said the man, gazing at me narrowly. "You must be careful going home. Do they pain you at all now? It's a bad sign, if they do."

"No doubt, Sir," answered I, "when once I have got out of the Devil's Dungeon, I shall feel them mending."

"Ah, yes; the winter air in valleys, or gorges, or any sunken place, is far colder and more bitter than elsewhere. You would hardly believe it now, but it is colder here than at the top of Woedolor Mountain."

"I dare say it is, Sir. But time presses me; I must depart."

With that, remuffling myself in dread-naught and tippet, thrusting my hands into my huge seal-skin mittens, I sallied out into the nipping air, and found poor Black, my horse, all cringing and doubled up with the cold.

Soon, wrapped in furs and meditations, I ascended from the Devil's Dungeon.

At the Black Notch I paused, and once more bethought me of Temple-Bar. Then, shooting through the pass, all alone with inscrutable nature, I exclaimed—Oh! Paradise of Bachelors! and oh! Tartarus of Maids!

1855

FITZ-JAMES O'BRIEN

(1828–1862)

What Was It?

A Mystery

IT is, I confess, with considerable diffidence that I approach the strange narrative which I am about to relate. The events which I purpose detailing are of so extraordinary and unheard-of a character that I am quite prepared to meet with an unusual amount of incredulity and scorn. I accept all such beforehand. I have, I trust, the literary courage to face unbelief. I have, after mature consideration, resolved to narrate, in as simple and straightforward a manner as I can compass, some facts that passed under my observation in the month of July last, and which, in the annals of the mysteries of physical science, are wholly unparalleled.

I live at No. — Twenty-sixth Street, in this city. The house is in some respects a curious one. It has enjoyed for the last two years the reputation of being haunted. It is a large and stately residence, surrounded by what was once a garden, but which is now only a green inclosure used for bleaching clothes. The dry basin of what has been a fountain, and a few fruit-trees, ragged and unpruned, indicate that this spot, in past days, was a pleasant, shady retreat, filled with fruits and flowers and the sweet murmur of waters.

The house is very spacious. A hall of noble size leads to a vast spiral staircase winding through its centre; while the various apartments are of imposing dimensions. It was built some fifteen or twenty years since by Mr. A——, the well-known New York merchant, who five years ago threw the commercial world into convulsions by a stupendous bank fraud. Mr. A——, as every one knows, escaped to Europe, and died not long after of a broken heart. Almost immediately after the news of his decease reached this country, and was verified, the report spread in Twenty-sixth Street that No. — was haunted. Legal

63

measures had dispossessed the widow of its former owner, and it was inhabited merely by a care-taker and his wife, placed there by the house-agent into whose hands it had passed for purposes of renting or sale. These people declared that they were troubled with unnatural noises. Doors were opened without any visible agency. The remnants of furniture scattered through the various rooms were, during the night, piled one upon the other by unknown hands. Invisible feet passed up and down the stairs in broad daylight, accompanied by the rustle of unseen silk dresses and the gliding of viewless hands along the massive balusters. The care-taker and his wife declared they would live there no longer. The house-agent laughed, dismissed them, and put others in their place. The noises and supernatural manifestations continued. The neighborhood caught up the story, and the house remained untenanted for three years. Several parties negotiated for it; but somehow, always before the bargain was closed, they heard the unpleasant rumors, and declined to treat any further.

It was in this state of things that my landlady—who at that time kept a boarding-house in Bleecker Street, and who wished to move farther up town—conceived the bold idea of renting No. — Twenty-sixth Street. Happening to have in her house rather a plucky and philosophical set of boarders, she laid her scheme before us, stating candidly every thing she had heard respecting the ghostly qualities of the establishment to which she wished to remove us. With the exception of one or two timid persons—a sea-captain and a returned Californian, who immediately gave notice that they would leave—every one of Mrs. Moffat's guests declared that they would accompany her in her chivalric incursion into the abode of spirits.

Our removal was effected in the month of May, and we were all charmed with our new residence. The portion of Twenty-sixth Street where our house is situated—between Seventh and Eighth Avenues—is one of the pleasantest localities in New York. The gardens back of the houses, running down nearly to the Hudson, form, in the summer time, a perfect avenue of verdure. The air is pure and invigorating, sweeping, as it does, straight across the river from the Weehawken heights, and even the ragged garden which surrounded the house on two sides, although displaying on washing-days rather too much clothesline, still gave us a piece of green sward to look at, and a cool retreat in the summer evenings, where we smoked our cigars in the dusk, and watched the fire-flies flashing their dark-lanterns in the long grass.

Of course we had no sooner established ourselves at No. — than we began to expect the ghosts. We absolutely awaited their advent with eagerness. Our dinner conversation was supernatural. One of the boarders, who had purchased Mrs. Crowe's "Night Side of Nature" for his own private delectation, was regarded as a public enemy by the entire household for not having bought twenty copies. The man led a life of supreme wretchedness while he was perusing the volume. A system of espionage was established, of which he was the victim. If he incautiously laid the book down for an instant and left the room, it was immediately seized and read aloud in secret places to a select few. I found myself a person of immense importance, it having leaked out that I was tolerably well versed in the history of supernaturalism, and had once written a story, entitled "The Pot of Tulips," for *Harper's Monthly*, the foundation of which was a ghost. If a table or a wainscot panel happened to warp when we were assembled in the large drawing-room, there was an instant silence, and every one was prepared for an immediate clanking of chains and a spectral form.

After a month of psychological excitement, it was with the utmost dissatisfaction that we were forced to acknowledge that nothing in the remotest degree approaching the supernatural had manifested itself. Once the black butler asseverated that his candle had been blown out by some invisible agency while in the act of undressing himself for the night; but as I had more than once discovered this colored gentleman in a condition when one candle must have appeared to him like two, I thought it possible that, by going a step farther in his potations, he might have reversed this phenomenon, and seen no candle at all where he ought to have beheld one.

Things were in this state when an incident took place so awful and inexplicable in its character that my reason fairly reels at the bare memory of the occurrence. It was the 10th of July. After dinner was over I repaired, with my friend Dr. Hammond, to the garden to smoke my evening pipe. Independent of certain mental sympathies which existed between the Doctor and myself, we were linked together by a secret vice. We both smoked opium. We knew each other's secret, and respected it. We enjoyed together that wonderful expansion of thought; that marvelous intensifying of the perceptive faculties; that boundless feeling of existence when we seem to have points of contact with the whole universe; in short, that unimaginable spiritual bliss, which I would not surrender for a throne, and which I hope you, reader, will never—never taste.

Those hours of opium happiness which the Doctor and I spent together in secret were regulated with a scientific accuracy. We did not blindly smoke the drug of Paradise, and leave our dreams to chance. While smoking we carefully steered our conversation through the brightest and calmest channels of thought. We talked of the East, and endeavored to recall the magical panorama of its glowing scenery. We criticised the most sensuous poets, those who painted life ruddy with health, brimming with passion, happy in the possession of youth, and strength, and beauty. If we talked of Shakspeare's "Midsummer Night's Dream," we lingered over Ariel and avoided Caliban. Like the Gebers, we turned our faces to the East, and saw only the sunny side of the world.

This skillful coloring of our train of thought produced in our subsequent visions a corresponding tone. The splendors of Arabian fairy-land dyed our dreams. We paced that narrow strip of grass with the tread and port of kings. The song of the *Rana arborea* while he clung to the bark of the ragged plumtree sounded like the strains of divine orchestras. Houses, walls, and streets melted like rain-clouds, and vistas of unimaginable glory stretched away before us. It was a rapturous companionship. We each of us enjoyed the vast delight more perfectly because, even in our most ecstatic moments, we were ever conscious of each other's presence. Our pleasures, while individual, were still twin, vibrating and moving in musical accord.

On the evening in question, the 10th of July, the Doctor and myself found ourselves in an unusually metaphysical mood. We lit our large meerschaums, filled with fine Turkish tobacco, in the core of which burned a little black nut of opium, that, like the nut in the fairy tale, held within its narrow limits wonders beyond the reach of kings; we paced to and fro, conversing. A strange perversity dominated the currents of our thought. They would *not* flow through the sun-lit channels into which we strove to divert them. For some unaccountable reason they constantly diverged into dark and lonesome beds, where a continual gloom brooded. It was in vain that, after our old fashion, we flung ourselves on the shores of the East, and talked of its gay bazaars, of the splendors of the time of Haroun, of harems and golden palaces. Black afreets continually arose from the depths of our talk, and expanded, like the one the fisherman released from the copper vessel, until they blotted every thing bright from our vision. Insensibly we yielded to the occult force that swayed us, and indulged in gloomy speculation. We had talked some time upon the proneness of the human mind to mysticism and the almost universal love of the Terrible, when Hammond suddenly said to me:

"What do you consider to be the greatest element of Terror?"

The question, I own, puzzled me. That many things were terrible, I knew. Stumbling over a corpse in the dark; beholding, as I once did, a woman floating down a deep and rapid river, with wildly-lifted arms and awful, upturned face, uttering, as she sank, shrieks that rent one's heart, while we, the spectators, stood frozen at a window which overhung the river at a height of sixty feet, unable to make the slightest effort to save her, but dumbly watching her last supreme agony and her disappearance. A shattered wreck, with no life visible, encountered floating listlessly on the ocean, is a terrible object, for it suggests huge terror, the proportions of which are vailed. But it now struck me for the first time that there must be one great and ruling embodiment of fear, a King of Terrors to which all others must succumb. What might it be? To what train of circumstances would it owe its existence?

"I confess, Hammond," I replied to my friend, "I never considered the subject before. That there must be one Something more terrible than any other thing, I feel. I can not attempt, however, even the most vague definition."

"I am somewhat like you, Harry," he answered. "I feel my capacity to experience a terror greater than any thing yet conceived by the human mind. Something combining in fearful and unnatural amalgamation hitherto supposed incompatible elements. The calling of the voices in Brockden Brown's novel of 'Wieland' is awful; so is the picture of the Dweller of the Threshold in Bulwer's 'Zanoni;' but," he added, shaking his head gloomily, "there is something more horrible still than these."

"Look here, Hammond," I rejoined; "let us drop this kind of talk for Heaven's sake. We shall suffer for it, depend on it."

"I don't know what's the matter with me to-night," he replied, "but my brain is running upon all sorts of weird and awful thoughts. I feel as if I could write a story like Hoffman to-night, if I were only master of a literary style."

"Well, if we are going to be Hoffmanesque in our talk I'm off to bed. Opium and nightmares should never be brought together. How sultry it is! Good-night, Hammond."

"Goodnight, Harry. Pleasant dreams to you."

"To you, gloomy wretch, afreets, ghouls, and enchanters."

We parted, and each sought his respective chamber. I undressed quickly and got into bed, taking with me, according to my usual custom, a book, over which I generally read myself to sleep. I opened the volume as soon as I had laid my head upon the pillow, and instantly flung it to the other side of the room. It was Goudon's "History of Monsters"—a curious French work, which I had lately imported from Paris, but which, in the state of mind I was then in, was any thing but an agreeable companion. I resolved to go to sleep at once; so turning down my gas until nothing but a little blue point of light glimmered on the top of the tube, I composed myself to rest once more.

The room was in total darkness. The atom of gas that still remained lighted did not illuminate a distance of three inches round the burner. I desperately drew my arm across my eyes, as if to shut out even the darkness, and tried to think of nothing. It was in vain. The confounded themes touched on by Hammond in the garden kept obtruding themselves on my brain. I battled against them. I erected ramparts of would-be blankness of intellect to keep them out. They still crowded upon me. While I was lying still as a corpse, hoping that by a perfect physical inaction I would hasten mental repose, an awful incident occurred. A Something dropped, as it seemed, from the ceiling, plumb upon my chest, and the next instant I felt two bony hands encircling my throat, endeavoring to choke me.

I am no coward, and am possessed of considerable physical strength. The suddenness of the attack instead of stunning me strung every nerve to its highest tension. My body acted from instinct, before my brain had time to realize the terrors of my position. In an instant I wound two muscular arms around the creature, and squeezed it, with all the strength of despair, against my chest. In a few seconds the bony hands that had fastened on my throat loosened their hold, and I was free to breathe once more. Then commenced a struggle of awful intensity. Immersed in the most profound darkness, totally ignorant of the nature of the Thing by which I was so suddenly attacked, finding my grasp slipping every moment by reason, it seemed to me, of the entire nakedness of my assailant, bitten with sharp teeth in the shoulder, neck, and chest, having every moment to protect my throat against a pair of sinewy, agile hands, which my utmost efforts could not confine—these were a combination of circumstances to combat which required all the strength and skill and courage that I possessed.

At last, after a silent, deadly, exhausting struggle, I got my assailant under by a series of incredible efforts of strength. Once pinned, with my knee on what I made out to be its chest, I knew that I was victor. I rested for a moment to breathe. I heard the creature beneath me panting in the darkness, and felt the violent throbbing of a heart. It was apparently as exhausted as I was, that was one comfort. At this moment I remembered that I usually placed under my pillow, before going to bed, a large, yellow silk pocket-handkerchief, for use during the night. I felt for it instantly; it was there. In a few seconds more I had, after a fashion, pinioned the creature's arms.

I now felt tolerably secure. There was nothing more to be done but to turn on the gas, and, having first seen what my midnight assailant was like, arouse the household. I will confess to being actuated by a certain pride in not giving the alarm before; I wished to make the capture alone and unaided.

Never loosing my hold for an instant, I slipped from the bed to the floor, dragging my captive with me. I had but a few steps to make to reach the gas-burner; these I made with the greatest caution, holding the creature in a grip like a vice. At last I got within arm's-length of the tiny speck of blue light, which told me where the gas-burner lay. Quick as lightning I released my grasp with one hand and let on the full flood of light. Then I turned to look at my captive.

I can not even attempt to give any definition of my sensations the instant after I turned on the gas. I suppose I must have shrieked with terror, for in less than a minute afterward my room was crowded with the inmates of the house. I shudder now as I think of that awful moment. *I saw nothing!* Yes; I had one arm firmly clasped round a breathing, panting, corporeal shape, my other hand gripped with all its strength a throat as warm, and apparently fleshly, as my own; and yet, with this living substance in my grasp, with its body pressed against my own, and all in the bright glare of a large jet of gas, I absolutely beheld nothing! Not even an outline—a vapor!

I do not, even at this hour, realize the situation in which I found myself. I can not recall the astounding incident thoroughly. Imagination in vain tries to compass the awful paradox.

It breathed. I felt its warm breath upon my cheek. It struggled fiercely. It had hands. They clutched me. Its skin was smooth, just like my own. There it lay, pressed close up against me, solid as stone—and yet utterly invisible!

I wonder that I did not faint or go mad on the instant. Some wonderful instinct must have sustained me; for, absolutely, in place of loosening my hold on the terrible Enigma, I seemed to gain an additional strength in my moment of horror, and tightened my grasp with such wonderful force that I felt the creature shivering with agony.

Just then Hammond entered my room at the head of the household. As soon as he beheld my face—which, I suppose, must have been an awful sight to look at—he hastened forward, crying,

"Great Heaven, Harry! what has happened?"

"Hammond! Hammond!" I cried, "come here. Oh! this is awful! I have been attacked in bed by something or other, which I have hold of; but I can't see it—I can't see it!"

Hammond, doubtless struck by the unfeigned horror expressed in my countenance, made one or two steps forward with an anxious yet puzzled expression. A very audible titter burst from the remainder of my visitors. This suppressed laughter made me furious. To laugh at a human being in my position! It was the worst species of cruelty. *Now*, I can understand why the appearance of a man struggling violently, as it would seem, with an airy nothing, and calling for assistance against a vision, should have appeared ludicrous. *Then*, so great was my rage against the mocking crowd that had I the power I would have stricken them dead where they stood.

"Hammond! Hammond!" I cried again, despairingly, "for God's sake come to me. I can hold the—the Thing but a short while longer. It is overpowering me. Help me. Help me!"

"Harry," whispered Hammond, approaching me, "you have been smoking too much opium."

"I swear to you Hammond that this is no vision," I answered, in the same low tone. "Don't you see how it shakes my whole frame with its struggles? If you don't believe me convince yourself. Feel it—touch it."

Hammond advanced and laid his hand in the spot I indicated. A wild cry of horror burst from him. He had felt it!

In a moment he had discovered somewhere in my room a long piece of cord, and was the next instant winding it, and knotting it about the body of the unseen being that I clasped in my arms.

"Harry," he said, in a hoarse, agitated voice, for, though he preserved his presence of mind, he was deeply moved, "Harry, it's all safe now. You may let go, old fellow, if you're tired. The Thing can't move."

I was utterly exhausted, and I gladly loosed my hold.

Hammond stood holding the ends of the cord that bound the Invisible, twisted round his hand, while before him, self-supporting, as it were, he beheld a rope laced and interlaced, and stretching tightly around a vacant space. I never saw a man look so thoroughly stricken with awe. Nevertheless his face expressed all the courage and determination which I knew him to possess. His lips, although white, were set firmly, and one could perceive at a glance that, although stricken with fear, he was not daunted.

The confusion that ensued among the guests of the house, who were witnesses of this extraordinary scene between Hammond and myself—who beheld the pantomime of binding this struggling Something—who beheld me almost sinking from physical exhaustion when my task of jailer was over—the confusion and terror that took possession of the by-standers, when they saw all this, was beyond description. Many of the weaker ones fled from the apartment. The few who remained behind clustered near the door, and could not be induced to approach Hammond and his Charge. Still incredulity broke out through their terror. They had not the courage to satisfy themselves, and yet they doubted. It was in vain that I begged of some of the men to come near and convince themselves by touch of the existence of a living being in that room which was invisible. They were incredulous, but did not dare to undeceive themselves. How could a solid, living, breathing body be invisible? they asked. My reply was this. I gave a sign to Hammond, and both of us—conquering our fearful repugnance to touching the invisible creature—lifted it from the ground, manacled as it was, and took it to my bed. Its weight was about that of a boy of fourteen.

"Now my friends," I said, as Hammond and myself held the creature suspended over the bed, "I can give you self-evident proof that here is a solid, ponderable body which, nevertheless, you can not see. Be good enough to watch the surface of the bed attentively."

I was astonished at my own courage in treating this strange event so calmly; but I had recovered from my first terror, and felt a sort of scientific pride in the affair which dominated every other feeling.

The eyes of the by-standers were immediately fixed on my bed. At a given signal Hammond and I let the creature fall. There was the dull sound of a heavy body alighting on a soft mass. The timbers of the bed creaked. A deep impression marked itself distinctly on the pillow, and on the bed itself. The crowd who witnessed this gave a sort of low, universal cry, and rushed from the room. Hammond and I were left alone with our Mystery.

We remained silent for some time, listening to the low, irregular breathing of the creature on the bed, and watching the rustle of the bedclothes as it impotently struggled to free itself from confinement. Then Hammond spoke.

"Harry, this is awful."

"Ay, awful."

"But not unaccountable."

"Not unaccountable! What do you mean? Such a thing has never occurred since the birth of the world. I know not what to think, Hammond. God grant that I am not mad, and that this is not an insane fantasy!"

"Let us reason a little, Harry. Here is a solid body which we touch, but which we can not see. The fact is so unusual that it strikes us with terror. Is there no parallel, though, for such a phenomenon? Take a piece of pure glass. It is tangible and transparent. A certain chemical coarseness is all that prevents its being so entirely transparent as to be totally invisible. It is not *theoretically impossible*, mind you, to fabricate a glass which shall not reflect a single ray of light—a glass so pure and homogeneous in its atoms that the rays from the sun shall pass through it as they do through the air, refracted but not reflected. We do not see the air, and yet we feel it."

"That's all very well, Hammond, but these are inanimate substances. Glass does not breathe, air does not breathe. *This* thing has a heart that palpitates. A will that moves it. Lungs that play and inspire and respire."

"You forget the strange phenomena of which we have so often heard of late," answered the Doctor, gravely. "At the meetings called 'spirit circles,' invisible hands have been thrust into the hands of those persons round the table—warm, fleshly hands that seemed to pulsate with mortal life."

"What? Do you think, then, that this thing is—"

"I don't know what it is," was the solemn reply; "but please the gods I will, with your assistance, thoroughly investigate it."

We watched together, smoking many pipes, all night long by the bedside of the unearthly being that tossed and panted until it was apparently wearied out. Then we learned by the low, regular breathing that it slept.

The next morning the house was all astir. The boarders congregated on the landing outside my room, and Hammond and myself were lions. We had to answer a thousand questions as to the state of our extraordinary prisoner, for as yet not one person in the house except ourselves could be induced to set foot in the apartment.

The creature was awake. This was evidenced by the convulsive manner in which the bed-clothes were moved in its efforts to escape. There was something truly terrible in beholding, as it were, those second-hand indications of the terrible writhings and agonized struggles for liberty, which themselves were invisible.

Hammond and myself had racked our brains during the long night to discover some means by which we might realize the shape and general appearance of the Enigma. As well as we could make out by passing our hands over the creature's form, its outlines and lineaments were human. There was a mouth; a round, smooth head without hair; a nose, which, however, was little elevated above the cheeks; and its hands and feet felt like those of a boy. At first we thought of placing the being on a smooth surface and tracing its outline with chalk, as shoe-makers trace the outline of the foot. This plan was given up as being of no value. Such an outline would give not the slightest idea of its conformation.

A happy thought struck me. We would take a cast of it in plaster of Paris. This would give us the solid figure, and satisfy all our wishes. But how to do it? The movements of the creature would disturb the setting of the plastic covering, and distort the mould. Another thought. Why not give it chloroform? It had respiratory organs—that was evident by its breathing. Once reduced to a state of insensibility, we could do with it what we would. Doctor X—— was sent for; and after the worthy physician had recovered from the first shock of amazement, he proceeded to administer the chloroform. In three minutes afterward we were enabled to remove the fetters from the creature's body, and a well-known modeler of this city was busily engaged in covering the invisible form with the moist clay. In five minutes more we had a mould, and before evening a rough *fac-simile* of the Mystery. It was shaped like a man. Distorted, uncouth, and horrible, but still a man. It was small, not over four feet and some inches in height, and its limbs betrayed a muscular development that was unparalleled. Its face surpassed in hideousness any thing I had ever seen. Gustave Doré, or Callot, or Tony Johannot never conceived any thing so horrible. There is a face in one of the latter's illustrations to "*Un voyage ou il vous plaira*," which somewhat approaches the

countenance of this creature, but does not equal it. It was the
physiognomy of what I should have fancied a ghoul to be. It
looked as if it was capable of feeding on human flesh.

Having satisfied our curiosity, and bound every one in the
house over to secrecy, it became a question what was to be
done with our Enigma? It was impossible that we should keep
such a horror in our house; it was equally impossible that such
an awful being should be let loose upon the world. I confess
that I would have gladly voted for the creature's destruction.
But who would shoulder the responsibility? Who would undertake the execution of this horrible semblance of a human
being? Day after day this question was deliberated gravely. The
boarders all left the house. Mrs. Moffat was in despair, and
threatened Hammond and myself with all sorts of legal penal-
ties if we did not remove the Horror. Our answer was, "We
will go if you like, but we decline taking this creature with us.
Remove it yourself if you please. It appeared in your house. On
you the responsibility rests." To this there was, of course, no
answer. Mrs. Moffat could not obtain for love or money a person who would even approach the Mystery.

The most singular part of the transaction was, that we were
entirely ignorant of what the creature habitually fed on. Every
thing in the way of nutriment that we could think of was
placed before it, but was never touched. It was awful to stand
by, day after day, and see the clothes lost and hear the hard
breathing, and know that it was starving.

Ten, twelve days, a fortnight passed, and it still lived. The
pulsations of the heart, however, were daily growing fainter,
and had now nearly ceased altogether. It was evident that the
creature was dying for want of sustenance. While this terrible
life-struggle was going on I felt miserable. I could not sleep of
nights. Horrible as the creature was, it was pitiful to think of
the pangs it was suffering.

At last it died. Hammond and I found it cold and stiff one
morning in the bed. The heart had ceased to beat, the lungs to
inspire. We hastened to bury it in the garden. It was a strange
funeral, the dropping of that viewless corpse into the damp
hole. The cast of its form I gave to Doctor X——, who keeps
it in his museum in Tenth Street.

As I am on the eve of a long journey from which I may not return, I have drawn up this narrative of an event the most singular that has ever come to my knowledge.

HARRY ESCOTT.

[NOTE.—It is rumored that the proprietors of a well-known museum in this city have made arrangements with Dr. X—— to exhibit to the public the singular cast which Mr. Escott deposited with him. So extraordinary a history can not fail to attract universal attention.]

1859

BRET HARTE

(1836–1902)

The Legend of Monte del Diablo

THE cautious reader will detect a lack of authenticity in the following pages. I am not a cautious reader myself, yet I confess with some concern to the absence of much documentary evidence in support of the singular incident I am about to relate. Disjointed memoranda, the proceedings of ayuntamientos and early departmental juntas, with other records of a primitive and superstitious people, have been my inadequate authorities. It is but just to state, however, that though this particular story lacks corroboration, in ransacking the Spanish archives of Upper California I have met with many more surprising and incredible stories, attested and supported to a degree that would have placed this legend beyond a cavil or doubt. I have, also, never lost faith in the legend myself, and in so doing have profited much from the examples of divers grant-claimants, who have often jostled me in their more practical researches, and who have my sincere sympathy at the skepticism of a modern hard-headed and practical world.

For many years after Father Junipero Serro first rang his bell in the wilderness of Upper California, the spirit which animated that adventurous priest did not wane. The conversion of the heathen went on rapidly in the establishment of missions throughout the land. So sedulously did the good Fathers set about their work, that around their isolated chapels there presently arose adobe huts, whose mud-plastered and savage tenants partook regularly of the provisions, and occasionally of the Sacrament, of their pious hosts. Nay, so great was their progress, that one zealous Padre is reported to have administered the Lord's Supper one Sabbath morning to "over three hundred heathen salvages." It was not to be wondered that the Enemy of Souls, being greatly incensed thereat, and alarmed at his decreasing popularity, should have grievously tempted and embarrassed these holy Fathers, as we shall presently see.

Yet they were happy, peaceful days for California. The vagrant keels of prying Commerce had not as yet ruffled the lordly gravity of her bays. No torn and ragged gulch betrayed the suspicion of golden treasure. The wild oats drooped idly in the morning heat or wrestled with the afternoon breezes. Deer and antelope dotted the plain. The watercourses brawled in their familiar channels, nor dreamed of ever shifting their regular tide. The wonders of the Yosemite and Calaveras were as yet unrecorded. The holy Fathers noted little of the landscape beyond the barbaric prodigality with which the quick soil repaid the sowing. A new conversion, the advent of a saint's day, or the baptism of an Indian baby, was at once the chronicle and marvel of their day.

At this blissful epoch there lived at the Mission of San Pablo Father José Antonio Haro, a worthy brother of the Society of Jesus. He was of tall and cadaverous aspect. A somewhat romantic history had given a poetic interest to his lugubrious visage. While a youth, pursuing his studies at famous Salamanca, he had become enamored of the charms of Doña Carmen de Torrencevara, as that lady passed to her matutinal devotions. Untoward circumstances, hastened, perhaps, by a wealthier suitor, brought this amour to a disastrous issue, and Father José entered a monastery, taking upon himself the vows of celibacy. It was here that his natural fervor and poetic enthusiasm conceived expression as a missionary. A longing to convert the uncivilized heathen succeeded his frivolous earthly passion, and a desire to explore and develop unknown fastnesses continually possessed him. In his flashing eye and sombre exterior was detected a singular commingling of the discreet Las Casas and the impetuous Balboa.

Fixed by this pious zeal, Father José went forward in the van of Christian pioneers. On reaching Mexico he obtained authority to establish the Mission of San Pablo. Like the good Junipero, accompanied only by an acolyte and muleteer, he unsaddled his mules in a dusky cañon, and rang his bell in the wilderness. The savages—a peaceful, inoffensive, and inferior race—presently flocked around him. The nearest military post was far away, which contributed much to the security of these pious pilgrims, who found their open trustfulness and amiability better fitted to repress hostility than the presence of an

armed, suspicious, and brawling soldiery. So the good Father
José said matins and prime, mass and vespers, in the heart of
sin and heathenism, taking no heed to himself, but looking
only to the welfare of the Holy Church. Conversions soon followed, and on the 7th of July, 1760, the first Indian baby was
baptized,—an event which, as Father José piously records, "ex-
ceeds the richnesse of gold or precious jewels or the chancing
upon the Ophir of Solomon." I quote this incident as best
suited to show the ingenious blending of poetry and piety
which distinguished Father José's record.

The Mission of San Pablo progressed and prospered, until
the pious founder thereof, like the infidel Alexander, might
have wept that there were no more heathen worlds to conquer.
But his ardent and enthusiastic spirit could not long brook an
idleness that seemed begotten of sin; and one pleasant August
morning in the year of grace 1770 Father José issued from the
outer court of the mission building, equipped to explore the
field for new missionary labors.

Nothing could exceed the quiet gravity and unpretentious-
ness of the little cavalcade. First rode a stout muleteer, leading
a pack-mule laden with the provisions of the party, together
with a few cheap crucifixes and hawks' bells. After him came
the devout Padre José, bearing his breviary and cross, with a
black serapa thrown around his shoulders; while on either side
trotted a dusky convert, anxious to show a proper sense of his
regeneration by acting as guide into the wilds of his heathen
brethren. Their new condition was agreeably shown by the
absence of the usual mud-plaster, which in their unconverted
state they assumed to keep away vermin and cold. The
morning was bright and propitious. Before their departure,
mass had been said in the chapel, and the protection of St.
Ignatius invoked against all contingent evils, but especially
against bears, which, like the fiery dragons of old, seemed to
cherish unconquerable hostility to the Holy Church.

As they wound through the cañon, charming birds dis-
ported upon boughs and sprays, and sober quails piped from
the alders; the willowy watercourses gave a musical utterance,
and the long grass whispered on the hillside. On entering the
deeper defiles, above them towered dark green masses of pine,
and occasionally the madroño shook its bright scarlet berries.

As they toiled up many a steep ascent, Father José sometimes picked up fragments of scoria, which spake to his imagination of direful volcanoes and impending earthquakes. To the less scientific mind of the muleteer Ignacio they had even a more terrifying significance; and he once or twice snuffed the air suspiciously, and declared that it smelt of sulphur. So the first day of their journey wore away, and at night they encamped without having met a single heathen face.

It was on this night that the Enemy of Souls appeared to Ignacio in an appalling form. He had retired to a secluded part of the camp and had sunk upon his knees in prayerful meditation, when he looked up and perceived the Arch-Fiend in the likeness of a monstrous bear. The Evil One was seated on his hind legs immediately before him, with his fore paws joined together just below his black muzzle. Wisely conceiving this remarkable attitude to be in mockery and derision of his devotions, the worthy muleteer was transported with fury. Seizing an arquebus, he instantly closed his eyes and fired. When he had recovered from the effects of the terrific discharge, the apparition had disappeared. Father José, awakened by the report, reached the spot only in time to chide the muleteer for wasting powder and ball in a contest with one whom a single ave would have been sufficient to utterly discomfit. What further reliance he placed on Ignacio's story is not known; but, in commemoration of a worthy Californian custom, the place was called "La Cañada de la Tentacion del Pio Muletero," or "The Glen of the Temptation of the Pious Muleteer," a name which it retains to this day.

The next morning the party, issuing from a narrow gorge, came upon a long valley, sear and burnt with the shadeless heat. Its lower extremity was lost in a fading line of low hills, which, gathering might and volume toward the upper end of the valley, upheaved a stupendous bulwark against the breezy north. The peak of this awful spur was just touched by a fleecy cloud that shifted to and fro like a banneret. Father José gazed at it with mingled awe and admiration. By a singular coincidence, the muleteer Ignacio uttered the simple ejaculation "Diablo!"

As they penetrated the valley, they soon began to miss the agreeable life and companionable echoes of the cañon they had quitted. Huge fissures in the parched soil seemed to gape as with thirsty mouths. A few squirrels darted from the earth and disappeared as mysteriously before the jingly mules. A gray wolf trotted leisurely along just ahead. But whichever way Father José turned, the mountain always asserted itself and arrested his wandering eye. Out of the dry and arid valley it seemed to spring into cooler and bracing life. Deep cavernous shadows dwelt along its base; rocky fastnesses appeared midway of its elevation; and on either side huge black hills diverged like massy roots from a central trunk. His lively fancy pictured these hills peopled with a majestic and intelligent race of savages; and looking into futurity, he already saw a monstrous cross crowning the dome-like summit. Far different were the sensations of the muleteer, who saw in those awful solitudes only fiery dragons, colossal bears, and breakneck trails. The converts, Concepcion and Incarnacion, trotting modestly beside the Padre, recognized, perhaps, some manifestation of their former weird mythology.

At nightfall they reached the base of the mountain. Here Father José unpacked his mules, said vespers, and, formally ringing his bell, called upon the Gentiles within hearing to come and accept the holy faith. The echoes of the black frowning hills around him caught up the pious invitation and repeated it at intervals; but no Gentiles appeared that night. Nor were the devotions of the muleteer again disturbed, although he afterward asserted that, when the Father's exhortation was ended, a mocking peal of laughter came from the mountain. Nothing daunted by these intimations of the near hostility of the Evil One, Father José declared his intention to ascend the mountain at early dawn, and before the sun rose the next morning he was leading the way.

The ascent was in many places difficult and dangerous. Huge fragments of rock often lay across the trail, and after a few hours' climbing they were forced to leave their mules in a little gully and continue the ascent afoot. Unaccustomed to such exertion, Father José often stopped to wipe the perspiration from his thin cheeks. As the day wore on a strange silence oppressed them. Except the occasional pattering of a squirrel, or a rustling in the chimisal bushes, there were no signs of life. The half-human print of a bear's foot sometimes appeared before them, at which Ignacio always crossed himself piously. The eye was sometimes cheated by a dripping from the rocks, which on closer inspection proved to be a resinous oily liquid with an abominable sulphurous smell. When they were within a short distance of the summit, the discreet Ignacio, selecting a sheltered nook for the camp, slipped aside and busied himself in preparations for the evening, leaving the holy Father to continue the ascent alone. Never was there a more thoughtless act of prudence, never a more imprudent piece of caution. Without noticing the desertion, buried in pious reflection, Father José pushed mechanically on, and, reaching the summit, cast himself down and gazed upon the prospect.

Below him lay a succession of valleys opening into each other like gentle lakes, until they were lost to the southward. Westerly the distant range hid the bosky cañada which sheltered the Mission of San Pablo. In the farther distance the Pacific Ocean stretched away, bearing a cloud of fog upon its bosom, which crept through the entrance of the bay, and rolled thickly between him and the northeastward; the same fog hid the base of the mountain and the view beyond. Still from time to time the fleecy veil parted, and timidly disclosed charming glimpses of mighty rivers, mountain defiles, and rolling plains, sear with ripened oats and bathed in the glow of the setting sun. As father José gazed, he was penetrated with a pious longing. Already his imagination, filled with enthusiastic conceptions, beheld all that vast expanse gathered under the mild sway of the holy faith and peopled with zealous converts. Each little knoll in fancy became crowned with a chapel; from each dark cañon gleamed the white walls of a mission building. Growing bolder in his enthusiasm and looking farther into futurity, he beheld a new Spain rising on these savage shores. He already saw the spires of stately cathedrals, the domes of palaces, vineyards, gardens, and groves. Convents, half hid among the hills, peeping from plantations of branching limes, and long processions of chanting nuns wound through the defiles. So completely was the good Father's conception of the future confounded with the past, that even in their choral strain the well-remembered accents of Carmen struck his ear. He was busied in these fanciful imaginings, when suddenly over that extended prospect the faint distant tolling of a bell rang sadly out and died. It was the Angelus. Father José listened with superstitious exaltation.

The Mission of San Pablo was far away, and the sound must have been some miraculous omen. But never before, to his enthusiastic sense, did the sweet seriousness of this angelic symbol come with such strange significance. With the last faint peal his glowing fancy seemed to cool; the fog closed in below him, and the good Father remembered he had not had his supper. He had risen and was wrapping his serapa around him, when he perceived for the first time that he was not alone.

Nearly opposite, and where should have been the faithless Ignacio, a grave and decorous figure was seated. His appearance was that of an elderly hidalgo, dressed in mourning, with mustaches of iron-gray carefully waxed and twisted round a pair of lantern-jaws. The monstrous hat and prodigious feather, the enormous ruff and exaggerated trunk-hose, contrasted with a frame shriveled and wizened, all belonged to a century previous. Yet Father José was not astonished. His adventurous life and poetic imagination, continually on the lookout for the marvelous, gave him a certain advantage over the practical and material-minded. He instantly detected the diabolical quality of his visitant, and was prepared. With equal coolness and courtesy he met the cavalier's obeisance.

"I ask your pardon, Sir Priest," said the stranger, "for disturbing your meditations. Pleasant they must have been, and right fanciful, I imagine, when occasioned by so fair a prospect.

"Worldly, perhaps, Sir Devil,—for such I take you to be," said the holy Father, as the stranger bowed his black plumes to the ground; "worldly, perhaps; for it hath pleased Heaven to retain even in our regenerated state much that pertaineth to the flesh, yet still, I trust, not without some speculation for the welfare of the Holy Church. In dwelling upon yon fair expanse, mine eyes have been graciously opened with prophetic inspiration, and the promise of the heathen as an inheritance hath marvelously recurred to me. For there can be none lack such diligence in the true faith but may see that even the conversion of these pitiful salvages hath a meaning. As the blessed St. Ignatius discreetly observes," continued Father José, clearing his throat and slightly elevating his voice, "'the heathen is given to the warriors of Christ, even as the pearls of rare discovery which gladden the hearts of shipmen.' Nay, I might say"—

But here the stranger, who had been wrinkling his brows

and twisting his mustaches with well-bred patience, took advantage of an oratorical pause.

"It grieves me, Sir Priest, to interrupt the current of your eloquence as discourteously as I have already broken your meditations; but the day already waneth to night. I have a matter of serious import to make with you, could I entreat your cautious consideration a few moments."

Father José hesitated. The temptation was great, and the prospect of acquiring some knowledge of the Great Enemy's plans not the least trifling object. And, if the truth must be told, there was a certain decorum about the stranger that interested the Padre. Though well aware of the Protean shapes the Arch-Fiend could assume, and though free from the weaknesses of the flesh, Father José was not above the temptations of the spirit. Had the Devil appeared, as in the case of the pious St. Anthony, in the likeness of a comely damsel, the good Father, with his certain experience of the deceitful sex, would have whisked her away in the saying of a paternoster. But there was, added to the security of age, a grave sadness about the stranger, —a thoughtful consciousness, as of being at a great moral disadvantage, which at once decided him on a magnanimous course of conduct.

The stranger then proceeded to inform him that he had been diligently observing the holy Father's triumphs in the valley. That, far from being greatly exercised thereat, he had been only grieved to see so enthusiastic and chivalrous an antagonist wasting his zeal in a hopeless work. For, he observed, the issue of the great battle of Good and Evil had been otherwise settled, as he would presently show him. "It wants but a few moments of night," he continued, "and over this interval of twilight, as you know, I have been given complete control. Look to the west."

As the Padre turned, the stranger took his enormous hat from his head and waved it three times before him. At each sweep of the prodigious feather the fog grew thinner, until it melted impalpably away, and the former landscape returned, yet warm with the glowing sun. As Father José gazed a strain of martial music arose from the valley, and issuing from a deep cañon the good Father beheld a long cavalcade of gallant cavaliers, habited like his companion. As they swept down the plain, they were joined by like processions, that slowly defiled from every ravine and cañon of the mysterious mountain. From time to time the peal of a trumpet swelled fitfully upon the breeze; the cross of Santiago glittered, and the royal banners of Castile and Aragon waved over the moving column. So they moved on solemnly toward the sea, where, in the distance, Father José saw stately caravels, bearing the same familiar banner, awaiting them. The good Padre gazed with conflicting emotions, and the serious voice of the stranger broke the silence.

"Thou hast beheld, Sir Priest, the fading footprints of adventurous Castile. Thou hast seen the declining glory of old Spain,—declining as yonder brilliant sun. The sceptre she hath wrested from the heathen is fast dropping from her decrepit and fleshless grasp. The children she hath fostered shall know her no longer. The soil she hath acquired shall be lost to her as irrevocably as she herself hath thrust the Moor from her own Granada."

The stranger paused, and his voice seemed broken by emotion; at the same time, Father José, whose sympathizing heart yearned toward the departing banners, cried in poignant accents,—

"Farewell, ye gallant cavaliers and Christian soldiers! Farewell, thou, Nuñes de Balboa! thou, Alonzo de Ojeda! and thou, most venerable Las Casas! farewell, and may Heaven prosper still the seed ye left behind!"

Then turning to the stranger, Father José beheld him gravely draw his pocket-handkerchief from the basket-hilt of his rapier and apply it decorously to his eyes.

"Pardon this weakness, Sir Priest," said the cavalier apologetically; "but these worthy gentlemen were ancient friends of mine, and have done me many a delicate service,—much more, perchance, than these poor sables may signify," he added, with a grim gesture toward the mourning suit he wore.

Father José was too much preoccupied in reflection to notice the equivocal nature of this tribute, and, after a few moments' silence, said, as if continuing his thought,—

"But the seed they have planted shall thrive and prosper on this fruitful soil."

As if answering the interrogatory, the stranger turned to the opposite direction, and, again waving his hat, said, in the same serious tone, "Look to the east!"

The Father turned, and, as the fog broke away before the waving plume, he saw that the sun was rising. Issuing with its bright beams through the passes of the snowy mountains beyond appeared a strange and motley crew. Instead of the dark and romantic visages of his last phantom train, the Father beheld with strange concern the blue eyes and flaxen hair of a Saxon race. In place of martial airs and musical utterance, there rose upon the ear a strange din of harsh gutturals and singular sibilation. Instead of the decorous tread and stately mien of the cavaliers of the former vision, they came pushing, bustling, panting, and swaggering. And as they passed, the good Father noticed that giant trees were prostrated as with the breath of a tornado, and the bowels of the earth were torn and rent as with a convulsion. And Father José looked in vain for holy cross or Christian symbol; there was but one that seemed an ensign, and he crossed himself with holy horror as he perceived it bore the effigy of a bear.

"Who are these swaggering Ishmaelites?" he asked, with something of asperity in his tone.

The stranger was gravely silent.

"What do they here, with neither cross nor holy symbol?" he again demanded.

"Have you the courage to see, Sir Priest?" responded the stranger quietly.

Father José felt his crucifix, as a lonely traveler might his rapier, and assented.

"Step under the shadow of my plume," said the stranger.

Father José stepped beside him and they instantly sank through the earth.

When he opened his eyes, which had remained closed in prayerful meditation during his rapid descent, he found himself in a vast vault, bespangled overhead with luminous points like the starred firmament. It was also lighted by a yellow glow that seemed to proceed from a mighty sea or lake that occupied the centre of the chamber. Around this subterranean sea dusky figures flitted, bearing ladles filled with the yellow fluid, which they had replenished from its depths. From this lake diverging streams of the same mysterious flood penetrated like mighty rivers the cavernous distance. As they walked by the banks of this glittering Styx, Father José perceived how the liquid stream at certain places became solid. The ground was strewn with glittering flakes. One of these the Padre picked up and curiously examined. It was virgin gold.

An expression of discomfiture overcast the good Father's face at this discovery; but there was trace neither of malice nor satisfaction in the stranger's air, which was still of serious and fateful contemplation. When Father José recovered his equanimity, he said bitterly,—

"This, then, Sir Devil, is your work! This is your deceitful lure for the weak souls of sinful nations! So would you replace the Christian grace of Holy Spain!"

"This is what must be," returned the stranger gloomily. "But listen, Sir Priest. It lies with you to avert the issue for a time. Leave me here in peace. Go back to Castile, and take with you your bells, your images, and your missions. Continue here, and you only precipitate results. Stay! promise me you will do this, and you shall not lack that which will render your old age an ornament and a blessing;" and the stranger motioned significantly to the lake.

It was here, the legend discreetly relates, that the Devil showed—as he always shows sooner or later—his cloven hoof. The worthy Padre, sorely perplexed by this threefold vision, and, if the truth must be told, a little nettled at this wresting away of the glory of holy Spanish discovery, had shown some hesitation. But the unlucky bribe of the Enemy of Souls touched his Castilian spirit. Starting back in deep disgust, he brandished his crucifix in the face of the unmasked Fiend, and in a voice that made the dusky vault resound cried,—

"Avaunt thee, Sathanas! Diabolus, I defy thee! What! wouldst thou bribe me,—me, a brother of the Sacred Society of the Holy Jesus, Licentiate of Cordova and Inquisitor of Guadalaxara? Thinkest thou to buy me with thy sordid treasure? Avaunt!"

What might have been the issue of this rupture, and how complete might have been the triumph of the holy Father over the Arch-Fiend, who was recoiling aghast at these sacred titles and the flourishing symbol, we can never know, for at that moment the crucifix slipped through his fingers.

Scarcely had it touched the ground before Devil and holy Father simultaneously cast themselves toward it. In the struggle they clinched, and the pious José, who was as much the superior of his antagonist in bodily as in spiritual strength, was about to treat the Great Adversary to a back somersault, when he suddenly felt the long nails of the stranger piercing his flesh. A new fear seized his heart, a numbing chillness crept through his body, and he struggled to free himself, but in vain. A strange roaring was in his ears; the lake and cavern danced before his eyes and vanished, and with a loud cry he sank senseless to the ground.

When he recovered his consciousness, he was aware of a gentle swaying motion of his body. He opened his eyes, and saw it was high noon, and that he was being carried in a litter through the valley. He felt stiff, and looking down, perceived that his arm was tightly bandaged to his side.

He closed his eyes, and, after a few words of thankful prayer, thought how miraculously he had been preserved, and made a vow of candlesticks to the blessed Saint José. He then called in a faint voice, and presently the penitent Ignacio stood beside him.

The joy the poor fellow felt at his patron's returning consciousness for some time choked his utterance. He could only ejaculate, "A miracle! Blessed Saint José, he lives!" and kiss the Padre's bandaged hand. Father José, more intent on his last night's experience, waited for his emotion to subside, and asked where he had been found.

"On the mountain, your Reverence, but a few varas from where he attacked you."

"How?—you saw him then?" asked the Padre in unfeigned astonishment,

"Saw him, your Reverence! Mother of God! I should think I did! And your Reverence shall see him too, if he ever comes again within range of Ignacio's arquebus."

"What mean you, Ignacio?" said the Padre, sitting bolt-upright in his litter.

"Why, the bear, your Reverence,—the bear, holy Father, who attacked your worshipful person while you were meditating on the top of yonder mountain."

"Ah!" said the holy Father, lying down again. "Chut, child! I would be at peace."

When he reached the mission he was tenderly cared for, and in a few weeks was enabled to resume those duties from which, as will be seen, not even the machinations of the Evil One could divert him. The news of his physical disaster spread over the country, and a letter to the Bishop of Guadalaxara contained a confidential and detailed account of the good Father's spiritual temptation. But in some way the story leaked out; and long after José was gathered to his fathers, his mysterious encounter formed the theme of thrilling and whispered narrative. The mountain was generally shunned. It is true that Señor Joaquin Pedrillo afterward located a grant near the base of the mountain; but as Señora Pedrillo was known to be a termagant half-breed, the señor was not supposed to be over-fastidious.

Such is the legend of Monte del Diablo. As I said before, it may seem to lack essential corroboration. The discrepancy between the Father's narrative and the actual climax has given rise to some skepticism on the part of ingenious quibblers. All such I would simply refer to that part of the report of Señor Julio Serro, Sub-Prefect of San Pablo, before whom attest of the above was made. Touching this matter, the worthy Prefect observes, "That although the body of Father José doth show evidence of grievous conflict in the flesh, yet that is no proof that the Enemy of Souls, who could assume the figure of a decorous elderly caballero, could not at the same time transform himself into a bear for his own vile purposes."

1863

HARRIET PRESCOTT SPOFFORD

(1835–1921)

The Moonstone Mass

THERE was a certain weakness possessed by my ancestors, though in nowise peculiar to them, and of which, in common with other more or less undesirable traits, I have come into the inheritance.

It was the fear of dying in poverty. That, too, in the face of a goodly share of pelf stored in stocks, and lands, and copper-bottomed clippers, or what stood for copper-bottomed clippers, or rather sailed for them, in the clumsy commerce of their times.

There was one old fellow in particular—his portrait is hanging over the hall stove to-day, leaning forward, somewhat blistered by the profuse heat and wasted fuel there, and as if as long as such an outrageous expenditure of caloric was going on he meant to have the full benefit of it—who is said to have frequently shed tears over the probable price of his dinner, and on the next day to have sent home a silver dish to eat it from at a hundred times the cost. I find the inconsistencies of this individual constantly cropping out in myself; and although I could by no possibility be called a niggard, yet I confess that even now my prodigalities make me shiver.

Some years ago I was the proprietor of the old family estate, unencumbered by any thing except timber, that is worth its weight in gold yet, as you might say; alone in the world, save for an unloved relative; and with a sufficiently comfortable income, as I have since discovered, to meet all reasonable wants. I had, moreover, promised me in marriage the hand of a woman without a peer, and which, I believe now, might have been mine on any day when I saw fit to claim it.

That I loved Eleanor tenderly and truly you can not doubt; that I desired to bring her home, to see her flitting here and there in my dark old house, illuminating it with her youth and beauty, sitting at the head of my table that sparkled with its gold and silver heir-looms, making my days and nights like one delightful dream, was just as true.

And yet I hesitated. I looked over my bank-book—I cast up my accounts. I have enough for one, I said; I am not sure that it is enough for two. Eleanor, daintily nurtured, requires as dainty care for all time to come; moreover, it is not two alone to be considered, for should children come, there is their education, their maintenance, their future provision and portion to be found. All this would impoverish us, and unless we ended by becoming mere dependents, we had, to my excited vision, only the cold charity of the world and the work-house to which to look forward. I do not believe that Eleanor thought me right in so much of the matter as I saw fit to explain, but in maiden pride her lips perforce were sealed. She laughed though, when I confessed my work-house fear, and said that for her part she was thankful there was such a refuge at all, standing as it did on its knoll in the midst of green fields, and shaded by broad-limbed oaks—she had always envied the old women sitting there by their evening fireside, and mumbling over their small affairs to one another. But all her words seemed merely idle badinage—so I delayed. I said—when this ship sails in, when that dividend is declared, when I see how this speculation turns out—the days were long that added up the count of years, the nights were dreary; but I believed that I was actuated by principle, and took pride to myself for my strength and self-denial.

Moreover, old Paul, my great-uncle on my mother's side, and the millionaire of the family, was a bitter misogynist, and regarded women and marriage and household cares as the three remediless mistakes of an overruling Providence. He knew of my engagement to Eleanor, but so long as it remained in that stage he had nothing to say. Let me once marry, and my share of his million would be best represented by a cipher. However, he was not a man to adore, and he could not live forever.

Still, with all my own effort, I amassed wealth but slowly, according to my standard; my various ventures had various luck; and one day my old Uncle Paul, always intensely interested in the subject, both scientifically and from a commercial point of view, too old and feeble to go himself, but fain to send a proxy, and desirous of money in the family, made me an offer of that portion of his wealth on my return which would be mine on his demise, funded safely subject to my order, provided I made one of those who sought the discovery of the Northwest Passage.

I went to town, canvassed the matter with the experts—I had always an adventurous streak, as old Paul well knew—and having given many hours to the pursuit of the smaller sciences, had a turn for danger and discovery as well. And when the *Albatross* sailed—in spite of Eleanor's shivering remonstrance and prayers and tears, in spite of the grave looks of my friends —I was one of those that clustered on her deck, prepared for either fate. They—my companions—it is true, were led by nobler lights; but as for me, it was much as I told Eleanor—my affairs were so regulated that they would go on uninterrupt-edly in my absence; I should be no worse off for going, and if I returned, letting alone the renown of the thing, my Uncle Paul's donation was to be appropriated; every thing then was assured, and we stood possessed of lucky lives. If I had any keen or eager desire of search, any purpose to aid the growth of the world or to penetrate the secrets of its formation, as in-deed I think I must have had, I did not at that time know any thing about it. But I was to learn that death and stillness have no kingdom on this globe, and that even in the extremest bit-terness of cold and ice perpetual interchange and motion is taking place. So we went, all sails set on favorable winds, bounding over blue sea, skirting frowning coasts, and ever pushing our way up into the dark mystery of the North.

I shall not delay here to tell of Danish posts and the hospi-tality of summer settlements in their long afternoon of arctic daylight; nor will I weary you with any description of the suc-culence of the radishes that grew under the panes of glass in the Governor's scrap of moss and soil, scarcely of more size than a lady's parlor fernery, and which seemed to our dry mouths full of all the earth's cool juices—but advance, as we ourselves hastened to do, while that chill and crystalline sun shone, up into the ice-cased dens and caverns of the Pole. By the time that the long, blue twilight fell, when the rough and rasping cold sheathed all the atmosphere, and the great stars pricked themselves out on the heavens like spears' points, the *Albatross* was hauled up for winter-quarters, banked and boarded, heaved high on fields of ice; and all her inmates, during the wintry dark, led the life that prepared them for further exploits in higher latitudes the coming year, learning the dialects of the Esquimaux, the tricks of the seal and walrus, making long explorations with the dogs and Glipnu, their master, breaking ourselves in for business that had no play about it.

Then, at last, the August suns set us free again; inlets of tumultuous water traversed the great ice-floes; the *Albatross*, refitted, ruffled all her plumage and spread her wings once more for the North—for the secret that sat there domineering all its substance.

It was a year since we had heard from home; but who staid to think of that while our keel spurned into foam the sheets of steely seas, and day by day brought us nearer to the hidden things we sought? For myself I confess that, now so close to the end as it seemed, curiosity and research absorbed every other faculty; Eleanor might be mouldering back to the parent earth—I could not stay to meditate on such a possibility; my Uncle Paul's donation might enrich itself with gold-dust instead of the gathered dust of idle days—it was nothing to me. I had but one thought, one ambition, one desire in those days —the discovery of the clear seas and open passage. I endured all our hardships as if they had been luxuries: I made light of scurvy, banqueted off train-oil, and met that cold for which there is no language framed, and which might be a new element; or which, rather, had seemed in that long night like the vast void of ether beyond the uttermost star, where was neither air nor light nor heat, but only bitter negation and emptiness. I was hardly conscious of my body; I was only a concentrated search in myself.

The recent explorers had announced here, in the neighborhood of where our third summer at last found us, the existence of an immense space of clear water. One even declared that he had seen it.

My Uncle Paul had pronounced the declaration false, and the sight an impossibility. The North he believed to be the breeder of icebergs, an ever-welling fountain of cold; the great glaciers there forever form, forever fall; the ice-packs line the gorges from year to year unchanging; peaks of volcanic rock drop their frozen mantles like a scale only to display the fresher one beneath. The whole region, said he, is Plutonic, blasted by a primordial convulsion of the great forces of creation; and though it may be a few miles nearer to the central fires of the earth, allowing that there are such things, yet that would not in itself detract from the frigid power of its sunless solitudes, the more especially when it is remembered that the spinning of the earth, while in its first plastic material, which gave it greater circumference and thinness of shell at its equator, must have thickened the shell correspondingly at the poles; and the character of all the waste and wilderness there only signifies the impenetrable wall between its surface and centre, through which wall no heat could enter or escape. The great rivers, like the White and the Mackenzie, emptying to the north of the continents, so far from being enough in themselves to form any body of ever fresh and flowing water, can only pierce the opposing ice-fields in narrow streams and bays and inlets as they seek the Atlantic and the Pacific seas. And as for the theory of the currents of water heated in the tropics and carried by the rotary motion of the planet to the Pole, where they rise and melt the ice-floes into this great supposititious sea, it is simply an absurdity on the face of it, he argued, when you remember that warm water being in its nature specifically lighter than cold it would have risen to the surface long before it reached there. No, thought my Uncle Paul, who took nothing for granted; it is as I said, an absurdity on the face of it; my nephew shall prove it, and I stake half the earnings of my life upon it.

To tell the truth, I thought much the same as he did; and now that such a mere trifle of distance intervened, between me and the proof, I was full of a feverish impatience that almost amounted to insanity.

We had proceeded but a few days, coasting the crushing capes of rock that every where seemed to run out in a diablerie of tusks and horns to drive us from the region that they warded, now cruising through a runlet of blue water just wide enough for our keel, with silver reaches of frost stretching away into a ghastly horizon—now plunging upon tossing seas, the sun wheeling round and round, and never sinking from the strange, weird sky above us, when again to our look-out a glimmer in the low horizon told its awful tale—a sort of smoky lustre like that which might ascend from an army of spirits—the fierce and fatal spirits tented on the terrible field of the ice-floe.

We were alone, our single little ship speeding ever upward in the midst of that untraveled desolation. We spoke seldom to one another, oppressed with the sense of our situation. It was a loneliness that seemed more than a death in life, a solitude that was supernatural. Here and now it was clear water; ten hours later and we were caught in the teeth of the cold, wedged in the ice that had advanced upon us and surrounded us, fettered by another winter in latitudes where human life had never before been supported.

We found, before the hands of the dial had taught us the lapse of a week, that this would be something not to be endured. The sun sank lower every day behind the crags and silvery horns; the heavens grew to wear a hue of violet, almost black, and yet unbearably dazzling; as the notes of our voices fell upon the atmosphere they assumed a metallic tone, as if the air itself had become frozen from the beginning of the world and they tinkled against it; our sufferings had mounted in their intensity till they were too great to be resisted.

It was decided at length—when the one long day had given place to its answering night, and in the jet-black heavens the stars, like knobs of silver, sparkled so large and close upon us that we might have grasped them in our hands—that I should take a sledge with Glipnu and his dogs, and see if there were any path to the westward by which, if the *Albatross* were forsaken, those of her crew that remained might follow it, and find an escape to safety. Our path was on a frozen sea; if we discovered land we did not know that the foot of man had ever trodden it; we could hope to find no *caché* of snow-buried food—neither fish nor game lived in this desert of ice that was so devoid of life in any shape as to seem dead itself. But, well provisioned, furred to the eyes, and essaying to nurse some hopefulness of heart, we set out on our way through this Valley of Death, relieving one another, and traveling day and night.

Still night and day to the west rose the black coast, one interminable height; to the east extended the sheets of unbroken ice; sometimes a huge glacier hung pendulous from the precipice; once we saw, by the starlight, a white, foaming, rushing river arrested and transformed to ice in its flight down that steep. A south wind began to blow behind us; we traveled on the ice; three days, perhaps, as days are measured among

men, had passed, when we found that we made double progress, for the ice traveled too; the whole field, carried by some
northward-bearing current, was afloat; it began to be crossed
and cut by a thousand crevasses; the cakes, an acre each, tilted
up and down, and made wide waves with their ponderous
plashing in the black body of the sea; we could hear them
grinding distantly in the clear dark against the coast, against
each other. There was no retreat—there was no advance; we
were on the ice, and the ice was breaking up. Suddenly we
rounded a tongue of the primeval rock, and recoiled before a
narrow gulf—one sharp shadow, as deep as despair, as full of
aguish fears. It was just wide enough for the sledge to span.
Glipnu made the dogs leap; we could be no worse off if they
drowned. They touched the opposite block; it careened; it
went under; the sledge went with it; I was left alone where I
had stood. Two dogs broke loose, and scrambled up beside me;
Glipnu and the others I never saw again. I sank upon the ice;
the dogs crouched beside me; sometimes I think they saved
my brain from total ruin, for without them I could not have
withstood the enormity of that loneliness, a loneliness that it
was impossible should be broken—floating on and on with that
vast journeying company of spectral ice. I had food enough to
support life for several days to come, in the pouch at my belt;
the dogs and I shared it—for, last as long as it would, when it
should be gone there was only death before us—no reprieve—
sooner or later that; as well sooner as later—the living terrors
of this icy hell were all about us, and death could be no worse.

Still the south wind blew, the rapid current carried us, the
dark skies grew deep and darker, the lanes and avenues
between the stars were crowded with forebodings—for the air
seemed full of a new power, a strange and invisible influence,
as if a king of unknown terrors here held his awful state. Sometimes the dogs stood up and growled and bristled their shaggy
hides; I, prostrate on the ice, in all my frame was stung with a
universal tingle. I was no longer myself. At this moment my
blood seemed to sing and bubble in my veins; I grew giddy with
a sort of delirious and inexplicable ecstasy; with another moment unutterable horror seized me; I was plunged and
weighed down with a black and suffocating load, while evil
things seemed to flap their wings in my face, to breathe in my

mouth, to draw my soul out of my body and carry it careering through the frozen realm of that murky heaven, to restore it with a shock of agony. Once as I lay there, still floating, floating northward, out of the dim dark rim of the water-world, a lance of piercing light shot up the zenith; it divided the heavens like a knife; they opened out in one blaze, and the fire fell sheetingly down before my face—cold fire, curdingly cold—light robbed of heat, and set free in a preternatural anarchy of the elements; its fringes swung to and fro before my face, pricked it with flaming spiculæ, dissolving in a thousand colors that spread every where over the low field, flashing, flickering, creeping, reflecting, gathering again in one long serpentine line of glory that wavered in slow convolutions across the cuts and crevasses of the ice, wreathed ever nearer, and, lifting its head at last, became nothing in the darkness but two great eyes like glowing coals, with which it stared me to a stound, till I threw myself face down to hide me in the ice; and the whining, bristling dogs cowered backward, and were dead.

I should have supposed myself to be in the region of the magnetic pole of the sphere, if I did not know that I had long since left it behind me. My pocket-compass had become entirely useless, and every scrap of metal that I had about me had become a loadstone. The very ice, as if it were congealed from water that held large quantities of iron in solution; iron escaping from whatever solid land there was beneath or around, the Plutonic rock that such a region could have alone veined and seamed with metal. The very ice appeared to have a magnetic quality; it held me so that I changed my position upon it with difficulty, and, as if it established a battery by the aid of the singular atmosphere above it, frequently sent thrills quivering through and through me till my flesh seemed about to resolve into all the jarring atoms of its original constitution; and again soothed me, with a velvet touch, into a state which, if it were not sleep, was at least haunted by visions that I dare not believe to have been realities, and from which I always awoke with a start to find myself still floating, floating. My watch had long since ceased to beat. I felt an odd persuasion that I had died when that stood still, and only this slavery of the magnet, of the cold, this power that locked every thing in invisible fetters and let nothing loose again, held my soul still in the bonds of my body. Another idea, also, took possession of me, for my mind was open to whatever visitant chose to enter, since utter despair of safety or release had left it vacant of a hope or fear. These enormous days and nights, swinging in their arc six months long, were the pendulum that dealt time in another measure than that dealt by the sunlight of lower zones; they told the time of what interminable years, the years of what vast generations far beyond the span that covered the age of the primeval men of Scripture—they measured time on this gigantic and enduring scale for what wonderful and mighty beings, old as the everlasting hills, as destitute as they of mortal sympathy, cold and inscrutable, handling the two-edged javelins of frost and magnetism, and served by all the unknown polar agencies. I fancied that I saw their far-reaching cohorts, marshaling and manœuvring at times in the field of an horizon that was boundless, the glitter of their spears and casques, the sheen of their white banners; and again, sitting in fearful circle with their phantasmagoria they shut and hemmed me in and watched me writhe like a worm before them.

I had a fancy that the perpetual play of magnetic impulses here gradually disintegrated myself to any further fear, I cowered beneath the stare of those dead and icy eyes. Slowly we rounded, and ever rounded; the inside, on which my place was, moving less slowly than the outer circle of the sheeted mass in its viscid flow; and as we moved, by some fate my eye was caught by the substance on which this figure sat. It was no figure at all now, but a bare jag of rock rising in the centre of this solid whirlpool, and carrying on its summit something which held a light that not one of these icy freaks, pranking in the dress of gems and flowers, had found it possible to assume. It was a thing so real, so genuine, my breath became suspended; my heart ceased to beat; my brain, that had been a lump of ice, seemed to move in its skull; hope, that had deserted me, suddenly sprung up like a second life within me; the old passion was not dead, if I was. It rose stronger than life or death or than myself. If I could but snatch that mass of moonstone, that inestimable wealth! It was nothing deceptive, I declared to myself. What more natural home could it have than this region, thrown up here by the old Plutonic powers of the planet, as the same substance in smaller shape was thrown up on the peaks of the Mount St. Gothard, when the Alpine aiguilles first sprang into the day? There it rested, limpid with its milky pearl, casting out flakes of flame and azure, of red and leaf-green light, and holding yet a sparkle of silver in the reflections and refractions of its inner axis—the splendid Turk's-eye of the lapidaries, the cousin of the water-opal and the girasole, the precious essence of feldspar. Could I break it, I would find clusters of great hemitrope crystals. Could I obtain it, I should have a jewel in that mass of moonstone such as the world never saw! The throne of Jemschid could not cast a shadow beside it.

Then the bitterness of my fate overwhelmed me. Here, with this treasure of a kingdom, this jewel that could not be priced, this wealth beyond an Emperor's—and here only to die! My stolid apathy vanished, old thoughts dominated once more, old habits, old desires. I thought of Eleanor then in her warm, sunny home, the blossoms that bloomed around her, the birds that sang, the cheerful evening fires, the longing thoughts for one who never came, who never was to come. But I would! I cried, where human voice had never cried before. I would re-turn! I would take this treasure with me! I would not be de-frauded! Should not I, a man, conquer this inanimate blind matter? I reached out my hands to seize it. Slowly it receded—slowly, and less slowly; or was the motion of the ice still carrying me onward? Had we encircled this apex? and were we driving out into the open and uncovered North, and so down the seas and out to the open main of black water again? If so—if I could live through it—I must have this thing!

I rose, and as well as I could, with my cramped and stiffened limbs, I moved to go back for it. It was useless; the current that carried us was growing invincible, the gaping gulfs of the outer seas were sucking us toward them. I fell; I scrambled to my feet; I would still have gone back, but, as I attempted it, the ice whereon I was inclined ever so slightly, tipped more boldly, gave way, and rose in a billow, broke, and piled over on another mass beneath. Then the cavern was behind us, and I compre-hended that this ice-stream, having doubled its central point, now in its outward movement encountered the still incoming body, and was to pile above and pass over it, the whole expanse bending, cracking, breaking, crowding, and compressing, till its rearing tumult made bergs more mountainous than the

offshot glaciers of the Greenland continent, that should ride
safely down to crumble in the surging seas below. As block after
block of the rent ice rose in the air, lighted by the blue and bristling aurora-points, toppled and mounted higher, it seemed to
me that now indeed I was battling with those elemental agencies in the dreadful fight I had desired—one man against the
might of matter. I sprang from that block to another; I gained
my balance on a third, climbing, shouldering, leaping, struggling, holding with my hands, catching with my feet, crawling,
stumbling, tottering, rising high and higher with the mountain
ever making underneath; a power unknown to my foes coming
to my aid, a blessed rushing warmth that glowed on all the surface of my skin, that set the blood to racing in my veins, that
made my heart beat with newer hope, sink with newer despair,
rise buoyant with new determination. Except when the shaft of
light pierced the shivering sky I could not see or guess the
height that I had gained. I was vaguely aware of chasms that
were bottomless, of precipices that opened on them, of pinnacles rising round me in aerial spires, when suddenly the shelf,
on which I must have stood, yielded, as if it were pushed by
great hands, swept down a steep incline like an avalanche,
stopped half-way, but sent me flying on, sliding, glancing, like a
shooting-star, down, down the slippery side, breathless, dizzy,
smitten with blistering pain by awful winds that whistled by me,
far out upon the level ice below that tilted up and down again
with the great resonant plash of open water, and conscious for a
moment that I lay at last upon a fragment that the mass behind
urged on, I knew and I remembered nothing more.

Faces were bending over me when I opened my eyes again,
rough, uncouth, and bearded faces, but no monsters of the
pole. Whalemen rather, smelling richly of train-oil, but I could
recall nothing in all my life one fraction so beautiful as they;
the angels on whom I hope to open my eyes when Death has
really taken me will scarcely seem sights more blest than did
those rude whalers of the North Pacific Sea. The North Pacific
Sea—for it was there that I was found, explain it how you
may—whether the *Albatross* had pierced farther to the west
than her sailing-master knew, and had lost her reckoning with
a disordered compass-needle under new stars—or whether I
had really been the sport of the demoniac beings of the ice,

tossed by them from zone to zone in a dozen hours. The whalers, real creatures enough, had discovered me on a block of ice, they said; nor could I, in their opinion, have been many days undergoing my dreadful experience, for there was still food in my wallet when they opened it. They would never believe a word of my story, and so far from regarding me as one who had proved the Northwest Passage in my own person, they considered me a mere idle maniac, as uncomfortable a thing to have on shipboard as a ghost or a dead body, wrecked and unable to account for myself, and gladly transferred me to a homeward-bound Russian man-of-war, whose officers afforded me more polite but quite as decided skepticism. I have never to this day found any one who believed my story when I told it—so you can take it for what it is worth. Even my Uncle Paul flouted it, and absolutely refused to surrender the sum on whose expectation I had taken ship; while my old ancestor, who hung peeling over the hall fire, dropped from his frame in disgust at the idea of one of his hard-cash descendants turning romancer. But all I know is that the *Albatross* never sailed into port again, and that if I open my knife to-day and lay it on the table it will wheel about till the tip of its blade points full at the North Star.

I have never found any one to believe me, did I say? Yes, there is one—Eleanor never doubted a word of my narration, never asked me if cold and suffering had not shaken my reason. But then, after the first recital, she has never been willing to hear another word about it, and if I ever allude to my lost treasure or the possibility of instituting search for it, she asks me if I need more lessons to be content with the treasure that I have, and gathers up her work and gently leaves the room. So that, now I speak of it so seldom, if I had not told the thing to you it might come to pass that I should forget altogether the existence of my mass of moonstone. My mass of moonshine, old Paul calls it. I let him have his say; he can not have that nor any thing else much longer; but when all is done I recall Galileo and I mutter to myself, "*Per si muove*—it *was* a mass of moonstone! With these eyes I saw it, with these hands I touched it, with this heart I longed for it, with this will I mean to have it yet!"

1868

W. C. MORROW

(1854–1923)

His Unconquerable Enemy

I WAS summoned from Calcutta to the heart of India to perform a difficult surgical operation on one of the women of a
great rajah's household. I found the rajah a man of a noble
character, but possessed, as I afterwards discovered, of a sense
of cruelty purely Oriental and in contrast to the indolence of
his disposition. He was so grateful for the success that attended my mission that he urged me to remain a guest at the
palace as long as it might please me to stay, and I thankfully accepted the invitation.

One of the male servants early attracted my notice for his
marvellous capacity of malice. His name was Neranya, and I
am certain that there must have been a large proportion of
Malay blood in his veins, for, unlike the Indians (from whom
he differed also in complexion), he was extremely alert, active,
nervous, and sensitive. A redeeming circumstance was his love
for his master. Once his violent temper led him to the commission of an atrocious crime,—the fatal stabbing of a dwarf. In
punishment for this the rajah ordered that Neranya's right arm
(the offending one) be severed from his body. The sentence
was executed in a bungling fashion by a stupid fellow armed
with an axe, and I, being a surgeon, was compelled, in order to
save Neranya's life, to perform an amputation of the stump,
leaving not a vestige of the limb remaining.

After this he developed an augmented fiendishness. His love
for the rajah was changed to hate, and in his mad anger he flung
discretion to the winds. Driven once to frenzy by the rajah's
scornful treatment, he sprang upon the rajah with a knife, but,
fortunately, was seized and disarmed. To his unspeakable dismay
the rajah sentenced him for this offence to suffer amputation
of the remaining arm. It was done as in the former instance.
This had the effect of putting a temporary curb on Neranya's
spirit, or, rather, of changing the outward manifestations of his

diabolism. Being armless, he was at first largely at the mercy of those who ministered to his needs,—a duty which I undertook to see was properly discharged, for I felt an interest in this strangely distorted nature. His sense of helplessness, combined with a damnable scheme for revenge which he had secretly formed, caused Neranya to change his fierce, impetuous, and unruly conduct into a smooth, quiet, insinuating bearing, which he carried so artfully as to deceive those with whom he was brought in contact, including the rajah himself.

Neranya, being exceedingly quick, intelligent, and dexterous, and having an unconquerable will, turned his attention to the cultivating of an enlarged usefulness of his legs, feet, and toes, with so excellent effect that in time he was able to perform wonderful feats with those members. Thus his capability, especially for destructive mischief, was considerably restored.

One morning the rajah's only son, a young man of an uncommonly amiable and noble disposition, was found dead in bed. His murder was a most atrocious one, his body being mutilated in a shocking manner, but in my eyes the most significant of all the mutilations was the entire removal and disappearance of the young prince's arms.

The death of the young man nearly brought the rajah to the grave. It was not, therefore, until I had nursed him back to health that I began a systematic inquiry into the murder. I said nothing of my own discoveries and conclusions until after the rajah and his officers had failed and my work had been done; then I submitted to him a written report, making a close analysis of all the circumstances and closing by charging the crime to Neranya. The rajah, convinced by my proof and argument, at once ordered Neranya to be put to death, this to be accomplished slowly and with frightful tortures. The sentence was so cruel and revolting that it filled me with horror, and I implored that the wretch be shot. Finally, through a sense of gratitude to me, the rajah relaxed. When Neranya was charged with the crime he denied it, of course, but, seeing that the rajah was convinced, he threw aside all restraint, and, dancing, laughing, and shrieking in the most horrible manner, confessed his guilt, gloated over it, and reviled the rajah to his teeth, —this, knowing that some fearful death awaited him.

The rajah decided upon the details of the matter that night, and in the morning he informed me of his decision. It was that Neranya's life should be spared, but that both of his legs should be broken with hammers, and that then I should amputate the limbs at the trunk! Appended to this horrible sentence was a provision that the maimed wretch should be kept and tortured at regular intervals by such means as afterwards might be devised.

Sickened to the heart by the awful duty set out for me, I nevertheless performed it with success, and I care to say nothing more about that part of the tragedy. Neranya escaped death very narrowly and was a long time in recovering his wonted vitality. During all these weeks the rajah neither saw him nor made inquiries concerning him, but when, as in duty bound, I made official report that the man had recovered his strength, the rajah's eyes brightened, and he emerged with deadly activity from the stupor into which he so long had been plunged.

The rajah's palace was a noble structure, but it is necessary here to describe only the grand hall. It was an immense chamber, with a floor of polished, inlaid stone and a lofty, arched ceiling. A soft light stole into it through stained glass set in the roof and in high windows on one side. In the middle of the room was a rich fountain, which threw up a tall, slender column of water, with smaller and shorter jets grouped around it. Across one end of the hall, half-way to the ceiling, was a balcony, which communicated with the upper story of a wing, and from which a flight of stone stairs descended to the floor of the hall. During the hot summers this room was delightfully cool; it was the rajah's favorite lounging-place, and when the nights were hot he had his cot taken thither, and there he slept.

This hall was chosen for Neranya's permanent prison; here was he to stay so long as he might live, with never a glimpse of the shining world or the glorious heavens. To one of his nervous, discontented nature such confinement was worse than death. At the rajah's order there was constructed for him a small pen of open iron-work, circular, and about four feet in diameter, elevated on four slender iron posts, ten feet above the floor, and placed between the balcony and the fountain. Such was Neranya's prison. The pen was about four feet in depth, and the pen-top was left open for the convenience of the servants whose duty it should be to care for him. These precautions for his safe confinement were taken at my suggestion, for, although the man was now deprived of all four of his limbs, I still feared that he might develop some extraordinary, unheard-of power for mischief. It was provided that the attendants should reach his cage by means of a movable ladder.

All these arrangements having been made and Neranya hoisted into his cage, the rajah emerged upon the balcony to see him for the first time since the last amputation. Neranya had been lying panting and helpless on the floor of his cage, but when his quick ear caught the sound of the rajah's footfall he squirmed about until he had brought the back of his head against the railing, elevating his eyes above his chest, and enabling him to peer through the open-work of the cage. Thus the two deadly enemies faced each other. The rajah's stern face paled at sight of the hideous, shapeless thing which met his gaze; but he soon recovered, and the old hard, cruel, sinister look returned. Neranya's black hair and beard had grown long, and they added to the natural ferocity of his aspect. His eyes blazed upon the rajah with a terrible light, his lips parted, and he gasped for breath; his face was ashen with rage and despair, and his thin, distended nostrils quivered.

The rajah folded his arms and gazed down from the balcony upon the frightful wreck that he had made. Oh, the dreadful pathos of that picture; the inhumanity of it; the deep and dismal tragedy of it! Who might look into the wild, despairing heart of the prisoner and see and understand the frightful turmoil there; the surging, choking passion; unbridled but impotent ferocity; frantic thirst for a vengeance that should be deeper than hell! Neranya gazed, his shapeless body heaving, his eyes aflame; and then, in a strong, clear voice, which rang throughout the great hall, with rapid speech he hurled at the rajah the most insulting defiance, the most awful curses. He cursed the womb that had conceived him, the food that should nourish him, the wealth that had brought him power; cursed him in the name of Buddha and all the wise men; cursed by the sun, the moon, and the stars; by the continents, mountains, oceans, and rivers; by all things living; cursed his head, his heart, his entrails; cursed in a whirlwind of unmentionable words; heaped unimaginable insults and contumely upon him; called him a knave, a beast, a fool, a liar, an infamous and unspeakable coward.

The rajah heard it all calmly, without the movement of a muscle, without the slightest change of countenance; and when the poor wretch had exhausted his strength and fallen helpless and silent to the floor, the rajah, with a grim, cold smile, turned and strode away.

The days passed. The rajah, not deterred by Neranya's curses often heaped upon him, spent even more time than formerly in the great hall, and slept there oftener at night; and finally Neranya wearied of cursing and defying him, and fell into a sullen silence. The man was a study for me, and I observed every change in his fleeting moods. Generally his condition was that of miserable despair, which he attempted bravely to conceal. Even the boon of suicide had been denied him, for when he would wriggle into an erect position the rail of his pen was a foot above his head, so that he could not clamber over and break his skull on the stone floor beneath; and when he had tried to starve himself the attendants forced food down his throat; so that he abandoned such attempts. At times his eyes would blaze and his breath would come in gasps, for imaginary vengeance was working within him; but steadily he became quieter and more tractable, and was pleasant and responsive when I would converse with him. Whatever might have been the tortures which the rajah had decided on, none as yet had been ordered; and although Neranya knew that they were in contemplation, he never referred to them or complained of his lot.

The awful climax of this situation was reached one night, and even after this lapse of years I cannot approach its description without a shudder.

It was a hot night, and the rajah had gone to sleep in the great hall, lying on a high cot placed on the main floor just underneath the edge of the balcony. I had been unable to sleep in my own apartment, and so I had stolen into the great hall through the heavily curtained entrance at the end farthest from the balcony. As I entered I heard a peculiar, soft sound above the patter of the fountain. Neranya's cage was partly concealed from my view by the spraying water, but I suspected that the unusual sound came from him. Stealing a little to one side, and crouching against the dark hangings of the wall, I could see him in the faint light which dimly illuminated the hall, and then I discovered that my surmise was correct—Neranya was quietly at work. Curious to learn more, and knowing that only mischief could have been inspiring him, I sank into a thick robe on the floor and watched him.

To my great astonishment Neranya was tearing off with his teeth the bag which served as his outer garment. He did it cautiously, casting sharp glances frequently at the rajah, who, sleeping soundly on his cot below, breathed heavily. After starting a strip with his teeth, Neranya, by the same means, would attach it to the railing of his cage and then wriggle away, much after the manner of a caterpillar's crawling, and this would cause the strip to be torn out the full length of his garment. He repeated this operation with incredible patience and skill until his entire garment had been torn into strips. Two or three of these he tied end to end with his teeth, lips, and tongue, tightening the knots by placing one end of the strip under his body and drawing the other taut with his teeth. In this way he made a line several feet long, one end of which he made fast to the rail with his mouth. It then began to dawn upon me that he was going to make an insane attempt—impossible of achievement without hands, feet, arms, or legs—to escape from his cage! For what purpose? The rajah was asleep in the hall—ah! I caught my breath. Oh, the desperate, insane thirst for revenge which could have unhinged so clear and firm a mind! Even though he should accomplish the impossible feat of climbing over the railing of his cage that he might fall to the floor below (for how could he slide down the rope?), he would be in all probability killed or stunned; and even if he should escape these dangers it would be impossible for him to clamber upon the cot without rousing the rajah, and impossible even though the rajah were dead! Amazed at the man's daring, and convinced that his sufferings and brooding had destroyed his reason, nevertheless I watched him with breathless interest.

With other strips tied together he made a short swing across one side of his cage. He caught the long line in his teeth at a point not far from the rail; then, wriggling with great effort to an upright position, his back braced against the rail, he put his chin over the swing and worked toward one end. He tightened the grasp of his chin on the swing, and with tremendous exertion, working the lower end of his spine against the railing, he

began gradually to ascend the side of his cage. The labor was
so great that he was compelled to pause at intervals, and his
breathing was hard and painful; and even while thus resting he
was in a position of terrible strain, and his pushing against the
swing caused it to press hard against his windpipe and nearly
strangle him.

After amazing effort he had elevated the lower end of his
body until it protruded above the railing, the top of which was
now across the lower end of his abdomen. Gradually he
worked his body over, going backward, until there was sufficient excess of weight on the outer side of the rail; and then,
with a quick lurch, he raised his head and shoulders and swung
into a horizontal position on top of the rail. Of course, he
would have fallen to the floor below had it not been for the
line which he held in his teeth. With so great nicety had he estimated the distance between his mouth and the point where
the rope was fastened to the rail, that the line tightened and
checked him just as he reached the horizontal position on the
rail. If one had told me beforehand that such a feat as I had just
seen this man accomplish was possible, I should have thought
him a fool.

Neranya was now balanced on his stomach across the top of
the rail, and he eased his position by bending his spine and
hanging down on either side as much as possible. Having
rested thus for some minutes, he began cautiously to slide off
backward, slowly paying out the line through his teeth, finding
almost a fatal difficulty in passing the knots. Now, it is quite
possible that the line would have escaped altogether from his
teeth laterally when he would slightly relax his hold to let it
slip, had it not been for a very ingenious plan to which he had
resorted. This consisted in his having made a turn of the line
around his neck before he attacked the swing, thus securing a
threefold control of the line,—one by his teeth, another by
friction against his neck, and a third by his ability to compress
it between his cheek and shoulder. It was quite evident now
that the minutest details of a most elaborate plan had been carefully worked out by him before beginning the task, and that
possibly weeks of difficult theoretical study had been consumed in the mental preparation. As I observed him I was reminded of certain hitherto unaccountable things which he had

been doing for some weeks past—going through certain hitherto inexplicable motions, undoubtedly for the purpose of
training his muscles for the immeasurably arduous labor which
he was now performing.

A stupendous and seemingly impossible part of his task had
been accomplished. Could he reach the floor in safety? Gradually he worked himself backward over the rail, in imminent
danger of falling; but his nerve never wavered, and I could see
a wonderful light in his eyes. With something of a lurch, his body
fell against the outer side of the railing, to which he was hanging
by his chin, the line still held firmly in his teeth. Slowly he
slipped his chin from the rail, and then hung suspended by the
line in his teeth. By almost imperceptible degrees, with infinite
caution, he descended the line, and, finally, his unwieldy body
rolled upon the floor, safe and unhurt!

What miracle would this superhuman monster next accomplish? I was quick and strong, and was ready and able to intercept any dangerous act; but not until danger appeared would I
interfere with this extraordinary scene.

I must confess to astonishment upon having observed that
Neranya, instead of proceeding directly toward the sleeping
rajah, took quite another direction. Then it was only escape, after
all, that the wretch contemplated, and not the murder of the
rajah. But how could he escape? The only possible way to reach
the outer air without great risk was by ascending the stairs to
the balcony and leaving by the corridor which opened upon it,
and thus fall into the hands of some British soldiers quartered
thereabout, who might conceive the idea of hiding him; but
surely it was impossible for Neranya to ascend that long flight
of stairs! Nevertheless, he made directly for them, his method of
progression this: He lay upon his back, with the lower end of
his body toward the stairs; then bowed his spine upward, thus
drawing his head and shoulders a little forward; straightened,
and then pushed the lower end of his body forward a space
equal to that through which he had drawn his head; repeating
this again and again, each time, while bending his spine, pre-
venting his head from slipping by pressing it against the floor.
His progress was laborious and slow, but sensible; and, finally,
he arrived at the foot of the stairs.

It was manifest that his insane purpose was to ascend them.

The desire for freedom must have been strong within him! Wriggling to an upright position against the newel-post, he looked up at the great height which he had to climb and sighed; but there was no dimming of the light in his eyes. How could he accomplish the impossible task?

His solution of the problem was very simple, though daring and perilous as all the rest. While leaning against the newel-post he let himself fall diagonally upon the bottom step, where he lay partly hanging over, but safe, on his side. Turning upon his back, he wriggled forward along the step to the rail and raised himself to an upright position against it as he had against the newel-post, fell as before, and landed on the second step. In this manner, with inconceivable labor, he accomplished the ascent of the entire flight of stairs.

It being apparent to me that the rajah was not the object of Neranya's movements, the anxiety which I had felt on that account was now entirely dissipated. The things which already he had accomplished were entirely beyond the nimblest imagination. The sympathy which I had always felt for the wretched man was now greatly quickened; and as infinitesimally small as I knew his chances for escape to be, I nevertheless hoped that he would succeed. Any assistance from me, however, was out of the question; and it never should be known that I had witnessed the escape.

Neranya was now upon the balcony, and I could dimly see him wriggling along toward the door which led out upon the balcony. Finally he stopped and wriggled to an upright position against the rail, which had wide openings between the balusters. His back was toward me, but he slowly turned and faced me and the hall. At that great distance I could not distinguish his features, but the slowness with which he had worked, even before he had fully accomplished the ascent of the stairs, was evidence all too eloquent of his extreme exhaustion. Nothing but a most desperate resolution could have sustained him thus far, but he had drawn upon the last remnant of his strength. He looked around the hall with a sweeping glance, and then down upon the rajah, who was sleeping immediately beneath him, over twenty feet below. He looked long and earnestly, sinking lower, and lower, and lower upon the rail. Suddenly, to my inconceivable astonishment and dismay, he toppled through and shot downward from his lofty height! I held my breath, expecting to see him crushed upon the stone floor beneath; but instead of that he fell full upon the rajah's breast, driving him through the cot to the floor. I sprang forward with a loud cry for help, and was instantly at the scene of the catastrophe. With indescribable horror I saw that Neranya's teeth were buried in the rajah's throat! I tore the wretch away, but the blood was pouring from the rajah's arteries, his chest was crushed in, and he was gasping in the agony of death. People came running in, terrified. I turned to Neranya. He lay upon his back, his face hideously smeared with blood. Murder, and not escape, had been his intentions from the beginning; and he had employed the only method by which there was ever a possibility of accomplishing it. I knelt beside him, and saw that he too was dying; his back had been broken by the fall. He smiled sweetly into my face, and a triumphant look of accomplished revenge sat upon his face even in death.

1889

SARAH ORNE JEWETT

(1849–1909)

In Dark New England Days

I.

THE last of the neighbors was going home; officious Mrs. Peter Downs had lingered late and sought for additional house-work with which to prolong her stay. She had talked incessantly, and buzzed like a busy bee as she helped to put away the best crockery after the funeral supper, while the sisters Betsey and Hannah Knowles grew every moment more forbidding and unwilling to speak. They lighted a solitary small oil lamp at last, as if for Sunday evening idleness, and put it on the side table in the kitchen.

"We ain't intending to make a late evening of it," announced Betsey, the elder, standing before Mrs. Downs in an expectant, final way, making an irresistible opportunity for saying good-night. "I'm sure we're more than obleeged to ye,—ain't we, Hannah?—but I don't feel 's if we ought to keep ye longer. We ain't going to do no more to-night, but set down a spell and kind of collect ourselves, and then make for bed."

Susan Downs offered one more plea. "I'd stop all night with ye an' welcome; 't is gettin' late—an' dark," she added plaintively; but the sisters shook their heads quickly, while Hannah said that they might as well get used to staying alone, since they would have to do it first or last. In spite of herself Mrs. Downs was obliged to put on her funeral best bonnet and shawl and start on her homeward way.

"Closed-mouthed old maids!" she grumbled as the door shut behind her all too soon and denied her the light of the lamp along the footpath. Suddenly there was a bright ray from the window, as if some one had pushed back the curtain and stood with the lamp close to the sash. "That's Hannah," said the retreating guest. "She'd told me somethin' about things, I know, if it hadn't 'a' been for Betsey. Catch me workin' myself

112

to pieces again for 'em." But, however grudgingly this was said, Mrs. Downs's conscience told her that the industry of the past two days had been somewhat selfish on her part; she had hoped that in the excitement of this unexpected funeral season she might for once be taken into the sisters' confidence. More than this, she knew that they were certain of her motive, and had deliberately refused the expected satisfaction. "'T ain't as if I was one o' them curious busy-bodies anyway," she said to herself pityingly; "they might 'a' neighbored with somebody for once, I do believe." Everybody would have a question ready for her the next day, for it was known that she had been slaving herself devotedly since the news had come of old Captain Knowles's sudden death in his bed from a stroke, the last of three which had in the course of a year or two changed him from a strong old man to a feeble, chair-bound cripple.

Mrs. Downs stepped bravely along the dark country road; she could see a light in her own kitchen window half a mile away, and did not stop to notice either the penetrating dampness, or the shadowy woods at her right. It was a cloudy night, but there was a dim light over the open fields. She had a disposition of mind towards the exciting circumstances of death and burial, and was in request at such times among her neighbors; in this she was like a city person who prefers tragedy to comedy, but not having the semblance within her reach, she made the most of looking on at real griefs and departures.

Some one was walking towards her in the road; suddenly she heard footsteps. The figure stopped, then it came forward again.

"Oh, 't is you, ain't it?" with a tone of disappointment. "I cal'lated you'd stop all night, 't had got to be so late, an' I was just going over to the Knowles gals'; well, to kind o' ask how they be, an'"—Mr. Peter Downs was evidently counting on his visit.

"They never passed me the compliment," replied the wife. "I declare I didn't covet the walk home; I'm most beat out, bein' on foot so much. I was 'most put out with 'em for letten' of me see quite so plain that my room was better than my company. But I don't know 's I blame 'em; they want to look an' see what they've got, an' kind of git by theirselves, I expect. 'T was natural."

Mrs. Downs knew that her husband would resent her first statements, being a sensitive and grumbling man. She had formed a pacific habit of suiting her remarks to his point of view, to save an outburst. He contented himself with calling the Knowles girls hoggish, and put a direct question as to whether they had let fall any words about their situation, but Martha Downs was obliged to answer in the negative.

"Was Enoch Holt there after the folks come back from the grave?"

"He wa'n't; they never give him no encouragement neither."

"He appeared well, I must say," continued Peter Downs. "He took his place next but one behind us in the procession, 'long of Melinda Dutch, an' walked to an' from with her, give her his arm, and then I never see him after we got back; but I thought he might be somewhere in the house, an' I was out about the barn an' so on."

"They was civil to him. I was by when he come, just steppin' out of the bedroom after we'd finished layin' the old Cap'n into his coffin. Hannah looked real pleased when she see Enoch, as if she hadn't really expected him, but Betsey stuck out her hand 's if 't was an eend o' board, an' drawed her face solemner 'n ever. There, they had natural feelin's. He was their own father when all was said, the Cap'n was, an' I don't know but he was clever to 'em in his way, 'ceptin' when he disappointed Hannah about her marryin' Jake Good'in. She l'arned to respect the old Cap'n's foresight, too."

"Sakes alive, Marthy, how you do knock folks down with one hand an' set 'em up with t' other," chuckled Mr. Downs. They next discussed the Captain's appearance as he lay in state in the front room, a subject which, with its endless ramifications, would keep the whole neighborhood interested for weeks to come.

An hour later the twinkling light in the Downs house suddenly disappeared. As Martha Downs took a last look out of doors through her bedroom window she could see no other light; the neighbors had all gone to bed. It was a little past nine, and the night was damp and still.

II.

The Captain Knowles place was eastward from the Downs's, and a short turn in the road and the piece of hard-wood growth hid one house from the other. At this unwontedly late hour the elderly sisters were still sitting in their warm kitchen; there were bright coals under the singing tea-kettle which hung from the crane by three or four long pothooks. Betsey Knowles objected when her sister offered to put on more wood.

"Father never liked to leave no great of a fire, even though he slept right here in the bedroom. He said this floor was one that would light an' catch easy, you r'member."

"Another winter we can move down and take the bedroom ourselves—'t will be warmer for us," suggested Hannah; but Betsey shook her head doubtfully. The thought of their old father's grave, unwatched and undefended in the outermost dark field, filled their hearts with a strange tenderness. They had been his dutiful, patient slaves, and it seemed like disloyalty to have abandoned the poor shape; to be sitting there disregarding the thousand requirements and services of the past. More than all, they were facing a free future; they were their own mistresses at last, though past sixty years of age. Hannah was still a child at heart. She chased away a dread suspicion, when Betsey forbade the wood, lest this elder sister, who favored their father's looks, might take his place as stern ruler of the household.

"Betsey," said the younger sister suddenly, "we'll have us a cook stove, won't we, next winter? I expect we're going to have something to do with?"

Betsey did not answer; it was impossible to say whether she truly felt grief or only assumed it. She had been sober and silent for the most part since she routed neighbor Downs, though she answered her sister's prattling questions with patience and sympathy. Now, she rose from her chair and went to one of the windows, and, pushing back the sash curtain, pulled the wooden shutter across and hasped it.

"I ain't going to bed just yet," she explained. "I've been a-waiting to make sure nobody was coming in. I don't know 's there 'll be any better time to look in the chest and see what we've got to depend on. We never 'll get no chance to do it by day."

Hannah looked frightened for a moment, then nodded, and turned to the opposite window and pulled that shutter with much difficulty; it had always caught and hitched and been provoking—a warped piece of red oak, when even-grained white pine would have saved strength and patience to three generations of the Knowles race. Then the sisters crossed the kitchen and opened the bedroom door. Hannah shivered a little as the colder air struck her, and her heart beat loudly. Perhaps it was the same with Betsey.

The bedroom was clean and orderly for the funeral guests. Instead of the blue homespun there was a beautifully quilted white coverlet which had been part of their mother's wedding furnishing, and this made the bedstead with its four low posts look unfamiliar and awesome. The lamplight shone through the kitchen door behind them, not very bright at best, but Betsey reached under the bed, and with all the strength she could muster pulled out the end of a great sea chest. The sisters tugged together and pushed, and made the most of their strength before they finally brought it through the narrow door into the kitchen. The solemnity of the deed made them both whisper as they talked, and Hannah did not dare to say what was in her timid heart—that she would rather brave discovery by daylight than such a feeling of being disapprovingly watched now, in the dead of night. There came a slight sound outside the house which made her look anxiously at Betsey, but Betsey remained tranquil.

"It's nothing but a stick falling down the woodpile," she answered in a contemptuous whisper, and the younger woman was reassured.

Betsey reached deep into her pocket and found a great key which was worn smooth and bright like silver, and never had been trusted willingly into even her own careful hands. Hannah held the lamp, and the two thin figures bent eagerly over the lid as it opened. Their shadows were waving about the low walls, and looked like strange shapes bowing and dancing behind them.

The chest was stoutly timbered, as if it were built in some ship-yard, and there were heavy wrought-iron hinges and a large escutcheon for the keyhole that the ship's blacksmith might have hammered out. On the top somebody had scratched deeply the crossed lines for a game of fox and geese, which had a trivial, irreverent look, and might have been the unforgiven fault of some idle ship's boy. The sisters had hardly dared look at the chest or to signify their knowledge of its existence, at unwary times. They had swept carefully about it year after year, and wondered if it were indeed full of gold as the neighbors used to hint; but no matter how much found a way in, little had found the way out. They had been hampered all their lives for money, and in consequence had developed a wonderful facility for spinning and weaving, mending and making. Their small farm was an early example of intensive farming; they were allowed to use its products in a niggardly way, but the money that was paid for wool, for hay, for wood, and for summer crops had all gone into the chest. The old captain was a hard master; he rarely commended and often blamed. Hannah trembled before him, but Betsey faced him sturdily, being amazingly like him, with a feminine difference; as like as a ruled person can be to a ruler, for the discipline of life had taught the man to aggress, the woman only to defend. In the chest was a fabled sum of prize-money, besides these slender earnings of many years; all the sisters' hard work and self-sacrifice were there in money and a mysterious largess besides. All their lives they had been looking forward to this hour of ownership.

There was a solemn hush in the house; the two sisters were safe from their neighbors, and there was no fear of interruption at such an hour in that hard-working community, tired with a day's work that had been early begun. If any one came knocking at the door, both door and windows were securely fastened.

The eager sisters bent above the chest, they held their breath and talked in softest whispers. With stealthy tread a man came out of the woods near by.

He stopped to listen, came nearer, stopped again, and then crept close to the old house. He stepped upon the banking, next the window with the warped shutter; there was a knothole in it high above the women's heads, towards the top. As they leaned over the chest, an eager eye watched them. If they had turned that way suspiciously, the eye might have caught the flicker of the lamp and betrayed itself. No, they were too busy: the eye at the shutter watched and watched.

There was a certain feeling of relief in the sisters' minds because the contents of the chest were so commonplace at first sight. There were some old belongings dating back to their father's early days of seafaring. They unfolded a waistcoat pattern or two of figured stuff which they had seen him fold and put away again and again. Once he had given Betsey a gay China silk handkerchief, and here were two more like it. They had not known what a store of treasures might be waiting for them, but the reality so far was disappointing; there was much spare room to begin with, and the wares within looked pinched and few. There were bundles of papers, old receipts, some letters in two not very thick bundles, some old account books with worn edges, and a blackened silver can which looked very small in comparison with their anticipation, being an heirloom and jealously hoarded and secreted by the old man. The women began to feel as if his lean angry figure were bending with them over the sea chest.

They opened a package wrapped in many layers of old soft paper—a worked piece of Indian muslin, and an embroidered red scarf which they had never seen before. "He must have brought them home to mother," said Betsey with a great outburst of feeling. "He never was the same man again; he never would let nobody else have them when he found she was dead, poor old father!"

Hannah looked wistfully at the treasures. She rebuked herself for selfishness, but she thought of her pinched girlhood and the delight these things would have been. Ah yes! it was too late now for many things besides the sprigged muslin. "If I was young as I was once there's lots o' things I'd like to do now I'm free," said Hannah with a gentle sigh; but her sister checked her anxiously—it was fitting that they should preserve a semblance of mourning even to themselves.

The lamp stood in a kitchen chair at the chest's end and shone full across their faces. Betsey looked intent and sober as she turned over the old man's treasures. Under the India mull was an antique pair of buff trousers, a waistcoat of strange old-fashioned foreign stuff, and a blue coat with brass buttons, brought home from over seas, as the women knew, for their father's wedding clothes. They had seen him carry them out at long intervals to hang them in the spring sunshine; he had been very feeble the last time, and Hannah remembered that she had longed to take them from his shaking hands.

"I declare for 't I wish't we had laid him out in 'em, 'stead o' the robe," she whispered; but Betsey made no answer. She was kneeling still, but held herself upright and looked away. It was evident that she was lost in her own thoughts.

"I can't find nothing else by eyesight," she muttered. "This chest never 'd be so heavy with them old clothes. Stop! Hold that light down, Hannah; there's a place underneath here. Them papers in the till takes a shallow part. Oh, my gracious! See here, will ye? Hold the light, hold the light!"

There was a hidden drawer in the chest's side—a long, deep place, and it was full of gold pieces. Hannah had seated herself in the chair to be out of her sister's way. She held the lamp with one hand and gathered her apron on her lap with the other, while Betsey, exultant and hawk-eyed, took out handful after handful of heavy coins, letting them jingle and chink, letting them shine in the lamp's rays, letting them roll across the floor—guineas, dollars, doubloons, old French and Spanish and English gold!

Now, now! Look! The eye at the window!

At last they have found it all; the bag of silver, the great roll of bank bills, and the heavy weight of gold—the prize-money that had been like Robinson Crusoe's in the cave. They were rich women that night; their faces grew young again as they sat side by side and exulted while the old kitchen grew cold. There was nothing they might not do within the range of their timid ambitions; they were women of fortune now and their own mistresses. They were beginning at last to live.

The watcher outside was cramped and chilled. He let himself down softly from the high step of the winter banking, and crept toward the barn, where he might bury himself in the hay and think. His fingers were quick to find the peg that opened the little barn door; the beasts within were startled and stumbled to their feet, then went back to their slumbers. The night wore on; the light spring rain began to fall, and the sound of it on the house roof close down upon the sisters' bed lulled them quickly to sleep. Twelve, one, two o'clock passed by.

They had put back the money and the clothes and the minor goods and treasures and pulled the chest back into the bedroom so that it was out of sight from the kitchen; the bedroom door was always shut by day. The younger sister wished to carry the money to their own room, but Betsey disdained such precaution. The money had always been safe in the old chest, and there it should stay. The next week they would go to Riverport and put it into the bank; it was no use to lose the interest any longer. Because their father had lost some invested money in his early youth, it did not follow that every bank was faithless. Betsey's self-assertion was amazing, but they still whispered to each other as they got ready for bed. With strange forgetfulness Betsey had laid the chest key on the white coverlet in the bedroom and left it there.

III.

In August of that year the whole countryside turned out to go to court.

The sisters had been rich for one night; in the morning they waked to find themselves poor with a bitter pang of poverty of which they had never dreamed. They had said little, but they grew suddenly pinched and old. They could not tell how much money they had lost, except that Hannah's lap was full of gold, a weight she could not lift nor carry. After a few days of stolid misery they had gone to the chief lawyer of their neighborhood to accuse Enoch Holt of the robbery. They dressed in their best and walked solemnly side by side across the fields and along the road, the shortest way to the man of law. Enoch Holt's daughter saw them go as she stood in her doorway, and felt a cold shiver run through her frame as if in foreboding. Her father was not at home; he had left for Boston late on the afternoon of Captain Knowles's funeral. He had had notice the day before of the coming in of a ship in which he owned a thirty-second; there was talk of selling the ship, and the owners' agent had summoned him. He had taken pains to go to the funeral, because he and the old captain had been on bad terms ever since they had bought a piece of woodland together, and the captain declared himself wronged at the settling of accounts. He was growing feeble even then, and had left the business to the younger man. Enoch Holt was not a trusted man, yet he had never before been openly accused of dishonesty. He was not a professor of religion, but foremost on the secular side of church matters. Most of the men in that region were hard men; it was difficult to get money, and there was little real comfort in a community where the sterner, stingier, forbidding side of New England life was well exemplified.

The proper steps had been taken by the officers of the law, and in answer to the writ Enoch Holt appeared, much shocked and very indignant, and was released on bail which covered the sum his shipping interest had brought him. The weeks had dragged by; June and July were long in passing, and here was court day at last, and all the townsfolk hastening by high-roads and by-roads to the court-house. The Knowles girls themselves had risen at break of day and walked the distance steadfastly, like two of the three Fates: who would make the third, to cut the thread for their enemy's disaster? Public opinion was divided. There were many voices ready to speak on the accused man's side; a sharp-looking acquaintance left his business in Boston to swear that Holt was in his office before noon on the day following the robbery, and that he had spent most of the night in Boston, as proved by several minor details of their interview. As for Holt's young married daughter, she was a favorite with the townsfolk, and her husband was away at sea overdue these last few weeks. She sat on one of the hard court benches with a young child in her arms, born since its father sailed; they had been more or less unlucky, the Holt family, though Enoch himself was a man of brag and bluster.

All the hot August morning, until the noon recess, and all the hot August afternoon, fly-teased and wretched with the heavy air, the crowd of neighbors listened to the trial. There was not much evidence brought; everybody knew that Enoch Holt left the funeral procession hurriedly, and went away on horseback towards Boston. His daughter knew no more than this. The Boston man gave his testimony impatiently, and one or two persons insisted that they saw the accused on his way at nightfall, several miles from home.

As the testimony came out, it all tended to prove his innocence, though public opinion was to the contrary. The Knowles
sisters looked more stern and gray hour by hour; their
vengeance was not to be satisfied; their accusation had been
listened to and found wanting, but their instinctive knowledge
of the matter counted for nothing. They must have been
watched through the knot-hole of the shutter; nobody had
noticed it until, some years before, Enoch Holt himself had
spoken of the light's shining through on a winter's night as he
came towards the house. The chief proof was that nobody else
could have done the deed. But why linger over *pros* and *cons*?
The jury returned directly with a verdict of "not proven," and
the tired audience left the court-house.

But not until Hannah Knowles with angry eyes had risen to
her feet.

The sterner elder sister tried to pull her back; every one said
that they should have looked to Betsey to say the awful words
that followed, not to her gentler companion. It was Hannah,
broken and disappointed, who cried in a strange high voice as
Enoch Holt was passing by without a look:

"You stole it, you thief! You know it in your heart!"

The startled man faltered, then he faced the women. The
people who stood near seemed made of eyes as they stared to
see what he would say.

"I swear by my right hand I never touched it."

"Curse your right hand, then!" cried Hannah Knowles,
growing tall and thin like a white flame drawing upward.
"Curse your right hand, yours and all your folks' that follow
you! May I live to see the day!"

The people drew back, while for a moment accused and ac-
cuser stood face to face. Then Holt's flushed face turned white,
and he shrank from the fire in those wild eyes, and walked
away clumsily down the courtroom. Nobody followed him,
nobody shook hands with him, or told the acquitted man that
they were glad of his release. Half an hour later, Betsey and
Hannah Knowles took their homeward way, to begin their
hard round of work again. The horizon that had widened with
such glory for one night, had closed round them again like an
iron wall.

Betsey was alarmed and excited by her sister's uncharacteristic behavior, and she looked at her anxiously from time to time. Hannah had become the harder-faced of the two. Her disappointment was the keener, for she had kept more of the unsatisfied desires of her girlhood until that dreary morning when they found the sea-chest rifled and the treasure gone.

Betsey said inconsequently that it was a pity she did not have that black silk gown that would stand alone. They had planned for it over the open chest, and Hannah's was to be a handsome green. They might have worn them to court. But even the pathetic facetiousness of her elder sister did not bring a smile to Hannah Knowles's face, and the next day one was at the loom and the other at the wheel again. The neighbors talked about the curse with horror; in their minds a fabric of sad fate was spun from the bitter words.

The Knowles sisters never had worn silk gowns and they never would. Sometimes Hannah or Betsey would stealthily look over the chest in one or the other's absence. One day when Betsey was very old and her mind had grown feeble, she tied her own India silk handkerchief about her neck, but they never used the other two. They aired the wedding suit once every spring as long as they lived. They were both too old and forlorn to make up the India mull. Nobody knows how many times they took everything out of the heavy old clamped box, and peered into every nook and corner to see if there was not a single gold piece left. They never answered any one who made bold to speak of their misfortune.

IV.

Enoch Holt had been a seafaring man in his early days, and there was news that the owners of a Salem ship in which he held a small interest wished him to go out as super-cargo. He was brisk and well in health, and his son-in-law, an honest but an unlucky fellow, had done less well than usual, so that nobody was surprised when Enoch made ready for his voyage. It was nearly a year after the theft, and nothing had come so near to restoring him to public favor as his apparent lack of ready money. He openly said that he put great hope in his adventure to the Spice Islands, and when he said farewell one Sunday to some members of the dispersing congregation, more than one person wished him heartily a pleasant voyage and safe return. He had an insinuating tone of voice and an imploring look that day, and this fact, with his probable long absence and the dangers of the deep, won him much sympathy. It is a shameful thing to accuse a man wrongfully, and Enoch Holt had behaved well since the trial; and, what is more, had shown no accession to his means of living. So away he went, with a fair amount of good wishes, though one or two persons assured remonstrating listeners that they thought it likely Enoch would make a good voyage, better than common, and show himself forwarded when he came to port. Soon after his departure, Mrs. Peter Downs and an intimate acquaintance discussed the ever-exciting subject of the Knowles robbery over a friendly cup of tea.

They were in the Downs kitchen, and quite by themselves. Peter Downs himself had been drawn as a juror, and had been for two days at the county town. Mrs. Downs was giving herself to social interests in his absence, and Mrs. Forder, an asthmatic but very companionable person, had arrived by two o'clock that afternoon with her knitting work, sure of being welcome. The two old friends had first talked over varied subjects of immediate concern, but when supper was nearly finished, they fell back upon the lost Knowles gold, as has been already said.

"They got a dreadful blow, poor gals," wheezed Mrs. Forder, with compassion. "'T was harder for them than for most folks; they'd had a long stent with the ol' gentleman; very arbitrary, very arbitrary."

"Yes," answered Mrs. Downs, pushing back her tea-cup, then lifting it again to see if it was quite empty. "Yes, it took holt o' Hannah, the most. I should 'a' said Betsey was a good deal the most set in her ways an' would 'a' been most tore up, but 't wa'n't so."

"Lucky that Holt's folks sets on the other aisle in the meetin'-house, I do consider, so 't they needn't face each other sure as Sabbath comes round."

"I see Hannah an' him come face to face two Sabbaths afore Enoch left. So happened he dallied to have a word 'long o' Deacon Good'in, an' him an' Hannah stepped front of each other 'fore they knowed what they 's about. I sh'd thought her eyes 'd looked right through him. No one of 'em took the word; Enoch he slinked off pretty quick."

"I see 'em too," said Mrs. Forder; "made my blood run cold."

"Nothin' ain't come of the curse yit,"—Mrs. Downs lowered the tone of her voice,—"least, folks says so. It kind o' worries pore Phœbe Holt—Mis' Dow, I would say. She was narved all up at the time o' the trial, an' when her next baby come into the world, first thin' she made out t' ask me was whether it seemed likely, an' she gived me a pleadin' look as if I'd got to tell her what she hadn't heart to ask. 'Yes, dear,' says I, 'put up his little hands to me kind of wonted'; an' she turned a look on me like another creatur', so pleased an' contented."

"I s'pose you don't see no great of the Knowles gals?" inquired Mrs. Forder, who lived two miles away in the other direction.

"They stepped to the door yisterday when I was passin' by, an' I went in an' set a spell long of 'em," replied the hostess. "They'd got pestered with that ol' loom o' theirn. 'Fore I thought, says I, ''T is all worn out, Betsey,' says I. 'Why on airth don't ye git somebody to git some o' your own wood an' season it well so 't won't warp, same 's mine done, an' build ye a new one?' But Betsey muttered an' twitched away; 't wa'n't like her, but they're dis'p'inted at every turn, I s'pose, an' feel poor where they've got the same 's ever to do with. Hannah's a-coughin' this spring 's if somethin' ailed her. I asked her if she had bad feelin's in her pipes, an' she said yis, she had, but not to speak of 't before Betsey. I'm goin' to fix her up some hoarhound an' elecampane quick 's the ground 's nice an' warm an' roots livens up a grain more. They're limp an' wizened 'long to the fust of the spring. Them would be service'ble, simmered away to a syrup 'long o' molasses; now don't you think so, Mis' Forder?"

"Excellent," replied the wheezing dame. "I covet a portion myself, now you speak. Nothin' cures my complaint, but a new remedy takes holt clever sometimes, an' eases me for a spell." And she gave a plaintive sigh, and began to knit again.

Mrs. Downs rose and pushed the supper-table to the wall and drew her chair nearer to the stove. The April nights were chilly.

"The folks is late comin' after me," said Mrs. Forder, ostentatiously. "I may 's well confess that I told 'em if they was late

with the work they might let go o' fetchin' o' me an' I'd walk
home in the mornin'; take it easy when I was fresh. Course I
mean ef 't wouldn't put you out: I knowed you was all alone,
an' I kind o' wanted a change."

"Them words was in my mind to utter while we was to
table," avowed Mrs. Downs, hospitably. "I ain't reelly afeared,
but 't is sort o' creepy fastenin' up an' goin' to bed alone. Nobody can't help hearkin', an' every common noise starts you. I
never used to give nothin' a thought till the Knowleses was
robbed, though."

"'Twas mysterious, I do maintain," acknowledged Mrs.
Forder. "Comes over me sometimes p'raps 't wasn't Enoch;
he'd 'a' branched out more in course o' time. I'm waitin' to
see if he does extry well to sea 'fore I let my mind come to bear
on his bein' clean handed."

"Plenty thought 't was the ole Cap'n come back for it an'
sperited it away. Enough said that 't wasn't no honest gains;
most on 't was prize-money o' slave ships, an' all kinds o' devil's
gold was mixed in. I s'pose you've heard that said?"

"Time an' again," responded Mrs. Forder; "an' the worst
on 't was simple old Pappy Flanders went an' told the Knowles
gals themselves that folks thought the ole Cap'n come back
an' got it, and Hannah done wrong to cuss Enoch Holt an' his
ginerations after him the way she done."

"I think it took holt on her ter'ble after all she'd gone
through," said Mrs. Downs, compassionately. "He ain't near
so simple as he is ugly, Pappy Flanders ain't. I've seen him set
here an' read the paper sober 's anybody when I've been goin'
about my mornin's work in the shed-room, an' when I'd come
in to look about he'd twist it with his hands an' roll his eyes an'
begin to git off some o' his gable. I think them wanderin'
cheap-wits likes the fun on 't an' 'scapes stiddy work, an' gits
the rovin' habit so fixed, it sp'iles 'em."

"My gran'ther was to the South Seas in his young days," related Mrs. Forder, impressively, "an' he said cussin' was common there. I mean sober spitin' with a cuss. He seen one o'
them black folks git a gredge against another an' go an' set
down an' look stiddy at him in his hut an' cuss him in his mind
an' set there an' watch, watch, until the other kind o' took sick
an' died, all in a fortnight, I believe he said; 't would make

your blood run cold to hear gran'ther describe it, 't would so. He never done nothin' but set an' look, an' folks would give him somethin' to eat now an' then, as if they thought 't was all right, an' the other one 'd try to go an' come, an' at last he hived away altogether an' died. I don't know what you'd call it that ailed him. There 's suthin' in cussin' that 's bad for folks, now I tell ye, Mis Downs."

"Hannah's eyes always makes me creepy now," Mrs. Downs confessed uneasily. "They don't look pleadin' an' childish same 's they used to. Seems to me as if she'd had the worst on 't."

"We ain't seen the end on 't yit," said Mrs. Forder, impressively. "I feel it within me, Marthy Downs, an' it 's a terrible thing to have happened right amon'st us in Christian times. If we live long enough we're goin' to have plenty to talk over in our old age that 's come o' that cuss. Some seed 's shy o' sproutin' till a spring when the s'ile 's jest right to breed it."

"There 's lobeely now," agreed Mrs. Downs, pleased to descend to prosaic and familiar levels. "They ain't a good crop one year in six, and then you find it in a place where you never observed none to grow afore, like 's not; ain't it so, reelly?" And she rose to clear the table, pleased with the certainty of a guest that night. Their conversation was not reassuring to the heart of a timid woman, alone in an isolated farmhouse on a dark spring evening, especially so near the anniversary of old Captain Knowles's death.

v.

Later in these rural lives by many years two aged women were crossing a wide field together, following a footpath such as one often finds between widely separated homes of the New England country. Along these lightly traced thoroughfares, the children go to play, and lovers to plead, and older people to companion one another in work and pleasure, in sickness and sorrow; generation after generation comes and goes again by these country by-ways.

The footpath led from Mrs. Forder's to another farmhouse half a mile beyond, where there had been a wedding. Mrs. Downs was there, and in the June weather she had been easily persuaded to go home to tea with Mrs. Forder with the promise of being driven home later in the evening. Mrs. Downs's husband had been dead three years, and her friend's large family was scattered from the old nest; they were lonely at times in their later years, these old friends, and found it very pleasant now to have a walk together. Thin little Mrs. Forder, with all her wheezing, was the stronger and more active of the two; Mrs. Downs had grown heavier and weaker with advancing years.

They paced along the footpath slowly, Mrs. Downs rolling in her gait like a sailor, and availing herself of every pretext to stop and look at herbs in the pasture ground they crossed, and at the growing grass in the mowing fields. They discussed the wedding minutely, and then where the way grew wider they walked side by side instead of following each other, and their voices sank to the low tone that betokens confidence.

"You don't say that you really put faith in all them old stories?"

"It ain't accident altogether, noways you can fix it in your mind," maintained Mrs. Downs. "Needn't tell me that cussin' don't do neither good nor harm. I shouldn't want to marry amon'st the Holts if I was young ag'in! I r'member when this young man was born that 's married to-day, an' the fust thing his poor mother wanted to know was about his hands bein' right. I said yes they was, but las' year he was twenty year old and come home from the frontier with one o' them hands— his right one—shot off in a fight. They say 't happened to sights o' other fellows, an' their laigs gone too, but I count 'em over on my fingers, them Holts, an' he 's the third. May say that 't was all an accident his mother's gittin' throwed out o' her waggin comin' home from meetin', an' her wrist not bein' set good, an' she, bein' run down at the time, 'most lost it altogether, but thar' it is, stiffened up an' no good to her. There was the second. An' Enoch Holt hisself come home from the Chiny seas, made a good passage an' a sight o' money in the pepper trade, jest 's we expected, an' goin' to build him a new house, an' the frame gives a kind o' lurch when they was raisin' of it an' surges over on to him an' nips him under. 'Which arm?' says everybody along the road when they was comin' an' goin' with the doctor. 'Right one—got to lose it,' says the doctor to 'em, an' next time Enoch Holt got out to meetin' he stood up in the house o' God with the hymn-book in his left hand, an' no right hand to turn his leaf with. He knowed what we was all a-thinkin'."

"Well," said Mrs. Forder, very short-breathed with climbing the long slope of the pasture hill, "I don't know but I'd as soon be them as the Knowles gals. Hannah never knowed no peace again after she spoke them words in the co't-house. They come back an' harnted her, an' you know, Miss Downs, better 'n I do, being door-neighbors as one may say, how they lived their lives out like wild beasts into a lair."

"They used to go out some by night to git the air," pursued Mrs. Downs with interest. "I used to open the door an' step right in, an' I used to take their yarn an' stuff 'long o' mine an' sell 'em, an' do for the poor stray creatur 's long 's they'd let me. They'd be grateful for a mess o' early pease or potatoes as ever you see, an' Peter he allays favored 'em with pork, fresh an' salt, when we slaughtered. The old Cap'n kept 'em child'n long as he lived, an' then they was too old to l'arn different. I allays liked Hannah the best till that change struck her. Betsey she held out to the last jest about the same. I don't know, now I come to think of it, but what she felt it the most o' the two."

"They'd never let me 's much as git a look at 'em," complained Mrs. Forder. "Folks got awful stories a-goin' one time. I've heard it said, an' it allays creeped me cold all over, that there was somethin' come an' lived with 'em—a kind o' black shadder, a cobweb kind o' a man-shape that followed 'em about the house an' made a third to them; but they got hardened to it theirselves, only they was afraid 't would follow if they went anywheres from home. You don't believe no such piece o' nonsense?—But there, I've asked ye times enough before."

"They'd got shadders enough, poor creatur's," said Mrs. Downs with reserve. "Wasn't no kind o' need to make 'em up no spooks, as I know on. Well, here's these young folks a-startin'; I wish 'em well, I'm sure. She likes him with his one hand better than most gals likes them as has a good sound pair. They looked prime happy; I hope no curse won't foller 'em."

The friends stopped again—poor, short-winded bodies—on the crest of the low hill and turned to look at the wide landscape, bewildered by the marvelous beauty and the sudden flood of golden sunset light that poured out of the western sky. They could not remember that they had ever observed the wide view before; it was like a revelation or an outlook towards the celestial country, the sight of their own green farms and the countryside that bounded them. It was a pleasant country indeed, their own New England: their petty thoughts and vain imaginings seemed futile and unrelated to so fair a scene of things. But the figure of a man who was crossing the meadow below looked like a malicious black insect. It was an old man, it was Enoch Holt; time had worn and bent him enough to have satisfied his bitterest foe. The women could see his empty coat-sleeve flutter as he walked slowly and unexpectantly in that glorious evening light.

1890

CHARLOTTE PERKINS GILMAN
(1860–1935)

The Yellow Wall Paper

I<small>T</small> is very seldom that mere ordinary people like John and my-self secure ancestral halls for the summer.

A colonial mansion, a hereditary estate, I would say a haunted house, and reach the height of romantic felicity,—but that would be asking too much of fate!

Still I will proudly declare that there is something queer about it.

Else, why should it be let so cheaply? And why have stood so long untenanted?

John laughs at me, of course, but one expects that in marriage.

John is practical in the extreme. He has no patience with faith, an intense horror of superstition, and he scoffs openly at any talk of things not to be felt and seen and put down in figures.

John is a physician, and *perhaps*—(I would not say it to a living soul, of course, but this is dead paper and a great relief to my mind)—*perhaps* that is one reason I do not get well faster.

You see, he does not believe I am sick!

And what can one do?

If a physician of high standing, and one's own husband, as-sures friends and relatives that there is really nothing the matter with one but temporary nervous depression,—a slight hysterical tendency,—what is one to do?

My brother is also a physician, and also of high standing, and he says the same thing.

So I take phosphates or phosphites,—whichever it is,—and tonics, and journeys, and air, and exercise, and am absolutely forbidden to "work" until I am well again.

Personally I disagree with their ideas.

Personally I believe that congenial work, with excitement and change, would do me good.

But what is one to do?

I did write for a while in spite of them; but it *does* exhaust me a good deal—having to be so sly about it, or else meet with heavy opposition.

I sometimes fancy that in my condition if I had less opposition and more society and stimulus—but John says the very worst thing I can do is to think about my condition, and I confess it always makes me feel bad.

So I will let it alone and talk about the house.

The most beautiful place! It is quite alone, standing well back from the road, quite three miles from the village. It makes me think of English places that you read about, for there are hedges and walls and gates that lock, and lots of separate little houses for the gardeners and people.

There is a *delicious* garden! I never saw such a garden—large and shady, full of box-bordered paths, and lined with long grape-covered arbors with seats under them.

There were greenhouses, too, but they are all broken now.

There was some legal trouble, I believe, something about the heirs and co-heirs; anyhow, the place has been empty for years.

That spoils my ghostliness, I am afraid; but I don't care— there is something strange about the house—I can feel it.

I even said so to John one moonlight evening, but he said what I felt was a *draught* and shut the window.

I get unreasonably angry with John sometimes. I'm sure I never used to be so sensitive. I think it is due to this nervous condition.

But John says if I feel so I shall neglect proper self-control; so I take pains to control myself,—before him, at least,—and that makes me very tired.

I don't like our room a bit. I wanted one downstairs that opened on the piazza and had roses all over the window, and such pretty, old-fashioned chintz hangings! but John would not hear of it.

He said there was only one window and not room for two beds, and no near room for him if he took another.

He is very careful and loving, and hardly lets me stir without special direction.

I have a schedule prescription for each hour in the day; he takes all care from me, and so I feel basely ungrateful not to value it more.

He said we came here solely on my account, that I was to have perfect rest and all the air I could get. "Your exercise depends on your strength, my dear," said he, "and your food somewhat on your appetite; but air you can absorb all the time." So we took the nursery, at the top of the house.

It is a big, airy room, the whole floor nearly, with windows that look all ways, and air and sunshine galore. It was nursery first and then playground and gymnasium, I should judge; for the windows are barred for little children, and there are rings and things in the walls.

The paint and paper look as if a boys' school had used it. It is stripped off—the paper—in great patches all around the head of my bed, about as far as I can reach, and in a great place on the other side of the room low down. I never saw a worse paper in my life.

One of those sprawling flamboyant patterns committing every artistic sin.

It is dull enough to confuse the eye in following, pronounced enough to constantly irritate, and provoke study, and when you follow the lame, uncertain curves for a little distance they suddenly commit suicide—plunge off at outrageous angles, destroy themselves in unheard-of contradictions.

The color is repellant, almost revolting; a smouldering, unclean yellow, strangely faded by the slow-turning sunlight.

It is a dull yet lurid orange in some places, a sickly sulphur tint in others.

No wonder the children hated it! I should hate it myself if I had to live in this room long.

There comes John, and I must put this away,—he hates to have me write a word.

We have been here two weeks, and I haven't felt like writing before, since that first day.

I am sitting by the window now, up in this atrocious nursery, and there is nothing to hinder my writing as much as I please, save lack of strength.

John is away all day, and even some nights when his cases are serious.

I am glad my case is not serious!

But these nervous troubles are dreadfully depressing.

John does not know how much I really suffer. He knows there is no *reason* to suffer, and that satisfies him.

Of course it is only nervousness. It does weigh on me so not to do my duty in any way!

I meant to be such a help to John, such a real rest and comfort, and here I am a comparative burden already!

Nobody would believe what an effort it is to do what little I am able—to dress and entertain, and order things.

It is fortunate Mary is so good with the baby. Such a dear baby!

And yet I *cannot* be with him, it makes me so nervous.

I suppose John never was nervous in his life. He laughs at me so about this wall paper!

At first he meant to repaper the room, but afterwards he said that I was letting it get the better of me, and that nothing was worse for a nervous patient than to give way to such fancies.

He said that after the wall paper was changed it would be the heavy bedstead, and then the barred windows, and then that gate at the head of the stairs, and so on.

"You know the place is doing you good," he said, "and really, dear, I don't care to renovate the house just for a three months' rental."

"Then do let us go downstairs," I said, "there are such pretty rooms there."

Then he took me in his arms and called me a blessed little goose, and said he would go down cellar if I wished, and have it whitewashed into the bargain.

But he is right enough about the beds and windows and things.

It is as airy and comfortable a room as any one need wish, and, of course, I would not be so silly as to make him uncomfortable just for a whim.

I'm really getting quite fond of the big room, all but that horrid paper.

Out of one window I can see the garden, those mysterious

deep-shaded arbors, the riotous old-fashioned flowers, and bushes and gnarly trees.

Out of another I get a lovely view of the bay and a little private wharf belonging to the estate. There is a beautiful shaded lane that runs down there from the house. I always fancy I see people walking in these numerous paths and arbors, but John has cautioned me not to give way to fancy in the least. He says that with my imaginative power and habit of story-making a nervous weakness like mine is sure to lead to all manner of excited fancies, and that I ought to use my will and good sense to check the tendency. So I try.

I think sometimes that if I were only well enough to write a little it would relieve the press of ideas and rest me.

But I find I get pretty tired when I try.

It is so discouraging not to have any advice and companionship about my work. When I get really well John says we will ask Cousin Henry and Julia down for a long visit; but he says he would as soon put fire-works in my pillow-case as to let me have those stimulating people about now.

I wish I could get well faster.

But I must not think about that. This paper looks to me as if it *knew* what a vicious influence it had!

There is a recurrent spot where the pattern lolls like a broken neck and two bulbous eyes stare at you upside-down.

I got positively angry with the impertinence of it and the everlastingness. Up and down and sideways they crawl, and those absurd, unblinking eyes are everywhere. There is one place where two breadths didn't match, and the eyes go all up and down the line, one a little higher than the other.

I never saw so much expression in an inanimate thing before, and we all know how much expression they have! I used to lie awake as a child and get more entertainment and terror out of blank walls and plain furniture than most children could find in a toy-store.

I remember what a kindly wink the knobs of our big old bureau used to have, and there was one chair that always seemed like a strong friend.

I used to feel that if any of the other things looked too fierce I could always hop into that chair and be safe.

The furniture in this room is no worse than inharmonious,

however, for we had to bring it all from downstairs. I suppose when this was used as a playroom they had to take the nursery things out, and no wonder! I never saw such ravages as the children have made here.

The wall paper, as I said before, is torn off in spots, and it sticketh closer than a brother—they must have had perseverance as well as hatred.

Then the floor is scratched and gouged and splintered, the plaster itself is dug out here and there, and this great heavy bed, which is all we found in the room, looks as if it had been through the wars.

But I don't mind it a bit—only the paper.

There comes John's sister. Such a dear girl as she is, and so careful of me! I must not let her find me writing.

She is a perfect, an enthusiastic housekeeper, and hopes for no better profession. I verily believe she thinks it is the writing which made me sick!

But I can write when she is out, and see her a long way off from these windows.

There is one that commands the road, a lovely, shaded, winding road, and one that just looks off over the country. A lovely country, too, full of great elms and velvet meadows.

This wall paper has a kind of sub-pattern in a different shade, a particularly irritating one, for you can only see it in certain lights, and not clearly then.

But in the places where it isn't faded, and where the sun is just so, I can see a strange, provoking, formless sort of figure, that seems to sulk about behind that silly and conspicuous front design.

There's sister on the stairs!

Well, the Fourth of July is over! The people are all gone and I am tired out. John thought it might do me good to see a little company, so we just had mother and Nellie and the children down for a week.

Of course I didn't do a thing. Jennie sees to everything now.

But it tired me all the same.

John says if I don't pick up faster he shall send me to Weir Mitchell in the fall.

But I don't want to go there at all. I had a friend who was in his hands once, and she says he is just like John and my brother, only more so!

Besides, it is such an undertaking to go so far.

I don't feel as if it was worth while to turn my hand over for anything, and I'm getting dreadfully fretful and querulous.

I cry at nothing, and cry most of the time.

Of course I don't when John is here, or anybody else, but when I am alone.

And I am alone a good deal just now. John is kept in town very often by serious cases, and Jennie is good and lets me alone when I want her to.

So I walk a little in the garden or down that lovely lane, sit on the porch under the roses, and lie down up here a good deal.

I'm getting really fond of the room in spite of the wall paper. Perhaps *because* of the wall paper.

It dwells in my mind so!

I lie here on this great immovable bed—it is nailed down, I believe—and follow that pattern about by the hour. It is as good as gymnastics, I assure you. I start, we'll say, at the bottom, down in the corner over there where it has not been touched, and I determine for the thousandth time that I *will* follow that pointless pattern to some sort of a conclusion.

I know a little of the principles of design, and I know this thing was not arranged on any laws of radiation, or alternation, or repetition, or symmetry, or anything else that I ever heard of.

It is repeated, of course, by the breadths, but not otherwise.

Looked at in one way, each breadth stands alone, the bloated curves and flourishes—a kind of "debased Romanesque" with *delirium tremens*—go waddling up and down in isolated columns of fatuity.

But, on the other hand, they connect diagonally, and the sprawling outlines run off in great slanting waves of optic horror, like a lot of wallowing seaweeds in full chase.

The whole thing goes horizontally, too, at least it seems so, and I exhaust myself in trying to distinguish the order of its going in that direction.

They have used a horizontal breadth for a frieze, and that adds wonderfully to the confusion.

There is one end of the room where it is almost intact, and there, when the cross-lights fade and the low sun shines directly upon it, I can almost fancy radiation, after all,—the interminable grotesques seem to form around a common centre and rush off in head-long plunges of equal distraction.

It makes me tired to follow it. I will take a nap, I guess.

I don't know why I should write this.

I don't want to.

I don't feel able.

And I know John would think it absurd. But I *must* say what I feel and think in some way—it is such a relief!

But the effort is getting to be greater than the relief.

Half the time now I am awfully lazy, and lie down ever so much.

John says I mustn't lose my strength, and has me take cod-liver oil and lots of tonics and things, to say nothing of ale and wine and rare meat.

Dear John! He loves me very dearly, and hates to have me sick. I tried to have a real earnest reasonable talk with him the other day, and tell him how I wished he would let me go and make a visit to Cousin Henry and Julia.

But he said I wasn't able to go, nor able to stand it after I got there; and I did not make out a very good case for myself, for I was crying before I had finished.

It is getting to be a great effort for me to think straight. Just this nervous weakness, I suppose.

And dear John gathered me up in his arms, and just carried me upstairs and laid me on the bed, and sat by me and read to me till he tired my head.

He said I was his darling and his comfort and all he had, and that I must take care of myself for his sake, and keep well.

He says no one but myself can help me out of it, that I must use my will and self-control and not let my silly fancies run away with me.

There's one comfort, the baby is well and happy, and does not have to occupy this nursery with the horrid wall paper.

If we had not used it that blessed child would have! What a fortunate escape! Why, I wouldn't have a child of mine, an impressionable little thing, live in such a room for worlds.

I never thought of it before, but it is lucky that John kept me here, after all. I can stand it so much easier than a baby, you see.

Of course I never mention it to them any more,—I am too wise,—but I keep watch of it all the same.

There are things in that paper that nobody knows but me, or ever will.

Behind that outside pattern the dim shapes get clearer every day.

It is always the same shape, only very numerous.

And it is like a woman stooping down and creeping about behind that pattern. I don't like it a bit. I wonder—I begin to think—I wish John would take me away from here!

It is so hard to talk with John about my case, because he is so wise, and because he loves me so.

But I tried it last night.

It was moonlight. The moon shines in all around, just as the sun does.

I hate to see it sometimes, it creeps so slowly, and always comes in by one window or another.

John was asleep and I hated to waken him, so I kept still and watched the moonlight on that undulating wall paper till I felt creepy.

The faint figure behind seemed to shake the pattern, just as if she wanted to get out.

I got up softly and went to feel and see if the paper *did* move, and when I came back John was awake.

"What is it, little girl?" he said. "Don't go walking about like that—you'll get cold."

I thought it was a good time to talk, so I told him that I really was not gaining here, and that I wished he would take me away.

"Why, darling!" said he, "our lease will be up in three weeks, and I can't see how to leave before.

"The repairs are not done at home, and I cannot possibly leave town just now. Of course if you were in any danger I could and would, but you really are better, dear, whether you can see it or not. I am a doctor, dear, and I know. You are gaining flesh and color, your appetite is better. I feel really much easier about you."

"I don't weigh a bit more," said I, "nor as much; and my appetite may be better in the evening, when you are here, but it is worse in the morning, when you are away."

"Bless her little heart!" said he with a big hug; "she shall be as sick as she pleases. But now let's improve the shining hours by going to sleep, and talk about it in the morning."

"And you won't go away?" I asked gloomily.

"Why, how can I, dear? It is only three weeks more and then we will take a nice little trip of a few days while Jennie is getting the house ready. Really, dear, you are better!"

"Better in body, perhaps"—I began, and stopped short, for he sat up straight and looked at me with such a stern, reproachful look that I could not say another word.

"My darling," said he, "I beg of you, for my sake and for our child's sake, as well as for your own, that you will never for one instant let that idea enter your mind! There is nothing so dangerous, so fascinating, to a temperament like yours. It is a false and foolish fancy. Can you not trust me as a physician when I tell you so?"

So of course I said no more on that score, and we went to sleep before long. He thought I was asleep first, but I wasn't,— I lay there for hours trying to decide whether that front pattern and the back pattern really did move together or separately.

On a pattern like this, by daylight, there is a lack of sequence, a defiance of law, that is a constant irritant to a normal mind.

The color is hideous enough, and unreliable enough, and infuriating enough, but the pattern is torturing.

You think you have mastered it, but just as you get well under way in following, it turns a back somersault, and there you are. It slaps you in the face, knocks you down, and tramples upon you. It is like a bad dream.

The outside pattern is a florid arabesque, reminding one of a fungus. If you can imagine a toadstool in joints, an interminable string of toadstools, budding and sprouting in endless convolutions,—why, that is something like it.

That is, sometimes!

There is one marked peculiarity about this paper, a thing nobody seems to notice but myself, and that is that it changes as the light changes.

When the sun shoots in through the east window—I always watch for that first long, straight ray—it changes so quickly that I never can quite believe it.

That is why I watch it always.

By moonlight—the moon shines in all night when there is a moon—I wouldn't know it was the same paper.

At night in any kind of light, in twilight, candlelight, lamp-light, and worst of all by moonlight, it becomes bars! The outside pattern, I mean, and the woman behind it is as plain as can be.

I didn't realize for a long time what the thing was that showed behind,—that dim sub-pattern,—but now I am quite sure it is a woman.

By daylight she is subdued, quiet. I fancy it is the pattern that keeps her so still. It is so puzzling. It keeps me quiet by the hour.

I lie down ever so much now. John says it is good for me, and to sleep all I can.

Indeed, he started the habit by making me lie down for an hour after each meal.

It is a very bad habit, I am convinced, for, you see, I don't sleep.

And that cultivates deceit, for I don't tell them I'm awake,—oh, no!

The fact is, I am getting a little afraid of John.

He seems very queer sometimes, and even Jennie has an inexplicable look.

It strikes me occasionally, just as a scientific hypothesis, that perhaps it is the paper!

I have watched John when he did not know I was looking, and come into the room suddenly on the most innocent excuses, and I've caught him several times *looking at the paper!* And Jennie too. I caught Jennie with her hand on it once.

She didn't know I was in the room, and when I asked her in a quiet, a very quiet voice, with the most restrained manner possible, what she was doing with the paper she turned around as if she had been caught stealing, and looked quite angry— asked me why I should frighten her so!

Then she said that the paper stained everything it touched, that she had found yellow smooches on all my clothes and John's, and she wished we would be more careful!

Did not that sound innocent? But I know she was studying that pattern, and I am determined that nobody shall find it out but myself!

*

Life is very much more exciting now than it used to be. You see I have something more to expect, to look forward to, to watch. I really do eat better, and am more quiet than I was.

John is so pleased to see me improve! He laughed a little the other day, and said I seemed to be flourishing in spite of my wall paper.

I turned it off with a laugh. I had no intention of telling him it was *because* of the wall paper—he would make fun of me. He might even want to take me away.

I don't want to leave now until I have found it out. There is a week more, and I think that will be enough.

I'm feeling ever so much better! I don't sleep much at night, for it is so interesting to watch developments; but I sleep a good deal in the daytime.

In the daytime it is tiresome and perplexing.

There are always new shoots on the fungus, and new shades of yellow all over it. I cannot keep count of them, though I have tried conscientiously.

It is the strangest yellow, that wall paper! It makes me think of all the yellow things I ever saw—not beautiful ones like buttercups, but old foul, bad yellow things.

But there is something else about that paper—the smell! I noticed it the moment we came into the room, but with so much air and sun it was not bad. Now we have had a week of fog and rain, and whether the windows are open or not the smell is here.

It creeps all over the house.

I find it hovering in the dining-room, skulking in the parlor, hiding in the hall, lying in wait for me on the stairs.

It gets into my hair.

Even when I go to ride, if I turn my head suddenly and surprise it—there is that smell!

Such a peculiar odor, too! I have spent hours in trying to analyze it, to find what it smelled like.

It is not bad—at first, and very gentle, but quite the subtlest, most enduring odor I ever met.

In this damp weather it is awful. I wake up in the night and find it hanging over me.

It used to disturb me at first. I thought seriously of burning the house—to reach the smell.

But now I am used to it. The only thing I can think of that it is like is the *color* of the paper—a yellow smell!

There is a very funny mark on this wall, low down, near the mopboard. A streak that runs around the room. It goes behind every piece of furniture, except the bed, a long, straight, even *smooch*, as if it had been rubbed over and over.

I wonder how it was done and who did it, and what they did it for. Round and round and round—round and round and round—it makes me dizzy!

I really have discovered something at last.

Through watching so much at night, when it changes so, I have finally found out.

The front pattern *does* move—and no wonder! The woman behind shakes it!

Sometimes I think there are a great many women behind, and sometimes only one, and she crawls around fast, and her crawling shakes it all over.

Then in the very bright spots she keeps still, and in the very shady spots she just takes hold of the bars and shakes them hard.

And she is all the time trying to climb through. But nobody could climb through that pattern—it strangles so; I think that is why it has so many heads.

They get through, and then the pattern strangles them off and turns them upside-down, and makes their eyes white!

If those heads were covered or taken off it would not be half so bad.

I think that woman gets out in the daytime!

And I'll tell you why—privately—I've seen her!

I can see her out of every one of my windows!

It is the same woman, I know, for she is always creeping, and most women do not creep by daylight.

I see her in that long shaded lane, creeping up and down. I see her in those dark grape arbors, creeping all around the garden.

I see her on that long road under the trees, creeping along, and when a carriage comes she hides under the blackberry vines.

I don't blame her a bit. It must be very humiliating to be caught creeping by daylight!

I always lock the door when I creep by daylight. I can't do it at night, for I know John would suspect something at once.

And John is so queer, now, that I don't want to irritate him. I wish he would take another room! Besides, I don't want anybody to get that woman out at night but myself.

I often wonder if I could see her out of all the windows at once.

But, turn as fast as I can, I can only see out of one at one time.

And though I always see her she *may* be able to creep faster than I can turn!

I have watched her sometimes away off in the open country, creeping as fast as a cloud shadow in a high wind.

If only that top pattern could be gotten off from the under one! I mean to try it, little by little.

I have found out another funny thing, but I shan't tell it this time! It does not do to trust people too much.

There are only two more days to get this paper off, and I believe John is beginning to notice. I don't like the look in his eyes.

And I heard him ask Jennie a lot of professional questions about me. She had a very good report to give.

She said I slept a good deal in the daytime.

John knows I don't sleep very well at night, for all I'm so quiet!

He asked me all sorts of questions, too, and pretended to be very loving and kind.

As if I couldn't see through him!

Still, I don't wonder he acts so, sleeping under this paper for three months.

It only interests me, but I feel sure John and Jennie are secretly affected by it.

Hurrah! This is the last day, but it is enough. John is to stay in town over night, and won't be out until this evening.

Jennie wanted to sleep with me—the sly thing! but I told her I should undoubtedly rest better for a night all alone.

That was clever, for really I wasn't alone a bit! As soon as it was moonlight, and that poor thing began to crawl and shake the pattern, I got up and ran to help her.

I pulled and she shook, I shook and she pulled, and before morning we had peeled off yards of that paper.

A strip about as high as my head and half around the room.

And then when the sun came and that awful pattern began to laugh at me I declared I would finish it to-day!

We go away to-morrow, and they are moving all my furniture down again to leave things as they were before.

Jennie looked at the wall in amazement, but I told her merrily that I did it out of pure spite at the vicious thing.

She laughed and said she wouldn't mind doing it herself, but I must not get tired.

How she betrayed herself that time!

But I am here, and no person touches this paper but me—not *alive*!

She tried to get me out of the room—it was too patent! But I said it was so quiet and empty and clean now that I believed I would lie down again and sleep all I could; and not to wake me even for dinner—I would call when I woke.

So now she is gone, and the servants are gone, and the things are gone, and there is nothing left but that great bedstead nailed down, with the canvas mattress we found on it.

We shall sleep downstairs to-night, and take the boat home to-morrow.

I quite enjoy the room, now it is bare again.

How those children did tear about here!

This bedstead is fairly gnawed!

But I must get to work.

I have locked the door and thrown the key down into the front path.

I don't want to go out, and I don't want to have anybody come in, till John comes.

I want to astonish him.

I've got a rope up here that even Jennie did not find. If that woman does get out, and tries to get away, I can tie her!

But I forgot I could not reach far without anything to stand on!

This bed will *not* move!

I tried to lift and push it until I was lame, and then I got so angry I bit off a little piece at one corner—but it hurt my teeth.

Then I peeled off all the paper I could reach standing on the floor. It sticks horribly and the pattern just enjoys it! All those strangled heads and bulbous eyes and waddling fungus growths just shriek with derision!

I am getting angry enough to do something desperate. To jump out of the window would be admirable exercise, but the bars are too strong even to try.

Besides, I wouldn't do it. Of course not. I know well enough that a step like that is improper and might be misconstrued.

I don't like to *look* out of the windows even—there are so many of those creeping women, and they creep so fast.

I wonder if they all come out of that wall paper, as I did?

But I am securely fastened now by my well-hidden rope— you don't get *me* out in the road there!

I suppose I shall have to get back behind the pattern when it comes night, and that is hard!

It is so pleasant to be out in this great room and creep around as I please!

I don't want to go outside. I won't, even if Jennie asks me to.

For outside you have to creep on the ground, and everything is green instead of yellow.

But here I can creep smoothly on the floor, and my shoulder just fits in that long smooch around the wall, so I cannot lose my way.

Why, there's John at the door!

It is no use, young man, you can't open it!

How he does call and pound!

Now he's crying for an axe.

It would be a shame to break down that beautiful door!

"John, dear!" said I in the gentlest voice, "the key is down by the front steps, under a plantain leaf!"

That silenced him for a few moments.

Then he said—very quietly indeed, "Open the door, my darling!"

"I can't," said I. "The key is down by the front door, under a plantain leaf!"

And then I said it again, several times, very gently and

slowly, and said it so often that he had to go and see, and he got it, of course, and came in. He stopped short by the door.

"What is the matter?" he cried.

"For God's sake, what are you doing?"

I kept on creeping just the same, but I looked at him over my shoulder.

"I've got out at last," said I, "in spite of you and Jane! And I've pulled off most of the paper, so you can't put me back!"

Now why should that man have fainted? But he did, and right across my path by the wall, so that I had to creep over him every time!

1892

STEPHEN CRANE

(1871–1900)

The Black Dog

THERE was a ceaseless rumble in the air as the heavy raindrops battered upon the laurel-thickets and the matted moss and haggard rocks beneath. Four water-soaked men made their difficult ways through the drenched forest. The little man stopped and shook an angry finger at where night was stealthily following them. "Cursed be fate and her children and her children's children! We are everlastingly lost!" he cried. The panting procession halted under some dripping, drooping hemlocks and swore in wrathful astonishment.

"It will rain for forty days and forty nights," said the pudgy man, moaningly, "and I feel like a wet loaf of bread, now. We shall never find our way out of this wilderness until I am made into a porridge."

In desperation, they started again to drag their listless bodies through the watery bushes. After a time, the clouds withdrew from above them and great winds came from concealment and went sweeping and swirling among the trees. Night also came very near and menaced the wanderers with darkness. The little man had determination in his legs. He scrambled among the thickets and made desperate attempts to find a path or road. As he climbed a hillock, he espied a small clearing upon which sat desolation and a venerable house, wept over by wind-waved pines.

"Ho," he cried, "here's a house."

His companions straggled painfully after him as he fought the thickets between him and the cabin. At their approach, the wind frenziedly opposed them and skirled madly in the trees. The little man boldly confronted the weird glances from the crannies of the cabin and rapped on the door. A score of timbers answered with groans and, within, something fell to the floor with a clang.

"Ho," said the little man. He stepped back a few paces.

Somebody in a distant part started and walked across the floor toward the door with an ominous step. A slate-colored man appeared. He was dressed in a ragged shirt and trousers, the latter stuffed into his boots. Large tears were falling from his eyes.

"How-d'-do, my friend?" said the little man, affably.

"My ol' uncle, Jim Crocker, he's sick ter death," replied the slate-colored person.

"Ho," said the little man. "Is that so?"

The latter's clothing clung desperately to him and water sogged in his boots. He stood patiently on one foot for a time.

"Can you put us up here until to-morrow?" he asked, finally.

"Yes," said the slate-colored man.

The party passed into a little unwashed room, inhabited by a stove, a stairway, a few precarious chairs and a misshapen table.

"I'll fry yer some po'k and make yer some coffee," said the slate-colored man to his guests.

"Go ahead, old boy," cried the little man cheerfully from where he sat on the table, smoking his pipe and dangling his legs.

"My ol' uncle, Jim Crocker, he's sick ter death," said the slate-colored man.

"Think he'll die?" asked the pudgy man, gently.

"No!"

"No?"

"He won't die! He's an ol' man, but he won't die, yit! The black dorg hain't been around yit!"

"The black dog?" said the little man, feebly. He struggled with himself for a moment.

"What's the black dog?" he asked at last.

"He's a sperrit," said the slate-colored man in a voice of sombre hue.

"Oh, he is? Well?"

"He hants these parts, he does, an' when people are goin' ter die, he comes an' sets an' howls."

"Ho," said the little man. He looked out of the window and saw night making a million shadows.

The little man moved his legs nervously.

"I don't believe in these things," said he, addressing the slate-colored man, who was scuffling with a side of pork.

"Wot things?" came incoherently from the combatant.

"Oh, these-er-phantoms and ghosts and what not. All rot, I say."

"That's because you have merely a stomach and no soul," grunted the pudgy man.

"Ho, old pudgkins!" replied the little man. His back curved with passion. A tempest of wrath was in the pudgy man's eye. The final epithet used by the little man was a carefully-studied insult, always brought forth at a crisis. They quarrelled.

"All right, pudgkins, bring on your phantom," cried the little man in conclusion.

His stout companion's wrath was too huge for words. The little man smiled triumphantly. He had staked his opponent's reputation.

The visitors sat silent. The slate-colored man moved about in a small personal atmosphere of gloom.

Suddenly, a strange cry came to their ears from somewhere. It was a low, trembling call which made the little man quake privately in his shoes. The slate-colored man bounded at the stairway, and disappeared with a flash of legs through a hole in the ceiling. The party below heard two voices in conversation, one belonging to the slate-colored man, and the other in the quavering tones of age. Directly the slate-colored man reappeared from above and said: "The ol' man is took bad for his supper."

He hurriedly prepared a mixture with hot water, salt and beef. Beef-tea, it might be called. He disappeared again. Once more the party below heard, vaguely, talking over their heads. The voice of age arose to a shriek.

"Open the window, fool! Do you think I can live in the smell of your soup?"

Mutterings by the slate-colored man and the creaking of a window were heard.

The slate-colored man stumbled down the stairs, and said with intense gloom, "The black dorg'll be along soon."

The little man started, and the pudgy man sneered at him. They ate a supper and then sat waiting. The pudgy man listened so palpably that the little man wished to kill him. The wood-fire became excited and sputtered frantically. Without, a thousand spirits of the winds had become entangled in the pine branches and were lowly pleading to be loosened. The slate-colored man tiptoed across the room and lit a timid candle. The men sat waiting.

The phantom dog lay cuddled to a round bundle, asleep down the roadway against the windward side of an old shanty. The spectre's master had moved to Pike County. But the dog lingered as a friend might linger at the tomb of a friend. His fur was like a suit of old clothes. His jowls hung and flopped, exposing his teeth. Yellow famine was in his eyes. The wind-rocked shanty groaned and muttered, but the dog slept. Suddenly, however, he got up and shambled to the roadway. He cast a long glance from his hungry, despairing eyes in the direction of the venerable house. The breeze came full to his nostrils. He threw back his head and gave a long, low howl and started intently up the road. Maybe he smelled a dead man.

The group around the fire in the venerable house were listening and waiting. The atmosphere of the room was tense. The slate-colored man's face was twitching and his drabbed hands were gripped together. The little man was continually looking behind his chair. Upon the countenance of the pudgy man appeared conceit for an approaching triumph over the little man, mingled with apprehension for his own safety. Five pipes glowed as rivals of the timid candle. Profound silence drooped heavily over them. Finally the slate-colored man spoke.

"My ol' uncle, Jim Crocker, he's sick ter death."

The four men started and then shrank back in their chairs.

"Damn it!" replied the little man, vaguely.

Again there was a long silence. Suddenly it was broken by a wild cry from the room above. It was a shriek that struck upon them with appalling swiftness, like a flash of lightning. The walls whirled and the floor rumbled. It brought the men together with a rush. They huddled in a heap and stared at the white terror in each other's faces. The slate-colored man grasped the candle and flared it above his head. "The black dorg," he howled, and plunged at the stairway. The maddened four men followed frantically, for it is better to be in the presence of the awful than only within hearing.

Their ears still quivering with the shriek, they bounded through the hole in the ceiling, and into the sick room.

With quilts drawn closely to his shrunken breast for a shield, his bony hand gripping the cover, an old man lay, with glazing

eyes fixed on the open window. His throat gurgled and a froth
appeared at his mouth.

From the outer darkness came a strange, unnatural wail,
burdened with weight of death and each note filled with foreboding. It was the song of the spectral dog.

"God!" screamed the little man. He ran to the open
window. He could see nothing at first save the pine-trees, engaged in a furious combat tossing back and forth and struggling. The moon was peeping cautiously over the rims of some
black clouds. But the chant of the phantom guided the little
man's eyes, and he at length perceived its shadowy form on the
ground under the window. He fell away gasping at the sight.
The pudgy man crouched in a corner, chattering insanely. The
slate-colored man, in his fear, crooked his legs and looked like
a hideous Chinese idol. The man upon the bed was turned to
stone, save the froth, which pulsated.

In the final struggle, terror will fight the inevitable. The
little man roared maniacal curses, and, rushing again to the
window, began to throw various articles at the spectre.

A mug, a plate, a knife, a fork, all crashed or clanged on the
ground, but the song of the spectre continued. The bowl of
beef-tea followed. As it struck the ground the phantom ceased
its cry.

The men in the chamber sank limply against the walls, with
the unearthly wail still ringing in their ears and the fear un-
faded from their eyes. They waited again.

The little man felt his nerves vibrate. Destruction was better
than another wait. He grasped a candle and, going to the
window, held it over his head and looked out.

"Ho!" he said.

His companions crawled to the window and peered out with
him.

"He's eatin' the beef-tea," said the slate-colored man, faintly.

"The damn dog was hungry," said the pudgy man.

"There's your phantom," said the little man to the pudgy
man.

On the bed, the old man lay dead. Without, the spectre was
wagging its tail.

1892

KATE CHOPIN
(1850–1904)

Ma'ame Pélagie

I.

WHEN the war began, there stood on Côte Joyeuse an imposing mansion of red brick, shaped like the Pantheon. A
grove of majestic live-oaks surrounded it.

Thirty years later, only the thick walls were standing, with
the dull red brick showing here and there through a matted
growth of clinging vines. The huge round pillars were intact;
so to some extent was the stone flagging of hall and portico.
There had been no home so stately along the whole stretch of
Côte Joyeuse. Every one knew that, as they knew it had cost
Philippe Valmêt sixty thousand dollars to build, away back in
1840. No one was in danger of forgetting that fact, so long as
his daughter Pélagie survived. She was a queenly, white-haired
woman of fifty. "Ma'ame Pélagie," they called her, though she
was unmarried, as was her sister Pauline, a child in Ma'ame
Pélagie's eyes; a child of thirty-five.

The two lived alone in a three-roomed cabin, almost within
the shadow of the ruin. They lived for a dream, for Ma'ame
Pélagie's dream, which was to rebuild the old home.

It would be pitiful to tell how their days were spent to accomplish this end; how the dollars had been saved for thirty
years and the picayunes hoarded; and yet, not half enough
gathered! But Ma'ame Pélagie felt sure of twenty years of life
before her, and counted upon as many more for her sister. And
what could not come to pass in twenty—in forty—years?

Often, of pleasant afternoons, the two would drink their black
coffee, seated upon the stone-flagged portico whose canopy
was the blue sky of Louisiana. They loved to sit there in the silence, with only each other and the sheeny, prying lizards for
company, talking of the old times and planning for the new;

153

while light breezes stirred the tattered vines high up among the columns, where owls nested.

"We can never hope to have all just as it was, Pauline," Ma'ame Pélagie would say; "perhaps the marble pillars of the salon will have to be replaced by wooden ones, and the crystal candelabra left out. Should you be willing, Pauline?"

"Oh, yes, Sesoeur, I shall be willing." It was always, "Yes, Sesoeur," or "No, Sesoeur," "Just as you please, Sesoeur," with poor little Mam'selle Pauline. For what did she remember of that old life and that old splendor? Only a faint gleam here and there; the half-consciousness of a young, uneventful existence; and then a great crash. That meant the nearness of war; the revolt of slaves; confusion ending in fire and flame through which she was borne safely in the strong arms of Pélagie, and carried to the log cabin which was still their home. Their brother, Léandre, had known more of it all than Pauline, and not so much as Pélagie. He had left the management of the big plantation with all its memories and traditions to his older sister, and had gone away to dwell in cities. That was many years ago. Now, Léandre's business called him frequently and upon long journeys from home, and his motherless daughter was coming to stay with her aunts at Côte Joyeuse.

They talked about it, sipping their coffee on the ruined portico. Mam'selle Pauline was terribly excited; the flush that throbbed into her pale, nervous face showed it; and she locked her thin fingers in and out incessantly.

"But what shall we do with La Petite, Sesoeur? Where shall we put her? How shall we amuse her? Ah, Seigneur!"

"She will sleep upon a cot in the room next to ours," responded Ma'ame Pélagie, "and live as we do. She knows how we live, and why we live; her father has told her. She knows we have money and could squander it if we chose. Do not fret, Pauline; let us hope La Petite is a true Valmêt."

Then Ma'ame Pélagie rose with stately deliberation and went to saddle her horse, for she had yet to make her last daily round through the fields; and Mam'selle Pauline threaded her way slowly among the tangled grasses toward the cabin.

The coming of La Petite, bringing with her as she did the pungent atmosphere of an outside and dimly known world, was a shock to these two, living their dream-life. The girl was quite as tall as her aunt Pélagie, with dark eyes that reflected joy as a still pool reflects the light of stars; and her rounded cheek was tinged like the pink crèpe myrtle. Mam'selle Pauline kissed her and trembled. Ma'ame Pélagie looked into her eyes with a searching gaze, which seemed to seek a likeness of the past in the living present.

And they made room between them for this young life.

II.

La Petite had determined upon trying to fit herself to the strange, narrow existence which she knew awaited her at Côte Joyeuse. It went well enough at first. Sometimes she followed Ma'ame Pélagie into the fields to note how the cotton was opening, ripe and white; or to count the ears of corn upon the hardy stalks. But oftener she was with her aunt Pauline, assisting in household offices, chattering of her brief past, or walking with the older woman arm-in-arm under the trailing moss of the giant oaks.

Mam'selle Pauline's steps grew very buoyant that summer, and her eyes were sometimes as bright as a bird's, unless La Petite were away from her side, when they would lose all other light but one of uneasy expectancy. The girl seemed to love her well in return, and called her endearingly Tan'tante. But as the time went by, La Petite became very quiet,—not listless, but thoughtful, and slow in her movements. Then her cheeks began to pale, till they were tinged like the creamy plumes of the white crèpe myrtle that grew in the ruin.

One day when she sat within its shadow, between her aunts, holding a hand of each, she said: "Tante Pélagie, I must tell you something, you and Tan'tante." She spoke low, but clearly and firmly. "I love you both,—please remember that I love you both. But I must go away from you. I can't live any longer here at Côte Joyeuse."

A spasm passed through Mam'selle Pauline's delicate frame. La Petite could feel the twitch of it in the wiry fingers that were intertwined with her own. Ma'ame Pélagie remained unchanged and motionless. No human eye could penetrate so

deep as to see the satisfaction which her soul felt. She said:
"What do you mean, Petite? Your father has sent you to us,
and I am sure it is his wish that you remain."

"My father loves me, tante Pélagie, and such will not be his
wish when he knows. Oh!" she continued with a restless movement, "it is as though a weight were pressing me backward here.
I must live another life; the life I lived before. I want to know
things that are happening from day to day over the world, and
hear them talked about. I want my music, my books, my companions. If I had known no other life but this one of privation,
I suppose it would be different. If I had to live this life, I should
make the best of it. But I do not have to; and you know, tante
Pélagie, you do not need to. It seems to me," she added in a
whisper, "that it is a sin against myself. Ah, Tan'tante!—what
is the matter with Tan'tante?"

It was nothing; only a slight feeling of faintness, that would
soon pass. She entreated them to take no notice; but they
brought her some water and fanned her with a palmetto leaf.

But that night, in the stillness of the room, Mam'selle Pauline
sobbed and would not be comforted. Ma'ame Pélagie took her
in her arms.

"Pauline, my little sister Pauline," she entreated, "I never
have seen you like this before. Do you no longer love me? Have
we not been happy together, you and I?"

"Oh, yes, Sesoeur."

"Is it because La Petite is going away?"

"Yes, Sesoeur."

"Then she is dearer to you than I!" spoke Ma'ame Pélagie
with sharp resentment. "Than I, who held you and warmed
you in my arms the day you were born; than I, your mother,
father, sister, everything that could cherish you. Pauline, don't
tell me that."

Mam'selle Pauline tried to talk through her sobs.

"I can't explain it to you, Sesoeur. I don't understand it myself. I love you as I have always loved you; next to God. But if
La Petite goes away I shall die. I can't understand,—help me,
Sesoeur. She seems—she seems like a saviour; like one who had
come and taken me by the hand and was leading me somewhere
—somewhere I want to go."

Ma'ame Pélagie had been sitting beside the bed in her

peignoir and slippers. She held the hand of her sister who lay there, and smoothed down the woman's soft brown hair. She said not a word, and the silence was broken only by Ma'mselle Pauline's continued sobs. Once Ma'ame Pélagie arose to drink of orange-flower water, which she gave to her sister, as she would have offered it to a nervous, fretful child. Almost an hour passed before Ma'ame Pélagie spoke again. Then she said:—

"Pauline, you must cease that sobbing, now, and sleep. You will make yourself ill. La Petite will not go away. Do you hear me? Do you understand? She will stay, I promise you."

Mam'selle Pauline could not clearly comprehend, but she had great faith in the word of her sister, and soothed by the promise and the touch of Ma'ame Pélagie's strong, gentle hand, she fell asleep.

III.

Ma'ame Pélagie, when she saw that her sister slept, arose noiselessly and stepped outside upon the low-roofed narrow gallery. She did not linger there, but with a step that was hurried and agitated, she crossed the distance that divided her cabin from the ruin.

The night was not a dark one, for the sky was clear and the moon resplendent. But light or dark would have made no difference to Ma'ame Pélagie. It was not the first time she had stolen away to the ruin at night-time, when the whole plantation slept; but she never before had been there with a heart so nearly broken. She was going there for the last time to dream her dreams; to see the visions that hitherto had crowded her days and nights, and to bid them farewell.

There was the first of them, awaiting her upon the very portal; a robust old white-haired man, chiding her for returning home so late. There are guests to be entertained. Does she not know it? Guests from the city and from the near plantations. Yes, she knows it is late. She had been abroad with Félix, and they did not notice how the time was speeding. Félix is there; he will explain it all. He is there beside her, but she does not want to hear what he will tell her father.

Ma'ame Pélagie had sunk upon the bench where she and

her sister so often came to sit. Turning, she gazed in through
the gaping chasm of the window at her side. The interior of
the ruin is ablaze. Not with the moonlight, for that is faint
beside the other one—the sparkle from the crystal candelabra,
which negroes, moving noiselessly and respectfully about, are
lighting, one after the other. How the gleam of them reflects
and glances from the polished marble pillars!

The room holds a number of guests. There is old Monsieur
Lucien Santien, leaning against one of the pillars, and laughing
at something which Monsieur Lafirme is telling him, till his fat
shoulders shake. His son Jules is with him—Jules, who wants
to marry her. She laughs. She wonders if Félix has told her
father yet. There is young Jerome Lafirme playing at checkers
upon the sofa with Léandre. Little Pauline stands annoying
them and disturbing the game. Léandre reproves her. She
begins to cry, and old black Clémentine, her nurse, who is not
far off, limps across the room to pick her up and carry her
away. How sensitive the little one is! But she trots about and
takes care of herself better than she did a year or two ago,
when she fell upon the stone hall floor and raised a great
"bobo" on her forehead. Pélagie was hurt and angry enough
about it; and she ordered rugs and buffalo robes to be brought
and laid thick upon the tiles, till the little one's steps were
surer.

"Il ne faut pas faire mal à Pauline." She was saying it
aloud—"faire mal à Pauline."

But she gazes beyond the salon, back into the big dining
hall, where the white crèpe myrtle grows. Ha! how low that
bat has circled. It has struck Ma'ame Pélagie full on the breast.
She does not know it. She is beyond there in the dining hall,
where her father sits with a group of friends over their wine. As
usual they are talking politics. How tiresome! She has heard
them say "la guerre" oftener than once. La guerre. Bah! She and
Félix have something pleasanter to talk about, out under the
oaks, or back in the shadow of the oleanders.

But they were right! The sound of a cannon, shot at Sumter,
has rolled across the Southern States, and its echo is heard
along the whole stretch of Côte Joyeuse.

Yet Pélagie does not believe it. Not till La Ricaneuse stands before her with bare, black arms akimbo, uttering a volley of vile abuse and of brazen impudence. Pélagie wants to kill her. But yet she will not believe. Not till Félix comes to her in the chamber above the dining hall—there where that trumpet vine hangs—comes to say good-by to her. The hurt which the big brass buttons of his new gray uniform pressed into the tender flesh of her bosom has never left it. She sits upon the sofa, and he beside her, both speechless with pain. That room would not have been altered. Even the sofa would have been there in the same spot, and Ma'ame Pélagie had meant all along, for thirty years, all along, to lie there upon it some day when the time came to die.

But there is no time to weep, with the enemy at the door. The door has been no barrier. They are clattering through the halls now, drinking the wines, shattering the crystal and glass, slashing the portraits.

One of them stands before her and tells her to leave the house. She slaps his face. How the stigma stands out red as blood upon his blanched cheek!

Now there is a roar of fire and the flames are bearing down upon her motionless figure. She wants to show them how a daughter of Louisiana can perish before her conquerors. But little Pauline clings to her knees in an agony of terror. Little Pauline must be saved.

"Il ne faut pas faire mal à Pauline."

Again she is saying it aloud—"faire mal à Pauline."

The night was nearly spent; Ma'ame Pélagie had glided from the bench upon which she had rested, and for hours lay prone upon the stone flagging, motionless. When she dragged herself to her feet it was to walk like one in a dream. About the great, solemn pillars, one after the other, she reached her arms, and pressed her cheek and her lips upon the senseless brick.

"Adieu, adieu!" whispered Ma'ame Pélagie.

There was no longer the moon to guide her steps across the familiar pathway to the cabin. The brightest light in the sky was Venus, that swung low in the east. The bats had ceased to beat their wings about the ruin. Even the mockingbird that had warbled for hours in the old mulberry-tree had sung himself asleep. That darkest hour before the day was mantling the earth. Ma'ame Pélagie hurried through the wet, clinging grass, beating aside the heavy moss that swept across her face, walking on toward the cabin—toward Pauline. Not once did she look back upon the ruin that brooded like a huge monster—a black spot in the darkness that enveloped it.

IV.

Little more than a year later the transformation which the old Valmêt place had undergone was the talk and wonder of Côte Joyeuse. One would have looked in vain for the ruin; it was no longer there; neither was the log cabin. But out in the open, where the sun shone upon it, and the breezes blew about it, was a shapely structure fashioned from woods that the forests of the State had furnished. It rested upon a solid foundation of brick.

Upon a corner of the pleasant gallery sat Léandre smoking his afternoon cigar, and chatting with neighbors who had called. This was to be his *pied à terre* now; the home where his sisters and his daughter dwelt. The laughter of young people was heard out under the trees, and within the house where La Petite was playing upon the piano. With the enthusiasm of a young artist she drew from the keys strains that seemed marvelously beautiful to Mam'selle Pauline, who stood enraptured near her. Mam'selle Pauline had been touched by the re-creation of Valmêt. Her cheek was as full and almost as flushed as La Petite's. The years were falling away from her.

Ma'ame Pélagie had been conversing with her brother and his friends. Then she turned and walked away; stopping to listen awhile to the music which La Petite was making. But it was only for a moment. She went on around the curve of the veranda, where she found herself alone. She stayed there, erect, holding to the banister rail and looking out calmly in the distance across the fields.

She was dressed in black, with the white kerchief she always wore folded across her bosom. Her thick, glossy hair rose like a silver diadem from her brow. In her deep, dark eyes smouldered the light of fires that would never flame. She had grown very old. Years instead of months seemed to have passed over her since the night she bade farewell to her visions.

Poor Ma'ame Pélagie! How could it be different! While the outward pressure of a young and joyous existence had forced her footsteps into the light, her soul had stayed in the shadow of the ruin.

1893

JOHN KENDRICK BANGS

(1862–1922)

Thurlow's Christmas Story

I

(Being the Statement of Henry Thurlow, Author,
to George Currier, Editor of the "Idler,"
a Weekly Journal of Human Interest.)

I HAVE always maintained, my dear Currier, that if a man wishes to be considered sane, and has any particular regard for his reputation as a truth-teller, he would better keep silent as to the singular experiences that enter into his life. I have had many such experiences myself; but I have rarely confided them in detail, or otherwise, to those about me, because I know that even the most trustful of my friends would regard them merely as the outcome of an imagination unrestrained by conscience, or of a gradually weakening mind subject to hallucinations. I know them to be true, but until Mr. Edison or some other modern wizard has invented a search-light strong enough to lay bare the secrets of the mind and conscience of man, I cannot prove to others that they are not pure fabrications, or at least the conjurings of a diseased fancy. For instance, no man would believe me if I were to state to him the plain and indisputable fact that one night last month, on my way up to bed shortly after midnight, having been neither smoking nor drinking, I saw confronting me upon the stairs, with the moonlight streaming through the windows back of me, lighting up its face, a figure in which I recognized my very self in every form and feature. I might describe the chill of terror that struck to the very marrow of my bones, and wellnigh forced me to stagger backward down the stairs, as I noticed in the face of this confronting figure every indication of all the bad qualities which I know myself to possess, of every evil instinct which by no easy effort I have repressed heretofore, and realized that that *thing* was, as far as I knew, entirely independent of my true self, in which I hope at least the moral has made an honest fight against the immoral always. I might describe this chill, I say, as vividly as I felt it at that moment, but it would be of no use to do so, because, however realistic it might prove as a bit of description, no man would believe that the incident really happened; and yet it did happen as truly as I write, and it has happened a dozen times since, and I am certain that it will happen many times again, though I would give all that I possess to be assured that never again should that disquieting creation of mind or matter, whichever it may be, cross my path. The experience has made me afraid almost to be alone, and I have found myself unconsciously and uneasily glancing at my face in mirrors, in the plate-glass of show-windows on the shopping streets of the city, fearful lest I should find some of those evil traits which I have struggled to keep under, and have kept under so far, cropping out there where all the world, all *my* world, can see and wonder at, having known me always as a man of right doing and right feeling. Many a time in the night the thought has come to me with prostrating force, what if that thing were to be seen and recognized by others, myself and yet not my whole self, my unworthy self unrestrained and yet recognizable as Henry Thurlow.

I have also kept silent as to that strange condition of affairs which has tortured me in my sleep for the past year and a half; no one but myself has until this writing known that for that period of time I have had a continuous, logical dream-life; a life so vivid and so dreadfully real to me that I have found myself at times wondering which of the two lives I was living and which I was dreaming; a life in which that other wicked self has dominated, and forced me to a career of shame and horror; a life which, being taken up every time I sleep where it ceased with the awakening from a previous sleep, has made me fear to close my eyes in forgetfulness when others are near at hand, lest, sleeping, I shall let fall some speech that, striking on their ears, shall lead them to believe that in secret there is some wicked mystery connected with my life. It would be of no use for me to tell these things. It would merely serve to make my family and my friends uneasy about me if they were told in their awful detail, and so I have kept silent about them. To you alone, and now for the first time, have I hinted as to the troubles which have oppressed me for many days, and to you they are confided only because of the demand you have made that I explain to you the extraordinary complication in which the Christmas story sent you last week has involved me. You know that I am a man of dignity; that I am not a school-boy and a lover of childish tricks; and knowing that, your friendship, at least, should have restrained your tongue and pen when, through the former, on Wednesday, you accused me of perpetrating a trifling, and to you excessively embarrassing, practical joke—a charge which, at the moment, I was too overcome to refute; and through the latter, on Thursday, you reiterated the accusation, coupled with a demand for an explanation of my conduct satisfactory to yourself, or my immediate resignation from the staff of the *Idler*. To explain is difficult, for I am certain that you will find the explanation too improbable for credence, but explain I must. The alternative, that of resigning from your staff, affects not only my own welfare, but that of my children, who must be provided for; and if my post with you is taken from me, then are all resources gone. I have not the courage to face dismissal, for I have not sufficient confidence in my powers to please elsewhere to make me easy in my mind, or, if I could please elsewhere, the certainty of finding the immediate employment of my talents which is necessary to me, in view of the at present overcrowded condition of the literary field.

To explain, then, my seeming jest at your expense, hopeless as it appears to be, is my task; and to do so as completely as I can, let me go back to the very beginning.

In August you informed me that you would expect me to provide, as I have heretofore been in the habit of doing, a story for the Christmas issue of the *Idler*; that a certain position in the make-up was reserved for me, and that you had already taken steps to advertise the fact that the story would appear. I undertook the commission, and upon seven different occasions set about putting the narrative into shape. I found great difficulty, however, in doing so. For some reason or other I could not concentrate my mind upon the work. No sooner would I start in on one story than a better one, in my estimation, would suggest itself to me; and all the labor expended on the story already begun would be cast aside, and the new story set in motion. Ideas were plenty enough, but to put them properly upon paper seemed beyond my powers. One story, however, I did finish; but after it had come back to me from my typewriter I read it, and was filled with consternation to discover that it was nothing more nor less than a mass of jumbled sentences, conveying no idea to the mind—a story which had seemed to me in the writing to be coherent had returned to me as a mere bit of incoherence—formless, without ideas—a bit of raving. It was then that I went to you and told you, as you remember, that I was worn out, and needed a month of absolute rest, which you granted. I left my work wholly, and went into the wilderness, where I could be entirely free from everything suggesting labor, and where no summons back to town could reach me. I fished and hunted. I slept; and although, as I have already said, in my sleep I found myself leading a life that was not only not to my taste, but horrible to me in many particulars, I was able at the end of my vacation to come back to town greatly refreshed, and, as far as my feelings went, ready to undertake any amount of work. For two or three days after my return I was busy with other things. On the fourth day after my arrival you came to me, and said that the story must be finished at the very latest by October 15th, and I assured you that you should have it by that time. That night I set about it. I mapped it out, incident by incident, and before starting up to bed had actually written some twelve or fifteen hundred words of the opening chapter—it was to be told in four chapters. When I had gone thus far I experienced a slight return of one of my nervous chills, and, on consulting my watch, discovered that it was after midnight, which was a sufficient explanation of my nervousness: I was merely tired. I arranged my manuscripts on my table so that I might easily take up the work the following morning. I locked up the windows and doors, turned out the lights, and proceeded up-stairs to my room.

It was then that I first came face to face with myself—that other self, in which I recognized, developed to the full, every bit of my capacity for an evil life.

Conceive of the situation if you can. Imagine the horror of it, and then ask yourself if it was likely that when next morning came I could by any possibility bring myself to my work-table in fit condition to prepare for you anything at all worthy of publication in the *Idler*. I tried. I implore you to believe that I did not hold lightly the responsibilities of the commission you had intrusted to my hands. You must know that if any of your writers has a full appreciation of the difficulties which are strewn along the path of an editor, I, who have myself had an editorial experience, have it, and so would not, in the nature of things, do anything to add to your troubles. You cannot but believe that I have made an honest effort to fulfil my promise to you. But it was useless, and for a week after that visitation was it useless for me to attempt the work. At the end of the week I felt better, and again I started in, and the story developed satisfactorily until—*it* came again. That figure which was my own figure, that face which was the evil counterpart of my own countenance, again rose up before me, and once more was I plunged into hopelessness.

Thus matters went on until the 14th day of October, when I received your peremptory message that the story must be forthcoming the following day. Needless to tell you that it was not forthcoming; but what I must tell you, since you do not know it, is that on the evening of the 15th day of October a strange thing happened to me, and in the narration of that incident, which I almost despair of your believing, lies my explanation of the discovery of October 16th, which has placed my position with you in peril.

At half-past seven o'clock on the evening of October 15th I was sitting in my library trying to write. I was alone. My wife and children had gone away on a visit to Massachusetts for a week. I had just finished my cigar, and had taken my pen in hand, when my front-door bell rang. Our maid, who is usually prompt in answering summonses of this nature, apparently did not hear the bell, for she did not respond to its clanging. Again the bell rang, and still did it remain unanswered, until finally, at the third ringing, I went to the door myself. On opening it I saw standing before me a man of, I should say, fifty odd years of age, tall, slender, pale-faced, and clad in sombre black. He was entirely unknown to me. I had never seen him before, but he had about him such an air of pleasantness and wholesomeness that I instinctively felt glad to see him, without knowing why or whence he had come.

"Does Mr. Thurlow live here?" he asked.

You must excuse me for going into what may seem to you to

be petty details, but by a perfectly circumstantial account of all that happened that evening alone can I hope to give a semblance of truth to my story, and that it must be truthful I realize as painfully as you do.

"I am Mr. Thurlow," I replied.

"Henry Thurlow, the author?" he said, with a surprised look upon his face.

"Yes," said I; and then, impelled by the strange appearance of surprise on the man's countenance, I added, "don't I look like an author?"

He laughed, and candidly admitted that I was not the kind of looking man he had expected to find from reading my books, and then he entered the house in response to my invitation that he do so. I ushered him into my library, and, after asking him to be seated, inquired as to his business with me.

His answer was gratifying at least. He replied that he had been a reader of my writings for a number of years, and that for some time past he had had a great desire, not to say curiosity, to meet me and tell me how much he had enjoyed certain of my stories.

"I'm a great devourer of books, Mr. Thurlow," he said, "and I have taken the keenest delight in reading your verses and humorous sketches. I may go further, and say to you that you have helped me over many a hard place in my life by your work. At times when I have felt myself worn out with my business, or face to face with some knotty problem in my career, I have found much relief in picking up and reading your books at random. They have helped me to forget my weariness or my knotty problems for the time being; and to-day, finding myself in this town, I resolved to call upon you this evening and thank you for all that you have done for me."

Thereupon we became involved in a general discussion of literary men and their works, and I found that my visitor certainly did have a pretty thorough knowledge of what has been produced by the writers of to-day. I was quite won over to him by his simplicity, as well as attracted to him by his kindly opinion of my own efforts, and I did my best to entertain him, showing him a few of my little literary treasures in the way of autograph letters, photographs, and presentation copies of well-known books from the authors themselves. From this we drifted naturally and easily into a talk on the methods of work adopted by literary men. He asked me many questions as to my own methods; and when I had in a measure outlined to him the manner of life which I had adopted, telling him of my days at home, how little detail office-work I had, he seemed much interested with the picture—indeed, I painted the picture of my daily routine in almost too perfect colors, for, when I had finished, he observed quietly that I appeared to him to lead the ideal life, and added that he supposed I knew very little unhappiness.

The remark recalled to me the dreadful reality, that through some perversity of fate I was doomed to visitations of an uncanny order which were practically destroying my usefulness in my profession and my sole financial resource.

"Well," I replied, as my mind reverted to the unpleasant predicament in which I found myself, "I can't say that I know little unhappiness. As a matter of fact, I know a great deal of that undesirable thing. At the present moment I am very much embarrassed through my absolute inability to fulfil a contract into which I have entered, and which should have been filled this morning. I was due to-day with a Christmas story. The presses are waiting for it, and I am utterly unable to write it."

He appeared deeply concerned at the confession. I had hoped, indeed, that he might be sufficiently concerned to take his departure, that I might make one more effort to write the promised story. His solicitude, however, showed itself in another way. Instead of leaving me, he ventured the hope that he might aid me.

"What kind of a story is it to be?" he asked.

"Oh, the usual ghostly tale," I said, "with a dash of the Christmas flavor thrown in here and there to make it suitable to the season."

"Ah," he observed. "And you find your vein worked out?"

It was a direct and perhaps an impertinent question; but I thought it best to answer it, and to answer it as well without giving him any clew as to the real facts. I could not very well take an entire stranger into my confidence, and describe to him the extraordinary encounters I was having with an uncanny other self. He would not have believed the truth, hence I told him an untruth, and assented to his proposition.

"Yes," I replied, "the vein is worked out. I have written ghost stories for years now, serious and comic, and I am to-day at the end of my tether—compelled to move forward and yet held back."

"That accounts for it," he said, simply. "When I first saw you to-night at the door I could not believe that the author who had provided me with so much merriment could be so pale and worn and seemingly mirthless. Pardon me, Mr. Thurlow, for my lack of consideration when I told you that you did not appear as I had expected to find you."

I smiled my forgiveness, and he continued:

"It may be," he said, with a show of hesitation—"it may be that I have come not altogether inopportunely. Perhaps I can help you."

I smiled again. "I should be most grateful if you could," I said.

"But you doubt my ability to do so?" he put in. "Oh—well —yes—of course you do; and why shouldn't you? Nevertheless, I have noticed this: At times when I have been baffled in my work a mere hint from another, from one who knew nothing of my work, has carried me on to a solution of my problem. I have read most of your writings, and I have thought over some of them many a time, and I have even had ideas for stories, which, in my own conceit, I have imagined were good enough for you, and I have wished that I possessed your facility with the pen that I might make of them myself what I thought you would make of them had they been ideas of your own."

The old gentleman's pallid face reddened as he said this, and while I was hopeless as to anything of value resulting from his ideas, I could not resist the temptation to hear what he had to say further, his manner was so deliciously simple, and his desire to aid me so manifest. He rattled on with suggestions for a half-hour. Some of them were good, but none were new. Some were irresistibly funny, and did me good because they made me laugh, and I hadn't laughed naturally for a period so long that it made me shudder to think of it, fearing lest I should forget how to be mirthful. Finally I grew tired of his persistence, and, with a very ill-concealed impatience, told him plainly that I could do nothing with his suggestions, thanking him, however, for the spirit of kindliness which had prompted him to offer them. He appeared somewhat hurt, but immediately desisted, and when nine o'clock came he rose up to go. As he walked to the door he seemed to be undergoing some mental struggle, to which, with a sudden resolve, he finally succumbed, for, after having picked up his hat and stick and donned his overcoat, he turned to me and said:

"Mr. Thurlow, I don't want to offend you. On the contrary, it is my dearest wish to assist you. You have helped me, as I have told you. Why may I not help you?"

"I assure you, sir—" I began, when he interrupted me.

"One moment, please," he said, putting his hand into the inside pocket of his black coat and extracting from it an envelope addressed to me. "Let me finish: it is the whim of one who has an affection for you. For ten years I have secretly been at work myself on a story. It is a short one, but it has seemed good to me. I had a double object in seeking you out to-night. I wanted not only to see you, but to read my story to you. No one knows that I have written it; I had intended it as a surprise to my—to my friends. I had hoped to have it published somewhere, and I had come here to seek your advice in the matter. It is a story which I have written and rewritten and rewritten time and time again in my leisure moments during the ten years past, as I have told you. It is not likely that I shall ever write another. I am proud of having done it, but I should be prouder yet if it—if it could in some way help you. I leave it with you, sir, to print or to destroy; and if you print it, to see it in type will be enough for me; to see your name signed to it will be a matter of pride to me. No one will ever be the wiser, for, as I say, no one knows I have written it, and I promise you that no one shall know of it if you decide to do as I not only suggest but ask you to do. No one would believe me after it has appeared as *yours*, even if I should forget my promise and claim it as my own. Take it. It is yours. You are entitled to it as a slight measure of repayment for the debt of gratitude I owe you."

He pressed the manuscript into my hands, and before I could reply had opened the door and disappeared into the darkness of the street. I rushed to the sidewalk and shouted out to him to return, but I might as well have saved my breath and spared the neighborhood, for there was no answer. Holding his story in my hand, I re-entered the house and walked back into my library, where, sitting and reflecting upon the curious interview, I realized for the first time that I was in entire ignorance as to my visitor's name and address.

I opened the envelope hoping to find them, but they were not there. The envelope contained merely a finely written manuscript of thirty odd pages, unsigned.

And then I read the story. When I began it was with a half-smile upon my lips, and with a feeling that I was wasting my time. The smile soon faded, however; after reading the first paragraph there was no question of wasted time. The story was a masterpiece. It is needless to say to you that I am not a man of enthusiasms. It is difficult to arouse that emotion in my breast, but upon this occasion I yielded to a force too great for me to resist. I have read the tales of Hoffmann and of Poe, the wondrous romances of De La Motte Fouque, the unfortunately little-known tales of the lamented Fitz-James O'Brien, the weird tales of writers of all tongues have been thoroughly sifted by me in the course of my reading, and I say to you now that in the whole of my life I never read one story, one paragraph, one line, that could approach in vivid delineation, in weirdness of conception, in anything, in any quality which goes to make up the truly great story, that story which came into my hands as I have told you. I read it once and was amazed. I read it a second time and was—tempted. It was mine. The writer himself had authorized me to treat it as if it were my own; had voluntarily sacrificed his own claim to its authorship that he might relieve me of my very pressing embarrassment. Not only this; he had almost intimated that in putting my name to his work I should be doing him a favor. Why not do so, then, I asked myself; and immediately my better self rejected the idea as impossible. How could I put out as my own another man's work and retain my self-respect? I resolved on another and better course—to send you the story in lieu of my own with a full statement of the circumstances under which it had come into my possession, when that demon rose up out of the floor at my side, this time more evil of aspect than before, more commanding in its manner. With a groan I shrank back into the cushions of my chair, and by passing my hands over my eyes tried to obliterate forever the offending sight; but it was useless. The uncanny thing approached me, and as truly as I write sat upon the edge of my couch, where for the first time it addressed me.

"Fool!" it said, "how can you hesitate? Here is your position: you have made a contract which must be filled; you are already behind, and in a hopeless mental state. Even granting that between this and to-morrow morning you could put together the necessary number of words to fill the space allotted to you, what kind of a thing do you think that story would make? It would be a mere raving like that other precious effort of August. The public, if by some odd chance it ever reached them, would think your mind was utterly gone; your reputation would go with that verdict. On the other hand, if you do not have the story ready by to-morrow, your hold on the *Idler* will be destroyed. They have their announcements printed, and your name and portrait appear among those of the prominent contributors. Do you suppose the editor and publisher will look leniently upon your failure?"

"Considering my past record, yes," I replied. "I have never yet broken a promise to them."

"Which is precisely the reason why they will be severe with you. You, who have been regarded as one of the few men who can do almost any kind of literary work at will—you, of whom it is said that your 'brains are on tap'—will they be lenient with *you*? Bah! Can't you see that the very fact of your invariable readiness heretofore is going to make your present unreadiness a thing incomprehensible?"

"Then what shall I do?" I asked. "If I can't, I can't, that is all."

"You can. There is the story in your hands. Think what it will do for you. It is one of the immortal stories—"

"You have read it, then?" I asked.

"Haven't you?"

"Yes—but—"

"It is the same," it said, with a leer and a contemptuous shrug. "You and I are inseparable. Aren't you glad?" it added, with a laugh that grated on every fibre of my being. I was too overwhelmed to reply, and it resumed: "It is one of the immortal stories. We agree to that. Published over your name, your name will live. The stuff you write yourself will give you present glory; but when you have been dead ten years people won't remember your name even—unless I get control of you, and in that case there is a very pretty though hardly a literary record in store for you."

Again it laughed harshly, and I buried my face in the pillows of my couch, hoping to find relief there from this dreadful vision.

"Curious," it said. "What you call your decent self doesn't dare look me in the eye! What a mistake people make who say that the man who won't look you in the eye is not to be trusted! As if mere brazenness were a sign of honesty; really, the theory of decency is the most amusing thing in the world. But come, time is growing short. Take that story. The writer gave it to you. Begged you to use it as your own. It is yours. It will make your reputation, and save you with your publishers. How can you hesitate?"

"I shall not use it!" I cried, desperately.

"You must—consider your children. Suppose you lose your connection with these publishers of yours?"

"But it would be a crime."

"Not a bit of it. Whom do you rob? A man who voluntarily came to you, and gave you that of which you rob him. Think of it as it is—and act, only act quickly. It is now midnight."

The tempter rose up and walked to the other end of the room, whence, while he pretended to be looking over a few of my books and pictures, I was aware he was eying me closely, and gradually compelling me by sheer force of will to do a thing which I abhorred. And I—I struggled weakly against the temptation, but gradually, little by little, I yielded, and finally succumbed altogether. Springing to my feet, I rushed to the table, seized my pen, and signed my name to the story.

"There!" I said. "It is done. I have saved my position and made my reputation, and am now a thief!"

"As well as a fool," said the other, calmly. "You don't mean to say you are going to send that manuscript in as it is?"

"Good Lord!" I cried. "What under heaven have you been trying to make me do for the last half hour?"

"Act like a sane being," said the demon. "If you send that

manuscript to Currier he'll know in a minute it isn't yours. He knows you haven't an amanuensis, and that handwriting isn't yours. Copy it."

"True!" I answered. "I haven't much of a mind for details to-night. I will do as you say."

I did so. I got out my pad and pen and ink, and for three hours diligently applied myself to the task of copying the story. When it was finished I went over it carefully, made a few minor corrections, signed it, put it in an envelope, addressed it to you, stamped it, and went out to the mail-box on the corner, where I dropped it into the slot, and returned home. When I had returned to my library my visitor was still there.

"Well," it said, "I wish you'd hurry and complete this affair. I am tired, and wish to go."

"You can't go too soon to please me," said I, gathering up the original manuscripts of the story and preparing to put them away in my desk.

"Probably not," it sneered. "I'll be glad to go too, but I can't go until that manuscript is destroyed. As long as it exists there is evidence of your having appropriated the work of an-other. Why, can't you see that? Burn it!"

"I can't see my way clear in crime!" I retorted. "It is not in my line."

Nevertheless, realizing the value of his advice, I thrust the pages one by one into the blazing log fire, and watched them as they flared and flamed and grew to ashes. As the last page disappeared in the embers the demon vanished. I was alone, and throwing myself down for a moment's reflection upon my couch, was soon lost in sleep.

It was noon when I again opened my eyes, and, ten minutes after I awakened, your telegraphic summons reached me.

"Come down at once," was what you said, and I went; and then came the terrible *dénouement*, and yet a *dénouement* which was pleasing to me since it relieved my conscience. You handed me the envelope containing the story.

"Did you send that?" was your question.

"I did—last night, or rather early this morning. I mailed it about three o'clock," I replied.

"I demand an explanation of your conduct," said you.

"Of what?" I asked.

"Look at your so-called story and see. If this is a practical joke, Thurlow, it's a damned poor one."

I opened the envelope and took from it the sheets I had sent you—twenty-four of them.

They were every one of them as blank as when they left the paper-mill!

You know the rest. You know that I tried to speak; that my utterance failed me; and that, finding myself unable at the time to control my emotions, I turned and rushed madly from the office, leaving the mystery unexplained. You know that you wrote demanding a satisfactory explanation of the situation or my resignation from your staff.

This, Currier, is my explanation. It is all I have. It is absolute truth. I beg you to believe it, for if you do not, then is my condition a hopeless one. You will ask me perhaps for a *résumé* of the story which I thought I had sent you.

It is my crowning misfortune that upon that point my mind is an absolute blank. I cannot remember it in form or in substance. I have racked my brains for some recollection of some small portion of it to help to make my explanation more credible, but, alas! it will not come back to me. If I were dishonest I might fake up a story to suit the purpose, but I am not dishonest. I came near to doing an unworthy act; I did do an unworthy thing, but by some mysterious provision of fate my conscience is cleared of that.

Be sympathetic, Currier, or, if you cannot, be lenient with me this time. *Believe, believe, believe*, I implore you. Pray let me hear from you at once.

(Signed)   HENRY THURLOW.

II

*(Being a Note from George Currier,
Editor of the "Idler," to Henry Thurlow, Author.)*

Your explanation has come to hand. As an explanation it isn't worth the paper it is written on, but we are all agreed here that it is probably the best bit of fiction you ever wrote. It is accepted for the Christmas issue. Enclosed please find check for one hundred dollars.

Dawson suggests that you take another month up in the Adirondacks. You might put in your time writing up some account of that dream-life you are leading while you are there. It seems to me there are possibilities in the idea. The concern will pay all expenses. What do you say?

(Signed)   Yours ever,   G. C.

1894

ROBERT W. CHAMBERS

(1865–1933)

> *"Along the shore the cloud waves break,*
> *The twin suns sink behind the lake,*
> *The shadows lengthen*
>> *In Carcosa.*
>
> *"Strange is the night where black stars rise*
> *And strange moons circle through the skies,*
> *But stranger still is*
>> *Lost Carcosa.*
>
> *"Songs that the Hyades shall sing.*
> *Where flap the tatters of the King,*
> *Must die unheard in*
>> *Dim Carcosa.*
>
> *"Song of my soul, my voice is dead,*
> *Die thou, unsung, as tears unshed*
> *Shall dry and die in*
>> *Lost Carcosa."*

—Cassilda's song in "The King in Yellow,"
act i., scene 2.

The Repairer of Reputations

I

"Ne raillons pas les fous; leur folie dure plus longtemps que la nôtre. . . .
Voilà toute la différence."

TOWARDS the end of the year 1920 the government of the
United States had practically completed the programme
adopted during the last months of President Winthrop's
administration. The country was apparently tranquil. Everybody knows how the Tariff and Labor questions were settled.
The war with Germany, incident on that country's seizure of
the Samoan Islands, had left no visible scars upon the republic,
and the temporary occupation of Norfolk by the invading army

177

had been forgotten in the joy over repeated naval victories and the subsequent ridiculous plight of General Von Gartenlaube's forces in the State of New Jersey. The Cuban and Hawaiian investments had paid one hundred per cent., and the territory of Samoa was well worth its cost as a coaling station. The country was in a superb state of defence. Every coast city had been well supplied with land fortifications; the army, under the parental eye of the general staff, organized according to the Prussian system, had been increased to three hundred thousand men, with a territorial reserve of a million; and six magnificent squadrons of cruisers and battle-ships patrolled the six stations of the navigable seas, leaving a steam reserve amply fitted to control home waters. The gentlemen from the West had at last been constrained to acknowledge that a college for the training of diplomats was as necessary as law schools are for the training of barristers; consequently we were no longer represented abroad by incompetent patriots. The nation was prosperous. Chicago, for a moment paralyzed after a second great fire, had risen from its ruins, white and imperial, and more beautiful than the white city which had been built for its plaything in 1893. Everywhere good architecture was replacing bad, and even in New York a sudden craving for decency had swept away a great portion of the existing horrors. Streets had been widened, properly paved, and lighted, trees had been planted, squares laid out, elevated structures demolished, and underground roads built to replace them. The new government buildings and barracks were fine bits of architecture, and the long system of stone quays which completely surrounded the island had been turned into parks, which proved a godsend to the population. The subsidizing of the state theatre and state opera brought its own reward. The United States National Academy of Design was much like European institutions of the same kind. Nobody envied the Secretary of Fine Arts either his cabinet position or his portfolio. The Secretary of Forestry and Game Preservation had a much easier time, thanks to the new system of National Mounted Police. We had profited well by the latest treaties with France and England; the exclusion of foreign-born Jews as a measure of national self-preservation, the settlement of the new independent negro state of Suanee, the checking of immigration, the new laws concerning natural-

ization, and the gradual centralization of power in the executive all contributed to national calm and prosperity. When the
government solved the Indian problem and squadrons of Indian cavalry scouts in native costume were substituted for the
pitiable organizations tacked on to the tail of skeletonized reg-
iments by a former Secretary of War, the nation drew a long
sigh of relief. When, after the colossal Congress of Religions,
bigotry and intolerance were laid in their graves, and kindness
and charity began to draw warring sects together, many
thought the millennium had arrived, at least in the new world,
which, after all, is a world by itself.

But self-preservation is the first law, and the United States had
to look on in helpless sorrow as Germany, Italy, Spain, and Belgium writhed in the throes of anarchy, while Russia, watching
from the Caucasus, stooped and bound them one by one.

In the city of New York the summer of 1910 was signalized
by the dismantling of the Elevated Railroads. The summer of 1911
will live in the memories of New York people for many a cycle;
the Dodge statue was removed in that year. In the following
winter began that agitation for the repeal of the laws prohibiting
suicide, which bore its final fruit in the month of April, 1920,
when the first Government Lethal Chamber was opened on
Washington Square.

I had walked down that day from Dr. Archer's house on
Madison Avenue, where I had been as a mere formality. Ever
since that fall from my horse, four years before, I had been
troubled at times with pains in the back of my head and neck,
but now for months they had been absent, and the doctor sent
me away that day saying there was nothing more to be cured
in me. It was hardly worth his fee to be told that; I knew it myself. Still I did not grudge him the money. What I minded was
the mistake which he made at first. When they picked me up
from the pavement where I lay unconscious, and somebody had
mercifully sent a bullet through my horse's head, I was carried
to Dr. Archer, and he, pronouncing my brain affected, placed
me in his private asylum, where I was obliged to endure treatment for insanity. At last he decided that I was well, and I,
knowing that my mind had always been as sound as his, if not
sounder, "paid my tuition," as he jokingly called it, and left. I
told him, smiling, that I would get even with him for his mistake,

and he laughed heartily, and asked me to call once in a while. I did so, hoping for a chance to even up accounts, but he gave me none, and I told him I would wait.

The fall from my horse had fortunately left no evil results; on the contrary, it had changed my whole character for the better. From a lazy young man about town, I had become active, energetic, temperate, and, above all—oh, above all else— ambitious. There was only one thing which troubled me: I laughed at my own uneasiness, and yet it troubled me.

During my convalescence I had bought and read for the first time "The King in Yellow." I remember after finishing the first act that it occurred to me that I had better stop. I started up and flung the book into the fireplace; the volume struck the barred grate and fell open on the hearth in the fire-light. If I had not caught a glimpse of the opening words in the second act I should never have finished it, but as I stooped to pick it up my eyes became riveted to the open page, and with a cry of terror, or perhaps it was of joy so poignant that I suffered in every nerve, I snatched the thing from the hearth and crept shaking to my bedroom, where I read it and reread it, and wept and laughed and trembled with a horror which at times assails me yet. This is the thing that troubles me, for I cannot forget Carcosa, where black stars hang in the heavens, where the shadows of men's thoughts lengthen in the afternoon, when the twin suns sink into the Lake of Hali, and my mind will bear forever the memory of the Pallid Mask. I pray God will curse the writer, as the writer has cursed the world with this beautiful, stupendous creation, terrible in its simplicity, irresistible in its truth—a world which now trembles before the King in Yellow. When the French government seized the translated copies which had just arrived in Paris, London, of course, became eager to read it. It is well known how the book spread like an infectious disease, from city to city, from continent to continent, barred out here, confiscated there, denounced by press and pulpit, censured even by the most advanced of literary anarchists. No definite principles had been violated in those wicked pages, no doctrine promulgated, no convictions outraged. It could not be judged by any known standard, yet, although it was acknowledged that the supreme note of art had been struck in "The King in Yellow," all felt that human nature could not bear the strain nor thrive on words in which the essence of purest poison lurked. The very banality and innocence of the first act only allowed the blow to fall afterwards with more awful effect.

It was, I remember, the 13th day of April, 1920, that the first Government Lethal Chamber was established on the south side of Washington Square, between Wooster Street and South Fifth Avenue. The block, which had formerly consisted of a lot of shabby old buildings, used as cafés and restaurants for foreigners, had been acquired by the government in the winter of 1913. The French and Italian cafés and restaurants were torn down; the whole block was enclosed by a gilded iron railing, and converted into a lovely garden, with lawns, flowers, and fountains. In the centre of the garden stood a small, white building, severely classical in architecture, and surrounded by thickets of flowers. Six Ionic columns supported the roof, and the single door was of bronze. A splendid marble group of "The Fates" stood before the door, the work of a young American sculptor, Boris Yvain, who had died in Paris when only twenty-three years old.

The inauguration ceremonies were in progress as I crossed University Place and entered the square. I threaded my way through the silent throng of spectators, but was stopped at Fourth Street by a cordon of police. A regiment of United States Lancers were drawn up in a hollow square around the Lethal Chamber. On a raised tribune facing Washington Park stood the Governor of New York, and behind him were grouped the Mayor of Greater New York, the Inspector-General of Police, the commandant of the State troops, Colonel Livingston (military aid to the President of the United States), General Blount (commanding at Governor's Island), Major-General Hamilton (commanding the garrison of Greater New York), Admiral Buffby (of the fleet in the North River), Surgeon-General Lanceford, the staff of the National Free Hospital, Senators Wyse and Franklin, of New York, and the Commissioner of Public Works. The tribune was surrounded by a squadron of hussars of the National Guard.

The Governor was finishing his reply to the short speech of the Surgeon-General. I heard him say: "The laws prohibiting suicide and providing punishment for any attempt at self-destruction have been repealed. The government has seen fit to acknowledge the right of man to end an existence which may have become intolerable to him, through physical suffering or mental despair. It is believed that the community will be benefited by the removal of such people from their midst. Since the passage of this law, the number of suicides in the United States has not increased. Now that the government has determined to establish a Lethal Chamber in every city, town, and village in the country, it remains to be seen whether or not that class of human creatures from whose desponding ranks new victims of self-destruction fall daily will accept the relief thus provided." He paused, and turned to the white Lethal Chamber. The silence in the street was absolute. "There a painless death awaits him who can no longer bear the sorrows of this life. If death is welcome, let him seek it there." Then, quickly turning to the military aid of the President's household, he said, "I declare the Lethal Chamber open"; and again facing the vast crowd, he cried, in a clear voice: "Citizens of New York and of the United States of America, through me the government declares the Lethal Chamber to be open."

The solemn hush was broken by a sharp cry of command, the squadron of hussars filed after the Governor's carriage, the lancers wheeled and formed along Fifth Avenue to wait for the commandant of the garrison, and the mounted police followed them. I left the crowd to gape and stare at the white marble death-chamber, and, crossing South Fifth Avenue, walked along the western side of that thoroughfare to Bleecker Street. Then I turned to the right and stopped before a dingy shop which bore the sign,

HAWBERK, ARMORER.

I glanced in at the door-way and saw Hawberk busy in his little shop at the end of the hall. He looked up, and, catching sight of me, cried, in his deep, hearty voice, "Come in, Mr. Castaigne!" Constance, his daughter, rose to meet me as I crossed the threshold, and held out her pretty hand, but I saw the blush of disappointment on her cheeks, and knew that it was another Castaigne she had expected, my cousin Louis. I smiled at her confusion and complimented her on the banner which she was embroidering from a colored plate. Old Hawberk sat riveting the worn greaves of some ancient suit of armor, and the ting! ting! ting! of his little hammer sounded pleasantly in the quaint shop. Presently he dropped his hammer and fussed about for a moment with a tiny wrench. The soft clash of the mail sent a thrill of pleasure through me. I loved to hear the music of steel brushing against steel, the mellow shock of the mallet on thigh-pieces, and the jingle of chain armor. That was the only reason I went to see Hawberk. He had never interested me personally, nor did Constance, except for the fact of her being in love with Louis. This did occupy my attention, and sometimes even kept me awake at night. But I knew in my heart that all would come right, and that I should arrange their future as I expected to arrange that of my kind doctor, John Archer. However, I should never have troubled myself about visiting them just then had it not been, as I say, that the music of the tinkling hammer had for me this strong fascination. I would sit for hours, listening and listening, and when a stray sunbeam struck the inlaid steel, the sensation it gave me was almost too keen to endure. My eyes would become fixed, dilating with a pleasure that stretched every nerve almost to breaking, until some movement of the old armorer cut off the ray of sunlight, then, still thrilling secretly, I leaned back and listened again to the sound of the polishing rag—swish! swish! —rubbing rust from the rivets.

Constance worked with the embroidery over her knees, now and then pausing to examine more closely the pattern in the colored plate from the Metropolitan Museum.

"Who is this for?" I asked.

Hawberk explained that in addition to the treasures of armor in the Metropolitan Museum, of which he had been appointed armorer, he also had charge of several collections belonging to rich amateurs. This was the missing greave of a famous suit which a client of his had traced to a little shop in Paris on the Quai d'Orsay. He, Hawberk, had negotiated for and secured the greave, and now the suit was complete. He laid down his hammer and read me the history of the suit, traced since 1450 from owner to owner until it was acquired by Thomas Stainbridge. When his superb collection was sold, this client of Hawberk's bought the suit, and since then the search for the missing greave had been pushed until it was, almost by accident, located in Paris.

"Did you continue the search so persistently without any certainty of the greave being still in existence?" I demanded.

"Of course," he replied, coolly.

Then for the first time I took a personal interest in Hawberk.

"It was worth something to you," I ventured.

"No," he replied, laughing, "my pleasure in finding it was my reward."

"Have you no ambition to be rich?" I asked, smiling.

"My one ambition is to be the best armorer in the world," he answered, gravely.

Constance asked me if I had seen the ceremonies at the Lethal Chamber. She herself had noticed cavalry passing up Broadway that morning, and had wished to see the inauguration, but her father wanted the banner finished, and she had stayed at his request.

"Did you see your cousin, Mr. Castaigne, there?" she asked, with the slightest tremor of her soft eyelashes.

"No," I replied, carelessly. "Louis' regiment is manœuvring out in Westchester County." I rose and picked up my hat and cane.

"Are you going up-stairs to see the lunatic again?" laughed old Hawberk. If Hawberk knew how I loathe that word "lunatic," he would never use it in my presence. It rouses certain feelings within me which I do not care to explain. However, I answered him quietly:

"I think I shall drop in and see Mr. Wilde for a moment or two."

"Poor fellow," said Constance, with a shake of her head, "it must be hard to live alone year after year, poor, crippled, and almost demented. It is very good of you, Mr. Castaigne, to visit him as often as you do."

"I think he is vicious," observed Hawberk, beginning again with his hammer. I listened to the golden tinkle on the greave-plates; when he had finished I replied:

"No, he is not vicious, nor is he in the least demented. His mind is a wonder chamber, from which he can extract treasures that you and I would give years of our lives to acquire."

Hawberk laughed.

I continued, a little impatiently: "He knows history as no one else could know it. Nothing, however trivial, escapes his search, and his memory is so absolute, so precise in details, that were it known in New York that such a man existed the people could not honor him enough."

"Nonsense!" muttered Hawberk, searching on the floor for a fallen rivet.

"Is it nonsense," I asked, managing to suppress what I felt— "is it nonsense when he says that the tassets and cuissards of the enamelled suit of armor commonly known as the 'Prince's Emblazoned' can be found among a mass of rusty theatrical properties, broken stoves, and rag-picker's refuse in a garret in Pell Street?"

Hawberk's hammer fell to the ground, but he picked it up and asked, with a great deal of calm, how I knew that the tassets and left cuissard were missing from the "Prince's Emblazoned."

"I did not know until Mr. Wilde mentioned it to me the other day. He said they were in the garret of 998 Pell Street."

"Nonsense!" he cried; but I noticed his hand trembling under his leathern apron.

"Is this nonsense, too?" I asked, pleasantly. "Is it nonsense when Mr. Wilde continually speaks of you as the Marquis of Avonshire, and of Miss Constance—"

I did not finish, for Constance had started to her feet with terror written on every feature. Hawberk looked at me and slowly smoothed his leathern apron. "That is impossible," he observed. "Mr. Wilde may know a great many things—"

"About armor, for instance, and the 'Prince's Emblazoned,'" I interposed, smiling.

"Yes," he continued, slowly, "about armor also—maybe— but he is wrong in regard to the Marquis of Avonshire, who, as you know, killed his wife's traducer years ago, and went to Australia, where he did not long survive his wife."

"Mr. Wilde is wrong," murmured Constance. Her lips were blanched, but her voice was sweet and calm.

"Let us agree, if you please, that in this one circumstance Mr. Wilde is wrong," I said.

II

I climbed the three dilapidated flights of stairs which I had so often climbed before, and knocked at a small door at the end of the corridor. Mr. Wilde opened the door and I walked in.

When he had double-locked the door and pushed a heavy chest against it, he came and sat down beside me, peering up into my face with his little, light-colored eyes. Half a dozen new scratches covered his nose and cheeks, and the silver wires which supported his artificial ears had become displaced. I thought I had never seen him so hideously fascinating. He had no ears. The artificial ones, which now stood out at an angle from the fine wire, were his one weakness. They were made of wax and painted a shell pink; but the rest of his face was yellow. He might better have revelled in the luxury of some artificial fingers for his left hand, which was absolutely fingerless, but it seemed to cause him no inconvenience, and he was satisfied with his wax ears. He was very small, scarcely higher than a child of ten, but his arms were magnificently developed, and his thighs as thick as any athlete's. Still, the most remarkable thing about Mr. Wilde was that a man of his marvellous intelligence and knowledge should have such a head. It was flat and pointed, like the heads of many of those unfortunates whom people imprison in asylums for the weak-minded. Many called him insane, but I knew him to be as sane as I was.

I do not deny that he was eccentric; the mania he had for keeping that cat and teasing her until she flew at his face like a demon was certainly eccentric. I never could understand why he kept the creature, nor what pleasure he found in shutting himself up in his room with the surly, vicious beast. I remember once glancing up from the manuscript I was studying by the light of some tallow dips and seeing Mr. Wilde squatting motionless on his high chair, his eyes fairly blazing with excitement, while the cat, which had risen from her place before the stove, came creeping across the floor right at him. Before I could move she flattened her belly to the ground, crouched, trembled, and sprang into his face. Howling and foaming, they rolled over and over on the floor, scratching and clawing, until the cat screamed and fled under the cabinet, and Mr. Wilde turned over on his back, his limbs contracting and curling up like the legs of a dying spider. He *was* eccentric.

Mr. Wilde had climbed into his high chair, and, after studying my face, picked up a dog's-eared ledger and opened it.

"Henry B. Matthews," he read, "book-keeper with Whysot Whysot & Company, dealers in church ornaments. Called April 3d. Reputation damaged on the race-track. Known as a welcher. Reputation to be repaired by August 1st. Retainer, Five Dollars." He turned the page and ran his fingerless knuckles down the closely written columns.

"P. Greene Dusenberry, Minister of the Gospel, Fairbeach, New Jersey. Reputation damaged in the Bowery. To be repaired as soon as possible. Retainer, $100."

He coughed and added, "Called, April 6th."

"Then you are not in need of money, Mr. Wilde," I inquired.

"Listen"—he coughed again.

"Mrs. C. Hamilton Chester, of Chester Park, New York City, called April 7th. Reputation damaged at Dieppe, France. To be repaired by October 1st. Retainer, $500.

"Note.—C. Hamilton Chester, Captain U.S.S. *Avalanche*, ordered home from South Sea Squadron October 1st."

"Well," I said, "the profession of a Repairer of Reputations is lucrative."

His colorless eyes sought mine. "I only wanted to demonstrate that I was correct. You said it was impossible to succeed as a Repairer of Reputations; that even if I did succeed in certain cases, it would cost me more than I would gain by it. Today I have five hundred men in my employ, who are poorly paid, but who pursue the work with an enthusiasm which possibly may be born of fear. These men enter every shade and grade of society; some even are pillars of the most exclusive social temples; others are the prop and pride of the financial world; still others hold undisputed sway among the 'Fancy and the Talent.' I choose them at my leisure from those who reply to my advertisements. It is easy enough—they are all cowards. I could treble the number in twenty days if I wished. So, you see, those who have in their keeping the reputations of their fellow-citizens, *I* have in my pay."

"They may turn on you," I suggested.

He rubbed his thumb over his cropped ears and adjusted the wax substitutes. "I think not," he murmured, thoughtfully, "I seldom have to apply the whip, and then only once. Besides, they like their wages."

"How do you apply the whip?" I demanded.

His face for a moment was awful to look upon. His eyes dwindled to a pair of green sparks.

"I invite them to come and have a little chat with me," he said, in a soft voice.

A knock at the door interrupted him, and his face resumed its amiable expression.

"Who is it?" he inquired.

"Mr. Steylette," was the answer.

"Come to-morrow," replied Mr. Wilde.

"Impossible," began the other; but was silenced by a sort of bark from Mr. Wilde.

"Come to-morrow," he repeated.

We heard somebody move away from the door and turn the corner by the stair-way.

"Who is that?" I asked.

"Arnold Steylette, owner and editor-in-chief of the great New York daily."

He drummed on the ledger with his fingerless hand, adding, "I pay him very badly, but he thinks it a good bargain."

"Arnold Steylette!" I repeated, amazed.

"Yes," said Mr. Wilde, with a self-satisfied cough.

The cat, which had entered the room as he spoke, hesitated, looked up at him, and snarled. He climbed down from the chair, and, squatting on the floor, took the creature into his arms and caressed her. The cat ceased snarling and presently began a loud purring, which seemed to increase in timbre as he stroked her.

"Where are the notes?" I asked. He pointed to the table, and for the hundredth time I picked up the bundle of manuscript entitled

"THE IMPERIAL DYNASTY OF AMERICA."

One by one I studied the well-worn pages, worn only by my own handling, and, although I knew all by heart, from the beginning, "When from Carcosa, the Hyades, Hastur, and Aldebaran," to "Castaigne, Louis de Calvados, born December 19, 1887," I read it with an eager, rapt attention, pausing to repeat parts of it aloud, and dwelling especially on "Hildred de Calvados, only son of Hildred Castaigne and Edythe Landes Castaigne, first in succession," etc., etc.

When I finished, Mr. Wilde nodded and coughed.

"Speaking of your legitimate ambition," he said, "how do Constance and Louis get along?"

"She loves him," I replied, simply.

The cat on his knee suddenly turned and struck at his eyes, and he flung her off and climbed on to the chair opposite me.

"And Dr. Archer? But that's a matter you can settle any time you wish," he added.

"Yes," I replied, "Dr. Archer can wait, but it is time I saw my cousin Louis."

"It is time," he repeated. Then he took another ledger from the table and ran over the leaves rapidly.

"We are now in communication with ten thousand men," he muttered. "We can count on one hundred thousand within the first twenty-eight hours, and in forty-eight hours the State will rise *en masse*. The country follows the State, and the portion that will not, I mean California and the Northwest, might better never have been inhabited. I shall not send them the Yellow Sign."

The blood rushed to my head, but I only answered, "A new broom sweeps clean."

"The ambition of Cæsar and of Napoleon pales before that which could not rest until it had seized the minds of men and controlled even their unborn thoughts," said Mr. Wilde.

"You are speaking of the King in Yellow," I groaned, with a shudder.

"He is a king whom emperors have served."

"I am content to serve him," I replied.

Mr. Wilde sat rubbing his ears with his crippled hand. "Perhaps Constance does not love him," he suggested.

I started to reply, but a sudden burst of military music from the street below drowned my voice. The Twentieth Dragoon Regiment, formerly in garrison at Mount St. Vincent, was returning from the manœuvres in Westchester County to its new

barracks on East Washington Square. It was my cousin's regiment. They were a fine lot of fellows, in their pale-blue, tight-
fitting jackets, jaunty busbies, and white riding-breeches, with
the double yellow stripe, into which their limbs seemed
moulded. Every other squadron was armed with lances, from
the metal points of which fluttered yellow-and-white pennons.
The band passed, playing the regimental march, then came the
colonel and staff, the horses crowding and trampling, while
their heads bobbed in unison, and the pennons fluttered from
their lance points. The troopers, who rode with the beautiful
English seat, looked brown as berries from their bloodless campaign among the farms of Westchester, and the music of their
sabres against the stirrups, and the jingle of spurs and carbines
was delightful to me. I saw Louis riding with his squadron. He
was as handsome an officer as I have ever seen. Mr. Wilde, who
had mounted a chair by the window, saw him, too, but said
nothing. Louis turned and looked straight at Hawberk's shop
as he passed, and I could see the flush on his brown cheeks. I
think Constance must have been at the window. When the last
troopers had clattered by, and the last pennons vanished into
South Fifth Avenue, Mr. Wilde clambered out of his chair and
dragged the chest away from the door.

"Yes," he said, "it is time that you saw your cousin Louis."

He unlocked the door and I picked up my hat and stick and
stepped into the corridor. The stairs were dark. Groping about,
I set my foot on something soft, which snarled and spit, and I
aimed a murderous blow at the cat, but my cane shivered to
splinters against the balustrade, and the beast scurried back
into Mr. Wilde's room.

Passing Hawberk's door again, I saw him still at work on the
armor, but I did not stop, and, stepping out into Bleecker
Street, I followed it to Wooster, skirted the grounds of the
Lethal Chamber, and, crossing Washington Park, went straight
to my rooms in the Benedick. Here I lunched comfortably, read
the *Herald* and the *Meteor*, and finally went to the steel safe in
my bedroom and set the time combination. The three and
three-quarter minutes which it is necessary to wait, while the
time lock is opening, are to me golden moments. From the instant I set the combination to the moment when I grasp the
knobs and swing back the solid steel doors, I live in an ecstacy

of expectation. Those moments must be like moments passed in paradise. I know what I am to find at the end of the time limit. I know what the massive safe holds secure for me, for me alone, and the exquisite pleasure of waiting is hardly enhanced when the safe opens and I lift, from its velvet crown, a diadem of purest gold, blazing with diamonds. I do this every day, and yet the joy of waiting and at last touching again the diadem only seems to increase as the days pass. It is a diadem fit for a king among kings, an emperor among emperors. The King in Yellow might scorn it, but it shall be worn by his royal servant.

I held it in my arms until the alarm on the safe rang harshly, and then tenderly, proudly I replaced it and shut the steel doors. I walked slowly back into my study, which faces Washington Square, and leaned on the window-sill. The afternoon sun poured into my windows, and a gentle breeze stirred the branches of the elms and maples in the park, now covered with buds and tender foliage. A flock of pigeons circled about the tower of the Memorial Church; sometimes alighting on the purple-tiled roof, sometimes wheeling downward to the lotos fountain in front of the marble arch. The gardeners were busy with the flower-beds around the fountain, and the freshly turned earth smelled sweet and spicy. A lawn-mower, drawn by a fat, white horse, clinked across the greensward, and watering-carts poured showers of spray over the asphalt drives. Around the statue of Peter Stuyvesant, which in 1906 had replaced the monstrosity supposed to represent Garibaldi, children played in the spring sunshine, and nurse girls wheeled elaborate baby-carriages with a reckless disregard for the pasty-faced occupants, which could probably be explained by the presence of half a dozen trim dragoon troopers languidly lolling on the benches. Through the trees the Washington Memorial Arch glistened like silver in the sunshine, and beyond, on the eastern extremity of the square, the gray-stone barracks of the dragoons and the white-granite artillery stables were alive with color and motion.

I looked at the Lethal Chamber on the corner of the square opposite. A few curious people still lingered about the gilded iron railing, but inside the grounds the paths were deserted. I watched the fountains ripple and sparkle; the sparrows had already found this new bathing nook, and the basins were crowded with the dusty-feathered little things. Two or three white peacocks picked their way across the lawns, and a drab-colored pigeon sat so motionless on the arm of one of the Fates that it seemed to be a part of the sculptured stone.

As I was turning carelessly away, a slight commotion in the group of curious loiterers around the gates attracted my attention. A young man had entered, and was advancing with nervous strides along the gravel path which leads to the bronze doors of the Lethal Chamber. He paused a moment before the Fates, and as he raised his head to those three mysterious faces, the pigeon rose from its sculptured perch, circled about for a moment, and wheeled to the east. The young man pressed his hands to his face, and then, with an undefinable gesture, sprang up the marble steps, the bronze doors closed behind him, and half an hour later the loiterers slouched away and the frightened pigeon returned to its perch in the arms of Fate.

I put on my hat and went out into the park for a little walk before dinner. As I crossed the central driveway a group of officers passed, and one of them called out, "Hello, Hildred!" and came back to shake hands with me. It was my cousin Louis, who stood smiling and tapping his spurred heels with his riding-whip.

"Just back from Westchester," he said; "been doing the bucolic; milk and curds, you know; dairy-maids in sunbonnets, who say 'haeow' and 'I don't think' when you tell them they are pretty. I'm nearly dead for a square meal at Delmonico's. What's the news?"

"There is none," I replied, pleasantly. "I saw your regiment coming in this morning."

"Did you? I didn't see you. Where were you?"

"In Mr. Wilde's window."

"Oh, hell!" he began, impatiently, "that man is stark mad! I don't understand why you—"

He saw how annoyed I felt by this outburst, and begged my pardon.

"Really, old chap," he said, "I don't mean to run down a man you like, but for the life of me I can't see what the deuce you find in common with Mr. Wilde. He's not well bred, to put it generously; he's hideously deformed; his head is the head of a criminally insane person. You know yourself he's been in an asylum—"

"So have I," I interrupted, calmly.

Louis looked startled and confused for a moment, but recovered and slapped me heartily on the shoulder.

"You were completely cured," he began; but I stopped him again.

"I suppose you mean that I was simply acknowledged never to have been insane."

"Of course that—that's what I meant," he laughed.

I disliked his laugh, because I knew it was forced; but I nodded gayly and asked him where he was going. Louis looked after his brother officers, who had now almost reached Broadway.

"We had intended to sample a Brunswick cocktail, but, to tell you the truth, I was anxious for an excuse to go and see Hawberk instead. Come along; I'll make you my excuse."

We found old Hawberk, neatly attired in a fresh spring suit, standing at the door of his shop and sniffing the air.

"I had just decided to take Constance for a little stroll before dinner," he replied to the impetuous volley of questions from Louis. "We thought of walking on the park terrace along the North River."

At that moment Constance appeared and grew pale and rosy by turns as Louis bent over her small, gloved fingers. I tried to excuse myself, alleging an engagement up-town, but Louis and Constance would not listen, and I saw I was expected to remain and engage old Hawberk's attention. After all, it would be just as well if I kept my eye on Louis, I thought, and, when they hailed a Spring Street electric-car, I got in after them and took my seat beside the armorer.

The beautiful line of parks and granite terraces overlooking the wharves along the North River, which were built in 1910 and finished in the autumn of 1917, had become one of the most popular promenades in the metropolis. They extended from the Battery to One Hundred and Ninetieth Street, overlooking the noble river, and affording a fine view of the Jersey shore and the Highlands opposite. Cafés and restaurants were scattered here and there among the trees, and twice a week military bands from the garrison played in the kiosques on the parapets.

We sat down in the sunshine on the bench at the foot of the equestrian statue of General Sheridan. Constance tipped her sunshade to shield her eyes, and she and Louis began a murmuring conversation which was impossible to catch. Old Hawberk, leaning on his ivory-headed cane, lighted an excellent cigar, the mate to which I politely refused, and smiled at vacancy. The sun hung low above the Staten Island woods, and the bay was dyed with golden hues reflected from the sun-warmed sails of the shipping in the harbor.

Brigs, schooners, yachts, clumsy ferry-boats, their decks swarming with people, railroad transports carrying lines of brown, blue, and white freight-cars, stately Sound steamers, *déclassé* tramp steamers, coasters, dredgers, scows, and everywhere pervading the entire bay impudent little tugs puffing and whistling officiously—these were the craft which churned the sunlit waters as far as the eye could reach. In calm contrast to the hurry of sailing vessel and steamer, a silent fleet of white war-ships lay motionless in midstream.

Constance's merry laugh aroused me from my reverie.

"What *are* you staring at?" she inquired.

"Nothing—the fleet." I smiled.

Then Louis told us what the vessels were, pointing out each by its relative position to the old red fort on Governor's Island.

"That little cigar-shaped thing is a torpedo-boat," he explained; "there are four more lying close together. They are the *Tarpon*, the *Falcon*, the *Sea Fox*, and the *Octopus*. The gunboats just above are the *Princeton*, the *Champlain*, the *Still Water*, and the *Erie*. Next to them lie the cruisers *Farragut* and *Los Angeles*, and above them the battle-ships *California* and *Dakota*, and the *Washington*, which is the flagship. Those two squatty-looking chunks of metal which are anchored there off Castle William are the double-turreted monitors *Terrible* and *Magnificent*; behind them lies the ram *Osceola*."

Constance looked at him with deep approval in her beautiful eyes. "What loads of things you know for a soldier," she said, and we all joined in the laugh which followed.

Presently Louis rose with a nod to us and offered his arm to Constance, and they strolled away along the river-wall. Hawberk watched them for a moment, and then turned to me.

"Mr. Wilde was right," he said. "I have found the missing

tassets and left cuissard of the 'Prince's Emblazoned,' in a vile old junk garret in Pell Street."

"998?" I inquired, with a smile.

"Yes."

"Mr. Wilde is a very intelligent man," I observed.

"I want to give him the credit of this most important discovery," continued Hawberk. "And I intend it shall be known that he is entitled to the fame of it."

"He won't thank you for that," I answered, sharply; "please say nothing about it."

"Do you know what it is worth?" said Hawberk.

"No—fifty dollars, perhaps."

"It is valued at five hundred, but the owner of the 'Prince's Emblazoned' will give two thousand dollars to the person who completes his suit; that reward also belongs to Mr. Wilde."

"He doesn't want it! He refuses it!" I answered, angrily. "What do you know about Mr. Wilde? He doesn't need the money. He is rich—or will be—richer than any living man except myself. What will we care for money then—what will we care, he and I, when—when—"

"When what?" demanded Hawberk, astonished.

"You will see," I replied, on my guard again.

He looked at me narrowly, much as Dr. Archer used to, and I knew he thought I was mentally unsound. Perhaps it was fortunate for him that he did not use the word lunatic just then.

"No," I replied to his unspoken thought, "I am not mentally weak; my mind is as healthy as Mr. Wilde's. I do not care to explain just yet what I have on hand, but it is an investment which will pay more than mere gold, silver, and precious stones. It will secure the happiness and prosperity of a continent—yes, a hemisphere!"

"Oh," said Hawberk.

"And eventually," I continued, more quietly, "it will secure the happiness of the whole world."

"And incidentally your own happiness and prosperity as well as Mr. Wilde's?"

"Exactly." I smiled, but I could have throttled him for taking that tone.

He looked at me in silence for a while, and then said, very

gently: "Why don't you give up your books and studies, Mr. Castaigne, and take a tramp among the mountains somewhere or other? You used to be fond of fishing. Take a cast or two at the trout in the Rangelys."

"I don't care for fishing any more," I answered, without a shade of annoyance in my voice.

"You used to be fond of everything," he continued— "athletics, yachting, shooting, riding—"

"I have never cared to ride since my fall," I said, quietly.

"Ah, yes, your fall," he repeated, looking away from me.

I thought this nonsense had gone far enough, so I turned the conversation back to Mr. Wilde; but he was scanning my face again in a manner highly offensive to me.

"Mr. Wilde," he repeated; "do you know what he did this afternoon? He came down-stairs and nailed a sign over the hall door next to mine; it read:

Mr. Wilde,
Repairer of Reputations.
3d Bell.

Do you know what a Repairer of Reputations can be?"

"I do," I replied, suppressing the rage within.

"Oh," he said again.

Louis and Constance came strolling by and stopped to ask if we would join them. Hawberk looked at his watch. At the same moment a puff of smoke shot from the casemates of Castle William, and the boom of the sunset gun rolled across the water and was re-echoed from the Highlands opposite. The flag came running down from the flag-pole, the bugles sounded on the white decks of the war-ships, and the first electric light sparkled out from the Jersey shore.

As I turned into the city with Hawberk I heard Constance murmur something to Louis which I did not understand; but Louis whispered "My darling!" in reply; and again, walking ahead with Hawberk through the square, I heard a murmur of "sweetheart!" and "my own Constance!" and I knew the time had nearly arrived when I should speak of important matters with my cousin Louis.

III

One morning early in May I stood before the steel safe in my bedroom, trying on the golden jewelled crown. The diamonds flashed fire as I turned to the mirror, and the heavy beaten gold burned like a halo about my head. I remembered Camilla's agonized scream and the awful words echoing through the dim streets of Carcosa. They were the last lines in the first act, and I dared not think of what followed—dared not, even in the spring sunshine, there in my own room, surrounded with familiar objects, reassured by the bustle from the street and the voices of the servants in the hall-way outside. For those poisoned words had dropped slowly into my heart, as death-sweat drops upon a bed-sheet and is absorbed. Trembling, I put the diadem from my head and wiped my forehead, but I thought of Hastur and of my own rightful ambition, and I remembered Mr. Wilde as I had last left him, his face all torn and bloody from the claws of that devil's creature, and what he said—ah, what he said! The alarm-bell in the safe began to whir harshly, and I knew my time was up; but I would not heed it, and, replacing the flashing circlet upon my head, I turned defiantly to the mirror. I stood for a long time absorbed in the changing expression of my own eyes. The mirror reflected a face which was like my own, but whiter, and so thin that I hardly recognized it. And all the time I kept repeating between my clinched teeth, "The day has come! the day has come!" while the alarm in the safe whirred and clamored, and the diamonds sparkled and flamed above my brow. I heard a door open, but did not heed it. It was only when I saw two faces in the mirror; it was only when another face rose over my shoulder, and two other eyes met mine. I wheeled like a flash and seized a long knife from my dressing-table, and my cousin sprang back very pale, crying: "Hildred! for God's sake!" Then, as my hand fell, he said: "It is I, Louis; don't you know me?" I stood silent. I could not have spoken for my life. He walked up to me and took the knife from my hand.

"What is all this?" he inquired, in a gentle voice. "Are you ill?"

"No," I replied. But I doubt if he heard me.

"Come, come, old fellow," he cried, "take off that brass

crown and toddle into the study. Are you going to a masquerade? What's all this theatrical tinsel anyway?"

I was glad he thought the crown was made of brass and
paste, yet I didn't like him any the better for thinking so. I let
him take it from my hand, knowing it was best to humor him.
He tossed the splendid diadem in the air, and, catching it,
turned to me smiling.

"It's dear at fifty cents," he said. "What's it for?"

I did not answer, but took the circlet from his hands, and,
placing it in the safe, shut the massive steel door. The alarm
ceased its infernal din at once. He watched me curiously, but
did not seem to notice the sudden ceasing of the alarm. He did,
however, speak of the safe as a biscuit-box. Fearing lest he might
examine the combination, I led the way into my study. Louis
threw himself on the sofa and flicked at flies with his eternal
riding-whip. He wore his fatigue uniform, with the braided
jacket and jaunty cap, and I noticed that his riding-boots were
all splashed with red mud.

"Where have you been?" I inquired.

"Jumping mud creeks in Jersey," he said. "I haven't had time
to change yet; I was rather in a hurry to see you. Haven't you
got a glass of something? I'm dead tired; been in the saddle
twenty-four hours."

I gave him some brandy from my medicinal store, which he
drank with a grimace.

"Damned bad stuff," he observed. "I'll give you an address
where they sell brandy that is brandy."

"It's good enough for my needs," I said, indifferently. "I use
it to rub my chest with." He stared and flicked at another fly.

"See here, old fellow," he began, "I've got something to suggest to you. It's four years now that you've shut yourself up here
like an owl, never going anywhere, never taking any healthy exercise, never doing a damn thing but poring over those books
up there on the mantel-piece."

He glanced along the row of shelves. "Napoleon, Napoleon,
Napoleon!" he read. "For Heaven's sake, have you nothing
but Napoleons there?"

"I wish they were bound in gold," I said. "But wait—yes,
there is another book, 'The King in Yellow.'" I looked him
steadily in the eye.

"Have you never read it?" I asked.

"I? No, thank God! I don't want to be driven crazy."

I saw he regretted his speech as soon as he had uttered it. There is only one word which I loathe more than I do lunatic, and that word is crazy. But I controlled myself and asked him why he thought "The King in Yellow" dangerous.

"Oh, I don't know," he said, hastily. "I only remember the excitement it created and the denunciations from pulpit and press. I believe the author shot himself after bringing forth this monstrosity, didn't he?"

"I understand he is still alive," I answered.

"That's probably true," he muttered; "bullets couldn't kill a fiend like that."

"It is a book of great truths," I said.

"Yes," he replied, "of 'truths' which send men frantic and blast their lives. I don't care if the thing is, as they say, the very supreme essence of art. It's a crime to have written it, and I for one shall never open its pages."

"Is that what you have come to tell me?" I asked.

"No," he said, "I came to tell you that I am going to be married."

I believe for a moment my heart ceased to beat, but I kept my eyes on his face.

"Yes," he continued, smiling happily, "married to the sweetest girl on earth."

"Constance Hawberk," I said, mechanically.

"How did you know?" he cried, astonished. "I didn't know it myself until that evening last April, when we strolled down to the embankment before dinner."

"When is it to be?" I asked.

"It was to have been next September; but an hour ago a despatch came, ordering our regiment to the Presidio, San Francisco. We leave at noon to-morrow. To-morrow," he repeated. "Just think, Hildred, tomorrow I shall be the happiest fellow that ever drew breath in this jolly world, for Constance will go with me."

I offered him my hand in congratulation, and he seized and shook it like the good-natured fool he was—or pretended to be.

"I am going to get my squadron as a wedding present," he rattled on. "Captain and Mrs. Louis Castaigne—eh, Hildred?"

Then he told me where it was to be and who were to be there, and made me promise to come and be best man. I set my teeth and listened to his boyish chatter without showing what I felt, but—

I was getting to the limit of my endurance, and when he jumped up, and, switching his spurs till they jingled, said he must go, I did not detain him.

"There's one thing I want to ask of you," I said, quietly.

"Out with it—it's promised," he laughed.

"I want you to meet me for a quarter of an hour's talk to-night."

"Of course, if you wish," he said, somewhat puzzled. "Where?"

"Anywhere—in the park there."

"What time, Hildred?"

"Midnight."

"What in the name of—" he began, but checked himself and laughingly assented. I watched him go down the stairs and hurry away, his sabre banging at every stride. He turned into Bleecker Street, and I knew he was going to see Constance. I gave him ten minutes to disappear and then followed in his footsteps, taking with me the jewelled crown and the silken robe embroidered with the Yellow Sign. When I turned into Bleecker Street and entered the doorway which bore the sign,

MR. WILDE,

REPAIRER OF REPUTATIONS,

3d Bell,

I saw old Hawberk moving about in his shop, and imagined I heard Constance's voice in the parlor; but I avoided them both and hurried up the trembling stair-ways to Mr. Wilde's apartment. I knocked, and entered without ceremony. Mr. Wilde lay groaning on the floor, his face covered with blood, his clothes torn to shreds. Drops of blood were scattered about over the carpet, which had also been ripped and frayed in the evidently recent struggle.

"It's that cursed cat," he said, ceasing his groans and turning his colorless eyes to me; "she attacked me while I was asleep. I believe she will kill me yet."

This was too much, so I went into the kitchen and, seizing a hatchet from the pantry, started to find the infernal beast and settle her then and there. My search was fruitless, and after a while I gave it up and came back to find Mr. Wilde squatting on his high chair by the table. He had washed his face and changed his clothes. The great furrows which the cat's claws had ploughed up in his face he had filled with collodion, and a rag hid the wound in his throat. I told him I should kill the cat when I came across her, but he only shook his head and turned to the open ledger before him. He read name after name of the people who had come to him in regard to their reputation, and the sums he had amassed were startling.

"I put on the screws now and then," he explained.

"One day or other some of these people will assassinate you," I insisted.

"Do you think so?" he said, rubbing his mutilated ears.

It was useless to argue with him, so I took down the manuscript entitled Imperial Dynasty of America for the last time I should ever take it down in Mr. Wilde's study. I read it through, thrilling and trembling with pleasure. When I had finished, Mr. Wilde took the manuscript, and, turning to the dark passage which leads from his study to his bedchamber, called out, in a loud voice, "Vance." Then for the first time I noticed a man crouching there in the shadow. How I had overlooked him during my search for the cat I cannot imagine.

"Vance, come in!" cried Mr. Wilde.

The figure rose and crept towards us, and I shall never forget the face that he raised to mine as the light from the window illuminated it.

"Vance, this is Mr. Castaigne," said Mr. Wilde. Before he had finished speaking, the man threw himself on the ground before the table, crying and gasping, "Oh, God! Oh, my God! Help me! Forgive me— Oh, Mr. Castaigne, keep that man away! You cannot, you cannot mean it! You are different—save me! I am broken down—I was in a madhouse, and now—when all was coming right—when I had forgotten the King—the King in Yellow, and—but I shall go mad again—I shall go mad—"

His voice died into a choking rattle, for Mr. Wilde had leaped on him, and his right hand encircled the man's throat. When Vance fell in a heap on the floor, Mr. Wilde clambered nimbly into his chair again, and, rubbing his mangled ears with the stump of his hand, turned to me and asked me for the ledger. I reached it down from the shelf and he opened it. After a moment's searching among the beautifully written pages, he coughed complacently and pointed to the name Vance.

"Vance," he read, aloud—"Osgood Oswald Vance." At the sound of his name the man on the floor raised his head and turned a convulsed face to Mr. Wilde. His eyes were injected with blood, his lips tumefied. "Called April 28th," continued Mr. Wilde. "Occupation, cashier in the Seaforth National Bank; has served a term for forgery at Sing Sing, whence he was transferred to the Asylum for the Criminal Insane. Pardoned by the Governor of New York, and discharged from the Asylum January 19, 1918. Reputation damaged at Sheepshead Bay. Rumors that he lives beyond his income. Reputation to be repaired at once. Retainer, $1500.

"Note.—Has embezzled sums amounting to $30,000 since March 20, 1919. Excellent family, and secured present position through uncle's influence. Father, President of Seaforth Bank."

I looked at the man on the floor.

"Get up, Vance," said Mr. Wilde, in a gentle voice. Vance rose as if hypnotized. "He will do as we suggest now," observed Mr. Wilde, and, opening the manuscript, he read the entire history of the Imperial Dynasty of America. Then, in a kind and soothing murmur, he ran over the important points with Vance, who stood like one stunned. His eyes were so blank and vacant that I imagined he had become half-witted, and remarked it to Mr. Wilde, who replied that it was of no consequence anyway. Very patiently we pointed out to Vance what his share in the affair would be, and he seemed to understand after a while. Mr. Wilde explained the manuscript, using several volumes on Heraldry to substantiate the result of his researches. He mentioned the establishment of the Dynasty in Carcosa, the lakes which connected Hastur, Aldebaran, and the mystery of the Hyades. He spoke of Cassilda and Camilla, and sounded the cloudy depths of Demhe and the Lake of Hali. "The scalloped tatters of the King in Yellow must hide Yhtill forever," he muttered, but I do not believe Vance heard him. Then by degrees he led Vance along the ramifications of the imperial family to Uoht and Thale, from Naotalba and Phantom of Truth to Aldones, and then, tossing aside his manuscript and notes, he began the wonderful story of the Last King. Fascinated and thrilled, I watched him. He threw up his head, his long arms were stretched out in a magnificent gesture of pride and power, and his eyes blazed deep in their sockets like two emeralds. Vance listened, stupefied. As for me, when at last Mr. Wilde had finished, and, pointing to me, cried, "The cousin of the King," my head swam with excitement.

Controlling myself with a superhuman effort, I explained to Vance why I alone was worthy of the crown, and why my cousin must be exiled or die. I made him understand that my cousin must never marry, even after renouncing all his claims, and how that, least of all, he should marry the daughter of the Marquis of Avonshire and bring England into the question. I showed him a list of thousands of names which Mr. Wilde had drawn up; every man whose name was there had received the Yellow Sign, which no living human being dared disregard. The city, the State, the whole land, were ready to rise and tremble before the Pallid Mask.

The time had come, the people should know the son of Hastur, and the whole world bow to the black stars which hang in the sky over Carcosa.

Vance leaned on the table, his head buried in his hands. Mr. Wilde drew a rough sketch on the margin of yesterday's *Herald* with a bit of lead-pencil. It was a plan of Hawberk's rooms. Then he wrote out the order and affixed the seal, and, shaking like a palsied man, I signed my first writ of execution with my name Hildred-Rex.

Mr. Wilde clambered to the floor and, unlocking the cabinet, took a long, square box from the first shelf. This he brought to the table and opened. A new knife lay in the tissue-paper inside, and I picked it up and handed it to Vance, along with the order and the plan of Hawberk's apartment. Then Mr. Wilde told Vance he could go; and he went, shambling like an outcast of the slums.

I sat for a while watching the daylight fade behind the square tower of the Judson Memorial Church, and finally, gathering up the manuscript and notes, took my hat and started for the door.

Mr. Wilde watched me in silence. When I had stepped into the hall I looked back; Mr. Wilde's small eyes were still fixed on me. Behind him the shadows gathered in the fading light. Then I closed the door behind me and went out into the darkening streets.

I had eaten nothing since breakfast, but I was not hungry. A wretched, half-starved creature, who stood looking across the street at the Lethal Chamber, noticed me and came up to tell me a tale of misery. I gave him money—I don't know why—and he went away without thanking me. An hour later another outcast approached and whined his story. I had a blank bit of paper in my pocket, on which was traced the Yellow Sign, and I handed it to him. He looked at it stupidly for a moment, and then, with an uncertain glance at me, folded it with what seemed to me exaggerated care and placed it in his bosom.

The electric lights were sparkling among the trees, and the new moon shone in the sky above the Lethal Chamber. It was tiresome waiting in the square; I wandered from the marble arch to the artillery stables, and back again to the lotos fountain. The flowers and grass exhaled a fragrance which troubled me. The jet of the fountain played in the moonlight, and the musical splash of falling drops reminded me of the tinkle of chained mail in Hawberk's shop. But it was not so fascinating, and the dull sparkle of the moonlight on the water brought no such sensations of exquisite pleasure as when the sunshine played over the polished steel of a corselet on Hawberk's knee. I watched the bats darting and turning above the water plants in the fountain basin, but their rapid, jerky flight set my nerves on edge, and I went away again to walk aimlessly to and fro among the trees.

The artillery stables were dark, but in the cavalry barracks the officers' windows were brilliantly lighted, and the sally-port was constantly filled with troopers in fatigue, carrying straw and harness and baskets filled with tin dishes.

Twice the mounted sentry at the gates was changed while I wandered up and down the asphalt walk. I looked at my watch. It was nearly time. The lights in the barracks went out one by one, the barred gate was closed, and every minute or two an officer passed in through the side wicket, leaving a rattle of accoutrements and a jingle of spurs on the night air. The square had become very silent. The last homeless loiterer had been driven away by the gray-coated park policeman, the car tracks along Wooster Street were deserted, and the only sound which broke the stillness was the stamping of the sentry's horse and the ring of his sabre against the saddle pommel. In the barracks the officers' quarters were still lighted, and military servants passed and repassed before the bay-windows. Twelve o'clock sounded from the new spire of St. Francis Xavier, and at the last stroke of the sad-toned bell a figure passed through the wicket beside the portcullis, returned the salute of the sentry, and, crossing the street, entered the square and advanced towards the Benedick apartment house.

"Louis," I called.

The man pivoted on his spurred heels and came straight towards me.

"Is that you, Hildred?"

"Yes, you are on time."

I took his offered hand and we strolled towards the Lethal Chamber.

He rattled on about his wedding and the graces of Constance and their future prospects, calling my attention to his captain's shoulder-straps and the triple gold arabesque on his sleeve and fatigue cap. I believe I listened as much to the music of his spurs and sabre as I did to his boyish babble, and at last we stood under the elms on the Fourth Street corner of the square opposite the Lethal Chamber. Then he laughed and asked me what I wanted with him. I motioned him to a seat on a bench under the electric light, and sat down beside him. He looked at me curiously, with that same searching glance which I hate and fear so in doctors. I felt the insult of his look, but he did not know it, and I carefully concealed my feelings.

"Well, old chap," he inquired, "what can I do for you?"

I drew from my pocket the manuscript and notes of the Imperial Dynasty of America, and, looking him in the eye, said:

"I will tell you. On your word as a soldier, promise me to read this manuscript from beginning to end without asking me a question. Promise me to read these notes in the same way, and promise me to listen to what I have to tell later."

"I promise, if you wish it," he said, pleasantly. "Give me the paper, Hildred."

He began to read, raising his eyebrows with a puzzled,

whimsical air, which made me tremble with suppressed anger. As he advanced, his eyebrows contracted, and his lips seemed to form the word "rubbish."

Then he looked slightly bored, but apparently for my sake read, with an attempt at interest, which presently ceased to be an effort. He started when, in the closely written pages he came to his own name, and when he came to mine he lowered the paper and looked sharply at me for a moment. But he kept his word, and resumed his reading, and I let the half-formed question die on his lips unanswered. When he came to the end and read the signature of Mr. Wilde, he folded the paper carefully and returned it to me. I handed him the notes, and he settled back, pushing his fatigue cap up to his forehead with a boyish gesture which I remembered so well in school. I watched his face as he read, and when he finished I took the notes, with the manuscript, and placed them in my pocket. Then I unfolded a scroll marked with the Yellow Sign. He saw the sign, but he did not seem to recognize it, and I called his attention to it somewhat sharply.

"Well," he said, "I see it. What is it?"

"It is the Yellow Sign," I said, angrily.

"Oh, that's it, is it?" said Louis, in that flattering voice which Dr. Archer used to employ with me, and would probably have employed again, had I not settled his affair for him.

I kept my rage down and answered as steadily as possible, "Listen, you have engaged your word?"

"I am listening, old chap," he replied, soothingly.

I began to speak very calmly: "Dr. Archer, having by some means become possessed of the secret of the Imperial Succession, attempted to deprive me of my right, alleging that, because of a fall from my horse four years ago, I had become mentally deficient. He presumed to place me under restraint in his own house in hopes of either driving me insane or poisoning me. I have not forgotten it. I visited him last night and the interview was final."

Louis turned quite pale, but did not move. I resumed, triumphantly: "There are yet three people to be interviewed in the interests of Mr. Wilde and myself. They are my cousin Louis, Mr. Hawberk, and his daughter Constance."

Louis sprang to his feet, and I arose also, and flung the paper marked with the Yellow Sign to the ground.

"Oh, I don't need that to tell you what I have to say," I cried, with a laugh of triumph. "You must renounce the crown to me—do you hear, to *me*?"

Louis looked at me with a startled air, but, recovering himself, said kindly, "Of course I renounce the—what is it I must renounce?"

"The crown," I said, angrily.

"Of course," he answered, "I renounce it. Come, old chap, I'll walk back to your rooms with you."

"Don't try any of your doctor's tricks on me," I cried, trembling with fury. "Don't act as if you think I am insane."

"What nonsense!" he replied. "Come, it's getting late, Hildred."

"No," I shouted, "you must listen. You cannot marry; I forbid it. Do you hear? I forbid it. You shall renounce the crown, and in reward I grant you exile; but if you refuse you shall die."

He tried to calm me, but I was roused at last, and, drawing my long knife, barred his way.

Then I told him how they would find Dr. Archer in the cellar with his throat open, and I laughed in his face when I thought of Vance and his knife, and the order signed by me.

"Ah, you are the King," I cried, "but I shall be King. Who are you to keep me from empire over all the habitable earth! I was born the cousin of a king, but I shall be King!"

Louis stood white and rigid before me. Suddenly a man came running up Fourth Street, entered the gate of the Lethal Temple, traversed the path to the bronze doors at full speed, and plunged into the death-chamber with the cry of one demented, and I laughed until I wept tears, for I had recognized Vance, and knew that Hawberk and his daughter were no longer in my way.

"Go," I cried to Louis, "you have ceased to be a menace. You will never marry Constance now, and if you marry any one else in your exile, I will visit you as I did my doctor last night. Mr. Wilde takes charge of you to-morrow." Then I turned and darted into South Fifth Avenue, and with a cry of terror Louis dropped his belt and sabre and followed me like the wind. I heard him close behind me at the corner of Bleecker Street, and I dashed into the door-way under Hawberk's sign. He cried, "Halt, or I fire!" but when he saw that I flew up the stairs leaving Hawberk's shop below, he left me, and I heard him hammering and shouting at their door as though it were possible to arouse the dead.

Mr. Wilde's door was open, and I entered, crying: "It is done, it is done! Let the nations rise and look upon their King!" but I could not find Mr. Wilde, so I went to the cabinet and took the splendid diadem from its case. Then I drew on the white silk robe, embroidered with the Yellow Sign, and placed the crown upon my head. At last I was King, King by my right in Hastur, King because I knew the mystery of the Hyades, and my mind had sounded the depths of the Lake of Hali. I was King! The first gray pencillings of dawn would raise a tempest which would shake two hemispheres. Then as I stood, my every nerve pitched to the highest tension, faint with the joy and splendor of my thought, without, in the dark passage, a man groaned.

I seized the tallow dip and sprang to the door. The cat passed me like a demon, and the tallow dip went out, but my long knife flew swifter than she, and I heard her screech, and I knew that my knife had found her. For a moment I listened to her tumbling and thumping about in the darkness, and then, when her frenzy ceased, I lighted a lamp and raised it over my head. Mr. Wilde lay on the floor with his throat torn open. At first I thought he was dead, but as I looked a green sparkle came into his sunken eyes, his mutilated hand trembled, and then a spasm stretched his mouth from ear to ear. For a moment my terror and despair gave place to hope, but as I bent over him his eyeballs rolled clean around in his head, and he died. Then, while I stood transfixed with rage and despair, seeing my crown, my empire, every hope and every ambition, my very life, lying prostrate there with the dead master, *they* came, seized me from behind and bound me until my veins stood out like cords, and my voice failed with the paroxysms of my frenzied screams. But I still raged, bleeding and infuriated, among them, and more than one policeman felt my sharp teeth. Then when I could no longer move they came nearer; I saw old Hawberk, and behind him my cousin Louis' ghastly face, and farther away, in the corner, a woman, Constance, weeping softly.

"Ah! I see it now!" I shrieked. "You have seized the throne and the empire. Woe! woe to you who are crowned with the crown of the King in Yellow!"

[EDITOR'S NOTE.—Mr. Castaigne died yesterday in the Asylum for Criminal Insane.]

1895

RALPH ADAMS CRAM

(1863–1942)

The Dead Valley

I HAVE a friend, Olof Ehrensvärd, a Swede by birth, who yet, by reason of a strange and melancholy mischance of his early boyhood, has thrown his lot with that of the New World. It is a curious story of a headstrong boy and a proud and relentless family: the details do not matter here, but they are sufficient to weave a web of romance around the tall yellow-bearded man with the sad eyes and the voice that gives itself perfectly to plaintive little Swedish songs remembered out of childhood. In the winter evenings we play chess together, he and I, and after some close, fierce battle has been fought to a finish—usually with my own defeat—we fill our pipes again, and Ehrensvärd tells me stories of the far, half-remembered days in the fatherland, before he went to sea: stories that grow very strange and incredible as the night deepens and the fire falls together, but stories that, nevertheless, I fully believe.

One of them made a strong impression on me, so I set it down here, only regretting that I cannot reproduce the curiously perfect English and the delicate accent which to me increased the fascination of the tale. Yet, as best I can remember it, here it is.

"I never told you how Nils and I went over the hills to Hallsberg, and how we found the Dead Valley, did I? Well, this is the way it happened. I must have been about twelve years old, and Nils Sjöberg, whose father's estate joined ours, was a few months younger. We were inseparable just at that time, and whatever we did, we did together.

"Once a week it was market day in Engelholm, and Nils and I went always there to see the strange sights that the market gathered from all the surrounding country. One day we quite lost our hearts, for an old man from across the Elfborg had brought a little dog to sell, that seemed to us the most beautiful dog in all the world. He was a round, woolly puppy, so funny that Nils and I sat down on the ground and laughed at him, until he came and played with us in so jolly a way that we felt that there was only one really desirable thing in life, and that was the little dog of the old man from across the hills. But alas! we had not half money enough wherewith to buy him, so we were forced to beg the old man not to sell him before the next market day, promising that we would bring the money for him then. He gave us his word, and we ran home very fast and implored our mothers to give us money for the little dog.

"We got the money, but we could not wait for the next market day. Suppose the puppy should be sold! The thought frightened us so that we begged and implored that we might be allowed to go over the hills to Hallsberg where the old man lived, and get the little dog ourselves, and at last they told us we might go. By starting early in the morning we should reach Hallsberg by three o'clock, and it was arranged that we should stay there that night with Nils's aunt, and, leaving by noon the next day, be home again by sunset.

"Soon after sunrise we were on our way, after having received minute instructions as to just what we should do in all possible and impossible circumstances, and finally a repeated injunction that we should start for home at the same hour the next day, so that we might get safely back before nightfall.

"For us, it was magnificent sport, and we started off with our rifles, full of the sense of our very great importance: yet the journey was simple enough, along a good road, across the big hills we knew so well, for Nils and I had shot over half the territory this side of the dividing ridge of the Elfborg. Back of Engelholm lay a long valley, from which rose the low mountains, and we had to cross this, and then follow the road along the side of the hills for three or four miles, before a narrow path branched off to the left, leading up through the pass.

"Nothing occurred of interest on the way over, and we reached Hallsberg in due season, found to our inexpressible joy that the little dog was not sold, secured him, and so went to the house of Nils's aunt to spend the night.

"Why we did not leave early on the following day, I can't quite remember; at all events, I know we stopped at a shooting range just outside of the town, where most attractive pasteboard pigs were sliding slowly through painted foliage, serving so as beautiful marks. The result was that we did not get fairly started for home until afternoon, and as we found ourselves at last pushing up the side of the mountain with the sun dangerously near their summits, I think we were a little scared at the prospect of the examination and possible punishment that awaited us when we got home at midnight.

"Therefore we hurried as fast as possible up the mountain side, while the blue dusk closed in about us, and the light died in the purple sky. At first we had talked hilariously, and the little dog had leaped ahead of us with the utmost joy. Latterly, however, a curious oppression came on us; we did not speak or even whistle, while the dog fell behind, following us with hesitation in every muscle.

"We had passed through the foothills and the low spurs of the mountains, and were almost at the top of the main range, when life seemed to go out of everything, leaving the world dead, so suddenly silent the forest became, so stagnant the air. Instinctively we halted to listen.

"Perfect silence,—the crushing silence of deep forests at night; and more, for always, even in the most impenetrable fastnesses of the wooded mountains, is the multitudinous murmur of little lives, awakened by the darkness, exaggerated and intensified by the stillness of the air and the great dark: but here and now the silence seemed unbroken even by the turn of a leaf, the movement of a twig, the note of night bird or insect. I could hear the blood beat through my veins; and the crushing of the grass under our feet as we advanced with hesitating steps sounded like the falling of trees.

"And the air was stagnant,—dead. The atmosphere seemed to lie upon the body like the weight of sea on a diver who has ventured too far into its awful depths. What we usually call silence seems so only in relation to the din of ordinary experience. This was silence in the absolute, and it crushed the mind while it intensified the senses, bringing down the awful weight of inextinguishable fear.

"I know that Nils and I stared towards each other in abject terror, listening to our quick, heavy breathing, that sounded to our acute senses like the fitful rush of waters. And the poor little dog we were leading justified our terror. The black oppression seemed to crush him even as it did us. He lay close on the ground, moaning feebly, and dragging himself painfully and slowly closer to Nils's feet. I think this exhibition of utter animal fear was the last touch, and must inevitably have blasted our reason—mine anyway; but just then, as we stood quaking on the bounds of madness, came a sound, so awful, so ghastly, so horrible, that it seemed to rouse us from the dead spell that was on us.

"In the depth of the silence came a cry, beginning as a low, sorrowful moan, rising to a tremulous shriek, culminating in a yell that seemed to tear the night in sunder and rend the world as by a cataclysm. So fearful was it that I could not believe it had actual existence: it passed previous experience, the powers of belief, and for a moment I thought it the result of my own animal terror, an hallucination born of tottering reason.

"A glance at Nils dispelled this thought in a flash. In the pale light of the high stars he was the embodiment of all possible human fear, quaking with an ague, his jaw fallen, his tongue out, his eyes protruding like those of a hanged man. Without a word we fled, the panic of fear giving us strength, and together, the little dog caught close in Nils's arms, we sped down the side of the cursed mountains,—anywhere, goal was of no account: we had but one impulse—to get away from that place.

"So under the black trees and the far white stars that flashed through the still leaves overhead, we leaped down the mountain side, regardless of path or landmark, straight through the tangled underbrush, across mountain streams, through fens and copses, anywhere, so only that our course was downward.

"How long we ran thus, I have no idea, but by and by the forest fell behind, and we found ourselves among the foothills, and fell exhausted on the dry short grass, panting like tired dogs.

"It was lighter here in the open, and presently we looked around to see where we were, and how we were to strike out in order to find the path that would lead us home. We looked in vain for a familiar sign. Behind us rose the great wall of black forest on the flank of the mountain: before us lay the undulating mounds of low foothills, unbroken by trees or rocks, and beyond, only the fall of black sky bright with multitudinous stars that turned its velvet depth to a luminous gray.

"As I remember, we did not speak to each other once: the terror was too heavy on us for that, but by and by we rose simultaneously and started out across the hills.

"Still the same silence, the same dead, motionless air—air that was at once sultry and chilling: a heavy heat struck through with an icy chill that felt almost like the burning of frozen steel. Still carrying the helpless dog, Nils pressed on through the hills, and I followed close behind. At last, in front of us, rose a slope of moor touching the white stars. We climbed it wearily, reached the top, and found ourselves gazing down into a great, smooth valley, filled half way to the brim with—what?

"As far as the eye could see stretched a level plain of ashy white, faintly phosphorescent, a sea of velvet fog that lay like motionless water, or rather like a floor of alabaster, so dense did it appear, so seemingly capable of sustaining weight. If it were possible, I think that sea of dead white mist struck even greater terror into my soul than the heavy silence or the deadly cry—so ominous was it, so utterly unreal, so phantasmal, so impossible, as it lay there like a dead ocean under the steady stars. Yet through that mist *we must go!* there seemed no other way home, and, shattered with abject fear, mad with the one desire to get back, we started down the slope to where the sea of milky mist ceased, sharp and distinct around the stems of the rough grass.

"I put one foot into the ghostly fog. A chill as of death struck through me, stopping my heart, and I threw myself backward on the slope. At that instant came again the shriek, close, close, right in our ears, in ourselves, and far out across that damnable sea I saw the cold fog lift like a water-spout and toss itself high in writhing convolutions towards the sky. The stars began to grow dim as thick vapor swept across them, and in the growing dark I saw a great, watery moon lift itself slowly above the palpitating sea, vast and vague in the gathering mist.

"This was enough: we turned and fled along the margin of the white sea that throbbed now with fitful motion below us, rising, rising, slowly and steadily, driving us higher and higher up the side of the foothills.

"It was a race for life; that we knew. How we kept it up I cannot understand, but we did, and at last we saw the white sea fall behind us as we staggered up the end of the valley, and then down into a region that we knew, and so into the old path. The last thing I remember was hearing a strange voice, that of

Nils, but horribly changed, stammer brokenly, 'The dog is dead!' and then the whole world turned around twice, slowly and resistlessly, and consciousness went out with a crash.

"It was some three weeks later, as I remember, that I awoke in my own room, and found my mother sitting beside the bed. I could not think very well at first, but as I slowly grew strong again, vague flashes of recollection began to come to me, and little by little the whole sequence of events of that awful night in the Dead Valley came back. All that I could gain from what was told me was that three weeks before I had been found in my own bed, raging sick, and that my illness grew fast into brain fever. I tried to speak of the dread things that had happened to me, but I saw at once that no one looked on them save as the hauntings of a dying frenzy, and so I closed my mouth and kept my own counsel.

"I must see Nils, however, and so I asked for him. My mother told me that he also had been ill with a strange fever, but that he was now quite well again. Presently they brought him in, and when we were alone I began to speak to him of the night on the mountain. I shall never forget the shock that struck me down on my pillow when the boy denied everything: denied having gone with me, ever having heard the cry, having seen the valley, or feeling the deadly chill of the ghostly fog. Nothing would shake his determined ignorance, and in spite of myself I was forced to admit that his denials came from no policy of concealment, but from blank oblivion.

"My weakened brain was in a turmoil. Was it all but the floating phantasm of delirium? Or had the horror of the real thing blotted Nils's mind into blankness so far as the events of the night in the Dead Valley were concerned? The latter explanation seemed the only one, else how explain the sudden illness which in a night had struck us both down? I said nothing more, either to Nils or to my own people, but waited, with a growing determination that, once well again, I would find that valley if it really existed.

"It was some weeks before I was really well enough to go, but finally, late in September, I chose a bright, warm, still day, the last smile of the dying summer, and started early in the morning along the path that led to Hallsberg. I was sure I knew where the trail struck off to the right, down which we had come from the valley of dead water, for a great tree grew by the Hallsberg path at the point where, with a sense of salvation, we had found the home road. Presently I saw it to the right, a little distance ahead.

"I think the bright sunlight and the clear air had worked as a tonic to me, for by the time I came to the foot of the great pine, I had quite lost faith in the verity of the vision that haunted me, believing at last that it was indeed but the nightmare of madness. Nevertheless, I turned sharply to the right, at the base of the tree, into a narrow path that led through a dense thicket. As I did so I tripped over something. A swarm of flies sung into the air around me, and looking down I saw the matted fleece, with the poor little bones thrusting through, of the dog we had bought in Hallsberg.

"Then my courage went out with a puff, and I knew that it all was true, and that now I was frightened. Pride and the desire for adventure urged me on, however, and I pressed into the close thicket that barred my way. The path was hardly visible: merely the worn road of some small beasts, for, though it showed in the crisp grass, the bushes above grew thick and hardly penetrable. The land rose slowly, and rising grew clearer, until at last I came out on a great slope of hill, unbroken by trees or shrubs, very like my memory of that rise of land we had topped in order that we might find the dead valley and the icy fog. I looked at the sun; it was bright and clear, and all around insects were humming in the autumn air, and birds were darting to and fro. Surely there was no danger, not until nightfall at least; so I began to whistle, and with a rush mounted the last crest of brown hill.

"There lay the Dead Valley! A great oval basin, almost as smooth and regular as though made by man. On all sides the grass crept over the brink of the encircling hills, dusty green on the crests, then fading into ashy brown, and so to a deadly white, this last color forming a thin ring, running in a long line around the slope. And then? Nothing. Bare, brown, hard earth, glittering with grains of alkali, but otherwise dead and barren. Not a tuft of grass, not a stick of brushwood, not even a stone, but only the vast expanse of beaten clay.

"In the midst of the basin, perhaps a mile and a half away, the level expanse was broken by a great dead tree, rising leafless and gaunt into the air. Without a moment's hesitation I started down into the valley and made for this goal. Every particle of fear seemed to have left me, and even the valley itself did not look so very terrifying. At all events, I was driven by an over-whelming curiosity, and there seemed to be but one thing in the world to do,—to get to that Tree! As I trudged along over the hard earth, I noticed that the multitudinous voices of birds and insects had died away. No bee or butterfly hovered through the air, no insects leaped or crept over the dull earth. The very air itself was stagnant.

"As I drew near the skeleton tree, I noticed the glint of sun-light on a kind of white mound around its roots, and I won-dered curiously. It was not until I had come close that I saw its nature.

"All around the roots and barkless trunk was heaped a wilderness of little bones. Tiny skulls of rodents and of birds, thousands of them, rising about the dead tree and streaming off for several yards in all directions, until the dreadful pile ended in isolated skulls and scattered skeletons. Here and there a larger bone appeared,—the thigh of a sheep, the hoofs of a horse, and to one side, grinning slowly, a human skull.

"I stood quite still, staring with all my eyes, when suddenly the dense silence was broken by a faint, forlorn cry high over my head. I looked up and saw a great falcon turning and sailing downward just over the tree. In a moment more she fell mo-tionless on the bleaching bones.

"Horror struck me, and I rushed for home, my brain whirling, a strange numbness growing in me. I ran steadily, on and on. At last I glanced up. Where was the rise of hill? I looked around wildly. Close before me was the dead tree with its pile of bones. I had circled it round and round, and the valley wall was still a mile and a half away.

"I stood dazed and frozen. The sun was sinking, red and dull, towards the line of hills. In the east the dark was growing fast. Was there still time? *Time!* It was not *that* I wanted, it was *will!* My feet seemed clogged as in a nightmare. I could hardly drag them over the barren earth. And then I felt the slow chill creeping through me. I looked down. Out of the earth a thin mist was rising, collecting in little pools that grew ever larger until they joined here and there, their currents swirling slowly like thin blue smoke. The western hills halved the copper sun.

When it was dark I should hear that shriek again, and then I should die. I knew that, and with every remaining atom of will I staggered towards the red west through the writhing mist that crept clammily around my ankles, retarding my steps.

"And as I fought my way off from the Tree, the horror grew, until at last I thought I was going to die. The silence pursued me like dumb ghosts, the still air held my breath, the hellish fog caught at my feet like cold hands.

"But I won! though not a moment too soon. As I crawled on my hands and knees up the brown slope, I heard, far away and high in the air, the cry that already had almost bereft me of reason. It was faint and vague, but unmistakable in its horrible intensity. I glanced behind. The fog was dense and pallid, heaving undulously up the brown slope. The sky was gold under the setting sun, but below was the ashy gray of death. I stood for a moment on the brink of this sea of hell, and then leaped down the slope. The sunset opened before me, the night closed behind, and as I crawled home weak and tired, darkness shut down on the Dead Valley."

1895

MADELINE YALE WYNNE

(1847–1918)

The Little Room

'How would it do for a smoking-room?'

'Just the very place! only, you know, Roger, you must not think of smoking in the house. I am almost afraid that having just a plain, common man around, let alone a smoking man, will upset Aunt Hannah. She is New England—Vermont New England—boiled down.'

'You leave Aunt Hannah to me; I'll find her tender side. I'm going to ask her about the old sea-captain and the yellow calico.'

'Not yellow calico—blue chintz.'

'Well, yellow *shell* then.'

'No, no! don't mix it up so; you won't know yourself what to expect, and that's half the fun.'

'Now you tell me again exactly what to expect; to tell the truth, I didn't half hear about it the other day; I was wool-gathering. It was something queer that happened when you were a child, wasn't it?'

'Something that began to happen long before that, and kept happening, and may happen again; but I hope not.'

'What was it?'

'I wonder if the other people in the car can hear us?'

'I fancy not; we don't hear them—not consecutively, at least.'

'Well, mother was born in Vermont, you know; she was the only child by a second marriage. Aunt Hannah and Aunt Maria are only half-aunts to me, you know.'

'I hope they are half as nice as you are.'

'Roger, be still; they certainly will hear us.'

'Well, don't you want them to know we are married?'

'Yes, but not just married. There's all the difference in the world.'

'You are afraid we look too happy!'

'No; only I want my happiness all to myself.'

'Well, the little room?'

'My aunts brought mother up; they were nearly twenty years older than she. I might say Hiram and they brought her up. You see, Hiram was bound out to my grandfather when he was a boy, and when grandfather died Hiram said he "s'posed he went with the farm, long o' the critters," and he has been there ever since. He was my mother's only refuge from the decorum of my aunts. They are simply workers. They make me think of the Maine woman who wanted her epitaph to be: "She was a *hard* working woman."'

'They must be almost beyond their working-days. How old are they?'

'Seventy, or thereabouts; but they will die standing; or, at least, on a Saturday night, after all the house-work is done up. They were rather strict with mother, and I think she had a lonely childhood. The house is almost a mile away from any neighbors, and off on top of what they call Stony Hill. It is bleak enough up there, even in summer.

'When mamma was about ten years old they sent her to cousins in Brooklyn, who had children of their own, and knew more about bringing them up. She staid there till she was married; she didn't go to Vermont in all that time, and of course hadn't seen her sisters, for they never would leave home for a day. They couldn't even be induced to go to Brooklyn to her wedding, so she and father took their wedding trip up there.'

'And that's why we are going up there on our own?'

'Don't, Roger; you have no idea how loud you speak.'

'You never say so except when I am going to say that one little word.'

'Well, don't say it, then, or say it very, very quietly.'

'Well, what was the queer thing?'

'When they got to the house, mother wanted to take father right off into the little room; she had been telling him about it, just as I am going to tell you, and she had said that of all the rooms, that one was the only one that seemed pleasant to her. She described the furniture and the books and paper and everything, and said it was on the north side, between the front and back room. Well, when they went to look for it, there was no little room there; there was only a shallow china-closet. She asked her sisters when the house had been altered and a closet made of the room that used to be there. They both said the house was exactly as it had been built—that they had never made any changes, except to tear down the old wood-shed and build a smaller one.

'Father and mother laughed a good deal over it, and when anything was lost they would always say it must be in the little room, and any exaggerated statement was called "little-roomy." When I was a child I thought that was a regular English phrase, I heard it so often.

'Well, they talked it over, and finally they concluded that my mother had been a very imaginative sort of a child, and had read in some book about such a little room, or perhaps even dreamed it, and then had "made believe," as children do, till she herself had really thought the room was there.'

'Why, of course, that might easily happen.'

'Yes, but you haven't heard the queer part yet; you wait and see if you can explain the rest as easily.

'They staid at the farm two weeks, and then went to New York to live. When I was eight years old my father was killed in the war, and mother was broken-hearted. She never was quite strong afterwards, and that summer we decided to go up to the farm for three months.

'I was a restless sort of a child, and the journey seemed very long to me; and finally, to pass the time, mamma told me the story of the little room, and how it was all in her own imagination, and how there really was only a china-closet there.

'She told it with all the particulars; and even to me, who knew beforehand that the room wasn't there, it seemed just as real as could be. She said it was on the north side, between the front and back rooms; that it was very small, and they sometimes called it an entry. There was a door also that opened out-of-doors, and that one was painted green, and was cut in the middle like the old Dutch doors, so that it could be used for a window by opening the top part only. Directly opposite the door was a lounge or couch; it was covered with blue chintz—India chintz—some that had been brought over by an old Salem sea-captain as a "venture." He had given it to Hannah when she was a young girl. She was sent to Salem for two years to school. Grandfather originally came from Salem.'

'I thought there wasn't any room or chintz.'

'*That is just it.* They had decided that mother had imagined it all, and yet you see how exactly everything was painted in her mind, for she had even remembered that Hiram had told her that Hannah could have married the sea-captain if she had wanted to!

'The India cotton was the regular blue stamped chintz, with the peacock figure on it. The head and body of the bird were in profile, while the tail was full front view behind it. It had seemed to take mamma's fancy, and she drew it for me on a piece of paper as she talked. Doesn't it seem strange to you that she could have made all that up, or even dreamed it?

'At the foot of the lounge were some hanging shelves with some old books on them. All the books were leather-colored except one; that was bright red, and was called the *Ladies' Album*. It made a bright break between the other thicker books.

'On the lower shelf was a beautiful pink sea-shell, lying on a mat made of balls of red shaded worsted. This shell was greatly coveted by mother, but she was only allowed to play with it when she had been particularly good. Hiram had shown her how to hold it close to her ear and hear the roar of the sea in it.

'I know you will like Hiram, Roger; he is quite a character in his way.

'Mamma said she remembered, or *thought* she remembered, having been sick once, and she had to lie quietly for some days on the lounge; then was the time she had become so familiar with everything in the room, and she had been allowed to have the shell to play with all the time. She had had her toast brought to her in there, with make-believe tea. It was one of her pleasant memories of her childhood; it was the first time she had been of any importance to anybody, even herself.

'Right at the head of the lounge was a light-stand, as they called it, and on it was a very brightly polished brass candle-stick and a brass tray, with snuffers. That is all I remember of her describing, except that there was a braided rag rug on the floor, and on the wall was a beautiful flowered paper—roses and morning-glories in a wreath on a light blue ground. The same paper was in the front room.'

'And all this never existed except in her imagination?'

'She said that when she and father went up there, there wasn't any little room at all like it anywhere in the house; there was a china-closet where she had believed the room to be.'

'And your aunts said there had never been any such room.'

'That is what they said.'

'Wasn't there any blue chintz in the house with a peacock figure?'

'Not a scrap, and Aunt Hannah said there had never been any that she could remember; and Aunt Maria just echoed her—she always does that. You see, Aunt Hannah is an up-and-down New England woman. She looks just like herself; I mean, just like her character. Her joints move up and down or backward and forward in a plain square fashion. I don't believe she ever leaned on anything in her life, or sat in an easy-chair. But Maria is different; she is rounder and softer; she hasn't any ideas of her own; she never had any. I don't believe she would think it right or becoming to have one that differed from Aunt Hannah's, so what would be the use of having any? She is an echo, that's all.

'When mamma and I got there, of course I was all excitement to see the china-closet, and I had a sort of feeling that it would be the little room after all. So I ran ahead and threw open the door, crying, "Come and see the little room."'

'And Roger,' said Mrs. Grant, laying her hand in his, 'there really was a little room there, exactly as mother had remembered it. There was the lounge, the peacock chintz, the green door, the shell, the morning-glory, and rose paper, *everything exactly as she had described it to me.*'

'What in the world did the sisters say about it?'

'Wait a minute and I will tell you. My mother was in the front hall still talking with Aunt Hannah. She didn't hear me at first, but I ran out there and dragged her through the front room, saying, "The room *is* here—it is all right."

'It seemed for a minute as if my mother would faint. She clung to me in terror. I can remember now how strained her eyes looked and how pale she was.

'I called out to Aunt Hannah and asked her when they had had the closet taken away and the little room built; for in my excitement I thought that that was what had been done.

' "That little room has always been there," said Aunt Hannah, "ever since the house was built."

' "But mamma said there wasn't any little room here, only a china-closet, when she was here with papa," said I.

' "No, there has never been any china-closet there; it has always been just as it is now," said Aunt Hannah.

'Then mother spoke; her voice sounded weak and far off. She said, slowly, and with an effort, "Maria, don't you remember that you told me that there had *never been any little room here*? and Hannah said so too, and then I said I must have dreamed it?"

' "No, I don't remember anything of the kind," said Maria, without the slightest emotion. "I don't remember you ever said anything about any china-closet. The house has never been altered; you used to play in this room when you were a child, don't you remember?"

' "I know it," said mother, in that queer slow voice that made me feel frightened. "Hannah, don't you remember my finding the china-closet here, with the gilt-edged china on the shelves, and then *you* said that the *china-closet* had always been here?"

' "No," said Hannah, pleasantly but unemotionally—"no, I don't think you ever asked me about any china-closet, and we haven't any gilt-edged china that I know of."

'And that was the strangest thing about it. We never could make them remember that there had ever been any question about it. You would think they could remember how surprised mother had been before, unless she had imagined the whole thing. Oh, it was so queer! They were always pleasant about it, but they didn't seem to feel any interest or curiosity. It was always this answer: "The house is just as it was built; there have never been any changes, so far as we know."

'And my mother was in an agony of perplexity. How cold their gray eyes looked to me! There was no reading anything in them. It just seemed to break my mother down, this queer thing. Many times that summer, in the middle of the night, I have seen her get up and take a candle and creep softly downstairs. I could hear the steps creak under her weight. Then she would go through the front room and peer into the darkness, holding her thin hand between the candle and her eyes. She seemed to think the little room might vanish. Then she would come back to bed and toss about all night, or lie still and shiver; it used to frighten me.

'She grew pale and thin, and she had a little cough; then she did not like to be left alone. Sometimes she would make errands in order to send me to the little room for something—a book, or her fan, or her handkerchief; but she would never sit there or let me stay in there long, and sometimes she wouldn't let me go in there for days together. Oh, it was pitiful!'

'Well, don't talk any more about it, Margaret, if it makes you feel so,' said Mr. Grant.

'Oh yes, I want you to know all about it, and there isn't much more—no more about the room.

'Mother never got well, and she died that autumn. She used often to sigh, and say, with a wan little laugh, "There is one thing I am glad of, Margaret: your father knows now all about the little room." I think she was afraid I distrusted her. Of course, in a child's way, I thought there was something queer about it, but I did not brood over it. I was too young then, and took it as a part of her illness. But, Roger, do you know, it really did affect me. I almost hate to go there after talking about it; I somehow feel as if it might, you know, be a china-closet again.'

'That's an absurd idea.'

'I know it; of course it can't be. I saw the room, and there isn't any china-closet there, and no gilt-edged china in the house, either.'

And then she whispered: 'But, Roger, you may hold my hand as you do now, if you will, when we go to look for the little room.'

'And you won't mind Aunt Hannah's gray eyes?'

'I won't mind *anything*.'

It was dusk when Mr. and Mrs. Grant went into the gate under the two old Lombardy poplars and walked up the narrow path to the door, where they were met by the two aunts.

Hannah gave Mrs. Grant a frigid but not unfriendly kiss; and Maria seemed for a moment to tremble on the verge of an emotion, but she glanced at Hannah, and then gave her greeting in exactly the same repressed and non-committal way.

Supper was waiting for them. On the table was the *gilt-edged china*. Mrs. Grant didn't notice it immediately, till she saw her husband smiling at her over his teacup; then she felt fidgety, and couldn't eat. She was nervous, and kept wondering what was behind her, whether it would be a little room or a closet.

After supper she offered to help about the dishes, but, mercy! she might as well have offered to help bring the seasons round; Maria and Hannah couldn't be helped.

So she and her husband went to find the little room, or closet, or whatever was to be there.

Aunt Maria followed them, carrying the lamp, which she set down, and then went back to the dish-washing.

Margaret looked at her husband. He kissed her, for she seemed troubled; and then, hand in hand, they opened the door. It opened into a *china-closet*. The shelves were neatly draped with scalloped paper; on them was the gilt-edged china, with the dishes missing that had been used at the supper, and which at that moment were being carefully washed and wiped by the two aunts.

Margaret's husband dropped her hand and looked at her. She was trembling a little, and turned to him for help, for some explanation, but in an instant she knew that something was wrong. A cloud had come between them; he was hurt; he was antagonized.

He paused for an appreciable instant, and then said, kindly enough, but in a voice that cut her deeply:

'I am glad this ridiculous thing is ended; don't let us speak of it again.'

'Ended!' said she. 'How ended?' And somehow her voice sounded to her as her mother's voice had when she stood there and questioned her sisters about the little room. She seemed to have to drag her words out. She spoke slowly: 'It seems to me to have only just begun in my case. It was just so with mother when she—'

'I really wish, Margaret, you would let it drop. I don't like to hear you speak of your mother in connection with it. It—' He hesitated, for was not this their wedding-day? 'It doesn't seem quite the thing, quite delicate, you know, to use her name in the matter.'

She saw it all now: *he didn't believe her.* She felt a chill sense of withering under his glance.

'Come,' he added, 'let us go out, or into the dining-room, somewhere, anywhere, only drop this nonsense.'

He went out; he did not take her hand now—he was vexed, baffled, hurt. Had he not given her his sympathy, his attention, his belief—and his hand?—and she was fooling him. What did it mean?—she so truthful, so free from morbidness—a thing he hated. He walked up and down under the poplars, trying to get into the mood to go and join her in the house.

Margaret heard him go out; then she turned and shook the shelves; she reached her hand behind them and tried to push the boards away; she ran out of the house on to the north side and tried to find in the darkness, with her hands, a door, or some steps leading to one. She tore her dress on the old rose-trees, she fell and rose and stumbled, then she sat down on the ground and tried to think. What could she think—was she dreaming?

She went into the house and out into the kitchen, and begged Aunt Maria to tell her about the little room—what had become of it, when had they built the closet, when had they bought the gilt-edged china?

They went on washing dishes and drying them on the spotless towels with methodical exactness; and as they worked they said that there had never been any little room, so far as they knew; the china-closet had always been there, and the gilt-edged china had belonged to their mother, it had always been in the house.

'No, I don't remember that your mother ever asked about any little room,' said Hannah. 'She didn't seem very well that summer, but she never asked about any changes in the house; there hadn't ever been any changes.'

There it was again: not a sign of interest, curiosity, or annoyance, not a spark of memory.

She went out to Hiram. He was telling Mr. Grant about the farm. She had meant to ask him about the room, but her lips were sealed before her husband.

Months afterwards, when time had lessened the sharpness of their feelings, they learned to speculate reasonably about the phenomenon, which Mr. Grant had accepted as something not to be scoffed away, not to be treated as a poor joke, but to be put aside as something inexplicable on any ordinary theory.

Margaret alone in her heart knew that her mother's words carried a deeper significance than she had dreamed of at the time. 'One thing I am glad of, your father knows now,' and she wondered if Roger or she would ever know.

Five years later they were going to Europe. The packing was done; the children were lying asleep, with their travelling things ready to be slipped on for an early start.

Roger had a foreign appointment. They were not to be back in America for some years. She had meant to go up to say good-by to her aunts; but a mother of three children intends to do a great many things that never get done. One thing she had done that very day, and as she paused for a moment between the writing of two notes that must be posted before she went to bed, she said:

'Roger, you remember Rita Lash? Well, she and Cousin Nan go up to the Adirondacks every autumn. They are clever girls, and I have intrusted to them something I want done very much.'

'They are the girls to do it, then, every inch of them.'

'I know it, and they are going to.'

'Well?'

'Why, you see, Roger, that little room—'

'Oh—'

'Yes, I was a coward not to go myself, but I didn't find time, because I hadn't the courage.'

'Oh! *that* was it, was it?'

'Yes, just that. They are going, and they will write us about it.'

'Want to bet?'

'No; I only want to know.'

Rita Lash and Cousin Nan planned to go to Vermont on their way to the Adirondacks. They found they would have three hours between trains, which would give them time to drive up to the Keys farm, and they could still get to the camp that night. But, at the last minute, Rita was prevented from going. Nan had to go to meet the Adirondack party, and she promised to telegraph her when she arrived at the camp. Imagine Rita's amusement when she received this message: 'Safely arrived; went to the Keys farm; it is a little room.'

Rita was amused, because she did not in the least think Nan had been there. She thought it was a hoax; but it put it into her mind to carry the joke further by really stopping herself when she went up, as she meant to do the next week.

She did stop over. She introduced herself to the two maiden ladies, who seemed familiar, as they had been described by Mrs. Grant.

They were, if not cordial, at least not disconcerted at her visit, and willingly showed her over the house. As they did not speak of any other stranger's having been to see them lately, she became confirmed in her belief that Nan had not been there.

In the north room she saw the roses and morning-glory paper on the wall, and also the door that should open into— what?

She asked if she might open it.

'Certainly,' said Hannah; and Maria echoed, 'Certainly.'

She opened it, and found the china-closet. She experienced a certain relief; she at least was not under any spell. Mrs. Grant left it a china-closet; she found it the same. Good.

But she tried to induce the old sisters to remember that there had at various times been certain questions relating to a confusion as to whether the closet had always been a closet. It was no use; their stony eyes gave no sign.

Then she thought of the story of the sea-captain, and said, 'Miss Keys, did you ever have a lounge covered with India chintz, with a figure of a peacock on it, given to you in Salem by a sea-captain, who brought it from India?'

'I dun'no' as I ever did,' said Hannah. That was all. She thought Maria's cheeks were a little flushed, but her eyes were like a stone wall.

She went on that night to the Adirondacks. When Nan and she were alone in their room she said, 'By-the-way, Nan, what did you see at the farm-house? and how did you like Maria and Hannah?'

Nan didn't mistrust that Rita had been there, and she began excitedly to tell her all about her visit. Rita could almost have believed Nan had been there if she hadn't known it was not so. She let her go on for some time, enjoying her enthusiasm, and the impressive way in which she described her opening the door and finding the 'little room.' Then Rita said: 'Now, Nan, that is enough fibbing. I went to the farm myself on my way up yesterday, and there is *no* little room, and there *never* has been any; it is a china-closet, just as Mrs. Grant saw it last.'

She was pretending to be busy unpacking her trunk, and did not look up for a moment; but as Nan did not say anything, she glanced at her over her shoulder. Nan was actually pale, and it was hard to say whether she was most angry or frightened. There was something of both in her look. And then Rita began to explain how her telegram had put her in the spirit of going up there alone. She hadn't meant to cut Nan out. She only thought— Then Nan broke in: 'It isn't that; I am sure you can't think it is that. But I went myself, and you did not go; you can't have been there, for *it is a little room.*'

Oh, what a night they had! They couldn't sleep. They talked and argued, and then kept still for a while, only to break out again, it was so absurd. They both maintained that they had been there, but both felt sure the other one was either crazy or obstinate beyond reason. They were wretched; it was perfectly ridiculous, two friends at odds over such a thing; but there it was—'little room,' 'china-closet,'—'china-closet,' 'little room.'

The next morning Nan was tacking up some tarlatan at a window to keep the midges out. Rita offered to help her, as she had done for the past ten years. Nan's 'No, thanks,' cut her to the heart.

'Nan,' said she, 'come right down from that step-ladder and pack your satchel. The stage leaves in just twenty minutes. We can catch the afternoon express train, and we will go together to the farm. I am either going there or going home. You better go with me.'

Nan didn't say a word. She gathered up the hammer and tacks, and was ready to start when the stage came round.

It meant for them thirty miles of staging and six hours of train, besides crossing the lake; but what of that, compared with having a lie lying round loose between them! Europe would have seemed easy to accomplish, if it would settle the question.

At the little junction in Vermont they found a farmer with a wagon full of meal-bags. They asked him if he could not take them up to the old Keys farm and bring them back in time for the return train, due in two hours.

They had planned to call it a sketching trip, so they said, 'We have been there before, we are artists, and we might find some views worth taking; and we want also to make a short call upon the Misses Keys.'

'Did ye calculate to paint the old *house* in the picture?'

They said it was possible they might do so. They wanted to see it, anyway.

'Waal, I guess you are too late. The *house* burnt down last night, and everything in it.'

1895

GERTRUDE ATHERTON

(1857–1948)

The Striding Place

WEIGALL, continental and detached, tired early of grouse-shooting. To stand propped against a sod fence while his host's workmen routed up the birds with long poles and drove them towards the waiting guns, made him feel himself a parody on the ancestors who had roamed the moors and forests of this West Riding of Yorkshire in hot pursuit of game worth the killing. But when in England in August he always accepted whatever proffered for the season, and invited his host to shoot pheasants on his estates in the South. The amusements of life, he argued, should be accepted with the same philosophy as its ills.

It had been a bad day. A heavy rain had made the moor so spongy that it fairly sprang beneath the feet. Whether or not the grouse had haunts of their own, wherein they were immune from rheumatism, the bag had been small. The women, too, were an unusually dull lot, with the exception of a new-minded *débutante* who bothered Weigall at dinner by demanding the verbal restoration of the vague paintings on the vaulted roof above them.

But it was no one of these things that sat on Weigall's mind as, when the other men went up to bed, he let himself out of the castle and sauntered down to the river. His intimate friend, the companion of his boyhood, the chum of his college days, his fellow-traveller in many lands, the man for whom he possessed stronger affection than for all men, had mysteriously disappeared two days ago, and his track might have sprung to the upper air for all trace he had left behind him. He had been a guest on the adjoining estate during the past week, shooting with the fervor of the true sportsman, making love in the intervals to Adeline Cavan, and apparently in the best of spirits. As far as was known there was nothing to lower his mental

232

mercury, for his rent-roll was a large one, Miss Cavan blushed whenever he looked at her, and, being one of the best shots in England, he was never happier than in August. The suicide theory was preposterous, all agreed, and there was as little reason to believe him murdered. Nevertheless, he had walked out of March Abbey two nights ago without hat or overcoat, and had not been seen since.

The country was being patrolled night and day. A hundred keepers and workmen were beating the woods and poking the bogs on the moors, but as yet not so much as a handkerchief had been found.

Weigall did not believe for a moment that Wyatt Gifford was dead, and although it was impossible not to be affected by the general uneasiness, he was disposed to be more angry than frightened. At Cambridge Gifford had been an incorrigible practical joker, and by no means had outgrown the habit; it would be like him to cut across the country in his evening clothes, board a cattle-train, and amuse himself touching up the picture of the sensation in West Riding.

However, Weigall's affection for his friend was too deep to companion with tranquillity in the present state of doubt, and, instead of going to bed early with the other men, he determined to walk until ready for sleep. He went down to the river and followed the path through the woods. There was no moon, but the stars sprinkled their cold light upon the pretty belt of water flowing placidly past wood and ruin, between green masses of overhanging rocks or sloping banks tangled with tree and shrub, leaping occasionally over stones with the harsh notes of an angry scold, to recover its equanimity the moment the way was clear again.

It was very dark in the depths where Weigall trod. He smiled as he recalled a remark of Gifford's: "An English wood is like a good many other things in life—very promising at a distance, but a hollow mockery when you get within. You see daylight on both sides, and the sun freckles the very bracken. Our woods need the night to make them seem what they ought to be—what they once were, before our ancestors' descendants demanded so much more money, in these so much more various days."

Weigall strolled along, smoking, and thinking of his friend,

his pranks—many of which had done more credit to his imagination than this—and recalling conversations that had lasted
the night through. Just before the end of the London season
they had walked the streets one hot night after a party, discussing the various theories of the soul's destiny. That afternoon they had met at the coffin of a college friend whose mind
had been a blank for the past three years. Some months previously they had called at the asylum to see him. His expression
had been senile, his face imprinted with the record of de-
bauchery. In death the face was placid, intelligent, without
ignoble lineation—the face of the man they had known at college. Weigall and Gifford had had no time to comment there,
and the afternoon and evening were full; but, coming forth
from the house of festivity together, they had reverted almost
at once to the topic.

"I cherish the theory," Gifford had said, "that the soul
sometimes lingers in the body after death. During madness, of
course, it is an impotent prisoner, albeit a conscious one.
Fancy its agony, and its horror! What more natural than that,
when the life-spark goes out, the tortured soul should take
possession of the vacant skull and triumph once more for a few
hours while old friends look their last? It has had time to re-
pent while compelled to crouch and behold the result of its
work, and it has shrived itself into a state of comparative purity.
If I had my way, I should stay inside my bones until the coffin
had gone into its niche, that I might obviate for my poor old
comrade the tragic impersonality of death. And I should like
to see justice done to it, as it were—to see it lowered among its
ancestors with the ceremony and solemnity that are its due. I
am afraid that if I dissevered myself too quickly, I should yield
to curiosity and hasten to investigate the mysteries of space."

"You believe in the soul as an independent entity, then—
that it and the vital principle are not one and the same?"

"Absolutely. The body and soul are twins, life comrades—
sometimes friends, sometimes enemies, but always loyal in the
last instance. Some day, when I am tired of the world, I shall
go to India and become a mahatma, solely for the pleasure of
receiving proof during life of this independent relationship."

"Suppose you were not sealed up properly, and returned
after one of your astral flights to find your earthly part unfit for

habitation? It is an experiment I don't think I should care to try, unless even juggling with soul and flesh had palled."

"That would not be an uninteresting predicament. I should rather enjoy experimenting with broken machinery."

The high wild roar of water smote suddenly upon Weigall's ear and checked his memories. He left the wood and walked out on the huge slippery stones which nearly close the River Wharfe at this point, and watched the waters boil down into the narrow pass with their furious untiring energy. The black quiet of the woods rose high on either side. The stars seemed colder and whiter just above. On either hand the perspective of the river might have run into a rayless cavern. There was no lonelier spot in England, nor one which had the right to claim so many ghosts, if ghosts there were.

Weigall was not a coward, but he recalled uncomfortably the tales of those that had been done to death in the Strid.* Wordsworth's Boy of Egremond had been disposed of by the practical Whitaker; but countless others, more venturesome than wise, had gone down into that narrow boiling course, never to appear in the still pool a few yards beyond. Below the great rocks which form the walls of the Strid was believed to be a natural vault, on to whose shelves the dead were drawn. The spot had an ugly fascination. Weigall stood, visioning skeletons, uncoffined and green, the home of the eyeless things which had devoured all that had covered and filled that rattling symbol of man's mortality; then fell to wondering if any one had attempted to leap the Strid of late. It was covered with slime; he had never seen it look so treacherous.

He shuddered and turned away, impelled, despite his manhood, to flee the spot. As he did so, something tossing in the foam below the fall—something as white, yet independent of it—caught his eye and arrested his step. Then he saw that it was describing a contrary motion to the rushing water—an upward backward motion. Weigall stood rigid, breathless; he fancied he heard the crackling of his hair. Was that a hand? It

*"This striding place is called the 'Strid,'
   A name which it took of yore;
 A thousand years hath it borne the name,
   And it shall a thousand more."

thrust itself still higher above the boiling foam, turned sidewise, and four frantic fingers were distinctly visible against the
black rock beyond.

Weigall's superstitious terror left him. A man was there,
struggling to free himself from the suction beneath the Strid,
swept down, doubtless, but a moment before his arrival, perhaps as he stood with his back to the current.

He stepped as close to the edge as he dared. The hand doubled as if in imprecation, shaking savagely in the face of that
force which leaves its creatures to immutable law; then spread
wide again, clutching, expanding, crying for help as audibly as
the human voice.

Weigall dashed to the nearest tree, dragged and twisted off a
branch with his strong arms, and returned as swiftly to the
Strid. The hand was in the same place, still gesticulating as
wildly; the body was undoubtedly caught in the rocks below,
perhaps already half-way along one of those hideous shelves.
Weigall let himself down upon a lower rock, braced his shoulder against the mass beside him, then, leaning out over the
water, thrust the branch into the hand. The fingers clutched it
convulsively. Weigall tugged powerfully, his own feet dragged
perilously near the edge. For a moment he produced no impression, then an arm shot above the waters.

The blood sprang to Weigall's head; he was choked with
the impression that the Strid had him in her roaring hold, and
he saw nothing. Then the mist cleared. The hand and arm
were nearer, although the rest of the body was still concealed
by the foam. Weigall peered out with distended eyes. The
meagre light revealed in the cuffs links of a peculiar device.
The fingers clutching the branch were as familiar.

Weigall forgot the slippery stones, the terrible death if he
stepped too far. He pulled with passionate will and muscle.
Memories flung themselves into the hot light of his brain,
trooping rapidly upon each other's heels, as in the thought of
the drowning. Most of the pleasures of his life, good and bad,
were identified in some way with this friend. Scenes of college
days, of travel, where they had deliberately sought adventure
and stood between one another and death upon more occasions
than one, of hours of delightful companionship among the
treasures of art, and others in the pursuit of pleasure, flashed

like the changing particles of a kaleidoscope. Weigall had loved several women; but he would have flouted in these moments the thought that he had ever loved any woman as he loved Wyatt Gifford. There were so many charming women in the world, and in the thirty-two years of his life he had never known another man to whom he had cared to give his intimate friendship.

He threw himself on his face. His wrists were cracking, the skin was torn from his hands. The fingers still gripped the stick. There was life in them yet.

Suddenly something gave way. The hand swung about, tearing the branch from Weigall's grasp. The body had been liberated and flung outward, though still submerged by the foam and spray.

Weigall scrambled to his feet and sprang along the rocks, knowing that the danger from suction was over and that Gifford must be carried straight to the quiet pool. Gifford was a fish in the water and could live under it longer than most men. If he survived this, it would not be the first time that his pluck and science had saved him from drowning.

Weigall reached the pool. A man in his evening clothes floated on it, his face turned towards a projecting rock over which his arm had fallen, upholding the body. The hand that had held the branch hung limply over the rock, its white reflection visible in the black water. Weigall plunged into the shallow pool, lifted Gifford in his arms and returned to the bank. He laid the body down and threw off his coat that he might be the freer to practise the methods of resuscitation. He was glad of the moment's respite. The valiant life in the man might have been exhausted in that last struggle. He had not dared to look at his face, to put his ear to the heart. The hesitation lasted but a moment. There was no time to lose.

He turned to his prostrate friend. As he did so, something strange and disagreeable smote his senses. For a half-moment he did not appreciate its nature. Then his teeth clacked together, his feet, his outstretched arms pointed towards the woods. But he sprang to the side of the man and bent down and peered into his face. There was no face.

1896

EMMA FRANCIS DAWSON

(1851–1926)

An Itinerant House

"Eternal longing with eternal pain,
Want without hope, and memory saddening all,
All congregated failure and despair
Shall wander there through some old maze of wrong."

"His *wife?*" cried Felipa.

"Yes," I answered, unwillingly; for until the steamer brought Mrs. Anson I believed in this Mexican woman's right to that name. I felt sorry for the bright eyes and kind heart that had cheered Anson's lodgers through weary months of early days in San Francisco.

She burst into tears. None of us knew how to comfort her. Dering spoke first: "Beauty always wins friends."

Between her sobs she repeated one of the pithy sayings of her language: "It is as easy to find a lover as to keep a friend, but as hard to find a friend as to keep a lover."

"Yes," said Volz, "a new friendship is like a new string to your guitar—you are not sure what its tone may prove, nor how soon it may break."

"But at least its falsity is learned at once," she sobbed.

"Is it possible," I asked, "that you had no suspicion?"

"None. He told me—" She ended in a fresh gust of tears.

"The old story," muttered Dering. "Marryatt's skipper was right in thinking everything that once happened would come again somewhere."

Anson came. He had left the new-comer at the Niantic, on pretense of putting his house in order. Felipa turned on him before we could go.

"Is this true?" she cried.

Without reply he went to the window and stood looking out. She sprang toward him, with rage distorting her face.

"Coward!" she screamed, in fierce scorn.

Then she fell senseless. Two doctors were called. One said

238

she was dead. The other, at first doubtful, vainly tried hot sealing-wax and other tests. After thirty-six hours her funeral was planned. Yet Dering, once medical student, had seen an electric current used in such a case in Vienna, and wanted to try it. That night, he, Volz, and I offered to watch. When all was still, Dering, who had smuggled in the simple things needed, began his weird work.

"Is it not too late?" I asked.

"Every corpse," said he, "can be thus excited soon after death, for a brief time only, and but once. If the body is not lifeless, the electric current has power at any time."

Volz, too nervous to stay near, stood in the door open to the dark hall. It was a dreadful sight. The dead woman's breast rose and fell; smiles and frowns flitted across her face.

"The body begins to react finely," cried Dering, making Volz open the windows, while I wrapped hot blankets round Felipa, and he instilled clear coffee and brandy.

"It seems like sacrilege! Let her alone!" I exclaimed. "Better dead than alive!"

"My God! say not that!" cried Volz; "the nerve which hears is last to die. She may know all we say."

"Musical bosh!" I muttered.

"Perhaps not," said Dering; "in magnetic sleep that nerve can be roused."

The night seemed endless. The room gained an uncanny look, the macaws on the gaudy, old-fashioned wall-paper seemed fluttering and changing places. Volz crouched in a heap near the door. Dering stood by Felipa, watching closely. I paced the shadowy room, looked at the gleam of the moon on the bay, listened to the soughing wind in the gum-trees mocking the sea, and tried to recall more cheerful scenes, but always bent under the weight of that fearful test going on beside me. Where was her soul? Beyond the stars, in the room with us, or "like trodden snowdrift melting in the dark?" Volz came behind, startling me by grasping my elbow.

"Shall I not play?" he whispered. "Familiar music is remembrance changed to sound—it brings the past as perfume does. Gypsy music in her ear would be like holding wild flowers to her nostrils."

"Ask Dering," I said; "he will know best."

I heard him urging Dering.

"She has gypsy blood," he said; "their music will rouse her."

Dering unwillingly agreed. "But nothing abrupt—begin low," said he.

Vaguely uneasy, I turned to object; but Volz had gone for his violin. Far off arose a soft, wavering, sleepy strain, like a wind blowing over a field of poppies. He passed, in slow, dramatic style, through the hall, playing on the way. As he came in, oddly sustained notes trembled like sighs and sobs; these were by degrees subdued, though with spasmodic outbursts, amid a grand movement as of phantom shapes through cloud-land. One heart-rending phrase recurring as of one of the shadowy host striving to break loose, but beaten back by impalpable throngs, numberless grace-notes trailing their sparks like fireworks. No music of our intervals and our rhythms, but perplexing in its charm like a draught that maddens. Time, space, our very identities, were consumed in this white heat of sound. I held my breath. I caught his arm.

"It is too bold and distracting," I cried. "It is enough to kill us! Do you expect to torment her back? How can it affect us so?"

"Because," he answered, laying down his violin and wiping his brow, "in the gypsy minor scale the fourth and seventh are augmented. The sixth is diminished. The frequent augmentation of the fourth makes that sense of unrest."

"Bah! Technical terms make it no plainer," I said, returning to the window.

He played a whispered, merry discordance, resolving into click of castanets, laugh, and dance of a gypsy camp. Out of the whirl of flying steps and tremolo of tambourines rose a tender voice, asking, denying, sighing, imploring, passing into an over-ruling, long-drawn call that vibrated in widening rings to reach the farthest horizon—nay, beyond land or sea, "east of the sun, west of the moon." With a rush returned the wild jollity of men's bass laughter, women's shrill reply, the stir of the gypsy camp. This dropped behind vague, rolling measures of clouds and chaos, where to and fro floated grotesque goblins of grace-notes like the fancies of a madman; struggling, rising, falling, vain-reaching strains; fierce cries like commands. The music seemed another vital essence thrilling us with its own emotion.

"No more, no more!" I cried, half gasping, and grasping Volz's arm. "What is it, Dering?"

He had staggered from the bed and was trying to see his watch. "It is just forty-four hours!" he said, pointing to Felipa.

Her eyes were open! We were alarmed as if doing wrong and silently watched her. Fifteen minutes later her lips formed one word:

"Idiots!"

Half an hour after she flung the violin from bed to floor, but would not speak. People began to stir about the house. The prosaic sounds jarred on our strained nerves. We felt brought from another sphere. Volz and I were going, but Felipa's up-raised hand kept us. She sat up, looking a ghastly vision. Turning first toward me she quoted my words:

" 'Better dead than alive!' True. You knew I would be glad to die. What right had you to bring me back? God's curses on you! I was dead. Then came agony. I heard your voices. I thought we were all in hell. Then I found how by your evil cunning I was to be forced to live. It was like an awful night-mare. I shall not forget you, nor you me. These very walls shall remember—here, where I have been so tortured no one shall have peace! Fools! Leave me! Never come in this room again!"

We went, all talking at once, Dering angry at her mood; Volz, sorry he had not reached a soothing *pianissimo* passage; I, owning we had no right to make the test. We saw her but once more, when with a threatening nod toward us she left the house.

From that time a gloom settled over the place. Mrs. Anson proved a hard-faced, cold-hearted, Cape Cod woman, a scold and drudge, who hated us as much as we disliked her. Home-sick and unhappy, she soon went East and died. Within a year, Anson was found dead where he had gone hunting in the Saucelito woods, supposed a suicide; Dering was hung by the Vigilantes, and the rest were scattered on the four winds. Volz and I were last to go. The night before we sailed, he for Aus-tralia, I for New York, he said:

"I am sorry for those who come after us in this house."

"Not knowing of any tragedy here," I said, "they will not feel its influence."

"They must feel it," he insisted; "it is written in the Proverbs, 'Evil shall not depart from his house.' "

Some years later, I was among passengers embarking at New York for California, when there was a cry of "Man overboard!" In the confusion of his rescue, among heartless and pitiful talk, I overheard one man declare that the drowned might be revived.

"Oh, yes!" cried a well-known voice behind me. "But they might not thank you."

I turned—to find Volz! He was coming out with Wynne, the actor. Enjoying our comradeship on the voyage, on reaching San Francisco we took rooms together, on Bush Street, in an old house with a large garden. Volz became leader of the orchestra, and Wynne, leading man at the same theatre. Lest my folks, a Maine deacon's family, should think I was on the road to ruin, I told in letters home only of the city missionary in the house.

Volz was hard worked. Wynne was not much liked. My business went wrong. It rained for many weeks; to this we laid the discomfort that grew to weigh on us. Volz wreaked his sense of it on his violin, adding to the torment of Wynne and myself, for to lonesome anxious souls "the demon in music" shows horns and cloven foot in the trying sounds of practice. One Sunday Volz played the "Witches Dance," the "Dream," and "The long, long weary day."

"I can bear it no longer!" said Wynne. "I feel like the haunted Matthias in 'The Bells.' If I could feel so when acting such parts, it would make my fortune. But I feel it only here."

"I think," said Volz, "it is the *gloria fonda* bush near the window; the scent is too strong." He dashed off Strauss' fretful, conflicting "Hurry and Delay."

"There, there! It is too much," said I. "You express my feelings."

He looked doubtful. "Put it in words," said he.

"How can I?" I said. "When our firm sent me abroad, I went sight-seeing among old palaces, whose Gobelin tapestries framed in their walls were faded to gray phantoms of pictures, but out of some the thrilling eyes followed me till I could not stay in their range. My feeling here is the uneasy one of being watched."

"Ha!" said Volz. "You remind me of Heine, when he wrote

from Livorno. He knew no Italian, but the old palaces whispered secrets unheard by day. The moon was interpreter, knew the lapidary style, translated to dialect of his heart."

"'Strange effects after the moon,'" mused Wynne. "That gives new meaning to Kent's threat: 'I'll make a sop o' the moonshine of you!'"

Volz went on: "Heine wrote: 'The stones here speak to me, and I know their mute language. Also, they seem deeply to feel what I think. So a broken column of the old Roman times, an old tower of Lombardy, a weather-beaten Gothic piece of a pillar understands me well. But I am a ruin myself, wandering among ruins.'"

"Perhaps, like Poe's hero," said I, "'I have imbibed shadows of fallen columns at Balbec, and Tadmor, and Persepolis, until my very soul has become a ruin.'"

"But I, too," said Wynne, "feel the unrest of Tannhauser:

'Alas! what seek I here, or anywhere,
Whose way of life is like the crumbled stair
That winds and winds about a ruined tower,
And leads no whither.'"

"I am oppressed," Volz owned, "as if some one in my presence was suffering deeply."

"I feel," said Wynne, "as if the scene was not set right for the performance now going on. There is a hitch and drag somewhere—scene-shifters on a strike. Happy are you poets and musicians, who can express what is vague."

Volz laughed. "As in Liszt's oratorio of 'Christus,'" said he, "where a sharp, ear-piercing *sostenuto* on the piccolo-flute shows the shining of the star of Bethlehem." He turned to me. "Schubert's 'Wanderer' always recalls to me a house you and I know to be under a ban."

"Haunted?" asked Wynne. "Of all speculative theories, St. Martin's sends the most cold thrills up one's back. He said none of the dead come back, but some stay."

"What we Germans call *gebannt*—tied to one spot," said Volz. "But this is no ghost, only a proof of what a German psychologist holds, that the magnetic man is a spirit."

"Go on, 'and tell quaint lies'—I like them," said Wynne.

I told in brief outline, with no names, the tale Volz and I

knew, while we strolled to Telegraph Hill, passing five streets blocked by the roving houses common to San Francisco.

Wynne said: "They seem to have minds of their own, with their entrances and exits in a *moving* drama."

"Sort of 'Poor Jo's,'" said I.

"Castles in chess," said Volz.

"Io-like," said Wynne, "with a gad in their hearts that forever drives them on."

A few foreign sailors lounged on the hill top, looking at the view. The wind blew such a gale we did not stay. The steps we had known, cut in the side, were gone. Where the old house used to be, goats were browsing.

"Perchance we do inhabit it but now," mockingly cried Wynne; "methinks it must be so."

"Then," said Volz, thoughtfully, "it might be what Germans call 'far-working'—acted in distance—that affects us."

"What do you mean?" I asked. "Do you know anything of her now?"

"I know she went to Mexico," said he; "that is all."

"What is 'far-working?'" asked Wynne. "If I could act in the distance, and here too—'what larks!'"

"Yes—'if,'" said I. "Think how all our lives turn on that pivot. Suppose Hawthorne's offer to join Wilkes' exploring expedition had been taken!"

"Only to wills that know no 'if' is 'far-working' possible," said Volz. "Substance or space can no more hinder this force than the one of mineral magnetism. Passavent joins it with pictures falling, or watches stopping at the time of a death. In sleep-walking, some kinds of illness, or nearness of death, the nervous ether is not so closely allied to its material conductors, the nerves, and may be loosened to act from afar, the surest where blood or feeling makes attraction or repulsion."

Wynne in the two voices of the play repeated:

> "VICTOR.—Where is the gentleman?
> CHISPE.—As the old song says:
> > 'His body is in Segovia,
> > His soul is in Madrid.'"

We could learn about the house we were in only that five families had moved in and out during the last year. Wynne resolved to shake off the gloom that wrapped us. In struggles to defy it, he on the strength of a thousand-dollar benefit, made one payment on the house and began repairs.

On an off-night he was vainly trying to study a new part. Volz advised the relief to his nerves of reciting the dream scene from "The Bells," reminding him he had compared it with his restlessness there. Wynne denied it.

"Yes," said Volz, "where the mesmerizer forces Matthias to confess."

But Wynne refused, as if vexed, till Volz offered to show in music his own mood, and I agreed to read some rhymes about mine. Volz was long tuning his violin.

"I feel," he said, "as if the passers-by would hear a secret. Music is such a subtle expression of emotion—like flower-odor rolls far and affects the stranger. Hearken! In Heine's 'Reise-bilder,' as the cross was thrown ringing on the banquet table of the gods, they grew dumb and pale, and even paler till they melted in mist. So shall you at the long-drawn wail of my violin grow breathless, and fade from each other's sight."

The music closed round us, and we waited in its deep solitude. One brief, sad phrase fell from airy heights to lowest depths into a sea of sound, whose harmonious eddies as they widened breathed of passion and pain, now swooning, now reviving, with odd pauses and sighs that rose to cries of despair, but the tormenting first strain recurring fainter and fainter, as if drowning, drowning, drowned—yet floating back for repeated last plaint, as if not to be quelled, and closing, as it began, the whole.

As I read the name of my verses, Volz murmured: "*Les Nuits Blanches*. No. 4. Stephen Heller."

SLEEPLESS NIGHTS.

Against the garden's mossy paling
  I lean, and wish the night away,
Whose faint, unequal shadows trailing
  Seem but a dream of those of day.

Sleep burdens blossom, bud, and leaf,
  My soul alone aspires, dilates,

Yearns to forget its care and grief—
    No bath of sleep its pain abates.

How dread these dreams of wide-eyed nights!
    What is, and is not, both I rue,
My wild thoughts fly like wand'ring kites,
    No peace falls with this balmy dew.

Through slumb'rous stillness, scarcely stirred
    By sudden trembles, as when shifts
O'er placid pool some skimming bird,
    Its Lethean bowl a poppy lifts.

If one deep draught my doubts could solve,
    The world might bubble down its brim,
Like Cleopatra's pearl dissolve,
    With all my dreams within its rim.

What should I know but calm repose?
    How feel, recalling this lost sphere?
Alas! the fabled poppy shows
    Upon its bleeding heart—a tear!

Wynne unwillingly began to recite: "'I fear nothing, but dreams are dreams—'"

He stammered, could not go on, and fell to the floor. We got him to bed. He never spoke sanely after. His wild fancies appalled us watching him all night.

"Avaunt Sathanas! That's not my cue," he muttered. "A full house to-night. How could Talma forget how the crowd looked, and fancy it a pack of skeletons? Tell Volz to keep the violins playing through this scene, it works me up as well as thrills the audience. Oh, what tiresome nights I have lately, always dreaming of scenes where rival women move, as in 'Court and Stage,' where, all masked, the king makes love to Frances Stewart before the queen's face! How do I try to cure it? 'And being thus frighted, swear a prayer or two and sleep again.' Madame, you're late; you've too little rouge; you'll look ghastly. We're not called yet; let's rehearse our scene. Now, then, I enter left, pass to the window. You cry 'is this true?' and faint. All crowd about. Quick curtain."

Volz and I looked at each other.

"Can our magnetism make his senses so sharp that he knows what is in our minds?" he asked me.

"Nonsense!" I said. "Memory, laudanum, and whisky."

"There," Wynne went on, "the orchestra is stopping. They've rung up the curtain. Don't hold me. The stage waits, yet how can I go outside my door to step on dead bodies? Street and sidewalk are knee-deep with them. They rise and curse me for disturbing them. I lift my cane to strike. It turns to a snake, whose slimy body writhes in my hand. Trying to hold it from biting me, my nails cut my palm till blood streams to drown the snake."

He awed us not alone from having no control of his thoughts, but because there came now and then a strange influx of emotion as if other souls passed in and out of his body.

"Is this hell?" he groaned. "What blank darkness! Where am I? What is that infernal music haunting me through all space? If I could only escape it I need not go back to earth—to that room where I feel choked, where the very wall paper frets me with its flaunting birds flying to and fro, mocking my fettered state. 'Here, here in the very den of the wolf!' Hallo, Benvolio, call-boy's hunting you. Romeo's gone on.

'See where he steals—
Locked in some gloomy covert under key
Of cautionary silence, with his arms
Threaded, like these cross-boughs, in sorrow's knot.'

What is this dread that weighs like a nightmare? 'I do not fear; like Macbeth, I only inhabit trembling.' 'For one of them—she is in hell already, and burns, poor soul! For the other'—Ah! must I die here, alone in the woods, felled by a coward, Indian-like, from behind a tree? None of the boys will know. 'I just now come from a whole world of mad women that had almost—what, is she dead?' Poor Felipa!"

"Did you tell him her name?" I asked Volz.

"No," said he. "Can one man's madness be another's real life?"

"Blood was spilt—the avenger's wing hovered above my house," raved Wynne. "What are these lights, hundreds of them—serpent's eyes? Is it the audience—coiled, many-headed monster, following me round the world? Why do they hiss? I've played this part a hundred times. 'Taught by Rage, and Hunger, and Despair?' Do they, full-fed, well-clothed, light-hearted, know how to judge me? 'A plague on both your houses!' What is that flame? Fire that consumes my vitals—spon-ta-neous combustion! It is then possible. Water! water!"

The doctor said there had been some great strain on Wynne's mind. He sank fast, though we did all we could. Toward morning I turned to Volz with the words:

"He is dead."

The city missionary was passing the open door. He grimly muttered:

"Better dead than alive!"

"My God! say not that!" cried Volz. "The nerve which hears is last to die. He may know——"

He faltered. We stood aghast. The room grew suddenly familiar. I tore off a strip of the gray tint on the walls. Under it we found the old paper with its bright macaws.

"Ah, ha!" Volz said; "will you now deny my theory of 'far-working?'"

Dazed, I could barely murmur: "Then people *can* be affected by it!"

"Certainly," said he, "as rubbed glasses gain electric power."

Within a week we sailed—he for Brazil, I for New York.

Several years after, at Sacramento, Arne, an artist I had known abroad, found me on the overland train, and on reaching San Francisco urged me to go where he lodged.

"I am low-spirited here," he said; "I don't know why."

I stopped short on the crowded wharf. "Where do you live?" I asked.

"Far up Market Street," said he.

"What sort of a house?" I insisted.

"Oh—nothing modern—over a store," he answered.

Reassured, I went with him. He lived in a jumble of easels, portfolios, paint, canvas, bits of statuary, casts, carvings, foils, red curtains, Chinese goatskins, woodcuts, photographs, sketches, and unfinished pictures. On the wall hung a scene from "The Wandering Jew," as we saw it at the Adelphi, in London, where in the Arctic regions he sees visions foreshadowing the future of his race. Under it was quoted:

——"All in my mind is confused, nor can I dissever
The mould of the visible world from the shape of my
      thought in me—
The Inward and Outward are fused, and through them
      murmur forever
The sorrow whose sound is the wind and the roar of the
      limitless sea."

"Do you remember," Arne asked, "when we saw that play? Both younger and more hopeful. How has the world used you? As for me, I have done nothing since I came here but that sketch, finished months ago. I have not lost ambition, but I feel fettered."

"Absinthe?—opium?—tobacco?" I hinted.

"Neither," he answered. "I try to work, but visions, widely different from what I will, crowd on me, as on the Jew in the play. Not the unconscious brain action all thinkers know, but a dictation from without. No rush of creative impulses, but a dragging sense of something else I ought to paint."

"Briefly," I said, "you are a 'Haunted Man.'"

"Haunted by a willful design," said he. "I feel as if something had happened somewhere which I *must* show."

"What is it like?" I asked.

"I wish I could tell you," he replied. "But only odd bits change places, like looking in a kaleidoscope; yet all cluster around one centre."

One day, looking over his portfolios, I found an old *Temple Bar*, which he said he kept for this passage—which he read to me—from T. A. Trollope's "Artist's Tragedy:"

"The old walls and ceilings and floors must be saturated with the exhalations of human emotions! These lintels, doorways, and stairs have become, by long use and homeliness, dear to human hearts, and have become so intimately blended a portion of the mental furniture of human lives, that they have contributed their part to the formation of human characters. Such facts and considerations have gone to the fashioning of the mental habitudes of all of us. If all could have been recorded! If emotion had the property of photographing itself on the surfaces of the walls which had witnessed it! Even if only passion, when translated into acts, could have done so! Ah, what palimpsests! What deciphering of tangled records! What skillful separation of successive layers of 'passionography!'"

"I know a room," said Arne, "thronged with acts that elbow me from my work and fill me with unrest."

I looked at him in mute surprise.

"I suppose," he went on, "such things do not interest you."

"No—yes," I stammered. "I have marked in traveling how lonely houses change their expression as you come near, pass, and leave them. Some frown, others smile. The Bible buildings had life of their own and human diseases; the priests cursed or blessed them as men."

"Houses seem to remember," said he. "Some rooms oppress us with a sense of lives that have been lived in them."

"That," I said, "is like Draper's theory of shadows on walls always staying. He shows how after a breath passes over a coin or key, its spectral outline remains for months after the substance is removed. But can the mist of circumstance sweeping over us make our vacant places hold any trace of us?"

"Why not? Who can deny it? Why do you look at me so?" he asked.

I could not tell him the sad tale. I hesitated; then said: "I was thinking of Volz, a friend I had, who not only believed in what Bulwer calls 'a power akin to mesmerism and superior to it, once called Magic, and that it might reach over the dead, so far as their experience on earth,' but also in animal magnetism from any distance."

Arne grew queerly excited. "If Time and Space exist but in our thoughts, why should it not be true?" said he. "Macdonald's lover cries, 'That which has been is, and the Past can never cease. She is mine, and I shall find her—what matters it when, or where, or how?'" He sighed. "In Acapulco, a year ago, I saw a woman who has been before me ever since—the centre of the circling, changing, crude fancies that trouble me."

"Did you know her?" I asked.

'No, nor anything about her, not even her name. It is like a spell. I must paint her before anything else, but I cannot yet decide how. I feel sure she has played a tragic part in some life-drama."

"Swinburne's queen of panthers," I hinted.

"Yes. But I was not in love. Love I must forego. I am not a man with an income."

"I know you are not a nincompoop!" I said, always trying to

change such themes by a jest. I could not tell him I knew a place which had the influence he talked of. I could not re-visit that house.

Soon after he told me he had begun his picture, but would not show it. He complained that one figure kept its back toward him. He worked on it till he fell ill. Even then he hid it. "Only a layer of passionography," he said.

I grew restless. I thought his mood affected mine. It was a torment as well as a puzzle to me that his whole talk should be of the influence of houses, rooms, even personal property that had known other owners. Once I asked him if he had anything like the brown coat Sheridan swore drew ill-luck to him.

"Sometimes I think," he answered, "it is this special brown paint artists prize which affects me. It is made from the best as-phaltum, and that can be got only from Egyptian mummy-cloths. Very likely dust of the mummies is ground in it. I ought to feel their ill-will."

One day I went to Saucelito. In the still woods I forgot my unrest till coming to the stream where, as I suddenly remem-bered, Anson was found dead, a dread took me which I tried to lose by putting into rhyme. Turning my pockets at night, I crumpled the page I had written on, and threw it on the floor.

In uneasy sleep I dreamed I was again in Paris, not where I liked to recall being, but at "Bullier's," and in war-time. The bald, spectacled leader of the orchestra, leaning back, sham-ming sleep, while a dancing, stamping, screaming crowd wave tri-colored flags, and call for the "Chant du Depart." Three thousand voices in a rushing roar that makes the twenty thou-sand lights waver, in spasmodic but steady chorus:

> "Les departs—parts—parts!
> Les departs—parts—parts!
> Les departs—parts—parts!"

Roused, I supposed by passing rioters, I did not try to sleep again, but rose to write a letter for the early mail. As I struck a light I saw, smoothed out on the table, the wrinkled page I had cast aside. The ink was yet wet on two lines added to each verse. A chill crept over me as I read:

FOREST MURMURS.

Across the woodland bridge I pass,
   And sway its three long, narrow planks,
To mark how gliding waters glass
   Bright blossoms doubled ranks on ranks;
And how through tangle of the ferns
Floats incense from veiled flower-urns,
What would the babbling brook reveal?
What may these trembling depths conceal?
Dread secret of the dense woods, held
With restless shudders horror-spelled!

How shift the shadows of the wood,
   As if it tossed in troubled sleep!
Strange whispers, vaguely understood,
   Above, below, around me creep;
While in the sombre-shadowed stream
Great scarlet splashes far down gleam,
The odd-reflected, stately shapes
Of cardinals in crimson capes;
Not those—but spectral pools of blood
That stain these sands through strongest flood!

Like blare of trumpets through black nights—
   Or sunset clouds before a storm—
Are these red phantom water-sprites
   That mock me with fantastic form;
With flitting of the last year's bird
Fled ripples that its low flight stirred—
How should these rushing waters learn
Aught but the bend of this year's fern?
The lonesome wood, with bated breath,
Hints of a hidden blow—and death!

I could not stay alone. I ran to Arne's room. As I knocked,
the falling of some light thing within made me think he was
stirring. I went in. He sat in the moonlight, back to me before
his easel. The picture on it might be the one he kept secret. I
would not look. I went to his side and touched him. He had
been dead for hours! I turned the unseen canvas to the wall.

Next day I packed and planned to go East. I paid the landlady not to send Arne's body to the morgue, and watched it that
night, when a sudden memory swept over me like a tidal wave.
There was a likeness in the room to one where I had before
watched the dead. Yes—there were the windows, there the
doors—just here stood the bed, in the same spot I sat. What
wildness was in the air of San Francisco!

To put such crazy thoughts to flight I would look at Arne's
last work. Yet I wavered, and more than once turned away
after laying my hand on it. At last I snatched it, placed it on the
easel and lighted the nearest gas-burner before looking at it.
Then—great heavens! How had this vision come to Arne? It
was the scene where Felipa cursed us. Every detail of the room
reproduced, even the gay birds on the wall-paper, and her
flower-pots. The figures and faces of Dering and Volz were
true as hers, and in the figure with averted face which Arne had
said kept its back to him, I knew—myself! What strange insight had he gained by looking at Felipa? It was like the man
who trembled before the unknown portrait of the Marquise de
Brinvilliers.

How long I gazed at the picture I do not know. I heard,
without heeding, the doorbell ring and steps along the hall.
Voices. Some one looking at rooms. The landlady, saying this
room was to let, but unwilling to show it, forced to own its last
tenant lay there dead. This seemed no shock to the stranger.

"Well," said her shrill tones, "poor as he was he's better
dead than alive!"

The door opened as a well-known voice cried: "My God!
say not that! The nerve which hears is last to die—"

Volz stood before me! Awe-struck, we looked at each other
in silence. Then he waved his hand to and fro before his eyes.

"Is this a dream?" he said. "There," pointing to the bed;
"you"—to me; "the same words—the very room! Is it our
fate?"

I pointed to the picture and to Arne. "The last work of this
man, who thought it a fancy sketch?"

While Volz stood dumb and motionless before it, the landlady spoke:

"Then you know the place. Can you tell what ails it? There

have been suicides in this room. No one prospers in the house. My cousin, who is a house-mover, warned me against taking it. He says before the store was put under it here it stood on Bush Street, and before that on Telegraph Hill."

Volz clutched my arm. "It is 'The Flying Dutchman' of a house!" he cried, and drew me fast down stairs and out into a dense fog which made the world seem a tale that was told, blotting out all but our two slanting forms, bent as by what poor Wynne would have called "a blast from hell," hurrying blindly away. I heard the voice of Volz as if from afar: "The magnetic man *is* a spirit!"

1897

MARY WILKINS FREEMAN

(1852–1930)

Luella Miller

CLOSE to the village street stood the one-story house in which Luella Miller, who had an evil name in the village, had dwelt. She had been dead for years, yet there were those in the village who, in spite of the clearer light which comes on a vantage-point from a long-past danger, half believed in the tale which they had heard from their childhood. In their hearts, although they scarcely would have owned it, was a survival of the wild horror and frenzied fear of their ancestors who had dwelt in the same age with Luella Miller. Young people even would stare with a shudder at the old house as they passed, and children never played around it as was their wont around an untenanted building. Not a window in the old Miller house was broken: the panes reflected the morning sunlight in patches of emerald and blue, and the latch of the sagging front door was never lifted, although no bolt secured it. Since Luella Miller had been carried out of it, the house had had no tenant except one friendless old soul who had no choice between that and the far-off shelter of the open sky. This old woman, who had survived her kindred and friends, lived in the house one week, then one morning no smoke came out of the chimney, and a body of neighbours, a score strong, entered and found her dead in her bed. There were dark whispers as to the cause of her death, and there were those who testified to an expression of fear so exalted that it showed forth the state of the departing soul upon the dead face. The old woman had been hale and hearty when she entered the house, and in seven days she was dead; it seemed that she had fallen a victim to some uncanny power. The minister talked in the pulpit with covert severity against the sin of superstition; still the belief prevailed. Not a soul in the village but would have chosen the almshouse rather than that dwelling. No vagrant, if he heard the tale, would seek shelter beneath that old roof, unhallowed by nearly half a century of superstitious fear.

There was only one person in the village who had actually known Luella Miller. That person was a woman well over eighty, but a marvel of vitality and unextinct youth. Straight as an arrow, with the spring of one recently let loose from the bow of life, she moved about the streets, and she always went to church, rain or shine. She had never married, and had lived alone for years in a house across the road from Luella Miller's.

This woman had none of the garrulousness of age, but never in all her life had she ever held her tongue for any will save her own, and she never spared the truth when she essayed to present it. She it was who bore testimony to the life, evil, though possibly wittingly or designedly so, of Luella Miller, and to her personal appearance. When this old woman spoke—and she had the gift of description, although her thoughts were clothed in the rude vernacular of her native village—one could seem to see Luella Miller as she had really looked. According to this woman, Lydia Anderson by name, Luella Miller had been a beauty of a type rather unusual in New England. She had been a slight, pliant sort of creature, as ready with a strong yielding to fate and as unbreakable as a willow. She had glimmering lengths of straight, fair hair, which she wore softly looped round a long, lovely face. She had blue eyes full of soft pleading, little slender, clinging hands, and a wonderful grace of motion and attitude.

"Luella Miller used to sit in a way nobody else could if they sat up and studied a week of Sundays," said Lydia Anderson, "and it was a sight to see her walk. If one of them willows over there on the edge of the brook could start up and get its roots free of the ground, and move off, it would go just the way Luella Miller used to. She had a green shot silk she used to wear, too, and a hat with green ribbon streamers, and a lace veil blowing across her face and out sideways, and a green ribbon flyin' from her waist. That was what she came out bride in when she married Erastus Miller. Her name before she was married was Hill. There was always a sight of 'l's' in her name, married or single. Erastus Miller was good lookin', too, better lookin' than Luella. Sometimes I used to think that Luella wa'n't so handsome after all. Erastus just about worshiped her.

I used to know him pretty well. He lived next door to me, and we went to school together. Folks used to say he was waitin' on me, but he wa'n't. I never thought he was except once or twice when he said things that some girls might have suspected meant somethin'. That was before Luella came here to teach the district school. It was funny how she came to get it, for folks said she hadn't any education, and that one of the big girls, Lottie Henderson, used to do all the teachin' for her, while she sat back and did embroidery work on a cambric pocket-handkerchief. Lottie Henderson was a real smart girl, a splendid scholar, and she just set her eyes by Luella, as all the girls did. Lottie would have made a real smart woman, but she died when Luella had been here about a year—just faded away and died: nobody knew what ailed her. She dragged herself to that schoolhouse and helped Luella teach till the very last minute. The committee all knew how Luella didn't do much of the work herself, but they winked at it. It wa'n't long after Lottie died that Erastus married her. I always thought he hurried it up because she wa'n't fit to teach. One of the big boys used to help her after Lottie died, but he hadn't much government, and the school didn't do very well, and Luella might have had to give it up, for the committee couldn't have shut their eyes to things much longer. The boy that helped her was a real honest, innocent sort of fellow, and he was a good scholar, too. Folks said he overstudied, and that was the reason he was took crazy the year after Luella married, but I don't know. And I don't know what made Erastus Miller go into consumption of the blood the year after he was married: consumption wa'n't in his family. He just grew weaker and weaker, and went almost bent double when he tried to wait on Luella, and he spoke feeble, like an old man. He worked terrible hard till the last trying to save up a little to leave Luella. I've seen him out in the worst storms on a wood-sled—he used to cut and sell wood—and he was hunched up on top lookin' more dead than alive. Once I couldn't stand it: I went over and helped him pitch some wood on the cart—I was always strong in my arms. I wouldn't stop for all he told me to, and I guess he was glad enough for the help. That was only a week before he died. He fell on the kitchen floor while he was gettin' breakfast. He always got the breakfast and let Luella lay abed. He did all the sweepin' and the washin' and the ironin' and most of the cookin'. He couldn't bear to have Luella lift her finger, and she let him do for her. She lived like a queen for all the work she did. She didn't even do her sewin'. She said it made her shoulder ache to sew, and poor Erastus's sister Lily used to do all her sewin'. She wa'n't able to, either; she was never strong in her back, but she did it beautifully. She had to, to suit Luella, she was so dreadful particular. I never saw anythin' like the fagottin' and hemstitchin' that Lily Miller did for Luella. She made all Luella's weddin' outfit, and that green silk dress, after Maria Babbit cut it. Maria she cut it for nothin', and she did a lot more cuttin' and fittin' for nothin' for Luella, too. Lily Miller went to live with Luella after Erastus died. She gave up her home, though she was real attached to it and wa'n't a mite afraid to stay alone. She rented it and she went to live with Luella right away after the funeral."

Then this old woman, Lydia Anderson, who remembered Luella Miller, would go on to relate the story of Lily Miller. It seemed that on the removal of Lily Miller to the house of her dead brother, to live with his widow, the village people first began to talk. This Lily Miller had been hardly past her first youth, and a most robust and blooming woman, rosy-cheeked, with curls of strong, black hair overshadowing round, candid temples and bright dark eyes. It was not six months after she had taken up her residence with her sister-in-law that her rosy colour faded and her pretty curves became wan hollows. White shadows began to show in the black rings of her hair, and the light died out of her eyes, her features sharpened, and there were pathetic lines at her mouth, which yet wore always an expression of utter sweetness and even happiness. She was devoted to her sister; there was no doubt that she loved her with her whole heart, and was perfectly content in her service. It was her sole anxiety lest she should die and leave her alone.

"The way Lily Miller used to talk about Luella was enough to make you mad and enough to make you cry," said Lydia Anderson. "I've been in there sometimes toward the last when she was too feeble to cook and carried her some blanc-mange or custard—somethin' I thought she might relish, and she'd thank me, and when I asked her how she was, say she felt better than she did yesterday, and asked me if I didn't think

she looked better, dreadful pitiful, and say poor Luella had an
awful time takin' care of her and doin' the work—she wa'n't
strong enough to do anythin'—when all the time Luella wa'n't
liftin' her finger and poor Lily didn't get any care except what
the neighbours gave her, and Luella eat up everythin' that was
carried in for Lily. I had it real straight that she did. Luella used
to just sit and cry and do nothin'. She did act real fond of Lily,
and she pined away considerable, too. There was those that
thought she'd go into a decline herself. But after Lily died, her
Aunt Abby Mixter came, and then Luella picked up and grew
as fat and rosy as ever. But poor Aunt Abby begun to droop
just the way Lily had, and I guess somebody wrote to her married daughter, Mrs. Sam Abbot, who lived in Barre, for she
wrote her mother that she must leave right away and come and
make her a visit, but Aunt Abby wouldn't go. I can see her
now. She was a real good-lookin' woman, tall and large, with a
big, square face and a high forehead that looked of itself kind
of benevolent and good. She just tended out on Luella as if she
had been a baby, and when her married daughter sent for her
she wouldn't stir one inch. She'd always thought a lot of her
daughter, too, but she said Luella needed her and her married
daughter didn't. Her daughter kept writin' and writin', but it
didn't do any good. Finally she came, and when she saw how
bad her mother looked, she broke down and cried and all but
went on her knees to have her come away. She spoke her mind
out to Luella, too. She told her that she'd killed her husband
and everybody that had anythin' to do with her, and she'd
thank her to leave her mother alone. Luella went into hysterics, and Aunt Abby was so frightened that she called me after
her daughter went. Mrs. Sam Abbot she went away fairly cryin'
out loud in the buggy, the neighbours heard her, and well she
might, for she never saw her mother again alive. I went in that
night when Aunt Abby called for me, standin' in the door with
her little green-checked shawl over her head. I can see her now.
'Do come over here, Miss Anderson,' she sung out, kind of
gasping for breath. I didn't stop for anythin'. I put over as fast
as I could, and when I got there, there was Luella laughin' and
cryin' all together, and Aunt Abby trying to hush her, and all
the time she herself was white as a sheet and shakin' so she
could hardly stand. 'For the land sakes, Mrs. Mixter,' says I,

'you look worse than she does. You ain't fit to be up out of
your bed.'

" 'Oh, there ain't anythin' the matter with me,' says she.
Then she went on talkin' to Luella. 'There, there, don't, don't,
poor little lamb,' says she. 'Aunt Abby is here. She ain't goin'
away and leave you. Don't, poor little lamb.'

" 'Do leave her with me, Mrs. Mixter, and you get back to
bed,' says I, for Aunt Abby had been layin' down considerable
lately, though somehow she contrived to do the work.

" 'I'm well enough,' says she. 'Don't you think she had
better have the doctor, Miss Anderson?'

" 'The doctor,' says I, 'I think *you* had better have the doctor. I think you need him much worse than some folks I could
mention.' And I looked right straight at Luella Miller laughin'
and cryin' and goin' on as if she was the centre of all creation.
All the time she was actin' so—seemed as if she was too sick to
sense anythin'—she was keepin' a sharp lookout as to how we
took it out of the corner of one eye. I see her. You could never
cheat me about Luella Miller. Finally I got real mad and I run
home and I got a bottle of valerian I had, and I poured some
boilin' hot water on a handful of catnip, and I mixed up that
catnip tea with most half a wineglass of valerian, and I went
with it over to Luella's. I marched right up to Luella, a-holdin'
out of that cup, all smokin'. 'Now,' says I, 'Luella Miller, '*you
swallar this!*'

" 'What is—what is it, oh, what is it?' she sort of screeches
out. Then she goes off a-laughin' enough to kill.

" 'Poor lamb, poor little lamb,' says Aunt Abby, standin'
over her, all kind of tottery, and tryin' to bathe her head with
camphor.

" '*You swaller this right down*,' says I. And I didn't waste any
ceremony. I just took hold of Luella Miller's chin and I tipped
her head back, and I caught her mouth open with laughin',
and I clapped that cup to her lips, and I fairly hollered at her:
'Swaller, swaller, swaller!' and she gulped it right down. She
had to, and I guess it did her good. Anyhow, she stopped
cryin' and laughin' and let me put her to bed, and she went to
sleep like a baby inside of half an hour. That was more than
poor Aunt Abby did. She lay awake all that night and I stayed
with her, though she tried not to have me; said she wa'n't sick

enough for watchers. But I stayed, and I made some good cornmeal gruel and I fed her a teaspoon every little while all night long. It seemed to me as if she was jest dyin' from bein' all wore out. In the mornin' as soon as it was light I run over to the Bisbees and sent Johnny Bisbee for the doctor. I told him to tell the doctor to hurry, and he come pretty quick. Poor Aunt Abby didn't seem to know much of anythin' when he got there. You couldn't hardly tell she breathed, she was so used up. When the doctor had gone, Luella came into the room lookin' like a baby in her ruffled nightgown. I can see her now. Her eyes were as blue and her face all pink and white like a blossom, and she looked at Aunt Abby in the bed sort of innocent and surprised. 'Why,' says she, 'Aunt Abby ain't got up yet?'

" 'No, she ain't,' says I, pretty short.

" 'I thought I didn't smell the coffee,' says Luella.

" 'Coffee,' says I. 'I guess if you have coffee this mornin' you'll make it yourself.'

" 'I never made the coffee in all my life,' says she, dreadful astonished. 'Erastus always made the coffee as long as he lived, and then Lily she made it, and then Aunt Abby made it. I don't believe I *can* make the coffee, Miss Anderson.'

" 'You can make it or go without, jest as you please,' says I.

" 'Ain't Aunt Abby goin' to get up?' says she.

" 'I guess she won't get up,' says I, 'sick as she is.' I was gettin' madder and madder. There was somethin' about that little pink-and-white thing standin' there and talkin' about coffee, when she had killed so many better folks than she was, and had jest killed another, that made me feel 'most as if I wished somebody would up and kill her before she had a chance to do any more harm.

" 'Is Aunt Abby sick?' says Luella, as if she was sort of aggrieved and injured.

" 'Yes,' says I, 'she's sick, and she's goin' to die, and then you'll be left alone, and you'll have to do for yourself and wait on yourself, or do without things.' I don't know but I was sort of hard, but it was the truth, and if I was any harder than Luella Miller had been I'll give up. I ain't never been sorry that I said it. Well, Luella, she up and had hysterics again at that, and I jest let her have 'em. All I did was to bundle her

into the room on the other side of the entry where Aunt Abby
couldn't hear her, if she wa'n't past it—I don't know but she
was—and set her down hard in a chair and told her not to
come back into the other room, and she minded. She had her
hysterics in there till she got tired. When she found out that
nobody was comin' to coddle her and do for her she stopped.
At least I suppose she did. I had all I could do with poor Aunt
Abby tryin' to keep the breath of life in her. The doctor had
told me that she was dreadful low, and give me some very
strong medicine to give to her in drops real often, and told me
real particular about the nourishment. Well, I did as he told
me real faithful till she wa'n't able to swaller any longer. Then
I had her daughter sent for. I had begun to realize that she
wouldn't last any time at all. I hadn't realized it before,
though I spoke to Luella the way I did. The doctor he came,
and Mrs. Sam Abbot, but when she got there it was too late;
her mother was dead. Aunt Abby's daughter just give one look
at her mother layin' there, then she turned sort of sharp and
sudden and looked at me.

   " 'Where is she?' says she, and I knew she meant Luella.

   " 'She's out in the kitchen,' says I. 'She's too nervous to see
folks die. She's afraid it will make her sick.'

   "The Doctor he speaks up then. He was a young man. Old
Doctor Park had died the year before, and this was a young fellow just out of college. 'Mrs. Miller is not strong,' says he,
kind of severe, 'and she is quite right in not agitating herself.'

   " 'You are another, young man; she's got her pretty claw on
you,' thinks I, but I didn't say anythin' to him. I just said over
to Mrs. Sam Abbot that Luella was in the kitchen, and Mrs.
Sam Abbot she went out there, and I went, too, and I never
heard anythin' like the way she talked to Luella Miller. I felt
pretty hard to Luella myself, but this was more than I ever
would have dared to say. Luella she was too scared to go into
hysterics. She jest flopped. She seemed to jest shrink away to
nothin' in that kitchen chair, with Mrs. Sam Abbot standin'
over her and talkin' and tellin' her the truth. I guess the truth
was most too much for her and no mistake, because Luella
presently actually did faint away, and there wa'n't any sham
about it, the way I always suspected there was about them hys-

terics. She fainted dead away and we had to lay her flat on the floor, and the Doctor he came runnin' out and he said somethin' about a weak heart dreadful fierce to Mrs. Sam Abbot, but she wa'n't a mite scared. She faced him jest as white as even Luella was layin' there lookin' like death and the Doctor feelin' of her pulse.

" 'Weak heart,' says she, 'weak heart; weak fiddlesticks! There ain't nothin' weak about that woman. She's got strength enough to hang onto other folks till she kills 'em. Weak? It was my poor mother that was weak: this woman killed her as sure as if she had taken a knife to her.'

"But the Doctor he didn't pay much attention. He was bendin' over Luella layin' there with her yellow hair all streamin' and her pretty pink-and-white face all pale, and her blue eyes like stars gone out, and he was holdin' onto her hand and smoothin' her forehead, and tellin' me to get the brandy in Aunt Abby's room, and I was sure as I wanted to be that Luella had got somebody else to hang onto, now Aunt Abby was gone, and I thought of poor Erastus Miller, and I sort of pitied the poor young Doctor, led away by a pretty face, and I made up my mind I'd see what I could do.

"I waited till Aunt Abby had been dead and buried about a month, and the Doctor was goin' to see Luella steady and folks were beginnin' to talk; then one evenin', when I knew the Doctor had been called out of town and wouldn't be round, I went over to Luella's. I found her all dressed up in a blue muslin with white polka dots on it, and her hair curled jest as pretty, and there wa'n't a young girl in the place could compare with her. There was somethin' about Luella Miller seemed to draw the heart right out of you, but she didn't draw it out of *me*. She was settin' rocking in the chair by her sittin'-room window, and Maria Brown had gone home. Maria Brown had been in to help her, or rather to do the work, for Luella wa'n't helped when she didn't do anythin'. Maria Brown was real capable and she didn't have any ties; she wa'n't married, and lived alone, so she'd offered. I couldn't see why she should do the work any more than Luella; she wa'n't any too strong; but she seemed to think she could and Luella seemed to think so, too, so she went over and did all the work—washed, and ironed, and baked, while Luella sat and rocked. Maria didn't live long afterward. She began to fade away just the same fashion the others had. Well, she was warned, but she acted real mad when folks said anythin': said Luella was a poor, abused woman, too delicate to help herself, and they'd ought to be ashamed, and if she died helpin' them that couldn't help themselves she would—and she did.

" 'I s'pose Maria has gone home,' says I to Luella, when I had gone in and sat down opposite her.

" 'Yes, Maria went half an hour ago, after she had got supper and washed the dishes,' says Luella, in her pretty way.

" 'I suppose she has got a lot of work to do in her own house to-night,' says I, kind of bitter, but that was all thrown away on Luella Miller. It seemed to her right that other folks that wa'n't any better able than she was herself should wait on her, and she couldn't get it through her head that anybody should think it *wa'n't* right.

" 'Yes,' says Luella, real sweet and pretty, 'yes, she said she had to do her washin' to-night. She has let it go for a fortnight along of comin' over here.'

" 'Why don't she stay home and do her washin' instead of comin' over here and doin' *your* work, when you are just as well able, and enough sight more so, than she is to do it?' says I.

"Then Luella she looked at me like a baby who has a rattle shook at it. She sort of laughed as innocent as you please. 'Oh, I can't do the work myself, Miss Anderson,' says she. 'I never did. Maria *has* to do it.'

"Then I spoke out: 'Has to do it!' says I. 'Has to do it!' She don't have to do it, either. Maria Brown has her own home and enough to live on. She ain't beholden to you to come over here and slave for you and kill herself.'

"Luella she jest set and stared at me for all the world like a doll-baby that was so abused that it was comin' to life.

" 'Yes,' says I, 'she's killin' herself. She's goin' to die just the way Erastus did, and Lily, and your Aunt Abby. You're killin' her jest as you did them. I don't know what there is about you, but you seem to bring a curse,' says I. 'You kill everybody that is fool enough to care anythin' about you and do for you.'

"She stared at me and she was pretty pale.

" 'And Maria ain't the only one you're goin' to kill,' says I.

'You're goin' to kill Doctor Malcom before you're done with him.'

"Then a red colour came flamin' all over her face. 'I ain't goin' to kill him, either,' says she, and she begun to cry.

"'Yes, you *be*!' says I. Then I spoke as I had never spoke before. You see, I felt it on account of Erastus. I told her that she hadn't any business to think of another man after she'd been married to one that had died for her: that she was a dreadful woman; and she was, that's true enough, but sometimes I have wondered lately if she knew it—if she wa'n't like a baby with scissors in its hand cuttin' everybody without knowin' what it was doin'.

"Luella she kept gettin' paler and paler, and she never took her eyes off my face. There was somethin' awful about the way she looked at me and never spoke one word. After awhile I quit talkin' and I went home. I watched that night, but her lamp went out before nine o'clock, and when Doctor Malcom came drivin' past and sort of slowed up he see there wa'n't any light and he drove along. I saw her sort of shy out of meetin' the next Sunday, too, so he shouldn't go home with her, and I begun to think mebbe she did have some conscience after all. It was only a week after that that Maria Brown died—sort of sudden at the last, though everybody had seen it was comin'. Well, then there was a good deal of feelin' and pretty dark whispers. Folks said the days of witchcraft had come again, and they were pretty shy of Luella. She acted sort of offish to the Doctor and he didn't go there, and there wa'n't anybody to do anythin' for her. I don't know how she *did* get along. I wouldn't go in there and offer to help her—not because I was afraid of dyin' like the rest, but I thought she was just as well able to do her own work as I was to do it for her, and I thought it was about time that she did it and stopped killin' other folks. But it wa'n't very long before folks began to say that Luella herself was goin' into a decline jest the way her husband, and Lily, and Aunt Abby and the others had, and I saw myself that she looked pretty bad. I used to see her goin' past from the store with a bundle as if she could hardly crawl, but I remembered how Erastus used to wait and 'tend when he couldn't hardly put one foot before the other, and I didn't go out to help her.

"But at last one afternoon I saw the Doctor come drivin' up like mad with his medicine chest, and Mrs. Babbit came in after supper and said that Luella was real sick.

" 'I'd offer to go in and nurse her,' says she, 'but I've got my children to consider, and mebbe it ain't true what they say, but it's queer how many folks that have done for her have died.'

"I didn't say anythin', but I considered how she had been Erastus's wife and how he had set his eyes by her, and I made up my mind to go in the next mornin', unless she was better, and see what I could do; but the next mornin' I see her at the window, and pretty soon she came steppin' out as spry as you please, and a little while afterward Mrs. Babbit came in and told me that the Doctor had got a girl from out of town, a Sarah Jones, to come there, and she said she was pretty sure that the Doctor was goin' to marry Luella.

"I saw him kiss her in the door that night myself, and I knew it was true. The woman came that afternoon, and the way she flew around was a caution. I don't believe Luella had swept since Maria died. She swept and dusted, and washed and ironed; wet clothes and dusters and carpets were flyin' over there all day, and every time Luella set her foot out when the Doctor wa'n't there there was that Sarah Jones helpin' of her up and down the steps, as if she hadn't learned to walk.

"Well, everybody knew that Luella and the Doctor were goin' to be married, but it wa'n't long before they began to talk about his lookin' so poorly, jest as they had about the others; and they talked about Sarah Jones, too.

"Well, the Doctor did die, and he wanted to be married first, so as to leave what little he had to Luella, but he died before the minister could get there, and Sarah Jones died a week afterward.

"Well, that wound up everything for Luella Miller. Not another soul in the whole town would lift a finger for her. There got to be a sort of panic. Then she began to droop in good earnest. She used to have to go to the store herself, for Mrs. Babbit was afraid to let Tommy go for her, and I've seen her goin' past and stoppin' every two or three steps to rest. Well, I stood it as long as I could, but one day I see her comin' with her arms full and stoppin' to lean against the Babbit fence, and I run out and took her bundles and carried them to her house.

Then I went home and never spoke one word to her though she called after me dreadful kind of pitiful. Well, that night I was taken sick with a chill, and I was sick as I wanted to be for two weeks. Mrs. Babbit had seen me run out to help Luella and she came in and told me I was goin' to die on account of it. I didn't know whether I was or not, but I considered I had done right by Erastus's wife.

"That last two weeks Luella she had a dreadful hard time, I guess. She was pretty sick, and as near as I could make out nobody dared go near her. I don't know as she was really needin' anythin' very much, for there was enough to eat in her house and it was warm weather, and she made out to cook a little flour gruel every day, I know, but I guess she had a hard time, she that had been so petted and done for all her life.

"When I got so I could go out, I went over there one morning. Mrs. Babbit had just come in to say she hadn't seen any smoke and she didn't know but it was somebody's duty to go in, but she couldn't help thinkin' of her children, and I got right up, though I hadn't been out of the house for two weeks, and I went in there, and Luella she was layin' on the bed, and she was dyin'.

"She lasted all that day and into the night. But I sat there after the new doctor had gone away. Nobody else dared to go there. It was about midnight that I left her for a minute to run home and get some medicine I had been takin', for I begun to feel rather bad.

"It was a full moon that night, and just as I started out of my door to cross the street back to Luella's, I stopped short, for I saw something."

Lydia Anderson at this juncture always said with a certain defiance that she did not expect to be believed, and then proceeded in a hushed voice:

"I saw what I saw, and I know I saw it, and I will swear on my death bed that I saw it. I saw Luella Miller and Erastus Miller, and Lily, and Aunt Abby, and Maria, and the Doctor, and Sarah, all goin' out of her door, and all but Luella shone white in the moonlight, and they were all helpin' her along till she seemed to fairly fly in the midst of them. Then it all disappeared. I stood a minute with my heart poundin', then I went over there. I thought of goin' for Mrs. Babbit, but I thought she'd be afraid. So I went alone, though I knew what had happened. Luella was layin' real peaceful, dead on her bed."

This was the story that the old woman, Lydia Anderson, told, but the sequel was told by the people who survived her, and this is the tale which has become folklore in the village.

Lydia Anderson died when she was eighty-seven. She had continued wonderfully hale and hearty for one of her years until about two weeks before her death.

One bright moonlight evening she was sitting beside a window in her parlour when she made a sudden exclamation, and was out of the house and across the street before the neighbour who was taking care of her could stop her. She followed as fast as possible and found Lydia Anderson stretched on the ground before the door of Luella Miller's deserted house, and she was quite dead.

The next night there was a red gleam of fire athwart the moonlight and the old house of Luella Miller was burned to the ground. Nothing is now left of it except a few old cellar stones and a lilac bush, and in summer a helpless trail of morning glories among the weeds, which might be considered emblematic of Luella herself.

1902

FRANK NORRIS

(1870–1902)

Grettir at Thorhall-stead

I—Glamr

Thorhall the bonder had been to the great Thingvalla, or
annual fair of Iceland, to engage a shepherd, and was now returning. It had been a good two-days' journey home, for his
shaggy little pony, though sure footed, was slow. For the
better part of three hours on the evening of the second day he
had been picking his way cautiously among the great boulders
of black basalt that encumbered the path. At length, on the
summit of a low hill, he brought the little animal to a standstill
and paused a moment, looking off to the northward, a smile of
satisfaction spreading over his broad, sober face. For he had
just passed the white stone that marked the boundary of his
own land. Below him opened the little valley named the Vale
of Shadows, and in its midst, overshadowed by a single Norway pine, black, wind-distorted, was the stone farmhouse, the
byre, Thorhall's home.

Only an Icelander could have found pleasure in that prospect.
It was dreary beyond expression. Save only for the deformed
pine, tortured and warped by its unending battle with the wintry gales, no other tree relieved the monotony of the landscape. To the west, mountains barred the horizon—volcanic
mountains, gashed, cragged, basaltic, and still blackened with
primeval fires. Bare of vegetation they were—somber, solitary,
empty of life. To the eastward, low, rolling sand dunes, sprinkled thinly with gorse, bore down to the sea. They shut off a
view of the shore, but farther on the horizon showed itself, a
bitter, inhospitable waste of gray water, blotted by fogs and
murk and sudden squalls. Though the shore was invisible, it
none the less asserted itself. With the rushing of the wind was
mingled the prolonged, everlasting thunder of the surf, while
the taint of salt, of decaying kelp, of fish, of seaweed, of all the
pungent aromas of the sea, pervaded the air on every hand.

Black gulls, sharply defined against the gray sky, slanted in long tacking flights hither and thither over sea and land. The raucous bark of the seal hunting mackerel off the shore made itself occasionally heard. Otherwise there was no sign of life. Veils of fine rain, half fog, drove across the scene between ocean and mountain. The wind blew incessantly from off the sea with a steady and uninterrupted murmur.

Thorhall rode on, inclining his head against the gusts and driving wind. Soon he had come to the farmhouse. The servants led the pony to the stables and in the doorway Thorhall found his wife waiting for him. They embraced one another and—for they were pious folk—thanked God for the bonder's safe journey and speedy return. Before the roaring fire of drift that evening Thorhall told his wife of all that had passed at the Thingvalla, of the wrestling, and of the stallion fights.

"And did you find a shepherd to your liking?" asked his wife.

"Yes; a great fellow with white teeth and black hair. Rather surly, I believe, but strong as a troll. He promised to be with me by the beginning of the Winter night. His name is Glamr."

But the Summer passed, the sun dipped below the horizon not to reappear for six months, the Winter night drew on, snow buried all the landscape, hurricanes sharp as boar-spears descended upon the Vale of Shadows; in their beds the dwellers in the byre heard the grind and growl of the great bergs careering onward through the ocean, and many a night the howl of hunger-driven wolves startled Thorhall from his sleep; yet Glamr did not come.

Then at length and of a sudden he appeared; and Thorhall on a certain evening, called hastily by a frightened servant, beheld the great figure of him in the midst of the kitchen floor, his eyebrows frosted yet scowling, his white teeth snapping with cold, while in a great hoarse voice, like the grumble of a bear, he called for meat and drink.

From thenceforward Glamr became a member of Thorhall's household. Yet seldom was he found in the byre. By day he was away with the sheep; by night he slept in the stables. The servants were afraid of him, though he rarely addressed them a word. He was not only feared, but disliked. This aversion was partly explained by Glamr's own peculiar disposition—gloomy, solitary, uncanny, and partly by a fact that came to light within the first month of his coming to the Vale of Shadows.

He was an unbeliever. Never did his broad bulk darken the lich-gate of the kirk; the knolling of matin and vesper-bell put him in a season of even deeper gloom than usual. It was noticed that he could not bear to look upon a cross; the priest he abhorred as a pestilence. On holy days he kept far from home, absenting himself upon one pretext or another, withdrawing up into the chasms and gorges of the hills.

So passed the first months of the Winter.

Christmas Day came, and Christmas Night. It was bitter, bitter cold. Snow had fallen since second cockcrow the day before, and as night closed in such a gale as had not been known for years gathered from off the Northern Ocean and whirled shrieking over the Vale of Shadows. All day long Glamr was in the hills with the sheep, and even above the roaring of the wind his bell-toned voice had occasionally been heard as he called and shouted to his charges. At candle-lighting time he had not returned. The bonder and his family busked themselves to attend the Christmas mass.

Some two hours later they were returning. The wind was going down, but even yet shreds of torn seaweed and scud of foam, swept up by the breath of the gale, drove landward across the valley. The clouds overhead were breaking up, and between their galloping courses one saw the sky, the stars glittering like hoar frost.

The bonder's party drew near the farmhouse, and the servants, going before with lanthorns and pine torches, undid the fastenings of the gate. The wind lapsed suddenly, and in the stillness between two gusts the plunge of the surf made itself heard.

Then all at once Thorhall and his wife stopped and her hand clutched quickly at his wrist.

"Hark! what was that?"

What, indeed? Was it an echo of the storm sounding hollow and faint from some thunder-split crag far off there in those hills toward which all eyes were suddenly turned; was it the cry of a wolf, the clamor of a falcon, or was it the horrid scream of human agony and fury, vibrating to a hoarse and bell-like note that sounded familiar in their ears?

"Glamr! Where is Glamr?" shouted Thorhall, as he entered

the byre. But those few servants who had been left in charge of the house reported he had not yet returned.

Night passed and no Glamr; and in the morning the search-party set out toward the hills. Half way up the slope, the sheep —a few of them—were found, scattered, half buried in drifts; then a dog, dead and frozen hard as wood. From it led a track up into the higher mountains, a strange track indeed, not human certainly, yet whether of wolf or bear no one could determine. Some had started to follow when a lad who had looked behind the shoulder of a great rock raised a cry.

There was the body of Glamr. The shepherd was stretched upon his back, dead, rigid. The open eyes were glazed, the face livid; the tongue protruding from the mouth had been bitten through in the last agony. All about the snow was trampled down, and the bare bushes crushed and flattened out. Even the massive boulder near which the body had been found was moved a little from its place. A fearful struggle had been wrought out here, yet upon the body of Glamr was no trace of a wound, no mark of claw or hand. Only among his footprints was mingled that strange track that had been noticed before, and as before it led straight up toward the high part of the mountains.

The young men raised the body of the shepherd and the party moved off toward the kirk and the graveyard. Even though Glamr had shunned the mass, the priest might be prevailed upon to bury him in consecrated ground. But soon the young men had to pause to rest. The body was unexpectedly heavy. Once again, after stopping to breathe, they raised the bier upon their shoulders. Soon another helper was summoned, then another; even Thorhall aided. Ten strong men though they were, they staggered and trembled under that unearthly weight. Even in that icy air the perspiration streamed from them. Heavier and still heavier grew the burden; it bore them to the earth. Their knees bowed out from under them, their backs bent. They were obliged to give over.

Later in the day they returned with oxen and a sledge. They repaired to the spot where the body had been left; then stared at each other with paling faces. In the snow at their feet there was the impression made by the great frame of the shepherd. But that was all; the body was gone, nor was there any foot-print in the snow other than they themselves had made.

A cairn was erected over the spot, and for many a long day the strange death of the shepherd of the Vale of Shadows was the talk of the country side. But about a month or so after the death of Glamr a strange sense of uneasiness seemed to invade the household of the byre. By degrees it took possession of first one and then another of the servants and family. No one spoke about this. It was not a thing that could be reduced to words, and for the matter of that, each one believed that he or she was the only one affected. This one thought himself sick; that one believed herself merely nervous. But nevertheless a certain perplexity, a certain disturbance of spirit was in the air.

One evening Thorhall and his wife met accidentally in the passage between the main body of the house and the dairy. They paused and looked at each other for no reason that they could imagine. Thus they stood for several seconds.

"Well," said Thorhall at length, "what is it?"

"Ay," responded his wife. "Ay, what *is* it?"

"Nothing," he replied; and she, echoing his words, also answered "Nothing."

Then they laughed nervously, yet still looking fixedly into each other's eyes for all that.

"I believe," said Thorhall the next day, "that I am to be sick. I cannot tell—I feel no pain—no fever—and yet——"

"And I, too," declared his wife. "I am—no, not sick—but distressed. I—I am troubled. I cannot tell what it is. I sometimes think I am *afraid*."

A week later, on a certain evening just after curfew, the whole family was aroused by a wild shriek as of some one in mortal terror. Thorhall and his wife rushed into the dairy whence the cry came and found one of the maids in a fit upon the floor.

When she recovered she cried out that she had seen at one of the windows the face of Glamr.

II—*Grettir*

The cold, bright Icelandic Summer shone over Thorhall's byre and the Vale of Shadows. There was no cloud in the sky. The void and lonely ocean was indigo blue. But still the prospect was barren, inhospitable. Only a few pallid flowers, hardy bluebells

and buttercups, appeared here and there on the sand dunes in
the hollows beneath the gorse and bracken. In the lower hills,
on the far side of the valley, a tenuous skim of verdure appeared. At times a ptarmigan fluttered in and out of the crevices
of these hills searching for blueberries; at times on the surfaces
of the waste of dunes a sandpiper uttered its shrill and feeble
piping. Always, as ever, the wind blew from off the ocean;
always, as ever, the solitary pine by the farmhouse writhed and
tossed its gaunt arms; always the gorse and bracken billowed
and weltered under it. The sand drifted like snow, encroaching
forever upon the cultivated patches around the house. Always
the surf—surge on surge—boomed and thundered on the shore,
casting up broken kelp and jetsam of wreck. Always, always
forever and forever, the monotony remained. The bleakness,
the wild, solitary stretches of sea and sky and land turned to
the eye their staring emptiness. At long intervals the figure of a
servant, a herdsman or at times Thorhall himself moved—a
speck of black on the illimitable gray of nature—across the
landscape. Ponies, shagged, half wild, their eyes hidden under
tangled forelocks, sometimes wandered down upon the shore
—their thick hair roughing in the wind—to snuff at the salty
seaweeds. The males sometimes fought here on the shore,
their hoofs thudding on the resounding beach, their screams
mingling with the incessant roar of the breakers.

Once even, at Easter-tide, during a gale, an empty galley
drove ashore, a *snekr* with dragon prow, the broken oars dangling from the thole-pins; and in the waist of her a Viking
chieftain, dead, the salt rime rusting on his helmet.

With the advent of Summer the mysterious trouble at the
farmhouse in the Vale of Shadows disappeared. But the fall
equinox drew on, the nights became longer; soon the daylight
lasted but a few hours and the sun set before it could be said to
have actually risen.

As the Winter darkness descended upon the farmhouse the
trouble recommenced. During the night the tread of footsteps
could be heard making the rounds of the byre. The fumbling
of unseen fingers could be distinguished at the locks. The low
eaves of the house were seized in the grip of strong hands and
wrenched and pulled till the rafters creaked. Outhouses were

plucked apart and destroyed, fences uprooted. After nightfall no one dared venture abroad.

Thorhall had engaged a new shepherd, one Thorgaut, a young man, who professed himself fearless of the haunted sheep-walks and farmyard. He was as popular as Glamr had been disliked. He made love to the housemaids, helped in the butter-making and rode the children on his back. As to the Vampire, he snapped his fingers and asked only to meet him in the open.

The snow came in August, and was followed by sleet and icy rains and blotting sea-fogs. As the time went on the nightly manifestations increased. Windows were broken in; iron bars shaken and wrenched; sheep and even horses killed.

At length one night a terrible commotion broke out in the stables—the shrill squealing of the horses and the tramping and bellowing of cows, mingled with deep tones of a dreadful voice. Thorhall and his people rushed out. They found that the stable door had been riven and splintered, and they entered the stable itself across the wreckage. The cattle were goring each other, and across the stone partition between the stalls was the body of Thorgaut, the shepherd, his head upon one side, his feet on the other, and his spine snapped in twain.

It chanced that about this time Grettir, well known and well beloved throughout all Iceland, came into that part of the country and one eventide drew rein at Thorhall's farmhouse. This was before Grettir had been hunted from the island by the implacable Thorbjorn, called The Hook, and driven to an asylum and practical captivity upon the rock of Drangey.

He was at this time in the prime of his youth and of a noble appearance. His shoulders were broad, his arms long, his eye a bright blue and his flaxen hair braided like a Viking's. For cloak he wore a bearskin, while as for weapons he carried nothing but a short sword.

Thorhall, as may be easily understood, welcomed the famous outlaw, but warned him of Glamr.

Grettir, however, was not to be dissuaded from remaining overnight at the byre.

"Vampire or troll, troll or vampire, here bide I till daybreak," he declared.

Yet despite the bonder's fears the night passed quietly. No sound broke the stillness but the murmur of the distant surf, no footfall sounded around the house, no fingers came groping at the doors.

"I have never slept easier," announced Grettir in the morning.

"Good; and Heaven be praised," declared the bonder fervently.

They walked together toward the stables, Thorhall instructing Grettir as to the road he should follow that day. As they drew near, Grettir whistled for his horse, but no answering whicker responded.

"How is this?" he muttered, frowning.

Thorhall and the outlaw hurried into the building, and Grettir, who was in the advance, stopped stock-still in the midst of the floor and swore a great oath.

His horse lay prone in the straw of his stall, his eyeballs protruding, the foam stiff upon his lips. He was dead. Grettir approached and examined him. Between shoulder and withers, the back—as if it had been a wheat-straw—was broken.

"Never mind," cried the bonder eagerly, "I have another animal for you, a piebald stallion of Norway stock, just the beast for your weight. Here is your saddle. On with it. Up you go and a speedy journey to you."

"Never!" exclaimed Grettir, his blue eyes flashing. "Here will I stay till I meet Glamr face to face. No man did me an injury that he did not rue it. I sleep at the byre another night."

Dark as a wolf's mouth, silent as his footfalls, the night closed down. There was no moon as yet, but the heavens were bright. Steadily as the blast of some great huntsman's horn, the wind held from the northeast. The sand skimming over the dunes and low hills near the coast was caught up and carried landward and drifted in at crevice and door-chink of the farmhouse. A young seal—lost, no doubt, from the herd that had all day been feeding in the offing—barked and barked incessantly from a rock in the breakers. In the pine tree by the house a huge night-bird, owl or hawk, stirred occasionally with a prolonged note. By and by the weather grew colder, the ground began to freeze and crack. Inside in the main hall of the house, covered by his bearskin cloak, Grettir lay wakeful and watching.

He reclined in such a manner—his head pillowed on his arm—
that he could see the door. At the other end of the hall the fire
of drift was dying down upon the flags. On the other side of
the partition, in the next room, lay the bonder, alternately
dozing and waking.

The time passed heavily, slowly. From far off toward the
shore could be heard the lost seal raising from time to time his
hoarse, sobbing bark.

Then at length a dog howled, and an instant after the bonder
spoke aloud. He had risen from his bed and stood in the door
of his room.

"Hark! Did you not hear something?"

"I hear the barking of the seal," said Grettir, "the baying of
the hound, the cry of the night-bird, and the break of the
surges; nothing else."

"No. This was a footstep. There. Listen!"

A heavy footfall sounded crunching in the snow from without and close by. It passed around and in front of the house;
and the wooden shutter of a window of the hall was plucked at
and shaken. Then an outhouse was attacked—a shed where in
Summer time the calves were fed. Grettir could hear the snap
and rasp of splintering boards.

"It has a strong arm," he muttered.

Once more the tread encircled the house. In a very short
time it sounded again in the front of the byre.

"It has a long stride," said Grettir.

The tread ceased. For a long moment there was silence, while
the scurrying sand rattled delicately against the house like
minute hailstones. Suddenly a corner eave was seized. Something tugged at it, wrenching, and the thatch gave with the
long swish of rent linen.

"It has a tall figure," said Grettir.

For nearly a quarter of an hour these different sounds continued, now distinct, now confused, now distant, now near at
hand. Suddenly from overhead there came a jar and a crash,
and Grettir felt the dust from the rafters descend upon his face;
the Vampire was on the roof. But soon he leaped down and now
the footsteps came straight to the door of the hall. The door
itself was gripped with colossal strength. In the crescent-shaped
openings of the upper panels a hand appeared, black against

the faint outside light, groping, picking. It seized upon the edge of the board in the lower bend of the crescent and pulled. The board gave way, ripped to the very door-sill; then an arm followed the hand, reaching for one of the two iron bars with which the door was fenced. Evidently it could not find these, for the effort was soon abandoned and another panel was split and torn away. The cross-panel followed, the nails shrieking as they were drawn from out the wood. Then at last the door, shattered to its very hinges, gave way, leaving only the bars set in the stone sockets of the jamb, and against the square of gray light of the entrance stood, silhouetted, the figure of a monster. Stood but for a moment, for almost at once the bars were pulled out.

The Vampire was within the house, the light from the smoldering logs illuminating the face.

Glamr's face was livid. The pupils of the eyes were white, the hair matted and thick. The whole figure was monstrously enlarged, bulked like a *jotun*, and the vast hands, white as those of the drowned, swung heavily at his sides.

Once in the hall, he stood for a long moment looking from side to side, then moved slowly forward, reaching his great arms overhead, feeling and fumbling with the roof-beams with his fingers, and guiding himself thus from beam to beam.

Grettir, watching, alert, never moved, but lay in his place, his eyes fixed upon the monster.

But at length Glamr made out the form stretched upon the couch and came up and laid hold of a flap of the bearskin under Grettir's shoulders and tugged at it. But Grettir, bracing his feet against the foot-board of the couch, held back with all his strength. Glamr seized the flap in both hands and set his might to the pull, till the tough hide fetched away, and he staggered back, the corner of skin still in his grip. He looked at it stupidly, wondering, bewildered.

Then suddenly the bonder, listening from within his bolted door, heard the muffled crashing shock of the onset. The rafters cracked, the byre shook, the shutters rocked in their grooves, and Grettir, eyes alight, hair flying like a torch, thews rigid as iron, leaped to the attack.

Down upon the hero's arms came the numbing, crushing grip of the dead man's might. One instant of that inhuman embrace and Grettir knew that now peril of his life was toward. Never in all his days of battle and strength had such colossal might risen to match his own. Back bore the wrestlers, back, back toward the sides of the hall. Benches ironed to the wall were overturned, wrenched like paper from their fastenings. The great table crashed and splintered beneath their weight. The floor split with their tramping, and the fire was scattered upon the hearth. Now forward, now back, from side to side and from end to end of the wrecked hall drove the fight. Great of build though the fighters were, huge of bone, big of muscle, they yet leaped and writhed with the agility, the rapidity of young lambs.

But fear was not in Grettir. Never in his life had he been afraid. Only anger shook him, and fine, above-board fury, and the iron will to beat his enemy.

All at once Grettir, his arms gripped about the Vampire's middle, his head beneath the armpit, realized that the creature was dragging him toward the door. He fought back from this till the effort sent the blood surging in his ears, for he knew well that ill as the fight had fared within the house it must go worse without. But it was all one that he braced his feet against the broken benches, the wreck of the table, the every unevenness of the floor. The Vampire had gripped him close and dragged and clutched and heaved at his body, so that the white nails drove into his flesh, and the embrace of those arms of steel shut in the ribs till the breath gushed from the nostrils in long gasps of agony.

And now they swayed and grappled in the doorway. Grettir's back was bent like a bow, and Grettir's arms at fullest stretch strained to their sockets, till it seemed as though the very tendons must tear from off the bones. And ever the foul thing above him drew him farther and yet farther from out the entrance-way of the house.

"God save you, Grettir!" cried the bonder, "God save you, brave man and true. Never was such fight as this in all Iceland. Are you spent, Grettir?"

Muffled under the arms of his foe, the voice of Grettir shouted: "Stand from us. I am much spent, but I fear not."

Then with the words, feeling the half-sunk stone of the threshold beneath his feet, he bowed his knees, and with his shoulder against the Vampire's breast drove, not, as hitherto, back, but forward, and that with all the power of limb and loin.

The Vampire reeled from the attack. His shoulder crashed against the outer door-case, and with that gigantic shock the roof burst asunder. Down crushed and roared the frozen thatch, and then in that hideous ruin of splintering rafters, grinding stones and wreck of panel and beam the Vampire fell backward and prone to the ground, while Grettir toppled down upon him till his face was against the dead man's face, his eye to his dead eye, his forehead against his front, and the gray bristle of his beard between his teeth.

The moon was bright outside, and all at once, lighted by her rays, Grettir for the first time saw the Vampire's face.

Then the soul of him shrank and sank, and the fear that all his days he had not known leaped to life in his heart. Terror of that glare of the dead man's gaze caught him by the throat, till his grip relaxed, and his strength dwindled away and he crouched there motionless but for his trembling, looking, looking into those blind, white, dead eyes.

And then the Vampire began to speak:

"Eagerly hast thou striven to match thyself with me, and ill hast thou done this night. Now thou art weak with the fear and the rigor of this fight, yet never henceforth shalt thou be stronger than at this moment. Till now thou hast won much fame by great deeds, yet henceforth ill-luck shall follow thee and woe and man-slayings and untoward fortune. Outlawed shalt thou be, and thy lot shall be cast in lands far from thine home. Alone shalt thou dwell, and in that loneliness, this weird I lay upon thee: Ever to see these eyes with thine eyes, till the terror of the Dark shall come upon thee and the fear of night, and the twain shall drag thee to thy death and thy undoing."

As the voice ceased, Grettir's wits and strength returned, and suddenly seizing the hair of the creature in one hand and his short sword in the other, he hewed off the head.

But within the heart of him he knew that the Vampire had said true words, and as he stood looking down upon the great body of his enemy and saw the glazed and fish-like eyes beneath the lids, he could for one instant look ahead to the days of his life yet to be, to the ill-fortune that should dog him from henceforth, and knew that at the gathering of each night's dusk the eyes of Glamr would look into his.

Thorhall came out when the fight was done, praising God for the issue, and he and Grettir together burned the body and, wrapping the ashes in a skin, buried them in a far corner of the sheep-walks.

In the morning Thorhall gave Grettir the piebald horse and new clothes and set him a mile on his road. They rode through the Vale of Shadows and kissed each other farewell on the shore where the road led away toward Waterdale.

The clouds had gathered again during the dawn and the rain was falling, driven landward by the incessant wind. The seals again barked and hunted in the offing, and the rough-haired ponies once more wandered about on the beach snuffing at the kelp and seaweed.

Long time Thorhall stood on the ridge watching the figure of Grettir grow small and indistinct in the waste of north country and under the blur of the rain. Then at last he turned back to the byre.

But Grettir after these things rode on to Biarg, to his mother's house, and sat at home through the winter.

1903

LAFCADIO HEARN

(1850–1904)

Yuki-Onna

IN a village of Musashi Province, there lived two woodcutters:
Mosaku and Minokichi. At the time of which I am speaking,
Mosaku was an old man; and Minokichi, his apprentice, was a
lad of eighteen years. Every day they went together to a forest
situated about five miles from their village. On the way to that
forest there is a wide river to cross; and there is a ferry-boat.
Several times a bridge was built where the ferry is; but the
bridge was each time carried away by a flood. No common
bridge can resist the current there when the river rises.

Mosaku and Minokichi were on their way home, one very
cold evening, when a great snowstorm overtook them. They
reached the ferry; and they found that the boatman had gone
away, leaving his boat on the other side of the river. It was no
day for swimming; and the woodcutters took shelter in the
ferryman's hut,—thinking themselves lucky to find any shelter
at all. There was no brazier in the hut, nor any place in which
to make a fire: it was only a two-mat* hut, with a single door,
but no window. Mosaku and Minokichi fastened the door, and
lay down to rest, with their straw rain-coats over them. At first
they did not feel very cold; and they thought that the storm
would soon be over.

The old man almost immediately fell asleep; but the boy,
Minokichi, lay awake a long time, listening to the awful wind,
and the continual slashing of the snow against the door. The
river was roaring; and the hut swayed and creaked like a junk at
sea. It was a terrible storm; and the air was every moment becoming colder; and Minokichi shivered under his raincoat. But
at last, in spite of the cold, he too fell asleep.

He was awakened by a showering of snow in his face. The

*That is to say, with a floor-surface of about six feet square.

door of the hut had been forced open; and, by the snow-light (*yuki-akari*), he saw a woman in the room,—a woman all in white. She was bending above Mosaku, and blowing her breath upon him;—and her breath was like a bright white smoke. Almost in the same moment she turned to Minokichi, and stooped over him. He tried to cry out, but found that he could not utter any sound. The white woman bent down over him, lower and lower, until her face almost touched him; and he saw that she was very beautiful,—though her eyes made him afraid. For a little time she continued to look at him;—then she smiled, and she whispered:—"I intended to treat you like the other man. But I cannot help feeling some pity for you,— because you are so young. . . . You are a pretty boy, Mino-kichi; and I will not hurt you now. But, if you ever tell anybody —even your own mother—about what you have seen this night, I shall know it; and then I will kill you. . . . Remember what I say!"

With these words, she turned from him, and passed through the doorway. Then he found himself able to move; and he sprang up, and looked out. But the woman was nowhere to be seen; and the snow was driving furiously into the hut. Mino-kichi closed the door, and secured it by fixing several billets of wood against it. He wondered if the wind had blown it open; —he thought that he might have been only dreaming, and might have mistaken the gleam of the snow-light in the door-way for the figure of a white woman: but he could not be sure. He called to Mosaku, and was frightened because the old man did not answer. He put out his hand in the dark, and touched Mosaku's face, and found that it was ice! Mosaku was stark and dead. . . .

By dawn the storm was over; and when the ferryman re-turned to his station, a little after sunrise, he found Minokichi lying senseless beside the frozen body of Mosaku. Minokichi was promptly cared for, and soon came to himself; but he re-mained a long time ill from the effects of the cold of that terri-ble night. He had been greatly frightened also by the old man's death; but he said nothing about the vision of the woman in white. As soon as he got well again, he returned to his calling, —going alone every morning to the forest, and coming back

at nightfall with his bundles of wood, which his mother helped
him to sell.

One evening, in the winter of the following year, as he was
on his way home, he overtook a girl who happened to be traveling by the same road. She was a tall, slim girl, very good-
looking; and she answered Minokichi's greeting in a voice as
pleasant to the ear as the voice of a song-bird. Then he walked
beside her; and they began to talk. The girl said that her name
was O-Yuki;* that she had lately lost both of her parents; and
that she was going to Yedo, where she happened to have some
poor relations, who might help her to find a situation as servant. Minokichi soon felt charmed by this strange girl; and the
more that he looked at her, the handsomer she appeared to be.
He asked her whether she was yet betrothed; and she answered, laughingly, that she was free. Then, in her turn, she
asked Minokichi whether he was married, or pledged to marry;
and he told her that, although he had only a widowed mother
to support, the question of an "honorable daughter-in-law"
had not yet been considered, as he was very young. . . . After
these confidences, they walked on for a long while without
speaking; but, as the proverb declares, *Ki ga aréba, mé mo
kuchi hodo ni mono wo iu:* "When the wish is there, the eyes
can say as much as the mouth." By the time they reached the
village, they had become very much pleased with each other;
and then Minokichi asked O-Yuki to rest awhile at his house.
After some shy hesitation, she went there with him; and his
mother made her welcome, and prepared a warm meal for her.
O-Yuki behaved so nicely that Minokichi's mother took a sudden fancy to her, and persuaded her to delay her journey to
Yedo. And the natural end of the matter was that Yuki never
went to Yedo at all. She remained in the house, as an "honorable daughter-in-law."

O-Yuki proved a very good daughter-in-law. When Minokichi's mother came to die,—some five years later,—her last
words were words of affection and praise for the wife of her

*This name, signifying "Snow," is not uncommon. On the subject of Japa-
nese female names, see my paper in the volume entitled *Shadowings.*

son. And O-Yuki bore Minokichi ten children, boys and girls,—handsome children all of them, and very fair of skin.

The country-folk thought O-Yuki a wonderful person, by nature different from themselves. Most of the peasant-women age early; but O-Yuki, even after having become the mother of ten children, looked as young and fresh as on the day when she had first come to the village.

One night, after the children had gone to sleep, O-Yuki was sewing by the light of a paper lamp; and Minokichi, watching her, said:—

"To see you sewing there, with the light on your face, makes me think of a strange thing that happened when I was a lad of eighteen. I then saw somebody as beautiful and white as you are now—indeed, she was very like you." . . .

Without lifting her eyes from her work, O-Yuki responded:—

"Tell me about her. . . . Where did you see her?"

Then Minokichi told her about the terrible night in the ferryman's hut,—and about the White Woman that had stooped above him, smiling and whispering,—and about the silent death of old Mosaku. And he said:—

"Asleep or awake, that was the only time that I saw a being as beautiful as you. Of course, she was not a human being; and I was afraid of her,—very much afraid,—but she was so white! . . . Indeed, I have never been sure whether it was a dream that I saw, or the Woman of the Snow." . . .

O-Yuki flung down her sewing, and arose, and bowed above Minokichi where he sat, and shrieked into his face:—

"It was I—I—I! Yuki it was! And I told you then that I would kill you if you ever said one word about it! . . . But for those children asleep there, I would kill you this moment! And now you had better take very, very good care of them; for if ever they have reason to complain of you, I will treat you as you deserve!" . . .

Even as she screamed, her voice became thin, like a crying of wind;—then she melted into a bright white mist that spired to the roof-beams, and shuddered away through the smoke-hole. . . . Never again was she seen.

1904

F. MARION CRAWFORD

(1854–1909)

For the Blood Is the Life

WE had dined at sunset on the broad roof of the old tower, because it was cooler there during the great heat of summer. Besides, the little kitchen was built at one corner of the great square platform, which made it more convenient than if the dishes had to be carried down the steep stone steps, broken in places and everywhere worn with age. The tower was one of those built all down the west coast of Calabria by the Emperor Charles V. early in the sixteenth century, to keep off the Barbary pirates, when the unbelievers were allied with Francis I. against the Emperor and the Church. They have gone to ruin, a few still stand intact, and mine is one of the largest. How it came into my possession ten years ago, and why I spend a part of each year in it, are matters which do not concern this tale. The tower stands in one of the loneliest spots in Southern Italy, at the extremity of a curving rocky promontory, which forms a small but safe natural harbour at the southern extremity of the Gulf of Policastro, and just north of Cape Scalea, the birthplace of Judas Iscariot, according to the old local legend. The tower stands alone on this hooked spur of the rock, and there is not a house to be seen within three miles of it. When I go there I take a couple of sailors, one of whom is a fair cook, and when I am away it is in charge of a gnome-like little being who was once a miner and who attached himself to me long ago.

My friend, who sometimes visits me in my summer solitude, is an artist by profession, a Scandinavian by birth, and a cosmopolitan by force of circumstances. We had dined at sunset; the sunset glow had reddened and faded again, and the evening purple steeped the vast chain of the mountains that embrace the deep gulf to eastward and rear themselves higher and higher toward the south. It was hot, and we sat at the landward corner of the platform, waiting for the night breeze to come down from the lower hills. The colour sank out of the air, there was a little interval of deep-grey twilight, and a lamp sent a yellow streak from the open door of the kitchen, where the men were getting their supper.

Then the moon rose suddenly above the crest of the promontory, flooding the platform and lighting up every little spur of rock and knoll of grass below us, down to the edge of the motionless water. My friend lighted his pipe and sat looking at a spot on the hillside. I knew that he was looking at it, and for a long time past I had wondered whether he would ever see anything there that would fix his attention. I knew that spot well. It was clear that he was interested at last, though it was a long time before he spoke. Like most painters, he trusts to his own eyesight, as a lion trusts his strength and a stag his speed, and he is always disturbed when he cannot reconcile what he sees with what he believes that he ought to see.

"It's strange," he said. "Do you see that little mound just on this side of the boulder?"

"Yes," I said, and I guessed what was coming.

"It looks like a grave," observed Holger.

"Very true. It does look like a grave."

"Yes," continued my friend, his eyes still fixed on the spot. "But the strange thing is that I see the body lying on the top of it. Of course," continued Holger, turning his head on one side as artists do, "it must be an effect of light. In the first place, it is not a grave at all. Secondly, if it were, the body would be inside and not outside. Therefore, it's an effect of the moonlight. Don't you see it?"

"Perfectly; I always see it on moonlight nights."

"It doesn't seem to interest you much," said Holger.

"On the contrary, it does interest me, though I am used to it. You're not so far wrong, either. The mound is really a grave."

"Nonsense!" cried Holger, incredulously. "I suppose you'll tell me what I see lying on it is really a corpse!"

"No," I answered, "it's not. I know, because I have taken the trouble to go down and see."

"Then what is it?" asked Holger.

"It's nothing."

"You mean that it's an effect of light, I suppose?"

"Perhaps it is. But the inexplicable part of the matter is that it makes no difference whether the moon is rising or setting, or waxing or waning. If there's any moonlight at all, from east or west or overhead, so long as it shines on the grave you can see the outline of the body on top."

Holger stirred up his pipe with the point of his knife, and then used his finger for a stopper. When the tobacco burned well he rose from his chair.

"If you don't mind," he said, "I'll go down and take a look at it."

He left me, crossed the roof, and disappeared down the dark steps. I did not move, but sat looking down until he came out of the tower below. I heard him humming an old Danish song as he crossed the open space in the bright moonlight, going straight to the mysterious mound. When he was ten paces from it, Holger stopped short, made two steps forward, and then three or four backward, and then stopped again. I know what that meant. He had reached the spot where the Thing ceased to be visible—where, as he would have said, the effect of light changed.

Then he went on till he reached the mound and stood upon it. I could see the Thing still, but it was no longer lying down; it was on its knees now, winding its white arms round Holger's body and looking up into his face. A cool breeze stirred my hair at that moment, as the night wind began to come down from the hills, but it felt like a breath from another world.

The Thing seemed to be trying to climb to its feet, helping itself up by Holger's body while he stood upright, quite unconscious of it and apparently looking toward the tower, which is very picturesque when the moonlight falls upon it on that side.

"Come along!" I shouted. "Don't stay there all night!"

It seemed to me that he moved reluctantly as he stepped from the mound, or else with difficulty. That was it. The Thing's arms were still round his waist, but its feet could not leave the grave. As he came slowly forward it was drawn and lengthened like a wreath of mist, thin and white, till I saw distinctly that Holger shook himself, as a man does who feels a chill. At the same instant a little wail of pain came to me on the breeze—it might have been the cry of the small owl that lives among the rocks—and the misty presence floated swiftly back from Holger's advancing figure and lay once more at its length upon the mound.

Again I felt the cool breeze in my hair, and this time an icy thrill of dread ran down my spine. I remembered very well that I had once gone down there alone in the moonlight; that presently, being near, I had seen nothing; that, like Holger, I had gone and had stood upon the mound; and I remembered how, when I came back, sure that there was nothing there, I had felt the sudden conviction that there was something after all if I would only look behind me. I remembered the strong temptation to look back, a temptation I had resisted as unworthy of a man of sense, until, to get rid of it, I had shaken myself just as Holger did.

And now I knew that those white, misty arms had been round me too; I knew it in a flash, and I shuddered as I remembered that I had heard the night owl then too. But it had not been the night owl. It was the cry of the Thing.

I refilled my pipe and poured out a cup of strong southern wine; in less than a minute Holger was seated beside me again.

"Of course there's nothing there," he said, "but it's creepy, all the same. Do you know, when I was coming back I was so sure that there was something behind me that I wanted to turn round and look? It was an effort not to."

He laughed a little, knocked the ashes out of his pipe, and poured himself out some wine. For a while neither of us spoke, and the moon rose higher, and we both looked at the Thing that lay on the mound.

"You might make a story about that," said Holger after a long time.

"There is one," I answered. "If you're not sleepy, I'll tell it to you."

"Go ahead," said Holger, who likes stories.

Old Alario was dying up there in the village behind the hill. You remember him, I have no doubt. They say that he made his money by selling sham jewellery in South America, and escaped with his gains when he was found out. Like all those fellows, if they bring anything back with them, he at once set to work to enlarge his house, and as there are no masons here, he sent all the way to Paola for two workmen. They were a

rough-looking pair of scoundrels—a Neapolitan who had lost
one eye and a Sicilian with an old scar half an inch deep across
his left cheek. I often saw them, for on Sundays they used to
come down here and fish off the rocks. When Alario caught
the fever that killed him the masons were still at work. As he
had agreed that part of their pay should be their board and
lodging, he made them sleep in the house. His wife was dead,
and he had an only son called Angelo, who was a much better
sort than himself. Angelo was to marry the daughter of the
richest man in the village, and, strange to say, though the marriage was arranged by their parents, the young people were
said to be in love with each other.

For that matter, the whole village was in love with Angelo,
and among the rest a wild, good-looking creature called
Cristina, who was more like a gipsy than any girl I ever saw
about here. She had very red lips and very black eyes, she was
built like a greyhound, and had the tongue of the devil. But
Angelo did not care a straw for her. He was rather a simple-
minded fellow, quite different from his old scoundrel of a
father, and under what I should call normal circumstances I
really believe that he would never have looked at any girl except the nice plump little creature, with a fat dowry, whom his
father meant him to marry. But things turned up which were
neither normal nor natural.

On the other hand, a very handsome young shepherd from
the hills above Maratea was in love with Cristina, who seems to
have been quite indifferent to him. Cristina had no regular
means of subsistence, but she was a good girl and willing to do
any work or go on errands to any distance for the sake of a loaf
of bread or a mess of beans, and permission to sleep under
cover. She was especially glad when she could get something
to do about the house of Angelo's father. There is no doctor in
the village, and when the neighbours saw that old Alario was
dying they sent Cristina to Scalea to fetch one. That was late in
the afternoon, and if they had waited so long, it was because
the dying miser refused to allow any such extravagance while
he was able to speak. But while Cristina was gone matters grew
rapidly worse, the priest was brought to the bedside, and when
he had done what he could he gave it as his opinion to the by-
standers that the old man was dead, and left the house.

You know these people. They have a physical horror of death. Until the priest spoke, the room had been full of people. The words were hardly out of his mouth before it was empty. It was night now. They hurried down the dark steps and out into the street.

Angelo, as I have said, was away, Cristina had not come back —the simple woman-servant who had nursed the sick man fled with the rest, and the body was left alone in the flickering light of the earthen oil lamp.

Five minutes later two men looked in cautiously and crept forward toward the bed. They were the one-eyed Neapolitan mason and his Sicilian companion. They knew what they wanted. In a moment they had dragged from under the bed a small but heavy iron-bound box, and long before any one thought of coming back to the dead man they had left the house and the village under cover of the darkness. It was easy enough, for Alario's house is the last toward the gorge which leads down here, and the thieves merely went out by the back door, got over the stone wall, and had nothing to risk after that except the possibility of meeting some belated country-man, which was very small indeed, since few of the people use that path. They had a mattock and shovel, and they made their way here without accident.

I am telling you this story as it must have happened, for, of course, there were no witnesses to this part of it. The men brought the box down by the gorge, intending to bury it until they should be able to come back and take it away in a boat. They must have been clever enough to guess that some of the money would be in paper notes, for they would otherwise have buried it on the beach in the wet sand, where it would have been much safer. But the paper would have rotted if they had been obliged to leave it there long, so they dug their hole down there, close to that boulder. Yes, just where the mound is now.

Cristina did not find the doctor in Scalea, for he had been sent for from a place up the valley, halfway to San Domenico. If she had found him, he would have come on his mule by the upper road, which is smoother but much longer. But Cristina took the short cut by the rocks, which passes about fifty feet above the mound, and goes round that corner. The men were digging when she passed, and she heard them at work. It would not have been like her to go by without finding out what the noise was, for she was never afraid of anything in her life, and, besides, the fishermen sometimes come ashore here at night to get a stone for an anchor or to gather sticks to make a little fire. The night was dark, and Cristina probably came close to the two men before she could see what they were doing. She knew them, of course, and they knew her, and understood instantly that they were in her power. There was only one thing to be done for their safety, and they did it. They knocked her on the head, they dug the hole deep, and they buried her quickly with the iron-bound chest. They must have understood that their only chance of escaping suspicion lay in getting back to the village before their absence was noticed, for they returned immediately, and were found half an hour later gossiping quietly with the man who was making Alario's coffin. He was a crony of theirs, and had been working at the repairs in the old man's house. So far as I have been able to make out, the only persons who were supposed to know where Alario kept his treasure were Angelo and the one woman-servant I have mentioned. Angelo was away; it was the woman who discovered the theft.

It is easy enough to understand why no one else knew where the money was. The old man kept his door locked and the key in his pocket when he was out, and did not let the woman enter to clean the place unless he was there himself. The whole village knew that he had money somewhere, however, and the masons had probably discovered the whereabouts of the chest by climbing in at the window in his absence. If the old man had not been delirious until he lost consciousness, he would have been in frightful agony of mind for his riches. The faithful woman-servant forgot their existence only for a few moments when she fled with the rest, overcome by the horror of death. Twenty minutes had not passed before she returned with the two hideous old hags who are always called in to prepare the dead for burial. Even then she had not at first the courage to go near the bed with them, but she made a pretence of dropping something, went down on her knees as if to find it, and looked under the bedstead. The walls of the room were newly whitewashed down to the floor, and she saw at a glance that the chest was gone. It had been there in the afternoon, it had therefore been stolen in the short interval since she had left the room.

There are no carabineers stationed in the village; there is not so much as a municipal watchman, for there is no municipality. There never was such a place, I believe. Scalea is supposed to look after it in some mysterious way, and it takes a couple of hours to get anybody from there. As the old woman had lived in the village all her life, it did not even occur to her to apply to any civil authority for help. She simply set up a howl and ran through the village in the dark, screaming out that her dead master's house had been robbed. Many of the people looked out, but at first no one seemed inclined to help her. Most of them, judging her by themselves, whispered to each other that she had probably stolen the money herself. The first man to move was the father of the girl whom Angelo was to marry; having collected his household, all of whom felt a personal interest in the wealth which was to have come into the family, he declared it to be his opinion that the chest had been stolen by the two journeyman masons who lodged in the house. He headed a search for them, which naturally began in Alario's house and ended in the carpenter's workshop, where the thieves were found discussing a measure of wine with the carpenter over the half-finished coffin, by the light of one earthen lamp filled with oil and tallow. The search party at once accused the delinquents of the crime, and threatened to lock them up in the cellar till the carabineers could be fetched from Scalea. The two men looked at each other for one moment, and then without the slightest hesitation they put out the single light, seized the unfinished coffin between them, and using it as a sort of battering ram, dashed upon their assailants in the dark. In a few moments they were beyond pursuit.

That is the end of the first part of the story. The treasure had disappeared, and as no trace of it could be found the people naturally supposed that the thieves had succeeded in carrying it off. The old man was buried, and when Angelo came back at last he had to borrow money to pay for the miserable funeral, and had some difficulty in doing so. He hardly needed to be told that in losing his inheritance he had lost his bride. In this part of the world marriages are made on strictly business principles, and if the promised cash is not forthcoming on the appointed day the bride or the bridegroom whose parents have failed to produce it may as well take themselves off, for there will be no wedding. Poor Angelo knew that well enough. His father had been possessed of hardly any land, and now that the hard cash which he had brought from South America was gone, there was nothing left but debts for the building materials that were to have been used for enlarging and improving the old house. Angelo was beggared, and the nice plump little creature who was to have been his turned up her nose at him in the most approved fashion. As for Cristina, it was several days before she was missed, for no one remembered that she had been sent to Scalea for the doctor, who had never come. She often disappeared in the same way for days together, when she could find a little work here and there at the distant farms among the hills. But when she did not come back at all, people began to wonder, and at last made up their minds that she had connived with the masons and had escaped with them.

I paused and emptied my glass.

"That sort of thing could not happen anywhere else," observed Holger, filling his everlasting pipe again. "It is wonderful what a natural charm there is about murder and sudden death in a romantic country like this. Deeds that would be simply brutal and disgusting anywhere else become dramatic and mysterious because this is Italy and we are living in a genuine tower of Charles V. built against genuine Barbary pirates."

"There's something in that," I admitted. Holger is the most romantic man in the world inside of himself, but he always thinks it necessary to explain why he feels anything.

"I suppose they found the poor girl's body with the box," he said presently.

"As it seems to interest you," I answered, "I'll tell you the rest of the story."

The moon had risen high by this time; the outline of the Thing on the mound was clearer to our eyes than before.

The village very soon settled down to its small, dull life. No one missed old Alario, who had been away so much on his voyages to South America that he had never been a familiar figure in his native place. Angelo lived in the half-finished house, and because he had no money to pay the old woman-servant she would not stay with him, but once in a long time she would come and wash a shirt for him for old acquaintance' sake. Besides the house, he had inherited a small patch of ground at some distance from the village; he tried to cultivate it, but he had no heart in the work, for he knew he could never pay the taxes on it and on the house, which would certainly be confiscated by the Government, or seized for the debt of the building material, which the man who had supplied it refused to take back.

Angelo was very unhappy. So long as his father had been alive and rich, every girl in the village had been in love with him; but that was all changed now. It had been pleasant to be admired and courted, and invited to drink wine by fathers who had girls to marry. It was hard to be stared at coldly, and some-times laughed at because he had been robbed of his inheri-tance. He cooked his miserable meals for himself, and from being sad became melancholy and morose.

At twilight, when the day's work was done, instead of hanging about in the open space before the church with young fellows of his own age, he took to wandering in lonely places on the outskirts of the village till it was quite dark. Then he slunk home and went to bed to save the expense of a light. But in those lonely twilight hours he began to have strange waking dreams. He was not always alone, for often when he sat on the stump of a tree, where the narrow path turns down the gorge, he was sure that a woman came up noiselessly over the rough stones, as if her feet were bare; and she stood under a clump of chestnut trees only half a dozen yards down the path, and beckoned to him without speaking. Though she was in the shadow he knew that her lips were red, and that when they parted a little and smiled at him she showed two small sharp teeth. He knew this at first rather than saw it, and he knew that it was Cristina, and that she was dead. Yet he was not afraid; he only wondered whether it was a dream, for he thought that if he had been awake he should have been frightened.

Besides, the dead woman had red lips, and that could only happen in a dream. Whenever he went near the gorge after sunset she was already there waiting for him, or else she very soon appeared, and he began to be sure that she came a little nearer to him every day. At first he had only been sure of her blood-red mouth, but now each feature grew distinct, and the pale face looked at him with deep and hungry eyes.

It was the eyes that grew dim. Little by little he came to know that some day the dream would not end when he turned away to go home, but would lead him down the gorge out of which the vision rose. She was nearer now when she beckoned to him. Her cheeks were not livid like those of the dead, but pale with starvation, with the furious and unappeased physical hunger of her eyes that devoured him. They feasted on his soul and cast a spell over him, and at last they were close to his own and held him. He could not tell whether her breath was as hot as fire or as cold as ice; he could not tell whether her red lips burned his or froze them, or whether her five fingers on his wrists seared scorching scars or bit his flesh like frost; he could not tell whether he was awake or asleep, whether she was alive or dead, but he knew that she loved him, she alone of all creatures, earthly or unearthly, and her spell had power over him.

When the moon rose high that night the shadow of that Thing was not alone down there upon the mound.

Angelo awoke in the cool dawn, drenched with dew and chilled through flesh, and blood, and bone. He opened his eyes to the faint grey light, and saw the stars still shining overhead. He was very weak, and his heart was beating so slowly that he was almost like a man fainting. Slowly he turned his head on the mound, as on a pillow, but the other face was not there. Fear seized him suddenly, a fear unspeakable and unknown; he sprang to his feet and fled up the gorge, and he never looked behind him until he reached the door of the house on the outskirts of the village. Drearily he went to his work that day, and wearily the hours dragged themselves after the sun, till at last he touched the sea and sank, and the great sharp hills above Maratea turned purple against the dove-coloured eastern sky.

Angelo shouldered his heavy hoe and left the field. He felt less tired now than in the morning when he had begun to work, but he promised himself that he would go home without lingering by the gorge, and eat the best supper he could get himself, and sleep all night in his bed like a Christian man. Not again would he be tempted down the narrow way by a shadow with red lips and icy breath; not again would he dream that dream of terror and delight. He was near the village now; it was half an hour since the sun had set, and the cracked church bell sent little discordant echoes across the rocks and ravines to tell all good people that the day was done. Angelo stood still a moment where the path forked, where it led toward the village on the left, and down to the gorge on the right, where a clump of chestnut trees overhung the narrow way. He stood still a minute, lifting his battered hat from his head and gazing at the fast-fading sea westward, and his lips moved as he silently repeated the familiar evening prayer. His lips moved, but the words that followed them in his brain lost their meaning and turned into others, and ended in a name that he spoke aloud—Cristina! With the name, the tension of his will relaxed suddenly, reality went out and the dream took him again, and bore him on swiftly and surely like a man walking in his sleep, down, down, by the steep path in the gathering darkness. And as she glided beside him, Cristina whispered strange, sweet things in his ear, which somehow, if he had been awake, he knew that he could not quite have understood; but now they were the most wonderful words he had ever heard in his life. And she kissed him also, but not upon his mouth. He felt her sharp kisses upon his white throat, and he knew that her lips were red. So the wild dream sped on through twilight and darkness and moonrise, and all the glory of the summer's night. But in the chilly dawn he lay as one half dead upon the mound down there, recalling and not recalling, drained of his blood, yet strangely longing to give those red lips more. Then came the fear, the awful nameless panic, the mortal horror that guards the confines of the world we see not, neither know of as we know of other things, but which we feel when its icy chill freezes our bones and stirs our hair with the touch of a ghostly hand. Once more Angelo sprang from the mound and fled up the gorge in the breaking day, but his step was less sure this time, and he panted for breath as he ran; and when he came to the bright spring of water that rises halfway up the hillside, he dropped upon his knees and hands and plunged his whole face in and drank as he had never drunk before—for it was the thirst of the wounded man who has lain bleeding all night long upon the battle-field.

She had him fast now, and he could not escape her, but would come to her every evening at dusk until she had drained him of his last drop of blood. It was in vain that when the day was done he tried to take another turning and to go home by a path that did not lead near the gorge. It was in vain that he made promises to himself each morning at dawn when he climbed the lonely way up from the shore to the village. It was all in vain, for when the sun sank burning into the sea, and the coolness of the evening stole out as from a hiding-place to delight the weary world, his feet turned toward the old way, and she was waiting for him in the shadow under the chestnut trees; and then all happened as before, and she fell to kissing his white throat even as she flitted lightly down the way, winding one arm about him. And as his blood failed, she grew more hungry and more thirsty every day, and every day when he awoke in the early dawn it was harder to rouse himself to the effort of climbing the steep path to the village; and when he went to his work his feet dragged painfully, and there was hardly strength in his arms to wield the heavy hoe. He scarcely spoke to any one now, but the people said he was "consuming himself" for love of the girl he was to have married when he lost his inheritance; and they laughed heartily at the thought, for this is not a very romantic country. At this time, Antonio, the man who stays here to look after the tower, returned from a visit to his people, who live near Salerno. He had been away all the time since before Alario's death and knew nothing of what had happened. He has told me that he came back late in the afternoon and shut himself up in the tower to eat and sleep, for he was very tired. It was past midnight when he awoke, and when he looked out the waning moon was rising over the shoulder of the hill. He looked out toward the mound, and he saw something, and he did not sleep again that night. When he went out again in the morning it was broad daylight, and there was nothing to be seen on the mound but loose stones and driven sand. Yet he did not go very near it; he went straight up the path to the village and directly to the house of the old priest.

"I have seen an evil thing this night," he said; "I have seen how the dead drink the blood of the living. And the blood is the life."

"Tell me what you have seen," said the priest in reply.

Antonio told him everything he had seen.

"You must bring your book and your holy water to-night," he added. "I will be here before sunset to go down with you, and if it pleases your reverence to sup with me while we wait, I will make ready."

"I will come," the priest answered, "for I have read in old books of these strange beings which are neither quick nor dead, and which lie ever fresh in their graves, stealing out in the dusk to taste life and blood."

Antonio cannot read, but he was glad to see that the priest understood the business; for, of course, the books must have instructed him as to the best means of quieting the half-living Thing for ever.

So Antonio went away to his work, which consists largely in sitting on the shady side of the tower, when he is not perched upon a rock with a fishing-line catching nothing. But on that day he went twice to look at the mound in the bright sunlight, and he searched round and round it for some hole through which the being might get in and out; but he found none. When the sun began to sink and the air was cooler in the shadows, he went up to fetch the old priest, carrying a little wicker basket with him; and in this they placed a bottle of holy water, and the basin, and sprinkler, and the stole which the priest would need; and they came down and waited in the door of the tower till it should be dark. But while the light still lingered very grey and faint, they saw something moving, just there, two figures, a man's that walked, and a woman's that flitted beside him, and while her head lay on his shoulder she kissed his throat. The priest has told me that, too, and that his teeth chattered and he grasped Antonio's arm. The vision passed and disappeared into the shadow. Then Antonio got the leathern flask of strong liquor, which he kept for great occasions, and poured such a draught as made the old man feel almost young again; and he got the lantern, and his pick and shovel, and gave the priest his stole to put on and the holy water to carry, and they went out together toward the spot

where the work was to be done. Antonio says that in spite of
the rum his own knees shook together, and the priest stumbled over his Latin. For when they were yet a few yards from
the mound the flickering light of the lantern fell upon Angelo's white face, unconscious as if in sleep, and on his upturned throat, over which a very thin red line of blood trickled
down into his collar; and the flickering light of the lantern
played upon another face that looked up from the feast—upon
two deep, dead eyes that saw in spite of death—upon parted
lips redder than life itself—upon two gleaming teeth on which
glistened a rosy drop. Then the priest, good old man, shut his
eyes tight and showered holy water before him, and his cracked
voice rose almost to a scream; and then Antonio, who is no
coward after all, raised his pick in one hand and the lantern in
the other, as he sprang forward, not knowing what the end
should be; and then he swears that he heard a woman's cry,
and the Thing was gone, and Angelo lay alone on the mound
unconscious, with the red line on his throat and the beads of
deathly sweat on his cold forehead. They lifted him, half-dead
as he was, and laid him on the ground close by; then Antonio
went to work, and the priest helped him, though he was old
and could not do much; and they dug deep, and at last Antonio, standing in the grave, stooped down with his lantern to
see what he might see.

His hair used to be dark brown, with grizzled streaks about
the temples; in less than a month from that day he was as grey
as a badger. He was a miner when he was young, and most of
these fellows have seen ugly sights now and then, when accidents have happened, but he had never seen what he saw that
night—that Thing which is neither alive nor dead, that Thing
that will abide neither above ground nor in the grave. Antonio
had brought something with him which the priest had not noticed. He had made it that afternoon—a sharp stake shaped
from a piece of tough old driftwood. He had it with him now,
and he had his heavy pick, and he had taken the lantern down
into the grave. I don't think any power on earth could make
him speak of what happened then, and the old priest was too
frightened to look in. He says he heard Antonio breathing like
a wild beast, and moving as if he were fighting with something
almost as strong as himself; and he heard an evil sound also,

with blows, as of something violently driven through flesh and bone; and then the most awful sound of all—a woman's shriek, the unearthly scream of a woman neither dead nor alive, but buried deep for many days. And he, the poor old priest, could only rock himself as he knelt there in the sand, crying aloud his prayers and exorcisms to drown these dreadful sounds. Then suddenly a small iron-bound chest was thrown up and rolled over against the old man's knee, and in a moment more Antonio was beside him, his face as white as tallow in the flickering light of the lantern, shovelling the sand and pebbles into the grave with furious haste, and looking over the edge till the pit was half full; and the priest said that there was much fresh blood on Antonio's hands and on his clothes.

I had come to the end of my story. Holger finished his wine and leaned back in his chair.

"So Angelo got his own again," he said. "Did he marry the prim and plump young person to whom he had been betrothed?"

"No; he had been badly frightened. He went to South America, and has not been heard of since."

"And that poor thing's body is there still, I suppose," said Holger. "Is it quite dead yet, I wonder?"

I wonder, too. But whether it be dead or alive, I should hardly care to see it, even in broad daylight. Antonio is as grey as a badger, and he has never been quite the same man since that night.

1905

AMBROSE BIERCE

(1842–1914?)

The Moonlit Road

I

STATEMENT OF JOEL HETMAN, JR.

I AM the most unfortunate of men. Rich, respected, fairly well educated and of sound health—with many other advantages usually valued by those having them and coveted by those who have them not—I sometimes think that I should be less unhappy if they had been denied me, for then the contrast between my outer and my inner life would not be continually demanding a painful attention. In the stress of privation and the need of effort I might sometimes forget the somber secret ever baffling the conjecture that it compels.

I am the only child of Joel and Julia Hetman. The one was a well-to-do country gentleman, the other a beautiful and accomplished woman to whom he was passionately attached with what I now know to have been a jealous and exacting devotion. The family home was a few miles from Nashville, Tennessee, a large, irregularly built dwelling of no particular order of architecture, a little way off the road, in a park of trees and shrubbery.

At the time of which I write I was nineteen years old, a student at Yale. One day I received a telegram from my father of such urgency that in compliance with its unexplained demand I left at once for home. At the railway station in Nashville a distant relative awaited me to apprise me of the reason for my recall: my mother had been barbarously murdered—why and by whom none could conjecture, but the circumstances were these:

My father had gone to Nashville, intending to return the next afternoon. Something prevented his accomplishing the business in hand, so he returned on the same night, arriving just before the dawn. In his testimony before the coroner he explained that having no latchkey and not caring to disturb the sleeping servants, he had, with no clearly defined intention, gone round to the rear of the house. As he turned an angle of the building, he heard a sound as of a door gently closed, and saw in the darkness, indistinctly, the figure of a man, which instantly disappeared among the trees of the lawn. A hasty pursuit and brief search of the grounds in the belief that the trespasser was some one secretly visiting a servant proving fruitless, he entered at the unlocked door and mounted the stairs to my mother's chamber. Its door was open, and stepping into black darkness he fell headlong over some heavy object on the floor. I may spare myself the details; it was my poor mother, dead of strangulation by human hands!

Nothing had been taken from the house, the servants had heard no sound, and excepting those terrible finger-marks upon the dead woman's throat—dear God! that I might forget them!—no trace of the assassin was ever found.

I gave up my studies and remained with my father, who, naturally, was greatly changed. Always of a sedate, taciturn disposition, he now fell into so deep a dejection that nothing could hold his attention, yet anything—a footfall, the sudden closing of a door—aroused in him a fitful interest; one might have called it an apprehension. At any small surprise of the senses he would start visibly and sometimes turn pale, then relapse into a melancholy apathy deeper than before. I suppose he was what is called a "nervous wreck." As to me, I was younger then than now—there is much in that. Youth is Gilead, in which is balm for every wound. Ah, that I might again dwell in that enchanted land! Unacquainted with grief, I knew not how to appraise my bereavement; I could not rightly estimate the strength of the stroke.

One night, a few months after the dreadful event, my father and I walked home from the city. The full moon was about three hours above the eastern horizon; the entire countryside had the solemn stillness of a summer night; our footfalls and the ceaseless song of the katydids were the only sound aloof. Black shadows of bordering trees lay athwart the road, which, in the short reaches between, gleamed a ghostly white. As we

approached the gate to our dwelling, whose front was in
shadow, and in which no light shone, my father suddenly
stopped and clutched my arm, saying, hardly above his breath:

"God! God! what is that?"

"I hear nothing," I replied.

"But see—see!" he said, pointing along the road, directly
ahead.

I said: "Nothing is there. Come, father, let us go in—you
are ill."

He had released my arm and was standing rigid and motionless in the center of the illuminated roadway, staring like one
bereft of sense. His face in the moonlight showed a pallor and
fixity inexpressibly distressing. I pulled gently at his sleeve, but
he had forgotten my existence. Presently he began to retire
backward, step by step, never for an instant removing his eyes
from what he saw, or thought he saw. I turned half round to
follow, but stood irresolute. I do not recall any feeling of fear,
unless a sudden chill was its physical manifestation. It seemed
as if an icy wind had touched my face and enfolded my body
from head to foot; I could feel the stir of it in my hair.

At that moment my attention was drawn to a light that suddenly streamed from an upper window of the house: one of
the servants, awakened by what mysterious premonition of evil
who can say, and in obedience to an impulse that she was never
able to name, had lit a lamp. When I turned to look for my
father he was gone, and in all the years that have passed no
whisper of his fate has come across the borderland of conjecture from the realm of the unknown.

II

STATEMENT OF CASPAR GRATTAN

To-day I am said to live; to-morrow, here in this room, will
lie a senseless shape of clay that all too long was I. If anyone lift
the cloth from the face of that unpleasant thing it will be in
gratification of a mere morbid curiosity. Some, doubtless, will
go further and inquire, "Who was he?" In this writing I supply
the only answer that I am able to make—Caspar Grattan. Surely,
that should be enough. The name has served my small need
for more than twenty years of a life of unknown length. True,

I gave it to myself, but lacking another I had the right. In this world one must have a name; it prevents confusion, even when it does not establish identity. Some, though, are known by numbers, which also seem inadequate distinctions.

One day, for illustration, I was passing along a street of a city, far from here, when I met two men in uniform, one of whom, half pausing and looking curiously into my face, said to his companion, "That man looks like 767." Something in the number seemed familiar and horrible. Moved by an uncontrollable impulse, I sprang into a side street and ran until I fell exhausted in a country lane.

I have never forgotten that number, and always it comes to memory attended by gibbering obscenity, peals of joyless laughter, the clang of iron doors. So I say a name, even if self-bestowed, is better than a number. In the register of the potter's field I shall soon have both. What wealth!

Of him who shall find this paper I must beg a little consideration. It is not the history of my life; the knowledge to write that is denied me. This is only a record of broken and apparently unrelated memories, some of them as distinct and sequent as brilliant beads upon a thread, others remote and strange, having the character of crimson dreams with interspaces blank and black—witch-fires glowing still and red in a great desolation.

Standing upon the shore of eternity, I turn for a last look landward over the course by which I came. There are twenty years of footprints fairly distinct, the impressions of bleeding feet. They lead through poverty and pain, devious and unsure, as of one staggering beneath a burden—

Remote, unfriended, melancholy, slow.

Ah, the poet's prophecy of Me—how admirable, how dreadfully admirable!

Backward beyond the beginning of this *via dolorosa*—this epic of suffering with episodes of sin—I see nothing clearly; it comes out of a cloud. I know that it spans only twenty years, yet I am an old man.

One does not remember one's birth—one has to be told. But with me it was different; life came to me full-handed and dowered me with all my faculties and powers. Of a previous existence I know no more than others, for all have stammering intimations that may be memories and may be dreams. I know only that my first consciousness was of maturity in body and mind—a consciousness accepted without surprise or conjecture. I merely found myself walking in a forest, half-clad, foot-sore, unutterably weary and hungry. Seeing a farmhouse, I approached and asked for food, which was given me by one who inquired my name. I did not know, yet knew that all had names. Greatly embarrassed, I retreated, and night coming on, lay down in the forest and slept.

The next day I entered a large town which I shall not name. Nor shall I recount further incidents of the life that is now to end—a life of wandering, always and everywhere haunted by an overmastering sense of crime in punishment of wrong and of terror in punishment of crime. Let me see if I can reduce it to narrative.

I seem once to have lived near a great city, a prosperous planter, married to a woman whom I loved and distrusted. We had, it sometimes seems, one child, a youth of brilliant parts and promise. He is at all times a vague figure, never clearly drawn, frequently altogether out of the picture.

One luckless evening it occurred to me to test my wife's fidelity in a vulgar, commonplace way familiar to everyone who has acquaintance with the literature of fact and fiction. I went to the city, telling my wife that I should be absent until the following afternoon. But I returned before daybreak and went to the rear of the house, purposing to enter by a door with which I had secretly so tampered that it would seem to lock, yet not actually fasten. As I approached it, I heard it gently open and close, and saw a man steal away into the darkness. With murder in my heart, I sprang after him, but he had vanished without even the bad luck of identification. Sometimes now I cannot even persuade myself that it was a human being.

Crazed with jealousy and rage, blind and bestial with all the elemental passions of insulted manhood, I entered the house and sprang up the stairs to the door of my wife's chamber. It was closed, but having tampered with its lock also, I easily entered and despite the black darkness soon stood by the side of her bed. My groping hands told me that although disarranged it was unoccupied.

"She is below," I thought, "and terrified by my entrance has evaded me in the darkness of the hall."

With the purpose of seeking her I turned to leave the room, but took a wrong direction—the right one! My foot struck her, cowering in a corner of the room. Instantly my hands were at her throat, stifling a shriek, my knees were upon her struggling body; and there in the darkness, without a word of accusation or reproach, I strangled her till she died!

There ends the dream. I have related it in the past tense, but the present would be the fitter form, for again and again the somber tragedy reenacts itself in my consciousness—over and over I lay the plan, I suffer the confirmation, I redress the wrong. Then all is blank; and afterward the rains beat against the grimy window-panes, or the snows fall upon my scant attire, the wheels rattle in the squalid streets where my life lies in poverty and mean employment. If there is ever sunshine I do not recall it; if there are birds they do not sing.

There is another dream, another vision of the night. I stand among the shadows in a moonlit road. I am aware of another presence, but whose I cannot rightly determine. In the shadow of a great dwelling I catch the gleam of white garments; then the figure of a woman confronts me in the road—my murdered wife! There is death in the face; there are marks upon the throat. The eyes are fixed on mine with an infinite gravity which is not reproach, nor hate, nor menace, nor anything less terrible than recognition. Before this awful apparition I retreat in terror—a terror that is upon me as I write. I can no longer rightly shape the words. See! they—

Now I am calm, but truly there is no more to tell: the incident ends where it began—in darkness and in doubt.

Yes, I am again in control of myself: "the captain of my soul." But that is not respite; it is another stage and phase of expiation. My penance, constant in degree, is mutable in kind: one of its variants is tranquillity. After all, it is only a life-sentence. "To Hell for life"—that is a foolish penalty: the culprit chooses the duration of his punishment. To-day my term expires.

To each and all, the peace that was not mine.

III

STATEMENT OF THE LATE JULIA HETMAN,
THROUGH THE MEDIUM BAYROLLES

I had retired early and fallen almost immediately into a peaceful sleep, from which I awoke with that indefinable sense of peril which is, I think, a common experience in that other, earlier life. Of its unmeaning character, too, I was entirely persuaded, yet that did not banish it. My husband, Joel Hetman, was away from home; the servants slept in another part of the house. But these were familiar conditions; they had never before distressed me. Nevertheless, the strange terror grew so insupportable that conquering my reluctance to move I sat up and lit the lamp at my bedside. Contrary to my expectation this gave me no relief; the light seemed rather an added danger, for I reflected that it would shine out under the door, disclosing my presence to whatever evil thing might lurk outside. You that are still in the flesh, subject to horrors of the imagination, think what a monstrous fear that must be which seeks in darkness security from malevolent existences of the night. That is to spring to close quarters with an unseen enemy—the strategy of despair!

Extinguishing the lamp I pulled the bed-clothing about my head and lay trembling and silent, unable to shriek, forgetful to pray. In this pitiable state I must have lain for what you call hours—with us there are no hours, there is no time.

At last it came—a soft, irregular sound of footfalls on the stairs! They were slow, hesitant, uncertain, as of something that did not see its way; to my disordered reason all the more terrifying for that, as the approach of some blind and mindless malevolence to which is no appeal. I even thought that I must have left the hall lamp burning and the groping of this creature proved it a monster of the night. This was foolish and inconsistent with my previous dread of the light, but what would you have? Fear has no brains; it is an idiot. The dismal witness that it bears and the cowardly counsel that it whispers are unrelated. We know this well, we who have passed into the Realm of Terror, who skulk in eternal dusk among the scenes of our former lives, invisible even to ourselves and one another, yet hiding forlorn in lonely places; yearning for speech with our loved ones, yet dumb, and as fearful of them as they of us. Sometimes the disability is removed, the law suspended: by the deathless power of love or hate we break the spell—we are seen by those whom we would warn, console, or punish. What form we seem to them to bear we know not; we know only that we terrify even those whom we most wish to comfort, and from whom we most crave tenderness and sympathy.

Forgive, I pray you, this inconsequent digression by what was once a woman. You who consult us in this imperfect way —you do not understand. You ask foolish questions about things unknown and things forbidden. Much that we know and could impart in our speech is meaningless in yours. We must communicate with you through a stammering intelligence in that small fraction of our language that you yourselves can speak. You think that we are of another world. No, we have knowledge of no world but yours, though for us it holds no sunlight, no warmth, no music, no laughter, no song of birds, nor any companionship. O God! what a thing it is to be a ghost, cowering and shivering in an altered world, a prey to apprehension and despair!

No, I did not die of fright: the Thing turned and went away. I heard it go down the stairs, hurriedly, I thought, as if itself in sudden fear. Then I rose to call for help. Hardly had my shaking hand found the doorknob when—merciful heaven!—I heard it returning. Its footfalls as it remounted the stairs were rapid, heavy and loud; they shook the house. I fled to an angle of the wall and crouched upon the floor. I tried to pray. I tried to call the name of my dear husband. Then I heard the door thrown open. There was an interval of unconsciousness, and when I revived I felt a strangling clutch upon my throat—felt my arms feebly beating against something that bore me backward—felt my tongue thrusting itself from between my teeth! And then I passed into this life.

No, I have no knowledge of what it was. The sum of what we knew at death is the measure of what we know afterward of all that went before. Of this existence we know many things, but no new light falls upon any page of that; in memory is written all of it that we can read. Here are no heights of truth overlooking the confused landscape of that dubitable domain. We still dwell in the Valley of the Shadow, lurk in its desolate places, peering from brambles and thickets at its mad, malign inhabitants. How should we have new knowledge of that fading past?

What I am about to relate happened on a night. We know when it is night, for then you retire to your houses and we can venture from our places of concealment to move unafraid about our old homes, to look in at the windows, even to enter and gaze upon your faces as you sleep. I had lingered long near the dwelling where I had been so cruelly changed to what I am, as we do while any that we love or hate remain. Vainly I had sought some method of manifestation, some way to make my continued existence and my great love and poignant pity understood by my husband and son. Always if they slept they would wake, or if in my desperation I dared approach them when they were awake, would turn toward me the terrible eyes of the living, frightening me by the glances that I sought from the purpose that I held.

On this night I had searched for them without success, fearing to find them; they were nowhere in the house, nor about the moonlit lawn. For, although the sun is lost to us forever, the moon, full-orbed or slender, remains to us. Sometimes it shines by night, sometimes by day, but always it rises and sets, as in that other life.

I left the lawn and moved in the white light and silence along the road, aimless and sorrowing. Suddenly I heard the voice of my poor husband in exclamations of astonishment, with that of my son in reassurance and dissuasion; and there by the shadow of a group of trees they stood—near, so near! Their faces were toward me, the eyes of the elder man fixed upon mine. He saw me—at last, at last, he saw me! In the consciousness of that, my terror fled as a cruel dream. The death-spell was broken: Love had conquered Law! Mad with exultation I shouted —I *must* have shouted, "He sees, he sees: he will understand!" Then, controlling myself, I moved forward, smiling and consciously beautiful, to offer myself to his arms, to comfort him with endearments, and, with my son's hand in mine, to speak words that should restore the broken bonds between the living and the dead.

Alas! alas! his face went white with fear, his eyes were as

those of a hunted animal. He backed away from me, as I advanced, and at last turned and fled into the wood—whither, it is not given to me to know.

To my poor boy, left doubly desolate, I have never been able to impart a sense of my presence. Soon he, too, must pass to this Life Invisible and be lost to me forever.

1907

EDWARD LUCAS WHITE

(1866–1934)

Lukundoo

"It stands to reason," said Twombly, "that a man must accept the evidence of his own eyes, and when eyes and ears agree, there can be no doubt. He has to believe what he has both seen and heard."

"Not always," put in Singleton, softly.

Every man turned toward Singleton. Twombly was standing on the hearth-rug, his back to the grate, his legs spread out, with his habitual air of dominating the room. Singleton, as usual, was as much as possible effaced in a corner. But when Singleton spoke he said something. We faced him in that flattering spontaneity of expectant silence which invites utterance.

"I was thinking," he said, after an interval, "of something I both saw and heard in Africa."

Now, if there was one thing we had found impossible it had been to elicit from Singleton anything definite about his African experiences. As with the Alpinist in the story, who could tell only that he went up and came down, the sum of Singleton's revelations had been that he went there and came away. His words now riveted our attention at once. Twombly faded from the hearth-rug, but not one of us could ever recall having seen him go. The room readjusted itself, focused on Singleton, and there was some hasty and furtive lighting of fresh cigars. Singleton lit one also, but it went out immediately, and he never relit it.

I

We were in the Great Forest, exploring for pigmies. Van Rieten had a theory that the dwarfs found by Stanley and others were a mere cross-breed between ordinary negroes and the real pigmies. He hoped to discover a race of men three feet tall at most, or shorter. We had found no trace of any such beings.

Natives were few; game scarce; food, except game, there was none; and the deepest, dankest, drippingest forest all about. We were the only novelty in the country, no native we met had even seen a white man before, most had never heard of white men. All of a sudden, late one afternoon, there came into our camp an Englishman, and pretty well used up he was, too. We had heard no rumor of him; he had not only heard of us but had made an amazing five-day march to reach us. His guide and two bearers were nearly as done up as he. Even though he was in tatters and had five days' beard on, you could see he was naturally dapper and neat and the sort of man to shave daily. He was small, but wiry. His face was the sort of British face from which emotion has been so carefully banished that a foreigner is apt to think the wearer of the face incapable of any sort of feeling; the kind of face which, if it has any expression at all, expresses principally the resolution to go through the world decorously, without intruding upon or annoying anyone.

His name was Etcham. He introduced himself modestly, and ate with us so deliberately that we should never have suspected, if our bearers had not had it from his bearers, that he had had but three meals in the five days, and those small. After we had lit up he told us why he had come.

"My chief is ve'y seedy," he said between puffs. "He is bound to go out if he keeps this way. I thought perhaps. . . ."

He spoke quietly in a soft, even tone, but I could see little beads of sweat oozing out on his upper lip under his stubby mustache, and there was a tingle of repressed emotion in his tone, a veiled eagerness in his eye, a palpitating inward solicitude in his demeanor that moved me at once. Van Rieten had no sentiment in him; if he was moved he did not show it. But he listened. I was surprised at that. He was just the man to refuse at once. But he listened to Etcham's halting, diffident hints. He even asked questions.

"Who is your chief?"

"Stone," Etcham lisped.

That electrified both of us.

"Ralph Stone?" we ejaculated together.

Etcham nodded.

For some minutes Van Rieten and I were silent. Van Rieten had never seen him, but I had been a classmate of Stone's, and

Van Rieten and I had discussed him over many a camp-fire. We had heard of him two years before, south of Luebo in the Balunda country, which had been ringing with his theatrical strife against a Balunda witch-doctor, ending in the sorcerer's complete discomfiture and the abasement of his tribe before Stone. They had even broken the fetish-man's whistle and given Stone the pieces. It had been like the triumph of Elijah over the prophets of Baal, only more real to the Balunda.

We had thought of Stone as far off, if still in Africa at all, and here he turned up ahead of us and probably forestalling our quest.

II

Etcham's naming of Stone brought back to us all his tantalizing story, his fascinating parents, their tragic death; the brilliance of his college days; the dazzle of his millions; the promise of his young manhood; his wide notoriety, so nearly real fame; his romantic elopement with the meteoric authoress whose sudden cascade of fiction had made her so great a name so young, whose beauty and charm were so much heralded; the frightful scandal of the breach-of-promise suit that followed; his bride's devotion through it all; their sudden quarrel after it was all over; their divorce; the too much advertised announcement of his approaching marriage to the plaintiff in the breach-of-promise suit; his precipitate remarriage to his divorced bride; their second quarrel and second divorce; his departure from his native land; his advent in the dark continent. The sense of all this rushed over me and I believe Van Rieten felt it, too, as he sat silent.

Then he asked:

"Where is Werner?"

"Dead," said Etcham. "He died before I joined Stone."

"You were not with Stone above Luebo?"

"No," said Etcham, "I joined him at Stanley Falls."

"Who is with him?" Van Rieten asked.

"Only his Zanzibar servants and the bearers," Etcham replied.

"What sort of bearers?" Van Rieten demanded.

"Mang-Battu men," Etcham responded simply.

Now that impressed both Van Rieten and myself greatly. It

bore out Stone's reputation as a notable leader of men. For up to that time no one had been able to use Mang-Battu as bearers outside of their own country, or to hold them for long or difficult expeditions.

"Were you long among the Mang-Battu?" was Van Rieten's next question.

"Some weeks," said Etcham. "Stone was interested in them and made up a fair-sized vocabulary of their words and phrases. He had a theory that they are an offshoot of the Balunda and he found much confirmation in their customs."

"What do you live on?" Van Rieten inquired.

"Game, mostly," Etcham lisped.

"How long has Stone been laid up?" Van Rieten next asked.

"More than a month," Etcham answered.

"And you have been hunting for the camp!" Van Rieten exclaimed.

Etcham's face, burnt and flayed as it was, showed a flush.

"I missed some easy shots," he admitted ruefully. "I've not felt ve'y fit myself."

"What's the matter with your chief?" Van Rieten inquired.

"Something like carbuncles," Etcham replied.

"He ought to get over a carbuncle or two," Van Rieten declared.

"They are not carbuncles," Etcham explained. "Nor one or two. He has had dozens, sometimes five at once. If they had been carbuncles he would have been dead long ago. But in some ways they are not so bad, though in others they are worse."

"How do you mean?" Van Rieten queried.

"Well," Etcham hesitated, "they do not seem to inflame so deep nor so wide as carbuncles, nor to be so painful, nor to cause so much fever. But then they seem to be part of a disease that affects his mind. He let me help him dress the first, but the others he has hidden most carefully, from me and from the men. He keeps his tent when they puff up, and will not let me change the dressings or be with him at all."

"Have you plenty of dressings?" Van Rieten asked.

"We have some," said Etcham doubtfully. "But he won't use them; he washes out the dressings and uses them over and over."

"How is he treating the swellings?" Van Rieten inquired.

"He slices them off clear down to flesh level, with his razor."

"What?" Van Rieten shouted.

Etcham made no answer but looked him steadily in the eyes.

"I beg pardon," Van Rieten hastened to say. "You startled me. They can't be carbuncles. He'd have been dead long ago."

"I thought I had said they are not carbuncles," Etcham lisped.

"But the man must be crazy!" Van Rieten exclaimed.

"Just so," said Etcham. "He is beyond my advice or control."

"How many has he treated that way?" Van Rieten demanded.

"Two, to my knowledge," Etcham said.

"Two?" Van Rieten queried.

Etcham flushed again.

"I saw him," he confessed, "through a crack in the hut. I felt impelled to keep a watch on him, as if he was not responsible."

"I should think not," Van Rieten agreed. "And you saw him do that twice?"

"I conjecture," said Etcham, "that he did the like with all the rest."

"How many has he had?" Van Rieten asked.

"Dozens," Etcham lisped.

"Does he eat?" Van Rieten inquired.

"Like a wolf," said Etcham. "More than any two bearers."

"Can he walk?" Van Rieten asked.

"He crawls a bit, groaning," said Etcham simply.

"Little fever, you say," Van Rieten ruminated.

"Enough and too much," Etcham declared.

"Has he been delirious?" Van Rieten asked.

"Only twice," Etcham replied; "once when the first swelling broke, and once later. He would not let anyone come near him then. But we could hear him talking, talking steadily, and it scared the natives."

"Was he talking their patter in delirium?" Van Rieten demanded.

"No," said Etcham, "but he was talking some similar lingo. Hamed Burghash said he was talking Balunda. I know too little Balunda. I do not learn languages readily. Stone learned more Mang-Battu in a week than I could have learned in a year. But I seemed to hear words like Mang-Battu words. Anyhow the Mang-Battu bearers were scared."

"Scared?" Van Rieten repeated, questioningly.

"So were the Zanzibar men, even Hamed Burghash, and so was I," said Etcham, "only for a different reason. He talked in two voices."

"In two voices," Van Rieten reflected.

"Yes," said Etcham, more excitedly than he had yet spoken. "In two voices, like a conversation. One was his own, one a small, thin, bleaty voice like nothing I ever heard. I seemed to make out, among the sounds the deep voice made, something like Mang-Battu words I knew, as *nedru*, *metebaba*, and *nedo*, their terms for 'head,' 'shoulder,' 'thigh,' and perhaps *kudra* and *nekere* ('speak' and 'whistle'); and among the noises of the shrill voice *matomipa*, *angunzi*, and *kamomami* ('kill,' 'death,' and 'hate'). Hamed Burghash said he also heard those words. He knew Mang-Battu far better than I."

"What did the bearers say?" Van Rieten asked.

"They said, '*Lukundoo, Lukundoo!*'" Etcham replied. "I did not know that word; Hamed Burghash said it was Mang-Battu for 'leopard.'"

"It's Mang-Battu for 'witchcraft,'" said Van Rieten.

"I don't wonder they thought so," said Etcham. "It was enough to make one believe in sorcery to listen to those two voices."

"One voice answering the other?" Van Rieten asked perfunctorily.

Etcham's face went gray under his tan.

"Sometimes both at once," he answered huskily.

"Both at once!" Van Rieten ejaculated.

"It sounded that way to the men, too," said Etcham. "And that was not all."

He stopped and looked helplessly at us for a moment.

"Could a man talk and whistle at the same time?" he asked.

"How do you mean?" Van Rieten queried.

"We could hear Stone talking away, his big, deep-chested baritone rumbling along, and through it all we could hear a high, shrill whistle, the oddest, wheezy sound. You know, no matter how shrilly a grown man may whistle, the note has a different quality from the whistle of a boy or a woman or little girl. They sound more treble, somehow. Well, if you can imagine the smallest girl who could whistle keeping it up tunelessly right along, that whistle was like that, only even more piercing, and it sounded right through Stone's bass tones."

"And you didn't go to him?" Van Rieten cried.

"He is not given to threats," Etcham disclaimed. "But he had threatened, not volubly, nor like a sick man, but quietly and firmly, that if any man of us (he lumped me in with the men), came near him while he was in his trouble, that man should die. And it was not so much his words as his manner. It was like a monarch commanding respected privacy for a death-bed. One simply could not transgress."

"I see," said Van Rieten shortly.

"He's ve'y seedy," Etcham repeated helplessly. "I thought perhaps. . . ."

His absorbing affection for Stone, his real love for him, shone out through his envelope of conventional training. Worship of Stone was plainly his master passion.

Like many competent men, Van Rieten had a streak of hard selfishness in him. It came to the surface then. He said we carried our lives in our hands from day to day just as genuinely as Stone; that he did not forget the ties of blood and calling between any two explorers, but that there was no sense in imperiling one party for a very problematical benefit to a man probably beyond any help; that it was enough of a task to hunt for one party; that if two were united, providing food would be more than doubly difficult; that the risk of starvation was too great. Deflecting our march seven full days' journey (he complimented Etcham on his marching powers) might ruin our expedition entirely.

III

Van Rieten had logic on his side and he had a way with him. Etcham sat there apologetic and deferential, like a fourth-form schoolboy before a head master. Van Rieten wound up.

"I am after pigmies, at the risk of my life. After pigmies I go."

"Perhaps, then, these will interest you," said Etcham, very quietly.

He took two objects out of the sidepocket of his blouse, and handed them to Van Rieten. They were round, bigger than big plums, and smaller than small peaches, about the right size to

enclose in an average hand. They were black, and at first I did
not see what they were.

"Pigmies!" Van Rieten exclaimed. "Pigmies, indeed! Why,
they wouldn't be two feet high! Do you mean to claim that
these are adult heads?"

"I claim nothing," Etcham answered evenly. "You can see
for yourself."

Van Rieten passed one of the heads to me. The sun was just
setting and I examined it closely. A dried head it was, perfectly
preserved, and the flesh as hard as Argentine jerked beef. A bit of
a vertebra stuck out where the muscles of the vanished neck had
shriveled into folds. The puny chin was sharp on a projecting
jaw, the minute teeth white and even between the retracted
lips, the tiny nose was flat, the little forehead retreating, there
were inconsiderable clumps of stunted wool on the Lilliputian
cranium. There was nothing babyish, childish or youthful
about the head, rather it was mature to senility.

"Where did these come from?" Van Rieten inquired.

"I do not know," Etcham replied precisely. "I found them
among Stone's effects while rummaging for medicines or drugs
or anything that could help me to help him. I do not know
where he got them. But I'll swear he did not have them when
we entered this district."

"Are you sure?" Van Rieten queried, his eyes big and fixed
on Etcham's.

"Ve'y sure," lisped Etcham.

"But how could he have come by them without your knowledge?" Van Rieten demurred.

"Sometimes we were apart ten days at a time hunting," said
Etcham. "Stone is not a talking man. He gave me no account
of his doings and Hamed Burghash keeps a still tongue and a
tight hold on the men."

"You have examined these heads?" Van Rieten asked.

"Minutely," said Etcham.

Van Rieten took out his notebook. He was a methodical
chap. He tore out a leaf, folded it and divided it equally into
three pieces. He gave one to me and one to Etcham.

"Just for a test of my impressions," he said, "I want each of
us to write separately just what he is most reminded of by these
heads. Then I want to compare the writings."

I handed Etcham a pencil and he wrote. Then he handed the pencil back to me and I wrote.

"Read the three," said Van Rieten, handing me his piece.

Van Rieten had written:

"An old Balunda witch-doctor."

Etcham had written:

"An old Mang-Battu fetish-man."

I had written:

"An old Katongo magician."

"There!" Van Rieten exclaimed. "Look at that! There is nothing Wagabi or Batwa or Wambuttu or Wabotu about these heads. Nor anything pigmy either."

"I thought as much," said Etcham.

"And you say he did not have them before?"

"To a certainty he did not," Etcham asserted.

"It is worth following up," said Van Rieten. "I'll go with you. And first of all, I'll do my best to save Stone."

He put out his hand and Etcham clasped it silently. He was grateful all over.

IV

Nothing but Etcham's fever of solicitude could have taken him in five days over the track. It took him eight days to re-trace with full knowledge of it and our party to help. We could not have done it in seven, and Etcham urged us on, in a re-pressed fury of anxiety, no mere fever of duty to his chief, but a real ardor of devotion, a glow of personal adoration for Stone which blazed under his dry conventional exterior and showed in spite of him.

We found Stone well cared for. Etcham had seen to a good, high thorn *zareeba* round the camp, the huts were well built and thatched and Stone's was as good as their resources would permit. Hamed Burghash was not named after two Seyyids for nothing. He had in him the making of a sultan. He had kept the Mang-Battu together, not a man had slipped off, and he had kept them in order. Also he was a deft nurse and a faithful servant.

The two other Zanzabaris had done some creditable hunt-ing. Though all were hungry, the camp was far from starvation.

Stone was on a canvas cot and there was a sort of collapsible camp-stool-table, like a Turkish tabouret, by the cot. It had a water-bottle and some vials on it and Stone's watch, also his razor in its case.

Stone was clean and not emaciated, but he was far gone; not unconscious, but in a daze; past commanding or resisting anyone. He did not seem to see us enter or to know we were there. I should have recognized him anywhere. His boyish dash and grace had vanished utterly, of course. But his head was even more leonine; his hair was still abundant, yellow and wavy; the close, crisped blond beard he had grown during his illness did not alter him. He was big and big-chested yet. His eyes were dull and he mumbled and babbled mere meaningless syllables, not words.

Etcham helped Van Rieten to uncover him and look him over. He was in good muscle for a man so long bedridden. There were no scars on him except about his knees, shoulders and chest. On each knee and above it he had a full score of roundish cicatrices, and a dozen or more on each shoulder, all in front. Two or three were open wounds and four or five barely healed. He had no fresh swellings except two, one on each side, on his pectoral muscles, the one on the left being higher up and farther out than the other. They did not look like boils or carbuncles, but as if something blunt and hard were being pushed up through the fairly healthy flesh and skin, not much inflamed.

"I should not lance those," said Van Rieten, and Etcham assented.

They made Stone as comfortable as they could, and just before sunset we looked in at him again. He was lying on his back, and his chest showed big and massive yet, but he lay as if in a stupor. We left Etcham with him and went into the next hut, which Etcham had resigned to us. The jungle noises were no different there than anywhere else for months past, and I was soon fast asleep.

V

Sometime in the pitch dark I found myself awake and listening. I could hear two voices, one Stone's, the other sibilant and wheezy. I knew Stone's voice after all the years that had passed since I heard it last. The other was like nothing I remembered. It had less volume than the wail of a new-born baby, yet there was an insistent carrying power to it, like the shrilling of an insect. As I listened I heard Van Rieten breathing near me in the dark, then he heard me and realized that I was listening, too. Like Etcham I knew little Balunda, but I could make out a word or two. The voices alternated with intervals of silence between.

Then suddenly both sounded at once and fast, Stone's baritone basso, full as if he were in perfect health, and that incredibly stridulous falsetto, both jabbering at once like the voices of two people quarreling and trying to talk each other down.

"I can't stand this," said Van Rieten. "Let's have a look at him."

He had one of those cylindrical electric night-candles. He fumbled about for it, touched the button and beckoned me to come with him. Outside of the hut he motioned me to stand still, and instinctively turned off the light, as if seeing made listening difficult.

Except for a faint glow from the embers of the bearers' fire we were in complete darkness, little starlight struggled through the trees, the river made but a faint murmur. We could hear the two voices together and then suddenly the creaking voice changed into a razor-edged, slicing whistle, indescribably cutting, continuing right through Stone's grumbling torrent of croaking words.

"Good God!" exclaimed Van Rieten.

Abruptly he turned on the light.

We found Etcham utterly asleep, exhausted by his long anxiety and the exertions of his phenomenal march and relaxed completely now that the load was in a sense shifted from his shoulders to Van Rieten's. Even the light on his face did not wake him.

The whistle had ceased and the two voices now sounded together. Both came from Stone's cot, where the concentrated white ray showed him lying just as we had left him, except that he had tossed his arms above his head and had torn the coverings and bandages from his chest.

The swelling on his right breast had broken. Van Rieten aimed the center line of the light at it and we saw it plainly. From his flesh, grown out of it, there protruded a head, such a head as the dried specimens Etcham had shown us, as if it were a miniature of the head of a Balunda fetishman. It was black, shining black as the blackest African skin; it rolled the whites of its wicked, wee eyes and showed its microscopic teeth between lips repulsively negroid in their red fullness, even in so diminutive a face. It had crisp, fuzzy wool on its minikin skull, it turned malignantly from side to side and chittered incessantly in that inconceivable falsetto. Stone babbled brokenly against its patter.

Van Rieten turned from Stone and waked Etcham, with some difficulty. When he was awake and saw it all, Etcham stared and said not one word.

"You saw him slice off two swellings?" Van Rieten asked.

Etcham nodded, chokingly.

"Did he bleed much?" Van Rieten demanded.

"Ve'y little," Etcham replied.

"You hold his arms," said Van Rieten to Etcham.

He took up Stone's razor and handed me the light. Stone showed no sign of seeing the light or of knowing we were there. But the little head mewled and screeched at us.

Van Rieten's hand was steady, and the sweep of the razor even and true. Stone bled amazingly little and Van Rieten dressed the wound as if it had been a bruise or scrape.

Stone had stopped talking the instant the excrescent head was severed. Van Rieten did all that could be done for Stone and then fairly grabbed the light from me. Snatching up a gun he scanned the ground by the cot and brought the butt down once and twice, viciously.

We went back to our hut, but I doubt if I slept.

VI

Next day, near noon, in broad daylight, we heard the two voices from Stone's hut. We found Etcham dropped asleep by his charge. The swelling on the left had broken, and just such another head was there miauling and spluttering. Etcham woke up and the three of us stood there and glared. Stone inter-jected hoarse vocables into the tinkling gurgle of the portent's utterance.

Van Rieten stepped forward, took up Stone's razor and knelt down by the cot. The atomy of a head squealed a wheezy snarl at him.

Then suddenly Stone spoke English.

"Who are you with my razor?"

Van Rieten started back and stood up.

Stone's eyes were clear now and bright, they roved about the hut.

"The end," he said; "I recognize the end. I seem to see Etcham, as if in life. But Singleton! Ah, Singleton! Ghosts of my boyhood come to watch me pass! And you, strange specter with the black beard, and my razor! Aroint ye all!"

"I'm no ghost, Stone," I managed to say. "I'm alive. So are Etcham and Van Rieten. We are here to help you."

"Van Rieten!" he exclaimed. "My work passes on to a better man. Luck go with you, Van Rieten."

Van Rieten went nearer to him.

"Just hold still a moment, old man," he said soothingly. "It will be only one twinge."

"I've held still for many such twinges," Stone answered quite distinctly. "Let me be. Let me die my own way. The hydra was nothing to this. You can cut off ten, a hundred, a thousand heads, but the curse you can not cut off, or take off. What's soaked into the bone won't come out of the flesh, any more than what's bred there. Don't hack me any more. Promise!"

His voice had all the old commanding tone of his boyhood and it swayed Van Rieten as it always had swayed everybody.

"I promise," said Van Rieten.

Almost as he said the word Stone's eyes filmed again.

Then we three sat about Stone and watched that hideous, gibbering prodigy grow up out of Stone's flesh, till two horrid, spindling little black arms disengaged themselves. The infini-tesimal nails were perfect to the barely perceptible moon at the quick, the pink spot on the palm was horridly natural. These arms gesticulated and the right plucked toward Stone's blond beard.

"I can't stand this," Van Rieten exclaimed and took up the razor again.

Instantly Stone's eyes opened, hard and glittering.

"Van Rieten break his word?" he enunciated slowly. "Never!"

"But we must help you," Van Rieten gasped.

"I am past all help and all hurting," said Stone. "This is my hour. This curse is not put on me; it grew out of me, like this horror here. Even now I go."

His eyes closed and we stood helpless, the adherent figure spouting shrill sentences.

In a moment Stone spoke again.

"You speak all tongues?" he asked thickly.

And the emergent minikin replied in sudden English:

"Yea, verily, all that you speak," putting out its microscopic tongue, writhing its lips and wagging its head from side to side. We could see the thready ribs on its exiguous flanks heave as if the thing breathed.

"Has she forgiven me?" Stone asked in a muffled strangle.

"Not while the moss hangs from the cypresses," the head squeaked. "Not while the stars shine on Lake Pontchartrain will she forgive."

And then Stone, all with one motion, wrenched himself over on his side. The next instant he was dead.

When Singleton's voice ceased the room was hushed for a space. We could hear each other breathing. Twombly, the tactless, broke the silence.

"I presume," he said, "you cut off the little minikin and brought it home in alcohol."

Singleton turned on him a stern countenance.

"We buried Stone," he said, "unmutilated as he died."

"But," said the unconscionable Twombly, "the whole thing is incredible."

Singleton stiffened.

"I did not expect you to believe it," he said; "I began by saying that although I heard and saw it, when I look back on it I cannot credit it myself."

1907

OLIVIA HOWARD DUNBAR

(1873–1953)

The Shell of Sense

It was intolerably unchanged, the dim, dark-toned room. In an agony of recognition my glance ran from one to another of the comfortable, familiar things that my earthly life had been passed among. Incredibly distant from it all as I essentially was, I noted sharply that the very gaps that I myself had left in my bookshelves still stood unfilled; that the delicate fingers of the ferns that I had tended were still stretched futilely toward the light; that the soft agreeable chuckle of my own little clock, like some elderly woman with whom conversation has become automatic, was undiminished.

Unchanged—or so it seemed at first. But there were certain trivial differences that shortly smote me. The windows were closed too tightly; for I had always kept the house very cool, although I had known that Theresa preferred warm rooms. And my work-basket was in disorder: it was preposterous that so small a thing should hurt me so. Then, for this was my first experience of the shadow-folded transition, the odd alternation of my emotions bewildered me. For at one moment the place seemed so humanly familiar, so distinctly my own proper envelope, that for love of it I could have laid my cheek against the wall; while in the next I was miserably conscious of strange new shrillnesses. How could they be endured—and had I ever endured them?—those harsh influences that I now perceived at the window; light and color so blinding that they obscured the form of the wind, tumult so discordant that one could scarcely hear the roses open in the garden below?

But Theresa did not seem to mind any of these things. Disorder, it is true, the dear child had never minded. She was sitting all this time at my desk—at *my* desk,—occupied, I could only too easily surmise how. In the light of my own habits of precision it was plain that that sombre correspondence should have been attended to before; but I believe that I did not really reproach Theresa, for I knew that her notes, when she did write them, were perhaps less perfunctory than mine. She finished the last one as I watched her, and added it to the heap of black-bordered envelopes that lay on the desk. Poor girl! I saw now that they had cost her tears. Yet, living beside her day after day, year after year, I had never discovered what deep tenderness my sister possessed. Toward each other it had been our habit to display only a temperate affection, and I remember having always thought it distinctly fortunate for Theresa, since she was denied my happiness, that she could live so easily and pleasantly without emotions of the devastating sort. . . . And now, for the first time, I was really to behold her. . . . Could it be Theresa, after all, this tangle of subdued turbulences? Let no one suppose that it is an easy thing to bear, the relentlessly lucid understanding that I then first exercised; or that, in its first enfranchisement, the timid vision does not yearn for its old screens and mists.

Suddenly, as Theresa sat there, her head, filled with its tender thoughts of me, held in her gentle hands, I felt Allan's step on the carpeted stair outside. Theresa felt it, too,—but how? for it was not audible. She gave a start, swept the black envelopes out of sight, and pretended to be writing in a little book. Then I forgot to watch her any longer in my absorption in Allan's coming. It was he, of course, that I was awaiting. It was for him that I had made this first lonely, frightened effort to return, to recover. . . . It was not that I had supposed he would allow himself to recognize my presence, for I had long been sufficiently familiar with his hard and fast denials of the invisible. He was so reasonable always, so sane—so blindfolded. But I had hoped that because of his very rejection of the ether that now contained me I could perhaps all the more safely, the more secretly, watch him, linger near him. He was near now, very near,—but why did Theresa, sitting there in the room that had never belonged to her, appropriate for herself his coming? It was so manifestly I who had drawn him, I whom he had come to seek.

The door was ajar. He knocked softly at it. "Are you there, Theresa?" he called. He expected to find her, then, there in my room? I shrank back, fearing, almost, to stay.

"I shall have finished in a moment," Theresa told him, and he sat down to wait for her.

No spirit still unreleased can understand the pang that I felt with Allan sitting almost within my touch. Almost irresistibly the wish beset me to let him for an instant feel my nearness. Then I checked myself, remembering—oh, absurd, piteous human fears!—that my too unguarded closeness might alarm him. It was not so remote a time that I myself had known them, those blind, uncouth timidities. I came, therefore, somewhat nearer—but I did not touch him. I merely leaned toward him and with incredible softness whispered his name. That much I could not have forborne; the spell of life was still too strong in me.

But it gave him no comfort, no delight. "Theresa!" he called, in a voice dreadful with alarm—and in that instant the last veil fell, and desperately, scarce believingly, I beheld how it stood between them, those two.

She turned to him that gentle look of hers.

"Forgive me," came from him hoarsely. "But I had suddenly the most—unaccountable sensation. Can there be too many windows open? There is such a—chill—about."

"There are no windows open," Theresa assured him. "I took care to shut out the chill. You are not well, Allan!"

"Perhaps not." He embraced the suggestion. "And yet I feel no illness apart from this abominable sensation that persists—persists. . . . Theresa, you must tell me: do I fancy it, or do you, too, feel—something—strange here?"

"Oh, there is something very strange here," she half sobbed. "There always will be."

"Good heavens, child, I didn't mean that!" He rose and stood looking about him. "I know, of course, that you have your beliefs, and I respect them, but you know equally well that I have nothing of the sort! So—don't let us conjure up anything inexplicable."

I stayed impalpably, imponderably near him. Wretched and bereft though I was, I could not have left him while he stood denying me.

"What I mean," he went on, in his low, distinct voice, "is a special, an almost ominous sense of cold. Upon my soul, Theresa,"—he paused—"if I *were* superstitious, if I *were* a woman, I should probably imagine it to seem—a presence!"

He spoke the last word very faintly, but Theresa shrank from it nevertheless.

"*Don't* say that, Allan!" she cried out. "Don't think it, I beg of you! I've tried so hard myself not to think it—and you must help me. You know it is only perturbed, uneasy spirits that wander. With her it is quite different. She has always been so happy—she must still be."

I listened, stunned, to Theresa's sweet dogmatism. From what blind distances came her confident misapprehensions, how dense, both for her and for Allan, was the separating vapor!

Allan frowned. "Don't take me literally, Theresa," he explained; and I, who a moment before had almost touched him, now held myself aloof and heard him with a strange untried pity, new born in me. "I'm not speaking of what you call—spirits. It's something much more terrible." He allowed his head to sink heavily on his chest. "If I did not positively know that I had never done her any harm, I should suppose myself to be suffering from guilt, from remorse. . . . Theresa, you know better than I, perhaps. Was she content, always? Did she believe in me?"

"Believe in you?—when she knew you to be so good!—when you adored her!"

"She thought that? She said it? Then what in Heaven's name ails me?—unless it is all as you believe, Theresa, and she knows now what she didn't know then, poor dear, and minds—"

"Minds what? What do you mean, Allan?"

I, who with my perhaps illegitimate advantage saw so clear, knew that he had not meant to tell her: I did him that justice, even in my first jealousy. If I had not tortured him so by clinging near him, he would not have told her. But the moment came, and overflowed, and he did tell her—passionate, tumultuous story that it was. During all our life together, Allan's and mine, he had spared me, had kept me wrapped in the white cloak of an unblemished loyalty. But it would have been kinder, I now bitterly thought, if, like many husbands, he had years ago found for the story he now poured forth some clandestine listener; I should not have known. But he was faithful and good, and so he waited till I, mute and chained, was there to hear him. So well did I know him, as I thought, so thoroughly had he once been mine, that I saw it in his eyes, heard it in his voice, before the words came. And yet, when it came, it lashed me with the whips of an unbearable humiliation. For I, his wife, had not known how greatly he could love.

And that Theresa, soft little traitor, should, in her still way, have cared too! Where was the iron in her, I moaned within my stricken spirit, where the steadfastness? From the moment he bade her, she turned her soft little petals up to him—and my last delusion was spent. It was intolerable; and none the less so that in another moment she had, prompted by some belated thought of me, renounced him. Allan was hers, yet she put him from her; and it was my part to watch them both.

Then in the anguish of it all I remembered, awkward, un-tutored spirit that I was, that I now had the Great Recourse. Whatever human things were unbearable, I had no need to bear. I ceased, therefore, to make the effort that kept me with them. The pitiless poignancy was dulled, the sounds and the light ceased, the lovers faded from me, and again I was merci-fully drawn into the dim, infinite spaces.

There followed a period whose length I cannot measure and during which I was able to make no progress in the difficult, dizzying experience of release. "Earth-bound" my jealousy re-lentlessly kept me. Though my two dear ones had forsworn each other, I could not trust them, for theirs seemed to me an affectation of a more than mortal magnanimity. Without a ghostly sentinel to prick them with sharp fears and recollec-tions, who could believe that they would keep to it? Of the efficacy of my own vigilance, so long as I might choose to ex-ercise it, I could have no doubt, for I had by this time come to have a dreadful exultation in the new power that lived in me. Repeated delicate experiment had taught me how a touch or a breath, a wish or a whisper, could control Allan's acts, could keep him from Theresa. I could manifest myself as palely, as transiently, as a thought. I could produce the merest necessary flicker, like the shadow of a just-opened leaf, on his trembling, tortured consciousness. And these unrealized perceptions of me he interpreted, as I had known that he would, as his soul's inevitable penance. He had come to believe that he had done evil in silently loving Theresa all these years, and it was my ven-geance to allow him to believe this, to prod him ever to believe it afresh.

I am conscious that this frame of mind was not continuous in me. For I remember, too, that when Allan and Theresa were safely apart and sufficiently miserable I loved them as dearly as I ever had, more dearly perhaps. For it was impossible that I should not perceive, in my new emancipation, that they were, each of them, something more and greater than the two beings I had once ignorantly pictured them. For years they had practised a selflessness of which I could once scarcely have conceived, and which even now I could only admire without entering into its mystery. While I had lived solely for myself, these two divine creatures had lived exquisitely for me. They had granted me everything, themselves nothing. For my undeserving sake their lives had been a constant torment of renunciation—a torment they had not sought to alleviate by the exchange of a single glance of understanding. There were even marvellous moments when, from the depths of my newly informed heart, I pitied them:—poor creatures, who, withheld from the infinite solaces that I had come to know, were still utterly within that

> Shell of sense
> So frail, so piteously contrived for pain.

Within it, yes; yet exercising qualities that so sublimely transcended it. Yet the shy, hesitating compassion that thus had birth in me was far from being able to defeat the earlier, earthlier emotion. The two, I recognized, were in a sort of conflict; and I, regarding it, assumed that the conflict would never end; that for years, as Allan and Theresa reckoned time, I should be obliged to withhold myself from the great spaces and linger suffering, grudging, shamed, where they lingered.

It can never have been explained, I suppose, what, to devitalized perception such as mine, the contact of mortal beings with each other appears to be. Once to have exercised this sense-freed perception is to realize that the gift of prophecy, although the subject of such frequent marvel, is no longer mysterious. The merest glance of our sensitive and uncloyed vision can detect the strength of the relation between two beings, and therefore instantly calculate its duration. If you see a heavy weight suspended from a slender string, you can know, without any wizardry, that in a few moments the string will snap; well, such, if you admit the analogy, is prophecy, is foreknowledge. And it was thus that I saw it with Theresa and Allan. For it was perfectly visible to me that they would very little longer have the strength to preserve, near each other, the denuded impersonal relation that they, and that I, behind them, insisted on; and that they would have to separate. It was my sister, perhaps the more sensitive, who first realized this. It had now become possible for me to observe them almost constantly, the effort necessary to visit them had so greatly diminished; so that I watched her, poor, anguished girl, prepare to leave him. I saw each reluctant movement that she made. I saw her eyes, worn from self-searching; I heard her step grown timid from inexplicable fears; I entered her very heart and heard its pitiful, wild beating. And still I did not interfere.

For at this time I had a wonderful, almost demoniacal sense of disposing of matters to suit my own selfish will. At any moment I could have checked their miseries, could have restored happiness and peace. Yet it gave me, and I could weep to admit it, a monstrous joy to know that Theresa thought she was leaving Allan of her own free intention, when it was I who was contriving, arranging, insisting. . . . And yet she wretchedly felt my presence near her; I am certain of that.

A few days before the time of her intended departure my sister told Allan that she must speak with him after dinner. Our beautiful old house branched out from a circular hall with great arched doors at either end; and it was through the rear doorway that always in summer, after dinner, we passed out into the garden adjoining. As usual, therefore, when the hour came, Theresa led the way. That dreadful daytime brilliance that in my present state I found so hard to endure was now becoming softer. A delicate, capricious twilight breeze danced inconsequently through languidly whispering leaves. Lovely pale flowers blossomed like little moons in the dusk, and over them the breath of mignonette hung heavily. It was a perfect place—and it had so long been ours, Allan's and mine. It made me restless and a little wicked that those two should be there together now.

For a little they walked about together, speaking of common, daily things. Then suddenly Theresa burst out:

"I am going away, Allan. I have stayed to do everything that needed to be done. Now your mother will be here to care for you, and it is time for me to go."

He stared at her and stood still. Theresa had been there so long, she so definitely, to his mind, belonged there. And she was, as I also had jealously known, so lovely there, the small, dark, dainty creature, in the old hall, on the wide staircases, in the garden. . . . Life there without Theresa, even the intentionally remote, the perpetually renounced Theresa—he had not dreamed of it, he could not, so suddenly, conceive of it.

"Sit here," he said, and drew her down beside him on a bench, "and tell me what it means, why you are going. Is it because of something that I have been—have done?"

She hesitated. I wondered if she would dare tell him. She looked out and away from him, and he waited long for her to speak.

The pale stars were sliding into their places. The whispering of the leaves was almost hushed. All about them it was still and shadowy and sweet. It was that wonderful moment when, for lack of a visible horizon, the not yet darkened world seems infinitely greater—a moment when anything can happen, anything be believed in. To me, watching, listening, hovering, there came a dreadful purpose and a dreadful courage. Suppose, for one moment, Theresa should not only feel, but *see* me—would she dare to tell him then?

There came a brief space of terrible effort, all my fluttering, uncertain forces strained to the utmost. The instant of my struggle was endlessly long and the transition seemed to take place outside me—as one sitting in a train, motionless, sees the leagues of earth float by. And then, in a bright, terrible flash I knew I had achieved it—I had *attained visibility*. Shuddering, insubstantial, but luminously apparent, I stood there before them. And for the instant that I maintained the visible state I looked straight into Theresa's soul.

She gave a cry. And then, thing of silly, cruel impulses that I was, I saw what I had done. The very thing that I wished to avert I had precipitated. For Allan, in his sudden terror and pity, had bent and caught her in his arms. For the first time they were together; and it was I who had brought them.

Then, to his whispered urging to tell the reason of her cry, Theresa said:

"Frances was here. You did not see her, standing there, under the lilacs, with no smile on her face?"

"My dear, my dear!" was all that Allan said. I had so long now lived invisibly with them, he knew that she was right.

"I suppose you know what it means?" she asked him, calmly.

"Dear Theresa," Allan said, slowly, "if you and I should go away somewhere, could we not evade all this ghostliness? And will you come with me?"

"Distance would not banish her," my sister confidently asserted. And then she said, softly: "Have you thought what a lonely, awesome thing it must be to be so newly dead? Pity her, Allan. We who are warm and alive should pity her. She loves you still,—that is the meaning of it all, you know—and she wants us to understand that for that reason we must keep apart. Oh, it was so plain in her white face as she stood there. And you did not see her?"

"It was your face that I saw," Allan solemnly told her—oh, how different he had grown from the Allan that I had known!— "and yours is the only face that I shall ever see." And again he drew her to him.

She sprang from him. "You are defying her, Allan!" she cried. "And you must not. It is her right to keep us apart, if she wishes. It must be as she insists. I shall go, as I told you. And, Allan, I beg of you, leave me the courage to do as she demands!"

They stood facing each other in the deep dusk, and the wounds that I had dealt them gaped red and accusing. "We must pity her," Theresa had said. And as I remembered that extraordinary speech, and saw the agony in her face, and the greater agony in Allan's, there came the great irreparable cleavage between mortality and me. In a swift, merciful flame the last of my mortal emotions—gross and tenacious they must have been—was consumed. My cold grasp of Allan loosened and a new unearthly love of him bloomed in my heart.

I was now, however, in a difficulty with which my experience in the newer state was scarcely sufficient to deal. How could I make it plain to Allan and Theresa that I wished to bring them together, to heal the wounds that I had made?

Pityingly, remorsefully, I lingered near them all that night and the next day. And by that time I had brought myself to the point of a great determination. In the little time that was left, before Theresa should be gone and Allan bereft and desolate, I saw the one way that lay open to me to convince them of my acquiescence in their destiny.

In the deepest darkness and silence of the next night I made a greater effort than it will ever be necessary for me to make again. When they think of me, Allan and Theresa, I pray now that they will recall what I did that night, and that my thousand frustrations and selfishnesses may shrivel and be blown from their indulgent memories.

Yet the following morning, as she had planned, Theresa appeared at breakfast dressed for her journey. Above in her room there were the sounds of departure. They spoke little during the brief meal, but when it was ended Allan said:

"Theresa, there is half an hour before you go. Will you come up-stairs with me? I had a dream that I must tell you of."

"Allan!" She looked at him, frightened, but went with him. "It was of Frances you dreamed," she said, quietly, as they entered the library together.

"Did I say it was a dream? But I was awake—thoroughly awake. I had not been sleeping well, and I heard, twice, the striking of the clock. And as I lay there, looking out at the stars, and thinking—thinking of you, Theresa,—she came to me, stood there before me, in my room. It was no sheeted spectre, you understand; it was Frances, literally she. In some inexplicable fashion I seemed to be aware that she wanted to make me know something, and I waited, watching her face. After a few moments it came. She did not speak, precisely. That is, I am sure I heard no sound. Yet the words that came from her were definite enough. She said: 'Don't let Theresa leave you. Take her and keep her.' Then she went away. Was that a dream?"

"I had not meant to tell you," Theresa eagerly answered, "but now I must. It is too wonderful. What time did your clock strike, Allan?"

"One, the last time."

"Yes; it was then that I awoke. And she had been with me. I had not seen her, but her arm had been about me and her kiss was on my cheek. Oh, I knew; it was unmistakable. And the sound of her voice was with me."

"Then she bade you, too—"

"Yes, to stay with you. I am glad we told each other." She smiled tearfully and began to fasten her wrap.

"But you are not going—*now*!" Allan cried. "You know that you cannot, now that she has asked you to stay."

"Then you believe, as I do, that it was she?" Theresa demanded.

"I can never understand, but I know," he answered her. "And now you will not go?"

I am freed. There will be no further semblance of me in my old home, no sound of my voice, no dimmest echo of my earthly self. They have no further need of me, the two that I have brought together. Theirs is the fullest joy that the dwellers in the shell of sense can know. Mine is the transcendent joy of the unseen spaces.

1908

HENRY JAMES

(1843–1916)

The Jolly Corner

"Every one asks me what I 'think' of everything," said Spencer Brydon; "and I make answer as I can—begging or dodging the question, putting them off with any nonsense. It wouldn't matter to any of them really," he went on, "for, even were it possible to meet in that stand-and-deliver way so silly a demand on so big a subject, my 'thoughts' would still be almost altogether about something that concerns only myself." He was talking to Miss Staverton, with whom for a couple of months now he had availed himself of every possible occasion to talk; this disposition and this resource, this comfort and sup-port, as the situation in fact presented itself, having promptly enough taken the first place in the considerable array of rather unattenuated surprises attending his so strangely belated re-turn to America. Everything was somehow a surprise; and that might be natural when one had so long and so consistently neglected everything, taken pains to give surprises so much margin for play. He had given them more than thirty years—thirty-three, to be exact; and they now seemed to him to have organised their performance quite on the scale of that licence. He had been twenty-three on leaving New York—he was fifty-six to-day: unless indeed he were to reckon as he had some-times, since his repatriation, found himself feeling; in which case he would have lived longer than is often allotted to man. It would have taken a century, he repeatedly said to himself, and said also to Alice Staverton, it would have taken a longer absence and a more averted mind than those even of which he had been guilty, to pile up the differences, the newnesses, the queernesses, above all the bignesses, for the better or the worse, that at present assaulted his vision wherever he looked.

The great fact all the while however had been the incalcula-bility; since he *had* supposed himself, from decade to decade, to be allowing, and in the most liberal and intelligent manner,

337

for brilliancy of change. He actually saw that he had allowed
for nothing; he missed what he would have been sure of finding,
he found what he would never have imagined. Proportions and
values were upside-down; the ugly things he had expected, the
ugly things of his far-away youth, when he had too promptly
waked up to a sense of the ugly—these uncanny phenomena
placed him rather, as it happened, under the charm; whereas
the "swagger" things, the modern, the monstrous, the famous
things, those he had more particularly, like thousands of in-
genuous enquirers every year, come over to see, were exactly
his sources of dismay. They were as so many set traps for displeasure, above all for reaction, of which his restless tread was
constantly pressing the spring. It was interesting, doubtless,
the whole show, but it would have been too disconcerting
hadn't a certain finer truth saved the situation. He had distinctly not, in this steadier light, come over *all* for the monstrosities; he had come, not only in the last analysis but quite
on the face of the act, under an impulse with which they had
nothing to do. He had come—putting the thing pompously—
to look at his "property," which he had thus for a third of a
century not been within four thousand miles of; or, expressing
it less sordidly, he had yielded to the humour of seeing again
his house on the jolly corner, as he usually, and quite fondly,
described it—the one in which he had first seen the light, in
which various members of his family had lived and had died, in
which the holidays of his overschooled boyhood had been
passed and the few social flowers of his chilled adolescence
gathered, and which, alienated then for so long a period, had,
through the successive deaths of his two brothers and the termination of old arrangements, come wholly into his hands. He
was the owner of another, not quite so "good"—the jolly corner having been, from far back, superlatively extended and
consecrated; and the value of the pair represented his main
capital, with an income consisting, in these later years, of their
respective rents which (thanks precisely to their original excellent type) had never been depressingly low. He could live in
"Europe," as he had been in the habit of living, on the product of these flourishing New York leases, and all the better
since, that of the second structure, the mere number in its

long row, having within a twelvemonth fallen in, renovation at a high advance had proved beautifully possible.

These were items of property indeed, but he had found himself since his arrival distinguishing more than ever between them. The house within the street, two bristling blocks westward, was already in course of reconstruction as a tall mass of flats; he had acceded, some time before, to overtures for this conversion—in which, now that it was going forward, it had been not the least of his astonishments to find himself able, on the spot, and though without a previous ounce of such experience, to participate with a certain intelligence, almost with a certain authority. He had lived his life with his back so turned to such concerns and his face addressed to those of so different an order that he scarce knew what to make of this lively stir, in a compartment of his mind never yet penetrated, of a capacity for business and a sense for construction. These virtues, so common all round him now, had been dormant in his own organism—where it might be said of them perhaps that they had slept the sleep of the just. At present, in the splendid autumn weather—the autumn at least was a pure boon in the terrible place—he loafed about his "work" undeterred, secretly agitated; not in the least "minding" that the whole proposition, as they said, was vulgar and sordid, and ready to climb ladders, to walk the plank, to handle materials and look wise about them, to ask questions, in fine, and challenge explanations and really "go into" figures.

It amused, it verily quite charmed him; and, by the same stroke, it amused, and even more, Alice Staverton, though perhaps charming her perceptibly less. She wasn't however going to be better-off for it, as *he* was—and so astonishingly much: nothing was now likely, he knew, ever to make her better-off than she found herself, in the afternoon of life, as the delicately frugal possessor and tenant of the small house in Irving Place to which she had subtly managed to cling through her almost unbroken New York career. If he knew the way to it now better than to any other address among the dreadful multiplied numberings which seemed to him to reduce the whole place to some vast ledger-page, overgrown, fantastic, of ruled and criss-crossed lines and figures—if he had formed, for his

consolation, that habit, it was really not a little because of the
charm of his having encountered and recognised, in the vast
wilderness of the wholesale, breaking through the mere gross
generalisation of wealth and force and success, a small still
scene where items and shades, all delicate things, kept the
sharpness of the notes of a high voice perfectly trained, and
where economy hung about like the scent of a garden. His old
friend lived with one maid and herself dusted her relics and
trimmed her lamps and polished her silver; she stood off, in
the awful modern crush, when she could, but she sallied forth
and did battle when the challenge was really to "spirit," the
spirit she after all confessed to, proudly and a little shyly, as to
that of the better time, that of *their* common, their quite far-
away and antediluvian social period and order. She made use of
the street-cars when need be, the terrible things that people
scrambled for as the panic-stricken at sea scramble for the
boats; she affronted, inscrutably, under stress, all the public
concussions and ordeals; and yet, with that slim mystifying
grace of her appearance, which defied you to say if she were a
fair young woman who looked older through trouble, or a fine
smooth older one who looked young through successful indifference; with her precious reference, above all, to memories
and histories into which he could enter, she was as exquisite
for him as some pale pressed flower (a rarity to begin with),
and, failing other sweetnesses, she was a sufficient reward of
his effort. They had communities of knowledge, "their" knowledge (this discriminating possessive was always on her lips) of
presences of the other age, presences all overlaid, in his case,
by the experience of a man and the freedom of a wanderer,
overlaid by pleasure, by infidelity, by passages of life that were
strange and dim to her, just by "Europe" in short, but still un-
obscured, still exposed and cherished, under that pious visitation of the spirit from which she had never been diverted.

She had come with him one day to see how his "apartment-
house" was rising; he had helped her over gaps and explained
to her plans, and while they were there had happened to have,
before her, a brief but lively discussion with the man in charge,
the representative of the building-firm that had undertaken his
work. He had found himself quite "standing-up" to this personage over a failure on the latter's part to observe some detail

of one of their noted conditions, and had so lucidly argued his case that, besides ever so prettily flushing, at the time, for sympathy in his triumph, she had afterwards said to him (though to a slightly greater effect of irony) that he had clearly for too many years neglected a real gift. If he had but stayed at home he would have anticipated the inventor of the sky-scraper. If he had but stayed at home he would have discovered his genius in time really to start some new variety of awful architectural hare and run it till it burrowed in a goldmine. He was to remember these words, while the weeks elapsed, for the small silver ring they had sounded over the queerest and deepest of his own lately most disguised and most muffled vibrations.

It had begun to be present to him after the first fortnight, it had broken out with the oddest abruptness, this particular wanton wonderment: it met him there—and this was the image under which he himself judged the matter, or at least, not a little, thrilled and flushed with it—very much as he might have been met by some strange figure, some unexpected occupant, at a turn of one of the dim passages of an empty house. The quaint analogy quite hauntingly remained with him, when he didn't indeed rather improve it by a still intenser form: that of his opening a door behind which he would have made sure of finding nothing, a door into a room shuttered and void, and yet so coming, with a great suppressed start, on some quite erect confronting presence, something planted in the middle of the place and facing him through the dusk. After that visit to the house in construction he walked with his companion to see the other and always so much the better one, which in the eastward direction formed one of the corners, the "jolly" one precisely, of the street now so generally dishonoured and disfigured in its westward reaches, and of the comparatively conservative Avenue. The Avenue still had pretensions, as Miss Staverton said, to decency; the old people had mostly gone, the old names were unknown, and here and there an old association seemed to stray, all vaguely, like some very aged person, out too late, whom you might meet and feel the impulse to watch or follow, in kindness, for safe restoration to shelter.

They went in together, our friends; he admitted himself with his key, as he kept no one there, he explained, preferring, for his reasons, to leave the place empty, under a simple arrangement with a good woman living in the neighbourhood and who came for a daily hour to open windows and dust and sweep. Spencer Brydon had his reasons and was growingly aware of them; they seemed to him better each time he was there, though he didn't name them all to his companion, any more than he told her as yet how often, how quite absurdly often, he himself came. He only let her see for the present, while they walked through the great blank rooms, that absolute vacancy reigned and that, from top to bottom, there was nothing but Mrs. Muldoon's broomstick, in a corner, to tempt the burglar. Mrs. Muldoon was then on the premises, and she loquaciously attended the visitors, preceding them from room to room and pushing back shutters and throwing up sashes—all to show them, as she remarked, how little there was to see. There was little indeed to see in the great gaunt shell where the main dispositions and the general apportionment of space, the style of an age of ampler allowances, had nevertheless for its master their honest pleading message, affecting him as some good old servant's, some lifelong retainer's appeal for a character, or even for a retiring-pension; yet it was also a remark of Mrs. Muldoon's that, glad as she was to oblige him by her noonday round, there was a request she greatly hoped he would never make of her. If he should wish her for any reason to come in after dark she would just tell him, if he "plased," that he must ask it of somebody else.

The fact that there was nothing to see didn't militate for the worthy woman against what one *might* see, and she put it frankly to Miss Staverton that no lady could be expected to like, could she? "craping up to thim top storeys in the ayvil hours." The gas and the electric light were off the house, and she fairly evoked a gruesome vision of her march through the great grey rooms—so many of them as there were too!—with her glimmering taper. Miss Staverton met her honest glare with a smile and the profession that she herself certainly would recoil from such an adventure. Spencer Brydon meanwhile held his peace—for the moment; the question of the "evil" hours in his old home had already become too grave for him. He had begun some time since to "crape," and he knew just why a packet of candles addressed to that pursuit had been stowed by his own hand, three weeks before, at the back of a drawer of the fine old sideboard that occupied, as a "fixture," the deep recess in the dining-room. Just now he laughed at his companions—quickly however changing the subject; for the reason that, in the first place, his laugh struck him even at that moment as starting the odd echo, the conscious human resonance (he scarce knew how to qualify it) that sounds made while he was there alone sent back to his ear or his fancy; and that, in the second, he imagined Alice Staverton for the instant on the point of asking him, with a divination, if he ever so prowled. There were divinations he was unprepared for, and he had at all events averted enquiry by the time Mrs. Muldoon had left them, passing on to other parts.

There was happily enough to say, on so consecrated a spot, that could be said freely and fairly; so that a whole train of declarations was precipitated by his friend's having herself broken out, after a yearning look round: "But I hope you don't mean they want you to pull *this* to pieces!" His answer came, promptly, with his re-awakened wrath: it was of course exactly what they wanted, and what they were "at" him for, daily, with the iteration of people who couldn't for their life understand a man's liability to decent feelings. He had found the place, just as it stood and beyond what he could express, an interest and a joy. There were values other than the beastly rent-values, and in short, in short—! But it was thus Miss Staverton took him up. "In short you're to make so good a thing of your sky-scraper that, living in luxury on *those* ill-gotten gains, you can afford for a while to be sentimental here!" Her smile had for him, with the words, the particular mild irony with which he found half her talk suffused; an irony without bitterness and that came, exactly, from her having so much imagination—not, like the cheap sarcasms with which one heard most people, about the world of "society," bid for the reputation of cleverness, from nobody's really having any. It was agreeable to him at this very moment to be sure that when he had answered, after a brief demur, "Well yes: so, precisely, you may put it!" her imagination would still do him justice. He explained that even if never a dollar were to come to him from the other house he would nevertheless cherish this one; and he

dwelt, further, while they lingered and wandered, on the fact
of the stupefaction he was already exciting, the positive mystification he felt himself create.

He spoke of the value of all he read into it, into the mere
sight of the walls, mere shapes of the rooms, mere sound of
the floors, mere feel, in his hand, of the old silver-plated knobs
of the several mahogany doors, which suggested the pressure of
the palms of the dead; the seventy years of the past in fine that
these things represented, the annals of nearly three generations, counting his grandfather's, the one that had ended there,
and the impalpable ashes of his long-extinct youth, afloat in
the very air like microscopic motes. She listened to everything;
she was a woman who answered intimately but who utterly
didn't chatter. She scattered abroad therefore no cloud of
words; she could assent, she could agree, above all she could
encourage, without doing that. Only at the last she went a
little further than he had done himself. "And then how do you
know? You may still, after all, want to live here." It rather indeed pulled him up, for it wasn't what he had been thinking,
at least in her sense of the words. "You mean I may decide to
stay on for the sake of it?"

"Well, *with* such a home—!" But, quite beautifully, she had
too much tact to dot so monstrous an *i*, and it was precisely an
illustration of the way she didn't rattle. How could any one—
of any wit—insist on any one else's "wanting" to live in New
York?

"Oh," he said, "I *might* have lived here (since I had my opportunity early in life); I might have put in here all these years.
Then everything would have been different enough—and, I
dare say, 'funny' enough. But that's another matter. And then
the beauty of it—I mean of my perversity, of my refusal to
agree to a 'deal'—is just in the total absence of a reason. Don't
you see that if I had a reason about the matter at all it would
have to be the other way, and would then be inevitably a reason of dollars? There are no reasons here *but* of dollars. Let us
therefore have none whatever—not the ghost of one."

They were back in the hall then for departure, but from
where they stood the vista was large, through an open door,
into the great square main saloon, with its almost antique felicity of brave spaces between windows. Her eyes came back

from that reach and met his own a moment. "Are you very sure the 'ghost' of one doesn't, much rather, serve—?"

He had a positive sense of turning pale. But it was as near as they were then to come. For he made answer, he believed, between a glare and a grin: "Oh ghosts—of course the place must swarm with them! I should be ashamed of it if it didn't. Poor Mrs. Muldoon's right, and it's why I haven't asked her to do more than look in."

Miss Staverton's gaze again lost itself, and things she didn't utter, it was clear, came and went in her mind. She might even for the minute, off there in the fine room, have imagined some element dimly gathering. Simplified like the death-mask of a handsome face, it perhaps produced for her just then an effect akin to the stir of an expression in the "set" commemorative plaster. Yet whatever her impression may have been she produced instead a vague platitude. "Well, if it were only furnished and lived in—!"

She appeared to imply that in case of its being still furnished he might have been a little less opposed to the idea of a return. But she passed straight into the vestibule, as if to leave her words behind her, and the next moment he had opened the house-door and was standing with her on the steps. He closed the door and, while he re-pocketed his key, looking up and down, they took in the comparatively harsh actuality of the Avenue, which reminded him of the assault of the outer light of the Desert on the traveller emerging from an Egyptian tomb. But he risked before they stepped into the street his gathered answer to her speech. "For me it *is* lived in. For me it *is* furnished." At which it was easy for her to sigh "Ah yes—!" all vaguely and discreetly; since his parents and his favourite sister, to say nothing of other kin, in numbers, had run their course and met their end there. That represented, within the walls, ineffaceable life.

It was a few days after this that, during an hour passed with her again, he had expressed his impatience of the too flattering curiosity—among the people he met—about his appreciation of New York. He had arrived at none at all that was socially producible, and as for that matter of his "thinking" (thinking the better or the worse of anything there) he was wholly taken up with one subject of thought. It was mere vain egoism, and it was moreover, if she liked, a morbid obsession. He found all things come back to the question of what he personally might have been, how he might have led his life and "turned out," if he had not so, at the outset, given it up. And confessing for the first time to the intensity within him of this absurd speculation —which but proved also, no doubt, the habit of too selfishly thinking—he affirmed the impotence there of any other source of interest, any other native appeal. "What would it have made of me, what would it have made of me? I keep for ever wondering, all idiotically; as if I could possibly know! I see what it has made of dozens of others, those I meet, and it positively aches within me, to the point of exasperation, that it would have made something of me as well. Only I can't make out *what*, and the worry of it, the small rage of curiosity never to be satisfied, brings back what I remember to have felt, once or twice, after judging best, for reasons, to burn some important letter unopened. I've been sorry, I've hated it—I've never known what was in the letter. You may of course say it's a trifle—!"

"I don't say it's a trifle," Miss Staverton gravely interrupted.

She was seated by her fire, and before her, on his feet and restless, he turned to and fro between this intensity of his idea and a fitful and unseeing inspection, through his single eye-glass, of the dear little old objects on her chimney-piece. Her interruption made him for an instant look at her harder. "I shouldn't care if you did!" he laughed, however; "and it's only a figure, at any rate, for the way I now feel. *Not* to have followed my perverse young course—and almost in the teeth of my father's curse, as I may say; not to have kept it up, so, 'over there,' from that day to this, without a doubt or a pang; not, above all, to have liked it, to have loved it, so much, loved it, no doubt, with such an abysmal conceit of my own preference: some variation from *that*, I say, must have produced some different effect for my life and for my 'form.' I should have stuck here—if it had been possible; and I was too young, at twenty-three, to judge, *pour deux sous*, whether it *were* possible. If I had waited I might have seen it was, and then I might have been, by staying here, something nearer to one of these types who have been hammered so hard and made so keen by their conditions. It isn't that I admire them so much—the question of any charm in them, or of any charm, beyond that of the rank money-passion, exerted by their conditions *for* them, has nothing to do with the matter: it's only a question of what fantastic, yet perfectly possible, development of my own nature I mayn't have missed. It comes over me that I had then a strange *alter ego* deep down somewhere within me, as the full-blown flower is in the small tight bud, and that I just took the course, I just transferred him to the climate, that blighted him for once and for ever."

"And you wonder about the flower," Miss Staverton said. "So do I, if you want to know; and so I've been wondering these several weeks. I believe in the flower," she continued, "I feel it would have been quite splendid, quite huge and monstrous."

"Monstrous above all!" her visitor echoed; "and I imagine, by the same stroke, quite hideous and offensive."

"You don't believe that," she returned; "if you did you wouldn't wonder. You'd know, and that would be enough for you. What you feel—and what I feel *for* you—is that you'd have had power."

"You'd have liked me that way?" he asked.

She barely hung fire. "How should I not have liked you?"

"I see. You'd have liked me, have preferred me, a billionaire!"

"How should I not have liked you?" she simply again asked.

He stood before her still—her question kept him motionless. He took it in, so much there was of it; and indeed his not otherwise meeting it testified to that. "I know at least what I am," he simply went on; "the other side of the medal's clear enough. I've not been edifying—I believe I'm thought in a hundred quarters to have been barely decent. I've followed strange paths and worshipped strange gods; it must have come to you again and again—in fact you've admitted to me as much —that I was leading, at any time these thirty years, a selfish frivolous scandalous life. And you see what it has made of me."

She just waited, smiling at him. "You see what it has made of *me*."

"Oh you're a person whom nothing can have altered. You were born to be what you are, anywhere, anyway: you've the perfection nothing else could have blighted. And don't you see how, without my exile, I shouldn't have been waiting till now—?" But he pulled up for the strange pang.

"The great thing to see," she presently said, "seems to me to be that it has spoiled nothing. It hasn't spoiled your being here at last. It hasn't spoiled this. It hasn't spoiled your speaking—" She also however faltered.

He wondered at everything her controlled emotion might mean. "Do you believe then—too dreadfully!—that I *am* as good as I might ever have been?"

"Oh no! Far from it!" With which she got up from her chair and was nearer to him. "But I don't care," she smiled.

"You mean I'm good enough?"

She considered a little. "Will you believe it if I say so? I mean will you let that settle your question for you?" And then as if making out in his face that he drew back from this, that he had some idea which, however absurd, he couldn't yet bargain away: "Oh you don't care either—but very differently: you don't care for anything but yourself."

Spencer Brydon recognised it—it was in fact what he had absolutely professed. Yet he importantly qualified. "*He* isn't myself. He's the just so totally other person. But I do want to see him," he added. "And I can. And I shall."

Their eyes met for a minute while he guessed from something in hers that she divined his strange sense. But neither of them otherwise expressed it, and her apparent understanding, with no protesting shock, no easy derision, touched him more deeply than anything yet, constituting for his stifled perversity, on the spot, an element that was like breatheable air. What she said however was unexpected. "Well, *I've* seen him."

"You—?"

"I've seen him in a dream."

"Oh a 'dream'—!" It let him down.

"But twice over," she continued. "I saw him as I see you now."

"You've dreamed the same dream——?"

"Twice over," she repeated. "The very same."

This did somehow a little speak to him, as it also gratified him. "You dream about me at that rate?"

"Ah about *him*!" she smiled.

His eyes again sounded her. "Then you know all about him." And as she said nothing more: "What's the wretch like?"

She hesitated, and it was as if he were pressing her so hard that, resisting for reasons of her own, she had to turn away. "I'll tell you some other time!"

II

It was after this that there was most of a virtue for him, most of a cultivated charm, most of a preposterous secret thrill, in the particular form of surrender to his obsession and of address to what he more and more believed to be his privilege. It was what in these weeks he was living for—since he really felt life to begin but after Mrs. Muldoon had retired from the scene and, visiting the ample house from attic to cellar, making sure he was alone, he knew himself in safe possession and, as he tacitly expressed it, let himself go. He sometimes came twice in the twenty-four hours; the moments he liked best were those of gathering dusk, of the short autumn twilight; this was the time of which, again and again, he found himself hoping most. Then he could, as seemed to him, most intimately wander and wait, linger and listen, feel his fine attention, never in his life before so fine, on the pulse of the great vague place: he preferred the lampless hour and only wished he might have prolonged each day the deep crepuscular spell. Later—rarely much before midnight, but then for a considerable vigil—he watched with his glimmering light; moving slowly, holding it high, playing it far, rejoicing above all, as much as he might, in open vistas, reaches of communication between rooms and by passages; the long straight chance or show, as he would have called it, for the revelation he pretended to invite. It was a practice he found he could perfectly "work" without exciting remark; no one was in the least the wiser for it; even Alice Staverton, who was moreover a well of discretion, didn't quite fully imagine.

He let himself in and let himself out with the assurance of calm proprietorship; and accident so far favoured him that, if a fat Avenue "officer" had happened on occasion to see him entering at eleven-thirty, he had never yet, to the best of his belief, been noticed as emerging at two. He walked there on the crisp November nights, arrived regularly at the evening's end; it was as easy to do this after dining out as to take his way to a club or to his hotel. When he left his club, if he hadn't been dining out, it was ostensibly to go to his hotel; and when he left his hotel, if he had spent a part of the evening there, it was ostensibly to go to his club. Everything was easy in fine; everything conspired and promoted: there was truly even in the

strain of his experience something that glossed over, something that salved and simplified, all the rest of consciousness.
He circulated, talked, renewed, loosely and pleasantly, old
relations—met indeed, so far as he could, new expectations
and seemed to make out on the whole that in spite of the career, of such different contacts, which he had spoken of to
Miss Staverton as ministering so little, for those who might have
watched it, to edification, he was positively rather liked than
not. He was a dim secondary social success—and all with people
who had truly not an idea of him. It was all mere surface
sound, this murmur of their welcome, this popping of their
corks—just as his gestures of response were the extravagant
shadows, emphatic in proportion as they meant little, of some
game of *ombres chinoises.* He projected himself all day, in
thought, straight over the bristling line of hard unconscious
heads and into the other, the real, the waiting life; the life that,
as soon as he had heard behind him the click of his great
house-door, began for him, on the jolly corner, as beguilingly
as the slow opening bars of some rich music follows the tap of
the conductor's wand.

   He always caught the first effect of the steel point of his stick
on the old marble of the hall pavement, large black-and-white
squares that he remembered as the admiration of his childhood
and that had then made in him, as he now saw, for the growth
of an early conception of style. This effect was the dim reverberating tinkle as of some far-off bell hung who should say
where?—in the depths of the house, of the past, of that mystical other world that might have flourished for him had he not,
for weal or woe, abandoned it. On this impression he did ever
the same thing; he put his stick noiselessly away in a corner—
feeling the place once more in the likeness of some great glass
bowl, all precious concave crystal, set delicately humming by
the play of a moist finger round its edge. The concave crystal
held, as it were, this mystical other world, and the indescribably fine murmur of its rim was the sigh there, the scarce audible pathetic wail to his strained ear, of all the old baffled
forsworn possibilities. What he did therefore by this appeal of
his hushed presence was to wake them into such measure of
ghostly life as they might still enjoy. They were shy, all but un-
appeasably shy, but they weren't really sinister; at least they

weren't as he had hitherto felt them—before they had taken
the Form he so yearned to make them take, the Form he at
moments saw himself in the light of fairly hunting on tiptoe,
the points of his evening-shoes, from room to room and from
storey to storey.

That was the essence of his vision—which was all rank folly,
if one would, while he was out of the house and otherwise occupied, but which took on the last verisimilitude as soon as he
was placed and posted. He knew what he meant and what he
wanted; it was as clear as the figure on a cheque presented in
demand for cash. His *alter ego* "walked"—that was the note of
his image of him, while his image of his motive for his own
odd pastime was the desire to waylay him and meet him. He
roamed, slowly, warily, but all restlessly, he himself did—Mrs.
Muldoon had been right, absolutely, with her figure of their
"craping"; and the presence he watched for would roam restlessly too. But it would be as cautious and as shifty; the conviction of its probable, in fact its already quite sensible, quite
audible evasion of pursuit grew for him from night to night,
laying on him finally a rigour to which nothing in his life had
been comparable. It had been the theory of many superficially-
judging persons, he knew, that he was wasting that life in a surrender to sensations, but he had tasted of no pleasure so fine as
his actual tension, had been introduced to no sport that demanded at once the patience and the nerve of this stalking of a
creature more subtle, yet at bay perhaps more formidable, than
any beast of the forest. The terms, the comparisons, the very
practices of the chase positively came again into play; there
were even moments when passages of his occasional experience as a sportsman, stirred memories, from his younger time,
of moor and mountain and desert, revived for him—and to the
increase of his keenness—by the tremendous force of analogy.
He found himself at moments—once he had placed his single
light on some mantel-shelf or in some recess—stepping back
into shelter or shade, effacing himself behind a door or in an
embrasure, as he had sought of old the vantage of rock and
tree; he found himself holding his breath and living in the joy
of the instant, the supreme suspense created by big game alone.

He wasn't afraid (though putting himself the question as he
believed gentlemen on Bengal tiger-shoots or in close quarters

with the great bear of the Rockies had been known to confess
to having put it); and this indeed—since here at least he might
be frank!—because of the impression, so intimate and so
strange, that he himself produced as yet a dread, produced certainly a strain, beyond the liveliest he was likely to feel. They
fell for him into categories, they fairly became familiar, the signs,
for his own perception, of the alarm his presence and his vigilance created; though leaving him always to remark, porten-
tously, on his probably having formed a relation, his probably
enjoying a consciousness, unique in the experience of man.
People enough, first and last, had been in terror of apparitions,
but who had ever before so turned the tables and become himself, in the apparitional world, an incalculable terror? He might
have found this sublime had he quite dared to think of it; but
he didn't too much insist, truly, on that side of his privilege.
With habit and repetition he gained to an extraordinary degree
the power to penetrate the dusk of distances and the darkness
of corners, to resolve back into their innocence the treacheries
of uncertain light, the evil-looking forms taken in the gloom
by mere shadows, by accidents of the air, by shifting effects of
perspective; putting down his dim luminary he could still wander on without it, pass into other rooms and, only knowing it
was there behind him in case of need, see his way about, visually project for his purpose a comparative clearness. It made
him feel, this acquired faculty, like some monstrous stealthy
cat; he wondered if he would have glared at these moments
with large shining yellow eyes, and what it mightn't verily be,
for the poor hard-pressed *alter ego*, to be confronted with such
a type.

He liked however the open shutters; he opened everywhere
those Mrs. Muldoon had closed, closing them as carefully afterwards, so that she shouldn't notice: he liked—oh this he did like,
and above all in the upper rooms!—the sense of the hard silver
of the autumn stars through the window-panes, and scarcely
less the flare of the street-lamps below, the white electric lustre
which it would have taken curtains to keep out. This was
human actual social; this was of the world he had lived in, and
he was more at his ease certainly for the countenance, coldly
general and impersonal, that all the while and in spite of his
detachment it seemed to give him. He had support of course

mostly in the rooms at the wide front and the prolonged side; it failed him considerably in the central shades and the parts at the back. But if he sometimes, on his rounds, was glad of his optical reach, so none the less often the rear of the house affected him as the very jungle of his prey. The place was there more subdivided; a large "extension" in particular, where small rooms for servants had been multiplied, abounded in nooks and corners, in closets and passages, in the ramifications especially of an ample back staircase over which he leaned, many a time, to look far down—not deterred from his gravity even while aware that he might, for a spectator, have figured some solemn simpleton playing at hide-and-seek. Outside in fact he might himself make that ironic *rapprochement*; but within the walls, and in spite of the clear windows, his consistency was proof against the cynical light of New York.

It had belonged to that idea of the exasperated consciousness of his victim to become a real test for him; since he had quite put it to himself from the first that, oh distinctly! he could "cultivate" his whole perception. He had felt it as above all open to cultivation—which indeed was but another name for his manner of spending his time. He was bringing it on, bringing it to perfection, by practice; in consequence of which it had grown so fine that he was now aware of impressions, attestations of his general postulate, that couldn't have broken upon him at once. This was the case more specifically with a phenomenon at last quite frequent for him in the upper rooms, the recognition—absolutely unmistakeable, and by a turn dating from a particular hour, his resumption of his campaign after a diplomatic drop, a calculated absence of three nights—of his being definitely followed, tracked at a distance carefully taken and to the express end that he should the less confidently, less arrogantly, appear to himself merely to pursue. It worried, it finally quite broke him up, for it proved, of all the conceivable impressions, the one least suited to his book. He was kept in sight while remaining himself—as regards the essence of his position—sightless, and his only recourse then was in abrupt turns, rapid recoveries of ground. He wheeled about, retracing his steps, as if he might so catch in his face at least the stirred air of some other quick revolution. It was indeed true that his fully dislocalised thought of these manœuvres recalled to him

Pantaloon, at the Christmas farce, buffeted and tricked from behind by ubiquitous Harlequin; but it left intact the influence of the conditions themselves each time he was re-exposed to them, so that in fact this association, had he suffered it to become constant, would on a certain side have but ministered to his intenser gravity. He had made, as I have said, to create on the premises the baseless sense of a reprieve, his three absences; and the result of the third was to confirm the after-effect of the second.

On his return, that night—the night succeeding his last intermission—he stood in the hall and looked up the staircase with a certainty more intimate than any he had yet known. "He's *there*, at the top, and waiting—not, as in general, falling back for disappearance. He's holding his ground, and it's the first time—which is a proof, isn't it? that something has happened for him." So Brydon argued with his hand on the banister and his foot on the lowest stair; in which position he felt as never before the air chilled by his logic. He himself turned cold in it, for he seemed of a sudden to know what now was involved. "Harder pressed?—yes, he takes it in, with its thus making clear to him that I've come, as they say, 'to stay.' He finally doesn't like and can't bear it, in the sense, I mean, that his wrath, his menaced interest, now balances with his dread. I've hunted him till he has 'turned': that, up there, is what has happened—he's the fanged or the antlered animal brought at last to bay." There came to him, as I say—but determined by an influence beyond my notation!—the acuteness of this certainty; under which however the next moment he had broken into a sweat that he would as little have consented to attribute to fear as he would have dared immediately to act upon it for enterprise. It marked none the less a prodigious thrill, a thrill that represented sudden dismay, no doubt, but also represented, and with the selfsame throb, the strangest, the most joyous, possibly the next minute almost the proudest, duplication of consciousness.

"He has been dodging, retreating, hiding, but now, worked up to anger, he'll fight!"—this intense impression made a single mouthful, as it were, of terror and applause. But what was wondrous was that the applause, for the felt fact, was so eager, since, if it was his other self he was running to earth, this ineffable identity was thus in the last resort not unworthy of him. It bristled there—somewhere near at hand, however unseen still—as the hunted thing, even as the trodden worm of the adage *must* at last bristle; and Brydon at this instant tasted probably of a sensation more complex than had ever before found itself consistent with sanity. It was as if it would have shamed him that a character so associated with his own should triumphantly succeed in just skulking, should to the end not risk the open; so that the drop of this danger was, on the spot, a great lift of the whole situation. Yet with another rare shift of the same subtlety he was already trying to measure by how much more he himself might now be in peril of fear; so rejoicing that he could, in another form, actively inspire that fear, and simultaneously quaking for the form in which he might passively know it.

The apprehension of knowing it must after a little have grown in him, and the strangest moment of his adventure perhaps, the most memorable or really most interesting, afterwards, of his crisis, was the lapse of certain instants of concentrated conscious *combat*, the sense of a need to hold on to something, even after the manner of a man slipping and slipping on some awful incline; the vivid impulse, above all, to move, to act, to charge, somehow and upon something—to show himself, in a word, that he wasn't afraid. The state of "holding-on" was thus the state to which he was momentarily reduced; if there had been anything, in the great vacancy, to seize, he would presently have been aware of having clutched it as he might under a shock at home have clutched the nearest chairback. He had been surprised at any rate—of this he *was* aware —into something unprecedented since his original appropriation of the place; he had closed his eyes, held them tight, for a long minute, as with that instinct of dismay and that terror of vision. When he opened them the room, the other contiguous rooms, extraordinarily, seemed lighter—so light, almost, that at first he took the change for day. He stood firm, however that might be, just where he had paused; his resistance had helped him—it was as if there were something he had tided over. He knew after a little what this was—it had been in the imminent danger of flight. He had stiffened his will against going; without this he would have made for the stairs, and it

seemed to him that, still with his eyes closed, he would have
descended them, would have known how, straight and swiftly,
to the bottom.

Well, as he had held out, here he was—still at the top, among
the more intricate upper rooms and with the gauntlet of the
others, of all the rest of the house, still to run when it should
be his time to go. He would go at his time—only at his time:
didn't he go every night very much at the same hour? He took
out his watch—there was light for that: it was scarcely a quarter
past one, and he had never withdrawn so soon. He reached his
lodgings for the most part at two—with his walk of a quarter
of an hour. He would wait for the last quarter—he wouldn't
stir till then; and he kept his watch there with his eyes on it, reflecting while he held it that this deliberate wait, a wait with an
effort, which he recognised, would serve perfectly for the at-
testation he desired to make. It would prove his courage—
unless indeed the latter might most be proved by his budging
at last from his place. What he mainly felt now was that, since
he hadn't originally scuttled, he had his dignities—which had
never in his life seemed so many—all to preserve and to carry
aloft. This was before him in truth as a physical image, an image almost worthy of an age of greater romance. That remark
indeed glimmered for him only to glow the next instant with a
finer light; since what age of romance, after all, could have
matched either the state of his mind or, "objectively," as they
said, the wonder of his situation? The only difference would
have been that, brandishing his dignities over his head as in a
parchment scroll, he might then—that is in the heroic time—
have proceeded downstairs with a drawn sword in his other
grasp.

At present, really, the light he had set down on the mantel of
the next room would have to figure his sword; which utensil,
in the course of a minute, he had taken the requisite number
of steps to possess himself of. The door between the rooms was
open, and from the second another door opened to a third.
These rooms, as he remembered, gave all three upon a common corridor as well, but there was a fourth, beyond them,
without issue save through the preceding. To have moved, to
have heard his step again, was appreciably a help; though even
in recognising this he lingered once more a little by the chim-

ney-piece on which his light had rested. When he next moved,
just hesitating where to turn, he found himself considering a
circumstance that, after his first and comparatively vague apprehension of it, produced in him the start that often attends
some pang of recollection, the violent shock of having ceased
happily to forget. He had come into sight of the door in which
the brief chain of communication ended and which he now
surveyed from the nearer threshold, the one not directly facing
it. Placed at some distance to the left of this point, it would
have admitted him to the last room of the four, the room without other approach or egress, had it not, to his intimate conviction, been closed *since* his former visitation, the matter
probably of a quarter of an hour before. He stared with all his
eyes at the wonder of the fact, arrested again where he stood
and again holding his breath while he sounded its sense. Surely
it had been *subsequently* closed—that is it had been on his previous passage indubitably open!

He took it full in the face that something had happened
between—that he couldn't not have noticed before (by which
he meant on his original tour of all the rooms that evening)
that such a barrier had exceptionally presented itself. He had
indeed since that moment undergone an agitation so extraordinary that it might have muddled for him any earlier view;
and he tried to convince himself that he might perhaps then
have gone into the room and, inadvertently, automatically, on
coming out, have drawn the door after him. The difficulty was
that this exactly was what he never did; it was against his whole
policy, as he might have said, the essence of which was to keep
vistas clear. He had them from the first, as he was well aware,
quite on the brain: the strange apparition, at the far end of one
of them, of his baffled "prey" (which had become by so sharp
an irony so little the term now to apply!) was the form of success his imagination had most cherished, projecting into it
always a refinement of beauty. He had known fifty times the
start of perception that had afterwards dropped; had fifty times
gasped to himself "There!" under some fond brief hallucination. The house, as the case stood, admirably lent itself; he might
wonder at the taste, the native architecture of the particular
time, which could rejoice so in the multiplication of doors—
the opposite extreme to the modern, the actual almost complete

proscription of them; but it had fairly contributed to provoke this obsession of the presence encountered telescopically, as he might say, focussed and studied in diminishing perspective and as by a rest for the elbow.

It was with these considerations that his present attention was charged—they perfectly availed to make what he saw portentous. He *couldn't*, by any lapse, have blocked that aperture; and if he hadn't, if it was unthinkable, why what else was clear but that there had been another agent? Another agent?—he had been catching, as he felt, a moment back, the very breath of him; but when had he been so close as in this simple, this logical, this completely personal act? It was so logical, that is, that one might have *taken* it for personal; yet for what did Brydon take it, he asked himself, while, softly panting, he felt his eyes almost leave their sockets. Ah this time at last they *were*, the two, the opposed projections of him, in presence; and this time, as much as one would, the question of danger loomed. With it rose, as not before, the question of courage—for what he knew the blank face of the door to say to him was "Show us how much you have!" It stared, it glared back at him with that challenge; it put to him the two alternatives: should he just push it open or not? Oh to have this consciousness was to *think*— and to think, Brydon knew, as he stood there, was, with the lapsing moments, not to have acted! Not to have acted—that was the misery and the pang—was even still not to act; was in fact *all* to feel the thing in another, in a new and terrible way. How long did he pause and how long did he debate? There was presently nothing to measure it; for his vibration had already changed—as just by the effect of its intensity. Shut up there, at bay, defiant, and with the prodigy of the thing palpably proveably *done*, thus giving notice like some stark signboard—under that accession of accent the situation itself had turned; and Brydon at last remarkably made up his mind on what it had turned to.

It had turned altogether to a different admonition; to a supreme hint, for him, of the value of Discretion! This slowly dawned, no doubt—for it could take its time; so perfectly, on his threshold, had he been stayed, so little as yet had he either advanced or retreated. It was the strangest of all things that now when, by his taking ten steps and applying his hand to a

latch, or even his shoulder and his knee, if necessary, to a
panel, all the hunger of his prime need might have been met,
his high curiosity crowned, his unrest assuaged—it was amazing, but it was also exquisite and rare, that insistence should
have, at a touch, quite dropped from him. Discretion—he
jumped at that; and yet not, verily, at such a pitch, because it
saved his nerves or his skin, but because, much more valuably,
it saved the situation. When I say he "jumped" at it I feel the
consonance of this term with the fact that—at the end indeed
of I know not how long—he did move again, he crossed
straight to the door. He wouldn't touch it—it seemed now
that he might *if* he would: he would only just wait there a
little, to show, to prove, that he wouldn't. He had thus another station, close to the thin partition by which revelation
was denied him; but with his eyes bent and his hands held off
in a mere intensity of stillness. He listened as if there had been
something to hear, but this attitude, while it lasted, was his
own communication. "If you won't then—good: I spare you
and I give up. You affect me as by the appeal positively for pity:
you convince me that for reasons rigid and sublime—what do I
know?—we both of us should have suffered. I respect them
then, and, though moved and privileged as, I believe, it has
never been given to man, I retire, I renounce—never, on my
honour, to try again. So rest for ever—and let *me!*"

That, for Brydon was the deep sense of this last demonstration—solemn, measured, directed, as he felt it to be. He
brought it to a close, he turned away; and now verily he knew
how deeply he had been stirred. He retraced his steps, taking
up his candle, burnt, he observed, well-nigh to the socket, and
marking again, lighten it as he would, the distinctness of his
footfall; after which, in a moment, he knew himself at the other
side of the house. He did here what he had not yet done at
these hours—he opened half a casement, one of those in the
front, and let in the air of the night; a thing he would have
taken at any time previous for a sharp rupture of his spell. His
spell was broken now, and it didn't matter—broken by his con-
cession and his surrender, which made it idle henceforth that
he should ever come back. The empty street—its other life so
marked even by the great lamplit vacancy—was within call,
within touch; he stayed there as to be in it again, high above

it though he was still perched; he watched as for some comforting common fact, some vulgar human note, the passage of
a scavenger or a thief, some night-bird however base. He would
have blessed that sign of life; he would have welcomed positively the slow approach of his friend the policeman, whom he
had hitherto only sought to avoid, and was not sure that if the
patrol had come into sight he mightn't have felt the impulse to
get into relation with it, to hail it, on some pretext, from his
fourth floor.

The pretext that wouldn't have been too silly or too com-
promising, the explanation that would have saved his dignity
and kept his name, in such a case, out of the papers, was not definite to him: he was so occupied with the thought of recording
his Discretion—as an effect of the vow he had just uttered to
his intimate adversary—that the importance of this loomed large
and something had overtaken all ironically his sense of proportion. If there had been a ladder applied to the front of the house,
even one of the vertiginous perpendiculars employed by
painters and roofers and sometimes left standing overnight, he
would have managed somehow, astride of the window-sill, to
compass by outstretched leg and arm that mode of descent. If
there had been some such uncanny thing as he had found in
his room at hotels, a workable fire-escape in the form of
notched cable or a canvas shoot, he would have availed himself
of it as a proof—well, of his present delicacy. He nursed that
sentiment, as the question stood, a little in vain, and even—at
the end of he scarce knew, once more, how long—found it, as
by the action on his mind of the failure of response of the
outer world, sinking back to vague anguish. It seemed to him
he had waited an age for some stir of the great grim hush; the
life of the town was itself under a spell—so unnaturally, up and
down the whole prospect of known and rather ugly objects,
the blankness and the silence lasted. Had they ever, he asked
himself, the hard-faced houses, which had begun to look livid
in the dim dawn, had they ever spoken so little to any need of
his spirit? Great builded voids, great crowded stillnesses put on,
often, in the heart of cities, for the small hours, a sort of sinister mask, and it was of this large collective negation that Brydon presently became conscious—all the more that the break

of day was, almost incredibly, now at hand, proving to him what a night he had made of it.

He looked again at his watch, saw what had become of his time-values (he had taken hours for minutes—not, as in other tense situations, minutes for hours) and the strange air of the streets was but the weak, the sullen flush of a dawn in which everything was still locked up. His choked appeal from his own open window had been the sole note of life, and he could but break off at last as for a worse despair. Yet while so deeply demoralised he was capable again of an impulse denoting—at least by his present measure—extraordinary resolution; of retracing his steps to the spot where he had turned cold with the extinction of his last pulse of doubt as to there being in the place another presence than his own. This required an effort strong enough to sicken him; but he had his reason, which overmastered for the moment everything else. There was the whole of the rest of the house to traverse, and how should he screw himself to that if the door he had seen closed were at present open? He could hold to the idea that the closing had practically been for him an act of mercy, a chance offered him to descend, depart, get off the ground and never again profane it. This conception held together, it worked; but what it meant for him depended now clearly on the amount of forbearance his recent action, or rather his recent inaction, had engendered. The image of the "presence," whatever it was, waiting there for him to go—this image had not yet been so concrete for his nerves as when he stopped short of the point at which certainty would have come to him. For, with all his resolution, or more exactly with all his dread, he did stop short—he hung back from really seeing. The risk was too great and his fear too definite: it took at this moment an awful specific form.

He knew—yes, as he had never known anything—that, *should* he see the door open, it would all too abjectly be the end of him. It would mean that the agent of his shame—for his shame was the deep abjection—was once more at large and in general possession; and what glared him thus in the face was the act that this would determine for him. It would send him straight about to the window he had left open, and by that window, be long ladder and dangling rope as absent as they would, he saw himself uncontrollably insanely fatally take his way to the street. The hideous chance of this he at least could avert; but he could only avert it by recoiling in time from assurance. He had the whole house to deal with, this fact was still there; only he now knew that uncertainty alone could start him. He stole back from where he had checked himself—merely to do so was suddenly like safety—and, making blindly for the greater stair-case, left gaping rooms and sounding passages behind. Here was the top of the stairs, with a fine large dim descent and three spacious landings to mark off. His instinct was all for mildness, but his feet were harsh on the floors, and, strangely, when he had in a couple of minutes become aware of this, it counted somehow for help. He couldn't have spoken, the tone of his voice would have scared him, and the common conceit or re-source of "whistling in the dark" (whether literally or figura-tively) have appeared basely vulgar; yet he liked none the less to hear himself go, and when he had reached his first landing —taking it all with no rush, but quite steadily—that stage of success drew from him a gasp of relief.

The house, withal, seemed immense, the scale of space again inordinate; the open rooms, to no one of which his eyes de-flected, gloomed in their shuttered state like mouths of cav-erns; only the high skylight that formed the crown of the deep well created for him a medium in which he could advance, but which might have been, for queerness of colour, some watery under-world. He tried to think of something noble, as that his property was really grand, a splendid possession; but this nobleness took the form too of the clear delight with which he was finally to sacrifice it. They might come in now, the builders, the destroyers—they might come as soon as they would. At the end of two flights he had dropped to another zone, and from the middle of the third, with only one more left, he recog-nised the influence of the lower windows, of half-drawn blinds, of the occasional gleam of streetlamps, of the glazed spaces of the vestibule. This was the bottom of the sea, which showed an illumination of its own and which he even saw paved—when at a given moment he drew up to sink a long look over the banisters—with the marble squares of his childhood. By that time indubitably he felt, as he might have said in a commoner cause, better; it had allowed him to stop and draw breath, and the ease increased with the sight of the old black-and-white slabs. But what he most felt was that now surely, with the element of impunity pulling him as by hard firm hands, the case was settled for what he might have seen above had he dared that last look. The closed door, blessedly remote now, was still closed—and he had only in short to reach that of the house.

He came down further, he crossed the passage forming the access to the last flight; and if here again he stopped an instant it was almost for the sharpness of the thrill of assured escape. It made him shut his eyes—which opened again to the straight slope of the remainder of the stairs. Here was impunity still, but impunity almost excessive; inasmuch as the sidelights and the high fan-tracery of the entrance were glimmering straight into the hall; an appearance produced, he the next instant saw, by the fact that the vestibule gaped wide, that the hinged halves of the inner door had been thrown far back. Out of that again the *question* sprang at him, making his eyes, as he felt, half-start from his head, as they had done, at the top of the house, before the sign of the other door. If he had left that one open, hadn't he left this one closed, and wasn't he now in *most* immediate presence of some inconceivable occult activity? It was as sharp, the question, as a knife in his side, but the answer hung fire still and seemed to lose itself in the vague darkness to which the thin admitted dawn, glimmering archwise over the whole outer door, made a semicircular margin, a cold silvery nimbus that seemed to play a little as he looked—to shift and expand and contract.

It was as if there had been something within it, protected by indistinctness and corresponding in extent with the opaque surface behind, the painted panels of the last barrier to his escape, of which the key was in his pocket. The indistinctness mocked him even while he stared, affected him as somehow shrouding or challenging certitude, so that after faltering an instant on his step he let himself go with the sense that here *was* at last something to meet, to touch, to take, to know— something all unnatural and dreadful, but to advance upon which was the condition for him either of liberation or of supreme defeat. The penumbra, dense and dark, was the virtual screen of a figure which stood in it as still as some image erect in a niche or as some black-vizored sentinel guarding a treasure. Brydon was to know afterwards, was to recall and make out, the particular thing he had believed during the rest of his descent. He saw, in its great grey glimmering margin, the central vagueness diminish, and he felt it to be taking the very form toward which, for so many days, the passion of his curiosity had yearned. It gloomed, it loomed, it was something, it was somebody, the prodigy of a personal presence.

Rigid and conscious, spectral yet human, a man of his own substance and stature waited there to measure himself with his power to dismay. This only could it be—this only till he recognised, with his advance, that what made the face dim was the pair of raised hands that covered it and in which, so far from being offered in defiance, it was buried as for dark deprecation. So Brydon, before him, took him in; with every fact of him now, in the higher light, hard and acute—his planted stillness, his vivid truth, his grizzled bent head and white masking hands, his queer actuality of evening-dress, of dangling double eye-glass, of gleaming silk lappet and white linen, of pearl button and gold watch-guard and polished shoe. No portrait by a great modern master could have presented him with more intensity, thrust him out of his frame with more art, as if there had been "treatment," of the consummate sort, in his every shade and salience. The revulsion, for our friend, had become, before he knew it, immense—this drop, in the act of apprehension, to the sense of his adversary's inscrutable manœuvre. That meaning at least, while he gaped, it offered him; for he could but gape at his other self in this other anguish, gape as a proof that *he*, standing there for the achieved, the enjoyed, the triumphant life, couldn't be faced in his triumph. Wasn't the proof in the splendid covering hands, strong and completely spread?—so spread and so intentional that, in spite of a special verity that surpassed every other, the fact that one of these hands had lost two fingers, which were reduced to stumps, as if accidentally shot away, the face was effectually guarded and saved.

"Saved," though, *would* it be?—Brydon breathed his wonder till the very impunity of his attitude and the very insistence of his eyes produced, as he felt, a sudden stir which showed the next instant as a deeper portent, while the head raised itself, the betrayal of a braver purpose. The hands, as he looked, began to move, to open; then, as if deciding in a flash, dropped from the face and left it uncovered and presented. Horror, with the sight, had leaped into Brydon's throat, gasping there in a sound he couldn't utter; for the bared identity was too hideous as *his*, and his glare was the passion of his protest. The face, *that* face, Spencer Brydon's?—he searched it still, but looking away from it in dismay and denial, falling straight from his height of sublimity. It was unknown, inconceivable, awful, disconnected from any possibility—! He had been "sold," he inwardly moaned, stalking such game as this: the presence before him was a presence, the horror within him a horror, but the waste of his nights had been only grotesque and the success of his adventure an irony. Such an identity fitted his at *no* point, made its alternative monstrous. A thousand times yes, as it came upon him nearer now—the face was the face of a stranger. It came upon him nearer now, quite as one of those expanding fantastic images projected by the magic lantern of childhood; for the stranger, whoever he might be, evil, odious, blatant, vulgar, had advanced as for aggression, and he knew himself give ground. Then harder pressed still, sick with the force of his shock, and falling back as under the hot breath and the roused passion of a life larger than his own, a rage of personality before which his own collapsed, he felt the whole vision turn to darkness and his very feet give way. His head went round; he was going; he had gone.

III

What had next brought him back, clearly—though after how long?—was Mrs. Muldoon's voice, coming to him from quite near, from so near that he seemed presently to see her as kneeling on the ground before him while he lay looking up at her; himself not wholly on the ground, but half-raised and upheld—conscious, yes, of tenderness of support and, more particularly, of a head pillowed in extraordinary softness and fainly refreshing fragrance. He considered, he wondered, his wit but half at his service; then another face intervened, bending more directly over him, and he finally knew that Alice Staverton had made her lap an ample and perfect cushion to him, and that she had to this end seated herself on the lowest degree of the staircase,

the rest of his long person remaining stretched on his old
black-and-white slabs. They were cold, these marble squares
of his youth; but *he* somehow was not, in this rich return of
consciousness—the most wonderful hour, little by little, that he
had ever known, leaving him, as it did, so gratefully, so abysmally passive, and yet as with a treasure of intelligence waiting
all round him for quiet appropriation; dissolved, he might call
it, in the air of the place and producing the golden glow of a
late autumn afternoon. He had come back, yes—come back
from further away than any man but himself had ever travelled;
but it was strange how with this sense what he had come back
to seemed really the great thing, and as if his prodigious journey had been all for the sake of it. Slowly but surely his consciousness grew, his vision of his state thus completing itself:
he had been miraculously *carried* back—lifted and carefully
borne as from where he had been picked up, the uttermost
end of an interminable grey passage. Even with this he was suffered to rest, and what had now brought him to knowledge
was the break in the long mild motion.

It had brought him to knowledge, to knowledge—yes, this
was the beauty of his state; which came to resemble more and
more that of a man who has gone to sleep on some news of a
great inheritance, and then, after dreaming it away, after pro-
faning it with matters strange to it, has waked up again to
serenity of certitude and has only to lie and watch it grow. This
was the drift of his patience—that he had only to let it shine on
him. He must moreover, with intermissions, still have been lifted
and borne; since why and how else should he have known himself, later on, with the afternoon glow intenser, no longer at the
foot of his stairs—situated as these now seemed at that dark
other end of his tunnel—but on a deep window-bench of his
high saloon, over which had been spread, couch-fashion, a
mantle of soft stuff lined with grey fur that was familiar to his
eyes and that one of his hands kept fondly feeling as for its
pledge of truth. Mrs. Muldoon's face had gone, but the other,
the second he had recognised, hung over him in a way that
showed how he was still propped and pillowed. He took it all
in, and the more he took it the more it seemed to suffice: he
was as much at peace as if he had had food and drink. It was

the two women who had found him, on Mrs. Muldoon's having plied, at her usual hour, her latch-key—and on her having above all arrived while Miss Staverton still lingered near the house. She had been turning away, all anxiety, from worrying the vain bell-handle—her calculation having been of the hour of the good woman's visit; but the latter, blessedly, had come up while she was still there, and they had entered together. He had then lain, beyond the vestibule, very much as he was lying now—quite, that is, as he appeared to have fallen, but all so wondrously without bruise or gash; only in a depth of stupor. What he most took in, however, at present, with the steadier clearance, was that Alice Staverton had for a long un-speakable moment not doubted he was dead.

"It must have been that I *was*." He made it out as she held him. "Yes—I can only have died. You brought me literally to life. Only," he wondered, his eyes rising to her, "only, in the name of all the benedictions, how?"

It took her but an instant to bend her face and kiss him, and something in the manner of it, and in the way her hands clasped and locked his head while he felt the cool charity and virtue of her lips, something in all this beatitude somehow an-swered everything. "And now I keep you," she said.

"Oh keep me, keep me!" he pleaded while her face still hung over him: in response to which it dropped again and stayed close, clingingly close. It was the seal of their situation—of which he tasted the impress for a long blissful moment in si-lence. But he came back. "Yet how did you know—?"

"I was uneasy. You were to have come, you remember—and you had sent no word."

"Yes, I remember—I was to have gone to you at one today." It caught on to their "old" life and relation—which were so near and so far. "I was still out there in my strange darkness—where was it, what was it? I must have stayed there so long." He could but wonder at the depth and the duration of his swoon.

"Since last night?" she asked with a shade of fear for her pos-sible indiscretion.

"Since this morning—it must have been: the cold dim dawn of to-day. Where have I been," he vaguely wailed, "where have

I been?" He felt her hold him close, and it was as if this helped
him now to make in all security his mild moan. "What a long
dark day!"

All in her tenderness she had waited a moment. "In the cold
dim dawn?" she quavered.

But he had already gone on piecing together the parts of the
whole prodigy. "As I didn't turn up you came straight—?"

She barely cast about. "I went first to your hotel—where
they told me of your absence. You had dined out last evening
and hadn't been back since. But they appeared to know you
had been at your club."

"So you had the idea of *this*—?"

"Of what?" she asked in a moment.

"Well—of what has happened."

"I believed at least you'd have been here. I've known, all
along," she said, "that you've been coming."

" 'Known' it—?"

"Well, I've believed it. I said nothing to you after that talk
we had a month ago—but I felt sure. I knew you *would*," she
declared.

"That I'd persist, you mean?"

"That you'd see him."

"Ah but I didn't!" cried Brydon with his long wail. "There's
somebody—an awful beast; whom I brought, too horribly, to
bay. But it's not me."

At this she bent over him again, and her eyes were in his eyes.
"No—it's not you." And it was as if, while her face hovered,
he might have made out in it, hadn't it been so near, some particular meaning blurred by a smile. "No, thank heaven," she
repeated—"it's not you! Of course it wasn't to have been."

"Ah but it *was*," he gently insisted. And he stared before
him now as he had been staring for so many weeks. "I was to
have known myself."

"You couldn't!" she returned consolingly. And then reverting, and as if to account further for what she had herself
done, "But it wasn't only *that*, that you hadn't been at home,"
she went on. "I waited till the hour at which we had found Mrs.
Muldoon that day of my going with you; and she arrived, as
I've told you, while, failing to bring any one to the door, I lingered in my despair on the steps. After a little, if she hadn't

come, by such a mercy, I should have found means to hunt her up. But it wasn't," said Alice Staverton, as if once more with her fine intention—"it wasn't only that."

His eyes, as he lay, turned back to her. "What more then?"

She met it, the wonder she had stirred. "In the cold dim dawn, you say? Well, in the cold dim dawn of this morning I too saw you."

"Saw *me*—?"

"Saw *him*," said Alice Staverton. "It must have been at the same moment."

He lay an instant taking it in—as if he wished to be quite reasonable. "At the same moment?"

"Yes—in my dream again, the same one I've named to you. He came back to me. Then I knew it for a sign. He had come to you."

At this Brydon raised himself; he had to see her better. She helped him when she understood his movement, and he sat up, steadying himself beside her there on the window-bench and with his right hand grasping her left. "*He* didn't come to me."

"You came to yourself," she beautifully smiled.

"Ah I've come to myself now—thanks to you, dearest. But this brute, with his awful face—this brute's a black stranger. He's none of *me*, even as I *might* have been," Brydon sturdily declared.

But she kept the clearness that was like the breath of infallibility. "Isn't the whole point that you'd have been different?"

He almost scowled for it. "As different as *that*—?"

Her look again was more beautiful to him than the things of this world. "Haven't you exactly wanted to know *how* different? So this morning," she said, "you appeared to me."

"Like *him*?"

"A black stranger!"

"Then how did you know it was I?"

"Because, as I told you weeks ago, my mind, my imagination, had worked so over what you might, what you mightn't have been—to show you, you see, how I've thought of you. In the midst of that you came to me—that my wonder might be answered. So I knew," she went on; "and believed that, since the question held you too so fast, as you told me that day, you too would see for yourself. And when this morning I again saw

I knew it would be because you had—and also then, from the first moment, because you somehow wanted me. *He* seemed to tell me of that. So why," she strangely smiled, "shouldn't I like him?"

It brought Spencer Brydon to his feet. "You 'like' that horror—?"

"I *could* have liked him. And to me," she said, "he was no horror. I had accepted him."

"'Accepted'—?" Brydon oddly sounded.

"Before, for the interest of his difference—yes. And as *I* didn't disown him, as *I* knew him—which you at last, confronted with him in his difference, so cruelly didn't, my dear—well, he must have been, you see, less dreadful to me. And it may have pleased him that I pitied him."

She was beside him on her feet, but still holding his hand—still with her arm supporting him. But though it all brought for him thus a dim light, "You 'pitied' him?" he grudgingly, resentfully asked.

"He has been unhappy, he has been ravaged," she said.

"And haven't I been unhappy? Am not I—you've only to look at me!—ravaged?"

"Ah I don't say I like him *better*," she granted after a thought. "But he's grim, he's worn—and things have happened to him. He doesn't make shift, for sight, with your charming monocle."

"No"—it struck Brydon: "I couldn't have sported mine 'downtown.' They'd have guyed me there."

"His great convex pince-nez—I saw it, I recognised the kind —is for his poor ruined sight. And his poor right hand—!"

"Ah!" Brydon winced—whether for his proved identity or for his lost fingers. Then, "He has a million a year," he lucidly added. "But he hasn't you."

"And he isn't—no, he isn't—*you!*" she murmured as he drew her to his breast.

1908

ALICE BROWN

(1857–1948)

Golden Baby

WE were in the *Sycorax* smoking-room, within an hour of turning the lights out for the night. The air was gray with smoke, and everybody, even the men that made it, looked dulled by it. The scion of one of our oldest families, who had seized the occasion of an ocean voyage for extravagant over-indulgence, sat at a little table, monotonously repeating, "She was the fairest of all the country round," in a tone of eccentric rhetorical emphasis. Nobody took any notice of him, because we had ceased doing that when he introduced us, one by one, to the aura of his ancestor who had "preceded Sir Philip Sidney at the battle of Zutphen." What he meant by that initiatory phrase we never knew. We were merely convinced, one after another, by the sound of it, that we weren't strong enough to hear it again. The man who was travelling round the globe on his own private fortune to discover a parasite for hostile bugs was absorbedly making diagrams of larvæ and what he called winged coleoptera for a buyer of seersucker, who was not listening to him, and the big fellow with the grizzled beard and the William Morris look of the eyes was sunk in some private reverie of his own. Suddenly the clerical young fellow opposite him asked him a question, whereupon he leaned back in his chair, gripped the beer glass before him as if he might sling it, and began, in a voice like a bell:

"Logic is a fool. The mystery your calling is founded on is no more a mystery than a million others. You simply fail to get the connections. I could tell you a dozen tales more unaccountable than that, because they're just ripped out of the air and made manifest. It's as if you should go out there on deck and see a film of some kind of impalpable parchment hanging from the topmast. You'd send up a man, he'd bring it down to you, and you'd find on it characters you could seem to read; but the story they made would say nothing whatever to you. I

371

mean, it couldn't be hitched on to the general course of things. Now I'll give you a case in point."

He had given us no cases in point throughout the voyage. He had simply rowed about labor and capital, and said one was as bad as the other, capital being only labor reversed, and we thought we had discovered his pet nursling of a fad and just what road it was leading him. Now two or three other men looked up, and then moved a little nearer. They scented story as you do when you buy the new magazine and are lotting on having it to go to bed on. The scion of the noble family leaned back in his chair, regarded us haughtily, and said, "What's all this?" in a loud tone nobody noticed except discouragingly because he was making more noise. We left him to the solace of it, and drew up in a circle about the William Morris man. He had put the tip of his blunt finger—the kind of digit artisans work wonders with—delicately into a little pond of beer on the table and drawn out a line from it like a peninsula. Then he dabbled his finger again and put it down in another place, to make an island, and another. A merchant of many sorts of goods, who sailed all seas, burst out there, with a sudden recognition:

"Why, you're making islands!"

A white-faced young man of no breadth and inconsiderable stature, who, we understood, had some reputation as a poet of the minor variety, bent over the table and put on his large horn-bowed spectacles to look. He, too, spoke with an irrational quickness, as if everything the William Morris man did suddenly bore a meaning. It seemed as if the man had turned on his battery and we had become aware of his voltage.

"Do you suppose that's how God did it?" asked the little poet. "Before He 'came to the making of man'?"

But the William Morris man never answered him. He did look up at the merchant.

"Yes," he said, "it's the West Indies." Then he hunched his big frame back in his chair and began speaking, rather slowly and in a quiet voice, as if what he had to tell bore for him a significance of a particular and really a solemn nature.

"It was a week before Christmas when we sailed. Some company—it was a bum company and went to pieces afterward when its unseaworthy boats had all gone cranky, one

way or another, and the public had turned back to the old
standbys that rule the wave and sap the pocket—this company
—I forget the name—had bought an old boat for a song and a
promise, knocked out bulkheads, furbished up some dog-holes
for new staterooms, put in red velvet and gilding, called her
the *Siren*, and advertised a grand excursion to the West Indies.
Somehow the idea took. It had been a nasty winter, there was
easy money, and without much delay the *Siren's* list was full. I
was among the first to take passage. I was done up that winter
with statistics and the deviltry of the rich and, besides, I'd
always wanted a sniff of sugar, rum and spices on their own
ground. When I went on board there was a great copper sunset; it looked as if it belonged to the land exclusively and we
might never have a whack at such another when we'd left New
York behind us. I turned to look at it, as I'd been turning all
the way along, and I stood there till the splendors and banners
of it blinded me. So when I went aboard things were dark
before me momentarily, in queer shapes, the outlines of warehouses and such, and I didn't feel that I'd really seen anything,
until, on the deck at the end of the gangplank, I came face to
face with a coolie woman, the thinnest of her sort, with bare
feet and legs, bare arms, the slightest possible garment, and a
weight of silver bangles on her wrists and collars round her
neck. She stood there holding a child, a baby with a queer expression of maturity, and her eyes as she looked at me were
black and solemn. They seemed to talk in a language of their
own, to sing things maybe, chant 'em—talking wasn't good
enough—and they made me shiver. The child sat there supported on the crook of her arm and looked at me as seriously
as she did, but with a kind of well-wishing, too, as if he said:

"'Old man, you're tired, aren't you? Everybody's tired.
Glad you're shut of little old New York for a spell. Wish all of
'em could do the same.'

"What came into my mind—I don't see why—was that he
was a kind of golden baby. Maybe it was because he had bright
hair—an image to be worshipped—and my mind said inside, as
plain as your lips might speak it, 'Golden Baby!' I felt I liked
him, too, better than any piece of littleness I'd ever seen. And
then, in the same minute—for it all passed as quickly as you
might set your foot on deck and lift the other foot to keep it

company—the coolie woman and the golden baby were gone, and there was a spot of blackness where he'd been.

"A sailor was passing me with an end of a rope.

"'Where's the woman?' I asked, before I could stop myself.

"He gave me a glance, and said, 'Sir?' without stopping, because he was evidently on business of the ship.

"'The woman and the child,' I called after him.

"I felt I'd got to know. But he shook his head and went along, and I felt disappointed, as if I'd lost something. But there was one queer thing. A darkness in the outline of the child stood before my eyes until I'd got into my stateroom and after. I couldn't rub it away.

"Well, gentlemen, that voyage was a corker for sheer madness of the human creature let loose. We hadn't been a day out before I knew what we'd got aboard—mothers that regarded the boat as a summer hotel and had fitted out their daughters with every rag known to milliners, to sell 'em in the market of some rich man's desire. That was the first—exhibit A. Then there were copper kings whose copper queens hadn't any chance to show off their diamonds and pearls and loot of the earth and sea in the regulation manner, and brought it all on board to flout the moon and stars, I guess, and the Creator of the moon and stars, and the other folks He'd made that had more or hadn't so many, each in a different way. It was all money and class hatred and scorn and contumely."

Here the scion of a noble stock broke in, his dreary drone addressed to none of us in particular:

"Sir Philip Sidney, let me inform you. Sir Philip Sidney! Battle of Zutphen!"

"That's it," said the William Morris man, quietly. "That just it. There were a few of 'em on board just like him. They'd had ancestors at Zutphen, and they wouldn't speak to the Semitic walking diamond-shops, nor me because I said I'd been in a foundry, nor the captain even, because he wasn't a *von*. Intercourse was restricted because they could only speak to one another, and they'd trodden that ground so long that they had only common recollections to go on, and I felt they were the best bored set on the boat. But in spite of all the hatreds and mildew of exclusiveness, the same old farce obtained that they were all enjoying themselves immensely. The decks were canvassed in nearly every night and the stars shut out, so that those apes of various degrees could put on their gimcracks borrowed from the earth and sea, and dance and strut under the light of electric bulbs with backgrounds of flags and paper garlands. Great Israel! I wonder the Lord of all don't turn His face away from the whole bloomin' show sometimes and say, 'I'm sick of vaudeville.'

"Well, as days went on, I can't tell you how or why, I began to be conscious of hate, hate everywhere. Whether it was the heat and madness of the tropics that got into our blood and set it seething, I don't know, or whether it was the revenge of big nature rising up against fool civilization—we were separated into as many little cliques and parties as the factions in a South-American state. I was out of the whole thing, not because I was better, but because I was worse. They hated one another, and I hated them all with a glorious impartiality. We'd gone due south, struck Jamaica, steamed on to the Isthmus, and then skirted the coast to Trinidad and dipped down beyond the mouth of the Orinoco, with the Southern Cross dominant now and the Dipper selling short. And suddenly one night about eleven, when the band was whanging away at a popular waltz and girls were swishing their muslins and laces round the deck in time, the boat stopped. You know there's always an underconsciousness of danger at sea, in the thickest-hided. No man forgets he's over an unplumbed abyss, except maybe he's in his cups and taking the return trip to Zutphen. So when the motion—there wasn't much of it on that sea— when it fell into a calm, the dancing grigs stopped, I suppose as the dancers did in 'Belgium's capital' when George Osborne got his summons to go and be killed, and wondered what the god of the machinery was going to do to them. We stopped, and we stayed so. I was on the hurricane-deck, and I came down with that same premonition of panic in me—I'm an old sailor, but I did feel actual panic—and the first man I met, making his thirty-six-inch strides along the deck, was the second officer. He was a good fellow; I hadn't hated him. We'd chummed together quite a lot on the voyage. I've grinned since to think how I greeted him inanely.

"'We've stopped,' said I.

"'Yes,' said he, two paces away from me.

"'What for?' I called, knowing I shouldn't be told.

"'Don't know, sir,' he returned. I knew he was entrenched in official reserve and not the accessible fellow I'd smoked my pipe with.

"Well, gentlemen, we had stopped, and there we hung all that night, and the next morning we were there still, a little motion under us, the very least, like the sound, so far as motion might be, of tiny ripples lapping on the beach. Everybody came haggard to breakfast. Nobody had slept, except some of the rummies who were in that condition of tissue where you might call 'em permanently asleep. The crew, such of them as I saw at intervals, seemed also to be in a state of tension. Then the questions began, fired by the broadside and popping like guerrilla warfare, always to the same tune: What was the matter? The answer reassured us briefly. It was no longer, 'We don't know.' 'Some trouble with the engine,' we were assured. 'The engineer's at it now.' So we went on eating, and fault-finding when our toast varied in brownness, and hating one another; but the day, the sulky, burning tropical day, went by, and the tropical night with its quick onrush of stars, and still we hadn't moved. That next morning I met the wireless man at the rail, where he's gone to lean both arms and, it seemed, throw some problem of his own at the bright horizon-line. He was a little, round, oily, dark fellow with curly hair, and in spite of his fatness his face looked funnily tragic with anxiety, as if he were going to cry. At once I felt he was pretty well shaken, and he'd tell me what's the matter.

"'Have you tried wireless?' I asked, in the fatuous way we have of baiting with a commonplace when we mean to fish up something that might dart and elude us unless it thought it was snapping at the same old fly. He shook his head as if he shook me off. I'd thought he knew nothing but wireless, but it was evident he sized me up for the ass I was.

"'Tried it?' he said. 'What else?'

"'Well, don't you get anything?'

"He shook his head again.

"'Why don't you keep on trying? There must be stations down here—there must be ships—'

"'They don't answer,' he said. It was almost as if with

another word he might break down actually. 'I've changed my tune, and changed it—changed it. I can't get them.'

"He turned abruptly as if he were really concealing tears now, and ran up the ladder to his post. Then I went away to think. I was afraid, sheer afraid, and wondered at myself. You see, I've no more pluck than any man of my inches, but I'd been about a good bit. I'd seen adventure and heard other fellows talk it over, and I knew you're pretty sure to get out of everything with a whole skin till that last particular time when you don't—so what's the use of grizzling? But this time there was panic in my left waistcoat pocket, neatly sewed in to stay, and I knew it and hated it for being there. There was foul weather all over the ship. Nobody sang, nobody strummed the light guitar as one girl had been doing till we wished she was at home in the kitchen with a consignment of pots and pans to wash. New York hated Jerusalem more frankly than ever, and Jerusalem wagged its fat chin and openly put up its beak at New York. Hate! Talk about the wars of nations! If that ship couldn't have made use of a whole Hague conference all to herself, it wasn't because she wasn't sick for it and only needed diagnosis to have it prescribed. Toward night I climbed up to the door of the little wireless cage, and stopped there, hat in hand, if you'll believe me. I don't know what kind of besetment made me feel as if every Jack on board that ship was in as tight a place as he could breathe in, and that every lubber that spoke to them had got to walk Spanish. He looked up at me. His tired little eyes were set in a bed of wrinkles. It hadn't been long, this universal panic of the ship, but it had had time to eat into him and change him, from a fat little manipulator who'd learned to do a certain thing, to a crying, hungering soul in trouble, beseeching—maybe with no voice, only with those eyes and that quiver of a mouth—beseeching the Lord of things big and little to lift him out of the pit he's stumbled into. I don't know whether the wireless chap ever heard of the Psalmist, but if he had, I bet he was tuning his own little pipe to him that minute.

"'Go down,' said he, looking at me as if I were in pinafores.

"That was all. But I felt I must speak. I had an ass's desire to bray and a meddler's insane push to help on somehow.

I'd got to help the ship on. We all felt so. One man in the smoking-room—we kept it all of a cloud now, we smoked so hard and universally—he told me he felt as if he must get out and push, even if he drowned in doing it. He gave a queer little catch in his throat when he said it. If it had been a woman that gave that sound, you'd have said it was a sob. 'That's it,' two or three other men had said, and looked the same way, and it was ten to one that, give them a lead, they'd have sobbed, too. It was then I had lighted out. I was afraid we should all be in hysterics together like a girls' boarding-school. But the wireless man:

" 'I beg pardon,' I said to him.

" 'Go down,' said he.

" 'I beg your pardon,' I said again, 'but mightn't there be—isn't there—some sort of magnetic field, and mightn't we be inside it?'

"He laughed a little—a shrill hoot all scorn and tiredness.

" 'Magnetic grandmother!' said he. 'Go down.'

"Then I went.

"Well, whatever it was that stopped stayed stopped. Life hung fire. Electricity hadn't played us false. There were plenty of lights, as faithful as the night. It wasn't true that according to the old tune—it ran in my head all the time then—'water wouldn't quench fire, fire wouldn't burn axe,' and the rest of it. Fire was faithful and cooked us three—no, by George! six times a day the most elaborate and embroidered and sinful meals for richness the tropics ever saw. But we simply didn't move, and now the mischief was so patent, the whole thing grew so upsetting and queer, that the usual disciplinary silence cracked and broke. The captain made no secret of it. The mate made none, nor the chief engineer. He, I found out, was spending his time digging into his engine, prying into her heart to find out whether she'd got some deadly secret he hadn't shared. At last he was crying over her, the chief electrician told me afterward. But they made no secret, any of them. There was nothing the matter anywhere. The engine simply would not go. And we saw no ship and we saw no land, and wireless wouldn't talk. The only creatures on the ship that showed any animation because they hadn't time to break, were the stewards and I suppose the *chef*, though I never saw him, and the band. For according to the notion that you can ensure a man against panic by making a noise or stuffing him, they kept the band playing the last comic-opera airs, and the stewards brought on more food, food, food, and offered it up to the god that's in every man's belly. I'll say right here that I never knew stewards so overworked as those poor devils had been from the start, and by now they were so pasty-pale it made you ashamed of yourself, if you were an able-bodied man, to ring a bell and see 'em totter out and start into that perfunctory sprightliness—you know it. See it here on this very ship; but these boys look better, a heap better. The stewards on the *Siren* made you want to say, 'For God's sake, give me the key of the pantry and I'll get it myself.'

"Well, one night, as if a great bubble burst in the air, something happened. Don't you know how it feels when your head's sort of muffled and woozy, and suddenly something clicks in your ear, and everything clears and lightens, and you find yourself out in the open? This was exactly that way. We were all on deck, packed into our rows of steamer chairs—I believe we were afraid of going below, and besides it was hot—and the band was dashing along from:

> " 'Oh, I am the King of Gold,
>   And I made it all myself;
>   My heart and brain I sold
>   In accumulating pelf,'

to the Sylvia ballet music, when a man down the line of chairs somewhere—I never knew who he was—burst out into a kind of screech: 'Stop that band! For God's sake, stop that band!'

"We didn't have to. The band stopped. I believe it knew, instruments and all, that we had had every hair's weight we could endure, and that it had blared out all the breath it could spare, and had got either to scream or die dead from tiredness and fear. And then I turned my head a little—I don't know why: I felt as if I had been called—and in a veil of darkness by the rail pretty well aft I saw them, the coolie woman and the baby. 'Golden Baby!' I caught myself saying, under my breath, 'Golden Baby!'

"And at once my fear passed away from me as the shadow passes when the cloud moves on. Something snapped—that same lightening like a bubble's breaking—and something came up in me that was like summer mornings and being young. I felt it going all over the ship, as if there'd been long breaths— what the stories call breaths of relief—and I knew I was in the midst of a flood of the same kind of sudden happiness. I had time to ask myself why, why, and to wonder a little, because the ship hadn't started and we were in exactly as bad case as before. But that I couldn't stop to think of, for my eyes were on the Golden Baby, and I seemed to be wanting to learn everything I could about him by heart, for fear I should never see him again. You know some minutes warn you they're going to be mighty short and you'd better take a snapshot of 'em while you can. The coolie woman stood there exactly as she'd stood on deck the first minute I saw her. She had on the same scanty, dignified garment down to her bare knees and thin legs, and the silver round her neck and on her arms shone out there in the dark. It seemed to shine like moonlight. The electric lights didn't touch her or the child. They were there in a darkness of their own, and it seemed as if they made their own light. The child sat on her arm and looked toward us and smiled. His hair was bright. His face was bright. Afterward I had a kind of feeling that he stretched out his arms toward us, but that I couldn't swear to. His smile was queer, too. Or, no, it wasn't queer. It was pretty much what you'd see in any baby, only more so. It wasn't—well, it wasn't benignant, you know; spiritual, you might call it, same as it is in pictures of—" He hesitated here, being, we thought, diffident about matters of accepted religion.

"Madonnas," said the little poet, raptly. He had hung on every word.

"Exactly, Madonnas. No, it was the way you'd like to have your own baby look, if he'd come in from play with his hands full of flowers. But the coolie woman smiled. She held out her arms toward us, and him in them. And all along the line I knew women were holding out their arms toward the child; and the men—well, I guess they did what I did. I brought my feet down to the deck and sat up straight and bent forward. That's all the way I know how to express it. I wanted to get there, somewhere near the baby, and same time I knew I mustn't go any nearer, not a step. And the only relief I had was muttering, just as you'd breathe hard, 'Golden Baby!' Then the woman spoke. It was a kind of voice—well, I don't know exactly, a cool voice, smooth, kind of like a silver horn. Something shaking in it, too, something that trembled and yet had a power of its own, a vibration—I've never been able to describe it to myself, all the times I've tried, and I'm not having any better luck now. But there wasn't any mistake about what she said. 'You're keeping him back, and he's got to be there. Oh, don't! You mustn't keep him back.'"

"What language did she speak in?" asked the man that sought the parasites. He'd been listening very seriously, not in any spirit of unbelief, I could see, but with the gravity due a marvel.

The William Morris man nodded at him.

"I knew that would come," he said. "It came that very night, before we turned in. 'What language did she speak?' says the wireless man to me, and I carried the question on to the first mate. 'God, man, I don't know,' says he. 'She spoke, that's all I can say.'

"And a Frenchman that was going to write up Martinique as he saw it from the deck swore she spoke in French, and the German that played the trombone said it was the best Hanoverian German. I knew well enough it wasn't either, but I didn't know what it was, and I didn't care. I only know she spoke and we understood. I didn't have much eyesight to spare from looking at the baby; but somehow I did realize that everything round me was different, and different all over the ship. Mrs.—I forget her condemned and sacred name—she was one of your Boston Apocalypse people, the kind that got transfigured on some mount or other and haven't spoken to anybody since—why, up to now she hadn't accepted anybody's being on that boat but herself and her two long-footed daughters and their following. And now she sat there with her hand on a bedizened Jewess's fat knee, and her daughters had hold of a school-teacher from the West—not with a ten-foot pole and a hook on the end of it, mind you, but as if they were constrained to hug somebody and it didn't matter whom. It was the same all over the ship. Something had lubricated us.

Something had washed us clean. I understood, and at the same minute I knew they all understood, too. Hate had passed away, and in its place was the other word that's just as big. 'Golden Baby!' I says to myself. I saw he had done it, though I didn't know how. That didn't concern us somehow.

"The coolie woman seemed to come forward. I say seemed, though she didn't move a step, but we all knew she was nearer, every one of us, and that it wasn't important except as she brought the child. Anyhow, he seemed nearer, and if everybody felt as I did it was as if the child was warm and bright right in the midst of us. She spoke again.

" 'That's it,' she said. 'That's good. When you feel like this it doesn't keep him back. Don't keep him back. He's needed so.'

"And then something happened. It was so gradual and so natural that at first we didn't realize what it was, only that everything in general was all right, and the sun would rise to-morrow on the good old practical world with no fear in it, and God was up there in His heavens wishing us well and not playing tricks on us. The ship was moving, that's what it was. There was the beat of the engine and the little heaving motion of a ship that begins to feel herself, though on smooth water. Then somebody began to cry and somebody else laughed, and we hugged each other, I guess, nobody particularly anxious to know whether he was hugging out of his class or not, and somehow or other the coolie woman and the Golden Baby were gone. But that night it seemed no more incredible to have them go than it did to have them come. And the engine was beating and the wireless man suddenly appeared among us, his flabby round face all puffed out again with satisfaction in his box of tricks, and he says:

" 'There's a revolution in Haiti!'

"And we laughed louder and more foolishly, not because there was a revolution, but because it was such a joyful thing to have wireless say anything at all.

" 'Let's have something to eat,' says somebody then, because we'd got used to eating as a kind of expression of emotion of any sort; but somebody else roared out: 'Let the stewards rest, can't you? Poor devils!'

" 'Poor devils!' said somebody else, and then I understood,

and I guess everybody else did, that we not only impossibly loved one another, but we loved the pasty stewards, too.

"And we bunked down quietly that night, and there was no eating or drinking, only a kind of prayerful yearning over the engine that kept beating on, and thoughts we didn't dare to put into words about the Baby. And next day the engines were still going, and there was a breeze, and in some queer way we were a quiet, happy crew of people. And everybody spoke to everybody else."

"Where were the woman and the baby?" asked the parasite man. He was frowning a good deal and beating a forefinger silently on the table.

"I don't know."

"Don't know? Didn't you ask for them?"

"No."

"Didn't anybody?"

"No."

"Why didn't you ask?"

The William Morris man paused a long time here, and seemed to study the question in many aspects. Then he answered slowly:

"We knew we were not to ask. We knew they'd come for a special purpose. What it was didn't concern us, and we felt—we felt a loyalty to the child, a loyalty bigger than anything I'd ever felt before. I guess it was so with all of 'em."

"Did you ever see them again?"

"Oh, yes. We sailed north, touching at an island now and then, contented as you please, but solemn, changed in a way. I was changed. I guess they all were. I haven't been the same man since. It was the pasty stewards on that trip that set me thinking labor and capital wasn't an institution to be sworn over. There was something to be done about it. Well, we kept our course north, and then we slid along the coast of Haiti, and the wireless man picked up more about the revolution. Hot as pepper it was, black as ink. And then one night off that coast—I never knew whether there was a harbor or not—the engines slowed down and we stopped. But queer as it was to stop again we didn't feel a breath of our old panic, only a solemn expectation. And we heard a stroke of oars, and before

I knew what was doing there was the coolie woman, Golden
Baby in her arms, going over the side. They seemed to make
their own light—the child did. His hair was bright almost like
flame. His face—I never saw—"

Here he stopped a moment, as if the memory were too
blinding to be borne.

"I heard a woman say—it wasn't as if she was afraid, but
only awed and wondering—'Don't let them go there into that
island in the dark. Don't let them go!' And somebody else
said:

" 'Hush!'

"I jumped to the rail and looked over, and I got a glimpse—
I swear I did—of a boat full of blacks and the stern seat vacant
for a passenger. And the boat moved away, and there was a
light in it there hadn't been before. It was bright, like the
baby's hair. We put on steam again, and that was all."

Nobody spoke for a while, and the steward, perking out the
curtains at the port-holes, to give himself pretence for lingering while our talk shut down, ventured to look at us im-
ploringly, like a tired clock striking the hour. The parasite man
began to feel his way cautiously through a sentence, evidently
not knowing where he was to come out.

"It's your theory, is it, that—that the spirit of those on
board ship delayed—well, it's absurd to say it—stopped the
machinery?"

The William Morris man nodded.

"When you put in that way," he owned, "of course there's
nothing for it but to laugh. But there were evil passions aboard
that ship, envy, pride, covetousness, lust, hate—chiefly hate.
Now if you should ask me if hate could stop an engine, I
should say, 'No, it can't,' and so would you. Still, the hate was
there and the engine stopped."

"Ah!" This was a breath in unison from us all, not a breath
of understanding, but of concurrence. The scion of a noble
stock, who'd been cooling off a little, got on his wobbly pins
and stretched himself cautiously, with regard to equipoise.

"Look here, old chap," said he, "I've heard that story
before."

The William Morris man was too much absorbed in the after-

tang of his renewed memory of it to notice who spoke, or he
wouldn't have answered. Nobody answered the Sidney man.

"Not likely," said he. He spoke briefly, absently. "None of us
who were there were likely to tell it. I never told it before in
my life."

"But I've heard it," said the little poet.

"Have you?'" asked the William Morris man. He looked up
at him and spoke as if in that quarter something might be doing.
"Have you?"

"Yes," said the little poet. His eyes shone. His hair seemed
to bristle and come alive with some new excitement under his
poll. "Oh yes, I've heard it."

"When d' you hear it?"

"Long ago—oh, long ago!"

"Who told you?"

"A man named Coleridge. He called it 'The Ancient
Mariner'."

1910

EDITH WHARTON

(1862–1937)

Afterward

"Oʜ, there *is* one, of course, but you'll never know it."

The assertion, laughingly flung out six months earlier in a bright June garden, came back to Mary Boyne with a new perception of its significance as she stood, in the December dusk, waiting for the lamps to be brought into the library.

The words had been spoken by their friend Alida Stair, as they sat at tea on her lawn at Pangbourne, in reference to the very house of which the library in question was the central, the pivotal "feature." Mary Boyne and her husband, in quest of a country place in one of the southern or southwestern counties, had, on their arrival in England, carried their problem straight to Alida Stair, who had successfully solved it in her own case; but it was not until they had rejected, almost capriciously, several practical and judicious suggestions that she threw out: "Well, there's Lyng, in Dorsetshire. It belongs to Hugo's cousins, and you can get it for a song."

The reason she gave for its being obtainable on these terms —its remoteness from a station, its lack of electric light, hot-water pipes, and other vulgar necessities—were exactly those pleading in its favour with two romantic Americans perversely in search of the economic drawbacks which were associated, in their tradition, with unusual architectural felicities.

"I should never believe I was living in an old house unless I was thoroughly uncomfortable," Ned Boyne, the more extravagant of the two, had jocosely insisted; "the least hint of 'convenience' would make me think it had been bought out of an exhibition, with the pieces numbered, and set up again." And they had proceeded to enumerate, with humorous precision, their various doubts and demands, refusing to believe that the house their cousin recommended was *really* Tudor till they learned it had no heating system, or that the village church was literally in the grounds till she assured them of the deplorable uncertainty of the water-supply.

"It's too uncomfortable to be true!" Edward Boyne had continued to exult as the avowal of each disadvantage was successively wrung from her; but he had cut short his rhapsody to ask, with a relapse to distrust: "And the ghost? You've been concealing from us the fact that there is no ghost!"

Mary, at the moment, had laughed with him, yet almost with her laugh, being possessed of several sets of independent perceptions, had been struck by a note of flatness in Alida's answering hilarity.

"Oh, Dorsetshire's full of ghosts, you know."

"Yes, yes; but that won't do. I don't want to have to drive ten miles to see somebody else's ghost. I want one of my own on the premises. *Is* there a ghost at Lyng?"

His rejoinder had made Alida laugh again, and it was then that she had flung back tantalisingly: "Oh, there *is* one, of course, but you'll never know it."

"Never know it?" Boyne pulled her up. "But what in the world constitutes a ghost except the fact of its being known for one?"

"I can't say. But that's the story."

"That there's a ghost, but that nobody knows it's a ghost?"

"Well—not till afterward, at any rate."

"Till afterward?"

"Not till long long afterward."

"But if it's once been identified as an unearthly visitant, why hasn't its *signalement* been handed down in the family? How has it managed to preserve its incognito?"

Alida could only shake her head. "Don't ask me. But it has."

"And then suddenly—" Mary spoke up as if from cavernous depths of divination— "suddenly, long afterward, one says to one's self *'That was it?'*"

She was startled at the sepulchral sound with which her question fell on the banter of the other two, and she saw the shadow of the same surprise flit across Alida's pupils. "I suppose so. One just has to wait."

"Oh, hang waiting!" Ned broke in. "Life's too short for a ghost who can only be enjoyed in retrospect. Can't we do better than that, Mary?"

But it turned out that in the event they were not destined
to, for within three months of their conversation with Mrs.
Stair they were settled at Lyng, and the life they had yearned
for, to the point of planning it in advance in all its daily details,
had actually begun for them.

It was to sit, in the thick December dusk, by just such a
wide-hooded fireplace, under just such black oak rafters, with
the sense that beyond the mullioned panes the downs were
darkened to a deeper solitude: it was for the ultimate indulgence of such sensations that Mary Boyne, abruptly exiled
from New York by her husband's business, had endured for
nearly fourteen years the soul-deadening ugliness of a Middle
Western town, and that Boyne had ground on doggedly at his
engineering till, with a suddenness that still made her blink,
the prodigious windfall of the Blue Star Mine had put them at
a stroke in possession of life and the leisure to taste it. They
had never for a moment meant their new state to be one of
idleness; but they meant to give themselves only to harmonious activities. She had her vision of painting and gardening
(against a background of grey walls), he dreamed of the production of his long-planned book on the "Economic Basis of
Culture"; and with such absorbing work ahead no existence
could be too sequestered: they could not get far enough from
the world, or plunge deep enough into the past.

Dorsetshire had attracted them from the first by an air of remoteness out of all proportion to its geographical position.
But to the Boynes it was one of the ever-recurring wonders of
the whole incredibly compressed island—a nest of counties, as
they put it—that for the production of its effects so little of a
given quality went so far: that so few miles made a distance,
and so short a distance a difference.

"It's that," Ned had once enthusiastically explained, "that
gives such depth to their effects, such relief to their contrasts.
They've been able to lay the butter so thick on every delicious
mouthful."

The butter had certainly been laid on thick at Lyng: the old
house hidden under a shoulder of the downs had almost all the
finer marks of commerce with a protracted past. The mere fact
that it was neither large nor exceptional made it, to the Boynes,
abound the more completely in its special charm—the charm

of having been for centuries a deep dim reservoir of life. The life had probably not been of the most vivid order: for long periods, no doubt, it had fallen as noiselessly into the past as the quiet drizzle of autumn fell, hour after hour, into the fish-pond between the yews; but these backwaters of existence sometimes breed, in their sluggish depths, strange acuities of emotion, and Mary Boyne had felt from the first the mysterious stir of intenser memories.

The feeling had never been stronger than on this particular afternoon when, waiting in the library for the lamps to come, she rose from her seat and stood among the shadows of the hearth. Her husband had gone off, after luncheon, for one of his long tramps on the downs. She had noticed of late that he preferred to go alone; and, in the tried security of their personal relations, had been driven to conclude that his book was bothering him, and that he needed the afternoons to turn over in solitude the problems left from the morning's work. Certainly the book was not going as smoothly as she had thought it would, and there were lines of perplexity between his eyes such as had never been there in his engineering days. He had often, then, looked fagged to the verge of illness, but the native demon of "worry" had never branded his brow. Yet the few pages he had so far read to her—the introduction, and a summary of the opening chapter—showed a firm hold on his subject, and an increasing confidence in his powers.

The fact threw her into deeper perplexity, since, now that he had done with "business" and its disturbing contingencies, the one other possible source of anxiety was eliminated. Unless it were his health, then? But physically he had gained since they had come to Dorsetshire, grown robuster, ruddier and fresher-eyed. It was only within the last week that she had felt in him the undefinable change which made her restless in his absence, and as tongue-tied in his presence as though it were *she* who had a secret to keep from him!

The thought that there *was* a secret somewhere between them struck her with a sudden rap of wonder, and she looked about her down the long room.

"Can it be the house?" she mused.

The room itself might have been full of secrets. They seemed to be piling themselves up, as evening fell, like the layers and layers of velvet shadow dropping from the low ceiling, the rows of books, the smoke-blurred sculpture of the hearth.

"Why, of course—the house is haunted!" she reflected.

The ghost—Alida's imperceptible ghost—after figuring largely in the banter of their first month or two at Lyng, had been gradually left aside as too ineffectual for imaginative use. Mary had, indeed, as became the tenant of a haunted house, made the customary inquiries among her rural neighbours, but, beyond a vague "They dü say so, Ma'am," the villagers had nothing to impart. The elusive spectre had apparently never had sufficient identity for a legend to crystallise about it, and after a time the Boynes had set the matter down to their profit-and-loss account, agreeing that Lyng was one of the few houses good enough in itself to dispense with supernatural enhancements.

"And I suppose, poor ineffectual demon, that's why it beats its beautiful wings in vain in the void," Mary had laughingly concluded.

"Or, rather," Ned answered in the same strain, "why, amid so much that's ghostly, it can never affirm its separate existence as *the* ghost." And thereupon their invisible housemate had finally dropped out of their references, which were numerous enough to make them soon unaware of the loss.

Now, as she stood on the hearth, the subject of their earlier curiosity revived in her with a new sense of its meaning—a sense gradually acquired through daily contact with the scene of the lurking mystery. It was the house itself, of course, that possessed the ghost-seeing faculty, that communed visually but secretly with its own past; if one could only get into close enough communion with the house, one might surprise its secret, and acquire the ghost-sight on one's own account. Perhaps, in his long hours in this very room, where she never trespassed till the afternoon, her husband *had* acquired it already, and was silently carrying about the weight of whatever it had revealed to him. Mary was too well versed in the code of the spectral world not to know that one could not talk about the ghosts one saw: to do so was almost as great a breach of taste as to name a lady in a club. But this explanation did not really satisfy her. "What, after all, except for the fun of the shudder," she reflected, "would he really care for any of their old ghosts?"

And thence she was thrown back once more on the fundamental dilemma: the fact that one's greater or less susceptibility to spectral influences had no particular bearing on the case, since, when one *did* see a ghost at Lyng, one did not know it.

"Not till long afterward," Alida Stair had said. Well, supposing Ned *had* seen one when they first came, and had known only within the last week what had happened to him? More and more under the spell of the hour, she threw back her thoughts to the early days of their tenancy, but at first only to recall a lively confusion of unpacking, settling, arranging of books, and calling to each other from remote corners of the house as, treasure after treasure, it revealed itself to them. It was in this particular connection that she presently recalled a certain soft afternoon of the previous October, when, passing from the first rapturous flurry of exploration to a detailed inspection of the old house, she had pressed (like a novel heroine) a panel that opened on a flight of corkscrew stairs leading to a flat ledge of the roof—the roof which, from below, seemed to slope away on all sides too abruptly for any but practised feet to scale.

The view from this hidden coign was enchanting, and she had flown down to snatch Ned from his papers and give him the freedom of her discovery. She remembered still how, standing at her side, he had passed his arm about her while their gaze flew to the long tossed horizon-line of the downs, and then dropped contentedly back to trace the arabesque of yew hedges about the fish-pond, and the shadow of the cedar on the lawn.

"And now the other way," he had said, turning her about within his arm; and closely pressed to him, she had absorbed, like some long satisfying draught, the picture of the grey-walled court, the squat lions on the gates, and the lime-avenue reaching up to the highroad under the downs.

It was just then, while they gazed and held each other, that she had felt his arm relax, and heard a sharp "Hullo!" that made her turn to glance at him.

Distinctly, yes, she now recalled that she had seen, as she glanced, a shadow of anxiety, of perplexity, rather, fall across his face; and, following his eyes, had beheld the figure of a man —a man in loose greyish clothes, as it appeared to her—who was sauntering down the lime-avenue to the court with the doubtful gait of a stranger who seeks his way. Her short-sighted eyes had given her but a blurred impression of slightness and greyishness, with something foreign, or at least unlocal, in the cut of the figure or its dress; but her husband had apparently seen more—seen enough to make him push past her with a hasty "Wait!" and dash down the stairs without pausing to give her a hand.

A slight tendency to dizziness obliged her, after a provisional clutch at the chimney against which they had been leaning, to follow him first more cautiously; and when she had reached the landing she paused again, for a less definite reason, leaning over the banister to strain her eyes through the silence of the brown sun-flecked depths. She lingered there till, somewhere in those depths, she heard the closing of a door; then, mechanically impelled, she went down the shallow flights of steps till she reached the lower hall.

The front door stood open on the sunlight of the court, and hall and court were empty. The library door was open, too, and after listening in vain for any sound of voices within, she crossed the threshold, and found her husband alone, vaguely fingering the papers on his desk.

He looked up, as if surprised at her entrance, but the shadow of anxiety had passed from his face, leaving it even, as she fancied, a little brighter and clearer than usual.

"What was it? Who was it?" she asked.

"Who?" he repeated, with the surprise still all on his side.

"The man we saw coming toward the house."

He seemed to reflect. "The man? Why, I thought I saw Peters; I dashed after him to say a word about the stable drains, but he had disappeared before I could get down."

"Disappeared? But he seemed to be walking so slowly when we saw him."

Boyne shrugged his shoulders. "So I thought; but he must have got up steam in the interval. What do you say to our trying a scramble up Meldon Steep before sunset?"

That was all. At the time the occurrence had been less than nothing, had, indeed, been immediately obliterated by the magic of their first vision from Meldon Steep, a height which they had dreamed of climbing ever since they had first seen its bare spine rising above the roof of Lyng. Doubtless it was the

mere fact of the other incident's having occurred on the very
day of their ascent to Meldon that had kept it stored away in
the fold of memory from which it now emerged; for in itself it
had no mark of the portentous. At the moment there could
have been nothing more natural than that Ned should dash
himself from the roof in the pursuit of dilatory tradesmen. It
was the period when they were always on the watch for one or
the other of the specialists employed about the place; always
lying in wait for them, and rushing out at them with questions,
reproaches or reminders. And certainly in the distance the grey
figure had looked like Peters.

Yet now, as she reviewed the scene, she felt her husband's
explanation of it to have been invalidated by the look of anxiety on his face. Why had the familiar appearance of Peters
made him anxious? Why, above all, if it was of such prime necessity to confer with him on the subject of the stable drains,
had the failure to find him produced such a look of relief?
Mary could not say that any one of these questions had occurred to her at the time, yet, from the promptness with which
they now marshalled themselves at her summons, she had a
sense that they must all along have been there, waiting their
hour.

II

Weary with her thoughts, she moved to the window. The
library was now quite dark, and she was surprised to see how
much faint light the outer world still held.

As she peered out into it across the court, a figure shaped itself far down the perspective of bare limes: it looked a mere
blot of deeper grey in the greyness, and for an instant, as it
moved toward her, her heart thumped to the thought "It's the
ghost!"

She had time, in that long instant, to feel suddenly that the
man of whom, two months earlier, she had had a distant vision
from the roof, was now, at his predestined hour, about to reveal himself as *not* having been Peters; and her spirit sank
under the impending fear of the disclosure. But almost with
the next tick of the clock the figure, gaining substance and character, showed itself even to her weak sight as her husband's;

and she turned to meet him, as he entered, with the confession of her folly.

"It's really too absurd," she laughed out, "but I never *can* remember!"

"Remember what?" Boyne questioned as they drew together.

"That when one sees the Lyng ghost one never knows it."

Her hand was on his sleeve, and he kept it there, but with no response in his gesture or in the lines of his preoccupied face.

"Did you think you'd seen it?" he asked, after an appreciable interval.

"Why, I actually took *you* for it, my dear, in my mad determination to spot it!"

"Me—just now?" His arm dropped away, and he turned from her with a faint echo of her laugh. "Really, dearest, you'd better give it up, if that's the best you can do."

"Oh, yes, I give it up. Have *you*?" she asked, turning round on him abruptly.

The parlour-maid had entered with letters and a lamp, and the light struck up into Boyne's face as he bent above the tray she presented.

"Have *you*?" Mary perversely insisted, when the servant had disappeared on her errand of illumination.

"Have I what?" he rejoined absently, the light bringing out the sharp stamp of worry between his brows as he turned over the letters.

"Given up trying to see the ghost." Her heart beat a little at the experiment she was making.

Her husband, laying his letters aside, moved away into the shadow of the hearth.

"I never tried," he said, tearing open the wrapper of a newspaper.

"Well, of course," Mary persisted, "the exasperating thing is that there's no use trying, since one can't be sure till so long afterward."

He was unfolding the paper as if he had hardly heard her; but after a pause, during which the sheets rustled spasmodically between his hands, he looked up to ask, "Have you any idea *how long*?"

Mary had sunk into a low chair beside the fireplace. From

her seat she glanced over, startled, at her husband's profile, which was projected against the circle of lamplight.

"No; none. Have *you*?" she retorted, repeating her former phrase with an added stress of intention.

Boyne crumpled the paper into a bunch, and then, inconsequently, turned back with it toward the lamp.

"Lord, no! I only meant," he explained, with a faint tinge of impatience, "is there any legend, any tradition, as to that?"

"Not that I know of," she answered; but the impulse to add "What makes you ask?" was checked by the reappearance of the parlour-maid, with tea and a second lamp.

With the dispersal of shadows, and the repetition of the daily domestic office, Mary Boyne felt herself less oppressed by that sense of something mutely imminent which had darkened her afternoon. For a few moments she gave herself to the details of her task, and when she looked up from it she was struck to the point of bewilderment by the change in her husband's face. He had seated himself near the farther lamp, and was absorbed in the perusal of his letters; but was it something he had found in them, or merely the shifting of her own point of view, that had restored his features to their normal aspect? The longer she looked the more definitely the change affirmed itself. The lines of tension had vanished, and such traces of fatigue as lingered were of the kind easily attributable to steady mental effort. He glanced up, as if drawn by her gaze, and met her eyes with a smile.

"I'm dying for my tea, you know; and here's a letter for you," he said.

She took the letter he held out in exchange for the cup she proffered him, and, returning to her seat, broke the seal with the languid gesture of the reader whose interests are all enclosed in the circle of one cherished presence.

Her next conscious motion was that of starting to her feet, the letter falling to them as she rose, while she held out to her husband a newspaper clipping.

"Ned! What's this? What does it mean?"

He had risen at the same instant, almost as if hearing her cry before she uttered it; and for a perceptible space of time he and she studied each other, like adversaries watching for an advantage, across the space between her chair and his desk.

"What's what? You fairly made me jump!" Boyne said at length, moving toward her with a sudden half-exasperated laugh. The shadow of apprehension was on his face again, not now a look of fixed foreboding, but a shifting vigilance of lips and eyes that gave her the sense of his feeling himself invisibly surrounded.

Her hand shook so that she could hardly give him the clipping.

"This article—from the *Waukesha Sentinel*—that a man named Elwell has brought suit against you—that there was something wrong about the Blue Star Mine. I can't understand more than half."

They continued to face each other as she spoke, and to her astonishment she saw that her words had the almost immediate effect of dissipating the strained watchfulness of his look.

"Oh, *that!*" He glanced down the printed slip, and then folded it with the gesture of one who handles something harmless and familiar. "What's the matter with you this afternoon, Mary? I thought you'd got bad news."

She stood before him with her undefinable terror subsiding slowly under the reassurance of his tone.

"You knew about this, then—it's all right?"

"Certainly I knew about it; and it's all right."

"But what *is* it? I don't understand. What does this man accuse you of?"

"Pretty nearly every crime in the calendar." Boyne had tossed the clipping down, and thrown himself into an armchair near the fire. "Do you want to hear the story? It's not particularly interesting—just a squabble over interests in the Blue Star."

"But who is this Elwell? I don't know the name."

"Oh, he's a fellow I put into it—gave him a hand up. I told you all about him at the time."

"I daresay. I must have forgotten." Vainly she strained back among her memories. "But if you helped him, why does he make this return?"

"Probably some shyster lawyer got hold of him and talked him over. It's all rather technical and complicated. I thought that kind of thing bored you."

His wife felt a sting of compunction. Theoretically, she deprecated the American wife's detachment from her husband's professional interests, but in practice she had always found it difficult to fix her attention on Boyne's report of the transactions in which his varied interests involved him. Besides, she had felt during their years of exile, that, in a community where the amenities of living could be obtained only at the cost of efforts as arduous as her husband's professional labours, such brief leisure as he and she could command should be used as an escape from immediate preoccupations, a flight to the life they always dreamed of living. Once or twice, now that this new life had actually drawn its magic circle about them, she had asked herself if she had done right; but hitherto such conjectures had been no more than the retrospective excursions of an active fancy. Now, for the first time, it startled her a little to find how little she knew of the material foundation on which her happiness was built.

She glanced at her husband, and was again reassured by the composure of his face; yet she felt the need of more definite grounds for her reassurance.

"But doesn't this suit worry you? Why have you never spoken to me about it?"

He answered both questions at once. "I didn't speak of it at first because it *did* worry me—annoyed me, rather. But it's all ancient history now. Your correspondent must have got hold of a back number of the *Sentinel*."

She felt a quick thrill of relief. "You mean it's over? He's lost his case?"

There was a just perceptible delay in Boyne's reply. "The suit's been withdrawn—that's all."

But she persisted, as if to exonerate herself from the inward charge of being too easily put off. "Withdrawn it because he saw he had no chance?"

"Oh, he had no chance," Boyne answered.

She was still struggling with a dimly felt perplexity at the back of her thoughts.

"How long ago was it withdrawn?"

He paused, as if with a slight return of his former uncertainty. "I've just had the news now; but I've been expecting it."

"Just now—in one of your letters?"

"Yes; in one of my letters."

She made no answer, and was aware only, after a short interval of waiting, that he had risen, and, strolling across the room,
had placed himself on the sofa at her side. She felt him, as he
did so, pass an arm about her, she felt his hand seek hers and
clasp it, and turning slowly, drawn by the warmth of his cheek,
she met his smiling eyes.

"It's all right—it's all right?" she questioned, through the
flood of her dissolving doubts; and "I give you my word it was
never righter!" he laughed back at her, holding her close.

III

One of the strangest things she was afterward to recall out
of all the next day's strangeness was the sudden and complete
recovery of her sense of security.

It was in the air when she woke in her low-ceiled, dusky room;
it went with her down-stairs to the breakfast-table, flashed out
at her from the fire, and reduplicated itself from the flanks of
the urn and the sturdy flutings of the Georgian teapot. It was
as if, in some roundabout way, all her diffused fears of the previous day, with their moment of sharp concentration about the
newspaper article—as if this dim questioning of the future, and
startled return upon the past, had between them liquidated
the arrears of some haunting moral obligation. If she had indeed been careless of her husband's affairs, it was, her new state
seemed to prove, because her faith in him instinctively justified
such carelessness; and his right to her faith had now affirmed
itself in the very face of menace and suspicion. She had never
seen him more untroubled, more naturally and unconsciously
himself, than after the cross-examination to which she had subjected him: it was almost as if he had been aware of her doubts,
and had wanted the air cleared as much as she did.

It was as clear, thank Heaven! as the bright outer light that
surprised her almost with a touch of summer when she issued
from the house for her daily round of the gardens. She had left
Boyne at his desk, indulging herself, as she passed the library
door, by a last peep at his quiet face, where he bent, pipe in
mouth, above his papers; and now she had her own morning's
task to perform. The task involved, on such charmed winter days,
almost as much happy loitering about the different quarters of

her demesne as if spring were already at work there. There were such endless possibilities still before her, such opportunities to bring out the latent graces of the old place, without a single irreverent touch of alteration, that the winter was all too short to plan what spring and autumn executed. And her recovered sense of safety gave, on this particular morning, a peculiar zest to her progress through the sweet still place. She went first to the kitchen-garden, where the espaliered pear-trees drew complicated patterns on the walls, and pigeons were fluttering and preening about the silvery-slated roof of their cot. There was something wrong about the piping of the hot-house, and she was expecting an authority from Dorchester, who was to drive out between trains and make a diagnosis of the boiler. But when she dipped into the damp heat of the green-houses, among the spiced scents and waxy pinks and reds of old-fashioned exotics—even the flora of Lyng was in the note! —she learned that the great man had not arrived, and, the day being too rare to waste in an artificial atmosphere, she came out again and paced along the springy turf of the bowling-green to the gardens behind the house. At their farther end rose a grass terrace, looking across the fish-pond and yew hedges to the long house-front with its twisted chimney-stacks and blue roof angles all drenched in the pale gold moisture of the air.

Seen thus, across the level tracery of the gardens, it sent her, from open windows and hospitably smoking chimneys, the look of some warm human presence, of a mind slowly ripened on a sunny wall of experience. She had never before had such a sense of her intimacy with it, such a conviction that its secrets were all beneficent, kept, as they said to children, "for one's good," such a trust in its power to gather up her life and Ned's into the harmonious pattern of the long long story it sat there weaving in the sun.

She heard steps behind her, and turned, expecting to see the gardener accompanied by the engineer from Dorchester. But only one figure was in sight, that of a youngish slightly built man, who, for reasons she could not on the spot have given, did not remotely resemble her notion of an authority on hot-house boilers. The new-comer, on seeing her, lifted his hat, and paused with the air of a gentleman—perhaps a traveller—who wishes to make it known that his intrusion is involuntary. Lyng

occasionally attracted the more cultivated traveller, and Mary
half-expected to see the stranger dissemble a camera, or justify
his presence by producing it. But he made no gesture of any sort,
and after a moment she asked, in a tone responding to the
courteous hesitation of his attitude: "Is there any one you wish
to see?"

"I came to see Mr. Boyne," he answered. His intonation,
rather than his accent, was faintly American, and Mary, at the
note, looked at him more closely. The brim of his soft felt hat
cast a shade on his face, which, thus obscured, wore to her short-
sighted gaze a look of seriousness, as of a person arriving "on
business," and civilly but firmly aware of his rights.

Past experience had made her equally sensible to such claims;
but she was jealous of her husband's morning hours, and doubtful of his having given any one the right to intrude on them.

"Have you an appointment with my husband?" she asked.

The visitor hesitated, as if unprepared for the question.

"I think he expects me," he replied.

It was Mary's turn to hesitate. "You see this is his time for
work: he never sees any one in the morning."

He looked at her a moment without answering; then, as if
accepting her decision, he began to move away. As he turned,
Mary saw him pause and glance up at the peaceful house-front.
Something in his air suggested weariness and disappointment,
the dejection of the traveller who has come from far off and
whose hours are limited by the time-table. It occurred to her
that if this were the case her refusal might have made his errand
vain, and a sense of compunction caused her to hasten after him.

"May I ask if you have come a long way?"

He gave her the same grave look. "Yes—I have come a long
way."

"Then, if you'll go to the house, no doubt my husband will
see you now. You'll find him in the library."

She did not know why she had added the last phrase, except
from a vague impulse to atone for her previous inhospitality.
The visitor seemed about to express his thanks, but her attention was distracted by the approach of the gardener with a
companion who bore all the marks of being the expert from
Dorchester.

"This way," she said, waving the stranger to the house; and

an instant later she had forgotten him in the absorption of her meeting with the boiler-maker.

The encounter led to such far-reaching results that the engineer ended by finding it expedient to ignore his train, and Mary was beguiled into spending the remainder of the morning in absorbed confabulation among the flower-pots. When the colloquy ended, she was surprised to find that it was nearly luncheon-time, and she half expected, as she hurried back to the house, to see her husband coming out to meet her. But she found no one in the court but an under-gardener raking the gravel, and the hall, when she entered it, was so silent that she guessed Boyne to be still at work.

Not wishing to disturb him, she turned into the drawing-room, and there, at her writing-table, lost herself in renewed calculations of the outlay to which the morning's conference had pledged her. The fact that she could permit herself such follies had not yet lost its novelty; and somehow, in contrast to the vague fears of the previous days, it now seemed an element of her recovered security, of the sense that, as Ned had said, things in general had never been "righter."

She was still luxuriating in a lavish play of figures when the parlour-maid, from the threshold, roused her with an enquiry as to the expediency of serving luncheon. It was one of their jokes that Trimmle announced luncheon as if she were divulging a state secret and Mary, intent upon her papers, merely murmured an absent-minded assent.

She felt Trimmle wavering doubtfully on the threshold, as if in rebuke of such unconsidered assent; then her retreating steps sounded down the passage, and Mary, pushing away her papers, crossed the hall and went to the library door. It was still closed, and she wavered in her turn, disliking to disturb her husband, yet anxious that he should not exceed his usual measure of work. As she stood there, balancing her impulses, Trimmle returned with the announcement of luncheon, and Mary, thus impelled, opened the library door.

Boyne was not at his desk, and she peered about her, expecting to discover him before the book-shelves, somewhere down the length of the room; but her call brought no response, and gradually it became clear to her that he was not there.

She turned back to the parlour-maid.

"Mr. Boyne must be up-stairs. Please tell him that luncheon is ready."

Trimmle appeared to hesitate between the obvious duty of obedience and an equally obvious conviction of the foolishness of the injunction laid on her. The struggle resulted in her saying: "If you please, Madam, Mr. Boyne's not up-stairs."

"Not in his room? Are you sure?"

"I'm sure, Madam."

Mary consulted the clock. "Where is he, then?"

"He's gone out," Trimmle announced, with the superior air of one who has respectfully waited for the question that a well-ordered mind would have put first.

Mary's conjecture had been right, then. Boyne must have gone to the gardens to meet her, and since she had missed him, it was clear that he had taken the shorter way by the south door, instead of going round to the court. She crossed the hall to the French window opening directly on the yew garden, but the parlour-maid, after another moment of inner conflict, decided to bring out: "Please, Madam, Mr. Boyne didn't go that way."

Mary turned back. "Where *did* he go? And when?"

"He went out of the front door, up the drive, Madam." It was a matter of principle with Trimmle never to answer more than one question at a time.

"Up the drive? At this hour?" Mary went to the door herself, and glanced across the court through the tunnel of bare limes. But its perspective was as empty as when she had scanned it on entering.

"Did Mr. Boyne leave no message?"

Trimmle seemed to surrender herself to a last struggle with the forces of chaos.

"No, Madam. He just went out with the gentleman."

"The gentleman? What gentleman?" Mary wheeled about, as if to front this new factor.

"The gentleman who called, Madam," said Trimmle resignedly.

"When did a gentleman call? Do explain yourself, Trimmle!"

Only the fact that Mary was very hungry, and that she wanted to consult her husband about the greenhouses, would have caused her to lay so unusual an injunction on her atten-

dant; and even now she was detached enough to note in
Trimmle's eye the dawning defiance of the respectful subordi-
nate who has been pressed too hard.

"I couldn't exactly say the hour, Madam, because I didn't
let the gentleman in," she replied, with an air of discreetly ignoring the irregularity of her mistress's course.

"You didn't let him in?"

"No, Madam. When the bell rang I was dressing, and
Agnes——"

"Go and ask Agnes, then," said Mary.

Trimmle still wore her look of patient magnanimity. "Agnes
would not know, Madam, for she had unfortunately burnt her
hand in trimming the wick of the new lamp from town"
—Trimmle, as Mary was aware, had always been opposed to
the new lamp— "and so Mrs. Dockett sent the kitchen-maid
instead."

Mary looked again at the clock. "It's after two! Go and ask
the kitchen-maid if Mr. Boyne left any word."

She went into luncheon without waiting, and Trimmle presently brought her there the kitchen-maid's statement that the
gentleman had called about eleven o'clock, and that Mr. Boyne
had gone out with him without leaving any message. The
kitchen-maid did not even know the caller's name, for he had
written it on a slip of paper, which he had folded and handed
to her, with the injunction to deliver it at once to Mr. Boyne.

Mary finished her luncheon, still wondering, and when it was
over, and Trimmle had brought the coffee to the drawing-room,
her wonder had deepened to a first faint tinge of disquietude. It
was unlike Boyne to absent himself without explanation at so
unwonted an hour, and the difficulty of identifying the visitor
whose summons he had apparently obeyed made his disappearance the more unaccountable. Mary Boyne's experience as
the wife of a busy engineer, subject to sudden calls and compelled to keep irregular hours, had trained her to the philosophic
acceptance of surprises; but since Boyne's withdrawal from
business he had adopted a Benedictine regularity of life. As if
to make up for the dispersed and agitated years, with their
"stand-up" lunches, and dinners rattled down to the joltings
of the dining-cars, he cultivated the last refinements of punctuality and monotony, discouraging his wife's fancy for the

unexpected, and declaring that to a delicate taste there were infinite gradations of pleasure in the recurrences of habit.

Still, since no life can completely defend itself from the unforeseen, it was evident that all Boyne's precautions would sooner or later prove unavailable, and Mary concluded that he had cut short a tiresome visit by walking with his caller to the station, or at least accompanying him for part of the way.

This conclusion relieved her from farther preoccupation, and she went out herself to take up her conference with the gardener. Thence she walked to the village post-office, a mile or so away; and when she turned toward home the early twilight was setting in.

She had taken a foot-path across the downs, and as Boyne, meanwhile, had probably returned from the station by the highroad, there was little likelihood of their meeting. She felt sure, however, of his having reached the house before her; so sure that, when she entered it herself, without even pausing to inquire of Trimmle, she made directly for the library. But the library was still empty, and with an unwonted exactness of visual memory she observed that the papers on her husband's desk lay precisely as they had lain when she had gone in to call him to luncheon.

Then of a sudden she was seized by a vague dread of the unknown. She had closed the door behind her on entering, and as she stood alone in the long silent room, her dread seemed to take shape and sound, to be there breathing and lurking among the shadows. Her short-sighted eyes strained through them, half-discerning an actual presence, something aloof, that watched and knew; and in the recoil from that intangible presence she threw herself on the bell-rope and gave it a sharp pull.

The sharp summons brought Trimmle in precipitately with a lamp, and Mary breathed again at this sobering reappearance of the usual.

"You may bring tea if Mr. Boyne is in," she said, to justify her ring.

"Very well, Madam. But Mr. Boyne is not in," said Trimmle, putting down the lamp.

"Not in? You mean he's come back and gone out again?"

"No, Madam. He's never been back."

The dread stirred again, and Mary knew that now it had her fast.

"Not since he went out with—the gentleman?"

"Not since he went out with the gentleman."

"But who *was* the gentleman?" Mary insisted, with the shrill note of some one trying to be heard through a confusion of noises.

"That I couldn't say, Madam." Trimmle, standing there by the lamp, seemed suddenly to grow less round and rosy, as though eclipsed by the same creeping shade of apprehension.

"But the kitchen-maid knows—wasn't it the kitchen-maid who let him in?"

"She doesn't know either, Madam, for he wrote his name on a folded paper."

Mary, through her agitation, was aware that they were both designating the unknown visitor by a vague pronoun, instead of the conventional formula which, till then, had kept their allusions within the bounds of conformity. And at the same moment her mind caught at the suggestion of the folded paper.

"But he must have a name! Where's the paper?"

She moved to the desk, and began to turn over the documents that littered it. The first that caught her eye was an unfinished letter in her husband's hand, with his pen lying across it, as though dropped there at a sudden summons.

"My dear Parvis"—who was Parvis?— "I have just received your letter announcing Elwell's death, and while I suppose there is now no farther risk of trouble, it might be safer——"

She tossed the sheet aside, and continued her search; but no folded paper was discoverable among the letters and pages of manuscript which had been swept together in a heap, as if by a hurried or a startled gesture.

"But the kitchen-maid *saw* him. Send her here," she commanded, wondering at her dulness in not thinking sooner of so simple a solution.

Trimmle vanished in a flash, as if thankful to be out of the room, and when she reappeared, conducting the agitated underling, Mary had regained her self-possession, and had her questions ready.

The gentleman was a stranger, yes—that she understood.

But what had he said? And, above all, what had he looked like? The first question was easily enough answered, for the disconcerting reason that he had said so little—had merely asked for Mr. Boyne, and, scribbling something on a bit of paper, had requested that it should at once be carried in to him.

"Then you don't know what he wrote? You're not sure it *was* his name?"

The kitchen-maid was not sure, but supposed it was, since he had written it in answer to her inquiry as to whom she should announce.

"And when you carried the paper in to Mr. Boyne, what did he say?"

The kitchen-maid did not think that Mr. Boyne had said anything, but she could not be sure, for just as she had handed him the paper and he was opening it, she had become aware that the visitor had followed her into the library, and she had slipped out, leaving the two gentlemen together.

"But then, if you left them in the library, how do you know that they went out of the house?"

This question plunged the witness into a momentary inarticulateness, from which she was rescued by Trimmle, who, by means of ingenious circumlocutions, elicited the statement that before she could cross the hall to the back passage she had heard the two gentlemen behind her, and had seen them go out of the front door together.

"Then, if you saw the strange gentleman twice, you must be able to tell me what he looked like."

But with this final challenge to her powers of expression it became clear that the limit of the kitchen-maid's endurance had been reached. The obligation of going to the front door to "show in" a visitor was in itself so subversive of the fundamental order of things that it had thrown her faculties into hopeless disarray, and she could only stammer out, after various panting efforts: "His hat, mum, was different-like, as you might say——"

"Different? How different?" Mary flashed out, her own mind, in the same instant, leaping back to an image left on it that morning, and then lost under layers of subsequent impressions.

"His hat had a wide brim, you mean? and his face was pale— a youngish face?" Mary pressed her, with a white-lipped inten-

sity of interrogation. But if the kitchen-maid found any adequate answer to this challenge, it was swept away for her listener down the rushing current of her own convictions. The
stranger—the stranger in the garden! Why had Mary not
thought of him before? She needed no one now to tell her that
it was he who had called for her husband and gone away with
him. But who was he, and why had Boyne obeyed him?

IV

It leaped out at her suddenly, like a grin out of the dark, that
they had often called England so little—"such a confoundedly
hard place to get lost in."

A confoundedly hard place to get lost in! That had been her
husband's phrase. And now, with the whole machinery of official investigation sweeping its flash-lights from shore to shore,
and across the dividing straits; now, with Boyne's name blazing
from the walls of every town and village, his portrait (how that
wrung her!) hawked up and down the country like the image
of a hunted criminal; now the little compact populous island,
so policed, surveyed and administered, revealed itself as a
Sphinx-like guardian of abysmal mysteries, staring back into his
wife's anguished eyes as if with the wicked joy of knowing
something they would never know!

In the fortnight since Boyne's disappearance there had been
no word of him, no trace of his movements. Even the usual
misleading reports that raise expectancy in tortured bosoms
had been few and fleeting. No one but the kitchen-maid had
seen Boyne leave the house, and no one else had seen "the
gentleman" who accompanied him. All enquiries in the neighbourhood failed to elicit the memory of a stranger's presence
that day in the neighbourhood of Lyng. And no one had met
Edward Boyne, either alone or in company, in any of the neighbouring villages, or on the road across the downs, or at either
of the local railway-stations. The sunny English noon had swallowed him as completely as if he had gone out into Cimmerian
night.

Mary, while every official means of investigation was working
at its highest pressure, had ransacked her husband's papers for
any trace of antecedent complications, of entanglements or

obligations unknown to her, that might throw a ray into the
darkness. But if any such had existed in the background of
Boyne's life, they had vanished like the slip of paper on which
the visitor had written his name. There remained no possible
thread of guidance except—if it were indeed an exception—the
letter which Boyne had apparently been in the act of writing
when he received his mysterious summons. That letter, read
and reread by his wife, and submitted by her to the police,
yielded little enough to feed conjecture.

"I have just heard of Elwell's death, and while I suppose there
is now no farther risk of trouble, it might be safer——" That
was all. The "risk of trouble" was easily explained by the newspaper clipping which had apprised Mary of the suit brought
against her husband by one of his associates in the Blue Star
enterprise. The only new information conveyed by the letter
was the fact of its showing Boyne, when he wrote it, to be still
apprehensive of the results of the suit, though he had told his
wife that it had been withdrawn, and though the letter itself
proved that the plaintiff was dead. It took several days of ca-
bling to fix the identity of the "Parvis" to whom the fragment
was addressed, but even after these enquiries had shown him to
be a Waukesha lawyer, no new facts concerning the Elwell suit
were elicited. He appeared to have had no direct concern in it,
but to have been conversant with the facts merely as an acquaintance, and possible intermediary; and he declared himself
unable to guess with what object Boyne intended to seek his
assistance.

This negative information, sole fruit of the first fortnight's
search, was not increased by a jot during the slow weeks that
followed. Mary knew that the investigations were still being
carried on, but she had a vague sense of their gradually slackening, as the actual march of time seemed to slacken. It was as
though the days, flying horror-struck from the shrouded image of the one inscrutable day, gained assurance as the distance
lengthened, till at last they fell back into their normal gait. And
so with the human imaginations at work on the dark event. No
doubt it occupied them still, but week by week and hour by
hour it grew less absorbing, took up less space, was slowly but
inevitably crowded out of the foreground of consciousness by

the new problems perpetually bubbling up from the cloudy caldron of human experience.

Even Mary Boyne's consciousness gradually felt the same lowering of velocity. It still swayed with the incessant oscillations of conjecture; but they were slower, more rhythmical in their beat. There were even moments of weariness when, like the victim of some poison which leaves the brain clear, but holds the body motionless, she saw herself domesticated with the Horror, accepting its perpetual presence as one of the fixed conditions of life.

These moments lengthened into hours and days, till she passed into a phase of stolid acquiescence. She watched the routine of daily life with the incurious eye of a savage on whom the meaningless processes of civilisation make but the faintest impression. She had come to regard herself as part of the routine, a spoke of the wheel, revolving with its motion; she felt almost like the furniture of the room in which she sat, an insensate object to be dusted and pushed about with the chairs and tables. And this deepening apathy held her fast at Lyng, in spite of the entreaties of friends and the usual medical recommendation of "change." Her friends supposed that her refusal to move was inspired by the belief that her husband would one day return to the spot from which he had vanished, and a beautiful legend grew up about this imaginary state of waiting. But in reality she had no such belief: the depths of anguish enclosing her were no longer lighted by flashes of hope. She was sure that Boyne would never come back, that he had gone out of her sight as completely as if Death itself had waited that day on the threshold. She had even renounced, one by one, the various theories as to his disappearance which had been advanced by the press, the police, and her own agonised imagination. In sheer lassitude her mind turned from these alternatives of horror, and sank back into the blank fact that he was gone.

No, she would never know what had become of him—no one would ever know. But the house *knew*; the library in which she spent her long lonely evenings knew. For it was here that the last scene had been enacted, here that the stranger had come, and spoken the word which had caused Boyne to rise and follow him. The floor she trod had felt his tread; the books on the shelves had seen his face; and there were moments when the intense consciousness of the old dusky walls seemed about to break out into some audible revelation of their secret. But the revelation never came, and she knew it would never come. Lyng was not one of the garrulous old houses that betray the secrets entrusted to them. Its very legend proved that it had always been the mute accomplice, the incorruptible custodian, of the mysteries it had surprised. And Mary Boyne, sitting face to face with its silence, felt the futility of seeking to break it by any human means.

V

"I don't say it *wasn't* straight, and yet I don't say it *was* straight. It was business."

Mary, at the words, lifted her head with a start, and looked intently at the speaker.

When, half an hour before, a card with "Mr. Parvis" on it had been brought up to her, she had been immediately aware that the name had been a part of her consciousness ever since she had read it at the head of Boyne's unfinished letter. In the library she had found awaiting her a small sallow man with a bald head and gold eye-glasses, and it sent a tremor through her to know that this was the person to whom her husband's last known thought had been directed.

Parvis, civilly, but without vain preamble—in the manner of a man who has his watch in his hand—had set forth the object of his visit. He had "run over" to England on business, and finding himself in the neighbourhood of Dorchester, had not wished to leave it without paying his respects to Mrs. Boyne; and without asking her, if the occasion offered, what she meant to do about Bob Elwell's family.

The words touched the spring of some obscure dread in Mary's bosom. Did her visitor, after all, know what Boyne had meant by his unfinished phrase? She asked for an elucidation of his question, and noticed at once that he seemed surprised at her continued ignorance of the subject. Was it possible that she really knew as little as she said?

"I know nothing—you must tell me," she faltered out; and her visitor thereupon proceeded to unfold his story. It threw, even to her confused perceptions, and imperfectly initiated vision, a lurid glare on the whole hazy episode of the Blue Star Mine. Her husband had made his money in that brilliant speculation at the cost of "getting ahead" of some one less alert to seize the chance; and the victim of his ingenuity was young Robert Elwell, who had "put him on" to the Blue Star scheme.

Parvis, at Mary's first cry, had thrown her a sobering glance through his impartial glasses.

"Bob Elwell wasn't smart enough, that's all; if he had been, he might have turned round and served Boyne the same way. It's the kind of thing that happens every day in business. I guess it's what the scientists call the survival of the fittest— see?" said Mr. Parvis, evidently pleased with the aptness of his analogy.

Mary felt a physical shrinking from the next question she tried to frame: it was as though the words on her lips had a taste that nauseated her.

"But then—you accuse my husband of doing something dishonourable?"

Mr. Parvis surveyed the question dispassionately. "Oh, no, I don't. I don't even say it wasn't straight." He glanced up and down the long lines of books, as if one of them might have supplied him with the definition he sought. "I don't say it *wasn't* straight, and yet I don't say it *was* straight. It was business." After all, no definition in his category could be more comprehensive than that.

Mary sat staring at him with a look of terror. He seemed to her like the indifferent emissary of some evil power.

"But Mr. Elwell's lawyers apparently did not take your view, since I suppose the suit was withdrawn by their advice."

"Oh, yes; they knew he hadn't a leg to stand on, technically. It was when they advised him to withdraw the suit that he got desperate. You see, he'd borrowed most of the money he lost in the Blue Star, and he was up a tree. That's why he shot himself when they told him he had no show."

The horror was sweeping over Mary in great deafening waves.

"He shot himself? He killed himself because of *that*?"

"Well, he didn't kill himself, exactly. He dragged on two months before he died." Parvis emitted the statement as unemotionally as a gramophone grinding out its "record."

"You mean that he tried to kill himself, and failed? And tried again?"

"Oh, he didn't have to *try* again," said Parvis grimly.

They sat opposite each other in silence, he swinging his eye-glasses thoughtfully about his finger, she, motionless, her arms stretched along her knees in an attitude of rigid tension.

"But if you knew all this," she began at length, hardly able to force her voice above a whisper, "how is it that when I wrote you at the time of my husband's disappearance you said you didn't understand his letter?"

Parvis received this without perceptible embarrassment: "Why, I didn't understand it—strictly speaking. And it wasn't the time to talk about it, if I had. The Elwell business was settled when the suit was withdrawn. Nothing I could have told you would have helped you to find your husband."

Mary continued to scrutinise him. "Then why are you telling me now?"

Still Parvis did not hesitate. "Well, to begin with, I supposed you knew more than you appear to—I mean about the circumstances of Elwell's death. And then people are talking of it now; the whole matter's been raked up again. And I thought if you didn't know you ought to."

She remained silent, and he continued: "You see, it's only come out lately what a bad state Elwell's affairs were in. His wife's a proud woman, and she fought on as long as she could, going out to work, and taking sewing at home when she got too sick—something with the heart, I believe. But she had his mother to look after, and the children, and she broke down under it, and finally had to ask for help. That called attention to the case, and the papers took it up, and a subscription was started. Everybody out there liked Bob Elwell, and most of the prominent names in the place are down on the list, and people began to wonder why——"

Parvis broke off to fumble in an inner pocket. "Here," he continued, "here's an account of the whole thing from the *Sentinel*—a little sensational, of course. But I guess you'd better look it over."

He held out a newspaper to Mary, who unfolded it slowly, remembering, as she did so, the evening when, in that same room, the perusal of a clipping from the *Sentinel* had first shaken the depths of her security.

As she opened the paper, her eyes, shrinking from the glaring headlines, "Widow of Boyne's Victim Forced to Appeal for Aid," ran down the column of text to two portraits inserted in it. The first was her husband's, taken from a photograph made the year they had come to England. It was the picture of him that she liked best, the one that stood on the writing-table upstairs in her bedroom. As the eyes in the photograph met hers, she felt it would be impossible to read what was said of him, and closed her lids with the sharpness of the pain.

"I thought if you felt disposed to put your name down——" she heard Parvis continue.

She opened her eyes with an effort, and they fell on the other portrait. It was that of a youngish man, slightly built, with features somewhat blurred by the shadow of a projecting hat-brim. Where had she seen that outline before? She stared at it confusedly, her heart hammering in her ears. Then she gave a cry.

"This is the man—the man who came for my husband!"

She heard Parvis start to his feet, and was dimly aware that she had slipped backward into the corner of the sofa, and that he was bending above her in alarm. She straightened herself, and reached out for the paper, which she had dropped.

"It's the man! I should know him anywhere!" she persisted in a voice that sounded to her own ears like a scream.

Parvis's answer seemed to come to her from far off, down endless fog-muffled windings.

"Mrs. Boyne, you're not very well. Shall I call somebody? Shall I get a glass of water?"

"No, no, no!" She threw herself toward him, her hand frantically clutching the newspaper. "I tell you, it's the man! I *know* him! He spoke to me in the garden!"

Parvis took the journal from her, directing his glasses to the portrait. "It can't be, Mrs. Boyne. It's Robert Elwell."

"Robert Elwell?" Her white stare seemed to travel into space. "Then it was Robert Elwell who came for him."

"Came for Boyne? The day he went away from here?" Parvis's voice dropped as hers rose. He bent over, laying a fraternal hand on her, as if to coax her gently back into her seat. "Why, Elwell was dead! Don't you remember?"

Mary sat with her eyes fixed on the picture, unconscious of what he was saying.

"Don't you remember Boyne's unfinished letter to me—the one you found on his desk that day? It was written just after he'd heard of Elwell's death." She noticed an odd shake in Parvis's unemotional voice. "Surely you remember!" he urged her.

Yes, she remembered: that was the profoundest horror of it. Elwell had died the day before her husband's disappearance; and this was Elwell's portrait; and it was the portrait of the man who had spoken to her in the garden. She lifted her head and looked slowly about the library. The library could have borne witness that it was also the portrait of the man who had come in that day to call Boyne from his unfinished letter. Through the misty surgings of her brain she heard the faint boom of half-forgotten words—words spoken by Alida Stair on the lawn at Pangbourne before Boyne and his wife had ever seen the house at Lyng, or had imagined that they might one day live there.

"This was the man who spoke to me," she repeated.

She looked again at Parvis. He was trying to conceal his disturbance under what he probably imagined to be an expression of indulgent commiseration; but the edges of his lips were blue. "He thinks me mad; but I'm not mad," she reflected; and suddenly there flashed upon her a way of justifying her strange affirmation.

She sat quiet, controlling the quiver of her lips, and waiting till she could trust her voice; then she said, looking straight at Parvis: "Will you answer me one question, please? When was it that Robert Elwell tried to kill himself?"

"When—when?" Parvis stammered.

"Yes; the date. Please try to remember."

She saw that he was growing still more afraid of her. "I have a reason," she insisted.

"Yes, yes. Only I can't remember. About two months before, I should say."

"I want the date," she repeated.

Parvis picked up the newspaper. "We might see here," he said, still humouring her. He ran his eyes down the page. "Here it is. Last October—the——"

She caught the words from him. "The 20th, wasn't it?" With a sharp look at her, he verified. "Yes, the 20th. Then you *did* know?"

"I know now." Her gaze continued to travel past him. "Sunday, the 20th—that was the day he came first."

Parvis's voice was almost inaudible. "Came *here* first?"

"Yes."

"You saw him twice, then?"

"Yes, twice." She just breathed it at him. "He came first on the 20th of October. I remember the date because it was the day we went up Meldon Steep for the first time." She felt a faint gasp of inward laughter at the thought that but for that she might have forgotten.

Parvis continued to scrutinise her, as if trying to intercept her gaze.

"We saw him from the roof," she went on. "He came down the lime-avenue toward the house. He was dressed just as he is in that picture. My husband saw him first. He was frightened, and ran down ahead of me; but there was no one there. He had vanished."

"Elwell had vanished?" Parvis faltered.

"Yes." Their two whispers seemed to grope for each other. "I couldn't think what had happened. I see now. He *tried* to come then; but he wasn't dead enough—he couldn't reach us. He had to wait for two months to die; and then he came back again—and Ned went with him."

She nodded at Parvis with the look of triumph of a child who has worked out a difficult puzzle. But suddenly she lifted her hands with a desperate gesture, pressing them to her temples.

"Oh, my God! I sent him to Ned—I told him where to go! I sent him to this room!" she screamed.

She felt the walls of books rush toward her, like inward falling ruins; and she heard Parvis, a long way off, through the ruins, crying to her, and struggling to get at her. But she was numb to his touch, she did not know what he was saying. Through the tumult she heard but one clear note, the voice of Alida Stair, speaking on the lawn at Pangbourne.

"You won't know till afterward," it said. "You won't know till long, long afterward."

1910

WILLA CATHER

(1873–1947)

Consequences

HENRY EASTMAN, a lawyer, aged forty, was standing beside the Flatiron building in a driving November rain-storm, signaling frantically for a taxi. It was six-thirty, and everything on wheels was engaged. The streets were in confusion about him, the sky was in turmoil above him, and the Flatiron building, which seemed about to blow down, threw water like a mill-shoot. Suddenly, out of the brutal struggle of men and cars and machines and people tilting at each other with umbrellas, a quiet, well-mannered limousine paused before him, at the curb, and an agreeable, ruddy countenance confronted him through the open window of the car.

"Don't you want me to pick you up, Mr. Eastman? I'm running directly home now."

Eastman recognized Kier Cavenaugh, a young man of pleasure, who lived in the house on Central Park South, where he himself had an apartment.

"Don't I?" he exclaimed, bolting into the car. "I'll risk getting your cushions wet without compunction. I came up in a taxi, but I didn't hold it. Bad economy. I thought I saw your car down on Fourteenth Street about half an hour ago."

The owner of the car smiled. He had a pleasant, round face and round eyes, and a fringe of smooth, yellow hair showed under the rim of his soft felt hat. "With a lot of little broilers fluttering into it? You did. I know some girls who work in the cheap shops down there. I happened to be down-town and I stopped and took a load of them home. I do sometimes. Saves their poor little clothes, you know. Their shoes are never any good."

Eastman looked at his rescuer. "Aren't they notoriously afraid of cars and smooth young men?" he inquired.

Cavenaugh shook his head. "They know which cars are safe and which are chancy. They put each other wise. You have to take a bunch at a time, of course. The Italian girls can never come along; their men shoot. The girls understand, all right; but their fathers don't. One gets to see queer places, sometimes, taking them home."

Eastman laughed drily. "Every time I touch the circle of your acquaintance, Cavenaugh, it's a little wider. You must know New York pretty well by this time."

"Yes, but I'm on my good behavior below Twenty-third Street," the young man replied with simplicity. "My little friends down there would give me a good character. They're wise little girls. They have grand ways with each other, a romantic code of loyalty. You can find a good many of the lost virtues among them."

The car was standing still in a traffic block at Fortieth Street, when Cavenaugh suddenly drew his face away from the window and touched Eastman's arm. "Look, please. You see that hansom with the bony gray horse—driver has a broken hat and red flannel around his throat. Can you see who is inside?"

Eastman peered out. The hansom was just cutting across the line, and the driver was making a great fuss about it, bobbing his head and waving his whip. He jerked his dripping old horse into Fortieth Street and clattered off past the Public Library grounds toward Sixth Avenue. "No, I couldn't see the passenger. Someone you know?"

"Could you see whether there was a passenger?" Cavenaugh asked.

"Why, yes. A man, I think. I saw his elbow on the apron. No driver ever behaves like that unless he has a passenger."

"Yes, I may have been mistaken," Cavenaugh murmured absent-mindedly. Ten minutes or so later, after Cavenaugh's car had turned off Fifth Avenue into Fifty-eighth Street, Eastman exclaimed, "There's your same cabby, and his cart's empty. He's headed for a drink now, I suppose." The driver in the broken hat and the red flannel neck cloth was still brandishing the whip over his old gray. He was coming from the west now, and turned down Sixth Avenue, under the elevated.

Cavenaugh's car stopped at the bachelor apartment house between Sixth and Seventh Avenues where he and Eastman lived, and they went up in the elevator together. They were still talking when the lift stopped at Cavenaugh's floor, and

Eastman stepped out with him and walked down the hall, finishing his sentence while Cavenaugh found his latch-key. When he opened the door, a wave of fresh cigarette smoke greeted them. Cavenaugh stopped short and stared into his hallway. "Now how in the devil—!" he exclaimed angrily.

"Someone waiting for you? Oh, no, thanks. I wasn't coming in. I have to work to-night. Thank you, but I couldn't." Eastman nodded and went up the two flights to his own rooms.

Though Eastman did not customarily keep a servant he had this winter a man who had been lent to him by a friend who was abroad. Rollins met him at the door and took his coat and hat.

"Put out my dinner clothes, Rollins, and then get out of here until ten o'clock. I've promised to go to a supper tonight. I shan't be dining. I've had a late tea and I'm going to work until ten. You may put out some kumiss and biscuit for me."

Rollins took himself off, and Eastman settled down at the big table in his sitting-room. He had to read a lot of letters submitted as evidence in a breach of contract case, and before he got very far he found that long paragraphs in some of the letters were written in German. He had a German dictionary at his office, but none here. Rollins had gone, and anyhow, the bookstores would be closed. He remembered having seen a row of dictionaries on the lower shelf of one of Cavenaugh's bookcases. Cavenaugh had a lot of books, though he never read anything but new stuff. Eastman prudently turned down his student's lamp very low—the thing had an evil habit of smoking—and went down two flights to Cavenaugh's door.

The young man himself answered Eastman's ring. He was freshly dressed for the evening, except for a brown smoking jacket, and his yellow hair had been brushed until it shone. He hesitated as he confronted his caller, still holding the door knob, and his round eyes and smooth forehead made their best imitation of a frown. When Eastman began to apologize, Cavenaugh's manner suddenly changed. He caught his arm and jerked him into the narrow hall. "Come in, come in. Right along!" he said excitedly. "Right along," he repeated as he pushed Eastman before him into his sitting-room. "Well I'll—" he stopped short at the door and looked about his own room with an air of complete mystification. The back window was wide open and a strong wind was blowing in. Cavenaugh walked over to the window and stuck out his head, looking up and down the fire escape. When he pulled his head in, he drew down the sash.

"I had a visitor I wanted you to see," he explained with a nervous smile. "At least I thought I had. He must have gone out that way," nodding toward the window.

"Call him back. I only came to borrow a German dictionary, if you have one. Can't stay. Call him back."

Cavenaugh shook his head despondently. "No use. He's beat it. Nowhere in sight."

"He must be active. Has he left something?" Eastman pointed to a very dirty white glove that lay on the floor under the window.

"Yes, that's his." Cavenaugh reached for his tongs, picked up the glove, and tossed it into the grate, where it quickly shriveled on the coals. Eastman felt that he had happened in upon something disagreeable, possibly something shady, and he wanted to get away at once. Cavenaugh stood staring at the fire and seemed stupid and dazed; so he repeated his request rather sternly, "I think I've seen a German dictionary down there among your books. May I have it?"

Cavenaugh blinked at him. "A German dictionary? Oh, possibly! Those were my father's. I scarcely know what there is." He put down the tongs and began to wipe his hands nervously with his handkerchief.

Eastman went over to the bookcase behind the Chesterfield, opened the door, swooped upon the book he wanted and stuck it under his arm. He felt perfectly certain now that something shady had been going on in Cavenaugh's rooms, and he saw no reason why he should come in for any hangover. "Thanks. I'll send it back to-morrow," he said curtly as he made for the door.

Cavenaugh followed him. "Wait a moment. I wanted you to see him. You did see his glove," glancing at the grate.

Eastman laughed disagreeably. "I saw a glove. That's not evidence. Do your friends often use that means of exit? Somewhat inconvenient."

Cavenaugh gave him a startled glance. "Wouldn't you think so? For an old man, a very rickety old party? The ladders are steep, you know, and rusty." He approached the window again and put it up softly. In a moment he drew his head back with a jerk. He caught Eastman's arm and shoved him toward the window. "Hurry, please. Look! Down there." He pointed to the little patch of paved court four flights down.

The square of pavement was so small and the walls about it were so high, that it was a good deal like looking down a well. Four tall buildings backed upon the same court and made a kind of shaft, with flagstones at the bottom, and at the top a square of dark blue with some stars in it. At the bottom of the shaft Eastman saw a black figure, a man in a caped coat and a tall hat stealing cautiously around, not across the square of pavement, keeping close to the dark wall and avoiding the streak of light that fell on the flagstones from a window in the opposite house. Seen from that height he was of course fore-shortened and probably looked more shambling and decrepit than he was. He picked his way along with exaggerated care and looked like a silly old cat crossing a wet street. When he reached the gate that led into an alley way between two buildings, he felt about for the latch, opened the door a mere crack, and then shot out under the feeble lamp that burned in the brick arch over the gateway. The door closed after him.

"He'll get run in," Eastman remarked curtly, turning away from the window. "That door shouldn't be left unlocked. Any crook could come in. I'll speak to the janitor about it, if you don't mind," he added sarcastically.

"Wish you would." Cavenaugh stood brushing down the front of his jacket, first with his right hand and then with his left. "You saw him, didn't you?"

"Enough of him. Seems eccentric. I have to see a lot of buggy people. They don't take me in any more. But I'm keeping you and I'm in a hurry myself. Good night."

Cavenaugh put out his hand detainingly and started to say something; but Eastman rudely turned his back and went down the hall and out of the door. He had never felt anything shady about Cavenaugh before, and he was sorry he had gone down for the dictionary. In five minutes he was deep in his papers; but in the half hour when he was loafing before he dressed to go out, the young man's curious behavior came into his mind again.

Eastman had merely a neighborly acquaintance with Cavenaugh. He had been to a supper at the young man's rooms once, but he didn't particularly like Cavenaugh's friends; so the next time he was asked, he had another engagement. He liked Cavenaugh himself, if for nothing else than because he was so cheerful and trim and ruddy. A good complexion is always at a premium in New York, especially when it shines reassuringly on a man who does everything in the world to lose it. It encourages fellow mortals as to the inherent vigor of the human organism and the amount of bad treatment it will stand for. "Footprints that perhaps another," etc.

Cavenaugh, he knew, had plenty of money. He was the son of a Pennsylvania preacher, who died soon after he discovered that his ancestral acres were full of petroleum, and Kier had come to New York to burn some of the oil. He was thirty-two and was still at it; spent his life, literally, among the breakers. His motor hit the Park every morning as if it were the first time ever. He took people out to supper every night. He went from restaurant to restaurant, sometimes to half-a-dozen in an evening. The head waiters were his hosts and their cordiality made him happy. They made a life-line for him up Broadway and down Fifth Avenue. Cavenaugh was still fresh and smooth, round and plump, with a lustre to his hair and white teeth and a clear look in his round eyes. He seemed absolutely unwearied and unimpaired; never bored and never carried away.

Eastman always smiled when he met Cavenaugh in the entrance hall, serenely going forth to or returning from gladiatorial combats with joy, or when he saw him rolling smoothly up to the door in his car in the morning after a restful night in one of the remarkable new roadhouses he was always finding. Eastman had seen a good many young men disappear on Cavenaugh's route, and he admired this young man's endurance.

To-night, for the first time, he had got a whiff of something unwholesome about the fellow—bad nerves, bad company, something on hand that he was ashamed of, a visitor old and vicious, who must have had a key to Cavenaugh's apartment, for he was evidently there when Cavenaugh returned at seven o'clock. Probably it was the same man Cavenaugh had seen in the hansom. He must have been able to let himself in, for Cavenaugh kept no man but his chauffeur; or perhaps the janitor had been instructed to let him in. In either case, and whoever he was, it was clear enough that Cavenaugh was ashamed of him and was mixing up in questionable business of some kind.

Eastman sent Cavenaugh's book back by Rollins, and for the next few weeks he had no word with him beyond a casual greeting when they happened to meet in the hall or the elevator. One Sunday morning Cavenaugh telephoned up to him to ask if he could motor out to a roadhouse in Connecticut that afternoon and have supper; but when Eastman found there were to be other guests he declined.

On New Year's eve Eastman dined at the University Club at six o'clock and hurried home before the usual manifestations of insanity had begun in the streets. When Rollins brought his smoking coat, he asked him whether he wouldn't like to get off early.

"Yes, sir. But won't you be dressing, Mr. Eastman?" he inquired.

"Not to-night." Eastman handed him a bill. "Bring some change in the morning. There'll be fees."

Rollins lost no time in putting everything to rights for the night, and Eastman couldn't help wishing that he were in such a hurry to be off somewhere himself. When he heard the hall door close softly, he wondered if there were any place, after all, that he wanted to go. From his window he looked down at the long lines of motors and taxis waiting for a signal to cross Broadway. He thought of some of their probable destinations and decided that none of those places pulled him very hard. The night was warm and wet, the air was drizzly. Vapor hung in clouds about the *Times* Building, half hid the top of it, and made a luminous haze along Broadway. While he was looking down at the army of wet, black carriage-tops and their reflected headlights and tail-lights, Eastman heard a ring at his door. He deliberated. If it were a caller, the hall porter would have telephoned up. It must be the janitor. When he opened the door, there stood a rosy young man in a tuxedo, without a coat or hat.

"Pardon. Should I have telephoned? I half thought you wouldn't be in."

Eastman laughed. "Come in, Cavenaugh. You weren't sure whether you wanted company or not, eh, and you were trying to let chance decide it? That was exactly my state of mind. Let's accept the verdict." When they emerged from the narrow hall into his sitting-room, he pointed out a seat by the fire to his guest. He brought a tray of decanters and soda bottles and placed it on his writing table.

Cavenaugh hesitated, standing by the fire. "Sure you weren't starting for somewhere?"

"Do I look it? No, I was just making up my mind to stick it out alone when you rang. Have one?" He picked up a tall tumbler.

"Yes, thank you. I always do."

Eastman chuckled. "Lucky boy! So will I. I had a very early dinner. New York is the most arid place on holidays," he continued as he rattled the ice in the glasses. "When one gets too old to hit the rapids down there, and tired of gobbling food to heathenish dance music, there is absolutely no place where you can get a chop and some milk toast in peace, unless you have strong ties of blood brotherhood on upper Fifth Avenue. But you, why aren't you starting for somewhere?"

The young man sipped his soda and shook his head as he replied:

"Oh, I couldn't get a chop, either. I know only flashy people, of course." He looked up at his host with such a grave and candid expression that Eastman decided there couldn't be anything very crooked about the fellow. His smooth cheeks were positively cherubic.

"Well, what's the matter with them? Aren't they flashing to-night?"

"Only the very new ones seem to flash on New Year's eve. The older ones fade away. Maybe they are hunting a chop, too."

"Well"—Eastman sat down—"holidays do dash one. I was just about to write a letter to a pair of maiden aunts in my old home town, up-state; old coasting hill, snow-covered pines, lights in the church windows. That's what you've saved me from."

Cavenaugh shook himself. "Oh, I'm sure that wouldn't have been good for you. Pardon me," he rose and took a photograph from the bookcase, a handsome man in shooting clothes. "Dudley, isn't it? Did you know him well?"

"Yes. An old friend. Terrible thing, wasn't it? I haven't got over the jolt yet."

"His suicide? Yes, terrible! Did you know his wife?"

"Slightly. Well enough to admire her very much. She must be terribly broken up. I wonder Dudley didn't think of that."

Cavenaugh replaced the photograph carefully, lit a cigarette, and standing before the fire began to smoke. "Would you mind telling me about him? I never met him, but of course I'd read a lot about him, and I can't help feeling interested. It was a queer thing."

Eastman took out his cigar case and leaned back in his deep chair. "In the days when I knew him best he hadn't any story, like the happy nations. Everything was properly arranged for him before he was born. He came into the world happy, healthy, clever, straight, with the right sort of connections and the right kind of fortune, neither too large nor too small. He helped to make the world an agreeable place to live in until he was twenty-six. Then he married as he should have married. His wife was a Californian, educated abroad. Beautiful. You have seen her picture?"

Cavenaugh nodded. "Oh, many of them."

"She was interesting, too. Though she was distinctly a person of the world, she had retained something, just enough of the large Western manner. She had the habit of authority, of calling out a special train if she needed it, of using all our ingenious mechanical contrivances lightly and easily, without over-rating them. She and Dudley knew how to live better than most people. Their house was the most charming one I have ever known in New York. You felt freedom there, and a zest of life, and safety—absolute sanctuary—from everything sordid or petty. A whole society like that would justify the creation of man and would make our planet shine with a soft, peculiar radiance among the constellations. You think I'm putting it on thick?"

The young man sighed gently. "Oh, no! One has always felt there must be people like that. I've never known any."

"They had two children, beautiful ones. After they had been married for eight years, Rosina met this Spaniard. He must have amounted to something. She wasn't a flighty woman. She came home and told Dudley how matters stood. He persuaded her to stay at home for six months and try to pull up. They were both fair-minded people, and I'm as sure as if I were the Almighty, that she did try. But at the end of the time, Rosina went quietly off to Spain, and Dudley went to hunt in the Canadian Rockies. I met his party out there. I didn't know his wife had left him and talked about her a good deal. I noticed that he never drank anything, and his light used to shine through the log chinks of his room until all hours, even after a hard day's hunting. When I got back to New York, rumors were creeping about. Dudley did not come back. He bought a ranch in Wyoming, built a big log house and kept splendid dogs and horses. One of his sisters went out to keep house for him, and the children were there when they were not in school. He had a great many visitors, and everyone who came back talked about how well Dudley kept things going.

"He put in two years out there. Then, last month, he had to come back on business. A trust fund had to be settled up, and he was administrator. I saw him at the club; same light, quick step, same gracious handshake. He was getting gray, and there was something softer in his manner; but he had a fine red tan on his face and said he found it delightful to be here in the season when everything is going hard. The Madison Avenue house had been closed since Rosina left it. He went there to get some things his sister wanted. That, of course, was the mistake. He went alone, in the afternoon, and didn't go out for dinner—found some sherry and tins of biscuit in the sideboard. He shot himself sometime that night. There were pistols in his smoking-room. They found burnt out candles beside him in the morning. The gas and electricity were shut off. I suppose there, in his own house, among his own things, it was too much for him. He left no letters."

Cavenaugh blinked and brushed the lapel of his coat. "I suppose," he said slowly, "that every suicide is logical and reasonable, if one knew all the facts."

Eastman roused himself. "No, I don't think so. I've known too many fellows who went off like that—more than I deserve, I think—and some of them were absolutely inexplicable. I can understand Dudley; but I can't see why healthy bachelors, with money enough, like ourselves, need such a device. It reminds me of what Dr. Johnson said, that the most discouraging thing about life is the number of fads and hobbies and fake religions it takes to put people through a few years of it."

"Dr. Johnson? The specialist? Oh, the old fellow!" said Cavenaugh imperturbably. "Yes, that's interesting. Still, I fancy if one knew the facts— Did you know about Wyatt?"

"I don't think so."

"You wouldn't, probably. He was just a fellow about town who spent money. He wasn't one of the *forestieri*, though. Had connections here and owned a fine old place over on Staten Island. He went in for botany, and had been all over, hunting things; rusts, I believe. He had a yacht and used to take a gay crowd down about the South Seas, botanizing. He really did botanize, I believe. I never knew such a spender—only not flashy. He helped a lot of fellows and he was awfully good to girls, the kind who come down here to get a little fun, who don't like to work and still aren't really tough, the kind you see talking hard for their dinner. Nobody knows what becomes of them, or what they get out of it, and there are hundreds of new ones every year. He helped dozens of 'em; it was he who got me curious about the little shop girls. Well, one afternoon when his tea was brought, he took prussic acid instead. He didn't leave any letters, either; people of any taste don't. They wouldn't leave any material reminder if they could help it. His lawyers found that he had just $314.72 above his debts when he died. He had planned to spend all his money, and then take his tea; he had worked it out carefully."

Eastman reached for his pipe and pushed his chair away from the fire. "That looks like a considered case, but I don't think philosophical suicides like that are common. I think they usually come from stress of feeling and are really, as the newspapers call them, desperate acts; done without a motive. You remember when Anna Karenina was under the wheels, she kept saying, 'Why am I here?'"

Cavenaugh rubbed his upper lip with his pink finger and made an effort to wrinkle his brows. "May I, please?" reaching for the whiskey. "But have you," he asked, blinking as the soda flew at him, "have you ever known, yourself, cases that were really inexplicable?"

"A few too many. I was in Washington just before Captain Jack Purden was married and I saw a good deal of him. Popular army man, fine record in the Philippines, married a charming girl with lots of money; mutual devotion. It was the gayest wedding of the winter, and they started for Japan. They stopped in San Francisco for a week and missed their boat because, as the bride wrote back to Washington, they were too happy to move. They took the next boat, were both good sailors, had exceptional weather. After they had been out for two weeks, Jack got up from his deck chair one afternoon, yawned, put down his book, and stood before his wife. 'Stop reading for a moment and look at me.' She laughed and asked him why. 'Because you happen to be good to look at.' He nodded to her, went back to the stern and was never seen again. Must have gone down to the lower deck and slipped overboard, behind the machinery. It was the luncheon hour, not many people about; steamer cutting through a soft green sea. That's one of the most baffling cases I know. His friends raked up his past, and it was as trim as a cottage garden. If he'd so much as dropped an ink spot on his fatigue uniform, they'd have found it. He wasn't emotional or moody; wasn't, indeed, very interesting; simply a good soldier, fond of all the pompous little formalities that make up a military man's life. What do you make of that, my boy?"

Cavenaugh stroked his chin. "It's very puzzling, I admit. Still, if one knew everything——"

"But we do know everything. His friends wanted to find something to help them out, to help the girl out, to help the case of the human creature."

"Oh, I don't mean things that people could unearth," said Cavenaugh uneasily. "But possibly there were things that couldn't be found out."

Eastman shrugged his shoulders. "It's my experience that when there are 'things' as you call them, they're very apt to be found. There is no such thing as a secret. To make any move at all one has to employ human agencies, employ at least one human agent. Even when the pirates killed the men who buried their gold for them, the bones told the story."

Cavenaugh rubbed his hands together and smiled his sunny smile.

"I like that idea. It's reassuring. If we can have no secrets, it means that we can't, after all, go so far afield as we might," he hesitated, "yes, as we might."

Eastman looked at him sourly. "Cavenaugh, when you've

practised law in New York for twelve years, you find that people can't go far in any direction, except—" He thrust his forefinger sharply at the floor. "Even in that direction, few people can do anything out of the ordinary. Our range is limited. Skip a few baths, and we become personally objectionable. The slightest carelessness can rot a man's integrity or give him ptomaine poisoning. We keep up only by incessant cleansing operations, of mind and body. What we call character, is held together by all sorts of tacks and strings and glue."

Cavenaugh looked startled. "Come now, it's not so bad as that, is it? I've always thought that a serious man, like you, must know a lot of Launcelots." When Eastman only laughed, the younger man squirmed about in his chair. He spoke again hastily, as if he were embarrassed. "Your military friend may have had personal experiences, however, that his friends couldn't possibly get a line on. He may accidentally have come to a place where he saw himself in too unpleasant a light. I believe people can be chilled by a draft from outside, somewhere."

"Outside?" Eastman echoed. "Ah, you mean the far out-side! Ghosts, delusions, eh?"

Cavenaugh winced. "That's putting it strong. Why not say tips from the outside? Delusions belong to a diseased mind, don't they? There are some of us who have no minds to speak of, who yet have had experiences. I've had a little something in that line myself and I don't look it, do I?"

Eastman looked at the bland countenance turned toward him. "Not exactly. What's your delusion?"

"It's not a delusion. It's a haunt."

The lawyer chuckled. "Soul of a lost Casino girl?"

"No; an old gentleman. A most unattractive old gentleman, who follows me about."

"Does he want money?"

Cavenaugh sat up straight. "No. I wish to God he wanted anything—but the pleasure of my society! I'd let him clean me out to be rid of him. He's a real article. You saw him yourself that night when you came to my rooms to borrow a dictio-nary, and he went down the fire-escape. You saw him down in the court."

"Well, I saw somebody down in the court, but I'm too cautious to take it for granted that I saw what you saw. Why, any-how, should I see your haunt? If it was your friend I saw, he impressed me disagreeably. How did you pick him up?"

Cavenaugh looked gloomy. "That was queer, too. Charley Burke and I had motored out to Long Beach, about a year ago, sometime in October, I think. We had supper and stayed until late. When we were coming home, my car broke down. We had a lot of girls along who had to get back for morning rehearsals and things; so I sent them all into town in Charley's car, and he was to send a man back to tow me home. I was driving myself, and didn't want to leave my machine. We had not taken a direct road back; so I was stuck in a lonesome, woody place, no houses about. I got chilly and made a fire, and was putting in the time comfortably enough, when this old party steps up. He was in shabby evening clothes and a top hat, and had on his usual white gloves. How he got there, at three o'clock in the morning, miles from any town or railway, I'll leave it to you to figure out. *He* surely had no car. When I saw him coming up to the fire, I disliked him. He had a silly, apolo-getic walk. His teeth were chattering, and I asked him to sit down. He got down like a clothes-horse folding up. I offered him a cigarette, and when he took off his gloves I couldn't help noticing how knotted and spotty his hands were. He was asthmatic, and took his breath with a wheeze. 'Haven't you got anything—refreshing in there?' he asked, nodding at the car. When I told him I hadn't, he sighed. 'Ah, you young fel-lows are greedy. You drink it all up. You drink it all up, all up—up!' he kept chewing it over."

Cavenaugh paused and looked embarrassed again. "The thing that was most unpleasant is difficult to explain. The old man sat there by the fire and leered at me with a silly sort of admiration that was—well, more than humiliating. 'Gay boy, gay dog!' he would mutter, and when he grinned he showed his teeth, worn and yellow—shells. I remembered that it was better to talk casually to insane people; so I remarked carelessly that I had been out with a party and got stuck.

" 'Oh yes, I remember,' he said, 'Flora and Lottie and May-belle and Marcelline, and poor Kate.'

"He had named them correctly; so I began to think I had been hitting the bright waters too hard.

"Things I drank never had seemed to make me woody; but you can never tell when trouble is going to hit you. I pulled my hat down and tried to look as uncommunicative as possible; but he kept croaking on from time to time, like this: 'Poor Kate! Splendid arms, but dope got her. She took up with Eastern religions after she had her hair dyed. Got to going to a Swami's joint, and smoking opium. Temple of the Lotus, it was called, and the police raided it.'

"This was nonsense, of course; the young woman was in the pink of condition. I let him rave, but I decided that if something didn't come out for me pretty soon, I'd foot it across Long Island. There wasn't room enough for the two of us. I got up and took another try at my car. He hopped right after me.

" 'Good car,' he wheezed, 'better than the little Ford.'

"I'd had a Ford before, but so has everybody; that was a safe guess.

" 'Still,' he went on, 'that run in from Huntington Bay in the rain wasn't bad. Arrested for speeding, he-he.'

"It was true I had made such a run, under rather unusual circumstances, and had been arrested. When at last I heard my life-boat snorting up the road, my visitor got up, sighed, and stepped back into the shadow of the trees. I didn't wait to see what became of him, you may believe. That was visitation number one. What do you think of it?"

Cavenaugh looked at his host defiantly. Eastman smiled.

"I think you'd better change your mode of life, Cavenaugh. Had many returns?" he inquired.

"Too many, by far." The young man took a turn about the room and came back to the fire. Standing by the mantel he lit another cigarette before going on with his story:

"The second visitation happened in the street, early in the evening, about eight o'clock. I was held up in a traffic block before the Plaza. My chauffeur was driving. Old Nibbs steps up out of the crowd, opens the door of my car, gets in and sits down beside me. He had on wilted evening clothes, same as before, and there was some sort of heavy scent about him. Such an unpleasant old party! A thorough-going rotter; you knew it at once. This time he wasn't talkative, as he had been when I first saw him. He leaned back in the car as if he owned

it, crossed his hands on his stick and looked out at the crowd
—sort of hungrily.

"I own I really felt a loathing compassion for him. We got
down the avenue slowly. I kept looking out at the mounted
police. But what could I do? Have him pulled? I was afraid to.
I was awfully afraid of getting him into the papers.

" 'I'm going to the New Astor,' I said at last. 'Can I take you
anywhere?'

" 'No, thank you,' says he. 'I get out when you do. I'm due
on West 44th. I'm dining to-night with Marcelline—all that is
left of her!'

"He put his hand to his hat brim with a grewsome salute.
Such a scandalous, foolish old face as he had! When we pulled
up at the Astor, I stuck my hand in my pocket and asked him if
he'd like a little loan.

" 'No, thank you, but'—he leaned over and whispered, ugh!
—'but save a little, save a little. Forty years from now—a little—
comes in handy. Save a little.'

"His eyes fairly glittered as he made his remark. I jumped
out. I'd have jumped into the North River. When he tripped
off, I asked my chauffeur if he'd noticed the man who got into
the car with me. He said he knew someone was with me, but
he hadn't noticed just when he got in. Want to hear any more?"

Cavenaugh dropped into his chair again. His plump cheeks
were a trifle more flushed than usual, but he was perfectly
calm. Eastman felt that the young man believed what he was
telling him.

"Of course I do. It's very interesting. I don't see quite
where you are coming out though."

Cavenaugh sniffed. "No more do I. I really feel that I've
been put upon. I haven't deserved it any more than any other
fellow of my kind. Doesn't it impress you disagreeably?"

"Well, rather so. Has anyone else seen your friend?"

"You saw him."

"We won't count that. As I said, there's no certainty that you
and I saw the same person in the court that night. Has anyone
else had a look in?"

"People sense him rather than see him. He usually crops
up when I'm alone or in a crowd on the street. He never

approaches me when I'm with people I know, though I've seen him hanging about the doors of theatres when I come out with a party; loafing around the stage exit, under a wall; or across the street, in a doorway. To be frank, I'm not anxious to introduce him. The third time, it was I who came upon him. In November my driver, Harry, had a sudden attack of appendicitis. I took him to the Presbyterian Hospital in the car, early in the evening. When I came home, I found the old villain in my rooms. I offered him a drink, and he sat down. It was the first time I had seen him in a steady light, with his hat off.

"His face is lined like a railway map, and as to color—Lord, what a liver! His scalp grows tight to his skull, and his hair is dyed until it's perfectly dead, like a piece of black cloth."

Cavenaugh ran his fingers through his own neatly trimmed thatch, and seemed to forget where he was for a moment.

"I had a twin brother, Brian, who died when we were sixteen. I have a photograph of him on my wall, an enlargement from a kodak of him, doing a high jump, rather good thing, full of action. It seemed to annoy the old gentleman. He kept looking at it and lifting his eyebrows, and finally he got up, tiptoed across the room, and turned the picture to the wall.

" 'Poor Brian! Fine fellow, but died young,' says he.

"Next morning, there was the picture, still reversed."

"Did he stay long?" Eastman asked interestedly.

"Half an hour, by the clock."

"Did he talk?"

"Well, he rambled."

"What about?"

Cavenaugh rubbed his pale eyebrows before answering.

"About things that an old man ought to want to forget. His conversation is highly objectionable. Of course he knows me like a book; everything I've ever done or thought. But when he recalls them, he throws a bad light on them, somehow. Things that weren't much off color, look rotten. He doesn't leave one a shred of self-respect, he really doesn't. That's the amount of it." The young man whipped out his handkerchief and wiped his face.

"You mean he really talks about things that none of your friends know?"

"Oh, dear, yes! Recalls things that happened in school. Anything disagreeable. Funny thing, he always turns Brian's picture to the wall."

"Does he come often?"

"Yes, oftener, now. Of course I don't know how he gets in down-stairs. The hall boys never see him. But he has a key to my door. I don't know how he got it, but I can hear him turn it in the lock."

"Why don't you keep your driver with you, or telephone for me to come down?"

"He'd only grin and go down the fire escape as he did before. He's often done it when Harry's come in suddenly. Everybody has to be alone sometimes, you know. Besides, I don't want anybody to see him. He has me there."

"But why not? Why do you feel responsible for him?"

Cavenaugh smiled wearily. "That's rather the point, isn't it? Why do I? But I absolutely do. That identifies him, more than his knowing all about my life and my affairs."

Eastman looked at Cavenaugh thoughtfully. "Well, I should advise you to go in for something altogether different and new, and go in for it hard; business, engineering, metallurgy, something this old fellow wouldn't be interested in. See if you can make him remember logarithms."

Cavenaugh sighed. "No, he has me there, too. People never really change; they go on being themselves. But I would never make much trouble. Why can't they let me alone, damn it! I'd never hurt anybody, except, perhaps——"

"Except your old gentleman, eh?" Eastman laughed. "Seriously, Cavenaugh, if you want to shake him, I think a year on a ranch would do it. He would never be coaxed far from his favorite haunts. He would dread Montana."

Cavenaugh pursed up his lips. "So do I!"

"Oh, you think you do. Try it, and you'll find out. A gun and a horse beats all this sort of thing. Besides losing your haunt, you'd be putting ten years in the bank for yourself. I know a good ranch where they take people, if you want to try it."

"Thank you. I'll consider. Do you think I'm batty?"

"No, but I think you've been doing one sort of thing too long. You need big horizons. Get out of this."

Cavenaugh smiled meekly. He rose lazily and yawned behind his hand. "It's late, and I've taken your whole evening." He strolled over to the window and looked out. "Queer place, New York; rough on the little fellows. Don't you feel sorry for them, the girls especially? I do. What a fight they put up for a little fun! Why, even that old goat is sorry for them, the only decent thing he kept."

Eastman followed him to the door and stood in the hall, while Cavenaugh waited for the elevator. When the car came up Cavenaugh extended his pink, warm hand. "Good night."

The cage sank and his rosy countenance disappeared, his round-eyed smile being the last thing to go.

Weeks passed before Eastman saw Cavenaugh again. One morning, just as he was starting for Washington to argue a case before the Supreme Court, Cavenaugh telephoned him at his office to ask him about the Montana ranch he had recommended; said he meant to take his advice and go out there for the spring and summer.

When Eastman got back from Washington, he saw dusty trunks, just up from the trunk room, before Cavenaugh's door. Next morning, when he stopped to see what the young man was about, he found Cavenaugh in his shirt sleeves, packing.

"I'm really going; off to-morrow night. You didn't think it of me, did you?" he asked gaily.

"Oh, I've always had hopes of you!" Eastman declared. "But you are in a hurry, it seems to me."

"Yes, I am in a hurry." Cavenaugh shot a pair of leggings into one of the open trunks. "I telegraphed your ranch people, used your name, and they said it would be all right. By the way, some of my crowd are giving a little dinner for me at Rector's to-night. Couldn't you be persuaded, as it's a farewell occasion?" Cavenaugh looked at him hopefully.

Eastman laughed and shook his head. "Sorry, Cavenaugh, but that's too gay a world for me. I've got too much work lined up before me. I wish I had time to stop and look at your guns, though. You seem to know something about guns. You've more than you'll need, but nobody can have too many good ones." He put down one of the revolvers regretfully. "I'll drop in to see you in the morning, if you're up."

"I shall be up, all right. I've warned my crowd that I'll cut away before midnight."

"You won't, though," Eastman called back over his shoulder as he hurried down-stairs.

The next morning, while Eastman was dressing, Rollins came in greatly excited.

"I'm a little late, sir. I was stopped by Harry, Mr. Cave-naugh's driver. Mr. Cavenaugh shot himself last night, sir."

Eastman dropped his vest and sat down on his shoe-box. "You're drunk, Rollins," he shouted. "He's going away to-day!"

"Yes, sir. Harry found him this morning. Ah, he's quite dead, sir. Harry's telephoned for the coroner. Harry don't know what to do with the ticket."

Eastman pulled on his coat and ran down the stairway. Cavenaugh's trunks were strapped and piled before the door. Harry was walking up and down the hall with a long green railroad ticket in his hand and a look of complete stupidity on his face.

"What shall I do about this ticket, Mr. Eastman?" he whispered. "And what about his trunks? He had me tell the transfer people to come early. They may be here any minute. Yes, sir. I brought him home in the car last night, before twelve, as cheerful as could be."

"Be quiet, Harry. Where is he?"

"In his bed, sir."

Eastman went into Cavenaugh's sleeping-room. When he came back to the sitting-room, he looked over the writing table; railway folders, time-tables, receipted bills, nothing else. He looked up for the photograph of Cavenaugh's twin brother. There it was, turned to the wall. Eastman took it down and looked at it; a boy in track clothes, half lying in the air, going over the string shoulders first, above the heads of a crowd of lads who were running and cheering. The face was somewhat blurred by the motion and the bright sunlight. Eastman put the picture back, as he found it. Had Cavenaugh entertained his visitor last night, and had the old man been more convincing than usual? "Well, at any rate, he's seen to it that the old man can't establish identity. What a soft lot they are, fellows like poor Cavenaugh!" Eastman thought of his office as a delightful place.

ELLEN GLASGOW

(1873–1945)

The Shadowy Third

WHEN the call came I remember that I turned from the telephone in a romantic flutter. Though I had spoken only once to the great surgeon, Roland Maradick, I felt on that December afternoon that to speak to him only once—to watch him in the operating-room for a single hour—was an adventure which drained the colour and the excitement from the rest of life. After all these years of work on typhoid and pneumonia cases, I can still feel the delicious tremor of my young pulses; I can still see the winter sunshine slanting through the hospital windows over the white uniforms of the nurses.

"He didn't mention me by name. Can there be a mistake?" I stood, incredulous yet ecstatic, before the superintendent of the hospital.

"No, there isn't a mistake. I was talking to him before you came down." Miss Hemphill's strong face softened while she looked at me. She was a big, resolute woman, a distant Canadian relative of my mother's, and the kind of nurse I had discovered in the month since I had come up from Richmond, that Northern hospital boards, if not Northern patients, appear instinctively to select. From the first, in spite of her hardness, she had taken a liking—I hesitate to use the word "fancy" for a preference so impersonal—to her Virginia cousin. After all, it isn't every Southern nurse, just out of training, who can boast a kinswoman in the superintendent of a New York hospital.

"And he made you understand positively that he meant me?" The thing was so wonderful that I simply couldn't believe it.

"He asked particularly for the nurse who was with Miss Hudson last week when he operated. I think he didn't even remember that you had a name. When I asked if he meant Miss Randolph, he repeated that he wanted the nurse who had been with Miss Hudson. She was small, he said, and

436

cheerful-looking. This, of course, might apply to one or two of
the others, but none of these was with Miss Hudson."

"Then I suppose it is really true?" My pulses were tingling.
"And I am to be there at six o'clock?"

"Not a minute later. The day nurse goes off duty at that
hour, and Mrs. Maradick is never left by herself for an instant."

"It is her mind, isn't it? And that makes it all the stranger
that he should select me, for I have had so few mental cases."

"So few cases of any kind," Miss Hemphill was smiling, and
when she smiled I wondered if the other nurses would know
her. "By the time you have gone through the treadmill in New
York, Margaret, you will have lost a good many things besides
your inexperience. I wonder how long you will keep your sympathy and your imagination? After all, wouldn't you have
made a better novelist than a nurse?"

"I can't help putting myself into my cases. I suppose one
ought not to?"

"It isn't a question of what one ought to do, but of what
one must. When you are drained of every bit of sympathy and
enthusiasm, and have got nothing in return for it, not even
thanks, you will understand why I try to keep you from wasting
yourself."

"But surely in a case like this—for Doctor Maradick?"

"Oh, well, of course—for Doctor Maradick." She must have
seen that I implored her confidence, for, after a minute, she let
fall carelessly a gleam of light on the situation: "It is a very sad
case when you think what a charming man and a great surgeon
Doctor Maradick is."

Above the starched collar of my uniform I felt the blood leap
in bounds to my cheeks. "I have spoken to him only once," I
murmured, "but he is charming, and so kind and handsome,
isn't he?"

"His patients adore him."

"Oh, yes, I've seen that. Everyone hangs on his visits." Like
the patients and the other nurses, I also had come by delightful, if imperceptible, degrees to hang on the daily visits of Doctor Maradick. He was, I suppose, born to be a hero to women.
From my first day in his hospital, from the moment when I
watched, through closed shutters, while he stepped out of his

car, I have never doubted that he was assigned to the great
part in the play. If I had been ignorant of his spell—of the
charm he exercised over his hospital—I should have felt it in
the waiting hush, like a drawn breath, which followed his ring
at the door and preceded his imperious footstep on the stairs.
My first impression of him, even after the terrible events of the
next year, records a memory that is both careless and splendid.
At that moment, when, gazing through the chinks in the shutters, I watched him, in his coat of dark fur, cross the pavement
over the pale streaks of sunshine, I knew beyond any doubt—I
knew with a sort of infallible prescience—that my fate was irre-
trievably bound up with his in the future. I knew this, I repeat,
though Miss Hemphill would still insist that my foreknowledge was merely a sentimental gleaning from indiscriminate
novels. But it wasn't only first love, impressionable as my kinswoman believed me to be. It wasn't only the way he looked.
Even more than his appearance—more than the shining dark
of his eyes, the silvery brown of his hair, the dusky glow in his
face—even more than his charm and his magnificence, I think,
the beauty and sympathy in his voice won my heart. It was a
voice, I heard someone say afterwards, that ought always to
speak poetry.

So you will see why—if you do not understand at the beginning, I can never hope to make you believe impossible things!
—so you will see why I accepted the call when it came as an
imperative summons. I couldn't have stayed away after he sent
for me. However much I may have tried not to go, I know that
in the end I must have gone. In those days, while I was still
hoping to write novels, I used to talk a great deal about "destiny" (I have learned since then how silly all such talk is), and I
suppose it was my "destiny" to be caught in the web of Roland
Maradick's personality. But I am not the first nurse to grow
love-sick about a doctor who never gave her a thought.

"I am glad you got the call, Margaret. It may mean a great
deal to you. Only try not to be too emotional." I remember
that Miss Hemphill was holding a bit of rose-geranium in
her hand while she spoke—one of the patients had given it to
her from a pot she kept in her room, and the scent of the flower
is still in my nostrils—or my memory. Since then—oh, long since
then—I have wondered if she also had been caught in the web.

"I wish I knew more about the case." I was pressing for light. "Have you ever seen Mrs. Maradick?"

"Oh, dear, yes. They have been married only a little over a year, and in the beginning she used to come sometimes to the hospital and wait outside while the doctor made his visits. She was a very sweet-looking woman then—not exactly pretty, but fair and slight, with the loveliest smile, I think, I have ever seen. In those first months she was so much in love that we used to laugh about it among ourselves. To see her face light up when the doctor came out of the hospital and crossed the pavement to his car, was as good as a play. We never tired of watching her—I wasn't superintendent then, so I had more time to look out of the window while I was on day duty. Once or twice she brought her little girl in to see one of the patients. The child was so much like her that you would have known them anywhere for mother and daughter."

I had heard that Mrs. Maradick was a widow, with one child, when she first met the doctor, and I asked now, still seeking an illumination I had not found, "There was a great deal of money, wasn't there?"

"A great fortune. If she hadn't been so attractive, people would have said, I suppose, that Doctor Maradick married her for her money. Only," she appeared to make an effort of memory, "I believe I've heard somehow that it was all left in trust away from Mrs. Maradick if she married again. I can't, to save my life, remember just how it was; but it was a queer will, I know, and Mrs. Maradick wasn't to come into the money unless the child didn't live to grow up. The pity of it——"

A young nurse came into the office to ask for something— the keys, I think, of the operating-room, and Miss Hemphill broke off inconclusively as she hurried out of the door. I was sorry that she left off just when she did. Poor Mrs. Maradick! Perhaps I was too emotional, but even before I saw her I had begun to feel her pathos and her strangeness.

My preparations took only a few minutes. In those days I always kept a suitcase packed and ready for sudden calls; and it was not yet six o'clock when I turned from Tenth Street into Fifth Avenue, and stopped for a minute, before ascending the steps, to look at the house in which Doctor Maradick lived. A fine rain was falling, and I remember thinking, as I turned the corner, how depressing the weather must be for Mrs. Maradick. It was an old house, with damp-looking walls (though that may have been because of the rain) and a spindle-shaped iron railing which ran up the stone steps to the black door, where I noticed a dim flicker through the old-fashioned fanlight. Afterwards I discovered that Mrs. Maradick had been born in the house—her maiden name was Calloran—and that she had never wanted to live anywhere else. She was a woman —this I found out when I knew her better—of strong attachments to both persons and places; and though Doctor Maradick had tried to persuade her to move uptown after her marriage, she had clung, against his wishes, to the old house in lower Fifth Avenue. I dare say she was obstinate about it in spite of her gentleness and her passion for the doctor. Those sweet, soft women, especially when they have always been rich, are sometimes amazingly obstinate. I have nursed so many of them since—women with strong affections and weak intellects —that I have come to recognize the type as soon as I set eyes upon it.

My ring at the bell was answered after a little delay, and when I entered the house I saw that the hall was quite dark except for the waning glow from an open fire which burned in the library. When I gave my name, and added that I was the night nurse, the servant appeared to think my humble presence unworthy of illumination. He was an old negro butler, inherited perhaps from Mrs. Maradick's mother, who, I learned afterwards, was from South Carolina; and while he passed me on his way up the staircase, I heard him vaguely muttering that he "wa'n't gwinter tu'n on dem lights twel de chile had done playin'."

To the right of the hall, the soft glow drew me into the library, and crossing the threshold timidly, I stooped to dry my wet coat by the fire. As I bent there, meaning to start up at the first sound of a footstep, I thought how cosy the room was after the damp walls outside to which some bared creepers were clinging; and I was watching the strange shapes and patterns the firelight made on the old Persian rug, when the lamps of a slowly turning motor flashed on me through the white shades at the window. Still dazzled by the glare, I looked round in the dimness and saw a child's ball of red and blue rubber roll towards me out of the gloom of the adjoining room. A moment later, while I made a vain attempt to capture the toy as it spun past me, a little girl darted airily, with peculiar lightness and grace, through the doorway, and stopped quickly, as if in surprise at the sight of a stranger. She was a small child—so small and slight that her footsteps made no sound on the polished floor of the threshold; and I remember thinking while I looked at her that she had the gravest and sweetest face I had ever seen. She couldn't—I decided this afterwards—have been more than six or seven years old, yet she stood there with a curious prim dignity, like the dignity of an elderly person, and gazed up at me with enigmatical eyes. She was dressed in Scotch plaid, with a bit of red ribbon in her hair, which was cut in a fringe over her forehead and hung very straight to her shoulders. Charming as she was, from her uncurled brown hair to the white socks and black slippers on her little feet, I recall most vividly the singular look in her eyes, which appeared in the shifting light to be of an indeterminate colour. For the odd thing about this look was that it was not the look of childhood at all. It was the look of profound experience, of bitter knowledge.

"Have you come for your ball?" I asked; but while the friendly question was still on my lips, I heard the servant returning. In my confusion I made a second ineffectual grasp at the play-thing, which had rolled away from me into the dusk of the drawing-room. Then, as I raised my head, I saw that the child also had slipped from the room; and without looking after her I followed the old negro into the pleasant study above, where the great surgeon awaited me.

Ten years ago, before hard nursing had taken so much out of me, I blushed very easily, and I was aware at the moment when I crossed Doctor Maradick's study that my cheeks were the colour of peonies. Of course, I was a fool—no one knows this better than I do—but I had never been alone, even for an instant, with him before, and the man was more than a hero to me, he was—there isn't any reason now why I should blush over the confession—almost a god. At that age I was mad about the wonders of surgery, and Roland Maradick in the operating-room was magician enough to have turned an older and more sensible head than mine. Added to his great reputation and his marvelous skill, he was, I am sure of this, the most splendid-looking man, even at forty-five, that one could imagine. Had he been ungracious—had he been positively rude to me, I should still have adored him; but when he held out his hand, and greeted me in the charming way he had with women, I felt that I would have died for him. It is no wonder that a saying went about the hospital that every woman he operated on fell in love with him. As for the nurses—well, there wasn't a single one of them who had escaped his spell—not even Miss Hemphill, who could have been scarcely a day under fifty.

"I am glad you could come, Miss Randolph. You were with Miss Hudson last week when I operated?"

I bowed. To save my life I couldn't have spoken without blushing the redder.

"I noticed your bright face at the time. Brightness, I think, is what Mrs. Maradick needs. She finds her day nurse depressing." His eyes rested so kindly upon me that I have suspected since that he was not entirely unaware of my worship. It was a small thing, heaven knows, to flatter his vanity—a nurse just out of a training-school—but to some men no tribute is too insignificant to give pleasure.

"You will do your best, I am sure." He hesitated an instant —just long enough for me to perceive the anxiety beneath the genial smile on his face—and then added gravely, "We wish to avoid, if possible, having to send her away."

I could only murmur in response, and after a few carefully chosen words about his wife's illness, he rang the bell and directed the maid to take me upstairs to my room. Not until I was ascending the stairs to the third storey did it occur to me that he had really told me nothing. I was as perplexed about the nature of Mrs. Maradick's malady as I had been when I entered the house.

I found my room pleasant enough. It had been arranged— at Doctor Maradick's request, I think—that I was to sleep in the house, and after my austere little bed at the hospital, I was agreeably surprised by the cheerful look of the apartment into which the maid led me. The walls were papered in roses, and there were curtains of flowered chintz at the window, which looked down on a small formal garden at the rear of the house. This the maid told me, for it was too dark for me to distinguish more than a marble fountain and a fir-tree, which looked

old, though I afterwards learned that it was replanted almost
every season.

In ten minutes I had slipped into my uniform and was ready
to go to my patient; but for some reason—to this day I have
never found out what it was that turned her against me at the
start—Mrs. Maradick refused to receive me. While I stood
outside her door I heard the day nurse trying to persuade her
to let me come in. It wasn't any use, however, and in the end I
was obliged to go back to my room and wait until the poor lady
got over her whim and consented to see me. That was long
after dinner—it must have been nearer eleven than ten o'clock
—and Miss Peterson was quite worn out by the time she came
for me.

"I'm afraid you'll have a bad night," she said as we went
downstairs together. That was her way, I soon saw, to expect
the worst of everything and everybody.

"Does she often keep you up like this?"

"Oh, no, she is usually very considerate. I never knew a
sweeter character. But she still has this hallucination——"

Here again, as in the scene with Doctor Maradick, I felt that
the explanation had only deepened the mystery. Mrs. Maradick's
hallucination, whatever form it assumed, was evidently a subject for evasion and subterfuge in the household. It was on the
tip of my tongue to ask, "What is her hallucination?"—but
before I could get the words past my lips we had reached Mrs.
Maradick's door, and Miss Peterson motioned me to be silent.
As the door opened a little way to admit me, I saw that Mrs.
Maradick was already in bed, and that the lights were out except for a night-lamp burning on a candle-stand beside a book
and a carafe of water.

"I won't go in with you," said Miss Peterson in a whisper;
and I was on the point of stepping over the threshold when I
saw the little girl, in the dress of Scotch plaid, slip by me from
the dusk of the room into the electric light of the hall. She
held a doll in her arms, and as she went by she dropped a doll's
work-basket in the doorway. Miss Peterson must have picked
up the toy, for when I turned in a minute to look for it I found
that it was gone. I remember thinking that it was late for a child
to be up—she looked delicate, too—but, after all, it was no
business of mine, and four years in a hospital had taught me

never to meddle in things that do not concern me. There is nothing a nurse learns quicker than not to try to put the world to rights in a day.

When I crossed the floor to the chair by Mrs. Maradick's bed, she turned over on her side and looked at me with the sweetest and saddest smile.

"You are the night nurse," she said in a gentle voice; and from the moment she spoke I knew that there was nothing hysterical or violent about her mania—or hallucination, as they called it. "They told me your name, but I have forgotten it."

"Randolph—Margaret Randolph." I liked her from the start, and I think she must have seen it.

"You look very young, Miss Randolph."

"I am twenty-two, but I suppose I don't look quite my age. People usually think I am younger."

For a minute she was silent, and while I settled myself in the chair by the bed, I thought how strikingly she resembled the little girl I had seen first in the afternoon, and then leaving her room a few moments before. They had the same small, heart-shaped faces, coloured ever so faintly; the same straight, soft hair, between brown and flaxen; and the same large, grave eyes, set very far apart under arched eyebrows. What surprised me most, however, was that they both looked at me with that enigmatical and vaguely wondering expression—only in Mrs. Maradick's face the vagueness seemed to change now and then to a definite fear—a flash, I had almost said, of startled horror.

I sat quite still in my chair, and until the time came for Mrs. Maradick to take her medicine not a word passed between us. Then, when I bent over her with the glass in my hand, she raised her head from the pillow and said in a whisper of suppressed intensity:

"You look kind. I wonder if you could have seen my little girl?"

As I slipped my arm under the pillow I tried to smile cheerfully down on her. "Yes, I've seen her twice. I'd know her anywhere by her likeness to you."

A glow shone in her eyes, and I thought how pretty she must have been before illness took the life and animation out of her features. "Then I know you're good." Her voice was so strained and low that I could barely hear it. "If you weren't good you couldn't have seen her."

I thought this queer enough, but all I answered was, "She looked delicate to be sitting up so late."

A quiver passed over her thin features, and for a minute I thought she was going to burst into tears. As she had taken the medicine, I put the glass back on the candle-stand, and bending over the bed, smoothed the straight brown hair, which was as fine and soft as spun silk, back from her forehead. There was something about her—I don't know what it was—that made you love her as soon as she looked at you.

"She always had that light and airy way, though she was never sick a day in her life," she answered calmly after a pause. Then, groping for my hand, she whispered passionately, "You must not tell him—you must not tell any one that you have seen her!"

"I must not tell any one?" Again I had the impression that had come to me first in Doctor Maradick's study, and afterwards with Miss Peterson on the staircase, that I was seeking a gleam of light in the midst of obscurity.

"Are you sure there isn't any one listening—that there isn't any one at the door?" she asked, pushing aside my arm and raising herself on the pillows.

"Quite, quite sure. They have put out the lights in the hall."

"And you will not tell him? Promise me that you will not tell him." The startled horror flashed from the vague wonder of her expression. "He doesn't like her to come back, because he killed her."

"Because he killed her!" Then it was that light burst on me in a blaze. So this was Mrs. Maradick's hallucination! She believed that her child was dead—the little girl I had seen with my own eyes leaving her room; and she believed that her husband—the great surgeon we worshipped in the hospital—had murdered her. No wonder they veiled the dreadful obsession in mystery! No wonder that even Miss Peterson had not dared to drag the horrid thing out into the light! It was the kind of hallucination one simply couldn't stand having to face.

"There is no use telling people things that nobody believes," she resumed slowly, still holding my hand in a grasp that would have hurt me if her fingers had not been so fragile. "Nobody believes that he killed her. Nobody believes that she comes back every day to the house. Nobody believes—and yet you saw her——"

"Yes, I saw her—but why should your husband have killed her?" I spoke soothingly, as one would speak to a person who was quite mad. Yet she was not mad, I could have sworn this while I looked at her.

For a moment she moaned inarticulately, as if the horror of her thoughts were too great to pass into speech. Then she flung out her thin, bare arm with a wild gesture.

"Because he never loved me!" she said. "He never loved me!"

"But he married you," I urged gently while I stroked her hair. "If he hadn't loved you, why should he have married you?"

"He wanted the money—my little girl's money. It all goes to him when I die."

"But he is rich himself. He must make a fortune from his profession."

"It isn't enough. He wanted millions." She had grown stern and tragic. "No, he never loved me. He loved someone else from the beginning—before I knew him."

It was quite useless, I saw, to reason with her. If she wasn't mad, she was in a state of terror and despondency so black that it had almost crossed the border-line into madness. I thought once that I would go upstairs and bring the child down from her nursery; but, after a moment's hesitation, I realized that Miss Peterson and Doctor Maradick must have long ago tried all these measures. Clearly, there was nothing to do except soothe and quiet her as much as I could; and this I did until she dropped into a light sleep which lasted well into the morning.

By seven o'clock I was worn out—not from work but from the strain on my sympathy—and I was glad, indeed, when one of the maids came in to bring me an early cup of coffee. Mrs. Maradick was still sleeping—it was a mixture of bromide and chloral I had given her—and she did not wake until Miss Peterson came on duty an hour or two later. Then, when I went downstairs, I found the dining-room deserted except for the old housekeeper, who was looking over the silver. Doctor

Maradick, she explained to me presently, had his breakfast served in the morning-room on the other side of the house.

"And the little girl? Does she take her meals in the nursery?"

She threw me a startled glance. Was it, I questioned afterwards, one of distrust or apprehension?

"There isn't any little girl. Haven't you heard?"

"Heard? No. Why, I saw her only yesterday."

The look she gave me—I was sure of it now—was full of alarm.

"The little girl—she was the sweetest child I ever saw—died just two months ago of pneumonia."

"But she couldn't have died." I was a fool to let this out, but the shock had completely unnerved me. "I tell you I saw her yesterday."

The alarm in her face deepened. "That is Mrs. Maradick's trouble. She believes that she still sees her."

"But don't you see her?" I drove the question home bluntly.

"No." She set her lips tightly. "I never see anything."

So I had been wrong, after all, and the explanation, when it came, only accentuated the terror. The child was dead—she had died of pneumonia two months ago—and yet I had seen her, with my own eyes, playing ball in the library; I had seen her slipping out of her mother's room, with her doll in her arms.

"Is there another child in the house? Could there be a child belonging to one of the servants?" A gleam had shot through the fog in which I was groping.

"No, there isn't any other. The doctors tried bringing one once, but it threw the poor lady into such a state she almost died of it. Besides, there wouldn't be any other child as quiet and sweet-looking as Dorothea. To see her skipping along in her dress of Scotch plaid used to make me think of a fairy, though they say that fairies wear nothing but white or green."

"Has any one else seen her—the child, I mean—any of the servants?"

"Only old Gabriel, the coloured butler, who came with Mrs. Maradick's mother from South Carolina. I've heard that negroes often have a kind of second sight—though I don't know that that is just what you would call it. But they seem to believe in the supernatural by instinct, and Gabriel is so old and doty—he does no work except answer the door-bell and clean the silver—that nobody pays much attention to anything that he sees——"

"Is the child's nursery kept as it used to be?"

"Oh, no. The doctor had all the toys sent to the children's hospital. That was a great grief to Mrs. Maradick; but Doctor Brandon thought, and all the nurses agreed with him, that it was best for her not to be allowed to keep the room as it was when Dorothea was living."

"Dorothea? Was that the child's name?"

"Yes, it means the gift of God, doesn't it? She was named after the mother of Mrs. Maradick's first husband, Mr. Ballard. He was the grave, quiet kind—not the least like the doctor."

I wondered if the other dreadful obsession of Mrs. Maradick's had drifted down through the nurses or the servants to the housekeeper; but she said nothing about it, and since she was, I suspected, a garrulous person, I thought it wiser to assume that the gossip had not reached her.

A little later, when breakfast was over and I had not yet gone upstairs to my room, I had my first interview with Doctor Brandon, the famous alienist who was in charge of the case. I had never seen him before, but from the first moment that I looked at him I took his measure almost by intuition. He was, I suppose, honest enough—I have always granted him that, bitterly as I have felt towards him. It wasn't his fault that he lacked red blood in his brain, or that he had formed the habit, from long association with abnormal phenomena, of regarding all life as a disease. He was the sort of physician—every nurse will understand what I mean—who deals instinctively with groups instead of with individuals. He was long and solemn and very round in the face; and I hadn't talked to him ten minutes before I knew he had been educated in Germany, and that he had learned over there to treat every emotion as a pathological manifestation. I used to wonder what he got out of life —what any one got out of life who had analyzed away everything except the bare structure.

When I reached my room at last, I was so tired that I could barely remember either the questions Doctor Brandon had asked or the directions he had given me. I fell asleep, I know, almost as soon as my head touched the pillow; and the maid who came to inquire if I wanted luncheon decided to let me finish my nap. In the afternoon, when she returned with a cup of tea, she found me still heavy and drowsy. Though I was used to night nursing, I felt as if I had danced from sunset to daybreak. It was fortunate, I reflected, while I drank my tea, that every case didn't wear on one's sympathies as acutely as Mrs. Maradick's hallucination had worn on mine.

Through the day I did not see Doctor Maradick; but at seven o'clock when I came up from my early dinner on my way to take the place of Miss Peterson, who had kept on duty an hour later than usual, he met me in the hall and asked me to come into his study. I thought him handsomer than ever in his evening clothes, with a white flower in his buttonhole. He was going to some public dinner, the housekeeper told me, but, then, he was always going somewhere. I believe he didn't dine at home a single evening that winter.

"Did Mrs. Maradick have a good night?" He had closed the door after us, and turning now with the question, he smiled kindly, as if he wished to put me at ease in the beginning.

"She slept very well after she took the medicine. I gave her that at eleven o'clock."

For a minute he regarded me silently, and I was aware that his personality—his charm—was focussed upon me. It was almost as if I stood in the centre of converging rays of light, so vivid was my impression of him.

"Did she allude in any way to her—to her hallucination?" he asked.

How the warning reached me—what invisible waves of sense-perception transmitted the message—I have never known; but while I stood there, facing the splendour of the doctor's presence, every intuition cautioned me that the time had come when I must take sides in the household. While I stayed there I must stand either with Mrs. Maradick or against her.

"She talked quite rationally," I replied after a moment.

"What did she say?"

"She told me how she was feeling, that she missed her child, and that she walked a little every day about her room."

His face changed—how I could not at first determine.

"Have you seen Doctor Brandon?"

"He came this morning to give me his directions."

"He thought her less well to-day. He has advised me to send her to Rosedale."

I have never, even in secret, tried to account for Doctor Maradick. He may have been sincere. I tell only what I know —not what I believe or imagine—and the human is sometimes as inscrutable, as inexplicable, as the supernatural.

While he watched me I was conscious of an inner struggle, as if opposing angels warred somewhere in the depths of my being. When at last I made my decision, I was acting less from reason, I knew, than in obedience to the pressure of some secret current of thought. Heaven knows, even then, the man held me captive while I defied him.

"Doctor Maradick," I lifted my eyes for the first time frankly to his, "I believe that your wife is as sane as I am—or as you are."

He started. "Then she did not talk freely to you?"

"She may be mistaken, unstrung, piteously distressed in mind"—I brought this out with emphasis—"but she is not—I am willing to stake my future on it—a fit subject for an asylum. It would be foolish—it would be cruel to send her to Rosedale."

"Cruel, you say?" A troubled look crossed his face, and his voice grew very gentle. "You do not imagine that I could be cruel to her?"

"No, I do not think that." My voice also had softened.

"We will let things go on as they are. Perhaps Doctor Brandon may have some other suggestion to make." He drew out his watch and compared it with the clock—nervously, I observed, as if his action were a screen for his discomfiture or perplexity. "I must be going now. We will speak of this again in the morning."

But in the morning we did not speak of it, and during the month that I nursed Mrs. Maradick I was not called again into her husband's study. When I met him in the hall or on the staircase, which was seldom, he was as charming as ever; yet, in spite of his courtesy, I had a persistent feeling that he had taken my measure on that evening, and that he had no further use for me.

As the days went by Mrs. Maradick seemed to grow stronger.

Never, after our first night together, had she mentioned the child to me; never had she alluded by so much as a word to her dreadful charge against her husband. She was like any woman recovering from a great sorrow, except that she was sweeter and gentler. It is no wonder that everyone who came near her loved her; for there was a mysterious loveliness about her like the mystery of light, not of darkness. She was, I have always thought, as much of an angel as it is possible for a woman to be on this earth. And yet, angelic as she was, there were times when it seemed to me that she both hated and feared her husband. Though he never entered her room while I was there, and I never heard his name on her lips until an hour before the end, still I could tell by the look of terror in her face whenever his step passed down the hall that her very soul shivered at his approach.

During the whole month I did not see the child again, though one night, when I came suddenly into Mrs. Maradick's room, I found a little garden, such as children make out of pebbles and bits of box, on the window-sill. I did not mention it to Mrs. Maradick, and a little later, as the maid lowered the shades, I noticed that the garden had vanished. Since then I have often wondered if the child were invisible only to the rest of us, and if her mother still saw her. But there was no way of finding out except by questioning, and Mrs. Maradick was so well and patient that I hadn't the heart to question. Things couldn't have been better with her than they were, and I was beginning to tell myself that she might soon go out for an airing, when the end came so suddenly.

It was a mild January day—the kind of day that brings the fore-taste of spring in the middle of winter, and when I came down-stairs in the afternoon, I stopped a minute by the window at the end of the hall to look down on the box maze in the garden. There was an old fountain, bearing two laughing boys in marble, in the centre of the gravelled walk, and the water, which had been turned on that morning for Mrs. Maradick's pleasure, sparkled now like silver as the sunlight splashed over it. I had never before felt the air quite so soft and springlike in January; and I thought, as I gazed down on the garden, that it would be a good idea for Mrs. Maradick to go out and bask for an hour or so in the sunshine. It seemed strange to me that she was never allowed to get any fresh air except the air that came through her windows.

When I went into her room, however, I found that she had no wish to go out. She was sitting, wrapped in shawls, by the open window, which looked down on the fountain; and as I entered she glanced up from a little book she was reading. A pot of daffodils stood on the window-sill—she was very fond of flowers and we tried always to keep some growing in her room.

"Do you know what I am reading, Miss Randolph?" she asked in her soft voice; and she read aloud a verse while I went over to the candle-stand to measure out a dose of medicine.

" 'If thou hast two loaves of bread, sell one and buy daffodils, for bread nourisheth the body, but daffodils delight the soul.' That is very beautiful, don't you think so?"

I said "Yes," that it was beautiful; and then I asked her if she wouldn't go downstairs and walk about in the garden.

"He wouldn't like it," she answered; and it was the first time she had mentioned her husband to me since the night I came to her. "He doesn't want me to go out."

I tried to laugh her out of the idea; but it was no use, and after a few minutes I gave up and began talking of other things. Even then it did not occur to me that her fear of Doctor Maradick was anything but a fancy. I could see, of course, that she wasn't out of her head; but sane persons, I knew, sometimes have unaccountable prejudices, and I accepted her dislike as a mere whim or aversion. I did not understand then and—I may as well confess this before the end comes—I do not understand any better to-day. I am writing down the things I actually saw, and I repeat that I have never had the slightest twist in the direction of the miraculous.

The afternoon slipped away while we talked—she talked brightly when any subject came up that interested her—and it was the last hour of day—that grave, still hour when the movement of life seems to droop and falter for a few precious minutes—that brought us the thing I had dreaded silently since my first night in the house. I remember that I had risen to close the window, and was leaning out for a breath of the mild air, when there was the sound of steps, consciously softened, in the hall outside, and Doctor Brandon's usual knock fell on my ears. Then, before I could cross the room, the door opened, and the doctor entered with Miss Peterson. The day nurse, I knew, was a stupid woman; but she had never appeared to me so stupid, so armoured and encased in her professional manner, as she did at that moment.

"I am glad to see that you are taking the air." As Doctor Brandon came over to the window, I wondered maliciously what devil of contradictions had made him a distinguished specialist in nervous diseases.

"Who was the other doctor you brought this morning?" asked Mrs. Maradick gravely; and that was all I ever heard about the visit of the second alienist.

"Someone who is anxious to cure you." He dropped into a chair beside her and patted her hand with his long, pale fingers. "We are so anxious to cure you that we want to send you away to the country for a fortnight or so. Miss Peterson has come to help you to get ready, and I've kept my car waiting for you. There couldn't be a nicer day for a trip, could there?"

The moment had come at last. I knew at once what he meant, and so did Mrs. Maradick. A wave of colour flowed and ebbed in her thin cheeks, and I felt her body quiver when I moved from the window and put my arms on her shoulders. I was aware again, as I had been aware that evening in Doctor Maradick's study, of a current of thought that beat from the air around into my brain. Though it cost me my career as a nurse and my reputation for sanity, I knew that I must obey that invisible warning.

"You are going to take me to an asylum," said Mrs. Maradick.

He made some foolish denial or evasion; but before he had finished I turned from Mrs. Maradick and faced him impulsively. In a nurse this was flagrant rebellion, and I realized that the act wrecked my professional future. Yet I did not care—I did not hesitate. Something stronger than I was driving me on.

"Doctor Brandon," I said, "I beg you—I implore you to wait until to-morrow. There are things I must tell you."

A queer look came into his face, and I understood, even in

my excitement, that he was mentally deciding in which group he should place me—to which class of morbid manifestations I must belong.

"Very well, very well, we will hear everything," he replied soothingly; but I saw him glance at Miss Peterson, and she went over to the wardrobe for Mrs. Maradick's fur coat and hat.

Suddenly, without warning, Mrs. Maradick threw the shawls away from her, and stood up. "If you send me away," she said, "I shall never come back. I shall never live to come back."

The grey of twilight was just beginning, and while she stood there, in the dusk of the room, her face shone out as pale and flower-like as the daffodils on the window-sill. "I cannot go away!" she cried in a sharper voice. "I cannot go away from my child!"

I saw her face clearly; I heard her voice; and then—the horror of the scene sweeps back over me!—I saw the door open slowly and the little girl run across the room to her mother. I saw the child lift her little arms, and I saw the mother stoop and gather her to her bosom. So closely locked were they in that passionate embrace that their forms seemed to mingle in the gloom that enveloped them.

"After this can you doubt?" I threw out the words almost savagely—and then, when I turned from the mother and child to Doctor Brandon and Miss Peterson, I knew breathlessly— oh, there was a shock in the discovery!—that they were blind to the child. Their blank faces revealed the consternation of ignorance, not of conviction. They had seen nothing except the vacant arms of the mother and the swift, erratic gesture with which she stooped to embrace some invisible presence. Only my vision—and I have asked myself since if the power of sympathy enabled me to penetrate the web of material fact and see the spiritual form of the child—only my vision was not blinded by the clay through which I looked.

"After this can you doubt?" Doctor Brandon had flung my words back to me. Was it his fault, poor man, if life had granted him only the eyes of flesh? Was it his fault if he could see only half of the thing there before him?

But they couldn't see, and since they couldn't see I realized that it was useless to tell them. Within an hour they took Mrs.

Maradick to the asylum; and she went quietly, though when the time came for parting from me she showed some faint trace of feeling. I remember that at the last, while we stood on the pavement, she lifted her black veil, which she wore for the child, and said: "Stay with her, Miss Randolph, as long as you can. I shall never come back."

Then she got into the car and was driven off, while I stood looking after her with a sob in my throat. Dreadful as I felt it to be, I didn't, of course, realize the full horror of it, or I couldn't have stood there quietly on the pavement. I didn't realize it, indeed, until several months afterwards when word came that she had died in the asylum. I never knew what her illness was, though I vaguely recall that something was said about "heart failure"—a loose enough term. My own belief is that she died simply of the terror of life.

To my surprise Doctor Maradick asked me to stay on as his office nurse after his wife went to Rosedale; and when the news of her death came there was no suggestion of my leaving. I don't know to this day why he wanted me in the house. Perhaps he thought I should have less opportunity to gossip if I stayed under his roof; perhaps he still wished to test the power of his charm over me. His vanity was incredible in so great a man. I have seen him flush with pleasure when people turned to look at him in the street, and I know that he was not above playing on the sentimental weakness of his patients. But he was magnificent, heaven knows! Few men, I imagine, have been the objects of so many foolish infatuations.

The next summer Doctor Maradick went abroad for two months, and while he was away I took my vacation in Virginia. When we came back the work was heavier than ever—his reputation by this time was tremendous—and my days were so crowded with appointments, and hurried flittings to emergency cases, that I had scarcely a minute left in which to remember poor Mrs. Maradick. Since the afternoon when she went to the asylum the child had not been in the house; and at last I was beginning to persuade myself that the little figure had been an optical illusion—the effect of shifting lights in the gloom of the old rooms—not the apparition I had once believed it to be. It does not take long for a phantom to fade from the memory—especially when one leads the active and methodical life I was forced into that winter. Perhaps—who knows?—(I remember telling myself) the doctors may have been right, after all, and the poor lady may have actually been out of her mind. With this view of the past, my judgment of Doctor Maradick insensibly altered. It ended, I think, in my acquitting him altogether. And then, just as he stood clear and splendid in my verdict of him, the reversal came so precipitately that I grow breathless now whenever I try to live it over again. The violence of the next turn in affairs left me, I often fancy, with a perpetual dizziness of the imagination.

It was in May that we heard of Mrs. Maradick's death, and exactly a year later, on a mild and fragrant afternoon, when the daffodils were blooming in patches around the old fountain in the garden, the housekeeper came into the office, where I lingered over some accounts, to bring me news of the doctor's approaching marriage.

"It is no more than we might have expected," she concluded rationally. "The house must be lonely for him—he is such a sociable man. But I can't help feeling," she brought out slowly after a pause in which I felt a shiver pass over me, "I can't help feeling that it is hard for that other woman to have all the money poor Mrs. Maradick's first husband left her."

"There is a great deal of money, then?" I asked curiously.

"A great deal." She waved her hand, as if words were futile to express the sum. "Millions and millions!"

"They will give up this house, of course?"

"That's done already, my dear. There won't be a brick left of it by this time next year. It's to be pulled down and an apartment-house built on the ground."

Again the shiver passed over me. I couldn't bear to think of Mrs. Maradick's old home falling to pieces.

"You didn't tell me the name of the bride," I said. "Is she someone he met while he was in Europe?"

"Dear me, no! She is the very lady he was engaged to before he married Mrs. Maradick, only she threw him over, so people said, because he wasn't rich enough. Then she married some lord or prince from over the water; but there was a divorce, and now she has turned again to her old lover. He is rich enough now, I guess, even for her!"

It was all perfectly true, I suppose; it sounded as plausible as a story out of a newspaper; and yet while she told me I felt, or dreamed that I felt, a sinister, an impalpable hush in the air. I was nervous, no doubt; I was shaken by the suddenness with which the housekeeper had sprung her news on me; but as I sat there I had quite vividly an impression that the old house was listening—that there was a real, if invisible, presence somewhere in the room or the garden. Yet, when an instant afterwards I glanced through the long window which opened down to the brick terrace, I saw only the faint sunshine over the deserted garden, with its maze of box, its marble fountain, and its patches of daffodils.

The housekeeper had gone—one of the servants, I think, came for her—and I was sitting at my desk when the words of Mrs. Maradick on that last evening floated into my mind. The daffodils brought her back to me; for I thought, as I watched them growing, so still and golden in the sunshine, how she would have enjoyed them. Almost unconsciously I repeated the verse she had read to me:

"If thou hast two loaves of bread, sell one and buy daffodils" —and it was at this very instant, while the words were still on my lips, that I turned my eyes to the box maze, and saw the child skipping rope along the gravelled path to the fountain. Quite distinctly, as clear as day, I saw her come, with what children call the dancing step, between the low box borders to the place where the daffodils bloomed by the fountain. From her straight brown hair to her frock of Scotch plaid and her little feet, which twinkled in white socks and black slippers over the turning rope, she was as real to me as the ground on which she trod or the laughing marble boys under the splashing water. Starting up from my chair, I made a single step to the terrace. If I could only reach her—only speak to her—I felt that I might at last solve the mystery. But with the first flutter of my dress on the terrace, the airy little form melted into the quiet dusk of the maze. Not a breath stirred the daffodils, not a shadow passed over the sparkling flow of the water; yet, weak and shaken in every nerve, I sat down on the brick step of the terrace and burst into tears. I must have known that something terrible would happen before they pulled down Mrs. Maradick's home.

The doctor dined out that night. He was with the lady he

was going to marry, the housekeeper told me; and it must have been almost midnight when I heard him come in and go upstairs to his room. I was downstairs because I had been unable to sleep, and the book I wanted to finish I had left that afternoon in the office. The book—I can't remember what it was—had seemed to me very exciting when I began it in the morning; but after the visit of the child I found the romantic novel as dull as a treatise on nursing. It was impossible for me to follow the lines, and I was on the point of giving up and going to bed, when Doctor Maradick opened the front door with his latch-key and went up the staircase. "There can't be a bit of truth in it," I thought over and over again as I listened to his even step ascending the stairs. "There can't be a bit of truth in it." And yet, though I assured myself that "there couldn't be a bit of truth in it," I shrank, with a creepy sensation, from going through the house to my room in the third storey. I was tired out after a hard day, and my nerves must have reacted morbidly to the silence and the darkness. For the first time in my life I knew what it was to be afraid of the unknown, of the unseen; and while I bent over my book, in the glare of the electric light, I became conscious presently that I was straining my senses for some sound in the spacious emptiness of the rooms overhead. The noise of a passing motor-car in the street jerked me back from the intense hush of expectancy; and I can recall the wave of relief that swept over me as I turned to my book again and tried to fix my distracted mind on its pages.

I was still sitting there when the telephone on my desk rang, with what seemed to my overwrought nerves a startling abruptness, and the voice of the superintendent told me hurriedly that Doctor Maradick was needed at the hospital. I had become so accustomed to these emergency calls in the night that I felt reassured when I had rung up the doctor in his room and had heard the hearty sound of his response. He had not yet undressed, he said, and would come down immediately while I ordered back his car, which must just have reached the garage.

"I'll be with you in five minutes!" he called as cheerfully as if I had summoned him to his wedding.

I heard him cross the floor of his room; and before he could reach the head of the staircase, I opened the door and went out into the hall in order that I might turn on the light and have his hat and coat waiting. The electric button was at the end of the hall, and as I moved towards it, guided by the glimmer that fell from the landing above, I lifted my eyes to the staircase, which climbed dimly, with its slender mahogany balustrade, as far as the third storey. Then it was, at the very moment when the doctor, humming gaily, began his quick descent of the steps, that I distinctly saw—I will swear to this on my deathbed—a child's skipping-rope lying loosely coiled, as if it had dropped from a careless little hand, in the bend of the staircase. With a spring I had reached the electric button, flooding the hall with light; but as I did so, while my arm was still outstretched behind me, I heard the humming voice change to a cry of surprise or terror, and the figure on the staircase tripped heavily and stumbled with groping hands into emptiness. The scream of warning died in my throat while I watched him pitch forward down the long flight of stairs to the floor at my feet. Even before I bent over him, before I wiped the blood from his brow and felt for his silent heart, I knew that he was dead.

Something—it may have been, as the world believes, a misstep in the dimness, or it may have been, as I am ready to bear witness, an invisible judgment—something had killed him at the very moment when he most wanted to live.

1916

JULIAN HAWTHORNE

(1846–1934)

Absolute Evil

I

I was half-way between twenty and thirty when I joined the
Pleasances' house-boat party on their adventure to Thirteen-
Mile Beach. Nobody—no society women, at any rate—had been
there before, and we called ourselves pioneers.

What made it our objective was the tale of its being
haunted. Haunted houses were a fashionable subject of polite
investigation at that period; and to test out a haunted island
was an enterprise even more engaging.

Our route lay along that chain of sounds or inland seas
which extend from Chesapeake to below Hatteras. The island
was one of those long, narrow sand-bars that form outlying but-
tresses against Atlantic storms. That, apart from legend, was all
that any of us knew about it at starting. And even legend did
not inform us by whom it was haunted, or why.

Two years after our expedition I was led by circumstances,
chiefly subjective, to repeat the trip; this time alone. It is of this
last occasion that I am to tell you; but first I must say a little
more about our pioneering.

II

The house-boat belonged to the Pleasances, very nice, middle-
aged Philadelphia people, of Quaker stock, but reconciled to
the world, while still retaining between each other their thee-
and-thy locution. They were rich, of course, and childless; but
they brought along their ward, Ann Marlowe, a pretty girl of
demure bearing, but with fire in her eye.

To amuse her came Jack Peters, a gilded youth of that
epoch, with many suits of wonderful clothes, including two
yachting-suits, in anticipation of maritime vicissitudes.

Of somewhat older years than Jack was Topham Brent, an old friend of my own, already a distinguished surgeon. Topham ought not to have come, for I had refused his offer of marriage not long before; but he was of the persistent sort, and, I admit, the finest sort of fellow.

Then there was the Rev. Nathaniel Tyler, a young New England divine, high-bred and learned, with a fine pulpit reputation, but suffering from nervous breakdown, owing to too assiduous study, no doubt. This did not prevent him from being very seriously interested in me, and we spent much of our time in intimate conversations about original sin and esoteric philosophy, with sentiment never far off; while Topham rambled about the craft, smoking cigars and trying to look indifferent.

Finally, there was myself, Martha Klemm, a handsome spinster, of the Beacon Street, Boston, brand. After this rather long interval I am a spinster still.

The house-boat was sixty or seventy feet long and more than half as wide, luxuriously decorated and furnished, with a chef and two other servants, and an inexhaustible supply of good things to eat and drink. Philadelphia Quakers know how to live.

III

I was interested in original sin, and had dabbled in esoteric philosophy; my remote ancestors had been Salem witches. So, on these grounds at least, I was ready to meet Nat Tyler half-way.

He was magnetic, fine-looking, and anything but a fool. He was tall, spare, dark-browed, with deep-set, gray eyes rather near together. His long hands were very sensitive and expressive. His lips were thin, but sharply curved, implying eloquence and secret voluptuousness. There was a conspicuous black mole on his left cheek, close to the furrow that went from the arched nostril to the corner of the mouth. His voice was a deep barytone, agreeably modulated, with reserves of power. I had heard him preach, and he could send forth notes like an organ.

Every once in a while something peeped forth from the shadows of those eyes of his that made me jump—interiorly, of

course; I was woman of the world enough to betray nothing.
It was as if somebody I knew very well had suddenly peeped
out at me from a window in a strange place, where that face
was the last I should have expected to see.

It seemed to have nothing to do with the personality of Nat
Tyler himself; he was a clergyman, and this was suggestive of
anything but divinity. It conveyed a profound, fascinating
wickedness. It was as old as the pyramids, yet riotous with vitality. Perhaps I ought not to speak in this way of a thing which
belonged to imagination; this reverend young gentleman's life
had always been open as daylight, and more than blameless—
apostolic. His family was as old-established as my own, and I
had known of him long, though our first personal meeting was
recent.

Nothing diabolic, therefore, could justly be inferred from
what I have mentioned. Call it just a grotesque notion of mine.
I'm sure nobody but I had noticed it, not even Topham Brent,
who might have been not unwilling to detect anything objectionable in my reverend crony.

Topham was not so wise then as he is now, and may not
have known that women are often attracted by what ought to
repel them—some women! I confess I was on the lookout for
that satanic drama in Tyler's eyes, and enjoyed the little fillip it
gave me. By no word or gesture did Tyler himself betray consciousness of his peculiarity.

We discovered that we both had queer books—antique lore
about witchcraft and the like. This gave us common ground,
and, what was more to the point, uncommon, too.

Imagine us side by side in our reclining chairs on a moonlight evening, with the calm, watery expanse far and near, and
a dark line of low shore on the horizon. Yonder the red, reflected light of a fisherman's dory; around one corner of the
deck-house the giggle and babble of Jack Peters entertaining
Ann, and her brief rejoinders; round the other occasional
smoke-drifts from the excellent cigar Topham was smoking;
inside the house was the placid silence of the benign old Pleasances reading magazines to themselves.

Tyler, in his agreeable murmur, is speculating in my ear on
the origin of evil.

"Thomas Aquinas says that angels, white and black, can

change men into beasts permanently; enchanters could do it, too, but not for long. Seventeenth century witchcraft affirmed that certain natural objects and rites could produce strange effects without aid of God or devil. But the operator must renounce God and Christ, be re-baptised, trample on the cross, and be marked in a certain way—a symbolic transaction. The person could then do only evil—good was forbidden to him, or her!"

"Do you believe people can be changed into beasts?" I inquired, as if we were talking of the weather to-morrow.

"Spiritually, I know they can be, and we often notice the resemblance of some one to an animal. Well, if, as the poet Spencer says, 'Soul is form and doth the body make,' why mightn't the body of a man with the soul of a hog assume, under favorable conditions, hoggish lineaments?"

"I wonder. But what are the favorable conditions?"

"His own persistent will, or dominating suggestion from another."

Here there was the creaking of a chair and Jack came grinning round the corner.

"Say, parson, here's Ann says there are ghosts, and I'll leave it to you; are there?"

Ann, with her inscrutable smile, appeared in the background.

"Ghosts, yes; but can we see them?" returned Tyler. "Ask Dr. Brent?"

"How about it, doc?" Jack called out.

"We're on our way to Thirteen-Mile Beach to find out," answered Topham's voice, with a whiff of cigar-smoke.

"I'll bet a dozen pairs of gloves to a cigarette we don't see one."

Mr. Pleasance put his head out of the window.

"Quarter of twelve, folks; wife and I are going to bed."

"Run along, Mr. Peters," said Ann.

The currents were mixed, and we all stood up. Tyler and I, however, found ourselves leaning over the taffrail at the front of our old vehicle, as it slowly pushed its way through the liquid wilderness. The moonlight fell upon his aquiline features, as he faced toward me, and I involuntarily watched for Satan.

"I wish we could have met sooner," he remarked. "I have

longed for stimulus and companionship in my researches; such things are perilous when one goes alone. The absolute evil!— is there such a thing? Until we know, how can we understand and combat it?"

"The difficulty seems to be," I said, "that those who know it don't care to combat it. We'll assume, for the sake of argument, that witches really existed, as well as ghosts. But, for my part, I don't feel sure that we ought to combat it—that is, if we felt any assurance of extirpating it. Evil is as necessary an ingredient of life as red pepper is of an epicure's menu—it stimulates one to enjoy the banquet of life."

Out peeped Beelzebub for a moment. "You are incomparable!" murmured the parson.

"It's a fine night for a broomstick ride," I said; "but we'd better go in."

" 'The bridal of the earth and sky!'" he quoted, from Herbert, I think, looking round admiringly on the tranquil prospect. When he turned back the devil had vanished, and we went inside like two Christians.

IV

No place to compare with a house-boat for being bored, or for a flirtation, has been invented; and when the youth of one flirtation is complicated by the animated corpse of a former one, the resources of the situation might keep anyone awake. But I shall not adduce further illustrations; and I am free to confess that although I afforded my reverend friend adequate opportunities, he did not come to a technical issue. Something kept him back at the critical juncture; whether it was Satan, or whether Satan lacked power to bring on the avowal, I won't decide.

Or maybe that the fatuity of poor Jack being slowly eviscerated by that demure little devil of an Ann Marlowe deterred me from putting forth all my spells; or, possibly, it may have been a stroke of altruistic conscience about Topham Brent, who vainly and intemperately sought an anodyne in tobacco.

Howbeit, neither Ann nor I was engaged when we arrived at Thirteen-Mile Beach and set forth in quest of the ghost.

All we found there was endless prolongation of sand, with a

low backbone of tussocks tufted with beach-grass, and a few groups of storm-stunted cedars. Nothing seemed farther from any taint of the supernatural as we four young people tramped hither and yon, and the Pleasance pair sat in their beach-chairs and contemplated the incoming or withdrawing tides.

The place was not wholly destitute of incarnate human beings, however. I must give a word to the Duckworths.

What a spot for a man to bring his bride to! Old Tom Duckworth had been a sailor originally, and after giving up the Seven Seas had become a sort of beach-comber. He had put together a hut on the highest part of the beach, at its hither end; had fished the Sound and the ocean, and had salvaged flotsam and jetsam from wrecks, of which there was always a tolerable supply after a gale. He had a little garden, and kept goats, pigs, and poultry. And there he dwelt in a solitude more unmitigated than Alexander Selkirk's.

One or twice a year, though, he rowed across the ten miles of Sound, and made his way to a neighboring town for provisions.

And it chanced, on an excursion of this kind, that he encountered an elderly female.

Jane—I never learned her maiden name—had been a schoolteacher in the vicinity for half a lifetime, but had been recently retired by the school board in favor of some younger and postdiluvian rival. She was thrown upon her own resources, which was exactly nothing, for either from inability or from moral principle she had contracted no debts.

Tom proposed marriage, she accepted him; and here they were, and for the past ten years had been, contented with their environment and each other.

Tom had added to his mansion (made of old ships' timbers) two more rooms, and a fence circumventing the building, five feet high, and sunk at least as far into the sand, as a protection against storm-tides. The enclosure was about forty feet square; the pigs had their sty, and the goats and the hens wandered at will.

I once spent a summer at Étretat, on the Normandy coast, where the old sailors' huts are made of overturned boats with windows cut in the sides, a flue sticking up at one end, and a hole at the other by way of a door. They have been painted by

a thousand artists, but were less picturesque than Tom Duckworth's contrivance. Within, the rooms were kept rigorously
neat by Jane, and she did much useful domestic knitting in addition to her other household duties.

They were a healthy, wholesome old couple, and may have
been more than a hundred and twenty years old, combined.
They had no children, and both seemed to be sorry for it.

After a first shyness they allowed us to become well acquainted with them. You might think there wasn't much of
them or theirs for us to get acquainted with; but the natures of
solitary people are apt to have more unmapped country in
them than worldly folk imagine. They see and think and do
things peculiar to themselves, and one may turn up buried
treasure in them at any moment.

Our house-boat was moored off their garden for three days
while we explored the island. Sea, sand, and sky—that was all,
a portentous, desolate monotony. But I began to feel the spell
of it, and so, I think, did Tyler.

On our last day he and I, both good walkers, tramped to the
other end of the island and back, a long twenty-five miles. We
had gone pretty deep into each other's minds before we returned; but, as I said, nothing ever took place. Our only substantial discovery was another hut, or shack, perched on a
hummock in a kind of marsh near the southern extremity of
the beach. It was uninhabited.

Tyler observed: "What a chance for a hermit!"

The Duckworths told us on our return that legend said it
had been occupied many years before by a fugitive negro murderer, and was supposed to be haunted. So here was what we
had come for, after all!

But the dear old Pleasances wanted to be heading for Philadelphia, and it was agreed that Jack had won his cigarettes by
default. A twenty-five-mile journey and a night in the shack
was voted to be too high a price to pay to decide the problem
of the supernatural. We left the ghost on the fence.

At Beaufort, on our way back, we met our forwarded mail,
and Tyler, after reading his, said he would have to leave us
there and get home by rail.

"I hope, Martha," he said, as he held my hand at parting—

we had got as far as first names—"that we may soon meet again, and arrive at more definite conclusions."

"As to the origin of evil?" I inquired with simplicity.

I felt his eyes for a moment, but I happened to be facing the sun, and could not be sure whether or not that interesting hobby of his made its appearance.

"So far as I am concerned," he replied after a little, "intimacy with you could be only a source of good."

It was a clever turn, and now I saw that his glance was as innocent as a child's. Topham, with his broad shoulders and square face, was puffing his cigar near by, leaning back against the rail and looking quite happy. He was to stick to the ship until the last. Jack, who was dejected, suddenly resolved to accompany Tyler, and his two big trunks and four suit-cases went over the side, Ann Marlowe looking serenely on. She afterwards married Philip Bramwell, a banker of fifty.

Between Topham and me during the rest of the voyage, nothing important transpired. In Boston I learned that the Rev. Nathaniel Tyler had resigned his pastorate, and would spend some years in Europe, especially Palestine.

I had meditations over that news, but could make nothing of it. I dreamed of him several times, vividly, a most unusual thing for me. In these dreams we were always traveling somewhere at great speed, I reluctantly, he with eagerness. We never arrived.

I will end this prologue, as I might term it, here. After two years I went back to Thirteen-Mile Beach, alone, and making no one privy to my destination.

V

Not only did I tell no one, not even Topham, where I was going, but I could not myself reasonably account for my escapade. If you are indulging the notion that some hypnotic influence was involved, dismiss it immediately.

I have said that I am a descendant of witches. My exterior motive was an intense craving for solitude. Many good-looking and affluent young women in society might feel the same, after too much social dissipation. I thought of that endless, desolate beach with a longing which at last became irresistible.

It did not occur to me that absence of human companionship does not assure solitude. It may, on the contrary, plunge one into an environment compared with which New York or London would appear deserts. For we take memory and imagination with us. The seabirds that scream overhead or waddle along the margins of the surf; the grotesque forms of twisted cedars; the rustle of sea-grass in the wind; the interminable percussion of the breakers; the dead infinity of the sand itself—there can be no solitude, in the sense of freedom from disturbances of thought, in the presence of such things. They draw us back into the maelstrom.

I meant to spend a month on Thirteen-Mile Beach, and sent a message to the Duckworths asking shelter with them, and naming the date of my arrival. Should they refuse it—which I was confident they would not—I was prepared to camp out on the sands; the weather was warm and I was hardy.

I remitted money to cover extra expenses for board and lodging. I took with me a trunk full of necessities, my bicycle (a chainless one), and a revolver; not for self-defense, but I am a good shot, and might amuse myself by practising at the gulls.

After leaving the train I had to drive forty miles in an open wagon over the preposterous roads; and then, not finding Duckworth as I had expected, was obliged to hunt up a local clam-digger and get him to row me across. He explained Duckworth's failure to appear; the poor fellow had been drowned in a great storm that winter. But Jane, he said, was still there, and he believed there was "a little gal" with her.

It was near sunset when the dory stuck its nose in the mud at the end of the Duckworths' thin-legged little pier. Jane was waiting there; she had seen our approach from afar. She greeted me with a sober countenance and words, but the grip of her lean old hand was expressive of a dreary kind of satisfaction. I asked if the young woman could help us up with the trunk. She stared; young woman?

Just then the gate of the fence was pushed open, and a child of four came trudging down the path. I understood.

My clam-digger got his bony back under the trunk and

plodded up with it. Jane had made ready my room for me; she gave the clam-digger a slice of pork and some baked beans as refreshment after his trip. I glanced at myself in the crooked bit of looking-glass and shook down my hair and combed it out, and changed my traveling-dress for a jersey and a pair of loose knee-breeches, which was to be my costume in this retirement, and then came into the combination kitchen and sitting-room to drink a dish of tea, as Jane called it.

The little gal stood between my knees all the while and stared up in my face. She had taken to me at first sight, and was interested in my black stream of hair. When I asked her name she puffed out her mouth and said something like "Puhd!" Jane explained:

"I named her Perdita; she was lost, you see, and my Tom, he was lost getting her ashore."

The child was sturdy, and had thick, yellow hair, cut square off at the back, like a fourteenth century page's.

My room being on the side of the sea, I had already seen through the window the ribs of the wrecked vessel—a schooner —sticking up outside the breakers and deeply embedded in the sand. Jane told me the story, not consecutively, but a little now and then, day after day. The gale—"Tom called it a hurricane, and I reckon he knew"—had blown two days, and the evening of the third was approaching when the vessel was sighted, driving straight on the beach, only the stumps of the masts left, and nobody, as it turned out, on board.

When she struck, the wind stopped, as if it had done its job and quit. The surf was too high to go out to her, however; the clouds broke away overhead, and the full moon shone down, it being then midnight.

As the two old people stood watching, Jane had fancied she heard a sound of crying from the wreck—the crying of a child. Tom had finally agreed he heard something, too, in the intervals of the breakers. He got out his old binoculars, but could make out nothing on the deck; but the name of the vessel, painted in white letters on her bows, was discernible—"Jane— New Orleans."

"Tom looks at me," said the old woman, "and says he: 'Jane —and a child crying! Looks like the Lord sent us a baby, after all!' And when that idee struck him, Miss Klemm, there was nothing could hold him. 'Tide's goin' out,' says he, 'and sea calmin' down; I got to get that kid!'"

The stout old mariner brought out the life-belt and line, hitched one end of the line to the post and went in. Jane stood by the post and watched. Tom passed the breakers safely and struck out for the ship. He would disappear in the trough of the seas and then reappear when she thought him lost.

But as he approached the side of the vessel, which lay broadside-on, a big comber lapped over her from seaward and came on, bearing something with it from the deck. It was an impromptu raft, made of heavy timbers, and the child had been made fast to it. A corner of the structure, carried on the crest of the wave, was dashed against Tom Duckworth's head. Jane ran down into the froth of the breakers and received the raft, with the little child upon it, still living, and her husband's dead body.

I suppose such things are not uncommon on this treacherous coast. But what a simple, appalling drama! There was nothing dramatic in Jane's temperament, and no gift of expression but might have been beggared in portraying such a catastrophe. She told me the thing without emphasis or gesture—doing her knitting or stirring the contents of the saucepan on the kitchen stove. There had been no one present to sympathize with her agony—only the thunder of the waves upon the sand, the screaming sea-gulls, the moon staring down from the cloud-rifts.

She drew the body up beyond the reach of the waves, and took the child into the cabin, fed it, and warmed it. The next day men came over from the mainland.

"It wasn't any use hating the child; it wasn't to blame, so I got fond of it," she remarked. The Lord had sent it to her, a substitute for what He had taken away! That was her interpretation. Perdita was not a marvel of beauty, but she was an active, smiling, affectionate little thing, and kept Jane busy looking after her.

"She keeps the loneliness off," Jane observed.

VI

I took up my regimen of life immediately. The sand was hard and elastic, just the consistency for bicycle-riding. It was September, and warm for the season. I had the freedom of the island—nobody ever visited it. I would ride out before breakfast eight or ten miles down the beach, and then take a surf bath, unimpeded by a bathing-dress. Coming out I would get on my wheel again and enjoy a wild witch-ride to and fro till my skin was dry and glowing.

What a tonic for body and mind! No born savage could have had a tithe my delight in it. The sun, the sea, the sand, the gulls were my sole playmates. I would throw a long wreath of kelp over my shoulder and speed till it flew out behind me, mingling with the fluttering flag of my hair. Nature seems to welcome defiance of conventions, and to say, with a smile, 'So, the truant has come back again!'"

How men and women interfere with and imprison one another!

After breakfast and washing up the things, in which I collaborated with Jane, though she didn't wish it, I would go out and sprawl in the sun and play with Perdita and feed the pigs and chickens and have fun with the goat. An hour or two of this and then, with a little bundle of lunch at my belt, I would jump on the wheel again and be off till late afternoon. Dismounting, I would make ready for another bath of sun and air, if not of sea, and seldom resumed my riding-dress till it was time to go home.

It was not many days before I might have been taken for a wild Indian: I was golden brown from head to feet.

Why not live this way always? The thought of going back to Boston was intolerable! Nature and I were one thing.

One evening, after Perdita had been got to her crib and was asleep, and Jane and I were sitting beside the driftwood fire, and all was still except the deep, soft rhythm of the surf, a strange, remote sound came vibrating to my ears. Jane gave a slight movement, but did not look up from her knitting. The sound came again.

"Are there dogs on the island?" I asked.

"Best not notice it, Miss Klemm," said Jane; she seemed embarrassed. "Gulls, maybe."

This evasion roused my curiosity. No sea-bird could emit a call like that. It had reminded me of the coyotes, as I had heard them on the western deserts at night; but, of course, it couldn't be that! It must be a dog, running wild. But how had a dog got over here? Some man must have brought it; but the idea of a man coming to the island was disquieting. It would be an invasion of my liberties!

The sound came once more—now further off.

"Just not mind it—that's my plan," repeated Jane. "My mother, she was born in Ireland, and used to tell us about the banshee. I reckon this is something in that way. Nothing there —only the sound. I heard it first after Tom died!"

"Never before that?"

"No, miss; and if you're agreeable I'd sooner not talk of it. Things like that comes oftener if you worry about 'em."

"I thought you had more sense, Jane!" I said. "I know all about banshees; but we're not children—we're two women out here alone. A wild dog like that might kill one of your pigs or chickens. Besides, where there's a dog a man is apt to be not far off. The creature ought to be hunted down and killed, and I'll do it to-morrow!" I added, remembering my revolver at the bottom of my trunk. "Its howling is disagreeable, and its being here interferes with my privacy."

Jane heaved a sigh, and went on with her knitting in silence; and there was no further disturbance that night. Next morning there was a northerly wind, with gusts of rain, and I omitted my early ride. But going out, during an intermission of the showers, I met Perdita at the seaward gate of the palisade, crying lustily.

In explanation she pointed over to Tom Duckworth's grave, which had been made about thirty yards south of the enclosure; it was surrounded with a little picket, and Jane had planted flowers on it.

But mischief had been at work there the night before. The flowers had been violently dug up and scattered about, and a hole of some depth hollowed out, as if to get at what lay beneath. There were no marks of spade or pickax, but there were other traces that left no doubt as to the perpetrator—it was the howling beast of the foregoing evening. Perdita, going out to pluck a flower and finding the destruction, had been smitten with indignation and grief.

I would have kept knowledge of it from Jane, but the child's lamentations had drawn her out of the kitchen—she came, wiping her hands on her apron, and beheld the desecration. She stood rigid a minute, her meager old face twisted with horror; then her lips trembled, and she said, "I didn't know I'd an enemy in the world!"

"Enemy? It's that damned hound!" I answered in wrath. "Clear your imagination of enemies and banshees, woman. The plundering beast has lived too long."

But Jane's reticence being thus broken she became almost voluble, and her supernatural fears came out. The howling, she told me, had begun soon after Tom's death—it was an evil spirit! The physical attack upon the grave seemed to confirm her in that conviction. Once, she declared, when she had gone out at night to bring in a skirt that had been blown over the fence, and the thing had made a swoop at her through the air! No, not a gull, nor a hawk—no mortal creature went on such wings!

She didn't know whether the things were the souls of the folks that had been swept off the ship before she struck, and had been carried away in the sea and never had burial; or whether the persecution was aimed at poor Tom for something he might have done when he was a sailor before the mast; or whether it was something about Perdita, who had appeared miraculously, as one might say; or whether, finally, she herself were the person concerned.

In short, to my surprise, the old schoolmistress confessed herself a prey to the rankest superstition, and reason and ridicule were alike wasted on her. The only thing to do was to kill the dog and show her its remains.

The rain-clouds drifted away during the night, and the sun rose clear for a day of perfect beauty and radiance. I awoke betimes and hastened to get abroad, not delaying to delve into my trunk for the revolver; neither concrete dogs nor ghosts were likely to be out so early. I swept down the beach as swiftly as I could drive; reached the point where I was accustomed to take my dip, threw off my clothes and ran in, eager to feel the thrill of the breakers on my body.

I came out breathing hard and tingling with joy of life. I had been carried down some distance by the set of the current; and as I debouched beyond the reach of the sliding surf I saw something which startled me not a little—a man's bare footprint in the sand!

VII

Without staying to examine it, I scuttled to my jersey and breeches and huddled them on in a jiffy. Then my panic changed to anger: I regretted not having brought my revolver, and went back to investigate.

There were several of them; they emerged from below the surf line and proceeded diagonally inland till they were lost in the loose, grass-grown sand. The tide was ebbing; they might be two or three hours old. They were long and narrow.

Where was the man?

From the little elevation, where I now stood, the surface of the island was visible for miles in all directions; but no living creature was in sight. My eyes are good, and I could have seen any moving object in that clear atmosphere, with the sun standing an hour high above the sea at a great distance. Of course the fellow might be hiding behind one of the little clumps of cedars that dotted the expanse.

A man and a dog on my island! Howlings by night and footprints in the morning! There were no dog footprints, to be sure, but it was inevitable to associate the evidences to ear and eye. They must have a habitation—where was it?

I recalled, for the first time, the little abandoned shack at the further end of the island, said to have been the refuge of the negro murderer of old times. I had never yet ridden more than ten or twelve miles from the Duckworth cabin. Had the shack a new tenant? If so, he could hardly be a desirable neighbor. Thirteen miles was, indeed, a considerable distance to go and return, for a man, if not for a dog. But, if the man were a "wild man," distance might be no hindrance to him. There had been no indications, however, that he had accompanied his dog on the nocturnal excursions.

I was now much nearer his abode than the Duckworths.

I took another look at the footprints and noticed their great distance apart—more than five feet. Thirty inches is a good average stride for a man, walking on sand. The sixty-inch intervals showed that he must have been running. Perhaps there was nothing singular in that; but it gave me an unpleasant sensation—a naked man running insanely along the beach! But I laughed at myself—I was giving imagination too much rein. The tracks could not be traced more than thirty or forty yards, and a barefoot man is not necessarily bare all over. Possibly he had been merely taking a bath, like myself, and had run out of the water, as I had, under a natural stimulus.

After all, too, he had as much ostensible right to be on the island as I had.

Nevertheless—and I am sensitive to such impressions—there was an evil "vibration," as the saying is, from the footprints. And, at any rate, their presence destroyed my freedom. I determined to get my gun and explore. Meanwhile I would say nothing to Jane. She had enough to tax her nerves as it was!

As I rode home my fancy pictured a big, shambling negro, with an ugly dog, roaming about the place; an outlaw, doubtless, subsisting on clams—what else was there for him to eat? He must be ripe for robbery and violence. And to oppose him, two lone women and a child, forty miles from help! I was glad of my revolver.

On my arrival at the cabin I took a look at the place as a post of defense. The palisade completely surrounded it, and was five feet in height; made of massive pieces of ship-timber, planted deep and firm in the sand. This strength had been designed to resist the onset of the waves in case they should come up so far; but, of course, an athletic man could easily vault over it—unless he were shot down in the act!

The cabin itself was also very strongly constructed, as strong as an ordinary blockhouse. I was confident I could defend it against any single assailant, especially were he unarmed, as the negro would most likely be. A surprise assault was the thing to be guarded against. A small dog of our own would have been useful—to give the alarm at night. Perhaps we could procure one.

After breakfast I spent an hour cleaning my revolver and trying my skill at a target. Jane shook her head, probably thinking that bullets were vain against demonic powers. But Perdita was hugely delighted with the shining little instrument, and wanted it for a plaything; women of all ages will play with death! When

I fired it the explosion didn't frighten her; her little heart had never learned to tremble, but she couldn't grasp the connection between the sharp, sudden noise, and the hole in the plank thirty yards distant. I took a shot at a gull on the wing, and by chance cut a piece of a feather from its tail; Perdita shouted with astonishment and delight; it was wondrous magic to her.

About ten o'clock I mounted my wheel again and set off down the beach—the gun in my belt. In the broad sunshine, beside the sparkling sea, I felt secure and adventurous; after all, there was good New England fighting blood in my veins!

It was my purpose to ride to the end of the beach and take a look at the negro's shack. My apprehensions might prove groundless. The owner of the footprints might be a harmless hunter in quest of ducks, or even a wandering tourist on a vacation hike. Old Jane's supernatural gossip had perhaps caused me to take too romantic a view of the situation. I would solve the problem forthwith.

The tide, since my early excursion, had passed its low mark, and was now making again. But when I got to the place where I had bathed the footprints were still uncovered. They were three inches longer than my own beside them. The fellow must be immense!

I rode on slowly, pondering, but, under the genial moisture of exercise on my body, neither uneasy nor as much irritated as before. The Atlantic coast of the United States was long enough to accommodate two persons without crowding. Very likely this was the first, and would be the last time the invader would leave his trail on this part of it!

But a mile or so beyond I halted sharply. The trail again—and something more!

I dismounted. The footsteps, still indicating a running gait, came down toward the sea again; but after going parallel with the surf-line for a little began circling around, as if the crazy negro—such I now imagined him—were in a fit. Some of the prints were deep driven. At first I thought there were two sets of prints. But, no! All were made by the same pair of feet. The circuits they traced were narrow and irregular; the marks often crossed one another—a sort of insane dance.

But there was something else, and it turned me cold when I realized what it meant.

The footprints didn't go on beyond the general circle in any direction! Where, then, was the man—unless a balloon had swooped down and borne him away?

That was one bad thing; the other was quite as bad.

The human footprints were intermingled with others, not human—the marks of the four paws of an enormous dog! But this beast had not entered the circle from any point outside of it—at least, if he had, the man must have carried him in his arms. But this was unthinkable; and if the man had carried him in the beast had left the circle on its own foot, continuing at full speed down the beach, leaving behind it—what? Nothing at all!

I was armed, and am far from being a timorous person. But this weird thing crawled into my nerves with a sensation, compared with which the threat of impending death would have seemed trivial.

A man had entered that circle and had vanished there. A beast had run out of that circle without having entered it.

As I rode slowly homeward, beside the sparkling sea, under the cloudless sky, that was all I could make of it; and I didn't like it.

VIII

But the creeping paralysis of helpless dismay—helpless against I knew not what—presently changed into a passion of black anger. I would have it out with this thing and be done with it—one way or another. To flinch from it would be to lose nerve and self-respect forever.

At the cabin I was monosyllabic with Jane, and in no mood to respond to Perdita's invitations to play with her, or give her the shining toy to play with. I wanted to take counsel with myself—by myself. I would have dismissed even Topham Brent, though I was used to think of him as a counselor. I would rather have discussed the matter with that very different person, the Rev. Nathaniel Tyler, with whom, as I have said, I had ground in common.

Upon second thought, however, I dismissed him, too; he would be too refined and fastidious to take hold of this brutal event efficiently. I must deal with it alone!

But thinking about it only made it worse. I must act. I must hunt the enigma down, solve it, and destroy it, or be destroyed by it. Still I stayed in my room, unable to decide how to go about the adventure. I sat listening to the surf and to the gulls and to the occasional voices of the child and Jane; once or twice the rap of soft little knuckles came on my door, but I kept silence.

When, later, Jane summoned me to dinner, I declined to come out. I wasn't hungry, I told her; had a headache.

Through my uneasy preoccupation I was sensible by familiar sounds that Perdita was being put to bed. I had usually helped at this ceremony, and the child asked after me. "I want Aunt Martha"—such was my title in her list of friends. Jane and I were the only persons represented there. I had an impulse to go to her, but resisted it. After she had gone to sleep the silence in the cabin was complete; there was only the heavy chanting of the surf coming through my open window.

A couple of hours passed and it was now dark—the moon had not yet risen. Jane's voice at my door; she hoped I was feeling better, she had put a dish of victuals on the stove for me, in case I got an appetite; she was going to bed.

"Good night, Jane; I'll be all right tomorrow!" I said.

Should I too turn in? What was the use of sitting up?

But I was in no condition to sleep, and it was better to be awake standing than lying down. I leaned out of the window and breathed in the soft air from the sea; there was a light breeze from the south. I could see the long, level line of the horizon, and part of the black ribs of the wrecked schooner, thrusting up against the sky.

All at once, between the ribs, appeared a pyramid of bright red light—the gibbous moon rising in the east. A moment after I thought I heard, very far away, a long ululation, which crisped my nerves.

The dog was abroad!

Since childhood I have always been affected by the changes of the moon, sometimes very much so. As the light of the satellite fell on my face my mind cleared, and I knew what was to be done. I had partly undressed; I pulled on my sweater again and buckled on the revolver. I had left my bicycle under the lean-to outside; to avoid disturbing Jane I slipped out of the window. One of the hens uttered an interrogative croak as I passed the coop.

I got my wheel, opened the gate of the palisade, closed it behind me, and ran the wheel down to the firm sand of the beach, where I mounted; it was just past eleven o'clock. I set off in the old direction, glad to be in action and strung up to meet anything.

The horizon line had been clear a few minutes before; but now I observed a low, gray fog moving in toward the coast, with the mysteriously slow yet swift movement characteristic of sea fogs. It had seemed distant, yet now it had reached out a long, silent arm, and had touched the beach ahead. The moon hung a little way above it. The fog clung close to the surface of the scene—seemed hardly more than a man's height in thickness.

In another minute it had swathed me in its gray impalpability; and at the same time I heard again the howl of the dog, much more distinct than at first. My pedals revolved more swiftly, and the revolver thumped against my hip; I hoped the negro was with his dog. My only fear was lest they should pass me in the obscurity of the flowing mist.

The line of the beach was not straight; there were wide, shallow bays and projections, and the mist confused me, so that occasionally I found myself running close to the surf, or away from it. But the sea was a safeguard against losing my direction entirely, and I kept on at a fast pace. But was that which I sought coming toward me, or fleeing before me? If the latter, my best speed would be needed to catch up with it. I bent over the handlebars; speed in either case!

Three short barks, followed by a long howl, sounded not fifty yards away. In the few seconds that followed I halted, leaped off the wheel, snatched the revolver from my belt, and held it ready in my right hand, standing behind the wheel. I could not risk a shot while mounted; but afoot I was confident of my aim, and could use the saddle as a rest.

Then, at last, the beast disclosed itself. It was alone. Itself gray, it seemed formed out of the fog. The cantering movement was what I first discerned; but when within a dozen yards it stopped, plunging its forepaws in the sand, its head extended forward.

Shreds of mist drifted past it, and perhaps exaggerated its apparent size, but it seemed much bigger than I had anticipated. And the long, dripping jaws, the short, thick ears, the build of the chest and shoulders, and the shaggy tail flung out behind, showed me at a glance that this was no dog of any breed; it was a wolf!

Unaccountable though its presence in this region might be, there could be no doubt of that. I had to deal with a savage wild beast—a giant of its kind.

For an instant a perplexing thought of its association with a human being, even a crazy negro, flashed across my brain; but the present emergency was enough, and I gripped myself to meet it.

"*The absolute evil—is there such a thing?*" This saying of Tyler's recurred to my mind as I faced the creature, challenging the glare of its close-set eyes down the barrel of my weapon. The aspect of the monster answered the question. Hell could engender nothing more diabolical than this!

My hand did not tremble as I sighted to a point between the glaring eyes and touched the trigger. The detonation sounded flat in the boundless gray expanse that surrounded us.

The beast gave a lurch of the head, uttered a harsh bark, swung round in its tracks, and was out of sight in a moment. I had missed it clean!

I sent a second bullet after it at hazard. Another long howl was the answer, and already it seemed to be a mile away.

The fog thickened and now obscured the moon. I had sprung to my saddle, but almost immediately gave up the pursuit. There wasn't a chance in a million that I would set eyes upon the creature again that night.

I turned and rode back, feeling upon the whole glad of the encounter. I had met the thing and knew what it was; and though I had incredibly missed killing it, I had put it to flight, and perhaps driven it off the island entirely.

But there was a feeling in me that I should meet it again. I didn't believe that an incident so out of the ordinary would have no sequel.

IX

Time passed on, however, and there was no more baying at the moon or alarms in our household, nor did I find any more tracks on the beach. The weather was the most exhilarating I had ever known, and Diana, the goddess—to whom fanciful admirers had often compared me—couldn't have felt more of the elixir of immortality in her than I did.

The moon, after her brief retirement, appeared once more, a lovely crescent, in the west, and, gradually attaining her full splendor, shone at last transcendent in the pallid sky. I was in the pink of condition, as the young fellows in training for a race say. I had ceased thinking of the wolf, and had never told Jane of my meeting with it. Either she had forgotten her misgivings, or some odd reluctance prevented her mentioning them. Perdita and I had become sworn play-fellows—her innocence and confidence had made me love her.

"Absolute evil" seemed a grotesque hallucination. Absolute good was more real and near.

One thing only marred my tranquillity—though the wolf never occurred to my mind in waking hours, I dreamed of it several times at night. I was alone in some desolate place, deeply preoccupied, and suddenly felt that I had lost my way. Looking up, I saw the wolf before me. Nothing but its head was clearly visible, however. And in this head the terrible, glaring, close-set eyes drew mine irresistibly till, after a moment, the eyes alone seemed there. Behind them spread a region of darkness, out of which the beast had emerged, and into which it seemed striving to entice me, as a snake fascinates a bird.

I struggled against the hideous lure, but felt I was yielding —at which juncture I awoke.

This dream, almost the same in details, visited me three or four times. In sleep only the nature of the sleeper is active; what belongs to acquired character no longer exists. And the nature possesses impulse, but not will. My resistance could never have been overcome in my waking state.

There was one other feature of this experience to which I will merely allude; I didn't understand it at the time. It was the most revolting of all. The eyes of the beast reminded me of eyes that I had seen before. Not the eyes themselves, either, but the look that came from them. I could not trace this impression back to its source, though that seemed only just beyond my reach. It disturbed me.

But by the time the moon had filled her circle, this obsession, too, left me, and there was no cloud on my sky except regret at my approaching departure from the beach. When I spoke of it to Jane, her face fell.

"I'd be thankful if you'd stay longer, miss," she said. "And the child—what'll *she* do?" She pressed her lips together, as if trying to keep something back; but it came. She bent forward and whispered, "I'm afeared of the dog!"

I laughed with ruddy-cheeked assurance.

"I think the dog, as you call it, won't trouble you again." Then I told her my story. "I fancy I must have wounded it," I said; "it's either dead or gone for good. I've been down and back scores of times since, and seen no trace of it. Put it out of your mind."

I did not tell her of that insoluble enigma of the mingled tracks of the beast and the man. In truth, I preferred to keep away from it. There must have been some error in my observation; impossibilities don't happen.

Jane said no more, and after sitting in a brown study for a while, got up and went about her domestic affairs. Perdita, from outside, called me to come and have some fun with the goat. But the goat was perverse that day, and I, being in my bathing-dress—it was the forenoon—proposed to take the child in with me for a bath.

The sea was as smooth as a pond and the sun warm. Perdita was fearless, and could swim well. The tide was low, and we managed to get out to the wreck, where we amused ourselves with the sea anemones and shells sticking to the old timbers.

Children, brought up naturally and in freedom, not only have imagination, but live in a world of imagination more real to them than our reality. Perdita, perched on one of the cross-pieces, with her small feet dabbling in the water, and a ribbon of green seaweed twisted round her head for a crown, said: "This ship mine. By 'n' by, when I'm big, I make it all new and sail to Boston!"

"This is a much nicer place than Boston," said I.

"No!" She insisted. "Sail to Boston and get away from naughty dog."

I hadn't supposed that she knew anything about the dog. "There is no dog," I said, "and dogs don't hurt little children."

But she looked at me, rounding her blue eyes and holding up her arms to express something vast and intimidating, and repeated, "Bi-ig dog! Make noise—so!"—she threw back her head and gave an absurd imitation of a howl—"and bite poor Pudh."

Then her mood changed, and she burst into uproarious laughter. I caught her up in my arms and kissed her.

The weather changed that afternoon, with the abruptness peculiar to this coast; a wind began blowing from the south, the temperature rose and became sticky and uncomfortable, and the sea "got up," as Jane expressed it.

States of the atmosphere pass into us as water through the meshes of a sieve, and storms occur in us before they break upon the world without, creating restless sensations. The cabin became oppressive, and we opened the doors and windows to let the air through. Perdita was so uneasy, after being put into her crib, that we drew the crib to the seaward door to give her the benefit of the draft.

Jane went to bed about nine o'clock as usual; but I remained sitting in the doorway, beside Perdita, who now seemed to sleep quietly. The moon, now riding high, broke through the hurrying clouds once in a while, and sent broad rays across the rough backs of the seas. The wind was not violent, except in gusts; but the heat of it was extraordinary—it seemed to come out of an oven.

I stood up at last out of patience, and going to my room, took off my skirt and waist and put on my pajamas, in which I returned to the doorway. It was some relief; but now, as I looked over to the breaking surf, an impulse came upon me to go down and take one dip in the cool waves and out again.

I didn't pause to debate the matter, but with a glance at the child, peaceful on her little pillow, I crossed the yard quickly and out at the gate of the palisade, which I left open behind me. I would let the sea just wet me as I was, and return; by the time the wind had dried my pajamas I should be cool enough to sleep.

As I stood upon the margin, the on-driving waves loomed gigantic, and the force of them appeared so great that I wouldn't venture far in: I stepped into the sliding tongues of water, and threw myself down at full length where the depth was not above my knees. Even there the drag of the withdrawing wave was very strong. But the coolness was delicious, and I may have lain wallowing there as much as five minutes. The thunder and rush of sound filled my ears. What an incomparable creature is the sea!

I got to my feet, thoroughly revived, and turned toward the cabin.

As I did so a shrill scream, which was more like a squeal, pierced my brain like a needle. It defined itself against the surf-roar like a slender stab of light against the dark. Almost simultaneously, out through the gate of the palisade, which my neglect had left open, plunged the gray shape of the wolf, bearing in its jaws a bundle of whiteness, partly trailing on the ground. He headed down the beach in a long, swinging canter, his pace hardly impeded by the weight he carried.

My knees weakened for an instant as if from a violent blow in the breast. An instant more I wavered, prompted to pursue on foot. That folly forced back, I leaped toward the cabin for my wheel and revolver.

I rushed against something in the doorway—Jane, distracted, frantically moaning—and we stumbled together over the overturned crib. In another breath I was in my room, had snatched the revolver from the dressing-table, was out again, and on my wheel. After a fierce interval of plowing through heavy sand, I felt the firm beach under my tires, and was off.

Beneath this frenzy of physical effort, some region far within me seemed to remain cold and unflurried, calculating chances, foreseeing obstacles, measuring advantages.

Be the strength of the beast what it might—and it appeared supernatural—I knew that I should overtake it. There was supernatural vigor in my limbs, too, and my heart was firm as granite and hot as fire. I would not miss my aim this time, but I clearly perceived the danger of sending a bullet through Perdita as well as through the beast.

There was another possibility—the child might be already

dead. I must accept these risks; get her, alive or dead, and deal out vengeance.

The wind, meanwhile, had backed to the north and blew much harder, but being more behind me than in front, aided rather than hindered my speed. There was great darkness, so that I could see nothing except the relative blanching of the breakers as they foamed up to me on my left hand. The temperature fell headlong, and I felt the sting of hail on the thin wet silk of my pajamas. But I was warm, and my body exulted, in spite of the wrath in my soul.

I was steering with my left hand only on the handlebars, my right being occupied with the revolver, but my arm felt as strong as a steel bar. No sound reached me from ahead; the beast could not bark, and Perdita had not screamed after the first. How far had I ridden?—miles probably; but distance seemed nothing, and I felt that nature, to which I so loved to give myself, was on my side. Absolute evil could not prevail.

The crisis came unawares, yet found me ready.

There—almost under my wheel! The beast, with its burden, was revealed suddenly in the darkness, huddled back upon its haunches, snarling, dripping froth, at bay. Before it lay the child on the wet sand, her arms tossed up beyond her head, her cheek resting on a roll of brown seaweed, as if asleep, swathed in her torn white wrappings. Gale, sea, and sky drove upon us.

The beast seemed to tower up, huge, hideous and fatal; it hurtled at me, snarling, and I fired.

I think I laughed aloud as I saw the bullet strike its left shoulder. The coarse, gray hair was dabbled with spurting blood. I leaped from my wheel, which fell to the left, and stepped forward to complete my work.

But the beast had vanished. The gale shrieked; in the blackness the gray form of a wave surged almost to my feet—gray and writhing like the beast itself. But the wind swept the spume away, and there was nothing visible but the white, precious bundle that was Perdita. From somewhere far off, against the gale, came faintly back the long-drawn howl. It sounded to my fancy like the despairing call of a damned soul.

I lifted the child from the sand, and holding her on my left arm, regained my seat and began to fight my way back to the cabin.

X

Perdita was alive. Hardly a scratch marred her little body; there were only a few bruises on her head and shoulder, which, combined with the shock of fear, had made her unconscious. She had stirred and whimpered before we reached home, and Jane and I ministered to her, and before morning she slept in comfort. Marvelous beings are little children!

These things went by like the figures of a magic lantern to which one pays but dim attention. I was reliving that wild hour, and answered Jane at random. I was content; the beast had not died on the spot, but I knew it must die. The corpse could be found later.

I felt no curiosity about it. I had done my part—saved Perdita, and freed Jane from the forebodings that had haunted her. The rest would take care of itself. Nature, through my agency, had been relieved of an ulcer that had been festering in her breast, and her wholesome law had been reestablished. I felt like a soldier returned from an honorable campaign, conscious of duty done, and indifferent to what fame rumored of the battle. Enough for him that the enemy was defeated; for me that the beast was no more.

I don't deny that this has a mystical sound. Probably our lives are full of symbols which only an unacknowledged sense perceives. Spiritual events assume a material guise, in accordance with some creative principle, but do not insist on recognition. The soul is wounded, or is healed, as the case may be, and the effect, echoed upon the mortal plane, exercises in silence its benign office as penalty or reward.

The storm continued for three days; it has happened twice or thrice to me that memorable events in my life have been ushered in or accompanied by great storms. When the turmoil and darkness passed away, a new, crisp brightness began, as of approaching winter. The black bones of the wreck upon the beach had been broken up by the waves, and lay scattered for miles along the shore. Jane congratulated herself on the supply of firewood, but Perdita was displeased; how was she to get to Boston?

That problem has since been solved in a less magical manner than her fancy had provided. I kept alive the link between myself and these two. Jane died after a few years; Perdita, after adventures not to be told here, is a fortunate and happy woman.

But why do I dilly-dally and gossip and procrastinate? I must tell the end of this story, great as is my unwillingness to do it. It is inhuman and incredible, but the truth has no concern with such adjectives. And you may give it lodging according to the character of your philosophy; you have your choice and opportunity.

But perhaps you know the end already. I thought, afterward, that I had known it. No secrets are better hidden than are those that we hide from ourselves.

I got back to Boston about the middle of November of that year, and was enjoying, I must admit, the various luxuries abounding in that most respectable old house of mine, which I had so well dispensed with, and with such a glow of fresh life, in the primitive cabin on Thirteen-Mile Beach. My friends in society had also returned from their holidays, and we were practising upon one another our old, urbane amenities.

One of the first to call on me was, of course, Topham Brent. I flirted artistically with him, as it is my fate to do with some men. He told me I looked tremendously fit, and wanted to know what adventures I had had. I answered "None," and inquired whether he had heard anything of the Rev. Nathaniel Tyler. "That man interested me," I remarked.

"Not really?—never should have imagined it!" was his ironic rejoinder. "Why, seems to me I heard somewhere that he was back from the Orient, or some such place. They said he was in bad health, too—worse than when we had the benefit of his company on the Pleasances' house-boat two years ago. But he hasn't called me in, so I'm unable to present any pathological details."

"I must drop him a line; I'd like to see him," said I.

But the next day I received a note from him. He wrote:

I've dwelt in the desert since we met, and while there sustained an injury which confines me to my house. I can never expect to appear in a pulpit again. It would afford me great pleasure if you would come to see me. I have never forgotten our talks on the house-boat, and I have reached some conclusions on the subjects we discussed which I would like to submit to you.

I was promised an invitation to a lunch next day, Tuesday, and to a reception the same evening. On Wednesday I had tickets for an afternoon concert, and a dinner later. On Thursday I was particularly desired to attend the meeting of the Homogeneity Club, and on Friday— No matter what; I made up my mind to give my Friday to the afflicted clergyman.

I found him in his study, which apparently adjoined his bedroom; a soothing brown effect of furniture and decoration, steel engravings of sacred subjects on the walls, shelves of books, old quartos, volumes of recent philosophical and scientific essays; on the table a portfolio of designs of "The Dance of Death," and several French and Russian novels; on the mantelpiece a bronze replica of the Venus Kallipygos, of Naples.

These things reported themselves to the corners of my eyes, the direct look of which, of course, was fixed upon Tyler. He reclined in an invalid's chair, fronting an open coal grate fire; his attitude reminded me of how he and I used to recline side by side in our deck chairs on the house-boat.

Otherwise he was strangely altered. His hair was gray and thin, and hung down to his neck. A thin gray beard was on his cheeks and chin and upper lip. His former spareness had become mere boniness; the sutures of his head, his cheek-bones, the angles of the jaw might have been a skull's, and his body, as indicated beneath the wrappings over him, was but a skeleton.

His eyes, sunken deep under the tufted eyebrows, appeared almost black in the subdued light of the room; they seemed to draw inward toward the narrow dividing ridge of his high nose, giving his gaze an intense concentration. His long hands rested on the arms of his chair; they were like talons, with prominent knuckles, and narrow, polished nails of a purplish hue. But his mouth had still its sharp, voluptuous curves, and smiled as he greeted me, though the eyes had no part in the smile. There was a sort of bunch over his left shoulder which the drapery didn't wholly conceal.

I said to myself, "The man will be dead in a few days." I felt this, quite as much as I inferred it from his aspect.

But the tones of his voice were firm and cheerful, with even a half-laughing accent of raillery in them.

"If you were a disciple of mine, Miss Klemm, summoned here for ghostly counsel, you'd need no better symbol of *memento mori* than myself, I fancy. But it is I who am under obligation to you—for this and other favors. I won't keep you long. I'm mortified at not being able to get up and fetch you a chair; will you pardon me, and be seated?"

As I sat down beside him he made a movement of the head, upon which the young woman in the attire of a professional nurse, who had been standing near his chair, silently withdrew into the bedroom and softly closed the door.

"As you've surmised," he then said, "I shall shortly lay aside this muddy vesture of decay; but I thought, in deference to your feelings and many social engagements that it would be more considerate to arrange our interview before than after that event; it was bound to take place one way or the other. You—er—enjoyed yourself last summer?"

"I'm feeling the better for it," I replied.

"You have the goddesslike quality of sweeping obstacles from your path, and punishing interlopers," he rejoined; and as he spoke that satanic presence sparkled in the depths of his eyes. "When Diana, your prototype, was surprised at her bath by Actæon, she didn't suffer him to live to boast of his enjoyment of her perfections. But I dare say he was as willing as I am to pay that price for the privilege."

"I hear you've been abroad," said I, not ready to understand him.

"Oh, that is for the vulgar ear. You and I are augurs, and have no subterfuges. Perhaps, in good old Cotton Mather's day, we may have bestridden a broomstick together. I've always had a notion that our acquaintance is of long standing."

I kept silence, instinctively shutting my mind.

"Abroad, yes: far abroad!—and in the desert, to which the Sahara or the plain of Nineveh would be populous." He pointed to his own breast with a light laugh. "There, like our friend Walt Whitman, I invited my soul, and we had it out *à outrance*—thanks to my friend, Miss Martha Klemm."

"What do you expect me to say, Mr Tyler?"

"My dear young lady, you are voluble! From the moment of

your entrance—if not before—you and I have been conversing like babbling brooks, though even had my clinical attendant not so discreetly retired, she couldn't have heard a syllable of it. The footprints perplexed you, possibly; but that first moonlight tryst, which ended so explosively—surely you've had no doubts since then?"

The sensation was as if he were throwing invisible nets around me. I stood up, with angry eyes. "Shall I call the nurse?"

"Ah, have a little patience! Give a poor moribund wretch the consolation of shriving himself. Don't let me perish quite alone in the world—alone—with the beast!"

At that word, and at that thought, I sat down again. I put out all my self-command to keep from trembling. He nodded thankfully, but for some moments, contending against the exhaustion which his assumption of mockery had, as I now perceived, cost him, he could not speak. When he did, it was in another vein.

"It needed a man like me—if I am a man—to conceive it and to do it. Learning, culture, the religious training and atmosphere, personal sanctity, esthetic sensitiveness, a heredity without blemish—I abounded in all that. I was vowed to God. To descend deep, you must first go high—touch the halo before polluting it. I can say that I went deep, at least. None has been lower. Yes, I went into the desert—but not to pray. It was a wonderful journey! Not for the elixir of life, not for gold, not for holiness. And, oh, if I could have gone with your hand in mine! It might have been, Martha, that if we'd gone on the quest together, we might not only have found what we sought, but have returned alive!"

"Am I a part of your confession, Mr Tyler?" I said with a coldness which was partly designed to chill him back to earth from this feverish flight.

"Ah, well, I ask your pardon!" he returned, his smile ghastly. "I shouldn't have ventured on the liberty if I hadn't thought my condition might excuse it. Really, though, as a rank outsider, which I certainly am now, I may say that you are the only woman with whom I ever desired an intimate connection. Possibly I led you to suspect as much on the boat; and I will add that I was withheld from proposing (as they say) by the very strength of the sentiment; that is, the risk of the enterprise I had undertaken. Had you happened to accept me, you see, and braved the desert with me, we might, so far from getting back alive, have shared in the disaster—made it even worse, if possible!"

"Put what you have to say in plain words," I said, not trusting myself to a longer speech.

"Thank you! Yes, it's the pulpiteer's vice—phrases, circumlocutions! Thank you! The quest of the absolute evil—that's a phrase, too." He set his teeth, and partly rose on his right elbow. "I went to find the devil, and I found him! He's all they say of him and more. I looked down—down; I thought away everything human, sacred, innocent, pure; I desecrated and profaned the Holy of Holies, burned every bridge, worshiped the black he-goat with the flame between his horns—ha, ha, ha! —and at last the beast was there! Squatting there in the little shack in the marsh, I felt the transformation—oh, the agony and triumph of it! The big, grizzled, shaggy body—the crooked thighs and sharp, pointed hocks behind—the clawed forepaws, the long, slavering grin, thick ears, and those eyes— those eyes! You recognized them, my dear Miss Klemm—yes, you did! And the odor—pah!"

"Stop!" I whispered. But he had gone too far.

"Then out I galloped into the moonlight, and howled— how I howled! You heard me; not quite the popular preacher's voice, but you recognized it! Fancy the Rev. Nathaniel Tyler cantering down the aisle of his church, and addressing his congregation with a howl—'Ha, ha, hoo!'"

I leaned forward and put my hand resolutely on his, bending my will to check his hysteria. He panted, gurgled in his throat, and presently expressed his gratitude in a look once more human. I didn't like to think what might have come to pass in another moment! Indeed, the next thing he said, speaking now very faintly, with closed eyes, "There was no telling when— where—!" confirmed my misgiving.

The flicker of life almost failed in him, but he feebly resisted my attempt to remove my hand. "You know," he said, with trembling eyelids, "persons fed on poisons are poisoned by the antidote. Your touch would have saved me at first—now it brings a delicious death! It finishes what your bullet began. I'm glad to die a—man!" The words were low, but distinct.

At last he lifted himself and gathered energy. "The—child—lived?"

"She was not hurt."

He relaxed, a convulsion that I couldn't interpret passed over his face. But I knew this was the end, and called sharply to the nurse. His grip on my hand had not loosened.

The nurse bent over him, and turned back the wrap on his left shoulder, and then loosened the bandage beneath. A puncture, not large, but with inflamed edges, was revealed; my bullet must have passed just above the heart.

"An odd case," said the woman. "He'd been away on a trip for several weeks, and came back wounded; wouldn't have a doctor, and acted strange about it. When he got weak, they had a surgeon in to examine him. Not a mortal wound at all, but his neglect of it, or something, gave it a bad turn; likely his vitality was low, too."

After death his lips gradually drew back in a sort of grimace, disclosing both the upper and lower teeth, which were remarkably perfect and white. Efforts to correct the contraction of the facial muscles were futile. It gave the narrow, lean face a sort of wolfish look.

Sometimes, even after so many years, I feel the grip of his fingers on my arm.

1918

FRANCIS STEVENS

Unseen—Unfeared

I HAD been dining with my ever-interesting friend, Mark Jenkins, at a little Italian restaurant near South Street. It was a chance meeting. Jenkins is too busy, usually, to make dinner engagements. Over our highly seasoned food and sour, thin, red wine, he spoke of little odd incidents and adventures of his profession. Nothing very vital or important, of course. Jenkins is not the sort of detective who first detects and then pours the egotistical and revealing details of achievement in the ears of every acquaintance, however appreciative.

But when I spoke of something I had seen in the morning papers, he laughed. "Poor old 'Doc' Holt! Fascinating old codger, to any one who really knows him. I've had his friendship for years—since I was first on the city force and saved a young assistant of his from jail on a false charge. And they had to drag him into the poisoning of this young sport, Ralph Peeler!"

"Why are you so sure he couldn't have been implicated?" I asked.

But Jenkins only shook his head, with a quiet smile. "I have reasons for believing otherwise," was all I could get out of him on that score. "But," he added, "the only reason he was suspected at all is the superstitious dread of these ignorant people around him. Can't see why he lives in such a place. I know for a fact he doesn't have to. Doc's got money of his own. He's an amateur chemist and dabbler in different sorts of research work, and I suspect he's been guilty of 'showing off.' Result, they all swear he has the evil eye and holds forbidden communion with invisible powers. Smoke?"

Jenkins offered me one of his invariably good cigars, which I accepted, saying thoughtfully: "A man has no right to trifle with the superstitions of ignorant people. Sooner or later, it spells trouble."

"Did in his case. They swore up and down that he sold love charms openly and poisons secretly, and that, together with his living so near to—somebody else—got him temporarily suspected. But my tongue's running away with me, as usual!"

"As usual," I retorted impatiently, "you open up with all the frankness of a Chinese diplomat."

He beamed upon me engagingly and rose from the table, with a glance at his watch. "Sorry to leave you, Blaisdell, but I have to meet Jimmy Brennan in ten minutes."

He so clearly did not invite my further company that I remained seated for a little while after his departure; then took my own way homeward. Those streets always held for me a certain fascination, particularly at night. They are so unlike the rest of the city, so foreign in appearance, with their little shabby stores, always open until late evening, their unbelievably cheap goods, displayed as much outside the shops as in them, hung on the fronts and laid out on tables by the curb and in the street itself. To-night, however, neither people nor stores in any sense appealed to me. The mixture of Italians, Jews and a few negroes, mostly bareheaded, unkempt and generally unhygienic in appearance, struck me as merely revolting. They were all humans, and I, too, was human. Some way I did not like the idea.

Puzzled a trifle, for I am more inclined to sympathize with poverty than accuse it, I watched the faces that I passed. Never before had I observed how stupid, how bestial, how brutal were the countenances of the dwellers in this region. I actually shuddered when an old-clothes man, a gray-bearded Hebrew, brushed me as he toiled past with his barrow.

There was a sense of evil in the air, a warning of things which it is wise for a clean man to shun and keep clear of. The impression became so strong that before I had walked two squares I began to feel physically ill. Then it occurred to me that the one glass of cheap Chianti I had drunk might have something to do with the feeling. Who knew how that stuff had been manufactured, or whether the juice of the grape entered at all into its ill-flavored composition? Yet I doubted if that were the real cause of my discomfort.

By nature I am rather a sensitive, impressionable sort of

chap. In some way to-night this neighborhood, with its sordid sights and smells, had struck me wrong.

My sense of impending evil was merging into actual fear. This would never do. There is only one way to deal with an imaginative temperament like mine—conquer its vagaries. If I left South Street with this nameless dread upon me, I could never pass down it again without a recurrence of the feeling. I should simply have to stay here until I got the better of it— that was all.

I paused on a corner before a shabby but brightly lighted little drug store. Its gleaming windows and the luminous green of its conventional glass show jars made the brightest spot on the block. I realized that I was tired, but hardly wanted to go in there and rest. I knew what the company would be like at its shabby, sticky soda fountain. As I stood there, my eyes fell on a long white canvas sign across from me, and its black-and-red lettering caught my attention.

SEE THE GREAT UNSEEN!
Come in! This Means You!
Free to All!

A museum of fakes, I thought, but also reflected that if it were a show of some kind I could sit down for a while, rest, and fight off this increasing obsession of nonexistent evil. That side of the street was almost deserted, and the place itself might well be nearly empty.

II.

I walked over, but with every step my sense of dread increased. Dread of I knew not what. Bodiless, inexplicable horror had me as in a net, whose strands, being intangible, without reason for existence, I could by no means throw off. It was not the people now. None of them were about me. There, in the open, lighted street, with no sight nor sound of terror to assail me, I was the shivering victim of such fear as I had never known was possible. Yet still I would not yield.

Setting my teeth, and fighting with myself as with some pet animal gone mad, I forced my steps to slowness and walked along the sidewalk, seeking entrance. Just here there were no shops, but several doors reached in each case by means of a few iron-railed stone steps. I chose the one in the middle beneath the sign. In that neighborhood there are museums, shops and other commercial enterprises conducted in many shabby old residences, such as were these. Behind the glazing of the door I had chosen I could see a dim, pinkish light, but on either side the windows were quite dark.

Trying the door, I found it unlocked. As I opened it a party of Italians passed on the pavement below and I looked back at them over my shoulder. They were gayly dressed, men, women and children, laughing and chattering to one another; probably on their way to some wedding or other festivity.

In passing, one of the men glanced up at me and involuntarily I shuddered back against the door. He was a young man, handsome after the swarthy manner of his race, but never in my life had I seen a face so expressive of pure, malicious cruelty, naked and unashamed. Our eyes met and his seemed to light up with a vile gleaming, as if all the wickedness of his nature had come to a focus in the look of concentrated hate he gave me.

They went by, but for some distance I could see him watching me, chin on shoulder, till he and his party were swallowed up in the crowd of marketers farther down the street.

Sick and trembling from that encounter, merely of eyes though it had been, I threw aside my partly smoked cigar and entered. Within there was a small vestibule, whose ancient tesselated floor was grimy with the passing of many feet. I could feel the grit of dirt under my shoes, and it rasped on my rawly quivering nerves. The inner door stood partly open, and going on I found myself in a bare, dirty hallway, and was greeted by the sour, musty, poverty-stricken smell common to dwellings of the very ill-to-do. Beyond there was a stairway, carpeted with ragged grass matting. A gas jet, turned low inside a very dusty pink globe, was the light I had seen from without.

Listening, the house seemed entirely silent. Surely, this was no place of public amusement of any kind whatever. More likely it was a rooming house, and I had, after all, mistaken the entrance.

To my intense relief, since coming inside, the worst agony of my unreasonable terror had passed away. If I could only get in some place where I could sit down and be quiet, probably I should be rid of it for good. Determining to try another entrance, I was about to leave the bare hallway when one of several doors along the side of it suddenly opened and a man stepped out into the hall.

"Well?" he said, looking at me keenly, but with not the least show of surprise at my presence.

"I beg your pardon," I replied. "The door was unlocked and I came in here, thinking it was the entrance to the exhibit —what do they call it?—the 'Great Unseen.' The one that is mentioned on that long white sign. Can you tell me which door is the right one?"

"I can."

With that brief answer he stopped and stared at me again. He was a tall, lean man, somewhat stooped, but possessing considerable dignity of bearing. For that neighborhood, he appeared uncommonly well dressed, and his long, smooth-shaven face was noticeable because, while his complexion was dark and his eyes coal-black, above them the heavy brows and his hair were almost silvery-white. His age might have been anything over the threescore mark.

I grew tired of being stared at. "If you can and—won't, then never mind," I observed a trifle irritably, and turned to go. But his sharp exclamation halted me.

"No!" he said. "No—no! Forgive me for pausing—it was not hesitation, I assure you. To think that one—one, even, has come! All day they pass my sign up there—pass and fear to enter. But you are different. *You* are not of these timorous, ignorant foreign peasants. You ask me to tell you the right door? Here it is! Here!"

And he struck the panel of the door, which he had closed behind him, so that the sharp yet hollow sound of it echoed up through the silent house.

Now it may be thought that after all my senseless terror in the open street, so strange a welcome from so odd a showman would have brought the feeling back, full force. But there is an emotion stronger, to a certain point, than fear. This queer old fellow aroused my curiosity. What kind of museum could it be that he accused the passing public of fearing to enter? Nothing really terrible, surely, or it would have been closed by the police. And normally I am not an unduly timorous person. "So, it's in there, is it?" I asked, coming toward him. "And I'm to be sole audience? Come, that will be an interesting experience." I was half laughing now.

"The most interesting in the world," said the old man, with a solemnity which rebuked my lightness.

With that he opened the door, passed inward and closed it again—in my very face. I stood staring at it blankly. The panels, I remember, had been originally painted white, but now the paint was flaked and blistered, gray with dirt and dirty finger marks. Suddenly it occurred to me that I had no wish to enter there. Whatever was behind it could be scarcely worth seeing, or he would not choose such a place for its exhibition. With the old man's vanishing my curiosity had cooled, but just as I again turned to leave, the door opened and this singular showman stuck his white-eyebrowed face through the aperture. He was frowning impatiently. "Come in—come in!" he snapped, and promptly withdrawing his head, once more closed the door.

"He has something in there he doesn't want should get out," was the very natural conclusion which I drew. "Well, since it can hardly be anything dangerous, and he's so anxious I should see it—here goes!"

With that I turned the soiled white porcelain handle, and entered.

The room I came into was neither very large nor very brightly lighted. In no way did it resemble a museum or lecture room. On the contrary, it seemed to have been fitted up as a quite well-appointed laboratory. The floor was linoleum-covered, there were glass cases along the walls whose shelves were filled with bottles, specimen jars, graduates, and the like. A large table in one corner bore what looked like some odd sort of camera, and a larger one in the middle of the room was fitted with a long rack filled with bottles and test tubes, and was besides littered with papers, glass slides, and various paraphernalia which my ignorance failed to identify. There were several cases of books, a few plain wooden chairs, and in the corner a large iron sink with running water.

My host of the white hair and black eyes was awaiting me, standing near the larger table. He indicated one of the wooden chairs with a thin forefinger that shook a little, either from age or eagerness. "Sit down—sit down! Have no fear but that you will be interested, my friend. Have no fear at all—of anything!"

As he said it he fixed his dark eyes upon me and stared harder than ever. But the effect of his words was the opposite of their meaning. I did sit down, because my knees gave under me, but if in the outer hall I had lost my terror, it now returned twofold upon me. Out there the light had been faint, dingily roseate, indefinite. By it I had not perceived how this old man's face was a mask of living malice—of cruelty, hate and a certain masterful contempt. Now I knew the meaning of my fear, whose warning I would not heed. Now I knew that I had walked into the very trap from which my abnormal sensitiveness had striven in vain to save me.

III.

Again I struggled within me, bit at my lip till I tasted blood, and presently the blind paroxysm passed. It must have been longer in going than I thought, and the old man must have all that time been speaking, for when I could once more control my attention, hear and see him, he had taken up a position near the sink, about ten feet away, and was addressing me with a sort of "platform" manner, as if I had been the large audience whose absence he had deplored.

"And so," he was saying, "I was forced to make these plates very carefully, to truly represent the characteristic hues of each separate organism. Now, in color work of every kind the film is necessarily extremely sensitive. Doubtless you are familiar in a general way with the exquisite transparencies produced by color photography of the single-plate type."

He paused, and, trying to act like a normal human being, I observed: "I saw some nice landscapes done in that way—last week at an illustrated lecture in Franklin Hall."

He scowled, and made an impatient gesture at me with his hand. "I can proceed better without interruptions," he said. "My pause was purely oratorical."

I meekly subsided, and he went on in his original loud, clear voice. He would have made an excellent lecturer before a much larger audience—if only his voice could have lost that eerie, ringing note. Thinking of that I must have missed some more, and when I caught it again he was saying:

"As I have indicated, the original plate is the final picture. Now, many of these organisms are extremely hard to photograph, and microphotography in color is particularly difficult. In consequence, to spoil a plate tries the patience of the photographer. They are so sensitive that the ordinary darkroom ruby lamp would instantly ruin them, and they must therefore be developed either in darkness or by a special light produced by interposing thin sheets of tissue of a particular shade of green and of yellow between lamp and plate, and even that will often cause ruinous fog. Now I, finding it hard to handle them so, made numerous experiments with a view to discovering some glass or fabric of a color which should add to the safety of the green, without robbing it of all efficiency. All proved equally useless, but intermittently I persevered—until last week."

His voice dropped to an almost confidential tone, and he leaned slightly toward me. I was cold from my neck to my feet, though my head was burning, but I tried to force an appreciative smile.

"Last week," he continued impressively, "I had a prescription filled at the corner drug store. The bottle was sent home to me wrapped in a piece of what I at first took to be whitish, slightly opalescent paper. Later I decided that it was some kind of membrane. When I questioned the druggist, seeking its source, he said it was a sheet of 'paper' that was around a bundle of herbs from South America. That he had no more, and doubted if I could trace it. He had wrapped my bottle so, because he was in haste and the sheet was handy.

"I can hardly tell you what first inspired me to try that membrane in my photographic work. It was merely dull white with a faint hint of opalescence, except when held against the light. Then it became quite translucent and quite brightly prismatic. For some reason it occurred to me that this refractive effect might help in breaking up the actinic rays—the rays which affect the sensitive emulsion. So that night I inserted it behind the sheets of green and yellow tissue, next the lamp, prepared my trays and chemicals, laid my plate holders to hand, turned off the white light and—turned on the green!"

There was nothing in his words to inspire fear. It was a

wearisomely detailed account of his struggles with photography. Yet, as he again paused impressively, I wished that he might never speak again. I was desperately, contemptibly in dread of the thing he might say next.

Suddenly he drew himself erect, the stoop went out of his shoulders, he threw back his head and laughed. It was a hollow sound, as if he laughed into a trumpet. "I won't tell you what I saw! Why should I? Your own eyes shall bear witness. But this much I'll say, so that you may better understand—later. When our poor, faultily sensitive vision can perceive a thing, we say that it is visible. When the nerves of touch can feel it, we say that it is tangible. Yet I tell you there are beings intangible to our physical sense, yet whose presence is felt by the spirit, and invisible to our eyes merely because those organs are not attuned to the light as reflected from their bodies. But light passed through the screen which we are about to use has a wave length novel to the scientific world, and by it you shall see with the eyes of the flesh that which has been invisible since life began. Have no fear!"

He stopped to laugh again, and his mirth was yellow-toothed—menacing.

"*Have no fear!*" he reiterated, and with that stretched his hand toward the wall, there came a click and we were in black, impenetrable darkness. I wanted to spring up, to seek the door by which I had entered and rush out of it, but the paralysis of unreasoning terror held me fast.

I could hear him moving about in the darkness, and a moment later a faint green glimmer sprang up in the room. Its source was over the large sink, where I suppose he developed his precious "color plates."

Every instant, as my eyes became accustomed to the dimness, I could see more clearly. Green light is peculiar. It may be far fainter than red, and at the same time far more illuminating. The old man was standing beneath it, and his face by that ghastly radiance had the exact look of a dead man's. Beside this, however, I could observe nothing appalling.

"That," continued the man, "is the simple developing light of which I have spoken—now watch, for what you are about to behold no mortal man but myself has ever seen before."

For a moment he fussed with the green lamp over the sink.

It was so constructed that all the direct rays struck downward. He opened a flap at the side, for a moment there was a streak of comforting white luminance from within, then he inserted something, slid it slowly in—and closed the flap.

The thing he put in—that South American "membrane" it must have been—instead of decreasing the light increased it—amazingly. The hue was changed from green to greenish-gray, and the whole room sprang into view, a livid, ghastly chamber, filled with—overcrawled by—what?

My eyes fixed themselves, fascinated, on something that moved by the old man's feet. It writhed there on the floor like a huge, repulsive starfish, an immense, armed, legged thing, that twisted convulsively. It was smooth, as if made of rubber, was whitish-green in color; and presently raised its great round blob of a body on tottering tentacles, crept toward my host and writhed upward—yes, climbed up his legs, his body. And he stood there, erect, arms folded, and stared sternly down at the thing which climbed.

But the room—the whole room was alive with other creatures than that. Everywhere I looked they were—centipedish things, with yard-long bodies, detestable, furry spiders that lurked in shadows, and sausage-shaped translucent horrors that moved—and floated through the air. They dived here and there between me and the light, and I could see its brighter greenness through their greenish bodies.

Worse, though, far worse than these were the *things with human faces*. Mask-like, monstrous, huge gaping mouths and slitlike eyes—I find I cannot write of them. There was that about them which makes their memory even now intolerable.

The old man was speaking again, and every word echoed in my brain like the ringing of a gong. "Fear nothing! Among such as these do you move every hour of the day and the night. Only you and I have seen, for God is merciful and has spared our race from sight. But I am not merciful! I loathe the race which gave these creatures birth—the race which might be so surrounded by invisible, unguessed but blessed beings—and chooses these for its companions! All the world shall see and know. One by one shall they come here, learn the truth, and perish. For who can survive the ultimate of terror? Then I, too, shall find peace, and leave the earth to its heritage of man-created horrors. Do you know what these are—whence they come?"

His voice boomed now like a cathedral bell. I could not answer him, but he waited for no reply. "Out of the ether—out of the omnipresent ether from whose intangible substance the mind of God made the planets, all living things, and man— man has made these! By his evil thoughts, by his selfish panics, by his lusts and his interminable, never-ending hate he has made them, and they are everywhere! Fear nothing—they cannot harm your body—but let your spirit beware! Fear nothing— but see where there comes to you, its creator, the shape and the body of your FEAR!"

And as he said it I perceived a great Thing coming toward me—a Thing—but consciousness could endure no more. The ringing, threatening voice merged in a roar within my ears, there came a merciful dimming of the terrible, lurid vision, and blank nothingness succeeded upon horror too great for bearing.

IV.

There was a dull, heavy pain above my eyes. I knew that they were closed, that I was dreaming, and that the rack full of colored bottles which I seemed to see so clearly was no more than a part of the dream. There was some vague but imperative reason why I should rouse myself. I wanted to awaken, and thought that by staring very hard indeed I could dissolve this foolish vision of blue and yellow-brown bottles. But instead of dissolving they grew clearer, more solid and substantial of appearance, until suddenly the rest of my senses rushed to the support of sight, and I became aware that my eyes were open, the bottles were quite real, and that I was sitting in a chair, fallen sideways so that my cheek rested most uncomfortably on the table which held the rack.

I straightened up slowly and with difficulty, groping in my dulled brain for some clew to my presence in this unfamiliar place, this laboratory that was lighted only by the rays of an arc light in the street outside its three large windows. Here I sat, alone, and if the aching of cramped limbs meant anything, here I had sat for more than a little time.

Then, with the painful shock which accompanies awakening to the knowledge of some great catastrophe, came memory. It was this very room, shown by the street lamp's rays to be empty of life, which I had seen thronged with creatures too loathsome for description. I staggered to my feet, staring fearfully about. There were the glass-doored cases, the bookshelves, the two tables with their burdens, and the long iron sink above which, now only a dark blotch of shadow, hung the lamp from which had emanated that livid, terrifically revealing illumination. Then the experience had been no dream, but a frightful reality. I was alone here now. With callous indifference my strange host had allowed me to remain for hours unconscious, with not the least effort to aid or revive me. Perhaps, hating me so, he had hoped that I would die there.

At first I made no effort to leave the place. Its appearance filled me with reminiscent loathing. I longed to go, but as yet felt too weak and ill for the effort. Both mentally and physically my condition was deplorable, and for the first time I realized that a shock to the mind may react upon the body as vilely as any debauch of self-indulgence.

Quivering in every nerve and muscle, dizzy with headache and nausea, I dropped back into the chair, hoping that before the old man returned I might recover sufficient self-control to escape him. I knew that he hated me, and why. As I waited, sick, miserable, I understood the man. Shuddering, I recalled the loathsome horrors he had shown me. If the mere desires and emotions of mankind were daily carnified in such forms as those, no wonder that he viewed his fellow beings with detestation and longed only to destroy them.

I thought, too, of the cruel, sensuous faces I had seen in the streets outside—seen for the first time, as if a veil had been withdrawn from eyes hitherto blinded by self-delusion. Fatuously trustful as a month-old puppy, I had lived in a grim, evil world, where goodness is a word and crude selfishness the only actuality. Drearily my thoughts drifted back through my own life, its futile purposes, mistakes and activities. All of evil that I knew returned to overwhelm me. Our gropings toward divinity were a sham, a writhing sunward of slime-covered beasts who claimed sunlight as their heritage, but in their hearts preferred the foul and easy depths.

Even now, though I could neither see nor feel them, this room, the entire world, was acrawl with the beings created by our real natures. I recalled the cringing, contemptible fear to which my spirit had so readily yielded, and the faceless Thing to which the emotion had given birth.

Then abruptly, shockingly, I remembered that every moment I was adding to the horde. Since my mind could conceive only repulsive incubi, and since while I lived I must think, feel, and so continue to shape them, was there no way to check so abominable a succession? My eyes fell on the long shelves with their many-colored bottles. In the chemistry of photography there are deadly poisons—I knew that. Now was the time to end it—now! Let him return and find his desire accomplished. One good thing I could do, if one only. I could abolish my monster-creating self.

V.

My friend Mark Jenkins is an intelligent and usually a very careful man. When he took from "Smiler" Callahan a cigar which had every appearance of being excellent, innocent Havana, the act denoted both intelligence and caution. By very clever work he had traced the poisoning of young Ralph Peeler to Mr. Callahan's door, and he believed this particular cigar to be the mate of one smoked by Peeler just previous to his demise. And if, upon arresting Callahan, he had not confiscated this bit of evidence, it would have doubtless been destroyed by its regrettably unconscientious owner.

But when Jenkins shortly afterward gave me that cigar, as one of his own, he committed one of those almost inconceivable blunders which, I think, are occasionally forced upon clever men to keep them from overweening vanity. Discovering his slight mistake, my detective friend spent the night searching for his unintended victim, myself, and that his search was successful was due to Pietro Marini, a young Italian of Jenkins' acquaintance, whom he met about the hour of two a.m. returning from a dance.

Now, Marini had seen me standing on the steps of the house where Doctor Frederick Holt had his laboratory and living rooms, and he had stared at me, not with any ill intent, but because he thought I was the sickest-looking, most ghastly specimen of humanity that he had ever beheld. And, sharing the superstition of his South Street neighbors, he wondered if the worthy doctor had poisoned me as well as Peeler. This suspicion he imparted to Jenkins, who, however, had the best of reasons for believing otherwise. Moreover, as he informed Marini, Holt was dead, having drowned himself late the previous afternoon. An hour or so after our talk in the restaurant news of his suicide reached Jenkins.

It seemed wise to search any place where a very sick-looking young man had been seen to enter, so Jenkins came straight to the laboratory. Across the fronts of those houses was the long sign with its mysterious inscription, "See the Great Unseen," not at all mysterious to the detective. He knew that next door to Doctor Holt's the second floor had been thrown together into a lecture room, where at certain hours a young man employed by settlement workers displayed upon a screen stereopticon views of various deadly bacilli, the germs of diseases appropriate to dirt and indifference. He knew, too, that Doctor Holt himself had helped the educational effort along by providing some really wonderful lantern slides, done by micro-color photography.

On the pavement outside, Jenkins found the two-thirds remnant of a cigar, which he gathered in and came up the steps, a very miserable and self-reproachful detective. Neither outer nor inner door was locked, and in the laboratory he found me, alive, but on the verge of death by another means than he had feared.

In the extreme physical depression following my awakening from drugged sleep, and knowing nothing of its cause, I believed my adventure fact in its entirety. My mentality was at too low an ebb to resist its dreadful suggestion. I was searching among Holt's various bottles when Jenkins burst in. At first I was merely annoyed at the interruption of my purpose, but before the anticlimax of his explanation the mists of obsession drifted away and left me still sick in body, but in spirit happy as any man may well be who has suffered a delusion that the world is wholly bad—and learned that its badness springs from his own poisoned brain.

The malice which I had observed in every face, including

young Marini's, existed only in my drug-affected vision. Last
week's "popular-science" lecture had been recalled to my subconscious mind—the mind that rules dreams and delirium—
by the photographic apparatus in Holt's workroom. "See the
Great Unseen" assisted materially, and even the corner drug
store before which I had paused, with its green-lit show vases,
had doubtless played a part. But presently, following something Jenkins told me, I was driven to one protest. "If Holt
was not here," I demanded, "if Holt is dead, as you say, how
do you account for the fact that I, who have never seen the man,
was able to give you an accurate description which you admit
to be that of Doctor Frederick Holt?"

He pointed across the room. "See that?" It was a life-size
bust portrait, in crayons, the picture of a white-haired man
with bushy eyebrows and the most piercing black eyes I had
ever seen—until the previous evening. It hung facing the door
and near the windows, and the features stood out with a
strangely lifelike appearance in the white rays of the arc lamp
just outside. "Upon entering," continued Jenkins, "the first
thing you saw was that portrait, and from it your delirium built
a living, speaking man. So, there are your white-haired showman, your unnatural fear, your color photography and your
pretty green golliwogs all nicely explained for you, Blaisdell,
and thank God you're alive to hear the explanation. If you had
smoked the whole of that cigar—well, never mind. You didn't.
And now, my very dear friend, I think it's high time that you
interviewed a real, flesh-and-blood doctor. I'll phone for a taxi."

"Don't," I said. "A walk in the fresh air will do me more
good than fifty doctors."

"Fresh air! There's no fresh air on South Street in July,"
complained Jenkins, but reluctantly yielded.

I had a reason for my preference. I wished to see people, to
meet face to face even such stray prowlers as might be about at
this hour, nearer sunrise than midnight, and rejoice in the goodness and kindliness of the human countenance—particularly as
found in the lower classes.

But even as we were leaving there occurred to me a curious
inconsistency.

"Jenkins," I said, "you claim that the reason Holt, when I
first met him in the hall, appeared to twice close the door in

my face, was because the door never opened until I myself un-
latched it."

"Yes," confirmed Jenkins, but he frowned, foreseeing my
next question.

"Then why, if it was from that picture that I built so solid, so
convincing a vision of the man, did I see Holt in the hall
before the door was open?"

"You confuse your memories," retorted Jenkins rather
shortly.

"Do I? Holt was dead at that hour, but—*I tell you I saw
Holt outside the door!* And what was his reason for committing
suicide?"

Before my friend could reply I was across the room, fumbling in the dusk there at the electric lamp above the sink. I
got the tin flap open and pulled out the sliding screen, which
consisted of two sheets of glass with fabric between, dark on
one side, yellow on the other. With it came the very thing I
dreaded—a sheet of whitish, parchmentlike, slightly opalescent stuff.

Jenkins was beside me as I held it at arm's length toward the
windows. Through it the light of the arc lamp fell—divided
into the most astonishingly brilliant rainbow hues. And instead
of diminishing the light, it was perceptibly increased in the
oddest way. Almost one thought that the sheet itself was luminous, and yet when held in shadow it gave off no light at all.

"Shall we—put it in the lamp again—and try it?" asked
Jenkins slowly, and in his voice there was no hint of mockery.

I looked him straight in the eyes. "No," I said, "we won't. I
was drugged. Perhaps in that condition I received a merciless
revelation of the discovery that caused Holt's suicide, but I
don't believe it. Ghost or no ghost, I refuse to ever again
believe in the depravity of the human race. If the air and the
earth are teeming with invisible horrors, they are *not* of our
making, and—the study of demonology is better let alone.
Shall we burn this thing, or tear it up?"

"We have no right to do either," returned Jenkins thoughtfully, "but you know, Blaisdell, there's a little too darn much
realism about some parts of your 'dream.' I haven't been
smoking any doped cigars, but when you held that up to the

light, I'll swear I saw—well, never mind. Burn it—send it back to the place it came from."

"South America?" said I.

"A hotter place than that. Burn it."

So he struck a match and we did. It was gone in one great white flash.

A large place was given by morning papers to the suicide of Doctor Frederick Holt, caused, it was surmised, by mental derangement brought about by his unjust implication in the Peeler murder. It seemed an inadequate reason, since he had never been arrested, but no other was ever discovered.

Of course, our action in destroying that "membrane" was illegal and rather precipitate, but, though he won't talk about it, I know that Jenkins agrees with me—doubt is sometimes better than certainty, and there are marvels better left unproved. Those, for instance, which concern the Powers of Evil.

1919

F. SCOTT FITZGERALD

(1896–1940)

The Curious Case of Benjamin Button

I

As long ago as 1860 it was the proper thing to be born at home. At present, so I am told, the high gods of medicine have decreed that the first cries of the young shall be uttered upon the anesthetic air of a hospital, preferably a fashionable one. So young Mr. and Mrs. Roger Button were fifty years ahead of style when they decided, one day in the summer of 1860, that their first baby should be born in a hospital. Whether this anachronism had any bearing upon the astonishing history I am about to set down will never be known.

I shall tell you what occurred, and let you judge for yourself.

The Roger Buttons held an enviable position, both social and financial, in ante-bellum Baltimore. They were related to the This Family and the That Family, which, as every Southerner knew, entitled them to membership in that enormous peerage which largely populated the Confederacy. This was their first experience with the charming old custom of having babies— Mr. Button was naturally nervous. He hoped it would be a boy so that he could be sent to Yale College in Connecticut, at which institution Mr. Button himself had been known for four years by the somewhat obvious nickname of "Cuff."

On the September morning consecrated to the enormous event he arose nervously at six o'clock, dressed himself, adjusted an impeccable stock, and hurried forth through the streets of Baltimore to the hospital, to determine whether the darkness of the night had borne in new life upon its bosom.

When he was approximately a hundred yards from the Maryland Private Hospital for Ladies and Gentlemen he saw Doctor Keene, the family physician, descending the front steps, rubbing his hands together with a washing movement—as all doctors are required to do by the unwritten ethics of their profession.

Mr. Roger Button, the president of Roger Button & Co., Wholesale Hardware, began to run toward Doctor Keene with much less dignity than was expected from a Southern gentleman of that picturesque period. "Doctor Keene!" he called. "Oh, Doctor Keene!"

The doctor heard him, faced around, and stood waiting, a curious expression settling on his harsh, medicinal face as Mr. Button drew near.

"What happened?" demanded Mr. Button, as he came up in a gasping rush. "What was it? How is she? A boy? Who is it? What——"

"Talk sense!" said Doctor Keene sharply. He appeared somewhat irritated.

"Is the child born?" begged Mr. Button.

Doctor Keene frowned. "Why, yes, I suppose so—after a fashion." Again he threw a curious glance at Mr. Button.

"Is my wife all right?"

"Yes."

"Is it a boy or a girl?"

"Here now!" cried Doctor Keene in a perfect passion of irritation, "I'll ask you to go and see for yourself. Outrageous!" He snapped the last word out in almost one syllable, then he turned away muttering: "Do you imagine a case like this will help my professional reputation? One more would ruin me—ruin anybody."

"What's the matter?" demanded Mr. Button, appalled. "Triplets?"

"No, not triplets!" answered the doctor cuttingly. "What's more, you can go and see for yourself. And get another doctor. I brought you into the world, young man, and I've been physician to your family for forty years, but I'm through with you! I don't want to see you or any of your relatives ever again! Good-by!"

Then he turned sharply, and without another word climbed into his phaeton, which was waiting at the curbstone, and drove severely away.

Mr. Button stood there upon the sidewalk, stupefied and

trembling from head to foot. What horrible mishap had occurred? He had suddenly lost all desire to go into the Maryland Private Hospital for Ladies and Gentlemen—it was with the greatest difficulty that, a moment later, he forced himself to mount the steps and enter the front door.

A nurse was sitting behind a desk in the opaque gloom of the hall. Swallowing his shame, Mr. Button approached her.

"Good-morning," she remarked, looking up at him pleasantly.

"Good-morning. I—I am Mr. Button."

At this a look of utter terror spread itself over the girl's face. She rose to her feet and seemed about to fly from the hall, restraining herself only with the most apparent difficulty.

"I want to see my child," said Mr. Button.

The nurse gave a little scream. "Oh—of course!" she cried hysterically. "Up-stairs. Right up-stairs. Go—*up!*"

She pointed the direction, and Mr. Button, bathed in a cool perspiration, turned falteringly, and began to mount to the second floor. In the upper hall he addressed another nurse who approached him, basin in hand. "I'm Mr. Button," he managed to articulate. "I want to see my——"

Clank! The basin clattered to the floor and rolled in the direction of the stairs. Clank! Clank! It began a methodical descent as if sharing in the general terror which this gentleman provoked.

"I want to see my child!" Mr. Button almost shrieked. He was on the verge of collapse.

Clank! The basin had reached the first floor. The nurse regained control of herself, and threw Mr. Button a look of hearty contempt.

"All *right*, Mr. Button," she agreed in a hushed voice. "Very *well!* But if you *knew* what state it's put us all in this morning! It's perfectly outrageous! The hospital will never have the ghost of a reputation after——"

"Hurry!" he cried hoarsely. "I can't stand this!"

"Come this way, then, Mr. Button."

He dragged himself after her. At the end of a long hall they reached a room from which proceeded a variety of howls—indeed, a room which, in later parlance, would have been known as the "crying-room." They entered. Ranged around the walls were half a dozen white-enameled rolling cribs, each with a tag tied at the head.

"Well," gasped Mr. Button, "which is mine?"

"There!" said the nurse.

Mr. Button's eyes followed her pointing finger, and this is what he saw. Wrapped in a voluminous white blanket, and partially crammed into one of the cribs, there sat an old man apparently about seventy years of age. His sparse hair was almost white, and from his chin dripped a long smoke-colored beard, which waved absurdly back and forth, fanned by the breeze coming in at the window. He looked up at Mr. Button with dim, faded eyes in which lurked a puzzled question.

"Am I mad?" thundered Mr. Button, his terror resolving into rage. "Is this some ghastly hospital joke?"

"It doesn't seem like a joke to us," replied the nurse severely. "And I don't know whether you're mad or not—but that is most certainly your child."

The cool perspiration redoubled on Mr. Button's forehead. He closed his eyes, and then, opening them, looked again. There was no mistake—he was gazing at a man of threescore and ten—a *baby* of threescore and ten, a baby whose feet hung over the sides of the crib in which it was reposing.

The old man looked placidly from one to the other for a moment, and then suddenly spoke in a cracked and ancient voice. "Are you my father?" he demanded.

Mr. Button and the nurse started violently.

"Because if you are," went on the old man querulously, "I wish you'd get me out of this place—or, at least, get them to put a comfortable rocker in here."

"Where in God's name did you come from? Who are you?" burst out Mr. Button frantically.

"I can't tell you *exactly* who I am," replied the querulous whine, "because I've only been born a few hours—but my last name is certainly Button."

"You lie! You're an impostor!"

The old man turned wearily to the nurse. "Nice way to welcome a new-born child," he complained in a weak voice. "Tell him he's wrong, why don't you?"

"You're wrong, Mr. Button," said the nurse severely. "This is your child, and you'll have to make the best of it. We're going to ask you to take him home with you as soon as possible—some time to-day."

"Home?" repeated Mr. Button incredulously.

"Yes, we can't have him here. We really can't, you know?"

"I'm right glad of it," whined the old man. "This is a fine place to keep a youngster of quiet tastes. With all this yelling and howling, I haven't been able to get a wink of sleep. I asked for something to eat"—here his voice rose to a shrill note of protest—"and they brought me a bottle of milk!"

Mr. Button sank down upon a chair near his son and concealed his face in his hands. "My heavens!" he murmured, in an ecstasy of horror. "What will people say? What must I do?"

"You'll have to take him home," insisted the nurse—"immediately!"

A grotesque picture formed itself with dreadful clarity before the eyes of the tortured man—a picture of himself walking through the crowded streets of the city with this appalling apparition stalking by his side. "I can't. I can't," he moaned.

People would stop to speak to him, and what was he going to say? He would have to introduce this—this septuagenarian: "This is my son, born early this morning." And then the old man would gather his blanket around him and they would plod on, past the bustling stores, the slave market—for a dark instant Mr. Button wished passionately that his son was black—past the luxurious houses of the residential district, past the home for the aged. . . .

"Come! Pull yourself together," commanded the nurse.

"See here," the old man announced suddenly, "if you think I'm going to walk home in this blanket, you're entirely mistaken."

"Babies always have blankets."

With a malicious crackle the old man held up a small white swaddling garment. "Look!" he quavered. "*This* is what they had ready for me."

"Babies always wear those," said the nurse primly.

"Well," said the old man, "this baby's not going to wear anything in about two minutes. This blanket itches. They might at least have given me a sheet."

"Keep it on! Keep it on!" said Mr. Button hurriedly. He turned to the nurse. "What'll I do?"

"Go down town and buy your son some clothes."

Mr. Button's son's voice followed him down into the hall: "And a cane, father. I want to have a cane."

Mr. Button banged the outer door savagely. . . .

II

"Good-morning," Mr. Button said, nervously, to the clerk in the Chesapeake Dry Goods Company. "I want to buy some clothes for my child."

"How old is your child, sir?"

"About six hours," answered Mr. Button, without due consideration.

"Babies' supply department in the rear."

"Why, I don't think—I'm not sure that's what I want. It's—he's an unusually large-size child. Exceptionally—ah—large."

"They have the largest child's sizes."

"Where is the boys' department?" inquired Mr. Button, shifting his ground desperately. He felt that the clerk must surely scent his shameful secret.

"Right here."

"Well—" He hesitated. The notion of dressing his son in men's clothes was repugnant to him. If, say, he could only find a *very* large boy's suit, he might cut off that long and awful beard, dye the white hair brown, and thus manage to conceal the worst, and to retain something of his own self-respect—not to mention his position in Baltimore society.

But a frantic inspection of the boys' department revealed no suits to fit the new-born Button. He blamed the store, of course—in such cases it is the thing to blame the store.

"How old did you say that boy of yours was?" demanded the clerk curiously.

"He's—sixteen."

"Oh, I beg your pardon. I thought you said six *hours*. You'll find the youths' department in the next aisle."

Mr. Button turned miserably away. Then he stopped, brightened, and pointed his finger toward a dressed dummy in the window display. "There!" he exclaimed. "I'll take that suit, out there on the dummy."

The clerk stared. "Why," he protested, "that's not a child's suit. At least it *is*, but it's for fancy dress. You could wear it yourself!"

"Wrap it up," insisted his customer nervously. "That's what I want."

The astonished clerk obeyed.

Back at the hospital Mr. Button entered the nursery and almost threw the package at his son. "Here's your clothes," he snapped out.

The old man untied the package and viewed the contents with a quizzical eye.

"They look sort of funny to me," he complained. "I don't want to be made a monkey of——"

"You've made a monkey of me!" retorted Mr. Button fiercely. "Never you mind how funny you look. Put them on— or I'll—or I'll *spank* you." He swallowed uneasily at the penultimate word, feeling nevertheless that it was the proper thing to say.

"All right, father"—this with a grotesque simulation of filial respect—"you've lived longer; you know best. Just as you say."

As before, the sound of the word "father" caused Mr. Button to start violently.

"And hurry."

"I'm hurrying, father."

When his son was dressed Mr. Button regarded him with depression. The costume consisted of dotted socks, pink pants, and a belted blouse with a wide white collar. Over the latter waved the long whitish beard, drooping almost to the waist. The effect was not good.

"Wait!"

Mr. Button seized a hospital shears and with three quick snaps amputated a large section of the beard. But even with this improvement the ensemble fell far short of perfection. The remaining brush of scraggly hair, the watery eyes, the ancient teeth, seemed oddly out of tone with the gayety of the costume. Mr. Button, however, was obdurate—he held out his hand. "Come along!" he said sternly.

His son took the hand trustingly. "What are you going to call me, dad?" he quavered as they walked from the nursery— "just 'baby' for a while? till you think of a better name?"

Mr. Button grunted. "I don't know," he answered harshly. "I think we'll call you Methuselah."

III

Even after the new addition to the Button family had had his hair cut short and then dyed to a sparse unnatural black, had had his face shaved so close that it glistened, and had been attired in small-boy clothes made to order by a flabbergasted tailor, it was impossible for Mr. Button to ignore the fact that his son was a poor excuse for a first family baby. Despite his aged stoop, Benjamin Button—for it was by this name they called him instead of by the appropriate but invidious Methuselah—was five feet eight inches tall. His clothes did not conceal this, nor did the clipping and dyeing of his eyebrows disguise the fact that the eyes underneath were faded and watery and tired. In fact, the baby-nurse who had been engaged in advance left the house after one look, in a state of considerable indignation.

But Mr. Button persisted in his unwavering purpose. Benjamin was a baby, and a baby he should remain. At first he declared that if Benjamin didn't like warm milk he could go without food altogether, but he was finally prevailed upon to allow his son bread and butter, and even oatmeal by way of a compromise. One day he brought home a rattle and, giving it to Benjamin, insisted in no uncertain terms that he should "play with it," whereupon the old man took it with a weary expression and could be heard jingling it obediently at intervals throughout the day.

There can be no doubt, though, that the rattle bored him, and that he found other and more soothing amusements when he was left alone. For instance, Mr. Button discovered one day that during the preceding week he had smoked more cigars than ever before—a phenomenon which was explained a few days later when, entering the nursery unexpectedly, he found the room full of faint blue haze and Benjamin, with a guilty expression on his face, trying to conceal the butt of a dark Havana. This, of course, called for a severe spanking, but Mr. Button found that he could not bring himself to administer it. He merely warned his son that he would "stunt his growth."

Nevertheless he persisted in his attitude. He brought home lead soldiers, he brought toy trains, he brought large pleasant animals made of cotton, and, to perfect the illusion which he was creating—for himself at least—he passionately demanded of the clerk in the toy-store whether "the paint would come off the pink duck if the baby put it in his mouth." But, despite all his father's efforts, Benjamin refused to be interested. He would steal down the back stairs and return to the nursery with a volume of the "Encyclopædia Britannica," over which he would pore through an afternoon, while his cotton cows and his Noah's ark were left neglected on the floor. Against such a stubbornness Mr. Button's efforts were of little avail.

The sensation created in Baltimore was, at first, prodigious. What the mishap would have cost the Buttons and their kinsfolk socially cannot be determined, for the outbreak of the Civil War drew the city's attention to other things. A few people who were unfailingly polite racked their brains for compliments to give to the parents—and finally hit upon the ingenious device of declaring that the baby resembled his grandfather, a fact which, due to the standard state of decay common to all men of seventy, could not be denied. Mr. and Mrs. Roger Button were not pleased, and Benjamin's grandfather was furiously insulted.

Benjamin, once he left the hospital, took life as he found it. Several small boys were brought to see him, and he spent a stiff-jointed afternoon trying to work up an interest in tops and marbles—he even managed, quite accidentally, to break a kitchen window with a stone from a sling shot, a feat which secretly delighted his father.

Thereafter Benjamin contrived to break something every day, but he did these things only because they were expected of him, and because he was by nature obliging.

When his grandfather's initial antagonism wore off, Benjamin and that gentleman took enormous pleasure in one another's company. They would sit for hours, these two so far apart in age and experience, and, like old cronies, discuss with tireless monotony the slow events of the day. Benjamin felt more at ease in his grandfather's presence than in his parents'—they seemed always somewhat in awe of him and, despite the dictatorial authority they exercised over him, frequently addressed him as "Mr."

He was as puzzled as any one else at the apparently advanced age of his mind and body at birth. He read up on it in the medical journal, but found that no such case had been previously recorded. At his father's urging he made an honest attempt to play with other boys, and frequently he joined in the milder games—football shook him up too much, and he feared that in case of a fracture his ancient bones would refuse to knit.

When he was five he was sent to kindergarten, where he was initiated into the art of pasting green paper on orange paper, of weaving colored maps and manufacturing eternal cardboard necklaces. He was inclined to drowse off to sleep in the middle of these tasks, a habit which both irritated and frightened his young teacher. To his relief she complained to his parents, and he was removed from the school. The Roger Buttons told their friends that they felt he was too young.

By the time he was twelve years old his parents had grown used to him. Indeed, so strong is the force of custom that they no longer felt that he was different from any other child—except when some curious anomaly reminded them of the fact. But one day a few weeks after his twelfth birthday, while looking in the mirror, Benjamin made, or thought he made, an astonishing discovery. Did his eyes deceive him, or had his hair turned in the dozen years of his life from white to iron-gray under its concealing dye? Was the network of wrinkles on his face becoming less pronounced? Was his skin healthier and firmer, with even a touch of ruddy winter color? He could not tell. He knew that he no longer stooped and that his physical condition had improved since the early days of his life.

"Can it be——?" he thought to himself, or, rather, scarcely dared to think.

He went to his father. "I am grown," he announced determinedly. "I want to put on long trousers."

His father hesitated. "Well," he said finally, "I don't know. Fourteen is the age for putting on long trousers—and you are only twelve."

"But you'll have to admit," protested Benjamin, "that I'm big for my age."

His father looked at him with illusory speculation. "Oh, I'm not so sure of that," he said. "I was as big as you when I was twelve."

This was not true—it was all part of Roger Button's silent agreement with himself to believe in his son's normality.

Finally a compromise was reached. Benjamin was to continue to dye his hair. He was to make a better attempt to play with boys of his own age. He was not to wear his spectacles or carry a cane in the street. In return for these concessions he was allowed his first suit of long trousers. . . .

IV

Of the life of Benjamin Button between his twelfth and twenty-first year I intend to say little. Suffice to record that they were years of normal ungrowth. When Benjamin was eighteen he was erect as a man of fifty; he had more hair and it was of a dark gray; his step was firm, his voice had lost its cracked quaver and descended to a healthy baritone. So his father sent him up to Connecticut to take examinations for entrance to Yale College. Benjamin passed his examination and became a member of the freshman class.

On the third day following his matriculation he received a notification from Mr. Hart, the college registrar, to call at his office and arrange his schedule. Benjamin, glancing in the mirror, decided that his hair needed a new application of its brown dye, but an anxious inspection of his bureau drawer disclosed that the dye bottle was not there. Then he remembered—he had emptied it the day before and thrown it away.

He was in a dilemma. He was due at the registrar's in five minutes. There seemed to be no help for it—he must go as he was. He did.

"Good-morning," said the registrar politely. "You've come to inquire about your son."

"Why, as a matter of fact, my name's Button—" began Benjamin, but Mr. Hart cut him off.

"I'm very glad to meet you, Mr. Button. I'm expecting your son here any minute."

"That's me!" burst out Benjamin. "I'm a freshman."

"What!"

"I'm a freshman."

"Surely you're joking."

"Not at all."

The registrar frowned and glanced at a card before him. "Why, I have Mr. Benjamin Button's age down here as eighteen."

"That's my age," asserted Benjamin, flushing slightly.

The registrar eyed him wearily. "Now surely, Mr. Button, you don't expect me to believe that."

Benjamin smiled wearily. "I am eighteen," he repeated.

The registrar pointed sternly to the door. "Get out," he said. "Get out of college and get out of town. You are a dangerous lunatic."

"I am eighteen."

Mr. Hart opened the door. "The idea!" he shouted. "A man of your age trying to enter here as a freshman. Eighteen years old, are you? Well, I'll give you eighteen minutes to get out of town."

Benjamin Button walked with dignity from the room, and half a dozen undergraduates, who were waiting in the hall, followed him curiously with their eyes. When he had gone a little way he turned around, faced the infuriated registrar, who was still standing in the doorway, and repeated in a firm voice: "I am eighteen years old."

To a chorus of titters which went up from the group of undergraduates, Benjamin walked away.

But he was not fated to escape so easily. On his melancholy walk to the railroad station he found that he was being followed by a group, then by a swarm, and finally by a dense mass of undergraduates. The word had gone around that a lunatic had passed the entrance examinations for Yale and attempted to palm himself off as a youth of eighteen. A fever of excitement permeated the college. Men ran hatless out of classes, the football team abandoned its practice and joined the mob, professors' wives with bonnets awry and bustles out of position, ran shouting after the procession, from which proceeded a continual succession of remarks aimed at the tender sensibilities of Benjamin Button.

"He must be the Wandering Jew!"

"He ought to go to prep school at his age!"

"Look at the infant prodigy!"

"He thought this was the old men's home."

"Go up to Harvard!"

Benjamin increased his gait, and soon he was running. He

would show them! He *would* go to Harvard, and then they would regret these ill-considered taunts!

Safely on board the train for Baltimore, he put his head from the window. "You'll regret this!" he shouted.

"Ha-ha!" the undergraduates laughed. "Ha-ha-ha!" It was the biggest mistake that Yale College had ever made. . . .

v

In 1880 Benjamin Button was twenty years old, and he signalized his birthday by going to work for his father in Roger Button & Co., Wholesale Hardware. It was in that same year that he began "going out socially"—that is, his father insisted on taking him to several fashionable dances. Roger Button was now fifty, and he and his son were more and more companionable—in fact, since Benjamin had ceased to dye his hair (which was still grayish) they appeared about the same age, and could have passed for brothers.

One night in August they got into the phaeton attired in their full-dress suits and drove out to a dance at the Shevlins' country house, situated just outside of Baltimore. It was a gorgeous evening. A full moon drenched the road to the lustreless color of platinum, and late-blooming harvest flowers breathed into the motionless air aromas that were like low, half-heard laughter. The open country, carpeted for rods around with bright wheat, was translucent as in the day. It was almost impossible not to be affected by the sheer beauty of the sky—almost.

"There's a great future in the dry-goods business," Roger Button was saying. He was not a spiritual man—his esthetic sense was rudimentary.

"Old fellows like me can't learn new tricks," he observed profoundly. "It's you youngsters with energy and vitality that have the great future before you."

Far up the road the lights of the Shevlins' country house drifted into view, and presently there was a sighing sound that crept persistently toward them—it might have been the fine plaint of violins or the rustle of the silver wheat under the moon.

They pulled up behind a handsome brougham whose passengers were disembarking at the door. A lady got out, then an elderly gentleman, then another young lady, beautiful as sin.

Benjamin started; an almost chemical change seemed to dissolve and recompose the very elements of his body. A rigor passed over him, blood rose into his cheeks, his forehead, and there was a steady thumping in his ears. It was first love.

The girl was slender and frail, with hair that was ashen under the moon and honey-colored under the sputtering gas-lamps of the porch. Over her shoulders was thrown a Spanish mantilla of softest yellow, butterflied in black; her feet were glittering buttons at the hem of her bustled dress.

Roger Button leaned over to his son. "That," he said, "is young Hildegarde Moncrief, the daughter of General Moncrief."

Benjamin nodded coldly. "Pretty little thing," he said indifferently. But when the negro boy had led the buggy away, he added: "Dad, you might introduce me to her."

They approached a group of which Miss Moncrief was the centre. Reared in the old tradition, she courtesied low before Benjamin. Yes, he might have a dance. He thanked her and walked away—staggered away.

The interval until the time for his turn should arrive dragged itself out interminably. He stood close to the wall, silent, inscrutable, watching with murderous eyes the young bloods of Baltimore as they eddied around Hildegarde Moncrief, passionate admiration in their faces. How obnoxious they seemed to Benjamin; how intolerably rosy! Their curling brown whiskers aroused in him a feeling equivalent to indigestion.

But when his own time came, and he drifted with her out upon the changing floor to the music of the latest waltz from Paris, his jealousies and anxieties melted from him like a mantle of snow. Blind with enchantment, he felt that life was just beginning.

"You and your brother got here just as we did, didn't you?" asked Hildegarde, looking up at him with eyes that were like bright blue enamel.

Benjamin hesitated. If she took him for his father's brother, would it be best to enlighten her? He remembered his experience at Yale, so he decided against it. It would be rude to contradict a lady; it would be criminal to mar this exquisite occasion with the grotesque story of his origin. Later, perhaps. So he nodded, smiled, listened, was happy.

"I like men of your age," Hildegarde told him. "Young boys are so idiotic. They tell me how much champagne they drink at college, and how much money they lose playing cards. Men of your age know how to appreciate women."

Benjamin felt himself on the verge of a proposal—with an effort he choked back the impulse.

"You're just the romantic age," she continued—"fifty. Twenty-five is too worldly-wise; thirty is apt to be pale from overwork; forty is the age of long stories that take a whole cigar to tell; sixty is—oh, sixty is too near seventy; but fifty is the mellow age. I love fifty."

Fifty seemed to Benjamin a glorious age. He longed passionately to be fifty.

"I've always said," went on Hildegarde, "that I'd rather marry a man of fifty and be taken care of than marry a man of thirty and take care of *him*."

For Benjamin the rest of the evening was bathed in a honey-colored mist. Hildegarde gave him two more dances, and they discovered that they were marvellously in accord on all the questions of the day. She was to go driving with him on the following Sunday, and then they would discuss all these questions further.

Going home in the phaeton just before the crack of dawn, when the first bees were humming and the fading moon glimmered in the cool dew, Benjamin knew vaguely that his father was discussing wholesale hardware.

". . . . And what do you think should merit our biggest attention after hammers and nails?" the elder Button was saying.

"Love," replied Benjamin absent-mindedly.

"Lugs?" exclaimed Roger Button. "Why, I've just covered the question of lugs."

Benjamin regarded him with dazed eyes just as the eastern sky was suddenly cracked with light, and an oriole yawned piercingly in the quickening trees. . . .

VI

When, six months later, the engagement of Miss Hildegarde Moncrief to Mr. Benjamin Button was made known (I say "made known," for General Moncrief declared he would rather fall upon his sword than announce it), the excitement in Balti-more society reached a feverish pitch. The almost forgotten story of Benjamin's birth was remembered and sent out upon the winds of scandal in picaresque and incredible forms. It was said that Benjamin was really the father of Roger Button, that he was his brother who had been in prison for forty years, that he was John Wilkes Booth in disguise—and, finally, that he had two small conical horns sprouting from his head.

The Sunday supplements of the New York papers played up the case with fascinating sketches which showed the head of Benjamin Button attached to a fish, to a snake, and, finally, to a body of solid brass. He became known, journalistically, as the Mystery Man of Maryland. But the true story, as is usually the case, had a very small circulation.

However, every one agreed with General Moncrief that it was "criminal" for a lovely girl who could have married any beau in Baltimore to throw herself into the arms of a man who was assuredly fifty. In vain Mr. Roger Button published his son's birth certificate in large type in the Baltimore *Blaze*. No one believed it. You had only to look at Benjamin and see.

On the part of the two people most concerned there was no wavering. So many of the stories about her fiancé were false that Hildegarde refused stubbornly to believe even the true one. In vain General Moncrief pointed out to her the high mortality among men of fifty—or, at least, among men who looked fifty; in vain he told her of the instability of the whole-sale hardware business. Hildegarde had chosen to marry for mellowness —and marry she did. . . .

VII

In one particular, at least, the friends of Hildegarde Moncrief were mistaken. The wholesale hardware business prospered amazingly. In the fifteen years between Benjamin Button's marriage in 1880 and his father's retirement in 1895, the family fortune was doubled—and this was due largely to the younger member of the firm.

Needless to say, Baltimore eventually received the couple to its bosom. Even old General Moncrief became reconciled to his son-in-law when Benjamin gave him the money to bring out his "History of the Civil War" in twenty volumes, which had been refused by nine prominent publishers.

In Benjamin himself fifteen years had wrought many changes. It seemed to him that the blood flowed with new vigor through his veins. It began to be a pleasure to rise in the morning, to walk with an active step along the busy, sunny street, to work untiringly with his shipments of hammers and his cargoes of nails. It was in 1890 that he executed his famous business coup: he brought up the suggestion that *all nails used in nailing up the boxes in which nails are shipped are the property of the shippee*, a proposal which became a statute, was approved by Chief Justice Fossile, and saved Roger Button and Company, Wholesale Hardware, more than *six hundred nails every year*.

In addition, Benjamin discovered that he was becoming more and more attracted by the gay side of life. It was typical of his growing enthusiasm for pleasure that he was the first man in the city of Baltimore to own and run an automobile. Meeting him on the street, his contemporaries would stare enviously at the picture he made of health and vitality.

"He seems to grow younger every year," they would remark. And if old Roger Button, now sixty-five years old, had failed at first to give a proper welcome to his son he atoned at last by bestowing on him what amounted to adulation.

And here we come to an unpleasant subject which it will be well to pass over as quickly as possible. There was only one thing that worried Benjamin Button: his wife had ceased to attract him.

At that time Hildegarde was a woman of thirty-five, with a son, Roscoe, fourteen years old. In the early days of their marriage Benjamin had worshipped her. But, as the years passed, her honey-colored hair became an unexciting brown, the blue enamel of her eyes assumed the aspect of cheap crockery—moreover, and most of all, she had become too settled in her ways, too placid, too content, too anemic in her excitements, and too sober in her taste. As a bride it had been she who had "dragged" Benjamin to dances and dinners—now conditions were reversed. She went out socially with him, but without enthusiasm, devoured already by that eternal inertia which comes to live with each of us one day and stays with us to the end.

Benjamin's discontent waxed stronger. At the outbreak of

the Spanish-American War in 1898 his home had for him so little charm that he decided to join the army. With his business influence he obtained a commission as captain, and proved so adaptable to the work that he was made a major, and finally a lieutenant-colonel just in time to participate in the celebrated charge up San Juan Hill. He was slightly wounded, and received a medal.

Benjamin had become so attached to the activity and excitement of army life that he regretted to give it up, but his business required attention, so he resigned his commission and came home. He was met at the station by a brass band and escorted to his house.

VIII

Hildegarde, waving a large silk flag, greeted him on the porch, and even as he kissed her he felt with a sinking of the heart that these three years had taken their toll. She was a woman of forty now, with a faint skirmish line of gray hairs in her head. The sight depressed him.

Up in his room he saw his reflection in the familiar mirror—he went closer and examined his own face with anxiety, comparing it after a moment with a photograph of himself in uniform taken just before the war.

"Good Lord!" he said aloud. The process was continuing. There was no doubt of it—he looked now like a man of thirty. Instead of being delighted, he was uneasy—he was growing younger. He had hitherto hoped that once he reached a bodily age equivalent to his age in years, the grotesque phenomenon which had marked his birth would cease to function. He shuddered. His destiny seemed to him awful, incredible.

When he came down-stairs Hildegarde was waiting for him. She appeared annoyed, and he wondered if she had at last discovered that there was something amiss. It was with an effort to relieve the tension between them that he broached the matter at dinner in what he considered a delicate way.

"Well," he remarked lightly, "everybody says I look younger than ever."

Hildegarde regarded him with scorn. She sniffed. "Do you think it's anything to boast about?"

"I'm not boasting," he asserted uncomfortably.

She sniffed again. "The idea," she said, and after a moment: "I should think you'd have enough pride to stop it."

"How can I?" he demanded.

"I'm not going to argue with you," she retorted. "But there's a right way of doing things and a wrong way. If you've made up your mind to be different from everybody else, I don't suppose I can stop you, but I really don't think it's very considerate."

"But, Hildegarde, I can't help it."

"You can too. You're simply stubborn. You think you don't want to be like any one else. You always have been that way, and you always will be. But just think how it would be if every one else looked at things as you do—what would the world be like?"

As this was an inane and unanswerable argument Benjamin made no reply, and from that time on a chasm began to widen between them. He wondered what possible fascination she had ever exercised over him.

To add to the breach, he found, as the new century gathered headway, that his thirst for gayety grew stronger. Never a party of any kind in the city of Baltimore but he was there, dancing with the prettiest of the young married women, chatting with the most popular of the débutantes, and finding their company charming, while his wife, a dowager of evil omen, sat among the chaperons, now in haughty disapproval, and now following him with solemn, puzzled, and reproachful eyes.

"Look!" people would remark. "What a pity! A young fellow that age tied to a woman of forty-five. He must be twenty years younger than his wife." They had forgotten—as people inevitably forget—that back in 1880 their mammas and papas had also remarked about this same ill-matched pair.

Benjamin's growing unhappiness at home was compensated for by his many new interests. He took up golf and made a great success of it. He went in for dancing: in 1906 he was an expert at "The Boston," and in 1908 he was considered proficient at the "Maxixe," while in 1909 his "Castle Walk" was the envy of every young man in town.

His social activities, of course, interfered to some extent with his business, but then he had worked hard at wholesale hardware for twenty-five years and felt that he could soon hand it on to his son, Roscoe, who had recently graduated from Harvard.

He and his son were, in fact, often mistaken for each other. This pleased Benjamin—he soon forgot the insidious fear which had come over him on his return from the Spanish-American War, and grew to take a naïve pleasure in his appearance. There was only one fly in the delicious ointment—he hated to appear in public with his wife. Hildegarde was almost fifty, and the sight of her made him feel absurd. . . .

IX

One September day in 1910—a few years after Roger Button & Co., Wholesale Hardware, had been handed over to young Roscoe Button—a man, apparently about twenty years old, entered himself as a freshman at Harvard University in Cambridge. He did not make the mistake of announcing that he would never see fifty again nor did he mention the fact that his son had been graduated from the same institution ten years before.

He was admitted, and almost immediately attained a prominent position in the class, partly because he seemed a little older than the other freshmen, whose average age was about eighteen.

But his success was largely due to the fact that in the football game with Yale he played so brilliantly, with so much dash and with such a cold, remorseless anger that he scored seven touchdowns and fourteen field goals for Harvard, and caused one entire eleven of Yale men to be carried singly from the field, unconscious. He was the most celebrated man in college.

Strange to say, in his third or junior year he was scarcely able to "make" the team. The coaches said that he had lost weight, and it seemed to the more observant among them that he was not quite as tall as before. He made no touchdowns—indeed, he was retained on the team chiefly in hope that his enormous reputation would bring terror and disorganization to the Yale team.

In his senior year he did not make the team at all. He had grown so slight and frail that one day he was taken by some sophomores for a freshman, an incident which humiliated him terribly. He became known as something of a prodigy—a senior who was surely no more than sixteen—and he was often shocked at the worldliness of some of his classmates. His studies seemed harder to him—he felt that they were too advanced. He had heard his classmates speak of St. Midas', the famous preparatory school, at which so many of them had prepared for college, and he determined after his graduation to enter himself at St. Midas', where the sheltered life among boys his own size would be more congenial to him.

Upon his graduation in 1914 he went home to Baltimore with his Harvard diploma in his pocket. Hildegarde was now residing in Italy, so Benjamin went to live with his son, Roscoe. But though he was welcomed in a general way, there was obviously no heartiness in Roscoe's feeling toward him—there was even perceptible a tendency on his son's part to think that Benjamin, as he moped about the house in adolescent mooniness, was somewhat in the way. Roscoe was married now and prominent in Baltimore life, and he wanted no scandal to creep out in connection with his family.

Benjamin, no longer persona grata with the débutantes and younger college set, found himself left much alone, except for the companionship of three or four fifteen-year-old boys in the neighborhood. His idea of going to St. Midas' school recurred to him.

"Say," he said to Roscoe one day, "I've told you over and over that I want to go to prep school."

"Well, go, then," replied Roscoe shortly. The matter was distasteful to him, and he wished to avoid a discussion.

"I can't go alone," said Benjamin helplessly. "You'll have to enter me and take me up there."

"I haven't got time," declared Roscoe abruptly. His eyes narrowed and he looked uneasily at his father. "As a matter of fact," he added, "you'd better not go on with this business much longer. You better pull up short. You better—you better"—he paused and his face crimsoned as he sought for words—"you better turn right around and start back the other way. This has gone too far to be a joke. It isn't funny any longer. You—you behave yourself!"

Benjamin looked at him, on the verge of tears.

"And another thing," continued Roscoe, "when visitors are

in the house I want you to call me 'Uncle'—not 'Roscoe,' but 'Uncle,' do you understand? It looks absurd for a boy of fifteen to call me by my first name. Perhaps you'd better call me 'Uncle' *all* the time, so you'll get used to it."

With a harsh look at his father, Roscoe turned away. . . .

X

At the termination of this interview, Benjamin wandered dismally up-stairs and stared at himself in the mirror. He had not shaved for three months, but he could find nothing on his face but a faint white down with which it seemed unnecessary to meddle. When he had first come home from Harvard, Roscoe had approached him with the proposition that he should wear eye-glasses and imitation whiskers glued to his cheeks, and it had seemed for a moment that the farce of his early years was to be repeated. But whiskers had itched and made him ashamed. He wept and Roscoe had reluctantly relented.

Benjamin opened a book of boys' stories, "The Boy Scouts in Bimini Bay," and began to read. But he found himself thinking persistently about the war. America had joined the Allied cause during the preceding month, and Benjamin wanted to enlist, but, alas, sixteen was the minimum age, and he did not look that old. His true age which was fifty-seven, would have disqualified him, anyway.

There was a knock at his door, and the butler appeared with a letter bearing a large official legend in the corner and addressed to Mr. Benjamin Button. Benjamin tore it open eagerly, and read the enclosure with delight. It informed him that many reserve officers who had served in the Spanish-American War were being called back into service with a higher rank, and it enclosed his commission as brigadier-general in the United States army with orders to report immediately.

Benjamin jumped to his feet fairly quivering with enthusiasm. This was what he had wanted. He seized his cap and ten minutes later he had entered a large tailoring establishment on Charles Street, and asked in his uncertain treble to be measured for a uniform.

"Want to play soldier, sonny?" demanded a clerk, casually.

Benjamin flushed. "Say! Never mind what I want!" he

retorted angrily. "My name's Button and I live on Mt. Vernon Place, so you know I'm good for it."

"Well," admitted the clerk, hesitantly, "if you're not, I guess your daddy is, all right."

Benjamin was measured, and a week later his uniform was completed. He had difficulty in obtaining the proper general's insignia because the dealer kept insisting to Benjamin that a nice Y.W.C.A. badge would look just as well and be much more fun to play with.

Saying nothing to Roscoe, he left the house one night and proceeded by train to Camp Mosby, in South Carolina, where he was to command an infantry brigade. On a sultry April day he approached the entrance to the camp, paid off the taxicab which had brought him from the station, and turned to the sentry on guard.

"Get some one to handle my luggage!" he said briskly.

The sentry eyed him reproachfully. "Say," he remarked, "where you goin' with the general's duds, sonny?"

Benjamin, veteran of the Spanish-American War, whirled upon him with fire in his eye, but with, alas, a changing treble voice.

"Come to attention!" he tried to thunder; he paused for breath—then suddenly he saw the sentry snap his heels together and bring his rifle to the present. Benjamin concealed a smile of gratification, but when he glanced around his smile faded. It was not he who had inspired obedience, but an imposing artillery colonel who was approaching on horseback.

"Colonel!" called Benjamin shrilly.

The colonel came up, drew rein, and looked coolly down at him with a twinkle in his eyes. "Whose little boy are you?" he demanded kindly.

"I'll soon darn well show you whose little boy I am!" retorted Benjamin in a ferocious voice. "Get down off that horse!"

The colonel roared with laughter.

"You want him, eh, general?"

"Here!" cried Benjamin desperately. "Read this." And he thrust his commission toward the colonel.

The colonel read it, his eyes popping from their sockets.

"Where'd you get this?" he demanded, slipping the document into his own pocket.

"I got it from the Government, as you'll soon find out!"

"You come along with me," said the colonel with a peculiar look. "We'll go up to headquarters and talk this over. Come along."

The colonel turned and began walking his horse in the direction of headquarters. There was nothing for Benjamin to do but follow with as much dignity as possible—meanwhile promising himself a stern revenge.

But this revenge did not materialize. Two days later, however, his son Roscoe materialized from Baltimore, hot and cross from a hasty trip, and escorted the weeping general, *sans* uniform, back to his home.

XI

In 1920 Roscoe Button's first child was born. During the attendant festivities, however, no one thought it "the thing" to mention that the little grubby boy, apparently about ten years of age who played around the house with lead soldiers and a miniature circus, was the new baby's own grandfather.

No one disliked the little boy whose fresh, cheerful face was crossed with just a hint of sadness, but to Roscoe Button his presence was a source of torment. In the idiom of his generation Roscoe did not consider the matter "efficient." It seemed to him that his father, in refusing to look sixty, had not behaved like a "red-blooded he-man"—this was Roscoe's favorite expression—but in a curious and perverse manner. Indeed, to think about the matter for as much as a half an hour drove him to the edge of insanity. Roscoe believed that "live wires" should keep young, but carrying it out on such a scale was—was—was inefficient. And there Roscoe rested.

Five years later Roscoe's little boy had grown old enough to play childish games with little Benjamin under the supervision of the same nurse. Roscoe took them both to kindergarten on the same day and Benjamin found that playing with little strips of colored paper, making mats and chains and curious and beautiful designs, was the most fascinating game in the world. Once he was bad and had to stand in the corner—then he cried —but for the most part there were gay hours in the cheerful room, with the sunlight coming in the windows and Miss

Bailey's kind hand resting for a moment now and then in his tousled hair.

Roscoe's son moved up into the first grade after a year, but Benjamin stayed on in the kindergarten. He was very happy. Sometimes when other tots talked about what they would do when they grew up a shadow would cross his little face as if in a dim, childish way he realized that those were things in which he was never to share.

The days flowed on in monotonous content. He went back a third year to the kindergarten, but he was too little now to understand what the bright shining strips of paper were for. He cried because the other boys were bigger than he and he was afraid of them. The teacher talked to him, but though he tried to understand he could not understand at all.

He was taken from the kindergarten. His nurse, Nana, in her starched gingham dress, became the centre of his tiny world. On bright days they walked in the park; Nana would point at a great gray monster and say "elephant," and Benjamin would say it after her, and when he was being undressed for bed that night he would say it over and over aloud to her: "Elyphant, elyphant, elyphant." Sometimes Nana let him jump on the bed, which was fun, because if you sat down exactly right it would bounce you up on your feet again, and if you said "Ah" for a long time while you jumped you got a very pleasing broken vocal effect.

He loved to take a big cane from the hatrack and go around hitting chairs and tables with it and saying: "Fight, fight, fight." When there were people there the old ladies would cluck at him, which interested him, and the young ladies would try to kiss him, which he submitted to with mild boredom. And when the long day was done at five o'clock he would go up-stairs with Nana and be fed oatmeal and nice soft mushy foods with a spoon.

There were no troublesome memories in his childish sleep; no token came to him of his brave days at college, of the glittering years when he flustered the hearts of many girls. There were only the white, safe walls of his crib and Nana and a man who came to see him sometimes, and a great big orange ball that Nana pointed at just before his twilight bed hour and called "sun." When the sun went his eyes were sleepy—there were no dreams, no dreams to haunt him.

The past—the wild charge at the head of his men up San Juan Hill; the first years of his marriage when he worked late into the summer dusk down in the busy city for young Hildegarde whom he loved; the days before that when he sat smoking far into the night in the gloomy old Button house on Monroe Street with his grandfather—all these had faded like unsubstantial dreams from his mind as though they had never been.

He did not remember. He did not remember clearly whether the milk was warm or cool at his last feeding or how the days passed—there was only his crib and Nana's familiar presence. And then he remembered nothing. When he was hungry he cried—that was all. Through the noons and nights he breathed and over him there were soft mumblings and murmurings that he scarcely heard, and faintly differentiated smells, and light and darkness.

Then it was all dark, and his white crib and the dim faces that moved above him, and the warm sweet aroma of the milk, faded out altogether from his mind.

1922

SEABURY QUINN

(1889–1969)

The Curse of Everard Maundy

"*Mort d'un chat!* I do not like this!" Jules de Grandin slammed the evening paper down upon the table and glared ferociously at me through the library lamplight.

"What's up now?" I asked, wondering vaguely what the cause of his latest grievance was. "Some reporter say something personal about you?"

"*Parbleu, non*, he would better not!" the little Frenchman replied, his round blue eyes flashing ominously. "Me, I would pull his nose and tweak his ears. But it is not of the reporter's insolence I speak, my friend; I do not like these suicides; there are too many of them."

"Of course there are," I conceded soothingly, "one suicide is that much too many; people have no right to——"

"Ah bah!" he cut in. "You do misapprehend me, *mon vieux*. Excuse me one moment, if you please." He rose hurriedly from his chair and left the room. A moment later I heard him rummaging about in the cellar.

In a few minutes he returned, the week's supply of discarded newspapers salvaged from the dust bin in his arms.

"Now, attend me," he ordered as he spread the sheets out before him and began scanning the columns hastily. "Here is an item from Monday's *Journal*:

Two Motorists Die While Driving Cars

The impulse to end their lives apparently attacked two automobile drivers on the Albemarle turnpike near Lonesome Swamp, two miles out of Harrisonville, last night. Carl Planz, thirty-one years old, of Martins Falls, took his own life by shooting himself in the head with a shotgun while seated in his automobile, which he had parked at the roadside where the pike passes nearest the swamp. His remains were identified by two letters, one addressed to his wife, the other to his father, Joseph Planz, with whom he was associated in the real estate business at Martins Falls. A check for three hundred dollars and several other papers found in his pockets completed identification. The letters, which merely declared his intention to kill himself, failed to establish any motive for the act.

Almost at the same time, and within a hundred yards of the spot where Planz's body was found by State Trooper Henry Anderson this morning, the body of Henry William Nixon, of New Rochelle, N.Y., was discovered partly sitting, partly lying on the rear seat of his automobile, an empty bottle of windshield cleaner lying on the floor beside him. It is thought this liquid, which contained a small amount of cyanide of potassium, was used to inflict death. Police Surgeon Stevens, who examined both bodies, declared that the men had been dead approximately the same length of time when brought to the station house.

"What think you of that, my friend, *hein*?" de Grandin demanded, looking up from the paper with one of his direct, challenging stares.

"Why—er——" I began, but he interrupted.

"Hear this," he commanded, taking up a second paper, "this is from the *News* of Tuesday:

Mother and Daughters Die in Death Pact

Police and heartbroken relatives are today trying to trace a motive for the triple suicide of Mrs. Ruby Westerfelt and her daughters, Joan and Elizabeth, who perished by leaping from the eighth floor of the Hotel Dolores, Newark, late yesterday afternoon. The women registered at the hotel under assumed names, went immediately to the room assigned them, and ten minutes later Miss Gladys Walsh, who occupied a room on the fourth floor, was startled to see a dark form hurtle past her window. A moment later a second body flashed past on its downward flight, and as Miss Walsh, horrified, rushed toward the window, a loud crash sounded outside. Looking out, Miss Walsh saw the body of a third woman partly impaled on the spikes of a balcony rail.

Miss Walsh sought to aid the woman. As she leaned from her window and reached out with a trembling arm she was greeted by a scream: "Don't try! I won't be saved; I must go with Mother and Sister!" A moment later the woman had managed to free herself from the restraining iron spikes and fell to the cement areaway four floors below.

"And here is still another account, this one from tonight's paper," he continued, unfolding the sheet which had caused his original protest:

High School Co-ed Takes Life in Attic

The family and friends of Edna May McCarty, fifteen-year-old co-ed of Harrisonville High School, are at a loss to assign a cause for her suicide early this morning. The girl had no love affairs, as far as is known, and had not failed in her examinations. On the contrary, she had passed the school's latest test with flying colors. Her mother told investigating police officials that overstudy might have temporarily unbalanced the child's mind. Miss McCarty's body was found suspended from the rafters of her father's attic by her mother this morning when the young woman did not respond to a call for breakfast and could not be found in her room on the second floor of the house. A clothesline, used to hang clothes which were dried inside the house in rainy weather, was used to form the fatal noose.

"Now then, my friend," de Grandin reseated himself and lighted a vile-smelling French cigarette, puffing furiously, till the smoke surrounded his sleek, blond head like a mephitic nimbus, "what have you to say to those reports? Am I not right? Are there not too many—*mordieu*, entirely too many!—suicides in our city?"

"All of them weren't committed here," I objected practically, "and besides, there couldn't very well be any connection between them. Mrs. Westerfelt and her daughters carried out a suicide pact, it appears, but they certainly could have had no understanding with the two men and the young girl——"

"Perhaps, maybe, possibly," he agreed, nodding his head so vigorously that a little column of ash detached itself from his cigarette and dropped unnoticed on the bosom of his stiffly starched evening shirt. "You may be right, Friend Trowbridge, but then, as is so often the case, you may be entirely wrong. One thing I know: I, Jules de Grandin, shall investigate these cases myself personally. *Cordieu*, they do interest me! I shall ascertain what is the what here."

"Go ahead," I encouraged. "The investigation will keep you out of mischief," and I returned to the second chapter of Haggard's *The Wanderer's Necklace*, a book which I have read at least half a dozen times, yet find as fascinating at each rereading as when I first perused its pages.

The matter of the six suicides still bothered him next morning. "Trowbridge, my friend," he asked abruptly as he disposed of

his second helping of coffee and passed his cup for replenish-
ment, "why is it that people destroy themselves?"

"Oh," I answered evasively, "different reasons, I suppose.
Some are crossed in love, some meet financial reverses and some
do it while temporarily deranged."

"Yes," he agreed thoughtfully, "yet every self-murderer has
a real or fancied reason for quitting the world, and there is apparently no reason why any of these six poor ones who hurled
themselves into outer darkness during the past week should have
done so. All, apparently, were well provided for, none of them,
as far as is known, had any reason to regret the past or fear the
future; yet"—he shrugged his narrow shoulders significantly—
"*voilà*, they are gone!

"Another thing: At the *Faculté de Médicine Légal* and the
Sûreté in Paris we keep most careful statistics, not only on the
number, but on the manner of suicides. I do not think your
Frenchman differs radically from your American when it comes
to taking his life, so the figures for one nation may well be a
signpost for the other. These self-inflicted deaths, they are not
right. They do not follow the rules. Men prefer to hang, slash
or shoot themselves; women favor drowning, poison or gas;
yet here we have one of the men taking poison, one of the
women hanging herself, and three of them jumping to death.
Nom d'un canard, I am not satisfied with it!"

"H'm, neither are the unfortunate parties who killed themselves, if the theologians are to be believed," I returned.

"You speak right," he returned, then muttered dreamily to
himself: "Destruction—destruction of body and imperilment
of soul—*mordieu*, it is strange, it is not righteous!" He disposed
of his coffee at a gulp and leaped from his chair. "I go!" he declared dramatically, turning toward the door.

"Where?"

"Where? Where should I go, if not to secure the history of
these so puzzling cases? I shall not rest nor sleep nor eat until
I have the string of the mystery's skein in my hands." He
paused at the door, a quick, elfin smile playing across his usually stern features. "And should I return before my work is
complete," he suggested, "I pray you, have the excellent Nora
prepare another of her so magnificent apple pies for dinner."

Forty seconds later the front door clicked shut, and from

the dining room's oriel window I saw his neat little figure, trimly encased in blue chinchilla and gray worsted, pass quickly down the sidewalk, his ebony cane hammering a rapid tattoo on the stones as it kept time to the thoughts racing through his active brain.

"I am desolated that my capacity is exhausted," he announced that evening as he finished his third portion of deep-dish apple pie smothered in pungent rum sauce and regarded his empty plate sadly. "*Eh bien*, perhaps it is as well. Did I eat more I might not be able to think clearly, and clear thought is what I shall need this night, my friend. Come; we must be going."

"Going where?" I demanded.

"To hear the reverend and estimable Monsieur Maundy deliver his sermon."

"Who? Everard Maundy?"

"But of course, who else?"

"But—but," I stammered, looking at him incredulously, "why should we go to the tabernacle to hear this man? I can't say I'm particularly impressed with his system, and—aren't you a Catholic, de Grandin?"

"Who can say?" he replied as he lighted a cigarette and stared thoughtfully at his coffee cup. "My father was a Huguenot of the Huguenots; a several times great-grandsire of his cut his way to freedom through the Paris streets on the fateful night of August 24, 1572. My mother was convent-bred, and as pious as anyone with a sense of humor and the gift of thinking for herself could well be. One of my uncles—he for whom I am named—was like a blood brother to Darwin the magnificent, and Huxley the scarcely less magnificent, also. Me, I am"—he elevated his eyebrows and shoulders at once and pursed his lips comically—"what should a man with such a heritage be, my friend? But come, we delay, we tarry, we lose time. Let us hasten. I have a fancy to hear what this Monsieur Maundy has to say, and to observe him. See, I have here tickets for the fourth row of the hall."

Very much puzzled, but never doubting that something more than the idle wish to hear a sensational evangelist urged the little Frenchman toward the tabernacle, I rose and accompanied him.

"*Parbleu*, what a day!" he sighed as I turned my car toward the downtown section. "From coroner's office to undertakers' I have run; and from undertakers' to hospitals. I have interviewed everyone who could shed the smallest light on these strange deaths, yet I seem no further advanced than when I began. What I have found out serves only to whet my curiosity; what I have not discovered——" He spread his hands in a world-embracing gesture and lapsed into silence.

The Jachin Tabernacle, where the Rev. Everard Maundy was holding his series of non-sectarian revival meetings, was crowded to overflowing when we arrived, but our tickets passed us through the jostling crowd of half-skeptical, half-believing people who thronged the lobby, and we were soon ensconced in seats where every word the preacher uttered could be heard with ease.

Before the introductory hymn had been finished, de Grandin mumbled a wholly unintelligible excuse in my ear and disappeared up the aisle, and I settled myself in my seat to enjoy the service as best I might.

The Rev. Mr. Maundy was a tall, hatchet-faced man in early middle life, a little inclined to rant and make use of worked-over platitudes, but obviously sincere in the message he had for his congregation. From the half-cynical attitude of a regularly-enrolled church member who looks on revivals with a certain disdain, I found myself taking keener and keener interest in the story of regeneration the preacher had to tell, my attention compelled not so much by his words as by the earnestness of his manner and the wonderful stage presence the man possessed. When the ushers had taken up the collection and the final hymn was sung, I was surprized to find we had been two hours in the tabernacle. If anyone had asked me, I should have said half an hour would have been nearer the time consumed by the service.

"Eh, my friend, did you find it interesting?" de Grandin asked as he joined me in the lobby and linked his arm in mine.

"Yes, very," I admitted, then, somewhat sulkily: "I thought you wanted to hear him, too—it was your idea that we came here—what made you run away?"

"I am sorry," he replied with a chuckle which belied his words, "but it was *necessaire* that I fry other fish while you listened to the reverend gentleman's discourse. Will you drive me home?"

The March wind cut shrewdly through my overcoat after the super-heated atmosphere of the tabernacle, and I felt myself shivering involuntarily more than once as we drove through the quiet streets. Strangely, too, I felt rather sleepy and ill at ease. By the time we reached the wide, tree-bordered avenue before my house I was conscious of a distinctly unpleasant sensation, a constantly-growing feeling of malaise, a sort of baseless, irritating uneasiness. Thoughts of years long forgotten seemed summoned to my memory without rime or reason. An incident of an unfair advantage I had taken of a younger boy while at public school, recollections of petty, useless lies and bits of naughtiness committed when I could not have been more than three came flooding back on my consciousness, finally an episode of my early youth which I had forgotten some forty years.

My father had brought a little stray kitten into the house, and I, with the tiny lad's unconscious cruelty, had fallen to teasing the wretched bundle of bedraggled fur, finally tossing it nearly to the ceiling to test the tale I had so often heard that a cat always lands on its feet. My experiment was the exception which demonstrated the rule, it seemed, for the poor, half-starved feline hit the hardwood floor squarely on its back, struggled feebly a moment, then yielded up its entire nine-fold expectancy of life.

Long after the smart of the whipping I received in consequence had been forgotten, the memory of that unintentional murder had plagued my boyish conscience, and many were the times I had awakened at dead of night, weeping bitter repentance out upon my pillow.

Now, some forty years later, the thought of that kitten's death came back as clearly as the night the unkempt little thing thrashed out its life upon our kitchen floor. Strive as I would, I could not drive the memory from me, and it seemed as though the unwitting crime of my childhood was assuming an enormity out of all proportion to its true importance.

I shook my head and passed my hand across my brow, as a sleeper suddenly wakened does to drive away the lingering memory of an unpleasant dream, but the kitten's ghost, like Banquo's, would not down.

"What is it, Friend Trowbridge?" de Grandin asked as he eyed me shrewdly.

"Oh, nothing," I replied as I parked the car before our door and leaped to the curb, "I was just thinking."

"Ah?" he responded on a rising accent. "And of what do you think, my friend? Something unpleasant?"

"Oh, no; nothing important enough to dignify by that term," I answered shortly, and led the way to the house, keeping well ahead of him, lest he push his inquiries farther.

In this, however, I did him wrong. Tactful women and Jules de Grandin have the talent of feeling without being told when conversation is unwelcome, and besides wishing me a pleasant good-night, he spoke not a word until we had gone upstairs to bed. As I was opening my door, he called down the hall, "Should you want me, remember, you have but to call."

"Humph!" I muttered ungraciously as I shut the door. "Want him? What the devil should I want him for?" And so I pulled off my clothes and climbed into bed, the thought of the murdered kitten still with me and annoying me more by its persistence than by the faint sting of remorse it evoked.

How long I had slept I do not know, but I do know I was wide-awake in a single second, sitting up in bed and staring through the darkened chamber with eyes which strove desperately to pierce the gloom.

Somewhere—whether far or near I could not tell—a cat had raised its voice in a long-drawn, wailing cry, kept silence a moment, then given tongue again with increased volume.

There are few sounds more eery to hear in the dead of night than the cry of a prowling feline, and this one was of a particularly sad, almost reproachful tone.

"Confound the beast!" I exclaimed angrily, and lay back on my pillow, striving vainly to recapture my broken sleep.

Again the wail sounded, indefinite as to location, but louder, more prolonged, even, it seemed, fiercer in its timbre than when I first heard it in my sleep.

I glanced toward the window with the vague thought of

hurling a book or boot or other handy missile at the disturber, then held my breath in sudden affright. Staring through the aperture between the scrim curtains was the biggest, most ferocious-looking tom-cat I had ever seen. Its eyes, seemingly as large as butter dishes, glared at me with the green phosphorescence of its tribe, and with an added demoniacal glow the like of which I had never seen. Its red mouth, opened to full compass in a venomous, soundless "spit," seemed almost as large as that of a lion, and the wicked, pointed ears above its rounded face were laid back against its head, as though it were crouching for combat.

"Get out! Scat!" I called feebly, but making no move toward the thing.

"S-s-s-sssh!" a hiss of incomparable fury answered me, and the creature put one heavy, padded paw tentatively over the windowsill, still regarding me with its unchanging, hateful stare.

"Get!" I repeated, and stopped abruptly. Before my eyes the great beast was *growing*, increasing in size till its chest and shoulders completely blocked the window. Should it attack me I would be as helpless in its claws as a Hindoo under the paws of a Bengal tiger.

Slowly, stealthily, its cushioned feet making no sound as it set them down daintily, the monstrous creature advanced into the room, crouched on its haunches and regarded me steadily, wickedly, malevolently.

I rose a little higher on my elbow. The great brute twitched the tip of its sable tail warningly, half lifted one of its forepaws from the floor, and set it down again, never shifting its sulfurous eyes from my face.

Inch by inch I moved my farther foot from the bed, felt the floor beneath it, and pivoted slowly in a sitting position until my other foot was free of the bedclothes. Apparently the cat did not notice my strategy, for it made no menacing move till I flexed my muscles for a leap, suddenly flung myself from the bedstead, and leaped toward the door.

With a snarl, white teeth flashing, green eyes glaring, ears laid back, the beast moved between me and the exit, and began slowly advancing on me, hate and menace in every line of its giant body.

I gave ground before it, retreating step by step and striving desperately to hold its eyes with mine, as I had heard hunters sometimes do when suddenly confronted by wild animals.

Back, back I crept, the ogreish visitant keeping pace with my retreat, never suffering me to increase the distance between us.

I felt the cold draft of the window on my back; the pressure of the sill against me; behind me, from the waist up, was the open night, before me the slowly advancing monster.

It was a thirty-foot drop to a cemented roadway, but death on the pavement was preferable to the slashing claws and grinding teeth of the terrible thing creeping toward me.

I threw one leg over the sill, watching constantly, lest the cat-thing leap on me before I could cheat it by dashing myself to the ground——

"Trowbridge, *mon Dieu*, Trowbridge, my friend! What is it you would do?" The frenzied hail of Jules de Grandin cut through the dark, and a flood of light from the hallway swept into the room as he flung the door violently open and raced across the room, seizing my arm in both hands and dragging me from the window.

"Look out, de Grandin!" I screamed. "The cat! It'll get you!"

"Cat?" he echoed, looking about him uncomprehendingly. "Do you say 'cat,' my friend? A cat will get *me*? *Mort d'un chou*, the cat which can make a mouse of Jules de Grandin is not yet whelped! Where is it, this cat of yours?"

"There! Th——" I began, then stopped, rubbing my eyes. The room was empty. Save for de Grandin and me there was nothing animate in the place.

"But it *was* here," I insisted. "I tell you, I saw it; a great, black cat, as big as a lion. It came in the window and crouched right over there, and was driving me to jump to the ground when you came——"

"*Nom d'un porc!* Do you say so?" he exclaimed, seizing my arm again and shaking me. "Tell me of this cat, my friend. I would learn more of this puss-puss who comes into Friend Trow-bridge's house, grows great as a lion and drives him to his death on the stones below. Ha, I think maybe the trail of these mysterious deaths is not altogether lost! Tell me more, *mon ami*; I would know all—all!"

"Of course, it was just a bad dream," I concluded as I finished the recital of my midnight visitation, "but it seemed terribly real to me while it lasted."

"I doubt it not," he agreed with a quick, nervous nod. "And on our way from the tabernacle tonight, my friend, I noticed you were much *distrait*. Were you, perhaps, feeling ill at the time?"

"Not at all," I replied. "The truth is, I was remembering something which occurred when I was a lad four or five years old; something which had to do with a kitten I killed," and I told him the whole wretched business.

"U'm?" he commented when I had done. "You are a good man, Trowbridge, my friend. In all your life, since you attained to years of discretion, I do not believe you have done a wicked or ignoble act."

"Oh, I wouldn't say that," I returned, "we all——"

"*Parbleu*, I have said it. That kitten incident, now, is probably the single tiny skeleton in the entire closet of your existence, yet sustained thought upon it will magnify it even as the cat of your dream grew from cat's to lion's size. *Pardieu*, my friend, I am not so sure you did dream of that abomination in the shape of a cat which visited you. Suppose——" he broke off, staring intently before him, twisting first one, then the other end of his trimly waxed mustache.

"Suppose what?" I prompted.

"*Non*, we will suppose nothing to-night," he replied. "You will please go to sleep once more, my friend, and I shall remain in the room to frighten away any more dream-demons which may come to plague you. Come, let us sleep. Here I do remain." He leaped into the wide bed beside me and pulled the down comforter snuggly up about his pointed chin.

". . . . and I'd like very much to have you come right over to see her, if you will," Mrs. Weaver finished. "I can't imagine whatever made her attempt such a thing—she's never shown any signs of it before."

I hung up the telephone receiver and turned to de Grandin. "Here's another suicide, or almost-suicide, for you," I told him half teasingly. "The daughter of one of my patients attempted her life by hanging in the bathroom this morning."

"*Par la tête bleu*, do you tell me so?" he exclaimed eagerly. "I go with you, *cher ami*. I see this young woman; I examine her. Perhaps I shall find some key to the riddle there. *Parbleu*, me, I itch, I burn, I am all on fire with this mystery! Certainly, there must be an answer to it; but it remains hidden like a peasant's pig when the tax collector arrives."

"Well, young lady, what's this I hear about you?" I demanded severely as we entered Grace Weaver's bedroom a few minutes later. "What on earth have you to die for?"

"I—I don't know what made me want to do it, Doctor," the girl replied with a wan smile. "I hadn't thought of it before —ever. But I just got to—oh, you know, sort of brooding over things last night, and when I went into the bathroom this morning, something—something inside my head, like those ringing noises you hear when you have a head-cold, you know —seemed to be whispering, 'Go on, kill yourself, you've nothing to live for. Go on, do it!' So I just stood on the scales and took the cord from my bathrobe and tied it over the transom, then knotted the other end about my neck. Then I kicked the scales away and"—she gave another faint smile—"I'm glad I hadn't locked the door before I did it," she admitted.

De Grandin had been staring unwinkingly at her with his curiously level glance throughout her recital. As she concluded he bent forward and asked: "This voice which you heard bidding you commit an unpardonable sin, *Mademoiselle*, did you, perhaps, recognize it?"

The girl shuddered. "No!" she replied, but a sudden paling of her face about the lips gave the lie to her word.

"*Pardonnez-moi, Mademoiselle*," the Frenchman returned. "I think you do not tell the truth. Now, whose voice was it, if you please?"

A sullen, stubborn look spread over the girl's features, to be replaced a moment later by the muscular spasm which preludes weeping. "It—it sounded like Fanny's," she cried, and turning her face to the pillow, fell to sobbing bitterly.

"And Fanny, who is she?" de Grandin began, but Mrs. Weaver motioned him to silence with an imploring gesture.

I prescribed a mild bromide and left the patient, wondering what mad impulse could have led a girl in the first flush of young womanhood, happily situated in the home of parents who idolized her, engaged to a fine young man, and without bodily or spiritual ill of any sort, to attempt her life. Outside, de Grandin seized the mother's arm and whispered fiercely: "Who is this Fanny, Madame Weaver? Believe me, I ask not from idle curiosity, but because I seek vital information!"

"Fanny Briggs was Grace's chum two years ago," Mrs. Weaver answered. "My husband and I never quite approved of her, for she was several years older than Grace, and had such pronounced modern ideas that we didn't think her a suitable companion for our daughter, but you know how girls are with their 'crushes'. The more we objected to her going with Fanny, the more she used to seek her company, and we were both at our wits' ends when the Briggs girl was drowned while swimming at Asbury Park. I hate to say it, but it was almost a positive relief to us when the news came. Grace was almost broken-hearted about it at first, but she met Charley this summer, and I haven't heard her mention Fanny's name since her engagement until just now."

"Ah?" de Grandin tweaked the tip of his mustache meditatively. "And perhaps Mademoiselle Grace was somewhere to be reminded of Mademoiselle Fanny last night?"

"No," Mrs. Weaver replied, "she went with a crowd of young folks to hear Maundy preach. There was a big party of them at the tabernacle—I'm afraid they went more to make fun than in a religious frame of mind, but he made quite an impression on Grace, she told us."

"*Feu de Dieu!*" de Grandin exploded, twisting his mustache furiously. "Do you tell me so, *Madame*? This is of the interest. *Madame*, I salute you," he bowed formally to Mrs. Weaver, then seized me by the arm and fairly dragged me away.

"Trowbridge, my friend," he informed me as we descended the steps of the Weaver portico, "this business, it has *l'odeur du poisson*—how is it you say?—the fishy smell."

"What do you mean?" I asked.

"*Parbleu*, what should I mean except that we go to interview this Monsieur Everard Maundy immediately, right away, at once? *Mordieu*, I damn think I have the tail of this mystery in my hand, and may the blight of prohibition fall upon France if I do not twist it!"

*

The Rev. Everard Maundy's rooms in the Tremont Hotel were not hard to locate, for a constant stream of visitors went to and from them.

"Have you an appointment with Mr. Maundy?" the secretary asked as we were ushered into the ante-room.

"Not we," de Grandin denied, "but if you will be so kind as to tell him that Dr. Jules de Grandin, of the Paris *Sûreté*, desires to speak with him for five small minutes, I shall be in your debt."

The young man looked doubtful, but de Grandin's steady, catlike stare never wavered, and he finally rose and took our message to his employer.

In a few minutes he returned and admitted us to the big room where the evangelist received his callers behind a wide, flat-topped desk.

"Ah, Mr. de Grandin," the exhorter began with a professionally bland smile as we entered, "you are from France, are you not, sir? What can I do to help you toward the light?"

"*Cordieu, Monsieur*," de Grandin barked, for once forgetting his courtesy and ignoring the preacher's outstretched hand, "you can do much. You can explain these so unexplainable suicides which have taken place during the past week—the time you have preached here. That is the light we do desire to see."

Maundy's face went masklike and expressionless. "Suicides? Suicides?" he echoed. "What should I know of——"

The Frenchman shrugged his narrow shoulders impatiently. "We do fence with words, *Monsieur*," he interrupted testily. "Behold the facts: Messieurs Planz and Nixon, young men with no reason for such desperate deeds, did kill themselves by violence; Madame Westerfelt and her two daughters, who were happy in their home, as everyone thought, did hurl themselves from an hotel window; a little schoolgirl hanged herself; last night my good friend Trowbridge, who never understandingly harmed man or beast, and whose life is dedicated to the healing of the sick, did almost take his life; and this very morning a young girl, wealthy, beloved, with every reason to be happy, did almost succeed in dispatching herself.

"Now, *Monsieur le prédicateur*, the only thing this miscellaneous assortment of persons had in common is the fact that *each of them did hear you preach the night before, or the same night, he attempted self-destruction.* That is the light we seek. Explain us the mystery, if you please."

Maundy's lean, rugged face had undergone a strange transformation while the little Frenchman spoke. Gone was his smug, professional smirk, gone the forced and meaningless expression of benignity, and in their place a look of such anguish and horror as might rest on the face of one who hears his sentence of damnation read.

"Don't—don't!" he besought, covering his writhing face with his hands and bowing his head upon his desk while his shoulders shook with deep, soul-racking sobs. "Oh, miserable me! My sin has found me out!"

For a moment he wrestled in spiritual anguish, then raised his stricken countenance and regarded us with tear-dimmed eyes. "I am the greatest sinner in the world," he announced sorrowfully. "There is no hope for me on earth or yet in heaven!"

De Grandin tweaked the ends of his mustache alternately as he gazed curiously at the man before us. "*Monsieur*," he replied at length, "I think you do exaggerate. There are surely greater sinners than you. But if you would shrive you of the sin which gnaws your heart, I pray you shed what light you can upon these deaths, for there may be more to follow, and who knows that I shall not be able to stop them if you will but tell me all?"

"*Mea culpa!*" Maundy exclaimed, and struck his chest with his clenched fists like a Hebrew prophet of old. "In my younger days, gentlemen, before I dedicated myself to the salvaging of souls, I was a scoffer. What I could not feel or weigh or measure, I disbelieved. I mocked at all religion and sneered at all the things which others held sacred.

"One night I went to a Spiritualistic séance, intent on scoffing, and forced my young wife to accompany me. The medium was an old colored woman, wrinkled, half-blind and unbelievably ignorant, but she had something—some secret power—which was denied the rest of us. Even I, atheist and derider of the truth that I was, could see that.

"As the old woman called on the spirits of the departed, I laughed out loud, and told her it was all a fake. The negress came out of her trance and turned her deep-set, burning old eyes on me. 'White man,' she said, 'yuh is gwine ter feel mighty sorry fo' dem words. Ah tells yuh de speerits can heah whut yuh says, an' dey will take deir revenge on yuh an' yours—yas, an' on dem as follers yuh—till yuh wishes yo' tongue had been cut out befo' yuh said dem words dis yere night.'

"I tried to laugh at her—to curse her for a sniveling old faker—but there was something so terrible in her wrinkled old face that the words froze on my lips, and I hurried away.

"The next night my wife—my young, lovely bride—drowned herself in the river, and I have been a marked man ever since. Wherever I go it is the same. God has seen fit to open my eyes to the light of Truth and give me words to place His message before His people, and many who come to sneer at me go away believers; but wherever throngs gather to hear me bear my testimony there are always these tragedies. Tell me, gentlemen" —he threw out his hands in a gesture of surrender—"must I forever cease to preach the message of the Lord to His people? I have told myself that these self-murders would have occurred whether I came to town or not, but—is this a judgment which pursues me forever?"

Jules de Grandin regarded him thoughtfully. "*Monsieur,*" he murmured, "I fear you make the mistakes we are all too prone to make. You do saddle *le bon Dieu* with all the sins with which the face of man is blackened. What if this were no judgment of heaven, but a curse of a very different sort, *hein?*"

"You mean the devil might be striving to overthrow the effects of my work?" the other asked, a light of hope breaking over his haggard face.

"U'm, perhaps; let us take that for our working hypothesis," de Grandin replied. "At present we may not say whether it be devil or devilkin which dogs your footsteps; but at the least we are greatly indebted to you for what you have told. Go, my friend; continue to preach the Truth as you conceive the Truth to be, and may the God of all peoples uphold your hands. Me, I have other work to do, but it may be scarcely less important." He bowed formally and, turning on his heel, strode quickly from the room.

"That's the most fantastic story I ever heard!" I declared as we entered the hotel elevator. "The idea! As if an ignorant old negress could put a curse on——"

"*Zut!*" de Grandin shut me off. "You are a most excellent physician in the State of New Jersey, Friend Trowbridge, but have you ever been in Martinique, or Haiti, or in the jungles of the Congo Belgique?"

"Of course not," I admitted, "but——"

"I have. I have seen things so strange among the *Voudois* people that you would wish to have me committed to a madhouse did I but relate them to you. However, as that Monsieur Kipling says, 'that is another story.' At the present we are pledged to the solving of another mystery. Let us go to your house. I would think, I would consider all this business-of-the-monkey. *Pardieu*, it has as many angles as a diamond cut in Amsterdam!"

"Tell me, Friend Trowbridge," he demanded as we concluded our evening meal, "have you perhaps among your patients some young man who has met with a great sorrow recently; someone who has sustained a loss of wife or child or parents?"

I looked at him in amazement, but the serious expression on his little heart-shaped face told me he was in earnest, not making some ill-timed jest at my expense.

"Why, yes," I responded. "There is young Alvin Spence. His wife died in childbirth last June, and the poor chap has been half beside himself ever since. Thank God I was out of town at the time and didn't have the responsibility of the case."

"Thank God, indeed," de Grandin nodded gravely. "It is not easy for us, though we do ply our trade among the dying, to tell those who remain behind of their bereavement. But this Monsieur Spence; will you call on him this evening? Will you give him a ticket to the lecture of Monsieur Maundy?"

"No!" I blazed, half rising from my chair. "I've known that boy since he was a little toddler—knew his dead wife from childhood, too; and if you're figuring on making him the subject of some experiment——"

"Softly, my friend," he besought. "There is a terrible Thing loose among us. Remember the noble martyrs of science, those so magnificent men who risked their lives that yellow fever and malaria should be no more. Was not their work a holy one? Certainly. I do but wish that this young man may attend the lecture tonight, and on my honor, I shall guard him until all danger of attempted self-murder is passed. You will do what I say?"

He was so earnest in his plea that, though I felt like an accessory before the fact in a murder, I agreed.

Meantime, his little blue eyes snapping and sparkling with the zest of the chase, de Grandin had busied himself with the telephone directory, looking up a number of addresses, culling through them, discarding some, adding others, until he had obtained a list of some five or six. "Now, *mon vieux*," he begged as I made ready to visit Alvin Spence on my treacherous errand, "I would that you convey me to the rectory of St. Benedict's Church. The priest in charge there is Irish, and the Irish have the gift of seeing things which you colder-blooded Saxons may not. I must have a confab with this good Father O'Brien before I can permit that you interview the young Monsieur Spence. *Mordieu*, me, I am a scientist; no murderer!"

I drove him past the rectory and parked my motor at the curb, waiting impatiently while he thundered at the door with the handle of his ebony walking stick. His knock was answered by a little old man in clerical garb and a face as round and ruddy as a winter apple.

De Grandin spoke hurriedly to him in a low voice, waving his hands, shaking his head, shrugging his shoulders, as was his wont when the earnestness of his argument bore him before it. The priest's round face showed first incredulity, then mild skepticism, finally absorbed interest. In a moment the pair of them had vanished inside the house, leaving me to cool my heels in the bitter March air.

"You were long enough," I grumbled as he emerged from the rectory.

"*Pardieu*, yes, just long enough," he agreed. "I did accomplish my purpose, and no visit is either too long or too short when you can say that. Now to the house of the good Monsieur Spence, if you will. *Mordieu*, but we shall see what we shall see this night!"

Six hours later de Grandin and I crouched shivering at the roadside where the winding, serpentine Albemarle Pike dips into the hollow beside the Lonesome Swamp. The wind which had been trenchant as a shrew's tongue earlier in the evening had died away, and a hard, dull bitterness of cold hung over the hills and hollows of the rolling country-side. From the wide salt marshes where the bay's tide crept up to mingle with the swamp's brackish waters twice a day there came great sheets of brumous, impenetrable vapor which shrouded the landscape and distorted commonplace objects into hideous, gigantic monstrosities.

"*Mort d'un petit bonhomme*, my friend," de Grandin commented between chattering teeth, "I do not like this place; it has an evil air. There are spots where the very earth does breathe of unholy deeds, and by the sacred name of a rooster, this is one such. Look you at this accursed fog. Is it not as if the specters of those drowned at sea were marching up the shore this night?"

"Umph!" I replied, sinking my neck lower in the collar of my ulster and silently cursing myself for a fool.

A moment's silence, then: "You are sure Monsieur Spence must come this way? There is no other road by which he can reach his home?"

"Of course not," I answered shortly. "He lives out in the new Weiss development with his mother and sister—you were there this evening—and this is the only direct motor route to the subdivision from the city."

"Ah, that is well," he replied, hitching the collar of his greatcoat higher about his ears. "You will recognize his car—surely?"

"I'll try to," I promised, "but you can't be sure of anything on a night like this. I'd not guarantee to pick out my own— there's somebody pulling up beside the road now," I interrupted myself as a roadster came to an abrupt halt and stood panting, its headlights forming vague, luminous spots in the haze.

"*Mais oui*," he agreed, "and no one stops at this spot for any good until *It* has been conquered. Come, let us investigate." He started forward, body bent, head advanced, like a motion picture conception of an Indian on the warpath.

Half a hundred stealthy steps brought us abreast of the parked car. Its occupant was sitting back on the driving seat, his hands resting listlessly on the steering wheel, his eyes up-turned, as though he saw a vision in the trailing wisps of fog before him. I needed no second chance to recognize Alvin Spence, though the rapt look upon his white, set face trans-figured it almost beyond recognition. He was like a poet be-holding the beatific vision of his mistress or a medieval eremite gazing through the opened portals of Paradise.

"A-a-ah!" de Grandin's whisper cut like a wire-edged knife through the silence of the fog-bound air, "do you behold it, Friend Trowbridge?"

"Wha——" I whispered back, but broke the syllable half uttered. Thin, tenuous, scarcely to be distinguished from the lazily drifting festoons of the fog itself, there was a *something* in midair before the car where Alvin Spence sat with his yearning soul looking from his eyes. I seemed to see clear through the thing, yet its outlines were plainly perceptible, and as I looked and looked again, I recognized the unmistakable features of Dorothy Spence, the young man's dead wife. Her body—if the tenuous, ethereal mass of static vapor could be called such—was bare of clothing, and seemed endued with a voluptuous grace and allure the living woman had never possessed, but her face was that of the young woman who had lain in Rosedale Cemetery for three-quarters of a year. If ever living man be-held the simulacrum of the dead, we three gazed on the wraith of Dorothy Spence that moment.

"Dorothy—my beloved, my dear, my dear!" the man half whispered, half sobbed, stretching forth his hands to the spirit-woman, then falling back on the seat as the vision seemed to elude his grasp when a sudden puff of breeze stirred the fog.

We could not catch the answer he received, close as we stood, but we could see the pale, curving lips frame the single word, "Come!" and saw the transparent arms stretched out to beckon him forward.

The man half rose from his seat, then sank back, set his face in sudden resolution and plunged his hand into the pocket of his overcoat.

Beside me de Grandin had been fumbling with something in his inside pocket. As Alvin Spence drew forth his hand and the dull gleam of a polished revolver shone in the light from his dashboard lamp, the Frenchman leaped forward like a panther. "Stop him, Friend Trowbridge!" he called shrilly, and to the hovering vision:

"Avaunt, accursed one! Begone, thou exile from heaven! Away, snake-spawn!"

As he shouted he drew a tiny pellet from his inner pocket and hurled it point-blank through the vaporous body of the specter.

Even as I seized Spence's hand and fought with him for possession of the pistol, I saw the transformation from the tail of my eye. As de Grandin's missile tore through its unsubstantial substance, the vision-woman seemed to shrink in upon herself, to become suddenly more compact, thinner, scrawny. Her rounded bosom flattened to mere folds of leatherlike skin stretched drum-tight above staring ribs, her slender graceful hands were horrid, claw-tipped talons, and the yearning, enticing face of Dorothy Spence became a mask of hideous, implacable hate, great-eyed, thin-lipped, beak-nosed—such a face as the demons of hell might show after a million million years of burning in the infernal fires. A screech like the keening of all the owls in the world together split the fog-wrapped stillness of the night, and the monstrous thing before us seemed suddenly to shrivel, shrink to a mere spot of baleful, phosphorescent fire, and disappear like a snuffed-out candle's flame.

Spence saw it, too. The pistol dropped from his nerveless fingers to the car's floor with a soft thud, and his arm went limp in my grasp as he fell forward in a dead faint.

"*Parbleu*," de Grandin swore softly as he climbed into the unconscious lad's car. "Let us drive forward, friend Trowbridge. We will take him home and administer a soporific. He must sleep, this poor one, or the memory of what we have shown him will rob him of his reason."

So we carried Alvin Spence to his home, administered a hypnotic and left him in the care of his wondering mother with instructions to repeat the dose if he should wake.

It was a mile or more to the nearest bus station, and we set out at a brisk walk, our heels hitting sharply against the frosty concrete of the road.

"What in the world was it, de Grandin?" I asked as we

marched in step down the darkened highway. "It was the most horrible———"

"*Parbleu*," he interrupted, "someone comes this way in a monstrous hurry!"

His remark was no exaggeration. Driven as though pursued by all the furies from pandemonium, came a light motor car with plain black sides and a curving top. "Look out!" the driver warned as he recognized me and came to a bumping halt. "Look out, Dr. Trowbridge, it's walking! It got out and walked!"

De Grandin regarded him with an expression of comic bewilderment. "Now what is it that walks, *mon brave?*" he demanded. "*Mordieu*, you chatter like a monkey with a handful of hot chestnuts! What is it that walks, and why must we look out for it, *hein?*"

"Sile Gregory," the young man answered. "He died this mornin', an' Mr. Johnson took him to th' parlors to fix 'im up, an' sent me an' Joe Williams out with him this evenin'. I was just drivin' up to th' house, an' Joe hopped out to give me a lift with th' casket, an' old Silas *got up an' walked away!* An' Mr. Johnson embalmed 'im this mornin', I tell you!"

"*Nom d'un chou-fleur!*" de Grandin shot back. "And where did this so remarkable demonstration take place, *mon vieux?* Also, what of the excellent Williams, your partner?"

"I don't know, an' I don't care," the other replied. "When a dead corpse I saw embalmed this mornin' gets outa its casket an' walks, I ain't gonna wait for nobody. Jump up here, if you want to go with me; I ain't gonna stay here no longer!"

"*Bien*," de Grandin acquiesced. "Go your way, my excellent one. Should we encounter your truant corpse, we will direct him to his waiting *bière*."

The young man waited no second invitation, but started his car down the road at a speed which would bring him into certain trouble if observed by a state trooper.

"Now, what the devil do you make of that?" I asked. "I know Johnson, the funeral director, well, and I always thought he had a pretty level-headed crowd of boys about his place, but if that lad hasn't been drinking some powerful liquor, I'll be———"

"Not necessarily, my friend," de Grandin interrupted. "I

think it not at all impossible that he tells but the sober truth. It may well be that the dead do walk this road tonight."

I shivered with something other than the night's chill as he made the matter-of-fact assertion, but forbore pressing him for an explanation. There are times when ignorance is a happier portion than knowledge.

We had marched perhaps another quarter-mile in silence when de Grandin suddenly plucked my sleeve. "Have you noticed nothing, my friend?" he asked.

"What d'ye mean?" I demanded sharply, for my nerves were worn tender by the night's events.

"I am not certain, but it seems to me we are followed."

"Followed? Nonsense! *Who* would be following us?" I returned, unconsciously stressing the personal pronoun, for I had almost said, "What would follow us," and the implication raised by the impersonal form sent tiny shivers racing along my back and neck.

De Grandin cast me a quick, appraising glance, and I saw the ends of his spiked mustache lift suddenly as his lips framed a sardonic smile, but instead of answering he swung round on his heel and faced the shadows behind us.

"*Holà, Monsieur le Cadavre!*" he called sharply. "Here we are, and—*sang du diable!*—here we shall stand."

I looked at him in open-mouthed amazement, but his gaze was turned stedfastly on something half seen in the mist which lay along the road.

Next instant my heart seemed pounding through my ribs and my breath came hot and choking in my throat, for a tall, gangling man suddenly emerged from the fog and made for us at a shambling gait.

He was clothed in a long, old-fashioned double-breasted frock coat and stiffly starched shirt topped by a standing collar and white, ministerial tie. His hair was neatly, though somewhat unnaturally, arranged in a central part above a face the color and smoothness of wax, and little flecks of talcum powder still clung here and there to his eyebrows. No mistaking it! Johnson, artist that he was, had arrayed the dead farmer in the manner of all his kind for their last public appearance before relatives and friends. One look told me the horrible, incredible truth. It was the body of old Silas Gregory which stumbled toward us through the fog. Dressed, greased and powdered for its last, long rest, the thing came toward us with faltering, uncertain strides, and I noticed, with the sudden ability for minute inventory fear sometimes lends our senses, that his old, sunburned skin showed more than one brand where the formaldehyde embalming fluid had burned it.

In one long, thin hand the horrible thing grasped the helve of a farmyard ax, the other hand lay stiffly folded across the midriff as the embalmer had placed it when his professional ministrations were finished that morning.

"My God!" I cried, shrinking back toward the roadside. But de Grandin ran forward to meet the charging horror with a cry which was almost like a welcome.

"Stand clear, Friend Trowbridge," he warned, "we will fight this to a finish, I and It!" His little, round eyes were flashing with the zest of combat, his mouth was set in a straight, uncompromising line beneath the sharply waxed ends of his diminutive mustache, and his shoulders hunched forward like those of a practised wrestler before he comes to grips with his opponent.

With a quick, whipping motion, he ripped the razor-sharp blade of his sword-cane from its ebony sheath and swung the flashing steel in a whirring circle about his head, then sank to a defensive posture, one foot advanced, one retracted, the leg bent at the knee, the triple-edged sword dancing before him like the darting tongue of an angry serpent.

The dead thing never faltered in its stride. Three feet or so from Jules de Grandin it swung the heavy, rust-encrusted ax above its shoulder and brought it downward, its dull, lack-luster eyes staring straight before it with an impassivity more terrible than any glare of hate.

"*Sa ha!*" de Grandin's blade flickered forward like a streak of storm lightning, and fleshed itself to the hilt in the corpse's shoulder.

He might as well have struck his steel into a bag of meal.

The ax descended with a crushing, devastating blow.

De Grandin leaped nimbly aside, disengaging his blade and swinging it again before him, but an expression of surprise—almost of consternation—was on his face.

I felt my mouth go dry with excitement, and a queer, weak

feeling hit me at the pit of the stomach. The Frenchman had driven his sword home with the skill of a practised fencer and the precision of a skilled anatomist. His blade had pierced the dead man's body at the junction of the short head of the biceps and the great pectoral muscle, at the coracoid process, inflicting a wound which should have paralyzed the arm—yet the terrible ax rose for a second blow as though de Grandin's steel had struck wide of the mark.

"Ah?" de Grandin nodded understandingly as he leaped backward, avoiding the ax-blade by the breadth of a hair. "*Bien. À la fin!*"

His defensive tactics changed instantly. Flickeringly his sword lashed forward, then came down and back with a sharp, whipping motion. The keen edge of the angular blade bit deeply into the corpse's wrist, laying bare the bone. Still the ax rose and fell and rose again.

Slash after slash de Grandin gave, his slicing cuts falling with almost mathematical precision in the same spot, shearing deeper and deeper into his dreadful opponent's wrist. At last, with a short, clucking exclamation, he drew his blade sharply back for the last time, severing the ax-hand from the arm.

The dead thing collapsed like a deflated balloon at his feet as hand and ax fell together to the cement roadway.

Quick as a mink, de Grandin thrust his left hand within his coat, drew forth a pellet similar to that with which he had transformed the counterfeit of Dorothy Spence, and hurled it straight into the upturned, ghastly-calm face of the mutilated body before him.

The dead lips did not part, for the embalmer's sutures had closed them forever that morning, but the body writhed upward from the road, and a groan which was a muted scream came from its flat chest. It twisted back and forth a moment, like a mortally stricken serpent in its death agony, then lay still.

Seizing the corpse by its grave-clothes, de Grandin dragged it through the line of roadside hazel bushes to the rim of the swamp, and busied himself cutting long, straight withes from the brushwood, then disappeared again behind the tangled branches. At last:

"It is finished," he remarked, stepping back to the road. "Let us go."

"Wha—what did you do?" I faltered.

"I did the needful, my friend. *Morbleu*, we had an evil, a very evil thing imprisoned in that dead man, and I took such precautions as were necessary to fix it in its prison. A stake through the heart, a severed head, and the whole firmly thrust into the ooze of the swamp—*voilà*. It will be long before other innocent ones are induced to destroy themselves by *that*."

"But——" I began.

"*Non, non*," he replied, half laughing. "*En avant, mon ami!* I would that we return home as quickly as possible. Much work creates much appetite, and I make small doubt that I shall consume the remainder of that so delicious apple pie which I could not eat at dinner."

Jules de Grandin regarded the empty plate before him with a look of comic tragedy. "May endless benisons rest upon your amiable cook, Friend Trowbridge," he pronounced, "but may the curse of heaven forever pursue the villain who manufactures the wofully inadequate pans in which she bakes her pies."

"Hang the pies, and the plate-makers, too!" I burst out. "You promised to explain all this hocus-pocus, and I've been patient long enough. Stop sitting there like a glutton, wailing for more pie, and tell me about it."

"Oh, the mystery?" he replied, stifling a yawn and lighting a cigarette. "That is simple, my friend, but these so delicious pies—however, I do digress:

"When first I saw the accounts of so many strange suicides within one little week I was interested, but not greatly puzzled. People have slain themselves since the beginning of time, and yet"—he shrugged his shoulders deprecatingly—"what is it that makes the hound scent his quarry, the war-horse sniff the battle afar off? Who can tell?

"I said to me: 'There is undoubtlessly more to these deaths than the newspapers have said. I shall investigate.'

"From the coroner's to the undertakers', and from the undertakers' to the physicians', yes, *parbleu!* and to the family residences, as well, I did go, gleaning here a bit and there a bit of information which seemed to mean nothing, but which might mean much did I but have other information to add to it.

"One thing I ascertained early: In each instance the suicides had been to hear this reverend Maundy the night before or the same night they did away with themselves. This was perhaps insignificant; perhaps it meant much. I determined to hear this Monsieur Maundy with my own two ears; but I would not hear him too close by.

"Forgive me, my friend, for I did make of you the guinea-pig for my laboratory experiment. You I left in a forward seat while the reverend gentleman preached, me, I stayed in the rear of the hall and used my eyes as well as my ears.

"What happened that night? Why, my good, kind Friend Trowbridge, who in all his life had done no greater wrong than thoughtlessly to kill a little, so harmless kitten, did almost *seemingly* commit suicide. But I was not asleep by the switch, my friend. Not Jules de Grandin! All the way home I saw you were *distrait*, and I did fear something would happen, and I did therefore watch beside your door with my eye and ear alternately glued to the keyhole. *Parbleu*, I entered the chamber not one little second too soon, either!

"'This is truly strange,' I tell me. 'My friend hears this preacher and nearly destroys himself. Six others have heard him, and have quite killed themselves. If Friend Trowbridge were haunted by the ghost of a dead kitten, why should not those others, who also undoubtlessly possessed distressing memories, have been hounded to their graves by them?'

"'There is no reason why they should not,' I tell me.

"Next morning comes the summons to attend the young Mademoiselle Weaver. She, too, have heard the preacher; she, too, have attempted her life. And what does she tell us? That she fancied the voice of her dead friend urged her to kill herself.

"'Ah, ha!' I say to me. 'This whatever-it-is which causes so much suicide may appeal by fear, or perhaps by love, or by whatever will most strongly affect the person who dies by his own hand. We must see this Monsieur Maundy. It is perhaps possible he can tell us much.'

"As yet I can see no light—I am still in darkness—but far ahead I already see the gleam of a promise of information. When we see Monsieur Everard Maundy and he tells us of his experience at that séance so many years ago—*parbleu*, I see it all, or almost all.

"Now, what was it acted as agent for that aged sorceress' curse?"

He elevated one shoulder and looked questioningly at me.

"How should I know?" I answered.

"Correct," he nodded, "how, indeed? Beyond doubt it were a spirit of some sort; what sort we do not know. Perhaps it were the spirit of some unfortunate who had destroyed himself and was earthbound as a consequence. There are such. And, as misery loves company in the proverb, so do these wretched ones seek to lure others to join them in their unhappy state. Or, maybe, it were an Elemental."

"A *what?*" I demanded.

"An Elemental—a Neutrarian."

"What the deuce is that?"

For answer he left the table and entered the library, return-ing with a small red-leather bound volume in his hand. "You have read the works of Monsieur Rossetti?" he asked.

"Yes."

"You recall his poem, *Eden Bowers*, perhaps?"

"H'm; yes, I've read it, but I never could make anything of it."

"Quite likely," he agreed, "its meaning is most obscure, but I shall enlighten you. *Attendez-moi!*"

Thumbing through the thin pages he began reading at random:

> It was Lilith, the wife of Adam,
> Not a drop of her blood was human,
> But she was made like a soft, sweet woman . . . .
>
> Lilith stood on the skirts of Eden,
> She was the first that thence was driven,
> With her was hell and with Eve was heaven . . . .
>
> What bright babes had Lilith and Adam,
> Shapes that coiled in the woods and waters,
> Glittering sons and radiant daughters . . . .

"You see, my friend?"

"No, I'm hanged if I do."

"Very well, then, according to the rabbinical lore, before Eve was created, Adam, our first father, had a demon wife named

Lilith. And by her he had many children, not human, nor yet wholly demon.

"For her sins Lilith was expelled from Eden's bowers, and Adam was given Eve to wife. With Lilith was driven out all her progeny by Adam, and Lilith and her half-man, half-demon brood declared war on Adam and Eve and their descendants for ever. These descendants of Lilith and Adam have ever since roamed the earth and air, incorporeal, having no bodies like men, yet having always a hatred for flesh and blood. Because they were the first, or elder race, they are sometimes called Elementals in the ancient lore; sometimes they are called Neutrarians, because they are neither wholly men nor wholly devils. Me, I do not take sides in the controversy; I care not what they are called, but I know what I have seen. I think it is highly possible those ancient Hebrews, misinterpreting the manifestations they observed, accounted for them by their so fantastic legends. We are told these Neutrarians or Elementals are immaterial beings. Absurd? Not necessarily. What is matter—material? Electricity, perhaps—a great system of law and order throughout the universe and all the millions of worlds extending throughout infinity.

"Very good, so far; but when we have said matter is electricity, what have we to say if asked, 'What is electricity?' Me, I think it a modification of the ether.

"'Very good,' you say; 'but what is ether?'

"*Parbleu*, I do not know. The matter—or material—of the universe is little, if anything, more than electrons flowing about in all directions. Now here, now there, the electrons coalesce and form what we call solids—rocks and trees and men and woman. But may they not coalesce at a different rate of speed, or vibration, to form beings which are real, with emotions and loves and hates similar to ours, yet for the most part invisible to us, as is the air? Why not? No man can truthfully say, 'I have seen the air,' yet no one is so great a fool as to doubt its existence for that reason."

"Yes, but we can see the effects of air," I objected. "Air in motion, for instance, becomes wind, and——"

"*Mort d'un crapaud!*" he burst out. "And have we not observed the effects of these Elementals—these Neutrarians, or whatsoever their name may be? How of the six suicides; how of that which tempted the young Mademoiselle Weaver and the young Monsieur Spence to self-murder? How of the cat which entered your room? Did we see no effects there, *hein*?"

"But the thing we saw with young Spence, and the cat, were visible," I objected.

"But of course. When you fancied you saw the cat, you were influenced from within, even as Mademoiselle Weaver was when she heard the voice of her dead friend. What we saw with the young Spence was the shadow of his desire—the intensified love and longing for his dead wife, plus the evil entity which urged him to unpardonable sin."

"Oh, all right," I conceded. "Go on with your theory."

He stared thoughtfully at the glowing tip of his cigarette a moment, then: "It has been observed, my friend, that he who goes to a Spiritualistic séance may come away with some evil spirit attached to him—whether it be a spirit which once inhabited human form or an Elemental, it is no matter; the evil ones swarm about the lowered lights of the Spiritualistic meeting as flies congregate at the honey-pot in summer. It appears such an one fastened to Everard Maundy. His wife was its first victim, afterward those who heard him preach were attacked.

"Consider the scene at the tabernacle when Monsieur Maundy preaches: Emotion, emotion—all is emotion; reason is lulled to sleep by the power of his words; and the minds of his hearers are not on their guard against the entrance of evil spirits; they are too intent on what he is saying. Their consciousness is absent. *Pouf!* The evil one fastens firmly on some unwary person, explores his innermost mind, finds out his weakest point of defense. With you it was the kitten; with young Mademoiselle Weaver, her dead friend; with Monsieur Spence, his lost wife. Even love can be turned to evil purposes by such an one.

"These things I did consider most carefully, and then I did enlist the services of young Monsieur Spence. You saw what you saw on the lonely road this night. Appearing to him in the form of his dead beloved, this wicked one had all but persuaded him to destroy himself when we intervened.

"*Très bien.* We triumphed then; the night before I had prevented your death. The evil one was angry at me; also it was frightened. If I continued, I would rob it of much prey, so it sought to do me harm. Me, I am ever on guard, for knowledge is power. It could not lead me to my death, and, being spirit, it could not directly attack me. It had recourse to its last resort. While the young undertaker's assistant was about to deliver the body of the old Monsieur Gregory, the spirit seized the corpse and animated it, then pursued me.

"Ha, almost, I thought, it had done for me at one time, for I forgot it was no living thing I fought, and attacked it as if it could be killed. But when I found my sword could not kill that which was already dead, I did cut off its so abominable hand. I am very clever, my friend. The evil spirit reaped small profits from fighting with me."

He made the boastful admission in all seriousness, entirely unaware of its sound, for to him it was but a straightforward statement of undisputed fact. I grinned in spite of myself, then curiosity got the better of amusement. "What were those little pellets you threw at the spirit when it was luring young Spence to commit suicide, and later at the corpse of Silas Gregory?" I asked.

"Ah"—his elfish smile flickered across his lips, then disappeared so quickly as it came—"it is better you do not ask me that, *mon cher*. Let it suffice when I tell you I convinced the good *Père* O'Brien that he should let me have what no layman is supposed to touch, that I might use the ammunition of heaven against the forces of hell."

"But how do we know this Elemental, or whatever it is, won't come back again?" I persisted.

"Little fear," he encouraged. "The resort to the dead man's body was its last desperate chance. Having elected to fight me physically, it must stand or fall by the result of the fight. Once inside the body, it could not quickly extricate itself. Half an hour, at least, must elapse before it could withdraw, and before that time had passed I had fixed it there for all time. The stake through the heart and the severed head makes that body as harmless as any other, and the wicked spirit which animated it must remain with the flesh it sought to pervert to its own evil ends henceforth and forever."

"But——"

"*Ah bah!*" He dropped his cigarette end into his empty coffee cup and yawned frankly. "We do talk too much, my friend. This night's work has made me heavy with sleep. Let us take a tiny sip of cognac, that the pie may not give us unhappy dreams, and then to bed. Tomorrow is another day, and who knows what new task lies before us?"

1927

STEPHEN VINCENT BENÉT

(1889–1943)

The King of the Cats

"But, my *dear*," said Mrs. Culverin, with a tiny gasp, "you can't actually mean—a *tail*!"

Mrs. Dingle nodded impressively. "Exactly. I've seen him. Twice. Paris, of course, and then, a command appearance at Rome—we were in the Royal box. He conducted—my dear, you've never heard such effects from an orchestra—and, my dear," she hesitated slightly, "he conducted *with it*."

"How perfectly, fascinatingly too horrid for words!" said Mrs. Culverin in a dazed but greedy voice. "We *must* have him to dinner as soon as he comes over—he is coming over, isn't he?"

"The twelfth," said Mrs. Dingle with a gleam in her eyes. "The New Symphony people have asked him to be guest-conductor for three special concerts—I do hope you can dine with *us* some night while he's here—he'll be very busy, of course —but he's promised to give us what time he can spare——"

"Oh, thank you, dear," said Mrs. Culverin, abstractedly, her last raid upon Mrs. Dingle's pet British novelist still fresh in her mind. "You're always so delightfully hospitable—but you mustn't wear yourself out—the rest of us must do *our* part—I know Henry and myself would be only too glad to——"

"That's very sweet of you, darling." Mrs. Dingle also remembered the larceny of the British novelist. "But we're just going to give Monsieur Tibault—sweet name, isn't it! They say he's descended from the Tybalt in 'Romeo and Juliet' and that's why he doesn't like Shakespeare—we're just going to give Monsieur Tibault the simplest sort of time—a little reception after his first concert, perhaps. He hates," she looked around the table, "large, mixed parties. And then, of course, his—er— little idiosyncrasy——" she coughed delicately. "It makes him feel a trifle shy with strangers."

"But I don't understand yet, Aunt Emily," said Tommy

Brooks, Mrs. Dingle's nephew. "Do you really mean this Tibault bozo has a tail? Like a monkey and everything?"

"Tommy dear," said Mrs. Culverin, crushingly, "in the first place Monsieur Tibault is not a bozo—he is a very distinguished musician—the finest conductor in Europe. And in the second place——"

"He has," Mrs. Dingle was firm. "He has a tail. He conducts with it."

"Oh, but honestly!" said Tommy, his ears pinkening. "I mean —of course, if you say so, Aunt Emily, I'm sure he has—but still, it sounds pretty steep, if you know what I mean! How about it, Professor Tatto?"

Professor Tatto cleared his throat. "Tck," he said, putting his fingertips together cautiously, "I shall be very anxious to see this Monsieur Tibault. For myself, I have never observed a genuine specimen of *homo caudatus*, so I should be inclined to doubt, and yet . . . In the Middle Ages, for instance, the belief in men—er—tailed or with caudal appendages of some sort, was both widespread and, as far as we can gather, well-founded. As late as the Eighteenth Century, a Dutch sea-captain with some character for veracity recounts the discovery of a pair of such creatures in the island of Formosa. They were in a low state of civilization, I believe, but the appendages in question were quite distinct. And in 1860, Dr. Grimbrook, the English surgeon, claims to have treated no less than three African natives with short but evident tails—though his testimony rests upon his unsupported word. After all, the thing is not impossible, though doubtless unusual. Web feet—rudimentary gills —these occur with some frequency. The appendix we have with us always. The chain of our descent from the ape-like form is by no means complete. For that matter," he beamed around the table, "what can we call the last few vertebrae of the normal spine but the beginnings of a concealed and rudimentary tail? Oh, yes—yes—it's possible—quite—that in an extraordinary case—a reversion to type—a survival—though, of course——"

"I told you so," said Mrs. Dingle triumphantly. "*Isn't* it fascinating? Isn't it, Princess?"

The Princess Vivrakanarda's eyes, blue as a field of larkspur, fathomless as the centre of heaven, rested lightly for a moment on Mrs. Dingle's excited countenance.

"Ve-ry fascinating," she said, in a voice like stroked, golden velvet. "I should like—I should like ve-ry much to meet this Monsieur Tibault."

"Well, *I* hope he breaks his neck!" said Tommy Brooks, under his breath—but nobody ever paid much attention to Tommy.

Nevertheless as the time for Mr. Tibault's arrival in these States drew nearer and nearer, people in general began to wonder whether the Princess had spoken quite truthfully—for there was no doubt of the fact that, up till then, she had been the unique sensation of the season—and you know what social lions and lionesses are.

It was, if you remember, a Siamese season, and genuine Siamese were at quite as much of a premium as Russian accents had been in the quaint old days when the Chauve-Souris was a novelty. The Siamese Art Theatre, imported at terrific expense, was playing to packed houses. "Gushuptzgu," an epic novel of Siamese farm life, in nineteen closely-printed volumes, had just been awarded the Nobel prize. Prominent pet-and-newt dealers reported no cessation in the appalling demand for Siamese cats. And upon the crest of this wave of interest in things Siamese, the Princess Vivrakanarda poised with the elegant nonchalance of a Hawaiian water-baby upon its surfboard. She was indispensable. She was incomparable. She was everywhere.

Youthful, enormously wealthy, allied on one hand to the Royal Family of Siam and on the other to the Cabots (and yet with the first eighteen of her twenty-one years shrouded from speculation in a golden zone of mystery), the mingling of races in her had produced an exotic beauty as distinguished as it was strange. She moved with a feline, effortless grace, and her skin was as if it had been gently powdered with tiny grains of the purest gold—yet the blueness of her eyes, set just a trifle slantingly, was as pure and startling as the sea on the rocks of Maine. Her brown hair fell to her knees—she had been offered extraordinary sums by the Master Barbers' Protective Association to have it shingled. Straight as a waterfall tumbling over brown rocks, it had a vague perfume of sandalwood and suave spices and held tints of rust and the sun. She did not talk very much—but then she did not have to—her voice had an odd, small, melodious huskiness that haunted the mind. She lived alone and was reputed to be very lazy—at least it was known that she slept during most of the day—but at night she bloomed like a moon-flower and a depth came into her eyes.

It was no wonder that Tommy Brooks fell in love with her. The wonder was that she let him. There was nothing exotic or distinguished about Tommy—he was just one of those pleasant, normal young men who seem created to carry on the bond business by reading the newspapers in the University Club during most of the day, and can always be relied upon at night to fill an unexpected hole in a dinner-party. It is true that the Princess could hardly be said to do more than tolerate any of her suitors—no one had ever seen those aloofly arrogant eyes enliven at the entrance of any male. But she seemed to be able to tolerate Tommy a little more than the rest—and that young man's infatuated day-dreams were beginning to be beset by smart solitaires and imaginary apartments on Park Avenue, when the famous M. Tibault conducted his first concert at Carnegie Hall.

Tommy Brooks sat beside the Princess. The eyes he turned upon her were eyes of longing and love, but her face was as impassive as a mask, and the only remark she made during the preliminary bustlings was that there seemed to be a number of people in the audience. But Tommy was relieved, if anything, to find her even a little more aloof than usual, for, ever since Mrs. Culverin's dinner-party, a vague disquiet as to the possible impression which this Tibault creature might make upon her had been growing in his mind. It shows his devotion that he was present at all. To a man whose simple Princetonian nature found in "Just a Little Love, a Little Kiss," the quintessence of musical art, the average symphony was a positive torture, and he looked forward to the evening's programme itself with a grim, brave smile.

"Ssh!" said Mrs. Dingle, breathlessly. "He's coming!" It seemed to the startled Tommy as if he were suddenly back in the trenches under a heavy barrage, as M. Tibault made his entrance to a perfect bombardment of applause.

Then the enthusiastic noise was sliced off in the middle and a gasp took its place—a vast, windy sigh, as if every person in that multitude had suddenly said, "Ah." For the papers had not lied about him. The tail was there.

They called him theatric—but how well he understood the uses of theatricalism! Dressed in unrelieved black from head to foot (the black dress-shirt had been a special token of Mussolini's esteem), he did not walk on, he strolled, leisurely, easily, aloofly, the famous tail curled nonchalantly about one wrist—a suave, black panther lounging through a summer garden with that little mysterious weave of the head that panthers have when they pad behind bars—the glittering darkness of his eyes unmoved by any surprise or elation. He nodded, twice, in regal acknowledgment, as the clapping reached an apogee of frenzy. To Tommy there was something dreadfully reminiscent of the Princess in the way he nodded. Then he turned to his orchestra.

A second and louder gasp went up from the audience at this point, for, as he turned, the tip of that incredible tail twined with dainty carelessness into some hidden pocket and produced a black baton. But Tommy did not even notice. He was looking at the Princess instead.

She had not even bothered to clap, at first, but now— He had never seen her moved like this, never. She was not applauding, her hands were clenched in her lap, but her whole body was rigid, rigid as a steel bar, and the blue flowers of her eyes were bent upon the figure of M. Tibault in a terrible concentration. The pose of her entire figure was so still and intense that for an instant Tommy had the lunatic idea that any moment she might leap from her seat beside him as lightly as a moth, and land, with no sound, at M. Tibault's side to—yes— to rub her proud head against his coat in worship. Even Mrs. Dingle would notice in a moment.

"Princess——" he said, in a horrified whisper, "Princess——"

Slowly the tenseness of her body relaxed, her eyes veiled again, she grew calm.

"Yes, Tommy?" she said, in her usual voice, but there was still something about her . . .

"Nothing, only—oh, hang—he's starting!" said Tommy, as M. Tibault, his hands loosely clasped before him, turned and *faced* the audience. His eyes dropped, his tail switched once impressively, then gave three little preliminary taps with his baton on the floor.

Seldom has Gluck's overture to "Iphigenie in Aulis" received such an ovation. But it was not until the Eighth Symphony that the hysteria of the audience reached its climax. Never before had the New Symphony played so superbly—and certainly never before had it been led with such genius. Three prominent conductors in the audience were sobbing with the despairing admiration of envious children toward the close, and one at least was heard to offer wildly ten thousand dollars to a well-known facial surgeon there present for a shred of evidence that tails of some variety could by any stretch of science be grafted upon a normally decaudate form. There was no doubt about it—no mortal hand and arm, be they ever so dexterous, could combine the delicate elan and powerful grace displayed in every gesture of M. Tibault's tail.

A sable staff, it dominated the brasses like a flicker of black lightning; an ebon, elusive whip, it drew the last exquisite breath of melody from the woodwinds and ruled the stormy strings like a magician's rod. M. Tibault bowed and bowed again—roar after roar of frenzied admiration shook the hall to its foundations—and when he finally staggered, exhausted, from the platform, the president of the Wednesday Sonata Club was only restrained by force from flinging her ninety-thousand-dollar string of pearls after him in an excess of aesthetic appreciation. New York had come and seen—and New York was conquered. Mrs. Dingle was immediately besieged by reporters, and Tommy Brooks looked forward to the "little party" at which he was to meet the new hero of the hour with feelings only a little less lugubrious than those that would have come to him just before taking his seat in the electric chair.

The meeting between his Princess and M. Tibault was worse and better than he expected. Better because, after all, they did not say much to each other—and worse because it seemed to him, somehow, that some curious kinship of mind between them made words unnecessary. They were certainly the most distinguished-looking couple in the room, as he bent over her hand. "So darlingly foreign, both of them, and yet so different," babbled Mrs. Dingle—but Tommy couldn't agree.

They were different, yes—the dark, lithe stranger with the bizarre appendage tucked carelessly in his pocket, and the blue-eyed, brown-haired girl. But that difference only accentuated what they had in common—something in the way they moved, in the suavity of their gestures, in the set of their eyes. Something deeper, even, than race. He tried to puzzle it out— then, looking around at the others, he had a flash of revelation. It was as if that couple were foreign, indeed—not only to New York but to all common humanity. As if they were polite guests from a different star.

Tommy did not have a very happy evening, on the whole. But his mind worked slowly, and it was not until much later that the mad suspicion came upon him in full force.

Perhaps he is not to be blamed for his lack of immediate comprehension. The next few weeks were weeks of bewildered misery for him. It was not that the Princess's attitude toward him had changed—she was just as tolerant of him as before, but M. Tibault was always there. He had a faculty of appearing as out of thin air—he walked, for all his height, as lightly as a butterfly—and Tommy grew to hate that faintest shuffle on the carpet that announced his presence.

And then, hang it all, the man was so smooth, so infernally, unrufflably smooth! He was never out of temper, never embarrassed. He treated Tommy with the extreme of urbanity, and yet his eyes mocked, deep-down, and Tommy could do nothing. And, gradually, the Princess became more and more drawn to this stranger, in a soundless communion that found little need for speech—and that, too, Tommy saw and hated, and that, too, he could not mend.

He began to be haunted not only by M. Tibault in the flesh, but by M. Tibault in the spirit. He slept badly, and when he slept, he dreamed—of M. Tibault, a man no longer, but a shadow, a spectre, the limber ghost of an animal whose words came purringly between sharp little pointed teeth. There was certainly something odd about the whole shape of the fellow —his fluid ease, the mould of his head, even the cut of his fingernails—but just what it was escaped Tommy's intensest cogitation. And when he did put his finger on it at length, at first he refused to believe.

A pair of petty incidents decided him, finally, against all reason. He had gone to Mrs. Dingle's, one winter afternoon, hoping to find the Princess. She was out with his aunt, but was expected back for tea, and he wandered idly into the library to wait. He was just about to switch on the lights, for the library was always dark even in summer, when he heard a sound of light breathing that seemed to come from the leather couch in the corner. He approached it cautiously and dimly made out the form of M. Tibault, curled up on the couch, peacefully asleep.

The sight annoyed Tommy so that he swore under his breath and was back near the door on his way out, when the feeling we all know and hate, the feeling that eyes we cannot see are watching us, arrested him. He turned back—M. Tibault had not moved a muscle of his body to all appearance—but his eyes were open now. And those eyes were black and human no longer. They were green—Tommy could have sworn it—and he could have sworn that they had no bottom and gleamed like little emeralds in the dark. It only lasted a moment, for Tommy pressed the light-button automatically—and there was M. Tibault, his normal self, yawning a little but urbanely apologetic, but it gave Tommy time to think. Nor did what happened a trifle later increase his peace of mind.

They had lit a fire and were talking in front of it—by now Tommy hated M. Tibault so thoroughly that he felt that odd yearning for his company that often occurs in such cases. M. Tibault was telling some anecdote and Tommy was hating him worse than ever for basking with such obvious enjoyment in the heat of the flames and the ripple of his own voice.

Then they heard the street-door open, and M. Tibault jumped up—and jumping, caught one sock on a sharp corner of the brass fire-rail and tore it open in a jagged flap. Tommy looked down mechanically at the tear—a second's glance, but enough—for M. Tibault, for the first time in Tommy's experience, lost his temper completely. He swore violently in some spitting, foreign tongue—his face distorted suddenly—he clapped his hand over his sock. Then, glaring furiously at Tommy, he fairly sprang from the room, and Tommy could hear him scaling the stairs in long, agile bounds.

Tommy sank into a chair, careless for once of the fact that he heard the Princess's light laugh in the hall. He didn't want to see the Princess. He didn't want to see anybody. There had been something revealed when M. Tibault had torn that hole in his sock—and it was not the skin of a man. Tommy had caught a glimpse of—black plush. Black velvet. And then had come M. Tibault's sudden explosion of fury. Good *Lord*—did the man wear black velvet stockings under his ordinary socks? Or could he—could he—but here Tommy held his fevered head in his hands.

He went to Professor Tatto that evening with a series of hypothetical questions, but as he did not dare confide his real suspicions to the Professor, the hypothetical answers he received served only to confuse him the more. Then he thought of Billy Strange. Billy was a good sort, and his mind had a turn for the bizarre. Billy might be able to help.

He couldn't get hold of Billy for three days and lived through the interval in a fever of impatience. But finally they had dinner together at Billy's apartment, where his queer books were, and Tommy was able to blurt out the whole disordered jumble of his suspicions.

Billy listened without interrupting until Tommy was quite through. Then he pulled at his pipe. "But, my dear *man*——" he said, protestingly.

"Oh, I know—I know——" said Tommy, and waved his hands, "I know I'm crazy—you needn't tell me that—but I tell you, the man's a cat all the same—no, I don't see how he could be, but he is—why, hang it, in the first place, everybody knows he's got a tail!"

"Even so," said Billy, puffing. "Oh, my dear Tommy, I don't doubt you saw, or think you saw, everything you say. But, even so——" He shook his head.

"But what about those other birds, werwolves and things?" said Tommy.

Billy looked dubious. "We-ll," he admitted, "you've got me there, of course. At least—a tailed man *is* possible. And the yarns about werwolves go back far enough, so that—well, I wouldn't say there aren't or haven't been werwolves—but then I'm willing to believe more things than most people. But a wer-cat—or a man that's a cat and a cat that's a man—honestly, Tommy——"

"If I don't get some real advice I'll go clean off my hinge. For Heaven's sake, tell me something to *do!*"

"Lemme think," said Billy. "First, you're pizen-sure this man is——"

"A cat. Yeah," and Tommy nodded violently.

"Check. And second—if it doesn't hurt your feelings, Tommy—you're afraid this girl you're in love with has—er—at least a streak of—felinity—in her—and so she's drawn to him?"

"Oh, Lord, Billy, if I only knew!"

"Well—er—suppose she really is, too, you know—would you still be keen on her?"

"I'd marry her if she turned into a dragon every Wednesday!" said Tommy, fervently.

Billy smiled. "H'm," he said, "then the obvious thing to do is to get rid of this M. Tibault. Lemme think."

He thought about two pipes full, while Tommy sat on pins and needles. Then, finally, he burst out laughing.

"What's so darn funny?" said Tommy, aggrievedly.

"Nothing, Tommy, only I've just thought of a stunt—something so blooming crazy—but if he is—h'm—what you think he is—it *might* work——" And, going to the bookcase, he took down a book.

"If you think you're going to quiet my nerves by reading me a bedtime story——"

"Shut up, Tommy, and listen to this—if you really want to get rid of your feline friend."

"What is it?"

"Book of Agnes Repplier's. About cats. Listen.

" 'There is also a Scandinavian version of the ever famous story which Sir Walter Scott told to Washington Irving, which Monk Lewis told to Shelley and which, in one form or another, we find embodied in the folklore of every land'—now, Tommy, pay attention—'the story of the traveller who saw within a ruined abbey, a procession of cats, lowering into a grave a little coffin with a crown upon it. Filled with horror, he hastened from the spot; but when he had reached his destination, he could not forbear relating to a friend the wonder he had seen. Scarcely had the tale been told when his friend's cat, who lay curled up tranquilly by the fire, sprang to its feet, cried out, "Then I am the King of the Cats!" and disappeared in a flash up the chimney.'

"Well?" said Billy, shutting the book.

"By gum!" said Tommy, staring. "By gum! Do you think there's a chance?"

"*I* think we're both in the booby-hatch. But if you want to try it——"

"Try it! I'll spring it on him the next time I see him. But—listen—I can't make it a ruined abbey——"

"Oh, use your imagination! Make it Central Park—anywhere. Tell it as if it happened to you—seeing the funeral procession and all that. You can lead into it somehow—let's see—some general line—oh, yes—'Strange, isn't it, how fact so often copies fiction. Why, only yesterday——' See?"

"Strange, isn't it, how fact so often copies fiction," repeated Tommy dutifully. "Why, only yesterday——"

"I happened to be strolling through Central Park when I saw something very odd."

"I happened to be strolling through—here, gimme that book!" said Tommy, "I want to learn the rest of it by heart!"

Mrs. Dingle's farewell dinner to the famous Monsieur Tibault, on the occasion of his departure for his Western tour, was looked forward to with the greatest expectations. Not only would everybody be there, including the Princess Vivrakanarda, but Mrs. Dingle, a hinter if there ever was one, had let it be known that at this dinner an announcement of very unusual interest to Society might be made. So everyone, for once, was almost on time, except for Tommy. He was at least fifteen minutes early, for he wanted to have speech with his aunt alone. Unfortunately, however, he had hardly taken off his overcoat when she was whispering some news in his ear so rapidly that he found it difficult to understand a word of it.

"And you mustn't breathe it to a soul!" she ended, beaming. "That is, not before the announcement—I think we'll have *that* with the salad—people never pay very much attention to salad——"

"Breathe what, Aunt Emily?" said Tommy, confused.

"The Princess, darling—the dear Princess and Monsieur Tibault—they just got engaged this afternoon, dear things! Isn't it *fascinating*?"

"Yeah," said Tommy, and started to walk blindly through the nearest door. His aunt restrained him.

"Not there, dear—not in the library. You can congratulate them later. They're just having a sweet little moment alone there now——" And she turned away to harry the butler, leaving Tommy stunned.

But his chin came up after a moment. He wasn't beaten yet.

"Strange, isn't it, how often fact copies fiction?" he repeated to himself in dull mnemonics, and, as he did so, he shook his fist at the library door.

Mrs. Dingle was wrong, as usual. The Princess and M. Tibault were not in the library—they were in the conservatory, as Tommy discovered when he wandered aimlessly past the glass doors.

He didn't mean to look, and after a second he turned away. But that second was enough.

Tibault was seated in a chair and she was crouched on a stool at his side, while his hand, softly, smoothly, stroked her brown hair. Black cat and Siamese kitten. Her face was hidden from Tommy, but he could see Tibault's face. And he could hear.

They were not talking, but there was a sound between them. A warm and contented sound like the murmur of giant bees in a hollow tree—a golden, musical rumble, deep-throated, that came from Tibault's lips and was answered by hers—a golden purr.

Tommy found himself back in the drawing-room, shaking hands with Mrs. Culverin, who said, frankly, that she had seldom seen him look so pale.

The first two courses of the dinner passed Tommy like dreams, but Mrs. Dingle's cellar was notable, and by the middle of the meat course, he began to come to himself. He had only one resolve now.

For the next few moments he tried desperately to break into the conversation, but Mrs. Dingle was talking, and even Gabriel will have a time interrupting Mrs. Dingle. At last, though, she paused for breath and Tommy saw his chance.

"Speaking of that," said Tommy, piercingly, without knowing in the least what he was referring to, "Speaking of that——"

"As I was saying," said Professor Tatto. But Tommy would not yield. The plates were being taken away. It was time for salad.

"Speaking of that," he said again, so loudly and strangely that Mrs. Culverin jumped and an awkward hush fell over the table. "Strange, isn't it, how often fact copies fiction?" There, he was started. His voice rose even higher. "Why, only to-day I was strolling through——" and, word for word, he repeated his lesson. He could see Tibault's eyes glowing at him, as he described the funeral. He could see the Princess, tense.

He could not have said what he had expected might happen when he came to the end; but it was not bored silence, everywhere, to be followed by Mrs. Dingle's acrid, "Well, Tommy, is that *quite* all?"

He slumped back in his chair, sick at heart. He was a fool and his last resource had failed. Dimly he heard his aunt's voice, saying, "Well, then——" and realized that she was about to make the fatal announcement.

But just then Monsieur Tibault spoke.

"One moment, Mrs. Dingle," he said, with extreme politeness, and she was silent. He turned to Tommy.

"You are—positive, I suppose, of what you saw this afternoon, Brooks?" he said, in tones of light mockery.

"Absolutely," said Tommy sullenly. "Do you think I'd——"

"Oh, no, no, no," Monsieur Tibault waved the implication aside, "but—such an interesting story—one likes to be sure of the details—and, of course, you *are* sure—*quite* sure—that the kind of crown you describe was on the coffin?"

"Of course," said Tommy, wondering, "but——"

"Then I'm the King of the Cats!" cried Monsieur Tibault in a voice of thunder, and, even as he cried it, the house-lights blinked—there was the soft thud of an explosion that seemed muffled in cotton-wool from the minstrel gallery—and the scene was lit for a second by an obliterating and painful burst of light that vanished in an instant and was succeeded by heavy, blinding clouds of white, pungent smoke.

"Oh, those *horrid* photographers," came Mrs. Dingle's voice in a melodious wail. "I *told* them not to take the flashlight picture till dinner was over, and now they've taken it *just* as I was nibbling lettuce!"

Someone tittered a little nervously. Someone coughed. Then, gradually the veils of smoke dislimned and the green-and-black spots in front of Tommy's eyes died away.

They were blinking at each other like people who have just come out of a cave into brilliant sun. Even yet their eyes stung with the fierceness of that abrupt illumination and Tommy found it hard to make out the faces across the table from him.

Mrs. Dingle took command of the half-blinded company with her accustomed poise. She rose, glass in hand. "And now, dear friends," she said in a clear voice, "I'm sure all of us are very happy to——" Then she stopped, open-mouthed, an expression of incredulous horror on her features. The lifted glass began to spill its contents on the tablecloth in a little stream of amber. As she spoke, she had turned directly to Monsieur Tibault's place at the table—and Monsieur Tibault was no longer there.

Some say there was a bursting flash of fire that disappeared up the chimney—some say it was a giant cat that leaped through the window at a bound, without breaking the glass. Professor Tatto puts it down to a mysterious chemical disturbance operating only over M. Tibault's chair. The butler, who is pious, believes the devil in person flew away with him, and Mrs. Dingle hesitates between witchcraft and a malicious ectoplasm dematerializing on the wrong cosmic plane. But be that as it may, one thing is certain—in the instant of fictive darkness which followed the glare of the flashlight, Monsieur Tibault, the great conductor, disappeared forever from mortal sight, tail and all.

Mrs. Culverin swears he was an international burglar and that she was just about to unmask him, when he slipped away under cover of the flashlight smoke, but no one else who sat at that historic dinner-table believes her. No, there are no sound explanations, but Tommy thinks he knows, and he will never be able to pass a cat again without wondering.

Mrs. Tommy is quite of her husband's mind regarding cats—she was Gretchen Woolwine, of Chicago—for Tommy told her his whole story, and while she doesn't believe a great deal of it, there is no doubt in her heart that one person concerned in the affair was a *perfect* cat. Doubtless it would have been more romantic to relate how Tommy's daring finally won him his Princess—but, unfortunately, it would not be veracious. For the Princess Vivrakanarda, also, is with us no longer. Her nerves, shattered by the spectacular denouement of Mrs. Dingle's dinner, required a sea-voyage, and from that voyage she has never returned to America.

Of course, there are the usual stories—one hears of her, a nun in a Siamese convent, or a masked dancer at Le Jardin de ma Soeur—one hears that she has been murdered in Patagonia or married in Trebizond—but, as far as can be ascertained, not one of these gaudy fables has the slightest basis of fact. I believe that Tommy, in his heart of hearts, is quite convinced that the sea-voyage was only a pretext, and that by some unheard-of means, she has managed to rejoin the formidable Monsieur Tibault, wherever in the world of the visible or the invisible he may be—in fact, that in some ruined city or subterranean palace they reign together now, King and Queen of all the mysterious Kingdom of Cats. But that, of course, is quite impossible.

1929

DAVID H. KELLER

(1880–1966)

The Jelly-Fish

"ALL space is relative. There is no such thing as size. The telescope and the microscope have produced a deadly leveling of great and small, far and near. The only little thing is sin, the only great thing is fear!"

For the hundredth time Professor Queirling repeated his statement, and for the hundredth time we listened in silence, afraid to enter into a controversy with him. It was not the fact that he knew more than we did that kept us quiet, but the haunting fear that filled us when we listened to him or watched him at work.

Working at an unsolved problem, he seemed a soul detached, a spirit separated from its earthly home, a being living only in the realm of thought. His body sat motionless, his eyes catatonic, unwinking stared until his mind, satisfied, deigned to return to bone-bound cell. Then in magnificent condescension he would talk freely in limpid phrases of the things he had considered and the conclusions he had deduced. We, chosen scientists, university graduates, hailed him as our master and hated him for admitting his mastery.

We hoped some evil might befall him, and yet we admitted that the success of the expedition depended upon his continued leadership. It was vitally necessary for our future: we were struggling young men with all life ahead of us, and if we failed in our first effort there would be no other opportunities for fame granted us.

In a specially constructed yacht, a veritable floating laboratory, we were south of Borneo, making a detailed study of microscopic sea life. In deep-sea nets we gathered the tiny organisms and then, with microscope, photography, and the cinema we observed them for the future instruction of the human race. There were hundreds of species, thousands of varieties, each to be identified, classified, described, studied, and photographed. We gathered in the morning, studied until midnight and slept restlessly until morning. The only thing in which we were agreed was ambition, our sole united emotion was hatred of the professor.

He knew how we felt and enjoyed taunting us: "I am your leader because I willed it so," he would say, speaking in a low restrained voice. "With me the will to attain is synonymous with accomplishment. I believe in myself and through this irreducible faith I succeed. There is nothing a strong man cannot do if he wills to do it and believes in his strength. Our ideas of space, size, and time are but the fanciful dreams of children. I am fifty-nine inches tall and fully clothed, weigh one hundred and ten pounds. If I desired I could make myself a colossus and swallow the earth as a child swallows a pill. If I willed it I could fly through space like a comet or hang suspended in the ether like the morning star. My will is greater than any other physical force, because I believe in it: I have confidence in my ability to do whatever I wish. So far I have conducted myself like an average man because I desire to so behave and not because of any limitations: Man has a soul and that ethereal force is greater than any law of nature that man ever thought of or any God ever created. He is purely and totally supreme—if he so desires."

It was after such a defiant declaration to us that our chemist, Bullard, gathered courage to challenge his power. He stated his opinion sharply and to the point, "I do not believe you."

"What is that to me?" answered the professor.

"Simply this: You make a statement that you have certain powers. I say that it is not true: Of what good to boast if you know we think you a liar? Can you do these things? If you can, do them for us, and I for one, will hail you as greater than God. Fail to do them and I will brand you a boasting poseur."

The professor looked steadily at the chemist. We waited breathlessly for the blow to fall, but he only laughed.

"You want a sign? A proof? I have thought of just such a thing and I would have proposed it myself had one of you not asked for it. The thing must be visible to all of you, something that I can demonstrate, a thing unheard of, an act all men consider impossible and yet I will do it. Listen to me.

"You have all seen the jellyfish called the Bishop's Miter.

When it is magnified three hundred times under the microscope it looks like a small balloon with a large opening at one end. It propels itself through the water by the flagellate movement of its cilia. The walls are translucent and transparent. At the top there are two specialized groups of nerve cells which we believe may serve as eyes. The opening at the bottom serves as a mouth. Smaller cells enter there and are absorbed. I describe it to refresh your memory, though you have all seen it. I will secure one in a hanging drop under the microscope and then we will attach the camera and cinema to it. We will project the picture on our screen. You will see the Miter move and live; you will observe the cilia move.

"While we have the actual specimen under observation I will look at it through the microscope. Then I will demonstrate to you that I am not the idle boaster you think me. I will force myself to pass through the glass eye-piece down into the brass tube. As I go, I will make myself grow smaller. Finally I will pass through the objective and jump into the hanging drop. I will swim in that drop—swim up to the jellyfish and touch it, make actual observations concerning its structure and functions. While I am in the drop of water you will be able to observe my every motion on the screen: Then I will disappear, pass through the microscope upwards and finally resume my original size and position in the room. I presume that if I do this you will be satisfied."

We were too astonished to reply. It was evident that the man had suddenly become insane. He smiled superciliously, as though we were children.

He waited for an answer, but we had none and then he began to prepare the apparatus for the experiment. Finally all was to his satisfaction. After examining several drops of water from our specimen-jar he was able to imprison a Bishop's Miter in the hanging drop under the microscope. He switched on the electricity and we saw the jellyfish move upon the screen.

The professor carefully adjusted the apparatus until the organism appeared with more than usual distinctness. We saw the little animal he had so carefully described to us. We even saw the little projections which we believed were its rudimentary visual organs.

Then Professor Queirling told the cinema operator what he

wanted done. He was to take a picture starting from the time the professor disappeared down the brass tube of the microscope and continue until he reappeared. No matter what happened, he was to go on taking pictures.

"It is all well enough," said our master, "for you children to see what is happening and to talk about it later on, but who would believe you? We know that the camera cannot lie. That is why it is important to take a consecutive picture of what occurs. Otherwise you might think that I have been able to hypnotize you. Now I will look down this tube. At the bottom of the hanging drop I see a transparent balloon. It is a pretty sight. Now watch me carefully as I will myself to shrink. I will go on talking as long as I can and you must listen carefully because the smaller I am the less audible will be my voice.

"Now I am twelve inches high. I am standing near the microscope. I grow still smaller and now I am only one inch tall and am standing on the eye-piece. No doubt you can barely hear me. Now I am smaller yet and am ready to will myself through the glass of the eye-piece."

The room became silent. Shivering, we looked at the microscope. The professor was gone. The chemist staggered over to the instrument, looked into it, and silently reeled back to his seat.

On the screen before us, the living inhabitants of the drop of water lived and moved and had their being. Largest of all was the transparent jellyfish, which was moving restlessly as though seeking a way of escape. The only sound in the room was the hum of the cinema and the stertorous breathing of the chemist.

Then on the screen came a new figure we were able to identify as the professor, swimming among the infusoria. Gaining his balance, at last he stood upright and waved his hand at us. It was easy to see his smile, that condescending smug smile that had so often driven us frantic. There was no doubt from his expression that he was highly pleased with his performance. None of us dared look at his fellow; not one of the audience thought for a second of taking his eyes off the silver screen. We were stunned, stupefied, and filled with a wild terror all the more horrible because of the silence.

The professor started to swim again and now approached

the jellyfish. He tapped the crystal walls. Then as though seized with a sudden impulse, he went to the bottom, jumped up through the mouth, and entered the translucent ball of protoplasm. He peered at us through the transparent walls. His arms made a series of peculiar movements and once again he smiled at us.

"My God!" exclaimed the artist. "He is wigwagging to us in army code. He says, 'I have done it, and now I will return to your world.' "

As though to keep his promise he started for the mouth of the jellyfish, and then—*the mouth closed.*

The professor circled the glasslike ball seeking a way of exit. Once he waved at us in a peculiar manner and then suddenly he sought the wall and with arms and feet tried to break through. On his face was now the look of ghastly despair. The things on top of the jellyfish began to glow—no doubt now that they were eyes, and bright ones.

Before our eyes the professor slowly disappeared into a globule of milky protoplasm. The jellyfish not only had made him a prisoner, but had actually dissolved and digested him. With a shriek the artist went over to the wall and turned on the electric lights. Trembling, the chemist looked down the tube of the microscope and told us that there was nothing in the hanging drop save the jellyfish.

The next day, after a conference, in which each of us said only part of what he thought, we decided to destroy the roll of film—and sent word to the university that the professor had disappeared from the ship and our only explanation was that he had been drowned.

1929

CONRAD AIKEN

(1889–1973)

Mr. Arcularis

Mr. Arcularis stood at the window of his room in the hospital and looked down at the street. There had been a light shower, which had patterned the sidewalks with large drops, but now again the sun was out, blue sky was showing here and there between the swift white clouds, a cold wind was blowing the poplar trees. An itinerant band had stopped before the building and was playing, with violin, harp, and flute, the finale of "Cavalleria Rusticana." Leaning against the window-sill— for he felt extraordinarily weak after his operation—Mr. Arcularis suddenly, listening to the wretched music, felt like crying. He rested the palm of one hand against a cold window-pane and stared down at the old man who was blowing the flute, and blinked his eyes. It seemed absurd that he should be so weak, so emotional, so like a child—and especially now that everything was over at last. In spite of all their predictions, in spite, too, of his own dreadful certainty that he was going to die, here he was, as fit as a fiddle—but what a fiddle it was, so out of tune!—with a long life before him. And to begin with, a voyage to England ordered by the doctor. What could be more delightful? Why should he feel sad about it and want to cry like a baby? In a few minutes Harry would arrive with his car to take him to the wharf; in an hour he would be on the sea, in two hours he would see the sunset behind him, where Boston had been, and his new life would be opening before him. It was many years since he had been abroad. June, the best of the year to come—England, France, the Rhine—how ridiculous that he should already be homesick!

There was a light footstep outside the door, a knock, the door opened, and Harry came in.

"Well, old man, I've come to get you. The old bus actually got here. Are you ready? Here, let me take your arm. You're tottering like an octogenarian!"

Mr. Arcularis submitted gratefully, laughing, and they made the journey slowly along the bleak corridor and down the stairs to the entrance hall. Miss Hoyle, his nurse, was there, and the Matron, and the charming little assistant with freckles who had helped to prepare him for the operation. Miss Hoyle put out her hand.

"Good-by, Mr. Arcularis," she said, "and *bon voyage.*"

"Good-by, Miss Hoyle, and thank you for everything. You were very kind to me. And I fear I was a nuisance."

The girl with the freckles, too, gave him her hand, smiling. She was very pretty, and it would have been easy to fall in love with her. She reminded him of some one. Who was it? He tried in vain to remember while he said good-by to her and turned to the Matron.

"And not too many latitudes with the young ladies, Mr. Arcularis!" she was saying.

Mr. Arcularis was pleased, flattered, by all this attention to a middle-aged invalid, and felt a joke taking shape in his mind, and no sooner in his mind than on his tongue.

"Oh, no latitudes," he said, laughing. "I'll leave the latitudes to the ship!"

"Oh, come now," said the Matron, "we don't seem to have hurt him much, do we?"

"I think we'll have to operate on him again and *really* cure him," said Miss Hoyle.

He was going down the front steps, between the potted palmettos, and they all laughed and waved. The wind was cold, very cold for June, and he was glad he had put on his coat. He shivered.

"Damned cold for June!" he said. "Why should it be so cold?"

"East wind," Harry said, arranging the rug over his knees. "Sorry it's an open car, but I believe in fresh air and all that sort of thing. I'll drive slowly. We've got plenty of time."

They coasted gently down the long hill toward Beacon Street, but the road was badly surfaced, and despite Harry's care Mr. Arcularis felt his pain again. He found that he could alleviate it a little by leaning to the right, against the arm-rest, and not breathing too deeply. But how glorious to be out again! How strange and vivid the world looked! The trees had innumerable green fresh leaves—they were all blowing and

shifting and turning and flashing in the wind; drops of rainwater fell downward sparkling; the robins were singing their
absurd, delicious little four-noted songs; even the street cars
looked unusually bright and beautiful, just as they used to look
when he was a child and had wanted above all things to be a
motorman. He found himself smiling foolishly at everything,
foolishly and weakly, and wanted to say something about it to
Harry. It was no use, though—he had no strength, and the mere
finding of words would be almost more than he could manage.
And even if he should succeed in saying it, he would then most
likely burst into tears. He shook his head slowly from side to
side.

"Ain't it grand?" he said.

"I'll bet it looks good," said Harry.

"Words fail me."

"You wait till you get out to sea. You'll have a swell time."

"Oh, swell! . . . I hope not. I hope it'll be calm."

"Tut tut."

When they passed the Harvard Club Mr. Arcularis made a
slow and somewhat painful effort to turn in his seat and look
at it. It might be the last chance to see it for a long time. Why
this sentimental longing to stare at it, though? There it was,
with the great flag blowing in the wind, the Harvard seal now
concealed by the swift folds and now revealed, and there were
the windows in the library, where he had spent so many delightful hours reading—Plato, and Kipling, and the Lord knows
what—and the balconies from which for so many years he had
watched the Marathon. Old Talbot might be in there now,
sleeping with a book on his knee, hoping forlornly to be interrupted by any one, for anything.

"Good-by to the old club," he said.

"The bar will miss you," said Harry, smiling with friendly
irony and looking straight ahead.

"But let there be no moaning," said Mr. Arcularis.

"What's *that* a quotation from?"

" 'The Odyssey.' "

In spite of the cold, he was glad of the wind on his face, for
it helped to dissipate the feeling of vagueness and dizziness that
came over him in a sickening wave from time to time. All of a
sudden everything would begin to swim and dissolve, the

houses would lean their heads together, he had to close his eyes, and there would be a curious and dreadful humming noise, which at regular intervals rose to a crescendo and then drawlingly subsided again. It was disconcerting. Perhaps he still had a trace of fever. When he got on the ship he would have a glass of whisky. . . . From one of these spells he opened his eyes and found that they were on the ferry, crossing to East Boston. It must have been the ferry's engines that he had heard. From another spell he woke to find himself on the wharf, the car at a standstill beside a pile of yellow packing-cases.

"We're here because we're here because we're here," said Harry.

"Because we're here," added Mr. Arcularis.

He dozed in the car while Harry—and what a good friend Harry was!—attended to all the details. He went and came with tickets and passports and baggage checks and porters. And at last he unwrapped Mr. Arcularis from the rugs and led him up the steep gangplank to the deck, and thence by devious windings to a small cold stateroom with a solitary porthole like the eye of a cyclops.

"Here you are," he said, "and now I've got to go. Did you hear the whistle?"

"No."

"Well, you're half asleep. It's sounded the all-ashore. Good-by, old fellow, and take care of yourself. Bring me back a spray of edelweiss. And send me a picture post-card from the Absolute."

"Will you have it finite or infinite?"

"Oh, infinite. But with your signature on it. Now you'd better turn in for a while and have a nap. Cheerio!"

Mr. Arcularis took his hand and pressed it hard, and once more felt like crying. Absurd! Had he become a child again?

"Good-by," he said.

He sat down in the little wicker chair, with his overcoat still on, closed his eyes, and listened to the humming of the air in the ventilator. Hurried footsteps ran up and down the corridor. The chair was not too comfortable, and his pain began to bother him again, so he moved, with his coat still on, to the narrow berth and fell asleep. When he woke up, it was dark, and the porthole had been partly opened. He groped for the switch and turned on the light. Then he rang for the steward.

"It's cold in here," he said. "Would you mind closing the port?"

The girl who sat opposite him at dinner was charming. Who was it she reminded him of? Why, of course, the girl at the hospital, the girl with the freckles. Her hair was beautiful, not quite red, not quite gold, nor had it been bobbed; arranged with a sort of graceful untidiness, it made him think of a Melozzo da Forli angel. Her face was freckled, she had a mouth which was both humorous and voluptuous. And she seemed to be alone.

He frowned at the bill of fare and ordered the thick soup.

"No hors d'œuvres?" asked the steward.

"I think not," said Mr. Arcularis. "They might kill me."

The steward permitted himself to be amused and deposited the menu card on the table against the water-bottle. His eyebrows were lifted. As he moved away, the girl followed him with her eyes and smiled.

"I'm afraid you shocked him," she said.

"Impossible," said Mr. Arcularis. "These stewards, they're dead souls. How could they be stewards otherwise? And they think they've seen and known everything. They suffer terribly from the *déjà vu*. Personally, I don't blame them."

"It must be a dreadful sort of life."

"It's because they're dead that they accept it."

"Do you think so?"

"I'm sure of it. I'm enough of a dead soul myself to know the signs!"

"Well, I don't know what you mean by that!"

"But nothing mysterious! I'm just out of hospital, after an operation. I was given up for dead. For six months I had given *myself* up for dead. If you've ever been seriously ill you know the feeling. You have a posthumous feeling—a mild, cynical tolerance for everything and every one. What is there you haven't seen or done or understood? Nothing."

Mr. Arcularis waved his hands and smiled.

"I wish I could understand you," said the girl, "but I've never been ill in my life."

"Never?"

"Never."

"Good God!"

The torrent of the unexpressed and inexpressible paralyzed him and rendered him speechless. He stared at the girl, wondering who she was and then, realizing that he had perhaps stared too fixedly, averted his gaze, gave a little laugh, rolled a pill of bread between his fingers. After a second or two he allowed himself to look at her again and found her smiling.

"Never pay any attention to invalids," he said, "or they'll drag you to the hospital."

She examined him critically, with her head tilted a little to one side, but with friendliness.

"You don't *look* like an invalid," she said.

Mr. Arcularis thought her charming. His pain ceased to bother him, the disagreeable humming disappeared, or rather, it was dissociated from himself and became merely, as it should be, the sound of the ship's engines, and he began to think the voyage was going to be really delightful. The parson on his right passed him the salt.

"I fear you will need this in your soup," he said.

"Thank you. Is it as bad as that?"

The steward, overhearing, was immediately apologetic and solicitous. He explained that on the first day everything was at sixes and sevens. The girl looked up at him and asked him a question.

"Do you think we'll have a good voyage?" she said.

He was passing the hot rolls to the parson, removing the napkins from them with a deprecatory finger.

"Well, madam, I don't like to be a Jeremiah, but——"

"Oh, come," said the parson, "I hope we have no Jeremiahs."

"What do you mean?" said the girl.

Mr. Arcularis ate his soup with gusto—it was nice and hot.

"Well, maybe I shouldn't say it, but there's a corpse on board, going to Ireland; and I never yet knew a voyage with a corpse on board that we didn't have bad weather."

"Why, steward, you're just superstitious! What nonsense!"

"That's a very ancient superstition," said Mr. Arcularis. "I've heard it many times. Maybe it's true. Maybe we'll be wrecked. And what does it matter, after all?" He was very bland.

"Then let's be wrecked," said the parson coldly.

Nevertheless, Mr. Arcularis felt a shudder go through him

on hearing the steward's remark. A corpse in the hold—a coffin? Perhaps it was true. Perhaps some disaster would befall them. There might be fogs. There might be icebergs. He thought of all the wrecks of which he had read. There was the *Titanic*, which he had read about in the warm newspaper room at the Harvard Club—it had seemed dreadfully real, even there. That band, playing "Nearer My God to Thee" on the after-deck while the ship sank! It was one of the darkest of his memories. And the *Empress of Ireland*—all those poor people trapped in the smoking-room, with only one door between them and life, and that door locked for the night by the deck-steward, and the deck-steward nowhere to be found! He shivered, feeling a draft, and turned to the parson.

"How do these strange delusions arise?" he said.

The parson looked at him searchingly, appraisingly—from chin to forehead, from forehead to chin—and Mr. Arcularis, feeling uncomfortable, straightened his tie.

"From nothing but fear," said the parson. "Nothing on earth but fear."

"How strange!" said the girl.

Mr. Arcularis again looked at her—she had lowered her face—and again tried to think of whom she reminded him. It wasn't only the little freckle-faced girl at the hospital—both of them had reminded him of some one else. Some one far back in his life: remote, beautiful, lovely. But he couldn't think. The meal came to an end, they all rose, the ship's orchestra played a feeble fox-trot, and Mr. Arcularis, once more alone, went to the bar to have his whisky. The room was stuffy, and the ship's engines were both audible and palpable. The humming and throbbing oppressed him, the rhythm seemed to be the rhythm of his own pain, and after a short time he found his way, with slow steps, holding on to the walls in his moments of weakness and dizziness, to his forlorn and white little room. The port had been—thank God!—closed for the night: it was cold enough anyway. The white and blue ribbons fluttered from the ventilator, the bottle and glasses clicked and clucked as the ship swayed gently to the long, slow motion of the sea. It was all very peculiar—it was all like something he had experienced somewhere before. What was it? Where was it? . . . He untied his tie, looking at his face in the glass, and won-

dered, and from time to time put his hand to his side to hold
in the pain. It wasn't at Portsmouth, in his childhood, nor at
Salem, nor in the rose-garden at his Aunt Julia's, nor in the
schoolroom at Cambridge. It was something very queer, very
intimate, very precious. The jackstones, the Sunday-school
cards which he had loved when he was a child . . . He fell
asleep.

The sense of time was already hopelessly confused. One hour
was like another, the sea looked always the same, morning was
indistinguishable from afternoon—and was it Tuesday or Wednesday? Mr. Arcularis was sitting in the smoking-room, in his
favorite corner, watching the parson teach Miss Dean to play
chess. On the deck outside he could see the people passing and
repassing in their restless round of the ship. The red jacket
went by, then the black hat with the white feather, then the
purple scarf, the brown tweed coat, the Bulgarian mustache,
the monocle, the Scotch cap with fluttering ribbons, and in no
time at all the red jacket again, dipping past the windows with
its own peculiar rhythm, followed once more by the black hat
and the purple scarf. How odd to reflect on the fixed little
orbits of these things—as definite and profound, perhaps, as
the orbits of the stars, and as important to God or the Absolute. There was a kind of tyranny in this fixedness, too—to
think of it too much made one uncomfortable. He closed his
eyes for a moment, to avoid seeing for the fortieth time the
Bulgarian mustache and the pursuing monocle. The parson
was explaining the movements of knights. Two forward and
one to the side. Eight possible moves, always to the opposite
color from that on which the piece stands. Two forward and
one to the side: Miss Dean repeated the words several times with
reflective emphasis. Here, too, was the terrifying fixed curve of
the infinite, the creeping curve of logic which at last must
become the final signpost at the edge of nothing. After that—
the deluge. The great white light of annihilation. The bright
flash of death. . . . Was it merely the sea which made these
abstractions so insistent, so intrusive? The mere notion of *orbit*
had somehow become extraordinarily naked; and to rid himself of the discomfort and also to forget a little the pain which
bothered his side whenever he sat down, he walked slowly and

carefully into the writing-room, and examined a pile of super-annuated magazines and catalogues of travel. The bright colors amused him, the photographs of remote islands and mountains, savages in sampans or sarongs or both—it was all very far off and delightful, like something in a dream or a fever. But he found that he was too tired to read and was incapable of concentration. Dreams! Yes, that reminded him. That rather alarming business—sleep-walking!

Later in the evening—at what hour he didn't know—he was telling Miss Dean about it, as he had intended to do. They were sitting in deck-chairs on the sheltered side. The sea was black, and there was a cold wind. He wished they had chosen to sit in the lounge.

Miss Dean was extremely pretty—no, beautiful. She looked at him, too, in a very strange and lovely way, with something of inquiry, something of sympathy, something of affection. It seemed as if, between the question and the answer, they had sat thus for a very long time, exchanging an unspoken secret, simply looking at each other quietly and kindly. Had an hour or two passed? And was it at all necessary to speak?

"No," she said, "I never have."

She breathed into the low words a note of interrogation and gave him a slow smile.

"That's the funny part of it. I never had either until last night. Never in my life. I hardly ever even dream. And it really rather frightens me."

"Tell me about it, Mr. Arcularis."

"I dreamed at first that I was walking, alone, in a wide plain covered with snow. It was growing dark, I was very cold, my feet were frozen and numb, and I was lost. I came then to a signpost—at first it seemed to me there was nothing on it. Nothing but ice. Just before it grew finally dark, however, I made out on it the one word 'Polaris.'"

"The Pole Star."

"Yes—and you see, I didn't myself know that. I looked it up only this morning. I suppose I must have seen it somewhere? And of course it rhymes with my name."

"Why, so it does!"

"Anyway, it gave me—in the dream—an awful feeling of despair, and the dream changed. This time, I dreamed I was standing *outside* my state-room in the little dark corridor, or *cul-de-sac*, and trying to find the door-handle to let myself in. I was in my pajamas, and again I was very cold. And at this point I woke up. . . . The extraordinary thing is that's exactly where I was!"

"Good heavens. How strange!"

"Yes. And now the question is, *where had I been?* I was frightened, when I came to—not unnaturally. For among other things I *did* have, quite definitely, the feeling that I *had been* somewhere. Somewhere where it was very cold. It doesn't sound very proper. Suppose I had been seen!"

"That might have been awkward," said Miss Dean.

"Awkward! It might indeed. It's very singular. I've never done such a thing before. It's this sort of thing that reminds one—rather wholesomely, perhaps, don't you think?"—and Mr. Arcularis gave a nervous little laugh—"how extraordinarily little we know about the workings of our own minds or souls. After all, what *do* we know?"

"Nothing—nothing—nothing—nothing," said Miss Dean slowly.

"*Absolutely* nothing."

Their voices had dropped, and again they were silent; and again they looked at each other gently and sympathetically, as if for the exchange of something unspoken and perhaps unspeakable. Time ceased. The orbit—so it seemed to Mr. Arcularis—once more became pure, became absolute. And once more he found himself wondering who it was that Miss Dean—Clarice Dean—reminded him of. Long ago and far away. Like those pictures of the islands and mountains. The little freckle-faced girl at the hospital was merely, as it were, the stepping-stone, the signpost, or, as in algebra, the "equals" sign. But what was it they both "equalled"? The jackstones came again into his mind and his Aunt Julia's rose-garden—at sunset; but this was ridiculous. It couldn't be simply that they reminded him of his childhood! And yet why not?

They went into the lounge. The ship's orchestra, in the oval-shaped balcony among faded palms, was playing the finale of "Cavalleria Rusticana," playing it badly.

"Good God!" said Mr. Arcularis, "can't I ever escape from that damned sentimental tune? It's the last thing I heard in America, and the last thing I *want* to hear."

"But don't you like it?"

"As music? No! It moves me too much, but in the wrong way."

"What, exactly, do you mean?"

"Exactly? Nothing. When I heard it at the hospital—when was it?—it made me feel like crying. Three old Italians tootling it in the rain. I suppose, like most people, I'm afraid of my feelings."

"Are they so dangerous?"

"Now then, young woman! Are you pulling my leg?"

The stewards had rolled away the carpets, and the passengers were beginning to dance. Miss Dean accepted the invitation of a young officer, and Mr. Arcularis watched them with envy. Odd, that last exchange of remarks—very odd; in fact, everything was odd. Was it possible that they were falling in love? Was that what it was all about—all these concealed references and recollections? He had read of such things. But at his age! And with a girl of twenty-two! It was ridiculous.

After an amused look at his old friend Polaris from the open door on the sheltered side, he went to bed.

The rhythm of the ship's engines was positively a persecution. It gave one no rest, it followed one like the Hound of Heaven, it drove one out into space and across the Milky Way and then back home by way of Betelgeuse. It was cold there, too. Mr. Arcularis, making the round trip by way of Betelgeuse and Polaris, sparkled with frost. He felt like a Christmas tree. Icicles on his fingers and icicles on his toes. He tinkled and spangled in the void, hallooed to the waste echoes, rounded the buoy on the verge of the Unknown, and tacked glitteringly homeward. The wind whistled. He was barefooted. Snowflakes and tinsel blew past him. Next time, by George, he would go farther still—for altogether it was rather a lark. Forward into the untrodden! as somebody said. Some intrepid explorer of his own backyard, probably, some middle-aged professor with an umbrella: those were the fellows for courage! But give us time, thought Mr. Arcularis, give us time, and we will bring back with us the night-rime of the Absolute. Or was it Abso-

lete? If only there weren't this perpetual throbbing, this iteration of sound, like a pain, these circles and repetitions of
light—the feeling as of everything coiling inward to a centre of
misery . . .

Suddenly it was dark, and he was lost. He was groping, he
touched the cold, white, slippery woodwork with his fingernails, looking for an electric switch. The throbbing, of course,
was the throbbing of the ship. But he was almost home—almost
home. Another corner to round, a door to be opened, and there
he would be. Safe and sound. Safe in his father's home.

It was at this point that he woke up: in the corridor that led
to the dining saloon. Such pure terror, such horror, seized him
as he had never known. His heart felt as if it would stop beating.
His back was toward the dining saloon; apparently he had just
come from it. He was in his pajamas. The corridor was dim, all
but two lights having been turned out for the night, and—
thank God!—deserted. Not a soul, not a sound. He was perhaps fifty yards from his room. With luck he could get to it
unseen. Holding tremulously to the rail that ran along the
wall, a brown, greasy rail, he began to creep his way forward.
He felt very weak, very dizzy, and his thoughts refused to concentrate. Vaguely he remembered Miss Dean—Clarice—and
the freckled girl, as if they were one and the same person. But
he wasn't in the hospital, he was on the ship. Of course. How
absurd. The Great Circle. Here we are, old fellow . . . steady
round the corner . . . hold hard to your umbrella . . .

In his room, with the door safely shut behind him, Mr. Arcularis broke into a cold sweat. He had no sooner got into his
bunk, shivering, than he heard the night watchman pass.

"But where—" he thought, closing his eyes in agony—
"have I been? . . ."

A dreadful idea had occurred to him.

"It's nothing serious—how could it be anything serious? Of
course it's nothing serious," said Mr. Arcularis.

"No, it's nothing serious," said the ship's doctor urbanely.

"I knew you'd think so. But just the same——"

"Such a condition is the result of worry," said the doctor.
"Are you worried—do you mind telling me—about something?
Just try to think."

"Worried?"

Mr. Arcularis knitted his brows. *Was* there something? Some little mosquito of a cloud disappearing into the southwest, the northeast? Some little gnat-song of despair? But no, that was all over. All over.

"Nothing," he said, "nothing whatever."

"It's very strange," said the doctor.

"Strange! I should say so. I've come to sea for a rest, not for a nightmare! What about a bromide?"

"Well, I can give you a bromide, Mr. Arcularis——"

"Then, please, if you don't mind, give me a bromide."

He carried the little phial hopefully to his stateroom, and took a dose at once. He could see the sun through his porthole. It looked northern and pale and small, like a little peppermint, which was only natural enough, for the latitude was changing with every hour. But why was it that doctors were all alike? and all, for that matter, like his father, or that other fellow at the hospital? Smythe, his name was. Doctor Smythe. A nice, dry little fellow, and they said he was a writer. Wrote poetry, or something like that. Poor fellow—disappointed. Like everybody else. Crouched in there, in his cabin, night after night, writing blank verse or something—all about the stars and flowers and love and death; ice and the sea and the infinite; time and tide—well, every man to his own taste.

"But it's nothing serious," said Mr. Arcularis, later, to the parson. "How could it be?"

"Why, of course not, my dear fellow," said the parson, patting his back. "How could it be?"

"I know it isn't and yet I worry about it."

"It would be ridiculous to think it serious," said the parson.

Mr. Arcularis shivered: it was colder than ever. It was said that they were near icebergs. For a few hours in the morning there had been a fog, and the siren had blown—devastatingly—at three-minute intervals. Icebergs caused fog—he knew that.

"These things always come," said the parson, "from a sense of guilt. You feel guilty about something. I won't be so rude as to inquire what it is. But if you could rid yourself of the sense of guilt——"

And later still, when the sky was pink:

"But is it anything to worry about?" said Miss Dean. "Really?"

"No, I suppose not."

"Then don't worry. We aren't children any longer!"

"Aren't we? I wonder!"

They leaned, shoulders touching, on the deck-rail, and looked at the sea, which was multitudinously incarnadined. Mr. Arcularis scanned the horizon in vain for an iceberg.

"Anyway," he said, "the colder we are the less we feel!"

"I hope that's no reflection on *you*," said Miss Dean.

"Here . . . feel my hand," said Mr. Arcularis.

"Heaven knows it's cold!"

"It's been to Polaris and back! No wonder."

"Poor thing, poor thing!"

"Warm it."

"May I?"

"You can."

"I'll try."

Laughing, she took his hand between both of hers, one palm under and one palm over, and began rubbing it briskly. The decks were deserted, no one was near them, every one was dressing for dinner. The sea grew darker, the wind blew colder.

"I wish I could remember who you are," he said.

"And you—who are you?"

"Myself."

"Then perhaps *I* am yourself."

"Don't be metaphysical!"

"But I *am* metaphysical!"

She laughed, withdrew, pulled the light coat about her shoulders.

The bugle blew the summons for dinner—"The Roast Beef of Old England"—and they walked together along the darkening deck toward the door, from which a shaft of soft light fell across the deck-rail. As they stepped over the brass door-sill Mr. Arcularis felt the throb of the engines again; he put his hand quickly to his side.

"*Auf wiedersehen*," he said. "*To-morrow and to-morrow and to-morrow.*"

Mr. Arcularis was finding it impossible, absolutely impossible, to keep warm. A cold fog surrounded the ship, had done so, it seemed, for days. The sun had all but disappeared, the transition from day to night was almost unnoticeable. The ship, too, seemed scarcely to be moving—it was as if anchored among walls of ice and rime. Monstrous, that merely because it was June, and supposed, therefore, to be warm, the ship's authorities should consider it unnecessary to turn on the heat! By day, he wore his heavy coat and sat shivering in the corner of the smoking-room. His teeth chattered, his hands were blue. By night, he heaped blankets on his bed, closed the port-hole's black eye against the sea, and drew the yellow curtains across it, but in vain. Somehow, despite everything, the fog crept in, and the icy fingers touched his throat. The steward, questioned about it, merely said, "Icebergs." Of course—any fool knew that. But how long, in God's name, was it going to last? They surely ought to be past the Grand Banks by this time! And surely it wasn't necessary to sail to England by way of Greenland and Iceland!

Miss Dean—Clarice—was sympathetic.

"It's simply because," she said, "your vitality has been lowered by your illness. You can't expect to be your normal self so soon after an operation! When *was* your operation, by the way?"

Mr. Arcularis considered. Strange—he couldn't be quite sure. It was all a little vague—his sense of time had disappeared.

"Heavens knows!" he said. "Centuries ago. When I was a tadpole and you were a fish. I should think it must have been at about the time of the Battle of Teutoburg Forest. Or perhaps when I was a Neanderthal man with a club!"

"Are you sure it wasn't farther back still?"

What did she mean by that?

"Not at all. Obviously, we've been on this damned ship for ages—for eras—for æons. And even on this ship, you must remember, I've had plenty of time, in my nocturnal wanderings, to go several times to Orion and back. I'm thinking, by the way, of going farther still. There's a nice little star off to the left, as you round Betelgeuse, which looks as if it might be right at the edge. The last outpost of the finite. I think I'll have a look at it and bring you back a frozen rime-feather."

"It would melt when you got it back."

"Oh, no, it wouldn't—not on *this* ship!"

Clarice laughed.

"I wish I could go with you," she said.

"If only you would! If only——"

He broke off his sentence and looked hard at her—how lovely she was, and how desirable! No such woman had ever before come into his life; there had been no one with whom he had at once felt so profound a sympathy and understanding. It was a miracle, simply—a miracle. No need to put his arm around her or to kiss her—delightful as such small vulgarities would be. He had only to look at her, and to feel, gazing into those extraordinary eyes, that she knew him, had always known him. It was as if, indeed, she might be his own soul.

But as he looked thus at her, reflecting, he noticed that she was frowning.

"What is it?" he said.

She shook her head, slowly.

"I don't know."

"Tell me."

"Nothing. It just occurred to me that perhaps you weren't looking quite so well."

Mr. Arcularis was startled. He straightened himself up.

"What nonsense! Of course this pain bothers me—and I feel astonishingly weak——"

"It's more than that—much more than that. Something is worrying you horribly." She paused, and then with an air of challenging him, added, "Tell me, did you——"

Her eyes were suddenly asking him blazingly the question he had been afraid of. He flinched, caught his breath, looked away. But it was no use, as he knew: he would have to tell her. He had known all along that he would have to tell her.

"Clarice," he said—and his voice broke in spite of his effort to control it—"It's killing me, it's ghastly! Yes, I did."

His eyes filled with tears, he saw that her own had done so also. She put her hand on his arm.

"I knew," she said. "I knew. But tell me."

"It's happened twice again—*twice*—and each time I was farther away. The same dream of going round a star, the same terrible coldness and helplessness. That awful whistling curve . . ." He shuddered.

"And when you woke up—" she spoke quietly— "where were you when you woke up? Don't be afraid!"

"The first time I was at the farther end of the dining saloon. I had my hand on the door that leads into the pantry."

"I see. Yes. And the next time?"

Mr. Arcularis wanted to close his eyes in terror—he felt as if he were going mad. His lips moved before he could speak, and when at last he did speak it was in a voice so low as to be almost a whisper.

"I was at the bottom of the stairway that leads down from the pantry to the hold, past the refrigerating-plant. It was dark, and I was crawling on my hands and knees . . . *Crawling on my hands and knees!* . . ."

"Oh!" she said, and again, "Oh!"

He began to tremble violently; he felt the hand on his arm trembling also. And then he watched a look of unmistakable horror come slowly into Clarice's eyes, and a look of understanding, as if she saw . . . She tightened her hold on his arm.

"Do you think . . ." she whispered.

They stared at each other.

"I know," he said. "And so do you . . . Twice more—three times—and I'll be looking down into an empty . . ."

It was then that they first embraced—then, at the edge of the infinite, at the last signpost of the finite. They clung together desperately, forlornly, weeping as they kissed each other, staring hard one moment and closing their eyes the next. Passionately, passionately, she kissed him, as if she were indeed trying to give him her warmth, her life.

"But what nonsense!" she cried, leaning back, and holding his face between her hands, her hands which were wet with his tears. "What nonsense! It can't be!"

"It is," said Mr. Arcularis slowly.

"But how do you know? . . . How do you know where the——"

For the first time Mr. Arcularis smiled.

"Don't be afraid, darling—you mean the coffin?"

"How could you know where it is?"

"I don't need to," said Mr. Arcularis . . . "I'm already almost there."

Before they separated for the night, in the smoking-room, they had several whisky cocktails.

"We must make it gay!" Mr. Arcularis said. "Above all, we must make it gay. Perhaps even now it will turn out to be nothing but a nightmare from which both of us will wake! And even at the worst, at my present rate of travel, I ought to need two more nights! It's a long way, still, to that little star."

The parson passed them at the door.

"What! turning in so soon?" he said. "I was hoping for a game of chess."

"Yes, both turning in. But to-morrow?"

"To-morrow, then, Miss Dean! And good night!"

"Good night."

They walked once round the deck, then leaned on the railing and stared into the fog. It was thicker and whiter than ever. The ship was moving barely perceptibly, the rhythm of the engines was slower, more subdued and remote, and at regular intervals, mournfully, came the long reverberating cry of the foghorn. The sea was calm, and lapped only very tenderly against the side of the ship, the sound coming up to them clearly, however, because of the profound stillness.

" 'On such a night as this—' " quoted Mr. Arcularis grimly.

" 'On such a night as this——' "

Their voices hung suspended in the night, time ceased for them, for an eternal instant they were happy. When at last they parted it was by tacit agreement on a note of the ridiculous.

"Be a good boy and take your bromide!" she said.

"Yes, mother, I'll take my medicine!"

In his stateroom, he mixed himself a strong potion of bromide, a very strong one, and got into bed. He would have no trouble in falling asleep: he felt more tired, more supremely exhausted, than he had ever been in his life; nor had bed ever seemed so delicious. And that long, magnificent, delirious swoop of dizziness . . . the Great Circle . . . the swift pathway to Arcturus . . .

It was all as before, but infinitely more rapid. Never had Mr. Arcularis achieved such phenomenal, such supernatural, speed. In no time at all he was beyond the moon, shot past the North Star as if it were standing still (which perhaps it was?), swooped in a long, bright curve round the Pleiades, shouted his frosty greetings to Betelgeuse, and was off to the little blue star which pointed the way to the Unknown. Forward into the untrodden! Courage, old man, and hold on to your umbrella! Have you got your garters on? Mind your hat! In no time at all we'll be back to Clarice with the frozen rime-feather, the rime-feather, the snowflake of the Absolute, the Obsolete. If only we don't wake . . . if only we needn't wake . . . if only we don't wake in that—in that—time and space . . . somewhere or nowhere . . . cold and dark . . . "Cavalleria Rusticana" sobbing among the palms; if a lonely . . . if only . . . the coffers of the poor—not coffers, not coffers, not coffers, Oh, God, not coffers, but light, delight, supreme white and brightness, whirling lightness above all—and freezing—freezing— freezing . . .

At this point in the void the surgeon's last effort to save Mr. Arcularis's life had failed. He stood back from the operating table and made a tired gesture with a rubber-gloved hand.

"It's all over," he said. "As I expected."

He looked at Miss Hoyle, whose gaze was downward, at the basin she held. There was a moment's stillness, a pause, a brief flight of unexchanged comment, and then the ordered life of the hospital was resumed.

1931

ROBERT E. HOWARD

(1906–1936)

The Black Stone

> *"They say foul beings of Old Times still lurk*
> *In dark forgotten corners of the world,*
> *And Gates still gape to loose, on certain nights,*
> *Shapes pent in Hell."*
>
> —JUSTIN GEOFFREY

I READ of it first in the strange book of Von Junzt, the German eccentric who lived so curiously and died in such grisly and mysterious fashion. It was my fortune to have access to his *Nameless Cults* in the original edition, the so-called Black Book, published in Düsseldorf in 1839, shortly before a hounding doom overtook the author. Collectors of rare literature are familiar with *Nameless Cults* mainly through the cheap and faulty translation which was pirated in London by Bridewall in 1845, and the carefully expurgated edition put out by the Golden Goblin Press of New York in 1909. But the volume I stumbled upon was one of the unexpurgated German copies, with heavy leather covers and rusty iron hasps. I doubt if there are more than half a dozen such volumes in the entire world today, for the quantity issued was not great, and when the manner of the author's demise was bruited about, many possessors of the book burned their volumes in panic.

Von Junzt spent his entire life (1795–1840) delving into forbidden subjects; he traveled in all parts of the world, gained entrance into innumerable secret societies, and read countless little-known and esoteric books and manuscripts in the original; and in the chapters of the Black Book, which range from startling clarity of exposition to murky ambiguity, there are statements and hints to freeze the blood of a thinking man. Reading what Von Junzt *dared* put in print arouses uneasy speculations as to what it was that he dared *not* tell. What dark matters, for instance, were contained in those closely written pages that formed the unpublished manuscript on which he worked unceasingly for months before his death, and which lay torn and scattered all over the floor of the locked and bolted chamber in which Von Junzt was found dead with the marks of taloned fingers on his throat? It will never be known, for the author's closest friend, the Frenchman Alexis Ladeau, after having spent a whole night piecing the fragments together and reading what was written, burnt them to ashes and cut his own throat with a razor.

But the contents of the published matter are shuddersome enough, even if one accepts the general view that they but represent the ravings of a madman. There among many strange things I found mention of the Black Stone, that curious, sinister monolith that broods among the mountains of Hungary, and about which so many dark legends cluster. Von Junzt did not devote much space to it—the bulk of his grim work concerns cults and objects of dark worship which he maintained existed in his day, and it would seem that the Black Stone represents some order or being lost and forgotten centuries ago. But he spoke of it as one of the *keys*—a phrase used many times by him, in various relations, and constituting one of the obscurities of his work. And he hinted briefly at curious sights to be seen about the monolith on midsummer's night. He mentioned Otto Dostmann's theory that this monolith was a remnant of the Hunnish invasion and had been erected to commemorate a victory of Attila over the Goths. Von Junzt contradicted this assertion without giving any refutory facts, merely remarking that to attribute the origin of the Black Stone to the Huns was as logical as assuming that William the Conqueror reared Stonehenge.

This implication of enormous antiquity piqued my interest immensely and after some difficulty I succeeded in locating a rat-eaten and moldering copy of Dostmann's *Remnants of Lost Empires* (Berlin, 1809, "Der Drachenhaus" Press). I was disappointed to find that Dostmann referred to the Black Stone even more briefly than had Von Junzt, dimmissing it with a few lines as an artifact comparatively modern in contrast with the Greco-Roman ruins of Asia Minor which were his pet theme. He admitted his inability to make out the defaced characters on the monolith but pronounced them unmistakably Mongoloid. However, little as I learned from Dostmann, he did mention the name of the village adjacent to the Black Stone—Stregoicavar —an ominous name, meaning something like Witch-Town.

A close scrutiny of guide-books and travel articles gave me no further information—Stregoicavar, not on any map that I could find, lay in a wild, little-frequented region, out of the path of casual tourists. But I did find subject for thought in Dornly's *Magyar Folklore*. In his chapter on *Dream Myths* he mentions the Black Stone and tells of some curious superstitions regarding it—especially the belief that if any one sleeps in the vicinity of the monolith, that person will be haunted by monstrous night- mares for ever after; and he cited tales of the peasants regarding too-curious people who ventured to visit the Stone on Mid- summer Night and who died raving mad because of *something* they saw there.

That was all I could gleam from Dornly, but my interest was even more intensely roused as I sensed a distinctly sinister aura about the Stone. The suggestion of dark antiquity, the recur- rent hint of unnatural events on Midsummer Night, touched some slumbering instinct in my being, as one senses, rather than hears, the flowing of some dark subterraneous river in the night.

And I suddenly saw a connection between this Stone and a certain weird and fantastic poem written by the mad poet Justin Geoffrey: *The People of the Monolith*. Inquiries led to the information that Geoffrey had indeed written that poem while traveling in Hungary, and I could not doubt that the Black Stone was the very monolith to which he referred in his strange verse. Reading his stanzas again, I felt once more the strange dim stirrings of subconscious promptings that I had noticed when first reading of the Stone.

I had been casting about for a place to spend a short vacation and I made up my mind. I went to Stregoicavar. A train of ob- solete style carried me from Temesvar to within striking dis- tance, at least, of my objective, and a three days' ride in a jouncing coach brought me to the little village which lay in a fertile valley high up in the fir-clad mountains. The journey it- self was uneventful, but during the first day we passed the old battlefield of Schomvaal where the brave Polish-Hungarian knight, Count Boris Vladinoff, made his gallant and futile stand against the victorious hosts of Suleiman the Magnificent, when the Grand Turk swept over eastern Europe in 1526.

The driver of the coach pointed out to me a great heap of crumbling stones on a hill near by, under which, he said, the bones of the brave Count lay. I remembered a passage from Larson's *Turkish Wars*: "After the skirmish" (in which the Count with his small army had beaten back the Turkish advance-guard) "the Count was standing beneath the half-ruined walls of the old castle on the hill, giving orders as to the disposition of his forces, when an aide brought to him a small lacquered case which had been taken from the body of the famous Turkish scribe and historian, Selim Bahadur, who had fallen in the fight. The Count took therefrom a roll of parchment and began to read, but he had not read far before he turned very pale and without saying a word, replaced the parchment in the case and thrust the case into his cloak. At that very instant a hidden Turkish battery suddenly opened fire, and the balls striking the old castle, the Hungarians were horrified to see the walls crash down in ruin, completely covering the brave Count. Without a leader the gallant little army was cut to pieces, and in the war-swept years which followed, the bones of the nobleman were never recovered. Today the natives point out a huge and moldering pile of ruins near Schomvaal beneath which, they say, still rests all that the centuries have left of Count Boris Vladinoff."

I found the village of Stregoicavar a dreamy, drowsy little village that apparently belied its sinister cognomen—a forgotten black-eddy that Progress had passed by. The quaint houses and the quainter dress and manners of the people were those of an earlier century. They were friendly, mildly curious but not inquisitive, though visitors from the outside world were extremely rare.

"Ten years ago another American came here and stayed a few days in the village," said the owner of the tavern where I had put up, "a young fellow and queer-acting—mumbled to himself—a poet, I think."

I knew he must mean Justin Geoffrey.

"Yes, he was a poet," I answered, "and he wrote a poem about a bit of scenery near this very village."

"Indeed?" mine host's interest was aroused. "Then, since all great poets are strange in their speech and actions, he must have achieved great fame, for his actions and conversations were the strangest of any man I ever knew."

"As is usual with artists," I answered, "most of his recognition has come since his death."

"He is dead, then?"

"He died screaming in a madhouse five years ago."

"Too bad, too bad," sighed mine host sympathetically. "Poor lad—he looked too long at the Black Stone."

My heart gave a leap, but I masked my keen interest and said casually: "I have heard something of this Black Stone; somewhere near this village, is it not?"

"Nearer than Christian folk wish," he responded. "Look!" He drew me to a latticed window and pointed up at the fir-clad slopes of the brooding blue mountains. "There beyond where you see the bare face of that jutting cliff stands that accursed Stone. Would that it were ground to powder and the powder flung into the Danube to be carried to the deepest ocean! Once men tried to destroy the thing, but each man who laid hammer or maul against it came to an evil end. So now the people shun it."

"What is there so evil about it?" I asked curiously.

"It is a demon-haunted thing," he answered uneasily and with the suggestion of a shudder. "In my childhood I knew a young man who came up from below and laughed at our traditions—in his foolhardiness he went to the Stone one Midsummer Night and at dawn stumbled into the village again, stricken dumb and mad. Something had shattered his brain and sealed his lips, for until the day of his death, which came soon after, he spoke only to utter terrible blasphemies or to slaver gibberish.

"My own nephew when very small was lost in the mountains and slept in the woods near the Stone, and now in his manhood he is tortured by foul dreams, so that at times he makes the night hideous with his screams and wakes with cold sweat upon him.

"But let us talk of something else, *Herr*; it is not good to dwell upon such things."

I remarked on the evident age of the tavern and he answered with pride: "The foundations are more than four hundred years old; the original house was the only one in the village which was not burned to the ground when Suleiman's devils swept through the mountains. Here, in the house that then stood on these same foundations, it is said, the scribe Selim Bahadur had his headquarters while ravaging the country hereabouts."

I learned then that the present inhabitants of Stregoicavar are not descendants of the people who dwelt there before the Turkish raid of 1526. The victorious Moslems left no living human in the village or the vicinity thereabouts when they passed over. Men, women and children they wiped out in one red holocaust of murder, leaving a vast stretch of country silent and utterly deserted. The present people of Stregoicavar are descended from hardy settlers from the lower valleys who came into the upper levels and rebuilt the ruined village after the Turk was thrust back.

Mine host did not speak of the extermination of the original inhabitants with any great resentment and I learned that his ancestors in the lower levels had looked on the mountaineers with even more hatred and aversion than they regarded the Turks. He was rather vague regarding the causes of this feud, but said that the original inhabitants of Stregoicavar had been in the habit of making stealthy raids on the lowlands and stealing girls and children. Moreover, he said that they were not exactly of the same blood as his own people; the sturdy, original Magyar-Slavic stock had mixed and intermarried with a degraded aboriginal race until the breeds had blended, producing an unsavory amalgamation. Who these aborigines were, he had not the slightest idea, but maintained that they were "pagans" and had dwelt in the mountains since time immemorial, before the coming of the conquering peoples.

I attached little importance to this tale; seeing in it merely a parallel to the amalgamation of Celtic tribes with Mediterranean aborigines in the Galloway hills, with the resultant mixed race which, as Picts, has such an extensive part in Scotch legendry. Time has a curiously foreshortening effect on folklore, and just as tales of the Picts became intertwined with legends of an older Mongoloid race, so that eventually the Picts were ascribed the repulsive appearance of the squat primitives, whose individuality merged, in the telling, into Pictish tales, and was forgotten; so, I felt, the supposed inhuman attributes of the first villagers of Stregoicavar could be traced to older, outworn myths with invading Huns and Mongols.

The morning after my arrival I received directions from my host, who gave them worriedly, and set out to find the Black Stone. A few hours' tramp up the fir-covered slopes brought me to the face of the rugged, solid stone cliff which jutted boldly from the mountainside. A narrow trail wound up it, and mounting this, I looked out over the peaceful valley of Stregoicavar, which seemed to drowse, guarded on either hand by the great blue mountains. No huts or any sign of human tenancy showed between the cliff whereon I stood and the village. I saw numbers of scattering farms in the valley but all lay on the other side of Stregoicavar, which itself seemed to shrink from the brooding slopes which masked the Black Stone.

The summit of the cliffs proved to be a sort of thickly wooded plateau. I made my way through the dense growth for a short distance and came into a wide glade; and in the center of the glade reared a gaunt figure of black stone.

It was octagonal in shape, some sixteen feet in height and about a foot and a half thick. It had once evidently been highly polished, but now the surface was thickly dinted as if savage efforts had been made to demolish it; but the hammers had done little more than to flake off small bits of stone and mutilate the characters which once had evidently marched in a spiraling line round and round the shaft to the top. Up to ten feet from the base these characters were almost completely blotted out, so that it was very difficult to trace their direction. Higher up they were plainer, and I managed to squirm part of the way up the shaft and scan them at close range. All were more or less defaced, but I was positive that they symbolized no language now remembered on the face of the earth. I am fairly familiar with all hieroglyphics known to researchers and philologists and I can say with certainty that those characters were like nothing of which I have ever read or heard. The nearest approach to them that I ever saw were some crude scratches on a gigantic and strangely symmetrical rock in a lost valley of Yucatan. I remember that when I pointed out these marks to the archeologist who was my companion, he maintained that they either represented natural weathering or the idle scratching of some Indian. To my theory that the rock was really the base of a long-vanished column, he merely laughed, calling my attention to the dimensions of it, which suggested, if it were built with any natural rules of architectural symmetry, a column a thousand feet high. But I was not convinced.

I will not say that the characters on the Black Stone were similar to those on that colossal rock in Yucatan; but one suggested the other. As to the substance of the monolith, again I was baffled. The stone of which it was composed was a dully gleaming black, whose surface, where it was not dinted and roughened, created a curious illusion of semi-transparency.

I spent most of the morning there and came away baffled. No connection of the Stone with any other artifact in the world suggested itself to me. It was as if the monolith had been reared by alien hands, in an age distant and apart from human ken.

I returned to the village with my interest in no way abated. Now that I had seen the curious thing, my desire was still more keenly whetted to investigate the matter further and seek to learn by what strange hands and for what strange purpose the Black Stone had been reared in the long ago.

I sought out the tavern-keeper's nephew and questioned him in regard to his dreams, but he was vague, though willing to oblige. He did not mind discussing them, but was unable to describe them with any clarity. Though he dreamed the same dreams repeatedly, and though they were hideously vivid at the time, they left no distinct impression on his waking mind. He remembered them only as chaotic nightmares through which huge whirling fires shot lurid tongues of flame and a black drum bellowed incessantly. One thing only he clearly remembered—in one dream he had seen the Black Stone, not on a mountain slope but set like a spire on a colossal black castle.

As for the rest of the villagers I found them not inclined to talk about the Stone, with the exception of the schoolmaster, a man of surprizing education, who spent much more of his time out in the world than any of the rest.

He was much interested in what I told him of Von Junzt's remarks about the Stone, and warmly agreed with the German author in the alleged age of the monolith. He believed that a coven had once existed in the vicinity and that possibly all of the original villagers had been members of that fertility cult which once threatened to undermine European civilization and gave rise to the tales of witchcraft. He cited the very name of the village to prove his point; it had not been originally named Stregoicavar, he said; according to legends the builders had called it Xuthltan, which was the aboriginal name of the site on which the village had been built many centuries ago.

This fact routed again an indescribable feeling of uneasiness. The barbarous name did not suggest connection with any Scythic, Slavic or Mongolian race to which an aboriginal people of these mountains would, under natural circumstances, have belonged.

That the Magyars and Slavs of the lower valleys believed the original inhabitants of the village to be members of the witch-craft cult was evident, the schoolmaster said, by the name they gave it, which name continued to be used even after the older settlers had been massacred by the Turks, and the village re-built by a cleaner and more wholesome breed.

He did not believe that the members of the cult erected the monolith but he did believe that they used it as a center of their activities, and repeating vague legends which had been handed down since before the Turkish invasion, he advanced the the-ory that the degenerate villagers had used it as a sort of altar on which they offered human sacrifices, using as victims the girls and babies stolen from his own ancestors in the lower valleys.

He discounted the myths of weird events on Midsummer Night, as well as a curious legend of a strange deity which the witch-people of Xuthltan were said to have invoked with chants and wild rituals of flagellation and slaughter.

He had never visited the Stone on Midsummer Night, he said, but he would not fear to do so; whatever *had* existed or taken place there in the past, had been long engulfed in the mists of time and oblivion. The Black Stone had lost its meaning save as a link to a dead and dusty past.

It was while returning from a visit with this schoolmaster one night about a week after my arrival at Stregoicavar that a sud-den recollection struck me—it was Midsummer Night! The very time that the legends linked with grisly implications to the Black Stone. I turned away from the tavern and strode swiftly through the village. Stregoicavar lay silent; the villagers retired early. I saw no one as I passed rapidly out of the village and up into the firs which masked the mountain slopes with whispering darkness. A broad silver moon hung above the valley, flooding the crags and slopes in a weird light and etching the shadows blackly. No wind blew through the firs, but a mysterious, intangible rustling and whispering was abroad. Surely on such nights in past centuries, my whimsical imagination told me, naked witches astride magic broomsticks had flown across this valley, pursued by jeering demoniac familiars.

I came to the cliffs and was somewhat disquieted to note that the illusive moonlight lent them a subtle appearance I had not noticed before—in the weird light they appeared less like natural cliffs and more like the ruins of cyclopean and Titan-reared battlements jutting from the mountain-slope.

Shaking off this hallucination with difficulty I came upon the plateau and hesitated a moment before I plunged into the brooding darkness of the woods. A sort of breathless tenseness hung over the shadows, like an unseen monster holding its breath lest it scare away its prey.

I shook off the sensation—a natural one, considering the eeriness of the place and its evil reputation—and made my way through the wood, experiencing a most unpleasant sensation that I was being followed, and halting once, sure that something clammy and unstable had brushed against my face in the darkness.

I came out into the glade and saw the tall monolith rearing its gaunt height above the sward. At the edge of the woods on the side toward the cliffs was a stone which formed a sort of natural seat. I sat down, reflecting that it was probably while there that the mad poet, Justin Geoffrey, had written his fantastic *People of the Monolith*. Mine host thought that it was the Stone which had caused Geoffrey's insanity, but the seeds of madness had been sown in the poet's brain long before he ever came to Stregoicavar.

A glance at my watch showed that the hour of midnight was close at hand. I leaned back, waiting whatever ghostly demonstration might appear. A thin night wind started up among the branches of the firs, with an uncanny suggestion of faint, unseen pipes whispering an eery and evil tune. The monotony of the sound and my steady gazing at the monolith produced a sort of self-hypnosis upon me; I grew drowsy. I fought this feeling, but sleep stole on me in spite of myself; the monolith seemed to sway and dance, strangely distorted to my gaze, and then I slept.

I opened my eyes and sought to rise, but lay still, as if an icy hand gripped me helpless. Cold terror stole over me. The glade was no longer deserted. It was thronged by a silent crowd of strange people, and my distended eyes took in strange barbaric details of costume which my reason told me were archaic and forgotten even in this backward land. Surely, I thought, these are villagers who have come here to hold some fantastic conclave—but another glance told me that these people were not of the folk of Stregoicavar. They were a shorter, more squat race, whose brows were lower, whose faces were broader and duller. Some had Slavic or Magyar features, but those features were degraded as from a mixture of some baser, alien strain I could not classify. Many wore the hides of wild beasts, and their whole appearance, both men and women, was one of sensual brutishness. They terrified and repelled me, but they gave me no heed. They formed in a vast half-circle in front of the monolith and began a sort of chant, flinging their arms in unison and weaving their bodies rythmically from the waist upward. All eyes were fixed on the top of the Stone which they seemed to be invoking. But the strangest of all was the dimness of their voices; not fifty yards from me hundreds of men and women were unmistakably lifting their voices in a wild chant, yet those voices came to me as a faint indistinguishable murmur as if from across vast leagues of Space —or *time*.

Before the monolith stood a sort of brazier from which a vile, nauseous yellow smoke billowed upward, curling curiously in an undulating spiral around the black shaft, like a vast unstable serpent.

On one side of this brazier lay two figures—a young girl, stark naked and bound hand and foot, and an infant, apparently only a few months old. On the other side of the brazier squatted a hideous old hag with a queer sort of black drum on her lap; this drum she beat with slow, light blows of her open palms, but I could not hear the sound.

The rhythm of the swaying bodies grew faster and into the space between the people and the monolith sprang a naked young woman, her eyes blazing, her long black hair flying loose. Spinning dizzily on her toes, she whirled across the open space and fell prostrate before the Stone, where she lay motionless. The next instant a fantastic figure followed her—a man from whose waist hung a goatskin, and whose features were entirely hidden by a sort of mask made from a huge wolf's head, so that he looked like a monstrous, nightmare being, horribly compounded of elements both human and bestial. In his hand he held a bunch of long fir switches bound together at the larger ends, and the moonlight glinted on a chain of heavy gold looped about his neck. A smaller chain depending from it suggested a pendant of some sort, but this was missing.

The people tossed their arms violently and seemed to redouble their shouts as this grotesque creature loped across the open space with many a fantastic leap and caper. Coming to the woman who lay before the monolith, he began to lash her with the switches he bore, and she leaped up and spun into the wild mazes of the most incredible dance I have ever seen. And her tormentor danced with her, keeping the wild rhythm, matching her every whirl and bond, while incessantly raining cruel blows on her naked body. And at every blow he shouted a single word, over and over, and all the people shouted it back. I could see the working of their lips, and now the faint far-off murmur of their voices merged and blended into one distant shout, repeated over and over with slobbering ecstasy. But what that one word was, I could not make out.

In dizzy whirls spun the wild dancers, while the lookers-on, standing still in their tracks, followed the rhythm of their dance with swaying bodies and weaving arms. Madness grew in the eyes of the capering votaress and was reflected in the eyes of the watchers. Wilder and more extravagant grew the whirling frenzy of that mad dance—it became a bestial and obscene thing, while the old hag howled and battered the drum like a crazy woman, and the switches cracked out a devil's tune.

Blood trickled down the dancer's limbs but she seemed not to feel the lashing save as a stimulus for further enormities of outrageous motion; bounding into the midst of the yellow smoke which now spread out tenuous tentacles to embrace both flying figures, she seemed to merge with that foul fog and

veil herself with it. Then emerging into plain view, closely followed by the beast-thing that flogged her, she shot into an indescribable, explosive burst of dynamic mad motion, and on the
very crest of that mad wave, she dropped suddenly to the sward,
quivering and panting as if completely overcome by her frenzied exertions. The lashing continued with unabated violence
and intensity and she began to wriggle toward the monolith
on her belly. The priest—or such I will call him—followed,
lashing her unprotected body with all the power of his arm as
she writhed along, leaving a heavy track of blood on the trampled earth. She reached the monolith, and gasping and panting,
flung both arms about it and covered the cold stone with fierce
hot kisses, as in frenzied and unholy adoration.

The fantastic priest bounded high in the air, flinging away
the red-dabbled switches, and the worshippers, howling and
foaming at the mouths, turned on each other with tooth and
nail, rending one another's garments and flesh in a blind passion of bestiality. The priest swept up the infant with a long
arm, and shouting again that Name, whirled the wailing babe
high in the air and dashed its brains out against the monolith,
leaving a ghastly stain on the black surface. Cold with horror I
saw him rip the tiny body open with his bare brutish fingers
and fling handfuls of blood on the shaft, then toss the red and
torn shape into the brazier, extinguishing flame and smoke in
a crimson rain, while the maddened brutes behind him howled
over and over that Name. Then suddenly they all fell prostrate,
writhing like snakes, while the priest flung wide his gory hands
as in triumph. I opened my mouth to scream my horror and
loathing, but only a dry rattle sounded; a huge monstrous toad-
like *thing* squatted on the top of the monolith!

I saw its bloated, repulsive and unstable outline against the
moonlight, and set in what would have been the face of a natural creature, its huge, blinking eyes which reflected all the lust,
abysmal greed, obscene cruelty and monstrous evil that has
stalked the sons of men since their ancestors mowed blind and
hairless in the tree-tops. In those grisly eyes were mirrored
all the unholy things and vile secrets that sleep in the cities
under the sea, and that skulk from the light of day in the blackness of primordial caverns. And so that ghastly thing that the

unhallowed ritual of cruelty and sadism and blood had evoked from the silence of the hills, leered and blinked down on its bestial worshippers, who groveled in abhorrent abasement before it.

Now the beast-masked priest lifted the bound and weakly writhing girl in his brutish hands and held her up toward that horror on the monolith. And as that monstrosity sucked in its breath, lustfully and slobberingly, something snapped in my brain and I fell into a merciful faint.

I opened my eyes on a still white dawn. All events of the night rushed back on me and I sprang up, then stared about me in amazement. The monolith brooded gaunt and silent above the sward which waved, green and untrampled, in the morning breeze. A few quick strides took me across the glade; here had the dancers leaped and bounded until the ground should have been trampled bare, and here had the votaress wriggled her painful way to the Stone, streaming blood on the earth. But no drop of crimson showed on the uncrushed sward. I looked, shudderingly, at the side of the monolith against which the bestial priest had brained the stolen baby—but no dark stain nor grisly clot showed there.

A dream! It had been a wild nightmare—or else—I shrugged my shoulders. What vivid clarity for a dream!

I returned quietly to the village and entered the inn without being seen. And there I sat meditating over the strange events of the night. More and more was I prone to discard the dream-theory. That what I had seen was illusion and without material substance, was evident. But I believed that I had looked on the mirrored shadow of a deed perpetrated in ghastly actuality in bygone days. But how was I to know? What proof to show that my vision had been a gathering of foul specters rather than a mere nightmare originating in my own brain?

As if for answer a name flashed into my mind—Selim Bahadur! According to legend this man, who had been a solider as well as a scribe, had commanded that part of Suleiman's army which had devastated Stregoicavar; it seemed logical enough; and if so, he had gone straight from the blotted-out country-side to the bloody field of Schomvaal, and his doom. I sprang up with a sudden shout—that manuscript which was taken

from the Turk's body, and which Count Boris shuddered over—
might it not contain some narration of what the conquering
Turks found in Stregoicavar? What else could have shaken the
iron nerves of the Polish adventurer? And since the bones of
the Count had never been recovered, what more certain than
that the lacquered case, with its mysterious contents, still lay
hidden beneath the ruins that covered Boris Vladinoff? I
began packing my bag with fierce haste.

Three days later found me ensconced in a little village a few
miles from the old battlefield, and when the moon rose I was
working with savage intensity on the great pile of crumbling
stone that crowned the hill. It was back-breaking toil—
looking back now I can not see how I accomplished it, though
I labored without a pause from moonrise to dawn. Just as the
sun was coming up I tore aside the last tangle of stones and
looked on all that was mortal of Count Boris Vladinoff—only
a few pitiful fragments of crumbling bone—and among them,
crushed out of all original shape, lay a case whose lacquered
surface had kept it from complete decay through the centuries.

I seized it with frenzied eagerness, and piling back some of
the stones on the bones I hurried away; for I did not care to be
discovered by the suspicious peasants in an act of apparent
desecration.

Back in my tavern chamber I opened the case and found the
parchment comparatively intact; and there was something else
in the case—a small squat object wrapped in silk. I was wild to
plumb the secrets of those yellowed pages, but weariness forbade me. Since leaving Stregoicavar I had hardly slept at all,
and the terrific exertions of the previous night combined to
overcome me. In spite of myself I was forced to stretch myself
on my bed, nor did I awake until sundown.

I snatched a hasty supper, and then in the light of a flickering
candle, I set myself to read the neat Turkish characters that
covered the parchment. It was difficult work, for I am not
deeply versed in the language and the archaic style of the narrative baffled me. But as I toiled through it a word or a phrase
here and there leaped at me and a dimly growing horror shook
me in its grip. I bent my energies fiercely to the task, and as the
tale grew clearer and took more tangible form my blood

chilled in my veins, my hair stood up and my tongue clove to my mouth. All external things partook of the grisly madness of that infernal manuscript until the night sounds of insects and creatures in the woods took the form of ghastly murmurings and stealthy treadings of ghoulish horrors and the sighing of the night wind changed to tittering obscene gloating of evil over the souls of men.

At last when gray dawn was stealing through the latticed window, I laid down the manuscript and took up and unwrapped the thing in the bit of silk. Staring at it with haggard eyes I knew the truth of the matter was clinched, even had it been possible to doubt the veractiy of that terrible manuscript.

And I replaced both obscene things in the case, nor did I rest or sleep or eat until that case containing them had been weighted with stones and flung into the deepest current of the Danube which, God grant, carried them back into the Hell from which they came.

It was no dream I dreamed on Midsummer Midnight in the hills above Stregoicavar. Well for Justin Geoffrey that he tarried there only in the sunlight and went his way, for had he gazed upon that ghastly conclave, his mad brain would have snapped before it did. How my own reason held, I do not know.

No—it was no dream—I gazed upon a foul rout of votaries long dead, come up from Hell to worship as of old; ghosts that bowed before a ghost. For Hell has long claimed their hideous god. Long, long he dwelt among the hills, a brain-shattering vestige of an outworn age, but no longer his obscene talons clutch for the souls of living men, and his kingdom is a dead kingdom, peopled only by the ghosts of those who served him in his lifetime and theirs.

By what foul alchemy or godless sorcery the Gates of Hell are opened on that one eery night I do not know, but mine own eyes have seen. And I know I looked on no living thing that night, for the manuscript written in the careful hand of Selim Bahadur narrated at length what he and his raiders found in the valley of Stregoicavar; and I read, set down in detail, the blasphemous obscenities that torture wrung from the lips of screaming worshippers; and I read, too, of the lost, grim black cavern high in the hills where the horrified Turks hemmed a monstrous, bloated, wallowing toad-like being and slew it with flame and ancient steel blessed in old times by Muhammad, and with incantations that were old when Arabia was young. And even staunch old Selim's hand shook as he recorded the cataclysmic, earth-shaking death-howls of the monstrosity, which died not alone; for a half-score of his slayers perished with him, in ways that Selim would not or could not describe.

And the squat idol carved of gold and wrapped in silk was an image of *himself*, and Selim tore it from the golden chain that looped the neck of the slain high priest of the mask.

Well that the Turks swept that foul valley with torch and cleanly steel! Such sights as those brooding mountains have looked on belong to the darkness and abysses of lost eons. No—it is not fear of the toad-thing that makes me shudder in the night. He is made fast in Hell with his nauseous horde, freed only for an hour on the most weird night of the year, as I have seen. And of his worshippers, none remains.

But it is the realization that such things once crouched beast-like above the souls of men which brings cold sweat to my brow; and I fear to peer again into the leaves of Von Junzt's abomination. For now I understand his repeated phrase of *keys!* —aye! Keys to Outer Doors—links with an abhorrent past and—who knows?—of abhorrent spheres of the *present*. And I understand why the cliffs look like battlements in the moonlight and why the tavern-keeper's nightmare-haunted nephew saw in his dream, the Black Stone like a spire on a cyclopean black castle. If men ever excavate among those mountains they may find incredible things below those masking slopes. For the cave wherein the Turks trapped the—*thing*—was not truly a cavern, and I shudder to contemplate the gigantic gulf of eons which must stretch between this age and the time when the earth shook herself and reared up, like a wave, those blue mountains that, rising, enveloped unthinkable things. May no man ever seek to uproot that ghastly spire men call the Black Stone!

A Key! Aye, it is a Key, symbol of a forgotten horror. That horror has faded into the limbo from which it crawled, loathsomely, in the black dawn of the earth. But what of the other fiendish possibilities hinted at by Von Junzt—what of the monstrous hand which strangled out his life? Since reading what Selim Bahadur wrote, I can no longer doubt anything in the Black Book. Man was not always master of the earth—*and is he now?*

And the thought recurs to me—if such a monstrous entity as the Master of the Monolith somehow survived its own unspeakably distant epoch so long—*what nameless shapes may even now lurk in the dark places of the world?*

1931

HENRY S. WHITEHEAD

(1882–1932)

Passing of a God

"You say that when Carswell came into your hospital over in Port au Prince his fingers looked as though they had been wound with string," said I, encouragingly.

"It is a very ugly story, that, Canevin," replied Doctor Pelletier, still reluctant, it appeared.

"You promised to tell me," I threw in.

"I know it, Canevin," admitted Doctor Pelletier of The U.S. Navy Medical Corps, now stationed here in the Virgin Islands. "But," he proceeded, "you couldn't use this story, anyhow. There are editorial *tabus*, aren't there? The thing is too—what shall I say?—too outrageous, too incredible."

"Yes," I admitted in turn, "there are *tabus*, plenty of them. Still, after hearing about those fingers, as though wound with string—why not give me the story, Pelletier; leave it to me whether or not I 'use' it. It's the story I want, mostly. I'm burning up for it!"

"I suppose it's your lookout," said my guest. "If you find it too gruesome for you, tell me and I'll quit."

I plucked up hope once more. I had been trying for this story, after getting little scraps of it which allured and intrigued me, for weeks.

"Start in," I ventured, soothingly, pushing the silver swizzel-jug after the humidor of cigarettes from which Pelletier was even now making a selection. Pelletier helped himself to the swizzel frowningly. Evidently he was torn between the desire to pour out the story of Arthur Carswell and some complication of feelings against doing so. I sat back in my wicker lounge-chair and waited.

Pelletier moved his large bulk about in his chair. Plainly now he was cogitating how to open the tale. He began, meditatively:

"I don't know as I ever heard public discussion of the malignant bodily growths except among medical people. Science knows little about them. The fact of such diseases, though, is well known to everybody, through campaigns of prevention, the life insurance companies, appeals for funds——

"Well, Carswell's case, primarily, is one of those cases."

He paused and gazed into the glowing end of his cigarette.

" 'Primarily?' " I threw in encouragingly.

"Yes. Speaking as a surgeon, that's where this thing begins, I suppose."

I kept still, waiting.

"Have you read Seabrook's book, *The Magic Island*, Canevin?" asked Pelletier suddenly.

"Yes," I answered. "What about it?"

"Then I suppose that from your own experience knocking around the West Indies and your study of it all, a good bit of that stuff of Seabrook's is familiar to you, isn't it?—the *vodu*, and the hill customs, and all the rest of it, especially over in Haiti—you could check up on a writer like Seabrook, couldn't you, more or less?"

"Yes," said I, "practically all of it was an old story to me—a very fine piece of work, however, the thing clicks all the way through—an honest and thorough piece of investigation."

"Anything in it new to you?"

"Yes—-Seabrook's statement that there was an exchange of personalities between the sacrificial goat—at the 'baptism'—and the young Black girl, the chapter he calls: *Girl-Cry—Goat-Cry*. That, at least, was a new one on me, I admit."

"You will recall, if you read it carefully, that he attributed that phenomenon to his own personal 'slant' on the thing. Isn't that the case, Canevin?"

"Yes," I agreed, "I think that is the way he put it."

"Then," resumed Doctor Pelletier, "I take it that all that material of his—I notice that there have been a lot of story-writers using his terms lately!—is sufficiently familiar to you so that you have some clear idea of the Haitian-African demi-gods, like Ogoun Badagris, Damballa, and the others, taking up their residence for a short time in some devotee?"

"The idea is very well understood," said I. "Mr. Seabrook mentions it among a number of other local phenomena. It was an old negro who came up to him while he was eating, thrust his soiled hands into the dishes of food, surprized him considerably—then was surrounded by worshippers who took him to the nearest *houmfort* or *vodu*-house, let him sit on the altar, brought him food, hung all their jewelry on him, worshipped him for the time being; then, characteristically, quite utterly ignored the original old fellow after the 'possession' on the part of the 'deity' ceased and reduced him to an unimportant old pantaloon as he was before."

"That summarizes it exactly," agreed Doctor Pelletier. "That, Canevin, that kind of thing, I mean, is the real starting-place of this dreadful matter of Arthur Carswell."

"You mean——?" I barged out at Pelletier, vastly intrigued. I had had no idea that there was *vodu* mixed in with the case.

"I mean that Arthur Carswell's first intimation that there was anything pressingly wrong with him was just such a 'possession' as the one you have recounted."

"But—but," I protested, "I had supposed—I had every reason to believe, that it was a surgical matter! Why, you just objected to telling about it on the ground that——"

"Precisely," said Doctor Pelletier, calmly. "It was such a surgical case, but, as I say, it *began* in much the same way as the 'occupation' of that old negro's body by Ogoun Badagris or whichever one of their devilish deities that happened to be, just as, you say, is well known to fellows like yourself who go in for such things, and just as Seabrook recorded it."

"Well," said I, "you go ahead in your own way, Pelletier. I'll do my best to listen. Do you mind an occasional question?"

"Not in the least," said Doctor Pelletier considerately, shifted himself to a still more pronouncedly recumbent position in my Chinese rattan lounge-chair, lit a fresh cigarette, and proceeded:

"Carswell had worked up a considerable intimacy with the snake-worship of interior Haiti, all the sort of thing familiar to you; the sort of thing set out, probably for the first time in English at least, in Seabrook's book; all the gatherings, and the 'baptism,' and the sacrifices of the fowls and the bull, and the goats; the orgies of the worshippers, the boom and thrill of the *rata* drums—all that strange, incomprehensible, rather silly-surfaced, deadly-underneathed worship of 'the Snake' which the Dahomeyans brought with them to old Hispaniola, now Haiti and the Dominican Republic.

"He had been there, as you may have heard, for a number of years; went there in the first place because everybody thought he was a kind of failure at home; made a good living, too, in a way nobody but an original-minded fellow like him would have thought of—shot ducks on the Léogane marshes, dried them, and exported them to New York and San Francisco to the United States' two largest Chinatowns!

"For a 'failure,' too, Carswell was a particularly smart-looking chap, smart, I mean, in the English sense of that word. He was one of those fellows who was always shaved, clean, freshly groomed, even under the rather adverse conditions of his living, there in Léogane by the salt marshes; and of his trade, which was to kill and dry ducks. A fellow can get pretty careless and let himself go at that sort of thing, away from 'home'; away, too, from such niceties as there are in a place like Port au Prince.

"He looked, in fact, like a fellow just off somebody's yacht the first time I saw him, there in the hospital in Port au Prince, and that, too, was right after a rather singular experience which would have unnerved or unsettled pretty nearly anybody.

"But not so old Carswell. No, indeed. I speak of him as 'Old Carswell,' Canevin. That, though, is a kind of affectionate term. He was somewhere about forty-five then; it was two years ago, you see, and, in addition to his being very spick and span, well groomed, you know, he looked surprizingly young, somehow. One of those faces which showed experience, but, along with the experience, a philosophy. The lines in his face were *good* lines, if you get what I mean—lines of humor and courage; no dissipation, no let-down kind of lines, nothing of slackness such as you would see in the face of even a comparatively young beach-comber. No, as he strode into my office, almost jauntily, there in the hospital, there was nothing, nothing whatever, about him, to suggest anything else but a prosperous fellow American, a professional chap, for choice, who might, as I say, have just come ashore from somebody's yacht.

"And yet—good God, Canevin, the story that came out——!"

Naval surgeon though he was, with service in Haiti, at sea,

in Nicaragua, and the China Station to his credit, Doctor Pelletier rose at this point, and, almost agitatedly, walked up and down my gallery. Then he sat down and lit a fresh cigarette.

"There is," he said, reflectively, and as though weighing his words carefully, "there is, Canevin, among various others, a somewhat 'wild' theory that somebody put forward several years ago, about the origin of malignant tumors. It never gained very much approval among the medical profession, but it has, at least, the merit of originality, and—it was new. Because of those facts, it had a certain amount of currency, and there are those, in and out of medicine, who still believe in it. It is that there are certain *nuclei*, certain masses, so to speak, of the bodily material which have persisted—not generally, you understand, but in certain cases—among certain persons, the kind who are 'susceptible' to this horrible disease, which, in the pre-natal state, did not develop fully or normally—little places in the bodily structure, that is—if I make myself clear?—which remain undeveloped.

"Something, according to this hypothesis, something like a sudden jar, or a bruise, a kick, a blow with the fist, the result of a fall, or whatnot, causes traumatism—physical injury, that is, you know—to one of the focus-places, and the undeveloped little mass of material *starts in to grow*, and so displaces the normal tissue which surrounds it.

"One objection to the theory is that there are at least two varieties, well-known and recognized scientifically; the carcinoma, which is itelf subdivided into two kinds, the hard and the soft carcinomæ, and the sarcoma, which is a soft thing, like what is popularly understood by a 'tumor.' Of course they are all 'tumors,' particular kinds of tumors, malignant tumors. What lends a certain credibility to the theory I have just mentioned is the malignancy, the growing element. For, whatever the underlying reason, they grow, Canevin, as is well recognized, and this explanation I have been talking about gives a reason for the growth. The 'malignancy' is, really, that one of the things seems to have, as it were, its own life. All this, probably, you know?"

I nodded. I did not wish to interrupt. I could see that this side-issue on a scientific by-path must have something to do with the story of Carswell.

"Now," resumed Pelletier, "notice this fact, Canevin. Let me put it in the form of a question, like this: To what kind, or type, of *vodu* worshipper, does the 'possession' by one of their deities occur—from your own knowledge of such things, what would you say?"

"To the incomplete; the abnormal, to an *old* man, or woman," said I, slowly, reflecting, "or—to a child, or, perhaps, to an idiot. Idiots, ancient crones, backward children, 'town-fools' and the like, all over Europe, are supposed to be in some mysterious way *en rapport* with deity—or with Satan! It is an established peasant belief. Even among the Mahometans, the moron or idiot is 'the afflicted of God.' There is no other better established belief along such lines of thought."

"Precisely!" exclaimed Pelletier, "and, Canevin, go back once more to Seabrook's instance that we spoke about. What type of person was 'possessed'?"

"An old doddering man," said I, "one well gone in his dotage apparently."

"Right once more! Note now, two things. First, I will admit to you, Canevin, that that theory I have just been expounding never made much of a hit with me. It might be true, but—very few first-rate men in our profession thought much of it, and I followed that negative lead and didn't think much of it, or, indeed, much about it. I put it down to the vaporings of the theorist who first thought it out and published it, and let it go at that. Now, Canevin, *I am convinced that it is true!* The second thing, then: When Carswell came into my office in the hospital over there in Port au Prince, the first thing I noticed about him —I had never seen him before, you see—was a peculiar, almost an indescribable, discrepancy. It was between his general appearance of weather-worn cleanliness, general fitness, his 'smart' appearance in his clothes—all that, which fitted together about the clean-cut, open character of the fellow; and what I can only describe as a pursiness. He seemed in good condition, I mean to say, and yet—there was something, somehow, *flabby* somewhere in his makeup. I couldn't put my finger on it, but—it was there, a suggestion of something that detracted from the impression he gave as being an upstanding fellow, a good-fellow-to-have-beside-you-in-a-pinch—that kind of person.

*

"The second thing I noticed, it was just after he had taken a chair beside my desk, was his fingers, and thumbs. They were swollen, Canevin, looked sore, as though they had been wound with string. That was the first thing I thought of, being wound with string. He saw me looking at them, held them out to me abruptly, laid them side by side, his hands I mean, on my desk, and smiled at me.

"'I see you have noticed them, Doctor,' he remarked, almost jovially. 'That makes it a little easier for me to tell you what I'm here for. It's—well, you might put it down as a "symptom".'

"I looked at his fingers and thumbs; every one of them was affected in the same way; and ended up with putting a magnifying glass over them.

"They were all bruised and reddened, and here and there on several of them, the skin was abraded, broken, *circularly*—it was a most curious-looking set of digits. My new patient was addressing me again:

"'I'm not here to ask you riddles, Doctor,' he said, gravely, this time, 'but—would you care to make a guess at what did that to those fingers and thumbs of mine?'

"'Well,' I came back at him, 'without knowing what's happened, it *looks* as if you'd been trying to wear about a hundred rings, all at one time, and most of them didn't fit!'

"Carswell nodded his head at me. 'Score one for the medico,' said he, and laughed. 'Even numerically you're almost on the dot, sir. The precise number was one hundred and six!'

"I confess, I stared at him then. But he wasn't fooling. It was a cold, sober, serious fact that he was stating; only, he saw that it had a humorous side, and that intrigued him, as anything humorous always did, I found out after I got to know Carswell a lot better than I did then."

"You said you wouldn't mind a few questions, Pelletier," I interjected.

"Fire away," said Pelletier. "Do you see any light, so far?"

"I was naturally figuring along with you, as you told about it all," said I. "Do I infer correctly that Carswell, having lived there—how long, four or five years or so?——"

"Seven, to be exact," put in Pelletier.

"——that Carswell, being pretty familiar with the native

doings, had mixed into things, got the confidence of his Black neighbors in and around Léogane, become somewhat 'adept', had the run of the *houmforts*, so to speak—'*votre bougie, M'sieu*' —the fortune-telling at the festivals, and so forth, and—had been 'visited' by one of the Black deities? That, apparently, if I'm any judge of tendencies, is what your account seems to be leading up to. Those bruised fingers—the one hundred and six rings—good heavens, man, is it really possible?"

"Carswell told me all about that end of it, a little later—yes, that was, precisely, what happened, but—that, surprizing, incredible as it seems, is only the small end of it all. You just wait——"

"Go ahead," said I, "I am all ears, I assure you!"

"Well, Carswell took his hands off the desk after I had looked at them through my magnifying glass, and then waved one of them at me in a kind of deprecating gesture.

" 'I'll go into all that, if you're interested to hear about it, Doctor,' he assured me, 'but that isn't what I'm here about.' His face grew suddenly very grave. 'Have you plenty of time?' he asked. 'I don't want to let my case interfere with anything.'

" 'Fire ahead,' says I, and he leaned forward in his chair.

" 'Doctor,' says he, 'I don't know whether or not you ever heard of me before. My name's Carswell, and I live over Léogane way. I'm an American, like yourself, as you can probably see, and, even after seven years of it, out there, duck-hunting, mostly, with virtually no White-man's doings for a pretty long time, I haven't "gone native" or anything of the sort. I wouldn't want you to think I'm one of those wasters.' He looked up at me inquiringly for my estimate of him. He had been by himself a good deal; perhaps too much. I nodded at him. He looked me in the eye, squarely, and nodded back. 'I guess we understand each other,' he said. Then he went on.

" 'Seven years ago, it was, I came down here. I've lived over there ever since. What few people know about me regard me as a kind of failure, I daresay. But—Doctor, there was a reason for that, a pretty definite reason. I won't go into it beyond your end of it—the medical end, I mean. I came down because of this.'

"He stood up then, and I saw what made that 'discrepancy' I spoke about, that 'flabbiness' which went so ill with the general cut of the man. He turned up the lower ends of his white drill jacket and put his hand a little to the left of the middle of his stomach. 'Just notice this,' he said, and stepped toward me.

"There, just over the left center of that area and extending up toward the spleen, on the left side, you know, there was a protuberance. Seen closely it was apparent that here was some sort of internal growth. It was that which had made him look flabby, stomachish.

"'This was diagnosed for me in New York,' Carswell explained, 'a little more than seven years ago. They told me it was inoperable then. After seven years, probably, I daresay it's worse, if anything. To put the thing in a nutshell, Doctor, I had to "let go" then. I got out of a promising business, broke off my engagement, came here. I won't expatiate on it all, but —it was pretty tough, Doctor, pretty tough. I've lasted all right, so far. It hasn't troubled me—until just lately. That's why I drove in this afternoon, to see you, to see if anything could be done.'

"'Has it been kicking up lately?' I asked him.

"'Yes,' said Carswell, simply. 'They said it would kill me, probably within a year or so, as it grew. It hasn't grown— much. I've lasted a little more than seven years, so far.'

"'Come in to the operating-room,' I invited him, 'and take your clothes off, and let's get a good look at it.'

"'Anything you say,' returned Carswell, and followed me back into the operating-room then and there.

"I had a good look at Carswell, first, superficially. That preliminary examination revealed a growth quite typical, the self-contained, not the 'fibrous' type, in the location I've already described, and about the size of an average man's head. It lay imbedded, fairly deep. It was what we call 'encapsulated.' That, of course, is what had kept Carswell alive.

"Then we put the X-rays on it, fore-and-aft, and sidewise. One of those things doesn't always respond very well to skiagraphic examination, to the X-ray, that is, but this one showed clearly enough. Inside it appeared a kind of dark, triangular mass, with the small end at the top. When Doctor Smithson and I had looked him over thoroughly, I asked Carswell whether or not he wanted to stay with us, to come into the hospital as a patient, for treatment.

"'I'm quite in your hands, Doctor,' he told me. 'I'll stay, or do whatever you want me to. But, first,' and for the first time he looked a trifle embarrassed, 'I think I'd better tell you the story that goes with my coming here! However, speaking plainly, do you think I have a chance?'

"'Well,' said I, 'speaking plainly, yes, there is a chance, maybe a "fifty-fifty" chance, maybe a little less. On the one hand, this thing has been let alone for seven years since original diagnosis. It's probably less operable than it was when you were in New York. On the other hand, we know a lot more, not about these things, Mr. Carswell, but about surgical technique, than they did seven years ago. On the whole, I'd advise you to stay and get ready for an operation, and, say about "forty-sixty" you'll go back to Léogane, or back to New York if you feel like it, several pounds lighter in weight and a new man. If it takes you, on the table, well, you've had a lot more time out there gunning for ducks in Léogane than those New York fellows allowed you.'

"'I'm with you,' said Carswell, and we assigned him a room, took his 'history', and began, to get him ready for his operation.

"We did the operation two days later, at ten-thirty in the morning, and in the meantime Carswell told me his 'story' about it.

"It seems that he had made quite a place for himself, there in Léogane, among the negroes and the ducks. In seven years a man like Carswell, with his mental and dispositional equipment, can go quite a long way, anywhere. He had managed to make quite a good thing out of his duck-drying industry, employed five or six 'hands' in his little wooden 'factory,' rebuilt a rather good house he had secured there for a song right after he had arrived, collected local antiques to add to the equipment he had brought along with him, made himself a real home of a peculiar, bachelor kind, and, above all, got in solid with the Black People all around him. Almost incidentally I gathered from him—he had no gift of narrative, and I had to question him a great deal—he had got onto, and into, the know in the *vodu* thing. There wasn't, as far as I could get it, any aspect of it all that he hadn't been in on, except, that is, '*la chevre sans cornes*'—the goat without horns, you know—the human sacrifice on great occasions. In fact, he strenuously denied that the *voduists* resorted to that; said it was a *canard* against them; that they never, really, did such things, never had, unless back in prehistoric times, in Guinea—Africa.

"But, there wasn't anything about it all that he hadn't at his very finger-ends, and at first-hand, too. The man was a walking encyclopedia of the native beliefs, customs, and practises. He knew, too, every turn and twist of their speech. He hadn't, as he had said at first, 'gone native' in the slightest degree, and yet, without lowering his White Man's dignity by a trifle, he had got it all.

"That brings us to the specific happening, the 'story' which, he had said, went along with his reason for coming in to the hospital in Port au Prince, to us.

"It appears that his sarcoma had never, practically, troubled. Beyond noting a very gradual increase in its size from year to year, he said, he 'wouldn't know he had one.' In other words, characteristically, it never gave him any pain or direct annoyance beyond the sense of the wretched thing being there, and increasing on him, and always drawing him closer to that end of life which the New York doctors had warned him about.

"Then, it had happened only three days before he came to the hospital, he had gone suddenly unconscious one afternoon, as he was walking down his shell path to his gateway. The last thing he remembered then was being 'about four steps from the gate.' When he woke up, it was dark. He was seated in a big chair on his own front gallery, and the first thing he noticed was that his fingers and thumbs were sore and ached very painfully. The next thing was that there were flares burning all along the edge of the gallery, and down in the front yard, and along the road outside the paling fence that divided his property from the road, and in the light of these flares, there swarmed literally hundreds of negroes, gathered about him and mostly on their knees; lined along the gallery and on the grounds below it; prostrating themselves, chanting, putting earth and sand on their heads; and, when he leaned back in his chair, something hurt the back of his neck, and he found that he was being nearly choked with the necklaces, strings of beads, gold and silver coin-strings, and other kinds, that had been draped over his head. His fingers, and the thumbs as well, were covered with gold and silver rings, many of them jammed on so as to stop the circulation.

"From his knowledge of their beliefs, he recognized what had happened to him. He had, he figured, probably fainted, although such a thing was not at all common with him, going down the pathway to the yard gate, and the Blacks had supposed him to be 'possessed' as he had several times seen Black people, children, old men and women, morons, chiefly, similarly 'possessed.' He knew that, now that he was recovered from whatever had happened to him, the 'worship' ought to cease and if he simply sat quiet and took what was coming to him, they would, as soon as they realized he was 'himself' once more, leave him alone and he would get some relief from this uncomfortable set of surroundings; get rid of the necklaces and the rings; get a little privacy.

"But—the queer part of it all was that they didn't quit. No, the mob around the house and on the gallery increased rather than diminished, and at last he was put to it, from sheer discomfort—he said he came to the point where he felt he couldn't stand it all another instant—to speak up and ask the people to leave him in peace.

"They left him, he says, at that, right off the bat, immediately, without a protesting voice, but—and here was what started him on his major puzzlement—they didn't take off the necklaces and rings. No—they left the whole set of that metallic drapery which they had hung and thrust upon him right there, and, after he had been left alone, as he had requested, and had gone into his house, and lifted off the necklaces and worked the rings loose, the *next* thing that happened was that old Pa'p Josef, the local *papaloi*, together with three or four other neighboring *papalois*, witch-doctors from nearby villages, and followed by a very old man who was known to Carswell as the *hougan*, or head witch-doctor of the whole countryside thereabouts, came in to him in a kind of procession, and knelt down all around him on the floor of his living-room, and laid down gourds of cream and bottles of red rum and cooked chickens, and even a big china bowl of Tannia soup—a dish he abominated, said it always tasted like soapy water to him!— and then backed out leaving him to these comestibles.

"He said that this sort of attention persisted in his case, right through the three days that he remained in his house in Léogane, before he started out for the hospital; would, apparently, be still going on if he hadn't come in to Port au Prince to us.

"But—his coming in was not, in the least, because of this. It had puzzled him a great deal, for there was nothing like it in his experience, nor, so far as he could gather from their attitude, in the experience of the people about him, of the *papalois*, or even of the *hougan* himself. They acted, in other words, precisely as though the 'deity' supposed to have taken up his abode within him had remained there, although there seemed no precedent for such an occurrence, and, so far as he knew, he felt precisely just as he had felt right along, that is, fully awake, and, certainly, not in anything like an abnormal condition, and, very positively, not in anything like a fainting-fit!

"That is to say—he felt precisely the same as usual except that—he attributed it to the probability that he must have fallen on the ground that time when he lost consciousness going down the pathway to the gate (he had been told that passers-by had picked him up and carried him to the gallery where he had awakened, later, these Good Samaritans meanwhile recognizing that one of the 'deities' had indwelt him)— he felt the same except for recurrent, almost unbearable pains in the vicinity of his lower abdominal region.

"There was nothing surprizing to him in this accession of the new painfulness. He had been warned that that would be the beginning of the end. It was in the rather faint hope that something might be done that he had come in to the hospital. It speaks volumes for the man's fortitude, for his strength of character, that he came in so cheerfully; acquiesced in what we suggested to him to do; remained with us, facing those comparatively slim chances with complete cheerfulness.

"For—we did not deceive Carswell—the chances were somewhat slim. 'Sixty-forty' I had said, but as I afterward made clear to him, the favorable chances, as gleaned from the mortality tables, were a good deal less than that.

"He went to the table in a state of mind quite unchanged from his accustomed cheerfulness. He shook hands good-bye with Doctor Smithson and me, 'in case,' and also with Doctor Jackson, who acted as anesthetist.

*

"Carswell took an enormous amount of ether to get him off. His consciousness persisted longer, perhaps, than that of any surgical patient I can remember. At last, however, Doctor Jackson intimated to me that I might begin, and, Doctor Smithson standing by with the retracting forceps, I made the first incision. It was my intention, after careful study of the X-ray plates, to open it up from in front, in an up-and-down direction, establish drainage directly, and, leaving the wound in the sound tissue in front of it open, to attempt to get it healed up after removing its contents. Such is the technique of the major portion of successful operations.

"It was a comparatively simple matter to expose the outer wall. This accomplished, and after a few words of consultation with my colleague, I very carefully opened it. We recalled that the X-ray had shown, as I mentioned, a triangular-shaped mass within. This apparent content we attributed to some obscure chemical coloration of the contents. I made my incisions with the greatest care and delicacy, of course. The critical part of the operation lay right at this point, and the greatest exactitude was indicated, of course.

"At last the outer coats of it were cut through, and retracted, and with renewed caution I made the incision through the inmost wall of tissue. To my surprize, and to Doctor Smithson's, the inside was comparatively dry. The gauze which the nurse attending had caused to follow the path of the knife, was hardly moistened. I ran my knife down below the original scope of that last incision, then upward from its upper extremity, greatly lengthening the incision as a whole, if you are following me.

"Then, reaching my gloved hand within this long up-and-down aperture, I felt about and at once discovered that I could get my fingers in around the inner containing wall quite easily. I reached and worked my fingers in farther and farther, finally getting both hands inside and at last feeling my fingers touch inside the posterior or rear wall. Rapidly, now, I ran the edges of my hands around inside, and, quite easily, lifted out the 'inside.' This, a mass weighing several pounds, of more or less solid material, was laid aside on the small table beside the operating-table, and, again pausing to consult with Doctor Smithson—the operation was going, you see, a lot better than either of us had dared to anticipate—and being encouraged by him to proceed to a radical step which we had not hoped to be able to take, I began the dissection from the surrounding, normal tissue, of the now collapsed walls. This, a long, difficult, and harassing job, was accomplished at the end of, perhaps, ten or twelve minutes of gruelling work, and the bag-like thing, now completely severed from the tissues in which it had been for so long imbedded, was placed also on the side table.

"Doctor Jackson reporting favorably on our patient's condition under the anesthetic, I now proceeded to dress the large aperture, and to close the body-wound. This was accomplished in a routine manner, and then, together, we bandaged Carswell, and he was taken back to his room to await awakening from the ether.

"Carswell disposed of, Doctor Jackson and Doctor Smithson left the operating-room and the nurse started in cleaning up after the operation; dropping the instruments into the boiler, and so on—a routine set of duties. As for me, I picked up the shell in a pair of forceps, turned it about under the strong electric operating-light, and laid it down again. It presented nothing of interest for a possible laboratory examination.

"Then I picked up the more or less solid contents which I had laid, very hastily, and without looking at it—you see, my actual removal of it had been done inside, in the dark for the most part and by the sense of feeling, with my hands, you will remember—I picked it up; I still had my operating-gloves on to prevent infection when looking over these specimens, and, still, not looking at it particularly, carried it out into the laboratory.

"Canevin"—Doctor Pelletier looked at me somberly through the very gradually fading light of late afternoon, the period just before the abrupt falling of our tropic dusk—"Canevin," he repeated, "honestly, I don't know how to tell you! Listen now, old man, do something for me, will you?"

"Why, yes—of course," said I, considerably mystified. "What is it you want me to do, Pelletier?"

"My car is out in front of the house. Come on home with me, up to my house, will you? Let's say I want to give you a cocktail! Anyhow, maybe you'll understand better when you are there, *I want to tell you the rest up at my house, not here.* Will you please come, Canevin?"

I looked at him closely. This seemed to me a very strange, an abrupt, request. Still, there was nothing whatever unreasonable about such a sudden whim on Pelletier's part.

"Why, yes, certainly I'll go with you, Pelletier, if you want me to."

"Come on, then," said Pelletier, and we started for his car.

The doctor drove himself, and after we had taken the first turn in the rather complicated route from my house to his, on the extreme airy top of Denmark Hill, he said, in a quiet voice:

"Put together, now, Canevin, certain points, if you please, in this story. Note, kindly, how the Black people over in Léogane acted, according to Carswell's story. Note, too, that theory I was telling you about; do you recollect it clearly?"

"Yes," said I, still more mystified.

"Just keep those two points in mind, then," added Doctor Pelletier, and devoted himself to navigating sharp turns and plodding up two steep roadways for the rest of the drive to his house.

We went in and found his houseboy laying the table for his dinner. Doctor Pelletier is unmarried, keeps a hospitable bachelor establishment. He ordered cocktails, and the houseboy departed on this errand. Then he led me into a kind of office, littered with medical and surgical paraphernalia. He lifted some papers off a chair, motioned me into it, and took another near by. "Listen, now!" he said, and held up a finger at me.

"I took that thing, as I mentioned, into the laboratory," said he. "I carried it in my hand, with my gloves still on, as aforesaid. I laid it down on a table and turned on a powerful light over it. It was only then that I took a good look at it. It weighed several pounds at least, was about the bulk and heft of a full-grown coconut, and about the same color as a hulled coconut, that is, a kind of medium brown. As I looked at it, I saw that it was, as the X-ray had indicated, vaguely triangular in shape. It lay over on one of its sides under that powerful light, and—Canevin, so help me God"—Doctor Pelletier leaned toward me, his face working, a great seriousness in his eyes—"it moved, Canevin," he murmured; "and, as I looked— the thing *breathed*! I was just plain dumfounded. A biological specimen like that—does not move, Canevin! I shook all over, suddenly. I felt my hair prickle on the roots of my scalp. I felt chills go down my spine. Then I remembered that here I was, after an operation, in my own biological laboratory. I came close to the thing and propped it up, on what might be called its logical base, if you see what I mean, so that it stood as nearly upright as its triangular conformation permitted.

"And then I saw that it had faint yellowish markings over the brown, and that what you might call its skin was moving, and—as I stared at the thing, Canevin—two things like little arms began to move, and the top of it gave a kind of convulsive shudder, and it opened straight at me, Canevin, a pair of eyes and looked me in the face.

"Those eyes—my God, Canevin, those eyes! They were eyes of something more than human, Canevin, something incredibly evil, something vastly old, sophisticated, cold, immune from anything except pure evil, the eyes of something that had been worshipped, Canevin, from ages and ages out of a past that went back before all known human calculation, eyes that showed all the deliberate, lurking wickedness that has ever been in the world. The eyes closed, Canevin, and the thing sank over onto its side, and heaved and shuddered convulsively.

"*It was sick, Canevin*; and now, emboldened, holding myself together, repeating over and over to myself that I had a case of the quavers, of post-operative 'nerves,' I forced myself to look closer, and as I did so I got from it a faint whiff of ether. Two tiny, ape-like nostrils, over a clamped-shut slit of a mouth, were exhaling and inhaling; drawing in the good, pure air, exhaling ether fumes. It popped into my head that Carswell had consumed a terrific amount of ether before he went under; we had commented on that, Doctor Jackson particularly. I put two and two together, Canevin, remembered we were in Haiti, where things are not like New York, or Boston, or Baltimore! Those negroes had believed that the 'deity' had not come out of Carswell, do you see? *That* was the thing that held the edge of my mind. The thing stirred uneasily, put out one of its 'arms,' groped about, stiffened.

"I reached for a near-by specimen-jar, Canevin, reasoning, almost blindly, that if this thing were susceptible to ether, it would be susceptible to—well, my gloves were still on my hands, and—now shuddering so that I could hardly move at all, I had to force every motion—I reached out and took hold of the thing—it felt like moist leather—and dropped it into the jar. Then I carried the carboy of preserving alcohol over to the table and poured it in till the ghastly thing was entirely covered, the alcohol near the top of the jar. It writhed once, then rolled over on its 'back,' and lay still, the mouth now open. Do you believe me, Canevin?"

"I have always said that I would believe anything, on proper evidence," said I, slowly, "and I would be the last to question a statement of yours, Pelletier. However, although I have, as you say, looked into some of these things perhaps more than most, it seems, well——"

Doctor Pelletier said nothing. Then he slowly got up out of his chair. He stepped over to a wall-cupboard and returned, a wide-mouthed specimen-jar in his hand. He laid the jar down before me, in silence.

I looked into it, through the slightly discolored alcohol with which the jar, tightly sealed with rubber-tape and sealing-wax, was filled nearly to the brim. There, on the jar's bottom, lay such a thing as Pelletier had described (a thing which, if it had been "seated," upright, would somewhat have resembled that representation of the happy little godling 'Billiken' which was popular twenty years ago as a desk ornament), a thing suggesting the sinister, the unearthly, even in this dessicated form. I looked long at the thing.

"Excuse me for even seeming to hesitate, Pelletier," said I, reflectively.

"I can't say that I blame you," returned the genial doctor. "It is, by the way, the first and only time I have ever tried to tell the story to anybody."

"And Carswell?" I asked. "I've been intrigued with that good fellow and his difficulties. How did he come out of it all?"

"He made a magnificent recovery from the operation," said Pelletier, "and afterward, when he went back to Léogane, he told me that the negroes, while glad to see him quite as usual, had quite lost interest in him as the throne of a 'divinity'."

"H'm," I remarked, "it would seem, that, to bear out——"

"Yes," said Pelletier, "I have always regarded that fact as absolutely conclusive. Indeed, how otherwise could one possibly account for—*this*?" He indicated the contents of the laboratory jar.

I nodded my head, in agreement with him. "I can only say that—if you won't feel insulted, Pelletier—that you are singularly open-minded, for a man of science! What, by the way, became of Carswell?"

The houseboy came in with a tray, and Pelletier and I drank to each other's good health.

"He came in to Port au Prince," replied Pelletier after he had done the honors. "He did not want to go back to the States, he said. The lady to whom he had been engaged had died a couple of years before; he felt that he would be out of touch with American business. The fact is—he had stayed out here too long, too continuously. But, he remains an 'authority' on Haitian native affairs, and is consulted by the High Commissioner. He knows, literally, more about Haiti than the Haitians themselves. I wish you might meet him; you'd have a lot in common."

"I'll hope to do that," said I, and rose to leave. The houseboy appeared at the door, smiling in my direction.

"The table is set for two, sar," said he.

Doctor Pelletier led the way into the dining-room, taking it for granted that I would remain and dine with him. We are informal in St. Thomas, about such matters. I telephoned home and sat down with him.

Pelletier suddenly laughed—he was half-way through his soup at the moment. I looked up inquiringly. He put down his soup spoon and looked across the table at me.

"It's a bit odd," he remarked, "when you stop to think of it! There's one thing Carswell doesn't know about Haiti and what happens there!"

"What's that?" I inquired.

"That—thing—in there," said Pelletier, indicating the office with his thumb in the way artists and surgeons do. "I thought he'd had troubles enough without *that* on his mind, too."

I nodded in agreement and resumed my soup. Pelletier has a cook in a thousand. . . .

1931

AUGUST DERLETH

(1909–1971)

The Panelled Room

WHEN Father Brauman could not change Mrs. Grant's mind, Miss Barbara Allen, seeing him come dolefully down the steps from the porch flung proudly across the face of the house Mrs. Grant had taken, thought she would try. People said that if Miss Barbara Allen could do nothing there was no use trying longer. But it was necessary to do everything possible to convince Mrs. Grant that the house on Main Street was not a healthy place to live in, because of the things that were whispered and sometimes openly said about it—since the murder some years back. So, after announcing her intention to the town through her friends, Miss Barbara Allen paid a visit to Mrs. Grant a week after that lady had moved into the house on Main Street with her sister and her sister's little daughter.

Her reception was not too cordial, and when she mentioned the house and spoke about what people said of it, Mrs. Grant put up her lorgnette and told the old lady that as she was a Freethinker she didn't believe in such things.

"I'm a Freethinker, too, Mrs. Grant," said Miss Barbara, "but I lived in this house once."

Mrs. Grant smiled politely and patiently and said, "Nothing seems to have happened to you," her inference clear and her manner no less so.

Miss Barbara blinked a little and said, "My sister died here," announcing it rather, as if this fact alone were incontestable proof of the strange rumors current about the house in which they sat.

Mrs. Grant thought, How provincial! and raised her eyebrows a little. "Surely you don't think this house had anything to do with that?" she asked, her voice more kind now.

The old lady was firm. "I know it did. If it wouldn't be for wanting to tell you, that being my duty, as I said to Elvira— that's my other sister—I'd never've set foot in this house

644

again. My sister was found dead in the panelled room, the parlor—at least, it was our parlor."

"Heart attack, I suppose?"

Miss Barbara shook her head. "There was never anything the matter with Abby. She was just found dead. Old Doctor Brown, he said it was shock—a scare, most likely. That was after poor Abby began to see things in that room."

"What things?"

The old lady picked at her shawl and looked at Mrs. Grant over her spectacles, as if trying to discover from Mrs. Grant's features how much she had already been told. "Fifty years ago, come next month, Peter Mason killed his wife in that room and then he killed himself. They found them both the next day, she choked to death, and he hanging there. Sometimes you can see him hanging there yet—and she a-lying on the floor pale and white."

"Why, Miss Allen, that's a childish invention!"

Miss Barbara smiled faintly. "Almost my very words, when Abby and I took this house. But I've seen Peter Mason hanging, myself—and I've seen his wife there, too." There was an intensity in her voice, but no flicker of emotion disturbed her face.

Mrs. Grant leaned forward a little, saying, "Yes?", still polite, still patient, urging her visitor to continue, though she did not wish to hear more.

"He was hanging from the cross-beam over the bookcase—just like they found him when I was a little girl. You don't know what it is to walk into that room and see him there all unexpected—you don't know, yet. And to see her like that again—all crumpled up on the floor, her face twisted! I wouldn't want to be in your place for anything. I'd move out right away, this very minute!"

Mrs. Grant sighed, having heard the admonition many times since she had come to the town and taken the house. Miss Barbara Allen began to feel uncomfortable and rose presently to go, feeling that she had done what she could.

"Will you promise me something, Mrs. Grant?" she asked.

Mrs. Grant hesitated. "That can be almost anything," she said, feeling her position becoming intolerable and wanting this woman to go away.

Miss Barbara said, "It's nothing unreasonable. Promise me

that when you see the panels moving in the parlor, you'll leave this house right away. There's a horror hanging over this house —and it may be too late to get away when you see the panels move."

Curiosity prompted Mrs. Grant to ask, "What do you mean, Miss Allen?"

"If you're staying, you'll see soon enough. But I hope you'll change your mind before then." Then she was gone, the door closing heavily behind her.

Mrs. Grant watched the old woman go down the outer steps, thinking, What a queer person! Then she turned away and went into the living room, where she sat down, aware of the critical eye her sister turned on her.

"The usual thing, Irma," said Mrs. Grant. "We are to move right away."

The child in one corner of the room took up the words. "I like moving, Mamma. When are we going to move?" She allowed her block building to tumble to the floor and jumped to her feet, clapping her hands.

"Do be quiet, Ellen," said her mother, fixing the child with her eyes while Mrs. Grant nodded stern but not unkind approval. "We aren't going to move, dear." Then she turned again to her older sister.

"But there's something new, this time," Mrs. Grant went on. "The panels in the parlor are said to move—that serpent design, I suppose Miss Allen meant."

Irma smiled. "An illusion, Lydia. Everyone knows that if you look at a design like that long enough, your eyes will seem to see movement."

Mrs. Grant nodded, clasping her fingers and looking down at them in a moment of silent speculation. Presently she spoke again. "True, Irma. Still, there was something about Miss Allen I didn't understand."

"What?"

"Why, I don't know. A peculiar earnestness—that's the best I can do by way of describing her attitude. She sat there telling me her story so simply, expecting me to believe every word of it. It was uncanny, Irma. I mean, she didn't look like the kind of woman who's very easily taken in by such things."

"I do believe the old lady's story has affected you," said

Irma, not without impatience. "But I shan't let you fall under her spell. I declare, Lydia, you're white as a sheet, just thinking about it."

Mrs. Grant felt considerably better on coming down to breakfast next morning, for indeed Miss Allen's simple earnestness had insidiously destroyed her confident superiority the evening before. The prattle of Irma's child this unusually bright morning took her mind away from Peter Mason and his unfortunate wife, and the unbelievable stories of weird hauntings that had been current since then.

In the afternoon Mrs. Grant let it be known that she would not welcome any more people, however well-intentioned, who came to warn her about the house. When she dropped this hint to her callers, she sensed immediately an air of restraint. Later, when she walked down Main Street at dusk, she felt a frightening air of waiting in the half-hidden faces peering out at her from behind the curtained windows of houses she passed.

In the evening she was afraid. With some reluctance, she said to her sister, "Really, the house *is* beginning to oppress me," and when Irma said, "Nonsense, Lydia!" she was afraid to say more. She sat in comparative silence for the rest of the evening, an obvious air of unnatural restraint cloaking her. For this she could not entirely account, Miss Allen's story being already too far in the past to explain it.

Mrs. Grant's strange oppression grew.

It crept upon her from all sides, day by day, and she felt it suddenly even when doing the most ordinary things—when dusting the room, or rearranging the furniture, things she trusted no maid with doing. She could not understand this oppression's growing in, building itself stronger about and within her, but when fear found her she knew.

Ten days after Miss Barbara Allen's call, Mrs. Grant walked into the panelled room one evening and saw a man hanging in the shadows where the bookcase was—and a crumpled shape oddly darkening the floor nearby. She fell back against the wall, but the thing was gone. She thought, It's nothing. There is nothing there at all. But it was two hours before she had convinced herself that she had seen nothing. When she came out of the parlor, Irma noticed her paleness.

"Well, I declare, Lydia, there's something the matter with you!" she exclaimed.

Mrs. Grant looked at her sister and knew she could not tell her, knew she could not face Irma's scornful skepticism. "I've got a terrible headache," she said.

Irma was surprised. "A headache—that's strange. You've never had one before, Lydia." She looked queerly at Mrs. Grant for a moment before she said, "You'll find aspirin tablets in my purse. You'd better take one. But I can't understand your having a headache like this."

Mrs. Grant did not reply. Irma did not notice that Mrs. Grant went directly upstairs, avoiding the purse on the side table. In the night, Mrs. Grant's sleep was haunted by dreams of the panelled room and what she had seen there, and in her dreams there was no illusion.

After Mrs. Grant had seen the man hanging and the form huddled on the floor beneath four times, she steeled herself to speak to her sister, thinking that this was the only way, for it must come some time. "I've seen him," she said abruptly one day while the two of them sat at the table.

Irma put down her cup of coffee and looked at her sister with a frown on her forehead. "You've seen him," she said. "What do you mean? Who is it you've seen?"

"Why, Peter Mason—the man who killed his wife. And I've seen her, too." Mrs. Grant made a vague and uncertain gesture in the direction of the panelled room.

A sudden comprehension came to Irma, and a strange gleam began to grow in her eyes. Mrs. Grant did not understand, but Irma was thinking, *If anything happens to her, I'll get everything!* The thought had come to her with startling suddenness, but she made no attempt to beat it down. It would mean freedom for her and Ellen. No more bending to Lydia's wish. With an effort she controlled her voice, for her abrupt excitement was beating in her. "You imagined it," she said calmly, but her fingers trembled as she took up a tea-cake.

"I think we *had* better give up this house," said Mrs. Grant.

Irma smiled in a superior fashion calculated to disarm her sister. "Nonsense, Lydia. I refuse to consider giving up this fine old house because of a few stories—like as not unfounded, my dear."

"*But Irma, I have seen him!*" Her voice was strong with the intensity of conviction that had grown in her during the past few days.

Irma stirred her coffee and said, "That is a peculiar arrangement of the shadows from the street-lamp, Lydia. I myself have got that impression several times—of someone hanging there. I had hoped you wouldn't see it because I knew you half-believed those stories."

Mrs. Grant said "Oh," weakly, and Irma thought, *If anything should happen to her: if anything . . .*

Abruptly Irma pressed the temporary advantage she had gained. "I'll go into the parlor with you, Lydia. Then we'll see." She got up immediately and took her sister's arm.

If Irma noticed the shadow, she gave no sign, even when Mrs. Grant clutched her arm in fright. "There's nothing there, Lydia," she said, patting her sister's hand.

"Oh, you can't see him," breathed Mrs. Grant. "And now he's gone . . . he's gone."

Irma said, "You're tired, Lydia, dear."

Mrs. Grant stared at her sister in the semi-dusk and said, "I want to go away." Her voice was thick and rough. Her hands were shuddering.

"You must face what's worrying you, Lydia; that's the only way."

Mrs. Grant nodded and said, "Yes. I will." She did not notice the strange fixity of Irma's eyes.

Miss Barbara Allen called the next day. She sat in the living room, fixing Mrs. Grant with her eyes. She looked tired, yet there was a curious alertness about her. The two of them—Irma had not come into the room—talked of everything but the house. Mrs. Grant did not want to give the old lady a chance to say anything; so she spoke a great deal and repeated many things she had said once already. And then, in spite of her talking, there came a lull in the conversation, and Miss Barbara said what she had come to say.

"Why are you staying here, Mrs. Grant?"

Mrs. Grant asked, "What do you mean?" She had meant her voice to be polite and calm; it was unsteady, alarmed.

"I know you've seen him," said the old lady, dropping her voice. "And I had hoped you would leave when you saw—

before the panels start moving. It's unbearable, it's awful, when they start. It works on your mind, Mrs. Grant."

"How did you know I'd seen him, Miss Allen?"

The old lady said, "It's in your eyes, Mrs. Grant. I know what it is to see him, because I've seen him, too—and her. And I remember Abby's eyes: waiting, always waiting, frightened."

Mrs. Grant made a nervous gesture with her hands as if seeking to brush the suggestion away like a tangible thing. "I've seen them both," she said, her words coming rapidly, "but it can't be real, because Irma can't see them."

Miss Barbara was obviously startled, for she jerked her head up and looked at her hostess as if she believed that Mrs. Grant was deliberately misleading her. Her eyes narrowed, her thin lips folded together, and abruptly she said, "Your sister lies!" her voice sharp and accusing.

Mrs. Grant was confused. "There's no reason why she should lie to me, Miss Allen."

"If your sister says she can't see them, it's because she wants you to stay here for a very strong reason. Does she go often into the panelled room?" Mrs. Grant's sudden start, her widened eyes, answered the old lady; she went on. "Are you sure there's no reason for her wanting you to stay, Mrs. Grant? Perhaps it would be better for her—if something happened to you? I understand she's entirely dependent on you, and as she's very young yet, I don't suppose she'd like that. Seems to me it's your sister who's keeping you here, Mrs. Grant."

Mrs. Grant's confusion became even more evident. "I don't know," she said. "I really don't. Irma doesn't go into the parlor at all. And she wouldn't want anything to happen to me. I know she wouldn't. No, no, it's unthinkable, Miss Allen. I feel bound to resent such a suggestion."

But the old lady paid no attention. "I think you'd better leave the house right away, Mrs. Grant. Tomorrow is a day no one should be in this house, an anniversary. It was seventeen years ago tomorrow . . ."

At this moment Irma swept into the room, eyeing the old lady in cold hostility. Miss Allen nodded politely, but she rose to go immediately. When she left the house, the old lady's eyes were pleading with Mrs. Grant to follow.

That afternoon Mrs. Grant called on Miss Barbara Allen. She had dropped all pretense and began to talk frankly about the house, admitting her inability to understand Irma's liking for it, and her being unable to see the man hanging—and what lay behind. Miss Barbara let her talk awhile before she advanced the plan which she had been formulating. She outlined it patiently, urging it upon Mrs. Grant as a means with which to test her sister—and to punish her if anything should happen. After a while the two women went downtown to the local lawyer, and Mrs. Grant made her will. In the evening Miss Barbara, having seen Mrs. Grant leave the house, made a short call on Irma.

"I don't know what you're up to," she said in her mild voice. "But I think you should know that Mrs. Grant has just made her will."

For a moment Irma was surprised. Then she drew herself together and said, "Really, Miss Allen, I don't understand." Her voice was edged and hostile.

"I think you do," the old lady went on, standing firmly before the younger woman. "I think you know as well as I do that Mrs. Grant should leave this house before anything happens— and I'm afraid something will happen."

"That's nonsense, Miss Allen, and you know it," Irma flung back. But her voice was not as firm as she would have liked it because she was thinking, *Then something will happen, something will happen* . . .

The old lady disregarded this. "Mrs. Grant has put in her will that if anything happens to her here, if she's not gone tomorrow because you've kept her back, then you'll get all she has—*providing you spend the rest of your life in this house!*"

Miss Barbara Allen went out of the house, and Irma stood in the dusk of the dimly lit room with her hands pressed to her breast. It was some moments before the full import of what the old lady had said broke in upon her, and then she thrust it blindly away, refusing to see it. It isn't true, she told herself. But she looked at her little girl in growing fear. Something will happen tomorrow, she thought. Something must happen— afterwards, we can go, Ellen and I.

Mrs. Grant got up early the next morning. She was definitely nervous and made little effort to hide it. At the breakfast table she said, "I must go away today. I can't stand this house any longer."

Irma steeled herself for combat. "Are you going to let children's tales and shadows affect you that way?" she demanded. Her voice was purposely very cold, and Mrs. Grant wavered in her resolve. Perhaps after all she *had* allowed herself to fall too easily a prey to unfounded fancies to which her imaginative mind had lent support by conjuring up before her suggestive hallucinations. And yet . . . Irma went on, "If you want, I shall send for a doctor. I can't help feeling that something's the matter with you. You've been acting so strangely of late, Lydia."

In the end, Mrs. Grant surrendered her resolve, so that when evening came, she was still in the house. Irma sat in the living room with her, waiting, wondering whether her sister would go into the parlor. In her own mind was forming a question of her right. But she crushed her conscience and said quickly, "Will you get my gold thimble from the parlor, Lydia?" Her voice was casual, and her question suggested that she had already been in the parlor during the day.

Mrs. Grant looked at her sister, sitting calmly near her with folds of embroidery over her knees. She conquered the abrupt apprehension that had risen in her with patient effort, and presently she said, "Yes, I'll go," her voice as casual as Irma's.

She took a lamp and lit it, and went slowly toward the closed double doors leading into the panelled room. She opened them and went into the room. A moment of breathless silence descended, hanging in the house. And then Irma heard a short, shrill scream of terror. She sat there half-paralyzed, thinking of Miss Barbara's accusing eyes. Then she sprang up with a cry and ran toward the panelled room, Ellen following.

Mrs. Grant was standing in the middle of the room, pointing at the walls. Little choking sounds came from her throat, and her hands went up to tear at her high collar. Then, before Irma could reach her, she fell in a heap on the floor. Irma came to her knees and caught up her sister's head.

"Lydia!—Lydia!" she moaned.

Even while she knelt there, she felt a horror such as she had never known, and she knew what it was that had stopped the beating of her sister's heart. She felt the brooding fear that came throbbing toward her from the walls, and she knew that unless she escaped, she too would be smothered and choked, this fear pressing in upon her with its icy hands until her life was gone. Her sister's collar came open, and Irma saw on her throat a faint line, red and bruised, as if the collar had strangled her. Irma's hands began to tremble, and her lips fell open and shut. She thought with sudden horror of Lydia's will and as she strove to push away the thought, she heard Ellen's voice coming it seemed from very far away.

"Mamma, will they do it again?"

The child was standing near her, pointing at the panels of the walls. Irma put one hand up to her throat, and her voice, as she answered the child, was little more than a whisper. "What?" she asked harshly. God, there's nothing, she thought. There's nothing.

The child continued to point at the panels, and she said, "I saw them move. I saw them."

There's nothing.—There's nothing there at all. Irma began to sway, and then suddenly she reached out and began to strike the child unmercifully, striking blindly, until at last the child's crying brought her to her senses. She crouched there on her knees looking with unseeing eyes at the crying child and screamed to her. "*You didn't see anything! You didn't see anything! You didn't—You didn't . . . !*"

1933

H. P. LOVECRAFT
(1890-1937)

The Thing on the Doorstep

I⊤ is true that I have sent six bullets through the head of my best friend, and yet I hope to shew by this statement that I am not his murderer. At first I shall be called a madman—madder than the man I shot in his cell at the Arkham Sanitarium. Later some of my readers will weigh each statement, correlate it with the known facts, and ask themselves how I could have believed otherwise than as I did after facing the evidence of that horror—that thing on the doorstep.

Until then I also saw nothing but madness in the wild tales I have acted on. Even now I ask myself whether I was misled— or whether I am not mad after all. I do not know—but others have strange things to tell of Edward and Asenath Derby, and even the stolid police are at their wits' end to account for that last terrible visit. They have tried weakly to concoct a theory of a ghastly jest or warning by discharged servants, yet they know in their hearts that the truth is something infinitely more terrible and incredible.

So I say that I have not murdered Edward Derby. Rather have I avenged him, and in so doing purged the earth of a horror whose survival might have loosed untold terrors on all mankind. There are black zones of shadow close to our daily paths, and now and then some evil soul breaks a passage through. When that happens, the man who knows must strike before reckoning the consequences.

I have known Edward Pickman Derby all his life. Eight years my junior, he was so precocious that we had much in common from the time he was eight and I sixteen. He was the most phenomenal child scholar I have ever known, and at seven was writing verse of a sombre, fantastic, almost morbid cast which astonished the tutors surrounding him. Perhaps his private education and coddled seclusion had something to do with his premature flowering. An only child, he had organic weaknesses which startled his doting parents and caused them to keep him closely chained to their side. He was never allowed out without his nurse, and seldom had a chance to play unconstrainedly with other children. All this doubtless fostered a strange, secretive inner life in the boy, with imagination as his one avenue of freedom.

At any rate, his juvenile learning was prodigious and bizarre; and his facile writings such as to captivate me despite my greater age. About that time I had leanings toward art of a somewhat grotesque cast, and I found in this younger child a rare kindred spirit. What lay behind our joint love of shadows and marvels was, no doubt, the ancient, mouldering, and subtly fearsome town in which we lived—witch-cursed, legend-haunted Arkham, whose huddled, sagging gambrel roofs and crumbling Georgian balustrades brood out the centuries beside the darkly muttering Miskatonic.

As time went by I turned to architecture and gave up my design of illustrating a book of Edward's daemoniac poems, yet our comradeship suffered no lessening. Young Derby's odd genius developed remarkably, and in his eighteenth year his collected nightmare-lyrics made a real sensation when issued under the title *Azathoth and Other Horrors*. He was a close correspondent of the notorious Baudelairean poet Justin Geoffrey, who wrote *The People of the Monolith* and died screaming in a madhouse in 1926 after a visit to a sinister, ill-regarded village in Hungary.

In self-reliance and practical affairs, however, Derby was greatly retarded because of his coddled existence. His health had improved, but his habits of childish dependence were fostered by overcareful parents; so that he never travelled alone, made independent decisions, or assumed responsibilities. It was early seen that he would not be equal to a struggle in the business or professional arena, but the family fortune was so ample that this formed no tragedy. As he grew to years of manhood he retained a deceptive aspect of boyishness. Blond and blue-eyed, he had the fresh complexion of a child; and his attempts to raise a moustache were discernible only with difficulty. His voice was soft and light, and his pampered, unexercised life gave him a juvenile chubbiness rather than the paunchiness of premature middle age. He was of good height, and his handsome face would have made him a notable gallant had not his shyness held him to seclusion and bookishness.

Derby's parents took him abroad every summer, and he was quick to seize on the surface aspects of European thought and expression. His Poe-like talents turned more and more toward the decadent, and other artistic sensitivenesses and yearnings were half-aroused in him. We had great discussions in those days. I had been through Harvard, had studied in a Boston architect's office, had married, and had finally returned to Arkham to practice my profession—settling in the family homestead in Saltonstall St. since my father had moved to Florida for his health. Edward used to call almost every evening, till I came to regard him as one of the household. He had a characteristic way of ringing the doorbell or sounding the knocker that grew to be a veritable code signal, so that after dinner I always listened for the familiar three brisk strokes followed by two more after a pause. Less frequently I would visit at his house and note with envy the obscure volumes in his constantly growing library.

Derby went through Miskatonic University in Arkham, since his parents would not let him board away from them. He entered at sixteen and completed his course in three years, majoring in English and French literature and receiving high marks in everything but mathematics and the sciences. He mingled very little with the other students, though looking enviously at the "daring" or "Bohemian" set—whose superficially "smart" language and meaninglessly ironic pose he aped, and whose dubious conduct he wished he dared adopt.

What he did do was to become an almost fanatical devotee of subterranean magical lore, for which Miskatonic's library was and is famous. Always a dweller on the surface of phantasy and strangeness, he now delved deep into the actual runes and riddles left by a fabulous past for the guidance or puzzlement of posterity. He read things like the frightful *Book of Eibon*, the *Unaussprechlichen Kulten* of von Junzt, and the forbidden *Necronomicon* of the mad Arab Abdul Alhazred, though he did not tell his parents he had seen them. Edward was twenty when my son and only child was born, and seemed pleased when I named the newcomer Edward Derby Upton, after him.

By the time he was twenty-five Edward Derby was a prodi-

giously learned man and a fairly well-known poet and fantai-
siste, though his lack of contacts and responsibilities had slowed
down his literary growth by making his products derivative
and overbookish. I was perhaps his closest friend—finding him
an inexhaustible mine of vital theoretical topics, while he relied
on me for advice in whatever matters he did not wish to refer
to his parents. He remained single—more through shyness,
inertia, and parental protectiveness than through inclination—
and moved in society only to the slightest and most perfunctory extent. When the war came both health and ingrained
timidity kept him at home. I went to Plattsburg for a commission, but never got overseas.

So the years wore on. Edward's mother died when he was
thirty-four, and for months he was incapacitated by some odd
psychological malady. His father took him to Europe, however, and he managed to pull out of his trouble without visible
effects. Afterward he seemed to feel a sort of grotesque exhilaration, as if of partial escape from some unseen bondage. He
began to mingle in the more "advanced" college set despite his
middle age, and was present at some extremely wild doings—
on one occasion paying heavy blackmail (which he borrowed
of me) to keep his presence at a certain affair from his father's
notice. Some of the whispered rumours about the wild Miskatonic set were extremely singular. There was even talk of black
magic and of happenings utterly beyond credibility.

II.

Edward was thirty-eight when he met Asenath Waite. She
was, I judge, about twenty-three at the time; and was taking a
special course in mediaeval metaphysics at Miskatonic. The
daughter of a friend of mine had met her before—in the Hall
School at Kingsport—and had been inclined to shun her
because of her odd reputation. She was dark, smallish, and
very good-looking except for overprotuberant eyes; but something in her expression alienated extremely sensitive people. It
was, however, largely her origin and conversation which caused
average folk to avoid her. She was one of the Innsmouth
Waites, and dark legends have clustered for generations about
crumbling, half-deserted Innsmouth and its people. There are

tales of horrible bargains about the year 1850, and of a strange element "not quite human" in the ancient families of the run-down fishing port—tales such as only old-time Yankees can devise and repeat with proper awesomeness.

Asenath's case was aggravated by the fact that she was Ephraim Waite's daughter—the child of his old age by an unknown wife who always went veiled. Ephraim lived in a half-decayed mansion in Washington Street, Innsmouth, and those who had seen the place (Arkham folk avoid going to Innsmouth whenever they can) declared that the attic windows were always boarded, and that strange sounds sometimes floated from within as evening drew on. The old man was known to have been a prodigious magical student in his day, and legend averred that he could raise or quell storms at sea according to his whim. I had seen him once or twice in my youth as he came to Arkham to consult forbidden tomes at the college library, and had hated his wolfish, saturnine face with its tangle of iron-grey beard. He had died insane—under rather queer circumstances—just before his daughter (by his will made a nominal ward of the principal) entered the Hall School, but she had been his morbidly avid pupil and looked fiendishly like him at times.

The friend whose daughter had gone to school with Asenath Waite repeated many curious things when the news of Edward's acquaintance with her began to spread about. Asenath, it seemed, had posed as a kind of magician at school; and had really seemed able to accomplish some highly baffling marvels. She professed to be able to raise thunderstorms, though her seeming success was generally laid to some uncanny knack at prediction. All animals markedly disliked her, and she could make any dog howl by certain motions of her right hand. There were times when she displayed snatches of knowledge and language very singular—and very shocking—for a young girl; when she would frighten her schoolmates with leers and winks of an inexplicable kind, and would seem to extract an obscene and zestful irony from her present situation.

Most unusual, though, were the well-attested cases of her influence over other persons. She was, beyond question, a genuine hypnotist. By gazing perculiarly at a fellow-student she would often give the latter a distinct feeling of *exchanged personality*—as if the subject were placed momentarily in the magician's body and able to stare half across the room at her real body, whose eyes blazed and protruded with an alien expression. Asenath often made wild claims about the nature of consciousness and about its independence of the physical frame —or at least from the life-processes of the physical frame. Her crowning rage, however, was that she was not a man; since she believed a male brain had certain unique and far-reaching cosmic powers. Given a man's brain, she declared, she could not only equal but surpass her father in mastery of unknown forces.

Edward met Asenath at a gathering of "intelligentsia" held in one of the students' rooms, and could talk of nothing else when he came to see me the next day. He had found her full of the interests and erudition which engrossed him most, and was in addition wildly taken with her appearance. I had never seen the young woman, and recalled casual references only faintly, but I knew who she was. It seemed rather regrettable that Derby should become so upheaved about her; but I said nothing to discourage him, since infatuation thrives on opposition. He was not, he said, mentioning her to his father.

In the next few weeks I heard of very little but Asenath from young Derby. Others now remarked Edward's autumnal gallantry, though they agreed that he did not look even nearly his actual age, or seem at all inappropriate as an escort for his bizarre divinity. He was only a trifle paunchy despite his indolence and self-indulgence, and his face was absolutely without lines. Asenath, on the other hand, had the premature crow's feet which come from the exercise of an intense will.

About this time Edward brought the girl to call on me, and I at once saw that his interest was by no means one-sided. She eyed him continually with an almost predatory air, and I perceived that their intimacy was beyond untangling. Soon afterward I had a visit from old Mr. Derby, whom I had always admired and respected. He had heard the tales of his son's new friendship, and had wormed the whole truth out of "the boy". Edward meant to marry Asenath, and had even been looking at houses in the suburbs. Knowing my usually great influence with his son, the father wondered if I could help to break the ill-advised affair off; but I regretfully expressed my doubts. This time it was not a question of Edward's weak will but of the woman's strong will. The perennial child had transferred his dependence from the parental image to a new and stronger image, and nothing could be done about it.

The wedding was performed a month later—by a justice of the peace, according to the bride's request. Mr. Derby, at my advice, offered no opposition; and he, my wife, my son, and I attended the brief ceremony—the other guests being wild young people from the college. Asenath had bought the old Crowninshield place in the country at the end of High Street, and they proposed to settle there after a short trip to Innsmouth, whence three servants and some books and household goods were to be brought. It was probably not so much consideration for Edward and his father as a personal wish to be near the college, its library, and its crowd of "sophisticates", that made Asenath settle in Arkham instead of returning permanently home.

When Edward called on me after the honeymoon I thought he looked slightly changed. Asenath had made him get rid of the undeveloped moustache, but there was more than that. He looked soberer and more thoughtful, his habitual pout of childish rebelliousness being exchanged for a look almost of genuine sadness. I was puzzled to decide whether I liked or disliked the change. Certainly, he seemed for the moment more normally adult than ever before. Perhaps the marriage was a good thing—might not the *change* of dependence form a start toward actual *neutralisation*, leading ultimately to responsible independence? He came alone, for Asenath was very busy. She had brought a vast store of books and apparatus from Innsmouth (Derby shuddered as he spoke the name), and was finishing the restoration of the Crowninshield house and grounds.

Her home in—that town—was a rather disquieting place, but certain objects in it had taught him some surprising things. He was progressing fast in esoteric lore now that he had Asenath's guidance. Some of the experiments she proposed were very daring and radical—he did not feel at liberty to describe them—but he had confidence in her powers and intentions. The three servants were very queer—an incredibly aged couple who had been with old Ephraim and referred occasionally to him and to Asenath's dead mother in a cryptic way, and a swarthy young wench who had marked anomalies of feature and seemed to exude a perpetual odour of fish.

III.

For the next two years I saw less and less of Derby. A fortnight would sometimes slip by without the familiar three-and-two strokes at the front door; and when he did call—or when, as happened with increasing infrequency, I called on him—he was very little disposed to converse on vital topics. He had become secretive about those occult studies which he used to describe and discuss so minutely, and preferred not to talk of his wife. She had aged tremendously since her marriage, till now —oddly enough—she seemed the elder of the two. Her face held the most concentratedly determined expression I had ever seen, and her whole aspect seemed to gain a vague, unplaceable repulsiveness. My wife and son noticed it as much as I, and we all ceased gradually to call on her—for which, Edward admitted in one of his boyishly tactless moments, she was unmitigatedly grateful. Occasionally the Derbys would go on long trips—ostensibly to Europe, though Edward sometimes hinted at obscurer destinations.

It was after the first year that people began talking about the change in Edward Derby. It was very casual talk, for the change was purely psychological; but it brought up some interesting points. Now and then, it seemed, Edward was observed to wear an expression and to do things wholly incompatible with his usual flabby nature. For example—although in the old days he could not drive a car, he was now seen occasionally to dash into or out of the old Crowninshield driveway with Asenath's powerful Packard, handling it like a master, and meeting traffic entanglements with a skill and determination utterly alien to his accustomed nature. In such cases he seemed always to be just back from some trip or just starting on one—what sort of trip, no one could guess, although he mostly favoured the old Innsmouth road.

Oddly, the metamorphosis did not seem altogether pleasing. People said he looked too much like his wife, or like old Ephraim Waite himself, in these moments—or perhaps these moments seemed unnatural because they were so rare. Sometimes, hours after starting out in this way, he would return listlessly sprawled on the rear seat of his car while an obviously hired chauffeur or mechanic drove. Also, his preponderant aspect on the streets during his decreasing round of social contacts (including, I may say, his calls on me) was the old-time indecisive one—its irresponsible childishness even more marked than in the past. While Asenath's face aged, Edward's—aside from those exceptional occasions—actually relaxed into a kind of exaggerated immaturity, save when a trace of the new sadness or understanding would flash across it. It was really very puzzling. Meanwhile the Derbys almost dropped out of the gay college circle—not through their own disgust, we heard, but because something about their present studies shocked even the most callous of the other decadents.

It was in the third year of the marriage that Edward began to hint openly to me of a certain fear and dissatisfaction. He would let fall remarks about things 'going too far', and would talk darkly about the need of 'saving his identity'. At first I ignored such references, but in time I began to question him guardedly, remembering what my friend's daughter had said about Asenath's hypnotic influence over the other girls at school—the cases where students had thought they were in her body looking across the room at themselves. This questioning seemed to make him at once alarmed and grateful, and once he mumbled something about having a serious talk with me later.

About this time old Mr. Derby died, for which I was afterward very thankful. Edward was badly upset, though by no means disorganised. He had seen astonishingly little of his parent since his marriage, for Asenath had concentrated in herself all his vital sense of family linkage. Some called him callous in his loss—especially since those jaunty and confident moods in the car began to increase. He now wished to move back into the old Derby mansion, but Asenath insisted on staying in the Crowninshield house, to which she had become well adjusted.

Not long afterward my wife heard a curious thing from a friend—one of the few who had not dropped the Derbys. She had been out to the end of High St. to call on the couple, and had seen a car shoot briskly out of the drive with Edward's oddly confident and almost sneering face above the wheel. Ringing the bell, she had been told by the repulsive wench that Asenath was also out; but had chanced to look up at the house in leaving. There, at one of Edward's library windows, she had glimpsed a hastily withdrawn face—a face whose expression of pain, defeat, and wistful hopelessness was poignant beyond description. It was—incredibly enough in view of its usual domineering cast—Asenath's; yet the caller had vowed that in that instant the sad, muddled eyes of poor Edward were gazing out from it.

Edward's calls now grew a trifle more frequent, and his hints occasionally became concrete. What he said was not to be believed, even in centuried and legend-haunted Arkham; but he threw out his dark lore with a sincerity and convincingness which made one fear for his sanity. He talked about terrible meetings in lonely places, of Cyclopean ruins in the heart of the Maine woods beneath which vast staircases lead down to abysses of nighted secrets, of complex angles that lead through invisible walls to other regions of space and time, and of hideous exchanges of personality that permitted explorations in remote and forbidden places, on other worlds, and in different space-time continua.

He would now and then back up certain crazy hints by exhibiting objects which utterly nonplussed me—elusively coloured and bafflingly textured objects like nothing ever heard of on earth, whose insane curves and surfaces answered no conceivable purpose and followed no conceivable geometry. These things, he said, came 'from outside'; and his wife knew how to get them. Sometimes—but always in frightened and ambiguous whispers—he would suggest things about old Ephraim Waite, whom he had seen occasionally at the college library in the old days. These adumbrations were never specific, but seemed to revolve around some especially horrible doubt as to whether the old wizard were really dead—in a spiritual as well as corporeal sense.

At times Derby would halt abruptly in his revelations, and I wondered whether Asenath could possibly have divined his speech at a distance and cut him off through some unknown sort of telepathic mesmerism—some power of the kind she had displayed at school. Certainly, she suspected that he told me things, for as the weeks passed she tried to stop his visits with words and glances of a most inexplicable potency. Only

with difficulty could he get to see me, for although he would
pretend to be going somewhere else, some invisible force
would generally clog his motions or make him forget his destination for the time being. His visits usually came when Asenath was away—'away in her own body', as he once oddly put
it. She always found out later—the servants watched his goings
and comings—but evidently she thought it inexpedient to do
anything drastic.

IV.

Derby had been married more than three years on that August day when I got the telegram from Maine. I had not seen
him for two months, but had heard he was away "on business". Asenath was supposed to be with him, though watchful
gossips declared there was someone upstairs in the house
behind the doubly curtained windows. They had watched the
purchases made by the servants. And now the town marshal of
Chesuncook had wired of the draggled madman who stumbled out of the woods with delirious ravings and screamed to
me for protection. It was Edward—and he had been just able
to recall his own name and my name and address.

Chesuncook is close to the wildest, deepest, and least explored forest belt in Maine, and it took a whole day of feverish
jolting through fantastic and forbidding scenery to get there in
a car. I found Derby in a cell at the town farm, vacillating
between frenzy and apathy. He knew me at once, and began
pouring out a meaningless, half-incoherent torrent of words in
my direction.

"Dan—for God's sake! The pit of the shoggoths! Down the
six thousand steps . . . the abomination of abominations . . .
I never would let her take me, and then I found myself there.
. . . Iä! Shub-Niggurath! . . . The shape rose up from the altar, and there were 500 that howled. . . . The Hooded Thing
bleated 'Kamog! Kamog!'—that was old Ephraim's secret
name in the coven. . . . I was there, where she promised she
wouldn't take me. . . . A minute before I was locked in the
library, and then I was there where she had gone with my
body—in the place of utter blasphemy, the unholy pit where
the black realm begins and the watcher guards the gate. . . .

I saw a shoggoth—it changed shape. . . . I can't stand it. . . . I won't stand it. . . . I'll kill her if she ever sends me there again. . . . I'll kill that entity . . . her, him, it . . . I'll kill it! I'll kill it with my own hands!"

It took me an hour to quiet him, but he subsided at last. The next day I got him decent clothes in the village, and set out with him for Arkham. His fury of hysteria was spent, and he was inclined to be silent; though he began muttering darkly to himself when the car passed through Augusta—as if the sight of a city aroused unpleasant memories. It was clear that he did not wish to go home; and considering the fantastic delusions he seemed to have about his wife—delusions un-doubtedly springing from some actual hypnotic ordeal to which he had been subjected—I thought it would be better if he did not. I would, I resolved, put him up myself for a time; no matter what unpleasantness it would make with Asenath. Later I would help him get a divorce, for most assuredly there were mental factors which made this marriage suicidal for him. When we struck open country again Derby's muttering faded away, and I let him nod and drowse on the seat beside me as I drove.

During our sunset dash through Portland the muttering commenced again, more distinctly than before, and as I lis-tened I caught a stream of utterly insane drivel about Asenath. The extent to which she had preyed on Edward's nerves was plain, for he had woven a whole set of hallucinations around her. His present predicament, he mumbled furtively, was only one of a long series. She was getting hold of him, and he knew that some day she would never let go. Even now she probably let him go only when she had to, because she couldn't hold on long at a time. She constantly took his body and went to nameless places for nameless rites, leaving him in her body and locking him upstairs—but sometimes she couldn't hold on, and he would find himself suddenly in his own body again in some far-off, horrible, and perhaps unknown place. Sometimes she'd get hold of him again and sometimes she couldn't. Of-ten he was left stranded somewhere as I had found him . . . time and again he had to find his way home from frightful dis-tances, getting somebody to drive the car after he found it.

The worst thing was that she was holding on to him longer

and longer at a time. She wanted to be a man—to be fully human—that was why she got hold of him. She had sensed the mixture of fine-wrought brain and weak will in him. Some day she would crowd him out and disappear with his body— disappear to become a great magician like her father and leave him marooned in that female shell that wasn't even quite human. Yes, he knew about the Innsmouth blood now. There had been traffick with things from the sea—it was horrible. . . . And old Ephraim—he had known the secret, and when he grew old did a hideous thing to keep alive . . . he wanted to live forever . . . Asenath would succeed—one successful demonstration had taken place already.

As Derby muttered on I turned to look at him closely, veri- fying the impression of change which an earlier scrutiny had given me. Paradoxically, he seemed in better shape than usual —harder, more normally developed, and without the trace of sickly flabbiness caused by his indolent habits. It was as if he had been really active and properly exercised for the first time in his coddled life, and I judged that Asenath's force must have pushed him into unwonted channels of motion and alertness. But just now his mind was in a pitiable state; for he was mum- bling wild extravagances about his wife, about black magic, about old Ephraim, and about some revelation which would convince even me. He repeated names which I recognised from bygone browsings in forbidden volumes, and at times made me shudder with a certain thread of mythological consistency—of convincing coherence—which ran through his maundering. Again and again he would pause, as if to gather courage for some final and terrible disclosure.

"Dan, Dan, don't you remember him—the wild eyes and the unkempt beard that never turned white? He glared at me once, and I never forgot it. Now *she* glares that way. *And I know why!* He found it in the *Necronomicon*—the formula. I don't dare tell you the page yet, but when I do you can read and understand. Then you will know what has engulfed me. On, on, on, on—body to body to body—he means never to die. The life-glow—he knows how to break the link . . . it can flicker on a while even when the body is dead. I'll give you hints, and maybe you'll guess. Listen, Dan—do you know why my wife always takes such pains with that silly backhand writing? Have you ever seen a manuscript of old Ephraim's? Do you want to know why I shivered when I saw some hasty notes Asenath had jotted down?

"Asenath . . . *is there such a person?* Why did they half think there was poison in old Ephraim's stomach? Why do the Gilmans whisper about the way he shrieked—like a frightened child—when he went mad and Asenath locked him up in the padded attic room where—the other—had been? *Was it old Ephraim's soul that was locked in? Who locked in whom?* Why had he been looking for months for someone with a fine mind and a weak will? Why did he curse that his daughter wasn't a son? Tell me, Daniel Upton—*what devilish exchange was perpetuated in the house of horror where that blasphemous monster had his trusting, weak-willed, half-human child at his mercy?* Didn't he make it permanent—as she'll do in the end with me? Tell me why that thing that calls itself Asenath writes differently when off guard, *so that you can't tell its script from . . .*"

Then the thing happened. Derby's voice was rising to a thin treble scream as he raved, when suddenly it was shut off with an almost mechanical click. I thought of those other occasions at my home when his confidences had abruptly ceased—when I had half fancied that some obscure telepathic wave of Asenath's mental force was intervening to keep him silent. This, though, was something altogether different—and, I felt, infinitely more horrible. The face beside me was twisted almost unrecognisably for a moment, while through the whole body there passed a shivering motion—as if all the bones, organs, muscles, nerves, and glands were readjusting themselves to a radically different posture, set of stresses, and general personality.

Just where the supreme horror lay, I could not for my life tell; yet there swept over me such a swamping wave of sickness and repulsion—such a freezing, petrifying sense of utter alienage and abnormality—that my grasp of the wheel grew feeble and uncertain. The figure beside me seemed less like a lifelong friend than like some monstrous intrusion from outer space— some damnable, utterly accursed focus of unknown and malign cosmic forces.

I had faltered only a moment, but before another moment was over my companion had seized the wheel and forced me

to change places with him. The dusk was now very thick, and
the lights of Portland far behind, so I could not see much of
his face. The blaze of his eyes, though, was phenomenal; and I
knew that he must now be in that queerly energised state—so
unlike his usual self—which so many people had noticed. It
seemed odd and incredible that listless Edward Derby—he who
could never assert himself, and who had never learned to
drive—should be ordering me about and taking the wheel of
my own car, yet that was precisely what had happened. He did
not speak for some time, and in my inexplicable horror I was
glad he did not.

In the lights of Biddeford and Saco I saw his firmly set
mouth, and shivered at the blaze of his eyes. The people were
right—he did look damnably like his wife and like old Ephraim
when in these moods. I did not wonder that the moods were
disliked—there was something unnatural and diabolic in them,
and I felt the sinister element all the more because of the wild
ravings I had been hearing. This man, for all my lifelong
knowledge of Edward Pickman Derby, was a stranger—an intrusion of some sort from the black abyss.

He did not speak until we were on a dark stretch of road,
and when he did his voice seemed utterly unfamiliar. It was
deeper, firmer, and more decisive than I had ever known it to
be; while its accent and pronunciation were altogether changed
—though vaguely, remotely, and rather disturbingly recalling
something I could not quite place. There was, I thought, a
trace of very profound and very genuine irony in the timbre—
not the flashy, meaninglessly jaunty pseudo-irony of the callow
"sophisticate", which Derby had habitually affected, but
something grim, basic, pervasive, and potentially evil. I mar-
velled at the self-possession so soon following the spell of
panic-struck muttering.

"I hope you'll forget my attack back there, Upton," he was
saying. "You know what my nerves are, and I guess you can
excuse such things. I'm enormously grateful, of course, for
this lift home.

"And you must forget, too, any crazy things I may have been
saying about my wife—and about things in general. That's
what comes from overstudy in a field like mine. My philosophy
is full of bizarre concepts, and when the mind gets worn out it

cooks up all sorts of imaginary concrete applications. I shall take a rest from now on—you probably won't see me for some time, and you needn't blame Asenath for it.

"This trip was a bit queer, but it's really very simple. There are certain Indian relics in the north woods—standing stones, and all that—which mean a good deal in folklore, and Asenath and I are following that stuff up. It was a hard search, so I seem to have gone off my head. I must send somebody for the car when I get home. A month's relaxation will put me back on my feet."

I do not recall just what my own part of the conversation was, for the baffling alienage of my seatmate filled my consciousness. With every moment my feeling of elusive cosmic horror increased, till at length I was in a virtual delirium of longing for the end of the drive. Derby did not offer to relinquish the wheel, and I was glad of the speed with which Portsmouth and Newburyport flashed by.

At the junction where the main highway runs inland and avoids Innsmouth I was half afraid my driver would take the bleak shore road that goes through that damnable place. He did not, however, but darted rapidly past Rowley and Ipswich toward our destination. We reached Arkham before midnight, and found the lights still on at the old Crowninshield house. Derby left the car with a hasty repetition of his thanks, and I drove home alone with a curious feeling of relief. It had been a terrible drive—all the more terrible because I could not quite tell why—and I did not regret Derby's forecast of a long absence from my company.

v.

The next two months were full of rumours. People spoke of seeing Derby more and more in his new energised state, and Asenath was scarcely ever in to her few callers. I had only one visit from Edward, when he called briefly in Asenath's car—duly reclaimed from wherever he had left it in Maine—to get some books he had lent me. He was in his new state, and paused only long enough for some evasively polite remarks. It was plain that he had nothing to discuss with me when in this condition—and I noticed that he did not even trouble to give the old three-and-two signal when ringing the doorbell. As on that evening in the car, I felt a faint, infinitely deep horror which I could not explain; so that his swift departure was a prodigious relief.

In mid-September Derby was away for a week, and some of the decadent college set talked knowingly of the matter—hinting at a meeting with a notorious cult-leader, lately expelled from England, who had established headquarters in New York. For my part I could not get that strange ride from Maine out of my head. The transformation I had witnessed had affected me profoundly, and I caught myself again and again trying to account for the thing—and for the extreme horror it had inspired in me.

But the oddest rumours were those about the sobbing in the old Crowninshield house. The voice seemed to be a woman's, and some of the younger people thought it sounded like Asenath's. It was heard only at rare intervals, and would sometimes be choked off as if by force. There was talk of an investigation, but this was dispelled one day when Asenath appeared in the streets and chatted in a sprightly way with a large number of acquaintances—apologising for her recent absences and speaking incidentally about the nervous breakdown and hysteria of a guest from Boston. The guest was never seen, but Asenath's appearance left nothing to be said. And then someone complicated matters by whispering that the sobs had once or twice been in a man's voice.

One evening in mid-October I heard the familiar three-and-two ring at the front door. Answering it myself, I found Edward on the steps, and saw in a moment that his personality was the old one which I had not encountered since the day of his ravings on that terrible ride from Chesuncook. His face was twitching with a mixture of odd emotions in which fear and triumph seemed to share dominion, and he looked furtively over his shoulder as I closed the door behind him.

Following me clumsily to the study, he asked for some whiskey to steady his nerves. I forbore to question him, but waited till he felt like beginning whatever he wanted to say. At length he ventured some information in a choking voice.

"Asenath has gone, Dan. We had a long talk last night while the servants were out, and I made her promise to stop preying on me. Of course I had certain—certain occult defences I never told you about. She had to give in, but got frightfully angry. Just packed up and started for New York—walked right out to catch the 8:20 in to Boston. I suppose people will talk, but I can't help that. You needn't mention that there was any trouble—just say she's gone on a long research trip.

"She's probably going to stay with one of her horrible groups of devotees. I hope she'll go west and get a divorce—anyhow, I've made her promise to keep away and let me alone. It was horrible, Dan—she was stealing my body—crowding me out—making a prisoner of me. I laid low and pretended to let her do it, but I had to be on the watch. I could plan if I was careful, for she can't read my mind literally, or in detail. All she could read of my planning was a sort of general mood of rebellion—and she always thought I was helpless. Never thought I could get the best of her . . . but I had a spell or two that worked."

Derby looked over his shoulder and took some more whiskey.

"I paid off those damned servants this morning when they got back. They were ugly about it, and asked questions, but they went. They're her kind—Innsmouth people—and were hand and glove with her. I hope they'll let me alone—I didn't like the way they laughed when they walked away. I must get as many of Dad's old servants again as I can. I'll move back home now.

"I suppose you think I'm crazy, Dan—but Arkham history ought to hint at things that back up what I've told you—and what I'm going to tell you. You've seen one of the changes, too—in your car after I told you about Asenath that day coming home from Maine. That was when she got me—drove me out of my body. The last thing of the ride I remember was when I was all worked up trying to tell you *what that she-devil is.* Then she got me, and in a flash I was back at the house—in the library where those damned servants had me locked up—and in that cursed fiend's body . . . that isn't even human. . . . You know, it was she you must have ridden home with . . . that preying wolf in my body. . . . You ought to have known the difference!"

I shuddered as Derby paused. Surely, I *had* known the

difference—yet could I accept an explanation as insane as this? But my distracted caller was growing even wilder.

"I had to save myself—I had to, Dan! She'd have got me for good at Hallowmass—they hold a Sabbat up there beyond Chesuncook, and the sacrifice would have clinched things. She'd have got me for good . . . she'd have been I, and I'd have been she . . . forever . . . too late. . . . My body'd have been hers for good. . . . She'd have been a man, and fully human, just as she wanted to be. . . . I suppose she'd have put me out of the way—killed her own ex-body with me in it, damn her, *just as she did before*—just as she, he, or it did before. . . ."

Edward's face was now atrociously distorted, and he bent it uncomfortably close to mine as his voice fell to a whisper.

"You must know what I hinted in the car—*that she isn't Asenath at all, but really old Ephraim himself.* I suspected it a year and a half ago, but I know it now. Her handwriting shews it when she's off guard—sometimes she jots down a note in writing that's just like her father's manuscripts, stroke for stroke —and sometimes she says things that nobody but an old man like Ephraim could say. He changed forms with her when he felt death coming—she was the only one he could find with the right kind of brain and a weak enough will—he got her body permanently, just as she almost got mine, and then poisoned the old body he'd put her into. Haven't you seen old Ephraim's soul glaring out of that she-devil's eyes dozens of times . . . and out of mine when she had control of my body?"

The whisperer was panting, and paused for breath. I said nothing, and when he resumed his voice was nearer normal. This, I reflected, was a case for the asylum, but I would not be the one to send him there. Perhaps time and freedom from Asenath would do its work. I could see that he would never wish to dabble in morbid occultism again.

"I'll tell you more later—I must have a long rest now. I'll tell you something of the forbidden horrors she led me into— something of the age-old horrors that even now are festering in out-of-the-way corners with a few monstrous priests to keep them alive. Some people know things about the universe that nobody ought to know, and can do things that nobody ought to be able to do. I've been in it up to my neck, but that's the end. Today I'd burn that damned *Necronomicon* and all the rest if I were librarian at Miskatonic.

"But she can't get me now. I must get out of that accursed house as soon as I can, and settle down at home. You'll help me, I know, if I need help. Those devilish servants, you know . . . and if people should get too inquisitive about Asenath. You see, I can't give them her address. . . . Then there are certain groups of searchers—certain cults, you know—that might misunderstand our breaking up . . . some of them have damnably curious ideas and methods. I know you'll stand by me if anything happens—even if I have to tell you a lot that will shock you. . . ."

I had Edward stay and sleep in one of the guest-chambers that night, and in the morning he seemed calmer. We discussed certain possible arrangements for his moving back into the Derby mansion, and I hoped he would lose no time in making the change. He did not call the next evening, but I saw him frequently during the ensuing weeks. We talked as little as possible about strange and unpleasant things, but discussed the renovation of the old Derby house, and the travels which Edward promised to take with my son and me the following summer.

Of Asenath we said almost nothing, for I saw that the subject was a peculiarly disturbing one. Gossip, of course, was rife; but that was no novelty in connexion with the strange ménage at the old Crowninshield house. One thing I did not like was what Derby's banker let fall in an overexpansive mood at the Miskatonic Club—about the cheques Edward was sending regularly to a Moses and Abigail Sargent and a Eunice Babson in Innsmouth. That looked as if those evil-faced servants were extorting some kind of tribute from him—yet he had not mentioned the matter to me.

I wished that the summer—and my son's Harvard vacation —would come, so that we could get Edward to Europe. He was not, I soon saw, mending as rapidly as I had hoped he would; for there was something a bit hysterical in his occasional exhilaration, while the moods of fright and depression were altogether too frequent. The old Derby house was ready by December, yet Edward constantly put off moving. Though he hated and seemed to fear the Crowninshield place, he was at the same time queerly enslaved by it. He could not seem to begin dismantling things, and invented every kind of excuse to postpone action. When I pointed this out to him he appeared unaccountably frightened. His father's old butler—who was there with other reacquired family servants—told me one day that Edward's occasional prowlings about the house, and especially down cellar, looked odd and unwholesome to him. I wondered if Asenath had been writing disturbing letters, but the butler said there was no mail which could have come from her.

VI.

It was about Christmas that Derby broke down one evening while calling on me. I was steering the conversation toward next summer's travels when he suddenly shrieked and leaped up from his chair with a look of shocking, uncontrollable fright—a cosmic panic and loathing such as only the nether gulfs of nightmare could bring to any sane mind.

"My brain! My brain! God, Dan—it's tugging—from beyond—knocking—clawing—that she-devil—even now— Ephraim—Kamog! Kamog!—The pit of the shoggoths—Iä! Shub-Niggurath! The Goat with a Thousand Young! . . .

"The flame—the flame . . . beyond body, beyond life . . . in the earth . . . oh, God! . . ."

I pulled him back to his chair and poured some wine down his throat as his frenzy sank to a dull apathy. He did not resist, but kept his lips moving as if talking to himself. Presently I realised that he was trying to talk to me, and bent my ear to his mouth to catch the feeble words.

". . . again, again . . . she's trying . . . I might have known . . . nothing can stop that force; not distance, nor magic, nor death . . . it comes and comes, mostly in the night . . . I can't leave . . . it's horrible . . . oh, God, Dan, *if you only knew as I do just how horrible it is. . . .*"

When he had slumped down into a stupor I propped him with pillows and let normal sleep overtake him. I did not call a doctor, for I knew what would be said of his sanity, and wished to give nature a chance if I possibly could. He waked at midnight, and I put him to bed upstairs, but he was gone by

morning. He had let himself quietly out of the house—and his
butler, when called on the wire, said he was at home pacing
restlessly about the library.

Edward went to pieces rapidly after that. He did not call
again, but I went daily to see him. He would always be sitting
in his library, staring at nothing and having an air of abnormal
listening. Sometimes he talked rationally, but always on trivial
topics. Any mention of his trouble, of future plans, or of Asenath would send him into a frenzy. His butler said he had
frightful seizures at night, during which he might eventually
do himself harm.

I had a long talk with his doctor, banker, and lawyer, and
finally took the physician with two specialist colleagues to visit
him. The spasms that resulted from the first questions were violent and pitiable—and that evening a closed car took his poor
struggling body to the Arkham Sanitarium. I was made his
guardian and called on him twice weekly—almost weeping to
hear his wild shrieks, awesome whispers, and dreadful, droning
repetitions of such phrases as "I had to do it—I had to do it . . .
it'll get me . . . it'll get me . . . down there . . . down
there in the dark. . . . Mother, mother! Dan! Save me. . . .
save me . . ."

How much hope of recovery there was, no one could say;
but I tried my best to be optimistic. Edward must have a home
if he emerged, so I transferred his servants to the Derby mansion, which would surely be his sane choice. What to do about
the Crowninshield place with its complex arrangements and
collections of utterly inexplicable objects I could not decide,
so left it momentarily untouched—telling the Derby household to go over and dust the chief rooms once a week, and
ordering the furnace man to have a fire on those days.

The final nightmare came before Candlemas—heralded, in
cruel irony, by a false gleam of hope. One morning late in January the sanitarium telephoned to report that Edward's reason
had suddenly come back. His continuous memory, they said,
was badly impaired; but sanity itself was certain. Of course he
must remain some time for observation, but there could
be little doubt of the outcome. All going well, he would surely
be free in a week.

I hastened over in a flood of delight, but stood bewildered

when a nurse took me to Edward's room. The patient rose to greet me, extending his hand with a polite smile; but I saw in an instant that he bore the strangely energised personality which had seemed so foreign to his own nature—the competent personality I had found so vaguely horrible, and which Edward himself had once vowed was the intruding soul of his wife. There was the same blazing vision—so like Asenath's and old Ephraim's—and the same firm mouth; and when he spoke I could sense the same grim, pervasive irony in his voice—the deep irony so redolent of potential evil. This was the person who had driven my car through the night five months before—the person I had not seen since that brief call when he had forgotten the old-time doorbell signal and stirred such nebulous fears in me—and now he filled me with the same dim feeling of blasphemous alienage and ineffable cosmic hideousness.

He spoke affably of arrangements for release—and there was nothing for me to do but assent, despite some remarkable gaps in his recent memories. Yet I felt that something was terribly, inexplicably wrong and abnormal. There were horrors in this thing that I could not reach. This was a sane person—but was it indeed the Edward Derby I had known? If not, who or what was it—*and where was Edward?* Ought it to be free or confined . . . or ought it to be extirpated from the face of the earth? There was a hint of the abysmally sardonic in everything the creature said—the Asenath-like eyes lent a special and baffling mockery to certain words about the 'early liberty earned by an *especially close confinement*'. I must have behaved very awkwardly, and was glad to beat a retreat.

All that day and the next I racked my brain over the problem. What had happened? What sort of mind looked out through those alien eyes in Edward's face? I could think of nothing but this dimly terrible enigma, and gave up all efforts to perform my usual work. The second morning the hospital called up to say that the recovered patient was unchanged, and by evening I was close to a nervous collapse—a state I admit, though others will vow it coloured my subsequent vision. I have nothing to say on this point except that no madness of mine could account for *all* the evidence.

VII.

It was in the night—after that second evening—that stark, utter horror burst over me and weighted my spirit with a black, clutching panic from which it can never shake free. It began with a telephone call just before midnight. I was the only one up, and sleepily took down the receiver in the library. No one seemed to be on the wire, and I was about to hang up and go to bed when my ear caught a very faint suspicion of sound at the other end. Was someone trying under great difficulties to talk? As I listened I thought I heard a sort of half-liquid bubbling noise—"*glub . . . glub . . . glub*"—which had an odd suggestion of inarticulate, unintelligible word and syllable divisions. I called, "Who is it?" But the only answer was "*glub-glub . . . glub-glub.*" I could only assume that the noise was mechanical; but fancying that it might be a case of a broken instrument able to receive but not to send, I added, "I can't hear you. Better hang up and try Information." Immediately I heard the receiver go on the hook at the other end.

This, I say, was just before midnight. When that call was traced afterward it was found to come from the old Crowninshield house, though it was fully half a week from the housemaid's day to be there. I shall only hint what was found at that house—the upheaval in a remote cellar storeroom, the tracks, the dirt, the hastily rifled wardrobe, the baffling marks on the telephone, the clumsily used stationery, and the detestable stench lingering over everything. The police, poor fools, have their smug little theories, and are still searching for those sinister discharged servants—who have dropped out of sight amidst the present furore. They speak of a ghoulish revenge for things that were done, and say I was included because I was Edward's best friend and adviser.

Idiots!—do they fancy those brutish clowns could have forged that handwriting? Do they fancy they could have brought what later came? Are they blind to the changes in that body that was Edward's? As for me, *I now believe all that Edward Derby ever told me.* There are horrors beyond life's edge that we do not suspect, and once in a while man's evil prying calls them just within our range. Ephraim—Asenath—that devil called them in, and they engulfed Edward as they are engulfing me.

Can I be sure that I am safe? Those powers survive the life of the physical form. The next day—in the afternoon, when I pulled out of my prostration and was able to walk and talk coherently—I went to the madhouse and shot him dead for Edward's and the world's sake, but can I be sure till he is cremated? They are keeping the body for some silly autopsies by different doctors—but I say he must be cremated. *He must be cremated—he who was not Edward Derby when I shot him.* I shall go mad if he is not, for I may be the next. But my will is not weak—and I shall not let it be undermined by the terrors I know are seething around it. One life—Ephraim, Asenath, and Edward—who now? I *will not* be driven out of my body . . . I *will not* change souls with that bullet-ridden lich in the madhouse!

But let me try to tell coherently of that final horror. I will not speak of what the police persistently ignored—the tales of that dwarfed, grotesque, malodorous thing met by at least three wayfarers in High St. just before two o'clock, and the nature of the single footprints in certain places. I will say only that just about two the doorbell and knocker waked me—doorbell and knocker both, plied alternately and uncertainly in a kind of weak desperation, *and each trying to keep to Edward's old signal of three-and-two strokes.*

Roused from sound sleep, my mind leaped into a turmoil. Derby at the door—and remembering the old code! That new personality had not remembered it . . . was Edward suddenly back in his rightful state? Why was he here in such evident stress and haste? Had he been released ahead of time, or had he escaped? Perhaps, I thought as I flung on a robe and bounded downstairs, his return to his own self had brought raving and violence, revoking his discharge and driving him to a desperate dash for freedom. Whatever had happened, he was good old Edward again, and I would help him!

When I opened the door into the elm-arched blackness a gust of insufferably foetid wind almost flung me prostrate. I choked in nausea, and for a second scarcely saw the dwarfed, humped figure on the steps. The summons had been Edward's, but who was this foul, stunted parody? Where had Edward had time to go? His ring had sounded only a second before the door opened.

The caller had on one of Edward's overcoats—its bottom almost touching the ground, and its sleeves rolled back yet still covering the hands. On the head was a slouch hat pulled low, while a black silk muffler concealed the face. As I stepped unsteadily forward, the figure made a semi-liquid sound like that I had heard over the telephone—"*glub . . . glub . . .*"—and thrust at me a large, closely written paper impaled on the end of a long pencil. Still reeling from the morbid and unaccountable foetor, I seized this paper and tried to read it in the light from the doorway.

Beyond question, it was in Edward's script. But why had he written when he was close enough to ring—and why was the script so awkward, coarse, and shaky? I could make out nothing in the dim half light, so edged back into the hall, the dwarf figure clumping mechanically after but pausing on the inner door's threshold. The odour of this singular messenger was really appalling, and I hoped (not in vain, thank God!) that my wife would not wake and confront it.

Then, as I read the paper, I felt my knees give under me and my vision go black. I was lying on the floor when I came to, that accursed sheet still clutched in my fear-rigid hand. This is what it said.

"Dan—go to the sanitarium and kill it. Exterminate it. It isn't Edward Derby any more. She got me—it's Asenath—*and she has been dead three months and a half.* I lied when I said she had gone away. I killed her. I had to. It was sudden, but we were alone and I was in my right body. I saw a candlestick and smashed her head in. She would have got me for good at Hallowmass.

"I buried her in the farther cellar storeroom under some old boxes and cleaned up all the traces. The servants suspected next morning, but they have such secrets that they dare not tell the police. I sent them off, but God knows what they—and others of the cult—will do.

"I thought for a while I was all right, and then I felt the tugging at my brain. I knew what it was—I ought to have remembered. A soul like hers—or Ephraim's—is half detached, and keeps right on after death as long as the body lasts. She was getting me—making me change bodies with her—*seizing my body and putting me in that corpse of hers buried in the cellar.*

"I knew what was coming—that's why I snapped and had to go to the asylum. Then it came—I found myself choked in the dark—in Asenath's rotting carcass down there in the cellar under the boxes where I put it. And I knew she must be in my body at the sanitarium—*permanently*, for it was after Hallowmass, and the sacrifice would work even without her being there—sane, and ready for release as a menace to the world. I was desperate, *and in spite of everything I clawed my way out.*

"I'm too far gone to talk—I couldn't manage to telephone—but I can still write. I'll get fixed up somehow and bring you this last word and warning. *Kill that fiend* if you value the peace and comfort of the world. *See that it is cremated.* If you don't, it will live on and on, body to body forever, and I can't tell you what it will do. Keep clear of black magic, Dan, it's the devil's business. Goodbye—you've been a great friend. Tell the police whatever they'll believe—and I'm damnably sorry to drag all this on you. I'll be at peace before long—this thing won't hold together much more. Hope you can read this. *And kill that thing—kill it.*

Yours—Ed."

It was only afterward that I read the last half of this paper, for I had fainted at the end of the third paragraph. I fainted again when I saw and smelled what cluttered up the threshold where the warm air had struck it. The messenger would not move or have consciousness any more.

The butler, tougher-fibred than I, did not faint at what met him in the hall in the morning. Instead, he telephoned the police. When they came I had been taken upstairs to bed, but the—other mass—lay where it had collapsed in the night. The men put handkerchiefs to their noses.

What they finally found inside Edward's oddly assorted clothes was mostly liquescent horror. There were bones, too—and a crushed-in skull. Some dental work positively identified the skull as Asenath's.

1933

CLARK ASHTON SMITH

(1893–1961)

Genius Loci

"It is a very strange place," said Amberville, "but I scarcely know how to convey the impression it made upon me. It will all sound so simple and ordinary. There is nothing but a sedgy meadow, surrounded on three sides by slopes of yellow pine. A dreary little stream flows in from the open end, to lose itself in a *cul-de-sac* of cat-tails and boggy ground. The stream, running slowly and more slowly, forms a stagnant pool of some extent, from which several sickly-looking alders seem to fling themselves backward, as if unwilling to approach it. A dead willow leans above the pool, tangling its wan, skeleton-like re-flection with the green scum that mottles the water. There are no blackbirds, no kildees, no dragon-flies even, such as one usually finds in a place of that sort. It is all silent and desolate. The spot is evil—it is unholy in a way that I simply can't de-scribe. I was compelled to make a drawing of it, almost against my will, since anything so outré is hardly in my line. In fact, I made two drawings. I'll show them to you, if you like."

Since I had a high opinion of Amberville's artistic abilities, and had long considered him one of the foremost landscape painters of his generation, I was naturally eager to see the drawings. He, however, did not even pause to await my avowal of interest, but began at once to open his portfolio. His facial expression, the very movements of his hands, were somehow eloquent of a strange mixture of compulsion and repugnance as he brought out and displayed the two watercolor sketches he had mentioned.

I could not recognize the scene depicted from either of them. Plainly it was one that I had missed in my desultory rambling about the foot-hill environs of the tiny hamlet of Bowman, where, two years before, I had purchased an uncul-tivated ranch and had retired for the privacy so essential to prolonged literary effort. Francis Amberville, in the one

fortnight of his visit, through his flair for the pictorial poten-
tialities of landscape, had doubtless grown more familiar with
the neighborhood than I. It had been his habit to roam about
in the forenoon, armed with sketching-materials; and in this
way he had already found the theme of more than one lovely
painting. The arrangement was mutually convenient, since I,
in his absence, was wont to apply myself assiduously to an antique Remington typewriter.

I examined the drawings attentively. Both, though of hurried execution, were highly meritorious, and showed the characteristic grace and vigor of Amberville's style. And yet, even
at first glance, I found a quality that was more alien to the
spirit of his work. The elements of the scene were those he had
described. In one picture, the pool was half hidden by a fringe
of mace-reeds, and the dead willow was leaning across it at a
prone, despondent angle, as if mysteriously arrested in its fall
toward the stagnant waters. Beyond, the alders seemed to
strain away from the pool, exposing their knotted roots as if in
eternal effort. In the other drawing, the pool formed the main
portion of the foreground, with the skeleton tree looming
drearily at one side. At the water's farther end, the cat-tails
seemed to wave and whisper among themselves in a dying
wind; and the steeply barring slope of pine at the meadow's
terminus was indicated as a wall of gloomy green that closed in
the picture, leaving only a pale margin of autumnal sky at the
top.

All this, as the painter had said, was ordinary enough. But I
was impressed immediately by a profound horror that lurked
in these simple elements and was expressed by them as if by the
balefully contorted features of some demoniac face. In both
drawings, this sinister character was equally evident, as if the
same face had been shown in profile and front view. I could
not trace the separate details that composed the impressions;
but ever, as I looked, the abomination of a strange evil, a spirit
of despair, malignity, desolation, leered from the drawing
more openly and hatefully. The spot seemed to wear a macabre
and Satanic grimace. One felt that it might speak aloud, might
utter the imprecations of some gigantic devil, or the raucous
derision of a thousand birds of ill omen. The evil conveyed was
something wholly outside of humanity—more ancient than

man. Somehow—fantastic as this will seem—the meadow had the air of a vampire, grown old and hideous with unutterable infamies. Subtly, indefinably, it thirsted for other things than the sluggish trickle of water by which it was fed.

"Where is the place?" I asked, after a minute or two of silent inspection. It was incredible that anything of the sort could really exist—and equally incredible that a nature so robust as Amberville should have been sensitive to its quality.

"It's in the bottom of that abandoned ranch, a mile or less down the little road toward Bear River," he replied. "You must know it. There's a small orchard about the house, on the upper hillside; but the lower portion, ending in that meadow, is all wild land."

I began to visualize the vicinity in question. "Guess it must be the old Chapman place," I decided. "No other ranch along that road would answer your specifications."

"Well, whoever it belongs to, that meadow is the most horrible spot I have ever encountered. I've known other landscapes that had something wrong with them, but never anything like this."

"Maybe it's haunted," I said, half in jest. "From your description, it must be the very meadow where old Chapman was found dead one morning by his youngest daughter. It happened a few months after I moved here. He was supposed to have died of heart failure. His body was quite cold, and he had probably been lying there all night, since the family had missed him at suppertime. I don't remember him very clearly, but I remember that he had a reputation for eccentricity. For some time before his death, people thought he was going mad. I forget the details. Anyway, his wife and children left, not long after he died, and no one has occupied the house or cultivated the orchard since. It was a commonplace rural tragedy."

"I'm not much of a believer in spooks," observed Amberville, who seemed to have taken my suggestion of haunting in a literal sense. "Whatever the influence is, it's hardly of human origin. Come to think of it, though, I received a very silly impression once or twice—the idea that some one was watching me while I did those drawings. Queer—I had almost forgotten that, till you brought up the possibility of haunting. I seemed to see him out of the tail of my eye, just beyond the radius that I was putting into the picture: a dilapidated old scoundrel with dirty gray whiskers and an evil scowl. It's odd, too, that I should have gotten such a definite conception of him, without ever seeing him squarely. I thought it was a tramp who had strayed into the meadow bottom. But when I turned to give him a level glance, he simply wasn't there. It was as if he melted into the miry ground, the cat-tails, the sedges."

"That isn't a bad description of Chapman," I said. "I remember his whiskers—they were almost white, except for the tobacco juice. A battered antique, if there ever was one—and very unamiable, too. He had a poisonous glare toward the end, which no doubt helped along the legend of his insanity. Some of the tales about him come back to me now. People said that he neglected the care of his orchard more and more. Visitors used to find him in that lower meadow, standing idly about and staring vacantly at the trees and water. Probably that was one reason they thought he was losing his mind. But I'm sure I never heard that there was anything unusual or queer about the meadow, either at the time of Chapman's death, or since. It's a lonely spot, and I don't imagine that any one ever goes there now."

"I stumbled on it quite by accident," said Amberville. "The place isn't visible from the road, on account of the thick pines. . . . But there's another odd thing: I went out this morning with a very strong and clear intuition that I might find something of uncommon interest. I made a bee-line for that meadow, so to speak; and I'll have to admit that the intuition justified itself. The place repels me—but it fascinates me, too. I've simply got to solve the mystery, if it has a solution," he added, with a slightly defensive air. "I'm going back early tomorrow, with my oils, to start a real painting of it."

I was surprised, knowing that predilection of Amberville for scenic brilliance and gayety which had caused him to be likened to Sorolla. "The painting will be a novelty for you," I commented. "I'll have to come and take a look at the place myself, before long. It should really be more in my line than yours. There ought to be a weird story in it somewhere, if it lives up to your drawings and description."

Several days passed. I was deeply preoccupied, at the time,

with the toilsome and intricate problems offered by the concluding chapters of a new novel; and I put off my proposed
visit to the meadow discovered by Amberville. My friend, on
his part, was evidently engrossed by his new theme. He sallied
forth each morning with his easel and oil-colors, and returned
later each day, forgetful of the luncheon-hour that had formerly brought him back from such expeditions. On the third
day, he did not reappear till sunset. Contrary to his custom, he
did not show me what he had done, and his answers to my
queries regarding the progress of the picture were somewhat
vague and evasive. For some reason, he was unwilling to talk
about it. Also, he was apparently loth to discuss the meadow
itself, and in answer to direct questions, merely reiterated in an
absent and perfunctory manner the account he had given me
following his discovery of the place. In some mysterious way
that I could not define, his attitude seemed to have changed.

There were other changes, too. He seemed to have lost his
usual blitheness. Often I caught him frowning intently, and
surprised the lurking of some equivocal shadow in his frank
eyes. There was a moodiness, a morbidity, which, as far as our
five years' friendship enabled me to observe, was a new aspect
of his temperament. Perhaps, if I had not been so preoccupied
with my own difficulties, I might have wondered more as to
the causation of his gloom, which I attributed readily enough
at first to some technical dilemma that was baffling him. He
was less and less the Amberville that I knew; and on the fourth
day, when he came back at twilight, I perceived an actual surliness that was quite foreign to his nature.

"What's wrong?" I ventured to inquire. "Have you struck a
snag? Or is old Chapman's meadow getting on your nerves
with its ghostly influences?"

He seemed, for once, to make an effort to throw off his
gloom, his taciturnity and ill humor.

"It's the infernal mystery of the thing," he declared. "I've
simply got to solve it, in one way or another. The place has an
entity of its own—an indwelling personality. It's there, like the
soul in a human body, but I can't pin it down or touch it. You
know that I'm not superstitious—but, on the other hand, I'm
not a bigoted materialist, either; and I've run across some odd
phenomena in my time. That meadow, perhaps, is inhabited by

what the ancients called a *Genius Loci*. More than once, before
this, I have suspected that such things might exist—might re-
side, inherent, in some particular spot. But this is the first time
that I've had reason to suspect anything of an actively malignant or inimical nature. The other influences, whose presence
I have felt, were benign in some large, vague, impersonal way
—or were else wholly indifferent to human welfare—perhaps
oblivious of human existence. This thing, however, is hatefully
aware and watchful: I feel that the meadow itself—or the force
embodied in the meadow—is scrutinizing me all the time. The
place has the air of a thirsty vampire, waiting to drink me in
somehow, if it can. It is a *cul-de-sac* of everything evil, in which
an unwary soul might well be caught and absorbed. But I tell
you, Murray, I can't keep away from it."

"It looks as if the place *were* getting you," I said, thoroughly
astonished by his extraordinary declaration, and by the air of
fearful and morbid conviction with which he uttered it.

Apparently he had not heard me, for he made no reply to
my observation. "There's another angle," he went on, with a
feverish tensity in his voice. "You remember my impression of
an old man lurking in the background and watching me, on
my first visit. Well, I have seen him again, many times, out of
the corner of my eye; and during the last two days, he has appeared more directly, though in a queer, partial way. Sometimes, when I am studying the dead willow very intently, I see
his scowling filthy-bearded face as a part of the bole. Then,
again, it will float among the leafless twigs, as if it had been
caught there. Sometimes a knotty hand, a tattered coat-sleeve,
will emerge through the mantling algae in the pool, as if a
drowned body were rising to the surface. Then, a moment
later—or simultaneously—there will be something of him
among the alders or the cat-tails. These apparitions are always
brief, and when I try to scutinize them closely, they melt like
films of vapor into the surrounding scene. But the old
scoundrel, whoever or whatever he may be, is a sort of fixture.
He is no less vile than everything else about the place, though
I feel that he isn't the main element of the vileness."

"Good Lord!" I exclaimed. "You certainly have been seeing
things. If you don't mind, I'll come down and join you for

a while, tomorrow afternoon. The mystery begins to inveigle me."

"Of course I don't mind. Come ahead." His manner, all at
once, for no tangible reason, had resumed the unnatural taciturnity of the past four days. He gave me a furtive look that
was sullen and almost unfriendly. It was as if an obscure barrier, temporarily laid aside, had again risen between us. The
shadows of his strange mood returned upon him visibly; and
my efforts to continue the conversation were rewarded only by
half-surly, half-absent monosyllables. Feeling an aroused concern, rather than any offense, I began to note, for the first
time, the unwonted pallor of his face, and the bright, febrile
luster of his eyes. He looked vaguely unwell, I thought, as if
something of his exuberant vitality had gone out of him, and
had left in its place an alien energy of doubtful and less healthy
nature. Tacitly, I gave up any attempt to bring him back from
the secretive twilight into which he had withdrawn. For the
rest of the evening, I pretended to read a novel, while Amberville maintained his singular abstraction. Somewhat inconclusively, I puzzled over the matter till bedtime. I made up my
mind, however, that I would visit Chapman's meadow. I did
not believe in the supernatural, but it seemed apparent that the
place was exerting a deleterious influence upon Amberville.

The next morning, when I arose, my Chinese servant informed me that the painter had already breakfasted and had
gone out with his easel and colors. This further proof of his
obsession troubled me; but I applied myself rigorously to a
forenoon of writing.

Immediately after luncheon, I drove down the highway, followed the narrow dirt road that branched off toward Bear
River, and left my car on the pine-thick hill above the old
Chapman place. Though I had never visited the meadow, I
had a pretty clear idea of its location. Disregarding the grassy,
half-obliterated road into the upper portion of the property,
I struck down through the woods into the little blind valley,
seeing more than once, on the opposite slope, the dying orchard of pear and apple trees, and the tumbledown shanty that
had belonged to the Chapmans.

It was a warm October day; and the serene solitude of the

forest, the autumnal softness of light and air, made the idea of anything malign or sinister seem impossible. When I came to the meadow bottom, I was ready to laugh at Amberville's notions; and the place itself, at first sight, merely impressed me as being rather dreary and dismal. The features of the scene were those that he had described so clearly, but I could not find the open evil that had leered from the pool, the willow, the alders and the cat-tails in his drawings.

Amberville, with his back toward me, was seated on a folding stool before his easel, which he had placed among the plots of dark green wire-grass in the open ground above the pool. He did not seem to be working, however, but was staring intently at the scene beyond him, while a loaded brush drooped idly in his fingers. The sedges deadened my footfalls; and he did not hear me as I drew near.

With much curiosity, I peered over his shoulder at the large canvas on which he had been engaged. As far as I could tell, the picture had already been carried to a consummate degree of technical perfection. It was an almost photographic rendering of the scummy water, the whitish skeleton of the leaning willow, the unhealthy, half-disrooted alders, and the cluster of nodding mace-reeds. But in it I found the macabre and demoniac spirit of the sketches: the meadow seemed to wait and watch like an evilly distorted face. It was a deadfall of malignity and despair, lying apart from the autumn world around it; a plague-spot of nature, for ever accursed and alone.

Again I looked at the landscape itself—and saw that the spot was indeed as Amberville had depicted it. It wore the grimace of a mad vampire, hateful and alert! At the same time, I became disagreeably conscious of the unnatural silence. There were no birds, no insects, as the painter had said; and it seemed that only spent and dying winds could ever enter that depressed valley-bottom. The thin stream that lost itself in the boggy ground was like a soul that went down to perdition. It was part of the mystery, too; for I could not remember any stream on the lower side of the barring hill that would indicate a subterranean outlet.

Amberville's intentness, and the very posture of his head and shoulders, were like those of a man who has been mesmerized. I was about to make my presence known to him; but at that instant there came to me the apperception that we were not alone in the meadow. Just beyond the focus of my vision, a figure seemed to stand in a furtive attitude, as if watching us both. I whirled about—and there was no one. Then I heard a startled cry from Amberville, and turned to find him staring at me. His features wore a wild look of terror and surprise, which had not wholly erased a hypnotic absorption.

"My God!" he said. "I thought you were the old man!"

I can not be sure whether anything more was said by either of us. I have, however, the impression of a blank silence. After his single exclamation of surprise, Amberville seemed to retreat into an impenetrable abstraction, as if he were no longer conscious of my presence; as if, having identified me, he had forgotten me at once. On my part, I felt a weird and overpowering constraint. That infamous, eery scene depressed me beyond measure. It seemed that the boggy bottom was trying to drag me down in some intangible way. The boughs of the sick alders beckoned. The pool, over which the bony willow presided like an arboreal death, was wooing me foully with its stagnant waters.

Moreover, apart from the ominous atmosphere of the scene itself, I was painfully aware of a further change in Amberville— a change that was an actual alienation. His recent mood, whatever it was, had strengthened upon him enormously: he had gone deeper into its morbid twilight, and was lost to the blithe and sanguine personality I had known. It was as if an incipient madness had seized him; and the possibility of this terrified me.

In a slow, somnambulistic manner, without giving me a second glance, he began to work at his painting, and I watched him for a while, hardly knowing what to do or say. For long intervals he would stop and peer with dreamy intentness at some feature of the landscape. I conceived the bizarre idea of a growing kinship, a mysterious *rapport* between Amberville and the meadow. In some intangible way, it seemed as if the place had taken something from his very soul—and had given something of itself in exchange. He wore the air of one who participates in some unholy secret, who has become the acolyte of an unhuman knowledge. In a flash of horrible definitude, I saw the place as an actual vampire, and Amberville as its willing victim.

How long I remained there, I can not say. Finally I stepped over to him and shook him roughly by the shoulder.

"You're working too hard," I said. "Take my advice, and lay off for a day or two."

He turned to me with the dazed look of one who is lost in some narcotic dream. This, very slowly, gave place to a sullen, evil anger.

"Oh, go to hell!" he snarled. "Can't you see that I'm busy?"

I left him then, for there seemed nothing else to do under the circumstances. The mad and spectral nature of the whole affair was enough to make me doubt my own reason. My impressions of the meadow—and of Amberville—were tainted with an insidious horror such as I had never before felt in any moment of waking life and normal consciousness.

At the bottom of the slope of yellow pine, I turned back with repugnant curiosity for a parting glance. The painter had not moved, he was still confronting the malignant scene like a charmed bird that faces a lethal serpent. Whether or not the impression was a double optic image, I have never been sure: but at that instant I seemed to discern a faint, unholy aura, neither light nor mist, that flowed and wavered about the meadow, preserving the outlines of the willow, the alders, the reeds, the pool. Stealthily it appeared to lengthen, reaching toward Amberville like ghostly arms. The whole image was extremely tenuous, and may well have been an illusion; but it sent me shuddering into the shelter of the tall, benignant pines.

The remainder of that day, and the evening that followed, were tinged with the shadowy horror I had found in Chapman's meadow. I believe that I spent most of the time in arguing vainly with myself, in trying to convince the rational part of my mind that all I had seen and felt was utterly preposterous. I could arrive at no conclusion, other than a conviction that Amberville's mental health was endangered by the damnable thing, whatever it was, that inhered in the meadow. The malign personality of the place, the impalpable terror, mystery and lure, were like webs that had been woven upon my brain, and which I could not dissipate by any amount of conscious effort.

I made two resolves, however: one was, that I should write immediately to Amberville's fiancée, Miss Avis Olcott, and invite her to visit me as a fellow-guest of the artist during the remainder of his stay at Bowman. Her influence, I thought, might help to counteract whatever was affecting him so perniciously. Since I knew her fairly well, the invitation would not seem out of the way. I decided to say nothing about it to Amberville: the element of surprise, I hoped, would be especially beneficial.

My second resolve was, that I should not again visit the meadow myself, if I could avoid it. Indirectly—for I knew the folly of trying to combat a mental obsession openly—I should also try to discourage the painter's interest in the place, and divert his attention to other themes. Trips and entertainments, too, could be devised, at the minor cost of delaying my own work.

The smoky autumn twilight overtook me in such meditations as these; but Amberville did not return. Horrible premonitions, without coherent shape or name, began to torment me as I waited for him. The night darkened; and dinner grew cold on the table. At last, about nine o'clock, when I was nerving myself to go out and hunt for him, he came in hurriedly. He was pale, dishevelled, out of breath; and his eyes held a painful glare, as if something had frightened him beyond endurance.

He did not apologize for his lateness; nor did he refer to my own visit to the meadow-bottom. Apparently he had forgotten the whole episode—had forgotten his rudeness to me.

"I'm through!" he cried. "I'll never go back again—never take another chance. That place is more hellish at night than in the daytime. I can't tell you what I've seen and felt—I must forget it, if I can. There's an emanation—something that comes out openly in the absence of the sun, but is latent by day. It lured me, it tempted me to remain this evening—and it nearly got me. . . . God! I didn't believe that such things were possible—that abhorrent compound of—" He broke off, and did not finish the sentence. His eyes dilated, as if with the memory of something too awful to be described. At that moment, I recalled the poisonously haunted eyes of old Chapman, whom I had sometimes met about the hamlet. He had not interested me particularly, since I had deemed him a common type of rural character, with a tendency to some obscure and unpleasant aberration. Now, when I saw the same look in the eyes of a sensitive artist, I began to wonder, with a shivering speculation, whether Chapman too had been aware of the weird evil that dwelt in his meadow. Perhaps, in some way that was beyond human comprehension, he had been its victim. . . . He had died there; and his death had not seemed at all mysterious. But perhaps, in the light of all that Amberville and I had perceived, there was more in the matter than any one had suspected.

"Tell me what you saw," I ventured to suggest.

At the question, a veil seemed to fall between us, impalpable but tenebrific. He shook his head morosely and made no reply. The human terror, which perhaps had driven him back toward his normal self, and had made him almost communicative for the nonce, fell away from Amberville. A shadow that was darker than fear, an impenetrable alien umbrage, again submerged him. I felt a sudden chill, of the spirit rather than the flesh; and once more there came to me the outré thought of his growing kinship with the ghoulish meadow. Beside me, in the lamplit room, behind the mask of his humanity, a thing that was not wholly human seemed to sit and wait.

Of the nightmarish days that followed, I shall offer only a summary. It would be impossible to convey the eventless, fantasmal horror in which we dwelt and moved.

I wrote immediately to Miss Olcott, pressing her to pay me a visit during Amberville's stay, and, in order to insure acceptance, I hinted obscurely at my concern for his health and my need of her coadjutation. In the meanwhile, waiting her answer, I tried to divert the artist by suggesting trips to sundry points of scenic interest in the neighborhood. These suggestions he declined, with an aloof curtness, an air that was stony and cryptic rather than deliberately rude. Virtually, he ignored my existence, and made it more than plain that he wished me to leave him to his own devices. This, in despair, I finally decided to do, pending the arrival of Miss Olcott. He went out early each morning, as usual, with his paints and easel, and returned about sunset or a little later. He did not tell me where he had been; and I refrained from asking.

Miss Olcott came on the third day following my letter, in the afternoon. She was young, lissome, ultra-feminine, and was altogether devoted to Amberville. In fact, I think she was a little in awe of him. I told her as much as I dared, and warned her of the morbid change in her fiancé, which I attributed to nervousness and overwork. I simply could not bring myself to mention Chapman's meadow and its baleful influence: the whole thing was too unbelievable, too fantasmagoric, to be offered as an explanation to a modern girl. When I saw the somewhat helpless alarm and bewilderment with which she listened to my story, I began to wish that she were of a more wilful and determined type, and were less submissive toward Amberville than I surmised her to be. A stronger woman might have saved him; but even then I began to doubt whether Avis could do anything to combat the imponderable evil that was engulfing him.

A heavy crescent moon was hanging like a blood-dipped horn in the twilight when he returned. To my immense relief, the presence of Avis appeared to have a highly salutary effect. The very moment that he saw her, Amberville came out of the singular eclipse that had claimed him, as I feared, beyond redemption, and was almost his former affable self. Perhaps it was all make-believe, for an ulterior purpose; but this, at the time, I could not suspect. I began to congratulate myself on having applied a sovereign remedy. The girl, on her part, was plainly relieved; though I saw her eyeing him in a slightly hurt and puzzled way, when he sometimes fell for a short interval into moody abstraction, as if he had temporarily forgotten her. On the whole, however, there was a transformation that appeared no less than magical, in view of his recent gloom and remoteness. After a decent interim, I left the pair together, and retired.

I rose very late the next morning, having overslept. Avis and Amberville I learned, had gone out together, carrying a lunch which my Chinese cook had provided. Plainly he was taking her along on one of his artistic expeditions; and I augured well for his recovery from this. Somehow, it never occurred to me that he had taken her to Chapman's meadow. The tenuous, malignant shadow of the whole affair had begun to lift from my mind; I rejoiced in a lightened sense of responsibility; and, for the first time in a week, was able to concentrate clearly on the ending of my novel.

The two returned at dusk, and I saw immediately that I had been mistaken on more points than one. Amberville had again retired into a sinister, saturnine reserve. The girl, beside his looming height and massive shoulders, looked very small, forlorn—and pitifully bewildered and frightened. It was as if she had encountered something altogether beyond her comprehension, something with which she was humanly powerless to cope.

Very little was said by either of them. They did not tell me where they had been; but, for that matter, it was unnecessary to inquire. Amberville's taciturnity, as usual, seemed due to an absorption in some dark mood or sullen revery. But Avis gave me the impression of a dual constraint—as if, apart from some enthralling terror, she had been forbidden to speak of the day's events and experiences. I knew that they had gone to that accursed meadow; but I was far from sure whether Avis had been personally conscious of the weird and baneful entity of the place, or had merely been frightened by the unwholesome change in her lover beneath its influence. In either case, it was obvious that she was wholly subservient to him. I began to damn myself for a fool in having invited her to Bowman—though the true bitterness of my regret was still to come.

A week went by, with the same daily excursions of the painter and his fiancée—the same baffling, sinister estrangement and secrecy in Amberville—the same terror, helplessness, constraint and submissiveness in the girl. How it would all end, I could not imagine; but I feared, from the ominous alteration of his character, that Amberville was heading for some form of mental alienation, if nothing worse. My offers of entertainment and scenic journeys were rejected by the pair; and several blunt efforts to question Avis were met by a wall of almost hostile evasion which convinced me that Amberville had enjoined her to secrecy—and had perhaps, in some sleightful manner, misrepresented my own attitude toward him.

"You don't understand him," she said, repeatedly. "He is very temperamental."

The whole affair was a maddening mystery, but it seemed more and more that the girl herself was being drawn, either directly or indirectly, into the same fantasmal web that had enmeshed the artist.

I surmised that Amberville had done several new pictures of the meadow; but he did not show them to me, nor even mention them. My own impressions of the place, as time went on, assumed an unaccountable vividness that was almost hallucinatory. The incredible idea of some inherent force or personality, malevolent and even vampirish, became an unavowed conviction against my will. The place haunted me like a fantasm, horrible but seductive. I felt an impelling morbid curiosity, an unwholesome desire to visit it again, and fathom, if possible, its enigma. Often I thought of Amberville's notion about a *Genius Loci* that dwelt in the meadow, and the hints of a human apparition that was somehow associated with the spot. Also, I wondered what it was that the artist had seen on the one occasion when he had lingered in the meadow after nightfall, and had returned to my house in driven terror. It seemed that he had not ventured to repeat the experiment, in spite of his obvious subjection to the unknown lure.

The end came, abruptly and without premonition. Business had taken me to the county seat, one afternoon, and I did not return till late in the evening. A full moon was high above the pine-dark hills. I expected to find Avis and the painter in my drawing-room; but they were not there. Li Sing, my factotum, told me that they had returned at dinnertime. An hour later, Amberville had gone out quietly while the girl was in her room. Coming down a few minutes later, Avis had shown excessive perturbation when she found him absent, and had also left the house, as if to follow him, without telling Li Sing where she was going or when she might return. All this had occurred three hours previously; and neither of the pair had yet reappeared.

A black and subtly chilling intuition of evil seized me as I listened to Li Sing's account. All too well I surmised that Amberville had yielded to the temptation of a second nocturnal visit to that unholy meadow. An occult attraction, somehow, had overcome the horror of his first experience, whatever it had been. Avis, knowing where he was, and perhaps fearful of his sanity—or safety—had gone out to find him. More and more, I felt an imperative conviction of some peril that threatened them both—some hideous and innominable thing to whose power, perhaps, they had already yielded.

Whatever my previous folly and remissness in the matter, I did not delay now. A few minutes of driving at precipitate speed through the mellow moonlight brought me to the piny edge of the Chapman property. There, as on my former visit, I left the car, and plunged headlong through the shadowy forest. Far down, in the hollow, as I went, I heard a single scream, shrill with terror, and abruptly terminated. I felt sure that the voice was that of Avis; but I did not hear it again.

Running desperately, I emerged in the meadow-bottom. Neither Avis nor Amberville was in sight; and it seemed to me, in my hasty scrutiny, that the place was full of mysteriously coiling and moving vapors that permitted only a partial view of the dead willow and the other vegetation. I ran on toward the scummy pool, and nearing it, was arrested by a sudden and twofold horror.

Avis and Amberville were floating together in the shallow pool, with their bodies half hidden by the mantling masses of algae. The girl was clasped tightly in the painter's arms, as if he had carried her with him, against her will, to that noisome death. Her face was covered by the evil, greenish scum; and I could not see the face of Amberville, which was averted against her shoulder. It seemed that there had been a struggle; but both were quiet now, and had yielded supinely to their doom.

It was not this spectacle alone, however, that drove me in mad and shuddering flight from the meadow, without making even the most tentative attempt to retrieve the drowned bodies. The true horror lay in the thing, which, from a little distance, I had taken for the coils of a slowly moving and rising mist. It was *not* vapor, nor anything else that could conceivably exist— that malign, luminous, pallid emanation that enfolded the entire scene before me like a restless and hungrily wavering extension of its outlines—a phantom projection of the pale and deathlike willow, the dying alders, the reeds, the stagnant pool and its suicidal victims. The landscape was visible through it, as through a film; but it seemed to curdle and thicken gradually in places, with some unholy, terrifying activity. Out of these curdlings, as if disgorged by the ambient exhalation, I saw the emergence of three human faces that partook of the same nebulous matter, neither mist nor plasm. One of these faces seemed to detach itself from the bole of the ghostly willow; the second and third swirled upward from the seething of the phantom pool, with their bodies trailing formlessly among the tenuous boughs. The faces were those of old Chapman, of Francis Amberville, and Avis Olcott.

Behind this eery, wraith-like projection of itself, the actual landscape leered with the same infernal and vampirish air which it had worn by day. But it seemed now that the place was no longer still—that it seethed with a malignant secret life—that it reached out toward me with its scummy waters, with the bony fingers of its trees, with the spectral faces it had spewed forth from its lethal deadfall.

Even terror was frozen within me for a moment. I stood watching, while the pale, unhallowed exhalation rose higher above the meadow. The three human faces, through a further agitation of the curdling mass, began to approach each other. Slowly, inexpressibly, they merged in one, becoming an androgynous face, neither young nor old, that melted finally into the lengthening phantom boughs of the willow—the hands of the arboreal death, that were reaching out to enfold me. Then, unable to bear the spectacle any longer, I started to run.

There is little more that need be told, for nothing that I could add to this narrative would lessen the abominable mystery of it all in any degree. The meadow—or the thing that dwells in the meadow—has already claimed three victims . . . and I sometimes wonder if it will have a fourth. I alone, it would seem, among the living, have guessed the secret of Chapman's death, and the death of Avis and Amberville; and no one else, apparently, has felt the malign genius of the meadow. I have not returned there, since the morning when the bodies of the artist and his fiancée were removed from the pool . . . nor have I summoned up the resolution to destroy or otherwise dispose of the four oil paintings and two water-color drawings of the spot that were made by Amberville. Perhaps . . . in spite of all that deters me . . . I shall visit it again.

1933

ROBERT BLOCH

(1917–1994)

The Cloak

THE sun was dying, and its blood spattered the sky as it crept into a sepulcher behind the hills. The keening wind sent the dry, fallen leaves scurrying toward the west, as though hastening them to the funeral of the sun.

"Nuts!" said Henderson to himself, and stopped thinking.

The sun was setting in a dingy red sky, and a dirty raw wind was kicking up the half-rotten leaves in a filthy gutter. Why should he waste time with cheap imagery?

"Nuts!" said Henderson, again.

It was probably a mood evoked by the day, he mused. After all, this was the sunset of Halloween. Tonight was the dreaded Allhallows Eve, when spirits walked and skulls cried out from their graves beneath the earth.

Either that, or tonight was just another rotten cold fall day. Henderson sighed. There was a time, he reflected, when the coming of this night meant something. A dark Europe, groaning in superstitious fear, dedicated this Eve to the grinning Unknown. A million doors had once been barred against the evil visitants, a million prayers mumbled, a million candles lit. There was something majestic about the idea, Henderson reflected. Life had been an adventure in those times, and men walked in terror of what the next turn of a midnight road might bring. They had lived in a world of demons and ghouls and elementals who sought their souls—and by Heaven, in those days a man's soul meant something. This new skepticism had taken a profound meaning away from life. Men no longer revered their souls.

"Nuts!" said Henderson again, quite automatically. There was something crude and twentieth-century about the coarse expression which always checked his introspective flights of fancy.

The voice in his brain that said "nuts" took the place of humanity to Henderson—common humanity which would

698

echo the same sentiment upon hearing his secret thoughts. So now Henderson uttered the word and endeavored to forget problems and purple patches alike.

He was walking down this street at sunset to buy a costume for the masquerade party tonight, and he had much better concentrate on finding the costumer's before it closed than waste his time daydreaming about Halloween.

His eyes searched the darkening shadows of the dingy buildings lining the narrow thoroughfare. Once again he peered at the address he had scribbled down after finding it in the phone book.

Why the devil didn't they light up the shops when it got dark? He couldn't make out numbers. This was a poor, run-down neighborhood, but after all—

Abruptly, Henderson spied the place across the street and started over. He passed the window and glanced in. The last rays of the sun slanted over the top of the building across the way and fell directly on the window and its display. Henderson drew a sharp intake of breath.

He was staring at a costumer's window—not looking through a fissure into hell. Then why was it all red fire, lighting the grinning visages of fiends?

"Sunset," Henderson muttered aloud. Of course it was, and the faces were merely clever masks such as would be displayed in this sort of place. Still, it gave the imaginative man a start. He opened the door and entered.

The place was dark and still. There was a smell of loneliness in the air—the smell that haunts all places long undisturbed; tombs, and graves in deep woods, and caverns in the earth, and—

"Nuts."

What the devil was wrong with him, anyway? Henderson smiled apologetically at the empty darkness. This was the smell of the costumer's shop, and it carried him back to college days of amateur theatricals. Henderson had known this smell of moth balls, decayed furs, grease paint and oils. He had played amateur Hamlet and in his hands he had held a smirking skull that hid all knowledge in its empty eyes—a skull, from the costumer's.

Well, here he was again, and the skull gave him the idea.

After all, Halloween night it was. Certainly in this mood of his he didn't want to go as a rajah, or a Turk, or a pirate—they all did that. Why not go as a fiend, or a warlock, or a werewolf? He could see Lindstrom's face when he walked into the elegant penthouse wearing rags of some sort. The fellow would have a fit, with his society crowd wearing their expensive Elsa Maxwell take-offs. Henderson didn't greatly care for Lindstrom's sophisticated friends anyway; a gang of amateur Noel Cowards and horsy women wearing harnesses of jewels. Why not carry out the spirit of Halloween and go as a monster?

Henderson stood there in the dusk, waiting for someone to turn on the lights, come out from the back room and serve him. After a minute or so he grew impatient and rapped sharply on the counter.

"Say in there! Service!"

Silence. And a shuffling noise from the rear, then—an unpleasant noise to hear in the gloom. There was a banging from downstairs and then the heavy clump of footsteps. Suddenly Henderson gasped. A black bulk was rising from the floor!

It was, of course, only the opening of the trapdoor from the basement. A man shuffled behind the counter, carrying a lamp. In that light his eyes blinked drowsily.

The man's yellowish face crinkled into a smile.

"I was sleeping, I'm afraid," said the man, softly. "Can I serve you, sir?"

"I was looking for a Halloween costume."

"Oh, yes. And what was it you had in mind?"

The voice was weary, infinitely weary. The eyes continued to blink in the flabby yellow face.

"Nothing usual, I'm afraid. You see, I rather fancied some sort of monster getup for a party—don't suppose you carry anything in that line?"

"I could show you masks."

"No. I meant werewolf outfits, something of the sort. More of the authentic."

"So. The *authentic*."

"Yes." Why did this old dunce stress the word?

"I might—yes. I might have just the. thing for you, sir." The eyes blinked, but the thin mouth pursed in a smile. "Just the thing for Halloween."

"What's that?"

"Have you ever considered the possibility of being a vampire?"

"Like Dracula ?"

"Ah—yes, I suppose—Dracula."

"Not a bad idea. Do you think I'm the type for that, though?"

The man appraised him with that tight smile. "Vampires are of all types, I understand. You would do nicely."

"Hardly a compliment," Henderson chuckled. "But why not? What's the outfit?"

"Outfit? Merely evening clothes, or what you wear. I will furnish you with the authentic cloak."

"Just a cloak—is that all?"

"Just a cloak. But it is worn like a shroud. It *is* shroud-cloth, you know. Wait, I'll get it for you."

The shuffling feet carried the man into the rear of the shop again. Down the trapdoor entrance he went, and Henderson waited. There was more banging, and presently the old man reappeared carrying the cloak. He was shaking dust from it in the darkness.

"Here it is—the genuine cloak."

"Genuine?"

"Allow me to adjust it for you—it will work wonders, I'm sure."

The cold, heavy cloth hung draped about Henderson's shoulders. The faint odor rose mustily in his nostrils as he stepped back and surveyed himself in the mirror. The lamp was poor, but Henderson saw that the cloak effected a striking transformation in his appearance. His long face seemed thinner, his eyes were accentuated in the facial pallor heightened by the somber cloak he wore. It was a big, black shroud.

"Genuine," murmured the old man. He must have come up suddenly, for Henderson hadn't noticed him in the glass.

"I'll take it," Henderson said. "How much?"

"You'll find it quite entertaining, I'm sure."

"How much?"

"Oh. Shall we say five dollars?"

"Here."

The old man took the money, blinking, and drew the cloak

from Henderson's shoulders. When it slid away he felt suddenly warm again. It must be cold in the basement—the cloth was icy.

The old man wrapped the garment, smiling, and handed it over.

"I'll have it back tomorrow," Henderson promised.

"No need. You purchased it. It is yours."

"But—"

"I am leaving business shortly. Keep it. You will find more use for it than I, surely."

"But—"

"A pleasant evening to you."

Henderson made his way to the door in confusion, then turned to salute the blinking old man in the dimness.

Two eyes were burning at him from across the counter—two eyes that did not blink.

"Good night," said Henderson, and closed the door quickly. He wondered if he were going just a trifle mad.

At eight, Henderson nearly called up Lindstrom to tell him he couldn't make it. The cold chills came the minute he put on the damned cloak, and when he looked at himself in the mirror his blurred eyes could scarcely make out the reflection.

But after a few drinks he felt better about it. He hadn't eaten, and the liquor warmed his blood. He paced the floor, attitudinizing with the cloak—sweeping it about him and scowling in what he thought was a ferocious manner. Damn it, he was going to be a vampire all right! He called a cab, went down to the lobby. The driver came in, and Henderson was waiting, black cloak furled.

"I wish you to drive me," he said in a low voice.

The cabman took one look at him in the cloak and turned pale.

"Whazzat?"

"I ordered you to come," said Henderson gutturally, while he quaked with inner mirth. He leered ferociously and swept the cloak back.

"Yeah, yeah. O.K."

The driver almost ran outside. Henderson stalked after him.

"Where to, boss—I mean, sir?"

The frightened face didn't turn as Henderson intoned the address and sat back.

The cab started with a lurch that set Henderson to chuckling deeply, in character. At the sound of the laughter the driver got panicky and raced his engine up to the limit set by the governor. Henderson laughed loudly, and the impressionable driver fairly quivered in his seat. It was quite a ride, but Henderson was entirely unprepared to open the door and find it slammed after him as the cabman drove hastily away without collecting a fare.

"I must look the part," he thought complacently, as he took the elevator up to the penthouse apartment.

There were three or four others in the elevator; Henderson had seen them before at other affairs Lindstrom had invited him to attend, but nobody seemed to recognize him. It rather pleased him to think how his wearing of an unfamiliar cloak and an unfamiliar scowl seemed to change his entire personality and appearance. Here the other guests had donned elaborate disguises—one woman wore the costume of a Watteau shepherdess, another was attired as a Spanish ballerina, a tall man dressed as Pagliacci, and his companion had donned a toreador outfit. Yet Henderson recognized them all; knew that their expensive habiliments were not truly disguises at all, but merely elaborations calculated to enhance their appearance. Most people at costume parties gave vent to suppressed desires. The women showed off their figures, the men either accentuated their masculinity as the toreador did, or clowned it. Such things were pitiful; these conventional fools eagerly doffing their dismal business suits and rushing off to a lodge, or amateur theatrical, or mask ball in order to satisfy their starving imaginations. Why didn't they dress in garish colors on the street? Henderson often pondered the question.

Surely, these society folk in the elevator were fine-looking men and women in their outfits—so healthy, so red-faced, and full of vitality. They had such robust throats and necks. Henderson looked at the plump arms of the woman next to him. He stared, without realizing it, for a long moment. And then, he saw that the occupants of the car had drawn away from him. They were standing in the corner, as though they feared his cloak and scowl, and his eyes fixed on the woman. Their chatter had ceased abruptly. The woman looked at him, as though she were about to speak, when the elevator doors opened and afforded Henderson a welcome respite.

What the devil was wrong? First the cab driver, then the woman. Had he drunk too much?

Well, no chance to consider that. Here was Marcus Lindstrom, and he was thrusting a glass into Henderson's hand.

"What have we here? Ah, a bogy-man!" It needed no second glance to perceive that Lindstrom, as usual at such affairs, was already quite bottle-dizzy. The fat host was positively swimming in alcohol.

"Have a drink, Henderson, my lad! I'll take mine from the bottle. That outfit of yours gave me a shock. Where'd you get the makeup?"

"Make-up? I'm not wearing any make-up."

"Oh. So you're not. How . . . silly of me."

Henderson wondered if he were crazy. Had Lindstrom really drawn back? Were his eyes actually filled with a certain dismay? Oh, the man was obviously intoxicated.

"I'll . . . I'll see you later," babbled Lindstrom, edging away and quickly turning to the other arrivals. Henderson watched the back of Lindstrom's neck. It was fat and white. It bulged over the collar of his costume and there was a vein in it. A vein in Lindstrom's fat neck. Frightened Lindstrom.

Henderson stood alone in the ante-room. From the parlor beyond came the sound of music and laughter; party noises. Henderson hesitated before entering. He drank from the glass in his hand—Bacardi rum, and powerful. On top of his other drinks it almost made the man reel. But he drank, wondering. What was wrong with him and his costume? Why did he frighten people? Was he unconsciously acting his vampire role? That crack of Lindstrom's about make-up now—

Acting on impulse, Henderson stepped over to the long panel mirror in the hall. He lurched a little, then stood in the harsh light before it. He faced the glass, stared into the mirror, and saw nothing.

He looked at himself in the mirror, and there was no one there!

Henderson began to laugh softly, evilly, deep in his throat.

And as he gazed into the empty, unreflecting glass, his laughter rose in black glee.

"*I'm drunk*," he whispered. "I must be drunk. Mirror in my apartment made me blurred. Now I'm so far gone I can't see straight. Sure I'm drunk. Been acting ridiculously, scaring people. Now I'm seeing hallucinations—or not seeing them, rather. Visions. Angels."

His voice lowered. "Sure, angels. Standing right in back of me, now. Hello, angel."

"Hello."

Henderson whirled. There she stood, in the dark cloak, her hair a shimmering halo above her white, proud face; her eyes celestial blue, and her lips infernal red.

"Are you real?" asked Henderson, gently. "Or am I a fool to believe in miracles?"

"This miracle's name is Sheila Darrly, and it would like to powder its nose if you please."

"Kindly use this mirror through the courtesy of Stephen Henderson," replied the cloaked man, with a grin. He stepped back a ways, eyes intent.

The girl turned her head and favored him with a slow, impish smile. "Haven't you ever seen powder used before?" she asked.

"Didn't know angels indulged in cosmetics," Henderson replied. "But then there's a lot I don't know about angels. From now on I shall make them a special study of mine. There's so much I want to find out. So you'll probably find me following you around with a notebook all evening."

"Notebooks for a vampire?"

"Oh, but I'm a very intelligent vampire—not one of those backwoods Transylvanian types. You'll find me charming, I'm sure."

"Yes, you look like the sure type," the girl mocked. "But an angel and a vampire—that's a queer combination."

"We can reform one another," Henderson pointed out. "Besides, I have a suspicion that there's a bit of the devil in you. That dark cloak over your angel costume; dark angel, you know. Instead of heaven you might hail from my home town."

Henderson was flippant, but underneath his banter cyclonic

thoughts whirled. He recalled discussions in the past; cynical observations he had made and believed.

Once, Henderson had declared that there was no such thing as love at first sight, save in books or plays where such a dramatic device served to speed up action. He asserted that people learned about romance from books and plays and accordingly adopted a belief in love at first sight when all one could possibly feel was desire.

And now this Sheila—this blond angel—had to come along and drive out all thoughts of morbidity, all thoughts of drunkenness and foolish gazings into mirrors, from his mind; had to send him madly plunging into dreams of red lips, ethereal blue eyes and slim white arms.

Something of his feelings had swept into his eyes, and as the girl gazed up at him she felt the truth.

"Well," she breathed, "I hope the inspection pleases."

"A miracle of understatement, that. But there was something I wanted to find out particularly about divinity. Do angels dance?"

"Tactful vampire! The next room?"

Arm in arm they entered the parlor. The merrymakers were in full swing. Liquor had already pitched gaiety at its height, but there was no dancing any longer. Boisterous little grouped couples laughed arm in arm about the room. The usual party gagsters were performing their antics in corners. The superficial atmosphere, which Henderson detested, was fully in evidence.

It was reaction which made Henderson draw himself up to full height and sweep the cloak about his shoulders. Reaction brought the scowl to his pale face, caused him to stalk along in brooding silence. Sheila seemed to regard this as a great joke.

"*Pull* a vampire act on them," she giggled, clutching his arm. Henderson accordingly scowled at the couples, sneered horrendously at the women. And his progress was marked by the turning of heads, the abrupt cessation of chatter. He walked through the long room like Red Death incarnate. Whispers trailed in his wake.

"Who is that man?"

"We came up with him in the elevator, and he—"

"His eyes—"

"Vampire!"

"Hello, Dracula!" It was Marcus Lindstrom and a sullen-looking brunette in Cleopatra costume who lurched toward Henderson. Host Lindstrom could scarcely stand, and his companion in cups was equally at a loss. Henderson liked the man when sober at the club, but his behavior at parties had always irritated him. Lindstrom was particularly objectionable in his present condition—it made him boorish.

"M'dear, I want you t' meet a very dear friend of mind. Yessir, it being Halloween and all, I invited Count Dracula here, t'gether with his daughter. Asked his grandmother, but she's busy tonight at a Black Sabbath—along with Aunt Jemima. Ha! Count, meet my little playmate."

The woman leered up at Henderson.

"Oooh Dracula, what big eyes you have! Oooh, what big teeth you have! Ooooh—"

"Really, Marcus," Henderson protested. But the host had turned and shouted to the room.

"Folks, meet the real goods—only genuine living vampire in captivity! Dracula Henderson, only existing vampire with false teeth."

In any other circumstance Henderson would have given Lindstrom a quick, efficient punch on the jaw. But Sheila was at his side, it was a public gathering; better to humor the man's clumsy jest. Why not be a vampire?

Smiling quickly at the girl, Henderson drew himself erect, faced the crowd, and frowned. His hands brushed the cloak. Funny, it still felt cold. Looking down he noticed for the first time that it was a little dirty at the edges; muddy or dusty. But the cold silk slid through his fingers as he drew it across his breast with one long hand. The feeling seemed to inspire him. He opened his eyes wide and let them blaze. His mouth opened. A sense of dramatic power filled him. And he looked at Marcus Lindstrom's soft, fat neck with the vein standing in the whiteness. He looked at the neck, saw the crowd watching him, and then the impulse seized him. He turned, eyes on that creasy neck—that wabbling, creasy neck of the fat man.

Hands darted out. Lindstrom squeaked like a frightened rat. He was a plump, sleek white rat, bursting with blood. Vampires liked blood. Blood from the rat, from the neck of the rat, from the vein in the neck of the squeaking rat.

"Warm blood."

The deep voice was Henderson's own.

The hands were Henderson's own.

The hands that went around Lindstrom's neck as he spoke, the hands that felt the warmth, that searched out the vein. Henderson's face was bending for the neck, and, as Lindstrom struggled, his grip tightened. Lindstrom's face was turning, turning purple. Blood was rushing to his head. That was good. Blood!

Henderson's mouth opened. He felt the air on his teeth. He bent down toward that fat neck, and then—

"Stop! That's plenty!"

The voice, the cooling voice of Sheila. Her fingers on his arm. Henderson looked up, startled. He released Lindstrom, who sagged with open mouth.

The crowd was staring, and their mouths were all shaped in the instinctive O of amazement.

Sheila whispered, "Bravo! Served him right—but you frightened him!"

Henderson struggled a moment to collect himself. Then he smiled and turned.

"Ladies and gentlemen," he said, "I have just given a slight demonstration to prove to you what our host said of me was entirely correct. I *am* a vampire. Now that you have been given fair warning, I am sure you will be in no further danger. If there is a doctor in the house I can, perhaps, arrange for a blood transfusion."

The O's relaxed and laughter came from startled throats. Hysterical laughter, in part, then genuine. Henderson had carried it off. Marcus Lindstrom alone still stared with eyes that held utter fear. *He* knew.

And then the moment broke, for one of the gagsters ran into the room from the elevator. He had gone downstairs and borrowed the apron and cap of a newsboy. Now he raced through the crowd with a bundle of papers under his arm.

"Extra! Extra! Read all about it! Big Halloween Horror! Extra!"

Laughing guests purchased papers. A woman approached Sheila, and Henderson watched the girl walk away in a daze.

"See you later," she called, and her glance sent fire through his veins. Still, he could not forget the terrible feeling that came over him when he had seized Lindstrom. Why?

Automatically, he accepted a paper from the shouting pseudo-news-boy. "Big Halloween Horror," he had shouted. What was that?

Blurred eyes searched the paper.

Then Henderson reeled back. That headline! It was an *Extra* after all. Henderson scanned the columns with mounting dread.

"Fire in costumer's . . . shortly after 8 p.m. firemen were summoned to the shop of . . . flames beyond control . . . completely demolished . . . damage estimated at . . . peculiarly enough, name of proprietor unknown . . . skeleton found in—"

"No!" gasped Henderson aloud.

He read, reread *that* closely. The skeleton had been found in a box of earth in the cellar beneath the shop. The box was a coffin. There had been two other boxes, empty. The skeleton had been wrapped in a cloak, undamaged by the flames—

And in the hastily penned box at the bottom of the column were eyewitness comments, written up under scareheads of heavy black type. Neighbors had feared the place. Hungarian neighborhood, hints of vampirism, of strangers who entered the shop. One man spoke of a cult believed to have held meetings in the place. Superstition about things sold there—love philters, outlandish charms and weird disguises.

Weird disguises—vampires—cloaks—*his eyes!*

"*This is an authentic cloak.*"

"*I will not be using this much longer. Keep it.*"

Memories of these words screamed through Henderson's brain. He plunged out of the room and rushed to the panel mirror.

A moment, then he flung one arm before his face to shield his eyes from the image that was not there—the missing reflection. *Vampires have no reflections.*

No wonder he looked strange. No wonder arms and necks invited him. He had wanted Lindstrom. Good God!

The cloak had done that, the dark cloak with the stains. The stains of earth, grave-earth. The wearing of the cloak, the cold cloak, had given him the feelings of a true vampire. It was a garment accursed, a thing that had lain on the body of one undead. The rusty stain along one sleeve was blood.

Blood. It would be nice to see blood. To taste its warmth, its red life, flowing.

No. That was insane. He was drunk, crazy.

"Ah. My pale friend, the vampire."

It was Sheila again. And above all horror rose the beating of Henderson's heart. As he looked at her shining eyes, her warm mouth shaped in red invitation, Henderson felt a wave of warmth. He looked at her white throat rising above her dark, shimmering cloak, and another kind of warmth rose. Love, desire, and a—hunger.

She must have seen it in his eyes, but she did not flinch. Instead, her own gaze burned in return.

Sheila loved him, too!

With an impulsive gesture, Henderson ripped the cloak from about his throat. The icy weight lifted. He was free. Somehow, he hadn't wanted to take the cloak off, but he had to. It was a cursed thing, and in another minute he might have taken the girl in his arms, taken her for a kiss and remained to—

But he dared not think of that.

"Tired of masquerading?" she asked. With a similar gesture she, too, removed her cloak and stood revealed in the glory of her angel robe. Her blond, statuesque perfection forced a gasp to Henderson's throat.

"Angel," he whispered.

"Devil," she mocked.

And suddenly they were embracing. Henderson had taken her cloak in his arm with his own. They stood with lips seeking rapture until Lindstrom and a group moved noisily into the anteroom.

At the sight of Henderson the fat host recoiled.

"You—" he whispered. "You are—"

"Just leaving," Henderson smiled. Grasping the girl's arm, he drew her toward the empty elevator. The door shut on Lindstrom's pale, fear-filled face.

"Were we leaving?" Sheila whispered, snuggling against his shoulder.

"We were. But not for earth. We do not go down into my realm, but up—into yours."

"The roof garden?"

"Exactly, my angelic one. I want to talk to you against the background of your own heavens, kiss you amidst the clouds, and—"

Her lips found his as the car rose.

"Angel and devil. What a match!"

"I thought so, too," the girl confessed. "Will our children have halos or horns?"

"Both, I'm sure."

They stepped out onto the deserted rooftop. And once again it was Halloween.

Henderson felt it. Downstairs it was Lindstrom and his society friends, in a drunken costume party. Here it was night, silence, gloom. No light, no music, no drinking, no chatter which made one party identical with another; one night like all the rest. This night was individual here.

The sky was not blue, but black. Clouds hung like the gray beards of hovering giants peering at the round orange globe of the moon. A cold wind blew from the sea, and filled the air with tiny murmurings from afar.

This was the sky that witches flew through to their Sabbath. This was the moon of wizardry, the sable silence of black prayers and whispered invocations. The clouds hid monstrous Presences shambling in summons from afar. It was Halloween.

It was also quite cold.

"Give me my cloak," Sheila whispered. Automatically, Henderson extended the garment, and the girl's body swirled under the dark splendor of the cloth. Her eyes burned up at Henderson with a call he could not resist. He kissed her, trembling.

"You're cold," the girl said. "Put on your cloak."

Yes, Henderson, he thought to himself. Put on your cloak while you stare at her throat. Then, the next time you kiss her you will want her throat and she will give it in love and you will take it in—hunger.

"Put it on, darling—I insist," the girl whispered. Her eyes were impatient, burning with an eagerness to match his own.

Henderson trembled.

Put on the cloak of darkness? The cloak of the grave, the cloak of death, the cloak of the vampire? The evil cloak, filled with a cold life of its own that transformed his face, transformed his mind, made his soul instinct with awful hunger?

"Here."

The girl's slim arms were about him, pushing the cloak onto his shoulders. Her fingers brushed his neck, caressingly, as she linked the cloak about his throat.

Henderson shivered.

Then he felt it—through him—that icy coldness turning to a more dreadful heat. He felt himself expand, felt the sneer cross his face. This was Power!

And the girl before him, her eyes taunting, inviting. He saw her ivory neck, her warm slim neck, waiting. It was waiting for him, for his lips.

For his teeth.

No—it couldn't be. He loved her. His love must conquer this madness. Yes, wear the cloak, defy its power, and take her in his arms as a man, not as a fiend. He must. It was the test.

"Sheila." Funny, how his voice deepened.

"Yes, dear."

"Sheila, I must tell you this."

Her eyes—so alluring. It would be easy!

"Sheila, please. You read the paper tonight."

"Yes."

"I . . . I got my cloak there. I can't explain it. You saw how I took Lindstrom. I wanted to go through with it. Do you understand me? I meant to . . . to bite him. Wearing this damnable thing makes me feel like one of those creatures."

Why didn't her stare change? Why didn't she recoil in horror? Such trusting innocence! Didn't she understand? Why didn't she run? Any moment now he might lose control, seize her.

"I love you, Sheila. Believe that. I love you."

"I know." Her eyes gleamed in the moonlight.

"I want to test it. I want to kiss you, wearing this cloak. I want to feel that my love is stronger than this—thing. If I weaken, promise me you'll break away and run, quickly. But don't misunderstand. I must face this feeling and fight it; I want my love for you to be that pure, that secure. Are you afraid?"

"No." Still she stared at him, just as he stared at her throat. If she knew what was in his mind!

"You don't think I'm crazy? I went to this costumer's—he was a horrible little old man—and he gave me the cloak. Actually told me it was a real vampire's. I thought he was joking, but tonight I didn't see myself in the mirror, and I wanted Lindstrom's neck, and I want you. But I must test it."

"You're not crazy. I know. I'm not afraid."

"Then—"

The girl's face mocked. Henderson summoned his strength. He bent forward, his impulses battling. For a moment he stood there under the ghastly orange moon, and his face was twisted in struggle.

And the girl lured.

Her odd, incredibly red lips parted in a silvery, chuckly laugh as her white arms rose from the black cloak she wore to circle his neck gently. "I know—I knew when I looked in the mirror. I knew you had a cloak like mine—got yours where I got mine—"

Queerly, her lips seemed to elude his as he stood frozen for an instant of shock. Then he felt the icy hardness of her sharp little teeth on his throat, a strangely soothing sting, and an engulfing blackness rising over him.

1939

BIOGRAPHICAL NOTES

NOTE ON THE TEXTS

NOTES

Biographical Notes

Conrad Aiken (August 5, 1889–August 17, 1973) b. Conrad Potter Aiken in Savannah, Georgia, first of four children of William Ford Aiken, a doctor, and Anna Aiken Potter. In February 1901, father shot mother and then killed himself; Aiken discovered the bodies moments later. Adopted by an uncle in Cambridge, Massachusetts. Attended Harvard (1907–11), where he formed close friendship with T. S. Eliot. First book of poetry, *Earth Triumphant* (1914), followed by many others including *The Jig of Forslin* (1916), *Senlin: A Biography* (1918), *The House of Dust* (1920), *Priapus and the Pool* (1922), *Preludes for Memnon* (1931), *Brownstone Eclogues* (1942), and *A Letter from Li Po* (1955). The first of his novels, *Blue Voyage*, appeared in 1927. He published his autobiography *Ushant* in 1952. Received Pulitzer Prize for *Selected Poems* (1930); was Poetry Consultant at the Library of Congress in 1950; won National Book Award for *Collected Poems* (1953) and National Medal for Literature in 1969.

Gertrude Atherton (October 30, 1857–June 14, 1948) b. Gertrude Franklin Horn in San Francisco. Raised by her maternal grandfather after parents separated; attended high school in California and college in Kentucky, but contracted tuberculosis and did not complete her studies. At 19, eloped with George H. Bowen Atherton and lived with him at his mother's estate, Valparaiso Park, in San Francisco. Her first book, *Randolph's of Redwood*, was published anonymously in a local newspaper in 1882. After husband's death, moved to New York and began a professional literary career. She subsequently resided for long periods of time in Germany and England. Over the course of her life, she wrote scores of books, many depicting the early history of California, including *What Dreams May Come* (1889), *Before the Gringo Came* (1894), *The Californians* (1898), *The Conqueror* (1902), *The Bell in the Fog and Other Stories* (1905), *Rézanov* (1906), and *The White Morning* (1918). *Black Oxen* (1923), a novel about a woman who undergoes surgery to make herself younger, became a bestseller. Her autobiography, *Adventures of a Novelist*, appeared in 1932.

John Kendrick Bangs (May 27, 1862–January 21, 1922) b. Yonkers, New York. He attended Columbia University, where he edited the literary magazine. Later he was an editor of *Life*, *Harper's Magazine*, and *Harper's Bazaar*, contributing articles, poems, and humorous stories. In later years he was an editor at *New Metropolitan Magazine* and *Puck* and a popular lecturer. He was a prolific author of satirical and whimsical fantasies, many set in the afterlife. His books included *Tiddledywink Tales* (1891), *Tappleton's Client: or, A Spirit in Exile* (1893), *A House-Boat on the Styx* (1895), *Mr. Bonaparte of Corsica* (1895), *Ghosts I Have Met and Some Others* (1898), *The Enchanted Type-Writer* (1899), and *Olympian Nights* (1902).

Stephen Vincent Benét (July 22, 1889–March 13, 1943) b. Bethlehem, Pennsylvania; siblings were the poets William Rose Benét and Laura Benét. Published his first two collections of poetry while he was at Yale. Received Guggenheim fellowship to write long poem on the Civil War, published as *John Brown's Body* (1928); it became a bestseller and won the Pulitzer Prize. In addition to poetry wrote fiction, radio plays, and film scripts. His fantasy stories included "The Devil and Daniel Webster" (1937), which was adapted into a film in 1941, "By the Waters of Babylon" (1937), and "Johnny Pye and the Fool Killer" (1938). His last book was *Western Star* (1943), intended as the first in a series of narrative poems on the history of the American West.

Ambrose Bierce (June 24, 1842–1914?) b. Ambrose Gwinnett Bierce on farm near Horse Cave Creek, Ohio, one of many children of poor but well-read farm family. Attended Kentucky Military Institute (1859–60) and subsequently enlisted in the 9th Indiana Infantry; fought at Shiloh, Murfreesboro, Chattanooga, Franklin, and was wounded at Kenesaw Mountain. Moved to San Francisco after the war, working at U.S. sub-treasury and beginning career in journalism, writing for *The Californian*, *The Overland Monthly*, and other publications. Lived in England and France before returning in 1875 to San Francisco, where he edited *The Wasp* and later became editor for William Randolph Hearst's *Examiner*. His books included *Tales of Soldiers and Civilians* (1892), *Can Such Things Be?* (1893), *Fantastic Fables* (1899), and *The Cynic's Word Book* (1906, later retitled *The Devil's Dictionary*). He disappeared into Mexico in 1913, writing to a friend: "If you hear of my being stood up against a Mexican stone wall and shot to rags please know that I think it a pretty good way to depart this life." Joined Pancho Villa's forces as an observer and died under circumstances that remain mysterious.

Robert Bloch (April 5, 1917–September 23, 1994) b. Chicago, Illinois, to a bank cashier and a social worker; developed an interest in fantastic stories as a teenager, and began corresponding with H. P.

Lovecraft, whose stories he had read and admired in *Weird Tales.*
With Lovecraft's encouragement and guidance, published two stories in *Weird Tales* at 17, and went on to become one of the magazine's most popular contributors. Wrote hundreds of stories,
including such frequently anthologized works as "Yours Truly, Jack
the Ripper," "The Opener of the Way," and "The Plot Is the
Thing," as well as novels including *The Scarf* (1947), *The Kidnapper*
(1954), *Spiderweb* (1954), and *Psycho* (1959), which was filmed the following year by Alfred Hitchcock. He also wrote many screenplays
and television scripts.

Alice Brown (December 5, 1857–June 21, 1948) b. Hampton Falls,
New Hampshire. She worked as a schoolteacher before moving to
Boston where she worked for *The Christian Register* and *Youth's
Companion* and wrote novels, poems, and plays. She was known for
stories of New England life, collected in *Meadow-Grass* (1895) and
Tiverton Tales (1899). Her many books included *Fools of Nature*
(1897), *The Rose of Hope* (1896), *Margaret Warraner* (1902), *The
One-Footed Fairy* (1911), *The Wind Between the Worlds* (1920), and
The Mysteries of Anne (1925). She was a friend of the poet Louise
Imogen Guiney, of whom she published a biography in 1921.

Charles Brockden Brown (January 17, 1771–February 22, 1810) b.
Philadelphia, son of James Brown, a prosperous merchant, and
Miriam Churchman Brown. Classically educated and a precocious
student, at an early age he began writing poetry. Studied law; began
to publish poems and essays in newspapers and magazines. Helped
found Society for the Attainment of Useful Knowledge. Abandoned
legal studies and embarked on literary career; read William Godwin,
Condorcet, and other social thinkers. In 1798 published *Alcuin,*
philosophical dialogue arguing for educational and professional
equality for women, and *Wieland; or the Transformation*, novel involving mesmerism, religious obsession, and murder. Subsequent
novels included *Ormond; or, the Secret Witness* (1799), *Edgar Huntly;
or, Memoirs of a Sleep-Walker* (1799), *Arthur Mervyn; or, Memoirs of
the Year 1793* (1799–1800), *Clara Howard* (1801), and *Jane Talbot*
(1801). Published journals *The American Review and Literary Journal* (1801–2) and *The Literary Magazine, and American Register*
(1803–9). Wrote series of political tracts critical of Jefferson administration. Married Elizabeth Linn in 1804. Died of tuberculosis.

Willa Cather (December 7, 1873–April 28, 1947) b. Back Creek Valley, near Winchester, Virginia. Daughter of Charles Cather, a sheep
farmer, and Mary Cather. The family moved to Nebraska in 1877 to

rejoin relatives successfully farming there; lived eventually in Red
Cloud. Cather read extensively from childhood. Attended University
of Nebraska (1891–95), where she began publishing stories, poems,
and criticism in school publications. Moved to Pittsburgh; worked as
editor and journalist; taught high school. Began publishing short
stories in *McClure's Magazine*; moved to New York when offered
editorial position at *McClure's*. Befriended many writers including
Sarah Orne Jewett. Story collection *The Troll Garden* published in
1905. First novel *Alexander's Bridge* (1911) was followed by *O Pioneers!*
(1913), *The Song of the Lark* (1915), and *My Ántonia* (1918). Later
novels included *A Lost Lady* (1923), *The Professor's House* (1925),
Death Comes for the Archbishop (1927), and *Shadows on the Rock*
(1931). Collected works published in 12 volumes by Houghton Mifflin, 1937–38.

Robert W. Chambers (May 26, 1865–December 16, 1933) b. Robert
William Chambers in Brooklyn, New York. Trained as an artist from
a young age, first at the Brooklyn Polytechnic Institute, then the Art
Student's League, where he was a classmate of Charles Dana Gibson.
Studied (1886–93) in Paris at the Ecole des Beaux-Arts and the Julien
Academy. Returned to the United States and published some of his
illustrations in *Life*, *Truth*, and *Vogue* before deciding to pursue a career as a writer. His many popular novels include *In the Quarter*
(1894), *The Red Republic* (1895), *Ashes of Empire* (1898), *Cardigan*
(1901), and *The Fighting Chance* (1906). His collection of linked
stories *The King in Yellow* (1895), revolving around a verse play that
brings madness and tragedy to all who read it, was exceptional in his
output for its fantastic elements.

Kate Chopin (February 8, 1850–August 22, 1904) b. Katherine
O'Flaherty in St. Louis, Missouri, daughter of Thomas O'Flaherty,
an Irish immigrant, and Catherine Reilhe, of an aristocratic but impoverished Creole family. Father was killed in a railroad accident
when she was five. Brother, a Confederate soldier, died of typhoid in
1863. Graduated from Sacred Heart Academy in 1868. Married busi-
nessman Oscar Chopin in 1870; couple traveled in Germany, Switzerland, and France on their honeymoon, then settled in New Orleans.
Husband participated in white supremacist insurrection of Crescent
City White League in 1874. Following business difficulties, family
moved to small town of Cloutierville in Natchitoches Parish, where
husband died of yellow fever in 1882. Inheriting debt-ridden estate,
Chopin operated husband's general store before moving back to
New Orleans. Began to publish stories and poems in literary magazines; published first novel, *At Fault*, at her own expense in 1890.

Short-story collections *Bayou Folk* (1894) and *A Night in Acadie* (1897) were followed by novel *The Awakening* (1899), widely attacked on moral grounds. Died of a stroke after attending St. Louis World's Fair.

Ralph Adams Cram (December 16, 1863–September 22, 1942) b. Hampton Falls, New Hampshire. He studied architecture in Boston and became a leading designer of buildings in the Gothic style. In 1887, during a stay in Rome, he experienced a religious conversion to Anglo-Catholicism. He married in 1900 and had two children. As an architect he was responsible for buildings at Cornell University, the University of Notre Dame, William College, the United States Military Academy, the University of Southern California, and Rice University. He was supervising architect at Princeton, 1907–29, and was head of the architecture department at M.I.T. He published a number of works on architecture—*Impressions of Japanese Architecture* (1905), *The Substance of Gothic* (1917)—and a volume of weird fiction, *Black Spirits and White: A Book of Ghost Stories* (1895), which was later praised by H. P. Lovecraft for its "subtleties of atmosphere and description."

Stephen Crane (November 1, 1871–June 5, 1900) b. Newark, New Jersey, youngest of 14 children of Mary Helen Peck and the Rev. Jonathan Townely Crane. Studied (1890–91) at Lafayette College and Syracuse University before leaving school to become a writer; wrote journalism, poetry, and stories. His novella *Maggie: A Girl of the Streets* (1893) was praised by Hamlin Garland and William Dean Howells. *The Red Badge of Courage* (1895) became a bestseller. Published other novels and stories, and the poetry collections *The Black Riders and Other Lines* (1895) and *War Is Kind* (1899). In 1896 met Cora Howorth Steward, brothel proprietress in Jacksonville, Florida, who became his lifelong partner. Traveled to Greece to cover Greek-Turkish War; settled in England, where friends included Joseph Conrad, Henry James, Ford Madox Ford, and H. G. Wells. Traveled to Cuba in 1898 to cover the Spanish-American War. Despite declining health continued to write stories collected in *The Open Boat and Other Tales of Adventure* (1898), *The Monster and Other Stories* (1899), and *Whilomville Stories* (1900). Died of tuberculosis at a sanatorium in the Black Forest, Germany.

F. Marion Crawford (August 2, 1854–April 9, 1909) b. Francis Marion Crawford in Bagni di Lucca, Italy. He was the son of the sculptor Thomas Crawford and Louisa Cutler Ward, and nephew of the poet and social activist Julia Ward Howe. He attended Cambridge, the University of Heidelberg, and Harvard; he studied Sanskrit in India, and settled permanently in Italy in 1883. His first novel, *Mr. Isaacs* (1882), was followed by over 40 others, including *A Roman Singer* (1884), *Saracinesca* (1887), *A Cigarette-maker's Romance* (1890), *Khaled: A Tale of Arabia* (1891), and *Don Orsino* (1892). He enjoyed great popularity and also published a number of historical works and a critical study, *The Novel: What It Is* (1893). His supernatural stories include "The Upper Berth" (1886) and "The Screaming Skull (1908).

Emma Francis Dawson (1851–February 6, 1926) A protégé of Ambrose Bierce, who described her as a writer "head and shoulders" above her contemporaries. She wrote for many periodicals in the 1880s and '90s, and was also a poet and translator. Worked at times as a music teacher. She lived reclusively on Russian Hill in San Francisco, caring for her invalid mother. She is said to have starved to death.

August Derleth (February 24, 1909–July 4, 1971) Raised in Sauk City, Wisconsin. Began writing for *Weird Tales* at 16. Was a prolific novelist and writer of short stories, much of his fiction having to do with Midwestern history. A correspondent of H. P. Lovecraft, he founded the press Arkham House in 1939 with Donald Wandrei in order to publish a collection of Lovecraft's fiction. Subsequently the imprint published work by other writers including Derleth. Derleth's fantastic stories are collected in *Someone in the Dark* (1941), *Something Near* (1945), *The Mask of Cthulhu* (1958), *The Trail of Cthulhu* (1962), and other volumes.

Olivia Howard Dunbar (1873–1953) b. West Bridgewater, Massachusetts. She graduated from Smith College in 1894 and subsequently became an editor for the *New York World*. Later she became a prolific contributor to magazines such as *Lippincott's*, *The Century*, *The Critic*, *Putnam's*, and *Scribner's*. She was married to the poet and playwright Ridgely Torrence from 1914 until his death in 1950. In a 1905 article in *The Dial* she called for "a renaissance of the literary ghost" and published many supernatural stories including "The Dream-Baby" (1904), "The Sycamore" (1910), and "The Long Chamber" (1914). She was a strong advocate of woman suffrage and with her husband was part of a social circle that included many poets and writers.

F. Scott Fitzgerald (September 24, 1896–December 21, 1940) b. St. Paul, Minnesota. After failure of father's furniture business, family moved to Buffalo and Syracuse before returning to St. Paul in 1908. Began writing stories and plays at an early age. Attended Princeton (1913–17), where he formed friendships with John Peale Bishop and Edmund Wilson. While undergoing military training, met Zelda Sayre at a country club in Montgomery, Alabama. Moved to New York, where he worked in advertising while publishing stories in *The Smart Set*, *The Saturday Evening Post*, and other magazines. Married Zelda in 1920 after publication of novel *This Side of Paradise*, which became a bestseller. Published story collections *Flappers and Philosophers* (1920) and *Tales of the Jazz Age* (1922) and second novel *The Beautiful and Damned* (1922). Sailed for France with Zelda in 1924 to complete novel published the following year as *The Great Gatsby*. In Paris met Ernest Hemingway, Gertrude Stein, Sylvia Beach, and many other literary figures. Story collection *All the Sad Young Men* appeared in 1926. In following years stayed frequently in Europe; Zelda's mental condition showed signs of deterioration and she attempted suicide in 1930, after which she was diagnosed as schizophrenic and was repeatedly hospitalized. Fitzgerald resided in Montgomery, Alabama, and subsequently Baltimore; novel *Tender Is the Night* published in 1934. Following suicide attempt in 1936, he underwent treatment at Johns Hopkins Hospital. Moved to Los Angeles to work on film scripts; fired by United Artists for drunkenness. Died of heart attack; uncompleted final novel published as *The Last Tycoon* (1941).

Mary E. Wilkins Freeman (October 31, 1852–March 13, 1930) b. Mary Eleanor Wilkins in Randolph, Massachusetts. Briefly attended Mount Holyoke College (1870–71). She began writing stories and verse while in her teens to help support her family. Her early stories of New England life, collected in *A Humble Romance* (1887) and *A New England Nun* (1891), established her as an important figure in the "local color" school of regional realism. Married Dr. Charles Freeman in 1902 and moved to New Jersey. Her more than two dozen books also include the novels *Jane Field* (1893), *Pembroke* (1894), *Jerome, a Poor Man* (1897), and *The Heart's Highway* (1900); the story collections *Silence* (1898) and *The Wind in the Rose-Bush* (1903) contain many of her stories of the supernatural. In April 1926 she was the first recipient of the William Dean Howells Medal for Distinction in Fiction from the American Academy of Arts and Letters.

Charlotte Perkins Gilman (July 3, 1860–August 17, 1935) b. Charlotte Anna Perkins in Hartford, Connecticut. Her father, Frederick Perkins, who was a nephew of Henry Ward Beecher and Harriet

Beecher Stowe, abandoned the family soon after her birth, and Gilman, with her mother and older brother, lived in near-poverty. Much of her early life was spent in Providence, Rhode Island. Married Charles Stetson, an artist, in 1884, and gave birth to a daughter, her only child, the following year. Depression following the birth led to a breakdown that was treated by Dr. Silas Weir Mitchell's "rest cure"; the effects of the treatment were fictionalized in "The Yellow Wall Paper." Separated from her husband in 1888, they were divorced in 1894. Moved to California where she was active as a writer and lecturer, and formed friendships with Edwin Markham, Ina Coolbrith, Joaquin Miller, and other writers; published poetry collection *In This World* (1893) and influential treatise *Women and Economics* (1898). Became prominent in support of women's rights and social reform. In 1900 married her second cousin George Houghton Gilman, an attorney, but the two ultimately lived apart. Edited magazine *The Forerunner* (1909–16). Later books include *Concerning Children* (1900), *Human Work* (1904), and *The Man-Made World* (1911). Committed suicide in 1935 while suffering from inoperable cancer. An autobiography, *The Living of Charlotte Perkins Gilman*, appeared after her death in 1935.

Ellen Glasgow (April 22, 1874–November 21, 1945). b. Ellen Anderson Gholson Glasgow in Richmond, Virginia, to a family of aristocratic heritage. She was sickly in her youth and was educated at home. Her novels, beginning with *The Descendant* in 1897, were steeped in Virginia history and traced social change from before the Civil War to the contemporary era. In her later books she turned increasingly to a vein of satirical comedy. Among her novels were *The Battle-Ground* (1902), *The Wheel of Life* (1906), *Virginia* (1913), *The Builders* (1919), *Barren Ground* (1925), *The Romantic Comedians* (1926), *They Stooped to Folly* (1929), *The Sheltered Life* (1932), and *Vein of Iron* (1935). She won the Pulitzer Prize for *In This Our Life* (1941). Her story collection *The Shadowy Third* appeared in 1923. An autobiography, *The Woman Within*, was published in 1954.

Bret Harte (August 25, 1836–May 5, 1902) b. Francis Brett Harte in Albany, New York. After several years in Brooklyn, moved to Oakland, California, with his family, in 1853. Gradually made his way to a small coastal town called Union where he got a job as a printer's devil and editorial assistant at the local newspaper, *The Northern Californian*. Forced to leave town after writing an editorial condemning the massacre of a group of Wiyots (mostly women and children) living nearby. Moved to San Francisco and began writing stories and poems for the newspaper *The Californian*. Formed friendships with Mark Twain and Ambrose Bierce. In 1868, became editor of *The Overland Monthly*, where he published his story "The Luck of Roaring Camp," which (along with his humorous poem "Plain Language from Truthful James") brought him nationwide fame. Early fiction collected in *The Luck of Roaring Camp and Other Sketches* (1870). Relocated to the East in 1871; his later writings found little favor and he struggled against accumulating debts. After the break-up of his marriage, settled in London, where he cultivated literary friendships and continued to publish prolifically. Served in several consular posts in Krefeld, Prussia, and Glasgow, but was dismissed from the latter for inattention to his duties.

Julian Hawthorne (June 22, 1846–1934) b. Boston, son of Nathaniel Hawthorne and Julia Peabody. Attended Harvard sporadically, then transferred to Cambridge's Lawrence Scientific School to study civil engineering; finished his studies in Dresden, where he moved in 1867. Married Mary Amelung and moved to New York in 1870 where he worked for the city as a hydrographic engineer; subsequently returned to Europe to live. His first novel, *Bressant* (1873), published serially in *Appleton's*, was followed by *Idolatry* (1874), *Garth* (1877), *Archibald Malmaison* (1879), and *Sebastian Strome* (1880). In 1882, moved back to the United States and, over the next 30 years, supported his wife and seven children by his successful career as editor, biographer, and journalist. Later books included the novels *The Professor's Sister* (1888), *David Poindexter's Disappearance* (1888), and *Sarah Was Judith* (1920), as well as nonfiction works such as *Nathaniel Hawthorne and His Wife* (1884), and *Hawthorne's History of the United States* (1898). Reported on the Spanish-American War for the *New York Journal*. Indicted in 1913 along with several associates on charges of mail fraud for tricking hundreds of investors into buying fake mining shares; was convicted and served a year in the Atlanta Federal Penitentiary. After his release wrote *The Subterranean Brotherhood* (1914), calling for an end to the incarceration of prisoners. He moved to San Francisco and after the death of his first wife married his long-time companion Edith Garrigues. He was honored on his 85th birthday with a banquet attended by a number of prominent literary and social figures.

Nathaniel Hawthorne (July 4, 1804–May 19, 1864) b. Salem, Massachusetts, second of three children of Nathaniel and Elizabeth Manning Hathorne. Father, a ship's captain, died of fever in Surinam when Hawthorne was four; with mother and sisters, lived with relatives thereafter. Educated at home for a number of years following a schoolyard injury. Attended Bowdoin College (1821–25), where he began first novel, *Fanshawe*. Devoted himself to writing short fiction, eventually collected in *Twice-Told Tales* (1837). Took job at Boston Custom House. Joined utopian community Brook Farm; left after eight months. Married Sophia Peabody in 1842; they settled in Concord, Massachusetts, where he became acquainted with Emerson, Thoreau, and their circle. Story collection *Mosses from an Old Manse* (1846) followed by *The Scarlet Letter* (1850), *The House of the Seven Gables* (1851), and *The Blithedale Romance* (1852). During residence in Lenox, Massachusetts, formed friendship with Herman Melville. Wrote campaign biography for presidential campaign of Bowdoin friend Franklin Pierce; appointed American consul at Liverpool after Pierce's election. Kept extensive notebooks of travels in England, France, and Italy. Last completed novel, *The Marble Faun*, published in 1860. Returned to America in 1860.

Lafcadio Hearn (June 27, 1850–September 26, 1904) b. Patrick Lafcadio Tessima Carlos Hearn on Lefkada, one of the Ionian Islands. His mother, Rosa Antonia Cassimati, was a native of Kythira; his father, Charles Bush Hearn, was an army surgeon of Irish origin. With mother, went to Dublin to live with father, but he soon left family and later had marriage annulled. Mother returned to Greece; Hearn lived with a relative of his father before being sent to school in France. Later attended a Catholic school in Durham, where he was blinded in one eye in a schoolyard accident. Sent to United States to seek help from friends of the family, but ended up penniless; began writing for Cincinnati newspapers. Married Alethea Foley, a former slave; fired from newspaper after marriage revealed; separated from wife and never saw her again. Settled in New Orleans in 1877, writing for *Daily City Item* and other papers; traveled in Louisiana coastal islands and West Indies. Published *Some Chinese Ghosts* (1887), the novels *Chita* (1889) and *Youma* (1890), and travel book *Two Years in the French West Indies* (1890). Traveled to Japan in 1890 and remained there for the remainder of his life. Hired as a teacher in a prefectural school in Matsue; married Koizumi Setsu, daughter of a local samurai family. Later moved to Kumamoto and to Tokyo, where in 1895 he became a professor of English language and literature at Tokyo Imperial University. Became Japanese citizen. Published many books on Japanese culture, society, and folklore, including *Glimpses of Unfamiliar Japan* (1894), *Out of the East* (1895), *Kokoro* (1896), *Gleanings in Buddha-Fields* (1897), *In Ghostly Japan* (1899), and *Japan: An Attempt at Interpretation* (1904). *Kwaidan: Stories and Studies of Strange Things*, containing some of his best-known versions of Japanese supernatural legends, was published posthumously in 1904.

Robert E. Howard (January 22, 1906–June 11, 1936) b. Robert Ervin Howard in Peaster, Texas. The son of an itinerant physician, he lived in many small Texas towns during his early childhood, settling with his parents in Cross Plains in 1919. At 15 he began submitting stories to pulp magazines, eventually becoming a prolific contributor of stories and poems to *Weird Tales*, *Fight Stories*, *Cowboy Stories*, and many others. For *Weird Tales* he created the characters King Kull, Bran Mak Morn, Solomon Kane, and, most successfully, Conan the Barbarian, who made his first appearance in "The Phoenix on the Sword" (December 1932). Howard corresponded regularly with H. P. Lovecraft, although the two never met. Howard, who had long suffered from depression, shot himself to death while his dying mother lay in a terminal coma.

Washington Irving (April 3, 1783–November 28, 1859) b. New York City, youngest of eight surviving children of William Irving, a successful merchant, and Sarah Sanders Irving. Studied law in desultory fashion while beginning to contribute sketches to the *Morning Chronicle* under pseudonym "Jonathan Oldstyle, Gent." Traveled to Europe where he befriended painter Washington Allston and met Madame de Staël. With James Kirke Paulding and brother William Irving, wrote *Salmagundi* (1807–8), a collection of comic pieces. *A History of New York* (1809), attributed to fictional author Diedrich Knickerbocker, became an instant success. Edited *Analectic Magazine* (1813–15). Traveled to England, where his brother Peter ran Liverpool office of family mercantile business; due in part to firm's difficulties extended stay for years. Wrote *The Sketch Book of Geoffrey Crayon, Gent.* (1819), including "Rip Van Winkle" and "The Legend of Sleepy Hollow"; book's success made him an international celebrity. Published *Bracebridge Hall* (1822) and *Tales of a Traveller* (1824); traveled to Spain, where in 1826 he became an attaché to the American legation in Madrid. Published *Life and Voyages of Columbus* (1828), *A Chronicle of the Conquest of Granada* (1829), *Voyages and Discoveries of the Companions of Columbus* (1830), and *The Alhambra* (1932). Returned to the United States in 1832 and made a trip west into Indian Territory, described in *A Tour on the Prairie* (1834). Settled in Tarrytown, New York, eventually building residence called Sunnyside. Served as minister to Spain, 1842–45. Later books included *Astoria* (1836), *Adventures of Captain Bonneville* (1837), and multi-volume biographies of Muhammad and George Washington.

Henry James (April 15, 1843–February 28, 1916) b. New York City, the second of five children of Henry James and Mary James; his siblings included the writers William James and Alice James. Family, living on father's inheritance, moved to Europe where father experienced nervous collapse and became proponent of Swedenborgian mysticism. Family moved between America and Europe, settling finally in Newport. James entered Harvard Law School but withdrew and began publishing short fiction and reviews. Toured Europe, 1869–70, returned there 1872–74. Published first novel, *Roderick Hudson* (1875). After brief residence in New York returned to Europe, living in France and publishing journalism; moved to London in 1876. Published novels including *The American* (1877), *The Europeans* (1898), *Washington Square* (1880), and *The Portrait of a Lady* (1881). After a few brief visits to America, settling family affairs, resided chiefly in London and Paris, and traveled extensively in Italy. Published *The Princess Casamassima* (1886), *The Aspern Papers* (1888), *The Tragic Muse* (1890). Made prolonged and unsuccessful attempt to write for the theater, culminating in raucous opening night of his play *Guy Domville* (1895). Settled permanently at Lamb House in Rye in 1897. Later novels included *The Spoils of Poynton* (1897), *What Maisie Knew* (1897), *The Awkward Age* (1899), *The Sacred Fount* (1901), *The Wings of the Dove* (1902), *The Ambassadors* (1903), and *The Golden Bowl* (1904). In 1904 made first trip to America in 20 years; described impressions in *The American Scene* (1907). Published autobiographical volumes *A Small Boy and Others* (1911) and *Notes of a Son and Brother* (1914). After 1914 participated in war relief projects, visiting wounded in hospitals. Became a British citizen in July 1915.

Sarah Orne Jewett (September 3, 1849–June 24, 1909) b. Theodora Sarah Orne Jewett in South Berwick, Maine. Her father was a wealthy physician and professor of medicine. After graduating from Berwick Academy she began to publish short fiction, chiefly about the lives of fishermen and farmers, which won the editorial support of William Dean Howells. Her first story collection, *Deephaven*, appeared in 1877. Following the death of publisher James T. Fields, she became the close companion of his widow, Annie Fields, traveling with her in Europe, Florida, and the Caribbean. Her later books included *A Country Doctor* (1884), *A White Heron* (1886), *Tales of New England* (1890), and *The Country of the Pointed Firs* (1896). She stopped writing after suffering spinal damage in a carriage accident in 1902. In later years she formed a friendship with Willa Cather.

David H. Keller (December 23, 1880–July 13, 1966) b. David Henry Keller in Philadelphia. A graduate from the medical school of the University of Pennsylvania, he worked at a mental institution in

Illinois beginning in 1915, and served as a psychiatrist in both world wars; in World War I he helped pioneer the treatment of shell-shock victims. After writing a number of pieces for college magazines, he published his first pulp story in *Amazing Stories* in February 1928, and thereafter contributed regularly to *Weird Tales, Science Wonder Stories,* and other publications. He also published novels including *The Human Termites* (1929), *The Metal Doom* (1932), *The Devil and the Doctor* (1940), and *The Homunculus* (1949).

H. P. Lovecraft (August 20, 1890–March 10, 1937) b. Howard Phillips Lovecraft in Providence, Rhode Island. Father was committed to an asylum in 1893 and died five years later. Began reading Poe at age eight; wrote story "The Beast in the Cave" at 15. Attended public school in Providence; suffered nervous breakdown and failed to graduate. Began writing astronomy column for *Pawtuxet Valley Gleaner* in 1906. Lived with mother until her death (following mental collapse) in 1921. Contributed to many small magazines and journals; elected editor of United Amateur Press Association in 1920. Began writing stories of fantasy and terror; deeply influenced by Irish fantasy writer Lord Dunsany. After first issue of *Weird Tales* appeared in 1923, submitted several stories, all of which were accepted, including "Dagon" and "The Statement of Randolph Carter"; became a regular contributor to the magazine. Married Sonia Greene, a milliner he had met through the Press Association, in 1924; they settled in Brooklyn; marriage gradually fell apart and the couple were divorced in 1929. Wrote stories including "The Shunned House," "The Horror at Red Hook," "Cool Air," "The Call of Cthulhu," and the novellas "The Dream-Quest of Unknown Kadath" and "The Case of Charles Dexter Ward." "The Colour Out of Space" (later described by Lovecraft as his favorite among his stories) published by *Amazing Stories* in 1927. In the same year published essay "Supernatural Horror in Literature' in *The Recluse*. Traveled extensively, visiting colonial sites in New England and the South. Corresponded extensively with other pulp writers including Robert E. Howard, Clark Ashton Smith, and the young Robert Bloch. Wrote "The Whisperer in Darkness," "The Shadow Over Innsmouth," "The Dreams in the Witch-House," "The Haunter of the Dark," and other stories; novellas "At the Mountains of Madness" and "The Shadow Out of Time." Died at Jane Brown Memorial Hospital in Providence.

Herman Melville (August 1, 1819–September 28, 1891) b. New York City, son of Maria Gansevoort (daughter of American Revolutionary hero General Peter Gansevoort) and Allan Melvill (importer and merchant). Father's business failed in financial panic of 1830; family forced to move to Albany where father died in 1832. Educated sporadically in New York City and upstate New York; worked as clerk, bookkeeper, and schoolteacher before joining crew of trading ship *St. Lawrence* in 1839, traveling to Liverpool and back. Sailed to South Seas on whaling ship *Acushnet* in 1841; deserted with a shipmate at Nuku Hiva in the Marquesas. After a month in Taipi valley, sailed on Australian whaling ship *Lucy Ann*, but sent ashore in Tahiti as mutineer; escaped, and explored Tahiti; sailed to Hawaii where he worked at various jobs in Honolulu before enlisting in U.S. Navy. Sailed to Boston on frigate *United States*; discharged October 1844. *Typee*, fictionalized account of Marquesas experiences, published to great success in 1846; *Omoo*, a sequel, appeared the following year. Married Elizabeth Shaw, daughter of Massachusetts Chief Justice Lemuel Shaw; they had four children. Published *Mardi* (1849), *Redburn* (1849), and *White-Jacket* (1850). Met Nathaniel Hawthorne, whose work he admired; bought farm Arrowhead near Pittsfield, Massachusetts. *Moby-Dick* was published in 1851; its indifferent reception was followed by the failure of *Pierre, or The Ambiguities* (1852), *Israel Potter* (1855), and *The Piazza Tales* (1856). Made year-long trip to Europe and the Holy Land with father-in-law's financial help. Last published novel, *The Confidence-Man*, appeared in 1857. Moved with family to New York City in 1863; collection of Civil War poems, *Battle-Pieces and Aspects of the War*, published in 1866. Worked as deputy inspector of customs at port of New York, 1866–85. Son Malcolm died of self-inflicted gunshot wound in 1867. Long poem *Clarel: A Poem and a Pilgrimage* published 1867. Left *Billy Budd, Sailor* in manuscript (first published 1924), along with a number of poems.

W. C. Morrow (July 7, 1854–1923) b. William Chambers Morris in Selma, Alabama. His father was a minister and hotel-keeper, and Morrow graduated from Howard College in Birmingham. Relocating to California, he became a contributor to *The Argonaut* and *The San Francisco Examiner*. His stories were collected in *The Ape, the Idiot, and Other People* (1897). He published a number of novels, including *Blood-Money* (1882) and *Lentala of the South Seas* (1908), as well as *The Art of Writing for Publication* (1901).

Frank Norris (March 5, 1870–October 25, 1902) b. Benjamin Franklin Norris, Jr., in Chicago, to Gertrude Doggett Norris, an actress, and Benjamin Franklin Norris, a successful jewelry wholesaler. Family moved to San Francisco in 1885; Norris showed early interest in painting and in 1887 began studying at Julien Academy in Paris.

Returned to America and enrolled at Berkeley; during his four years there began publishing stories in the *Argonaut*, *The Overland Monthly*, and other periodicals. Traveled to South Africa to report on Boer War for the *San Francisco Chronicle*; on returning to California became staff writer for *The Wave*. Published novel *Moran of the Lady Letty* (1898); moved to New York to work for Doubleday. Went to Cuba to cover Spanish-American War for *McClure's*. *McTeague* (1899) was attacked for "lurid" subject matter, but praised by William Dean Howells and others. Published *Vandover and the Brute* (1899), *Blix* (1899), and first two volumes of trilogy "The Epic of the Wheat": *The Octopus* (1901) and *The Pit* (1902). Returned to San Francisco; died of peritonitis before completing trilogy's third volume.

Fitz-James O'Brien (December 31, 1828–April 6, 1862) b. Michael O'Brien in County Cork, Ireland. Educated at the University of Dublin. Changed his name to "Fitz-James" after arriving penniless (having squandered an inheritance) in United States in 1852. He frequented Bohemian circles at Pfaff's Cellar in New York. Began contributing articles, stories, and poems to *Harper's Magazine*, *New York Saturday Press*, *Putnam's Magazine*, *Vanity Fair*, and *Atlantic Monthly*. To *Atlantic* he contributed two of his best-known stories, "The Diamond Lens" (1858), about a man who falls in love with a woman he sees in a drop of water under a microscope, and "The Wonder Smith" (1859), in which fractious toys rebel against their owners. He joined the 7th regiment of the New York National Guard at the outbreak of the Civil War, and after the regiment returned without seeing action, was appointed to the staff of General Frederick W. Lander. O'Brien was wounded in a skirmish in early 1862, and died soon after in Cumberland, Maryland. The critic William Winter, a friend of O'Brien, collected his *Poems and Stories* in 1881.

Edgar Allan Poe (January 19, 1809–October 7, 1849) b. Boston, Massachusetts, second of three children of Elizabeth Arnold and David Poe, traveling actors. Father abandoned family in 1809; mother moved frequently before her death in Richmond, Virginia, in December 1811. Poe was separated from his siblings and taken into the home of Richmond tobacco merchant John Allan and his wife, Frances; they served as foster parents but did not legally adopt him. Accompanying the Allans to Great Britain, attended schools in London (1815–20) before returning with family to Richmond. Entered University of Virginia; lost money while gambling, and Allan refused to honor debts. Moved to Boston; published anonymously first book of verse, *Tamerlane and Other Poems* (1827). Enlisted in U.S. Army; at request of dying foster mother was partially reconciled with Allan, who helped secure appointment to U.S. Military Academy at West Point; he was dismissed from West Point after eight months for neglect of duty. Lived in Baltimore with aunt Maria Clemm and her eight-year-old daughter Virginia; published *Al Aaraaf, Tamerlane and Minor Poems* (1829). Began to publish short fiction in magazines, and in 1833 "Ms. Found in a Bottle" won a competition. Obtained editorial position with the *Southern Literary Messenger*, contributing stories (including "Berenice" and "Morella"), reviews, and poems. Married Virginia (then 13) in 1835. Resigned from *Messenger* after quarreling with editor and moved with Virginia and Mrs. Clemm to New York, then to Philadelphia. Became co-editor of *Burton's Gentleman's Magazine*. In 1838–39 wrote "Ligeia," "The Fall of the House of Usher," and "William Wilson" among other stories. Novel *The Narrative of Arthur Gordon Pym* was published in 1838; story collection *Tales of the Grotesque and Arabesque* appeared in 1839. Became literary editor of *Graham's Magazine* (1841–42), where he published "The Murders in the Rue Morgue" and "The Masque of the Red Death." Moved back to New York in 1844, working for *New-York Evening Mirror* and as editor of *The Broadway Journal*. Achieved fame with publication of "The Raven" in 1845. Later stories included "The Tell-Tale Heart," "The Black Cat," "The Premature Burial," "The Purloined Letter," "The Facts in the Case of M. Valdemar," and "The Cask of Amontillado"; published collections *Prose Romances* (1843) and *Tales* (1845). After years of illness, Virginia died of tuberculosis in 1847. Published metaphysical treatise *Eureka* (1848); returned to Richmond. In October 1849 stopped in Baltimore on the way to New York on literary business; he was found in a delirious condition and died four days later on October 7.

Seabury Quinn (January 1, 1889–December 24, 1969) b. Seabury Grandin Quinn. in Washington, D.C. Attended law school at the National University. Moved to New York after serving in the army during World War I and began writing, editing, and teaching on medical jurisprudence, specializing in mortuary law. Edited the mortuary journal *Casket and Sunnyside*. After publishing several weird stories in various magazines, he wrote "The Horror on the Links," which was published in the October 1925 issue of *Weird Tales* and was the first story to feature the team of Dr. Trowbridge and psychic detective Jules de Grandin. From 1925 to 1951 Quinn wrote 93 such stories, making him the magazine's most prolific contributor.

Clark Ashton Smith (January 13, 1893–August 14, 1961) b. Long Valley, California. Grew up in a small cabin in Auburn, California. Various psychological disorders prevented him from going to high school, but he continued to study on his own, eventually learning French and Spanish. He started writing stories when he was 11 and drew the attention of San Francisco poet George Sterling, who helped him get his first poetry collection, *The Star-Treader*, published; it was followed by *Odes and Sonnets* (1918) and *Ebony and Crystal* (1922), the latter of which elicited a fan letter from H. P. Lovecraft, beginning a life-long correspondence and friendship between the two. From 1926 he began publishing stories regularly in *Weird Tales*, writing more than a hundred during a six-year period, most set in fantasy realms such as Zothique, Hyperborea, and Averoigne. A single collection, *The Double Shadow*, was published privately in 1933. He virtually stopped writing after 1936, living alone and devoting himself to sculpture. He married in 1954.

Harriet Prescott Spofford (April 3, 1835–August 14, 1921) b. Harriet Elizabeth Prescott in Calais, Maine. After graduating from Pinkerton Academy in Derry, New Hampshire, she worked to support her invalid parents through writing; her story "In the Cellar" was highly praised by other writers when published in *Atlantic Monthly* in 1859. The following year she published "The Amber Gods" and "Circumstance." Of the first of these stories, Emily Dickinson remarked that "it is the only thing I ever read in my life that I didn't think I could have imagined myself," and of the second: "It followed me, in the Dark." Published the novels *Sir Rohan's Ghost* (1860) and *Azarian* (1864). Married Richard Spofford, a Boston lawyer, in 1865 and moved with him to Deer Island in Amesbury, Massachusetts. Continued to publish fiction prolifically, but her later work was not as well received. Published a memoir, *A Little Book of Friends*, in 1916.

Francis Stevens (1883–1948) b. Gertrude Mabel Barrows in Minneapolis. Attended school through the eighth grade; later attended night school. After the death of her husband, Stewart Bennett, a British explorer who died on an expedition the year after they were married, she worked as a stenographer to support her daughter and invalid mother. Began to write fantasy and science fiction stories, publishing "The Nightmare," a novella about a shipwreck survivor who finds himself on an island of monsters, in *All Story Weekly* in 1917. "Friend Island" (1918), set in the 22nd century, concerned a world ruled entirely by women. She wrote a number of novels, including *The Citadel of Fear* (1918), *The Heads of Cerberus* (1919), a dystopian fantasy, and *Claimed* (1920), in which an ancient god was summoned to contemporary New Jersey by magical means, and which H. P. Lovecraft praised. In the 1920s, Stevens moved to San Francisco, where she lived until her death in 1948.

Edith Wharton (January 24, 1862–August 11, 1937) b. Edith Newbold Jones in New York City, daughter of George Frederic Jones and Lucretia Stevens Rhinelander, both from socially prominent New York families. As a child, lived with her family in England, Italy, France, and Germany; returning to the United States in 1872, they divided their time between Manhattan and Newport, Rhode Island. Married Edward Wharton in 1885, and they spent several months every year in Europe. Began to publish poems and short stories in *Scribner's*, *Harper's*, and *Century Magazine*. Published historical novel, *The Valley of Decision* (1902). In 1902 moved into The Mount, a house in Lenox, Massachusetts, which she helped design. Bought an automobile in 1904 and toured in England (with close friend Henry James) and France. Continued to publish fiction, focusing most often on New York society as she had observed it: *The House of Mirth* (1905), *The Fruit of the Tree* (1907), *Ethan Frome* (1911), *The Reef* (1912), and *The Custom of the Country* (1913). In 1908 she began an affair with journalist William Morton Fullerton. The following year her husband admitted to embezzling money from her trust funds, and she was granted a divorce in 1913 on grounds of adultery. During World War I established American Hostels for Refugees and organized the Children of Flanders Rescue Committee. Bought a house near Paris in 1918. Later fiction included *Summer* (1917), *The Age of Innocence* (1920), *The Old Maid* (1921), *The Glimpses of the Moon* (1922), *The Mother's Recompense* (1925), *Hudson River Bracketed* (1929), and *The Gods Arrive* (1932). Her autobiography, *A Backward Glance*, appeared in 1934.

Edward Lucas White (May 11, 1866–March 30, 1934) b. Bergen, New Jersey. Attended Johns Hopkins University in Baltimore, where he lived for the rest of his life. Taught at University School for Boys, 1915–30. Wrote a number of historical novels, including *El Supremo* (1916), *The Unwilling Vestal* (1918), *Andivius Hedulio* (1921), and *Helen* (1926), and fantasy stories, the most famous—"The Nightmare" and "Lukundoo"—based on his own nightmares. He published two story collections, *The Song of the Sirens* (1919) and *Lukundoo and Other Stories* (1927). He killed himself seven years to the day after his wife's death; his last book, *Matrimony* (1932), was a memoir of their marriage.

Henry S. Whitehead (March 5, 1882–November 23, 1932) b. Henry St. Clair Whitehead in Elizabeth, New Jersey. Graduated from Harvard in 1904. Studied at Berkeley Divinity School in Middleton, Connecticut, where he was ordained an Episcopal deacon in 1912. While serving in this capacity in the Virgin Islands (1921–29), gathered much of the voodoo-related folkloric material he was to use in his fantastic fiction. Published 25 stories in *Weird Tales*. Became a friend of H. P. Lovecraft, with whom he collaborated on the story "The Trap" (1931). His stories were later collected in *Jumbee* (1944) and *West India Lights* (1946).

Madeline Yale Wynne (1847–1918). Daughter of Linus Yale, Jr., inventor of the Yale lock. Active in the Arts and Crafts movement. Studied at the Museum School of the Museum of Fine Arts in Boston, 1877–78, and at Art Student's League in New York in the spring of 1880. Moved to Deerfield, Mass., and became president of Arts and Crafts society; highly regarded as a metalworker. Later moved to Chicago for the remainder of her life. Her story "The Little Room" first appeared in *Harper's Magazine* and was frequently anthologized thereafter. *The Little Room and Other Stories* (1895) was her only published book.

Note on the Texts

This volume contains 44 fantastic tales by American writers originally published between 1805 and 1939 and presents them in the
order of their original publication or, in a few instances, of their
composition. In the case of stories that were not collected in book
form during the author's lifetime, the texts are taken from periodical
versions.

The following is a list of the sources of the texts included in this
volume, listed in the order of their appearance in this volume.

Charles Brockden Brown: Somnambulism: A Fragment; *Literary
Magazine and American Register*, May 1805, pp. 335–47.

Washington Irving: The Adventure of the German Student; *Washington Irving: Bracebridge Hall, Tales of a Traveller, The Alhambra*, ed. Andrew Myers (New York: Library of America, 1991),
pp. 418–24; first published in *Tales of a Traveller* (London: John
Murray, 1824).

Edgar Allan Poe: Berenice; *Edgar Allan Poe: Poetry and Tales*, ed.
Patrick F. Quinn (New York: Library of America, 1984), pp. 225–
33. First published in *The Southern Literary Messenger*, March 1835,
and collected in revised form in *Tales of the Grotesque and
Arabesque* (Philadelphia: Lea and Blanchard, 1840).

Nathaniel Hawthorne: Young Goodman Brown. *Nathaniel
Hawthorne: Tales and Sketches*, ed. Roy Harvey Pearce (New York:
Library of America, 1982), pp. 276–89; first published in *New-
England Magazine*, 1835, and collected in *Mosses from an Old
Manse* (New York: Wiley and Putnam, 1846). Copyright © 1974 by
the Ohio State University Press. Reprinted by permission of the
publisher.

Herman Melville: The Tartarus of Maids; *Herman Melville: Pierre,
Israel Potter, The Confidence-Man, Tales & Billy Budd*, ed. Harri-
son Hayford (New York: Library of America, 1985), pp. 1265–79;
first published in *Harper's*, April 1855. Copyright © 1996. Reprinted by permission of the Northwestern University Press and
the Newberry Library.

Fitz-James O'Brien: What Was It?; *Harper's Monthly*, March, 1859,
pp. 504–9.

Bret Harte: The Legend of Monte del Diablo; *The Writings of Bret
Harte, Volume One: The Luck of Roaring Camp and Other Tales*

(Boston and New York: Houghton Mifflin, 1906), pp. 382–97; first published in *The Atlantic Monthly*, September 1863.

Harriet Prescott Spofford: The Moonstone Mass; *Harper's Monthly*, October 1868, pp. 655–61.

W. C. Morrow: His Unconquerable Enemy; *The Ape, the Idiot, and Other People* (Philadelphia: J. B. Lippincott Company, 1910), pp. 48–66; first published (as "The Rajah's Nemesis") in *The Argonaut*, March 11, 1889.

Sarah Orne Jewett: In Dark New England Days; *Strangers and Wayfarers* (Boston: Houghton Mifflin, 1899), pp. 220–56; first published in *The Century*, October 1890.

Charlotte Perkins Gilman: The Yellow Wall Paper; *The Yellow Wall Paper* (Boston: Small, Maynard & Co., 1899); first published in *New England Magazine*, January 1892.

Stephen Crane: The Black Dog; *Stephen Crane: Prose and Poetry*, ed. J. C. Levenson (New York: Library of America, 1984), pp. 501–5; first published in the *New York Tribune*, July 24, 1892.

Kate Chopin: Ma'ame Pélagie; *Kate Chopin: Complete Novels and Stories*, ed. Sandra M. Gilbert (New York: Library of America, 2002), pp. 294–301. First published in *New Orleans Times-Democrat*, December 24, 1893, and collected in *Bayou Folk* (Boston: Houghton Mifflin, 1894).

John Kendrick Bangs: Thurlow's Christmas Story; *Ghosts I Have Met and Some Others* (New York: Harper & Bros., 1898), pp. 109–39. First published in *Harper's Weekly*, December 15, 1894.

Robert W. Chambers: The Repairer of Reputations; *The King in Yellow* (New York: Harper & Bros., 1902), pp. 3–44; first edition 1895 (New York: F. T. Neely).

Ralph Adams Cram: The Dead Valley; *Black Spirits and White: A Book of Ghost Stories* (New York: Stone & Kimball, 1895), pp. 133–50.

Madeline Yale Wynne: The Little Room; *The Little Room and Other Stories* (Chicago: Walter M. Hill, 1895), pp. 7–39; first published in *Harper's*, August 1895.

Gertrude Atherton: The Striding Place; *The Bell in the Fog and Other Stories* (New York: Harper & Bros., 1905), pp. 47–57; first published (as "The Twins") in *The Speaker*, June 20, 1896.

Emma Francis Dawson: An Itinerant House; *An Itinerant House and Other Stories* (San Francisco: William Doxey, 1897), pp. 1–30; first published in *Overland Monthly*, 1897.

Mary Wilkins Freeman: Luella Miller; *The Wind in the Rosebush* (New York: Doubleday, Page & Co., 1903) pp. 75–104; first published in *Everybody's Magazine*, December 1902.

Frank Norris: Grettir at Thorhall-stead; *Everybody's Magazine,* April 1903, pp. 311–19.

Lafcadio Hearn: Yuki-Onna; *Kwaidan* (Boston: Houghton Mifflin, 1904), pp. 111–18.

F. Marion Crawford: For the Blood Is the Life; *Wandering Ghosts* (New York: Macmillan Company, 1911), pp. 167–94; first published in *Collier's,* December 1905.

Ambrose Bierce: The Moonlit Road; *Collected Works of Ambrose Bierce, Volume Three: Can Such Things Be?* (New York & Washington: The Neale Publishing Company, 1910), pp. 62–80; first published in *Cosmopolitan,* January 1907.

Edward Lucas White: Lukundoo; *Lukundoo and Other Stories* (New York: George H. Doran Company, 1927), pp. 9–28; written 1907.

Olivia Howard Dunbar: The Shell of Sense; *Harper's Monthly,* December 1908, pp. 69–74.

Henry James: The Jolly Corner; *Henry James: Complete Stories 1898–1910,* ed. Denis Donoghue (New York: Library of America, 1996), pp. 697–731. First published in *The English Review,* December 1908, and collected in volume 17 of *The Novels and Tales of Henry James* (New York: Scribner's, 1907–9).

Alice Brown: Golden Baby; *Vanishing Points* (New York: Macmillan Company, 1913), pp. 275–95; first published in *Harper's,* March 1910.

Edith Wharton: Afterward; *Edith Wharton: Collected Stories 1891–1910,* ed. Maureen Howard (New York: Library of America, 2001), pp. 830–60. First published in *Century Magazine,* January 1910, and collected in *Tales of Men and Ghosts* (New York: Scribner's, 1910).

Willa Cather: Consequences; *Willa Cather: Stories, Poems and Other Writings,* ed. Sharon O'Brien (New York: Library of America), pp.133–53; first published in *McClure's Magazine,* November 1915.

Ellen Glasgow: The Shadowy Third; *The Shadowy Third and Other Stories* (New York: Doubleday, Page & Co., 1923), pp. 3–43; first published in *Scribner's Magazine,* December 1916.

Julian Hawthorne: Absolute Evil; *All-Story Weekly,* April 13, 1918.

Francis Stevens (Gertrude Mabel Barrows): Unseen—Unfeared; *People's Favorite Magazine,* February 10, 1919, pp. 139–48.

F. Scott Fitzgerald: The Curious Case of Benjamin Button; *F. Scott Fitzgerald: Novels and Stories, 1920–1922,* ed. Jackson R. Bryer (New York: Library of America, 2000), pp. 954–79. First published in *Collier's,* May 27, 1922, and collected in *Tales of the Jazz Age* (New York: Scribner's, 1922).

Seabury Quinn: The Curse of Everard Maundy; *Weird Tales,* July 1927, pp. 49–68.

Stephen Vincent Benét: The King of the Cats; *Thirteen O'Clock: Stories of Several Worlds* (New York: Farrar & Rinehart, Inc., 1937), pp. 48–68; first published in *Harper's Bazaar*, February 1929. Copyright ©1929 by Stephen Vincent Benét; copyright renewed © 1957 by Rosemary Carr Benét. Reprinted by permission of Brandt & Hochman Literary Agents, Inc.

David H. Keller: The Jelly-Fish; *Tales from Underwood* (New York: Published for Arkham House by Pelligrini & Cudahy, 1952), pp. 244–48; first published in *Weird Tales*, January 1929.

Conrad Aiken: Mr. Arcularis; *Among the Lost People* (New York: C. Scribner's Sons, 1934), 12–43; first published in *Harper's*, March 1931. Copyright © Conrad Aiken. Reprinted by permission of Joseph I. Killorin for the Estate of Conrad Aiken.

Robert E. Howard: The Black Stone; *Weird Tales*, November 1931, pp. 500–11.

Henry S. Whitehead: Passing of a God; *Weird Tales*, January, 1931, pp. 98–110.

August Derleth: The Panelled Room; *Someone in the Dark* (Sauk City, WI: Arkham House, 1941), pp. 228–44; first published in *Westminster Magazine*, September 1933. Copyright © 1941 by August Derleth, renewed © 1969, 1997 by Arkham House, Publishers, Inc. Reprinted by permission of Arkham House Publishers, Inc.

H. P. Lovecraft: The Thing on the Doorstep; *Lovecraft: Tales*, Peter Straub, ed. (New York: Library of America, 2005), pp. 692–718; first published in *Weird Tales*, January 1937. Copyright © 1937. Used by permission of Lovecraft Properties, LLC.

Clark Ashton Smith: Genius Loci; *Genius Loci and Other Tales* (Sauk City, WI: Arkham House, 1945), pp. 3–20; first published in *Weird Tales*, June 1933.

Robert Bloch: The Cloak; *The Opener of the Way* (Sauk City, WI: Arkham House, 1945), pp. 3–18; first published in *Unknown*, May 1939. Copyright © 1945 by Robert Bloch. Reprinted by permission of The Estate of Robert Bloch c/o Ralph M. Vicinanza, Ltd.

This volume presents the texts listed here without change except for the correction of typographical errors, but it does not attempt to reproduce features of their typographic design. The following is a list of typographical errors, cited by page and line number: 13.12, de-/cling; 14.4, on?; 190.40, esctasy; 198.39, Yellow'"; 208.3, fire!'; 244.22, 'if,"; 248.4, 'A; 256.37, "l's"; 323.20, Ven; 374.3, A; 374.5, He; 376.36, He; 378.10, girl's; 449.39, see; 458.12, it."; 468.32, Duckworth's; 481.10, transcendant; 530.17, Roscie; 551.34, word; 570.14, are; 598.40, if; 610.21, noblemen; 610.37, Goeffrey; 612.27, aboriginies; 618.25, ecstacy; 623.19, "Have; 695.10, though.

Notes

In the notes below, the reference numbers refer to page and line of this volume (the line count includes titles and headings). Biblical quotations are keyed to the King James Version. Quotations from Shakespeare are keyed to G. Blakemore Evans, ed., *The Riverside Shakespeare* (Boston: Houghton Mifflin, 1974). The editor wishes to thank Stefan Dziemianowicz for his expert and deeply knowledgeable assistance in the preparation of these volumes and the selection of their contents.

21.18   Swedenborg] Emanuel Swedenborg (1688–1772), Swedish mystic.

24.5–6   statue of Henry the Fourth . . . overthrown by the populace] The statue was torn down in 1792 and restored in 1818.

25.12   Goddess of Reason] The worship of reason was promulgated during the French Revolution by Jacques Hébert and others; the Goddess of Reason was personified by Thérèse Momoro in an anti-Christian Festival of Liberty and Reason celebrated at Notre Dame Cathedral in November 1793.

27.4–5   *Dicebant . . . fore levatas.—Ebn Zaiat*] In Poe's translation, from a footnote he later deleted: "My companions told me I might find some little alleviation of my misery, in visiting the grave of my beloved." Ebn Zaiat (or more properly Abou Giafar Mohammed ben Abdalmalek ben Abban) was a poet of Baghdad who died around 218 C.E. The quotation is from a 10th-century poetry anthology, the *Kitab al-Aghani* (*Book of Songs*).

30.26–28   treatise of . . . "*de Carne Christi*,"] The treatise by Curio (1503–1569) was published in 1554; St. Augustine's *City of God* was finished in 426; Tertullian's *On the Flesh of Christ* dates from the early third century.

30.29–31   *Mortuus est . . . impossibile est*] That the Son of God died is to be believed because it is incredible; that He is risen is certain because it is impossible.

33.8   Mad'selle Sallé] Marie Sallé (1714–1756), a dancer.

33.8–9   "*que tous ses pas etaient des sentiments*,"] That all her steps were feelings.

33.9–10   *que tous ses dents etaient des idées*] That all her teeth were ideas.

33.30   preparations for the burial were completed.] In Poe's original version, published in *The Southern Literary Messenger* and collected in *Tales of the Grotesque and Arabesque* (1840), four paragraphs follow which Poe deleted when he reprinted the story in *The Broadway Journal* in 1845:

> With a heart full of grief, yet reluctantly, and oppressed with awe, I made my way to the bed-chamber of the departed. The room was large, and very dark, and at every step within its gloomy precincts I encountered the paraphernalia of the grave. The coffin, so a menial told me, lay surrounded by the curtains of yonder bed, and in that coffin, he whisperingly assured me, was all that remained of Berenice. Who was it asked me would I not look upon the corpse? I had seen the lips of no one move, yet the question had been demanded, and the echo of the syllables still lingered in the room. It was impossible to refuse; and with a sense of suffocation I dragged myself to the side of the bed. Gently I uplifted the draperies of the curtains.
>
> As I let them fall they descended upon my shoulders, and shutting me thus out from the living, enclosed me in the strictest communion with the deceased.
>
> The very atmosphere was redolent of death. The peculiar smell of the coffin sickened me; and I fancied a deleterious odor was already exhaling from the body. I would have given worlds to escape—to fly from the pernicious influence of mortality—to breathe once again the pure air of the eternal heavens. But I had no longer the power to move—my knees tottered beneath me—and I remained rooted to the spot, and gazing upon the frightful length of the rigid body as it lay outstretched in the dark coffin without a lid.
>
> God of heaven!—was it possible? Was it my brain that reeled—or was it indeed the finger of the enshrouded dead that stirred in the white cerement that bound it? Frozen with unutterable awe I slowly raised my eyes to the countenance of the corpse. There had been a band around the jaws, but, I know not how, it was broken asunder. The livid lips were wreathed into a species of smile, and, through the enveloping gloom, once again there glared upon me in too palpable reality, the white and glistening, and ghastly teeth of Berenice. I sprang convulsively from the bed, and, uttering no words, rushed forth a maniac from that apartment of triple horror, and mystery, and death.

37.27   King Philip's war]   Conflict (1675–76) between Native Americans and English settlers in southern New England. Metacom, the leader of the Wampanoag Indians, was known to the English as King Philip.

50.32   pung]   One-horse sleigh.

52.34   Paradise of Bachelors]   "The Paradise of Bachelors" was the companion piece to "The Tartarus of Maids"; the two sketches were published together in *Harper's*, April 1, 1855. The bachelors in question are residents of the Temple Bar in London.

55.9   Actæon]   Hunter who in Greek mythology was transformed into a stag and devoured by his own hounds after spying on Diana at her bath.

60.39   Saint Veronica]   In Christian tradition, a woman of Jerusalem who took pity on Jesus on his way to Golgotha and wiped his brow with her veil; the cloth thereafter bore a miraculous impression of his face.

65.8–9   Mrs. Crowe's "Night Side of Nature"]   Catherine Crowe, *The Night-Side of Nature, or Ghosts and Ghost-Seers* (New York: 1853).

65.18–19   "The Pot of Tulips,"]   An earlier story by Fitz-James O'Brien.

66.26   *Rana arborea*]   Tree frog.

67.7   Haroun]   Haroun al-Raschid, eighth-century caliph of Baghdad who plays a legendary role in *The Thousand and One Nights*.

67.8   afreets]   In Arabic mythology, demons or evil spirits.

68.1–2   Brockden Brown's novel of 'Wieland']   In Charles Brockden Brown's *Wieland, or The Transformation* (1798), the protagonist hears disembodied voices created through ventriloquism and mistakes them for divine commands.

68.3   Bulwer's 'Zanoni;']   Novel (1842) involving the achievement of eternal life through occult arts.

68.10   Hoffman]   E.T.W. Hoffmann (1776–1822), German writer, composer, and theatrical impresario, whose fantastic tales exerted widespread influence.

74.36–37 Gustave Doré, or Callot, or Tony Johannot]   Doré (1832–1883), artist and engraver known for his illustrations of Dante, Rabelais, Milton, and the Bible; Jacques Callot (c. 1592–1635), celebrated printmaker; Johannot (1803–1852), French engraver and illustrator.

74.39   *Un voyage ou il vous plaira*]   A trip to wherever you like.

99.10   Jemschid]   Or Jamshid; legendary Persian king.

101.36   *Per si muove*]   *Eppur si muove*: And yet it moves. The phrase was said to have been muttered by Galileo after his forced recantation in 1633 of the theory of heliocentrism.

136.38–39 Weir Mitchell]   Silas Weir Mitchell (1829–1914), physician and author whose works included the novel *Hugh Wynne, Free Quaker* (1897). Gilman underwent his experimental treatment for depression, involving isolation and inactivity, of which "The Yellow Wall Paper" is in part a description.

158.25   "Il ne . . . à Pauline."]   We mustn't let Pauline get hurt.

171.16   De La Motte Fouque]   Friedrich Heinrich Karl, Baron de la

Motte Fouqué (1777–1843), writer and officer in the Prussian cavalry; best known for his supernatural fantasy *Undine* (1811).

177.23–24   "*Ne raillons . . . la différence.*"] Let us not mock the mad; their madness lasts longer than ours. . . . That is the only difference.

191.25–26   the monstrosity . . . to represent Garibaldi] The statue, by Giovanni Turini, was erected in Washington Square Park in 1888.

201.7   Carcosa] Chambers derived the name Carcosa and many other details of the imaginary play "The King in Yellow" from Ambrose Bierce's story "An Inhabitant of Carcosa" (1886). The story is recounted by a man (later revealed to have already died) as he wanders through an unknown landscape.

235.16–17   Wordsworth's Boy of Egremond] Young Romilly, the heir of a noble family, who drowned in the Strid, as recounted in Wordsworth's poem "The Force of Prayer; or, the Founding of Bolton Priory. A Tradition" (1815). "The story is preserved," according to Wordsworth's later note, "in Dr. Whitaker's History of Craven." "The Boy of Egremond" (1819), a poem on the same subject, was written by Samuel Rogers.

238.4–7   *Eternal longing with eternal pain . . . through some old maze of wrong.*] From "The Wanderer" (1857) by Owen Meredith (pseudonym of Edward Robert Bulwer Lytton, 1831–1891).

238.25   Marryatt] Frederick Marryatt (1792–1848), English naval officer whose popular novels of the sea included *Peter Simple* (1833) and *Mr. Midshipman Easy* (1834).

241.40   'Evil shall not depart from his house.'] Proverbs 17:13: "Whoso rewardeth evil for good, evil shall not depart from his house."

242.25   'The Bells.'] Play (1871) by Leopold Lewis; Sir Henry Irving was celebrated for his portrayal of the conscience-racked murderer Mathias.

243.5–6   'I'll make . . . of you!'] *King Lear*, II.ii.32–33.

243.13–15   Poe's hero . . . and Persepolis, until my very soul has become a ruin.'] In "Ms. Found in a Bottle" (1833).

243.38   'and tell quaint lies'] *The Merchant of Venice*, III.iv.69.

244.5   'Poor Jo's,'] Poor Jo, chimney sweep in Charles Dickens' *Bleak House* (1852–53); he was a principal character in stage adaptations of the novel.

244.7   Io-like] In Greek mythology, Io was loved by Zeus and changed him into a heifer to elude the jealousy of Hera; eventually Hera sent a gadfly to torment her and keep her wandering until she reached Egypt where she was permitted to settle.

244.23–24   Hawthorne's offer . . . exploring expedition] Nathaniel Hawthorne applied unsuccessfully for the position of historian on the Great

Exploring Expedition (1838–42). Under the command of Charles Wilkes, the expedition surveyed areas of Antarctica, the Pacific Ocean, and the northwest coast of America.

244.27   Passavent] Johan Karl Passavant (1790–1857), German theologian and homeopathist, author of *Animal Magnetism* (1821).

244.34–38   VICTOR.—Where is the gentleman? . . . His soul is in Madrid.'] Henry Wadsworth Longfellow, *The Spanish Student* (1843), III.v.

245.15–16   Heine's 'Reisebilder,'] *Pictures of Travel* (1826–27).

246.25   Talma] François-Joseph Talma (1763–1826), actor who dominated the French stage from before the Revolution until after the Bourbon restoration.

246.30   'Court and Stage,'] Play (1854) by Charles Reade, originally titled *The King's Rival*.

247.22–25   'See where he steals . . . in sorrow's knot.'] The lines are from David Garrick's altered version of *Romeo and Juliet* (1750).

248.37–38   "The Wandering Jew,"] A play adapted from Eugène Sue's novel *Le Juif Errant* (1844).

249.1–7   "All in my mind is confused . . . the roar of the limitless sea."] From Owen Meredith, "The Shore" (see note 238.4–7).

249.28   T. A. Trollope's "Artist's Tragedy:"] Thomas Adolphus Trollope's story about Andrea del Sarto appeared in *The Temple Bar Magazine* in 1870.

250.26–29   Macdonald's lover cries . . . when, or where, or how?'] See George MacDonald, *The Portent* (1864).

250.37   Swinburne's queen of panthers] See Algernon Charles Swinburne, "At a Month's End": "But I, who leave my queen of panthers, / As a tired honey-heavy bee / Gilt with sweet dust from gold-grained anthers / Leaves the rose-chalice, what for me?"

251.27   "Chant du Depart."] Revolutionary song written around 1794.

253.19–20   Marquise de Brinvilliers] Marie-Madeleine-Marguerite d'Aubray, marquise de Brinvilliers (b. 1630), was beheaded and burned at the stake for the poisoning of her father, brother, and two sisters; she was also implicated in other poisonings.

269.3   *Grettir*] Outlawed protagonist of the Icelandic *Saga of Grettir the Strong*.

305.29   Remote, unfriended, melancholy, slow.] Oliver Goldsmith, *The Traveller* (1764), line 1.

314.7–8   triumph of Elijah over the prophets of Baal] See 1 Kings 18:21–39.

331.20–21   Shell of sense / So frail, so piteously contrived for pain,]   Cf.
William Vaughn Moody, *The Masque of Judgment* (1900): "My heart makes
question which were worthier state / For a free soul to choose,—angelic
calm, / Angelic vision, ebbless, increscent, / Or earth-life with its reachings
and recoils, / Its lewd harsh blood so swift to change and flower / At the
least touch of love, its shell of sense / So subtly made to minister them delight, / So frail, so piteously contrived for pain."

346.35   *pour deux sous*]   For two sous.

350.14   *ombres chinoises*]   Shadow-puppets.

371.13–14   Sir Philip Sidney . . . Zutphen]   Sidney was killed in 1586 while
leading an attack on a Spanish convoy near Zutphen in the Netherlands.

371.22   William Morris]   British artist, designer, and author (1834–1896).
As an artist he was associated with the Pre-Raphaelites.

372.31   'came to the making of man']   Algernon Charles Swinburne, *Ata-
lanta in Calydon* (1865): "Before the beginning of years / There came to the
making of man / Time with a gift of tears; / Grief with a glass that ran . . ."

375.29   George Osborne]   Self-indulgent character in Thackeray's *Vanity
Fair* (1847–48), a military officer who dies at the battle of Waterloo.

379.26   Sylvia]   Ballet (1876) with music by Léo Delibes.

426.6   *forestieri*]   Tourists.

463.13   Spencer . . . doth the body make,']   Edmund Spenser, "A
Hymn in Honour of Beauty" (1596), line 133.

464.16–17   'The bridal of the earth . . . Herbert]   George Herbert,
"Virtue": "Sweet day, so cool, so calm, so bright, / The bridal of the earth
and sky, / The dew shall weep thy fall tonight; / For thou must die."

489.24   Actæon]   See note 55.9.

489.37   I invited my soul]   See Walt Whitman, "Song of Myself": "I loafe
and invite my soul, / I lean and loafe at my ease observing a spear of summer grass."

489.37–38   *à outrance*]   Excessively.

527.6   charge up San Juan Hill]   On July 1, 1898, American troops assaulted and captured the San Juan heights east of Santiago, Cuba.

538.34–35   Haggard's *The Wanderer's Necklace*]   Short adventure novel
(1914) by Sir Henry Rider Haggard, recounted by the English reincarnation
of a Norse warrior.

552.9   Kipling . . . 'that is another story.']   "But that is another story"
became a catchphrase in the 1890's due to Rudyard Kipling's frequent use of
it in his early fiction.

563.17–33   Rossetti . . . *Eden Bowers* . . . Glittering sons and radiant daughters]   See Dante Gabriel Rossetti, "Eden's Bower" (1868).

573.4   "Iphigenie in Aulis"]   *Iphigénie en Aulide* (1774), opera by Christoph Willibald Gluck.

577.36   Monk Lewis]   Matthew Gregory Lewis (1775–1818), author of the Gothic novel *The Monk* (1796).

590.34   "But let there be no moaning,"]   See Alfred Tennyson, "Crossing the Bar," first stanza: "Sunset and evening star, / And one clear call for me! / And may there be no moaning of the bar, / When I put out to sea."

592.7–8   Melozzo da Forli]   Umbrian fresco painter (c. 1438–1494).

594.9   *Empress of Ireland*]   Canadian ocean liner that was sunk in the St. Lawrence River in 1914 after colliding with a coal freighter; over a thousand lives were lost.

598.25–26   the Hound of Heaven]   God, as personified in the poem by Francis Thompson (1859–1907).

601.29–30   "The Roast Beef of Old England"]   Patriotic ballad from Henry Fielding's *The Grub-Street Opera* (1731); the musical setting by Richard Leveridge was widely performed to introduce or close theatrical performances.

605.20   'On such a night as this—']   See *The Merchant of Venice*, V.i.1–22.

655.23   the notorious . . . Justin Geoffrey]   From Robert E. Howard's "The Black Stone," pages 607–24 in this volume.

657.11   Plattsburg]   A training camp for army officers was established at Plattsburg, New York, during World War I.

678.13   lich]   Corpse.

684.35   Sorolla]   Joaquín Sorolla y Bastide (1863–1923), Spanish painter.

700.6–7   Elsa Maxwell]   Gossip columnist and society hostess (1883–1963).

THE LIBRARY OF AMERICA SERIES

The Library of America fosters appreciation and pride in America's literary heritage by publishing, and keeping permanently in print, authoritative editions of America's best and most significant writing. An independent nonprofit organization, it was founded in 1979 with seed money from the National Endowment for the Humanities and the Ford Foundation.

To subscribe to the series or to order individual copies,
please visit www.loa.org or call (800) 964.5778.

*This book is set in 10 point Linotron Galliard,
a face designed for photocomposition by Matthew Carter
and based on the sixteenth-century face Granjon. The paper
is acid-free lightweight opaque and meets the requirements
for permanence of the American National Standards Institute.
The binding material is Brillianta, a woven rayon cloth made
by Van Heek-Scholco Textielfabrieken, Holland. Composition by Dedicated Business Services. Printing by
Malloy Incorporated. Binding by Dekker Book-
binding. Designed by Bruce Campbell.*